PENGUIN BOOKS

# U.S.A.

John Dos Passos was born in Chicago in 1896 of Portuguese descent. His father was an eminent lawyer, and he was educated at the Choate School and then at Harvard, graduating in 1916. After the First World War – during which he served in the US Army Medical Corps – he was a freelance correspondent in Spain and the Near East before settling down to the writing of books. In 1922 he published a volume of poetry and a collection of essays that explored the Spanish culture. In 1925 he published *Manhattan Transfer*, his first experimental novel in what was to become his peculiar style – a mixture of fact and fiction. He began his panoramic epics of American life with the *U.S.A.* trilogy written with the same technique and tracing, through interwoven biographies, the story of America from the early twentieth century to the onset of the Depression in 1929. Then came the *District of Columbia* trilogy, which is a fictionalized social history of America in the thirties and forties. During the Second World War Dos Passos became a war correspondent in the Pacific for *Life* magazine.

In later years John Dos Passos published a number of historical works dealing with the founding years of the United States: *The Ground We Stand On*, *The Head and Heart of Thomas Jefferson*, *The Men Who Made This Nation* and *The Shackles of Power*.

His most permanent home was his father's farm in Tidewater, Virginia. He died in 1970.

# JOHN DOS PASSOS

# *U.S.A.*

PENGUIN BOOKS

# PENGUIN BOOKS

Published by the Penguin Group
Penguin Books Ltd, 80 Strand, London WC2R 0RL, England
Penguin Putnam Inc., 375 Hudson Street, New York, New York 10014, USA
Penguin Books Australia Ltd, 250 Camberwell Road, Camberwell, Victoria 3124, Australia
Penguin Books Canada Ltd, 10 Alcorn Avenue, Toronto, Ontario, Canada M4V 3B2
Penguin Books India (P) Ltd, 11 Community Centre, Panchsheel Park, New Delhi – 110 017, India
Penguin Books (NZ) Ltd, Cnr Rosedale and Airborne Roads, Albany, Auckland, New Zealand
Penguin Books (South Africa) (Pty) Ltd, 24 Sturdee Avenue, Rosebank 2196, South Africa

Penguin Books Ltd, Registered Offices: 80 Strand, London WC2R 0RL, England

www.penguin.com

*The 42nd Parallel* first published in the U.S.A. 1930
*Nineteen Nineteen* first published in the U.S.A. 1932
*The Big Money* first published in the U.S.A. 1936
The collected trilogy, *U.S.A.*, first published in the U.S.A. 1938
Published in Great Britain by Constable 1938
Published in Penguin Books 1966
Reprinted in Penguin Classics 2001

013

Copyright 1930, 1932, 1933, 1934, 1935, 1936, 1937 by John Dos Passos
Copyright 1946 by John Dos Passos and Houghton Mifflin
Copyright © renewed John Dos Passos, 1958, 1960
All rights reserved

Printed in England by Clays Ltd, St Ives plc
Set in Linotype Times Roman

ISBN-13: 978-0-141-18581-1
ISBN-10: 0-141-18581-3

www.greenpenguin.co.uk

# U.S.A.

The young man walks fast by himself through the crowd that thins into the night streets; feet are tired from hours of walking; eyes greedy for warm curve of faces, answering flicker of eyes, the set of a head, the lift of a shoulder, the way hands spread and clench; blood tingles with wants; mind is a beehive of hopes buzzing and stinging; muscles ache for the knowledge of jobs, for the roadmender's pick and shovel work, the fisherman's knack with a hook when he hauls on the slithery net from the rail of the lurching trawler, the swing of the bridgeman's arm as he slings down the whitehot rivet, the engineer's slow grip wise on the throttle, the dirtfarmer's use of his whole body when, whoaing the mules, he yanks the plow from the furrow. The young man walks by himself searching through the crowd with greedy eyes, greedy ears taut to hear, by himself, alone.

The streets are empty. People have packed into subways, climbed into streetcars and buses; in the stations they've scampered for suburban trains; they've filtered into lodgings and tenements, gone up in elevators into apartmenthouses. In a showwindow two sallow windowdressers in their shirtsleeves are bringing out a dummy girl in a red evening dress, at a corner welders in masks lean into sheets of blue flame repairing a cartrack, a few drunk bums shamble along, a sad streetwalker fidgets under an arclight. From the river comes the deep rumbling whistle of a steamboat leaving dock. A tug hoots far away.

The young man walks by himself, fast but not fast enough, far but not far enough (faces slide out of sight, talk trails into tattered scraps, footsteps tap fainter in alleys); he must catch the last subway, the streetcar, the bus, run up the gangplanks of all the steamboats, register at all the hotels, work in the cities, answer the wantads, learn the trades, take up the jobs, live in all the boardinghouses, sleep in all

the beds. One bed is not enough, one job is not enough, one
life is not enough. At night, head swimming with wants, he
walks by himself alone.

No job, no woman, no house, no city.

Only the ears busy to catch the speech are not alone; the
ears are caught tight, linked tight by the tendrils of phrased
words, the turn of a joke, the singsong fade of a story, the
gruff fall of a sentence; linking tendrils of speech twine
through the city blocks, spread over pavements, grow out
along broad parked avenues, speed with the trucks leaving
on their long night runs over roaring highways, whisper
down sandy byroads past wornout farms, joining up cities
and fillingstations, roundhouses, steamboats, planes grop-
ing along airways; words call out on mountain pastures,
drift slow down rivers widening to the sea and the hushed
beaches.

It was not in the long walks through jostling crowds at
night that he was less alone, or in the training camp at
Allentown, or in the day on the docks at Seattle, or in the
empty reek of Washington City hot boyhood summer nights,
or in the meal on Market Street, or in the swim off the red
rocks at San Diego, or in the bed full of fleas in New
Orleans, or in the cold razorwind off the lake, or in the
gray faces trembling in the grind of gears in the street under
Michigan Avenue, or in the smokers of limited express-
trains, or walking across country, or riding up the dry mountain canyons, or the night without a sleepingbag among
frozen beartracks in the Yellowstone, or canoeing Sundays
on the Quinnipiac;

but in his mother's words telling about longago, in his
father's telling about when I was a boy, in the kidding
stories of uncles, in the lies the kids told at school, the hired
man's yarns, the tall tales the doughboys told after taps;

it was the speech that clung to the ears, the link that
tingled in the blood; U.S.A.

U.S.A. is the slice of a continent. U.S.A. is a group of
holding companies, some aggregations of trade unions, a
set of laws bound in calf, a radio network, a chain of moving picture theatres, a column of stockquotations rubbed

out and written in by a Western Union boy on a blackboard, a publiclibrary full of old newspapers and dogeared historybooks with protests scrawled on the margins in pencil. U.S.A. is the world's greatest rivervalley fringed with mountains and hills. U.S.A. is a set of bigmouthed officials with too many bankaccounts. U.S.A. is a lot of men buried in their uniforms in Arlington Cemetery. U.S.A. is the letters at the end of an address when you are away from home. But mostly U.S.A. is the speech of the people.

# Contents

## THE 42ND PARALLEL

# NINETEEN NINETEEN

## JOE WILLIAMS

## DAUGHTER

## EVELINE HUTCHINS

## RICHARD ELLSWORTH SAVAGE

## DAUGHTER

## BEN COMPTON

## RICHARD ELLSWORTH SAVAGE

# THE BIG MONEY

# The 42nd Parallel

# Newsreel 1

*It was that emancipated race*
*That was chargin' up the hill*
*Up to where them insurrectos*
*Was afightin' fit to kill*

## CAPITAL CITY'S CENTURY CLOSED

General Miles with his gaudy uniform and spirited charger was the center for all eyes, especially as his steed was extremely restless. Just as the band passed the Commanding General, his horse stood upon his hind legs and was almost erect. General Miles instantly reined in the frightened animal and dug in his spurs in an endeavor to control the horse which, to the horror of the spectators, fell over backwards and landed squarely on the Commanding General. Much to the gratification of the people, General Miles was not injured, but considerable skin was scraped off the flank of his horse. Almost every inch of General Miles's overcoat was covered with the dust of the street and between the shoulders a hole about an inch in diameter was punctured. Without waiting for anyone to brush the dust from his garments, General Miles remounted his horse and reviewed the parade as if it were an everyday occurrence.

The incident naturally attracted the attention of the crowd, and this brought to notice the fact that the Commanding General never permits a flag to be carried past him without uncovering and remaining so until the colors have passed

*And the Captain bold of Company B*
*Was afightin' in the lead*
*Just like a trueborn soldier he*
*Of them bullets took no heed*

OFFICIALS KNOW NOTHING OF VICE

Sanitary trustees turn water of Chicago River into drainage canal    LAKE MICHIGAN SHAKES HANDS WITH THE FATHER OF THE WATERS    German zuchterverein    singing contest for canarybirds opens    the fight for bimetallism at the ratio of 16 to 1 has not been lost, says Bryan

BRITISH BEATEN AT MAFEKING

*For there's many a man been murdered in Luzon*

CLAIMS ISLANDS FOR ALL TIME

Hamilton Club listens to Oratory by ex-Congressman Posey of Indiana

NOISE GREETS NEW CENTURY

LABOR GREETS NEW CENTURY

CHURCHES GREET NEW CENTURY

Mr McKinley is hard at work in his office when the new year begins.

NATION GREETS CENTURY'S DAWN

Responding to a toast, Hail Columbia! at the Columbia Club banquet in Indianapolis, Indiana, ex-President Benjamin Harrison said in part: I have no argument to make here or anywhere against territorial expansion; but I do not, as some do, look upon territorial expansion as the safest and most attractive avenue of national development. By the advantages of abundant and cheap coal and iron, of an enormous overproduction of food products and of invention and economy in production, we are now leading by the nose the original and the greatest of the colonizing nations.

Society Girls Shocked: Danced with Detectives

*For there's many a man been murdered in Luzon*
*and Mindanao*

GAIETY GIRLS MOBBED IN NEW JERSEY

One of the lithographs of the leading lady represented her in less than Atlantic City bathing costume, sitting on a red-hot stove; in one hand she held a brimming glass of wine, in the other ribbons drawn over a pair of rampant lobsters.

*For there's many a man been murdered in Luzon*
*and Mindanao*
*and in Samar*

In responding to the toast, 'The Twentieth Century,' Senator Albert J. Beveridge said in part: *The twentieth century will be American. American thought will dominate it. American progress will give it color and direction. American deeds will make it illustrious.*

*Civilization will never lose its hold on Shanghai. Civilization will never depart from Hongkong. The gates of Peking will never again be closed to the methods of modern man. The regeneration of the world, physical as well as moral, has begun, and revolutions never move backwards.*

*There's been many a good man murdered in the Philippines*
*Lies sleeping in some lonesome grave.*

## The Camera Eye (1)

when you walk along the street you have to step carefully always on the cobbles so as not to step on the bright anxious grassblades    easier if you hold Mother's hand and hang on it that way you can kick up your toes but walking fast you have to tread on too many grassblades the poor hurt green tongues shrink under your feet    maybe that's why those people are so angry and follow us shaking their fists    they're throwing stones grownup people throwing stones    She's walking fast and we're running her pointed toes sticking out sharp among the poor trodden grassblades under the shaking folds of the brown cloth dress    Englander    a pebble tinkles along the cobbles

Quick darling quick in the postcard shop it's quiet the angry people are outside and can't come in    non nein nicht englander amerikanisch americain    Hoch Amerika Vive l'Amérique She laughs My dear they had me right frightened war on the veldt Kruger Bloemfontein Ladysmith and Queen Victoria an old lady in a pointed lace cap sent chocolate to the soldiers at Christmas

under the counter it's dark and the lady the nice Dutch lady who loves Americans and has relations in Trenton shows you postcards that shine in the dark pretty hotels and palaces    O que c'est beau schön prittie prittie    and the moonlight ripple ripple under a bridge and the little reverbères are alight in the dark under the counter and the little windows of hotels around the harbor    O que c'est beau la lune

and the big moon

## *Mac*

When the wind set from the silver factories across the river the air of the gray fourfamily frame house where Fainy McCreary was born was choking all day with the smell of whaleoil soap. Other days it smelt of cabbage and babies and Mrs McCreary's washboilers. Fainy could never play at home because Pop, a lame cavechested man with a wispy blondgray mustache, was nightwatchman at the Chadwick Mills and slept all day. It was only round five o'clock that a curling whiff of tobaccosmoke would seep through from the front room into the kitchen. That was a sign that Pop was up and in good spirits, and would soon be wanting his supper.

Then Fainy would be sent running out to one of two corners of the short muddy street of identical frame houses where they lived.

To the right it was half a block to Finley's where he would have to wait at the bar in a forest of mudsplattered trouserlegs until all the rank brawling mouths of grownups had been stopped with beers and whiskies. Then he would walk home, making each step very carefully, with the handle of the pail of suds cutting into his hand.

To the left it was half a block to Maginnis's Fancy Groceries, Home and Imported Products. Fainy liked the cardboard Cream of Wheat darkey in the window, the glass case with different kinds of salami in it, the barrels of potatoes and cabbages, the brown smell of sugar, sawdust, ginger, kippered herring, ham, vinegar, bread, pepper, lard.

'A loaf of bread, please, Mister, a halfpound of butter, and a box of gingersnaps.'

Some evenings, when Mom felt poorly, Fainy had to go further; round the corner past Maginnis's, down Riverside Avenue where the trolley ran, and across the red bridge over the little river that flowed black between icy undercut snowbanks in winter, yellow and spuming in the spring thaws, brown and oily in summer. Across the river all the way to the corner of Riverside and Main, where the drugstore was, lived Bohunks and Polaks. Their kids were always fighting with the kids of the Murphys and O'Haras and O'Flanagans who lived on Orchard Street.

Fainy would walk along with his knees quaking, the medicine bottle in its white paper tight in one mittened hand. At the corner of Quince was a group of boys he'd have to pass. Passing wasn't so bad; it was when he was about twenty yards from them that the first snowball would hum by his ear. There was no comeback. If he broke into a run, they'd chase him. If he dropped the medicine bottle he'd be beaten up when he got home. A soft one would plunk on the back of his head and the snow began to trickle down his neck. When he was a half a block from the bridge he'd take a chance and run for it.

'Scared cat . . . Shanty Irish . . . Bowlegged Murphy . . . Running home to tell the cop' . . . would yell the Polak and Bohunk kids between snowballs. They made their snowballs hard by pouring water on them and leaving them to freeze overnight; if one of those hit him it drew blood.

The backyard was the only place you could really feel safe to play in. There were brokendown fences, dented garbage cans, old pots and pans too nearly sieves to mend, a vacant chickencoop that still had feathers and droppings on the floor, hogweed in summer, mud in winter; but the glory of the McCrearys' backyard was Tony Harriman's rabbit hutch, where he kept Belgian hares. Tony Harriman was a consumptive and lived with his mother on the groundfloor left. He wanted to raise all sorts of other small animals too, raccoons, otter, even silver fox, he'd get rich that way. The day he died nobody could find the key to the big padlock on the door of the rabbit hutch. Fainy fed the hares for several days by pushing in cabbage and lettuce leaves through the double thickness of chickenwire. Then came a week of sleet and rain when he didn't go out in the yard. The first day, when he went to look, one of the hares was dead. Fainy turned white; he tried to tell himself the hare was asleep, but it lay gawkily stiff, not asleep. The other hares were huddled in a corner looking about with twitching noses, their bag ears flopping helplessly over their backs. Poor hares; Fainy wanted to cry. He ran upstairs to his mother's kitchen, ducked under the ironing board and got the hammer out of the drawer in the kitchen table. The first time he tried he mashed his finger, but the second time he managed to jump the padlock. Inside the cage there was a funny, sour smell. Fainy picked the dead hare up by its ears. Its soft white belly was beginning to puff up, one dead eye was scaringly open. Something suddenly got hold of Fainy and made him drop the hare in the nearest garbage can and run upstairs. Still cold and trembling, he tiptoed out onto the back porch and looked down. Breathlessly he watched the other hares. By cautious hops they were getting near the door of the hutch into the yard. One of them was out. It sat up on its hind legs, limp ears suddenly stiff. Mom called him to bring her a flatiron from the stove. When he got back to the porch the hares were all gone.

That winter there was a strike in the Chadwick Mills and Pop lost his job. He would sit all day in the front room smoking and cursing:

'Ablebodied man, by Jesus, if I couldn't lick any one of those damn Polaks with my crutch tied behind my back ... I says so to Mr Barry; I ain't goin' to join no strike. Mr Barry, a sensible quiet man, a bit of an invalid, with a wife an' kiddies to think for. Eight years I've been watchman, an' now you give me the sack to take on a bunch of thugs from a detective agency. The dirty pugnosed sonofabitch.'

'If those damn lousy furreners hadn't a-walked out,' somebody would answer soothingly.

The strike was not popular on Orchard Street. It meant that Mom had to work harder and harder, doing bigger and bigger boilerfuls of wash, and that Fainy and his older sister Milly had to help when they came home from school. And then one day Mom got sick and had to go back to bed instead of starting in on the ironing, and lay with her round white creased face whiter than the pillow and her watercreased hands in a knot under her chin. The doctor came and the district nurse, and all three rooms of the flat smelt of doctors and nurses and drugs, and the only place Fainy and Milly could find to sit was on the stairs. There they sat and cried quietly together. Then Mom's face on the pillow shrank into a little creased white thing like a rumpled-up handkerchief and they said that she was dead and took her away.

The funeral was from the undertaking parlors on Riverside Avenue on the next block. Fainy felt very proud and important because everybody kissed him and patted his head and said he was behaving like a little man. He had a new black suit on, too, like a grownup suit with pockets and everything, except that it had short pants. There were all sorts of people at the undertaking parlors he had never been close to before, Mr Russell the butcher, and Father O'Donnell and Uncle Tim O'Hara who'd come on from Chicago, and it smelt of whiskey and beer like at Finley's. Uncle Tim was a skinny man with a knobbed red face and blurry blue eyes. He wore a loose black silk tie that worried Fainy, and kept leaning down suddenly, bending from the waist as if he was going to close up like a jackknife, and whispering in a thick voice in Fainy's ear.

'Don't you mind 'em, old sport, they're a bunch o' bums and hypocrytes, stewed to the ears most of 'em already. Look at Father O'Donnell the fat swine already figurin' up the burial fees. But don't you mind 'em, remember you're an O'Hara on your mother's side. I don't mind 'em, old sport, and she was my own sister by birth and blood.'

When they got home he was terribly sleepy and his feet were cold and wet. Nobody paid any attention to him. He sat whimpering on the edge of the bed in the dark. In the front room there were voices and a sound of knives and forks, but he didn't dare go in there. He curled up against the wall and went to sleep. Light in his eyes woke him up. Uncle Tim and Pop were standing over him talking loud. They looked funny and didn't seem to be standing very steady. Uncle Tim held the lamp.

'Well, Fainy, old sport,' said Uncle Tim giving the lamp a perilous wave over Fainy's head. 'Fenian O'Hara McCreary, sit up and take notice and tell us what you think of our proposed removal to the great and growing city of Chicago. Middletown's a terrible bitch of a dump if you ask me . . . Meanin' no offense, John . . . But Chicago . . . Jesus God, man, when you get there you'll think you've been dead and nailed up in a coffin all these years.'

Fainy was scared. He drew his knees up to his chin and looked tremblingly at the two big swaying figures of men lit by the swaying lamp. He tried to speak but the words dried up on his lips.

'The kid's asleep, Tim, for all your speechifyin' . . . Take your clothes off, Fainy, and get into bed and get a good night's sleep. We're leavin' in the mornin'.'

And late on a rainy morning, without any breakfast, with a big old swelltop trunk tied up with rope joggling perilously on the roof of the cab that Fainy had been sent to order from Hodgeson's Livery Stable, they set out. Milly was crying. Pop didn't say a word but sucked on an unlit pipe. Uncle Tim handled everything, making little jokes all the time that nobody laughed at, pulling a roll of bills out of his pocket at every juncture, or taking great gurgling sips out of the flask he had in his pocket. Milly cried and cried. Fainy looked out with big dry eyes at the familiar streets, all suddenly odd and lopsided, that rolled past the cab; the red bridge, the scabshingled houses where the Polaks lived, Smith's and Smith's corner drugstore . . . there was Billy Hogan just coming out with a package of chewing gum in his hand. Playing hookey again. Fainy had an impulse to yell at him, but something froze it . . . Main with its elms and streetcars, blocks of stores round the corner of Church, and then the fire department. Fainy looked for the last time into the dark cave where shone entrancingly the brass and copper curves of the engine, then past the cardboard fronts of the First Congregational Church, The Carmel Baptist Church, Saint Andrew's Episcopal Church built of brick and set cater-cornered on its lot instead of straight with a stern face to the street like the other churches, then the three castiron stags on the lawn in front of the Commercial House, and the residences, each with its lawn, each with its scrollsaw porch, each with its hydrangea bush. Then the houses got smaller, and the lawns disappeared; the cab trundled round past Simpson's Grain and Feed Warehouse, along a row of barbershops, saloons and lunchrooms, and they were all getting out at the station.

At the station lunchcounter Uncle Tim set everybody up to breakfast. He dried Milly's tears and blew Fainy's nose in a big new pockethandkerchief that still had the tag on the corner and set them to work on bacon and eggs and coffee. Fainy hadn't had coffee before, so the idea of sitting up like a man and drinking coffee made him feel pretty good. Milly didn't like hers, said it was bitter. They were left all alone in the lunchroom for some time with the empty plates and empty coffeecups under the beady eyes of a woman with the long neck and pointed face of a hen who looked at them disapprovingly from behind the counter. Then with an enormous, shattering rumble, sludgepuff sludge . . . puff, the train came into the station. They were scooped up and dragged across the platform and through a pipesmoky car and before they knew it the train was moving and the wintry russet Connecticut landscape was clattering by.

## The Camera Eye (2)

we hurry wallowing like in a boat in the musty stably-smelling herdic cab.     He kept saying What would you do Lucy if I were to invite one of them to my table? They're very lovely people Lucy the colored people and He had cloves in a little silver box and a rye whiskey smell on his breath hurrying to catch the cars to New York.

and She was saying Oh dolly I hope we won't be late and Scott was waiting with the tickets and we had to run up the platform of the Seventh Street Depot and all the little cannons kept falling out of the Olympia and everybody stooped to pick them up and the conductor Allaboard lady quick lady

they were little brass cannons and were bright in the sun on the platform of the Seventh Street Depot and Scott hoisted us all up and the train was moving and the engine bell was ringing and Scott put in your hand a little handful of brass tiny cannons just big enough to hold the smallest size red firecracker at the battle of Manila Bay and said Here's the artillery Jack

and He was holding forth in the parlor car Why Lucy if it were necessary for the cause of humanity I would walk out and be shot any day you would Jack wouldn't you? wouldn't you porter? who was bringing apollinaris and He had a flask in the brown grip where the silk initialed handkerchiefs always smelt of bay rum

and when we got to Havre de Grace He said Remember Lucy we used to have a ferry across the Susquehanna before the bridge was built

and across Gunpowder Creek too

## *Mac*

Russet hills, patches of woods, farmhouses, cows, a red colt kicking up its heels in a pasture, rail fences, streaks of marsh.

'Well, Tim, I feel like a whipped cur . . . So long as I've lived, Tim, I've tried to do the right thing,' Pop kept repeating in a rattling voice. 'And now what can they be sayin' about me?'

'Jesus God, man, there was nothin' else you could do, was there? What the devil can you do if you haven't any money and haven't any job and a lot o' doctors and undertakers and landlords come round with their bills and you with two children to support?'

'But I've been a quiet and respectable man, steady and misfortunate ever since I married and settled down. And now what'll they be thinkin' of me sneakin' out like a whipped cur?'

'John, take it from me that I'd be the last one to want to bring disrespect on the dead that was my own sister by birth and blood . . . But it ain't your fault and it ain't my fault . . . it's the fault of poverty, and poverty's the fault of the system . . . Fenian, you listen to Tim O'Hara for a minute and Milly, you listen too, cause a girl ought to know these things just as well as a man and for once in his life Tim O'Hara's tellin' the truth . . . It's the fault of the system that don't give a man the fruit of his labor . . . The only man that gets anything out of capitalism is a crook, an' he gets to be a millionaire in short order . . . But an honest workin' man like John or muself we can work a hundred years and not leave enough to bury us decent with.'

Smoke rolled white in front of the window shaking out of its folds trees and telegraph poles and little square shingleroofed houses and towns and trolleycars, and long rows of buggies with steaming horses standing in line.

'And who gets the fruit of our labor, the goddam businessmen, agents, middlemen who never did a productive piece of work in their life.'

Fainy's eyes are following the telegraph wires that sag and soar.

'Now, Chicago ain't no paradise, I can promise you that, John, but it's a better market for a workin'man's muscle and brains at present than the East is . . . And why, did you ask me why . . . ? Supply and demand, they need workers in Chicago.'

'Tim, I tellyer I feel like a whipped cur.'

'It's the system, John, it's the goddam lousy system.'

A great bustle in the car woke Fainy up. It was dark. Milly was crying again. He didn't know where he was.

'Well, gentlemen,' Uncle Tim was saying, 'we're about to arrive in little old New York.'

In the station it was light; that surprised Fainy, who thought it was already night. He and Milly were left a long time sitting on a suitcase in the waitingroom. The waitingroom was huge, full of unfamiliarlooking people, scary like people in picturebooks. Milly kept crying.

'Hey, Milly, I'll biff you one if you don't stop crying.'

'Why?' whined Milly, crying all the more.

Fainy stood as far away from her as possible so that people wouldn't think they were together. When he was about ready to cry himself, Pop and Uncle Tim came and took them and the suitcase into the restaurant. A strong smell of fresh whiskey came from their breaths, and they seemed very bright around the eyes. They all sat at a table with a white cloth and a sympathetic colored man in a white coat handed them a large card full of printing.

'Let's eat a good supper,' said Uncle Tim, 'if it's the last thing we do on this earth.'

'Damn the expense,' said Pop, 'it's the system that's to blame.'

'To hell with the pope,' said Uncle Tim. 'We'll make a Social Democrat out of you yet.'

They gave Fainy fried oysters and chicken and icecream and cake, and when they all had to run for the train he had a terrible stitch in his side. They got into a daycoach that smelt of coalgas and armpits. 'When are we going to bed?' Milly began to whine. 'We're not going to bed,' said Uncle Tim airily. 'We're going to sleep right here like little mice . . . like little mice in a cheese.' 'I doan like mice,' yelled Milly with a new flood of tears as the train started.

Fainy's eyes smarted; in his ears was the continuous roar, the clatter clatter over crossings, the sudden snarl under bridges. It was a tunnel; all the way to Chicago it was a tunnel. Opposite him Pop's and Uncle Tim's faces looked red and snarling, he didn't like the way they looked, and the light was smoky and jiggly and outside it was all a tunnel and his eyes hurt and wheels and rails roared in his ears and he fell asleep.

When he woke up it was a town and the train was running right through the main street. It was a sunny morning. He could

see people going about their business, stores, buggies and
springwagons standing at the curb, newsboys selling newspapers,
wooden Indians outside of cigarstores. At first he thought he
was dreaming, but then he remembered and decided it must
be Chicago. Pop and Uncle Tim were asleep on the seat opposite. Their mouths were open, their faces were splotched, and
he didn't like the way they looked. Milly was curled up with a
woolly shawl all over her. The train was slowing down, it was
a station. If it was Chicago they ought to get off. At that
moment the conductor passed, an old man who looked a little
like Father O'Donnell.

'Please, Mister, is this Chicago?'

'Chicago's a long way off yet, son,' said the conductor without smiling. 'This is Syracuse.'

And they all woke up, and for hours and hours the telephone
poles went by, and towns, frame houses, brick factories with
ranks and ranks of glittering windows, dumping grounds, trainyards, plowed land, pasture, and cows, and Milly got trainsick
and Fainy's legs felt like they would drop off from sitting in the
seat so long; some places it was snowing and some places it was
sunny, and Milly kept getting sick and smelt dismally of vomit
and it got dark and they all slept; and light again, and then the
towns and the frame houses and the factories all started drawing
together, humping into warehouses and elevators, and the
trainyards spread out as far as you could see and it was Chicago.

But it was so cold and the wind blew the dust so hard in his
face and his eyes were so stuck together by dust and tiredness
that he couldn't look at anything. After they had waited round
a long while, Milly and Fainy huddled together in the cold, they
got on a streetcar and rode and rode. They were so sleepy they
never knew exactly where the train ended and the streetcar
began. Uncle Tim's voice went on talking proudly excitedly,
Chicago, Chicago, Chicago. Pop sat with his chin on his crutch.
'Tim, I feel like a whipped cur.'

Fainy lived ten years in Chicago.

At first he went to school and played baseball on back lots on
Saturday afternoons, but then came his last commencement, and
all the children sang *My Country, 'Tis of Thee*, and school was
over and he had to go to work. Uncle Tim at that time had his
own jobprinting shop on a dusty side street off North Clark in
the groundfloor of a cranky old brick building. It only occupied
a small section of the building that was mostly used as a warehouse and was famous for its rats. It had a single wide plate-

glass window made resplendent by gold Old English lettering: Timothy O'Hara, Job Printer.

'Now, Fainy, old sport,' said Uncle Tim, 'you'll have a chance to learn the profession from the ground up.' So he ran errands, delivered packages of circulars, throwaways, posters, was always dodging trolleycars, ducking from under the foamy bits of big truckhorses, bumming rides on deliverywagons. When there were no errands to run he swept out under the presses, cleaned type, emptied the office wastepaper basket, or, during rush times, ran round the corner for coffee and sandwiches for the typesetter, or for a small flask of bourbon for Uncle Tim.

Pop puttered round on his crutch for several years, always looking for a job. Evenings he smoked his pipe and cursed his luck on the back stoop of Uncle Tim's house and occasionally threatened to go back to Middletown. Then one day he got pneumonia and died quietly at the Sacred Heart Hospital. It was about the same time that Uncle Tim bought a linotype machine.

Uncle Tim was so excited he didn't take a drink for three days. The floorboards were so rotten they had to build a brick base for the linotype all the way up from the cellar. 'Well, when we get another one we'll concrete the whole place,' Uncle Tim told everybody. For a whole day there was no work done. Everybody stood around looking at the tall black intricate machine that stood there like an organ in a church. When the machine was working and the printshop filled with the hot smell of molten metal, everybody's eyes followed the quivering inquisitive arm that darted and flexed above the keyboard. When they handed round the warm shiny slugs of type the old German typesetter who for some reason they called Mike pushed back his glasses on his forehead and cried. 'Fifty-five years a printer, and now when I'm old I'll have to carry hods to make a living.'

The first print Uncle Tim set up on the new machine was the phrase: *Workers of the world unite; you have nothing to lose but your chains.*

When Fainy was seventeen and just beginning to worry about skirts and ankles and girls' underwear when he walked home from work in the evening and saw the lights of the city bright against the bright heady western sky, there was a strike in the Chicago printing trades. Tim O'Hara had always run a union shop and did all the union printing at cost. He even got up a handbill signed, 'A Citizen,' entitled 'An Ernest Protest,' which Fainy was allowed to set up on the linotype one evening after the operator had gone home. One phrase stuck in Fainy's mind, and he repeated it to himself after he had gone to bed that night: *It is time for all honest men to band together to resist the ravages of greedy privilege.*

The next day was Sunday, and Fainy went along Michigan Avenue with a package of the handbills to distribute. It was a day of premature spring. Across the rotting yellow ice on the lake came little breezes that smelt unexpectedly of flowers. The girls looked terribly pretty and their skirts blew in the wind and Fainy felt the spring blood pumping hot in him, he wanted to kiss and to roll on the ground and to run out across the ice-cakes and to make speeches from the tops of telegraph poles and to vault over trolleycars; but instead he distributed hand-bills and worried about his pants being frayed and wished he had a swell looking suit and a swell looking girl to walk with.

'Hey, young feller, where's your permit to distribute them handbills?' It was a cop's voice growling in his ear. Fainy gave the cop one look over his shoulder, dropped the handbills and ran. He ducked through between the shiny black cabs and carriages, ran down a side street and walked and walked and didn't look back until he managed to get across a bridge just before the draw opened. The cop wasn't following him anyway.

He stood on the curb a long time with the whistle of a pea-nutstand shrilling derisively in his ear.

That night at supper his uncle asked him about the handbills.

'Sure I gave 'em out all along the lakeshore ... A cop tried to stop me, but I told him right where to get off.' Fainy turned burning red when a hoot went up from everybody at the table. He filled up his mouth with mashed potato and wouldn't say any more. His aunt and his uncle and their three daughters laughed and laughed.

'Well, it's a good thing you ran faster than the cop,' said Uncle Tim, 'else I should have had to bail you out and that would have cost money.'

The next morning early Fainy was sweeping out the office, when a man with a face like a raw steak walked up the steps; he was smoking a thin black stogy of a sort Fainy had never seen before. He knocked on the groundglass door.

'I want to speak to Mr O'Hara, Timothy O'Hara.'

'He's not here yet, be here any minute now, sir. Will you wait?'

'You bet I'll wait.' The man sat on the edge of a chair and

spat, first taking the chewed end of the stogy out of his mouth and looking at it meditatively for a long time.

When Tim O'Hara came the office door closed with a bang. Fainy hovered nervously around, a little bit afraid the man might be a detective following up the affair of the handbills. Voices rose and fell, the stranger's voice in short rattling tirades, O'Hara's voice in long expostulating clauses, now and then Fainy caught the word foreclose, until suddenly the door flew open and the stranger shot out, his face purpler than ever. On the iron stoop he turned and pulling a new stogy from his pocket, lit it from the old one; growling the words through the stogy and the blue puff of smoke, he said, 'Mr O'Hara, you have twentyfour hours to think it over . . . A word from you and proceedings stop immediately.' Then he went off down the street leaving behind him a long trail of rancid smoke.

A minute later, Uncle Tim came out of the office, his face white as paper. 'Fenian, old sport,' he said, 'you go get yourself a job. I'm going out of business . . . Keep a weather eye open. I'm going to have a drink.' And he was drunk for six days. By the end of that time a number of meeklooking men appeared with summonses, and Uncle Tim had to sober up enough to go down to the court and put in a plea of bankruptcy.

Mrs O'Hara scolded and stormed, 'Didn't I tell you, Tim O'Hara, no good'll ever come with your fiddlin' round with these godless labor unions and social-democrats and knights of labor, all of 'em drunk and loafin' bums like yourself, Tim O'Hara? Of course the master printers 'ud have to get together and buy up your outstandin' paper and squash you, and serve you right too, Tim O'Hara, you and your godless socialistic boozin' ways only they might have thought of your poor wife and her helpless wee babes, and now we'll starve all of us together, us and the dependents and hangerson you've brought into the house.'

'Well, I declare,' cried Fainy's sister Milly. 'If I haven't slaved and worked my fingers to the bone for every piece of bread I've eaten in this house,' and she got up from the breakfast table and flounced out of the room. Fainy sat there while the storm raged above his head; then he got up, slipping a corn muffin into his pocket as he went. In the hall he found the 'help wanted' section of the *Chicago Tribune*, took his cap and went out into a raw Sunday morning full of churchbells jangling in his ears. He boarded a streetcar and went out to Lincoln Park.

There he sat on a bench for a long time munching the muffin
and looking down the columns of advertisements: Boy Wanted.
But they none of them looked very inviting. One thing he was
bound, he wouldn't get another job in a printing shop until the
strike was over. Then his eye struck

Bright boy wanted with amb. and lit. taste, knowledge of
print. and pub. business. Conf. sales and distrib. proposition
$15 a week apply by letter P.O. Box 1256b

Fainy's head suddenly got very light. Bright boy, that's me,
ambition and literary taste . . . Gee, I must finish *Looking
Backward* . . . and jeez, I like reading fine, an' I could run a
linotype or set up print if anybody'd let me. Fifteen bucks a
week . . . pretty soft, ten dollars' raise. And he began to write
a letter in his head, applying for the job.

DEAR SIR (MY DEAR SIR)
          or maybe GENTLEMEN,
In applying for the position you offer in today's Sunday *Tribune*
I want to apply, (allow me to state) that I'm seventeen years old,
no, nineteen, with several years' experience in the printing and publishing trades, ambitious and with excellent knowledge and taste in
the printing and publishing trades,

no, I can't say that twice . . . And I'm very anxious for the
job . . . As he went along it got more and more muddled in his
head.

He found he was standing beside a peanut wagon. It was cold
as blazes, a razor wind was shrieking across the broken ice and
the black patches of water of the lake. He tore out the ad and
let the rest of the paper go with the wind. Then he bought
himself a warm package of peanuts.

# Newsreel 2

*Come on and hear*
*Come on and hear*
*Come on and hear*

In his address to the Michigan State Legislature the retiring governor, Hazen S. Pingree, said in part: I make the prediction that unless those in charge and in whose hands legislation is reposed do not change the present system of inequality, there will be a bloody revolution in less than a quarter of a century in this great country of ours.

### CARNEGIE TALKS OF HIS EPITAPH

*Alexander's Ragtime Band*
*It is the best*
*It is the best*

the luncheon which was served in the physical laboratory was replete with novel features. A miniature blastfurnace four feet high was on the banquet table and a narrowgauge railroad forty feet long ran round the edge of the table. Instead of molten metal the blastfurnace poured hot punch into small cars on the railroad. Icecream was served in the shape of railroad ties and bread took the shape of locomotives.

Mr Carnegie, while extolling the advantages of higher education in every branch of learning, came at last to this conclusion: Manual labor has been found to be the best foundation for the greatest work of the brain.

### VICE-PRESIDENT EMPTIES A BANK

*Come on and hear*
*Alexander's Ragtime Band*
*It is the best*
*It is the best*

brother of Jesse James declares play picturing him as bandit trainrobber and outlaw is demoralizing district battle ends with polygamy, according to an investigation by Salt Lake ministers, still practiced by Mormons clubwomen gasp

*It is the best band in the land*

say circus animals only eat Chicago horsemeat Taxsale of Indiana marks finale of World's Fair boom uses flag as ragbag killed on cannibal isle keeper falls into water and sealions attack him.

The launch then came alongside the halfdeflated balloon of the aerostat which threatened at any moment to smother Santos Dumont. The latter was half pulled and half clambered over the gunwale into the boat.

The Prince of Monaco urged him to allow himself to be taken on board the yacht to dry himself and change his clothes. Santos Dumont would not leave the launch until everything that could be saved had been taken ashore, then, wet but smiling and unconcerned, he landed amid the frenzied cheers of the crowd.

## The Camera Eye (3)

O qu'il a des beaux yeux said the lady in the seat opposite but She said that was no way to talk to children and the little boy felt all hot and sticky but it was dusk and the lamp shaped like half a melon was coming on dim red and the train rumbled and suddenly I've been asleep and it's black dark and the blue tassel bobs on the edge of the dark shade shaped like a melon and everywhere there are pointed curved shadows (the first time He came He brought a melon and the sun was coming in through the tall lace window-curtains and when we cut it the smell of melons filled the whole room) No don't eat the seeds deary they give you appendicitis

but you're peeking out of the window into the black

rumbling dark suddenly ranked with squat chimneys and you're scared of the black smoke and the puffs of flame that flare and fade out of the squat chimneys     Potteries dearie they work there all night Who works there all night? Workingmen and people like that laborers travailleurs greasers

you were scared

but now the dark was all black again the lamp in the train and the sky and everything had a blueback shade on it and She was telling a story about

Longago Beforetheworldsfair Beforeyouwereborn and they went to Mexico on a private car on the new international line and the men shot antelope off the back of the train and big rabbits jackasses they called them and once one night Longago Beforetheworldsfair Beforeyouwereborn one night Mother was so frightened on account of all the rifleshots but it was allright turned out to be nothing but a little shooting they'd been only shooting a greaser that was all

that was in the early days

## Lover of Mankind

Debs was a railroadman, born in a weatherboarded shack at Terre Haute.

He was one of ten children.

His father had come to America in a sailingship in '49,

an Alsatian from Colmar; not much of a moneymaker, fond of music and reading,

he gave his children a chance to finish public school and that was about all he could do.

At fifteen Gene Debs was already working as a machinist on the Indianapolis and Terre Haute Railway.

He worked as a locomotive fireman,

clerked in a store

joined the local of the Brotherhood of Locomotive Firemen, was elected secretary, traveled all over the country as organizer.

He was a tall shamblefooted man, had a sort of gusty rhetoric that set on fire the railroad workers in their pineboarded halls

made them want the world he wanted,
a world brothers might own
where everybody would split even:
*I am not a labor leader. I don't want you to follow me or
anyone else. If you are looking for a Moses to lead you out of
the capitalist wilderness you will stay right where you are. I
would not lead you into this promised land if I could, because
if I could lead you in, someone else would lead you out.*

That was how he talked to freighthandlers and gandywalkers, to firemen and switchmen and engineers, telling them
it wasn't enough to organize the railroadmen, that all workers
must be organized, that all workers must be organized in the
workers' co-operative commonwealth.

Locomotive fireman on many a long night's run,
under the smoke a fire burned him up, burned in gusty
words that beat in pineboarded halls; he wanted his brothers to
be free men.

That was what he saw in the crowd that met him at the Old
Wells Street Depot when he came out of jail after the Pullman
strike,
those were the men that chalked up nine hundred thousand
votes for him in nineteen-twelve and scared the frockcoats
and the tophats and diamonded hostesses at Saratoga Springs,
Bar Harbor, Lake Geneva with the bogy of a Socialist
president.

But where were Gene Debs's brothers in nineteen eighteen
when Woodrow Wilson had him locked up in Atlanta for
speaking against war,
where were the big men fond of whiskey and fond of each
other, gentle rambling tellers of stories over bars in small towns
in the Middle West,
quiet men who wanted a house with a porch to putter
around and a fat wife to cook for them, a few drinks and cigars,
a garden to dig in, cronies to chew the rag with
and wanted to work for it
and others to work for it;
where were the locomotive firemen and engineers when
they hustled him off to Atlanta Penitentiary?

And they brought him back to die in Terre Haute
to sit on his porch in a rocker with a cigar in his mouth,
beside him American Beauty roses his wife fixed in a bowl;
and the people of Terre Haute and the people in Indiana

and the people of the Middle West were fond of him and afraid of him and thought of him as an old kindly uncle who loved them, and wanted to be with him and to have him give them candy,

but they were afraid of him as if he had contracted a social disease, syphilis or leprosy, and thought it was too bad,

but on account of the flag
and prosperity
and making the world safe for democracy,

they were afraid to be with him,

or to think much about him for fear they might believe him;

for he said:

*While there is a lower class I am of it, while there is a criminal class I am of it, while there is a soul in prison I am not free.*


## The Camera Eye (4)

riding backwards through the rain in the rumbly cab looking at their two faces in the jiggly light of the four-wheeled cab and Her big trunks thumping on the roof and He reciting *Othello* in his lawyer's voice

> *Her father loved me, oft invited me*
> *Still questioned me the story of my life*
> *From year to year, the battles, sieges, fortunes*
> *That I have past.*
> *I ran it through, even from my boyish days,*
> *To th' very moment that he bade me tell it*
> *Wherein I spoke of the most disastrous chances*
> *Of moving accidents by flood and field*
> *Of hairbreadth 'scapes i' th' imminent deadly breach*

why that's the Schuylkill        the horse's hoofs rattle sharp on smooth wet asphalt after cobbles        through the gray streaks of rain the river shimmers ruddy with winter mud        When I was your age Jack I dove off this bridge through the rail of the bridge we can look way down into the cold rainyshimmery water        Did you have any clothes on?        Just my shirt

## *Mac*

Fainy stood near the door in the crowded elevated train; against the back of the fat man who held on to the strap in front of him, he kept rereading a letter on crisp watermarked stationery:

The Truthseeker Literary Distributing Co., Inc.
General Offices 1104 S. Hamlin Avenue
Chicago, Ill. April 14, 1904

Fenian O'H. McCreary
456 N. Wood Street
Chicago, Ill.
DEAR SIR,
We take the pleasure to acknowledge yours of the 10th inst.

In reference to the matter in hand we feel that much could be gained by a personal interview. If you will be so good as to step around to the above address on Monday April 16th at nine o'clock, we feel that the matter of your adaptability for the position for which you have applied can be thoroughly thrashed out.

Yours in search for Truth,
EMMANUEL R. BINGHAM, D.D.

Fainy was scared. The train got to his station too soon. He had fifteen minutes to walk two blocks in. He loafed along the street, looking in store windows. There was a golden pheasant, stuffed, in a taxidermist's; above it hung a big flat greenish fish with a sawtoothed bill from which dangled a label:

SAWFISH (*pristis perrotetti*)

*Habitat Gulf and Florida waters. Frequents shallow bays and inlets.*

Maybe he wouldn't go at all. In the back of the window was a lynx and on the other side a bobtailed cat, each on its limb of a tree. Suddenly he caught his breath. He'd be late. He went tearing off down the block.

He was breathless and his heart was pounding to beat the cars when he reached the top of the fourth flight of stairs. He studied the groundglass doors on the landing;

THE UNIVERSAL CONTACT COMPANY

F. W. Perkins

*Assurance*

THE WINDY CITY MAGIC AND NOVELTY COMPANY

### Dr Noble

*Hospital and Sickroom Supplies*

The last one was a grimy door in the back beside the toilet. The gold-leaf had come off the letters, but he was able to spell out from the outlines:

THE GENERAL OUTFITTING AND MERCHANDIZING
CORPORATION

Then he saw a card on the wall beside the door with a hand holding a torch drawn out on it and under it the words 'Truth-seeker Inc.' He tapped gingerly on the glass. No answer. He tapped again.

'Come in . . . Don't knock,' called out a deep voice. Fainy found himself stuttering as he opened the door and stepped into a dark, narrow room completely filled up by two huge rolltop desks:

'Please, I called to see Mr Bingham, sir.'

At the further desk, in front of the single window sat a big man with a big drooping jaw that gave him a little of the expression of a setter dog. His black hair was long and curled a little over each ear, on the back of his head was a broad black felt hat. He leaned back in his chair and looked Fainy up and down.

'How do you do, young man? What kind of books are you inclined to purchase this morning? What can I do for you this morning?' he boomed.

'Are you Mr Bingham, sir, please?'

'This is Doc Bingham right here before you.'

'Please, sir, I . . . I came about that job.'

Doc Bingham's expression changed. He twisted his mouth as if he'd just tasted something sour. He spun around in his swivelchair and spat into a brass spittoon in the corner of the room. Then he turned to Fainy again and leveled a fat finger at him, 'Young man, how do you spell experience?'

'E . . . x . . . p . . . er . . . er . . . er . . . i . . . a . . . n . . .'

'That'll do . . . No education . . . I thought as much . . . No culture, none of those finer feelings that distinguish the civilized man from the savage aborigines of the wilds . . . No enthusiasm for truth, for bringing light into dark places . . . Do you realize, young man, that it is not a job I'm offering you, it

is a great opportunity . . . a splendid opportunity for service
and self-improvement. I'm offering you an education gratis.'

Fainy shuffled his feet. He had a husk in his throat.

'If it's in the printin' line I guess I could do it.'

'Well, young man, during the brief interrogatory through
which I'm going to put you, remember that you stand on the
threshold of opportunity.'

Doc Bingham ferreted in the pigeonholes of his desk for a
long time, found himself a cigar, bit off the end, lit it, and then
turned again to Fainy, who was standing first on one foot and
then on the other.

'Well, if you'll tell me your name.'

'Fenian O'Hara McCreary . . .'

'Hum . . . Scotch and Irish . . . that's pretty good stock . . .
that's the stock I come from.'

'Religion?'

Fainy squirmed. 'Pop was a Catholic but . . .' He turned red.

Dr Bingham laughed, and rubbed his hands.

'Oh, religion, what crimes are committed in thy name. I'm an
agnostic myself . . . caring nothing for class or creed when
among friends; though sometimes, my boy, you have to bow
with the wind . . . No, sir, my God is the truth, that rising ever
higher in the hands of honest men will dispel the mists of ignorance and greed, and bring freedom and knowledge to mankind . . . Do you agree with me?'

'I've been working for my uncle. He's a social-democrat.'

'Ah, hotheaded youth . . . Can you drive a horse?'

'Why, yessir, I guess I could.'

'Well, I don't see why I shouldn't hire you.'

'The advertisement in the *Tribune* said fifteen dollars a week.'

Doc Bingham's voice assumed a particularly velvety tone.

'Why, Fenian, my boy, fifteen dollars a week will be the
minimum you will make . . . Have you ever heard of the co-
operative system? That is how I'm going to hire you . . . As
sole owner and representative of the Truthseeker Corporation,
I have here a magnificent line of small books and pamphlets
covering every phase of human knowledge and endeavor . . . I
am embarking immediately on a sales campaign to cover the
whole country. You will be one of my distributors. The books
sell at from ten to fifty cents. On each ten-cent book you make
a cent, on the fifty-cent books you make five cents . . .'

'And don't I get anything every week?' stammered Fainy.

'Would you be penny-wise and pound-foolish? Throwing

away the most magnificent opportunity of a lifetime for the
assurance of a paltry pittance. No, I can see by your flaming
eye, by your rebellious name out of old Ireland's history, that
you are a young man of spirit and determination . . . Are we
on? Shake hands on it then and by gad, Fenian, you shall never
regret it.'

Doc Bingham jumped to his feet and seized Fainy's hand
and shook it.

'Now, Fenian, come with me; we have an important preliminary errand to perform.' Doc Bingham pulled his hat forward on his head and they walked down the stairs to the front
door; he was a big man and the fat hung loosely on him as he
walked. Anyway, it's a job, Fainy told himself.

First they went to a tailorshop where a longnosed yellow
man whom Doc Bingham addressed as Lee shuffled out to meet
them. The tailorshop smelt of steamed cloth and cleansing
fluid. Lee talked as if he had no palate to his mouth.

' 'M pretty sick man,' he said. 'Spen' mor'n thou'an' dollarm
on doctor, no get well.'

'Well, I'll stand by you; you know that, Lee.'

'Hure, Mannie, hure, only you owe me too much money.'

Doctor Emmanuel Bingham glanced at Fainy out of the
corner of his eye.

'I can assure you that the entire financial situation will be
clarified within sixty days . . . But what I want you to do now
is to lend me two of your big cartons, those cardboard boxes
you send suits home in.'

'What you wan' to do?'

'My young friend and I have a little project.'

'Don't you do nothin' crooked with them cartons; my name's
on them.'

Doc Bingham laughed heartily as they walked out the door,
carrying under each arm one of the big flat cartons that had
LEVY AND GOLDSTEIN, RELIABLE TAILORING, written
on them in florid lettering.

'He's a great joker, Fenian,' he said. 'But let that man's
lamentable condition be a lesson to you . . . The poor unfortunate is suffering from the consequences of a horrible social
disease, contracted through some youthful folly.'

They were passing the taxidermist's store again. There were
the wildcats and the golden pheasant and the big sawfish . . . *Frequents shallow bays and inlets.* Fainy had a temptation to drop
the tailor's cartons and run for it. But anyhow, it was a job.

'Fenian,' said Doc Bingham confidentially, 'do you know the Mohawk House?'

'Yessir, we used to do their printing for them.'

'They don't know you there, do they?'

'Naw, they wouldn't know me from Adam . . . I just delivered some writin' paper there once.'

'That's superb . . . Now get this right; my room is 303. You wait and come in about five minutes. You're the boy from the tailor's, see, getting some suits to be cleaned. Then you come up to my room and get the suits and take 'em round to my office. If anybody asks you where you're goin' with 'em, you're goin' to Levy and Goldstein, see?'

Fainy drew a deep breath.

'Sure, I get you.'

When he reached the small room in the top of the Mohawk House, Doc Bingham was pacing the floor.

'Levy and Goldstein, sir,' said Fainy, keeping his face straight.

'My boy,' said Doc Bingham, 'you'll be an able assistant; I'm glad I picked you out. I'll give you a dollar in advance on your wages.' While he talked he was taking clothes, papers, old books, out of a big trunk that stood in the middle of the floor. He packed them carefully in one of the cartons. In the other he put a furlined overcoat. 'That coat cost two hundred dollars, Fenian, a remnant of former splendors . . . Ah, the autumn leaves at Vallombrosa . . . Et tu in Arcadia vixisti . . . That's Latin, a language of scholars.'

'My Uncle Tim who ran the printing shop where I worked knew Latin fine.'

'Do you think you can carry these, Fenian . . . they're not too heavy?'

'Sure I can carry 'em.' Fainy wanted to ask about the dollar.

'All right, you'd better run along . . . Wait for me at the office.'

In the office Fainy found a man sitting at the second rolltop desk. 'Vell, what's your business?' he yelled out in a rasping voice. He was a sharpnosed waxyskinned young man with straight black hair standing straight up. Fainy was winded from running up the stairs. His arms were stiff from carrying the heavy cartons. 'I suppose this is some more of Mannie's tomfoolishness. Tell him he's got to clear out of here; I've rented the other desk.'

'But Doctor Bingham has just hired me to work for the Truthseeker Literary Distributing Company.'

'The hell he has.'

'He'll be here in a minute.'

'Well, sit down and shut up; can't you see I'm busy?'

Fainy sat down glumly in the swivelchair by the window, the only chair in the office not piled high with small papercovered books. Outside the window he could see a few dusty roofs and fire escapes. Through grimy windows he could see other offices, other rolltop desks. On the desk in front of him were paperwrapped packages of books. Between them were masses of loose booklets. His eye caught a title:

### THE QUEEN OF THE WHITE SLAVES

*Scandalous revelations of Milly Meecham stolen from her parents at the age of sixteen, tricked by her vile seducer into a life of infamy and shame.*

He started reading the book. His tongue got dry and he felt sticky all over.

'Nobody said anything to you, eh?' Doc Bingham's booming voice broke in on his reading.

Before he could answer, the voice of the man at the other desk snarled out: 'Look here, Mannie, you've got to clear out of here . . . I've rented the desk.'

'Shake not thy gory locks at me, Samuel Epstein. My young friend and I are just preparing an expedition among the aborigines of darkest Michigan. We are leaving for Saginaw tonight. Within sixty days I'll come back and take the office off your hands. This young man is coming with me to learn the business.'

'Business, hell,' growled the other man, and shoved his face back down among his papers again.

'Procrastination, Fenian, is the thief of time,' said Doc Bingham, putting one fat hand Napoleonfashion into his doublebreasted vest. 'There is a tide in the affairs of men that taken at its full . . .' And for two hours Fainy sweated under his direction, packing booklets into brown paper packages, tying them and addressing them to Truthseeker Inc., Saginaw, Mich.

He begged off for an hour to go home to see his folks. Milly kissed him on the forehead with thin tight lips. Then she burst out crying. 'You're lucky; oh, I wish I was a boy,' she spluttered and ran upstairs. Mrs O'Hara said to be a good boy and always live at the Y.M.C.A. – that kept a boy out of temptation, and to let his Uncle Tim be a lesson to him, with his boozin' ways.

His throat was pretty tight when he went to look for his Uncle Tim. He found him in the back room at O'Grady's. His eyes were a flat bright blue and his lower lip trembled when he spoke, 'Have one drink with me, son, you're on your own now.' Fainy drank down a beer without tasting it.

'Fainy, you're a bright boy . . . I wish I could have helped you more; you're an O'Hara every inch of you. You read Marx . . . study all you can, remember that you're a rebel by birth and blood . . . Don't blame people for things . . . Look at that terrible forktongued virago I'm married to; do I blame her? No, I blame the system. And don't ever sell out to the sonsofbitches, son; it's women'll make you sell out every time. You know what I mean. All right, go on . . . better cut along or you'll miss your train.'

'I'll write you from Saginaw, Uncle Tim, honest, I will.'

Uncle Tim's lanky red face in the empty cigarsmoky room, the bar and its glint of brass and the pinkarmed barkeep leaning across it, the bottles and the mirrors and the portrait of Lincoln gave a misty half turn in his head and he was out in the shiny rainy street under the shiny clouds, hurrying for the Elevated station with his suitcase in his hand.

At the Illinois Central station he found Doc Bingham waiting for him, in the middle of a ring of brown paper parcels. Fen felt a little funny inside when he saw him, the greasy sallow jowls, the doublebreasted vest, the baggy black ministerial coat, the dusty black felt hat that made the hair stick out in a sudden fuzzycurl over the beefy ears. Anyway, it was a job.

'It must be admitted, Fenian,' began Doc Bingham as soon as Fainy had come up to him, 'that confident as I am of my knowledge of human nature I was a little afraid you wouldn't turn up. Where is it that the poet says that difficult is the first fluttering course of the fledgeling from the nest. Put these packages on the train while I go purchase tickets, and be sure it's a smoker.'

After the train had started and the conductor had punched the tickets, Doc Bingham leaned over and tapped Fainy on the knee with a chubby forefinger. 'I'm glad you're a neat dresser, my boy; you must never forget the importance of putting up a fine front to the world. Though the heart be as dust and ashes, yet must the outer man be sprightly and of good cheer. We will go sit for a while in the Pullman smoker up ahead to get away from the yokels.'

It was raining hard and the windows of the train were striped with transverse beaded streaks against the darkness. Fainy felt uneasy as he followed Doc Bingham lurching through the green-plush parlor car to the small leather upholstered smoking-compartment at the end. There Doc Bingham drew a large cigar from his pocket and began blowing a magnificent series of smoke rings. Fainy sat beside him with his feet under the seat trying to take up as little room as possible.

Gradually the compartment filled up with silent men and crinkly spiraling cigarsmoke. Outside the rain beat against the windows with a gravelly sound. For a long time nobody said anything. Occasionally a man cleared his throat and let fly towards the cuspidor with a big gob of phlegm or a jet of tobaccojuice.

'Well, sir,' a voice began, coming from nowhere in particular, addressed to nowhere in particular, 'it was a great old inauguration even if we did freeze to death.'

'Were you in Washington?'

'Yessir, I was in Washington.'

'Most of the trains didn't get in till the next day.'

'I know it; I was lucky, there was some of them snowed up for fortyeight hours.'

'Some blizzard all right.'

> All day the gusty northwind bore
> The lessening drift its breath before
> Low circling through its southern zone
> The sun through dazzling snowmist shone,

recited Doc Bingham coyly, with downcast eyes.

'You must have a good memory to be able to recite verses right off the reel like that.'

'Yessir, I have a memory that may I think, without undue violation of modesty, be called compendious. Were it a natural gift I should be forced to blush and remain silent, but since it is the result of forty years of study of what is best in the world's epic lyric and dramatic literatures, I feel that to call attention to it may sometimes encourage some other whose feet are also bound on the paths of enlightenment and selfeducation.' He turned suddenly to Fainy. 'Young man, would you like to hear Othello's address to the Venetian Senate?'

'Sure I would,' said Fainy, blushing.

'Well, at last Teddy has a chance to carry out his word about fighting the trusts.' 'I'm telling you the insurgent farmer vote of the great Northwest . . .' 'Terrible thing the wreck of those inauguration specials.'

But Doc Bingham was off:

> *Most potent grave and reverend signiors,*
> *My very noble and approved good masters,*
> *That I have ta'en away this old man's daughter*
> *It is most true; true, I have married her . . .*

'They won't get away with those antitrust laws, believe me they won't. You can't curtail the liberty of the individual liberty in that way.' 'It's the liberty of the individual business man that the progressive wing of the Republican party is trying to protect.'

But Doc Bingham was on his feet, one hand was tucked into his doublebreasted vest, with the other he was making broad circular gestures:

> *Rude am I in speech*
> *And little blessed with the soft phrase of peace,*
> *For since these arms of mine had seven years' pith*
> *Till now some nine moons wasted they have used*
> *Their dearest action in the tented field.*

'The farmer vote,' the other man began shrilly, but nobody was listening. Doc Bingham had the floor.

> *And little of the great world can I speak*
> *More than pertains to broils and battle*
> *And therefore little shall I grace my cause*
> *In speaking for myself.*

The train began to slacken speed. Doc Bingham's voice sounded oddly loud in the lessened noise. Fainy felt his back pushing into the back of the seat and then suddenly there was stillness and the sound of an engine bell in the distance and Doc Bingham's voice in a queasy whisper:

'Gentlemen, I have here in pamphlet form a complete and unexpurgated edition of one of the world's classics, the famous *Decameron* of Boccaccio, that for four centuries has been a byword for spicy wit and ribald humor . . .' He took a bundle of little books out of one of his sagging pockets and began dandling them in his hand. 'Just as an act of friendship I would be willing to part with some if any of you gentlemen care for them . . . Here, Fenian, take these and see if anybody wants one; they're two dollars apiece. My young friend here will attend to distribution . . . Goodnight, gentlemen.' And he went off and the train had started again and Fainy found himself standing with the little books in his hand in the middle of the lurching car with the suspicious eyes of all the smokers boring into him like so many gimlets.

'Let's see one,' said a little man with protruding ears who sat in the corner. He opened the book and started reading greedily. Fainy stood in the center of the car, feeling pins and needles all over. He caught a white glint in the corner of an eyeball as the little man looked down the line of cigars through the crinkly smoke. A touch of pink came into the protruding ears.

'Hot stuff,' said the little man, 'but two dollars is too much.'

Fainy found himself stuttering: 'They're nnnot mmmine, sir; I don't know . . .'

'Oh, well, what the hell . . .' The little man dropped two dollar bills in Fainy's hand and went back to his reading. Fainy had six dollars in his pocket and two books left when he started back to the daycoach. Halfway down the car he met the conductor. His heart almost stopped beating. The conductor looked at him sharply but said nothing.

Doc Bingham was sitting in his seat with his head in his hand and his eyes closed as if he were dozing. Fainy slipped into the seat beside him.

'How many did they take?' asked Doc Bingham, talking out of the corner of his mouth without opening his eyes.

'I got six bucks . . . Golly, the conductor scared me, the way he looked at me.'

'You leave the conductor to me, and remember that it's never a crime in the face of humanity and enlightenment to distribute the works of the great humanists among the merchants and moneychangers of this godforsaken country . . . You better slip me the dough.'

Fainy wanted to ask about the dollar he'd been promised, but Doc Bingham was off on Othello again.

> *If after every tempest the·e come such calms as this*
> *Then may the laboring bark climb hills of seas*
> *Olympus high.*

They slept late at the Commercial House in Saginaw, and ate a large breakfast, during which Doc Bingham discoursed on the theory and practice of book salesmanship. 'I am very much afraid that through the hinterland to which we are about to penetrate,' he said as he cut up three fried eggs and stuffed his mouth with bakingpowder biscuit, 'that we will find the yokels still hankering after Maria Monk.'

Fainy didn't know who Maria Monk was, but he didn't like to ask. He went with Doc Bingham round to Hummer's livery stable to hire a horse and wagon. There followed a long wrangle between the firm of Truthseeker Inc., and the management of Hummer's Livery Stable as to the rent of a springwagon and an elderly piebald horse with cruppers you could hang a hat on, so that it was late afternoon before they drove out of Saginaw with their packages of books piled behind them, bound for the road.

It was a chilly spring day. Sagging clouds moved in a gray blur over a bluish silvery sky. The piebald kept slackening to a walk; Fainy clacked the reins continually on his caving rump and clucked with his tongue until his mouth was dry. At the first whack the piebald would go into a lope that would immediately degenerate into an irregular jogtrot and then into a walk. Fainy cursed and clucked, but he couldn't get the horse to stay in the lope or the jogtrot. Meanwhile Doc Bingham sat beside him with his broad hat on the back of his head, smoking a cigar and discoursing: 'Let me say right now, Fenian, that the attitude of a man of enlightened ideas, is, *A plague on both your houses* . . . I myself am a pantheist . . . but even a pantheist . . . must eat, hence Maria Monk.' A few drops of rain, icy and stinging as hail, had begun to drive in their faces. 'I'll get pneumonia at this rate, and it'll be your fault, too; I thought you said you could drive a horse . . . Here, drive into that farmhouse on the left. Maybe they'll let us put the horse and wagon in their barn.'

As they drove up the lane towards the gray house and the big gray barn that stood under a clump of pines a little off from the road, the piebald slowed to a walk and began reaching for the bright green clumps of grass at the edge of the ditch. Fainy beat at him with the ends of the reins, and even stuck his foot over the dashboard and kicked him, but he wouldn't budge.

'Goddam it, give me the reins.'

Doc Bingham gave the horse's head a terrible yank, but all that happened was that he turned his head and looked at them, a green foam of partly chewed grass between his long yellow teeth. To Fainy it looked as if he were laughing. The rain had come on hard. They put their coat collars up. Fainy soon had a little icy trickle down the back of his neck.

'Get out and walk; goddam it to hell, lead it if you can't drive it,' sputtered Doc Bingham. Fainy jumped out and led the horse up to the back door of the farmhouse; the rain ran down his sleeve from the hand he held the horse by.

'Good afternoon, ma'am.' Doc Bingham was on his feet bowing to a little old woman who had come out of the door. He stood beside her on the stoop out of the rain. 'Do you mind if I put my horse and wagon in your barn for a few moments? I have valuable perishable materials in the wagon and no waterproof covering . . .' The old woman nodded a stringy white head. 'Well, that's very kind of you, I must say . . . All right, Fenian, put the horse in the barn and come here and bring in that little package under the seat . . . I was just saying to my young friend here that I was sure that some good samaritan lived in this house who would take in two weary wayfarers.' 'Come inside, mister . . . maybe you'd like to set beside the stove and dry yourself. Come inside, mister-er?' 'Doc Bingham's the name . . . the Reverend Doctor Bingham,' Fainy heard him say as he went in the house.

He was soaked and shivering when he went into the house himself, carrying a package of books under his arm. Doc Bingham was sitting large as life in a rocking chair in front of the kitchen stove. Beside him on the well-scrubbed deal table was a piece of pie and a cup of coffee. The kitchen had a warm cosy smell of apples and bacon grease and lamps. The old woman was leaning over the kitchen table listening intently to what Doc Bingham was saying. Another woman, a big scrawny woman with her scant sandy hair done up in a screw on top of her head, stood in the background with her redknuckled hands on her hips. A black and white cat, back arched and tail in the air, was rubbing against Doc Bingham's legs.

'Ah, Fenian, just in time,' he began in a voice that purred like the cat, 'I was just telling . . . relating to your kind hostesses the contents of our very interesting and educational library, the prime of the world's devotional and inspirational literature. They have been so kind to us during our little misfortune with the weather that I thought it would be only fair to let them see a few of our titles.'

The big woman was twisting her apron. 'I like a mite o' readin' fine,' she said, shyly, 'but I don't get much chanct for it. not till wintertime.'

Benignly smiling, Doc Bingham untied the string and pulled the package open on his knees. A booklet dropped to the floor. Fainy saw that it was *The Queen of the White Slaves*. A shade of sourness went over Doc Bingham's face. He put his foot on the dropped book. 'These are Gospel Talks, my boy,' he said.

'I wanted *Doctor Spikenard's Short Sermons for All Occasions.*'
He handed the halfopen package to Fainy, who snatched it to
him. Then he stooped and picked the book up from under his
foot with a slow sweeping gesture of the hand and slipped it
in his pocket. 'I suppose I'll have to go and find them myself,'
he went on in his purringest voice. When the kitchen door
closed behind them he snarled in Fainy's ear, 'Under the seat,
you little rat . . . If you play a trick like that again I'll break
every goddam bone in your body.' And he brought his knee
up so hard into the seat of Fainy's pants that his teeth clacked
together and he shot out into the rain towards the barn. 'Honest,
I didn't do it on purpose,' Fainy whined. But Doc Bingham
was already back in the house and his voice was burbling
comfortably out into the rainy dusk with the first streak of
lamplight.

This time Fainy was careful to open the package before he
brought it in. Doc Bingham took the books out of his hand
without looking at him and Fainy went round behind the stovepipe. He stood there in the soggy steam of his clothes listening
to Doc Bingham boom. He was hungry, but nobody seemed
to think of offering him a piece of pie.

'Ah, my dear friends, how can I tell you with what gratitude
to the Great Giver a lonely minister of the gospel of light,
wandering among the tares and troubles of this world, finds
ready listeners. I'm sure that these little books will be consol-
ing, interesting and inspirational to all that undertake the slight
effort of perusal. I feel this so strongly that I always carry a few
extra copies with me to dispose of for a moderate sum. It
breaks my heart that I can't yet give them away free gratis.'

'How much are they?' asked the old woman, a sudden sharp-
ness coming over her features. The scrawny woman let her
arms drop to her side and shook her head.

'Do you remember, Fenian,' asked Doc Bingham, leaning
genially back in his chair, 'what the cost price of these little
booklets was?' Fainy was sore. He didn't answer. 'Come here,
Fenian,' said Doc Bingham in honied tones, 'allow me to
remind you of the words of the immortal bard:

> *Lowliness is your ambition's ladder*
> *Whereto the climber upward turns his face*
> *But when he once attains the topmost round*
> *He then unto the ladder turns his back*

'You must be hungry. You can eat my pie.'

'I reckon we can find the boy a piece of pie,' said the old woman.

'Ain't they ten cents?' said Fainy, coming forward.

'Oh, if they're only ten cents I think I'd like one,' said the old woman quickly. The scrawny woman started to say something, but it was too late.

The pie had hardly disappeared into Fainy's gullet and the bright dime out of the old tobaccobox in the cupboard into Doc Bingham's vest pocket when there was a sound of clinking harness and the glint of a buggylamp through the rainy dark outside the window. The old woman got to her feet and looked nervously at the door, which immediately opened. A heavyset grayhaired man with a small goatee sprouting out of a round red face came in, shaking the rain off the flaps of his coat. After him came a skinny lad about Fainy's age.

'How do you do, sir; how do you do, son?' boomed Doc Bingham through the last of his pie and coffee.

'They asked if they could put their horse in the barn until it should stop rainin'. It's all right, ain't it, James?' asked the old woman nervously. 'I reckon so.' said the older man, sitting down heavily in the free chair. The old woman had hidden the pamphlet in the drawer of the kitchen table: 'Travelin' in books, I gather.' He stared hard at the open package of pamphlets. 'Well, we don't need any of that trash here, but you're welcome to stay the night in the barn. This is no night to throw a human being out inter.'

So they unhitched the horse and made beds for themselves in the hay over the cowstable. Before they left the house the older man made them give up their matches. 'Where there's matches there's danger of fire,' he said. Doc Bingham's face was black as thunder as he wrapped himself in a horseblanket, muttering about 'indignity to a wearer of the cloth.' Fainy was excited and happy. He lay on his back listening to the beat of the rain on the roof and its gurgle in the gutters, and the muffled stirring and champing of the cattle and horse, under them; his nose was full of the smell of the hay and the warm meadowsweetness of the cows. He wasn't sleepy. He wished he had someone his own age to talk to. Anyway, it was a job and he was on the road.

He had barely got to sleep when a light woke him. The boy he'd seen in the kitchen was standing over him with a lantern. His shadow hovered over them enormous against the rafters.

'Say, I wanner buy a book.'

'What kind of book?' Fainy yawned and sat up.

'You know . . . one o' them books about chorusgirls an' white slaves an' stuff like that.'

'How much do you want to pay, son?' came Doc Bingham's voice from under the horseblanket. 'We have a number of very interesting books stating the facts of life frankly and freely, describing the deplorable licentiousness of life in the big cities, ranging from a dollar to five dollars. *The Complete Sexology of Doctor Burnside*, is six-fifty.'

'I couldn't go higher'n a dollar . . . Say, you won't tell the ole man on me?' the young man said, turning from one to another. 'Seth Hardwick, he lives down the road, he went into Saginaw once an' got a book from a man at the hotel. Gosh, it was a pippin.' He tittered uneasily.

'Fenian, go down and get him *The Queen of the White Slaves* for a dollar,' said Doc Bingham, and settled back to sleep.

Fainy and the farmer's boy went down the rickety ladder.

'Say, is she pretty spicy? . . . Gosh, if pop finds it he'll give me a whalin' . . . Gosh, I bet you've read all them books.'

'Me?' said Fainy haughtily. 'I don't need to read books. I kin see life if I wanter. Here it is . . . it's about fallen women.'

'Ain't that pretty short for a dollar? I thought you could get a big book for a dollar.'

'This one's pretty spicy.'

'Well, I guess I'll take it before dad ketches me snoopin' around . . . Goodnight.' Fainy went back to his bed in the hay and fell fast asleep. He was dreaming that he was going up a rickety stair in a barn with his sister Milly who kept getting all the time bigger and white and fatter, and had on a big hat with ostrich plumes all round it and her dress began to split from the neck and lower and lower and Doc Bingham's voice was saying She's Maria Monk, the queen of the white slaves, and just as he was going to grab her, sunlight opened his eyes. Doc Bingham stood in front of him, his feet wide apart, combing his hair with a pocketcomb and reciting:

> Let us depart, the universal sun
> Confines not to one land his blessed beams
> Nor is man rooted like a tree . . .

'Come, Fenian,' he boomed, when he saw that Fainy was awake, 'let us shake the dust of this inhospitable farm, latcheting our shoes with a curse like philosophers of old . . . Hitch up the horse; we'll get breakfast down the road.'

This went on for several weeks until one evening they found themselves driving up to a neat yellow house in a grove of feathery dark tamaracks. Fainy waited in the wagon while Doc Bingham interviewed the people in the house. After a while Doc Bingham appeared in the door, a broad smile creasing his cheeks. 'We're going to be very handsomely treated, Fenian, as befits a wearer of the cloth and all that . . . You be careful how you talk, will you? Take the horse to the barn and unhitch.'

'Say, Mr Bingham, how about my money? It's three weeks now.' Fainy jumped down and went to the horse's head.

An expression of gloom passed over Doc Bingham's face. 'Oh, lucre, lucre . . .

> *Examine well*
> *His milkwhite hand, the palm is hardly clean*
> *But here and there an ugly smutch appears,*
> *Foh, 'twas a bribe that left it. . . .*

'I had great plans for a co-operative enterprise that you are spoiling by your youthful haste and greed . . . but if you must I'll hand over to you this very night everything due you and more. All right, unhitch the horse and bring me that little package with *Maria Monk*, and *The Popish Plot*.'

It was a warm day. There were robins singing round the barn. Everything smelt of sweetgrass and flowers. The barn was red and the yard was full of white leghorns. After he had unhitched the springwagon and put the horse in a stall, Fainy sat on a rail of the fence looking out over the silvergreen field of oats out back, and smoked a cigarette. He wished there was a girl there he could put his arm round or a fellow to talk to.

A hand dropped onto his shoulder. Doc Bingham was standing beside him.

'Fenian, my young friend, we are in clover,' he said. 'She is alone in the house, and her husband has gone to town for two days with the hired man. There'll be nobody there but her two little children, sweet bairns. Perhaps I shall play Romeo. You've never seen me in love. It's my noblest role. Ah, some day I'll tell you about my headstrong youth. Come and meet the sweet charmer.'

When they went in the kitchen door a dimplefaced pudgy woman in a lavender housecap greeted them coyly.

'This is my young assistant, ma'am,' said Doc Bingham, with a noble gesture. 'Fenian, this is Mrs Kovach.'

'You must be hungry. We're having supper right away.'

The last of the sun lit up a kitchen range that was crowded with saucepans and stewpots. Fragrant steam rose in little jets from round wellpolished lids. As she spoke Mrs Kovach leaned over so that her big blue behind with starched apronstrings tied in a bow above it stood up straight in the air, opened the oven door and pulled out a great pan of cornmuffins that she dumped into a dish on the dining table already set next the window. Their warm toasted smoke filled the kitchen. Fainy felt his mouth watering. Doc Bingham was rubbing his hands and rolling his eyes. They sat down, and the two blue-eyed smearyfaced children were sat down and started gobbling silently, and Mrs Kovach heaped their plates with stewed tomatoes, mashed potatoes, beef stew and limabeans with pork. She poured them out coffee and then said with moist eyes, as she sat down herself:

'I love to see men eat.'

Her face took on a crushed-pansy look that made Fainy turn away his eyes when he found himself looking at it. After supper she sat listening with a pleased, frightened expression while Doc Bingham talked and talked, now and then stopping to lean back and blow a smoke ring at the lamp.

'While not myself a Lutheran as you might say, ma'am, I myself have always admired, nay, revered, the great figure of Martin Luther as one of the lightbringers of mankind. Were it not for him we would be still groveling under the dread domination of the Pope of Rome.'

'They'll never get into this country; land sakes, it gives me the creeps to think of it.'

'Not while there's a drop of red blood in the viens of freeborn Protestants . . . but the way to fight darkness, ma'am, is with light. Light comes from education, reading of books and studies . . .'

'Land sakes, it gives me a headache to read most books, an' I don't get much time, to tell the truth. My husband, he reads books he gets from the Department of Agriculture. He tried to make me read one once, on raisin' poultry, but I couldn't make much sense out of it. His folks they come from the old country . . . I guess people feels different over there.'

'It must be difficult being married to a foreigner like that.'

'Sometimes I don't know how I stand it; 'course he was awful goodlookin' when I married him . . . I never could resist a goodlookin' man.'

Doc Bingham leaned further across the table. His eyes rolled as if they were going to drop out.

'I never could resist a goodlooking lady.'

Mrs Kovach sighed deeply.

Fainy got up and went out. He'd been trying to get in a word about getting paid, but what was the use? Outside it was chilly; the stars were bright above the roofs of the barns and outhouses. From the chickencoop came an occasional sleepy cluck or the rustle of feathers as a hen lost her balance on her perch. He walked up and down the barnyard cursing Doc Bingham and kicking at an occasional clod of manure.

Later he looked into the lamplit kitchen. Doc Bingham had his arm around Mrs Kovach's waist and was declaiming verses, making big gestures with his free hand:

> ... These things to hear
> Would Desdemona seriously incline
> But still the house affairs would draw her hence
> Which ever as she could with haste dispatch
> She'd come again and with a greedy ear ...

Fainy shook his fist at the window. 'Goddam your hide. I want my money,' he said aloud. Then he went for a walk down the road. When he came back he was sleepy and chilly. The kitchen was empty and the lamp was turned down low. He didn't know where to go to sleep, so he settled down to warm himself in a chair beside the fire. His head began to nod and he fell asleep.

A tremendous thump on the floor above and a woman's shrieks woke him. His first thought was that Doc Bingham was robbing and murdering the woman. But immediately he heard another voice cursing and shouting in broken English. He had half gotten up from the chair, when Doc Bingham dashed past him. He had on only his flannel unionsuit. In one hand were his shoes, in the other his clothes. His trousers floated after him at the end of his suspenders like the tail of a kite.

'Hey, what are we going to do?' Fainy called after him, but got no answer. Instead he found himself face to face with a tall dark man with a scraggly black beard who was coolly fitting shells into a doublebarreled shotgun.

'Buckshot. I shoot the sonabitch.'

'Hey, you can't do that,' began Fainy. He got the butt of the shotgun in the chest and went crashing down into the chair again. The man strode out the door with a long elastic stride, and there followed two shots that went rattling among the farm buildings. Then the woman's shrieks started up again, punctuating a longdrawnout hysterical tittering and sobbing.

Fainy sat in the chair by the stove as if glued to it.

He noticed a fiftycent piece on the kitchen floor that must have dropped out of Doc Bingham's pants as he ran. He grabbed it and had just gotten it in his pocket when the tall man with the shotgun came back.

'No more shells,' he said thickly. Then he sat down on the kitchen table among the uncleared supper dishes and began to cry like a child, the tears trickling through the knobbed fingers of his big dark hands. Fainy stole out of the door and went to the barn. 'Doc Bingham,' he called gently. The harness lay in a heap between the shafts of the wagon, but there was no trace of Doc Bingham or of the piebald horse. The frightened clucking of the hens disturbed in the hencoop mixed with the woman's shrieks that still came from upstairs in the farmhouse. 'What the hell shall I do?' Fainy was asking himself when he caught sight of a tall figure outlined in the bright kitchen door and pointing the shotgun at him. Just as the shotgun blazed away he ducked into the barn and out through the back door. Buckshot whined over his head. 'Gosh, he found shells.' Fainy was off as fast as his legs could carry him across the oatfield. At last, without any breath in his body, he scrambled over a railfence full of briars that tore his face and hands and lay flat in a dry ditch to rest. There was nobody following him.

# Newsreel 3

'IT TAKES NERVE TO LIVE IN THIS WORLD'
LAST WORDS OF GEORGE SMITH HANGED WITH
HIS BROTHER BY MOB IN KANSAS  MARQUIS
OF QUEENSBERRY DEAD   FLAMES WRECK
SPICE PLANT  COURT SETS ZOLA FREE

a few years ago the anarchists of New Jersey, wearing the McKinley button and the red badge of anarchy on their coats and supplied with beer by the Republicans, plotted the death of one of the crowned heads of Europe and it is likely that the plan to assassinate the President was hatched at the same time or soon afterward.

*It's moonlight fair tonight upon the Wabash*
*From the fields there comes the breath of newmown hay*
*Through the sycamores the candlelight is gleaming*
*On the banks of the Wabash far away*

OUT FOR BULLY GOOD TIME

Six Thousand Workmen at Smolensk Parade with
Placards Saying Death to Czar Assassin

Riots and Streetblockades Mark Opening of
Teamsters Strike

WORLD'S GREATEST SEA BATTLE NEAR

Madrid Police Clash with Five Thousand Workmen Carrying Black Flag

Spectators Become Dizzy While Dancer Eats
Orange Breaking Record that Made Man Insane

## The Camera Eye (5)

and we played the battle of Port Arthur in the bathtub

and the water leaked down through the drawingroom ceiling and it was altogether too bad but in Kew Gardens old Mr Garnet who was still hale and hearty although so very old came to tea and we saw him first through the window with his red face and John Bull whiskers and aunty said it was a sailor's rolling gait and he was carrying a box under his arm and Vickie and Pompon barked and here was Mr Garnet come to tea and he took a gramophone out of a black box and put a cylinder on the gramophone and they pushed back the teathings off the corner of the table. Be careful not to drop it now they scratch rather heasy    Why a hordinary sewin' needle would do maam but I 'ave special needles

and we got to talking about Hadmiral Togo and the Banyan and how the Roosians drank so much vodka and killed all those poor fisherlads in the North Sea and he wound it up very carefully so as not to break the spring and the needle went rasp rasp    Yes I was a bluejacket miself miboy from the time I was a little shayver not much bigger'n you rose to be bosun's mite on the first British hironclad the *Warrior* and I can dance a 'ornpipe yet maam    and he had a mariner's compass in red and blue on the back of his hand and his nails looked black and thick as he fumbled with the needle and the needle went rasp rasp and far away a band played and out of a grindy noise in the little black horn came *God Save the King* and the little dogs howled

# Newsreel 4

*I met my love in the Alamo*
*When the moon was on the rise*
*Her beauty quite bedimmed its light*
*So radiant were her eyes*

during the forenoon union pickets turned back a wagon loaded with fifty campchairs on its way to the fire engine house at Michigan Avenue and Washington street. The chairs, it is reported, were ordered for the convenience of policemen detailed on strike duty

### FLEETS MAY MEET IN BATTLE TODAY WEST OF LUZON

three big wolves were killed before the dinner.

A grand parade is proposed here in which President Roosevelt shall ride so that he can be seen by citizens. At the head will be a caged bear recently captured after killing a dozen dogs and injuring several men. The bear will be given an hour's start for the hills then the packs will be set on the trail and President Roosevelt and the guides will follow in pursuit.

### Three Columbia Students Start Auto Trip to Chicago on Wager

### GENERAL STRIKE NOW THREATENS

*It's moonlight fair tonight upon the Wa-abash*

### OIL KING'S HAPPYEST DAY

one cherub every five minutes   market for all classes of realestate continues to be healthy with good demand for factory sites residence and business properties   court bills break labor

BLOODY SUNDAY IN MOSCOW

lady angels are smashed     troops guard oilfields
America tends to become empire like in the days of the
Caesars five-dollar poem gets rich husband   eat less says
Edison   rich pokerplayer falls dead when he draws royal
flush   charges graft in Cicero

STRIKE MAY MEAN REVOLT IN RUSSIA

lake romance of two yachts   murder ends labor feud
Michigan runs all over Albion   red flags in St Petersburg

CZAR YIELDS TO PEOPLE

holds dead baby forty hours   families evicted by
bursting watermain

CZAR GRANTS CONSTITUTION

*From the fields there comes the breath of newmown hay*
*Through the sycamores the candlelight is gleaming*


## The Camera Eye (6)

Go it go it said Mr Linwood the headmaster when one
was running up the field kicking the round ball footer they
called it in Hampstead and afterwards it was time to walk
home and one felt good because Mr Linwood had said Go it

Taylor said There's another American come and he had
teeth like Teddy in the newspapers and a turnedup nose and
a Rough Rider suit and he said Who are you going to vote
for? and one said I dunno and he stuck his chest out and
said I mean who your folks for Roosevelt or Parker? and
one said Judge Parker

the other American's hair was very black and he stuck
his fists up and his nose turned up and he said I'm for
Roosevelt wanto fight? all trembly one said I'm for Judge
Parker but Taylor said Who's got tuppence for ginger beer?
and there wasn't any fight that time

# Newsreel 5

BUGS DRIVE OUT BIOLOGIST

elopers bind and gag; is released by dog

EMPEROR NICHOLAS II FACING REVOLT OF
EMPIRE GRANTS SUBJECTS LIBERTY

paralysis stops surgeon's knife   by the stroke of a pen
the last absolute monarchy of Europe passes into history
miner of Death Valley and freak advertiser of Santa Fe
Road may die   sent to bridewell for stealing plaster angel

*On the banks of the Wabash far away.*

## *Mac*

Next morning soon after daylight Fainy limped out of a
heavy shower into the railroad station at Gaylord. There was
a big swagbellied stove burning in the station waitingroom.
The ticket agent's window was closed. There was nobody in
sight. Fainy took off first one drenched shoe and then the other
and toasted his feet till his socks were dry. A blister had formed
and broken on each heel and the socks stuck to them in a grimy
scab. He put on his shoes again and stretched out on the
bench. Immediately he was asleep.

Somebody tall in blue was speaking to him. He tried to raise
his head but he was too sleepy.

'Hey, bo, you better not let the station agent find you,' said
a voice he'd been hearing before through his sleep. Fainy opened
his eyes and sat up. 'Jeez, I thought you were a cop.'

A squareshouldered young man in blue denim shirt and
overalls was standing over him. 'I thought I'd better wake you
up, station agent's so friggin' tough in this dump.'

'Thanks.' Fainy stretched his legs. His feet were so swollen
he could hardly stand on them. 'Golly, I'm stiff.'

'Say, if we each had a quarter I know a dump where we could
get a bully breakfast.'

'I gotta dollar an' a half,' said Fainy slowly. He stood with his hands in his pockets, his back to the warm stove looking carefully at the other boy's square bulljawed face and blue eyes. 'Where are you from?'

'I'm from Duluth . . . I'm on the bum more or less. Where are you from?'

'Golly, I wish I knew. I had a job till last night.'

'Resigned?'

'Say, suppose we go eat that breakfast.'

'That's slick. I didn't eat yesterday. . . . My name's George Hall . . . The fellers call me Ike. I ain't exactly on the bum, you know. I want to see the world.'

'I guess I'm going to have to see the world now,' said Fainy. 'My name's McCreary. I'm from Chi. But I was born back east in Middletown, Connecticut.'

As they opened the screen door of the railroadmen's boarding house down the road they were met by a smell of ham and coffee and roachpowder. A horsetoothed blond woman with a rusty voice set places for them.

'Where do you boys work? I don't remember seein' you before.'

'I worked down to the sawmill,' said Ike.

'Sawmill shet down two weeks ago because the superintendent blew out his brains.'

'Don't I know it?'

'Maybe you boys better pay in advance.'

'I got the money,' said Fainy, waving a dollar bill in her face.

'Well, if you got the money I guess you'll pay all right,' said the waitress, showing her long yellow teeth in a smile.

'Sure, peaches and cream, we'll pay like millionaires,' said Ike.

They filled up on coffee and hominy and ham and eggs and big heavy white bakingpowder biscuits, and by the end of breakfast they had gotten to laughing so hard over Fainy's stories of Doc Bingham's life and loves that the waitress asked them if they'd been drinking. Ike kidded her into bringing them each another cup of coffee without extra charge. Then he fished up two mashed cigarettes from the pocket of his overalls. 'Have a coffee nail, Mac?'

'You can't smoke here,' said the waitress. 'The missus won't stand for smokin'.'

'All right, bright eyes, we'll skidoo.'

'How far you goin'?'

'Well, I'm headed for Duluth myself. That's where my folks are . . .'

'So you're from Duluth, are you?'

'Well, what's the big joke about Duluth?'

'It's no joke, it's a misfortune.'

'You don't think you can kid me, do you?'

' 'Tain't worth my while, sweetheart.' The waitress tittered as she cleared off the table. She had big red hands and thick nails white from kitchenwork.

'Hey, got any noospapers? I want somethin' to read waitin' for the train.'

'I'll get you some. The missus takes the *American* from Chicago.'

'Gee, I ain't seen a paper in three weeks.'

'I like to read the paper, too,' said Mac. 'I like to know what's goin' on in the world.'

'A lot of lies most of it . . . all owned by the interests.'

'Hearst's on the side of the people.'

'I don't trust him any more'n the rest of 'em.'

'Ever read *The Appeal to Reason*?'

'Say, are you a Socialist?'

'Sure; I had a job in my uncle's printin' shop till the big interests put him outa business because he took the side of the strikers.'

'Gee, that's swell . . . put it there . . . me, too. . . . Say, Mac, this is a big day for me . . . I don't often meet a guy thinks like I do.'

They went out with a roll of newspapers and sat under a big pine a little way out of town. The sun had come out warm; big white marble clouds sailed through the sky. They lay on their backs with their heads on a piece of pinkish root with bark like an alligator. In spite of last night's rain the pineneedles were warm and dry under them. In front of them stretched the single-track line through thickets and clearings of wrecked woodland where fireweed was beginning to thrust up here and there a palegreen spike of leaves. They read sheets of the weekold paper turn and turn about and talked.

'Maybe in Russia it'll start; that's the most backward country where the people are oppressed worst . . . There was a Russian feller workin' down to the sawmill, an educated feller who's fled from Siberia . . . I used to talk to him a lot . . . That's what he thought. He said the social revolution would start in Russia an' spread all over the world. He was a swell guy. I bet he was somebody.'

'Uncle Tim thought it would start in Germany.'

'Oughter start right here in America . . . We got free institutions here already . . . All we have to do is get out from under the interests.'

'Uncle Tim says we're too well off in America . . . we don't know what oppression or poverty is. Him an' my other uncles was Fenians back in Ireland before they came to this country. That's what they named me Fenian . . . Pop didn't like it, I guess . . . he didn't have much spunk, I guess.'

'Ever read Marx?'

'No . . . golly, I'd like to though.'

'Me neither, I read Bellamy's *Looking Backward*, though; that's what made me a Socialist.'

'Tell me about it; I'd just started readin' it when I left home.'

'It's about a galoot that goes to sleep an' wakes up in the year two thousand and the social revolution's all happened and everything's socialistic an' there's no jails or poverty and nobody works for themselves an' there's no way anybody can get to be a rich bondholder or capitalist and life's pretty slick for the workingclass.'

'That's what I always thought . . . It's the workers who create wealth and they ought to have it instead of a lot of drones.'

'If you could do away with the capitalist system and the big trusts and Wall Street things 'ud be like that.'

'Gee.'

'All you'd need would be a general strike and have the workers refuse to work for a boss any longer . . . God damn it, if people only realized how friggin' easy it would be. The interests own all the press and keep knowledge and education from the workin'men.'

'I know printin', pretty good, an' linotypin'. . . . Golly, maybe some day I could do somethin'.'

Mac got to his feet. He was tingling all over. A cloud had covered the sun, but down the railroad track the scrawny woods were full of the goldgreen blare of young birch leaves in the sun. His blood was like fire. He stood with his feet apart looking down the railroad track. Round the bend in the far distance a handcar appeared with a section gang on it, a tiny cluster of brown and dark blue. He watched it come nearer. A speck of red flag fluttered in the front of the handcar; it grew bigger, ducking into patches of shadow, larger and more distinct each time it came out into a patch of sun.

'Say, Mac, we better keep out of sight if we want to hop that freight. There's some friggin' mean yard detectives on this road.'

'All right.'

They walked off a hundred yards into the young growth of scrub pine and birch. Beside a big greenlichened stump Mac stopped to make water. His urine flowed bright yellow in the sun, disappearing at once into the porous loam of rotten leaves and wood. He was very happy. He gave the stump a kick. It was rotten. His foot went through it and a little powder like smoke went up from it as it crashed over into the alderbushes behind.

Ike had sat down on a log and was picking his teeth with a little birchtwig.

'Say, ever been to the coast, Mac?'

'No.'

'Like to?'

'Sure.'

'Well, let's you an' me beat our way out to Duluth ... I want to stop by and say hello to the old woman, see. Haven't seen her in three months. Then we'll take in the wheat harvest and make Frisco or Seattle by fall. Tell me they have good free nightschools in Seattle. I want to do some studyin', see? I dunno a friggin' thing yet.'

'That's slick.'

'Ever hopped a freight or ridden blind baggage, Mac?'

'Well, not exactly.'

'You follow me and do what I do. You'll be all right."

Down the track they heard the hoot of a locomotive whistle.

'There is number three comin' round the bend now ... We'll hop her right after she starts outa the station. She'll take us into Mackinaw City this afternoon.'

Late that afternoon, stiff and cold, they went into a little shed on the steamboat wharf at Mackinaw City to get shelter. Everything was hidden in a driving rainstreaked mist off the lake. They had bought a ten-cent package of Sweet Caps, so that they only had ninety cents left between them. They were arguing about how much they ought to spend for supper when the steamboat agent, a thin man wearing a green eyeshade and a slicker, came out of his office.

'You boys lookin' for a job?' he asked. ' 'Cause there's a guy here from the Lakeview House lookin' for a coupla pearldivers.

Agency didn't send 'em enough help, I guess. They're openin' up tomorrer.'

'How much do they pay ye?' asked Ike.

'I don't reckon it's much, but the grub's pretty good.'

'How about it, Mac? We'll save up our fare an' then we'll go to Duluth like a coupla dudes on the boat.'

So they went over that night on the steamboat to Mackinac Island. It was pretty dull on Mackinac Island. There was a lot of small scenery with signs on it reading 'Devil's Cauldron,' 'Sugar Loaf,' 'Lover's Leap,' and wives and children of mediumpriced business men from Detroit, Saginaw and Chicago. The grayfaced woman who ran the hotel, known as The Management, kept them working from six in the morning till way after sundown. It wasn't only dishwashing, it was sawing wood, running errands, cleaning toilets, scrubbing floors, smashing baggage and a lot of odd chores. The waitresses were all old maids or else brokendown farmers' wives whose husbands drank. The only other male in the place was the cook, a hypochondriac French-Canadian halfbreed who insisted on being called Mr Chef. Evenings he sat in his little log shack back of the hotel drinking paregoric and mumbling about God.

When they got their first month's pay, they packed up their few belongings in a newspaper and sneaked on board the *Juniata* for Duluth. The fare took all their capital, but they were happy as they stood in the stern watching the spruce and balsamcovered hill of Mackinac disappear into the lake.

Duluth: girderwork along the waterfront, and the shackcovered hills and the tall thin chimneys and the huddle of hunchshouldered grain elevators under the smoke from the mills scrolled out dark against a huge salmoncolored sunset. Ike hated to leave the boat on account of a pretty darkhaired girl he'd meant all the time to speak to.

'Hell, she wouldn't pay attention to you, Ike, she's too swank for you,' Mac kept saying.

'The old woman'll be glad to see us anyway,' said Ike as they hurried off the gangplank. 'I half expected to see her at the dock, though I didn't write we was coming. Boy, I bet she'll give us a swell feed.'

'Where does she live?'

'Not far. I'll show you. Say, don't ask anythin' about my ole man, will ye; he don't amount to much. He's in jail, I guess. Ole woman's had pretty tough sleddin' bringin' up us kids ... I got two brothers in Buffalo ... I don't get along with 'em.

She does fancy needlework and preservin' an' bakes cakes an'
stuff like that. She used to work in a bakery but she's got the
lumbago too bad now. She'd 'a' been a real bright woman if we
hadn't always been so friggin' poor.'

They turned up a muddy street on a hill. At the top of the
hill was a little prim house like a schoolhouse.

'That's where we live . . . Gee, I wonder why there's no light.'

They went in by a gate in the picket fence. There was sweet-
william in bloom in the flowerbed in front of the house. They
could smell it though they could hardly see, it was so dark. Ike
knocked.

'Damn it, I wonder what's the matter.' He knocked again.
Then he struck a match. On the door was nailed a card 'FOR
SALE' and the name of a realestate agent. 'Jesus Christ, that's
funny, she musta moved. Now I think of it, I haven't had a
letter in a couple of months. I hope she ain't sick . . . I'll ask at
Bud Walker's next door.'

Mac sat down on the wooden step and waited. Overhead in
a gash in the clouds that still had the faintest stain of red from
the afterglow his eye dropped into empty black full of stars.
The smell of the sweetwilliams tickled his nose. He felt hungry.

A low whistle from Ike roused him. 'Come along,' he said
gruffly and started walking fast down the hill with his head
sunk between his shoulders.

'Hey, what's the matter?'

'Nothin'. The old woman's gone to Buffalo to live with my
brothers. The lousy bums got her to sell out so's they could
spend the dough, I reckon.'

'Jesus, that's hell, Ike.'

Ike didn't answer. They walked till they came to the corner
of a street with lighted stores and trolleycars. A tune from a
mechanical piano was tumbling out from a saloon. Ike turned
and slapped Mac on the back. 'Let's go have a drink, kid . . .
What the hell.'

There was only one other man at the long bar. He was a very
drunken tall elderly man in lumbermen's boots with a sou'-
wester on his head who kept yelling in an inaudible voice,
'Whoop her up, boys,' and making a pass at the air with a long
grimy hand. Mac and Ike drank down two whiskies each, so
strong and raw that it pretty near knocked the wind out of
them. Ike put the change from a dollar in his pocket and said:

'What the hell, let's get out of here.' In the cool air of the
street they began to feel lit. 'Jesus, Mac, let's get outa here to-

night . . . It's terrible to come back to a town where you was a kid . . . I'll be meetin' all the crazy galoots I ever knew and girls I had crushes on . . . I guess I always get the dirty end of the stick, all right.'

In a lunchroom down by the freight depot they got hamburger and potatoes and bread and butter and coffee for fifteen cents each. When they'd bought some cigarettes they still had eight-seventyfive between them.

'Golly, we're rich,' said Mac. 'Well, where do we go?'

'Wait a minute. I'll go scout round the freight depot. Used to be a guy I knowed worked there.'

Mac loafed round under a lamppost at the streetcorner and smoked a cigarette and waited. It was warmer since the wind had gone down. From a puddle somewhere in the freight yards came the peep peep peep of toads. Up on the hill an accordion was playing. From the yards came the heavy chugging of a freight locomotive and the clank of shunted freightcars and the singing rattle of the wheels.

After a while he heard Ike's whistle from the dark side of the street. He ran over.

'Say, Mac, we gotta hurry. I found the guy. He's goin' to open up a boxcar for us on the westbound freight. He says it'll carry us clear out to the coast if we stick to it.'

'How the hell will we eat if we're locked up in a freightcar?'

'We'll eat fine. You leave the eatin' to me.'

'But, Ike . . .'

'Keep your trap shut, can't you . . . Do you want everybody in the friggin' town to know what we're tryin' to do?'

They walked along tiptoe in the dark between two tracks of boxcars. Then Ike found a door half open and darted in. Mac followed and they shut the sliding door very gently after them.

'Now all we got to do is go to sleep,' whispered Ike, his lips touching Mac's ear. 'This here galoot, see, said there wasn't any yard dicks on duty tonight.'

In the end of the car they found hay from a broken bale. The whole car smelt of hay.

'Ain't this hunkydory?' whispered Ike.

'It's the cat's nuts, Ike.'

Pretty soon the train started, and they lay down to sleep side by side in the sparse hay. The cold night wind streamed in through the cracks in the floor. They slept fitfully. The train started and stopped and started and shunted back and forth on sidings and the wheels rattled and rumbled in their ears and

slambanged over crossings. Towards morning they fell into a
warm sleep and the thin layer of hay on the boards was suddenly soft and warm. Neither of them had a watch and the day
was overcast so they didn't know what time it was when they
woke up. Ike slid open the door a little so that they could peek
out; the train was running through a broad valley brimful-like
with floodwater, with the green ripple of full-grown wheat.
Now and then in the distance a clump of woodland stood up
like an island. At each station was the hunched blind bulk of
an elevator.

'Gee, this must be the Red River, but I wonder which way
we're goin',' said Ike.

'Golly, I could drink a cup of coffee,' said Mac.

'We'll have swell coffee in Seattle, damned if we won't, Mac.'

They went to sleep again, and when they woke up they were
thirsty and stiff. The train had stopped. There was no sound
at all. They lay on their backs stretching and listening. 'Gee, I
wonder where in hell we are.' After a long while they heard the
cinders crunching down the track and someone trying the fast-
enings of the boxcar doors down the train. They lay so still they
could hear both their hearts beating. The steps on the cinders
crunched nearer and nearer. The sliding door slammed open,
and their car was suddenly full of sunlight. They lay still. Mac
felt the rap of a stick on his chest and sat up blinking. A Scotch
voice was burring in his ears:

'I thought I'd find some Pullman passengerrs . . . All right,
byes, stand and deliver, or else you'll go to the constabulary.'

'Aw, hell,' said Ike, crawling forward.

'Currsin' and swearin' won't help ye . . . If you got a couple
o' quid you can ride on to Winnipeg an' take your chances
there . . . If not you'll be doin' a tidy bit on the roads before
you can say Jack Robinson.'

The brakeman was a small blackhaired man with a mean
quiet manner.

'Where are we, guv'ner?' asked Ike, trying to talk like an
Englishman.

'Gretna . . . You're in the Dominion of Canada. You can be
had up, too, for illegally crossin' Her Majesty's frontier as well
as for bein' vags.'

'Well, I guess we'd better shell out . . . You see we're a couple
of noblemen's sons out for a bit of a bloody lark, guv'ner.'

'No use currsin' and prevarricatin'. How much have you?'

'Coupla dollars.'

'Let's see it quick.'

Ike pulled first one dollar, then another, out of his pocket; folded in the second dollar was a five. The Scotchman swept the three bills up with one gesture and slammed the sliding door to. They heard him slip down the catch on the outside. For a long time they sat there quiet in the dark.

Finally Ike said, 'Hey, Mac, gimme a sock in the jaw. That was a damn fool thing to do . . . Never oughta had that in my jeans anyway . . . oughta had it inside my belt. That leaves us with about seventyfive cents. We're up shit creek now for fair . . . He'll probably wire ahead to take us outa here at the next big town."

'Do they have mounted police on the railroad, too?' asked Mac in a hollow whisper.

'Jeez, I don't know any more about it than you do.'

The train started again and Ike rolled over on his face and went glumly to sleep. Mac lay on his back behind him looking at the slit of sunlight that made its way in through the crack in the door and wondered what the inside of a Canadian jail would be like.

That night, after the train had lain still for some time in the middle of the hissing and clatter of a big freightyard, they heard the catch slipped off the door. After a while Ike got up his nerve to slide the door open and they dropped, stiff and terribly hungry, down to the cinders. There was another freight on the next track, so all they could see was a bright path of stars overhead. They got out of the freightyards without any trouble and found themselves walking through the deserted streets of a large widescattered city.

'Winnipeg's a pretty friggin' lonelylookin' place, take it from me,' said Ike.

'It must be after midnight.'

They tramped and tramped and at last found a little lunch-room kept by a Chink who was just closing up. They spent forty cents on some stew and potatoes and coffee. They asked the Chink if he'd let them sleep on the floor behind the counter, but he threw them out and they found themselves dogtired tramping through the broad deserted streets of Winnipeg again. It was too cold to sit down anywhere, and they couldn't find anyplace that looked as if it would give them a flop for thirtyfive cents, so they walked and walked, and anyway the sky was beginning to pale into a slow northern summer dawn. When it was fully day they went back to the Chink's and spent the thirtyfive cents on oatmeal and coffee. Then they went to the Canadian Pacific employment office and signed up for work in a construction camp at Banff. The hours they had to wait till traintime they spent in the public library. Mac read part of Bellamy's *Looking Backward*, and Ike, not being able to find a volume of Karl Marx, read an instalment of 'When the Sleeper Wakes' in the *Strand Magazine*. So when they got on the train they were full of the coming Socialist revolution and started talking it up to two lanky redfaced lumberjacks who sat opposite them.

One of them chewed tobacco silently all the while, but the other spat his quid out of the window and said, 'You blokes'll keep quiet with that kinder talk if you knows what's 'ealthy for ye.'

'Hell, this is a free country, ain't it? A guy's free to talk, ain't he?' said Ike.

'A bloke kin talk so long as his betters don't tell him to keep his mouth shut.'

'Hell, I'm not tryin' to pick a fight,' said Ike.

'Better not,' said the other man, and didn't speak again.

They worked for the C.P.R. all summer and by the first of October they were in Vancouver. They had new suitcases and new suits. Ike had fortynine dollars and fifty cents and Mac had eightythree fifteen in a brandnew pigskin wallet. Mac had more because he didn't play poker. They took a dollar and a half room between them and lay in bed like princes their first free morning. They were tanned and toughened and their hands were horny. After the smell of rank pipes and unwashed feet and the bedbugs in the railroad bunkhouses the small cleanboarded hotel room with its clean beds seemed like a palace.

When he was fully awake Mac sat up and reached for his Ingersoll. Eleven o'clock. The sunlight on the windowledge was ruddy from the smoke of forestfires up the coast. He got up and washed in cold water at the washbasin. He walked up and down the room wiping his face and arms in the towel. It made him feel good to follow the contours of his neck and the hollow between his shoulderblades and the muscles of his arms as he dried himself with the fresh coarse towel.

'Say, Ike, what do you think we oughta do? I think we oughta go down on the boat to Seattle, Washington, like a coupla dude passengers. I wanta settle down an' get a printin' job; there's good money in that. I'm goin' to study to beat hell this winter. What do you think, Ike? I want to get out of this limejuicy hole an' get back to God's country. What do you think, Ike?'

Ike groaned and rolled over in bed.

'Say, wake up, Ike, for crissake. We want to take a look at this burg an' then twentythree.'

Ike sat up in bed. 'God damn it, I need a woman.'

'I've heard tell there's swell broads in Seattle, honest, Ike.'

Ike jumped out of bed and began splattering himself from head to foot with cold water. Then he dashed into his clothes and stood looking out the window combing the water out of his hair.

'When does the friggin' boat go? Jeez, I had two wet dreams last night, did you?'

Mac blushed. He nodded his head.

'Jeez, we got to get us women. Wet dreams weakens a guy.'

'I wouldn't want to get sick.'

'Aw, hell, a man's not a man until he's had his three doses.'

'Aw, come ahead, let's go see the town.'

'Well, ain't I been waitin' for ye this halfhour?'

They ran down the stairs and out into the street. They walked round Vancouver, sniffing the winey smell of lumbermills along the waterfront, loafing under the big trees in the park. Then they got their tickets at the steamboat office and went to a haberdashery store and bought themselves striped neckties, colored socks and fourdollar silk shirts. They felt like millionaires when they walked up the gangplank of the boat for Victoria and Seattle, with their new suits and their new suitcases and their silk shirts. They strolled round the deck smoking cigarettes and looking at the girls. 'Gee, there's a couple looks kinda easy . . . I bet they're hookers at that,' Ike whispered in Mac's ear and gave him a dig in the ribs with his elbow as they passed two girls in Spring Maid hats who were walking round the deck the other way. 'Shit, let's try pick 'em up.'

They had a couple of beers at the bar, then they went on deck. The girls had gone. Mac and Ike walked disconsolately round the deck for a while, then they found the girls leaning over the rail in the stern. It was a cloudy moonlight night. The sea and the dark islands covered with spiring evergreens shone light and dark in a mottling silvery green. Both girls had frizzy hair and dark circles under their eyes. Mac thought they looked too old, but as Ike had gone sailing ahead it was too late to say anything. The girl he talked to was named Gladys. He liked the looks of the other one, whose name was Olive, better, but Ike got next to her first. They stayed on deck kidding and giggling

until the girls said they were cold, then they went in the saloon
and sat on a sofa and Ike went and bought a box of candy.

'We ate onions for dinner today,' said Olive. 'Hope you
fellers don't mind. Gladys, I told you we oughtn't to of eaten
them onions, not before comin' on the boat.'

'Gimme a kiss an' I'll tell ye if I mind or not,' said Ike.

'Kiddo, you can't talk fresh like that to us, not on this boat,'
snapped Olive, two mean lines appearing on either side of her
mouth.

'We have to be awful careful what we do on the boat,' explained Gladys. 'They're terrible suspicious of two girls
travelin' alone nowadays. Ain't it a crime?'

'It sure is.' Ike moved up a little closer on the seat.

'Quit that . . . Make a noise like a hoop an' roll away. I mean
it.' Olive went and sat on the opposite bench. Ike followed
her.

'In the old days it was liberty hall on these boats, but not so
any more,' Gladys said, talking to Mac in a low intimate voice.
'You fellers been workin' up in the canneries?'

'No, we been workin' for the C.P.R. all summer.'

'You must have made big money.' As she talked to him, Mac
noticed that she kept looking out of the corner of her eye at
her friend.

'Yare . . . not so big . . . I saved up pretty near a century.'

'An' now you're going to Seattle.'

'I want to get a job linotypist.'

'That's where we live, Seattle. Olive an' I've got an apartment . . . Let's go out on deck, it's too hot in here.'

As they passed Olive and Ike, Gladys leaned over and whispered something in Olive's ear. Then she turned to Mac with a
melting smile. The deck was deserted. She let him put his arm
round her waist. His fingers felt the bones of some sort of
corset. He squeezed. 'Oh, don't be too rough, kiddo,' she
whined in a funny little voice. He laughed. As he took his hand
away he felt the contour of her breast. Walking, his leg brushed
against her leg. It was the first time he'd been so close to a
girl.

After a while she said she had to go to bed. 'How about me
goin' down with ye?'

She shook her head. 'Not on this boat. See you tomorrow;
maybe you and your pal'll come and see us at our apartment.
We'll show you the town.'

'Sure,' said Mac. He walked on round the deck, his heart

beating hard. He could feel the pound of the steamboat's engines and the arrowshaped surge of broken water from the bow and he felt like that. He met Ike.

'My girl said she had to go to bed.'

'So did mine.'

'Get anywheres, Mac?'

'They got an apartment in Seattle.'

'I got a kiss off mine. She's awful hot. Jeez, I thought she was going to feel me up.'

'We'll get it tomorrow all right.'

The next day was sunny; the Seattle waterfront was sparkling, smelt of lumberyards, was noisy with rattle of carts and yells of drivers when they got off the boat. They went to the Y.M.C.A. for a room. They were through with being laborers and hobos. They were going to get clean jobs, live decently and go to school nights. They walked round the city all day, and in the evening met Olive and Gladys in front of the totempole on Pioneer Square.

Things happened fast. They went to a restaurant and had wine with a big feed and afterwards they went to a beergarden where there was a band, and drank whiskey-sours. When they went to the girls' apartment they took a quart of whiskey with them and Mac almost dropped it on the steps and the girls said, 'For crissake don't make so much noise or you'll have the cops on us,' and the apartment smelt of musk and face-powder and there was women's underwear around on all the chairs and the girls got fifteen bucks out of each of them first thing. Mac was in the bathroom with his girl and she smeared liprouge on his nose and they laughed and laughed until he got rough and she slapped his face. Then they all sat together round the table and drank some more and Ike danced a Salomeydance in his bare feet. Mac laughed, it was so very funny, but he was sitting on the floor and when he tried to get up he fell on his face and all of a sudden he was being sick in the bathtub and Gladys was cursing hell out of him. She got him dressed, only he couldn't find his necktie, and everybody said he was too drunk and pushed him out and he was walking down the street singing *Make a Noise Like a Hoop and Just Roll Away, Roll Away*, and asked a cop where the Y.M.C.A. was and the cop pushed him into a cell at the stationhouse and locked him up.

He woke up with his head like a big split millstone. There was vomit on his shirt and a rip in his pants. He went over all his pockets and couldn't find his pocketbook. A cop opened the cell door and told him to make himself scarce and he walked out into the dazzling sun that cut into his eyes like a knife. The man at the desk at the Y looked at him queerly when he went in, but he got up to his room and fell into bed without anybody saying anything to him. Ike wasn't back yet. He dozed off feeling his headache all through his sleep.

When he woke up Ike was sitting on the bed. Ike's eyes were bright and his cheeks were red. He was still a little drunk. 'Say, Mac, did they roll yer? I can't find my pocketbook an' I tried to go back, but I couldn't find the apartment. God, I'd have beat up the goddam flousies . . . Shit, I'm drunk as a pissant still. Say, the galoot at the desk said we'd have to clear out. Can't have no drunks in the Y.M.C.A.'

'But jeez, we paid for a week.'

'He'll give us part of it back . . . Aw, what the hell, Mac . . . We're flat, but I feel swell . . . Say, I had a rough time with your Jane after they'd thrown you out.'

'Hell, I feel sick as a dog.'

'I'm afraid to go to sleep for fear of getting a hangover. Come on out, it'll do you good.'

It was three in the afternoon. They went into a little Chinese restaurant on the waterfront and drank coffee. They had two dollars they got from hocking their suitcases. The pawnbroker wouldn't take the silk shirts because they were dirty. Outside it was raining pitchforks.

'Jesus, why the hell didn't we have the sense to keep sober? God, we're a coupla big stiffs, Ike.'

'We had a good party . . . Jeez, you looked funny with that liprouge all over your face.'

'I feel like hell . . . I wanta study an' work for things; you know what I mean, not to get to be a goddam slavedriver, but for socialism and the revolution an' like that, not work an' go on a bat an' work an' go on a bat like those damn yaps on the railroad.'

'Hell, another time we'll have more sense an' leave our wads somewhere safe . . . Gee, I'm beginning to sink by the bows myself.'

'If the damn house caught fire I wouldn't have the strength to walk out.'

They sat in the Chink place as long as they could and then they went out in the rain to find a thirtycent flophouse where they spent the night, and the bedbugs ate them up. In the morning they went round looking for jobs, Mac in the printing trades and Ike at the shipping agencies. They met in the evening without having had any luck and slept in the park, as it was a fine night. Eventually they both signed up to go to a lumbercamp up the Snake River. They were sent up by the agency on a car full of Swedes and Finns. Mac and Ike were the only ones who spoke English. When they got there they found the foreman so hardboiled and the grub so rotten and the bunkhouse so filthy that they lit out at the end of a couple of days, on the bum again. It was already cold in the Blue Mountains and they would have starved to death if they hadn't been able to beg food in the cookhouses of lumbercamps along the way. They hit the railroad at Baker City, managed to beat their way back to Portland on freights. In Portland, they couldn't find jobs because their clothes were so dirty, so they hiked southward along a big endless Oregon valley full of fruitranches, sleeping in barns and getting an occasional meal by cutting wood or doing chores around a ranchhouse.

In Salem, Ike found that he had a dose and Mac couldn't sleep nights worrying for fear he might have it too. They tried to go to a doctor in Salem. He was a big roundfaced man with a hearty laugh. When they said they didn't have any money, he guessed it was all right and that they could do some chores to pay for the consultation, but when he heard it was a venereal disease he threw them out with a hot lecture on the wages of sin.

They trudged along the road, hungry and footsore; Ike had fever and it hurt him to walk. Neither of them said anything. Finally they got to a small fruitshipping station where there were watertanks, on the main line of the Southern Pacific.

There Ike said he couldn't walk any further, that they'd have to wait for a freight. 'Jesus Christ, jail 'ud be better than this.'

'When you're outa luck in this man's country, you certainly are outa luck,' said Mac and for some reason they both laughed.

Among the bushes back of the station they found an old tramp boiling coffee in a tin can. He gave them some coffee and bread and baconrind and they told him their troubles. He said he was headed south for the winter and that the thing to cure it up was tea made out of cherry pits and stems. 'But where the hell am I going to get cherry pits and stems?' Anyway he said not to worry, it was no worse than a bad cold. He was a cheerful old man with a face so grimed with dirt it looked like a brown leather mask. He was going to take a chance on a freight that stopped there to water a little after sundown. Mac dozed off to sleep while Ike and the old man talked. When he woke up Ike was yelling at him and they were all running for the freight that had already started. In the dark Mac missed his footing and fell flat on the ties. He wrenched his knee and ground cinders into his nose and by the time he had got to his feet all he could see were the two lights on the end of the train fading into the November haze.

That was the last he saw of Ike Hall.

He got himself back on the road and limped along until he came to a ranchhouse. A dog barked at him and worried his ankles, but he was too down and out to care. Finally a stout woman came to the door and gave him some cold biscuits and applesauce and told him he could sleep in the barn if he gave her all his matches. He limped to the barn and snuggled into a pile of dry sweetgrass and went to sleep.

In the morning the rancher, a tall ruddy man named Thomas, with a resonant voice, went over to the barn and offered him work for a few days at the price of his board and lodging. They were kind to him, and had a pretty daughter named Mona that he kinder fell in love with. She was a plump rosy-cheeked girl, strong as a boy and afraid of nothing. She punched him and wrestled with him; and, particularly after he'd gotten fattened up a little and rested, he could hardly sleep nights for thinking of her. He lay in his bed of sweetgrass telling over the touch of her bare arm that rubbed along his when she handed him back the nozzle of the sprayer for the fruittrees, or was helping him pile up the pruned twigs to burn, and the roundness of her breasts and her breath sweet as a cow's on his neck when they romped and played tricks on each other evenings after supper. But the Thomases had other ideas for their daughter and told Mac that they didn't need him any more. They sent him off kindly with a lot of good advice, some old clothes and a cold lunch done up in newspaper, but no money. Mona ran after him as he walked off down the dustyrutted wagonroad and kissed him right in front of her parents. 'I'm stuck on you,' she said. 'You make a lot of money and come back and marry me.' 'By gum, I'll do that,' said Mac, and he walked off with tears in his eyes and feeling very good. He was particularly glad he hadn't got the clap off that girl in Seattle.

# Newsreel 6

PARIS SHOCKED AT LAST

HARRIMAN SHOWN AS RAIL COLOSSUS

NOTED SWINDLER RUN TO EARTH

TEDDY WIELDS BIG STICK

STRAPHANGERS DEMAND RELIEF

*We were sailing along*
> *On moonlight bay*
*You can hear the voices ringing*
*They seem to say*
*You have stolen my heart, now don't go away*
*Just as we sang*
> *love's*
>> *old*
>>> *sweet*
>>>> *songs*
>> *On moonlight bay*

MOB LYNCHES AFTER PRAYER

when the metal poured out of the furnace I saw the men running to a place of safety. To the right of the furnace I saw a party of ten men all of them running wildly and their clothes a mass of flames. Apparently some of them had been injured when the explosion occurred and several of them tripped and fell. The hot metal ran over the poor men in a moment.

PRAISE MONOPOLY AS BOON TO ALL

industrial foes work for peace at Mrs Potter Palmer's

> *love's*
>> *old*
>>> *sweet*
>>>> *song*

*We were sailing along*
*on moonlight bay*

## The Camera Eye (7)

skating on the pond next the silver company's mills
where there was a funny fuzzy smell from the dump whaleoil
soap somebody said it was that they used in cleaning the
silver knives and spoons and forks putting shine on them for
sale      there was shine on the ice early black ice that rang
like a sawblade just scratched white by the first skaters
I couldn't learn to skate and kept falling down look out for
the muckers everybody said      Bohunk and Polak kids put
stones in their snowballs write dirty words up on walls do
dirty things up alleys their folks work in the mills
we clean young American Rover Boys handy with tools
Deerslayers played hockey Boy Scouts and cut figure eights
on the ice Achilles Ajax Agamemnon I couldn't learn to
skate and kept falling down.

## The Plant Wizard

Luther Burbank was born in a brick farmhouse in Lancaster Mass.
he walked round the woods one winter
crunching through the shinycrusted snow
stumbled into a little dell where a warm spring was
and found the grass green and the weeds sprouting
and skunk cabbage pushing up a potent thumb,
He went home and sat by the stove and read Darwin
Struggle for Existence Origin of Species Natural
Selection that wasn't what they taught in church,
so Luther Burbank ceased to believe moved to Lunen-
burg,
found a seedball in a potato plant
sowed the seed and cashed in on Mr Darwin's Natural
Selection
on Spencer and Huxley
with the Burbank Potato.

*Young man go west;*
Luther Burbank went to Santa Rosa
full of his dream of green grass in winter everblooming flowers ever-
bearing berries; Luther Burbank
could cash in on Natural Selection Luther Burbank
carried his apocalyptic dream of green grass in winter
and seedless berries and stoneless plums and thornless
roses brambles cactus –
          winters were bleak in that bleak
          brick farmhouse in bleak Massachusetts –
out to sunny Santa Rosa;
and he was a sunny old man
where roses bloomed all year
everblooming everbearing
hybrids.

America was hybrid
America should cash in on Natural Selection.
He was an infidel he believed in Darwin and Natural
Selection and the influence of the mighty dead
and a good firm shipper's fruit
suitable for canning.
He was one of the grand old men until the churches
and the congregations
got wind that he was an infidel and believed
in Darwin.
Luther Burbank had never a thought of evil,
selecting improved hybrids for America
those sunny years in Santa Rosa.
But he brushed down a wasp's nest that time;
he wouldn't give up Darwin and Natural Selection
and they stung him and he died
puzzled.

They buried him under a cedartree.
His favorite photograph
was of a little tot
standing beside a bed of hybrid
everblooming double Shasta daisies
with never a thought of evil
And Mount Shasta
in the background, used to be a volcano
but they don't have volcanos
any more.

# Newsreel 7

SAYS THIS IS CENTURY WHERE BILLIONS AND
BRAINS ARE TO RULE

INFANT BORN IN MINNEAPOLIS COMES HERE
IN INCUBATOR

*Cheyenne Cheyenne*
*Hop on my pony*

SAYS JIM HILL HITS OIL TRUST ON 939 COUNTS

BIG FOUR TRAIN BLOWN TO PIECES

woman and children blotted out    admits he saw flog-
gings and even mutilations but no frightful outrages

TRUTH ABOUT THE CONGO FREE STATE

Find bad fault in Dreadnaught    Santos Dumont tells
of rival of bird of prey    wives, prime aim of Congo natives
extraordinary letter ordering away U.S. marines

WHITES IN CONGO LOSE MORAL SENSE

WOMAN HELD A CAPTIVE BY AMBULANCE CHASERS

THAW FACES JUDGE IN FATEFUL FIGHT

LABOR MENACE IN POLITICS

last of Salome seen in New York    heroism of mother
unavailing

*There's room here for two, dear*
*But after the ceremony*
*Two, dear, as one, dear, will ride back on my pony*
*From old Cheyenne*

## *The Camera Eye (8)*

you sat on the bed unlacing your shoes Hey Frenchie
yelled Tylor in the door you've got to fight the Kid    doan
wanna fight him    gotto fight him hasn't he got to fight

him fellers? Freddie pushed his face through the crack in the door and made a long nose Gotta fight him umpyaya and all the fellows on the top floor were there if not you're a girlboy and I had on my pyjamas and they pushed in the Kid and the Kid hit Frenchie and Frenchie hit the Kid and your mouth tasted bloody and everybody yelled Go it Kid except Gummer and he yelled Bust his jaw Jack and Frenchie had the Kid down on the bed and everybody pulled him off and they all had Frenchie against the door and he was slamming right an' left and he couldn't see who was hitting and Tylor and Freddie held his arms and told the Kid to come and hit him but the Kid wouldn't and the Kid was crying

the bloody sweet puky taste and then the bell rang for lights and everybody ran to their rooms and you got into bed with your head throbbing and you were crying when Gummer tiptoed in an' said you had him licked Jack it was a fucking shame it was Freddie hit you that time, but Hoppy was tiptoeing round the hall and caught Gummer trying to get back to his room and he got his

## Mac

By Thanksgiving Mac had beaten his way to Sacramento, where he got a job smashing crates in a driedfruit warehouse. By the first of the year he'd saved up enough to buy a suit of dark clothes and take the steamboat down the river to San Francisco.

It was around eight in the evening when he got in. With his suitcase in his hand, he walked up Market Street from the dock. The streets were full of lights. Young men and pretty girls in brightcolored dresses were walking fast through a big yanking wind that fluttered dresses and scarfs, slapped color into cheeks, blew grit and papers into the air. There were Chinamen, Wops, Portuguese, Japs in the street. People were hustling to shows and restaurants. Music came out of the doors of bars, frying, buttery foodsmells from restaurants, smells of winecasks and beer. Mac wanted to go on a party but he only had four dollars so he went and got a room at the Y and ate some soggy pie and coffee in the deserted cafeteria downstairs.

When he got up in the bare bedroom like something in a hospital he opened the window, but it only gave on an airshaft. The room smelt of some sort of cleaning fluid and when he lay down on the bed the blanket smelt of formaldehyde. He felt too well. He could feel the prancing blood steam all through him. He wanted to talk to somebody, to go to a dance or have a drink with a fellow he knew or kid a girl somewhere. The smell of rouge and musky facepowder in the room of those girls in Seattle came back to him. He got up and sat on the edge of the bed swinging his legs. Then he decided to go out, but before he went he put his money in his suitcase and locked it up. Lonely as a ghost he walked up and down the streets until he was deadtired; he walked fast not looking to the right or left, brushing past painted girls at streetcorners, touts that tried to put addresscards into his hand, drunks that tried to pick fights with him, panhandlers whining for a handout. Then, bitter and cold and tired, he went back to his room and fell into bed.

Next day he went out and got a job in a small printshop run and owned by a baldheaded Italian with big whiskers and a flowing black tie, named Bonello. Bonello told him he had been a redshirt with Garibaldi and was now an anarchist. Ferrer was his great hero; he hired Mac because he thought he might make a convert out of him. All that winter Mac worked at Bonello's, ate spaghetti and drank red wine and talked revolution with him and his friends in the evening, went to Socialist picnics or libertarian meetings on Sundays. Saturday nights he went round to whorehouses with a fellow named Miller, whom he'd met at the Y. Miller was studying to be a dentist. He got to be friends with a girl named Maisie Spencer who worked in the millinery department at the Emporium. Sundays she used to try to get him to go to church. She was a quiet girl with big blue eyes that she turned up to him with an unbelieving smile when he talked revolution to her. She had tiny regular pearly teeth and dressed prettily. After a while she got so that she did not bother him so much about church. She liked to have him take her to hear the band play at the Presidio or to look at the statuary in Sutro Park.

The morning of the earthquake Mac's first thought, when he got over his own terrible scare, was for Maisie. The house where her folks lived on Mariposa Street was still standing when he got there, but everyone had cleared out. It was not till the third day, three days of smoke and crashing timbers and dynamiting he spent working in firefighting squad, that he found her in a provision line at the entrance to Golden Gate Park. The Spencers were living in a tent near the shattered greenhouses.

She didn't recognize him because his hair and eyebrows were singed and his clothes were in tatters and he was soot from head to foot. He'd never kissed her before, but he took her in his arms before everybody and kissed her. When he let her go her face was all sooty from his. Some of the people in the line laughed and clapped, but the old woman right behind, who had her hair done in a pompadour askew so that the rat showed through and who wore two padded pink silk dressing gowns one above the other said spitefully, 'Now you'll have to go and wash your face.'

After that they considered themselves engaged, but they couldn't get married, because Bonello's printshop had been gutted with the rest of the block it stood in, and Mac was out of a job. Maisie used to let him kiss her and hug her in dark doorways when he took her home at night, but further than that he gave up trying to go.

In the fall he got a job on the *Bulletin*. That was night work and he hardly ever saw Maisie except Sundays, but they began to talk about getting married after Christmas. When he was away from her he felt somehow sore at Maisie most of the time, but when he was with her he melted absolutely. He tried to get her to read pamphlets on socialism, but she laughed and looked up at him with her big intimate blue eyes and said it was too deep for her. She liked to go to the theater and eat in restaurants where the linen was starched and there were waiters in dress suits.

About that time he went one night to hear Upton Sinclair speak about the Chicago stockyards. Next to him was a young man in dungarees. He had a nose like a hawk and gray eyes and deep creases under his cheekbones and talked in a slow drawl. His name was Fred Hoff. After the lecture they went and had a beer together and talked. Fred Hoff belonged to the new revolutionary organization called The Industrial Workers of the World. He read Mac the preamble over a second glass of beer. Fred Hoff had just hit town as donkeyengine man on a freighter. He was sick of the bum grub and hard life on the sea. He still had his pay in his pocket and he was bound he wouldn't blow it in on a bust. He'd heard that there was a miners' strike in Goldfield and he thought he'd go up there and

see what he could do. He made Mac feel that he was leading a
pretty stodgy life helping print lies against the workingclass.
'Godalmighty, man, you're just the kind o' stuff we need out
there. We're goin' to publish a paper in Goldfield, Nevada.'

That night Mac went round to the local and filled out a card,
and went home to his boardinghouse with his head swimming.
I was just on the point of selling out to the sonsofbitches, he
said to himself.

The next Sunday he and Maisie had been planning to go up
the Scenic Railway to the top of Mount Tamalpais. Mac was
terribly sleepy when his alarmclock got him out of bed. They
had to start early because he had to be on the job again that
night. As he walked to the ferry station where he was going to
meet her at nine the clank of the presses was still in his head,
and the sour smell of ink and paper bruised under the presses,
and on top of that the smell of the hall of the house he'd been
in with a couple of the fellows, the smell of moldy rooms and
sloppails and the smell of armpits and the dressingtable of the
frizzyhaired girl he'd had on the clammy bed and the taste of
the stale beer they'd drunk and the cooing mechanical voice,
'Goodnight, dearie, come round soon.'

'God, I'm a swine,' he said to himself.

For once it was a clear morning, all the colors in the street
shone like bits of glass. God, he was sick of whoring round. If
Maisie would only be a sport, if Maisie was only a rebel you
could talk to like you could to a friend. And how the hell was
he going to tell her he was throwing up his job?

She was waiting for him at the ferry looking like a Gibson
girl with her neat sailorblue dress and picture hat. They didn't
have time to say anything as they had to run for the ferry.
Once on the ferryboat she lifted up her face to be kissed. Her
lips were cool and her gloved hand rested so lightly on his. At
Sausalito they took the trolleycar and changed and she kept
smiling at him when they ran to get good places in the scenic
car and they felt so alone in the roaring immensity of tawny
mountain and blue sky and sea. They'd never been so happy
together. She ran ahead of him all the way to the top. At the
observatory they were both breathless. They stood against a
wall out of sight of the other people and she let him kiss her
all over her face, all over her face and neck.

Scraps of mist flew past cutting patches out of their view of
the bay and the valleys and the shadowed mountains. When
they went round to the seaward side an icy wind was shrilling

through everything. A churning mass of fog was welling up from the sea like a tidal wave. She gripped his arm. 'Oh, this scares me, Fainy!' Then suddenly he told her that he'd given up his job. She looked up at him frightened and shivering in the cold wind and little and helpless; tears began to run down either side of her nose. 'But I thought you loved me, Fenian ... Do you think it's been easy for me waitin' for you all this time, wantin' you and lovin' you? Oh, I thought you loved me!'

He put his arm round her. He couldn't say anything. They started walking towards the gravity car.

'I don't want all those people to see I've been crying. We were so happy before. Let's walk down to Muir Woods.'

'It's pretty far, Maisie.'

'I don't care; I want to.'

'Gee, you're a good sport, Maisie.'

They started down the footpath and the mist blotted out everything.

After a couple of hours they stopped to rest. They left the path and found a patch of grass in the middle of a big thicket of cistus. The mist was all round, but it was bright overhead and they could feel the warmth of the sun through it. 'Ouch, I've got blisters,' she said and made a funny face that made him laugh. 'It can't be so awful far now,' he said; 'honest, Maisie.' He wanted to explain to her about the strike and the wobblies and why he was going to Goldfield, but he couldn't. All he could do was kiss her. Her mouth clung to his lips and her arms were tight round his neck.

'Honest, it won't make any difference about our gettin' married; honest, it won't ... Maisie, I'm crazy about you ... Maisie, do let me ... You must let me ... Honest, you don't know how terrible it is for me, lovin' you like this and you never lettin' me.'

He got up and smoothed down her dress. She lay there with her eyes closed and her face white; he was afraid she had fainted. He kneeled down and kissed her gently on the cheek. She smiled ever so little and pulled his head down and ruffled his hair. 'Little husband,' she said. After a while they got to their feet and walked through the redwood grove, without seeing it, to the trolley station. Going home on the ferry they decided they'd get married inside of the week. Mac promised not to go to Nevada.

Next morning he got up feeling depressed. He was selling out. When he was shaving in the bathroom he looked at himself in the mirror and said, half aloud: 'You bastard, you're selling out to the sonsofbitches.'

He went back to his room and wrote Maisie a letter.

DEAR MAISIE:
Honestly you mustn't think for one minute I don't love you ever so much, but I promised to go to Goldfield to help the gang run that paper and I've got to do it. I'll send you my address as soon as I get there and if you really need me on account of anything, I'll come right back, honestly I will.

A whole lot of kisses and love
FAINY

He went down to the *Bulletin* office and drew his pay, packed his bag and went down to the station to see when he could get a train for Goldfield, Nevada.

## The Camera Eye (9)

all day the fertilizer factories smelt something awful and at night the cabin was full of mosquitoes fit to carry you away but it was Crisfield on the Eastern Shore and if we had a gasoline boat to carry them across the bay here we could ship our tomatoes and corn and early peaches ship 'em clear to New York instead of being gypped by the commission merchants in Baltimore we'd run a truck farm ship early vegetables irrigate fertilize enrich the tobacco-exhausted land of the Northern Neck if we had a gasoline boat we'd run oysters in her in winter raise terrapin for the market

but up on the freight siding I got talking to a young guy couldn't have been much older 'n me was asleep in one of the boxcars asleep right there in the sun and the smell of cornstalks and the reek of rotting menhaden from the fertilizer factories    he had curly hair and wisps of hay in it and through his open shirt you could see his body was burned brown to the waist I guess he wasn't much account but he'd bummed all way from Minnesota he was going south and when I told him about Chesapeake Bay he wasn't surprised but said I guess it's to fur to swim it I'll git a job in a menhaden boat

## Big Bill

Big Bill Haywood was born in sixtynine in a boarding-house in Salt Lake City.

He was raised in Utah, got his schooling in Ophir, a mining camp with shooting scrapes, faro Saturday nights, whiskey spilled on pokertables piled with new silver dollars.

When he was eleven his mother bound him out to a farmer, he ran away because the farmer lashed him with a whip. That was his first strike.

He lost an eye whittling a slingshot out of cruboak.

He worked for storekeepers, ran a fruitstand, ushered in the Salt Lake Theater, was a messengerboy, bellhop at the Continental Hotel.

When he was fifteen

he went out to the mines in Humboldt County, Nevada,

his outfit was overalls, a jumper, a blue shirt, miningboots, two pair of blankets, a set of chessmen, boxinggloves and a big lunch of plum pudding his mother fixed for him.

When he married he went to live in Fort McDermitt built in the old days against the Indians, abandoned now that there was no more frontier;

there his wife bore their first baby without doctor or midwife. Bill cut the navelstring, Bill buried the afterbirth;

the child lived. Bill earned money as he could surveying, haying in Paradise Valley, breaking colts, riding a wide rangy country.

One night at Thompson's Mill, he was one of five men who met by chance and stopped the night in the abandoned ranch. Each of them had lost an eye, they were the only oneeyed men in the county.

They lost the homestead, things went to pieces, his wife was sick, he had children to support. He went to work as a miner at Silver City.

At Silver City, Idaho, he joined the W.F.M., there he held his first union office; he was delegate to the Silver City miners to the convention of the Western Federation of Miners held in Salt Lake City in '98.

From then on he was an organizer, a speaker, an exhorter, the wants of all the miners were his wants; he fought Coeur D'Alenes, Telluride, Cripple Creek,

joined the Socialist Party, wrote and spoke through Idaho,

Utah, Nevada, Montana, Colorado to miners striking for an eighthour day, better living, a share of the wealth they hacked out of the hills.

In Chicago in January 1905 a conference was called that met at the same hall in Lake Street where the Chicago anarchists had addressed meetings twenty years before.

William D. Haywood was permanent chairman. It was this conference that wrote the manifesto that brought into being the I.W.W.

When he got back to Denver he was kidnapped to Idaho and tried with Moyer and Pettibone for the murder of the sheepherder Steunenberg, ex-Governor of Idaho, blown up by a bomb in his own home.

When they were acquitted at Boise (Darrow was their lawyer), Big Bill Haywood was known as a workingclass leader from coast to coast.

Now the wants of all the workers were his wants, he was the spokesman of the West, of the cowboys and the lumberjacks and the harvesthands and the miners.

(The steamdrill had thrown thousands of miners out of work; the steamdrill had thrown a scare into all the miners of the West.)

The W.F.M. was going conservative. Haywood worked with the I.W.W. *building a new society in the shell of the old,* campaigned for Debs for President in 1908 on the Red Special. He was in on all the big strikes in the East where revolutionary spirit was growing, Lawrence, Paterson, the strike of the Minnesota ironworkers.

They went over with the A.E.F. to save the Morgan loans, to save Wilsonian Democracy, they stood at Napoleon's tomb and dreamed empire, they had champagne cocktails at the Ritz bar and slept with Russian countesses in Montmartre and dreamed empire, all over the country at American legion posts and businessmen's luncheons it was worth money to make the eagle scream;

they lynched the pacifists and the pro-Germans and the wobblies and the reds and the bolsheviks.

Bill Haywood stood trial with the hundred and one at Chicago where Judge Landis the baseball czar

with the lack of formality of a traffic court

handed out his twenty-year sentences and thirty-thousand dollar fines.

After two years in Leavenworth they let them bail out Big

Bill (he was fifty years old a heavy broken man), the war was over, but they'd learned empire in the Hall of the Mirrors at Versailles;

the courts refused a new trial.

It was up to Haywood to jump his bail or to go back to prison for twenty years.

He was sick with diabetes, he had had a rough life, prison had broken down his health. Russia was a workers' republic; he went to Russia and was in Moscow a couple of years but he wasn't happy there, that world was too strange for him. He died there and they burned his big broken hulk of a body and buried the ashes under the Kremlin wall.

## The Camera Eye (10)

the old major who used to take me to the Capitol when the Senate and the House of Representatives were in session had been in the commissary of the Confederate Army and had very beautiful manners so the attendants bowed to the old major except for the pages who were little boys not much older than your brother was a page in the Senate once and occasionally a Representative or a Senator would look at him with slit eyes may be somebody and bow or shake hearty or raise a hand

the old major dressed very well in a morningcoat and had muttonchop whiskers and we would walk very slowly through the flat sunlight in the Botanical Gardens and look at the little labels on the trees and shrubs and see the fat robins and the starlings hop across the grass and walk up the steps and through the flat air of the rotunda with the dead statues of different sizes and the Senate Chamber flat red and the committee room and the House flat green and the committee rooms and the Supreme Court I've forgotten what color the Supreme Court was and the committee rooms

and whispering behind the door of the visitors' gallery and the dead air and a voice rattling under the glass skylights and desks slammed and the long corridors full of the dead air and our legs would get very tired and I thought of the starlings on the grass and the long streets full of dead air

and my legs were tired and I had a pain between the eyes and
the old men bowing with quick slit eyes

may be somebody and big slit unkind mouths and the
dusty black felt and the smell of coatclosets and dead air
and I wonder what the old major thought about and what
I thought about maybe about that big picture at the Corcoran
Art Gallery full of columns and steps and conspirators and
Caesar in purple fallen flat called Caesar dead

# *Mac*

Mac had hardly gotten off the train at Goldfield when a
lanky man in khaki shirt and breeches, wearing canvas army
leggins, went up to him. 'If you don't mind, what's your
business in this town, brother?'

'I'm travelin' in books.'

'What kinda books?'

'Schoolbooks and the like, for Truthseeker, Inc., of Chicago.'
Mac rattled it off very fast, and the man seemed impressed.

'I guess you're all right,' he said. 'Going up to the Eagle?'
Mac nodded. 'Plug'll take ye up, the feller with the team . . .
You see we're looking out for these goddam agitators, the I
Won't Work outfit.'

Outside the Golden Eagle Hotel there were two soldiers on
guard, toughlooking sawedoff men with their hats over their
eyes. When Mac went in everybody at the bar turned and
looked at him. He said 'Good evening, gents,' as snappily as
possible and went up to the proprietor to ask for a room. All
the while he was wondering who the hell he dared ask where
the office of the *Nevada Workman* was.

'I guess I can fix you up with a bed. Travelin' man?'

'Yes,' said Mac. 'In books.'

Down at the end a big man with walrus whiskers was standing
at the bar talking fast in a drunken whining voice, 'If they'd
only give me my head I'd run the bastards outa town soon
enough. Too goddam many lawyers mixed up in this. Run the
sonsobitches out. If they resists shoot 'em, that's what I says to
the Governor, but they're all these sonsobitches a lawyers
fussin' everythin' up all the time with warrants and habeas
corpus and longwinded rigmarole. My ass to habeas corpus.'

'All right, Joe, you tell 'em,' said the proprietor soothingly.

Mac bought a cigar and sauntered out. As the door closed behind him the big man was yelling out again, 'I said, My ass to habeas corpus.'

It was nearly dark. An icy wind blew through the ramshackle clapboard streets. His feet stumbling in the mud of the deep ruts, Mac walked round several blocks looking up at dark windows. He walked all over the town, but no sign of a newspaper office. When he found himself passing the same Chink hashjoint for the third time, he slackened his steps and stood irresolutely on the curb. At the end of the street the great jagged shank of a hill hung over the town. Across the street a young man, his head and ears huddled into the collar of a mackinaw, was loafing against the dark window of a hardware store. Mac decided he was a squarelooking stiff and went over to speak to him.

'Say, bo, where's the office of the *Nevada Workman*?'

'What the hell d'you wanter know for?'

Mac and the other man looked at each other. 'I want to see Fred Hoff . . . I came on from San Fran to help in the printin'.'

'Got a red card?'

Mac pulled out his I.W.W. membership card. 'I've got my union card, too, if you want to see that.'

'Hell, no . . . I guess you're all right, but, as the feller said, suppose I'd been a dick, you'd be in the bullpen now, bo.'

'I told 'em I was a friggin' bookagent to get into the damn town. Spent my last quarter on a cigar to keep up the burjwa look.'

The other man laughed. 'All right, fellowworker. I'll take you round.'

'What they got here, martial law?' asked Mac as he followed the man down an alley between two overgrown shanties.

'Every sonofabitchin' yellerleg in the State of Nevada right here in town . . . Lucky if you don't get run outa town with a bayonet in yer crotch, as the feller said.'

At the end of the alley was a small house like a shoebox with brightly lit windows. Young fellows in miners' clothes or overalls filled up the end of the alley and sat three deep on the rickety steps.

'What's this, a poolroom?' asked Mac.

'This is the *Nevada Workman* . . . Say, my name's Ben Evans; I'll introjuce you to the gang . . . Say, yous guys, this is fellowworker McCreary . . . he's come on from Frisco to set up type.'

'Put it there, Mac,' said a sixfooter who looked like a Swede lumberman, and gave Mac's hand a wrench that made the bones crack.

Fred Hoff had on a green eyeshade and sat behind a desk piled with galleys. He got up and shook hands. 'Oh, boy, you're just in time. There's hell to pay. They got the printer in the bullpen and we've got to get this sheet out.'

Mac took off his coat and went back to look over the press. He was leaning over the typesetter's 'stone' when Fred Hoff came back and beckoned him into a corner.

'Say, Mac, I want to explain the layout here . . . It's kind of a funny situation . . . The W.F.M.'s goin' yellow on us . . . It's a hell of a scrap. The Saint was here the other day and that bastard Mullany shot him through both arms and he's in hospital now . . . They're sore as a boil because we're instillin' ideas of revolutionary solidarity, see? We got the restaurant workers out and we got some of the minin' stiffs. Now the A.F. of L.'s gettin' wise and they've got a bonehead scab organizer in hobnobbin' with the mineowners at the Montezuma Club.'

'Hey, Fred, let me take this on gradually,' said Mac.

'Then there was a little shootin' the other day out in front of a restaurant down the line an' the stiff that owned the joint got plugged an' now they've got a couple of the boys in jail for that.'

'The hell you say.'

'And Big Bill Haywood's comin' to speak next week . . . That's about the way the situation is, Mac. I've got to tear off an article . . . You're boss printer an' we'll pay you seventeenfifty like we all get. Ever written any?'

'No.'

'It's a time like this a feller regrets he didn't work harder in school. Gosh, I wish I could write decent.'

'I'll take a swing at an article if I get a chance.'

'Big Bill'll write us some stuff. He writes swell.'

They set up a cot for Mac back of the press. It was a week before he could get time to go round to the Eagle to get his suitcase. Over the office and the presses was a long attic, with a stove in it, where most of the boys slept. Those that had blankets rolled up in their blankets, those that hadn't put their jackets over their heads, those that didn't have jackets slept as best they could. At the end of the room was a long sheet of paper where someone had printed out the Preamble in shaded block letters. On the plaster wall of the office someone had drawn a cartoon of a workingstiff labeled 'I.W.W.' giving a fat man in a stovepipe hat labeled 'mineowner' a kick in the seat of the pants. Above it they had started to letter 'solidarity' but had only gotten as far as 'SOLIDA.'

One November night Big Bill Haywood spoke at the miners' union. Mac and Fred Hoff went to report the speech for the paper. The town looked lonely as an old trashdump in the huge valley full of shrill wind and driving snow. The hall was hot and steamy with the steam of big bodies and plug tobacco and thick mountaineer clothes that gave off the shanty smell of oil lamps and charred firewood and greasy fryingpans and raw whiskey. At the beginning of the meeting men moved round uneasily, shuffling their feet and clearing the phlegm out of their throats. Mac was uncomfortable himself. In his pocket was a letter from Maisie. He knew it by heart:

DEAREST FAINY:
Everything has happened just as I was afraid of. You know what I mean, dearest little husband. It's two months already and I'm so frightened and there's nobody I can tell. Darling, you must come right back. I'll die if you don't. Honestly I'll die and I'm so lonely for you anyways and so afraid somebody'll notice. As it is we'll have to go away somewheres when we're married and not come back until plenty of time has elapsed. If I thought I could get work there I'd come to you to Goldfield. I think it would be nice if we went to San Diego. I have friends there and they say it's lovely and there we could tell people we'd been married a long time. Please come sweetest little husband. I'm so lonely for you and it's so terrible to stand this all alone. The crosses are kisses. Your loving wife,
                                          MAISIE
                    XXXXXXXXXXXXXXXX

Big Bill talked about solidarity and sticking together in the face of the masterclass and Mac kept wondering what Big Bill would do if he'd got a girl in trouble like that. Big Bill was saying the day had come to start building a new society in the shell of the old and for the workers to get ready to assume control of the industries they'd created out of their sweat and blood. When he said, 'We stand for the one big union,' there was a burst of cheering and clapping from all the wobblies in the hall. Fred Hoff nudged Mac as he clapped. 'Let's raise the roof, Mac.' The exploiting classes would be helpless against the solidarity of the whole workingclass. The militia and the yellowlegs were workingstiffs too. Once they realized the historic mission of solidarity the masterclass couldn't use them to shoot down their brothers any more. The workers must realize that every small fight, for higher wages, for free speech, for decent living conditions, was only significant as part of the big fight for the revolution and the co-operative commonwealth. Mac forgot about Maisie. By the time Big Bill had finished speaking his mind had run ahead of the speech so that he'd forgotten just what he said, but Mac was in a glow all over and was cheering to beat hell. He and Fred Hoff were cheering and the stocky Bohemian miner that smelt so bad next them was clapping and the oneeyed Pole on the other side was clapping and the bunch of Wops were clapping and the little Jap who was waiter at the Montezuma Club was clapping and the sixfoot ranchman who'd come in in hopes of seeing a fight was clapping. 'Ain't the sonofabitch some orator,' he was saying again and again. 'I tellyer, Utah's the state for mansized men. I'm from Ogden myself.'

After the meeting Big Bill was round at the office and he joked everybody and sat down and wrote an article right there for the paper. He pulled out a flask and everybody had a drink, except Fred Hoff who didn't like Big Bill's drinking, or any drinking, and they all went to bed with the next issue on the press, feeling tired and flushed and fine.

Next morning when Mac woke up he suddenly thought of Maisie and re-read her letter, and tears came to his eyes sitting on the edge of the cot before anybody was up yet. He stuck his head in a pail of icy water from the pump, that was frozen so hard he had to pour a kettleful of hot water off the stove into it to thaw it, but he couldn't get the worried stiff feeling out of his forehead. When he went over with Fred Hoff to the Chink joint for breakfast he tried to tell him he was going back to San Francisco to get married.

'Mac, you can't do it; we need you here.'

'But I'll come back, honest I will, Fred.'

'A man's first duty's to the workin'class,' said Fred Hoff.

'As soon as the kid's born an' she can go back to work I'll come back. But you know how it is, Fred. I can't pay the hospital expenses on seventeen-fifty a week.'

'You oughta been more careful.'

'But hell, Fred, I'm made of flesh and blood like everybody else. For crissake, what do you want us to be, tin saints?'

'A wobbly oughtn't to have any wife or children, not till after the revolution.'

'I'm not giving up the fight, Fred . . . I'm not sellin' out; I swear to God I'm not.'

Fred Hoff had gotten very pale. Sucking his lips in between his teeth he got up from the table and left the restaurant. Mac sat there a long time feeling gloomy as hell. Then he went back to the office of the *Workman*. Fred Hoff was at the desk writing hard. 'Say, Fred,' said Mac, 'I'll stay another month. I'll write Maisie right now.'

'I knew you'd stay, Mac; you're no quitter.'

'But Jesus God, man, you expect too much of a feller.'

'Too much is too damn little,' said Fred Hoff.

Mac started running the paper through the press.

For the next few weeks, when Maisie's letters came he put them in his pocket without reading them. He wrote her as reassuringly as he could, that he'd come as soon as the boys could get someone to take his place.

Then Christmas night he read all Maisie's letters. They were all the same; they made him cry. He didn't want to get married, but it was hell living up here in Nevada all winter without a girl, and he was sick of whoring around. He didn't want the boys to see him looking so glum, so he went down to have a drink at the saloon the restaurant workers went to. A great roaring steam of drunken singing came out of the saloon.

Going in the door he met Ben Evans. 'Hello, Ben, where you goin'?'

'I'm goin' to have a drink as the feller said.'

'Well, so am I.'

'What's the matter?'

'I'm blue as hell.'

Ben Evans laughed. 'Jesus, so am I . . . and it's Christmas, ain't it?'

They had three drinks each, but the bar was crowded and they didn't feel like celebrating; so they took a pint flask, which was all they could afford, up to Ben Evans's room. Ben Evans was a dark thickset young man with very black eyes and hair. He hailed from Louisville, Kentucky. He'd had considerable schooling and was an automobile mechanic. The room was icy cold. They sat on the bed, each of them wrapped in one of his blankets.

'Well, ain't this a way to spend Christmas?' said Mac.

'Holy Jesus, it's a good thing Fred Hoff didn't ketch us,' Mac snickered.

'Fred's a hell of a good guy, honest as the day an' all that, but he won't let a feller live.'

'I guess if the rest of us were more like Fred we'd get somewheres sooner.'

'We would at that . . . Say, Mac, I'm blue as hell about all
this business, this shootin' an' these fellers from the W.F.M.
goin' up to the Montezuma Club and playin' round with that
damn scab delegate from Washington.'

'Well, none of the wobbly crowd's done anything like
that.'

'No, but there's not enough of us . . .'

'What you need's a drink, Ben.'

'It's just like this goddam pint, as the feller said, if we had
enough of 'em, we'd get fried, but we haven't. If we had enough
boys like Fred Hoff, we'd have a revolution, but we haven't.'

They each had a drink from the pint and then Mac said:
'Say, Ben, did you ever get a girl in trouble, a girl you liked a
hellova lot?'

'Sure, hundreds of 'em.'

'Didn't it worry you?'

'For crissake, Mac, if a girl wasn't a goddam whore she
wouldn't let you, would she?'

'Jeez, I don't see it like that, Ben . . . But hell, I don't know
what to do about it . . . She's a good kid, anyways, gee . . .'

'I don't trust none of 'em . . . I know a guy onct married a
girl like that, carried on and bawled an' made out he'd knocked
her up. He married her all right an' she turned out to be a
goddam whore and he got the siph off'n her . . . You take it
from me, boy. . . . Love 'em and leave 'em, that's the only way
for stiffs like us.'

They finished up the pint. Mac went back to the *Workman*
office and went to sleep with the whiskey burning in his
stomach. He dreamed he was walking across a field with a girl
on a warm day. The whiskey was hotsweet in his mouth, buzzed
like bees in his ears. He wasn't sure if the girl was Maisie or
just a goddam whore, but he felt very warm and tender, and
she was saying in a little hotsweet voice, 'Love me up, kid,' and
he could see her body through her thin gauze dress as he leaned
over her and she kept crooning, 'Love me up, kid,' in a hotsweet
buzzing.

'Hey, Mac, ain't you ever goin' to get waked up?' Fred Hoff,
scrubbing his face and neck with a towel, was standing over
him. 'I want to get this place cleaned up before the gang gets
here.'

Mac sat up on the cot. 'Yare, what's the matter?' He didn't

have a hangover, but he felt depressed, he could tell that at once.

'Say, you certainly were stinkin' last night.'

'The hell I was, Fred . . . I had a coupla drinks, but, Jesus . . .'

'I heard you staggerin' round here goin' to bed like any goddam scissorbill.'

'Look here, Fred, you're not anybody's nursemaid. I can take care of myself.'

'You guys need nursemaids . . . You can't even wait till we won the strike before you start boozin' and whorin' around.'

Mac was sitting on the edge of the bed lacing his boots. 'What in God's name do you think we're all hangin' round here for . . . our health?'

'I don't know what the hell most of you are hangin' round for,' said Fred Hoff and went out slamming the door.

A couple of days later it turned out that there was another fellow around who could run a linotype and Mac left town. He sold his suitcase and his good clothes for five dollars and hopped a train of flatcars loaded with ore that took him down to Ludlow. In Ludlow he washed the alkali dust out of his mouth, got a meal and got cleaned up a little. He was in a terrible hurry to get to Frisco, all the time he kept thinking that Maisie might kill herself. He was crazy to see her, to sit beside her, to have her pat his hand gently while they were sitting side by side talking the way she used to do. After those bleak dusty months up in Goldfield he needed a woman. The fare to Frisco was $11.15 and he had only four dollars and some pennies left. He tried risking a dollar in a crapgame in the back of a saloon, but he lost it right away and got cold feet and left.

# Newsreel 8

Professor Ferrer, former director of the Modern School in Barcelona who has been on trial there on the charge of having been the principal instigator of the recent revolutionary movement has been sentenced to death and will be shot Wednesday unless

Cook still pins faith on Esquimaux says interior of the Island of Luzon most beautiful place on earth

QUIZZES WARM UP POLE TALK

*Oh bury me not on the lone prairie*
*Where the wild kiyotes will howl over me*
*Where the rattlesnakes hiss and the wind blows free*

GYPSY'S MARCHERS STORM SIN'S FORT

Nation's big men await trip   Englewood clubwomen move to uplift drama   Evangelist's host thousands strong pierces heart of crowded hushed levee has $3018 and is arrested

GIVE MILLION IN HOOKWORM WAR

gypsy smith's spectral parade through south side red-light region

with a bravery that brought tears to the eyes of the squad of twelve men who were detailed to shoot him Francisco Ferrer marched this morning to the trench that had been prepared to receive his body after the fatal volley

PLUNGE BY AUTO; DEATH IN RIVER

## The Camera Eye (11)

the Pennypackers went to the Presbyterian Church and the Pennypacker girls sang chilly shrill soprano in the choir

and everybody was greeted when they went into church
and outside the summer leaves on the trees wigwagged green-
blueyellow through the windows and we all filed into the
pew and I'd asked Mr Pennypacker he was a deacon in the
church who were the Molly Maguires?

a squirrel was scolding in the whiteoak but the Pennypacker girls all the young ladies in their best hats singing
the anthem who were the Molly Maguires? thoughts, bulletholes in an old barn abandoned mine pits black skeleton
tipples weedgrown dumps who were the Molly Maguires?
but it was too late you couldn't talk in church and all the
young ladies best hats and pretty pink green blue yellow
dresses and the squirrel scolding who were the Molly
Maguires?

and before I knew it it was communion and I wanted
to say I hadn't been baptized but all eyes looked shut up
when I started to whisper to Con

communion was grapejuice in little glasses and little
squares of stale bread and you had to gulp the bread and
put your handkerchief over your mouth and look holy and
the little glasses made a funny sucking noise and all the quiet
church in the middle of the sunny brightblue Sunday in the
middle of whiteoaks wigwagging and the smell of fries from
the white house and the blue quiet Sunday smoke of
chimneys from stoves where fried chicken sizzled and fritters
and brown gravy set back to keep hot

in the middle of squirrels and minetipples in the middle
of the blue Pennsylvania summer Sunday the little glasses
sucking to get the last drop of communion

and I felt itchy in the back of my neck would I be struck
by lightning eating the bread drinking the communion me
not believing or baptized or Presbyterian and who were the
Molly Maguires? masked men riding at night shooting
bullets into barns at night what were they after in the oldtime
night?

church was over and everybody was filing out and being
greeted as they went out and everybody had a good appetite
after communion but I couldn't eat much itchy in the back
of the neck scary with masked men riding Molly Maguires

# Newsreel 9

FORFEIT STARS BY DRINKING

*'Oh bury me not*
*on the lone prairie'*
*They heeded not his dying prayer*
*They buried him there on the lone prairie*

COLLEGE HEAD DENIES KISSES

then our courage returned, for we knew that rescue was
near at hand, we shouted and yelled again but did not know
whether we were heard. Then came the unsealing and I lost
consciousness. All the days and nights fell back and I
dropped into a sleep

VOTE AT MIDNIGHT ON ALTMAN'S FATE

*This is the fourth day we have been down here. That is what*
*I think, but our watches stopped. I have been waiting in the*
*dark because we have been eating the wax from our safety*
*lamps. I have also eaten a plug of tobacco, some bark and*
*some of my shoe. I could only chew it. I hope you can read*
*this. I am not afraid to die. O holy Virgin have mercy on me.*
*I think my time has come. You know what my property is.*
*We worked for it together and it is all yours. This is my will*
*and you must keep it. You have been a good wife. May the*
*Holy Virgin guard you. I hope this reaches you sometime*
*and you can read it. It has been very quiet down here and*
*I wonder what has become of our comrades. Goodbye until*
*heaven shall bring us together.*

GIRLS' ANNOYER LASHED IN PUBLIC
COVETS OSTRICHES

*In a little box just six by three*
*And his bones now rot on the lone prairie*

## *Mac*

Mac went down to the watertank beyond the yards to wait for a chance to hop a freight. The old man's hat and his ruptured shoes were ashen gray with dust; he was sitting all hunched up with his head between his knees and didn't make a move until Mac was right up to him. Mac sat down beside him. A rank smell of feverish sweat came from the old man. 'What's the trouble, daddy?'

'I'm through, that's all . . . I been a lunger all my life an' I guess it's got me now.' His mouth twisted in a spasm of pain. He let his head droop between his knees. After a minute he raised his head again, making little feeble gasps with his mouth like a dying fish. When he got his breath he said, 'It's a razor a-slicin' off my lungs every time. Stand by, will you, kid?'

'Sure I will,' said Mac.

'Listen, kid, I wanna go West to where there's trees an' stuff . . . You got to help me into one o' them cars. I'm too weak for the rods . . . Don't let me lay down . . . I'll start bleedin' if I lay down, see.' He choked again.

'I got a coupla bucks. I'll square it with the brakeman, maybe.'

'You don't talk like no vag.'

'I'm a printer. I wanta make San Francisco soon as I can.'

'A workin'man; I'll be a sonofabitch. Listen here, kid . . . I ain't worked in seventeen years.'

The train came in and the engine stood hissing by the watertank.

Mac helped the old man to his feet and got him propped in the corner of a flatcar that was loaded with machine parts covered with a tarpaulin. He saw the fireman and the engineer looking at them out of the cab, but they didn't say anything.

When the train started the wind was cold. Mac took off his coat and put it behind the old man's head to keep it from jiggling with the rattling of the car. The old man sat with his eyes closed and his head thrown back. Mac didn't know whether he was dead or not. It got to be night. Mac was terribly cold and huddled shivering in a fold of tarpaulin in the other end of the car.

In the gray of dawn Mac woke up from a doze with his teeth chattering. The train had stopped on a siding. His legs were so numb it was some time before he could stand on them.

He went to look at the old man, but he couldn't tell whether he was dead or not. It got a little lighter and the east began to glow like the edge of a piece of iron in a forge. Mac jumped to the ground and walked back along the train to the caboose.

The brakeman was drowsing beside his lantern. Mac told him that an old tramp was dying in one of the flatcars. The brakeman had a small flask of whiskey in his good coat that hung on a nail in the caboose. They walked together up the track again. When they got to the flatcar it was almost day. The old man had flopped over on his side. His face looked white and grave like the face of a statue of a Civil War general. Mac opened his coat and the filthy torn shirts and underclothes and put his hand on the old man's chest. It was cold and lifeless as a board. When he took his hand away there was sticky blood on it.

'Hemorrhage,' said the brakeman, making a perfunctory clucking noise in his mouth.

The brakeman said they'd have to get the body off the train. They laid him down flat in the ditch beside the ballast with his hat over his face. Mac asked the brakeman if he had a spade so that they could bury him, so that the buzzards wouldn't get him, but he said no, the gandywalkers would find him and bury him. He took Mac back to the caboose and gave him a drink and asked him all about how the old man had died.

Mac beat his way to San Francisco.

Maisie was cold and bitter at first, but after they'd talked a little while she said he looked thin and ragged as a bum and burst into tears and kissed him. They went to get her savings out of the bank and bought Mac a suit and went down to City Hall and got married without saying anything to her folks. They were both very happy going down on the train to San Diego, and they got a furnished room there with kitchen privileges and told the landlady they'd been married a year. They wired Maisie's folks that they were down there on their honeymoon and would be back soon.

Mac got work there at a job printer's and they started payments on a bungalow at Pacific Beach. The work wasn't bad and he was pretty happy in his quiet life with Maisie. After all, he'd had enough bumming for a while. When Maisie went to the hospital to have the baby, Mac had to beg a two months' advance of pay from Ed Balderston, his boss. Even at that they had to take out a second mortgage on the bungalow to pay the doctor's bill. The baby was a girl and had blue eyes and they named her Rose.

Life in San Diego was sunny and quiet. Mac went to work mornings on the steamcar and came back evenings on the steamcar and Sundays he puttered round the house or sometimes sat on one of the beaches with Maisie and the kid. It was understood between them now that he had to do everything that Maisie wanted because he'd given her such a tough time before they were married. The next year they had another kid and Maisie was sick and in hospital a long time after, so that now all that he could do with his pay each week was cover the interest on his debts, and he was always having to kid the grocerystore along and the milkman and the bakery to keep their charge-accounts going from week to week. Maisie read a lot of magazines and always wanted new things for the house, a pianola, or a new icebox, or a fireless cooker. Her brothers were making good money in the realestate business in Los Angeles and her folks were coming up in the world. Whenever she got a letter from them she'd worry Mac about striking his boss for more pay or moving to a better job.

When there was anybody of the wobbly crowd in town down on his uppers or when they were raising money for strike funds or anything like that, he'd help them out with a couple of dollars, but he never could do much for fear Maisie would find out about it. Whenever she found *The Appeal to Reason* or any other radical paper round the house she'd burn it up, and then they'd quarrel and be sulky and make each other's lives miserable for a few days, until Mac decided what was the use, and never spoke to her about it. But it kept them apart almost as if she thought he was going out with some other woman.

One Saturday afternoon Mac and Maisie had managed to get a neighbor to take care of the kids and were going into a vaudeville theater when they noticed a crowd at the corner in front of Marshall's drugstore. Mac elbowed his way through. A thin young man in blue denim was standing close to the corner lamppost where the firealarm was, reading the Declaration of Independence: *When in the course of human events . . .* A cop came up and told him to move on . . . *inalienable right . . . life, liberty, and the pursuit of happiness.*

Now there were two cops. One of them had the young man by the shoulders and was trying to pull him loose from the lamppost.

'Come on, Fainy, we'll be late for the show,' Maisie kept saying.

'Hey, get a file; the bastard's locked himself to the post,' he heard one cop say to the other. By that time Maisie had managed to hustle him to the theater boxoffice. After all, he'd promised to take her to the show and she hadn't been out all winter. The last thing he saw the cop had hauled off and hit the young guy in the corner of the jaw.

Mac sat there in the dark stuffy theater all afternoon. He didn't see the acts or the pictures between the acts. He didn't speak to Maisie. He sat there feeling sick in the pit of his stomach. The boys must be staging a free-speech fight right here in town. Now and then he glanced at Maisie's face in the dim glow from the stage. It had puffed out a little in well-satisfied curves like a cat sitting by a warm stove, but she was still a good looker. She'd already forgotten everything and was completely happy looking at the show, her lips parted, her eyes bright, like a little girl at a party. 'I guess I've sold out to the sonsobitches all right, all right,' he kept saying to himself.

The last number on the programme was Eva Tanguay. The nasal voice singing *I'm Eva Tanguay, I don't care* brought Mac out of his sullen trance. Everything suddenly looked bright and clear to him, the proscenium with its heavy gold fluting, the people's faces in the boxes, the heads in front of him, the tawdry powdery mingling of amber and blue lights on the stage, the scrawny woman flinging herself around inside the rainbow hoop of the spotlight.

> *The papers say that I'm insane*
> *But . . . I . . . don't . . . care.*

Mac got up. 'Maisie, I'll meet you at the house. You see the rest of the show. I feel kind of bum.' Before she could answer, he'd slipped out past the other people in the row, down the aisle and out. On the street there was nothing but the ordinary Saturday afternoon crowd. Mac walked round and round the downtown district. He didn't even know where I.W.W. headquarters was. He had to talk to somebody. As he passed the Hotel Brewster he caught a whiff of beer. What he needed was a drink. This way he was going nuts.

At the next corner he went into a saloon and drank four rye whiskies straight. The bar was lined with men drinking, treating each other, talking loud about baseball, prizefights, Eva Tanguay and her Salome dance.

Beside Mac was a big redfaced man with a widebrimmed felt hat on the back of his head. When Mac reached for his fifth drink this man put his hand on his arm and said, 'Pard, have that on me if you don't mind . . . I'm celebratin' today.'

'Thanks; here's lookin' at you,' said Mac.

'Pard, if you don't mind my sayin' so, you're drinkin' like you wanted to drink the whole barrel up at once and not leave any for the rest of us . . . Have a chaser.'

'All right, bo,' said Mac. 'Make it a beer chaser.'

'My name's McCreary,' said the big man. 'I just sold my fruit crop. I'm from up San Jacinto way.'

'So's my name McCreary, too,' said Mac.

They shook hands heartily.

'By the living jumbo, that's a coincidence . . . We must be kin or pretty near it . . . Where you from, pard?'

'I'm from Chicago, but my folks was Irish.'

'Mine was from East, Delaware . . . but it's the good old Scotch-Irish stock.'

They had more drinks on that. Then they went to another saloon where they sat in a corner at a table and talked. The big man talked about his ranch and his apricot crop and how his wife was bedridden since his last child had come. 'I'm awful fond of the old gal, but what can a feller do? Can't get gelded just to be true to your wife."

'I like my wife swell,' said Mac, 'and I've got swell kids. Rose is four and she's beginning to read already and Ed's about learnin' to walk. . . . But hell, before I was married I used to think I might amount to somethin' in the world . . . I don't mean I thought I was anythin' in particular . . . You know how it is.'

'Sure, pard, I used to feel that way when I was a young feller.'

'Maisie's a fine girl, too, and I like her better all the time,' said Mac, feeling a warm tearing wave of affection go over him, like sometimes a Saturday evening when he'd helped her bathe the kids and put them to bed and the room was still steamy from their baths and his eyes suddenly met Maisie's eyes and there was nowhere they had to go and they were just both of them there together.

The man from up San Jacinto way began to sing:

> *Oh my wife has gone to the country,*
> *Hooray, hooray.*
> *I love my wife, but oh you kid,*
> *My wife's gone away.*

'But God damn it to hell,' said Mac, 'a man's got to work for more than himself and his kids to feel right.'

'I agree with you absholootely, pard; every man for himself, and the devil take the hindmost.'

'Oh, hell,' said Mac, 'I wish I was on the bum again or up at Goldfield with the bunch.'

They drank and drank and ate free lunch and drank some more, all the time rye with beer chasers, and the man from up San Jacinto way had a telephone number and called up some girls and they bought a bottle of whiskey and went out to their apartment, and the rancher from up San Jacinto way sat with a girl on each knee singing *My wife has gone to the country*. Mac just sat belching in a corner with his head dangling over his chest; then suddenly he felt bitterly angry and got to his feet upsetting a table with a glass vase on it.

'McCreary,' he said, 'this is no place for a classconscious rebel . . . I'm a wobbly, damn you . . . I'm goin' out and get in this free-speech fight.'

The other McCreary went on singing and paid no attention. Mac went out and slammed the door. One of the girls followed him out jabbering about the broken vase, but he pushed her in the face and went out into the quiet street. It was moonlight. He'd lost the last steamcar and would have to walk home.

When he got to the house he found Maisie sitting on the porch in her kimono. She was crying. 'And I had such a nice supper for you,' she kept saying, and her eyes looked into him cold and bitter the way they'd been when he'd gotten back from Goldfield before they were married.

The next day he had a hammering headache and his stomach was upset. He figured up he'd spent fifteen dollars that he couldn't afford to waste. Maisie wouldn't speak to him. He stayed on in bed, rolling round, feeling miserable, wishing he could go to sleep and stay asleep forever. That Sunday evening Maisie's brother Bill came to supper. As soon as he got into the house Maisie started talking to Mac as if nothing had happened. It made him sore to feel that this was just in order to keep Bill from knowing they had quarreled.

Bill was a powerfullybuilt towhaired man with a red neck, just beginning to go to fat. He sat at the table, eating the potroast and cornbread Maisie had made, talking big about the real estate boom up in Los Angeles. He'd been a locomotive engineer and had been hurt in a wreck and had had the lucky breaks with a couple of options on lots he'd bought with his compensation money. He tried to argue Mac into giving up his job in San Diego and coming in with him. 'I'll get you in on the ground floor, just for Maisie's sake,' he said over and over again. 'And in ten years you'll be a rich man, like I'm goin' to be in less time than that . . . Now's the time, Maisie, for you folks to make a break, while you're young, or it'll be too late and Mac'll just be a workingman all his life.'

Maisie's eyes shone. She brought out a chocolate layer cake and a bottle of sweet wine. Her cheeks flushed and she kept laughing showing all her pearly teeth. She hadn't looked so pretty since she'd had her first baby. Bill's talk about money made her drunk.

'Suppose a feller didn't want to get rich . . . you know what Gene Debs said, "I want to rise with the ranks, not from the ranks," ' said Mac.

Maisie and Bill laughed. 'When a guy talks like that he's ripe for the nuthouse, take it from me," said Bill.

Mac flushed and said nothing.

Bill pushed back his chair and cleared his throat in a serious tone: 'Look here, Mac . . . I'm goin' to be around this town for a few days lookin' over the situation, but looks to me like things was pretty dead. Now what I propose is this . . . You know what I think of Maisie . . . I think she's about the sweetest little girl in the world. I wish my wife had half what Maisie's got . . . Well, anyway, here's my proposition: Out on Ocean View Avenue I've got several magnificent missionstyle bungalows I haven't disposed of yet, twentyfivefoot frontage on a refined residential street by a hundredfoot depth. Why, I've gotten as high as five grand in cold cash for 'em. In a year or two none of us fellers'll be able to stick our noses in there. It'll be millionaires' row . . . Now if you're willing to have the house in Maisie's name I'll tell you what I'll do . . . I'll swap properties with you, paying all the expenses of searching title and transfer and balance up the mortgages, that I'll hold so's to keep 'em in the family, so that you won't have to make substantially bigger payments than you do here, and will be launched on the road to success.'

'Oh, Bill, you darling!' cried Maisie. She ran over and kissed him on the top of the head and sat swinging her legs on the arm of the chair.

'Gee, I'll have to sleep on that,' said Mac; 'it's mighty white of you to make the offer.'

'Fainy, I'd think you'd be more grateful to Bill,' snapped Maisie. 'Of course we'll do it.'

'No, you're quite right,' said Bill. 'A man's got to think a proposition like that over. But don't forget the advantages offered, better schools for the kids, more refined surroundings, an upandcoming boom town instead of a dead one, chance to get ahead in the world instead of being a goddam wageslave.'

So a month later the McCrearys moved up to Los Angeles. The expenses of moving and getting the furniture installed put Mac five hundred dollars in debt. On top of that little Rose caught the measles and the doctor's bill started mounting. Mac couldn't get a job on any of the papers. Up at the union local that he transferred to they had ten men out of work as it was.

He spent a lot of time walking about town worrying. He didn't like to be at home any more. He and Maisie never got on now. Maisie was always thinking about what went on at brother Bill's house, what kind of clothes Mary Virginia, his wife, wore, how they brought up their children, the fine new victrola they'd bought. Mac sat on benches in parks round town, reading *The Appeal to Reason* and *The Industrial Worker* and the local papers.

One day he noticed *The Industrial Worker* sticking out of the pocket of the man beside him. They had both sat on the bench a long time when something made him turn to look at the man. 'Say, aren't you Ben Evans?'

'Well, Mac, I'll be goddamned . . . What's the matter, boy, you're lookin' thin?'

'Aw, nothin', I'm lookin' for a master, that's all.'

They talked for a long time. Then they went to have a cup of coffee in a Mexican restaurant where some of the boys hung out. A young blond fellow with blue eyes joined them there who talked English with an accent. Mac was surprised to find out that he was a Mexican. Everybody talked Mexico. Madero had started his revolution. The fall of Diaz was expected any day. All over the peons were taking to the hills, driving the rich cientificos off their ranches. Anarchist propaganda was spreading among the town workers. The restaurant had a warm smell of chiles and overroasted coffee. On each table there were niggerpink and vermilion paper flowers, an occasional flash of white teeth in bronze and brown faces talking low. Some of the Mexicans there belonged to the I.W.W., but most of them were anarchists. The talk of revolution and foreign places made him feel happy and adventurous again, as if he had a purpose in life, like when he'd been on the bum with Ike Hall.

'Say, Mac, let's go to Mexico and see if there's anything in this revoloossione talk,' Ben kept saying.

'If it wasn't for the kids . . . Hell, Fred Hoff was right when he bawled me out and said a revolutionist oughtn't to marry.'

Eventually Mac got a job as linotype operator on *The Times*, and things at the house were a little better, but he never had any spare money, as everything had to go into paying debts and interest on mortgages. It was night work again, and he hardly ever saw Maisie and the kids any more. Sundays Maisie would take little Ed to brother Bill's and he and Rose would go for walks or take trolleytrips. That was the best part of the week. Saturday nights he'd sometimes get to a lecture or go down to chat with the boys at the I.W.W. local, but he was scared to be seen round in radical company too much for fear of losing his job. The boys thought he was pretty yellow but put up with him because they thought of him as an oldtimer.

He got occasional letters from Milly telling him about Uncle Tim's health. She had married a man named Cohen who was a registered accountant and worked in one of the offices at the stockyards. Uncle Tim lived with them. Mac would have liked to bring him down to live with him in Los Angeles, but he knew that it would only mean squabbling with Maisie. Milly's letters were pretty depressing. She felt funny, she said, to be married to a Jew. Uncle Tim was always poorly. The doctor said it was the drink, but whenever they gave him any money he drank it right up. She wished she could have children. Fainy was lucky, she thought, to have such nice children. She was afraid that poor Uncle Tim wasn't long for this world.

The same day that the papers carried the murder of Madero in Mexico City, Mac got a wire from Milly that Uncle Tim was dead and please to wire money for the funeral. Mac went to the savingsbank and drew out $53.75 he had in an account for the children's schooling and took it down to the Western Union and wired fifty to her. Maisie didn't find out until the baby's birthday came around, when she went down to deposit five dollars birthday money from brother Bill.

That night when Mac let himself in by the latchkey he was surprised to find the light on in the hall. Maisie was sitting half asleep on the hall settee with a blanket wrapped round her waiting for him. He was pleased to see her and went up to kiss her. 'What's the matter, baby?' he said. She pushed him away from her and jumped to her feet.

'You thief,' she said. 'I couldn't sleep till I told you what I thought of you. I suppose you've been spending it on drink or on some other woman. That's why I never see you any more.'

'Maisie, calm down, old girl . . . What's the matter; let's talk about it quietly.'

'I'll get a divorce, that's what I'll do. Stealing money from your own children to make yourself a bum with . . . your own poor little . . .'

Mac drew himself up and clenched his fists. He spoke very quietly, although his lips were trembling.

'Maisie, I had an absolute right to take out that money. I'll deposit some more in a week or two, and it's none of your damn business.'

'A fat chance you saving up fifty dollars; you aren't man enough to make a decent living for your wife and children so you have to take it out of your poor little innocent children's bank account,' Maisie broke out into dry sobbing.

'Maisie, that's enough of that . . . I'm about through.'

'I'm the one that's through with you and your ungodly socialistic talk. That never got nobody anywheres, and the low-down bums you go around with . . . I wish to God I'd never married you. I never would have, you can be damn well sure of that if I hadn't got caught the way I did.'

'Maisie, don't talk like that.'

Maisie walked straight up to him, her eyes wide and feverish.

'This house is in my name; don't forget that.'

'All right, I'm through.'

Before he knew it he had slammed the door behind him and was walking down the block. It began to rain. Each raindrop made a splatter the size of a silver dollar in the dust of the street. It looked like stage rain round the arclight. Mac couldn't think where to go. Drenched, he walked and walked. At one corner there was a clump of palms in a yard that gave a certain amount of shelter. He stood there a long time shivering. He was almost crying thinking of the warm gentleness of Maisie when he used to pull the cover a little way back and slip into bed beside her asleep when he got home from work in the clanking sour printing plant; her breasts, the feel of the nipples through the thin nightgown; the kids in their cots out on the sleepingporch, him leaning over to kiss each of the little warm foreheads. 'Well, I'm through,' he said aloud as if he were speaking to somebody else. Then only did the thought come to him. 'I'm free to see the country now, to work for the movement, to go on the bum again.'

Finally he went to Ben Evans's boardinghouse. It was a long time before he could get anybody to come to the door. When he finally got in Ben sat up in bed and looked at him stupid with sleep. 'What the hell?'

'Say, Ben, I've just broken up housekeepin' . . . I'm goin' to Mexico.'

'Are the cops after you? For crissake, this wasn't any place to come.'

'No, it's just my wife.'

Ben laughed. 'Oh, for the love of Mike!'

'Say, Ben, do you want to come to Mexico and see the revolution?'

'What the hell could you do in Mexico? . . . Anyway, the boys elected me secretary of local 257 . . . I got to stay here an' earn my seventeen-fifty. Say, you're soaked; take your clothes off and put on my workclothes hangin' on the back of the door . . . You better get some sleep. I'll move over.'

Mac stayed in town two weeks until they could get a man to take his place at the linotype. He wrote Maisie that he was going away and that he'd send her money to help support the kids as soon as he was in a position to. Then one morning he got on the train with twentyfive dollars in his pocket and a ticket to Yuma, Arizona. Yuma turned out to be hotter'n the hinges of hell. A guy at the railroadmen's boardinghouse told him he'd sure die of thirst if he tried going into Mexico there, and nobody knew anything about the revolution, anyway. So he beat his way along the Southern Pacific to El Paso. Hell had broken loose across the border, everybody said. The bandits were likely to take Juarez at any moment. They shot Americans on sight. The bars of El Paso were full of ranchers and miningmen bemoaning the good old days when Porfirio Diaz was in power and a white man could make money in Mexico. So it was with beating heart that Mac walked across the international bridge into the dusty bustling adobe streets of Juarez.

Mac walked around looking at the small trolleycars and the mules and the walls daubed with seablue and the peon women squatting behind piles of fruit in the marketplace and the crumbling scrollface churches and the deep bars open to the street. Everything was strange and the air was peppery to his nostrils and he was wondering what he was going to do next.

It was late afternoon of an April day. Mac was sweating in his blue flannel shirt. His body felt gritty and itchy and he wanted a bath. 'Gettin' too old for this kinda stuff,' he told himself. At last he found the house of a man named Ricardo Perez whom one of the Mexican anarchists in Los Angeles had told him to look up. He had trouble finding him in the big house with an untidy courtyard, on the edge of town. None of the women hanging out clothes seemed to understand Mac's lingo. At last Mac heard a voice from above in carefully modulated English. 'Come up if you are looking for Ricardo Perez . . . please . . . I am Ricardo Perez.' Mac looked up and saw a tall bronzecolored grayhaired man in an old tan duster leaning from the top gallery of the courtyard. He went up the iron steps. The tall man shook hands with him.

'Fellowworker McCreary . . . My comrades wrote me you were coming.'

'That's me, all right . . . I'm glad you talk English.'

'I lived in Santa Fe many years and in Brockton, Massachusetts. Sit down . . . please . . . I am very happy to welcome an American revolutionary worker . . . Though our ideas probably do not entirely agree we have much in common. We are comrades in the big battle.' He patted Mac on the shoulder and pressed him into a chair. 'Please.' There were several little yellow children in torn shirts running round barefoot. Ricardo Perez sat down and took the smallest on his knee, a little girl with kinky pigtails and a smudged face. The place smelt of chile and scorched olive oil and children and washing. 'What are you going to do in Mexico, fellowworker?'

Mac blushed. 'Oh, I want to kinda get into things, into the revolution.'

'The situation is very confusing here . . . Our townworkers are organizing and are classconcious, but the peons, the peasants, are easily misled by unscrupulous leaders.'

'I want to see some action, Perez . . . I was living in Los Angeles an' gettin' to be a goddam booster like the rest of 'em. I can earn my keep in the printin' line, I guess.'

'I must introduce you to the comrades . . . Please . . . We will go now.'

Blue dusk was swooping down on the streets when they went out. Lights were coming out yellow. Mechanical pianos jinglejangled in bars. In a gateway a little outoftune orchestra was playing. The market was all lit up by flares, all kinds of shiny brightcolored stuff was for sale at booths. At a corner an old

Indian and an old broadfaced woman, both of them blind and heavily pockmarked, were singing a shrill endless song in the middle of a dense group of short thickset country people, the women with black shawls over their heads, the men in white cotton suits like pajamas.

'They sing about the murder of Madero . . . It is very good for the education of the people . . . You see they cannot read the papers so they get their news in songs . . . It was your ambassador murdered Madero. He was a bourgeois idealist but a great man . . . Please . . . Here is the hall. . . . You see that sign says "Viva the Revindicating Revolution prelude to the Social Revolution." This is the hall of the Anarchist Union of Industry and Agriculture. Huerta has a few federales here but they are so weak they dare not attack us. Ciudad Juarez is heart and soul with the revolution . . . Please . . . you will greet the comrades with a few words.'

The smoky hall and the platform were filled with swarthy men in blue denim workclothes; in the back were a few peons in white. Many hands shook Mac's, black eyes looked sharp into his, several men hugged him. He was given a campchair in the front row on the platform. Evidently Ricardo Perez was chairman. Applause followed in every pause in his speech. A feeling of big events hovered in the hall. When Mac got on his feet, somebody yelled 'Solidarity forever' in English. Mac stammered a few words about how he wasn't an official representative of the I.W.W., but that all the same classconscious American workers were watching the Mexican revolution with big hopes, and ended up with the wobbly catchword about building the new society in the shell of the old. The speech went big when Perez translated it and Mac felt pretty good. Then the meeting went on and on, more and more speeches and occasional songs. Mac found himself nodding several times. The sound of the strange language made him sleepy. He barely managed to keep awake until a small band in the open door of the hall broke into a tune and everybody sang and the meeting broke up.

'That's *Cuatro Milpas* . . . that means four cornfields . . . that's a song of the peons everybody's singin' now,' said Perez.

'I'm pretty hungry . . . I'd like to get a little something to eat somewheres,' said Mac. 'I haven't eaten since morning when I had a cup of coffee and a doughnut in El Paso.'

'We will eat at the house of our comrade,' said Perez. 'Please . . . this way.'

They went in off the street, now black and empty, through a tail door hung with a bead curtain, into a whitewashed room brightly lit by an acetylene flare that smelt strong of carbide. They sat down at the end of a long table with a spotted cloth on it. The table gradually filled with people from the meeting, mostly young men in blue workclothes, with thin sharp faces. At the other end sat an old dark man with the big nose and broad flat cheekbones of an Indian. Perez poured Mac out two glasses of funnytasting white drink that made his head spin. The food was very hot with pepper and chile and he choked on it a little bit. The Mexicans petted Mac like a child at his birthday party. He had to drink many glasses of beer and cognac. Perez went home early and left him in charge of a young fellow named Pablo. Pablo had a Colt automatic on a shoulder strap that he was very proud of. He spoke a little pidginenglish and sat with one hand round Mac's neck and the other on the buckle of his holster. 'Gringo bad . . . Kill him quick . . . Fellowworker good . . . internacional . . . hurray,' he kept saying. They sang the *International* several times and then the *Marseillaise* and the *Carmagnole*. Mac was carried along in a peppery haze. He sang and drank and ate and everything began to lose outline.

'Fellowworker marry nice girl,' said Pablo. They were standing at a bar somewhere. He made a gesture of sleeping with his two hands against his face. 'Come.'

They went to a dancehall. At the entrance everybody had to leave his gun on a table guarded by a soldier in a visored cap. Mac noticed that the men and girls drew away from him a little. Pablo laughed. 'They think you gringo . . . I tell them revolucionario internacional. There she, nice girl . . . Not goddam whore . . . not pay, she nice workinggirl . . . comrade.'

Mac found himself being introduced to a brown broadfaced girl named Encarnacion. She was neatly dressed and her hair was very shinyblack. She gave him a bright flash of a smile. He patted her on the cheek. They drank some beer at the bar and left. Pablo had a girl with him too. The others stayed on at the dancehall. Pablo and his girl walked round to Encarnacion's house with them. It was a room in a little courtyard. Beyond it was a great expanse of lightcolored desert land stretching as far as you could see under a waning moon. In the distance were some tiny specks of fires. Pablo pointed at them with his full hand and whispered, 'Revolucion.'

Then they said goodnight at the door of Encarnacion's little room that had a bed, a picture of the Virgin and a new photograph of Madero stuck up by a pin. Encarnacion closed the door, bolted it and sat down on the bed looking up at Mac with a smile.

## The Camera Eye (12)

when everybody went away for a trip Jeanne took us out to play every day in Farragut Square and told you about how in the Jura in winter the wolves come down and howl through the streets of the villages

and sometimes we'd see President Roosevelt ride by all alone on a bay horse and once we were very proud because when we took off our hats we were very proud because he smiled and showed his teeth like in the newspaper and touched his hat and we were very proud and he had an aide de camp

but we had a cloth duck that we used to play with on the steps until it began to get dark and the wolves howled ran with little children's blood dripping from their snout through the streets of the villages only it was summer and between dog and wolf we'd be put to bed and Jeanne was a young French girl from the Jura where the wolves howled ran through the streets and when everybody had gone to bed she would take you into her bed

and it was a very long scary story and the worst of the wolves howled through the streets gloaming to freeze little children's blood was the Loup Garou howling in the Jura and we were scared and she had breasts under her nightgown and the Loup Garou was terrible scary and black hair and rub against her and outside the wolves howled in the streets and it was wet there and she said it was nothing she had just washed herself

but the Loup Garou was really a man hold me close cheri a man howled through streets with a bloody snout that tore up the bellies of girls and little children Loup Garou

and afterwards you knew what girls were made like and she was very silly and made you promise not to tell but you wouldn't have anyway

# Newsreel 10

MOON'S PATENT IS FIZZLE

insurgents win at Kansas polls.  Oak Park soulmates part  Eight thousand to take autoride  says girl begged for her husband

PIT SENTIMENT FAVORS UPTURN

*Oh you be-eautiful doll*
*You great big beautiful doll*

the world cannot understand all that is involved in this, she said. It appears like an ordinary worldly affair with the trappings of what is low and vulgar but there is nothing of the sort. He is honest and sincere. I know him. I have fought side by side with him. My heart is with him now.

*Let me throw my arms around you*
*Honey ain't I glad I found you*

ALMOST MOTIONLESS IN MIDSUMMER LANGUOR ON BUSINESS SEAS ONE MILLION SEE DRUNKARDS BOUNCED

JURORS AT GATES OF BEEF BARONS

compare love with Vesuvius  emblazoned streets await tramp of paladins

*Honey ain't I glad I found you*
*Oh you beautiful doll*
*You great big beautiful doll*

TRADES WHITE HORSE FOR RED

Madero's troops defeat rebels in battle at Parral Roosevelt carries Illinois  oratory closes eyelids  Chicago pleads for more water

CONFESSED ANARCHISTS ON BENDED KNEES
KISS U.S. FLAG

THE SUNBEAM MOVEMENT IS SPREADING

BOMB NO. 4 IN LEVEE WAR SPLINTERS
WEST SIDE SALOON

*a report printed Wednesday that a patient in a private
pavilion in St Luke's Hospital undergoing an operation for
the extirpation of a cancerous growth at the base of the
tongue was General Grant was denied by both the hospital
authorities and Lieut. Howzes who characterized the story
as a deliberate fabrication*

## The Camera Eye (13)

he was a towboat captain and he knew the river blind-
fold from Indian Head to the Virginia Capes and the bay
and the Eastan Shoa up to Baltima' for that matter and he
lived in a redbrick house in Alexandria the pilothouse
smelt of a hundred burntout pipes.

that's the *Mayflower* the President's yacht and that
there's the *Dolphin* and that's the ole monitor *Tippecanoe*
and that there's the ravenoo cutter and we're just passin'
the po-lice boat

when Cap'n Keen reaches up to pull the whistle on the
ceiling of the pilothouse you can see the red and green
bracelet tattoed under the black hairs on his wrist

Ma soul an' body ole Cap'n Gifford used ter be a frien'
o' mahne many's the time we been oysterin' together on the
Eastan Shoa an' oysterpirates used to shanghai young fellers
in those days an' make 'em work all winter you couldn't
git away less you swam ashoa and the water was too damna-
tion cole an' the ole man used to take the fellers' clothes
away so's they couldn't git ashoa when they was anchored
up in a crik or near a house or somethin' boy they was mean
customers the oysterpirates ma soul and body onct there
was a young feller they worked till he dropped and then
they'd just sling him overboard tongin' for oysters or

dredgin' like them oysterpirates did's the meanest kinda
work in winter with the spray freezin' on the lines an' cuttin'
your hands to shreds an' the dredge foulin' every minute
an' us havin' to haul it up an' fix it with our hands in the
icy water hauled up a stiff onct    What's a stiff?   Ma
soul an' body a stiff's a dead man ma boy a young feller it
was too without a stitch on him an' the body looked like it
had been beat with a belayin' pin somethin' terrible or an'
oar mebbe reckon he wouldn't work or was sick or somethin' an' the ole man jus' beat him till he died sure couldn't
a been nothin' but an oysterpirate


## *Janey*

When Janey was little she lived in an old flatface brick house
a couple of doors up the hill from M Street in Georgetown.
The front part of the house was always dark because Mommer kept the heavy lace curtains drawn to and the yellow linen
shades with lace inset bands down. Sunday afternoons Janey
and Joe and Ellen and Francie had to sit in the front room and
look at pictures or read books. Janey and Joe read the funnypaper together because they were the oldest and the other two
were just babies and not old enough to know what was funny
anyway. They couldn't laugh out loud because Popper sat with
the rest of *The Sunday Star* on his lap and usually went to sleep
after dinner with the editorial section crumpled in one big
blueveined hand. Tiny curds of sunlight flickering through the
lace insets in the windowshade would lie on his bald head and
on one big red flange on his nose and on the droop of one
mustache and on his speckled Sundayvest and on the white
starched shirtsleeves with shiny cuffs, held up above the elbow
by a rubber band. Janey and Joe would sit on the same chair
feeling each other's ribs jiggle when they laughed about the
Katzenjammer kids setting off a cannoncracker under the captain's stool. The little ones would see them laughing and start
laughing too, 'Shut up, can't you,' Joe would hiss at them out
of the corner of his mouth. 'You don't know what we're laughing at.' Once in a while, if there was no sound from Mommer
who was taking her Sunday afternoon nap upstairs stretched
out in the back bedroom in a faded lilac sack with frills on it,

after they'd listened for a long time to the drawnout snort that
ended in a little hiss of Popper's snores, Joe would slip off his
chair and Janey would follow him without breathing into the
front hall and out the front door. Once they'd closed it very
carefully so that the knocker wouldn't bang, Joe would give her
a slap, yell 'You're it' and run off down the hill towards M
Street, and she'd have to run after him, her heart pounding, her
hands cold for fear he'd run away and leave her.

Winters the brick sidewalks were icy and there were colored
women out spreading cinders outside their doors when the
children went to school mornings. Joe never would walk with
the rest of them because they were girls, he lagged behind or
ran ahead. Janey wished she could walk with him, but she
couldn't leave her little sisters who held tight onto her hands.
One winter they got in the habit of walking up the hill with a
little yaller girl who lived directly across the street and whose
name was Pearl. Afternoons Janey and Pearl walked home together. Pearl usually had a couple of pennies to buy bullseyes
or candy bananas with at a little store on Wisconsin Avenue,
and she always gave Janey half, so Janey was very fond of her.
One afternoon she asked Pearl to come in and they played dolls
together under the big rose of sharon bush in the back yard.
When Pearl had gone Mommer's voice called from the kitchen.
Mommer had her sleeves rolled up on her faded pale arms and
a checked apron on and was rolling piecrust for supper so that
her hands were covered with flour.

'Janey, come here,' she said. Janey knew from the cold
quaver in her voice that something was wrong.

'Yes, Mommer.' Janey stood in front of her mother shaking
her head about so that the two stiff sandy pigtails lashed from
side to side.

'Stand still, child, for gracious sake . . . Jane, I want to talk
to you about something. That little colored girl you brought in
this afternoon . . .' Janey's heart was dropping. She had a sick
feeling and felt herself blushing, she hardly knew why. 'Now,
don't misunderstand me; I like and respect the colored people;
some of them are fine selfrespecting people in their place . . .
But you mustn't bring that little colored girl in the house again.
Treating colored people kindly and with respect is one of the
signs of good breeding . . . You mustn't forget that your
mother's people were wellborn every inch of them . . . Georgetown was very different in those days. We lived in a big house
with most lovely lawns . . . but you must never associate with

colored people on an equal basis. Living in this neighbourhood it's all the more important to be careful about those things ... Neither the whites nor the blacks respect those who do ... That's all, Janey, you understand; now run out and play, it'll soon be time for your supper.'

Janey tried to speak, but she couldn't. She stood stiff in the middle of the yard on the grating that covered the drainpipe, staring at the back fence. 'Niggerlover,' yelled Joe in her ear. 'Niggerlover ump-mya-mya ... Niggerlover niggerlover ump-mya-mya.' Janey began to cry.

Joe was an untalkative sandyhaired boy who could pitch a mean outcurve when he was still little. He learned to swim and dive in Rock Creek and used to say he wanted to be motorman on a streetcar when he grew up. For several years his best friend was Alec McPherson whose father was a locomotive engineer on the B. and O. After that Joe wanted to be a loco-motive engineer. Janey used to tag around after the two boys whenever they'd let her, to the carbarns at the head of Penn-sylvania Avenue where they made friends with some of the conductors and motormen who used to let them ride on the platform a couple of blocks sometimes if there wasn't any inspector around, down along the canal or up Rock Creek where they caught tadpoles and fell in the water and splashed each other with mud.

Summer evenings when the twilight was long after supper they played lions and tigers with other kids from the neighbor-hood in the long grass of some empty lots near Oak Hill Cemetery. There were long periods when there was measles or scarlet fever around and Mommer wouldn't let them out. Then Alec would come down and they'd play three-o-cat in the back yard. Those were the times Janey liked best. Then the boys treated her as one of them. Summer dusk would come down on them sultry and full of lightningbugs. If Popper was feeling in a good mood he'd send them up the hill to the drugstore on N Street to buy icecream, there'd be young men in their shirt-sleeves and straw hats strolling with girls who wore a stick of punk in their hair to keep off the mosquitoes, a rankness and a smell of cheap perfume from the colored families crowded on their doorsteps, laughing, talking softly with an occasional flash of teeth, rolling of a white eyeball. The dense sweaty night was scary, hummed, rumbled with distant thunder, with junebugs, with the clatter of traffic from M Street, the air of the street dense and breathless under the thick trees; but when she was with Alec and Joe she wasn't scared, not even of drunks or big shamblefooted coloredmen. When they got back Popper would smoke a cigar and they'd sit out in the back yard and the mosquitoes 'ud eat them up and Mommer and Aunt Francine and the kids 'ud eat the icecream and Popper would just smoke a cigar and tell them stories of when he'd been a towboat captain down on the Chesapeake in his younger days and he'd saved the barkentine *Nancy Q* in distress on the Kettlebottoms in a sou'west gale. Then it'd get time to go to bed and Alec 'ud be sent home and Janey'd have to go to bed in the stuffy little back room on the top floor with her two little sisters in their cribs against the opposite wall. Maybe a thunderstorm would come up and she'd lie awake staring up at the ceiling cold with fright, listening to her little sisters whimper as they slept until she heard the reassuring sound of Mommer scurrying about the house closing windows, the slam of a door, the whine of wind and rattle of rain and the thunder rolling terribly loud and near overhead like a thousand beertrucks roaring over the bridge. Times like that she thought of going down to Joe's room and crawling into bed with him, but for some reason she was afraid to, though sometimes she got as far as the landing. He'd laugh at her and call her a softie.

About once a week Joe would get spanked. Popper would come home from the Patent Office where he worked, angry and out of sorts, and the girls would be scared of him and go about the house quiet as mice; but Joe seemed to like to provoke him, he'd run whistling through the back hall or clatter up and down stairs making a tremendous racket with his stubtoed ironplated shoes. Then Popper would start scolding him and Joe would stand in front of him without saying a word glaring at the floor with bitter blue eyes. Janey's insides knotted up and froze when Popper would start up the stairs to the bathroom pushing Joe in front of him. She knew what would happen. He'd take down the razorstrop from behind the door and put the boy's head and shoulders under his arm and beat him. Joe would clench his teeth and flush and not say a word and when Popper was tired of beating him they'd look at each other and Joe would be sent up to his room and Popper would come down stairs trembling all over and pretend nothing had happened, and Janey would slip out into the yard with her fists clenched, whispering to herself, 'I hate him . . . I hate him . . . I hate him.'

Once a drizzling Saturday night she stood against the fence

in the dark looking up at the lighted window. She could hear Popper's voice and Joe's in an argument. She thought maybe she'd fall down dead at the first thwack of the razorstrop. She couldn't hear what they were saying. Then suddenly it came, the leather sound of blows and Joe stifling a gasp. She was eleven years old. Something broke loose. She rushed into the kitchen with her hair all wet from the rain, 'Mommer, he's killing Joe. Stop it.' Her mother turned up a withered helpless drooping face from a pan she was scouring. 'Oh, you can't do anything.' Janey ran upstairs and started beating on the bathroom door. 'Stop it, stop it,' her voice kept yelling. She was scared, but something stronger than she was had hold of her. The door opened; there was Joe looking sheepish and Popper with his face all flushed and the razorstrop in his hand.

'Beat me . . . it's me that's bad . . . I won't have you beating Joe like that.' She was scared. She didn't know what to do, tears stung in her eyes.

Popper's voice was unexpectedly kind:

'You go straight up to bed without any supper and remember that you have enough to do to fight your own battles, Janey.'

She ran up to her room and lay on the bed shaking. When she'd gone to sleep, Joe's voice woke her up with a start.

He was standing in his nightgown in the door. 'Say, Janey,' he whispered. 'Don't you do that again, see. I can take care of myself, see. A girl can't butt in between men like that. When I get a job and make enough dough I'll get me a gun and if Popper tries to beat me up I'll shoot him dead.' Janey began to sniffle. 'What you wanna cry for; this ain't no Johnstown flood.'

She could hear him tiptoe down the stairs again in his bare feet.

At highschool she took the commercial course and learned stenography and typewriting. She was a plain thinfaced sandyhaired girl, quiet and popular with the teachers. Her fingers were quick and she picked up typing and shorthand easily. She liked to read and used to get books like *The Inside of the Cup, The Battle of the Strong, The Winning of Barbara Worth* out of the library. Her mother kept telling her that she'd spoil her eyes if she read so much. When she read she used to imagine she was the heroine, that the weak brother who went to the bad but was a gentleman at core and capable of every sacrifice, like Sidney Carton in *A Tale of Two Cities*, was Joe and that the hero was Alec.

She thought Alec was the bestlooking boy in Georgetown

and the strongest. He had black closecropped hair and a very white skin with a few freckles and a strong squareshouldered way of walking. After him Joe was the bestlooking and strongest and the best baseball player anyway. Everybody said he ought to go on through highschool on account of being such a good baseball player, but at the end of his first year Popper said he had three girls to support and that Joe would have to get to work; so he got a job as a Western Union messenger. Janey was pretty proud of him in his uniform until the girls at highschool kidded her about it. Alec's folks had promised to put him through college if he made good in highschool, so Alec worked hard. He wasn't tough and dirtytalking like most of the boys Joe knew. He was always nice to Janey, though he never seemed to want to be left alone with her. She pretty well admitted to herself that she had a terrible crush on Alec.

The best day of her life was the sweltering summer Sunday they all went canoeing up to Great Falls. She had put up the lunch the night before. In the morning she added a steak she found in the icebox. There was blue haze at the end of every street of brick houses and dark summergreen trees when before anybody else was awake she and Joe crept out of the house round seven that morning.

They met Alec at the corner in front of the depot. He stood waiting for them with his feet wide apart and a skillet in his hand.

They all ran and caught the car that was just leaving for Cabin John's Bridge. They had the car all to themselves like it was a private car. The car hummed over the rails past whitewashed shanties and nigger cabins along the canal, skirting hillsides where the sixfoot tall waving corn marched in ranks like soldiers. The sunlight glanced in bluewhite glare on the wavingdrooping leaves of the tasseling corn; glare, and a whirring and tinkling of grasshoppers and dryflies rose in hot smoke into the pale sky round the clattering shaking electric car. They ate sweet summer-apples Joe had bought off a colored woman in the station and chased each other round the car and flopped down on top of each other in the cornerseats; and they laughed and giggled till they were weak. Then the car was running through woods; they could see the trestlework of the rollercoasters of Glen Echo through the trees and they piled off the car at Cabin John's having more fun than a barrel of monkeys.

They ran down to the bridge to look up and down the river brown and dark in the white glary morning between foliage-sodden banks; then they found the canoe that belonged to a friend of Alec's and some packages of neccos and started out. Alec and Joe paddled and Janey sat in the bottom with her sweater rolled round a thwart for a pillow. Alec was paddling in the bow. It was sweltering hot. The sweat made the shirt cling to the hollow of his chunky back that curved with every stroke of the paddle. After a while the boys stripped to their bathingsuits that they wore under their clothes. It made Janey's throat tremble to watch Alec's back and the bulging muscles of his arm as he paddled, made her feel happy and scared. She sat there in her white dimity dress, trailing her hand in the weedy browngreen water. They stopped to pick waterlilies and the white flowers of arrowhead that glistened like ice and everything smelt wet rank of the muddy roots of waterlilies. The cream soda got warm and they drank it that way and kidded each other back and forth and Alec caught a crab and covered Janey's dress with greenslimy splashes and Janey didn't care a bit and they called Joe skipper and he loosened up and said he was going to join the navy and Alec said he'd be a civil engineer and build a motorboat and take them all cruising and Janey was happy because they included her when they talked just like she was a boy too. At a place below the Falls where there were locks in the canal they had a long portage down to the river. Janey carried the grub and the paddles and the frying pan and the boys sweated and cussed under the canoe. Then they paddled across to the Virginia side and made a fire in a little hollow among gray rusty bowlders. Joe cooked the steak and Janey unpacked the sandwiches and cookies she'd made and nursed some murphies baking in the ashes. They roasted ears of corn too that they had swiped out of a field beside the canal. Everything turned out fine except that they hadn't brought enough butter. Afterwards they sat eating cookies and drinking rootbeer quietly talking round the embers. Alec and Joe brought out pipes and she felt pretty good sitting there at the Great Falls of the Potomac with two men smoking pipes.

'Geewhiz, Janey, Joe cooked that steak fine.'

'When we was kids we used to ketch frogs and broil 'em up in Rock Creek . . . Remember, Alec?'

'Damned if I don't, and Janey she was along once; geewhiz, the fuss you kicked up then, Janey.'

'I don't like seeing you skin them.'

'We thought we was regular wildwest hunters then. We had packs of fun then.'

'I like this better, Alec,' said Janey hesitatingly.

'So do I . . .' said Alec. 'Dod gast it, I wisht we had a water-melon.'

'Maybe we'll see some along the riverbank somewhere goin' home.'

'Jiminy crickets, what I couldn't do to a watermelon, Joe.'

'Mommer had a watermelon on ice,' said Janey; 'maybe there'll be some yet when we get home.'

'I don't never want to go home,' said Joe, suddenly bitter serious.

'Joe, you oughtn't to talk like that.' She felt girlish and frightened.

'I'll talk how I goddam please . . . Kerist, I hate the scrimpy dump.'

'Joe, you oughtn't to talk like that.' Janey felt she was going to cry.

'Dod gast it,' said Alec. 'It's time we shoved . . . What you say, bo . . .? We'll take one more dip and then make tracks for home.'

When the boys were through swimming they all went up to look at the Falls and then they started off. They went along fast in the swift stream under the steep treehung bank. The afternoon was very sultry, they went through layers of hot steamy air. Big cloudheads were piling up in the north. It wasn't fun any more for Janey. She was afraid it was going to rain. Inside she felt sick and drained out. She was afraid her period was coming on. She'd only had the curse a few times yet and the thought of it scared her and took all the strength out of her, made her want to crawl away out of sight like an old sick mangy cat. She didn't want Joe and Alec to notice how she felt. She thought how would it be if she turned the canoe over. The boys could swim ashore all right, and she'd drown and they'd drag the river for her body and everybody'd cry and feel so sorry about it.

Purplegray murk rose steadily and drowned the white summits of the cloudheads. Everything got to be livid white and purple. The boys paddled as hard as they could. They could hear the advancing rumble of thunder. The bridge was well in sight when the wind hit them, a hot stormwind full of dust and dead leaves and bits of chaff and straw, churning the riverwater.

They made the shore just in time. 'Dod gast it, this is goin' to be some storm,' said Alec; 'Janey, get under the boat.' They turned the canoe over on the pebbly shore in the lee of a big

bowlder and huddled up under it. Janey sat in the middle with
the waterlilies they had picked that morning all shriveled and
clammy from the heat in her hand. The boys lay in their damp
bathingsuits on either side of her. Alec's towsled black hair was
against her cheek. The other side of her Joe lay with his head
in the end of the canoe and his lean brown feet and legs in their
rolledup pants tucked under her dress. The smell of sweat and
riverwater and the warm boysmell of Alec's hair and shoulders
made her dizzy. When the rain came drumming on the bottom
of the canoe curtaining them in with lashing white spray, she
slipped her arm round Alec's neck and let her hand rest timidly
on his bare shoulder. He didn't move.

The rain passed after a while. 'Gee, that wasn't as bad as I
thought it would be,' said Alec. They were pretty wet and
chilly, but they felt good in the fresh rainwashed air. They put
the canoe back in the water and went on down as far as the
bridge. Then they carried it back to the house they'd gotten it
from, and went to the little shelter to wait for the electric car.
They were tired and sunburned and sticky. The car was packed
with a damp Sunday afternoon crowd, picnickers caught by
the shower at Great Falls and Glen Echo. Janey thought she'd
never stand it till she got home. Her belly was all knotted up
with a cramp. When they got to Georgetown the boys still had
fifty cents between them and wanted to go to a movie, but Janey
ran off and left them. Her only thought was to get to bed so
that she could put her face into the pillow and cry.

After that Janey never cried much; things upset her, but she
got a cold hard feeling all over instead. Highschool went by
fast, with hot thunderstormy Washington summers in between
terms, punctuated by an occasional picnic at Marshall Hall or
a party at some house in the neighborhood. Joe got a job at
the Adams Express. She didn't see him much, as he didn't eat
home any more. Alec had bought a motorcycle and although
he was still in highschool Janey heard little about him. Sometimes she sat up to get a word with Joe when he came home at
night. He smelt of tobacco and liquor, though he never seemed
to be drunk. He went to his job at seven and when he got out
in the evenings he went out with the bunch hanging round
poolrooms on 4½ Street or playing craps or bowling. Sundays
he played baseball in Maryland. Janey would sit up for him,
but when he came she'd ask how things were going where
he worked and he'd say 'Fine' and he'd ask her how things were
going at school and she'd say 'Fine' and then they'd both go off

to bed. Once in a while she'd ask if he'd seen Alec and he'd say 'Yes' with a scrap of a smile and she'd ask how Alec was and he'd say 'Fine.'

She had one friend, Alice Dick, a dark stubby girl with glasses who took all the same classes with her in highschool. Saturday afternoons they'd dress up in their best and go window-shopping down F Street way. They'd buy a few little things, stop in for a soda and come home on the streetcar feeling they'd had a busy afternoon. Once in a very long while they went to a matinee at Poli's and Janey would take Alice Dick home to supper. Alice Dick liked the Williamses and they liked her. She said it made her feel freer to spend a few hours with broadminded people. Her own folks were Southern Methodists and very narrow. Her father was a clerk in the Government Printing Office and was in daily dread that his job would come under the civil service regulations. He was a stout shortwinded man, fond of playing practical jokes on his wife and daughter, and suffered from chronic dyspepsia.

Alice Dick and Janey planned that as soon as they got through highschool they'd get jobs and leave home. They even picked out the house where they'd board, a greenstone house near Thomas Circle, run by a Mrs Jenks, widow of a naval officer, who was very refined and had Southern cooking and charged moderately for table-board.

One Sunday night during the spring of her last term in high-school Janey was in her room getting undressed. Francie and Ellen were still playing in the backyard. Their voices came in through the open window with a spicy waft of lilacs from the lilacbushes in the next yard. She had just let down her hair and was looking in the mirror imagining how she'd look if she was a peach and had auburn hair, when there was a knock at the door and Joe's voice outside. There was something funny about his voice.

'Come in,' she called. 'I'm just fixin' my hair.'

She first saw his face in the mirror. It was very white and the skin was drawn back tight over the cheekbones and round the mouth.

'Why, what's the matter, Joe?' She jumped up and faced him.

'It's like this, Janey,' said Joe, drawling his words out painfully. 'Alec was killed. He smashed up on his motorbike. I've just come from the hospital. He's dead, all right.'

Janey seemed to be writing the words on a white pad in her

mind. She couldn't say anything.

'He smashed up comin' home from Chevy Chase . . . He'd gone out to the ballgame to see me pitch. You oughter seen him all smashed to hell."

Janey kept trying to say something.

'He was your best . . .'

'He was the best guy I'll ever know,' Joe went on gently. 'Well, that's that, Janey . . . But I wanted to tell you I don't want to hang round this lousy dump now that Alec's gone. I'm goin' to enlist in the navy. You tell the folks, see . . . I don't wanna talk to 'em. That's it; I'll join the navy and see the world.'

'But, Joe . . .'

'I'll write you, Janey; honestly, I will . . . I'll write you a hell of a lot. You an' me . . . Well, goodbye, Janey.' He grabbed her by the shoulders and kissed her awkwardly on the nose and cheek. All she could do was whisper 'Do be careful, Joe,' and stand there in front of the bureau in the gust of lilacs and the yelling of the kids that came through the open window. She heard Joe's steps light quick down the stairs and heard the frontdoor shut. She turned out the light, took off her clothes in the dark, and got into bed. She lay there without crying.

Graduation came and commencement and she and Alice went out to parties and even once with a big crowd on one of the moonlight trips down the river to Indian Head on the steamboat *Charles McAlister*. The crowd was rougher than Janey and Alice liked. Some of the boys were drinking a good deal and there were couples kissing and hugging in every shadow; still the moonlight was beautiful rippling on the river and she and Janey put two chairs together and talked. There was a band and dancing, but they didn't dance on account of the rough men who stood round the dancefloor making remarks. They talked and on the way home up the river, Janey, talking very low and standing by the rail very close to Alice, told her about Alec. Alice had read about it in the paper, but hadn't dreamed that Janey had known him so well or felt that way about him. She began to cry and Janey felt very strong comforting her and they felt that they'd be very close friends after that. Janey whispered that she'd never be able to love anybody else and Alice said she didn't think she could ever love a man anyway, they all drank and smoked and talked dirty among themselves and had only one idea.

In July Alice and Janey got jobs in the office of Mrs Robin-

son, public stenographer in the Riggs Building, to replace girls
away on their vacations. Mrs Robinson was a small grayhaired
pigeonbreasted woman with a Kentucky shriek in her voice,
that made Janey think of a parrot's. She was very precise and
all the proprieties were observed in her office. 'Miss Williams,'
she would chirp, leaning back from her desk, 'that em ess of
Judge Roberts's has absolutely got to be finished today . . . My
dear, we've given our word and we'll deliver if we have to stay
till midnight. Noblesse oblige, my dear,' and the typewriters
would trill and jingle and all the girls' fingers would go like
mad typing briefs, manuscripts of undelivered speeches by
lobbyists, occasional overflow from a newspaperman or a
scientist, or prospectuses from realestate offices or patent promoters, dunning letters for dentists and doctors.

## The Camera Eye (14)

Sunday nights when we had fishballs and baked beans
and Mr Garfield read to us in a very beautiful reading voice
and everybody was so quiet you could have heard a pin
drop because he was reading *The Man Without a Country*
and it was a very terrible story and Aaron Burr had been
a very dangerous man and this poor young man had said
'Damn the United States; I never hope to hear her name
again' and it was a very terrible thing to say and the grayhaired judge was so kind and good

and the judge sentenced me and they took me far away
to foreign lands on a frigate and the officers were kind and
good and spoke in kind grave very sorry reading voices like
Mr Garfield and everything was very kind and grave and
very sorry and frigates and the blue Mediterranean and
islands and when I was dead I began to cry and I was afraid
the other boys would see I had tears in my eyes

American shouldn't cry he should look kind and grave
and very sorry when they wrapped me in the stars and
stripes and brought me home on a frigate to be buried I was
so sorry I never remembered whether they brought me home
or buried me at sea but anyway I was wrapped in Old Glory

# Newsreel 11

the government of the United States must insist and demand that American citizens who may be taken prisoner whether by one party or the other as participants in the present insurrectionary disturbances shall be dealt with in accordance with the broad principles of international law

### SOLDIERS GUARD CONVENTION

the *Titanic* left Southampton on April 10th on its maiden operation is to be performed against the wishes of the New York Life according to 'Kimmel' Why they know I'm Kimmel in Niles I'm George to everyone even mother and sister when we meet on the streets

> *I'm going to Maxim's*
> *Where fun and frolic beams*
> *With all the girls I'll chatter*
> *I'll laugh and kiss and flatter*
> *Lolo, Dodo, Joujou.*
> *Cloclo, Margot, Froufrou*

### TITANIC LARGEST SHIP IN THE WORLD SINKING

personally I am not sure that the twelvehour day is bad for employees especially when they insist on working that long in order to make more money

> *Still all my song shall be*
> *Nearer My God to thee*
> *Nearer to thee*

it was now about 1 A.M., a beautiful starlight night with no moon. The sea was as calm as a pond, just a gentle heave as the boat dipped up and down in the swell, an ideal night except for the bitter cold. In the distance the *Titanic* looked an enormous length, its great hulk outlined in black

against the starry sky, every porthole and saloon blazing
with light

### ASK METHODISM TO OUST TRINITY

*the bride's gown is of charmeuse satin with a chiffon
veiled lace waist. The veil is of crepe lisse edged with point
de venise a departure from the conventional bridal veil and
the bouquet is to be lilies of the valley and gardenias*

> *Lolo, Dodo, Joujou,*
> *Cloclo, Margot, Froufrou*
> *I'm going to Maxim's*
> *And you can go to . . .*

the *Titanic* slowly tilted straight on end with the stern
vertically upward and as it did so the lights in the cabins
and saloons which had not flickered for a moment since we
left, died out, came on again for a single flash and finally
went out altogether. Meanwhile the machinery rattled
through the vessel with a rattle and a groaning that could be
heard for miles. Then with a quiet slanting dive

## *Janey*

'But it's so interesting, Mommer,' Janey would say when her
mother bewailed the fact that she had to work.

'In my day it wasn't considered ladylike, it was thought to
be demeaning.'

'But it isn't now,' Janey would say, getting into a temper.

Then it would be a great relief to get out of the stuffy house
and the stuffy treeshaded streets of Georgetown and to stop by
for Alice Dick and go downtown to the moving pictures and to
see the pictures of foreign countries, and the crowds on F
Street and to stop in at a drugstore for a soda afterwards, before getting on the Georgetown car, and to sit up at the fountain talking about the picture they'd seen and Olive Thomas
and Charley Chaplin and John Bunny. She began to read the
paper every day and to take an interest in politics. She began
to feel that there was a great throbbing arclighted world somewhere outside and that only living in Georgetown where everything was so poky and oldfashioned, and Mommer and Pop-

per were so poky and oldfashioned, kept her from breaking into it.

Postcards from Joe made her feel like that too. He was a sailor on the battleship *Connecticut*. There'd be a picture of the waterfront at Havana or the harbor of Marseille or Villefranche or a photograph of a girl in peasant costume inside a tinsel horseshoe and a few lines hoping she was well and liked her job, never a word about himself. She wrote him long letters full of questions about himself and foreign countries, but he never answered them. Still it gave her a sort of feeling of adventure to get the postcards. Whenever she saw a navy man on the street or marines from Quantico she thought of Joe and wondered how he was getting on. The sight of a gob lurching along in blue with his cap on one side took a funny twist at her heart.

Sundays Alice almost always came out to Georgetown. The house was different now, Joe gone, her mother and father older and quieter, Francie and Ellen blooming out into pretty giggly highschool girls, popular with the boys in the neighborhood, going out to parties, all the time complaining because they didn't have any money to spend. Sitting at the table with them, helping Mommer with the gravy, bringing in the potatoes or the Brussels sprouts for Sunday dinner, Janey felt grownup, almost an old maid. She was on the side of her father and mother now against the sisters. Popper began to look old and shrunk-up. He talked often about retiring, and was looking forward to his pension.

When she'd been eight months with Mrs Robinson she got an offer from Dreyfus and Carroll, the patent lawyers up on the top floor of the Riggs Building to work for them for seventeen a week, which was five dollars more than she was getting from Mrs Robinson. It made her feel fine. She realized now that she was good at her work and that she could support herself whatever happened. On the strength of it she went down to Woodward and Lothrop's with Alice Dick to buy a dress. She wanted a silk grownup dress with embroidery on it. She was twentyone and was going to make seventeen dollars a week and thought she had a right to one nice dress. Alice said it ought to be a bronzy gold color to match her hair. They went in all the stores down F Street, but they couldn't find anything that suited that wasn't too expensive, so all they could do was buy some materials and some fashion magazines and take it home to Janey's mother to make up. It galled Janey still being dependent on her mother this way, but there was nothing for it; so Mrs Williams had to make up Janey's new dress the way she had made all her children's dresses since they were born. Janey had never had the patience to learn to sew the way Mommer could. They bought enough material so that Alice could have one too, so Mrs Williams had to make up two dresses.

Working at Dreyfus and Carroll's was quite different from working at Mrs Robinson's. There were mostly men in the office. Mr Dreyfus was a small thinfaced man with a small black mustache and small black twinkly eyes and a touch of accent that gave him a distinguished foreign diplomat manner. He carried yellow wash gloves and a yellow cane and had a great variety of very much-tailored overcoats. He was the brains of the firm, Jerry Burnham said. Mr Carroll was a stout redfaced man who smoked many cigars and cleared his throat a great deal and had a very oldtimey Southern Godblessmysoul way of talking. Jerry Burnham said he was the firm's bay window. Jerry Burnham was a wrinkledfaced young man with dissipated eyes who was the firm's adviser in technical and engineering matters. He laughed a great deal, always got into the office late, and for some reason took a fancy to Janey and used to joke about things to her while he was dictating. She liked him, though the dissipated look under his eyes scared her off a little. She'd have liked to have talked to him like a sister, and gotten him to stop burning the candle at both ends. Then there was an elderly accountant, Mr Sills, a shriveled man who lived in Anacostia and never said a word to anybody. At noon he didn't go out for lunch, but sat at his desk eating a sandwich and an apple wrapped in waxed paper which he carefully folded afterwards and put back in his pocket. Then there were two fresh errandboys and a little plainfaced typist named Miss Simonds who only got twelve a week. All sorts of people in every sort of seedyrespectable or Peacock Alley clothes came in during the day and stood round in the outer office listening to Mr Carroll's rich bloom from behind the groundglass door. Mr Dreyfus slipped in and out without a word, smiling faintly at his acquaintances, always in a great mysterious hurry. At lunch in the little cafeteria or at a sodafountain Janey 'ud tell Alice all about it and Alice would look up at her admiringly. Alice always waited for her in the vestibule at one. They'd arranged to go out then because there was less of a crowd. Neither of them ever spent more than twenty cents, so lunch didn't take

them very long and they'd have time to take a turn round
Lafayette Square or sometimes round the White House grounds
before going back to the office.

There was one Saturday night when she had to work late to
finish up typing the description of an outboard motor that had
to be in at the Patent Office first thing Monday morning. Everybody else had left the office. She was making out the complicated technical wording as best she could, but her mind was on
a postcard showing the Christ of the Andes she'd gotten from
Joe that day. All it said was:

'To hell with Uncle Sam's tin ships. Coming home soon.'

It wasn't signed but she knew the writing. It worried her.
Burnham sat at the telephone switchboard going over the pages
as she finished them. Now and then he went out to the washroom; when he came back each time a hot breath of whiskey
wafted across the office. Janey was nervous. She typed till the
little black letters squirmed before her eyes. She was worried
about Joe. How could he be coming home before his enlistment was up? Something must be the matter. And Jerry Burnham moving restlessly round on the telephone girl's seat made
her uncomfortable. She and Alice had talked about the danger
of staying in an office alone with a man like this. Late like this
and drinking, a man had just one idea.

When she handed him the next to the last sheet, his eye,
bright and moist, caught hers. 'I bet you're tired, Miss Williams,' he said. 'It's a darned shame to keep you in like this and
Saturday night too.'

'It's quite all right, Mr Burnham,' she said icily and her
fingers chirruped.

'It's the damned old baywindow's fault. He chewed the rag
so much about politics all day, nobody could get any work
done.'

'Well, it doesn't matter now,' said Janey.

'Nothing matters any more. . . . It's almost eight o'clock. I
had to pass up a date with my best girl . . . or thereabouts. I bet
you passed up a date too, Miss Williams.'

'I was going to meet another girl, that's all.'

'Now I'll tell one . . .' He laughed so easily that she found
herself laughing too.

When the last page was done and in the envelope, Janey
got up to get her hat. 'Look, Miss Williams, we'll drop this
in the mail and then you'd better come and have a bite with
me.'

Going down in the elevator Janey intended to excuse herself
and go home, but somehow she didn't and found herself, everything aflutter inside of her, sitting coolly down with him in a
French restaurant on H Street.

'Well, what do you think of the New Freedom, Miss Williams?' asked Jerry Burnham with a laugh after he'd sat down.
He handed her the menu. 'Here's the scorecard . . . Let your
conscience be your guide.'

'Why, I hardly know, Mr Burnham.'

'Well, I'm for it, frankly. I think Wilson's a big man . . .
Nothing like change anyway, the best thing in the world, don't
you think so? Bryan's a big bellowing blatherskite, but even he
represents something, and even Josephus Daniels filling the
navy with grapejuice. I think there's a chance we may get back
to being a democracy . . . Maybe there won't have to be a
revolution; what do you think?'

He never waited for her to answer a question, he just talked
and laughed all by himself.

When Janey tried to tell Alice about it afterwards the things
Jerry Burnham said didn't seem so funny, nor the food so good
nor everything so jolly. Alice was pretty bitter about it. 'Oh,
Janey, how could you go out late at night with a drunken man
and to a place like that, and here I was crazy anxious . . . You
know a man like that has only one idea . . . I declare I think it
was heartless and light . . . I wouldn't have thought you capable
of such a thing.' 'But, Alice, it wasn't like that at all,' Janey
kept saying, but Alice cried and went round looking hurt for a
whole week; so that after that Janey kept off the subject of
Jerry Burnham. It was the first disagreement she'd ever had
with Alice and it made her feel bad.

Still she got to be friends with Jerry Burnham. He seemed
to like taking her out and having her listen to him talk. Even
after he'd thrown up his job at Dreyfus and Carroll, he sometimes called for her Saturday afternoons to take her to Keith's.
Janey arranged a meeting with Alice out in Rock Creek Park,
but it wasn't much of a success. Jerry set the girls up to tea
at the old stone mill. He was working for an engineering paper
and writing a weekly letter for the *New York Sun*. He upset
Alice by calling Washington a cesspool and a sink of boredom
and saying he was rotting there and that most of the inhabitants
were dead from the neck up anyway. When he put them on the
car to go back to Georgetown, Alice said emphatically that
young Burnham was not the sort of boy a respectable girl

ought to know. Janey sat back happily in the seat of the open car, looking out at trees, girls in summer dresses, men in straw hats, mailboxes, storefronts sliding by and said, 'But Alice, he's smart as a whip. . . . Gosh, I like brainy people, don't you?' Alice looked at her and shook her head sadly and said nothing.

That same afternoon they went to the Georgetown hospital to see Popper. It was pretty horrible. Mommer and Janey and the doctor and the wardnurse knew that he had cancer of the bladder and couldn't live very long, but they didn't admit it even to themselves. They had just moved him into a private room where he would be more comfortable. It was costing lots of money and they'd had to put a second mortgage on the house. They'd already spent all Janey's savings that she had in a bankaccount of her own against a rainy day. That afternoon they had to wait a while. When the nurse came out with a glass urinal under a towel Janey went in alone.

'Hello, Popper,' she said with a forced smile. The smell of disinfectant in the room sickened her. Through the open window came warm air of sunwilted trees, drowsy Sundayafternoon noises, the caw of a crow, a distant sound of traffic. Popper's face was drawn in and twisted to one side. His big mustaches looked pathetically silky and white. Janey knew that she loved him better than anybody else in the world . . .

His voice was feeble but fairly firm. 'Janey, I'm in drydock, girl, and I guess I'll never . . . you know better'n I do, the sonsobitches won't tell me . . . Say, tell me about Joe. You hear from him, don't you? I wish he hadn't joined the navy; no future for a boy there without pull higher up; but I'm glad he went to sea, takes after me . . . I'd been three times round the Horn in the old days before I was twenty. That was before I settled down in the towboat business, you understand . . . But I been thinkin' here lyin' in bed that Joe done just what I'd 'a' done, a chip of the old block, and I'm glad of it. I don't worry about him, but I wish you girls was married an' off my hands. I'd feel easier. I don't trust girls nowadays with these here anklelength skirts an' all that.' Popper's eyes traveled all over her with a chilly feeble gleam that made her throat stiffen when she tried to speak.

'I guess I can take care of myself,' she said.

'You got to take care of me now. I done my best by you kids. You don't know what life is, none of you, been sheltered and now you ship me off to die in the hospital.'

'But, Popper, you said yourself you thought it would be best to go where you'd get better care.'

'I don't like that night nurse, Janey, she handles me too rough . . . You tell 'em down at the office.'

It was a relief when it was time to go. She and Alice walked along the street without saying anything. Finally Janey said, 'For goodness' sake, Alice, don't get sulky. If you only knew how I hate it all too . . . oh, goodness, I wish . . .'

'What do you wish, Janey?'

'Oh, I dunno.'

July was hot that summer, in the office they worked in a continual whir of electric fans, the men's collars wilted and the girls kept themselves overplastered with powder; only Mr Dreyfus still looked cool and crisply tailored as if he'd just stepped out of a bandbox. The last day of the month Janey was sitting a minute at her desk getting up energy to go home along the simmering streets when Jerry Burnham came in. He had his shirtsleeves rolled above the elbow and white duck pants on and carried his coat. He asked her how her father was and said he was all excited about the European news and would have to take her out to supper to talk to somebody soothing. 'I've got a car belongs to Bugs Dolan and I haven't any driver's license, but I guess we can sneak round the Speedway and get cooled off all the same.' She tried to refuse because she ought to go home to supper and Alice was always so sulky when she went out with Jerry, but he could see that she really wanted to come and insisted.

They both sat in the front seat of the Ford and dropped their coats in the back. They went once round the Speedway, but the asphalt was like a griddle. The trees and the brown stagnant river stewed in late afternoon murk like meat and vegetables in a pot. The heat from the engine suffocated them. Jerry, his face red, talked incessantly about war brewing in Europe and how it would be the end of civilization and the signal for a general workingclass revolution and how he didn't care and anything that got him out of Washington, where he was drinking himself silly with his brains addled by the heat and the *Congressional Record*, would be gravy to him, and how tired he was of women who didn't want anything but to get money out of him or parties or marriage or some goddam thing or other and how cool and soothing it was to talk to Janey who wasn't like that.

It was too hot, so they put off driving till later and went to

the Willard to get something to eat. He insisted on going to the
Willard because he said he had his pockets full of money and
would just spend it anyhow and Janey was very much awed
because she'd never been in a big hotel before and felt she wasn't
dressed for it and said she was afraid she'd disgrace him and
he laughed and said it couldn't be done. They sat in the big long
gilt dining room and Jerry said it looked like a millionaire
morgue and the waiter was very polite and Janey couldn't find
what she wanted to eat on the big bill-of-fare and took a salad.
Jerry made her take a gin fizz because he said it was cooling;
it made her feel lightheaded and tall and gawky. She followed
his talk breathless the way she used to tag along after Joe and
Alec down to the carbarns when she was little.

After supper they drove round some more and Jerry got
quiet and she felt constrained and couldn't think of what to say.
They went way out Rhode Island Avenue and circled round
back by the Old Soldiers' Home. There was no air anywhere
and the staring identical streetlights went by on either side,
lighting segments of monotonous unrustling trees. Even out
on the hills there was not a breath stirring.

Out in the dark roads beyond the streetlamps it was better.
Janey lost all sense of direction and lay back breathing in an
occasional patch of freshness from a cornfield or a copse of
woods. In a spot where a faint marshy dampness almost cool
drifted across the road Jerry suddenly stopped the car and
leaned over and kissed her. Her heart began to beat very fast.
She wanted to tell him not to, but she couldn't.

'I didn't mean to, but I can't help it,' he whispered. 'It's living
in Washington undermines the will . . . Or maybe I'm in love
with you, Janey. I don't know . . . Let's sit in the back seat
where it's cooler.'

Weakness started in the pit of her stomach and welled up
through her. As she stepped out he caught her in his arms. She
let her head droop on his shoulder, her lips against his neck.
His arms were burning hot round her shoulders, she could feel
his ribs through his shirt pressing against her. Her head started
going round in a reek of tobacco and liquor and male sweat.
His legs began pressing up to hers. She yanked herself away
and got into the back seat. She was trembling. He was right
after her. 'No, no,' she said. He sat down beside her with his
arm round her waist. 'Lez have a cigarette,' he said in a shaky
voice.

Smoking gave her something to do, made her feel even with

him. The two granulated red ends of the cigarettes glowed side by side.

'Do you mean you like me, Jerry?'

'I'm crazy about you, kid.'

'Do you mean you ...?'

'Want to marry you ... Why the hell not? I dunno ... Suppose we were engaged?'

'You mean you want me to marry you?'

'If you like ... But don't you understand the way a feller feels ... a night like this ... the smell of the swamp ... God, I'd give anything to have you.'

They'd smoked out their cigarettes. They sat a long time without saying a word. She could feel the hairs on his bare arm against her bare arm.

'I'm worried about my brother Joe ... He's in the navy, Jerry, and I'm afraid he's going to desert or something ... I think you'd like him. He's a wonderful baseball player.'

'What made you think of him? Do you feel that way towards me? Love's a swell thing; goddam it, don't you realize it's not the way you feel towards your brother?'

He put his hand on her knee. She could feel him looking at her in the dark. He leaned over and kissed her very gently. She liked his lips gentle against hers that way. She was kissing them. She was falling through centuries of swampy night. His hot chest was against her breast bearing her down. She would cling to him bearing her down through centuries of swampy night. Then all at once in a cold spasm she felt sick, choking for breath like drowning. She began to fight him. She got her leg up and pushed him hard in the groin with her knee.

He let go of her and got out of the car. She could hear him walking up and down the road in the dark behind her. She was trembling and scared and sick. After a while he got in, switched on the light and drove on without looking at her. He was smoking a cigarette and little sparks came from it as he drove.

When he got to the corner of M Street below the Williams house in Georgetown he stopped and got out and opened the door for her. She got out, not knowing what to say, afraid to look at him.

'I suppose you think I ought to apologize to you for being a swine,' he said.

'Jerry, I'm sorry,' she said.

'I'll be damned if I will ... I thought we were friends. I might have known there wouldn't be a woman in this muck hole

with a human spark in her . . . I suppose you think you ought
to hold out for the wedding bells. Go ahead; that's your
business. I can get what I want with any nigger prostitute down
the street here . . . Goodnight.' Janey didn't say anything. He
drove off. She went home and went to bed.

All that August her father was dying, full of morphine, in the
Georgetown hospital. The papers came out every day with big
headlines about war in Europe, Liège, Louvain, Mons. Dreyfus
and Carroll's was in a fever. Big lawsuits over munitions patents
were on. It began to be whispered about that the immaculate
Mr Dreyfus was an agent of the German government. Jerry
came to see Janey one noon to apologize for having been so
rude that night and to tell her that he had a job as a war
correspondent and was leaving in a week for the front. They had
a good lunch together. He talked about spies and British
intrigue and pan-Slavism and the assassination of Jaurès and the
Socialist revolution and laughed all the time and said everything
was well on its way to ballyhack. She thought he was wonderful and wanted to say something about their being engaged
and felt very tender towards him and scared he'd be killed, but
suddenly it was time for her to go back to the office and neither
of them had brought the matter up. He walked back to the
Riggs Building with her and said goodbye and gave her a big
kiss right there in front of everybody and ran off promising he'd
write from New York. At that moment Alice came up on
her way to Mrs Robinson's and Janey found herself telling her that she was engaged to be married to Jerry Burnham
and that he was going to Europe to the war as a war correspondent.

When her father died in early September, it was a great relief
to all concerned. Only, coming back from Oak Hill Cemetery
all the things she'd wanted as a girl came back to her, and the
thought of Alec, and everything seemed so unhappy that she
couldn't stand it. Her mother was very quiet and her eyes were
very red and she kept saying that she was so glad that there'd be
room on the lot for her to be buried in Oak Hill too. She'd
have hated for him to be buried in any other cemetery than
Oak Hill. It was so beautiful and all the nicest people in Georgetown were buried there.

With the insurance money Mrs Williams did over the house
and fixed up the two top floors to rent out as apartments. That
was the chance Janey had been waiting for for so long to get
a place of her own and she and Alice got a room in a house

on Massachusetts Avenue near the Carnegie Library, with cooking privileges. So one Saturday afternoon she phoned from the drugstore for a taxicab and set out with her suitcase and trunk and a pile of framed pictures from her room on the seat beside her. The pictures were two color prints of Indians by Remington, a Gibson girl, a photograph of the battleship *Connecticut* in the harbor of Villefranche that Joe had sent her and an enlarged photograph of her father in uniform standing at the wheel of an imaginary ship against a stormy sky furnished by a photographer in Norfolk, Virginia. Then there were two unframed colorprints by Maxfield Parrish that she'd bought recently and a framed snapshot of Joe in baseball clothes. The little picture of Alec she'd wrapped among her things in her suitcase. The cab smelt musty and rumbled along the streets. It was a crisp autumn day, the gutters were full of dry leaves. Janey felt scared and excited as if she were starting out all alone on a journey.

That fall she read a great many newspapers and magazines and *The Beloved Vagabond*, by W. J. Locke. She began to hate the Germans that were destroying art and culture, civilization, Louvain. She waited for a letter from Jerry, but a letter never came.

One afternoon she was coming out of the office a little late, who should be standing in the hall by the elevator but Joe. 'Hello, Janey,' he said. 'Gee, you look like a million dollars.' She was so glad to see him she could hardly speak, could only squeeze his arm tight. 'I just got paid off . . . I thought I better come up here and see the folks before I spent all my jack . . . I'll take you out and set you up to a big feed an' a show if you want . . .' He was sunburned and his shoulders were broader than when he left. His big hands and knotty wrists stuck out of a newlooking blue suit that was too tight for him at the waist. The sleeves were too short too.

'Did you go to Georgetown?' she asked him.

'Yare.'

'Did you go up to the cemetery?'

'Mommer wanted me to go, but what's the use?'

'Poor mother, she's so sentimental about it . . .'

They walked along, Joe didn't say anything. It was a hot day. Dust blew down the street.

Janey said: 'Joe, dear, you must tell me all about your adventures . . . You must have been to some wonderful places. It's thrilling having a brother in the navy.'

'Janey, pipe down about the navy, will you? ... I don't want to hear about it. I deserted in B.A., see, and shipped out East on a limey, on an English boat ... That's a dog's life too, but anything's better than the U.S.N.'

'But, Joe ...'

'Ain't nothin' to worry about ...'

'But, Joe, what happened?'

'You won't say a word to a livin' soul, will you, Janey? You see I got in a scrap with a petty officer tried to ride me too damn hard. I socked him in the jaw an' kinda mauled him, see, an' things looked pretty bad for me, so I made tracks for the tall timber.... That's all.'

'Oh, Joe, and I was hoping you'd get to be an officer.'

'A gob get to be an officer ...? A fat chance.'

She took him to the Mabillion, where Jerry had taken her. At the door Joe peered in critically. 'Is this the swellest joint you know, Janey? I got a hundred iron men in my pocket.'

'Oh, this is dreadfully expensive ... It's a French restaurant. And you oughtn't to spend all your money on me.'

'Who the hell else do you want me to spend it on?'

Joe sat down at a table and Janey went back to 'phone Alice that she wouldn't be home till late. When she got back to the table, Joe was pulling some little packages wrapped in red and greenstriped tissuepaper out of his pockets.

'Oh, what's that?'

'You open 'em, Janey ... It's yours.'

She opened the packages. They were some lace collars and an embroidered tablecloth.

'The lace is Irish and that other's from Madeira ... I had a Chinee vase for you too, but some sonofabit ... sonofagun snitched it on me.'

'That was awful sweet of you to think of me ... I appreciate it.'

Joe fidgeted with his knife and fork. 'We gotta git a move on, Janey, or we'll be late for the show ... I got tickets for *The Garden of Allah*.'

When they came out of the Belasco onto Lafayette Square that was cool and quiet with a rustle of wind in the trees, Joe said, 'Ain't so much; I seen a real sandstorm onct,' and Janey felt bad about her brother being so rough and uneducated. The play made her feel like when she was little, full of uneasy yearn for foreign countries and a smell of incense and dark eyes and dukes in tailcoats tossing money away on the gaming tables of

Monte Carlo, monks and the mysterious East. If Joe was only a little better educated he'd be able to really appreciate all the interesting ports he visited. He left her on the stoop of the house on Massachusetts Avenue.

'Where are you going to stay, Joe?' she asked.

'I guess I'll shove along back to New York an' pick up a berth. . . . Sailoring's a pretty good graft with this war on.'

'You mean tonight?' He nodded.

'I wish I had a bed for you, but I couldn't very well on account of Alice.'

'Naw, I doan want to hang round this dump . . . I jus' came up to say hello.'

'Well, goodnight, Joe, be sure and write.'

'Goodnight, Janey, I sure will.'

She watched him walk off down the street until he went out of sight in the shadows of the trees. It made her unhappy to see him go all alone down the shadowed street. It wasn't quite the shambling walk of a sailor, but he looked like a workingman all right. She sighed and went into the house. Alice was waiting up for her. She showed Alice the lace and they tried on the collars and agreed that it was very pretty and quite valuable.

Janey and Alice had a good time that winter. They took to smoking cigarettes and serving tea to their friends Sunday afternoons. They read novels by Arnold Bennett and thought of themselves as bachelor girls. They learned to play bridge and shortened their skirts. At Christmas Janey got a hundred-dollar bonus and a raise to twenty a week from Dreyfus and Carroll. She began telling Alice that she was an old stickinthemud to stay on at Mrs Robinson's. For herself she began to have ambitions of a business career. She wasn't afraid of men any more and kidded back and forth with young clerks in the elevator about things that would have made her blush the year before. When Johnny Edwards or Morris Byer took her out to the movies in the evening, she didn't mind having them put their arms around her, or having them kiss her once or twice while she was fumbling in her bag for her latchkey. She knew just how to catch a boy's hand by the wrist and push it away without making any scene when he tried to get too intimate. When Alice used to talking warningly about men having just one idea, she'd laugh and say, 'Oh, they're not so smart.' She discovered that just a little peroxide in the water when she washed her hair made it blonder and took away that mousey look. Sometimes when she was getting ready to go out in the evening, she'd put a speck of rouge on her little finger and rub it very carefully on her lips.

## The Camera Eye (15)

in the mouth of the Schuylkill Mr Pierce came on board ninetysix years old and sound as a dollar He'd been officeboy in Mr Pierce's office about the time He'd enlisted and missed the battle of Antietam on account of having dysentery so bad and Mr Pierce's daughter Mrs Black called Him Jack and smoked little brown cigarettes and we played *Fra Diavolo* on the phonograph and everybody was very jolly when Mr Pierce tugged at his dundrearies and took a toddy and Mrs Black lit cigarettes one after another and they talked about old days and about how His father had wanted Him to be a priest and His poor mother had had such trouble getting together enough to eat for that family of greedy boys and His father was a silent man and spoke mostly Portugee and when he didn't like the way a dish was cooked that came on the table he'd pick it up and sling it out of the window and He wanted to go to sea and studied law at the University and in Mr Pierce's office and He sang

> Oh who can tell the joy he feels
> As o'er the foam his vessel reels

and He mixed up a toddy and Mr Pierce pulled at his dundrearies and everybody was very jolly and they talked about the schooner *Mary Wentworth* and how Colonel Hodgeson and Father Murphy looked so hard on the cheery glass and He mixed up a toddy and Mr Pierce pulled at his dundrearies and Mrs Black smoked the little brown cigarettes one after another and everybody was very jolly with *Fra Diavolo* playing on the phonograph and the harbor smell and the ferryboats and the Delaware all silveryripply used to be all marshes over there where we used to go duckshooting and He sang *Vittoria* with the phonograph

and Father Murphy got a terrible attack of gout and had to be carried off on a shutter and Mr Pierce ninetysix years

old and sound as a dollar took a sip of toddy and tugged
at his dundrearies silveryripply and the harborsmell came
on the fresh wind and smoke from the shipyards in Camden
and lemon rye sugary smell of toddyglasses and everybody
was very jolly

# Newsreel 12

GREEKS IN BATTLE FLEE BEFORE COPS

PASSENGERS IN SLEEPING CAR AROUSED
AT POINT OF GUN

*Flow, river, flow*
*Down to the sea*
*Bright stream bring my loved one*
*Home to me*

FIGHTING AT TORREON

at the end of the last campaign, writes Champ Clark, Missouri's brilliant Congressman, I had about collapsed from overwork, nervous tension, loss of sleep and appetite and constant speaking, but three bottles of Electric Bitters made me allright

ROOSEVELT IS MADE LEADER OF NEW PARTY

BRYAN'S THROAT CUT BY CLARK; AIDS PARKER

*True, dear one, true*
*I'm trying hard to be*
*But hear me say*
*It's a very very long long way*
*From the banks of the Seine*

the crime for which Richardson was sentenced to die in the electric chair was the confessed murder of his former sweetheart nineteen-year-old Avis Linnell of Hyannis a pupil in the New England Conservatory of Music at Boston.

The girl stood in the way of the minister's marriage to a society girl and heiress of Brookline both through an engagement that still existed between the two and because of a condition in which Miss Linnell found herself.

The girl was deceived into taking a poison given her by Richardson which she believed would remedy that condition and died in her room at the Young Women's Christian Association.

ROOSEVELT TELLS FIRST TIME HOW US GOT
PANAMA

HUNDRED THOUSAND PEOPLE UNABLE TO
ENTER BIG HALL ECHO CHEERING

at dinnertime the Governor said he hadn't heard directly from Mr Bryan during the day. 'At the present rate of gain,' Mr Wilson said, 'after reading the results of the fifteenth ballot, I figure it'll take about 175 more ballots to land me'

Redhaired Youth Says Stories of Easy Money Led Him to Crime

interest in the case was intensified on December 20 when it became known that the ex-clergyman had mutilated himself in his cell at the Charles Street Jail.

FIVE MEN DIE AFTER GETTING TO SOUTH POLE

DIAZ TRAINS HEAVY GUNS ON BUSINESS
SECTION

*It's a very very long long way*
*From the banks of the Seine*
*For a girl to go and stay*
*On the banks of the Saskatchewan*

## *The Boy Orator of the Platte*

It was in the Chicago Convention in '96 that the prize-winning boy orator, the minister's son whose lips had never touched liquor, let out his silver voice so that it filled the gigantic hall, filled the ears of the plain people:

*Mr Chairman and gentlemen of the convention:*
*I would be presumptuous indeed*
        *to present myself against*
*the distinguished gentleman to whom you have listened, if*
*this were a mere measuring of abilities;*
        *but this is not a contest between persons.*
    *The humblest citizen in all the land,*

*when clad in the armor of a righteous cause,*
        *is stronger than all the hosts of error.*
*I come to speak to you in defence of a cause as holy as the cause*
    *of Liberty . . .*
    a youngish bigmouthed man in a white tie
    barnstormer, exhorter, evangelist,
    his voice charmed the mortgageridden farmers of the great
plains, rang through weatherboarded schoolhouses in the
Missouri Valley, was sweet in the ears of small storekeepers
hungry for easy credit, melted men's innards like the song of
a thrush or a mockin' in the gray quiet before sunup, or a
sudden soar in winter wheat or a bugler playing taps and the
flag flying;

    silver tongue of the plain people:

    *. . . the man who is employed for wages is as much a*
*businessman as his employer;*
        *the attorney in a country town is as much a businessman as*
*the corporation counsel in a giant metropolis;*
        *the merchant in a crossroads store is as much a business-*
*man as the merchant of New York;*
        *the farmer who goes forth in the morning and toils all day,*
*who begins in the spring and toils all summer, and who by the*
*application of brain and muscle to the natural resources of the*
*country creates wealth, is as much a businessman as the man*
*who goes upon the board of trade and bets upon the price of*
*grain;*
        *the miners who go down a thousand feet in the earth*
            *or climb two thousand feet upon the cliffs*
*and bring forth from their hidingplaces*
                *the precious metals*
                    *to be poured in the channels of trade,*
*are as much businessmen*
                *as the few financial magnates*
            *who*
                *in a back room*
                *corner the money of the world.*

The hired man and the country attorney sat up and listened.
    this was big talk for the farmer who'd mortgaged his
crop to buy fertilizer, big talk for the smalltown hardware
man, groceryman, feed and corn merchant, undertaker, truck-
gardener . . .

*Having behind us*
*the producing masses*
*of this nation and the world,*
*supported by the commercial interests, the laboring*
*interests, and the toilers everywhere*
*we will answer*
*their demand*
*for a gold standard*
*by saying to them:*
*You shall not press down upon the brow of labor this crown of*
*thorns, you shall not crucify mankind upon a cross of*
*gold.*

They roared their lungs out (*crown of thorns and cross of
gold*)
carried him round the hall on their shoulders, hugged him,
loved him, named their children after him, nominated him for
President,
boy orator of the Platte,
silver tongue of the plain people.
But McArthur and Forrest, two Scotchmen in the Rand,
had invented the cyanide process for extracting gold from ore,
South Africa flooded the gold market; there was no need for a
prophet of silver.

The silver tongue chanted on out of the big mouth, chanting Pacifism, Prohibition, Fundamentalism,
nibbling radishes on the lecture platform,
drinking grapejuice and water,
gorging big cornbelt meals;
Bryan grew gray in the hot air of Chautauqua
tents, in the applause, the handshakes, the backpattings, the
cigarsmoky air of committeerooms at Democratic conventions,
a silver tongue in a big mouth.
In Dayton he dreamed of turning the trick again,
of setting back the clocks for the plain people, branding, flaying, making a big joke
of Darwinism and the unbelieving outlook of city
folks, scientists, foreigners with beards and monkey morals.

In Florida he'd spoken every day at noon on a
float under an awning selling lots for Coral Gables . . . he had
to speak, to feel the drawling voices hush, feel the tense approv-
ing ears, the gust of handclaps.

Why not campaign again through the length
and breadth to set up again the tottering word for the
plain people who wanted the plain word of God?
                              (*crown of thorns and cross of gold*)
the plain prosperous comfortable word of God
for plain prosperous comfortable midamerican folks?

He was a big eater. It was hot. A stroke killed him.

Three days later down in Florida the company delivered
the electric horse he'd ordered to exercise on
when he'd seen the electric horse the President
exercised on in the White House.


## The Camera Eye (16)

it was hot as a bakeoven going through the canal from
Delaware City and turtles sunning themselves tumbled off
into the thick ocher ripple we made in passing and He was
very gay and She was feeling well for once and He made us
punch of tea and mint and a little Saint Croix rum but it was
hot as the hinges of Delaware and we saw scarlet tanagers
and redwing blackbirds and kingfishers cackled wrathfully
as the yellow wave from the white bow rustled the reeds and
the cattails and the sweetflag and He talked about law reform
and what politicians were like and where were the Good
Men in this country and said Why thinking the way I think
I couldn't get elected to be notary public in any county in
the state not with all the money in the world no not even
dogcatcher


## J. Ward Moorehouse

He was born in Wilmington, Delaware, on the Fourth of
July. Poor Mrs Moorehouse could hear the firecrackers popping
and crackling outside the hospital all through her laborpains.
And when she came to a little and they brought the baby to her,
she asked the nurse in a trembling husky whisper if she thought
it could have a bad effect on the baby all that noise, prenatal
influence you know. The nurse said the little boy ought to grow

up to be very patriotic and probably President, being born on the Glorious Fourth, and went on to tell a long story about a woman who'd been frightened by having a beggar stick his hand out suddenly right under her nose just before the child was born and the child had been born with six fingers, but Mrs Moorehouse was too weak to listen and went off to sleep. Later Mr Moorehouse came by on his way home from the depot where he worked as stationagent and they decided to call the kid John Ward after Mrs Moorehouse's father who was a farmer in Iowa and pretty well off. Then Mr Moorehouse went round to Healy's to get tanked up because he was a father and because it was the Glorious Fourth and Mrs Moorehouse went off to sleep again.

Johnny grew up in Wilmington. He had two brothers, Ben and Ed, and three sisters, Myrtle, Edith, and Hazel, but everybody said he was the bright boy of the family as well as the eldest. Ben and Ed were stronger and bigger than he was, but he was the marbles champion of the public school, getting considerable fame one term by a corner in agates he maneuvered with the help of a little Jewish boy named Ike Goldberg; they managed to rent out agates to other boys for a cent a week for ten.

When the Spanish War came on, everybody in Wilmington was filled with martial enthusiasm, all the boys bothered their parents to buy them Rough Rider suits and played filibuster and Pawnee Indian wars and Colonel Roosevelt and Remember the *Maine* and the White Fleet and the *Oregon* steaming through the Straits of Magellan. Johnny was down on the wharf one summer evening when Admiral Cervera's squadron was sighted in battle formation passing through the Delaware Capes by a detachment of the state militia who immediately opened fire on an old colored man crabbing out in the river. Johnny ran home like Paul Revere and Mrs Moorehouse gathered up her six children and, pushing two of them in a babycarriage and dragging the other four after her, made for the railway station to find her husband. By the time they'd decided to hop on the next train to Philadelphia, news went round that the Spanish squadron was just some boats fishing for menhaden and that the militiamen were being confined in barracks for drunkenness. When the old colored man had hauled in his last crabline, he sculled back to shore and exhibited to his cronies several splintery bulletholes in the side of his skiff.

When Johnny graduated from highschool as head of the

debating team, class orator, and winner of the prize essay contest with an essay entitled 'Roosevelt, the Man of the Hour,' everybody felt he ought to go to college. But the financial situation of the family was none too good, his father said, shaking his head. Poor Mrs Moorehouse, who had been sickly since the birth of her last child, had been taken to the hospital to have an operation and would stay there for some time to come. The younger children had had measles, whooping cough, scarlet fever, and mumps all year. The amortization on the house was due and Mr Moorehouse had not gotten the expected raise that New Year's. So instead of getting a job as assistant freight agent or picking peaches down near Dover, the way he had other summers, Johnny went round Delaware, Maryland, and Pennsylvania as agent for a bookdistributing firm. In September he received a congratulatory note from them saying that he was the first agent they had ever had who sold a hundred consecutive sets of Bryant's *History of the United States*. On the strength of it he went out to West Philadelphia and applied for a scholarship at the U. of P. He got the scholarship, passed the exams, and enrolled himself as a freshman, indicating B.S. as the degree he was working for. The first term he commuted from Wilmington to save the expense of a room. Saturdays and Sundays he picked up a little money taking subscriptions for Stoddard's *Lectures*. Everything would have gone right if his father hadn't slipped on the ice on the station steps one January morning in Johnny's sophomore year and broken his hip. He was taken to the hospital and one complication after another ensued. A little shyster lawyer, Ike Goldberg's father, in fact, went to see Moorehouse, who lay with his leg in the air in a Balkan frame and induced him to sue the railroad for a hundred thousand dollars under the employers' liability law. The railway lawyers got up witnesses to prove that Moorehouse had been drinking heavily and the doctor who had examined him testified that he showed traces of having used liquor the morning of the fall, so by midsummer he hobbled out of hospital on crutches, without a job and without any compensation. That was the end of Johnny's college education. The incident left in his mind a lasting bitterness against drink and against his father.

Mrs Moorehouse had to write for help from her father to save the house, but his answer took so long that the bank foreclosed before it came and it wouldn't have done much good anyway because it was only a hundred dollars in ten-dollar

bills in a registered envelope and just about paid the cost of
moving to a floor in a fourfamily frame house down by the
Pennsylvania freightyards. Ben left highschool and got a job
as assistant freightagent and Johnny went into the office of
Hillyard and Miller, Real Estate. Myrtle and her mother baked
pies evenings and made angelcake to send to the Woman's
Exchange and Mr Moorehouse sat in an invalid chair in the
front parlor cursing shyster lawyers and the lawcourts and the
Pennsylvania Railroad.

This was a bad year for Johnny Moorehouse. He was twenty
and didn't drink or smoke and was keeping himself clean for
the lovely girl he was going to marry, a girl in pink organdy
with golden curls and a sunshade. He'd sit in the musty little
office of Hillyard and Miller, listing tenements for rent, furnished rooms, apartments, desirable lots for sale, and think of
the Boer War and the Strenuous Life and prospecting for gold.
From his desk he could see a section of a street of frame houses
and a couple of elmtrees through a grimy windowpane. In front
of the window was in summer a conical wiremesh flytrap where
caught flies buzzed and sizzled, and in winter a little openface
gas-stove that had a peculiar feeble whistle all its own. Behind
him, back of a groundglass screen that went partway to the
ceiling, Mr Hillyard and Mr Miller sat facing each other at a
big double desk, smoking cigars and fiddling with papers. Mr
Hillyard was a sallowfaced man with black hair a little too long
who had been on the way to making a reputation for himself
as a criminal lawyer when, through some scandal that nobody
ever mentioned, as it was generally agreed in Wilmington that
he had lived it down, he had been disbarred. Mr Miller was a
little roundfaced man who lived with his elderly mother. He
had been forced into the realestate business by the fact that his
father had died leaving him building lots scattered over Wilmington and the outskirts of Philadelphia and nothing else to
make a living from. Johnny's job was to sit in the outer office
and be polite to prospective buyers, to list the properties, attend
to advertising, type the firm's letters, empty the wastebaskets
and the dead flies out of the flytrap, take customers to visit
apartments, houses, and buildinglots, and generally make himself useful and agreeable. It was on this job that he found out
that he had a pair of bright blue eyes and that he could put on
an engaging boyish look that people liked. Old ladies looking
for houses used to ask specially to have that nice young man
show them round, and business men who dropped in for a chat

with Mr Hillyard or Mr Miller would nod their heads and look wise and say, 'Bright boy, that.' He made eight dollars a week.

Outside of the Strenuous Life and a lovely girl to fall in love with him, there was one thing Johnny Moorehouse's mind dwelt on as he sat at his desk listing desirable five and seven-room dwelling-houses, drawingroom, diningroom, kitchen and butler's pantry, three master's bedrooms and bath, maid's room, water, electricity, gas, healthy location on gravelly soil in restricted residential area: He wanted to be a songwriter. He had a fair tenor voice and could carry *Larboard Watch Ahoy* or *I Dreamt I Dwelt in Marble Halls* or *Through Pleasures and Palaces Sadly I Roam* very adequately. Sunday afternoons he took music lessons with Miss O'Higgins, a shriveled little Irishwoman, unmarried, of about thirtyfive, who taught him the elements of the piano and listened with rapture to his original compositions that she took down for him on musicpaper that she had all ready ruled when he came. One song that began

> *Oh, show me the state where the peaches bloom*
> *Where maids are fair . . . It's Delaware*

she thought good enough to send to a music publisher in Philadelphia, but it came back, as did his next composition that Miss O'Higgins – he called her Marie by this time and she declared she couldn't take any money from him for her lessons, at least not until he was rich and had made a name for himself – that Marie cried over and said was as beautiful as MacDowell. It began

> *The silver bay of Delaware*
> *Rolls through peachblossoms to the sea*
> *And when my heart is bowed with care*
> *Its memory sweet comes back to me.*

Miss O'Higgins had a little parlor with gilt chairs in it where she gave her music lessons. It was very heavily hung with lace curtains and with salmoncolored brocaded portieres she had bought at an auction. In the center was a black walnut table piled high with worn black leather albums. Sunday afternoons after the lesson was over she'd bring out tea and cookies and cinnamon toast and Johnny would sit there sprawled in the horsehair armchair that had to have a flowered cover over it winter and summer on account of its being so worn and his eyes would be so blue and he'd talk about things he wanted to do and poke fun at Mr Hillyard and Mr Miller and she'd tell

him stories of great composers, and her cheeks would flush and
she'd feel almost pretty and feel that after all there wasn't such
a terrible disparity in their ages. She supported by her music
lessons an invalid mother and a father who had been a wellknown baritone and patriot in Dublin in his younger days but
who had taken to drink, and she was madly in love with Johnny
Moorehouse.

Johnny Moorehouse worked on at Hillyard and Miller's
sitting in the stuffy office, chafing when he had nothing to do
until he thought he'd go mad and run amok and kill somebody,
sending songs to the music publishers that they always sent
back, reading the *Success Magazine*, full of sick longing for the
future: to be away from Wilmington and his father's grumbling and pipesmoking and the racket his little brothers and
sisters made and the smell of corned beef and cabbage and his
mother's wrinkled crushed figure and her overworked hands.

But one day he was sent down to Ocean City, Maryland, to
report on some lots the firm had listed there. Mr Hillyard
would have gone himself only he had a carbuncle on his neck.
He gave Johnny the return ticket and ten dollars for the trip.

It was a hot July afternoon. Johnny ran home to get a bag
and to change his clothes and got down to the station just in
time to make the train. The ride was hot and sticky down
through peachorchards and pinebarrens under a blazing slaty
sky that flashed back off sandy patches in scraggly cornfields
and whitewashed shacks and strips of marshwater. Johnny had
taken off the jacket of his gray flannel suit and folded it on the
seat beside him to keep it from getting mussed and laid his
collar and tie on top of it so that they'd be fresh when he got
in, when he noticed a darkeyed girl in a ruffled pink dress and
a wide white leghorn hat sitting across the aisle. She was considerably older than he was and looked like the sort of fashionably dressed woman who'd be in a parlorcar rather than in a
daycoach. But Johnny reflected that there wasn't any parlorcar
on this train. Whenever he wasn't looking at her, he felt that
she was looking at him.

The afternoon grew overcast and it came on to rain, big
drops spattered against the car windows. The girl in pink
ruffles was struggling to put her window down. He jumped
over and put it down for her. 'Allow me,' he said. 'Thanks.'
She looked up and smiled into his eyes. 'Oh, it's so filthy on
this horrid train.' She showed him her white gloves all smudged
from the windowfastenings. He sat down again on the inside

edge of his seat. She turned her full face to him. It was an irregular brown face with ugly lines from the nose to the ends of the mouth, but her eyes set him tingling. 'You won't think it's too unconventional of me if we talk, will you?' she said. 'I'm bored to death on this horrid train, and there isn't any parlorcar though the man in New York swore that there was.'

'I bet you been traveling all day,' said Johnny, looking shy and boyish.

'Worse than that. I came down from Newport on the boat last night.'

The casual way she said Newport quite startled him. 'I'm going to Ocean City,' he said.

'So am I. Isn't it a horrid place? I wouldn't go there for a minute if it weren't for Dad. He pretends to like it.'

'They say that Ocean City has a great future . . . I mean in a kind of a realestate way,' said Johnny.

There was a pause.

'I got on in Wilmington,' said Johnny with a smile.

'A horrid place, Wilmington . . . I can't stand it.'

'I was born and raised there . . . I suppose that's why I like it,' said Johnny.

'Oh, I didn't mean there weren't awfully nice people in Wilmington . . . lovely old families . . . Do you know the Rawlinses?'

'Oh, that's all right . . . I don't want to spend all my life in Wilmington, anyway . . . Gosh, look at it rain.'

It rained so hard that a culvert was washed out and the train was four hours late into Ocean City. By the time they got in they were good friends; it had thundered and lightened and she'd been so nervous and he'd acted very strong and protecting and the car had filled up with mosquitoes and they had both been eaten up and they'd gotten very hungry together. The station was pitchblack and there was no porter and it took him two trips to get her bags out and even then they almost forgot her alligatorskin handbag and he had to go back into the car a third time to get it and his own suitcase. By that time an old darkey with a surrey had appeared who said he was from the Ocean House. 'I hope you're going there too,' she said. He said he was and they got in, though they had no place to put their feet because she had so many bags. There were no lights in Ocean City on account of the storm. The surreywheels ground through a deep sandbed; now and then that sound and the clucking of the driver at his horse were drowned by the

roar of the surf from the beach. The only light was from the
moon continually hidden by driving clouds. The rain had
stopped, but the tense air felt as if another downpour would
come any minute. 'I certainly would have perished in the storm
if it hadn't been for you,' she said; then suddenly she offered
him her hand like a man: 'My name's Strang . . . Annabelle
Marie Strang. . . . Isn't that a funny name?' He took her hand.
'John Moorehouse is mine . . . Glad to meet you, Miss Strang.'
The palm of her hand was hot and dry. It seemed to press into
his. When he let go he felt that she had expected him to hold
her hand longer. She laughed a husky low laugh. 'Now we're
introduced, Mr Moorehouse, and everything's quite all right
. . . I certainly shall give Dad a piece of my mind. The idea
of his not meeting his only daughter at the station.'

In the dark hotel lobby lit by a couple of smoked oillamps
he saw her, out of the corner of his eye, throw her arms round
a tall whitehaired man, but by the time he had scrawled John
W. Moorehouse in his most forceful handwriting in the register
and gotten his roomkey from the clerk, they had gone. Up in
the little pine bedroom it was very hot. When he pulled up the
window, the roar of the surf came in through the rusty screen
mingling with the rattle of rain on the roof. He changed his
collar and washed in tepid water he poured from the cracked
pitcher on the washstand and went down to the diningroom to
try to get something to eat. A goat-toothed waitress was just
bringing him soup when Miss Strang came in followed by the
tall man. As the only lamp was on the table he was sitting at,
they came towards it and he got up and smiled. 'Here he is,
Dad,' she said. 'And you owe him for the driver that brought
us from the station . . . Mr Morris, you must meet my father,
Doctor Strang . . . The name was Morris, wasn't it?' Johnny
blushed. 'Moorehouse, but it's quite all right. . . . I'm glad to
meet you, sir.'

Next morning Johnny got up early and went round to the
office of the Ocean City Improvement and Realty Company that
was in a new greenstained shingled bungalow on the freshly
laidout street back of the beach. There was no one there yet,
so he walked round the town. It was a muggy gray day and the
cottages and the frame stores and the unpainted shacks along
the railroad track looked pretty desolate. Now and then he
slapped a mosquito on his neck. He had on his last clean collar
and he was worried for fear it would get wilted. Whenever he
stepped off the board sidewalks he got sand in his shoes, and

sharp beachburrs stuck to his ankles. At last he found a stout
man in a white linen suit sitting on the steps of the realestate
office. 'Good morning, sir,' he said. 'Are you Colonel Wedgewood?' The stout man was too out of breath to answer and
only nodded. He had one big silk handkerchief stuck into his
collar behind and with another was mopping his face. Johnny
gave him the letter he had from his firm and stood waiting for
him to say something. The fat man read the letter with puckered brows and led the way into the office. 'It's this asthma,' he
gasped between great wheezing breaths. 'Cuts ma wind when
Ah trah to hurry. Glad to meet you, son.'

Johnny hung round old Colonel Wedgewood the rest of the
morning, looking blue-eyed and boyish, listening politely to
stories of the Civil War and General Lee and his white horse
Traveller and junketings befoa de woa on the Easten Shoa, ran
down to the store to get a cake of ice for the cooler, made a
little speech about the future of Ocean City as a summer resort – 'Why, what have they got at Atlantic City or Cape May
that we haven't got here?' roared the Colonel – went home
with him to his bungalow for lunch, thereby missing the train
he ought to have taken back to Wilmington, refused a mint
julep – he neither drank nor smoked – but stood admiringly by
while the Colonel concocted and drank two good stiff ones, for
his asthma, used his smile and his blue eyes and his boyish
shamble on the Colonel's colored cook Mamie and by four
o'clock he was laughing about the Governor of North Carolina
and the Governor of South Carolina and had accepted a job
with the Ocean City Improvement and Realty Company at
fifteen dollars a week, with a small furnished cottage thrown
in. He went back to the hotel and wrote Mr Hillyard, inclosing
the deeds for the lots and his expense account, apologized for
leaving the firm at such short notice, but explained that he
owed it to his family who were in great need to better himself
as much as he could; then he wrote to his mother that he was
staying on in Ocean City and please to send him his clothes by
express; he wondered whether to write Miss O'Higgins, but
decided not to. After all, bygones were bygones.

When he had eaten supper he went to the desk to ask for his
bill, feeling pretty nervous for fear he wouldn't have enough
money to pay it, and was just coming out with two quarters
in his pocket and his bag in his hand when he met Miss Strang.
She was with a short dark man in white flannels whom she
introduced as Monsieur de la Rochevillaine. He was a French-

man but spoke good English. 'I hope you're not leaving us,' she said. 'No, ma'am, I'm just moving down the beach to one of Colonel Wedgewood's cottages.' The Frenchman made Johnny uneasy; he stood smiling suave as a barber beside Miss Strang. 'Oh, you know our fat friend, do you? He's a great crony of Dad's. I think he's just too boring with his white horse Traveller.' Miss Strang and the Frenchman smiled both at once as if they had some secret in common. The Frenchman stood beside her swinging easily on the balls of his feet as if he were standing beside some piece of furniture he owned and was showing off to a friend. Johnny had a notion to paste him one right where the white flannel bulged into a pot belly. 'Well, I must go,' he said. 'Won't you come back later? There's going to be dancing. We'd love to have you.' 'Yes, come back by all means,' said the Frenchman. 'I will if I can,' said Johnny, and walked off with his suitcase in his hand, feeling sticky under the collar and sore. 'Drat that Frenchman,' he said aloud. Still, there was something about the way Miss Strang looked at him. He guessed he must be falling in love.

It was a hot August, the mornings still, the afternoons piling up sultry into thundershowers. Except when there were clients to show about the scorched sandlots and pinebarrens laid out into streets, Johnny sat in the office alone under the twoflanged electric fan. He was dressed in white flannels and a pink tennis shirt rolled up to the elbows, drafting the lyrical description of Ocean City (Maryland) that was to preface the advertising booklet that was the Colonel's pet idea: 'The lifegiving surges of the broad Atlantic beat on the crystalline beaches of Ocean City (Maryland) . . . the tonic breath of the pines brings relief to the asthmatic and the consumptive . . . nearby the sportsman's paradise of Indian River spreads out its broad estuary teeming with . . .' In the afternoon the Colonel would come in sweating and wheezing and Johnny would read him what he had written and he'd say, 'Bully, ma boy, bully,' and suggest that it be all done over. And Johnny would look up a new batch of words in a dogeared *Century Dictionary* and start off again.

It would have been a fine life except that he was in love. Evenings he couldn't keep away from the Ocean House. Each time he walked up the creaking porch steps past the old ladies rocking and fanning with palmleaf fans, and went through the screen doors into the lobby, he felt sure that this time he'd find Annabelle Marie alone, but each time the Frenchman was with her as smiling and cool and potbellied as ever. They both made

a fuss over Johnny and petted him like a little dog or a pre-
cocious child; she taught him to dance the 'Boston,' and the
Frenchman, who it turned out was a duke or a baron or something, kept offering him drinks and cigars and scented cigarettes. Johnny was shocked to death when he found out that
she smoked, but somehow it went with dukes and Newport
and foreign travel and that sort of thing. She used some kind
of musky perfume and the smell of it and the slight rankness
of cigarettesmoke in her hair made him dizzy and feverish
when he danced with her. Some nights he tried to tire out the
Frenchman playing pool, but then she'd disappear to bed and
he'd have to go off home cursing under his breath. While he undressed he could still feel a little tingle of musk in his nostrils.
He was trying to make up a song:

> *By the moonlight sea*
> *I pine for thee*
> *Annabelle Marie . . .*

Then it 'ud suddenly sound too damn silly and he'd stride up
and down his little porch in his pajamas, with the mosquitoes
shrilling about his head and the pound of the sea and the jeer
of the dryflies and katydids in his ears, cursing being young
and poor and uneducated and planning how he'd make a big
enough pile to buy out every damn Frenchman; then he'd be
the one she'd love and look up to and he wouldn't care if she
did have a few damn Frenchmen for mascots if she wanted
them. He'd clench his fits and stride around the porch muttering,
'By gum, I can do it.'

Then one evening he found Annabelle Marie alone. The
Frenchman had gone on the noon train. She seemed glad to see
Johnny, but there was obviously something on her mind. She
had too much powder on her face and her eyes looked red;
perhaps she'd been crying. It was moonlight. She put her hand
on his arm, 'Moorehouse, walk down the beach with me,' she
said. 'I hate the sight of all these old hens in rockingchairs.' On
the walk that led across a scraggly lawn down to the beach
they met Doctor Strang.

'What's the matter with Rochevillaine, Annie?' he said. He
was a tall man with a high forehead. His lips were compressed
and he look worried.

'He got a letter from his mother . . . She won't let him.'

'He's of age, isn't he?'

'Dad, you don't understand the French nobility . . . The

family council won't let him . . . They could tie up his income.'

'You'll have enough for two . . . I told him that.'

'Oh, shut up about it, can't you? . . .' She suddenly started to blubber like a child. She ran past Johnny and back to the hotel, leaving Johnny and Doctor Strang facing each other on the narrow boardwalk. Doctor Strang saw Johnny for the first time. 'H'm . . . excuse us,' he said as he brushed past and walked with long strides up the walk, leaving Johnny to go down to the beach and look at the moon all by himself.

But the nights that followed, Annabelle Marie did walk out along the beach with him and he began to feel that perhaps she hadn't loved the Frenchman so much after all. They would go far beyond the straggling cottages and build a fire and sit side by side looking into the flame. Their hands sometimes brushed against each other as they walked; when she'd want to get to her feet he'd take hold of her two hands and pull her up towards him and he always planned to pull her to him and kiss her, but he hadn't the nerve.

One night was very warm and she suddenly suggested they go in bathing.

'But we haven't our suits.'

'Haven't you ever been in without? It's much better . . . Why, you funny boy, I can see you blushing even in the moonlight.'

'Do you dare me?'

'I doubledare you.'

He ran up the beach a way and pulled off his clothes and went very fast into the water. He didn't dare look and only got a glimpse out of the corner of an eye of white legs and breasts and a wave spuming white at her feet. While he was putting his clothes on again, he was wondering if he wanted to get married to a girl who'd go in swimming with a fellow all naked like that, anyway. He wondered if she'd done it with that damn Frenchman. 'You were like a marble faun,' she said when he got back beside the fire where she was coiling her black hair round her head. She had hairpins in her mouth and spoke through them. 'Like a very nervous marble faun . . . I got my hair wet.'

He hadn't intended to, but he suddenly pulled her to him and kissed her. She didn't seem at all put out, but made herself little in his arms and put her face up to be kissed again. 'Would you marry a feller like me without any money?'

'I hadn't thought of it, darling, but I might.'

'You're pretty wealthy, I guess, and I haven't a cent, and I have to send home money to my folks . . . but I have prospects.'

'What kind of prospects?' She pulled his face down and ruffled his hair and kissed him.

'I'll make good in this realestate game. I swear I will.'

'Will it make good, poor baby?'

'You're not so much older'n me . . . How old are you, Annabelle?'

'Well, I admit to twentyfour, but you mustn't tell anybody, or about tonight or anything.'

'Who would I be telling about it, Annabelle Marie?'

Walking home, something seemed to be on her mind because she paid no attention to anything he said. She kept humming under her breath.

Another evening they were sitting on the porch of his cottage smoking cigarettes – he would occasionally smoke a cigarette now to keep her company – he asked her what it was worrying her. She put her hands on his shoulders and shook him: 'Oh, Moorehouse, you're such a fool . . . but I like it.'

'But there must be something worrying you, Annabelle . . . You didn't look worried the day we came down on the train together.'

'If I told you . . . Gracious, I can imagine your face.' She laughed her hard gruff laugh that always made him feel uncomfortable.

'Well, I wish I had the right to make you tell me . . . You ought to forget that damn Frenchman.'

'Oh, you're such a little innocent,' she said. Then she got up and walked up and down the porch.

'Won't you sit down, Annabelle? Don't you like me even a little bit?'

She rubbed her hand through his hair and down across his face. 'Of course I do, you little blue-eyed ninny . . . But can't you see it's everything driving me wild, all those old cats round the hotel talk about me as if I was a scarlet woman because I occasionally smoke a cigarette in my own room . . . Why, in England some of the most aristocratic women smoke right in public without anybody saying "boo" to them . . . And then I'm worried about Dad; he's sinking too much money in realestate. I think he's losing his mind.'

'But there's every indication of a big boom coming down here. It'll be another Atlantic City in time.'

'Now look here, 'fess up, how many lots have been sold this month?'

'Well, not so many . . . But there are some important sales pending . . . There's that corporation that's going to build the new hotel.'

'Dad'll be lucky if he gets fifty cents out on the dollar . . . and he keeps telling me how rattlebrained I am. He's a physician and not a financial wizard and he ought to realize it. It's all right for somebody like you who has nothing to lose and a way to make in the world to be messing around in realestate . . . As for that fat Colonel I don't know whether he's a fool or a crook.'

'What kind of a doctor is your father?'

'Do you mean to say you never heard of Doctor Strang? He's the bestknown nose and throat specialist in Philadelphia . . . Oh, it's so cute . . .' She kissed him on the cheek '. . . and ignorant . . .' she kissed him again . . . 'and pure.'

'I'm not so pure,' he said quickly and looked at her hard in the eyes. Their faces began to blush looking at each other. She let her head sink slowly on his shoulder.

His heart was pounding. He was dizzy with the smell of her hair and the perfume she wore. He pulled her to her feet with his arm round her shoulders. Tottering a little, her leg against his leg, the stiffness of her corset against his ribs, her hair against his face, he pulled her through the little livingroom into the bedroom and locked the door behind them. Then he kissed her as hard as he could on the lips. She sat down on the bed and began to take off her dress, a little coolly he thought, but he'd gone too far to pull back. When she took off her corset, she flung it in the corner of the room. 'There,' she said. 'I hate the beastly things.' She got up and walked towards him in her chemise and felt for his face in the dark.

'What's the matter, darling?' she whispered fiercely. 'Are you afraid of me?'

Everything was much simpler than Johnny expected. They giggled together while they were dressing. Walking back along the beach to the Ocean House, he kept thinking: 'Now she'll have to marry me."

In September a couple of cold northeasters right after Labor Day emptied the Ocean House and the cottages. The Colonel talked bigger about the coming boom and his advertising campaign, and drank more. Johnny took his meals with him now instead of at Mrs Ames's boardinghouse. The booklet was finished and approved and Johnny had made a couple of trips to Philadelphia with the text and the photographs to get estimates from printers. Running through Wilmington on the train without getting off there gave him a pleasant feeling of independence. Doctor Strang looked more and more worried and talked about protecting his investments. They had not talked of Johnny's engagement to his daughter, but it seemed to be understood. Annabelle's moods were unaccountable. She kept saying she was dying of boredom. She teased and nagged at Johnny continually. One night he woke suddenly to find her standing beside the bed. 'Did I scare you?' she said. 'I couldn't sleep . . . Listen to the surf.' The wind was shrilling round the cottage and a tremendous surf roared on the beach. It was almost daylight before he could get her to get out of bed and go back to the hotel. 'Let 'em see me . . . I don't care,' she said. Another time when they were walking along the beach she was taken with nausea and he had to stand waiting while she was sick behind a sanddune, then he supported her, white and trembling, back to the Ocean House. He was worried and restless. On one of his trips to Philadelphia he went round to the *Public Ledger* to see if he could get a job as a reporter.

One Saturday afternoon he sat reading the paper in the lobby of the Ocean House. There was no one else there, most of the guests had left. The hotel would close the fifteenth. Suddenly he found himself listening to a conversation. The two bellhops had come in and were talking in low voices on the bench against the wall.

'Well, I got mahn awright this summer, damned if I didn't, Joe.'

'I would of too if I hadn't gotten sick.'

'Didn't I tell you not to monkey round with that Lizzie? Man, I b'lieve every sonofabitch in town slep' with that jane, not excludin' niggers.'

'Say, did you . . . You know the blackeyed one? You said you would.'

Johnny froze. He held the paper rigid in front of him.

The bellhop gave out a low whistle. 'Hotstuff,' he said. 'Jeez, what these society dames gits away with 's got me beat.'

'Didye, honest?'

'Well, not exactly . . . 'Fraid I might ketch somethin'. But that Frenchman did . . . Jeez, he was in her room all the time.'

'I know he was. I caught him onct.' They laughed. 'They'd forgot to lock the door.'

'Was she all neked?'

'I guess she was . . . under her kimono . . . He's cool as a cucumber and orders icewater.'

'Whah didn't ye send up Mr Greeley?'

'Hell, why should I? Frenchman wasn't a bad scout. He gave me five bucks.'

'I guess she can do what she goddam pleases. Her dad about owns this dump, they tell me, him an ole Colonel Wedgewood.'

'I guess that young guy in the realestate office is gettin' it now . . . looks like he'd marry her.'

'Hell, I'd marry her maself if a girl had that much kale.'

Johnny was in a cold sweat. He wanted to get out of the lobby without their seeing him. A bell rang and one of the boys ran off. He heard the other one settling himself on the bench. Maybe he was reading a magazine or something. Johnny folded up the paper quietly and walked out onto the porch. He walked down the street without seeing anything. For a while he thought he'd go down to the station and take the first train out and throw the whole business to ballyhack, but there was the booklet to get out, and there was a chance that if the boom did come he might get in on the ground floor, and this connection with money and the Strangs; opportunity knocks but once at a young man's door. He went back to his cottage and locked himself in his bedroom. He stood a minute looking at himself in the glass of the bureau. The neatly parted light hair, the cleancut nose and chin; the image blurred. He found he was crying. He threw himself face down on the bed and sobbed.

When he went up to Philadelphia the next time to read proof on the booklet:

## OCEAN CITY (Maryland)

#### VACATIONLAND SUPREME

He also took up a draft of the wedding invitations to be engraved:

*Doctor Alonso B. Strang*
*announces the marriage of his daughter*
*Annabelle Marie*
*to Mr J. Ward Moorehouse*
*at Saint Stephen's Protestant Episcopal Church,*
*Germantown, Pennsylvania, on November fifteenth*
*nineteen hundred and nine at twelve noon*

Then there was an invitation to the reception to be sent to a special list. It was to be a big wedding because Doctor Strang had so many social obligations. Annabelle decided on J. Ward Moorehouse as more distinguished than John W. and began to call him Ward. When they asked him about inviting his family, he said his mother and father were both invalids and his brothers and sisters too little to enjoy it. He wrote his mother that he was sure she'd understand, but that as things were and with Dad the way he was ... he was sure she'd understand. Then one evening Annabelle told him she was going to have a baby.

'I thought maybe that was it.'

Her eyes were suddenly scaringly cold black in his. He hated her at that minute, then he smiled blue-eyed and boyish. 'I mean you being so nervous and everything.' He laughed and took her hand. 'Well, I'm goin' to make you an honest woman, ain't I?' He had the drop on her now. He kissed her.

She burst out crying.

'Oh, Ward, I wish you wouldn't say "ain't." '

'I was just teasing, dear . . . But isn't there some way?'

'I've tried everything . . . Dad would know, but I don't dare tell him. He knows I'm pretty independent . . . but . . .'

'We'll have to stay away for a year after we're married . . . It's rotten for me. I was just offered a job on the *Public Ledger*.'

'We'll go to Europe . . . Dad'll fix us up for our honeymoon . . . He's glad to get me off his hands and I've got money in my own right, mother's money.'

'Maybe it's all a mistake.'

'How can it be?'

'How long is it since you ... noticed ...?'

Her eyes were suddenly black and searching in his again. They stared at each other and hated each other. 'Quite long enough,' she said and pulled his ear as if he were a child, and went swishing upstairs to dress. The Colonel was tickled to death about the engagement and had invited them all to dinner to celebrate it.

The wedding came off in fine style and J. Ward Moorehouse found himself the center of all eyes in a wellfitting frock coat and a silk hat. People thought he was very handsome. His mother back in Wilmington let flatiron after flatiron cool while she pored over the account in the papers; finally she took off her spectacles and folded the papers carefully and laid them on the ironing board. She was very happy.

The young couple sailed the next day from New York on

the *Teutonic*. The crossing was so rough that only the last two days was it possible to go out on deck. Ward was sick and was taken care of by a sympathetic cockney steward who spoke of Annabelle as the 'Madam' and thought she was his mother. Annabelle was a good sailor, but the baby made her feel miserable and whenever she looked at herself in her handmirror she was so haggard that she wouldn't get out of her bunk. The stewardess suggested gin with a dash of bitters in it and it helped her over the last few days of the crossing. The night of the captain's dinner she finally appeared in the diningroom in an evening gown of black valenciennes and everybody thought her the bestlooking woman on the boat. Ward was in a fever for fear she'd drink too much champagne as he had seen her put away four ponies of gin and bitters and a Martini cocktail while dressing. He had made friends with an elderly banker, Mr Jarvis Oppenheimer, and his wife, and he was afraid that Annabelle would seem a little fast to them. The captain's dinner went off without a hitch, however, and Annabelle and Ward found that they made a good team. The captain, who had known Doctor Strang, came and sat with them in the smokingroom afterwards and had a glass of champagne with them and with Mr and Mrs Oppenheimer and they heard people asking each other who could that charming scintillating brilliant young couple be, somebody interesting surely, and when they went to bed after having seen the lighthouses in the Irish Sea, they felt that all the seasick days had been thoroughly worth while.

Annabelle didn't like it in London where the dark streets were dismal in a continual drizzle of sleet, so they only stayed a week at the Cecil before crossing to Paris. Ward was sick again on the boat from Folkestone to Boulogne and couldn't keep track of Annabelle whom he found in the diningsaloon drinking brandy and soda with an English army officer when the boat reached the calm water between the long jetties of Boulogne harbor. It wasn't so bad as he expected being in a country where he didn't know the language and Annabelle spoke French very adequately and they had a firstclass compartment and a basket with a cold chicken and sandwiches in it and some sweet wine that Ward drank for the first time – when in Rome do as the Romans do – and they were quite the honeymoon couple on the train going down to Paris. They drove in a cab from the station to the Hotel Wagram, with only their handbaggage because the hotel porter took care of the rest, through streets shimmering with green gaslight on wet pavements. The horse's

hoofs rang sharp on the asphalt and the rubbertired wheels
of the cab spun smoothly and the streets were crowded in spite
of the fact that it was a rainy winter night and there were
people sitting out at little marbletop tables round little stoves in
front of cafés and there were smells in the air of coffee and
wine and browning butter and baking bread. Annabelle's eyes
caught all the lights; she looked very pretty, kept nudging him
to show him things and patting his thigh with one hand.
Annabelle had written to the hotel, where she had stayed before
with her father, and they found a white bedroom and parlor
waiting for them and a roundfaced manager who was very
elegant and very affable to bow them into it and a fire in the
grate. They had a bottle of champagne and some pâté de foie
gras before going to bed and Ward felt like a king. She took
off her traveling clothes and put on a negligee and he put on
a smoking jacket that she had given him and that he hadn't
worn and all his bitter feelings of the last month melted away.

They sat a long time looking into the fire smoking Muratti
cigarettes out of a tin box. She kept fondling his hair and
rubbing her hand round his shoulders and neck. 'Why aren't
you more affectionate, Ward?' she said in low gruff tones. 'I'm
the sort of woman likes to be carried off her feet . . . Take care
. . . You may lose me . . . Over here the men know how to
make love to a woman.'

'Gimme a chance, won't you? . . . First thing I'm going to
get a job with some American firm or other. I think Mr Oppenheimer'll help me do that. I'll start in taking French lessons
right away. This'll be a great opportunity for me.'

'You funny boy.'

'You don't think I'm going to run after you like a poodledog,
do you, without making any money of my own? . . . Nosiree,
bobby.' He got up and pulled her to her feet. 'Let's go to bed.'

Ward went regularly to the Berlitz School for his French
lessons and went round to see Notre Dame and Napoleon's
tomb and the Louvre with old Mr Oppenheimer and his wife.
Annabelle, who said that museums gave her a headache, spent
her days shopping and having fittings with dressmakers. There
were not many American firms in Paris, so the only job Ward
could get, even with the help of Mr Oppenheimer who knew
everyone, was on Gordon Bennett's newspaper, the Paris edition
of the *New York Herald*. The job consisted of keeping track
of arriving American business men, interviewing them on the
beauties of Paris and on international relations. This was his

meat and enabled him to make many valuable contacts. Annabelle thought it was all too boring and refused to be told anything about it. She made him put on a dress suit every evening
and take her to the opera and theatres. This he was quite willing
to do as it was good for his French.

She went to a very famous specialist for women's diseases
who agreed that on no account should she have a baby at this
time. An immediate operation was necessary and would be a
little dangerous, as the baby was so far along. She didn't tell
Ward and only sent word from the hospital when it was over.
It was Christmas Day. He went immediately to see her. He
heard the details in chilly horror. He'd gotten used to the idea
of having a baby and thought it would have a steadying effect
on Annabelle. She lay looking very pale in the bed in the
private sanatorium and he stood beside the bed with his fists
clenched without saying anything. At length the nurse said to
him that he was tiring madame and he went away. When
Annabelle came back from the hospital after four or five days
announcing gaily that she was fit as a fiddle and was going to
the south of France, he said nothing. She got ready to go,
taking it for granted that he was coming, but the day she left
on the train to Nice he told her that he was going to stay on
in Paris. She looked at him sharply and then said with a laugh,
'You're turning me loose, are you?'

'I have my business and you have your pleasure,' he said.

'All right, young man, it's a go.'

He took her to the station and put her on the train, gave the
conductor five francs to take care of her and came away from
the station on foot. He'd had enough of the smell of musk and
perfume for a while.

Paris was better than Wilmington, but Ward didn't like it.
So much leisure and the sight of so many people sitting round
eating and drinking got on his nerves. He felt very homesick
the day the Ocean City booklet arrived inclosed with an
enthusiastic letter from Colonel Wedgewood. Things were
moving at last, the Colonel said; as for himself he was putting
every cent he could scrape up, beg or borrow, into options.
He even suggested that Ward send him a little money to invest
for him, now that he was in a position to risk a stake on the
surety of a big turnover; risk wasn't the word because the
whole situation was sewed up in a bag; nothing to do but shake
the tree and let the fruit fall into their mouths. Ward went
down the steps from the office of Morgan Harjes where he

got his mail and out onto Boulevard Haussmann. The heavy coated paper felt good to his fingers. He put the letter in his pocket and walked down the boulevard with the honk of horns and the ring of horses' hoofs and the shuffle of steps in his ears, now and then reading a phrase. Why, it almost made him want to go back to Ocean City (Maryland) himself. A little ruddy sunlight was warming the winter gray of the streets. A smell of roasting coffee came from somewhere; Ward thought of the white crackling sunlight of windswept days at home; days that lashed you full of energy and hope; the Strenuous Life. He had a date to lunch with Mr Oppenheimer at a very select little restaurant down in the slums somewhere called the Tour d'Argent. When he got into a redwheeled taximeter cab it made him feel good again that the driver understood his directions. After all it was educational, made up for those years of college he had missed. He had read through the booklet for the third time when he reached the restaurant.

He got out at the restaurant and was just paying the taxi when he saw Mr Oppenheimer and another man arriving down the quai on foot. Mr Oppenheimer wore a gray overcoat and a gray derby of the same pearly color as his moustaches; the other man was a steelgray individual with a thin nose and chin. When he saw them Ward decided that he must be more careful about his clothes in the future.

They ate lunch for a long time and a great many courses, although the steelgray man, whose name was McGill – he was manager of one of Jones and Laughlin's steel plants in Pittsburgh – said his stomach wouldn't stand anything but a chop and a baked potato and drank whiskey and soda instead of wine. Mr Oppenheimer enjoyed his food enormously and kept having long consultations about it with the head waiter. 'Gentlemen, you must indulge me a little . . . this for me is a debauch,' he said. 'Then, not being under the watchful eye of my wife, I can take certain liberties with my digestion . . . My wife has entered the sacred precincts of a fitting at her corsetière's and is not to be disturbed . . . You, Ward, are not old enough to realize the possibilities of food.' Ward looked embarrassed and boyish and said he was enjoying the duck very much. 'Food,' went on Mr Oppenheimer, 'is the last pleasure of an old man.'

When they were sitting over Napoleon brandy in big bowl-shaped glasses and cigars, Ward got up his nerve to bring out the Ocean City (Maryland) booklet that had been burning a hole in his pocket all through lunch. He laid it on the table modestly. 'I thought maybe you might like to glance at it, Mr Oppenheimer, as . . . as something a bit novel in the advertising line.'

Mr Oppenheimer took out his glasses and adjusted them on his nose, took a sip of brandy and looked through the book with a bland smile. He closed it, let a little curling blue cigarsmoke out through his nostrils and said, 'Why, Ocean City must be an earthly paradise indeed . . . Don't you lay it on . . . er . . . a bit thick?'

'But you see, sir, we've got to make the man in the street just crazy to go there . . . There's got to be a word to catch your eye the minute you pick it up.'

Mr McGill, who up to that time hadn't looked at Ward, turned a pair of hawkgray eyes on him in a hard stare. With a heavy red hand he reached for the booklet. He read it intently right through while Mr Oppenheimer went on to talk about the bouquet of the brandy and how you should warm the glass a little in your hand and take it in tiny sips, rather inhaling it than drinking it. Suddenly Mr McGill brought his fist down on the table and laughed a dry quick laugh that didn't move a muscle of his face. 'By gorry, that'll get 'em, too,' he said. 'I reckon it was Mark Twain said there was a sucker born every minute . . .' He turned to Ward and said, 'I'm sorry I didn't ketch your name, young feller; do you mind repeating it?'

'With pleasure . . . It's Moorehouse, J. Ward Moorehouse.'

'Where do you work?'

'I'm on the *Paris Herald* for the time being,' said Ward, blushing.

'Where do you live when you're in the States?'

'My home's in Wilmington, Delaware, but I don't guess I'll go back there when we go home. I've been offered some editorial work on the *Public Ledger* in Philly.'

Mr McGill took out a visiting card and wrote an address on it.

'Well, if you ever think of coming to Pittsburgh, look me up.'

'I'd be delighted to see you.'

'His wife,' put in Mr Oppenheimer, 'is the daughter of Doctor Strang, the Philadelphia nose and throat specialist . . . By the way, Ward, how is the dear girl? I hope Nice has cured her of her tonsillitis.'

'Yes, sir,' said Ward, 'she writes that she's much better.'

'She's a lovely creature . . . charming . . .' said Mr Oppenheimer, draining the last sip out of his brandyglass with upcast eyes.

Next day Ward got a wire from Annabelle that she was coming up to Paris. He met her at the train. She introduced a tall Frenchman with a black Vandyke beard, who was helping her off with her bags when Ward came up, as 'Monsieur Forelle, my traveling companion.' They didn't get a chance to talk until they got into the cab together. The cab smelt musty, as they had to keep the windows closed on account of the driving rain.

'Well, my dear,' Annabelle said, 'have you got over the pet you were in when I left? . . . I hope you have because I have bad news for you.'

'What's the trouble?'

'Dad's gotten himself in a mess financially . . . I knew it'd happen. He has no more idea of business than a cat... Well, that fine Ocean City boom of yours collapsed before it had started and Dad got scared and tried to unload his sandlots and naturally nobody'd buy them . . . Then the Improvement and Realty Company went bankrupt and that precious Colonel of yours has disappeared and Dad has got himself somehow personally liable for a lot of the concern's debts. . . And there you are. I wired him we were coming home as soon as we could get a sailing. I'll have to see what I can do . . . He's helpless as a child about business.'

'That won't make me mad. I wouldn't have come over here anyway if it wasn't for you.'

'Just all selfsacrifice, aren't you?'

'Let's not squabble, Annabelle.'

The last days in Paris Ward began to like it. They heard *La Bohème* at the opera and were both very much excited about it. Afterwards they went to a café and had some cold partridge and wine and Ward told Annabelle about how he'd wanted to be a songwriter and about Marie O'Higgins and how he'd started to compose a song about her and they felt very fond of each other. He kissed her again and again in the cab going home and the elevator going up to their room seemed terribly slow.

They still had a thousand dollars on the letter of credit Doctor Strang had given them as a wedding present, so that Annabelle bought all sorts of clothes and hats and perfumes and Ward went to an English tailor near the Church of the Madeleine and had four suits made. The last day Ward bought her a brooch in the shape of a rooster, made of Limoges enamel and set with garnets, out of his salary from the *Paris Herald*. Eating lunch after their baggage had gone to the boat train they felt very tender about Paris and each other and the brooch. They sailed from Havre on the *Touraine* and had a completely calm passage, a gray glassy swell all the way, although the month was February. Ward wasn't seasick. He walked round and round the firstclass every morning before Annabelle got up. He wore a Scotch tweed cap and a Scotch tweed overcoat to match, with a pair of fieldglasses slung over his shoulder, and tried to puzzle out some plan for the future. Wilmington anyway was far behind like a ship hull down on the horizon.

The steamer with tugboats chugging at its sides nosed its way through the barges and tugs and carferries and red whistling ferryboats of New York harbor against a howling icybright northwest wind.

Annabelle was grouchy and said it looked horrid, but Ward felt himself full of enthusiasm when a Jewish gentleman in a checked cap pointed out the Battery, the Custom House, the Aquarium, and Trinity Church.

They drove right from the dock to the ferry and ate in the redcarpeted diningroom at the Pennsylvania Station in Jersey City. Ward had fried oysters. The friendly darkey waiter in a white coat was like home. 'Home to God's country,' Ward said, and decided he'd have to go down to Wilmington and say hello to the folks. Annabelle laughed at him and they sat stiffly in the parlorcar of the Philadelphia train without speaking.

Doctor Strang's affairs were in very bad shape and, as he was busy all day with his practice, Annabelle took them over completely. Her skill in handling finance surprised both Ward and her father. They lived in Doctor Strang's big old house on Spruce Street. Ward, through a friend of Doctor Strang's, got a job on the *Public Ledger* and was rarely home. When he had any spare time he listened to lectures on economics and business at the Drexel Institute. Evenings Annabelle took to going out with a young architect named Joachim Beale who was very rich and owned an automobile. Beale was a thin young man with a taste for majolica and Bourbon whiskey and he called Annabelle 'my Cleopatra'.

Ward came in one night and found them both drunk sitting with very few clothes on in Annabelle's den in the top of the house. Doctor Strang had gone to a medical conference in

Kansas City. Ward stood in the doorway with his arms folded and announced that he was through and would sue for divorce and left the house, slamming the door behind him and went to the Y.M.C.A. for the night. Next afternoon when he got to the office he found a special delivery letter from Annabelle begging him to be careful what he did, as any publicity would be disastrous to her father's practice, and offering to do anything he suggested. He immediately answered it:

DEAR ANNABELLE

I now realize that you have intended all along to use me only as a screen for your disgraceful and unwomanly conduct. I now understand why you prefer the company of foreigners, bohemians, and such to that of ambitious young Americans.

I have no desire to cause you or your father any pain or publicity, but in the first place you must refrain from degrading the name of Moorehouse while you still legally bear it and also I shall feel that when the divorce is satisfactorily arranged, I shall be entitled to some compensation for the loss of time, etc, and the injury to my career that has come through your fault. I am leaving tomorrow for Pittsburgh where I have a position awaiting me and work that I hope will cause me to forget you and the great pain your faithlessness has caused me.

He wondered for a while how to end the letter, and finally wrote

                                          sincerely JWM

and mailed it.

He lay awake all night in the upper berth in the sleeper for Pittsburgh. Here he was twentythree years old and he hadn't a college degree and he didn't know any trade and he'd given up the hope of being a songwriter. God damn it, he'd never be valet to any society dame again. The sleeper was stuffy, the pillow kept going in a knot under his ear, snatches of the sales talk for Bancroft's or Bryant's histories, . . . 'Through peachorchards to the sea . . . ' Mr Hillyard's voice addressing the jury from the depths of the realestate office in Wilmington: 'Realestate, sir, is the one safe sure steady conservative investment, impervious to loss by flood and fire; the owner of realestate links himself by indissoluble bonds to the growth of his city or nation . . . improve or not at his leisure and convenience and sit at home in quiet and assurance letting the riches drop into his lap that are produced by the unavoidable and inalienable growth in wealth of a mighty nation . . .' 'For a young man with proper connections and if I may say so pleas-

ing manners and a sound classical education,' Mr Oppenheimer had said, 'banking should offer a valuable field for the
cultivation of the virtues of energy, diplomacy, and perhaps
industry. . . .' A hand was tugging at his bedclothes.

'Pittsburgh, sah, in fortyfive minutes,' came the colored
porter's voice. Ward pulled on his trousers, noticed with dismay that they were losing their crease, dropped from the berth,
stuck his feet in his shoes that were sticky from being hastily
polished with inferior polish, and stumbled along the aisle past
dishevelled people emerging from their bunks, to the men's
washroom. His eyes were glued together and he wanted a bath.
The car was unbearably stuffy and the washroom smelt of
underwear and of other men's shaving soap. Through the window he could see black hills powdered with snow, an occasional
coaltipple, rows of gray shacks all alike, a riverbed scarred
with minedumps and slagheaps, purple lacing of trees along the
hill's edge cut sharp against a red sun; then against the hill,
bright and red as the sun, a blob of flame from a smelter.
Ward shaved, cleaned his teeth, washed his face and neck as
best he could, parted his hair. His jaw and cheekbones were
getting a square look that he admired. 'Cleancut young executive,' he said to himself as he fastened his collar and tied his
necktie. It was Annabelle had taught him the trick of wearing
a necktie the same color as his eyes. As he thought of her
name a faint tactile memory of her lips troubled him, of the
musky perfume she used. He brushed the thought aside, started
to whistle, stopped for fear the other men dressing might think
it peculiar and went and stood on the platform. The sun was
well up now, the hills were pink and black and the hollows
blue where the smoke of breakfast fires collected. Everything
was shacks in rows, ironworks, coaltipples. Now and then a
hill threw a row of shacks or a group of furnaces up against
the sky. Stragglings of darkfaced men in dark clothes stood in
the slush at the crossings. Coalgrimed walls shut out the sky.
The train passed through tunnels under crisscrossed bridges,
through deep cuttings. 'Pittsburgh Union Station,' yelled the
porter. Ward put a quarter into the colored man's hand, picked
out his bag from a lot of other bags, and walked with a brisk
firm step down the platform, breathing deep the cold coal-
smoky air of the trainshed.

## *The Camera Eye (17)*

the spring you could see Halley's Comet over the elms
from the back topfloor windows of the Upper House Mr
Greenleaf said you would have to go to confirmation class
and be confirmed when the bishop came and next time you
went canoeing you told Skinny that you wouldn't be confirmed because you believed in camping and canoeing and
Halley's Comet and the Universe and the sound the rain
made on the tent the night you'd both read *The Hound of
the Baskervilles* and you'd hung out the steak on a tree and
a hound must have smelt it because he kept circling round
you and howling something terrible and you were so scared
(but you didn't say that, you don't know what you said)

and not in church and Skinny said if you'd never been
baptized you couldn't be confirmed and you went and told
Mr Greenleaf and he looked very chilly and said you'd better
not go to confirmation class any more and after that you
had to go to church Sundays but you could go to either one
you liked so sometimes you went to the Congregational and
sometimes to the Episcopalian and the Sunday the bishop
came you couldn't see Halley's Comet any more and you
saw the others being confirmed and it lasted for hours because there were a lot of little girls being confirmed too and
all you could hear was mumble mumble this thy child
mumble mumble this thy child and you wondered if you'd
be alive next time Halley's Comet came round

# Newsreel 13

I was in front of the national palace when the firing began. I ran across the Plaza with other thousands of scurrying men women and children scores of whom fell in their flight to cover

.NEW HIGH MOUNTAINS FOUND

*Oh Jim O'Shea was cast away upon an Indian Isle*
*The natives there they liked his hair*
*They liked his Irish smile*

BEDLAM IN ART

BANDITS AT HOME IN WILDS

Washington considers unfortunate illogical and unnatural the selection of General Huerta as provisional president of Mexico in succession to the overthrown president

THREE FLEE CITY FEAR WEB

He'd put sand in the hotel sugar writer says he came to America an exile and found only sordidness.

LUNG YU FORMER EMPRESS OF CHINA DIES IN THE FORBIDDEN CITY

*La cucaracha la cucaracha*
*Ya no quiere caminar*
*Porque no tiene*
*porque no tiene*
*Marijuana que fumar*

IGNORING OF LOWER CLASSES IN ORGANIZING OF REPUBLIC MAY CAUSE ANOTHER UPRISING

SIX HUNDRED AMERICANS FLEE CAPITAL

*You shall have rings on your fingers*
*And bells on your toes*
*Elephants to ride upon*
*My little Irish rose*
*So come to your nabob and on next Saint Patrick's day*
*Be Mrs Mumbo Jumbo Jijibhoy Jay O'Shea*

## Eleanor Stoddard

When she was small she hated everything. She hated her father, a stout redhaired man smelling of whiskers and stale pipetobacco. He worked in an office in the stockyards and came home with the stockyards stench on his clothes and told bloody jokes about butchering sheep and steers and hogs and men. Eleanor hated smells and the sight of blood. Nights she used to dream she lived alone with her mother in a big clean white house in Oak Park in winter when there was snow on the ground and she'd been setting a white linen tablecloth with bright white silver and she'd set white flowers and the white meat of chicken before her mother who was a society lady in a dress of white samite, but there'd suddenly be a tiny red speck on the table and it would grow and grow and her mother would make helpless fluttering motions with her hands and she'd try to brush it off but it would grow a spot of blood welling into a bloody blot spreading over the tablecloth and she'd wake up out of the nightmare smelling the stockyards and screaming.

When she was sixteen in highschool she and a girl named Isabelle swore together that if a boy ever touched them they'd kill themselves. But that fall the girl got pneumonia after scarlet fever and died.

The only other person Eleanor liked was Miss Oliphant, her English teacher. Miss Oliphant had been born in England. Her parents had come to Chicago when she was a girl in her teens. She was a great enthusiast for the English language, tried to get her pupils to use the broad 'a' and felt that she had a right to some authority in matters pertaining to English literature due to being distantly related to a certain Mrs Oliphant who'd been an English literary lady in the middle nineteenth century and had written so beautifully about Florence. So she'd occasionally have her more promising pupils, those who seemed the children of nicer parents, to tea in her little flat where she lived all alone with a sleepy blue Persian cat and a bullfinch, and talk to them about Goldsmith and Doctor Johnson's pithy sayings and Keats and *cor cordium* and how terrible it was he died so young and Tennyson and how rude he'd been to women and about how they changed the guard at Whitehall and the grapevine Henry the Eighth planted at Hampton Court and the ill-fated Mary Queen of Scots. Miss Oliphant's parents had been Catholics and had considered the Stuarts the rightful heirs to the British throne, and used to pass their wineglasses over the waterpitcher when they drank to the king. All this thrilled the boys and girls very much and particularly Eleanor and Isabelle, and Miss Oliphant used to give them high grades for their compositions and encourage them to read. Eleanor was very fond of her and very attentive in class. Just to hear Miss Oliphant pronounce a phrase like 'The Great Monuments of English Prose,' or 'The Little Princes in the Tower' or 'Saint George and Merrie England' made small chills go up and down her spine. When Isabelle died, Miss Oliphant was so lovely about it, had her to tea with her all alone and read her 'Lycidas' in a clear crisp voice and told her to read 'Adonais' when she got home, but that she couldn't read it to her because she knew she'd break down if she did. Then she talked about her best friend when she'd been a girl who'd been an Irish girl with red hair and a clear warm white skin like Crown Darby, my dear, and how she'd gone to India and died of the fever, and how Miss Oliphant had never thought to survive her grief and how Crown Darby had been invented and the inventor had spent his last penny working on the formula for this wonderful china and had needed some gold as the last ingredient, and they had been starving to death and there had been nothing left but his wife's wedding ring and how they kept the fire in the furnace going with their chairs and tables and at last he had produced this wonderful china that the royal family used exclusively.

It was Miss Oliphant who induced Eleanor to take courses at the Art Institute. She had reproductions on her walls of pictures by Rossetti and Burne-Jones and talked to Eleanor about the pre-Raphaelite Brotherhood. She made her feel that Art was something ivory white and very pure and noble and distant and sad.

When her mother died of pernicious anaemia Eleanor was a thin girl of eighteen, working days in a laceshop in the Loop and studying commercial art evenings at the Art Institute. After the funeral she went home and packed her belongings and moved to Moody House. She hardly ever went to see her father. He sometimes called her up on the phone, but whenever she could she avoided answering. She wanted to forget all about him.

In the laceshop they liked her because she was so refined and gave the place what old Mrs Lang who owned the store called 'an indefinable air of chic', but they only paid her ten dollars a week and five of that went for rent and board. She didn't eat much, but the food was so bad in the dininghall and she hated sitting with the other girls so that sometimes she had to get an extra bottle of milk to drink in her room and some weeks she'd find herself without money to buy pencils and drawingpaper with and would have to go by to see her father and get a couple of dollars from him. He gave it to her gladly enough, but somehow that made her hate him more than ever.

Evenings she used to sit in her little sordid cubbyhole of a room with its ugly bedspread and ugly iron bed, while a sound of hymnsinging came up from the common hall, reading Ruskin and Pater out of the public library. Sometimes she would let the book drop on her knees and sit all evening staring at the dim reddish electriclight bulb that was all the management allowed.

Whenever she asked for a raise Mrs Lang said, 'Why, you'll be marrying soon and leaving me, dear; a girl with your style, indefinable chic can't stay single long, and then you won't need it.'

Sundays she usually took the train out to Pullman where her mother's sister had a little house. Aunt Betty was a quiet housewifely little woman who laid all Eleanor's peculiarities to girlish fancies and kept a bright lookout for a suitable young man she could corral as a beau for her. Her husband, Uncle Joe, was foreman in a rolling mill. Many years in the rolling mill had made him completely deaf, but he claimed that actually in the mill he could hear what was said perfectly. If it was summer he spent Sunday hoeing his gardenpatch where he specialized in lettuce and asters. In winter or in bad weather he'd be sitting in the front room reading the *Railroad Man's Magazine*. Aunt Betty would cook an elaborate dinner from recipes out of the *Ladies' Home Journal* and they'd ask Eleanor to arrange the flowers for them on the dinnertable. After dinner Aunt Betty would wash the dishes and Eleanor would wipe them, and while the old people took their nap she would sit in the front room reading the society section of the *Chicago*

*Tribune.* After supper if it was fine the old people would walk down to the station with her and put her on the train, and Aunt Betty would say that it was a shocking shame for a lovely girl like her to be living all alone in the big city. Eleanor would smile a bright bitter smile and say that she wasn't afraid.

The cars going home would be crowded Sunday nights with young men and girls sticky and mussed up and sunburned from an outing in the country or on the dunes. Eleanor hated them and the Italian families with squalling brats that filled the air with a reek of wine and garlic and the Germans redfaced from a long afternoon's beerdrinking and the drunk Finn and Swedish workmen who stared at her with a blue alcoholic gleam out of wooden faces. Sometimes a man would try to start something and she'd have to move into another car.

Once, when the car was very crowded, a curlyhaired man rubbed himself up against her suggestively. The crowd was so thick she couldn't pull herself away from him. She could hardly keep from screaming out for help; it was only that she felt it was so vulgar to make a fuss. Uncontrollable dizziness came over her when she finally forced her way out at her station, and she had to stop at a drugstore on the way home for a little aromatic spirits of ammonia. She rushed through the hall of Moody House and up to her room still trembling. She was nauseated and one of the other girls found her being sick in the bathroom and looked at her so queerly. She was very unhappy at times like that and thought of suicide. She had painful cramps during her monthly periods and used to have to stay in bed at least one day every month. Often she felt miserable for a whole week.

One fall day she had phoned Mrs Lang that she was sick and would have to stay in bed. She went back up to her room and lay down on the bed and read *Romola*. She was reading through the complete works of George Eliot that were in the Moody House library. When the old scrubwoman opened the door to make the bed she said, 'Sick . . . I'll clean up, Mrs Koontz.' In the afternoon she got hungry and the sheets were all rumply under her back and although she felt rather ashamed of herself for feeling able to go out when she'd told Mrs Lang she was too sick to move, she suddenly felt she would suffocate if she stayed in her room another minute. She dressed carefully and went downstairs feeling a little furtive. 'So you're not so sick after all,' said Mrs Biggs, the matron, when she passed her in the hall. 'I just felt I needed a breath of air.' 'Too bad about you,' she heard Mrs Biggs say under her breath as she went out the door. Mrs Biggs was very suspicious of Eleanor because she was an art student.

Feeling a little faint she stopped at a drugstore and had some aromatic spirits of ammonia in water. Then she took a car down to Grant Park. A tremendous northwest wind was blowing grit and papers in whirls along the lakefront.

She went into the Art Institute and up into the Stickney Room to see the Whistlers. She liked the Art Institute better than anything else in Chicago, better than anything else in the world, the quiet, the absence of annoying men, the smooth smell of varnish from the paintings. Except on Sundays when the crowd came and it was horrid. Today there was no one in the Stickney Room but another girl welldressed in a gray fox neckpiece and a little gray hat with a feather in it. The other girl was looking fixedly at the portrait of Manet. Eleanor was interested; she rather pretended to look at the Whistlers than look at them. Whenever she could she looked at the other girl. She found herself standing beside the other girl also looking at the portrait of Manet. Suddenly their eyes met. The other girl had palebrown almondshaped eyes rather far apart.

'I think he's the best painter in the world,' she said combatively as if she wanted somebody to deny it.

'I think he's a lovely painter,' said Eleanor, trying to keep her voice from trembling. 'I love that picture.'

'You know that's not by Manet himself, that's by Fantin-Latour,' said the other girl.

'Oh, yes, of course,' said Eleanor.

There was a pause. Eleanor was afraid that would be all but the other girl said, 'What other pictures do you like?'

Eleanor looked carefully at the Whistler; then she said slowly, 'I like Whistler and Corot.'

'I do, too, but I like Millet best. He's so round and warm ... Have you ever been to Barbizon?'

'No, but I'd love to.' There was a pause. 'But I think Millet's a little coarse, don't you?' Eleanor ventured.

'You mean that chromo of the Angelus? Yes, I simply loathe and despise religious feeling in a picture, don't you?'

Eleanor didn't quite know what to say to that, so she shook her head and said, 'I love Whistler so; when I've been looking at them I can look out of the window and everything looks, you know, pastelly like that.'

'I have an idea,' said the other girl who had been looking at a little watch she had in her handbag. 'I don't have to be home till six. Why don't you come and have tea with me? I know a little place where you can get very good tea, a German pastry shop. I don't have to be home till six and we can have a nice long chat. You won't think it's unconventional of me asking you, will you? I like unconventionality, don't you? Don't you hate Chicago?'

Yes, Eleanor did hate Chicago and conventional people and all that. They went to the pastryshop and drank tea and the girl in gray, whose name was Eveline Hutchins, took hers with lemon in it. Eleanor talked a great deal and made the other girl laugh. Her father, Eleanor found herself explaining, was a painter who lived in Florence and whom she hadn't seen since she was a little girl. There had been a divorce and her mother had married again, a business man connected with Armour and Company, and now her mother was dead and she had only some relatives at Lake Forest; she studied at the Art Institute, but was thinking of giving it up because the teachers didn't suit her. She thought living in Chicago was just too horrible and wanted to go East.

'Why don't you go to Florence and live with your father?' asked Eveline Hutchins.

'Well, I might some day, when my ship comes in,' said Eleanor.

'Oh, well, I'll never be rich,' said Eveline. 'My father's a clergyman ... Let's go to Florence together, Eleanor, and call on your father. If we arrived there he couldn't very well throw us out.'

'I'd love to take a trip some day.'

'It's time I was home. By the way, where do you live? Let's meet tomorrow afternoon and look at all the pictures together.'

'I'm afraid I'll be busy tomorrow.'

'Well, maybe you can come to supper some night. I'll ask mother when I can have you. It's so rare to meet a girl you can talk to. We live on Drexel Boulevard. Here's my card. I'll send you a postcard and you'll promise to come, won't you?'

'I'd love to, if it's not earlier than seven ... You see I have an occupation that keeps me busy every afternoon except Sunday, and Sundays I usually go out to see my relatives in ...'

'In Lake Forest?'

'Yes ... When I'm in town I live at a sort of Y.W.C.A. place. Moody House; it's plebeian but convenient ... I'll write down the address on this card.' The card was of Mrs Lang's, 'Imported Laces and Hand-Embroidered Fabrics.' She wrote her address on it, scratched out the other side and handed it to Eveline.

'That's lovely,' she said, 'I'll drop you a card this very night and you'll promise to come, won't you?'

Eleanor saw her onto the streetcar and started to walk slowly along the street. She had forgotten all about feeling sick, but now that the other girl had gone she felt let down and shabbily dressed and lonely picking her way through the windy evening bustle of the streets.

Eleanor made several friends through Eveline Hutchins. The first time she went to the Hutchinses she was too awed to notice much, but later she felt freer with them, particularly as she discovered that they all thought her an interesting girl and very refined. There were Doctor and Mrs Hutchins and two daughters and a son away at college. Doctor Hutchins was a Unitarian minister and very broadminded and Mrs Hutchins did watercolors of flowers that were declared to show great talent. The elder daughter, Grace, had been at school in the East, at Vassar, and was thought to have shown ability in a literary way, the son was taking postgraduate Greek at Harvard, and Eveline was taking the most interesting courses right there at Northwestern. Doctor Hutchins was a softvoiced man with a large smooth pinkish face and large smooth white deadlooking hands. The Hutchinses were all planning to go abroad next year which would be Doctor Hutchins's sabbatical. Eleanor had never heard talk like that before and it thrilled her.

Then one evening Eveline took her to Mrs Shuster's. 'You mustn't say anything about Mrs Shuster at home, will you?' said Eveline as they were coming down from the Elevated. 'Mr Shuster is an art dealer and my father thinks they're a little too Bohemian . . . It's just because Annie Shuster came to our house one night and smoked all through dinner. . . . I said we'd go to the concert at the Auditorium.'

Eleanor had made herself a new dress, a very simple white dress, with a little green on it, not exactly an evening dress, but one she could wear any time, for the occasion, and when Annie Shuster, a dumpy little redhaired woman with a bouncy manner of walking and talking, helped them off with their wraps in the hall she exclaimed how pretty it was.

'Why, yes, it's lovely,' said Eveline. 'In fact, you're looking pretty as a peach tonight, Eleanor.'

'I bet that dress wasn't made in this town . . . Looks like Paris to me,' said Mrs Shuster.

Eleanor smiled deprecatingly and blushed a little and looked handsomer than ever.

There were a great many people packed into two small rooms and cigarette smoke and coffeecups and smell of some kind of punch. Mr Shuster was a whitehaired grayfaced man with a head too large for his body and a tired manner. He talked like an Englishman. There were several young men standing round him; one of them Eleanor had known casually when she had studied at the Art Institute. His name was Eric Egstrom and she had always liked him; he was towhaired and blue-eyed and had a little blond mustache. She could see that Mr Shuster thought a lot of him. Eveline took her around and introduced her to everybody and asked everybody questions that seemed sometimes disconcerting. Men and women both smoked and talked about books and pictures and about people Eleanor had never heard of. She looked around and didn't say much and noticed the Greek silhouettes on the orange lampshades and the pictures on the walls which looked very odd indeed and the two rows of yellowbacked French books on the shelves and felt that she might learn a great deal there.

They went away early because Eveline had to go by the Auditorium to see what the program at the concert was for fear she might be asked about it, and Eric and another young man took them home. After they'd left Eveline at her house, they asked Eleanor where she lived and she hated to say Moody House because it was in such a horridlooking street, so she made them walk with her to an Elevated station and ran up the steps quickly and wouldn't let them come with her, although it scared her to go home alone as late as it was.

Many of Mrs Lang's customers thought Eleanor was French, on account of her dark hair, her thin oval face and her transparent skin. In fact, one day when a Mrs McCormick that Mrs Lang suspected might be one of 'the' McCormicks asked after that lovely French girl who waited on her before, Mrs Lang got an idea. Eleanor would have to be French from now on; so she bought her twenty tickets at the Berlitz School and said she could have the hour off in the morning between nine and ten if she would go and take French lessons there. So all through December and January Eleanor studied French three times a week with an old man in a smelly alpaca jacket and began to slip a phrase in now and then as unconcernedly as she could when she was talking to the customers, and when there was anybody in the shop Mrs Lang always called her 'Mademoiselle.'

She worked hard and borrowed yellowbacked books from the Shusters to read in the evenings with a dictionary and soon she knew more French than Eveline did who had had a French governess when she was little. One day at the Berlitz School she found she had a new teacher. The old man had pneumonia and she had a young Frenchman instead. He was a thin young man with a sharp blue-shaved chin and large brown eyes with long lashes. Eleanor liked him at once, his thin aristocratic hands and his aloof manner. After half an hour they had forgotten all about the lesson and were talking English. He spoke English with a funny accent but fluently. She particularly liked the throaty way he pronounced 'r'.

Next time she was all tingling going up the stairs to see if it would be the same young man. It was. He told her that the old man had died. She felt she ought to be sorry but she wasn't. The young man noticed how she felt and screwed his face up into a funny half-laughing, half-crying expression and said, 'Vae victis.' Then he told her about his home in France and how he hated the conventional bourgeois life there and how he'd come to America because it was the land of youth and the future and skyscrapers and the Twentieth Century Limited and how beautiful he thought Chicago was. Eleanor had never heard anyone talk like that and told him he must have gone through Ireland and kissed the blarney stone. Then he looked very aggrieved and said, 'Mademoiselle, c'est la pure vérité,' and she said she believed him absolutely and how interesting it was to meet him and how she must introduce him to her friend Eveline Hutchins. Then he went on to tell her how he'd lived in New Orleans and how he'd come as a steward on a French Line boat and how he'd worked as dishwasher and busboy and played the piano in cabarets and worse places than that and how much he loved Negroes and how he was a painter and wanted so much to get a studio and paint but that he hadn't the money yet. Eleanor was a little chilled by the part about dishwashing and cabarets and colored people, but when he said he was interested in art she felt she really would have to introduce him to Eveline and she felt very bold and unconventional when she asked him to meet them at the Art Institute Sunday afternoon. After all if they decided against it they wouldn't have to go.

Eveline was thrilled to death, but they got Eric Egstrom to come along too, on account of Frenchmen having such a bad reputation. The Frenchman was very late and they began to be afraid he wasn't coming or that they'd missed him in the crowd, but at last Eleanor saw him coming up the big staircase. His name was Maurice Millet – no, no relation of the painter's – and he shocked them all very much by refusing to look at any paintings in the Art Institute and saying that he thought it ought to be burned down and used a lot of words like cubism and futurism that Eleanor had never heard before. But she could see at once that he had made a great hit with Eveline and Eric; in fact, they hung on his every word and all through tea neither of them paid any attention to Eleanor. Eveline invited Maurice to the house and they all went to supper to Drexel Boulevard, where Maurice was very polite to Doctor and Mrs Hutchins, and on to the Shusters' afterwards. They left the Shusters' together and Maurice said that the Shusters were impossible and had very bad paintings on their walls, 'Tout ça c'est affreusement pompier,' he said. Eleanor was puzzled, but Eveline and Eric said that they understood perfectly that he meant they knew as little about art as a firemen's convention, and they laughed a great deal.

The next time she saw Eveline, Eveline confessed that she was madly in love with Maurice and they both cried a good deal and decided that after all their beautiful friendship could stand even that. It was up in Eveline's room at Drexel Boulevard. On the mantel was a portrait Eveline was trying to do of him in pastels from memory. They sat side by side on the bed, very close, with their arms round each other and talked solemnly about each other and Eleanor told about how she felt about men; Eveline didn't feel quite that way, but nothing could ever break up their beautiful friendship and they'd always tell each other everything.

About that time Eric Egstrom got a job in the interior decorating department at Marshall Field's that paid him fifty a week. He got a fine studio with a northlight in an alley off North Clark Street and Maurice went to live with him there. The girls were there a great deal and they had many friends in and tea in glasses Russian style and sometimes a little Virginia Dare wine, so they didn't have to go to the Shusters' any more. Eleanor was always trying to get in a word alone with Eveline; and the fact that Maurice didn't like Eveline the way Eveline liked him made Eveline very unhappy, but Maurice and Eric seemed to be thoroughly happy. They slept in the same bed and were always together. Eleanor used to wonder about them sometimes, but it was so nice to know boys who weren't horrid about women. They all went to the opera together and to concerts and art exhibitions – it was Eveline or Eric who usually bought the tickets and paid when they ate in restaurants – and Eleanor had a better time those few months than she'd ever had in her life before. She never went out to Pullman any more and she and Eveline talked about getting a studio together when the Hutchinses came back from their trip abroad. The thought that every day brought June nearer and that then she would lose Eveline and have to face the horrid gritty dusty sweaty Chicago summer alone made Eleanor a little miserable sometimes, but Eric was trying to get her a job in his department at Marshall Field's, and she and Eveline were following a course of lectures on interior decorating at the University evenings, and that gave her something to look forward to.

Maurice painted the loveliest pictures in pale buffs and violets of longfaced boys with big luminous eyes and long lashes, and longfaced girls that looked like boys, and Russian wolfhounds with big luminous eyes, and always in the back there were a few girders or a white skyscraper and a big puff of white clouds and Eveline and Eleanor thought it was such a shame that he had to go on teaching at the Berlitz School.

The day before Eveline sailed for Europe they had a little party at Egstrom's place. Maurice's pictures were around the walls and they were all glad and sorry and excited and tittered a great deal. Then Egstrom came in with the news that he had told his boss about Eleanor and how she knew French and had studied art and was so goodlooking and everything and Mr Spotmann had said to bring her around at noon tomorrow, and that the job, if she could hold it down, would pay at least twenty-five a week. There had been an old lady in to see Maurice's paintings and she was thinking of buying one; they all felt very gay and drank quite a lot of wine, so that in the end when it was time for goodbyes it was Eveline who felt lonesome at going away from them all, instead of Eleanor feeling lonesome at being left behind as she had expected.

When Eleanor walked back alone the platform from seeing the Hutchinses all off for New York the next evening, and their bags all labeled for the steamship *Baltic* and their eyes all bright with the excitement of going East and going abroad and the smell of coalsmoke and the clang of engine bells and scurry of feet, she walked with her fists clenched and her sharppointed nails dug into the palms of her hands, saying to herself over and over again: 'I'll be going, too; it's only a question of time; I'll be going, too.'

## The Camera Eye (18)

she was a very fashionable lady and adored bullterriers and had a gentleman friend who was famous for his resemblance to King Edward.

she was a very fashionable lady and there were white lilies in the hall No my dear I can't bear the scent of them in the room and the bullterriers bit the trades people and the little newsy No my dear they never bite nice people and they're quite topping with Billy and his friends

we all went coaching in a fourinhand and the man in the back blew a long horn and that's where Dick Whittington stood with his cat and the bells   there were hampers full of luncheon and she had gray eyes and was very kind to her friend's little boy though she loathed simply loathed most children and her gentleman friend who was famous for his resemblance to King Edward couldn't bear them or the bullterriers and she kept asking Why do you call him that?

and you thought of Dick Whittington and the big bells of Bow, three times Lord Mayor of London, and looked into her gray eyes and said Maybe because I called him that the first time I saw him and I didn't like her and I didn't like the bullterriers and I didn't like the fourinhand but I wished Dick Whittington three times Lord Mayor of London boomed the big bells of Bow and I wished Dick Whittington I wished I was home but I hadn't any home and the man in the back blew a long horn

## Eleanor Stoddard

Working at Marshall Field's was very different from working at Mrs Lang's. At Mrs Lang's she had only one boss, but in the big store she seemed to have everybody in the department over her. Still she was so refined and cold and had such a bright definite little way of talking that, although people didn't like her much, she got along well. Even Mrs Potter and Mr Spotmann, the department heads, were a little afraid of her. News got around that she was a society girl and didn't really have to earn a living at all. She was very sympathetic with the customers about their problems of homemaking and had a little humble-condescending way with Mrs Potter and admired her clothes, so that at the end of a month Mrs Potter said to Mr Spotmann, 'I think we have quite a find in the Stoddard girl,' and Mr Spotmann, without opening his white trap of an old woman's mouth, said, 'I've thought so all along.'

When Eleanor stepped out on Randolph one sunny afternoon with her first week's pay envelope in her hand she felt pretty happy. She had such a sharp little smile on her thin lips that a couple of people turned to look at her as she walked along ducking her head into the gusty wind to keep her hat from being blown off. She turned down Michigan Avenue towards the Auditorium looking at the bright shop windows and the very-pale blue sky and the piles of dovegray fluffy clouds over the lake and the white blobs of steam from the locomotives. She went into the deep amberlit lobby of the Auditorium Annex, sat down all by herself at a wicker table in the corner of the lounge and sat there a long while all by herself drinking a cup of tea and eating buttered toast, ordering the waiter about with a crisp little refined monied voice.

Then she went to Moody House, packed her things and moved to the Eleanor Club, where she got a room for sevenfifty with board. But the room wasn't much better and everything still had the gray smell of a charitable institution, so the next week she moved again to a small residential hotel on the North Side where she got room and board for fifteen a week. As that only left her a balance of three-fifty – it had turned out that the job only paid twenty, which actually only meant eighteen-fifty when insurance was taken off – she had to go to see her father again. She so impressed him with her rise in the world and the chances of a raise that he promised her five a week, although he was only making twenty himself and was planning to marry again, to a Mrs O'Toole, a widow with five children who kept a boardinghouse out Elsdon Way.

Eleanor refused to go to see her future stepmother, and made her father promise to send her the money in a moneyorder each week, as he couldn't expect her to go all the way out to Elsdon to get it. When she left him she kissed him on the forehead and made him feel quite happy. All the time she was telling herself that this was the very last time.

Then she went back to the Hotel Ivanhoe and went up to her room and lay on her back on the comfortable brass bed looking round at her little room with its white woodwork and its pale yellow wallpaper with darker satiny stripes and the lace curtains in the window and the heavy hangings. There was a crack in the plaster of the ceiling and the carpet was worn, but the hotel was very refined, she could see that, full of old couples living on small incomes and the help were very elderly and polite and she felt at home for the first time in her life.

When Eveline Hutchins came back from Europe the next spring wearing a broad hat with a plume on it, full of talk of the Salon des Tuileries and the Rue de la Paix and museums and art exhibitions and the opera, she found Eleanor a changed girl. She looked older than she was, dressed quietly and fashionably, had a new bitter sharp way of talking. She was thoroughly established in the interior decorating department at Marshall Field's and expected a raise any day, but she wouldn't talk about it. She had given up going to classes or haunting the Art Institute and spent a great deal of time with an old maiden lady who also lived at the Ivanhoe who was reputed to be very rich and very stingy, a Miss Eliza Perkins.

The first Sunday she was back, Eleanor had Eveline to tea at the hotel and they sat in the stuffy lounge talking in refined whispers with the old lady. Eveline asked about Eric and Maurice, and Eleanor supposed that they were all right, but hadn't seen them much since Eric had lost his job at Marshall Field's. He wasn't turning out so well as she had hoped, she said. He and Maurice had taken to drinking a great deal and going round with questionable companions, and Eleanor rarely got a chance to see them. She had dinner every evening with Miss Perkins and Miss Perkins thought a great deal of her and bought her clothes and took her with her driving in the park and sometimes to the theater when there was something really worth while on, Minnie Maddern Fiske or Guy Bates Post in an interesting play. Miss Perkins was the daughter of a wealthy saloonkeeper and had been played false in her youth by a young lawyer whom she had trusted to invest some money for her and whom she had fallen in love with. He had run away with another girl and a number of cash certificates. Just how much she had left Eleanor hadn't been able to find out, but as she always took the best seats at the theater and liked going to dinner at expensive hotels and restaurants and hired a carriage by the half-day whenever she wanted one, she gathered that she must still be well off.

After they had left Miss Perkins to go to the Hutchinses for supper, Eveline said: 'Well, I declare – I don't see what you see in that . . . that little old maid . . . And here I was just bursting to tell you a million things and to ask you a million questions . . . I think it was mean of you.'

'I'm very devoted to her, Eveline. I thought you'd be interested in meeting any dear friend of mine.'

'Oh, of course I am, dear, but, gracious, I can't make you out.'

'Well, you won't have to see her again, though I could tell by her manner that she thought you were lovely.'

Walking from the Elevated station to the Hutchinses it was more like old times again. Eleanor told about the hard feelings that were growing between Mr Spotmann and Mrs Potter and how they both wanted her to be on their side, and made Eveline laugh, and Eveline confessed that on the *Kroonland* coming back she had fallen very much in love with a man from Salt Lake City, such a relief after all those foreigners, and Eleanor teased her about it and said he was probably a Mormon and Eveline laughed and said, No, he was a judge, and admitted that he was married already. 'You see,' said Eleanor, 'of course he's a Mormon.' But Eveline said that she knew he wasn't and that if he'd divorce his wife she'd marry him in a minute. Then Eleanor said she didn't believe in divorce and if they hadn't gotten to the door they would have started quarrelling.

That winter she didn't see much of Eveline. Eveline had many beaux and went out a great deal to parties and Eleanor used to read about her on the society page Sunday mornings. She was very busy and often too tired at night even to go to the theater with Miss Perkins. The row between Mrs Potter and Mr Spotmann had come to a head and the management had moved Mrs Potter to another department and she had let herself plunk into an old Spanish chair and had broken down and cried right in front of the customers and Eleanor had had to take her to the dressingroom and borrow smelling salts for her and help her do up her peroxide hair into the big pompadour again and consoled her by saying that she would probably like it much better over in the other building anyway. After that Mr Spotmann was very goodnatured for several months. He occasionally took Eleanor out to lunch with him and they had a little joke that they laughed about together about Mrs Potter's pompadour wobbling when she'd cried in front of the customers. He sent Eleanor out on many little errands to wealthy homes, and the customers liked her because she was so refined and sympathetic and the other employees in the department hated her and nickednamed her 'teacher's pet'. Mr Spotmann even said that he'd try to get her a percentage on commissions and talked often about giving her that raise to twentyfive a week.

Then one day Eleanor got home late to supper and the old clerk at the hotel told her that Miss Perkins had been stricken with heartfailure while eating steak and kidney pie for lunch and had died right in the hotel diningroom and that the body had been removed to the Irving Funeral Chapel and asked her if she knew any of her relatives that should be notified. Eleanor knew nothing except that her financial business was handled by the Corn Exchange Bank and that she thought that she had nieces in Mound City, but didn't know their names. Their clerk was very worried about who would pay for the removal of the body and the doctor and a week's unpaid hotel bill and said that all her things would be held under seal until some qualified person appeared to claim them. He seemed to think Miss Perkins had died especially to spite the hotel management.

Eleanor went up to her room and locked the door and threw herself on the bed and cried a little, because she'd been fond of Miss Perkins.

Then a thought crept into her mind that made her heart beat fast. Suppose Miss Perkins had left her a fortune in her will. Things like that happened. Young men who opened church pews, coachmen who picked up a handbag; old ladies were always leaving their fortunes to people like that.

She could see it in headlines—

MARSHALL FIELD EMPLOYEE INHERITS MILLION

She couldn't sleep all night and in the morning she found the manager of the hotel and offered to do anything she could. She called up Mr Spotmann and coaxed him to give her the day off, explaining that she was virtually prostrated by Miss Perkins's death. Then she called up the Corn Exchange Bank and talked to a Mr Smith who had been in charge of the Perkins estate. He assured her that the bank would do everything in its power to protect the heirs and the residuary legatees and said that the will was in Miss Perkins's safe-deposit box and that he was sure everything was in proper legal form.

Eleanor had nothing to do all day, so she got hold of Eveline for lunch and afterwards they went to Keith's together. She felt it wasn't just proper to go to the theater with her old friend still lying at the undertaker's, but she was so nervous and hysterical she had to do something to take her mind off this horrible shock. Eveline was very sympathetic and they felt closer than they had since the Hutchinses had gone abroad. Eleanor didn't say anything about her hopes.

At the funeral there were only Eleanor and the Irish chambermaid at the hotel, an old woman who sniffled and crossed herself a great deal, and Mr Smith and a Mr Sullivan who was representing the Mound City relatives. Eleanor wore black and the undertaker came up to her and said, 'Excuse me, miss, but I can't refrain from remarking how lovely you look, just like a Bermuda lily.' It wasn't as bad as she had expected and afterwards Eleanor and Mr Smith and Mr Sullivan, the representative of the law firm who had charge of the interests of the relatives, were quite jolly together coming out of the crematorium.

It was a sparkling October day and everybody agreed that October was the best month in the year and that the minister had read the funeral service very beautifully. Mr Smith asked Eleanor wouldn't she eat lunch with them as she was mentioned in the will, and Eleanor's heart almost stopped beating and she cast down her eyes and said she'd be very pleased.

They all got into a taxi. Mr Sullivan said it was pleasant to roll away from the funeral chapel and such gloomy thoughts. They went to lunch at de Yonghe's and Eleanor made them laugh telling them about how they'd acted at the hotel and what a scurry everybody had been in, but when they handed her the menu said that she couldn't eat a thing. Still when she saw the planked whitefish she said that she'd take just a little to pick to pieces on her plate. It turned out that the windy October air had made them all hungry and the long ride in the taxi. Eleanor enjoyed her lunch very much and after the whitefish she ate a little Waldorf salad and then a peach melba.

The gentlemen asked her whether she would mind if they smoked cigars and Mr Smith put on a rakish look and said would she have a cigarette and she blushed and said no, she never smoked and Mr Sullivan said he'd never respect a woman who smoked and Mr Smith said some of the girls of the best families in Chicago smoked and as for himself he didn't see the harm in it if they didn't make chimneys of themselves. After lunch they walked across the street and went up in the elevator to Mr Sullivan's office and there they sat down in big leather chairs and Mr Sullivan and Mr Smith put on solemn faces and Mr Smith cleared his throat and began to read the will. Eleanor couldn't make it out at first and Mr Smith had to explain to her that the bulk of the fortune of three million dollars was left to the Florence Crittenton home for wayward girls, but that the sum of one thousand dollars each was to the three nieces in Mound City and that a handsome diamond brooch in the form of a locomotive was left to Eleanor Stoddard and, 'If you call at the Corn Exchange Bank some time tomorrow, Miss Stoddard,' said Mr Smith, 'I shall be very glad to deliver it to you.'

Eleanor burst out crying.

They both were very sympathetic and so touched that Miss Stoddard should be so touched by the remembrance of her old friend. As she left the office, promising to call for the brooch tomorrow, Mr Sullivan was just saying in the friendliest voice, 'Mr Smith, you understand that I shall have to endeavour to break that will in the interests of the Mound City Perkinses,' and Mr Smith said in the friendliest voice, 'I suppose so, Mr Sullivan, but I don't see that you can get very far with it. It's an ironclad, copper-riveted document if I do say so as shouldn't, because I drew it up myself.'

So the next day at eight Eleanor was on her way down to Marshall Field's again and there she stayed for several years. She got the raise and the percentages on commissions and she and Mr Spotmann got to be quite thick, but he never tried to make love to her and their relations were always formal; that was a relief to Eleanor because she kept hearing stories about floorwalkers and department heads forcing their attentions on the young girl employees and Mr Elwood of the furniture department had been discharged for that very reason, when it came out that little Lizzie Dukes was going to have a baby, but perhaps that hadn't been all Mr Elwood's fault as Lizzie Dukes didn't look as if she was any better than she should be; anyway, it seemed to Eleanor as if she'd spend the rest of her life furnishing other people's new drawingrooms and diningrooms, matching curtains and samples of upholstery and wallpaper, smoothing down indignant women customers who'd been sent an Oriental china dog instead of an inlaid teak teatable or who even after they'd chosen it themselves weren't satisfied with the pattern on that cretonne.

She found Eveline Hutchins waiting for her one evening when the store closed. Eveline wasn't crying but was deathly pale. She said she hadn't had anything to eat for two days and wouldn't Eleanor have some tea with her over at the Sherman House or anywhere.

They went to the Auditorium Annex and sat in the lounge and ordered tea and cinnamon toast and then Eveline told her that she'd broken off her engagement with Dirk McArthur and that she'd decided not to kill herself but to go to work. 'I'll never fall in love with anybody again, that's all, but I've got to do something and you're just wasting yourself in that stuffy department store, Eleanor; you know you never get a chance to show what you can do; you're just wasting your ability.'

Eleanor said that she hated it like poison, but what was she to do? 'Why not do what we've been talking about all these years . . . Oh, people make me so mad, they never will have any nerve or do anything that's fun or interesting . . . I bet you if we started a decorating business we'd have lots of orders. Sally Emerson'll give us her new house to decorate and then everybody else'll just have to have us to be in the swim . . . I don't think people really want to live in the horrible stuffy places they live in; it's just that they don't know any better.'

Eleanor lifted her teacup and drank several little sips. She looked at her little white carefully manicured hand with pointed nails holding the teacup. Then she said, 'But where'd we get the capital? We'd have to have a little capital to start on.'

'Dad'll let us have something, I think, and maybe Sally Emerson might; she's an awfully good sport and then our first commission'll launch us . . . Oh, do come on, Eleanor, it'll be such fun.'

' "Hutchins and Stoddard, Interior Decorating," ' said Eleanor, putting down her teacup, 'or maybe "Miss Hutchins and Miss Stoddard"; why, my dear, I think it's a grand idea!'

'Don't you think just "Eleanor Stoddard and Eveline Hutchins" would be better?'

'Oh, well, we can decide on the name when we hire a studio and have put it in the telephone book. Why don't we put it this way, Eveline dear . . . if you can get your friend Mrs Emerson to give us the decorating of her new house, we'll go in for it, if not we'll wait until we have a genuine order to start off on.'

'All right; I know she will. I'll run right out and see her now.'
Eveline had a high color now. She got to her feet and leaned
over Eleanor and kissed her. 'Oh, Eleanor, you're a darling.'

'Wait a minute, we haven't paid for our tea,' said Eleanor.

The next month the office was unbearable, and the customers'
complaints and leaving the Ivanhoe in a hurry every morning
and being polite to Mr Spotmann and thinking up little jokes
to make him laugh. Her room at the Ivanhoe seemed small and
sordid and the smell of cooking that came up through the
window and the greasesmell of the old elevator. Several days
she called up that she was sick and then found that she couldn't
stay in her room and roamed about the city going to shops and
movingpicture shows and then getting suddenly dead tired and
having to come home in a taxi that she couldn't afford. She
even went back to the Art Institute once in a while, but she
knew all the pictures by heart and hadn't the patience to look
at them any more. Then at last Eveline got Mrs Phillip Paine
Emerson to feeling that her new house couldn't do without a
novel note in the diningroom and they got her up an estimate
much less than any of the established decorators was asking,
and Eleanor had the pleasure of watching Mr Spotmann's
astonished face when she refused to stay even with a raise to
forty a week and said that she had a commission with a
friend to decorate the new Paine Emerson mansion in Lake
Forest.

'Well, my dear,' said Mr Spotmann, snapping his square
white mouth, 'if you want to commit suicide of your career I
won't be the one to stop you. You can leave right this minute
if you want to. Of course you forfeit the Christmas bonus.'

Eleanor's heart beat fast. She looked at the gray light that
came through the office, and the yellow cardcatalogue case and
the letters on a file and the little samples dangling from them.
In the outer office Ella Bowen the stenographer had stopped
typing; she was probably listening. Eleanor sniffed the lifeless
air that smelt of chintz and furniturevarnish and steamheat
and people's breath and then she said, 'All right, Mr Spotmann,
I will.'

It took her all day to get her pay and to collect the insurance
money due her and she had a long wrangle with a cashier about
the amount, so that it was late afternoon before she stepped
out into the driving snow of the streets and went into a drugstore to call up Eveline.

Eveline had already rented two floors of an old Victorian

house off Chicago Avenue, and they were busy all winter decorating the office and showrooms downstairs and the apartment upstairs where they were going to live, and doing Sally Emerson's diningroom. They got a colored maid named Amelia who was a very good cook although she drank a little, and they had cigarettes and cocktails at the end of the afternoon and little dinners with wine, and found a downattheheels French dressmaker to make them evening gowns to wear when they went out with Sally Emerson and her set, and rode in taxis and got to know a lot of really interesting people. By spring when they finally got a check for five hundred dollars out of Philip Paine Emerson they were a thousand dollars in the hole but they were living the way they liked. The diningroom was considered a little extreme, but some people liked it, and a few more orders came. They made many friends and started going round with artists again and with special writers on the *Daily News* and the *American*, who took them out to dinner in foreign restaurants that were very smoky and where they talked a great deal about modern French painting and the Middle West and going to New York. They went to the Armory Show and had a photograph of Brancusi's Golden Bird over the desk in the office and copies of the *Little Review* and *Poetry* among the files of letters from clients and unpaid bills from wholesalers.

Eleanor went out a great deal with Tom Custis, who was an elderly redfaced man, fond of music, and chorusgirls and drinking, who belonged to all the clubs and for years had been a great admirer of Mary Garden. He had a box at the opera and a Stevens-Duryea and nothing to do except go to tailors and visit specialists and occasionally blackball a Jew or a newcomer applying for membership in some club he belonged to. The Armours had bought out his father's meatpacking concern when he was still a college athlete and he hadn't done a stroke of work since. He claimed to be thoroughly sick of social life and enjoyed taking an interest in the girls' decorating business. He kept in close touch with Wall Street and would occasionally turn over to Eleanor a couple of shares that he was trading in. If they rose it was her gain, if they fell it was his loss. He had a wife in a private sanitarium and he and Eleanor decided they'd be just friends. Sometimes he was a little too affectionate coming home in a taxicab in the evening, but Eleanor would scold him and he'd be very contrite the next day, and send her great boxes of white flowers.

Eveline had several beaux, writers and illustrators and people like that, but they never had any money and ate and drank everything in the house when they came to dinner. One of them, Freddy Seargeant, was an actor and producer temporarily stranded in Chicago. He had friends in the Shubert office and his great ambition was to put on a pantomime like Reinhardt's *Sumurun*, only based on Maya Indian stories. He had a lot of photographs of Maya ruins, and Eleanor and Eveline began to design costumes for it and settings. They hoped to get Tom Custis or the Paine Emersons to put up money for a production in Chicago.

The main trouble was with the music. A young pianist whom Tom Custis had sent to Paris to study began to write it and came and played it one night. They had quite a party for him. Sally Emerson came and a lot of fashionable people, but Tom Custis drank too many cocktails to be able to hear a note and Amelia the cook got drunk and spoiled the dinner and Eveline told the young pianist that his music sounded like movie music and he went off in a huff. When everybody had gone, Freddy Seargeant and Eveline and Eleanor roamed around the ravaged apartment feeling very bad indeed. Freddy Seargeant twisted his black hair, slightly splotched with gray, in his long hands and said he was going to kill himself, and Eleanor and Eveline quarrelled violently.

'But it did sound like movingpicture music and, after all, why shouldn't it?' Eveline kept saying. Then Freddy Seargeant got his hat and went out saying, 'You women are making life a hell for me,' and Eveline burst out crying and got hysterical and Eleanor had to send for a doctor.

The next day they scraped up fifty dollars to send Freddy back to New York, and Eveline went back to live at the house on Drexel Boulevard, leaving Eleanor to carry on the decorating business all alone.

Next spring Eleanor and Eveline sold for five hundred some chandeliers that they had picked up in a junk shop on the west side for twentyfive dollars and were just writing out checks for their more pressing debts when a telegram arrived.

SIGNED CONTRACT WITH SHUBERTS PRODUCTION RETURN OF THE NATIVE  WILL YOU DO SCENERY COSTUMES HUNDRED FIFTY A WEEK EACH  MUST COME ON NEW YORK IMMEDIATELY

MUST HAVE YOU WIRE IMMEDIATELY HOTEL
DES ARTISTES CENTRAL PARK SOUTH FREDDY

'Eleanor, we've got to do it,' said Eveline, taking a cigarette out of her handbag and walking round the room puffing at it furiously. 'It'll be a rush, but let's make the Twentieth Century this afternoon.' 'It's about noon now,' said Eleanor in a trembly voice. Without answering Eveline went to the phone and called up the Pullman office. That evening they sat in their section looking out of the window at the steelworks of Indiana Harbor, the big cement works belching puttycolored smoke, the flaring furnaces of Gary disappearing in smokeswirling winter dusk. Neither of them could say anything.

## The Camera Eye (19)

the methodist minister's wife was a tall thin woman who sang little songs at the piano in a spindly lost voice who'd heard you liked books and grew flowers and vegetables and was so interested because she'd once been an episcopalian and loved beautiful things and had had stories she had written published in a magazine and she was younger than her husband who was a silent blackhaired man with a mouth like a mousetrap and tobaccojuice on his chin and she wore thin white dresses and used perfume and talked in a bell-like voice about how things were lovely as a lily and the moon was bright as a bubble full to bursting behind the big pine when we walked back along the shore and you felt you ought to put your arm round her and kiss her only you didn't want to and anyway you wouldn't have had the nerve walking slow through the sand and the pine needles under the big moon swelled to bursting like an enormous drop of quicksilver and she talked awful sad about the things she had hoped for and you thought it was too bad

you liked books and Gibbon's *Decline and Fall of the Roman Empire* and Captain Marryat's novels and wanted to go away and to sea and to foreign cities Carcassonne Marakesh Isfahan and liked things to be beautiful and

wished you had the nerve to hug and kiss Martha the
colored girl they said was half Indian old Emma's daughter
and little redheaded Mary 1 taught how to swim if 1 only
had the nerve breathless nights when the moon was full but
Oh God not lilies

# Newsreel 14

colonel says Democrats have brought distress to nation
I'll resign when I die Huerta snarls in grim defi and half
Mexico will die with me   no flames were seen but the vast
plume of blackened steam from the crater waved a mile
high in the sky and volcanic ash fell on Macomber Flats
thirteen miles distant

Eggs Noisy? No Pokerchips.

> *Way down on the levee*
> *In old Alabamy*
> *There's daddy and mammy*
> *And Ephram and Sammy*

## MOONFAIRIES DANCE ON RAVINIA GREENS

## WILSON WILL TAKE ADVICE OF BUSINESS

admits he threw bomb   policewoman buys drinks after
one loses on wheat   slain as burglar

> *On a moonlight night*
> *You can find them all*
> *While they are waiting*
> *Banjoes are syncopating*
> *What's that they're all saying*
> *What's that they're all singing*

recognizing James scrawl the president seized the
cracker and pulled out the fuse. A stream of golden gum-
drops fell over the desk; then glancing at the paper the
Chief Executive read, 'Don't eat too many of them because
Mama says they'll make you sick if you do.'

## RIDING SEAWOLF IN MEXICAN WATERS

> *They all keep aswaying*
> *Ahumming and swinging*

*It's the good ship Robert E. Lee*
*That's come to carry the cotton away*

### ISADORA DUNCAN'S NEW HAPPINESS

I.W.W. troublemakers overran a Garibaldi birthday celebration at Rosebank Staten Island this afternoon, insulted the Italian flag, pummeled and clubbed members of the Italian Rifle Society and would have thrown the American flag to the dirt if

### SIX UNCLAD BATHING GIRLS BLACK EYES OF HORRID MAN

Indian divers search for drowned boy's body. Some of the witnesses say they saw a woman in the crowd. She was hit with a brick. The man in gray took refuge behind her skirts to fire. The upper decks and secluded parts of the boat are the spooners' paradise where liberties are often taken with intoxicated young girls whose mothers should not have permitted them to go on a public boat unescorted.

### MIDWEST MAY MAKE OR BREAK WILSON

### TELL CAUSES OF UNREST IN LABOR WORLD

'I'm a Swiss admiral proceeding to America,' and the copper called a taxi

*See them shuffling along*
*Hear their music and song*
*It's simply great, mate,*
*Waiting on the levee*
*Waiting*
      *for*
        *the*
          *Robert*
            *E.*
              *Lee.*

## *Emperor of the Caribbean*

When Minor C. Keith died all the newspapers carried his picture, a brighteyed man with a hawknose and a respectable bay window, and an uneasy look under the eyes.

Minor C. Keith was a rich man's son, born in a family that liked the smell of money, they could smell money halfway round the globe in that family.

His Uncle was Henry Meiggs, the Don Enrique of the West Coast. His father had a big lumber business and handled realestate in Brooklyn;

young Keith was a chip of the old block

Back in fortynine Don Enrique had been drawn to San Francisco by the gold rush. He didn't go prospecting in the hills, he didn't die of thirst sifting alkalidust in Death Valley. He sold outfits to the other guys. He stayed in San Francisco and played politics and high finance until he got in too deep and had to get aboard ship in a hurry.

The vessel took him to Chile. He could smell money in Chile.

He was the capitalista yanqui. He'd build the railroad from Santiago to Valparaiso. There were guano deposits on the Chincha Islands. Meiggs could smell money in guano. He dug himself a fortune out of guano, became a power on the West Coast, juggled figures, railroads, armies, the politics of the local caciques and politicos: they were all chips in a huge pokergame. Behind a big hand he heaped up the dollars.

He financed the unbelievable Andean railroads.

When Tomas Guardia got to be dictator of Costa Rica he wrote to Don Enrique to build him a railroad;

Meiggs was busy in the Andes, a $75,000 contract was hardly worth his while,

so he sent for his nephew Minor Keith.

They didn't let grass grow under their feet in that family.

at sixteen Minor Keith had been on his own, selling collars and ties in a clothingstore.

After that he was a lumber surveyor and ran a lumber business.

When his father bought Padre Island off Corpus Christi,

Texas, he sent Minor down to make money out of it.

Minor Keith started raising cattle on Padre Island and seining for fish,

but cattle and fish didn't turn over money fast enough

so he bought hogs and chopped up the steers and boiled the meat and fed it to the hogs and chopped up the fish and fed it to the hogs,

but hogs didn't turn over money fast enough,

so he was glad to be off to Limon.

Limon was one of the worst pestholes on the Carribbean, even the Indians died there of malaria, yellowjack, dysentery.

Keith went back up to New Orleans on the steamer *John G. Meiggs* to hire workers to build the railroad. He offered a dollar a day and grub and hired seven hundred men. Some of them had been down before in the filibustering days of William Walker.

Of that bunch about twentyfive came out alive.

The rest left their whiskey-scalded carcasses to rot in the swamps.

On another load he shipped down fifteen hundred; they all died to prove that only Jamaica Negroes could live in Limon.

Minor Keith didn't die.

In 1882 there were twenty miles of railroad built and Keith was a million dollars in the hole;

the railroad had nothing to haul.

Keith made them plant bananas so that the railroad might have something to haul, to market the bananas he had to go into the shipping business;

this was the beginning of the Caribbean fruittrade.

All the while the workers died of whiskey, malaria, yellowjack, dysentery.

Minor Keith's three brothers died.

Minor Keith didn't die.

He built railroads, opened retail stores up and down the coast in Bluefields, Belize, Limon, bought and sold rubber, vanilla, tortoiseshell, sarsaparilla, anything he could buy cheap he bought, anything he could sell dear he sold.

In 1898 in co-operation with the Boston Fruit Company he formed the United Fruit Company that has since become one the most powerful industrial units in the world.

In 1912 he incorporated the International Railroads of Central America;

all of it built out of bananas;

in Europe and the United States people had started to eat bananas,

so they cut down the jungles through Central America to plant bananas,

and built railroads to haul the bananas,

and every year more steamboats of the Great White Fleet steamed north loaded with bananas,

and that is the history of the American empire in the Caribbean,

and the Panama Canal and the future Nicaragua Canal and the marines and the battleships and the bayonets.

Why that uneasy look under the eyes, in the picture of Minor C. Keith the pioneer of the fruit trade, the railroad-builder, in all the pictures the newspapers carried of him when he died?

## The Camera Eye (20)

when the streetcarmen went out on strike in Lawrence in sympathy with what the hell they were a lot of wops anyway bohunks hunkies that didn't wash their necks ate garlic with squalling brats and fat oily wives the damn dagoes they put up a notice for volunteers good clean young

to man the streetcars and show the foreign agitators this was still a white man's

well this fellow lived in Matthews and he'd always wanted to be a streetcar conductor they said Mr Grover had been a streetcar conductor in Albany and drank and was seen on the street with floosies

well this fellow lived in Matthews and he went over to Lawrence with his roommate and they reported in Lawrence and people yelled at them Blacklegs Scabs but those that weren't wops were muckers a low element they liked each other a lot this fellow did and his roommate and he got up on the platform and twirled the bright brass handle and clanged the bell

it was in the carbarn his roommate was fiddling with

something between the bumpers and this fellow twirled the
shiny brass handle and the car started and he ran down his
roommate and his head was mashed just like that between
the bumpers killed him dead just like that right there in the
carbarn and now the fellow's got to face his roommate's
folks

# J. Ward Moorehouse

In Pittsburgh Ward Moorehouse got a job as a reporter on
the *Times Dispatch* and spent six months writing up Italian
weddings, local conventions of Elks, obscure deaths, murders
and suicides among Lithuanians, Albanians, Croats, Poles, the
difficulties over naturalization papers of Greek restaurant
keepers, dinners of the Sons of Italy. He lived in a big red frame
house, at the lower end of Highland Avenue, kept by a Mrs
Cook, a crotchety old woman from Belfast who had been forced
to take lodgers since her husband, who had been a foreman
in one of the Homestead mills, had been crushed by a crane
dropping a load of pigiron over him. She made Ward his break-
fasts and his Sunday dinners and stood over him while he was
eating them alone in the stuffy furniture-crowded diningroom
telling him about her youth in the north of Ireland and the
treachery of papists and the virtues of the defunct Mr Cook.

It was a bad time for Ward. He had no friends in Pittsburgh
and he had colds and sore throats all through the cold grimy
sleety winter. He hated the newspaper office and the inclines
and the overcast skies and the breakneck wooden stairs he was
always scrambling up and down, and the smell of poverty and
cabbage and children and washing in the rattletrap tenements
where he was always seeking out Mrs Piretti whose husband had
been killed in a rumpus in a saloon on Locust Street or Sam
Burkovich who'd been elected president of the Ukrainian singing
society, or some woman with sudsy hands whose child had been
slashed by a degenerate. He never got home to the house before
three or four in the morning and by the time he had breakfast
round noon there never seemed to be any time to do anything
before he had to call up the office for assignments again. When
he had first gotten to Pittsburgh he had called to see Mr McGill,
whom he'd met with Jarvis Oppenheimer in Paris. Mr McGill
remembered him and took down his address and told him to
keep in touch because he hoped to find an opening for him in

the new information bureau that was being organized by the Chamber of Commerce, but the weeks went by and he got no word from Mr McGill. He got an occasional dry note from Annabelle Marie about legal technicalities; she would divorce him charging nonsupport, desertion and cruelty. All he had to do was to refuse to go to Philadelphia when the papers were served on him. The perfume on the blue notepaper raised a faint rancor of desire for women in him. But he must keep himself clean and think of his career.

The worst time was his weekly day off. Often he'd stay all day sprawled on the bed, too depressed to go out into the black slush of the streets. He sent to correspondence schools for courses in journalism and advertising and even for a course in the care of fruit trees on the impulse to throw up everything and go West and get a job on a ranch or something; but he felt too listless to follow them and the little booklets accumulated week by week on the table in his room. Nothing seemed to be leading anywhere. He'd go over and over again his whole course of action since he'd left Wilmington that day on the train to go down to Ocean City. He must have made a mistake somewhere but he couldn't see where. He took to playing solitaire, but he couldn't even keep his mind on that. He'd forget the cards and sit at the table with a gingerbreadcolored velveteen cloth on it, looking past the pot of dusty artificial ferns ornamented with a crepe paper cover and a dusty pink bow off a candybox, down into the broad street where trolleycars went by continually scraping round the curve and where the arclights coming on in the midafternoon murk shimmered a little in the black ice of the gutters. He thought a lot about the old days at Wilmington and Marie O'Higgins and his piano lessons and fishing in an old skiff along the Delaware when he'd been a kid; he'd get so nervous that he'd have to go out and would go and drink a hot chocolate at the sodafountain on the next corner and then go downtown to a cheap movie or vaudeville show. He took to smoking three stogies a day, one after each meal. It gave him something he could vaguely look forward to.

He called once or twice to see Mr McGill at his office in the Frick Building. Each time he was away on a business trip. He'd have a little chat with the girl at the desk while waiting and then go away reluctantly, saying, 'Oh, yes, he said he was going on a trip,' or, 'He must have forgotten the appointment,' to cover his embarrassment when he had to go away. He was loath to leave the brightly lit office anteroom, with its great shiny mahogany chairs with lions' heads on the arms and the tables with lions' claws for feet and the chirrup of typewriters from behind partitions, and telephone bells ringing and welldressed clerks and executives bustling in and out. Down at the newspaper office it was noisy with clanging presses and smelt sour of printer's ink and moist rolls of paper and sweating copyboys running round in green eyeshades. And not to know any really nice people, never to get an assignment that wasn't connected with working people or foreigners or criminals; he hated it.

One day in the spring he went to the Schenley to interview a visiting travel lecturer. He felt good about it as he hoped to wheedle a by-line out of the city editor. He was picking his way through the lobby crowded by the arrival of a state convention of Kiwanians when he ran into Mr McGill.

'Why, hello, Moorehouse,' said Mr McGill, in a casual tone as if he'd been seeing him all along. 'I'm glad I ran into you. Those fools at the office mislaid your address. Have you a minute to spare?'

'Yes, indeed, Mr McGill,' said Ward. 'I have an appointment to see a man, but he can wait.'

'Never make a man wait if you have an appointment with him,' said Mr McGill.

'Well, this isn't a business appointment,' said Ward, looking up into Mr McGill's face with his boyish blue-eyed smile. 'He won't mind waiting a minute.'

They went into the writingroom and sat down on a tapestried sofa. Mr McGill explained that he had just been appointed temporary general manager to reorganize the Bessemer Metallic Furnishings and Products Company that handled a big line of byproducts of the Homestead Mills. He was looking for an ambitious and energetic man to handle the advertising and promotion.

'I remember that booklet you showed me in Paris, Moorehouse, and I think you're the man.'

Ward looked at the floor. 'Of course that would mean giving up my present work.'

'What's that?'

'Newspaper work.'

'Oh, drop that; there's no future in that . . . We'd have to make someone else nominal advertising manager for reasons we won't go into now . . . but you'll be the actual executive. What kind of a salary would you expect?'

Ward looked Mr McGill in the eyes, the blood stopped in his ears while he heard his own voice saying casually: 'How about a hundred a week?'

Mr McGill stroked his mustache and smiled. 'Well, we'll thrash that out later,' he said, getting to his feet. 'I think I can advise you strongly to give up your present work . . . I'll call up Mr Bateman about it . . . so that he'll understand why we're taking you away from him . . . No hard feelings, you understand, on account of your resigning suddenly . . . never want hard feelings . . . Come down and see me tomorrow at ten. You know the office in the Frick Building.'

'I think I've got some valuable ideas about advertising, Mr McGill. It's the work I'm most interested in doing,' said Ward.

Mr McGill wasn't looking at him any more. He nodded and went off. Ward went on up to interview his lecturer, afraid to let himself feel too jubilant yet.

The next day was his last in a newspaper office. He accepted a salary of seventyfive with a promise of a raise as soon as returns warranted it, took a room and bath at the Schenley, had an office of his own in the Frick Building where he sat at a desk with a young man named Oliver Taylor who was a nephew of one of the directors who was being worked up through the organization. Oliver Taylor was a firstrate tennis player and belonged to all the clubs and was only too glad to let Moorehouse do the work. When he found that Moorehouse had been abroad and had had his clothes made in England, he put him up at the Sewickley Country Club and took him out with him for drinks after officehours. Little by little Moorehouse got to know people and to be invited out as an eligible bachelor. He started to play golf with an instructor on a small course over in Allegheny where he hoped nobody he knew would go. When he could play a fair game he went over to Sewickley to try it out.

One Sunday afternoon Oliver Taylor went with him and pointed out all the big executives of the steel mills and the mining properties and the oil industry out on the links on a Sunday afternoon, making ribald remarks about each one that Ward tittered at a little bit, but that seemed to him in very bad taste. It was a sunny May afternoon and he could smell locustblossoms on the breeze off the fat lands along the Ohio, and there were the sharp whang of the golfballs and the flutter of bright dresses on the lawn round the clubhouse, and frazzles of laughter and baritone snatches of the safe talk of business men coming on the sunny breeze that still had a little scorch of furnace smoke in it. It was hard to keep the men he was introduced to from seeing how good he felt.

The rest of the time he did nothing but work. He got his stenographer, Miss Rodgers, a plainfaced spinster who knew the metal products business inside out from having worked fifteen years in Pittsburgh offices, to get him books on the industry that he read at his hotel in the evenings, so that at executive conferences he astonished them by his knowledge of the processes and products of the industry. His mind was full of augerbits, canthooks, mauls, sashweights, axes, hatchets, monkeywrenches; sometimes in the lunch hour he'd stop in to a hardware store on the pretext of buying a few brads or tacks and talk to the storekeeper. He read *Crowds Junior* and various books on psychology, tried to imagine himself a hardware merchant or the executive of Hammacher Schlemmer or some other big hardware house, and puzzled over what kind of literature from a factory would be appealing to him. Shaving while his bath was running in the morning, he would see long processions of andirons, grates, furnace fittings, pumps, sausage-grinders, drills, calipers, vises, casters, drawerpulls pass between his face and the mirror and wonder how they could be made attractive to the retail trade. He was shaving himself with a Gillette; why was he shaving with a Gillette instead of some other kind of razor? 'Bessemer' was a good name, smelt of money and mighty rolling mills and great executives stepping out of limousines. The thing to do was to interest the hardware buyer, to make him feel a part of something mighty and strong, he would think as he picked out a necktie. 'Bessemer,' he'd say to himself as he ate breakfast. Why should our cotterpins appeal more than any other cotterpins, he'd ask himself as he stepped on the streetcar. Jolting in the straphanging crowd on the way downtown, staring at the headlines in the paper without seeing them, chainlinks and anchors and ironcouplings and malleable elbows and unions and bushings and nipples and pipecaps would jostle in his head. 'Bessemer.'

When he asked for a raise he got it, to a hundred and twenty-five dollars.

At a country club dance he met a blond girl who danced very well. Her name was Gertrude Staple and she was the only daughter of old Horace Staple who was director of several corporations, and was reputed to own a big slice of Standard Oil stock. Gertrude was engaged to Oliver Taylor, though they did nothing but quarrel when they were together, so she confided to Ward while they were sitting out a dance. Ward's dress-suit fitted well and he looked much younger than most of the men at the dance. Gertrude said that the men in Pittsburgh had no allure. Ward talked about Paris and she said that she was bored to tears and would rather live in Nome, Alaska, than in Pittsburgh. She was awfully pleased that he knew Paris and he talked about the Tour d'Argent and the Hotel Wagram and the Ritz Bar and he felt very sore that he hadn't a car, because he noticed that she was making it easy for him to ask her to let him take her home. But next day he sent her some flowers with a little note in French that he thought would make her laugh. The next Saturday afternoon he went to an automobile school to take lessons in driving a car, and strolled past the Stutz sales agency to see what kind of terms he could get to buy a roadster on.

One day Oliver Taylor came into the office with a funny smile on his face and said, 'Ward, Gertrude's got a crush on you. She can't talk about anything else . . . Go ahead; I don't give a damn. She's too goddam much trouble for me to handle. She tires me out in a half an hour.'

'It's probably just because she doesn't know me,' said Ward, blushing a little .

'Too bad her old man won't let her marry anything but a millionaire. You might get some lovin' out of it, though.'

'I haven't got the time for that stuff,' said Ward.

'It don't leave me time for anything else,' said Taylor. 'Well, so long . . . You hold down the fort; I've got a luncheon date with a swell girl . . . she's a warm baby an' she's dancing in the *Red Mill*, first row, third from the left.' He winked, and slapped Ward on the back and went off.

The next time that Ward went to call at the big house of the Staples that lay back from the trees, he went in a red Stutz roadster that he'd taken out on trial. He handled it well enough, although he turned in too quickly at the drive and slaughtered some tulips in a flowerbed. Gertrude saw him from the library window and kidded him about it. He said he was a rotten driver, always had been and always would be. She gave him tea and a cocktail at a little table under an appletree back of the house and he wondered all the time he was talking to her whether he ought to tell her about his divorce. He told her about his unhappy life with Annabelle Strang. She was very sympathetic. She knew of Doctor Strang. 'And I was hoping you were

just an adventurer . . . from plowboy to president, you know
. . . that sort of thing.'

'But I am,' he said, and they both laughed and he could see
that she was really crazy about him.

That night they met at a dance and walked down to the end
of the conservatory where it was very steamy among the
orchids, and he kissed her and told her that she looked like a
pale yellow orchid. After that they always sneaked off whenever
they got a chance. She had a way of going limp suddenly in his
arms under his kisses that made him sure that she loved him.
But when he got home after those evenings, he'd be too nervous
and excited to sleep, and would pace up and down the room
wanting a woman to sleep with, and cursing himself out. Often
he'd take a cold bath and tell himself he must attend to business
and not worry about those things or let a girl get under his
skin that way. The streets in the lower part of the town were
full of prostitutes, but he was afraid of catching a disease or
being blackmailed. Then one night after a party Taylor took
him to a house that he said was thoroughly reliable where he
met a pretty dark Polish girl who couldn't have been more than
eighteen, but he didn't go there very often, as it cost fifty
dollars, and he was always nervous when he was in the place
for fear there'd be a police raid and he'd have blackmail to pay.

One Sunday afternoon Gertrude told him that her mother
had scolded her for being seen about with him so much on
account of his having a wife in Philadelphia. The notice of the
decree had come the morning before. Ward was in high spirits
and told her about it and asked her to marry him. They were
at the free organ recital in Carnegie Institute, a good place to
meet because nobody who was anybody ever went there. 'Come
over to the Schenley and I'll show you the decree.' The music had
started. She shook her head, but patted his hand that lay on
the plush seat beside her knee. They went out in the middle of
the number. The music got on their nerves. They stood talking
a long while in the vestibule. Gertrude looked miserable and
haggard. She said she was in wretched health and that her
father and mother would never consent to her marrying a man
who didn't have as much income as she did and she wished she
was a poor stenographer or telephone girl that could do as she
liked and that she loved him very much and would always love
him and thought she'd take to drink or dope or something
because life was just too terrible.

Ward was very cold and kept his jaw set square and said that she couldn't really care for him and that as far as he was concerned that was the end and that if they met they'd be good friends. He drove her out Highland Avenue in the Stutz that wasn't paid for yet and showed her the house he'd lived in when he first came to Pittsburgh and talked of going out West and starting an advertising business of his own and finally left her at a friend's house in Highland Park where she'd told her chauffeur to pick her up at six.

He went back to the Schenley and had a cup of black coffee sent up to his room and felt very bitter and settled down to work on some copy he was getting out, saying, 'To hell with the bitch,' all the time under his breath.

He didn't worry much about Gertrude in the months that followed because a strike came on at Homestead and there were strikers killed by the mine guards and certain writers from New York and Chicago who were sentimentalists began to take a good deal of space in the press with articles flaying the steel industry and the feudal conditions in Pittsburgh as they called them, and the Progressives in Congress were making a howl, and it was rumored that people wanting to make politics out of it were calling for a congressional investigation. Mr McGill and Ward had dinner together all alone at the Schenley to talk about the situation, and Ward said that what was necessary was an entirely new line in the publicity of the industry. It was the business of the industry to educate the public by carefully planned publicity extending over a term of years. Mr McGill was very much impressed and said he'd talk around at directors' meetings about the feasibility of founding a joint information bureau for the entire industry. Ward said he felt he ought to be at the head of it, because he was just wasting his time at the Bessemer Products; that had all simmered down to a routine job that anybody could take care of. He talked of going to Chicago and starting an advertising agency of his own. Mr McGill smiled and stroked his steelgray mustache and said, 'Not so fast, young man; you stay around here a while yet and on my honor you won't regret it,' and Ward said that he was willing, but here he'd been in Pittsburgh five years and where was he getting?

The information bureau was founded, and Ward was put in charge of the actual work at ten thousand dollars a year and began to play stocks a little with his surplus money, but there were several men over him earning higher salaries who didn't do anything but get in his way, and he was very restless. He

felt he ought to be married and have an establishment of his
own. He had many contacts in different branches of the casting
and steel and oil industries, and felt he ought to entertain.
Giving dinners at the Fort Pitt or the Schenley was expensive
and somehow didn't seem solid.

Then one morning he opened his newspaper to find that
Horace Staple had died of angina pectoris the day before while
going up in the elevator of the Carnegie Building, and that
Gertrude and her mother were prostrated at their palatial
residence in Sewickley. He immediately sat down in the writingroom, although it would make him late at the office, and wrote
Gertrude a note:

DEAREST GERTRUDE:
In this terrible moment of grief, allow me to remind you that I
think of you constantly. Let me know at once if I can be of any
use to you in any way. In the valley of the shadow of death we
must realize that the Great Giver to whom we owe all love and
wealth and all affection around the jocund fireside is also the Grim
Reaper...

After staring at the words, chewing the end of a pen a
minute, he decided that it was a bit thick about the Grim Reaper
and copied the note out again leaving out the last sentence,
signed it 'Your Devoted Ward,' and sent it out to Sewickley by
special messenger.

At noon he was just leaving for lunch when the office boy
told him there was a lady on his phone. It was Gertrude. Her
voice was trembly, but she didn't seem too terribly upset. She
begged him to take her out to dinner that night somewhere where
they wouldn't be seen because the house and everything gave her
the creeps and that she'd go mad if she heard any more condo-
lences. He told her to meet him in the lobby of the Fort Pitt and
he'd run her out to some little place where they could be quiet
and talk.

That evening there was an icy driving wind. The sky had
been leaden all day with inky clouds driving out of the northwest. She was so muffled up in furs that he didn't recognize her
when she came into the lobby. She held out her hand to him
and said, 'Let's get out of here,' as soon as she came up to him.
He said he knew a little roadhouse on the way to McKeesport,
but thought the drive would be too cold for her in his open
roadster. She said, 'Let's go; do let's ... I love a blizzard.' When
she got into the car she said in a trembling voice, 'Glad to see

your old flame, Ward?' and he said, 'God, Gertrude, I am; but are you glad to see me?' And then she said, 'Don't I look glad?' Then he started to mumble something about her father, but she said, 'Please let's not talk about that.'

The wind was howling behind them all the way up the Monongahela Valley, with occasional lashing flurries of snow. Tipples and bessemer furnaces and tall ranks of chimneys stood out inky black against a low woolly sky that caught all the glare of flaming metal and red slag and the white of arcs and of locomotive headlights. At one crossing they almost ran into a train of coalcars. Her hand tightened on his arm when the car skidded as he put on the brakes.

'That was a narrow squeak,' he said through clenched teeth.

'I don't care. I don't care about anything tonight,' she said.

He had to get out to crank the car as he had stalled the motor. 'It'll be all right if we don't freeze to death,' he said. When he'd clambered back into the car, she leaned over and kissed him on the cheek. 'Do you still want to marry me? I love you, Ward.' The motor raced as he turned and kissed her hard on the mouth the way he'd kissed Annabelle that day in the cottage at Ocean City. 'Of course I do, dear,' he said.

The roadhouse was kept by a French couple, and Ward talked French to them and ordered a chicken dinner and red wine and hot whiskey toddies to warm them up while they were waiting. There was no one else in the roadhouse and he had a table placed right in front of the gaslogs at the end of a pink and yellow diningroom, dimly lit, a long ghostly series of empty tables and long windows blocked with snow. Through dinner he told Gertrude about his plans to form an agency of his own and said he was only waiting to find a suitable partner and he was sure that he could make it the biggest in the country, especially with this new unexploited angle of the relations between capital and labor. 'Why, I'll be able to help you a lot with capital and advice and all sorts of things, once we're married,' she said, looking at him with flushed cheeks and sparkling eyes. 'Of course you can, Gertrude.'

She drank a great deal during dinner and wanted more hot whiskies afterwards, and he kissed her a great deal and ran his hand up her leg. She didn't seem to care what she did and kissed him right in front of the roadhouse keeper. When they went out to get in the car to go home, the wind was blowing sixty miles an hour and the snow had blotted out the road and Ward said it would be suicide to try to drive to Pittsburgh a night like that and the roadhouse keeper said that he had a room all ready for them and that monsieur et madame would be mad to start out, particularly as they'd have the wind in their faces all the way. At that Gertrude had a moment of panic and said she'd rather kill herself than stay. Then she suddenly crumpled up in Ward's arms sobbing hysterically, 'I want to stay, I want to stay, I love you so.'

They called up the Staple house and talked to the nightnurse who said that Mrs Staple was resting more easily, that she'd been given an opiate and was sleeping quietly as a child, and Gertrude told her that when her mother woke to tell her she was spending the night with her friend Jane English and that she'd be home as soon as the blizzard let them get a car on the road. Then she called up Jane English and told her that she was distracted with grief and had taken a room at the Fort Pitt to be alone. And if her mother called to tell her she was asleep. Then they called up the Fort Pitt and reserved a room in her name. Then they went up to bed. Ward was very happy and decided he loved her very much and she seemed to have done this sort of thing before because the first thing she said was: 'We don't want to make this a shotgun wedding, do we, darling?'

Six months later they were married, and Ward resigned his position with the information bureau. He'd had a streak of luck on the Street and decided to take a year off for a honeymoon in Europe. It turned out that the Staple fortune was all left to Mrs Staple in trust and that Gertrude would only have an annuity of fifteen thousand dollars until her mother died, but they were planning to meet the old lady at Carlsbad and hoped to coax some capital out of her for the new advertising agency. They sailed in the bridal suite on the *Deutschland* to Plymouth and had a fine passage and Ward was only seasick one day.

## The Camera Eye (21)

that August it never rained a drop and it had hardly rained in July   the truck garden was in a terrible state and all through the Northern Neck of Virginia it was no use pulling cornfodder because the lower leaves were all withered and curled up at the edges   only the tomatoes gave a crop.

when they weren't using Rattler on the farm you'd ride

him (he was a gelding sorrel threeyearold and stumbled) through the tall woods of white pine and the sandbed roads on fire with trumpetvine and through swamps dry and cracked crisscross like alligator hide

past the Morris's house where all the Morris children looked dry and dusty and brown.

and round along the rivershore past Harmony Hall where Sydnor a big sixfoot-six barefoot man with a long face and a long nose with a big wart on his nose 'ud be ashamblin' around and not knowin' what to do on account of the drought and his wife sick and ready to have another baby and the children with hoopin' cough and his stomach trouble

and past Sandy Pint agin past the big pine

and Miss Emily 'ud be alookin' over the fence astandin' beside the crapemyrtle (Miss Emily wore poke bonnets and always had a few flowers and a couple of broilers for sale and the best blood in the South flowed in her veins Tancheford that's how we spell it but we pronounce it Tofford if only the boys warnt so noaccount always drinkin' an' carryin' on down by the rivershoa an' runnin' whiskey over from Mar'land instead o' fishin' an' agoin' out blind drunk and gettin' the trapnets cut up or lost   Miss Emily took a drop herself now and then but she always put a good face on things lookin' over the picket fence astandin' by the crapemyrtle bush visitin' with the people passin' along the road)

then down to Lynch's Pint where old Bowie Franklin was (he warn't much account neither looked like a bantam rooster Bowie Franklin did with his long scrawny neck an' his ruptured walk couldn't do much work and he didn't have money to spend on liquor so he just fed his gray fowls that warn't much account and looked just like Bowie did and hung round the wharf and sometimes when the boat was in or there were some fisherman in the crick on account of it blowin' so hard down the bay somebody'd slip him a drink o' whiskey an' he'd be a whole day sleepin' it off)

Rattler sweat somethin' awful on account o' bein' fed corn in this hot weather and the old saddle stank and the horsedoctors buzzed round his flanks and it was time for supper and you'd ride slowly home hating the goddam exhausted land and the drought that wouldn't let the garden grow and the katydids and the dryflies jeering out of the sapling gums and persimmons ghostly with dust along the road and the sickleshaped beach where the seanettles stung you when you tried to swim out and the chiggers and the little scraps of talk about what was going on up to the Hague or Warsaw or Pekatone and the phone down at the cottage that kept ringing whenever any farmer's wife along the line took up the receiver to talk to any other farmer's wife and all down the line you could hear the receivers click as they all ran to the receiver to listen to what was said

and the land between the rivers was flat drained of all strength by tobacco in the early Walter Raleigh Captain John Smith Pocahontas days but what was it before the war that drained out the men and women?

and I rode Rattler the threeyearold sorrel gelding who stumbled so much and I hated the suncaked hardpan and the clay subsoil and the soughing pines and the noaccount gums and persimmonbushes and the brambles.

there was only the bay you could like sparkling to the horizon and the southeast wind that freshened every afternoon and the white sails of bugeyes

# Newsreel 15

lights go out as 'Home Sweet Home' is played to patrons low wages cause unrest, woman says

*There's a girl in the heart of Maryland*
*With a heart that belongs to me*

WANT BIG WAR OR NONE

the mannequin who is such a feature of the Paris racecourse surpasses herself in the launching of novelties. She will put on the most amazing costume and carry it with perfect sangfroid. Inconsistency is her watchword.

Three German staff officers who passed nearby were nearly mobbed by enthusiastic people who insisted on shaking their hands

GIRL STEPS ON MATCH; DRESS IGNITED; DIES

*And Mary-land*
*Was fairy-land*
*When she said that mine she'd be*

DANUBE SHOTS SIGNAL FOR EARLY STRIFE

I'm against capital punishment as are all levelminded women. I hate to think any woman would attend a hanging. It is a terrible thing for the state to commit murder

CZAR LOSES PATIENCE WITH AUSTRIA

panic in exodus from Carlsbad      disappearance of Major reveals long series of assassinations      décolleté in broad daylight lingerie frocks that by no possible means could be associated with the tub What shall be worn next? Paris cries choirboys go camping professor to tour woods Belgrade Falls

GENERAL WAR NEAR

ASSASSIN SLAYS DEPUTY JAURES

LIVES TWO HOURS AFTER HE'S DEAD

I lost a friend and a pal when Garros gave up his life but I expect to lose more friends in the profession before this war is over

LOST TRUNKS SHOW UP IN LONDON

conventions of one sort or another are inevitably sidestepped or trod upon during the languid or restful days of summer, and because of the relaxation just now there are several members of the younger set whose debutante days lie in the distance of two or even three seasons hence enjoying the glory of

BLACK POPE ALSO DEAD

large quantities of Virginia tobacco to be imported to England especially for the use of British troops on the continent

*There's a girl in the heart of Maryland*
*With a heart that belongs to me*

## Prince of Peace

Andrew Carnegie
was born in Dunfermline in Scotland
came over to the States in an immigrant
ship worked as bobbinboy in a textile factory
fired boilers
clerked in a bobbin factory at $2.50 a week
ran round Philadelphia with telegrams as a Western Union messenger
learned the Morse code was telegraph operator on the Pennsy lines
was a military telegraph operator in the Civil War and

always saved his pay;
whenever he had a dollar he invested it.
Andrew Carnegie started out buying Adams Express and Pullman stock when they were in a slump;
he had confidence in railroads,
he had confidence in communications,

he had confidence in transportation,
he believed in iron.
Andrew Carnegie believed in iron, built bridges Bessemer
plants blast furnaces rolling mills;
Andrew Carnegie believed in oil;
Andrew Carnegie believed in steel;
always saved his money
whenever he had a million dollars he invested it.
Andrew Carnegie became the richest man in the world
                                        and died.

Bessemer Duquesne Rankin Pittsburgh Bethlehem Gary
Andrew Carnegie gave millions for peace
and libraries and scientific institutes and endowments and
thrift
whenever he made a billion dollars he endowed an institution to promote universal peace
always
except in time of war.

## The Camera Eye (22)

all week the fog clung to the sea and the cliffs at noon
there was just enough warmth of the sun through the fog
to keep the salt cod drying on the flakes   gray flakes green
sea gray houses white fog   at noon there was just enough
sun to ripen bakeapple and wildpear on the moorlands to
warm the bayberry and sweetfern mealtimes in the boardinghouse everybody waited for the radio operators   the radio
operators could hardly eat   yes it was war
Will we go in? will Britain go in?
*Obligations according to the treaty of . . . handed the
ambassador his passports*   every morning they put out the
cod on the flakes spreading them even in the faint glow of
the sun through the fog
a steamer blowing in the distance the lap of the waves
against piles along the seaweedy rocks scream of gulls clatter
of boardinghouse dishes
*War declared expedit . . . Big battle in the North Sea
German Fleet Destroyed* BRITISH FLEET DESTROYED

GERMAN SQUADRON OFF CAPE RACE *loyal Newfoundlanders to the colors Port closed at St Johns Port aux Basques*

and every evening they brought in the cod off the flakes clatter of boardinghouse dishes and everybody waiting for the radio operators

lap of the waves against the piles of the wharf, scream of gulls circling and swooping white in the white fog a steamer blowing in the distance and every morning they spread out the cod on the flakes

# J. Ward Moorehouse

When Ward came back from his second honeymoon abroad he was thirtytwo, but he looked older. He had the capital and the connections and felt that the big moment had come. The war talk in July had decided him to cut short his trip. In London he'd picked up a young man named Edgar Robbins who was in Europe for International News. Edgar Robbins drank too much and was a fool about the women, but Ward and Gertrude took him around with them everywhere and confided in each other that they wanted to straighten him out. Then one day Robbins took Ward aside and said that he had syphilis and would have to follow the straight and narrow. Ward thought the matter over a little and offered him a job in the New York office that he was going to open as soon as he got home. They told Gertrude it was liver trouble and she scolded him like a child when he took a drink and on the boat back to America they felt he was completely devoted to both of them. Ward didn't have to write any copy after that and could put in all his time organizing the business. Old Mrs Staple had been induced to put fifty thousand dollars into the firm. Ward rented an office at 100 Fifth Avenue, fitted it up with Chinese porcelain vases and cloisonné ashtrays from Vantine's and had a tiger-skin rug in his private office. He served tea in the English style every afternoon and put himself in the telephone book as J. Ward Moorehouse, Public Relations Counsel. While Robbins was drafting the literature to be sent out, Ward went to Pittsburgh and Chicago and Bethlehem and Philadelphia to re-establish contacts.

In Philadelphia he was walking into the lobby of the Bellevue

Stratford when he met Annabelle Marie. She greeted him amiably and said she'd heard of him and his publicity business and they had dinner together, talking about old times. 'You certainly have improved,' Annabelle Marie kept saying. Ward could see that she regretted the divorce a little, but he felt he couldn't say the same for her. The lines on her face had deepened and she didn't finish her sentences, and had a parrot screech to her voice. She was tremendously made up and he wondered if she took drugs. She was busy divorcing Beale who she said had turned homosexual on her. Ward said dryly that he had married again and was very happy. 'Who wouldn't be with the Staple fortune back of them?' she said. Her little air of ownership irritated Ward and he excused himself right after dinner, saying he had work to do. Annabelle looked at him through halfclosed eyes with her head to one side, said 'I wish you luck,' and went up in the hotel elevator in a shrill cackle of laughter.

Next day he took the Pennsylvania to Chicago, traveling in a drawingroom. Miss Rosenthal, his secretary, and Morton, his English valet, went with him. He had his dinner in the drawingroom with Miss Rosenthal, a sallowfaced girl, shrewd and plain, who he felt was devoted to his interests. She had been with him in Pittsburgh with Bessemer Products. When the coffee had been cleared away and Morton had poured them each out a swallow of brandy that Miss Rosenthal giggled over a great deal declaring it would go to her head, he started to dictate. The train rumbled and lurched and now and then he could smell coalsmoke and the hot steamygreasy body of the engine up ahead, hot shiny steel charging through the dark Appalachians. He had to talk loudly to be heard. The rumble of the train made the cords of his voice vibrate. He forgot everything in his own words . . . American industry like a steamengine, like a highpower locomotive on a great express train charging through the night of old individualistic methods. . . . What does a steamengine require? Co-operation, co-ordination of the inventor's brain, the promoter's brain that made the development of these highpower products possible . . . Co-ordination of capital, the storedup energy of the race in the form of credit intelligently directed . . . labor, the prosperous contented American working man to whom the unprecedented possibilities of capital collected in great corporations had given the full dinnerpail, cheap motor transport, insurance, short working hours . . . a measure of comfort and prosperity unequaled before or since in the tragic procession of recorded history or in the known regions of the habitable globe.

But he had to stop dictating because he found he'd lost his voice. He sent Miss Rosenthal to bed and went to bed himself, but he couldn't sleep; words, ideas, plans, stock quotations kept unrolling in endless tickertape in his head.

Next afternoon at the LaSalle he had a call from Judge Bowie C. Planet. Ward sat waiting for him to come up, looking out at the very pale blue Lake Michigan sky. In his hand he had a little filing card on which was written:

Planet, Bowie C. . . . Tennessee Judge, married Elsie Wilson Denver; small copper lead interests. . . . Anaconda? unlucky oil speculator . . . member one-horse lawfirm Planet and Wilson, Springfield, Illinois.

'All right, Miss Rosenthal,' he said when there was a knock at the door. She went off into the other room with the filing card.

Morton opened the door to let in a roundfaced man with a black felt hat and a cigar.

'Hello, Judge,' Ward said, getting to his feet and holding out his hand. 'How's everything? Won't you sit down?'

Judge Planet advanced slowly into the room. He had a curious rolling gait as if his feet hurt him. They shook hands, and Judge Planet found himself sitting facing the steelbright light that came through the big windows back of Moorehouse's desk.

'Won't you have a cup of tea, sir?' asked Morton, who advanced slowly with a tray glittering with silver teathings. The judge was so surprised that he let the long ash that he'd been carrying on his cigar to prove to himself he was sober drop off on his bulging vest. The judge's face remained round and bland. It was the face of a mucker from which all the lines of muckerdom had been carefully massaged away. The judge found himself sipping a cup of lukewarm tea with milk in it.

'Clears the head, clears the head,' said Ward, whose cup was cooling untasted before him.

Judge Planet puffed silently on his cigar.

'Well, sir,' he said, 'I'm very glad to see you.'

At that moment Morton announced Mr Barrow, a skinny man with popeyes and a big adamsapple above a stringy necktie. He had a nervous manner of speaking and smoked too many cigarettes. He had the look of being stained with nicotine all over, face, fingers, teeth yellow.

On Ward's desk there was another little filing card that read:

Barrow, G. H., labor connections, reformer type. Once sec. Bro. locomotive engineers; unreliable.

As he got to his feet, he turned the card over. After he'd shaken hands with Mr Barrow, placed him facing the light and encumbered him with a cup of tea, he began to talk.

'Capital and labor,' he began in a slow careful voice as if dictating, 'as you must have noticed, gentlemen, in the course of your varied and useful careers, capital and labor, those two great forces of our national life neither of which can exist without the other are growing further and further apart; any cursory glance at the newspapers will tell you that. Well, it has occurred to me that one reason for this unfortunate state of affairs has been the lack of any private agency that might fairly present the situation to the public. The lack of properly distributed information is the cause of most of the misunderstandings in this world . . . The great leaders of American capital, as you probably realize, Mr Barrow, are firm believers in fairplay and democracy and are only too anxious to give the worker his share of the proceeds of industry if they can only see their way to do so in fairness to the public and the investor. After all, the public is the investor whom we all aim to serve.'

'Sometimes,' said Mr Barrow, 'but hardly . . .'

'Perhaps you gentlemen would have a whiskey and soda.' Morton stood sleekhaired between them with a tray on which were decanters, tall glasses full of ice and some open splits of Apollinaris.

'I don't mind if I do,' said Judge Planet.

Morton padded out, leaving them each with a clinking glass. Outside the sky was beginning to glow with evening a little. The air was winecolored in the room. The glasses made things chattier. The judge chewed on the end of a fresh cigar.

'Now, let's see if I'm getting you right, Mr Moorehouse. You feel that with your connections with advertising and big business you want to open up a new field in the shape of an agency to peaceably and in a friendly fashion settle labor disputes. Just how would you go about it?'

'I am sure that organized labor would co-operate in such a movement,' said G. H. Barrow, leaning forward on the edge of his chair. 'If only they could be sure that . . . well, that . . .'

'That they weren't getting the wool pulled over their eyes,' said the judge, laughing.

'Exactly.'

'Well, gentlemen, I'm going to put my cards right down on the table. The great motto upon which I have built up my business has always been co-operation.'

'I certainly agree with you there,' said the judge, laughing again and slapping his knee. 'The difficult question is how to bring about that happy state.'

'Well, the first step is to establish contact . . . Right at this moment under our very eyes we see friendly contact being established.'

'I must admit,' said G. H. Barrow with an uneasy laugh, 'I never expected to be drinking a highball with a member of the firm of Planet and Wilson.'

The judge slapped his fat thigh. 'You mean on account of the Colorado trouble . . . ? You needn't be afraid. I won't eat you, Mr Barrow . . . But frankly, Mr Moorehouse, this doesn't seem to me to be just the time to launch your little project.'

'This war in Europe . . .' began G. H. Barrow.

'Is America's great opportunity . . . You know the proverb about when thieves fall out . . . Just at present I admit we find ourselves in a moment of doubt and despair, but as soon as American business recovers from the first shock and begins to pull itself together . . . Why, gentlemen, I just came back from Europe; my wife and I sailed the day Great Britain declared war . . . I can tell you it was a narrow squeak . . . Of one thing I can assure you with comparative certainty, whoever wins, Europe will be economically ruined. This war is America's great opportunity. The very fact of our neutrality . . . '

'I don't see who will be benefited outside of the munitions-makers,' said G. H. Barrow.

Ward talked a long time, and then looked at his watch, that lay on the desk before him, and got to his feet. 'Gentlemen, I'm afraid you'll have to excuse me. I have just time to dress for dinner.' Morton was already standing beside the desk with their hats. It had gotten dark in the room. 'Lights, please, Morton,' snapped Ward.

As they went out Judge Planet said, 'Well, it's been a very pleasant chat, Mr Moorehouse, but I'm afraid your schemes are a little idealistic.'

'I've rarely heard a businessman speak with such sympathy and understanding of the labor situation,' said G. H. Barrow.

'I only voice the sentiments of my clients,' said Ward as he bowed them out.

Next day he spoke at a Rotary Club luncheon on 'Labor Troubles: A Way Out.' He sat at a long table in the big hotel banquet hall full of smells of food and cigarettes, and scurrying waiters. He spread the food a little round his plate with a fork, answering when he was spoken to, joking a little with Judge Planet, who sat opposite him, trying to formulate sentences out of the haze of phrases in his mind. At last it was time for him to get to his feet. He stood at the end of the long table with a cigar in his hand, looking at the two rows of heavyjowled faces turned towards him.

'When I was a boy down along the Delaware . . .' He stopped. A tremendous clatter of dishes was coming from behind the swinging doors through which waiters were still scuttling with trays. The man who had gone to the door to make them keep quiet came stealthily back. You could hear his shoes creak across the parquet floor. Men leaned forward along the table. Ward started off again. He was going on now; he hardly knew what he was saying, but he had raised a laugh out of them. The tension relaxed. 'American business has been slow to take advantage of the possibilities of modern publicity . . . education of the public and employers and employees, all equally servants of the public . . . Co-operation . . . stockownership giving the employee an interest in the industry . . . avoiding the grave dangers of socialism and demagoguery and worse . . . It is in such a situation that the public relations counsel can step in in a quiet manly way and say, Look here, men, let's talk this over eye to eye . . . But his main importance is in times of industrial peace . . . when two men are sore and just about to hit one another is not time to preach public service to them. . . The time for an educational campaign and an oral crusade that will drive home to the rank and file of the mighty Colossus of American uptodate industry is right now, today.'

There was a great deal of clapping. He sat down and sought out Judge Planet's face with his blue-eyed smile. Judge Planet looked impressed.

# Newsreel 16

The Philadelphian had completed the thirteenth lap and was two miles away on the fourteenth. His speed it is thought must have been between a hundred and a hundred and ten miles an hour. His car wavered for a flash and then careered to the left. It struck a slight elevation and jumped. When the car alighted it was on four wheels atop of a high embankment. Its rush apparently was unimpeded. Wishart turned the car off the embankment and attempted to regain the road. The speed would not permit the slight turn necessary, however, and the car plowed through the frontyard of a farmer residing on the course. He escaped one tree but was brought up sideways against another. The legs being impeded by the steering gear they were torn from the trunk as he was thrown through

> *I want to go*
> *To Mexico*
> *Under the Stars and Stripes to fight the foe*

#### SNAPS CAMERA; ENDS LIFE

gay little chairs and table stand forlornly on the sidewalk for there are few people feeling rich enough to take even a small drink

#### PLUMBER HAS HUNDRED LOVES

#### BRINGS MONKEYS HOME

missing rector located losses in U.S. crop report let baby go naked if you want it to be healthy if this mystery is ever solved you will find a woman at the bottom of the mystery said Patrolman E. B. Garfinkle events leading up to the present war run continuously back to the French Revolution

UNIVERSITY EXPELS GUM

they seemed to stagger like drunken men suddenly hit
between the eyes after which they made a run for us shouting some outlandish cry we could not make out

> *And the ladies of the harem*
> *Knew exactly how to wear 'em*
> *In Oriental Baghdad long ago.*

## The Camera Eye (23)

this friend of mother's was a very lovely woman with
lovely blond hair and she had two lovely daughters   the
blond one married an oil man who was bald as the palm of
your hand and went to live in Sumatra   the dark one
married a man from Bogota and it was a long trip in a dugout canoe up the Magdalena River and the natives were
Indians and slept in hammocks and had such horrible
diseases and when the woman had a baby it was the husband
who went to bed and used poisoned arrows and if you got a
wound in that country it never healed but festered white
and maturated and the dugout tipped over so easily into the
warm steamy water full of ravenous fish that if you had a
scratch on you or an unhealed wound it was the smell of
blood attracted them sometimes they tore people to pieces
    it was eight weeks up the Magdalena River in dugout
canoes and then you got to Bogota
    poor Jonas Fenimore came home from Bogota a very
sick man and they said it was elephantiasis   he was a good
fellow and told stories about the steamy jungle and the
thunderstorms and the crocodiles and the horrible diseases
and the ravenous fish and he drank up all the whiskey in the
sideboard and when he went swimming you could see that
there were thick blotches on his legs like the scale of an
apple and he liked to drink whiskey and he talked about
Colombia becoming one of the richest countries in the world
and oil and rare woods for veneering and tropical butterflies

but the trip up the Magdalena River was too long and
too hot and too dangerous and he died
they said it was whiskey and elephantiasis
and the Magdalena River

## Eleanor Stoddard

When they first arrived in New York, Eleanor, who'd never
been East before, had to rely on Eveline for everything. Freddy
met them at the train and took them to get rooms at the
Brevoort. He said it was a little far from the theater, but much
more interesting than an uptown hotel, all the artists and
radicals and really interesting people stayed there and it was
very French. Going down in the taxi he chattered about the
lovely magnificent play and his grand part, and what a fool the
director Ben Freelby was, and how one of the backers had only
put up half the money he'd promised; but that Josephine
Gilchrist, the business manager, had the sum virtually lined
up now and the Shuberts were interested and they would open
out of town at Greenwich exactly a month from today. Eleanor
looked out at Fifth Avenue and the chilly spring wind blowing
women's skirts, a man chasing a derby hat, the green buses,
taxicabs, the shine on shopwindows; after all, this wasn't so
very different from Chicago. But at lunch at the Brevoort it was
very different, Freddy seemed to know so many people and
introduced them to everybody as if he was very proud of them.
They were all names she had heard or read of in the book column
of the *Daily News*. Everybody seemed very friendly. Freddy
talked French to the waiter and the hollandaise sauce was the
most delicious she had ever eaten.

That afternoon on the way to rehearsal, Eleanor had her
first glimpse of Times Square out of the taxicab window. In the
dark theater they found the company sitting waiting for Mr
Freelby. It was very mysterious, with just a single big electric
light bulb hanging over the stage and the set for some other
play looking all flat and dusty.

A grayhaired man with a broad sad face and big circles under
his eyes came in. That was the famous Benjamin Freelby; he
had a tired fatherly manner and asked Eveline and Eleanor
up to his apartment to dinner with Freddy that night so that
they could talk at their ease about the settings and the costumes.

Eleanor was relieved that he was so kind and tired and thought that after all she and Eveline were much better dressed than any of those New York actresses. Mr Freelby made a great fuss about there being no lights; did they expect him to rehearse in the dark? The stagemanager with the manuscript in his hand ran round looking for the electrician and somebody was sent to call up the office. Mr Freelby walked about the stage and fretted and fumed and said, 'This is monstrous.' When the electrician arrived wiping his mouth with the back of his hand, and finally switched on the houselights and some spots, Mr Freelby had to have a table and chair and a reading light on the table. Nobody seemed to be able to find a chair the right height for him. He kept fuming up and down, tugging at his coarse gray hair and saying, 'This is monstrous.' At last he got settled and he said to Mr Stein, the stagemanager, a lanky man who sat in another chair near him, 'We'll start with act one, Mr Stein. Has everybody their parts?' Several actors got on the stage and stood round and the rest talked in low voices. Mr Freelby 'shushed' them and said, 'Please, children, we've got to be quiet,' and the rehearsal was in progress.

From that time on everything was a terrible rush. Eleanor never seemed to get to bed. The scenepainter, Mr Bridgeman, at whose studios the scenery was painted, found objections to everything; it turned out that someone else, a pale young man with glasses who worked for Mr Bridgeman, would have to design the scenery from their sketches and that they couldn't have their names in the program at all except for the costumes on account of not belonging to the scene designers' union. When they weren't wrangling at the Bridgeman Studios they were dashing about the streets in taxicabs with samples of materials. They never seemed to get to bed before four or five in the morning. Everybody was so temperamental and Eleanor had quite a siege each week to get a check out of Miss Gilchrist.

When the costumes were ready, all in early Victorian style, and Eleanor and Freddy and Mr Freelby went to see them at the costumers' they really looked lovely, but the costumers wouldn't deliver them without a check and nobody could find Miss Gilchrist, and everybody was running round in taxis, and at last late that night Mr Freelby said he'd give his personal check. The transfer company had its truck at the door with the scenery, but wouldn't let the flats be carried into the theater until they had a check. Mr Bridgeman was there, too, saying his check had come back marked *no funds* and he and Mr Freelby had words in the box office. At last Josephine Gilchrist appeared in a taxi with five hundred dollars in bills on account for Mr Bridgeman and for the transfer company. Everybody smiled when they saw the crisp orangebacked bills. It was a great relief.

When they had made sure that the scenery was going into the theater, Eleanor and Eveline and Freddy Seargeant and Josephine Gilchrist and Mr Freelby all went to Bustanoby's to get a bite to eat and Mr Freelby set them up to a couple of bottles of Pol Roger and Josephine Gilchrist said that she felt it in her bones that the play would be a hit and that didn't often happen with her, and Freddy said the stagehands liked it and that was always a good sign and Mr Freelby said Ike Gold, the Shuberts' officeboy, had sat through the run-through with the tears running down his cheeks, but nobody knew what theater they'd open in after a week in Greenwich and a week in Hartford and Mr Freelby said he'd go and talk to J. J. about it personally first thing in the morning.

Friends from Chicago called up who wanted to get into the dress rehearsal. It made Eleanor feel quite important, especially when Sally Emerson called up. The dress rehearsal dragged terribly, half the scenery hadn't come and the Wessex villagers didn't have any costumes, but everybody said that it was a good sign to have a bad dress rehearsal.

Opening night Eleanor didn't get any supper and had only a half an hour to dress in. She was icy all over with excitement. She hoped the new chartreuse tulle evening dress she'd charged at Tappé's looked well, but she didn't have time to worry. She drank a cup of black coffee and it seemed as if the taxi never would get up town. When she got to the theater the lobby was all lit up and full of silk hats and bare powdered backs and diamonds and eveningwraps and all the firstnighters looked at each other and waved to their friends and talked about who was there and kept trooping up the aisle halfway through the first act. Eleanor and Eveline stood stiffly side by side in the back of the theater and nudged each other when a costume looked good and agreed that the actors were too dreadful and that Freddy Seargeant was the worst. At the party that Sally Emerson gave for them afterwards at the duplex apartment of her friends the Careys everybody said that the scenery and costumes were lovely and that they were sure the play would be a great success. Eleanor and Eveline were the center of everything and Eleanor was annoyed because Eveline drank a little too much and was noisy. Eleanor met a great many interesting people and decided that she'd stay on in New York whatever happened.

The play failed after two weeks and Eleanor and Eveline never did get seven hundred and fifty dollars that the management owed them. Eveline went back to Chicago, and Eleanor rented an apartment on Eighth Street. Sally Emerson had decided that Eleanor had great talent and got her husband to put up a thousand dollars to start her New York decorating business on. Eveline Hutchins's father was sick, but she wrote from Chicago that she'd be on whenever she could.

While Sally Emerson was in New York that summer, Eleanor went out with her all the time and got to know many rich people. It was through Alexander Parsons that she got the job to decorate the house the J. Ward Moorehouses were building near Great Neck. Mrs Moorehouse walked round the unfinished house with her. She was a washedout blonde who kept explaining that she'd do the decorating herself only she hadn't the strength since her operation. She'd been in bed most of the time since her second child was born and told Eleanor all about her operation. Eleanor hated to hear about women's complaints and nodded coldly from time to time, making businesslike comments about furniture and draperies and now and then jotting notes on the decoration down on a piece of paper. Mrs Moorehouse asked her to stay to lunch in the little cottage where they were living until they got the house finished. The little cottage was a large house in Dutch Colonial style full of pekinese dogs and maids in flounced aprons and a butler. As they went into the diningroom, Eleanor heard a man's voice in an adjoining room and smelt cigarsmoke. At lunch she was introduced to Mr Moorehouse and a Mr Perry. They had been playing golf and were talking about Tampico and oilwells. Mr Moorehouse offered to drive her back to town after lunch and she was relieved to get away from Mrs Moorehouse. She hadn't had a chance to talk about her ideas for decorating the new house yet, but, going in, Mr Moorehouse asked her many questions about it and they laughed together about how ugly most people's houses were, and Eleanor thought that it was very interesting to find a business man who cared about those things. Mr Moorehouse suggested that she prepare the estimates and bring them to his office. 'How will Thursday do?' Thursday would be fine and he had no date that day and they'd have a bite of lunch together if she cared to. 'Mealtime's the

only time I get to devote to the things of the spirit,' he said with
a blue twinkle in his eye, so they both said 'Thursday' again
when he let Eleanor out at the corner of Eighth Street and
Fifth Avenue and Eleanor thought he looked as if he had a
sense of humor and thought she liked him much better than
Tom Custis.

Eleanor found that she had to have many interviews with
Ward Moorehouse as the work went on. She had him to dinner
at her place on Eighth Street and she had her Martinique maid
Augustine cook sauté chicken with red peppers and tomatoes.
They had cocktails with absinthe in them and a bottle of very
good burgundy and Ward Moorehouse enjoyed sitting back on
the sofa and talking and she enjoyed listening and began to call
him J. W. After that they were friends quite apart from the
work on the house at Great Neck.

He told Eleanor about how he'd been a boy in Wilmington,
Delaware, and the day the militia fired on the old darkey and
thought it was the Spanish fleet and about his unhappy first
marriage and about how his second wife was an invalid and
about his work as a newspaperman and in advertising offices,
and Eleanor, in a gray dress with just a touch of sparkly something on one shoulder and acting the discreet little homebody,
led him on to explain about the work he was doing keeping the
public informed about the state of relations between capital
and labor and stemming the propaganda of sentimentalists and
reformers, upholding American ideas against crazy German
socialistic ideas and the panaceas of discontented dirtfarmers in
the Northwest. Eleanor thought his ideas were very interesting,
but she liked better to hear about the stock exchange and how
the Steel Corporation was founded and the difficulties of the
oil companies in Mexico, and Hearst and great fortunes. She
asked him about some small investment she was making, and
he looked up at her with twinkly blue eyes in a white square
face where prosperity was just beginning to curve over the
squareness of the jowl and said, 'Miss Stoddard, may I have
the honor of being your financial adviser?'

Eleanor thought his slight Southern accent and oldschool
gentlemanly manners very attractive. She wished she had a
more distinctivelooking apartment and that she'd kept some of
the crystal chandeliers instead of selling them. It was twelve
o'clock before he left, saying he'd had a very pleasant evening,
but that he must go to answer some longdistance calls. Eleanor
sat before the mirror at her dressingtable rubbing cold cream

on her face by the light of two candles. She wished her neck wasn't so scrawny and wondered how it would be to start getting a henna rinse now and then when she got her hair washed.

## The Camera Eye (24)

    raining in historic Quebec    it was raining on the Château in historic Quebec where gallant Wolfe in a three-cornered hat sat in a boat in a lithograph and read Gray's 'Elegy' to his men gallant Wolfe climbing up the cliffs to meet gallant Montcalm in a threecornered hat on the plains of Abraham with elaborate bows and lace ruffles on the uniforms in the hollow squares and the gallantry and the command to fire and the lace ruffles ruined in the mud on the plains of Abraham

    but the Château was the Château Frontenac world-famous hostelry historic in the gray rain in historic gray Quebec and we were climbing up from the Saguenay River Scenic Steamer Greatest Scenic Route in the World the Chautauqua Lecturer and his wife and the baritone from Athens Kentucky where they have a hill called the Acro-polis exactly the way it is in Athens Greece and culture and a reproduction of the Parthenon exactly the way it is in Athens Greece

    stony rain on stony streets and out onto the platform and the St Lawrence people with umbrellas up walking back and forth on the broad wooden rainy platform looking over the slatepointed roofs of Quebec and the coal wharves and the grain elevators and the ferries and the *Empress of Ireland* with creamcolored funnels steaming in from the Other Side and Levis and green hills across the river and the Isle of Orléans green against green and the stony rain on the shining gray slatepointed roofs of Quebec.

    but the Chautauqua Lecturer wants his dinner and quarrels with his wife and makes a scene in the historic diningroom of the historic Château Frontenac and the head-waiter comes and the Chautauqua Lecturer's a big thick curlyhaired angry man with a voice used to bawling in tents about the Acropolis just like it is in Athens Greece and the Parthenon just like it is in Athens Greece and the Winged Victory and the baritone is too attentive to the small boy who wants to get away and wishes he hadn't said he'd come and wants to shake the whole bunch

but it's raining in historic Quebec and walking down the street alone with the baritone he kept saying about how there were bad girls in a town like this and boys shouldn't go with bad girls and the Acropolis and the bel canto and the Parthenon and voice culture and the beautiful statues of Greek boys and the Winged Victory and the beautiful statues

but I finally shook him and went out on the cars to see the Falls of Montmorency famous in song and story and a church full of crutches left by the sick in Sainte Anne de Beaupré

and the gray rainy streets full of girls

## Janey

In the second year of the European War Mr Carroll sold out his interest in the firm of Dreyfus and Carroll to Mr Dreyfus and went home to Baltimore. There was a chance that the state Democratic convention would nominate him for Governor. Janey missed him in the office and followed all the reports of Maryland politics with great interest. When Mr Carroll didn't get the nomination Janey felt quite sorry about it. Round the office there got to be more and more foreigners and talk there took on a distinctly pro-German trend that she didn't at all like. Mr Dreyfus was very polite and generous with his employees, but Janey kept thinking of the ruthless invasion of Belgium and the horrible atrocities and didn't like to be working for a Hun, so she began looking round for another job. Business was slack in Washington and she knew it was foolish to leave Mr Dreyfus, but she couldn't help it, so she went to work for Smedley Richards, a realestate operator on Connecticut Avenue, at a dollar less a week. Mr Richards was a stout man who talked a great deal about the gentleman's code and made love to her. For a couple of weeks she kept him off, but the third week he took to drinking and kept putting his big beefy hands on her and borrowed a dollar one day and at the end of the week said he wouldn't be able to pay her for a day or two, so she just didn't go back and there she was out of a job.

It was scary being out of a job; she dreaded having to go back to live at her mother's with the boarders and her sisters' noisy ways. She read the ads in *The Star* and *The Post* every day and answered any she saw, but someone had always been there ahead of her, although she got to the address the first thing in the morning. She even put her name down at an employment agency. The woman at the desk was a stout woman with bad teeth and a mean smile, she made Janey pay two dollars as a registration fee and showed her the waiting list of expert stenographers she had and said that girls ought to marry and that trying to earn their own living was stuff and nonsense because it couldn't be done. The bad air and the pinched faces of the girls waiting on benches made her feel quite sick so she went and sat a little while in the sun in Lafayette Square getting her courage up to tell Alice, who was still at Mrs Robinson's, that she hadn't found a job yet. A young man with a red face sat down beside her and tried to start talking to her, so she had to walk on. She went into a drugstore and had a chocolate milk, but the sodajerker tried to kid her a little, and she burst out crying. The sodajerker looked scared to death and said, 'Beg pardon, miss, I didn't mean no offence.' Her eyes were still red when she met Alice coming out of the Riggs Building; Alice insisted on paying for a thirtyfive-cent lunch for her at The Brown Teapot, although Janey couldn't eat a thing. Alice had an Itoldyouso manner that made Janey mad, and she said that it was too late now for her to try to go back to Mrs Robinson's because Mrs Robinson didn't have work for the girls she had there as it was. That afternoon Janey felt too discouraged to look for work and roamed round the Smithsonian Institution trying to interest herself in the specimens of Indian beadwork and war canoes and totempoles, but everything gave her the creeps and she went up to the room and had a good cry. She thought of Joe and Jerry Burnham and wondered why she never got letters from them, and thought of the poor soldiers in the trenches and felt very lonely. By the time Alice came home she'd washed her face and put on powder and rouge and was bustling briskly about their room; she joked

Alice about the business depression and said that if she couldn't get a job in Washington she'd go to Baltimore or New York or Chicago to get a job. Alice said that sort of talk made her miserable. They went out and ate a ham sandwich and a glass of milk for supper to save money.

All that fall Janey went round trying to get work. She got so the first thing she was conscious of in the morning when she woke up was the black depression of having nothing to do. She ate Christmas dinner with her mother and sisters and told them that she'd been promised twentyfive a week after the first of the year to keep them from sympathizing with her. She wouldn't give them the satisfaction.

At Christmas she got a torn paper package from Joe through the mail with an embroidered kimono in it. She went through the package again and again hoping to find a letter, but there was nothing but a little piece of paper with Merry Xmas scrawled on it. The package was postmarked St Nazaire in France and stamped OUVERT PAR LA CENSURE. It made the war seem very near to her and she hoped Joe wasn't in any danger over there.

One icy afternoon in January when Janey was lying on the bed reading *The Old Wives' Tale*, she heard the voice of Mrs Baghot, the landlady, calling her. She was afraid it was about the rent that they hadn't paid that month yet, but it was Alice on the phone. Alice said for her to come right over because there was a man calling up who wanted a stenographer for a few days and none of the girls were in and she thought Janey might just as well go over and see if she wanted the job. 'What's the address? I'll go right over.' Alice told her the address. Her voice was stuttering excitedly at the other end of the line. 'I'm so scared . . . if Mrs Robinson finds out she'll be furious.' 'Don't worry, and I'll explain it to the man,' said Janey.

The man was at the Hotel Continental on Pennsylvania Avenue. He had a bedroom and a parlor littered with typewritten sheets and papercovered pamphlets. He wore shellrimmed spectacles that he kept pulling off and putting on as if he wasn't sure whether he saw better with them or without them. He started to dictate without looking at Janey, as soon as she'd taken off her hat and gotten pad and pencil out of her handbag. He talked in jerks as if delivering a speech, striding back and forth on long thin legs all the while. It was some sort of article to be marked 'For immediate release,' all about

capital and labor and the eighthour day and the Brotherhood
of Locomotive Engineers. It was with a little feeling of worry
that she worked out that he must be a laborleader. When he'd
finished dictating he went out of the room abruptly and told
her please to type it out as soon as she could that he'd be back
in a minute. There was a Remington on the table, but she had
to change the ribbon, and typed in a great hurry for fear he
would come back and find her not finished. Then she sat there
waiting, with the article and the carbon copies all piled on the
table looking neat and crisp. An hour passed and he didn't
come. Janey got restless, roamed about the room, looked into
the pamphlets. They were all about labor and economics and
didn't interest her. Then she looked out of the window and
tried to crane her neck out to see what time it said by the clock
on the postoffice tower. But she couldn't see it, so she went
over to the phone to ask the office if Mr Barrow was in the
hotel please to tell him his manuscript was ready. The desk
said it was five o'clock and that Mr Barrow hadn't come in yet,
although he'd left word that he'd be back immediately. As she
set down the receiver she knocked a letter on lavender paper
off the stand. When she picked it up, as she had nothing to do
and was tired of playing naughts and crosses with herself, she
read it. She was ashamed of herself, but once she'd started she
couldn't stop.

DEAR G.H.

I hate to do this but honestly, kid, I'm in a hell of a fix for jack.
You've got to come across with two thousand iron men ($2000) or
else I swear I'll stop behaving like a lady and raise the roof. I hate
to do this, but I know you've got it or else I wouldn't plague you
like I do, I mean business this time

– the little girl you used to love
QUEENIE

Janey blushed and put the letter back exactly the way it had
been. Weren't men awful, always some skeleton in the closet.
It was dark outside and Janey was getting hungry and uneasy
when the telephone rang. It was Mr Barrow, who said that he
was sorry he'd kept her waiting and that he was at the Shoreham in Mr Moorehouse's suite and would she mind coming
right over – no, not to bring the manuscript – but he had some
more dictation for her right there, J. Ward Moorehouse it was,
she must know the name. Janey didn't know the name, but the
idea of going to take dictation at the Shoreham quite thrilled
her and this letter and everything. This was some excitement

like when she used to go round with Jerry Burnham. She put on her hat and coat, freshened up her face a little in the mirror over the mantel and walked through the stinging January evening to the corner of F and Fourteenth, where she stood waiting for the car. She wished she had a muff; the lashing wind bit into her hands in her thin gloves and into her legs just above the shoetops. She wished she was a wealthy married woman living in Chevy Chase and waiting for her limousine to come by and take her home to her husband and children and a roaring open fire. She remembered Jerry Burnham and wondered if she could have married him if she'd handled it right. Or Johnny Edwards; he'd gone to New York when she'd refused him, and was making big money in a broker's office. Or Morris Byer. But he was a Jew. This year she hadn't had any beaux. She was on the shelf; that was about the size of it.

At the corner before the Shoreham she got out of the car. The lobby was warm. Welldressed people stood around talking in welldressed voices. It smelt of hothouse flowers. At the desk they told her to go right up to apartment number eight on the first floor. A man with a wrinkled white face under a flat head of sleek black hair opened the door. He wore a sleek black suit and had a discreet skating walk. She said she was the stenographer for Mr Barrow and he beckoned her into the next room. She stood at the door waiting for someone to notice her. At the end of the room there was a big fireplace where two logs blazed. In front of it was a broad table piled with magazines, newspapers, and typewritten manuscripts. On one end stood a silver teaservice, on the other a tray with decanters, a cocktail shaker and glasses. Everything had a wellpolished silvery gleam, chairs, tables, teaset, and the watchchain and the teeth and sleek prematurely gray hair of the man who stood with his back to the fire.

Immediately she saw him Janey thought he must be a fine man. Mr Barrow and a little baldheaded man sat in deep chairs on either side of the fireplace listening to what he said with great attention.

'It's a very important thing for the future of this country,' he was saying in a low earnest voice. 'I can assure you that the great executives and the powerful interests in manufacturing and financial circles are watching these developments with the deepest interest. Don't quote me in this; I can assure you confidentially that the President himself . . .' His eye caught Janey's. 'I guess this is the stenographer. Come right in, Miss . . .'

'Williams is the name,' said Janey.

His eyes were the blue of alcoholflame, with a boyish flicker in them; this must be J. Ward Moorehouse whose name she ought to know.

'Have you a pencil and paper? That's fine; sit right down at the table. Morton, you'd better carry away those teathings.' Morton made the teathings disappear noiselessly. Janey sat down at the end of the table and brought out her pad and pencil. 'Hadn't you better take off your hat and coat, or you won't feel them when you go out?' There was something homey in his voice, different when he talked to her than when he talked to the men. She wished she could work for him. Anyway she was glad she had come.

'Now, Mr Barrow, what we want is a statement that will allay unrest. We must make both sides in this controversy understand the value of co-operation. That's a great word, co-operation . . . First we'll get it down in rough . . . You'll please make suggestions from the angle of organized labor, and you, Mr Jonas, from the juridical angle. Ready, Miss Williams . . . Released by J. Ward Moorehouse, Public Relations Counsel, Hotel Shoreham, Washington, D.C., January 15, 1916 . . .' Then Janey was too busy taking down the dictation to catch the sense of what was being said.

That evening when she got home she found Alice already in bed. Alice wanted to go to sleep, but Janey chattered like a magpie about Mr Barrow and labor troubles and J. Ward Moorehouse and what a fine man he was, and so kind and friendly and had such interesting ideas for collaboration between capital and labor, and spoke so familiarly about what the President thought and what Andrew Carnegie thought and what the Rockefeller interests or Mr Schick or Senator La Follette intended, and had such handsome boyish blue eyes, and was so nice, and the silver teaservice, and how young he looked in spite of his prematurely gray hair, and the open fire and the silver cocktail shaker and the crystal glasses.

'Why, Janey,' broke in Alice, yawning, 'I declare you must have a crush on him. I never heard you talk about a man that way in my life.'

Janey blushed and felt very sore at Alice. 'Oh, Alice, you're so silly . . . It's no use talking to you about anything.' She got undressed and turned out the light. It was only when she got to bed that she remembered that she hadn't had any supper. She didn't say anything about it because she was sure Alice would say something silly.

Next day she finished the job for Mr Barrow. All morning she wanted to ask him about Mr Moorehouse, where he lived, whether he was married or not, where he came from, but she reflected it wouldn't be much use. That afternoon, after she had been paid, she found herself walking along H Street past the Shoreham. She pretended to herself that she wanted to look in the storewindows. She didn't see him, but she saw a big shiny black limousine with a monogram that she couldn't make out without stooping and it would look funny if she stooped; she decided that was his car.

She walked down the street to the corner opposite the big gap in the houses where they were tearing down the Arlington. It was a clear sunny afternoon. She walked round Lafayette Square looking at the statue of Andrew Jackson on a rearing horse among the bare trees.

There were children and nursemaids grouped on the benches. A man with a grizzled vandyke with a black portfolio under his arm sat down on one of the benches and immediately got up again and strode off; foreign diplomat, thought Janey, and how fine it was to live in the Capital City where there were foreign diplomats and men like J. Ward Moorehouse. She walked once more round the statue of Andrew Jackson rearing green and noble on a green noble horse in the russet winter afternoon sunlight and then back towards the Shoreham, walking fast as if she were late to an appointment. She asked a bellboy where the public stenographer was. He sent her up to a room on the second floor where she asked an acideyed woman with a long jaw, who was typing away with her eyes on the little sector of greencarpeted hall she could see through the halfopen door, whether she knew of anyone who wanted a stenographer.

The acideyed woman stared at her. 'Well, this isn't an agency, you know.'

'I know; I just thought on the chance . . . ' said Janey, feeling everything go suddenly out of her. 'Do you mind if I sit down a moment?'

The acideyed woman continued staring at her.

'Now, where have I seen you before . . .? No, don't remind me . . . You . . . you were working at Mrs Robinson's the day I came in to take out her extra work. There, you see, I remember you perfectly.' The woman smiled a yellow smile.

'I'd have remembered you,' said Janey, 'only I'm so tired of going round looking for a job.'

'Don't I know?' sighed the woman.

'Don't you know anything I could get?'

'I'll tell you what you do . . . They were phoning for a girl to take dictation in number eight. They're using 'em up like . . . like sixty in there, incorporating some concern or something. Now, my dear, you listen to me, you go in there and take off your hat like you'd come from somewhere and start taking dictation and they won't throw you out, my dear, even if the other girl just came, they use 'em up too fast.'

Before Janey knew what she was doing, she'd kissed the acideyed woman on the edge of the jaw and had walked fast along the corridor to number eight and was being let in by the sleekhaired man who recognized her and asked 'Stenographer?'

'Yes,' said Janey, and in another minute she had taken out her pad and paper and taken off her hat and coat and was sitting at the end of the shinydark mahogany table in front of the crackling fire, and the firelight glinted on silver decanters and hotwater pitchers and teapots and on the black perfectly shined shoes and in the flameblue eyes of J. Ward Moorehouse.

There she was sitting taking dictation from J. Ward Moorehouse.

At the end of the afternoon the sleekhaired man came in and said, 'Time to dress for dinner, sir,' and J. Ward Moorehouse grunted and said, 'Hell.' The sleekhaired man skated a little nearer across the thick carpet. 'Beg pardon, sir, Miss Rosenthal's fallen down and broken 'er 'ip. Fell on the hice in front of the Treasury Buildin', sir.'

'The hell she has . . . Excuse me, Miss Williams,' he said and smiled. Janey looked up at him indulgent-understandingly and smiled too. 'Has she been fixed up all right?'

'Mr Mulligan took her to the orspital, sir.'

'That's right . . . You go downstairs, Morton, and send her some flowers. Pick out nice ones.'

'Yessir . . . About five dollars' worth, sir?'

'Two-fifty's the limit, Morton, and put my card in.'

Morton disappeared. J. Ward Moorehouse walked up and down in front of the fireplace for a while as if he were going to dictate. Janey's poised pencil hovered above the pad.

J. Ward Moorehouse stopped walking up and down and looked at Janey. 'Do you know anyone, Miss Williams . . . I want a nice smart girl as stenographer and secretary, someone I can repose confidence in . . . Damn that woman for breaking her hip.'

Janey's head swam. 'Well, I'm looking for a position of that sort myself.'

J. Ward Moorehouse was still looking at her with a quizzical blue stare. 'Do you mind telling me, Miss Williams, why you lost your last job?'

'Not at all. I left Dreyfus and Carroll, perhaps you know them . . . I didn't like what was going on round there. It would have been different if old Mr Carroll had stayed, though Mr Dreyfus was very kind, I'm sure.'

'He's an agent of the German government.'

'That's what I mean. I didn't like to stay after the President's proclamation.'

'Well, round here we're all for the Allies, so it'll be quite all right. I think you're just the person I like . . . Of course, can't be sure, but all my best decisions are made in a hurry. How about twentyfive a week to begin on?'

'All right, Mr Moorehouse; it's going to be very interesting work, I'm sure.'

'Tomorrow at nine please, and send these telegrams from me as you go out:

MRS J. WARD MOOREHOUSE
GREAT NECK LONG ISLAND NEW YORK
MAY HAVE TO GO MEXICO CITY EXPLAIN SALT-
WORTHS UNABLE ATTEND DINNER HOPE EVERY-
THING ALLRIGHT LOVE TO ALL

                                        WARD


MISS ELEANOR STODDARD
45 E 11TH STREET NEW YORK
WRITE ME WHAT YOU WANT BROUGHT BACK
FROM MEXICO AS EVER J.W.

'Do you mind traveling, Miss Williams?'

'I've never traveled, but I'm sure I'd like it.'

'I may have to take a small office force down with me . . . oil business. Let you know in a day or two . . .

JAMES FRUNZE C/O J. WARD MOOREHOUSE
100 FIFTH AVENUE NEW YORK
ADVISE ME IMMEDIATELY SHOREHAM DEVELOP-

MENT SITUATION A AND B BARROW RESTLESS
RELEASE STATEMENT ON UNITY OF INTEREST
AMERICANISM VERSUS FOREIGN SOCIALISTIC
RUBBISH. JWM...

'Thank you; that'll be all today. When you've typed those
out and sent the wires, you may go.'

J. Ward Moorehouse went through a door in the back, taking
his coat off as he went. When Janey had typed the articles and
was slipping out of the hotel lobby to send the wires at the
Western Union, she caught a glimpse of him in a dress-suit with
a gray felt hat on and a buffcolored overcoat over his arm. He
was hurrying into a taxi and didn't see her. It was very late
when she went home. Her cheeks were flushed, but she didn't
feel tired. Alice was sitting up reading on the edge of the bed.
'Oh, I was so worried . . .' she began, but Janey threw her arms
round her and told her she had a job as private secretary to
J. Ward Moorehouse and that she was going to Mexico. Alice
burst out crying, but Janey was feeling so happy she couldn't
stop to notice it, but went on to tell her everything about the
afternoon at the Shoreham.


# The Electrical Wizard

Edison was born in Milan, Ohio, in eighteen-fortyseven;

Milan was a little town on the Huron River that for a while
was the wheatshipping port of the whole Western Reserve; the
railroads took away the carrying trade, the Edison family
went up to Port Huron in Michigan to grow up with the
country;

his father was a shinglemaker who puttered round with
various small speculations; he dealt in grain and feed and
lumber and built a wooden tower a hundred feet high; tourists
and excursionists paid a quarter each to go up the tower and
look at the view over Lake Huron and the St Clair River and
Sam Edison became a solid and respected citizen of Port Huron.

Thomas Edison went to school for only three months
because the teacher thought he wasn't right bright. His mother
taught him what she knew at home and read eighteenth-century
writers with him, Gibbon and Hume and Newton, and let him
rig up a laboratory in the cellar.

Whenever he read about anything he went down cellar and tried it out.

When he was twelve he needed money to buy books and chemicals; he got a concession as newsbutcher on the daily train from Detroit to Port Huron. In Detroit there was a public library and he read it.

He rigged up a laboratory on the train and whenever he read about anything he tried it out. He rigged up a printing press and printed a paper called *The Herald*, when the Civil War broke out he organized a newsservice and cashed in on the big battles. Then he dropped a sick of phosphoros and set the car on fire and was thrown off the train.

By that time he had considerable fame in the country as the boy editor of the first newspaper to be published on a moving train. The London *Times* wrote him up.

He learned telegraphy and got a job as night operator at Stratford Junction in Canada, but one day he let a freighttrain get past a switch and had to move on.

(During the Civil War a man that knew telegraphy could get a job anywhere.)

Edison traveled round the country taking jobs and dropping them and moving on, reading all the books he could lay his hands on; whenever he read about a scientific experiment he tried it out, whenever he could get near an engine he'd tinker with it, whenever they left him alone in a telegraph office he'd do tricks with the wires. That often lost him the job and he had to move on.

He was tramp operator through the whole Middle West: Detroit, Cincinnati, Indianapolis, Louisville, New Orleans, always broke, his clothes stained with chemicals, always trying tricks with the telegraph.

He worked for the Western Union in Boston.

In Boston he doped out the model of his first patent, an automatic voterecorder for use in Congress, but they didn't want an automatic voterecorder in Congress, so Edison had the trip to Washington and made some debts and that was all he got out of that; he worked out a stockticker and burglar alarms and burned all the skin off his face with nitric acid.

But New York was already the big market for stocks and ideas and gold and greenbacks.

*(This part is written by Horatio Alger:)*

When Edison got to New York he was stony broke and had debts in Boston and Rochester. This was when gold was at a premium and Jay Gould was trying to corner the gold market. Wall Street was crazy. A man named Law had rigged up an electric indicator (Callahan's invention) that indicated the price of gold in brokers' offices. Edison, looking for a job, broke and with no place to go, had been hanging round the central office passing the time of day with the operators when the general transmitter stopped with a crash in the middle of a rush day of nervous trading; everybody in the office lost his head. Edison stepped up and fixed the machine and landed a job at three hundred dollars a month.

In sixtynine, the year of Black Friday, he started an electrical engineering firm with a man named Pope.

From then on he was on his own; he invented a stockticker and it sold. He had a machineshop and a laboratory; whenever he thought of a device he tried it out. He made forty thousand dollars out of the Universal Stock Ticker.

He rented a shop in Newark and worked on an automatic telegraph and on devices for sending two and four messages at the same time over the same wire.

In Newark he tinkered with Sholes on the first typewriter, and invented the mimeograph, the carbon rheostat, the microtasimeter, and first made paraffin paper.


Something he called etheric force worried him; he puzzled a lot about etheric force but it was Marconi who cashed in on the Hertzian waves. Radio was to smash the ancient universe. Radio was to kill the old Euclidian God, but Edison was never a man to worry about philosophical concepts;

he worked all day and all night tinkering with cogwheels and bits of copperwire and chemicals in bottles; whenever he thought of a device he tried it out. He made things work. He wasn't a mathematician. I can hire mathematicians but mathematicians can't hire me, he said.

In eighteen-seventysix he moved to Menlo Park where he invented the carbon transmitter that made the telephone a commercial proposition, that made the microphone possible

he worked all day and all night and produced

the phonograph

the incandescent electric lamp

and systems of generation, distribution, regulation and measurement of electric current, sockets, switches, insulators, manholes. Edison worked out the first systems of electric light using the direct current and small unit lamps and the multiple arc that were installed in London Paris New York and Sunbury Pennsylvania,

the three wire system,
the magnetic ore separator,
an electric railway.

He kept them busy at the Patent Office filing patents and caveats.

To find a filament for his electric lamp that would work, that would be a sound commercial proposition, he tried all kinds of paper and cloth, thread, fishline, fibre, celluloid, boxwood, coconutshells, spruce, hickory, bay, mapleshavings, rosewood, punk, cork, flax, bamboo, and the hair out of a redheaded Scotchman's beard;

whenever he got a hunch he tried it out.

In eighteen-eightyseven he moved to the huge laboratories at West Orange.

He invented rockcrushers and the fluoroscope and the reeled film for movie cameras and the alkaline storage battery and the long kiln for burning out portland cement and the kinetophone that was the first talking movie and the poured cement house that is to furnish cheap artistic identical sanitary homes for workers in the electrical age.

Thomas A. Edison at eightytwo worked sixteen hours a day;

he never worried about mathematics or the social system or generalized philosophical concepts;

in collaboration with Henry Ford and Harvey Firestone who never worried about mathematics or the social system or generalized philosophical concepts;

he worked sixteen hours a day trying to find a substitute for rubber; whenever he read about anything he tried it out; whenever he got a hunch he went to the laboratory and tried it out.

## The Camera Eye (25)

those spring nights the streetcar wheels screech grinding in a rattle of loose trucks round the curved tracks of Harvard Square dust hangs in the powdery arclight glare allnight till dawn can't sleep

haven't got the nerve to break out of the bellglass

four years under the ethercone breathe deep gently now that's the way be a good boy one two three four five six get A's in some courses but don't be a grind be interested in literature but remain a gentleman don't be seen with Jews or Socialists

and all the pleasant contacts will be useful in Later Life say hello pleasantly to everybody crossing the yard

sit looking out into the twilight of the pleasantest four years of your life

grow cold with culture like a cup of tea forgotten between an incenseburner and a volume of Oscar Wilde cold and not strong like a claret lemonade drunk at a Pop Concert in Symphony Hall

four years I didn't know you could do what you Michelangelo wanted say

    Marx

       to all

the professors with a small Swift break all the Greenoughs in the shooting gallery

but tossed with eyes smarting all the spring night reading *The Tragical History of Doctor Faustus* and went mad listening to the streetcar wheels screech grinding in a rattle of loose trucks round Harvard Square and the trains crying across the saltmarshes and the rumbling siren of a steamboat leaving dock and the blue peter flying and millworkers marching with a red brass band through the streets of Lawrence Massachusetts

it was like the Magdeburg spheres the pressure outside sustained the vacuum within

and I hadn't the nerve
                    to jump up and walk outofdoors and tell
them all to go take a flying
                         Rimbaud
                              at the moon

# Newsreel 17

an attack by a number of hostile airships developed before midnight. Bombs were dropped somewhat indiscriminately over localities possessing no military importance

### RAILROADS WON'T YIELD AN INCH

We shall have to make the passage under conditions not entirely advantageous to us, said Captain Koenig of the *Deutschland* ninety miles on his way passing Solomon's Island at 2:30. Every steamer passed blew his whistle in salute.

> *You made me what I am today*
> *I hope you're satisfied*
> *You dragged me down and down and down*
> *Until the soul within me died*

Sir Roger Casement was hanged in Pentonville Gaol at nine o'clock this morning.

### U-BOAT PASSES CAPES UNHINDERED

clad only in kimono girl bathers shock dairy lunch instead of firstclass café on amusement dock heavy losses shown in U.S. crop report Italians cheered as Austrians leave hot rolls in haste to get away giant wall of water rushes down valley professor says Beethoven gives the impression of a juicy steak

### PRISON'S MAGIC TURNS CITY JUNK INTO GOLD MINE

### MOON WILL HIDE PLANET SATURN FROM SIGHT TONIGHT

### BROTHERS FIGHT IN DARK

# *Mac*

The rebels took Juarez and Huerta fled and the steamboats to Europe were packed with cientificos making for Paris and Venustiano Carranza was president in Mexico City. Somebody got Mac a pass on the Mexican Central down to the capital. Encarnacion cried when he left and all the anarchists came down to the station to see him off. Mac wanted to join Zapata. He'd picked up a little Spanish from Encarnacion and a vague idea of the politics of the revolution. The train took five days. Five times it was held up while the section hands repaired the track ahead. Occasionally at night bullets came through the windows. Near Caballos a bunch of men on horses rode the whole length of the train waving their big hats and firing as they went. The soldiers in the caboose woke up and returned the fire and the men rode off in a driving dustcloud. The passengers had to duck under the seats when the firing began or lie flat in the aisle. After the attack had been driven off, an old woman started to shriek and it was found that a child had been hit through the head. The mother was a stout dark woman in a flowered dress. She went up and down the train with the tiny bloody body wrapped in a shawl asking for a doctor, but anybody could see that the child was dead.

Mac thought the trip would never end. He bought peppery food and lukewarm beer from old Indian women at stations, tried to drink pulque and to carry on conversations with his fellowpassengers. At last they passed Queretaro and the train began going fast down long grades in the cold bright air. Then the peaks of the great volcanos began to take shape in the blue beyond endless crisscrosspatterned fields of centuryplants and suddenly the train was rattling between garden walls, through feathery trees. It came to a stop with a clang of couplings: Mexico City.

Mac felt lost wandering round the bright streets among the lowvoiced crowds, the men all dressed in white and the women all in black or dark blue. The streets were dusty and sunny and quiet. There were stores open and cabs and trolleycars and polished limousines. Mac was worried. He had only two dollars. He'd been on the train so long he'd forgotten what he intended to do when he reached his destination. He wanted clean clothes and a bath. When he'd wandered round a good deal he saw a place marked 'American Bar.' His legs were tired. He sat down at a table. A waiter came over and asked him in English what he wanted. He couldn't think of anything else so he ordered a whiskey. He drank the whiskey and sat there with his head in his hands. At the bar were a lot of Americans and a couple of Mexicans in tengallon hats rolling dice for drinks. Mac ordered another whiskey.

A beefy redeyed man in a rumpled khaki shirt was roaming uneasily about the bar. His eye lit on Mac and he sat down at his table. 'Mind if I set here awhile, pardner?' he asked. 'Those sonsobitches too damn noisy. Here, sombrero . . . wheresat damn waiter? Gimme a glass-beer. Well, I got the old woman an' kids off today . . . When are you pullin' out?'

'Why, I just pulled in,' said Mac.

'The hell you say . . . This ain't no place for a white man . . . These bandits'll be on the town any day . . . It'll be horrible, I tell you. There won't be a white man left alive . . . I'll get some of 'em before they croak me, though . . . By God, I can account for twentyfive of 'em, no, twentyfour.' He pulled a Colt out of his pocket, emptied the chamber into his hand and started counting the cartridges, 'Eight,' then he started going through his pockets and ranged the cartridges in a row on the deal table. There were only twenty. 'Some sonvabitch robbed me.'

A tall lanky man came over from the bar and put his hand on the redeyed man's shoulder. 'Eustace, you'd better put that away till we need it . . . You know what to do, don't you?' He turned to Mac; 'as soon as the shooting begins, all American citizens concentrate at the Embassy. There we'll sell our lives to the last man.'

Somebody yelled from the bar, 'Hey, big boy, have another round,' and the tall man went back to the bar.

'You fellers seem to expect trouble,' said Mac.

'Trouble – my God! You don't know this country. Did you just come in?'

'Blew in from Juarez just now.'

'You can't have. Railroad's all tore up at Queretaro.'

'Well, they musta got it fixed,' said Mac. 'Say, what do they say round here about Zapata?'

'My God, he's the bloodthirstiest villain of the lot . . . They roasted a feller was foreman of a sugar mill down in Morelos on a slow fire and raped his wife and daughters right before his eyes . . . My God, pardner, you don't know what kind of country this is! Do you know what we ought to do . . . d'you know what we'd do if we had a man in the White House instead of a yellowbellied potatomouthed reformer? We'd get up an army of a hundred thousand men and clean this place up . . . It's a hell of a fine country, but there's not one of these damn greasers worth the powder and shot to shoot 'em . . . smoke 'em out like vermin, that's what I say . . . Every mother's sonvabitch of 'em 's a Zapata under the skin.'

'What business are you in?'

'I'm an oil prospector, and I've been in this lousy hole fifteen years and I'm through. I'd have gotten out on the train to Vera Cruz today only I have some claims to settle up an' my furniture to sell . . . You can't tell when they'll cut the railroad and then we won't be able to get out and President Wilson'll let us be shot down right here like rats in a trap . . . If the American public realized conditions down here . . . My God, we're the laughingstock of all the other nations . . . What's your line o' work, pardner?'

'Printer . . . linotype operator.'

'Looking for a job?'

Mac had brought out a dollar to pay for his drinks. 'I guess I'll have to,' he said. 'That's my last dollar but one.'

'Why don't you go round to the *Mexican Herald*? They're always needin' English language printers . . . They can't keep anybody down here . . . Ain't fit for a white man down here no more . . . Look here, pardner, that drink's on me.'

'Well, we'll have another then, on me.'

'The fat's in the fire in this country now, pardner . . . everything's gone to hell . . . might as well have a drink while we can.'

That evening, after he'd eaten some supper in a little American lunchroom, Mac walked round the Alameda to get the whiskey out of his head before going up to the *Mexican Herald* to see if he could get a job. It would only be for a couple of weeks, he told himself, till he could get wise to the lay of the land. The tall trees on the Alameda and the white statues and the fountains and the welldressed couples strolling round in the gloaming and the cabs clattering over the cobbles looked quiet enough, and the row of stoneyeyed Indian women selling fruit and nuts and pink and yellow and green candies in booths along the curb. Mac decided that the man he'd talked to in the bar had been stringing him along because he was a tenderfoot.

He got a job all right at the *Mexican Herald* at thirty mex dollars a week, but round the printing plant everybody talked just like the man in the bar. That night an old Polish American who was a proofreader there took him round to a small hotel to get him a flop and lent him a couple of cartwheels till payday.

'You get your wages in advance as much as you can,' said the old Pole; 'one of these days there will be a revolution and then goodbye *Mexican Herald* . . . unless Wilson makes intervention mighty quick.'

'Sounds all right to me; I want to see the social revolution,' said Mac.

The old Pole laid his fingers along his nose and shook his head in a peculiar way and left him.

When Mac woke up in the morning, he was in a small room calsomined bright yellow. The furniture was painted blue and there were red curtains in the window. Between the curtains the long shutters were barred with vivid violet sunlight that cut a warm path across the bedclothes. A canary was singing somewhere and he could hear the flap pat flap of a woman making tortillas. He got up and threw open the shutters. The sky was cloudless above the redtile roofs. The street was empty and full of sunlight. He filled his lungs with cool thin air and felt the sun burning his face and arms and neck as he stood there. It must be early. He went back to bed and fell asleep again.

When Wilson ordered the Americans out of Mexico several months later, Mac was settled in a little apartment in the Plaza del Carmen with a girl named Concha and two white Persian cats. Concha had been a stenographer and interpreter with an American firm and had been the mistress of an oilman for three years, so she spoke pretty good English. The oilman had jumped on the train for Vera Cruz in the panic at the time of the flight of Huerta, leaving Concha high and dry. She had taken a fancy to Mac from the moment she had first seen him going into the postoffice. She made him very comfortable, and when he talked to her about going out to join Zapata, she only laughed and said peons were ignorant savages and fit only to be ruled with the whip. Her mother, an old woman with a black shawl perpetually over her head, came to cook for them and Mac began to like Mexican food, turkey with thick chocolate brown sauce, and enchiladas with cheese. The cats were named Porfirio and Venustiano and always slept on the foot of their bed. Concha was very thrifty and made Mac's pay go much further than he could and never complained when he went out batting round town and came home late with a headache from drinking tequila. Instead of trying to get on the crowded trains to Vera Cruz, Mac took a little money he had saved up and bought up the office furniture that wildeyed American businessmen were selling out for anything they could get for it. He had it piled in the courtyard back of the house where they lived. Buying it had been Concha's idea in the first place and he used to tease her about how they'd never get rid of it again, but she'd nod her head and say, 'Wait a minute.'

Concha liked it very much when he'd have friends in to eat with him Sundays. She would wait on them very pleasantly and send her little brother Antonio round for beer and cognac and always have cakes in the house to bring out if anybody dropped in. Mac would sometimes think how much pleasanter this was than when he'd lived with Maisie in San Diego, and began to think less often about going out to join Zapata.

The Polish proofreader, whose name was Korski, turned out to be a political exile, a Socialist, and a wellinformed man. He would sit all afternoon over a half a glass of cognac talking about European politics; since the collapse of the European Socialist parties at the beginning of the war he had taken no part in anything; from now on he'd be an onlooker. He had a theory that civilization and a mixed diet were causing the collapse of the human race.

Then there was Ben Stowell, an independent oil promoter who was trying to put through a deal with Carranza's government to operate some oilwells according to the law. He was broke most of the time and Mac used to lend him money, but he always talked in millions. He called himself a progressive in politics and thought that Zapata and Villa were honest men. Ben Stowell would always take the opposite side of any argument from Korski and would infuriate the old man by his antisocial attitude. Mac wanted to make some money to send up to Maisie for the kids' schooling. It made him feel good to send Rose up a box of toys now and then. He and Ben would have long talks about the chances of making money in Mexico. Ben Stowell brought round a couple of young radical politicians who enjoyed sitting through the afternoon talking about socialism and drinking and learning English. Mac usually didn't say much, but sometimes he got sore and gave them a broadside of straight I.W.W. doctrine. Concha would finish all arguments by bringing on supper and saying with a shake of her head, 'Every poor man socialista . . . a como no? But when you get rich, quick you all very much capitalista.'

One Sunday Mac and Concha and some Mexican newspapermen and Ben Stowell and his girl, Angustias, who was a chorusgirl at the Lirico, went out on the trolley to Xochimilco. They hired a boat with a table in it and an awning and an Indian to pole them round through the poplarboarded canals among the rich flower patches and vegetable gardens. They drank pulque and they had a bottle of whiskey with them, and they bought the girls calla lilies. One of the Mexicans played a guitar and sang.

In the afternoon the Indian brought the boat back to a landing and they strolled off in couples into the woods. Mac suddenly felt very homesick and told Concha about his children in the U.S. and about Rose particularly, and she burst into tears and told him how much she loved children, but that when she was seventeen she had been very sick and they'd thought she was going to die and now she couldn't have any children, only Porfirio and Venustiano. Mac kissed her and told her that he'd always look after her.

When they got back to the trolley station, loaded down with flowers, Mac and Ben let the girls go home alone and went to a cantina to have a drink. Ben said he was pretty tired of this sort of thing and wished he could make his pile and go back to the States to marry and have a home and a family. 'You see, Mac,' he said, 'I'm forty years old. Christ, a man can't bat around all his life.' 'Well, I'm not far from it,' said Mac. They didn't say much, but Ben walked up with Mac as far as the office of the *Mexican Herald* and then went downtown to the Iturbide to see some oilmen who were staying there. 'Well, it's a great life if you don't weaken,' he said as he waved his hand at Mac and started down the street. He was a stocky bullnecked man with a bowlegged walk.

Several days later Ben came around to the Plaza del Carmen before Mac was out of bed. 'Mac, you come and eat with me this noon,' he said. 'There's a guy named G. H. Barrow here I want to kinda show the town a little bit. He might be useful to us . . . I want to know what he's after anyway.' The man was writing articles on the Mexican situation and was said to have some connection with the A.F. of L. At lunch he asked anxiously if the water was safe and whether it wasn't dangerous to walk round the streets after nightfall. Ben Stowell kidded him along a little and told him stories of generals and their friends breaking into a bar and shooting into the floor to make the customers dance and then using the place for a shooting gallery. 'The shooting gallery, that's what they call congress here,' said Mac. Barrow said he was going to a meeting of the Union Nacional de Trabajadores that afternoon and would they mind going with him to interpret for him. It was Mac's day off, so they said, 'All right.' He said he'd been instructed to try to make contacts with stable labor elements in Mexico with the hope of joining them up with the Pan-American Federation of Labor. Gompers would come down himself if something could be lined up. He said he'd been a shipping clerk and a Pullman conductor and had been in the office of the Railroad Brotherhood, but now he was working for the A.F. of L. He wished American workers had more ideas about the art of life. He'd been at the Second International meetings at Amsterdam and felt the European workers understood the art of life. When Mac asked him why the hell the Second International hadn't done something to stop the World War, he said the time wasn't ripe yet and spoke about German atrocities.

'The German atrocities are a Sunday school picnic to what goes on every day in Mexico,' said Ben.

Then Barrow went on to ask whether Mexicans were as immoral as it was made out. The beer they were drinking with their lunch was pretty strong and they all loosened up a little. Barrow wanted to know whether it wasn't pretty risky going out with girls here on account of the high percentage of syphilis. Mac said yes, but that he and Ben could show him some places that were all right if he wanted to look 'em over. Barrow tittered and looked embarrassed and said he'd just as soon look 'em over. 'A man ought to see every side of things when he's investigating conditions.'

Ben Stowell slapped his hand on the edge of the table and said that Mac was just the man to show him the backside of Mexico.

They went to the meeting that was crowded with slender dark men in blue denim. At first they couldn't get in on account of the crowd packed in the aisles and in the back of the hall, but Mac found an official he knew who gave them seats in a box. The hall was very stuffy and the band played and there was singing and the speeches were very long. Barrow said listening to a foreign language made him sleepy, and suggested that they walk around town; he'd heard that the red light district was ... he was interested in conditions.

Outside the hall they ran across Enrique Salvador, a news-paperman that Ben knew. He had a car and a chauffeur. He shook hands and laughed and said the car belonged to the chief of police who was a friend of his and wouldn't they like to ride out to San Angel? They went out the long avenue past Chapultepec, the Champs Elysées of Mexico, Salvador called it. Near Tacubaya Salvador pointed out the spot where Carranza's troops had had a skirmish with the Zapatistas the week before and a corner where a rich clothing merchant had been murdered by bandits, and G. H. Barrow kept asking was it quite safe to go so far out in the country, and Salvador said, 'I am a newspaperman. I am everybody's friend.'

Out at San Angel they had some drinks and when they got back to the city they drove round the Pajaritos district. G. H. Barrow got very quiet and his eyes got a watery look when he saw the little lighted cribhouses, each one with a bed and some paperflowers and a crucifix that you could see through the open door, past a red or blue curtain, and the dark quiet Indian girls in short chemises standing outside their doors or sitting on the sill.

'You see,' said Ben Stowell, 'it's easy as rolling off a log . . . But I don't advise you to get too careless round here . . . Salvador'll show us a good joint after supper. He ought to know because he's a friend of the chief of police and he runs most of them.'

But Barrow wanted to go into one of the cribs, so they got out and talked to one of the girls and Salvador sent the chauffeur to get a couple of bottles of beer. The girl received them very politely and Barrow tried to get Mac to ask her questions, but Mac didn't like asking her questions, so he let Salvador do it. When G. H. Barrow put his hand on her bare shoulder and tried to pull her chemise off and asked how much did she want to let him see her all naked, the girl didn't understand and tore herself away from him and yelled and cursed at him and Salvador wouldn't translate what she said. 'Let's get this bastard outa here,' said Ben in a low voice to Mac, 'before we have to get in a fight or somethin'.'

They had a tequila each before dinner at a little bar where nothing was sold but tequila out of varnished kegs. Salvador showed G. H. Barrow how to drink it, first putting salt on the hollow between his thumb and forefinger and then gulping the little glass of tequila, licking up the salt and swallowing some chile sauce to finish up with, but he got it down the wrong way and choked.

At supper they were pretty drunk and G. H. Barrow kept saying that Mexicans understood the art of life and that was meat for Salvador who talked about the Indian genius and the Latin genius and said that Mac and Ben were the only gringos he ever met he could get along with, and insisted on their not paying for their meal. He'd charge it to his friend the chief of police. Next they went to a cantina beside a theater where there were said to be French girls, but the French girls weren't there. There were three old men in the cantina playing a cello, a violin, and a piccolo. Salvador made them play *La Adelita* and everybody sang it and then *La Cucaracha*. There was an old man in a broadbrimmed hat with a huge shiny pistolholster on his back, who drank up his drink quickly when they came in and left the bar. Salvador whispered to Mac that he was General Gonzales and had left in order not to be seen drinking with gringos.

Ben and Barrow sat with their heads together at a table in the corner talking about the oil business. Barrow was saying that there was an investigator for certain oil interests coming down; he'd be at the Regis almost any day now and Ben was saying he wanted to meet him and Barrow put his arm around his shoulder and said he was sure Ben was just the man this investigator would want to meet to get an actual working knowledge of conditions. Meanwhile Mac and Salvador were dancing the Cuban danzon with the girls. Then Barrow got to his feet a little unsteadily and said he didn't want to wait for the French girls, but why not go to that place where they'd been and try some of the dark meat, but Salvador insisted on taking them to the house of Remedios near the American embassy. 'Quelque cosa de chic,' he'd say in bad French. It was a big house with a marble stairway and crystal chandeliers and salmonbrocaded draperies and lace curtains and mirrors everywhere. 'Personne que les henerales vieng aqui,' he said when he'd introduced them to the madam, who was a darkeyed grayhaired woman in black with a black shawl who looked rather like a nun. There was only one girl left unoccupied, so they fixed up Barrow with her and arranged about the price and left him. 'Whew, that's a relief,' said Ben when they came out. The air was cold and the sky was all stars.

Salvador had made the three old men with their instruments get back into the back of the car and said he felt romantic and wanted to serenade his novia and they went out towards Guadalupe speeding like mad along the broad causeway. Mac and the chauffeur and Ben and Salvador and the three old men singing *La Adelita* and the instruments chirping, all off key. In Guadalupe they stopped under some buttonball trees against the wall of a house with big grated windows and sang *Cielito lindo* and *La Adelita* and *Cuatro milpas*, and Ben and Mac sang *Just to keep her from the foggy dew* and were just starting *Oh, bury me not on the lone prairie* when a girl came to the window and talked a long time in low Spanish to Salvador.

Salvador said, 'Elle dit que nous make escandalo and must go away. Très chic.'

By that time a patrol of soldiers had come up and were about to arrest them all when the officer arrived and recognized the car and Salvador and took them to have a drink with him at his billet. When they all got home to Mac's place they were very drunk. Concha, whose face was drawn from waiting up, made up a mattress for Ben in the diningroom, and as they were all going to turn in Ben said, 'By heavens, Concha, you're a swell girl. When I make my pile I'll buy you the handsomest pair of diamond earrings in the Federal District.' The last they saw of Salvador he was standing up in the front seat of the car as it went round the corner on two wheels conducting the three old men in *La Adelita* with big gestures like an orchestra leader.

Before Christmas Ben Stowell came back from a trip to Tamaulipas feeling fine. Things were looking up for him. He'd made an arrangement with a local general near Tampico to run an oilwell on a fifty-fifty basis. Through Salvador he'd made friends with some members of Carranza's cabinet and was hoping to be able to turn over a deal with some of the big claimholders up in the States. He had plenty of cash and took a room at the Regis. One day he went round to the printing plant and asked Mac to step out in the alley with him for a minute.

'Look here, Mac,' he said, 'I've got an offer for you ... You know old Worthington's bookstore? Well, I got drunk last night and bought him out for two thousand pesos ... He's pulling up stakes and going home to blighty, he says.'

'The hell you did!'

'Well, I'm just as glad to have him out of the way.'

'Why, you old whoremaster, you're after Lisa.'

'Well, maybe she's just as glad to have him out of the way, too.'

'She's certainly a goodlooker.'

'I got a lot a news I'll tell you later . . . Ain't goin' to be healthy round the *Mexican Herald* maybe . . . I've got a proposition for you, Mac . . . Christ knows I owe you a hellova lot . . . You know that load of office furniture you have out back Concha made you buy that time?' Mac nodded. 'Well, I'll take it off your hands and give you a half interest in that bookstore. I'm opening an office. You know the book business . . . you told me yourself you did . . . the profits of the first year are yours and after that we split two ways, see? You certainly ought to make it pay. That old fool Worthington did, and kept Lisa into the bargain . . . Are you on?'

'Jeez, lemme think it over, Ben . . . but I got to go back to the daily bunksheet.'

So Mac found himself running a bookstore on the Calle Independencia with a line of stationery and a few typewriters. It felt good to be his own boss for the first time in his life. Concha, who was a storekeeper's daughter, was delighted. She kept the books and talked to the customers so that Mac didn't have much to do but sit in the back and read and talk to his friends. That Christmas Ben and Lisa, who was a tall Spanish girl said to have been a dancer in Malaga, with a white skin like a camellia and ebony hair, gave all sorts of parties in an apartment with Americanstyle bath and kitchen that Ben rented out in the new quarter towards Chapultepec. The day the Asociacion de Publicistas had its annual banquet, Ben stopped into the bookstore feeling fine and told Mac he wanted him and Concha to come up after supper and wouldn't Concha bring a couple of friends, nice wellbehaved girls not too choosy, like she knew. He was giving a party for G. H. Barrow who was back from Vera Cruz and a big contact man from New York who was wangling something, Ben didn't know just what. He'd seen Carranza yesterday and at the banquet everybody'd kowtowed to him.

'Jeez, Mac, you oughta been at that banquet; they took one of the streetcars and had a table the whole length of it and an orchestra and rode us out to San Angel and back and then all round town.'

'I saw 'em starting out,' said Mac, 'looked too much like a funeral to me.'

'Jeez, it was swell, though. Salvador an' everybody was there and this guy Moorehouse, the big hombre from New York, jeez, he looked like he didn't know if he was comin' or goin'.'

Looked like he expected a bomb to go off under the seat any minute . . . hellova good thing for Mexico if one had, when you come to think of it. All the worst crooks in town was there.' The party at Ben's didn't come off so well. J. Ward Moorehouse didn't make up to the girls as Ben had hoped. He brought his secretary, a tired blond girl, and they both looked scared to death. They had a dinner Mexican style and champagne and a great deal of cognac and a victrola played records by Victor Herbert and Irving Berlin and a little itinerant band attracted by the crowd played Mexican airs on the street outside. After dinner things were getting a little noisy inside, so Ben and Moorehouse took chairs out on the balcony and had a long talk about the oil situation over their cigars. J. Ward Moorehouse explained that he had come down in a purely unofficial capacity you understand to make contacts, to find out what the situation was and just what there was behind Carranza's stubborn opposition to American investors and that the big businessmen he was in touch with in the States desired only fair play and that he felt that if their point of view could be thoroughly understood through some information bureau or the friendly co-operation of Mexican newspapermen . . .

Ben went back into the diningroom and brought out Enrique Salvador and Mac. They all talked over the situation and J. Ward Moorehouse said that speaking as an old newspaperman himself he thoroughly understood the situation of the press, probably not so different in Mexico City from that in Chicago or Pittsburgh, and that all the newspapermen wanted was to give each fresh angle of the situation its proper significance in a spirit of fair play and friendly co-operation, but that he felt that the Mexican business in Mexico just as the American press was misinformed about the aims of Mexican politics. If Mr Enrique would call by the Regis he'd be delighted to talk to him more fully, or to any one of you gentlemen, and if he wasn't in, due to the great press of appointments and the very few days he had to spend in the Mexican capital, his secretary, Miss Williams, would be only too willing to give them any information they wanted and a few specially prepared strictly confidential notes on the attitude of the big American corporations with which he was purely informally in touch.

After that he said he was sorry, but he had telegrams waiting for him at the Regis, and Salvador took him and Miss Williams, his secretary, home in the chief of police's automobile.

'Jeez, Ben, that's a smooth bastard,' said Mac to Ben after J. Ward Moorehouse had gone.

'Mac,' said Ben, 'that baby's got a slick cream of millions all over him. By gum, I'd like to make some of these contacts he talks about . . . By gorry, I may do it yet . . . You just watch your Uncle Dudley, Mac. I'm goin' to associate with the big hombres after this.'

After that the party was not so refined. Ben brought out a lot more cognac and the men started taking the girls into the bedrooms and hallways and even into the pantry and kitchen. Barrow cottoned onto a blonde named Nadia who was half English and talked to her all evening about the art of life. After everybody had gone Ben found them locked up in his bedroom.

Mac got to like the life of a storekeeper. He got up when he wanted to and walked up the sunny streets past the cathedral and the façade of the National Palace and up Independencia where the sidewalks had been freshly sprinkled with water and a morning wind was blowing through, sweet with the smell of flowers and roasting coffee. Concha's little brother Antonio would have the shutters down and be sweeping out the store by the time he got there. Mac would sit in the back reading or would roam about the store chatting with people in English and Spanish. He didn't sell many books, but he kept all the American and European papers and magazines and they sold well, especially the *Police Gazette* and *La Vie Parisienne*. He started a bank account and was planning to take on some typewriter agencies. Salvador kept telling him he'd get a contract to supply stationery to some government department and make him a rich man.

One morning he noticed a big crowd in the square in front of the National Palace. He went into one of the cantinas under the arcade and ordered a glass of beer. The waiter told him that Carranza's troops had lost Torreón and that Villa and Zapata were closing in on the Federal District. When he got to the bookstore, news was going down the street that Carranza's government had fled and that the revolutionists would be in the city before night. The storekeepers began to put up their shutters. Concha and her mother came in crying, saying that it would be worse than the terrible week when Madero fell and that the revolutionists had sworn to burn and loot the city. Antonio ran in saying that the Zapatistas were bombarding Tacuba. Mac got a cab and went over to the Chamber of Deputies to see if he could find anybody he knew. All the doors were open to the street and there were papers littered along the corridors. There was nobody in the theater but an old Indian and his wife who were walking round hand in hand looking reverently at the gilded ceiling and the paintings and the tables covered with green plush. The old man carried his hat in his hand as if he were in church.

Mac told the cabman to drive to the paper where Salvador worked, but the janitor there told him with a wink that Salvador had gone to Vera Cruz with the chief of police. Then he went to the Embassy where he couldn't get a word with anybody. All the anterooms were full of Americans who had come in from ranches and concessions and who were cursing out President Wilson and giving each other the horrors with stories of the revolutionists. At the consulate Mac met a Syrian who offered to buy his stock of books. 'No, you don't,' said Mac and went back down Independencia.

When he got back to the store, newsboys were already running through the street crying, 'Viva la revolucion revindicadora.' Concha and her mother were in a panic and said they must get on the train to Vera Cruz or they'd all be murdered. The revolutionists were sacking convents and murdering priests and nuns. The old woman dropped on her knees in the corner of the room and began chanting Ave Marias.

'Aw, hell!' said Mac, 'let's sell out and go back to the States. Want to go to the States, Concha?' Concha nodded vigorously and began to smile through her tears. 'But what the devil can we do with your mother and Antonio?' Concha said she had a married sister in Vera Cruz. They could leave them there if they could ever get to Vera Cruz.

Mac, the sweat pouring off him, hurried back to the consulate to find the Syrian. They couldn't decide on the price. Mac was desperate because the banks were all closed and there was no way of getting any money. The Syrian said that he was from the Lebanon and an American citizen and a Christian and that he'd lend Mac a hundred dollars if Mac would give him a sixty-day note hypothecating his share in the bookstore for two hundred dollars. He said that he was an American citizen and a Christian and was risking his life to save Mac's wife and children. Mac was so flustered he noticed just in time that the Syrian was giving him a hundred dollars mex and that the note was made out in American dollars. The Syrian called upon Got to protect them both and said it was an error and Mac went off with two hundred pesos in gold.

He found Concha all packed. She had closed up the store and was standing on the pavement outside with some bundles, the two cats in a basket, and Antonio and her mother, each wrapped in a blanket.

They found the station so packed full of people and baggage they couldn't get in the door. Mac went round to the yards and found a man named McGrath he knew who worked for the railroad. McGrath said he could fix them up, but that they must hurry. He put them into a secondclass coach out in the yards and said he'd buy their tickets, but would probably have to pay double for them. Sweat was pouring from under Mac's hatband when he finally got the two women seated and the basket of cats and the bundles and Antonio stowed away. The train was already full, although it hadn't backed into the station yet. After several hours the train pulled out, a line of dusty soldiers fighting back the people on the platform who tried to rush the train as it left. Every seat was taken, the aisles were full of priests and nuns, there were welldressed people hanging onto the platforms.

Mac didn't have much to say sitting next to Concha in the dense heat of the slowmoving train. Concha sighed a great deal and her mother sighed, 'Ay, de mi dios,' and they gnawed on chickenwings and ate almond paste. The train was often stopped by groups of soldiers patrolling the line. On sidings were many boxcars loaded with troops, but nobody seemed to know what side they were on. Mac looked out at the endless crisscross ranks of centuryplants and the crumbling churches and watched the two huge snowy volcanoes, Popocatepetl and Ixtacihuatl, change places on the horizon; then there was another golden-brown cone of an extinct volcano slowly turning before the train; then it was the bluewhite peak of Orizaba in the distance growing up taller and taller into the cloudless sky.

After Huamantla they ran down through clouds. The rails rang under the merry clatter of the wheels curving down steep grades in the misty winding valley through moist forestgrowth. They began to feel easier. With every loop of the train the air became warmer and damper. They began to see orange and lemontrees. The windows were all open. At stations women came through selling beer and pulque and chicken and tortillas.

At Orizaba it was sunny again. The train stopped a long time. Mac sat drinking beer by himself in the station restaurant. The other passengers were laughing and talking, but Mac felt sore.

When the bell rang he didn't want to go back to Concha and her mother and their sighs and their greasy fingers and their chickenwings.

He got on another car. Night was coming on full of the smells of flowers and warm earth.

It was late the next day when they got into Vera Cruz. The town was full of flags and big red banners stretched from wall to wall of the orange and lemon and banana-colored streets with their green shutters and the palms waving in the seawind. The banners read: 'Viva Obregon,' 'Viva La Revolucion Revindicadora,' 'Viva El Partido Laborista.'

In the main square a band was playing and people were dancing. Sacred daws flew cawing among the dark umbrella-shaped trees.

Mac left Concha and her bundles and the old woman and Antonio on a bench and went to the Ward Line office to see about passage to the States. There everybody was talking about submarine warfare and America entering the Great War and German atrocities and Mac found that there was no boat for a week and that he didn't have enough cash even for two steerage passages. He bought himself a single steerage passage. He'd begun to suspect that he was making a damn fool of himself and decided to go without Concha.

When he got back to where she was sitting, she'd bought custardapples and mangos. The old woman and Antonio had gone off with the bundles to find her sister's house. The white cats were out of their basket and were curled up on the bench beside her. She looked up at Mac with a quick confident black-eyed smile and said that Porfirio and Venustiano were happy because they smelt fish. He gave her both hands to help her to her feet. At that moment he couldn't tell her he'd decided to go back to the States without her. Antonio came running up and said that they'd found his aunt and that she'd put them up and that everybody in Vera Cruz was for the revolution.

Going through the main square again, Concha said she was thirsty and wanted a drink. They were looking around for an empty table outside of one of the cafés when they caught sight of Salvador. He jumped to his feet and embraced Mac and cried, 'Viva Obregon,' and they had a mint julep American style. Salvador said that Carranza had been murdered in the mountains by his own staff officers and that onearmed Obregon had ridden into Mexico City dressed in white cotton like a peon wearing a big peon hat at the head of his Yaqui Indians and that there'd been no disorder and that the principles of Madero and Juarez were to be re-established and that a new era was to dawn.

They drank several mint juleps and Mac didn't say anything about going back to America.

He asked Salvador where his friend, the chief of police, was, but Salvador didn't hear him. Then Mac said to Concha suppose he went back to America without her, but she said he was only joking. She said she liked Vera Cruz and would like to live there. Salvador said that great days for Mexico were coming, that he was going back up the next day. That night they all ate supper at Concha's sister's house. Mac furnished the cognac. They all drank to the workers, to the tradeunions, to the partido laborista, to the social revolution and the agraristas.

Next morning Mac woke up early with a slight headache. He slipped out of the house alone and walked out along the breakwater. He was beginning to think it was silly to give up his bookstore like that. He went to the Ward Line office and took his ticket back. The clerk refunded him the money and he got back to Concha's sister's house in time to have chocolate and pastry with them for breakfast.


## *Proteus*

Steinmetz was a hunchback,
son of a hunchback lithographer.

He was born in Breslau in eighteen-sixtyfive, graduated with highest honors at seventeen from the Breslau Gymnasium, went to the University of Breslau to study mathematics;

mathematics to Steinmetz was muscular strength and long walks over the hills and the kiss of a girl in love and big evenings spent swilling beer with your friends;

on his broken back he felt the topheavy weight of society the way workingmen felt it on their straight backs, the way poor students felt it, was a member of a Socialist club, editor of a paper called *The People's Voice.*

Bismarck was sitting in Berlin like a big paperweight to keep the new Germany feudal, to hold down the empire for his bosses the Hohenzollerns.

Steinmetz had to run off to Zurich for fear of going to jail;

at Zurich his mathematics woke up all the professors at the Polytechnic;

but Europe in the eighties was no place for a penniless German student with a broken back and a big head filled with symbolic calculus and wonder about electricity that is mathematics made power

and a Socialist at that.

With a Danish friend he sailed for America steerage on an old French line boat *La Champagne*,

lived in Brooklyn at first and commuted to Yonkers where he had a twelvedollar a week job with Rudolph Eichemeyer, who was a German exile from fortyeight, an inventor and electrician and owner of a factory where he made hatmaking machinery and electrical generators.

In Yonkers he worked out the theory of the Third Harmonics and

the law of hysteresis which states in a formula the hundredfold relations between the metallic heat, density, frequency, when the poles change places in the core of a magnet under an alternating current.

It is Steinmetz's law of hysteresis that makes possible all the transformers that crouch in little boxes and gableroofed houses in all the hightension lines all over everywhere. The mathematical symbols of Steinmetz's law are the patterns of all transformers everywhere.

In eighteen-ninetytwo, when Eichemeyer sold out to the corporation that was to form General Electric. Steinmetz was entered in the contract along with other valuable apparatus. All his life Steinmetz was a piece of apparatus belonging to General Electric.

First his laboratory was at Lynn, then it was moved and the little hunchback with it to Schenectady, the electric city.

General Electric humored him, let him be a Socialist, let him keep a greenhouseful of cactuses lit up by mercury lights, let him have alligators, talking crows, and a gila monster for pets, and the publicity department talked up the wizard, the medicine man who knew the symbols that opened up the doors of Ali Baba's cave.

Steinmetz jotted a formula on his cuff and next morning a thousand new powerplants had sprung up and the dynamos sang dollars and the silence of the transformers was all dollars,

and the publicity department poured oily stories into the ears of the American public every Sunday and Steinmetz became the little parlor magician,

who made a toy thunderstorm in his laboratory and made all the toy trains run on time and the meat stay cold in the icebox and the lamp in the parlor and the great lighthouses and the searchlights and the revolving beams of light that guide airplanes at night towards Chicago, New York, St Louis, Los Angeles,

and they let him be a Socialist and believe that human society could be improved the way you can improve a dynamo, and they let him be pro-German and write a letter offering his services to Lenin because mathematicians are so impractical who make up formulas by which you can build powerplants, factories, subway systems, light, heat, air, sunshine, but not human relations that affect the stockholders' money and the directors' salaries.

Steinmetz was a famous magician and he talked to Edison tapping with the Morse code on Edison's knee

because Edison was so very deaf

and he went out West

to make speeches that nobody understood

and he talked to Bryan about God on a railroad train

and all the reporters stood round while he and Einstein met face to face,

but they couldn't catch what they said

and Steinmetz was the most valuable piece of apparatus General Electric had

until he wore out and died.

## *Janey*

The trip to Mexico and the private car the Mexican government put at the disposal of J. Ward Moorehouse to go back north in was lovely but a little tiresome, and it was so dusty going across the desert. Janey bought some very pretty things so cheap, some turquoise jewelry and pink onyx to take home to Alice and her mother and sisters as presents. Going up in the private car J. Ward kept her busy dictating and there was a big bunch of men always drinking and smoking cigars and laughing at smutty stories in the smokingroom or on the observation platform. One of them was that man Barrow she'd done some work for in Washington. He always stopped to talk to her now and she didn't like the way his eyes were when he stood over her table talking to her, still he was an interesting man and quite different from what she'd imagined a laborleader would be like, and it amused her to think that she knew about Queenie and how startled he'd be if he knew she knew. She kidded him a good deal and she thought maybe he was getting a crush on her, but he was the sort of man who'd be like that with any woman.

They didn't have a private car after Laredo and the trip wasn't so nice. They went straight through to New York. She had a lower in a different car from J. Ward and his friends, and in the upper berth there was a young fellow she took quite a fancy to. His name was Buck Saunders and he was from the Panhandle of Texas and talked with the funniest drawl. He'd punched cows and worked in the Oklahoma oilfields and saved up some money and was going to see Washington City. He was tickled to death when she said she was from Washington and she told him all about what he ought to see, the Capitol and the White House and the Lincoln Memorial and the Washington Monument and the Old Soldiers' Home and Mount Vernon. She said to be sure to go out to Great Falls and told him about canoeing on the canal and how she'd been caught in a terrible thunderstorm once near Cabin John's Bridge. They ate several meals together in the diningcar and he told her she was a dandy girl and awful easy to talk to and how he had a girl in Tulsa, Oklahoma, and how he was going to get a job in Venezuela, down at Maracaibo in the oilfields, because she'd thrown him over to marry a rich dirtfarmer who struck oil in his cowpasture. G. H. Barrow kidded Janey about her fine handsome pickup and she said what about him and the redheadedlady who got off in St Louis, and they laughed and she felt quite devilish and that G. H. Barrow wasn't so bad after all. When Buck got off the train in Washington, he gave her a snapshot of himself taken beside an oilderrick and said he'd write every day and would come to New York to see her if she'd let him, but she never heard from him.

She liked Morton, the cockney valet, too, because he always spoke to her so respectfully. Every morning he'd come and report on how J. Ward was feeling, ' 'E looks pretty black this mornin', Miss Williams,' or, ' 'E was whistlin' while 'e was shavin'. Is 'e feelin' good? Rath-er.'

When they got to the Pennsylvania Station, New York, she had to stay with Morton to see that the box of files was sent to the office at 100 Fifth Avenue and not out to Long Island where J. Ward's home was. She saw Morton off in a Pierce Arrow that had come all the way in from Great Neck to get the baggage, and went alone to the office in a taxicab with her typewriter and the papers and files. She felt scared and excited looking out of the taxicab window at the tall white buildings and the round watertanks against the sky and the puffs of steam way up and the sidewalks crowded with people and all the taxicabs and trucks and the shine and jostle and clatter. She wondered where she'd get a room to live, and how she'd find friends and where she'd eat. It seemed terribly scary being all alone in the big city like that and she wondered that she'd had the nerve to come. She decided she'd try to find Alice a job and that they'd take an apartment together, but where would she go tonight?

When she got to the office, everything seemed natural and reassuring and so handsomely furnished and polished so bright and typewriters going so fast and much more stir and bustle than there'd been in the offices of Dreyfus and Carroll; but everybody looked Jewish and she was afraid they wouldn't like her and afraid she wouldn't be able to hold down the job.

A girl named Gladys Compton showed her her desk, that she said had been Miss Rosenthal's desk. It was in a little passage just outside J. Ward's private office opposite the door to Mr Robbins's office. Gladys Compton was Jewish and was Mr Robbins's stenographer and said what a lovely girl Miss Rosenthal had been and how sorry they all were in the office about her accident and Janey felt that she was stepping into a dead man's shoes and would have a stiff row to hoe. Gladys Compton stared at her with resentful brown eyes that had a slight squint in them when she looked hard at anything and said she hoped she'd be able to get through the work, that sometimes the work was simply killing, and left her.

When things were closing up at five, J. Ward came out of his private office. Janey was so pleased to see him standing by her desk. He said he'd talked to Miss Compton and asked her to look out for Janey a little at first and that he knew it was hard for a young girl finding her way around a new city, finding a suitable place to live and that sort of thing, but that Miss

Compton was a very nice girl and would help her out and he was sure everything would work out fine. He gave her a blue-eyed smile and handed her a closely written packet of notes and said would she mind coming in the office a little early in the morning and having them all copied and on his desk by nine o'clock. He wouldn't usually ask her to do work like that, but all the typists were so stupid and everything was in confusion owing to his absence. Janey felt only too happy to do it and warm all over from his smile.

She and Gladys Compton left the office together. Gladys Compton suggested that seeing as she didn't know the city hadn't she better come home with her. She lived in Flatbush with her father and mother and of course it wouldn't be what Miss Williams was accustomed to, but they had a spare room that they could let her have until she could find her way around, and that it was clean at least and that was more than you could say about many places. They went by the station to get her bag. Janey felt relieved not to have to find her way alone in all that crowd. Then they went down into the subway and got on an expresstrain that was packed to the doors and Janey didn't think she could stand it being packed in close with so many people. She thought she'd never get there and the trains made so much noise in the tunnel she couldn't hear what the other girl was saying.

At last they got out into a wide street with an elevated running down it where the buildings were all one or two stories and the stores were groceries and vegetable and fruit stores. Gladys Compton said, 'We eat kosher, Miss Williams, on account of the old people. I hope you don't mind; of course Benny – Benny's my brudder – and I haven't any prejudices.' Janey didn't know what kosher was, but she said of course she didn't mind, and told the other girl about how funny the food was down in Mexico, so peppery you couldn't hardly eat it.

When they got to the house Gladys Compton began to pronounce her words less precisely and was very kind and thoughtful. Her father was a little old man with glasses on the end of his nose and her mother was a fat pearshaped woman in a wig. They talked Yiddish among themselves. They did everything they could to make Janey comfortable and gave her a nice room and said they'd give her board and lodging for ten dollars a week as long as she wanted to stay and when she wanted to move she could go away and no hard feelings. The house was a yellow two family frame house on a long block of houses all exactly alike, but it was well heated and the bed was comfortable. The old man was a watchmaker and worked at a Fifth Avenue jeweler's. In the old country their name had been Kompshchski, but they said that in New York nobody could pronounce it. The old man had wanted to take the name of Freedman, but his wife thought Compton sounded more refined. They had a good supper with tea in glasses and soup with dumplings and red caviar and gefültefisch, and Janey thought it was very nice knowing people like that. The boy Benny was still in highschool, a gangling youth with heavy glasses who ate with his head hung over his plate and had a rude way of contradicting anything anybody said. Gladys said not to mind him, that he was very good in his studies and was going to study law. When the strangeness had worn off a little, Janey got to like the Comptons, particularly old Mr Compton, who was very kind and treated everything that happened with gentle heartbroken humor.

The work at the office was so interesting. J. Ward was beginning to rely on her for things. Janey felt it was going to be a good year for her.

The worst thing was the threequarters of an hour ride in the subway to Union Square mornings. Janey would try to read the paper and to keep herself in a corner away from the press of bodies. She liked to get to the office feeling bright and crisp, with her dress feeling neat and her hair in nice order, but the long jolting ride fagged her out, made her feel as if she wanted to get dressed and take a bath all over again. She liked walking along Fourteenth Street, all garish and shimmering in the sunny early morning dust, and up Fifth Avenue to the office. She and Gladys were always among the first to get in. Janey kept flowers on her desk and would sometimes slip in and put a couple of roses in a silver vase on J. Ward's broad mahogany desk. Then she'd sort the mail, lay his personal letters in a neat pile on the corner of the blotter-pad that was in a sort of frame of red illuminated Italian leather, read the other letters, look over his engagement book and make up a small typewritten list of engagements, interviews, copy to be got out, statements to the press. She laid the list in the middle of the blotter under a rawcopper paperweight from the Upper Peninsula of Michigan, checking off with a neat W. the items she could attend to without consulting him.

By the time she was back at her desk correcting the spelling in the copy that had emanated from Mr Robbins's office the day before, she began to feel a funny tingle inside her; soon J. Ward would be coming in. She told herself it was all nonsense, but every time the outer office door opened she looked up expectantly. She began to worry a little; he might have had an accident driving in from Great Neck. Then, when she'd given up expecting him, he'd walk hurriedly through with a quick smile all around and the groundglass door of his private office would close behind him. Janey would notice whether he wore a dark or a light suit, what color his necktie was, whether he had a fresh haircut or not. One day he had a splatter of mud on the trouserleg of his blue serge suit and she couldn't keep her mind off it all morning trying to think of a pretext to go in and tell him about it. Rarely he'd look at her directly with a flash of blue eyes as he passed, or stop and ask her a question. Then she'd feel fine.

The work at the office was so interesting. It put her right in the midst of headlines like when she used to talk to Jerry Burnham back at Dreyfus and Carroll's. There was the Onondaga Salt Products account and literature about bathsalts and chemicals and the employees' baseball team and cafeteria and old-age pensions, and Marigold Copper and combating subversive tendencies among the miners who were mostly foreigners who had to be educated in the principles of Americanism, and the Citrus Center Chamber of Commerce's campaign to educate the small investors in the North in the stable building qualities of the Florida fruit industry, and the slogan to be launched, 'Put an Alligator Pear on Every Breakfast Table' for the Avocado Producers Co-operative. That concern occasionally sent up a case so that everybody in the office had an alligator pear to take home, except Mr Robbins, who wouldn't take his, but said they tasted like soap. Now the biggest account of all was Southwestern Oil campaign to counter the insidious anti-American propaganda of the British oilcompanies in Mexico and to oppose the intervention lobby of the Hearst interests in Washington.

In June Janey went to her sister Ellen's wedding. It was funny being in Washington again. Going on the train Janey looked forward a whole lot to seeing Alice, but when she saw her they couldn't seem to find much to talk about. She felt out of place at her mother's. Ellen was marrying a law student at Georgetown University who had been a lodger and the house was full of college boys and young girls after the wedding. They all laughed and giggled around and Mrs Williams and Francie seemed to enjoy it all right, but Janey was glad when it was time for her to go down to the station and take the train to New York again. When she said goodbye to Alice she didn't say anything about her coming down to New York to get an apartment.

She felt pretty miserable on the train sitting in the stuffy parlorcar looking out at towns and fields and signboards. Getting back to the office the next morning was like getting home.

It was exciting in New York. The sinking of the *Lusitania* had made everybody feel that America's going into the war was only a question of months. There were many flags up on Fifth Avenue. Janey thought a great deal about the war. She had a letter from Joe from Scotland that he'd been torpedoed on the steamer *Marchioness* and that they'd been ten hours in an open boat in a snowstorm off Pentland Firth with the current carrying them out to sea, but that they'd landed and he was feeling fine and that the crew had gotten bonuses and that he was making big money anyway. When she'd read the letter she went in to see J. Ward with a telegram that had just come from Colorado and told him about her brother being torpedoed and he was very much interested. He talked about being patriotic and saving civilization and the historic beauties of Rheims Cathedral. He said he was ready to do his duty when the time came, and that he thought America's entering the war was only a question of months.

A very welldressed woman came often to see J. Ward. Janey looked enviously at her lovely complexion and her neat dresses, not ostentatious but very chic, and her manicured nails and her tiny feet. One day the door swung open so that she could hear her and J. Ward talking familiarly together. 'But, J. W., my darling,' she was saying, 'this office is a fright. It's the way they used to have their offices in Chicago in the early eighties.' He was laughing. 'Well, Eleanor, why don't you redecorate it for me? Only the work would have to be done without interfering with business. I can't move, not with the press of important business just now.'

Janey felt quite indignant about it. The office was lovely the way it was, quite distinctive, everybody said so. She wondered who this woman was who was putting ideas into J. Ward's head. Next day when she had to make out a check for two hundred and fifty dollars on account to Stoddard and Hutchins, Interior Decorators, she almost spoke her mind, but after all it was hardly her business. After that Miss Stoddard seemed to be around the office all the time. The work was done at night so that every morning when Janey came in, she found something changed. It was all being done over in black and white with curtains and upholstery of a funny claret-color. Janey didn't like it at all, but Gladys said it was in the modern style and very interesting. Mr Robbins refused to have his private cubbyhole touched and he and J. Ward almost had words about it, but in the end he had his own way and the rumor went round that J. Ward had had to increase his salary to keep him from going to another agency.

Labor Day Janey moved. She was sorry to leave the Comptons, but she'd met a middleaged woman named Eliza Tingley who worked for a lawyer on the same floor as J. Ward's office. Eliza Tingley was a Baltimorean, had passed a bar examination herself, and Janey said to herself that she was a woman of the world. She and her twin brother, who was a certified accountant, had taken a floor of a house on West Twentythird Street in the Chelsea district and they asked Janey to come in with them. It meant being free from the subway and Janey felt that the little walk over to Fifth Avenue every morning would do her good. The minute she'd seen Eliza Tingley in the lunchcounter downstairs she'd taken a fancy to her. Things at the Tingleys were free and easy and Janey felt at home there. Sometimes they had a drink in the evening. Eliza was a good cook and they'd take a long time over dinner and play a couple of rubbers of threehanded bridge before going to bed. Saturday night they'd almost always go to the theater. Eddy Tingley would get the seats at a cutrate agency he knew. They subscribed to the *Literary Digest* and to the *Century* and the *Ladies' Home Journal* and Sundays they had roast chicken or duck and read the magazine section of the *New York Times*.

The Tingleys had a good many friends and they liked Janey and included her in everything and she felt that she was living the way she'd like to live. It was exciting too that winter with rumors of war all the time. They had a big map of Europe hung up on the livingroom wall and marked the positions of the Allied armies with little flags. They were heart and soul for the Allies, and names like Verdun or Chemin des Dames started little shivers running down their spines. Eliza wanted to travel and made Janey tell her over and over again every detail of her trip to Mexico; they began to plan a trip abroad together when the war was over and Janey began to save money for it. When Alice wrote from Washington that maybe she would pull up stakes in Washington and go down to New York, Janey wrote saying that it was so hard for a girl to get a job in New York just at present and that maybe it wasn't such a good idea.

All that fall J. Ward's face looked white and drawn. He got in the habit of coming into the office Sunday afternoons and Janey was only too glad to run around there after dinner to help him out. They'd talk over the events of the week in the office and J. Ward would dictate a lot of private letters to her and tell her she was a treasure and leave her there typing away happily. Janey was worried too. Although new accounts came in all the time the firm wasn't in a very good financial condition. J. Ward had made some unfortunate plunges in the Street and was having a hard time holding things together. He was anxious to buy out the large interest still held by old Mrs Staple and talked of notes his wife had gotten hold of and that he was afraid his wife would use unwisely. Janey could see that his wife was a disagreeable peevish woman trying to use her mother's money as a means of keeping a hold on J. Ward. She never said anything to the Tingleys about J. Ward personally, but she talked a great deal about the business and they agreed with her that the work was so interesting. She was looking forward to this Christmas because J. Ward had hinted that he would give her a raise.

A rainy Sunday afternoon she was typing off a confidential letter to Judge Planet inclosing a pamphlet from a detective agency describing the activities of labor agitators among the Colorado miners, and J. Ward was walking up and down in front of the desk staring with bent brows at the polished toes of his shoes when there was a knock on the outer office door. 'I wonder who that could be?' said J. Ward. There was something puzzled and nervous about the way he spoke. 'It may be Mr Robbins forgotten his key,' said Janey. She went to see. When she opened the door Mrs Moorehouse brushed past her. She wore a wet slicker and carried an umbrella, her face was pale and her nostrils were twitching. Janey closed the door gently and went to her own desk and sat down. She was worried. She took up a pencil and started drawing scrolls round the edge of a piece of typewriter paper. She couldn't help hearing what was going on in J. Ward's private office. Mrs Moorehouse had shot in slamming the groundglass door behind her. 'Ward, I can't stand it. . . . I won't stand it another minute,' she was screaming at the top of her voice. Janey's heart started beating very fast. She heard J. Ward's voice low and conciliatory, then Mrs Moorehouse's. 'I won't be treated like that, I tell you. I'm not a child to be treated like that ... You're taking advantage of my condition. My health won't stand being treated like that.'

'Now look here, Gertrude, on my honor as a gentleman,' J. Ward was saying. 'There's nothing in it, Gertrude. You lie there in bed imagining things and you shouldn't break in like this. I'm a very busy man. I have important transactions that demand my complete attention.'

Of course it's outrageous, Janey was saying to herself.

'You'd still be in Pittsburgh working for Bessemer Products, Ward, if it wasn't for me and you know it ... You may despise me, but you don't despise Dad's money ... but I'm through, I tell you. I'm going to start divorce ...'

'But, Gertrude, you know very well there's no other woman in my life.'

'How about this woman you're seen round with all the time ... what's her name ... Stoddard? You see, I know more than you think ... I'm not the kind of woman you think I am, Ward. You can't make a fool of me, do you hear?'

Mrs Moorehouse's voice rose into a rasping shriek. Then she seemed to break down and Janey could hear her sobbing. 'Now, Gertrude,' came Ward's voice soothingly, 'you've gotten yourself all wrought up over nothing ... Eleanor Stoddard and I have had a few business dealings ... She's a bright woman and I find her stimulating ... intellectually, you understand ... We've occasionally eaten dinner together, usually with mutual friends, and that's absolutely ...' Then his voice sunk so low that Janey couldn't hear what he was saying. She began to think she ought to slip out. She didn't know what to do.

She'd half gotten to her feet when Mrs Moorehouse's voice soared to a hysterical shriek again. 'Oh, you're cold as a fish ... You're just a fish. I'd like you better if it was true, if you were having an affair with her ... But I don't care; I won't be used as a tool to use Dad's money.'

The door of the private office opened and Mrs Moorehouse came out, gave Janey a bitter glare as if she suspected her relations with J. Ward too, and went out. Janey sat down at her desk again trying to look unconcerned. Inside the private office she could hear J. Ward striding up and down with a heavy step. When he called her his voice sounded weak:

'Miss Williams.'

She got up and went into the private office with her pencil

and pad in one hand. J. Ward started to dictate as if nothing had happened, but halfway through a letter to the president of the Ansonia Carbide Corporation he suddenly said, 'Oh, hell,' and gave the wastebasket a kick that sent it spinning against the wall.

'Excuse me, Miss Williams; I'm very much worried . . . Miss Williams, I'm sure I can trust you not to mention it to a soul . . . You understand, my wife is not quite herself; she'd been ill . . . the last baby . . . you know those things sometimes happen to women.'

Janey looked up at him. Tears had started into her eyes, 'Oh, Mr Moorehouse, how can you think I'd not understand? . . . Oh, it must be dreadful for you, and this is a great work and so interesting.' She couldn't say any more. Her lips couldn't form any words. 'Miss Williams,' J. Ward was saying, 'I . . . er . . . appreciate . . er.' Then he picked up the wastepaper basket. Janey jumped up and helped him pick up the crumpled papers and trash that had scattered over the floor. His face was flushed from stooping. 'Grave responsibilities . . . Irresponsible woman may do a hell of a lot of damage, you understand.' Jane nodded and nodded. 'Well, where were we? Let's finish up and get out of here.'

They set the wastebasket under the desk and started in on the letters again.

All the way home to Chelsea, picking her way through the slush and pools of water on the streets, Janey was thinking of what she'd like to have said to J. Ward to make him understand that everybody in the office would stand by him whatever happened.

When she got in the apartment, Eliza Tingley said a man had called her up. 'Sounded like a rather rough type; wouldn't give his name; just said to say Joe had called up and that he'd call up again.' Janey felt Eliza's eyes on her inquisitively.

'That's my brother Joe, I guess . . . He's a . . . he's in the merchant marine.'

Some friends of the Tingleys came in, they had two tables of bridge and were having a very jolly evening when the telephone rang again, and it was Joe. Janey felt herself blushing as she talked to him. She couldn't ask him up and still she wanted to see him. The others were calling to her to play her hand. He said he had just got in and that he had some presents for her and he'd been clear out to Flatbush and that the yids there had told him she lived in Chelsea now and he was in the cigarstore at the corner of Eighth Avenue. The others were calling to her to play her hand. She found herself saying that she was very busy doing some work and wouldn't he meet her at five tomorrow at the office building where she worked. She asked him again how he was and he said, 'Fine,' but he sounded disappointed. When she went back to her table they all kidded her about the boyfriend and she laughed and blushed, but inside she felt mean because she hadn't asked him to come up.

Next evening it snowed. When she stepped out of the elevator crowded to the doors at five o'clock, she looked eagerly round the vestibule. Joe wasn't there. As she was saying goodnight to Gladys she saw him through the door. He was standing outside with his hands deep in the pockets of a blue peajacket. Big blobs of snowflakes spun round his face that looked lined and red and weatherbeaten.

'Hello, Joe,' she said.

'Hello, Janey.'

'When did you get in?'

'A couple a days ago.'

'Are you in good shape, Joe? How do you feel?'

'I gotta rotten head today . . . Got stinkin' last night.'

'Joe, I was so sorry about last night, but there were a lot of people there and I wanted to see you alone so we could talk.' Joe grunted.

'That's awright, Janey . . . Gee, you're lookin' swell. If any of the guys saw me with you they'd think I'd picked up somethin' pretty swell awright.'

Janey felt uncomfortable. Joe had on heavy workshoes and there were splatters of gray paint on his trouserlegs. He had a package wrapped in newspaper under his arm.

'Let's go eat somewheres . . . Jeez, I'm sorry I'm not rigged up better. We lost all our duffle, see, when we was torpedoed.'

'Were you torpedoed again?'

Joe laughed, 'Sure, right off Cape Race. It's a great life . . . Well, that's strike two . . . I brought along your shawl, though, by God if I didn't . . . I know where we'll eat; we'll eat at Lüchow's.'

'Isn't Fourteenth Street a little . . .'

'Naw, they got a room for ladies . . . Janey, you don't think I'd take you to a dump wasn't all on the up an' up?'

Crossing Union Square a seedylooking young man in a red sweater said, 'Hi, Joe.' Joe dropped back of Janey for a minute and he and the young man talked with their heads together.

Then Joe slipped a bill in his hand, said, 'So long, Tex,' and ran after Janey, who was walking along feeling a little uncomfortable.

She didn't like Fourteenth Street after dark.

'Who was that, Joe?'

'Some damn AB or other. I knew him down New Orleans . . . I call him Tex. I don't know what his name is . . . He's down on his uppers.'

'Were you down in New Orleans?'

Joe nodded. 'Took a load a molasses out on the *Henry B. Higginbotham* . . . Piginbottom we called her. Well, she's layin' easy now on the bottom awright . . . on the bottom of the Grand Banks.'

When they went in the restaurant the headwaiter looked at them sharply and put them at a table in the corner of a little inside room. Joe ordered a big meal and some beer, but Janey didn't like beer, so he had to drink hers too. After Janey had told him all the news about the family and how she liked her job and expected a raise Christmas and was so happy living with the Tingleys who were so lovely to her, there didn't seem to be much to say. Joe had bought tickets to the Hippodrome, but they had plenty of time before that started. They sat silent over their coffee and Joe puffed at a cigar. Janey finally said it was a shame the weather was so mean and that it must be terrible for the poor soldiers in the trenches and she thought the Huns were just too barbarous and the *Lusitania* and how silly the Ford peace ship idea was. Joe laughed in the funny abrupt way he had of laughing now, and said, 'Pity the poor sailors out at sea on a night like this.' He got up to get another cigar.

Janey thought what a shame it was he'd had his neck shaved when he had a haircut; his neck was red and had little wrinkles in it and she thought of the rough life he must be leading, and when he came back she asked him why he didn't get a different job.

'You mean in a shipyard? They're making big money in shipyards, but hell, Janey, I'd rather knock around . . . It's all for the experience, as the feller said when they blew his block off.'

'No, but there are boys not half so bright as you are with nice clean jobs right in my office . . . and a future to look forward to.'

'All my future's behind me,' said Joe with a laugh. 'Might go down to Perth Amboy get a job in a munitions factory, but I rather be blowed up in the open, see?'

Janey went on to talk about the war and how she wished we were in it to save civilization and poor little helpless Belgium.

'Can that stuff, Janey,' said Joe. He made a cutting gesture with his big red hand above the tablecloth. 'You people don't understand it, see . . . The whole damn war's crooked from start to finish. Why don't they torpedo any French Line boats? Because the Frogs have it all set with the Jerries, see, that if the Jerries leave their boats alone they won't shell the German factories back of the front. What we wanta do 's sit back and sell 'em munitions and let 'em blow 'emselves to hell. An' those babies are makin' big money in Bordeaux and Toulouse or Marseilles while their own kin are shootin' daylight into each other at the front, and it's the same thing with the limeys . . . I'm tellin' ye, Janey, this war's crooked, like every other goddam thing.'

Janey started to cry. 'Well, you needn't curse and swear all the time.'

'I'm sorry, sister,' said Joe humbly, 'but I'm just a bum an' that's about the size of it an' not fit to associate with a nice-dressed girl like you.'

'No, I didn't mean that,' said Janey, wiping her eyes.

'Gee, but I forgot to show you the shawl.' He unwrapped the paper package. Two Spanish shawls spilled out on the table, one of black lace and the other green silk embroidered with big flowers.

'Oh, Joe, you oughtn't to give me both of them . . . You ought to give one to your best girl.'

'The kinda girls I go with ain't fit to have things like that . . . I bought those for you, Janey.'

Janey thought the shawls were lovely and decided she'd give one of them to Eliza Tingley.

They went to the Hippodrome, but they didn't have a very good time. Janey didn't like shows like that much and Joe kept falling asleep. When they came out of the theater it was bitterly cold. Gritty snow was driving hard down Sixth Avenue almost wiping the 'L' out of sight. Joe took her home in a taxi and left her at her door with an abrupt 'Solong, Janey.' She stood a moment on the step with her key in her hand and watched him walking west towards Tenth Avenue and the wharves, with his head sunk in his peajacket.

That winter the flags flew every day on Fifth Avenue. Janey

read the paper eagerly at breakfast; at the office there was talk of German spies and submarines and atrocities and propaganda. One morning a French military mission came to call on J. Ward, handsome pale officers with blue uniforms and red trousers and decorations. The youngest of them was on crutches. They'd all of them been severely wounded at the front. When they'd left, Janey and Gladys almost had words because Gladys said officers were a lot of lazy loafers and she'd rather see a mission of private soldiers. Janey wondered if she oughtn't to tell J. Ward about Gladys's pro-Germanism, whether it mightn't be her patriotic duty. The Comptons might be spies; weren't they going under an assumed name? Benny was a socialist or worse, she knew that. She decided she'd keep her eyes right open.

The same day G. H. Barrow came in. Janey was in the private office with them all the time. They talked about President Wilson and neutrality and the stockmarket and the delay in transmission in the *Lusitania* note. G. H. Barrow had had an interview with the President. He was a member of a committee endeavoring to mediate between the railroads and the Brotherhoods that were threatening a strike. Janey liked him better than she had on the private car coming up from Mexico, so that when he met her in the hall just as he was leaving the office she was quite glad to talk to him and when he asked her to come out to dinner with him, she accepted and felt very devilish.

All the time G. H. Barrow was in New York, he took Janey out to dinner and the theater. Janey had a good time and she could always kid him about Queenie if he tried to get too friendly going home in a taxi. He couldn't make out where she'd found out about Queenie and he told her the whole story and how the woman kept hounding him for money, but he said that now he was divorced from his wife and there was nothing she could do. After making Janey swear she'd never tell a soul, he explained that through a legal technicality he'd been married to two women at the same time and that Queenie was one of them and that now he'd divorced them both, and there was nothing on earth Queenie could do, but the newspapers were always looking for dirt and particularly liked to get something on a liberal like himself devoted to the cause of labor. Then he talked about the art of life and said American women didn't understand the art of life; at least women like Queenie didn't. Janey felt very sorry for him, but when he asked her to marry him she laughed and said she really would have to consult counsel before replying. He told her all about his life and how poor he'd been as a boy and then about jobs as stationagent and freightagent and conductor and the enthusiasm with which he'd gone into work for the Brotherhood and his muckraking articles on conditions in the railroads had made him a name and money so that all his old associates felt he'd sold out, but that, so help me, it wasn't true. Janey went home and told the Tingleys all about the proposal, only she was careful not to say anything about Queenie or bigamy, and they all laughed and joked about it, and it made Janey feel good to have been proposed to by such an important man and she wondered why it was such interesting men always fell for her and regretted they always had that dissipated look, but she didn't know whether she wanted to marry G. H. Barrow or not.

At the office next morning, she looked him up in *Who's Who* and there he was, *Barrow, George Henry, publicist* . . . but she didn't think she could ever love him. At the office that day J. Ward looked very worried and sick and Janey felt so sorry for him and quite forgot about G. H. Barrow. She was called into a private conference J. Ward was having with Mr Robbins and an Irish lawyer named O'Grady, and they said did she mind if they rented a safedeposit box in her name to keep certain securities in and started a private account for her at the Bankers Trust. They were forming a new corporation. There were business reasons why something of the sort might become imperative. Mr Robbins and J. Ward would own more than half the stock of a new concern and would work for it on a salary basis. Mr Robbins looked very worried and a little drunk and kept lighting cigarettes and forgetting them on the edge of the desk and kept saying, 'You know very well, J. W., that anything you do is O.K. by me.' J. Ward explained to Janey that she'd be an officer of the new corporation, but of course would in no way be personally liable. It came out that old Mrs Staple was suing J. Ward to recover a large sum of money, and that his wife had started divorce proceedings in Pennsylvania and that she was refusing to let him go home to see the children and that he was living at the McAlpin.

'Gertrude's lost her mind,' said Mr Robbins genially. Then he slapped J. Ward on the back. 'Looks like the fat was in the fire now,' he roared. 'Well, I'm goin' out to lunch; a man must eat . . . and drink . . . even if he's a putative bankrupt.'

J. Ward scowled and said nothing and Janey thought it was in very bad taste to talk like that and so loud too.

When she went home that evening she told the Tingleys that she was going to be a director of the new corporation and they thought it was wonderful that she was getting ahead so fast and that she really ought to ask for a raise even if business was in a depressed state. Janey smiled, and said, 'All in good time.' On the way home she had stopped in the telegraph office on Twentythird Street and wired G. H. Barrow, who had gone up to Washington: LET'S JUST BE FRIENDS.

Eddy Tingley brought out a bottle of sherry and at dinner he and Eliza drank a toast, 'To the new executive,' and Janey blushed crimson and was very pleased. Afterwards they played a rubber of dummy bridge.

## *The Camera Eye (26)*

the garden was crowded and outside Madison Square was full of cops that made everybody move on and the bombsquad all turned out

we couldn't get a seat so we ran up the stairs to the top gallery and looked down through the blue air at the faces thick as gravel and above them on the speakers' stand tiny black figures and a man was speaking and whenever he said war there were hisses and whenever he said Russia there was clapping on account of the revolution I didn't know who was speaking somebody said Max Eastman and some-body said another guy but we clapped and yelled for the revolution and hissed for Morgan and the capitalist war and there was a dick looking into our faces as if he was trying to remember them

then we went to hear Emma Goldman at the Bronx Casino but the meeting was forbidden and the streets around were very crowded and there were moving vans moving through the crowd and they said the moving vans were full of cops with machineguns and there were little police-department Fords with searchlights and they charged the crowd with the Fords and the searchlights everybody talked machineguns revolution civil liberty freedom of speech but occasionally somebody got into the way of a cop and was beaten up and shoved into a patrol wagon and the cops were scared and they said they were calling out the fire department to disperse the crowd and everybody said it was an outrage and what about Washington and Jeffe ɔn and Patrick Henry?

Afterwards we went to the Brevoort it was much nicer everybody who was anybody was there and there was Emma Goldman eating frankfurters and sauerkraut and everybody looked at Emma Goldman and at everybody else that was anybody and everybody was for peace and the co-operative commonwealth and the Russian revolution and we talked about red flags and barricades and suitable posts for machine-guns

and we had several drinks and welsh rabbits and paid our bill and went home, and opened the door with a latch-key and put on pajamas and went to bed and it was comfortable in bed

# Newsreel 18

*Goodbye, Piccadilly, farewell, Leicester Square*
*It's a long long way to Tipperary*

WOMAN TRAPS HUSBAND WITH GIRL IN HOTEL

to such a task we can dedicate our lives
and our fortunes, everything that we are,
and everything that we have, with the pride of those
who know
that the day has come when America is privileged to
spend her
blood and her might for the principles that gave her
birth
and happiness and the peace that she has treasured. God
helping her she can do no other

*It's a long way to Tipperary*
*It's a long way to go*
*It's a long way to Tipperary*
*And the sweetest girl I know*

TRAITORS BEWARE

FOUR MEN IN EVANSTON FINED FOR
KILLING BIRDS

WILSON WILL FORCE DRAFT

food gamblers raise price of canned foods   move for
dry U S in war   files charges when men ignore national air

JOFFRE ASKS TROOPS NOW

MOONEY CASE INCENTIVE

*Goodbye, Piccadilly, farewell, Leicester Square*
*It's a long long way to Tipperary*
*But my heart's right there.*

HOUSE REFUSES TO ALLOW T. R. TO
RAISE TROOPS

the American Embassy was threatened today with an attack by a mob of radical Socialists led by Nicolai Lenin an exile who recently returned from Switzerland via Germany.

ALLIES TWINE FLAGS ON TOMB OF
WASHINGTON

## *Eleanor Stoddard*

Eleanor thought that things were very exciting that winter. She and J. W. went out a great deal together, to all the French operas and to first nights. There was a little French restaurant where they ate hors d'oeuvres way east in Fiftysix Street. They went to see French paintings in the galleries up Madison Avenue. J. W. began to get interested in art, and Eleanor loved going round with him because he had such a romantic manner about everything and he used to tell her she was his inspiration and that he always got good ideas when he'd been talking to her. They often talked about how silly people were who said that a man and a woman couldn't have a platonic friendship. They wrote each other little notes in French every day. Eleanor often thought it was a shame J. W. had such a stupid wife who was an invalid too, but she thought that the children were lovely and it was nice that they both had lovely blue eyes like their father.

She had an office now all by herself and had two girls working with her to learn the business and had quite a lot of work to do. The office was in the first block above Madison Square on Madison Avenue and she had just had her own name on it. Eveline Hutchins didn't have anything to do with it any more as Doctor Hutchins had retired and the Hutchinses had all moved out to Santa Fe. Eveline sent her an occasional box of Indian curios or pottery and the watercolors the Indian children did in the schools, and Eleanor found they sold very well. In the afternoon she'd ride downtown in a taxi and look up at the Metropolitan Life tower and the Flatiron Building and the lights against the steely Manhattan sky and think of crystals and artificial flowers and gilt patterns on indigo and claretcolored brocade.

The maid would have tea ready for her and often there would be friends waiting for her, young architects or painters. Ther 'd always be flowers, calla lilies with the texture of icecream ι. a bowl of freesias. She'd talk a while before slipping off to dress for dinner. When J. W. phoned that he couldn't come she'd feel very bad. If there was still anybody there who'd come to tea she'd ask him to stay and have potluck with her.

The sight of the French flag excited her always or when a band played *Tipperary*; and one evening when they were going to see *The Yellow Jacket* for the third time, she had on a new furcoat that she was wondering how she was go:ng to pay for, and she thought of all the bills at her office and the house on Sutton Place she was remodeling on a speculation and wanted to ask J. W. about a thousand he'd said he'd invested for her and wondered if there'd been any turnover yet. They'd been talking about the air raids and poison gas and the effect of the war news downtown and the Bowmen of Mons and the Maid of Orleans and she said she believed in the supernatural, and J. W. was hinting something about reverses on the Street and his face looked drawn and worried; but they were crossing Times Square through the eighto'clock crowds and the skysigns flashing on and off. The fine little triangular men were doing exercises on the Wrigley sign and suddenly a grindorgan began to play *The Marseillaise* and it was too beautiful; she burst into tears and they talked about Sacrifice and Dedication and J. W. held her arm tight through the fur coat and gave the organgrinder man a dollar. When they got to the theater Eleanor hurried down to the ladies' room to see if her eyes had got red. But when she looked in the mirror they weren't red at all and there was a flash of heartfelt feeling in her eyes, so she just freshened up her face and went back up to the lobby, where J. W. was waiting for her with the tickets in his hand; her gray eyes were flashing and had tears in them.

Then one evening J. W. looked very worried indeed and said when he was taking her home from the opera where they'd seen *Manon* that his wife didn't understand their relations and was making scenes and threatening to divorce him. Eleanor was indignant and said she must have a very coarse nature not to understand that their relations were pure as driven snow. J. W. said she had and that he was very worried and he explained that most of the capital invested in his agency was his mother-

in-law's and that she could bankrupt him if she wanted to, which
was much worse than a divorce. At that Eleanor felt very cold
and crisp and said that she would rather go out of his life
entirely than break up his home and that he owed something to
his lovely children. J. W. said she was his inspiration and he
had to have her in his life and when they got back to Eighth
Street they walked back and forth in Eleanor's white glittering
drawingroom in the heavy smell of lilies wondering what could
be done. They smoked many cigarettes, but they couldn't seem
to come to any decision. When J. W. left he said with a sigh,
'She may have detectives shadowing me this very minute,' and
he went away very despondent.

After he'd gone, Eleanor walked back and forth in front
of the long Venetian mirror between the windows. She didn't
know what to do. The decorating business was barely breaking
even. She had the amortization to pay off on the house on
Sutton Place. The rent of her apartment was two months overdue and there was her fur coat to pay for. She'd counted on the
thousand dollars' worth of shares J. W. had said would be hers
if he made the killing he expected in that Venezuela Oil stock.
Something must have gone wrong or else he would have spoken
of it. When Eleanor went to bed she didn't sleep. She felt very
miserable and lonely. She'd have to go back to the drudgery of
a department store. She was losing her looks and her friends
and now if she had to give up J. W. it would be terrible. She
thought of her colored maid Augustine with her unfortunate
loves that she always told Eleanor about and she wished she'd
been like that. Maybe she'd been wrong from the start to want
everything so justright and beautiful. She didn't cry, but she
lay all night with her eyes wide and smarting staring at the
flowered molding round the ceiling that she could see in the
light that filtered in from the street through her lavender tulle
curtains.

A couple of days later at the office she was looking at some
antique Spanish chairs an old furniture dealer was trying to
sell her when a telegram came:

DISAGREEABLE DEVELOPMENTS MUST SEE YOU
INADVISABLE USE TELEPHONE MEET ME TEA
FIVE OCLOCK PRINCE GEORGE HOTEL

It wasn't signed. She told the man to leave the chairs and when
he'd gone stood a long time looking down at a pot of lavender
crocuses with yellow pistils she had on her desk. She was

wondering if it would do any good if she went out to Great Neck and talked to Gertrude Moorehouse. She called Miss Lee who was making up some curtains in the other room and asked her to take charge of the office and that she'd phone during the afternoon.

She got into a taxi and went up to the Pennsylvania Station. It was a premature spring day. People were walking along the street with their overcoats unbuttoned. The sky was a soft mauve with frail clouds like milkweed floss. In the smell of furs and overcoats and exhausts and bundledup bodies came an unexpected scent of birchbark. Eleanor sat bolt upright in the back of the taxi driving her sharp nails into the palms of her graygloved hands. She hated these treacherous days when winter felt like spring. They made the lines come out on her face, made everything seem to crumble about her, there seemed to be no firm footing any more. She'd go out and talk to Gertrude Moorehouse as one woman to another. A scandal would ruin everything. If she talked to her awhile she'd make her realize that there had never been anything between her and J. W. A divorce scandal would ruin everything. She'd lose her clients and have to go into bankruptcy and the only thing to do would be to go back to Pullman to live with her uncle and aunt.

She paid the taximan and went down the stairs to the Long Island Railroad. Her knees were shaky and she felt desperately tired as she pushed her way through the crowd to the information desk. No, she couldn't get a train to Great Neck till 2:13. She stood in line a long time for a ticket. A man stepped on her foot. The line of people moved maddeningly slowly past the ticketwindow. When she got to the window it was several seconds before she could remember the name of the place she wanted a ticket for. The man looked at her through the window, with peevish shoebutton eyes. He wore a green eyeshade and his lips were too red for his pale face. The people behind were getting impatient. A man with a tweed coat and a heavy suitcase was already trying to brush past her. 'Great Neck and return.' As soon as she'd bought the ticket the thought came to her that she wouldn't have time to get out there and back by five o'clock. She put the ticket in her gray silk purse that had a little design in jet on it. She thought of killing herself. She would take the subway downtown and go up in the elevator to the top of the Woolworth Building and throw herself off.

Instead she went out to the taxistation. Russet sunlight was pouring through the gray colonnade, the blue smoke of exhausts rose into it crinkled like watered silk. She got into a taxi and told the driver to take her round Central Park. Some of the twigs were red and there was a glint on the long buds of beeches, but the grass was still brown and there were piles of dirty snow in the gutters. A shivery raw wind blew across the ponds. The taximan kept talking to her. She couldn't catch what he said and got tired of making random answers and told him to leave her at the Metropolitan Art Museum. While she was paying him a newsboy ran by crying 'Extra!' Eleanor bought a paper for a nickel and the taximan bought a paper. 'I'll be a sonova . . .' she heard the taximan exclaim, but she ran up the steps fast for fear she'd have to talk to him. When she got into the quiet silvery light of the museum she opened up the paper. A rancid smell of printer's ink came from it; the ink was still sticky and came off on her gloves.

## DECLARATION OF WAR

A matter of hours now Washington observers declare.
*Germans' note thoroughly unsatisfactory.*

She left the newspaper on a bench and went to look at the Rodins. After she'd looked at the Rodins she went to the Chinese wing. By the time she was ready to go down Fifth Avenue in the bus – she felt she'd been spending too much on taxis – she felt elated. All the way downtown she kept remembering the Age of Bronze. When she made out J. W. in the stuffy pinkish light of the hotel lobby she went towards him with a springy step. His jaw was set and his blue eyes were on fire. He looked younger than last time she'd seen him. 'Well, it's come at last,' he said. 'I just wired Washington offering my services to the government. I'd like to see 'em try and pull a railroad strike now.' 'It's wonderful and terrible,' said Eleanor. 'I'm trembling like a leaf.'

They went to a little table in the corner behind some heavy draperies to have tea. They had hardly sat down before the orchestra started playing *The Star-Spangled Banner*, and they had to get to their feet. There was great bustle in the hotel. People kept running about with fresh editions of the papers, laughing and talking loud. Perfect strangers borrowed each other's newspapers, chatted about the war, lit cigarettes for each other.

'I have an idea, J. W.,' Eleanor was saying, holding a piece of cinnamontoast poised in her pointed fingers, 'that if I went out and talked to your wife as one woman to another, she'd understand the situation better. When I was decorating the house she was so kind and we got along famously.'

'I have offered my services to Washington,' said Ward. 'There may be a telegram at the office now. I'm sure that Gertrude will see that it is her simple duty.'

'I want to go J. W.,' said Eleanor. 'I feel I must go.'

'Where?'

'To France.'

'Don't do anything hasty, Eleanor.'

'No, I feel I must . . . I could be a very good nurse . . . I'm not afraid of anything; you ought to know that, J. W.'

The orchestra played *The Star-Spangled Banner* again; Eleanor sang some of the chorus in a shrill little treble voice. They were too excited to sit still long and went over to J. W.'s office in a taxi. The office was in great excitement. Miss Williams had had a flagpole put up in the center window and was just raising the flag on it. Eleanor went over to her and they shook hands warmly. The cold wind was rustling the papers on the desk and typewritten pages were sailing across the room, but nobody paid any attention. Down Fifth Avenue a band was coming near playing *Hail, Hail, the Gang's All Here*. All along office windows were brightly lit, flags were slapping against their poles in the cold wind, clerks and stenographers were leaning out and cheering, dropping out papers that sailed and whirled in the bitter eddying wind.

'It's the Seventh Regiment,' somebody said and they all clapped and yelled. The band was clanging loud under the window. They could hear the tramp of the militiamen's feet. All the automobiles in the stalled traffic tooted their horns. People on the tops of the busses were waving small flags. Miss Williams leaned over and kissed Eleanor on the cheek. J. W. stood by looking out over their heads with a proud smile on his face.

After the band had gone and traffic was running again they put the window down and Miss Williams went around picking up and arranging loose papers. J. W. had a telegram from Washington accepting his services on the Public Information Committee that Mr Wilson was gathering about him and said he'd leave in the morning. He called up Great Neck and asked Gertrude if he could come out to dinner and bring a friend. Gertrude said he might and that she hoped she'd be able to stay up to see them. She was excited by the warnews, but she said the thought of all that misery and slaughter gave her horrible pains in the back of the head.

'I have a hunch that if I take you out to dinner at Gertrude's, everything will be all right,' he said to Eleanor. 'I'm rarely wrong in my hunches.'

'Oh, I know she'll understand,' said Eleanor.

As they were leaving the office they met Mr Robbins in the hall. He didn't take his hat off or the cigar out of his mouth. He looked drunk. 'What the hell is this, Ward?' he said. 'Are we at war or not?'

'If we're not we will be before morning,' said J. W.

'It's the goddamnedest treason in history,' said Mr Robbins. 'What did we elect Wilson for instead of Old Fuzzywhiskers except to keep us out of the goddam mess?'

'Robbins, I don't agree with you for a minute,' said J. W. 'I think it's our duty to save . . .' But Mr Robbins had disappeared through the office door leaving a strong reek of whiskey behind him.

'I'd have given him a piece of my mind,' said Eleanor, 'if I hadn't seen that he was in no condition.'

Driving out to Great Neck in the Pierce Arrow it was thrilling. A long red afterglow lingered in the sky. Crossing the Queensboro Bridge with the cold wind back of them was like flying above lights and blocks of houses and the purple bulk of Blackwell's Island and the steamboats and the tall chimneys and the blue light of powerplants. They talked of Edith Cavell and airraids and flags and searchlights and the rumble of armies advancing and Joan of Arc. Eleanor drew the fur robe up to her chin and thought about what she'd say to Gertrude Moorehouse.

When they got to the house she felt a little afraid of a scene. She stopped in the hall to do up her face with a pocketmirror she had in her bag.

Gertrude Moorehouse was sitting in a long chair beside a crackling fire. Eleanor glanced around the room and was pleased at how lovely it looked. Gertrude Moorehouse went very pale when she saw her. 'I wanted to talk to you,' said Eleanor.

Gertrude Moorehouse held out her hand without getting up. 'Excuse me for not getting up, Miss Stoddard,' she said, 'but I'm absolutely prostrated by the terrible news.'

'Civilization demands a sacrifice . . . from all of us,' said Eleanor.

'Of course it is terrible what the Huns have done, cutting the hands off Belgian children and all that,' said Gertrude Moorehouse.

'Mrs Moorehouse,' said Eleanor. 'I want to speak to you about this unfortunate misunderstanding of my relations with your husband . . . Do you think I am the sort of woman who could come out here and face you if there was anything in these horrible rumors? Our relations are pure as driven snow.'

'Please don't speak of it, Miss Stoddard. I believe you.'

When J. W. came in they were sitting on either side of the fire talking about Gertrude's operation.

Eleanor got to her feet. 'Oh, I think it's wonderful of you, J. W.'

J. W. cleared his throat and looked from one to the other. 'It's little less than my duty,' he said.

'What is it?' asked Gertrude.

'I have offered my services to the government to serve in whatever capacity they see fit for the duration of the war.'

'Not at the front,' said Gertrude with a startled look.

'I'm leaving for Washington tomorrow . . . Of course I shall serve without pay.'

'Ward, that's noble of you,' said Gertrude. He walked over slowly until he stood beside her chair, then he leaned over and kissed her on the forehead. 'We must all make our sacrifices . . . My dear, I shall trust you and your mother . . .'

'Of course, Ward, of course . . . It's all been a silly misunderstanding.' Gertrude flushed red. She got to her feet. 'I've been a damn suspicious fool . . . but you mustn't go to the front, Ward. I'll talk mother around' . . . She went up to him and put her hands on his shoulders. Eleanor stood back against the wall looking at them. He wore a smoothfitting tuxedo. Gertrude's salmoncolored teagown stood out against the black. His light hair was ashgray in the light from the crystal chandelier against the tall ivorygray walls of the room. His face was in shadow and looked very sad. Eleanor thought how little people understood a man like that, how beautiful the room was, like a play, like a Whistler, like Sarah Bernhardt. Emotion misted her eyes.

'I'll join the Red Cross,' she said. 'I can't wait to get to France.'

# Newsreel 19

**U.S. AT WAR**

**UPHOLD NATION CITY'S CRY**

*Over there*
*Over there*

at the annual meeting of the stockholders of the Colt Patent Firearms Manufacturing Company a $2,500,000 melon was cut. The present capital stock was increased. The profits for the year were 259 per cent

**JOYFUL SURPRISE OF BRITISH**

*The Yanks are coming*
*We're coming o-o-o-ver*

**PLAN LEGISLATION TO KEEP COLORED PEOPLE FROM WHITE AREAS**

many millions paid for golf about Chicago Hindu agitators in nationwide scare Armour urges U.S. save earth from famine

**ABUSING FLAG TO BE PUNISHED**

Labor deputies peril to Russia acts have earmarks of dishonorable peace London hears

**BILLIONS FOR ALLIES**

*And we won't come home*
*Till it's over over there.*

## The Camera Eye (27)

there were priests and nuns on the *Espagne* the

Atlantic was glassgreen and stormy   covers were clamped on the portholes and all the decklights were screened and you couldn't light a match on deck

but the stewards were very brave and said the Boche wouldn't sink a boat of the Compagnie Générale anyway, because of the priests and nuns and the Jesuits and the Comité des Forges promising not to bombard the Bassin de la Briey where the big smelters were and stock in the company being owned by the Prince de Bourbon and the Jesuits and the priests and nuns

anyhow everybody was very brave except for Colonel and Mrs Knowlton of the American Red Cross who had waterproof coldproof submarineproof suits like eskimosuits and they wore them and they sat up on deck with the suits all blown up and only their faces showing and there were firstaid kits in the pockets and in the belt there was a waterproof container with milkchocolate and crackers and maltedmilk tablets.

and in the morning you'd walk round the deck and there would be Mr Knowlton blowing up Mrs Knowlton

or Mrs Knowlton blowing up Mr Knowlton

the Roosevelt boys were very brave in stiff visored new American army caps and sharpshooter medals on the khaki whipcord and they talked all day about We must come in We must come in

as if the war were a swimming pool

and the barman was brave and the stewards were brave they'd all been wounded and they were very glad that they were stewards and not in the trenches

and the pastry was magnificent

at last it was the zone and a zigzag course we sat quiet in the bar and then it was the mouth of the Gironde and a French torpedoboat circling round the ship in the early pearl soft morning and the steamers following the little patrolboat on account of the minefields   the sun was rising red over the ruddy winegrowing land and the Gironde was full of freighters and airplanes in the sun and battleships

the Garonne was red   it was autumn there were barrels of new wine and shellcases along the quays in front of the grayfaced houses and the masts of stocky sailboats packed against the great red iron bridge

at the Hotel of the Seven Sisters everybody was in mourning but business was brisk on account of the war and every minute they expected the government to come down from Paris

up north they were dying in the mud and the trenches but business was good in Bordeaux and the winegrowers and the shipping agents and the munitionsmakers crowded into the Chapon Fin and ate ortolans and mushrooms and truffles and there was a big sign

### MEFIEZ–VOUS
#### les oreilles ennemis vous écoutent

red wine twilight and yellowgravelled squares edged with winebarrels and a smell of chocolate in the park gray statues and the names of streets

Street of Lost Hopes, Street of the Spirit of the Laws, Street of Forgotten Footsteps

and the smell of burning leaves and the grayfaced Bourbon houses crumbling into red wine twilight

at the Hotel of the Seven Sisters after you were in bed late at night you suddenly woke up and there was a secret-serviceagent going through your bag

and he frowned over your passport and peeped in your books and said Monsieur c'est la petite visite


## Fighting Bob

La Follette was born in the town limits of Primrose; he worked on a farm in Dane County, Wisconsin, until he was nineteen.

At the University of Wisconsin he worked his way through. He wanted to be an actor, studied elocution and Robert Ingersoll and Shakespeare and Burke;

(who will ever explain the influence of Shakespeare in the last century, Marc Antony over Caesar's bier, Othello to the Venetian Senate, and Polonius, everywhere Polonius?)

riding home in a buggy after commencement he was Booth

and Wilkes writing the Junius papers and Daniel Webster and
Ingersoll defying God and the togaed great grave and incorruptible as statues magnificently spouting through the capitoline
centuries;

he was the star debater in his class,
and won an interstate debate with an oration on the
character of Iago.
He went to work in a law office and ran for district
attorney. His schoolfriends canvassed the county riding round
evenings. He bucked the machine and won the election.
It was the revolt of the young man against the state
republican machine
and Boss Keyes the postmaster in Madison who ran the
county was so surprised he about fell out of his chair.

That gave La Follette a salary to marry on. He was twentyfive years old.
Four years later he ran for Congress; the university was
with him again; he was the youngsters' candidate. When he was
elected he was the youngest representative in the house
He was introduced round Washington by Philetus Sawyer
the Wisconsin lumber king who was used to stacking and
selling politicians the way he stacked and sold cordwood.
He was a Republican and he'd bucked the machine. Now
they thought they had him. No man could stay honest in
Washington.
Booth played Shakespeare in Baltimore that winter. Booth
never would go to Washington on account of the bitter memory
of his brother. Bob La Follette and his wife went to every
performance.

In the parlor of the Plankinton Hotel in Milwaukee during
the state fair, Boss Sawyer the lumber king tried to bribe him
to influence his brother-in-law who was presiding judge over
the prosecution of the Republican state treasurer;
Bob La Follette walked out of the hotel in a white rage.
From that time it was war without quarter with the Republican
machine in Wisconsin until he was elected governor and
wrecked the Republican machine;
this was the tenyears war that left Wisconsin the model
state where the voters, orderloving Germans and Finns,

Scandinavians fond of their own opinion, learned to use the new leverage, direct primaries, referendum and recall.

La Follette taxed the railroads

John C. Payne said to a group of politicians in the lobby of the Ebbitt House in Washington 'La Follette's a damn fool if he thinks he can buck a railroad with five thousand miles of continuous track, he'll find he's mistaken . . . We'll take care of him when the time comes.'

But when the time came the farmers of Wisconsin and the young lawyers and doctors and businessmen just out of school

took care of him

and elected him governor three times

and then to the United States Senate,

where he worked all his life making long speeches full of statistics, struggling to save democratic government, to make a farmers' and small businessmen's commonwealth, lonely with his back to the wall, fighting corruption and big business and high finance and trusts and combinations of combinations and the miasmic lethargy of Washington.

He was one of 'the little group of willful men expressing no opinion but their own'

who stood out against Woodrow Wilson's armed ship bill that made war with Germany certain; they called it a filibuster, but it was six men with nerve straining to hold back a crazy steamroller with their bare hands;

the press pumped hatred into its readers against La Follette, the traitor;

they burned him in effigy in Illinois;

in Wheeling they refused to let him speak.

In nineteen-twentyfour La Follette ran for President and without money or political machine rolled up four and a half million votes

but he was a sick man, incessant work and the breathed out air of committee rooms and legislative chambers choked him

and the dirty smell of politicians,

and he died,

an orator haranguing from the capitol of a lost republic;

but we will remember

how he sat firm in March nineteen-seventeen while
Woodrow Wilson was being inaugurated for the second time,
and for three days held the vast machine at deadlock. They
wouldn't let him speak; the galleries glared hatred at him; the
Senate was a lynching party,

a stumpy man with a lined face, one leg stuck out in the
aisle and his arms folded and a chewed cigar in the corner of
his mouth

and an undelivered speech on his desk,

a willful man expressing no opinion but his own.

## Charley Anderson

Charley Anderson's mother kept a railroad boardinghouse
near the Northern Pacific station at Fargo, North Dakota. It
was a gabled frame house with porches all round, painted
mustard yellow with chocolatebrown trim, and out back there
was always washing hanging out on sagging lines that ran
from a pole near the kitchen door to a row of brokendown
chickenhouses. Mrs Anderson was a quietspoken grayhaired
woman with glasses; the boarders were afraid of her and did
their complaining about the beds, or the food, or that the eggs
weren't fresh to waddling bigarmed Lizzie Green from the
north of Ireland who was the help and cooked and did all the
housework. When any of the boys came home drunk, it was
Lizzie with a threadbare man's overcoat pulled over her nightgown who came out to make them shut up. One of the brake-
men tried to get fresh with Lizzie one night and got such a
sock in the jaw that he fell clear off the front porch. It was
Lizzie who washed and scrubbed Charley when he was little,
who made him get to school on time and put arnica on his
knees when he skinned them and soft soap on his chilblains and
mended the rents in his clothes. Mrs Anderson had already
raised three children who had grown up and left home before
Charley came, so that she couldn't seem to keep her mind on
Charley. Mr Anderson had also left home about the time
Charley was born; he'd had to go West on account of his weak
lungs, couldn't stand the hard winters, was how Mrs Anderson
put it. Mrs Anderson kept the accounts, preserved or canned
strawberries, peas, peaches, beans, tomatoes, pears, plums,
applesauce as each season came round, made Charley read a
chapter of the Bible every day and did a lot of churchwork.

Charley was a chunky little boy with untidy towhair and gray eyes. He was a pet with the boarders and liked things allright except Sundays when he'd have to go to church twice and to Sundayschool and then right after dinner his mother would read him her favorite sections of Matthew or Esther or Ruth and ask him questions about the chapters he'd been assigned for the week. This lesson took place at a table with a red tablecloth next to a window that Mrs Anderson kept banked with pots of patienceplant, wandering jew, begonias and ferns summer and winter. Charley would have pins and needles in his legs and the big dinner he'd eaten would have made him drowsy and he was terribly afraid of committing the sin against the Holy Ghost, which his mother hinted was inattention in church or in Sundayschool or when she was reading him the Bible. Winters the kitchen was absolutely quiet except for the faint roaring of the stove or Lizzie's heavy step or puffing breath as she stacked the dinnerdishes she'd just washed back in the cupboard. Summers it was much worse. The other kids would have told him about going swimming down in the Red River or fishing or playing follow my leader in the lumberyard or on the coalbunkers back of the roundhouse, and the caught flies would buzz thinly in the festooned tapes of flypaper and he'd hear the yardengine shunting freightcars or the through train for Winnipeg whistling for the station and the bell clanging, and he'd feel sticky and itchy in his stiff collar and he'd keep looking up at the loudticking porcelain clock on the wall. It made the time go too slowly to look up at the clock often, so he wouldn't let himself look until he thought fifteen minutes had gone by, but when he looked again it'd only be five minutes and he'd feel desperate. Maybe it'd be better to commit the sin against the Holy Ghost right there and be damned good and proper once and for all and run away with a tramp the way Dolphy Olsen did, but he didn't have the nerve.

By the time he was ready for highschool he began to find funny things in the Bible, things like the kids talked about when they got tired playing toad in the hole in the deep weeds back of the lumberyard fence, the part about Onan and the Levite and his concubine and the Song of Solomon, it made him feel funny and made his heart pound when he read it, like listening to scraps of talk among the railroadmen in the boardinghouse, and he knew what hookers were and what was happening when women got so fat in front and it worried him and he was care-

ful when he talked to his mother not to let her know he knew
about things like that.

Charley's brother Jim had married the daughter of a liverystable owner in Minneapolis. The spring Charley was getting
ready to graduate from the eighth grade they came to visit Mrs
Anderson. Jim smoked cigars right in the house and jollied his
mother and while he was there there was no talk of Bible-
reading. Jim took Charley fishing one Sunday up the Sheyenne
and told him that if he came down to the Twin Cities when
school was over he'd give him a job helping round the garage
he was starting up in part of his fatherinlaw's liverystable. It
sounded good when he told the other guys in school that he
had a job in the city for the summer. He was glad to get out, as
his sister Esther had just come back from taking a course in
nursing and nagged him all the time about talking slang and
not keeping his clothes neat and eating too much pie.

He felt fine the morning he went over to Moorhead all alone,
carrying a suitcase Esther had lent him, to take the train for the
Twin Cities. At the station he tried to buy a package of cigarettes, but the man at the newsstand kidded him and said he was
too young. When he started it was a fine spring day a little too
hot. There was sweat on the flanks of the big horses pulling the
long line of flourwagons that was crossing the bridge. While he
was waiting in the station the air became stifling and a steamy
mist came up. The sunlight shone red on the broad backs of the
grain elevators along the track. He heard one man say to
another, 'Looks to me like it might be a tornado,' and when he
got on the train he half leaned out of the open window watching purple thunderheads building up in the northwest beyond
the brightgreen wheat that stretched clear to the clouds. He
kinda hoped it would be a tornado because he'd never seen
one, but when the lightning began cracking like a whip out of
the clouds he felt a little scared, though being on the train with
the conductor and the other passengers made it seem safer. It
wasn't a tornado, but it was a heavy thundershower and the
wheatfields turned to zinc as great trampling hissing sheets of
rain advanced slowly across them. Afterwards the sun came
out and Charley opened the window and everything smelt like
spring and there were birds singing in all the birchwoods and
in the dark firs round all the little shining lakes.

Jim was there to meet him at the Union Depot in a Ford
truck. They stopped at the freight station and Charley had to
help load a lot of heavy packages of spare parts shipped from

Detroit and marked 'Vogel's Garage'. Charley tried to look as if he'd lived in a big city all his life, but the clanging trolleycars and the roughshod hoofs of truckhorses striking sparks out of the cobbles and the goodlooking blond girls and the stores and the big German beersaloons and the hum that came from mills and machineshops went to his head. Jim looked tall and thin in his overalls and had a new curt way of talking. 'Kid, you see you mind yourself a little up to the house; the old man's an old German, Hedwig's old man, an' a little pernickety, like all old Germans are,' said Jim when they'd filled the truck and were moving slowly through the heavy traffic. 'Sure, Jim,' said Charley, and he began to feel a little uneasy about what it 'ud be like living in Minneapolis. He wished Jim 'ud smile a little more.

Old man Vogel was a stocky redfaced man with untidy gray hair and a pot belly, fond of dumpling and stews with plenty of rich sauce on them and beer, and Jim's wife Hedwig was his only daughter. His wife was dead, but he had a middleaged German woman everybody addressed as Aunt Hartmann to keep house for him. She followed the men around all the time with a mop and between her and Hedwig, whose blue eyes had a peevish look because she was going to have a baby in the fall, the house was so spotless that you could have eaten a fried egg off the linoleum anywhere. They never let the windows be opened for fear of the dust coming in. The house was right on the street and the liverystable was in the yard behind, entered through an alley beyond which was the old saddler's shop that had just been done over as a garage. When Jim and Charley drove up the signpainters were on a stepladder out front putting up the new shiny red and white sign that read 'VOGEL'S GARAGE.' 'The old bastard,' muttered Jim. 'He said he'd call it Vogel and Anderson's, but what the hell!' Everything smelt of stables, and a colored man was leading a skinny horse around with a blanket over him.

All that summer Charley washed cars and drained transmissions and relined brakes. He was always dirty and greasy in greasy overalls, in the garage by seven every morning and not through till late in the evening when he was too tired to do anything but drop into the cot that had been fixed for him in the attic over the garage. Jim gave him a dollar a week for pocket money and explained that he was mighty generous to do it, as it was to Charley's advantage to learn the business. Saturday nights he was the last one to get a bath and there usually wasn't anything but lukewarm water left, so that he'd have a hard time getting cleaned up. Old man Vogel was a socialist and no churchgoer and spent all day Sunday drinking beer with his cronies. At Sunday dinner everybody talked German, and Jim and Charley sat at the table glumly without saying anything, but old Vogel plied them with beer and made jokes at which Hedwig and Aunt Hartmann always laughed uproariously, and after dinner Charley's head would be swimming from the beer that tasted awful bitter to him, but he felt he had to drink it, and old man Vogel would tease him to smoke a cigar and then tell him to go out and see the town. He'd walk out feeling overfed and a little dizzy and take the streetcar to St Paul to see the new state capitol or to Lake Harriet or go out to Big Island Park and ride on the rollercoaster or walk around the Parkway until his feet felt like they'd drop off. He didn't know any kids his own age at first, so he took to reading for company. He'd buy every number of *Popular Mechanics* and the *Scientific American* and *Adventure* and the *Wide World Magazine*. He had it all planned to start building a yawlboat from the plans in the *Scientific American* and to take a trip down the Mississippi River to the Gulf. He'd live by shooting ducks and fishing for catfish. He started saving up his dollars to buy himself a shotgun.

He liked it all right at old man Vogel's, though, on account of not having to read the Bible or go to church, and he liked tinkering with motors and learned to drive the Ford truck. After a while he got to know Buck and Slim Jones, two brothers about his age who lived down the block. He was a pretty big guy to them on account of working in a garage. Buck sold newspapers and had a system of getting into moving-picture shows by the exit doors and knew all the best fences to see ballgames from. Once Charley got to know the Jones boys he'd run round to their place as soon as he was through dinner Sundays and they'd have a whale of a time getting hitches all over the place on graintrucks, riding on the back bumpers of streetcars and getting chased by cops and going out on the lumber booms and going swimming and climbing round above the falls and he'd get back all sweaty and with his good suit dirty and be bawled out by Hedwig for being late for supper. Whenever old Vogel found the Jones boys hanging round the garage he'd chase them out, but when he and Jim were away, Gus the colored stableman would come over smelling of horses and tell them stories about horseraces and fast women and whiskey-drinking down at Louisville and the proper way to take a girl the first time and how he and his steady girl just did it all night without stopping not even for a minute.

Labor Day old man Vogel took Jim and his daughter and Aunt Hartmann out driving in the surrey behind a fine pair of bays that had been left with him to sell and Charley was left to take care of the garage in case somebody came along who wanted gas or oil. Buck and Slim came round and they all talked about how it was Labor Day and wasn't it hell to pay that they weren't going out anywhere. There was a double-header out at the Fair Grounds and lots of other ballgames around. The trouble started by Charley showing Buck how to drive the truck, then to show him better he had to crank her up, then before he knew it he was telling them he'd take them for a ride round the block. After they'd ridden round the block he went back and closed up the garage and they went joyriding out towards Minnehaha. Charley said to himself he'd drive very carefully and be home hours before the folks got back, but somehow he found himself speeding down an asphalt boulevard and almost ran into a ponycart full of little girls that turned in suddenly from a side road. Then on the way home they were drinking sarsaparilla out of the bottles and having a fine time when Buck suddenly said there was a cop on a motorcycle following them. Charley speeded up to get away from the cop, made a turn too sharp and stopped with a crash against a telegraph pole. Buck and Slim beat it as fast as they could run and there was Charley left to face the cop.

The cop was a Swede and cursed and swore and bawled him out and said he'd take him to the hoosegow for driving without a license, but Charley found his brother Jim's license under the seat and said his brother had told him to take the car back to the garage after they'd delivered a load of apples out at Minnehaha and the cop let him off and said to drive more carefully another time. The car ran all right except one fender was crumpled up and the steering wheel was a little funny. Charley drove home so slow that the radiator was boiling over when he got back and there was the surrey standing in front of the house and Gus holding the bays by the head and all the family just getting out.

There was nothing he could say. The first thing they saw was the crumpled fender. They all lit into him and Aunt Hartmann yelled the loudest and old Vogel was purple in the face and they all talked German at him and Hedwig yanked at his coat

and slapped his face and they all said Jim 'd have to give him a
licking. Charley got sore and said nobody was going to give
him a licking and then Jim said he reckoned he'd better go
back to Fargo anyway, and Charley went up and packed his
suitcase and went off without saying goodbye to any of them
that evening with his suitcase in one hand and five back numbers of the *Argosy* under his arm. He had just enough jack
saved up to get a ticket to Barnesville. After that he had to play
hide and seek with the conductor until he dropped off the train
at Moorhead. His mother was glad to see him and said he was
a good boy to get back in time to visit with her a little before
highschool opened and talked about his being confirmed.
Charley didn't say anything about the Ford truck and decided
in his mind he wouldn't be confirmed in any damned church.
He ate a big breakfast that Lizzie fixed for him and went into
his room and lay down on the bed. He wondered if not wanting
to be confirmed was the sin against the Holy Ghost, but the
thought didn't scare him as much as it used to. He was sleepy
from sitting up on the train all night and fell asleep right away.

Charley dragged through a couple of years of highschool,
making a little money helping round the Moorhead Garage
evenings, but he didn't like it home any more after he got back
from his trip to the Twin Cities. His mother wouldn't let him
work Sundays and nagged him about being confirmed and his
sister Esther nagged him about everything and Lizzie treated
him as if he was still a little kid, called him 'Pet' before the
boarders, and he was sick of schooling, so the spring when he
was seventeen, after commencement, he went down to Minneapolis again looking for a job on his own this time. As he had
money to keep him for a few days, the first thing he did was to
go down to Big Island Park. He wanted to ride on the rollercoasters and shoot in the shootinggalleries and go swimming
and pick up girls. He was through with hick towns like Fargo
and Moorhead where nothing ever happened.

It was almost dark when he got to the lake. As the little
steamboat drew up to the wharf, he could hear the jazzband
through the trees, and the rasp and rattle of the rollercoaster
and yells as a car took a dip. There were a dancing pavilion and
colored lights among the trees and a smell of girls' perfumery
and popcorn and molasses candy and powder from the shoot-
inggallery and the barkers were at it in front of their booths.
As it was Monday evening there weren't very many people.
Charley went round the rollercoaster a couple of times and got

to talking with the young guy who ran it about what the chances were of getting a job round there.

The guy said to stick around, Svenson the manager would be there when they closed up at eleven, and he thought he might be looking for a guy. The guy's name was Ed Walters; he said it wasn't much of a graft, but that Svenson was pretty straight; he let Charley take a couple of free rides to see how the roller-coaster worked and handed him out a bottle of cream soda and told him to keep his shirt on. This was his second year in the amusement game and he had a sharp foxface and a wise manner.

Charley's heart was thumping when a big hollowfaced man with coarse sandy hair came round to collect the receipts at the ticket booth. That was Svenson. He looked Charley up and down and said he'd try him out for a week and to remember that this was a quiet family amusement park and that he wouldn't stand for any rough stuff and told him to come round at ten the next morning. Charley said 'So long' to Ed Walters and caught the last boat and car back to town. When he got out of the car it was too late to take his bag out of the station parcelroom; he didn't want to spend money on a room or to go out to Jim's place, so he slept on a bench in front of the City Hall. It was a warm night and it made him feel good to be sleeping on a bench like a regular hobo. The arclights kept getting in his eyes, though, and he was nervous about the cop; it'd be a hell of a note to get pinched for a vag and lose the job out at the park. His teeth were chattering when he woke up in the gray early morning. The arclights spluttered pink against a pale lemonyellow sky; the big business blocks with all their empty windows looked funny and gray and deserted. He had to walk fast pounding the pavement with his heels to get the blood going through his veins again.

He found a stand where he could get a cup of coffee and a doughnut for five cents and went out to Lake Minnetonka on the first car. It was a bright summer day with a little north in the wind. The lake was very blue and the birchtrunks looked very white and the little leaves danced in the wind greenyellow against the dark evergreens and the dark blue of the sky. Charley thought it was the most beautiful place he'd ever seen. He waited a long time drowsing in the sun on the end of the wharf for the boat to start over to the island. When he got there the park was all locked up, there were shutters on all the booths and the motionless red and blue cars of the rollercoaster looked forlorn in the morning light. Charley roamed round for a while, but his eyes smarted and his legs ached and his suitcase was too heavy, so he found a place sheltered by the wall of a shack from the wind and lay down in the warm sun on the pineneedles and went to sleep with his suitcase beside him.

He woke up with a start. His Ingersoll said eleven. He had a cold sinking feeling. It'd be lousy to lose the job by being late. Svenson was there sitting in the ticket booth at the rollercoaster with a straw hat on the back of his head. He didn't say anything about the time. He just told Charley to take his coat off and help MacDonald the engineer oil up the motor.

Charley worked on that rollercoaster all summer until the park closed in September. He lived in a little camp over at Excelsior with Ed Walters and a wop named Spagnolo who had a candy concession.

In the next camp Svenson lived with his six daughters. His wife was dead. Anna the eldest was about thirty and was cashier at the amusement park, two of them were waitresses at the Tonka Bay Hotel and the others were in highschool and didn't work. They were all tall and blond and had nice complexions. Charley fell for the youngest, Emiscah, who was just about his age. They had a float and a springboard and they all went in swimming together. Charley wore a bathingsuit upper and a pair of khaki pants all summer and got very sunburned. Ed's girl was Zona and all four of them used to go out canoeing after the amusement park closed, particularly warm nights when there was a moon. They didn't drink, but they smoked cigarettes and played the phonograph and kissed and cuddled up together in the bottom of the canoe. When they'd got back to the boys' camp, Spagnolo would be in bed and they'd haze him a little and put junebugs under his blankets and he'd curse and swear and toss around. Emiscah was a great hand for making fudge, and Charley was crazy about her and she seemed to like him. She taught him how to frenchkiss and would stroke his hair and rub herself up against him like a cat, but she never let him go too far, and he wouldn't have thought it was right anyway. One night all four of them went out and built a fire under a pine in a patch of big woods up the hill back of the camps. They toasted marshmallows and sat round the fire telling ghoststories. They had blankets and Ed knew how to make a bed with hemlock twigs stuck in the ground and they all four of them slept in the same blankets and tickled each other and roughhoused around and it took them a long time to get to sleep. Part of the time Charley lay between the two girls and they cuddled up close to him, but he got a hardon and couldn't sleep and was worried for fear the girls would notice.

He learned to dance and to play poker and when Labor Day came he hadn't saved any money, but he felt he'd had a wonderful summer.

He and Ed got a room together in St Paul. He got a job as machinist's assistant in the Northern Pacific shops and made fair money. He learned to run an electric lathe and started a course in nightschool to prepare for civil engineering at the Mechanical Arts High. Ed didn't seem to have much luck about jobs, all he seemed to be able to do was pick up a few dollars now and then as attendant at a bowling alley. Sundays they often ate dinner with the Svensons. Mr Svenson was running a small movie house called the Leif Ericsson on Fourth Street, but things weren't going so well. He took it for granted that the boys were engaged to two of his daughters and was only too glad to see them come around. Charley took Emiscah out every Saturday night and spent a lot on candy and taking her to vaudeville shows and to a Chink restaurant where you could dance afterwards. At Christmas he gave her his seal ring and after that she admitted that she was engaged to him. They'd go back to the Svensons' and sit on the sofa in the parlor hugging and kissing.

She seemed to enjoy getting him all wrought up, then she'd run off and go and fix her hair or put some rouge on her face and be gone a long time and he'd hear her upstairs giggling with her sisters. He'd walk up and down in the parlor, where there was only one light in a flowered shade, feeling nervous and jumpy. He didn't know what to do. He didn't want to get married because that 'ud keep him from traveling round the country and getting ahead in studying engineering. The other guys at the shop who weren't married went down the line or picked up streetwalkers, but Charley was afraid of getting a disease, and he never seemed to have any time what with nightschool and all, and besides it was Emiscah he wanted.

After he'd given her a last rough kiss, feeling her tongue in his mouth and his nostrils full of her hair and the taste of her mouth in his mouth, he'd walk home with his ears ringing, feeling sick and weak; when he got to bed he couldn't sleep, but would toss around all night thinking he was going mad and Ed'd grunt at him from the other side of the bed for crissake to keep still.

In February Charley got a bad sore throat and the doctor he went to said it was diphtheria and sent him to the hospital. He was terribly sick for several days after they gave him the antitoxin. When he was getting better Ed and Emiscah came to see him and sat on the edge of his bed and made him feel good. Ed was all dressed up and said he had a new job and was making big money, but he wouldn't tell what it was. Charley got the idea that Ed and Emiscah were going round together a little since he'd been sick, but he didn't think anything of it.

The man in the next cot, who was also recovering from diphtheria, was a lean grayhaired man named Michaelson. He'd been working in a hardware store that winter and was having a hard time. Up to a couple of years before he'd had a farm in Iowa in the cornbelt, but a series of bad crops had ruined him, the bank had foreclosed and taken the farm and offered to let him work it as a tenant, but he'd said he'd be damned if he'd work as a tenant for any man and had pulled up his stakes and come to the city, and here he was fifty years old with a wife and three small children to support trying to start from the ground up again. He was a great admirer of Bob La Follette and had a theory that the Wall Street bankers were conspiring to seize the government and run the country by pauperizing the farmer. He talked all day in a thin wheezy voice until the nurse made him shut up, about the Non-Partisan League and the Farmer-Labor Party and the destiny of the great Northwest and the need for workingmen and farmers to stick together to elect honest men like Bob La Follette. Charley had joined a local of an A.F. of L. union that fall and Michaelson's talk, broken by spells of wheezing and coughing, made him feel excited and curious about politics. He decided he'd read the papers more and keep up with what was going on in the world. What with this war and everything you couldn't tell what might happen.

When Michaelson's wife and children came to see him he introduced them to Charley and said that being laid up next to a bright young fellow like that made being sick a pleasure. It made Charley feel bad to see how miserably pale and illfed they looked and what poor clothes they had on in this zero weather. He left the hospital before Michaelson did and the last thing Michaelson said when Charley leaned over him to shake his dry bony hand was 'Boy, you read Henry George, do you hear . . . ? He knows what's the trouble with this country; damme if he don't.'

Charley was so glad to be walking on his pins down the snowy street in the dry icecold wind and to get the smell of iodoform and sick people out of his head that he forgot all about it.

First thing he did was to go to Svensons'. Emiscah asked him where Ed Walters was. He said he hadn't been home and didn't know. She looked worried when he said that and he wondered about it. 'Don't Zona know?' asked Charley. 'No, Zona's got a new feller; that's all she thinks about.' Then she smiled and patted his hand and babied him a little bit and they sat on the sofa and she brought out some fudge she'd made and they held hands and gave each other sticky kisses and Charley felt happy. When Anna came in she said how thin he looked and that they'd have to feed him up, and he stayed to supper. Mr Svenson said to come and eat supper with them every night for a while until he was on his feet again. After supper they all played hearts in the front parlor and had a fine time.

When Charley got back to his lodginghouse, he met the landlady in the hall. She said his friend had left without paying the rent and that he'd pay up right here and now or else she wouldn't let him go up to his room. He argued with her and said he'd just come out of the hospital and she finally said she'd let him stay another week. She was a big softlooking woman with puckered cheeks and a yellow chintz apron full of little pockets. When Charley got up to the hall bedroom where he'd slept all winter with Ed, it was miserably cold and lonely. He got into the bed between the icy sheets and lay shivering, feeling weak and kiddish and almost ready to cry, wondering why the hell Ed had gone off without leaving him word and why Emiscah had looked so funny when he said he didn't know where Ed was.

Next day he went to the shop and got his old job back, though he was so weak he wasn't much good. The foreman was pretty decent about it and told him to go easy for a few days, but he wouldn't pay him for the time he was sick because he wasn't an old employee and hadn't gotten a certificate from the company doctor. That evening he went to the bowlingalley where Ed used to work. The barkeep upstairs said Ed had beaten it to Chi on account of some flimflam about raffling off a watch. 'Good riddance, if you ask me,' he said. 'That bozo has all the makin's of a bad egg.'

He had a letter from Jim saying that ma had written from Fargo that she was worried about him and that Charley had

better let Jim take a look at him, so he went over to the Vogels'
next Sunday. First thing he did when he saw Jim was to say
that busting up the Ford had been a damn fool kid's trick and
they shook hands on it and Jim said nobody would say anything about it and that he'd better stay and eat with them. The
meal was fine and the beer was fine. Jim's kid was darn cute;
it was funny to think that he was an uncle. Even Hedwig didn't
seem so peevish as before. The garage was making good money
and old man Vogel was going to give up the liverystable and
retire. When Charley said he was studying at nightschool, old
Vogel began to pay more attention to him. Somebody said
something about La Follette and Charley said he was a big
man.

'Vat is the use being a big man if you are wrong?' said
old Vogel with beersuds in his mustache. He took another
draft out of his stein and looked at Charley with sparkling blue
eyes. 'But dot's only a beginning . . . ve vill make a Sozialist out
of you yet.' Charley blushed and said, 'Well, I don't know
about that,' and Aunt Hartmann piled another helping
of hasenpfeffer and noodles and mashed potatoes on his
plate.

One raw March evening he took Emiscah to see *The Birth
of a Nation*. The battles and the music and the bugles made
them all jelly inside. They both had tears in their eyes when the
two boys met on the battlefield and died in each other's arms on
the battlefield. When the Ku Klux Klan charged across the
screen Charley had his leg against Emiscah's leg and she dug
her fingers into his knee so hard it hurt. When they came out
Charley said by heck he thought he wanted to go up to Canada
and enlist and go over and see the Great War. Emiscah said
not to be silly and then looked at him kinda funny and asked
him if he was pro-British. He said he didn't care and that the
only fellows that would gain would be the bankers, whoever
won. She said 'Isn't it terrible? Let's not talk about it any
more.'

When they got back to the Svensons', Mr Svenson was sitting
in the parlor in his shirtsleeves reading the paper. He got up
and went to meet Charley with a worried frown on his face and
was just about to say something when Emiscah shook her head.
He shrugged his shoulders and went out. Charley asked
Emiscah what was eating the old man. She grabbed hold of
him and put her head on his shoulder and burst out crying.
'What's the matter, kitten; what's the matter, kitten?' he kept

asking. She just cried and cried until he could feel her tears on his cheek and neck and said. 'For crissake, snap out of it, kitten; you're wilting my collar.'

She let herself drop on the sofa and he could see that she was working hard to pull herself together. He sat down beside her and kept patting her hand. Suddenly she got up and stood in the middle of the floor. He tried to put his arms around her to pet her, but she pushed him off. 'Charley,' she said in a hard strained voice, 'lemme tellye somethin' . . . I think I'm goin' to have a baby.'

'But you're crazy. We haven't ever . . .'

'Maybe it's somebody else . . . Oh, God, I'm going to kill myself.'

Charley took her by the arms and made her sit down on the sofa. 'Now pull yourself together, and tell me what the trouble is.'

'I wish you'd beat me up,' Emiscah said, laughing crazily. 'Go ahead; hit me with your fist.'

Charley went weak all over.

'Tell me what the trouble is,' he said. 'By Jeez, it couldn't be Ed.'

She looked up at him with scared eyes, her face drawn like an old woman's. 'No, no . . . Here's how it is. I'm a month past my time, see, and I don't know enough about things like that, so I asks Anna about it and she says I'm goin' to have a baby sure and that we've got to get married right away and she told dad, the dirty little sneak, and I couldn't tell 'em it wasn't you . . . They think it's you, see, and dad says it's all right, young folks bein' like that nowadays an' everythin' an' says we'll have to get married and I thought I wouldn't let on an' you'd never know, but, kid, I had to tell you.'

'Oh, Jeez,' said Charley. He looked at the flowered pink shade with a fringe over the lamp on the table beside him and the tablecover with a fringe and at his shoes and the roses on the carpet. 'Who was it?'

'It was when you were in the hospital, Charley. We had a lot of beer to drink an' he took me to a hotel. I guess I'm just bad, that's all. He was throw'n money around an' we went in a taxicab and I guess I was crazy. No, I'm a bad woman through and through, Charley. I went out with him every night when you were in the hospital.'

'By God, it was Ed.'

She nodded and then hid her face and started to cry again.

'The lousy little bastard,' Charley kept saying. She crumpled up on the sofa with her face in her hands.

'He's gone to Chicago . . . He's a bad egg allright,' said Charley.

He felt he had to get out in the air. He picked up his coat and hat and started to put them on. Then she got to her feet and threw herself against him. She held him close and her arms were tight round his neck. 'Honestly, Charley, I loved you all the time . . . I pretended to myself it was you.' She kissed him on the mouth. He pushed her away but he felt weak and tired and thought of the icy streets walking home and his cold hall-bedroom and thought, what the hell did it matter anyway? and took off his hat and coat again. She kissed him and loved him up and locked the parlor door and they loved each other up on the sofa and she let him do everything he wanted. Then after a while she turned on the light and straightened her clothes and went over to the mirror to fix her hair and he tied his necktie again and she smoothed down his hair as best she could with her fingers and they unlocked the parlor door very carefully and she went out in the hall to call dad. Her face was flushed and she looked very pretty again. Mr Svenson and Anna and all the girls were out in the kitchen and Emiscah said, 'Dad, Charley and I are going to get married next month,' and everybody said, 'Congratulations,' and all the girls kissed Charley and Mr Svenson broke out a bottle of whiskey and they had a drink all around and Charley went home feeling like a whipped dog.

There was a fellow named Hendriks at the shop seemed a pretty wise guy; Charley asked him next noon whether he didn't know of anything a girl could take and he said he had a prescription for some pills and next day he brought it and told Charley not to tell the druggist what he wanted them for. It was payday and Hendriks came round to Charley's room after he'd gotten cleaned up that night and asked him if he'd gotten the pills all right. Charley had the package right in his pocket and was going to cut nightschool that night to take it to Emiscah. First he and Hendriks went to have a drink at the corner. He didn't like whiskey straight and Hendriks said to take it with gingerale. It tasted great and Charley felt sore and miserable inside and didn't want to see Emiscah anyway. They had some more drinks and then went and bowled for a while. Charley beat him four out of five and Hendriks said the party was on him from now on.

Hendriks was a squareshouldered redheaded guy with a freckled face and a twisted nose and he began telling stories about funny things that had happened with the ribs and how that was his long suit anyway. He'd been all over and had had high yallers and sealskin browns down New Orleans and Chink girls in Seattle, Washington, and a fullblooded Indian squaw in Butte, Montana, and French girls and German Jewish girls in Colon and a Caribee woman more than ninety years old in Port of Spain. He said that the Twin Cities was the bunk and what a guy ought to do was to go down an' get a job in the oilfields at Tampico or in Oklahoma where you could make decent money and live like a white man. Charley said he'd pull out of St Paul in a minute if it wasn't that he wanted to finish his course in nightschool, and Hendriks told him he was a damn fool, that booklearnin' never got nobody nowhere and what he wanted was to have a good time when he had his strength and after that to hell wid 'em. Charley said he felt like saying to hell wid 'em anyway.

They went to several bars, and Charley who wasn't used to drinking anything much except beer began to reel a little, but it was swell barging round with Hendriks from bar to bar. Hendriks sang *My Mother Was a Lady* in one place and *The Bastard King of England* in another where an old redfaced guy with a cigar set them up to some drinks. Then they tried to get into a dancehall, but the guy at the door said they were too drunk and threw them out on their ear and that seemed funny as hell and they went to a back room of a place Hendriks knew and there were two girls there Hendriks knew and Hendriks fixed it up for ten dollars each for all night, then they had one more drink before going to the girls' place and Hendriks sang:

> *Two drummers sat at dinner in a grand hotel one day*
> *While dining they were chatting in a jolly sort of way*
> *And when a pretty waitress brought them a tray of food*
> *They spoke to her familiarly in a manner rather rude*

'He's a hot sketch,' said one of the girls to the other. But the other was a little soused and began to get a crying jag when Hendriks and Charley put their heads together and sang:

> *My mother was a lady like yours you will allow*
> *And you may have a sister who needs protection now*
> *I've come to this great city to find a brother dear*
> *And you wouldn't dare insult me, sir, if Jack were only here.*

They cried and the other one kept shoving her and saying, 'Dry your eyes deary you're maudlin,' and it was funny as hell.

The next few weeks Charley was uneasy and miserable. The pills made Emiscah feel awful sick, but they finally brought her around. Charley didn't go there much, though they still talked about 'When we're married,' and the Svensons treated Charley as a soninlaw. Emiscah nagged a little about Charley's drinking and running round with this fellow Hendriks. Charley had dropped out of nightschool and was looking for a chance to get a job that would take him away somewhere, he didn't much care where. Then one day he busted a lathe and the foreman fired him. When he told Emiscah about it she got sore and said she thought it was about time he gave up boozing and running round and he paid little attention to her and he said it was about time for him to butt out, and picked up his hat and coat and left. Afterwards when he was walking down the street he wished he'd remembered to ask her to give him back his seal ring, but he didn't go back to ask for it.

That Sunday he went to eat at old man Vogel's, but he didn't tell them he'd lost his job. It was a sudden hot spring day. He'd been walking round all morning, with a headache from getting tanked up with Hendriks the night before, looking at the crocuses and hyacinths in the parks and the swelling buds in the dooryards. He didn't know what to do with himself. He was a week overdue on his rent and he wasn't getting any schooling and he hadn't any girl and he felt like saying to hell with everything and joining up in the militia to go down to the Mexican border. His head ached and he was tired of dragging his feet over the pavements in the early heat. Welldressed men and women went by in limousines and sedans. A boy flashed by on a red motorbike. He wished he had the jack to buy a motorbike himself and go on a trip somewhere. Last night he'd tried to argue Hendriks into going South with him, but Hendriks said he'd picked up with a skirt that was a warm baby and he was getting his nookie every night and going to stay right with it. To hell with that, thought Charley; I want to see some country.

He looked so down in the mouth that Jim said, 'What's the trouble, Charley?' when he walked into the garage. 'Aw, nothing,' said Charley, and started to help clean the parts of the carburetor of a Mack truck Jim was tinkering with. The truckdriver was a young feller with closecropped black hair and a tanned face. Charley liked his looks. He said he was going to take a load of storefittings down to Milwaukee next day and was looking for a guy to go with him.

'Would you take me?' said Charley. The truckdriver looked puzzled.

'He's my kid brother, Fred; he'll be all right ... But what about your job?'

Charley colored up. 'Aw, I resigned.'

'Well, come round with me to see the boss,' said the truckdriver. 'And if it's all right by him it's all right by me.'

They left next morning before day. Charley felt bad about sneaking out on his landlady, but he left a note on the table saying he'd send her what he owed her as soon as he got a job. It was fine leaving the city and the mills and grainelevators behind in the gray chilly early morning light. The road followed the river and the bluffs and the truck roared along sloshing through puddles and muddy ruts. It was chilly, although the sun was warm when it wasn't behind the clouds. He and Fred had to yell at each other to make their voices heard, but they told stories and chewed the fat about one thing and another. They spent the night in LaCrosse.

They just got into the hashjoint in time to order hamburger steaks before it closed, and Charley felt he was making a hit with the waitress who was from Omaha and whose name was Helen. She was about thirty and had a tired look under the eyes that made him think maybe she was kind of easy. He hung round until she closed up and took her out walking and they walked along the river and the wind was warm and smelt winey of sawmills and there was a little moon behind fleecy clouds and they sat down in the new grass where it was dark behind stacks of freshcut lumber laid out to season. She let her head drop on his shoulder and called him 'baby boy'.

Fred was asleep in the truck rolled up in a blanket on top of the sacking when he got back. Charley curled up in his overcoat on the other side of the truck. It was cold and the packingcases were uncomfortable to lie on, but he was tired and his face felt windburned, and he soon fell asleep.

They were off before day.

The first thing Fred said was, 'Well, did you make her, kid?' Charley laughed and nodded. He felt good and thought to himself he was damn lucky to get away from the Twin Cities and Emiscah and that sonofabitchin' foreman. The whole world was laid out in front of him like a map, and the Mack truck roaring down the middle of it and towns were waiting for him everywhere where he could pick up jobs and make good money and find goodlooking girls waiting to call him their baby boy.

He didn't stay long in Milwaukee. They didn't need any help in any of the garages, so he got a job pearldiving in a lunchroom. It was a miserable greasy job with long hours. To save money he didn't get a room, but flopped in a truck in a garage where a friend of Jim's was working. He was planning to go over on the boat as soon as he got his first week's pay. One of the stiffs working in the lunchroom was a wobbly named Monte Davis. He got everybody to walk out on account of a freespeech fight the wobblies were running in town, so Charley worked a whole week and had not a cent to show for it and hadn't eaten for a day and a half when Fred came back with another load on his Mack truck and set him up to a feed. They drank some beer afterwards and had a big argument about strikes. Fred said all this wobbly agitation was damn foolishness and he thought the cops would be doing right if they jailed every last one of them. Charley said that working stiffs ought to stick together for decent living conditions and the time was coming when there'd be a big revolution like the American Revolution only bigger, and after that there wouldn't be any bosses and the workers would run industry. Fred said he talked like a damn foreigner and ought to be ashamed of himself and that a white man ought to believe in individual liberty and if he got a raw deal on one job he was goddam well able to find another. They parted sore, but Fred was a goodhearted guy and lent Charley five bucks to go over to Chi with.

Next day he went over on the boat. There were still some yellowish floes of rotting ice on the lake that was a very pale cold blue with a few whitecaps on it. Charley had never been out on a big body of water before and felt a little sick, but it was fine to see the chimneys and great blocks of buildings, pearly where the sun hit them, growing up out of the blur of factory smoke, and the breakwaters and the big oreboats plowing through the blue seas, and to walk down the wharf with everything new to him and to plunge into the crowd and the stream of automobiles and green and yellow buses blocked up by the drawbridge on Michigan Avenue, and to walk along in the driving wind looking at the shiny storewindows and goodlooking girls and windblown dresses.

Jim had told him to go to see a friend of his who worked in a Ford servicestation on Blue Island Avenue, but it was so far that by the time he got there the guy had gone. The boss was there, though, and he told Charley that if he came round next morning he'd have a job for him. As he didn't have anywhere to go and didn't like to tell the boss he was flat, he left his suitcase in the garage and walked around all night. Occasionally he got a few winks of sleep on a park bench, but he'd wake up stiff and chilled to the bone and would have to run around to warm up. The night seemed never to end and he didn't have a red to get a cup of coffee with in the morning, and he was there walking up and down outside an hour before anybody came to open up the servicestation in the morning.

He worked at the Ford servicestation several weeks until one Sunday he met Monte Davis on North Clark Street and went to a wobbly meeting with him in front of the Newberry Library. The cops broke up the meeting and Charley didn't walk away fast enough and before he knew what had happened to him he'd been halfstunned by a riotstick and shoved into the policewagon. He spent the night in a cell with two bearded men who were blind drunk and didn't seem to be able to talk English anyway. Next day he was questioned by a police magistrate and when he said he was a garage mechanic a dick called up the servicestation to check up on him; the magistrate discharged him, but when he got to the garage the boss said he'd have no goddam I Won't Works in this outfit and paid him his wages and discharged him too.

He hocked his suitcase and his good suit and made a little bundle of some socks and a couple of shirts and went round to see Monte Davis to tell him he was going to hitchhike to St Louis. Monte said there was a free-speech fight in Evansville and he guessed he'd come along to see what was doing. They went out on the train to Joliet. When they walked past the prison, Monte said the sight of a prison always made him feel sick and gave him a kind of a foreboding. He got pretty blue and said he guessed the bosses'd get him soon, but that there'd be others. Monte Davis was a sallow thinfaced youth from Muscatine, Iowa. He had a long crooked nose and stuttered and didn't remember a time when he hadn't sold papers or worked in a buttonfactory. He thought of nothing but the I.W.W. and the revolution. He bawled Charley out for a scissorbill because he laughed about how fast the wobblies ran when the cops broke up the meeting, and told him he ought to be class-conscious and take things serious.

At the citylimits of Joliet they hopped a truck that carried them to Peoria, where they separated because Charley found a truckdriver he'd known in Chicago who offered him a lift all the way to St Louis. In St Louis things didn't seem to be so good, and he got into a row with a hooker he picked up on Market Street who tried to roll him, so as a guy told him there were plenty jobs to be had in Louisville he began to beat his way East. By the time he got to New Albany it was hot as the hinges of hell; he'd had poor luck on hitches and his feet were swollen and blistered. He stood a long time on the bridge looking down into the swift brown current of the Ohio, too tired to go any further. He hated the idea of tramping round looking for a job. The river was the color of gingerbread; he started to think about the smell of gingercookies Lizzie Green used to make in his mother's kitchen and he thought he was a damn fool to be bumming round like this. He'd go home and plant himself among the weeds, that's what he'd do.

Just then a brokendown Ford truck came by running on a flat tire. 'Hey, you've got a flat,' yelled Charley.

The driver put on the brakes with a bang. He was a big bullet-headed man in a red sweater. 'What the hell is it to you?'

'Jeez, I just thought you might not a noticed.'

'Ah notice everythin', boy . . . ain't had nutten but trouble all day. Wanta lift?'

'Sure,' said Charley.

'Now, Ah can't park on de bridge nohow . . . Been same goddam thing all day. Here Ah gits up early in de mornin' b'fo' day and goes out to haul foa hawgsheads a tobacca and de goddam nigger done lost de warehouse key. Ah swear if Ah'd had a gun Ah'd shot de sonofabitch dead.'

At the end of the bridge he stopped and Charley helped him change the tire. 'Where you from, boy?' he said as he straightened up and brushed the dust off his pants.

'I'm from up in the Northwest,' said Charley.

'Ah reckon you're a Swede, ain't yez?'

Charley laughed. 'No; I'm a garage mechanic and lookin' for a job.'

'Pahl in, boy; we'll go an' see ole man Wiggins – he's ma boss – an' see what we can do.'

Charley stayed all summer in Louisville working at the Wiggins Repair Shops. He roomed with an Italian named Grassi who'd come over to escape military service. Grassi read the papers every day and was very much afraid the U. S. would go into the war. Then he said he'd have to hop across the border to Mexico. He was an anarchist and a quiet sort of guy who spent the evenings singing low to himself and playing the accordion on the lodginghouse steps. He told Charley about the big Fiat factories at Torino where he'd worked, and taught him to eat spaghetti and drink red wine and to play *Funiculi funicula* on the accordion. His big ambition was to be an airplane pilot. Charley picked up with a Jewish girl who worked as sorter in a tobacco warehouse. Her name was Sarah Cohen, but she made him call her Belle. He liked her well enough, but he was careful to make her understand that he wasn't the marrying kind. She said she was a radical and believed in free love, but that didn't suit him much either. He took her to shows and took her out walking in Cherokee Park and bought her an amethyst brooch when she said amethyst was her birthstone.

When he thought about himself he felt pretty worried. Here he was doing the same work day after day, with no chance of making better money or getting any schooling or seeing the country. When winter came on he got restless. He'd rescued an old Ford roadster that they were going to tow out to the junkheap and had patched it up with discarded spare parts.

He talked Grassi into going down to New Orleans with him. They had a little money saved up and they'd run down there and get a job and be there for the Mardi Gras. The first day that he'd felt very good since he left St Paul was the sleety January day they pulled out of Louisville with the engine hitting on all four cylinders and a pile of thirdhand spare tires in the back, headed south.

They got down through Nashville and Birmingham and Mobile, but the roads were terrible, and they had to remake the car as they went along and they almost froze to death in a blizzard near Guntersville and had to lay over for a couple of days, so that by the time they'd gotten down to Bay St Louis and were bowling along the shore road under a blue sky and feeling the warm sun and seeing palms and bananatrees and Grassi was telling about Vesuvio and Bella Napoli and his girl in Torino that he'd never see again on account of the bastardly capitalista war, their money had run out. They got into New Orleans with a dollar five between them and not more than a teacupful of gasoline in the tank, but by a lucky break Charley managed to sell the car as it stood for twentyfive dollars to a colored undertaker.

They got a room in a house near the levee for three dollars a week. The landlady was a yellowfaced woman from Panama and there was a parrot on the balcony outside their room and

the sun was warm on their shoulders walking along the street.
Grassi was very happy. 'This is lika the Italia,' he kept saying.
They walked around and tried to find out about jobs, but they
couldn't seem to find out about anything except that Mardi
Gras was next week. They walked along Canal Street that was
crowded with colored people, Chinamen, pretty girls in brightcolored dresses, racetrack hangerson, tall elderly men in palmbeach suits. They stopped to have a beer in a bar open to the
street with tables along the outside where all kinds of men
sat smoking cigars and drinking. When they came out Grassi
bought an afternoon paper. He turned pale and showed the
headline, WAR WITH GERMANY IMMINENT. 'If America
go to war with Germany cops will arrest all Italian men to
send back to Italy for fight, see? My friend tell who work in
consule's office; tell me, see? I will not go fight in capitalista
war.' Charley tried to kid him along, but a worried set look
came over Grassi's face and as soon as it was dark he left
Charley saying he was going back to the flop and going to bed.

Charley walked round the streets alone. There was a warm
molasses smell from the sugar refineries, whiffs of gardens and
garlic and pepper and oil cookery. There seemed to be women
everywhere, in bars, standing round streetcorners, looking out
invitingly behind shutters ajar in all the doors and windows;
but he had twenty dollars on him and was afraid one of them
might lift it off him, so he just walked around until he was
tired and then went back to the room, where he found Grassi
already asleep with the covers over his head.

It was late when he woke up. The parrot was squawking on
the gallery outside the window, hot sunlight filled the room.
Grassi was not there.

Charley had dressed and was combing his hair when Grassi
came in looking very much excited. He had taken a berth as
donkey-engineman on a freighter bound for South America.
'When I get Buenos Aires goodbye and no more war,' he said.
'If Argentina go to war, goodbye again.' He kissed Charley on
the mouth, and insisted on giving him his accordion and there
were tears in his eyes when he went off to join the boat that
was leaving at noon.

Charley walked all over town inquiring at garages and
machineshops if there was any chance of a job. The streets
were broad and dusty, bordered by low shuttered frame houses,
and distances were huge. He got tired and dusty and sweaty.
People he talked to were darned agreeable, but nobody seemed

to know where he could get a job. He decided he ought to stay
through the Mardi Gras anyway and then he would go up North
again. Men he talked to told him to go to Florida or Birmingham, Alabama, or up to Memphis or Little Rock, but everybody agreed that unless he wanted to ship as a seaman there
wasn't a job to be had in the city. The days dragged along warm
and slow and sunny and smelling of molasses from the refineries. He spent a great deal of time reading in the public
library or sprawled on the levee watching the niggers unload
the ships. He had too much time to think and he worried
about what he was going to do with himself. Nights he
couldn't sleep well because he hadn't done anything all day
to tire him.

One night he heard guitar music coming out of a joint called
'The Original Tripoli,' on Chartres Street. He went in and sat
down at a table and ordered drinks. The waiter was a Chink.
Couples were dancing in a kind of wrestling hug in the dark
end of the room. Charley decided that if he could get a girl
for less than five seeds he'd take one on.

Before long he found himself setting up a girl who said her
name was Liz to drinks and a feed. She said she hadn't had
anything to eat all day. He asked her about Mardi Gras and
she said it was a bum time because the cops closed everything
up tight. 'They rounded up all the waterfront hustlers last night,
sent every last one of them up the river.'

'What they do with 'em?'

'Take 'em up to Memphis and turn 'em loose . . . ain't a jail
in the state would hold all the floosies in this town.' They
laughed and had another drink and then they danced. Charley
held her tight. She was a skinny girl with little pointed breasts
and big hips.

'Jeez, baby, you've got some action,' he said after they'd
been dancing a little while.

'Ain't it ma business to give the boys a good time?'

He liked the way she looked at him. 'Say, baby, how much
do you get.'

'Five bucks.'

'Jeez, I ain't no millionnaire . . . and didn't I set you up to
some eats?'

'Awright, sugarpopper; make it three.'

They had another drink. Charley noticed that she took some
kind of lemonade each time. 'Don't you ever drink anything,
Liz?'

'You can't drink in this game, dearie; first thing you know I'd be givin' it away.'

There was a big drunken guy in a dirty undershirt looked like a ship's stoker reeling round the room. He got hold of Liz's hand and made her dance with him. His big arms tattooed blue and red folded right round her. Charley could see he was mauling and pulling at her dress as he danced with her. 'Quit that, you sonofabitch,' she was yelling. That made Charley sore and he went up and pulled the big guy away from her. The big guy turned and swung on him. Charley ducked and hopped into the center of the floor with his dukes up. The big guy was blind drunk, as he let fly another haymaker Charley put his foot out and the big guy tripped and fell on his face upsetting a table and a little dark man with a black mustache with it. In a second the dark man was on his feet and had whipped out a machete. The Chinks ran round mewing like a lot of damn gulls. The proprietor, a fat Spaniard in an apron, had come out from behind the bar and was yellin', 'Git out, every last one of you.' The man with the machete made a run at Charley. Liz gave him a yank one side and before Charley knew what had happened she was pulling him through the stinking latrines into a passage that led to a back door out into the street. 'Don't you know no better'n to git in a fight over a goddam whore?' she was saying in his ear.

Once out in the street Charley wanted to go back to get his hat and coat. Liz wouldn't let him. 'I'll get it for you in the mornin',' she said.

They walked along the street together. 'You're a damn good girl; I like you,' said Charley.

'Can't you raise ten dollars and make it all night?'

'Jeez, kid, I'm broke.'

'Well, I'll have to throw you out and do some more hustlin', I guess . . . There's only one feller in this world gets it for nothin' and you ain't him.'

They had a good time together. They sat on the edge of the bed talking. She looked flushed and pretty in a fragile sort of way in her pink shimmy shirt. She showed him a snapshot of her steady who was second engineer on a tanker. 'Ain't he handsome? I don't hustle when he's in town. He's that strong . . . He can crack a pecan with his biceps.' She showed him the place on his arm where her steady could crack a pecan.

'Where you from?' asked Charley.

'What's that to you?'

'You're from up North; I can tell by the way you talk.'

'Sure. I'm from Iowa, but I'll never go back there no more ... It's a hell of life, bo, and don't you forget ... "Women of pleasure" my foot. I used to think I was a classy dame up home and then I woke up one morning and found I was nothing but a goddam whore.'

'Ever been to New York?'

She shook her head. 'It ain't such a bad life if you keep away from drink and the pimps,' she said thoughtfully.

'I guess I'll shove off for New York right after Mardi Gras. I can't seem to find me a master in this man's town.'

'Mardi Gras ain't so much if you're broke.'

'Well, I came down here to see it and I guess I'd better see it.'

It was dawn when he left her. She came downstairs with him. He kissed her and told her he'd give her the ten bucks if she got his hat and coat back for him and she said to come around to her place that evening about six, but not to go back to the 'Tripoli' because that greaser was a bad egg and would be laying for him.

The streets of old stucco houses inset with lacy iron balconies were brimful of blue mist. A few mulatto women in bandanas were moving around in the courtyards. In the market old colored men were laying out fruit and green vegetables. When he got back to his flop the Panama woman was out on the gallery outside his room holding out a banana and calling 'Ven, Polly ... Ven, Polly,' in a little squeaky voice. The parrot sat on the edge of the tiled roof cocking a glassy eye at her and chuckling softly. 'Me here all right,' said the Panama woman with a tearful smile. 'Polly no quiere comer.' Charley climbed up by the shutter and tried to grab the parrot, but the parrot hitched away sideways up to the ridge of the roof and all Charley did was bring a tile down on his head. 'No quiere comer,' said the Panama woman sadly. Charley grinned at her and went into his room, where he dropped on the bed and fell asleep.

During Mardi Gras Charley walked round town till his feet were sore. There were crowds everywhere and lights and floats and parades and bands and girls running round in fancy dress. He picked up plenty of girls, but as soon as they found he was flat they dropped him. He was spending his money as slowly as he could. When he got hungry he'd drop into a bar and drink a glass of beer and eat as much free lunch as he dared.

The day after Mardi Gras the crowds began to thin out, and Charley didn't have any money for beer. He walked round feeling hungry and miserable; the smell of molasses and the absinthe smell from bars in the French Quarter in the heavy damp air made him feel sick. He didn't know what to do with himself. He didn't have the gumption to start off walking or hitchhiking again. He went to the Western Union and tried to wire Jim collect, but the guy said they wouldn't take a wire asking for money collect.

The Panama woman threw him out when he couldn't pay for another week in advance and there he was walking down Esplanade Avenue with Grassi's accordion on one arm and his little newspaper bundle of clothes under the other. He walked down the levee and sat down in a grassy place in the sun and thought for a long time. It was either throwing himself in the river or enlisting in the army. Then he suddenly thought of the accordion. An accordion was worth a lot of money. He left his bundle of clothes under some planks and walked around to all the hockshops he could find with the accordion, but they wouldn't give him more than fifteen bucks for it anywhere. By the time he'd been round to all the hockshops and musicstores, it was dark and everything had closed. He stumbled along the pavement feeling sick and dopy from hunger. At the corner of Canal and Rampart he stopped. Singing was coming out of a saloon. He got the hunch to go in and play *Funiculi funicula* on the accordion. He might get some free lunch and a glass of beer out of it.

He'd hardly started playing and the bouncer had just vaulted across the bar to give him the bum's rush, when a tall man sprawled at a table beckoned to him.

'Brother, you come right here an' set down.' It was a big man with a long broken nose and high cheekbones.

'Brother, you set down.' The bouncer went back behind the bar. 'Brother, you can't play that there accordeen no mor'n a rabbit. Ah'm nutten but a lowdown cracker from Okachobe City but if Ah couldn't play no better'n that . . .'

Charley laughed. 'I know I can't play it. That's all right.'

The Florida guy pulled out a big wad of bills. 'Brother, do you know what you're going to do? You're going to sell me the goddam thing. . . . Ah'm nothin' but a lowdown cracker, but, by Jesus Christ . . .'

'Hey, Doc, be yourself . . . You don't want the damn thing.' His friends tried to make him put his money back.

Doc swept his arm round with a gesture that shot three glasses onto the floor with a crash. 'You turkey-buzzards talk in your turn . . . Brother, how much do you want for the accordeen?' The bouncer had come back and was standing threateningly over the table. 'All right, Ben,' said Doc. 'It's all on your Uncle Henry . . . and let's have another round a that good rye whiskey. Brother, how much do you want for it?'

'Fifty bucks,' said Charley, thinking fast.

Doc handed him out five tens. Charley swallowed a drink, put the accordion on the table and went off in a hurry. He was afraid if he hung round the cracker 'ud sober up and try to get the money back, and besides he wanted to eat.

Next day he got a steerage passage on the steamer *Momus* bound for New York. The river was higher than the city. It was funny standing on the stern of the steamboat and looking down on the roofs and streets and trolleycars of New Orleans. When the steamer pulled out from the wharf Charley began to feel good. He found the colored steward and got him to give him a berth in the deckhouse. When he put his newspaper package under the pillow he glanced down into the berth below. There lay Doc, fast asleep, all dressed up in a light gray suit and a straw hat with a burntout cigar sticking out of the corner of his mouth and the accordion beside him.

They were passing between the Eads Jetties and feeling the seawind in their faces and the first uneasy swell of the Gulf under their feet when Doc came lurching on deck. He recognized Charley and went up to him with a big hand held out. 'Well, I'll be a sonofabitch if there ain't the musicmaker . . . That's a good accordeen, boy. Ah thought you'd imposed on me bein' only a poa country lad an' all that, but I'll be a sonofabitch if it ain't worth the money. Have a snifter on me?'

They went and sat on Doc's bunk and Doc broke out a bottle of Bacardi and they had some drinks and Charley told about how he'd been flat broke; if it wasn't for that fifty bucks he'd still be sitting on the levee and Doc said that if it wasn't for that fifty bucks he'd be riding firstclass.

Doc said he was going up to New York to sail for France in a volunteer ambulance corps; wasn't ever'day you got a chance to see a big war like that and he wanted to get in on it before the whole thing went bellyup; still he didn't like the idea of shooting a lot of whitemen he didn't have no quarrel with and reckoned this was the best way; if the Huns was niggers he'd feel different about it.

Charley said he was going to New York because he thought there were good chances of schooling in a big city like that and how he was an automobile mechanic and wanted to get to be a C.E. or something like that because there was no future for a working stiff without schooling.

Doc said that was all mahoula and what a boy like him ought to do was go and sign up as a mechanic in this here ambulance and they'd pay fifty dollars a month an' maybe more and that there was a lot of seeds on the other side and he'd ought to see the goddam war before the whole thing went bellyup.

Doc's name was William H. Rogers and he'd come from Michigan originally and his old man had been a grapefruit grower down at Frostproof and Doc had cashed in on a couple of good crops of vegetables off the Everglades muck and was going over to see the mademosels before the whole thing went bellyup.

They were pretty drunk by the time night fell and were sitting in the stern with a seedylooking man in a derby hat who said he was an Est from the Baltic. The Est and Doc and Charley got up on the little bridge above the afterhouse after supper; the wind had gone down and it was a starlight night with a slight roll and Doc said, 'By God, there's somethin' funny about this here boat . . . Befoa we went down to supper the Big Dipper was in the north and now it's gone right around to the southwest.'

'It is vat you vould expect of a kapitalistichesky society,' said the Est. When he found that Charley had a red card and that Doc didn't believe in shooting anything but niggers he made a big speech about how revolution had broken out in Russia and the Czar was being forced to abdicate and that was the beginning of the regeneration of mankind from the East. He said the Ests would get their independence and that soon all Europe would be the free sozialistichesky United States of Europe under the Red flag and Doc said, 'What did I tell yez, Charley? The friggin' business'll go bellyup soon . . . What you want to do is come with me an' see the war while it lasts.' And Charley said Doc was right and Doc said, 'I'll take you round with me, boy, an' all you need do's show your driver's license an' tell 'em you're a college student.'

The Est got sore at that and said that it was the duty of every classconscious worker to refuse to fight in this war and Doc said, 'We ain't goin' to fight, Esty old man. What we'll do is carry the boys out before they count out on 'em, see? I'd be a disappointed sonofabitch if the whole business had gone bellyup befoa we git there, wouldn't you, Charley?'

Then they argued some more about where the Dipper was and Doc kept saying it had moved to the south and when they'd finished the second quart, Doc was saying he didn't believe in white men shootin' each other up, only niggers, and started going round the boat lookin' for that damn shine steward to kill him just to prove it and the Est was singing *The Marseillaise* and Charley was telling everybody that what he wanted to do was to get in on the big war before it went belly-up. The Est and Charley had a hard time holding Doc down in his bunk when they put him to bed. He kept jumping out shouting he wanted to kill a couple of niggers.

They got into New York in a snowstorm. Doc said the Statue of Liberty looked like she had a white nightgown on. The Est looked around and hummed *The Marseillaise* and said American cities were not artistical because they did not have gables on the houses like in Baltic Europe.

When they got ashore Charley and Doc went to the Broadway Central Hotel together. Charley had never been in a big hotel like that and wanted to find a cheaper flop, but Doc insisted that he come along with him and said he had plenty of jack for both of them and that it was no use saving money because things would go bellyup soon. New York was full of grinding gears and clanging cars and the roar of the 'L' and newsboys crying extras. Doc lent Charley a good suit and took him down to the enlistment office of the ambulance corps that was in an important lawyer's office in a big shiny officebuilding down in the financial district. The gentleman who signed the boys up was a New York lawyer and he talked about their being gentlemen volunteers and behaving like gentlemen and being a credit to the cause of the Allies and the American flag and civilization that the brave French soldiers had been fighting for so many years in the trenches. When he found out Charley was a mechanic, he signed him up without waiting to write to the principal of the highschool and the pastor of the Lutheran church home in Fargo whose names he had given as references. He told them about getting antityphoid injections and a physical examination and said to call the next day to find out the sailing date. When they came out of the elevator there was a group of men in the shinymarble lobby with their heads bent over a newspaper; the U.S. was at war with Ger-

many. That night Charley wrote his mother that he was going
to the war and please send him fifty dollars. Then he and Doc
went out to look at the town.

There were flags on every building. They walked past business block after business block looking for Times Square.
Everywhere people were reading newspapers. At Fourteenth
they heard a drumbeat and a band and waited at the corner
to see what regiment it would be, but it was only the Salvation
Army. By the time they got to Madison Square it was the dinner
hour and the streets were deserted. It began to drizzle a little
and the flags up Broadway and Fifth Avenue hung limp from
their poles.

They went into the Hofbrau to eat. Charley thought it looked
too expensive, but Doc said it was his party. A man was on
a stepladder over the door screwing the bulbs into an electric
sign of an American flag. The restaurant was draped with
American flags inside and the band played *The Star-Spangled
Banner* every other number, so that they kept having to get
to their feet. 'What do they think this is, settin'up exercises?'
grumbled Doc.

There was one group at a round table in the corner that
didn't get up when the band played *The Star-Spangled Banner*,
but sat there quietly talking and eating as if nothing had
happened. People round the restaurant began to stare at them
and pass comments. 'I bet they're . . . Huns . . . German spies
. . . Pacifists.' There was an army officer at a table with a
girl who got red in the face whenever he looked at them.
Finally a waiter, an elderly German, went up to them and
whispered something.

'I'll be damned if I will,' came the voice from the table in the
corner. Then the army officer went over to them and said something about courtesy to our national anthem. He came away
redder in the face than ever. He was a little man with bowlegs
squeezed into brightly polished puttees. 'Dastardly pro-
Germans,' he sputtered as he sat down. Immediately he had
to get up because the band played *The Star-Spangled Banner*.
'Why don't you call the police, Cyril?' the girl who was with
him said. By this time people from all over the restaurant were
advancing on the round table.

Doc pulled Charley's chair around. 'Watch this; it's going to
be good.'

A big man with a Texas drawl yanked one of the men out
of his chair. 'You git up or git out.'

'You people have no right to interfere with us,' began one of the men at the round table. 'You express your approval of the war getting up, we express our disapproval by . . .'

There was a big woman with a red hat with a plume on it at the table who kept saying, 'Shut up; don't talk to 'em.' By this time the band had stopped. Everybody clapped as hard as he could and yelled, 'Play it again; that's right.' The waiters were running round nervously and the proprietor was in the center of the floor mopping his bald head.

The army officer went over to the orchestra leader and said, 'Please play our national anthem again.' At the first bar he came stiffly to attention. The other men rushed the round table. Doc and the man with the English accent were jostling each other. Doc squared off to hit him.

'Come outside if you want to fight,' the man with the English accent was saying.

'Leave 'em be, boys,' Doc was shouting. 'I'll take 'em on outside, two at a time.'

The table was upset and the party began backing off towards the door. The woman with the red hat picked up a bowl of lobster mayonnaise and was holding back the crowd by chucking handfuls of it in their faces. At that moment three cops appeared and arrested the damn pacifists. Everybody stood around wiping mayonnaise off his cothes. The band played *The Star-Spangled Banner* again and everybody tried to sing but it didn't make much of an effect because nobody knew the words.

After that Doc and Charley went to a bar to have a whiskey sour. Doc wanted to go to see a legshow and asked the barkeep. A little fat man with an American flag in the lapel of his coat overheard him and said the best legshow in New York was Minsky's on East Houston Street. He set them up to some drinks when Doc said they were going to see this here war, and said he'd take them down to Minsky's himself. His name was Segal and he said he'd been a Socialist up to the sinking of the *Lusitania*, but now he thought they ought to lick the Germans and destroy Berlin. He was in the cloak and suit business and was happy because he'd as good as landed a contract for army uniforms. 'Ve need the var to make men of us,' he'd say and strike himself on the chest. They went downtown in a taxi, but when they got to the burlesque show it was so full they couldn't get a seat.

'Standin' room, hell . . . Ah want women,' Doc was saying.

Mr Segal thought a little while with his head cocked to one side. 'Ve will go to "Little Hungary," ' he said.

Charley felt let down. He'd expected to have a good time in New York. He wished he was in bed. At 'Little Hungary' there were many German and Jewish and Russian girls. The wine came in funnylooking bottles upside down in a stand in the middle of each table. Mr Segal said it was his party from now on. The orchestra played foreign music. Doc was getting pretty drunk. They sat at a table crowded in among other tables. Charley roamed round and asked a girl to dance with him, but she wouldn't for some reason.

He got to talking to a young narrowfaced fellow at the bar who had just been to a peace meeting at Madison Square Garden. Charley pricked his ears up when the fellow said there'd be a revolution in New York if they tried to force conscription on the country. His name was Benny Compton and he'd been studying law at New York University. Charley went and sat with him at a table with another fellow who was from Minnesota and who was a reporter on *The Call*. Charley asked them about the chances of working his way through the engineering school. He'd about decided to back out of this ambulance proposition. But they didn't seem to think there was much chance if you hadn't any money saved up to start on. The Minnesota man said New York was no place for a poor man.

'Aw, hell; I guess I'll go to the war,' said Charley.

'It's the duty of every radical to go to jail first,' said Benny Compton. 'Anyway, there'll be a revolution. The workingclass won't stand for this much longer.'

'If you want to make some jack the thing to do is to go over to Bayonne and get a job in a munitions factory,' said the man from Minnesota in a tired voice.

'A man who does that is a traitor to his class,' said Benny Compton.

'A working stiff's in a hell of a situation,' said Charley. 'Damn it, I don't want to spend all my life patchin' up tin lizzies at seventyfive a month.'

'Didn't Eugene V. Debs say, "I want to rise with the ranks, not from them"?'

'After all, Benny, ain't you studyin' night an' day to get to be a lawyer an' get out of the workin'class?' said the man from Minnesota.

'That is so I can be of some use in the struggle . . . I want to be a wellsharpened instrument. We must fight capitalists with their own weapons.'

'I wonder what I'll do when they suppress *The Call*.'

'They won't dare suppress it.'

'Sure, they will. We're in this war to defend the Morgan loans . . . They'll use it to clear up opposition at home, sure as my name's Johnson.'

'Talking of that, I got some dope. My sister, see, she's a stenographer . . . She works for J. Ward Moorehouse, the public relations counsel, you know . . . he does propaganda for the Morgans and the Rockefellers. Well, she said that all this year he's been working with a French secret mission. The big interests are scared to death of a revolution in France. They paid him ten thousand dollars for his services. He runs pro-war stuff through a feature syndicate. And they call this a free country.'

'I wouldn't be surprised at anything,' said the man from Minnesota, pouring himself out the last of the bottle of wine. 'Why, any one of us may be a government agent or a spy right at this minute.' The three of them sat there looking at each other. It gave Charley chills down his spine.

'That's what I'm tryin' to tell ye . . . My sister, she knows all about it, see, on account of workin' in this guy's office . . . It's a plot of the big interests, Morgan an' them, to defeat the workers by sendin' 'em off to the war. Once they get you in the army you can't howl about civic liberty or the Bill of Rights . . . They can shoot you without trial, see?'

'It's an outrage . . . The people of the Northwest won't stand for it,' said the man from Minnesota. 'Look here, you've been out there more recently than I have. La Follette expresses the opinion of people out there, don't he?'

'Sure,' said Charley.

'Well, what the hell?'

'It's too deep for me,' said Charley, and started working his way among the closepacked tables to find Doc. Doc was pretty drunk, and Charley was afraid the evening would start running into money, so they said goodbye to Mr Segal who said please to kill a lot of Germans just for him, and they went out and started walking west along Houston Street. There were pushcarts all along the curb with flares that made the packed faces along the sidewalk glow red in the rainy darkness.

They came out at the end of a wide avenue crowded with people pouring out from a theater. In front of the Cosmopolitan Café a man was speaking on a soapbox. As the people came out of the theater they surged around him. Doc and Charley edged their way through to see what the trouble was. They could only catch scraps of what the man was shouting in a hoarse barking voice:

'A few days ago I was sittin' in the Cooper Institute listenin' to Eugene Victor Debs, and what was he sayin'? . . . "What is this civilization, this democracy that the bosses are asking you workers to give your lives to save, what does it mean to you except wageslavery, what is . . . ?" '

'Hey, shut up, youse . . . If you don't like it go back where you came from,' came voices from the crowd.

'Freedom to work so that the bosses can get rich . . . Opportunity to starve to death if you get fired from your job.'

Doc and Charley were shoved from behind. The man toppled off his box and disappeared. The whole end of the avenue filled with a milling crowd. Doc was sparring with a big man in overalls. A cop came between them hitting right and left with his billy. Doc hauled off to slam the cop, but Charley caught his arm and pulled him out of the scrimmage.

'Hey, for crissake, Doc, this ain't the war yet,' said Charley.

Doc was red in the face. 'Ah didn't like that guy's looks,' he said.

Behind the cops two policedepartment cars with big searchlights were charging the crowd. Arms, heads, hats, jostling shoulders, riotsticks rising and falling stood out black against the tremendous white of the searchlights. Charley pulled Doc against the plateglass window of the café.

'Say, Doc, we don't want to get in the can and lose the boat,' Charley whispered in his ear.

'What's the use?' said Doc. 'It'll all go bellyup before we get there.'

'Today the voikers run before the cops, but soon it will be the cops run before the voikers,' someone yelled. Someone else started singing *The Marseillaise*. Voices joined. Doc and Charley were jammed with their shoulders against the plateglass. Behind them the café was full of faces swimming in blue crinkly tobaccosmoke like fish in an aquarium. The plateglass suddenly smashed. People in the café were hopping to their feet. 'Look out for the Cossacks,' a voice yelled.

A cordon of cops was working down the avenue. The empty pavement behind them widened. The other way mounted police were coming out of Houston Street. In the open space a patrolwagon parked. Cops were shoving men and women into it.

Doc and Charley ducked past a mounted policeman who was trotting his horse with a great clatter down the inside of the sidewalk, and shot round the corner. The Bowery was empty and dark. They walked west towards the hotel.

'My God,' said Charley, 'you almost got us locked up that time . . . I'm all set to go to France now, and I wanter go.'

A week later they were on the *Chicago* of the French Line steaming out through the Narrows. They had hangovers from their farewell party and felt a little sick from the smell of the boat and still had the music of the jazzband on the wharf ringing through their heads. The day was overcast, with a low lid of leaden clouds, looked like it was going to snow. The sailors were French and the stewards were French. They had wine with their first meal. There was a whole tableful of other guys going over in the ambulance service.

After dinner Doc went down to the cabin to go to sleep. Charley roamed around the ship with his hands in his pockets without knowing what to do with himself. In the stern they were taking the canvas cover off the seventyfive gun. He walked round the lowerdeck full of barrels and packingcases and stumbled across coils of big fuzzy cable to the bow. In the bow there was a little pinkfaced French sailor with a red tassel on his cap stationed as a lookout.

The sea was glassy, with dirty undulating patches of weed and garbage. There were gulls sitting on the water or perched on bits of floating wood. Now and then a gull stretched its wings lazily and flew off crying.

The boat's bluff bow cut two even waves through dense glassgreen water. Charley tried to talk to the lookout. He pointed ahead. 'East,' he said, 'France.'

The lookout paid no attention. Charley pointed back towards the smoky west. 'West,' he said and tapped himself on the chest. 'My home Fargo, North Dakota.' But the lookout just shook his head and put his finger to his lips.

'France very far east . . . submarines . . . war,' said Charley. The lookout put his hand over his mouth. At last he made Charley understand that he wasn't supposed to talk to him.

# Nineteen Nineteen

# Newsreel 20

*Oh the infantree the infantree*
*With the dirt behind their ears*

## ARMIES CLASH AT VERDUN IN GLOBE'S GREATEST BATTLE

## 150,000 MEN AND WOMEN PARADE

but another question and a very important one is raised. The New York Stock Exchange is today the only free securities market in the world. If it maintains that position it is sure to become perhaps the world's greatest center for the marketing of

## BRITISH FLEET SENT TO SEIZE GOLDEN HORN

*The cavalree artilleree*
*And the goddammed engineers*
*Will never beat the infantree*
*In eleven thousand years*

## TURKS FLEE BEFORE TOMMIES AT GALLIPOLI

when they return home what will our war veterans think of the American who babbles about some vague new order, while dabbling in the sand of shoal water? From his weak folly they who lived through the spectacle will recall the vast new No Man's Land of Europe reeking with murder and the lust of rapine, aflame with the fires of revolution

## STRIKING WAITERS ASK AID OF WOMEN

*Oh the oak and the ash and the weeping willow tree*
*And green grows the grass in North Amerikee*

coincident with a position of that kind will be the

bringing from abroad of vast quantities of money for the purposes of maintaining balances in this country

*When I think of the flag which our ships carry, the only touch of color about them, the only thing that moves as if it had a settled spirit in it – in their solid structure; it seems to me I see alternate strips of parchment upon which are written the rights of liberty and justice and strips of blood spilt to vindicate these rights, and then – in the corner a prediction of the blue serene into which every nation may swim which stands for these things.*

*Oh we'll nail Old Glory to the top of the pole*
*And we'll all reenlist in the pig's a—h—*

## Joe Williams

Joe Williams put on the secondhand suit and dropped his uniform, with a cobblestone wrapped up in it, off the edge of the dock into the muddy water of the basin. It was noon. There was nobody around. He felt bad when he found he didn't have the cigarbox with him. Back in the shed he found it where he'd left it. It was a box that had once held Flor de Mayo cigars he'd bought when he was drunk in Guantanamo. In the box under the goldpaper lace were Janey's highschool graduation picture, a snapshot of Alec with his motorcycle, a picture with the signatures of the coach and all the players of the whole highschool junior team that he was captain of all in baseball clothes, an old pink almost faded snapshot of his dad's tug, the *Mary B. Sullivan*, taken off the Virginia Capes with a full-rigged ship in tow, an undressed postcard picture of a girl named Antoinette he'd been with in Villefranche, some safety-razor blades, a postcard photo of himself and two other guys, all gobs in white suits, taken against the background of a Moorish arch in Malaga, a bunch of foreign stamps, a package of Merry Widows, and ten little pink and red shells he'd picked up on the beach at Santiago. With the box tucked right under his arm, feeling crummy in the baggy civies, he walked slowly out to the beacon and watched the fleet in formation steaming down the River Plate. The day was overcast; the lean cruisers soon blurred into their trailing smokesmudges.

Joe stopped looking at them and watched a rusty tramp come in. She had a heavy list to port and you could see the hull below the waterline green and slimy with weed. There was a blue and white Greek flag on the stern and a dingy yellow quarantine flag halfway up the fore.

A man who had come up behind him said something to Joe in Spanish. He was a smiling ruddy man in blue denims and was smoking a cigar, but for some reason he made Joe feel panicky. 'No savvy,' Joe said and walked away and out between the warehouses into the streets back of the waterfront.

He had trouble finding Maria's place, all the blocks looked so much alike. It was by the mechanical violin in the window that he recognized it. Once he got inside the stuffy anisesmelling dump he stood a long time at the bar with one hand round a sticky beerglass looking out at the street he could see in bright streaks through the beadcurtain that hung in the door. Any minute he expected the white uniform and yellow holster of a marine to go past.

Behind the bar a yellow youth with a crooked nose leaned against the wall looking at nothing. When Joe made up his mind he jerked his chin up. The youth came over and craned confidentially across the bar, leaning on one hand and swabbing at the oilcloth with the rag he held in the other. The flies that had been grouped on the rings left by the beerglasses on the oilcloth flew up to join the buzzing mass on the ceiling. 'Say, bo, tell Maria I want to see her,' Joe said out of the corner of his mouth. The youth behind the bar held up two fingers. 'Dos pesos,' he said. 'Hell, no, I only want to talk to her.'

Maria beckoned to him from the door in back. She was a sallow woman with big eyes set far apart in bluish sacks. Through the crumpled pink dress tight over the bulge of her breasts Joe could make out the rings of crinkled flesh round the nipples. They sat down at a table in the back room.

'Gimme two beers,' Joe yelled through the door.

'Watta you wan', iho de mi alma?' asked Maria.

'You savvy Doc Sidner?'

'Sure me savvy all yanki. Watta you wan' you no go wid beeg sheep?'

'No go wid beeg sheep . . . Fight wid beeg sonofabeech, see?'

'Ché!' Maria's breasts shook like jelly when she laughed. She put a fat hand at the back of his neck and drew his face towards her. 'Poor baby . . . black eye.'

'Sure he gave me a black eye.' Joe pulled away from her. 'Petty officer. I knocked him cold, see . . . Navy's no place for me after that . . . I'm through. Say, Doc said you knew a guy could fake A.B. certificates . . . able seaman savvy? Me for the Merchant Marine from now on, Maria.'

Joe drank down his beer.

She sat shaking her head saying, 'Ché . . . pobrecito . . . Ché.' Then she said in a tearful voice, ' 'Ow much dollars you got?'

'Twenty,' said Joe.

'Heem want fiftee.'

'I guess I'm f — d for fair then.'

Maria walked round to the back of his chair and put a fat arm round his neck, leaning over him with little clucking noises. 'Wait a minute, we tink . . . sabes?' Her big breast pressing against his neck and shoulder made him feel itchy; he didn't like her touching him in the morning when he was sober like this. But he sat there until she suddenly let out a parrot screech. 'Paquito . . . ven acá.'

A dirty pearshaped man with a red face and neck came in from the back. They talked Spanish over Joe's head. At last she patted his cheek and said, 'Awright Paquito sabe where heem live . . . maybe heem take twenty, sabes?'

Joe got to his feet. Paquito took off the smudged cook's apron and lit a cigarette. 'You savvy A.B. papers?' said Joe walking up and facing him. He nodded, 'Awright.' Joe gave Maria a hug and a little pinch. 'You're a good girl, Maria.' She followed them grinning to the door of the bar.

Outside Joe looked sharply up and down the street. Not a uniform. At the end of the street a crane tilted black above the cement warehouse buildings. They got on a streetcar and rode a long time without saying anything. Joe sat staring at the floor with his hands dangling between his knees until Paquito poked him. They got out in a cheaplooking suburban section of new cement houses already dingy. Paquito rang at a door like all the other doors and after a while a man with redrimmed eyes and big teeth like a horse came and opened it. He and Paquito talked Spanish a long while through the halfopen door. Joe stood first on one foot and then on the other. He could tell that they were sizing up how much they could get out of him by the way they looked at him sideways as they talked.

He was just about to break in when the man in the door spoke to him in cracked cockney. 'You give the blighter five pesos for his trouble, mytey, an' we'll settle this hup between wahte men.' Joe shelled out what silver he had in his pocket and Paquito went.

Joe followed the limey into the front hall that smelt of cabbage and frying grease and wash day. When he got inside he put his hand on Joe's shoulder and said, blowing stale whiskeybreath in his face, 'Well, mytey, 'ow much can you afford?' Joe drew away. 'Twenty American dollars's all I got,' he said through his teeth. The limey shook his head, 'Only four quid . . . well, there's no 'arm in seein' what we can do, is there, mytey? Let's see it.' While the limey stood looking at him Joe took off his belt, picked out a couple of stitches with the small blade of his jackknife and pulled out two orangebacked American bills folded long. He unfolded them carefully and was about to hand them over when he thought better of it and put them in his pocket. 'Now let's take a look at the paper,' he said, grinning.

The limey's redrimmed eyes looked tearful; he said we ought to be 'elpful one to another and gryteful when a bloke risked a forger's hend to 'elp 'is fellow creature. Then he asked Joe his name, age and birthplace, how long he'd been to sea and all that and went into an inside room, carefully locking the door after him.

Joe stood in the hall. There was a clock ticking somewhere. The ticks dragged slower and slower. At last Joe heard the key turn in the lock and the limey came out with two papers in his hand. 'You oughter realize what I'm doin' for yez, mytey . . .' Joe took the paper. He wrinkled his forehead and studied it; looked all right to him. The other paper was a note authorizing Titterton's Marine Agency to garnishee Joe's pay monthly until the sum of ten pounds had been collected. 'But look here you,' he said, 'that makes seventy dollars I'm shelling out.' The limey said think of the risk he was tyking and 'ow times was 'ard and that arfter all he could tyke it or leave it. Joe followed him into the paperlittered inside room and leaned over the desk and signed with a fountain pen.

They went downtown on the streetcar and got off at Rivadavia Street. Joe followed the limey into a small office back of a warehouse. ' 'Ere's a smart young 'and for you, Mr McGregor,' the limey said to a biliouslooking Scotchman who was walking up and down chewing his nails.

Joe and Mr McGregor looked at each other. 'American?' 'Yes.' 'You're not expectin' American pay I'm supposin'?'

The limey went up to him and whispered something; Mc-

Gregor looked at the certificate and seemed satisfied. 'All right, sign in the book . . . Sign under the last name.' Joe signed and handed the limey the twenty dollars. That left him flat. 'Well, cheeryoh, mytey.' Joe hesitated a moment before he took the limey's hand. 'So long,' he said.

'Go get your dunnage and be back here in an hour,' said McGregor in a rasping voice. 'Haven't got any dunnage. I've been on the beach,' said Joe, weighing the cigarbox in his hand. 'Wait outside then and I'll take you aboard the *Argyle* by and by.' Joe stood for a while in the warehouse door looking out into the street. Hell, he'd seen enough of B.A. He sat on a packingcase marked Tibbett & Tibbett, Enameled Ware, Blackpool, to wait for Mr McGregor, wondering if he was the skipper or the mate. Time sure would drag all right till he got out of B.A.

## The Camera Eye (28)

when the telegram came that she was dying (the streetcar wheels screeched round the bellglass like all the pencils on all the slates in all the schools) walking around Fresh Pond the smell of puddlewater willowbuds in the raw wind shrieking streetcar wheels rattling on loose trucks through the Boston suburbs   grief isn't a uniform and go shock the Booch and drink wine for supper at the Lenox before catching the Federal

*I'm so tired of violets*
*Take them all away*

when the telegram came that she was dying the bellglass cracked in a screech of slate pencils   (have you ever never been able to sleep for a week in April?)   and He met me in the gray trainshed my eyes were stinging with vermillion bronze and chromegreen inks that oozed from the spinning April hills   His mustaches were white the tired droop of an old man's cheeks   She's gone Jack grief isn't a uniform and the   in the parlor   the waxen odor of lilies in the parlor   (He and I we must bury the uniform of grief)

then the riversmell the shimmering Potomac reaches
the little choppysilver waves at Indian Head   there were
mockingbirds in the graveyard and the roadsides steamed
with spring   April enough to shock the world

when the cable came that He was dead I walked
through the streets full of fiveoclock Madrid seething with
twilight in shivered cubes of aguardiente redwine gaslamp-
green sunsetpink tileochre   eyes lips red cheeks brown
pillar of the throat   climbed on the night train at the
Notre station without knowing why

> *I'm so tired of violets*
> *Take them all away*

the shattered iridescent bellglass the carefully copied
busts the architectural details the grammar of styles.
        it was the end of that book and I left Oxford poets in
the little noisy room that smelt of stale olive oil in the Pension Boston   Ahora   Now   Maintenant   Vita Nuova
but we
        who had heard Copey's beautiful reading voice and
read the handsomely bound books and breathed deep
(breathe deep one two three four) of the waxwork lilies
and the artificial parmaviolet scent under the ethercone and
sat breakfasting in the library where the bust was of
Octavius
        were now dead at the cableoffice
        on the rumblebumping wooden bench on the train
slamming through midnight climbing up from the steerage
to get a whiff of Atlantic on the lunging steamship (the
ovalfaced Swiss girl and her husband were my friends) she
had slightly popeyes and a little gruff way of saying *Zut
alors* and throwing us a little smile a fish to a sealion that
warmed our darkness   when the immigration officer came
for her passport he couldn't send her to Ellis Island la
grippe espagnole she was dead

washing those windows
K.P.

cleaning the sparkplugs with a pocketknife
A.W.O.L.

grinding the American Beauty roses to dust in that
whore's bed   (the foggy night flamed with proclamations
of the League of the Rights of Man)   the almond smell of
high explosives sending singing éclats through the sweetish
puking grandiloquence of the rotting dead

tomorrow I hoped would be the first day of the first
month of the first year

## *Playboy*

Jack Reed
was the son of a United States Marshal, a prominent
citizen of Portland Oregon
He was a likely boy
so his folks sent him East to school
and to Harvard.
Harvard stood for the broad 'a' and those contacts so
useful in later life and good English prose . . . if the hedgehog
can't be cultured at Harvard the hedgehog can't
at all and the Lowells only speak to the Cabots and the
Cabots
and the Oxford Book of Verse.
Reed was a likely youngster, he wasn't a Jew or a Socialist
and he didn't come from Roxbury; he was husky greedy had
appetite for everything: a man's got to like many things in his
life.
Reed was a man; he liked men he liked women he liked
eating and writing and foggy nights and drinking and foggy
nights and swimming and football and rhymed verse and being
cheerleader ivy orator making clubs (not the very best clubs,
his blood didn't run thin enough for the very best clubs)
and Copey's voice reading *The Man Who Would be King*,
the dying fall *Urnburial*, good English prose the lamps coming
on across the Yard, under the elms in the twilight
dim voices in lecturehalls,
the dying fall the elms the Discobulus the bricks of the
old buildings and the commemorative gates and the goodies

and the deans and the instructors all crying in thin voices refrain,

refrain; the rusty machinery creaked, the deans quivered under their mortarboards, the cogs turned to Class Day, and Reed was out in the world:

Washington Square!
Conventional turns out to be a cussword;
Villon seeking a lodging for the night in the Italian tenements on Sullivan Street, Bleecker, Carmine;
research proves R.L.S. to have been a great cocksman,
and as for the Elizabethans
to hell with them.
Ship on a cattleboat and see the world have adventures you can tell funny stories about every evening; a man's got to love . . . the quickening pulse the feel that today in foggy evenings footsteps taxicabs women's eyes . . . many things in his life.
Europe with a dash of horseradish, gulp Paris like an oyster;
but there's more to it than the Oxford Book of English Verse. Linc Steffens talked the co-operative commonwealth.
revolution in a voice as mellow as Copey's, Diogenes Steffens with Marx for a lantern going through the west looking for a good man, Socrates Steffens kept asking why not revolution?

Jack Reed wanted to live in a tub and write verses;
but he kept meeting bums workingmen husky guys he liked out of luck out of work why not revolution?
He couldn't keep his mind on his work with so many people out of luck;
in school hadn't he learned the Declaration of Independence by heart? Reed was a Westerner and words meant what they said; when he said something standing with a classmate at the Harvard Club bar, he meant what he said from the soles of his feet to the waves of his untidy hair (his blood didn't run thin enough for the Harvard Club and the Dutch Treat Club and respectable New York freelance Bohemia).
Life, liberty, and the pursuit of happiness;
not much of that round the silkmills when
in nineteen-thirteen,
he went over to Paterson to write up the strike, textile

workers parading beaten up by the cops, the strikers in jail;
before he knew it he was a striker parading beaten up by the
cops in jail;

> he wouldn't let the editor bail him out, he'd learn more
with the strikers in jail.

> He learned enough to put on the pageant of the Paterson
Strike in Madison Square Garden.

> He learned the hope of a new society where nobody would
be out of luck.

> why not revolution?

> The *Metropolitan Magazine* sent him to Mexico
to write up Pancho Villa.

> Pancho Villa taught him to write and the skeleton moun-
tains and the tall organ cactus and the armored trains and the
bands playing in little plazas full of dark girls in blue scarfs

> and the bloody dust and the ping of rifleshots

> in the enormous night of the desert, and the brown quiet-
voiced peons dying starving killing for liberty

> for land for water for schools.

> Mexico taught him to write.

> Reed was a Westerner and words meant what they said.

> The war was a blast that blew out all the Diogenes
lanterns;

> the good men began to gang up to call for machineguns.
Jack Reed was the last of the great race of warcorrespondents
who ducked under censorships and risked their skins for a
story.

> Jack Reed was the best American writer of his time, if
anybody had wanted to know about the war they could have
read about it in the articles he wrote

> about the German front,

> the Serbian retreat,

> Saloniki;

> behind the lines in the tottering empire of the Czar,

> dodging the secret police,

> jail in Cholm.

> The brasshats wouldn't let him go to France because they
said one night in the German trenches kidding with the Boche
guncrew he'd pulled the string on a Hun gun pointed at the
heart of France . . . playboy stuff but after all what did it

matter who fired the guns or which way they were pointed?
Reed was with the boys who were being blown to hell,
    with the Germans the French the Russians the Bulgarians
the seven little tailors in the Ghetto in Salonique,
      and in nineteen-seventeen
      he was with the soldiers and peasants
      in Petrograd in October:
      Smolny,
      *Ten Days That Shook the World;*


    no more Villa picturesque Mexico, no more Harvard
Club playboy stuff, plans for Greek theaters, rhyming verse,
good stories of an oldtime warcorrespondent,
    this wasn't fun anymore
    this was grim.


    Delegate,
    back in the States indictments, the Masses trial, the Wobbly
trial, Wilson cramming the jails,
    forged passports, speeches, secret documents, riding the
rods across the cordon sanitaire, hiding in the bunkers on
steamboats;
    jail in Finland all his papers stolen,
    no more chance to write verses now, no more warm chats
with every guy you met up with, the college boy with the nice
smile talking himself out of trouble with the judge;
    at the Harvard Club they're all in the Intelligence Service
making the world safe for the Morgan-Baker-Stillman combination of banks;
    that old tramp sipping his coffee out of a tomatocan's a
spy of the General Staff.
    The world's no fun anymore,
    only machinegunfire and arson
    starvation lice bedbugs cholera typhus
    no lint for bandages no chloroform or ether thousands
dead of gangrened wounds cordon sanitaire and everywhere
spies.
    The windows of Smolny glow whitehot like a bessemer,
    no sleep in Smolny,
    Smolny the giant rollingmill running twentyfour hours a
day rolling out men nations hopes millenniums impulses fears,
    rawmaterial

for the foundations
of a new society.

A man has to do many things in his life.
Reed was a Westerner words meant what they said.
He threw everything he had and himself into Smolny,
dictatorship of the proletariat;
U.S.S.R.
The first workers republic
was established and stands.
Reed wrote, undertook missions (there were spies everywhere), worked till he dropped,
     caught typhus and died in Moscow.

## Joe Williams

Twentyfive days at sea on the steamer *Argyle*, Glasgow, Captain Thompson, loaded with hides, chipping rust, daubing red lead on steel plates that were sizzling hot, griddles in the sun, painting the stack from dawn to dark, pitching and rolling in the heavy dirty swell; bedbugs in the bunks in the stinking fo'c'stle, slumgullion for grub, with potatoes full of eyes and moldy beans, cockroaches mashed on the messtable, but a tot of limejuice every day in accordance with the regulations; then sickening rainy heat and Trinidad blue in the mist across the ruddy water.

Going through the Boca it started to rain and the islands heaped with ferny parisgreen foliage went gray under the downpour. By the time they got her warped into the wharf at Port of Spain, everybody was soaked to the skin with rain and sweat. Mr McGregor, striding up and down in a sou'wester purple in the face, lost his voice from the heat and had to hiss out his orders in a mean whisper. Then the curtain of the rain lifted, the sun came out and everything steamed. Apart from the heat everybody was sore because there was talk that they were going up to the Pitch Lake to load asphaltum.

Next day nothing happened. The hides in the forward hold stank when they unbattened the hatches. Clothes and bedding, hung out to dry in the torrid glare of sun between showers, was always getting soaked again before they could get it in. While it was raining there was nowhere you could keep dry; the awning over the deck ripped continually.

In the afternoon, Joe's watch got off, though it wasn't much use going ashore because nobody had gotten any pay. Joe found himself sitting under a palmtree on a bench in a sort of a park near the waterfront staring at his feet. It began to rain and he ducked under an awning in front of a bar. There were electric fans in the bar; a cool whiff of limes and rum and whiskey in iced drinks wafted out through the open door. Joe was thirsty for a beer, but he didn't have a red cent. The rain hung like a beadcurtain at the edge of the awning.

Standing beside him was a youngish man in a white suit and a panama hat, who looked like an American. He glanced at Joe several times, then he caught his eye and smiled. 'Are you an Am-m-merican,' he said. He stuttered a little when he talked.

'I am that,' said Joe.

There was a pause. Then the man held out his hand. 'Welcome to our city,' he said.

Joe noticed that he had a slight edge on. The man's palm was soft when he shook his hand. Joe didn't like the way his handshake felt.

'You live here?' he asked.

The man laughed. He had blue eyes and a round poutlipped face that looked friendly. 'Hell no . . . I'm only here for a couple of days on this West India cruise. Much b-b-better have saved my money and stayed home. I wanted to go to Europe but you c-c-can't on account of the war.'

'Yare, that's all they talk about on the bloody limejuicer I'm on, the war.'

'Why they brought us to this hole I can't imagine and now there's something the matter with the boat and we can't leave for two days.'

'That must be the *Monterey*.'

'Yes. It's a terrible boat, nothing on board but women. I'm glad to run into a fellow I can talk to. Seems to be nothing but niggers down here.'

'Looks like they had 'em all colors in Trinidad.'

'Say, this rain isn't going to stop for a hell of a time. Come in and have a drink with me.'

Joe looked at him suspiciously. 'All right,' he said finally, 'but I might as well tell you right now I can't treat you back . . . I'm flat and those goddam Scotchmen won't advance us any pay.'

'You're a sailor, aren't you?' asked the man when they got to the bar.

'I work on a boat, if that's what you mean.'

'What'll you have . . . They make a fine Planter's punch here. Ever tried that?'

'I'll drink a beer . . . I usually drink beer.'

The barkeeper was a broadfaced Chink with a heartbroken smile like a very old monkey's. He put the drinks down before them very gently as if afraid of breaking the glasses.

The beer was cold and good in its dripping glass. Joe drank it off. 'Say, you don't know any baseball scores, do you? Last time I saw a paper looked like the Senators had a chance for the pennant.'

The man took off his panama hat and mopped his brow with a handkerchief. He had curly black hair. He kept looking at Joe as if he was making up his mind about something. Finally he said, 'Say, my name's . . . Wa-wa-wa . . . Warner Jones.'

'They call me Yank on the *Argyle* . . . In the navy they called me Slim.'

'So you were in the navy, were you? I thought you looked more like a jackie than a merchant seaman, Slim.'

'That so?'

The man who said his name was Jones ordered two more of the same. Joe was worried. But what the hell, they can't arrest a guy for a deserter on British soil. 'Say, did you say you knew anything about the baseball scores? The leagues must be pretty well under way by now.'

'I got the papers up at the hotel . . . like to look at them?'

'I sure would.'

The rain stopped. The pavement was already dry when they came out of the bar.

'Say, I'm going to take a ride around this island. Tell me you can see wild monkeys and all sorts of things. Why don't you come along? I'm bored to death of sightseeing by myself.'

Joe thought a minute. 'These clothes ain't fit . . .'

'What the hell, this isn't Fifth Avenue. Come ahead.' The man who said his name was Jones signaled a nicely polished Ford driven by a young Chinaman. The Chinaman wore glasses and a dark blue suit and looked like a college student; he talked with an English accent. He said he'd drive them round the town and out to the Blue Pool. As they were setting off the man who said his name was Jones said, 'Wait a minute,' and ran in the bar and got a flask of Planter's Punch.

He talked a blue streak all the time they were driving out past the British bungalows and brick institution buildings and after that out along the road through rubbery blue woods so dense and steamy it seemed to Joe there must be a glass roof overhead somewhere. He said how he liked adventure and travel and wished he was free to ship on boats and bum around and see the world and that it must be wonderful to depend only on your own sweat and muscle the way Joe was doing. Joe said, 'Yare?' But the man who said his name was Jones paid no attention and went right on and said how he had to take care of his mother and that was a great responsibility and sometimes he thought he'd go mad and he'd been to a doctor about it and the doctor had advised him to take a trip, but that the food wasn't any good on the boat and gave him indigestion and it was all full of old women with daughters they wanted to marry off and it made him nervous having women run after him like that. The worst of it was not having a friend to talk to about whatever he had on his mind when he got lonely. He wished he had a nice goodlooking fellow who'd been around and wasn't a softy and knew what life was and could appreciate beauty for a friend, a fellow like Joe in fact. His mother was awfully jealous and didn't like the idea of his having any intimate friends and would always get sick or try to hold out on his allowance when she found out about his having any friends, because she wanted him to be always tied to her apronstrings, but he was sick and tired of that and from now on he was going to do what he damn pleased, and she didn't have to know about everything he did anyway.

He kept giving Joe cigarettes and offering them to the Chinaman who said each time, 'Thank you very much, sir. I have forgone smoking.' Between them they had finished the flask of punch and the man who said his name was Jones was beginning to edge over towards Joe in the seat, when the Chinaman stopped the car at the end of a little path and said, 'If you wish to view the Blue Pool you must walk up there almost seven minutes, sir. It is the principal attraction of the island of Trinidad.'

Joe hopped out of the car and went to make water beside a big tree with shaggy red bark. The man who said his name was Jones came up beside him. 'Two minds with but a single thought,' he said. Joe said, 'Yare,' and went and asked the Chinaman where they could see some monkeys.

'The Blue Pool,' said the Chinaman, 'is one of their favorite resorts.' He got out of the car and walked around it looking intently with his black beads of eyes into the foliage over their heads. Suddenly he pointed. Something black was behind a shaking bunch of foliage. A screechy giggle came from behind it and three monkeys went off flying from branch to branch with long swinging leaps. In a second they were gone and all you could see was the branches stirring at intervals through the woods where they jumped. One of them had a pinkish baby monkey hanging on in front. Joe was tickled. He'd never seen monkeys really wild like that before. He went off up the path, walking fast so that the man who said his name was Jones had trouble keeping up to him. Joe wanted to see some more monkeys.

After a few minutes' walk uphill he began to hear a waterfall. Something made him think of Great Falls and Rock Creek and he went all soft inside. There was a pool under a waterfall hemmed in by giant trees.

'Dod gast it, I've got a mind to take me a dip,' he said.

'Wouldn't there be snakes, Slim?'

'Snakes won't bother you, 'less you bother 'em first.'

But when they got right up to the pool they saw that there were people picnicking there, girls in light pink and blue dresses, two or three men in white ducks, grouped under striped umbrellas. Two Hindoo servants were waiting on them, bringing dishes out of a hamper. Across the pool came the chirp-chirp of cultivated English voices.

'Shoot, we can't go swimmin' here and they won't be any monkeys either.'

'Suppose we joined them . . . I might introduce myself and you would be my kid brother. I've got a letter to a Colonel Somebody, but I felt too blue to present it.'

'What the hell do they want to be fartin' around here for?' said Joe and started back down the path again. He didn't see any more monkeys and by the time he'd got back to the car big drops had started to fall.

'That'll spoil their goddam picnic,' he said, grinning to the man who said his name was Jones when he came up, the sweat running in streams down his face.

'My, you're a fast walker, Slim.' He puffed and patted him on the back.

Joe got into the car. 'I guess we're goin' to get it.'

'Sirs,' said the Chinaman, 'I will return to the city, for I perceive that a downpour is imminent.'

By the time they'd gone half a mile it was raining so hard the Chinaman couldn't see to drive. He ran the car into a small shed on the side of the road. The rain pounding on the tin roof overhead sounded loud as a steamboat letting off steam. The man who said his name was Jones started talking; he had to yell to make himself heard above the rain. 'I guess you see some funny sights, Slim, leading the life you lead.'

Joe got out of the car and stood facing the sudden curtain of rain; the spray in his face felt almost cool. The man who said his name was Jones sidled up to him, holding out a cigarette. 'How do you like it in the navy?'

Joe took the cigarette, lit it and said, 'Not so good.'

'I've been friends with lots of navy boys . . . I suppose you liked raising cain on shore leave, didn't you?'

Joe said he didn't usually have much pay to raise cain with, used to play ball sometimes, that wasn't so bad.

'But, Slim, I thought sailors didn't care what they did when they got in port.'

'I guess some of the boys try to paint the town red, but they don't usually have enough jack to get very far.'

'Maybe you and I can paint the town red in Port of Spain, Slim.'

Joe shook his head. 'No, I gotta go back on board ship.'

The rain increased till the tin roof roared so Joe couldn't hear what the man who said his name was Jones was trying to say, then slackened and stopped entirely.

'Well, at least you come up to my room in the hotel, Slim, and we'll have a couple of drinks. Nobody knows me here. I can do anything I like.'

'I'd like to see the sports page of that paper from home if you don't mind.'

They got into the car and rode back to town along roads brimmed with water like canals. The sun came out hot and everything was in a blue steam. It was late afternoon. The streets of the town were crowded; Hindoos with turbans, Chinks in natty Hart Schaffner and Marx clothes, redfaced white men dressed in white, raggedy shines of all colors.

Joe felt uncomfortable going through the lobby of the hotel in his dungarees, pretty wet at that, and he needed a shave. The man who said his name was Jones put his arm over his shoulders going up the stairs. His room was big with tall narrow shuttered windows and smelt of bay rum.

'My, but I'm hot and wet,' he said. 'I'm going to take a

shower . . . but first we'd better ring for a couple of ginfizzes.
. . . Don't you want to take your clothes off and take it easy?
His skin's about as much clothes as a fellow can stand in this
weather.'

Joe shook his head, 'They stink too much,' he said. 'Say,
have you got them papers?'

The Hindoo servant came with the drinks while the man
who said his name was Jones was in the bathroom. Joe took
the tray. There was something about the expression of the
Hindoo's thin mouth and black eyes looking at something
behind you in the room that made Joe sore. He wanted to hit
the tobaccocolored bastard. The man who said his name was
Jones came back looking cool in a silk bathrobe.

'Sit down, Slim, and we'll have a drink and a chat.' The man
ran his fingers gently over his forehead as if it ached and
through his curly black hair and settled in an armchair. Joe
sat down in a straight chair across the room. 'My, I think this
heat would be the end of me if I stayed a week in this place. I
don't see how you stand it, doing manual work and everything.
You must be pretty tough!'

Joe wanted to ask about the newspapers, but the man who
said his name was Jones was talking again, saying how he
wished he was tough, seeing the world like that, meeting all
kinds of fellows, going to all kinds of joints, must see some
funny sights, must be funny all these fellows bunking together
all these days at sea, rough and tumble, hey? and then nights
ashore, raising cain, painting the town red, several fellows with
one girl. 'If I was living like that, I wouldn't care what I did, no
reputation to lose, no danger of somebody trying to blackmail
you, only have to be careful to keep out of jail, hay? Why,
Slim, I'd like to go along with you and lead a life like
that.'

'Yare?' said Joe.

The man who said his name was Jones rang for another
drink. When the Hindoo servant had gone Joe asked about
the papers. 'Honestly, Slim, I looked everywhere for them.
They must have been thrown out.'

'Well, I guess I'll be gettin' aboard my bloody limejuicer.'
Joe had his hand on the door.

The man who said his name was Jones came running over
and took his hand and said, 'No, you're not going. You said
you'd go on a party with me. You're an awful nice boy. You
won't be sorry. You can't go away like this, now you've got me

feeling all sort of chummy and, you know, amorous. Don't you ever feel that way, Slim? I'll do the handsome thing. I'll give you fifty dollars.'

Joe shook his head and pulled his hand away.

He had to give him a shove to get the door open; he ran down the white marble steps and out into the street.

It was, about dark; Joe walked along fast. The sweat was pouring off him. He was cussing under his breath as he walked along. He felt rotten and sore and he'd wanted real bad to see some papers from home.

He loafed up and down a little in the sort of park place where he'd sat that afternoon, then he started down towards the wharves. Might as well turn in. The smell of frying from eating joints reminded him he was hungry. He turned into one before he remembered he didn't have a cent in his pocket. He followed the sound of a mechanical piano and found himself in the redlight district. Standing in the doorways of the little shacks there were nigger wenches of all colors and shapes, halfbreed Chinese and Indian women, a few faded fat German or French women; one little mulatto girl who reached her hand out and touched his shoulder as he passed was damn pretty. He stopped to talk to her, but when he said he was broke, she laughed and said, 'Go long from here, Mister No-Money Man ... no room here for a No-Money Man.'

When he got back on board he couldn't find the cook to try and beg a little grub off him, so he took a chaw and let it go at that. The fo'c'stle was like an oven. He went up on deck with only a pair of overalls on and walked up and down with the watchman who was a pinkfaced youngster from Dover everybody called Tiny. Tiny said he'd heard the old man and Mr McGregor talking in the cabin about how they'd be off tomorrow to St Luce to load limes and then 'ome to blighty and would 'e be glad to see the tight little hile an' get off this bleedin' crahft, not 'arf. Joe said a hell of a lot of good it'd do him, his home was in Washington, D.C. 'I want to get out of the c— g life and get a job that pays something. This way every bastardly tourist with a little jack thinks he can hire you for his punk.' Joe told Tiny about the man who said his name was Jones and he laughed like he'd split. 'Fifty dollars, that's ten quid. I'd a 'ad 'arf a mind to let the toff 'ave a go at me for ten quid.'

The night was absolutely airless. The mosquitoes were beginning to get at Joe's bare neck and arms. A sweet hot haze

came up from the slack water round the wharves blurring the
lights down the waterfront. They took a couple of turns without saying anything.

'My eye, what did 'e want ye to do, Yank?' said Tiny,
giggling.

'Aw to hell with him,' said Joe. 'I'm goin' to get out of this
life. Whatever happens, wherever you are, the seaman gets the
s — y end of the stick. Ain't that true, Tiny?'

'Not 'arf . . . ten quid! Why, the bleedin' toff ought to be
ashymed of hisself. Corruptin' morals, that's what 'e's after.
Ought to go to 'is 'otel with a couple of shipmytes and myke
him pay blackmyl. There's many an old toff in Dover payin'
blackmyl for doin' less 'n 'e did. They comes down on a
vacation and goes after the bath'ouse boys. . . . Blackmyl 'im,
that's what I'd do, Yank.'

Joe didn't say anything. After a while he said, 'Jeez, an'
when I was a kid I thought I wanted to go to the tropics.'

'This ain't tropics, it's a bleedin' 'ell 'ole, that's what it is.'

They took another couple of turns. Joe went and leaned
over the side looking down into the greasy blackness. God
damn these mosquitoes. When he spat out his plug of tobacco
it made a light plunk in the water. He went down into the
fo'c'stle again, crawled into his bunk and pulled the blanket
over his head and lay there sweating. 'Darn it, I wanted to see
the baseball scores.'

Next day they coaled ship and the day after they had Joe
painting the officers' cabins while the *Argyle* nosed out through
the Boca again between the slimegreen ferny islands, and he
was sore because he had A.B. papers and here they were still
treating him like an ordinary seaman and he was going to
England and didn't know what he'd do when he'd get there,
and his shipmates said they'd likely as not run him into a
concentrytion camp; bein' an alien and landin' in England
without a passport, wat wit' war on and 'un spies everywhere,
an' all; but the breeze had salt in it now and when he peeked
out of the porthole he could see blue ocean instead of the
puddlewater off Trinidad and flying fish in hundreds skimming
away from the ship's side.

The harbor at St Luce's was clean and landlocked, white
houses with red roofs under the coconutpalms. It turned out
that it was bananas they were going to load; it took them a day
and a half knocking up partitions in the afterhold and scantlings
for the bananas to hang from. It was dark by the time they'd

come alongside the bananawharf and had rigged the two gangplanks and the little derrick for lowering the bunches into the
hold. The wharf was crowded with colored women laughing and
shrieking and yelling things at the crew, and big buck niggers
standing round doing nothing. The women did the loading.
After a while they started coming up one gangplank, each one
with a huge green bunch of bananas slung on her head and
shoulders; there were old black mammies and pretty young
mulatto girls; their faces shone with sweat under the big bunch-
lights, you could see their swinging breasts hanging down
through their ragged clothes, brown flesh through a rip in a
sleeve. When each woman got to the top of the gangplank two
big buck niggers lifted the bunch tenderly off her shoulders, the
foreman gave her a slip of paper, and she ran down the other
gangplank to the wharf again. Except for the donkeyengine
men the deck crew had nothing to do. They stood around
uneasy, watching the women, the glitter of white teeth and
eyeballs, the heavy breasts, the pumping motion of their thighs.
They stood around, looking at the women, scratching themselves, shifting their weight from one foot to the other; not even
much smut was passed. It was a black still night, the smell
of the bananas and the stench of niggerwoman sweat was hot
around them; now and then a little freshness came in a whiff
off some cases of limes piled on the wharf.

Joe caught on that Tiny was waving to him to come somewhere. He followed him into the shadow. Tiny put his mouth
against his ear, 'There's bleedin' tarts 'ere, Yank, come along.'
They went up the bow and slid down a rope to the wharf. The
rope scorched their hands. Tiny spat into his hands and rubbed
them together. Joe did the same. Then they ducked into the
warehouse. A rat scuttled past their feet. It was a guano warehouse and stank of fertilizer. Outside a little door in the back
it was pitchblack, sandy underfoot. A little glow from streetlights hit the upper part of the warehouse. There were women's
voices, a little laugh. Tiny had disappeared. Joe had his hand on a
woman's bare shoulder. 'But first you must give me a shilling,'
said a sweet cockney West India woman's voice. His voice had
gone hoarse, 'Sure, cutie, sure I will.'

When his eyes got used to the dark he could see that they
weren't the only ones. There were giggles, hoarse breathing
all around them. From the ship came the intermittent whir of
the winches, and a mixedup noise of voices from the women
loading bananas.

The woman was asking for money. 'Come on now, white boy, do like you say.'

Tiny was standing beside him buttoning up his pants. 'Be back in a jiff, girls.'

'Sure, we left our jack on board the boat.'

They ran back through the warehouse with the girls after them, up the jacobsladder somebody had let down over the side of the ship and landed on deck out of breath and doubled up with laughing. When they looked over the side the women were running up and down the wharf spitting and cursing at them like wildcats.

'Cheeryoh, lydies,' Tiny called down to them, taking off his cap. He grabbed Joe's arm and pulled him along the deck; they stood round awhile near the end of the gangplank.

'Say, Tiny, yours was old enough to be your grandmother, damned if she wasn't,' whispered Joe.

'Granny my eye, it was the pretty un I 'ad.'

'The hell you say . . . She musta been sixty.'

'Wot a bleedin' wopper . . . it was the pretty un I 'ad,' said Tiny walking off sore.

A moon had come up red from behind the fringed hills. The bananabunches the women were carrying up the gangplank made a twisting green snake under the glare of the working lights. Joe suddenly got to feeling disgusted and sleepy. He went down and washed himself carefully with soap and water before crawling into his bunk. He went to sleep listening to the Scotch and British voices of his shipmates, talking about the tarts out bàck of the wharfhouse, 'ow many they'd 'ad, 'ow many times, 'ow it stacked up with the Argentyne or Durban or Singapore. The loading kept up all night.

By noon they'd cleared for Liverpool with the Chief stoking her up to make a fast passage and all hands talking about blighty. They had bananas as much as they could eat that trip; every day the supercargo was bringing up overripe bunches and hanging them in the galley. Everybody was grousing about the ship not being armed, but the Old Man and Mr McGregor seemed to take on more about the bananas than about the raiders. They were always peeping down under the canvas cover over the hatch that had been rigged with a ventilator on the peak of it, to see if they were ripening too soon. There was a lot of guying about the blahsted banahnas down in the fo'c'stle.

After crossing the tropic they ran into a nasty norther that blew four days, after that the weather was dirty right along.

Joe didn't have much to do after his four hours at the wheel; in the fo'c'stle they were all grousing about the ship not being fumigated to kill the bugs and the cockroaches and not being armed and not picking up a convoy. Then word got around that there were German submarines cruising off the Lizard and everybody from the Old Man down got shorttempered as hell. They all began picking on Joe on account of America's not being in the war and he used to have long arguments with Tiny and an old fellow from Glasgow they called Haig. Joe said he didn't see what the hell business the States had in the war and that almost started a fight.

After they picked up the Scilly Island lights, Sparks said they were in touch with a convoy and would have a destroyer all to themselves up through the Irish Sea that wouldn't leave them until they were safe in the Mersey. The British had won a big battle at Mons. The Old Man served out a tot of rum all round and everybody was in fine shape except Joe who was worried about what'd happen to him getting into England without a passport. He was chilly all the time on account of not having any warm clothes.

That evening a destroyer loomed suddenly out of the foggy twilight, looking tall as a church above the great wave of white water curling from her bows. It gave them a great scare on the bridge because they thought at first it was a Hun. The destroyer broke out the Union Jack and slowed down to the *Argyle's* speed, keeping close and abreast of her. The crew piled out on deck and gave the destroyer three cheers. Some of them wanted to sing *God Save the King*, but the officer on the bridge of the destroyer began bawling out the Old Man through a megaphone asking him why in bloody f—g hell he wasn't steering a zigzag course and if he didn't jolly well know that it was prohibited making any kind of bloody f—g noise on a merchantship in wartime.

It was eight bells and the watches were changing and Joe and Tiny began to laugh coming along the deck just at the moment when they met Mr McGregor stalking by purple in the face. He stopped square in front of Joe and asked him what he found so funny? Joe didn't answer. Mr McGregor stared at him hard and began saying in his slow mean voice that he was probably not an American at all but a dirty 'un spy, and told him to report on the next shift in the stokehole. Joe said he'd signed on as an A.B. and they didn't have any right to work him as a stoker. Mr McGregor said he'd never struck a man yet in thirty years at sea, but if he let another word out he'd damn well knock him down. Joe felt burning hot, but he stood still with his fists clenched without saying anything. For several seconds Mr McGregor just stared at him, red as a turkey gobbler. Two of the watch passed along the deck. 'Turn this fellow over to the bosun and put him in irons. He may be a spy. . . . You go along quiet now or it'll be the worse for you.'

Joe spent that night hunched up in a little cubbyhole that smelt of bilge with his feet in irons. The next morning the bosun let him out and told him fairly kindly to go get cookee to give him some porridge, but to keep off the deck. He said they were going to turn him over to the Aliens Control as soon as they docked in Liverpool.

When he crossed the deck to go to the galley, his ankles still stiff from the irons, he noticed that they were already in the Mersey. It was a ruddy sunlit morning. In every direction there were ships at anchor, stumpylooking black sailboats and patrol-boats cutting through the palegreen ruffled water. Overhead the great pall of brown smoke was shot here and there with crisp white steam that caught the sun.

The cook gave him some porridge and a mug of bitter barely warm tea. When he came out of the galley they were further up the river, you could see towns on both sides, the sky was entirely overcast with brown smoke and fog. The *Argyle* was steaming under one bell.

Joe went below to the fo'c'stle and rolled into his bunk. His shipmates all stared at him without speaking and when he spoke to Tiny who was in the bunk below him, he didn't answer. That made Joe feel worse than anything. He turned his face to the wall, pulled the blanket over his head and went to sleep.

Somebody shaking him woke him up. 'Come on, my man,' said a tall English bobby with a blue helmet and varnished chinstrap who had hold of his shoulder.

'All right, just a sec,' Joe said. 'I'd like to get washed up.'

The bobby shook his head. 'The quieter and quicker you come the better it'll be for you.'

Joe pulled his cap over his eyes, took his cigarbox out from under his mattress, and followed the bobby out on deck. The *Argyle* was already tied up to the wharf. So without saying goodbye to anybody or getting paid off, he went down the gangplank with the bobby half a step behind. The bobby had a tight grip on the muscle of his arm. They walked across a flagstoned wharf and out through some big iron gates to where the Black Maria was waiting. A small crowd of loafers, red faces in the fog, black grimy clothes. 'Look at the filthy 'un,' one man said. A woman hissed, there were a couple of boos and a catcall and the shiny black doors closed behind him; the car started smoothly and he could feel it speeding through the cobbled streets.

Joe sat hunched up in the dark. He was glad he was alone in there. It gave him a chance to get hold of himself. His hands and feet were cold. He had hard work to keep from shivering. He wished he was dressed decently. All he had on was a shirt and pants spotted with paint and a pair of dirty felt slippers. Suddenly the car stopped, two bobbies told him to get out and he was hustled down a whitewashed corridor into a little room where a police inspector, a tall longfaced Englishman, sat at a yellow varnished table. The inspector jumped to his feet, walked towards Joe with his fists clenched as if he was going to hit him and suddenly said something in what Joe thought must be German. Joe shook his head, it struck him funny somehow and he grinned. 'No savvy,' he said.

'What's in that box?' the inspector, who had sat down at the desk again, suddenly bawled out at the bobbies. 'You'd oughter search these buggers before you bring 'em in here.'

One of the bobbies snatched the cigarbox out from under Joe's arm and opened it, looked relieved when he saw it didn't have a bomb in it and dumped everything out on the desk.

'So you pretend to be an American?' the man yelled at Joe.

'Sure I'm an American,' said Joe.

'What the hell do you want to come to England in wartime for?'

'I didn't want to come to . . .'

'Shut up,' the man yelled.

Then he motioned to the bobbies to go, and said, 'Send in Corporal Eakins.' 'Very good, sir,' said the two bobbies respectfully in unison. When they'd gone, he came towards Joe with his fists clenched again. 'You might as well make a clean breast of it, my lad. . . . We have all the necessary information.'

Joe had to keep his teeth clenched to keep them from chattering. He was scared.

'I was on the beach in B.A. you see . . . had to take the first berth I could get. You don't think anybody'd ship on a limejuicer if they could help it, do you?' Joe was getting sore; he felt warm again.

The plainclothes man took up a pencil and tapped with it

threateningly on the desk. 'Impudence won't help you, my lad
. . . you'd better keep a civil tongue in your head.' Then he
began looking over the photographs and stamps and newspaper clippings that had come out of Joe's cigarbox. Two men
in khaki came in. 'Strip him and search him,' the man at the
desk said without looking up.

Joe looked at the two men without understanding; they had
a little the look of hospital orderlies. 'Sharp now,' one of them
said. 'We don't want to 'ave to use force.' Joe took off his shirt.
It made him sore that he was blushing; he was ashamed because he didn't have any underwear. 'All right, breeches next.'
Joe stood naked in his slippers while the men in khaki went
through his shirt and pants. They found a bunch of clean
waste in one pocket, a battered Prince Albert can with a piece
of chewing tobacco in it and a small jackknife with a broken
blade. One of them was examining the belt and pointed out to
the other the place where it had been resewed. He slit it up
with a knife and they both looked eagerly inside. Joe grinned,
'I used to keep my bills in there,' he said. They kept their faces
stiff.

'Open your mouth.' One of them put a heavy hand on Joe's
jaw. 'Sergeant, shall we take out the fillin's? 'E's got two or
three fillin's in the back of 'is mouth.' The man behind the
desk shook his head. One of the men stepped out of the door
and came back with an oiled rubber glove on his hand. 'Lean
hover,' said the other man, putting his hand on Joe's neck and
shoving his head down while the man with the rubber glove
felt in his rectum. 'Hay, for Chris' sake,' hissed Joe through his
teeth.

'All right, me lad, that's all for the present,' said the man
who held his head, letting go. 'Sorry, but we 'ave to do it . . .
part of the regulations.'

The corporal walked up to the desk and stood at attention.
'All right, sir . . . Nothin' of interest on the prisoner's person.'

Joe was terribly cold. He couldn't keep his teeth from chattering.

'Look in his slippers, can't you?' growled the inspector. Joe
didn't like handing over his slippers because his feet were
dirty, but there was nothing he could do. The corporal slashed
them to pieces with his penknife. Then both men stood at attention and waited for the inspector to lift his eye. 'All right,
sir . . . nothin' to report. Shall I get the prisoner a blanket, sir?
'E looks chilly.'

The man behind the desk shook his head and beckoned to Joe, 'Come over here. Now are you ready to answer truthfully and give us no trouble it won't be worse than a concentrytion camp for durytion. . . . But if you give us trouble I can't say how serious it mightn't be. We're under the Defence of the Realm Act, don't forget that. . . . What's your name?'

After Joe had told his name, birthplace, father's and mother's names, names of ships he'd sailed on, the inspector suddenly shot a question in German at him. Joe shook his head, 'Hay, what do you think I know German for?'

'Shut the bugger up. . . . We know all about him anyway.'

'Shall we give him 'is kit, sir?' asked one of the men timidly.

'He won't need a kit if he isn't jolly careful.'

The corporal got a bunch of keys and opened a heavy wooden door on the side of the room. They pushed Joe into a little cell with a bench and no window. The door slammed behind him and Joe was there shivering in the dark. Well, you're in the pig's a. h. for fair, Joe Williams, he said aloud. He found he could warm himself by doing exercises and rubbing his arms and legs, but his feet stayed numb.

After a while he heard the key in the lock; the man in khaki threw a blanket into the cell and slammed the door to, without giving him a chance to say anything.

Joe curled up in the blanket on the bench and tried to go to sleep.

He woke in a sudden nightmare fright. It was cold. The watch had been called. He jumped off the bench. It was blind dark. For a second he thought he'd gone blind in the night. Where he was, and everything since they sighted the Scilly Island lights came back. He had a lump of ice in his stomach. He walked up and down from wall to wall of the cell for a while and then rolled up in the blanket again. It was a good clean blanket and smelt of lysol or something like that. He went to sleep.

He woke up again hungry as hell, wanting to make water. He shuffled around the square cell for a long time until he found an enamelled pail under the bench. He used it and felt better. He was glad it had a cover on it. He began wondering how he'd pass the time. He began thinking about Georgetown and good times he'd had with Alec and Janey and the gang that hung around Mulvaney's pool parlor and making pickups on moonlight trips on the *Charles McAlister* and went over all the good pitchers he'd ever seen or read about and tried to remember the batting averages of every man on the Washington ballteams.

He'd gotten back to trying to remember his highschool games, inning by inning, when the key was put into the lock. The corporal who'd searched him opened the door and handed him his shirt and pants. 'You can wash up if you want to,' he said. 'Better clean up smart. Orders is to take you to Captain Cooper-Trahsk.'

'Gosh, can't you get me somethin' to eat or some water. I'm about starved. . . . Say, how long have I been in here, anyway?' Joe was blinking in the bright white light that came in from the other room. He pulled on his shirt and pants.

'Come along,' said the corporal. 'Cahn't ahnswer no question till you've seen Captain Cooper-Trahsk.'

'But what about my slippers?'

'You keep a civil tongue in your mouth and ahnswer all questions you're harsked and it'll be all the better for you. . . . Come along.'

When he followed the corporal down the same corridor he'd come in by, all the English tommies stared at his bare feet. In the lavatory there was a shiny brass tap of cold water and a hunk of soap. First Joe took a long drink. He felt giddy and his knees were shaking. The cold water and washing his hands and face and feet made him feel better. The only thing he had to dry himself on was a roller towel already grimy.

'Say, I need a shave,' he said.

'You'll 'ave to come along now,' said the corporal sternly.

'But I got a Gillette somewheres . . .'

The corporal gave him an angry stare. They were going in the door of a nicely furnished office with a thick red and brown carpet on the floor. At a mahogany desk sat an elderly man with white hair and a round roastbeef face and lots of insignia on his uniform.

'Is that . . . ?' Joe began, but he saw that the corporal after clicking his heels and saluting had frozen into attention.

The elderly man raised his head and looked at them with a fatherly blue eye, 'Ah . . . quite so . . .' he said. 'Bring him up closer, corporal, and let's have a look at him. . . . Isn't he in rather a mess, corporal? You'd better give the poor beggar some shoes and stockings. . . .'

'Very good, sir,' said the corporal in a spiteful tone, stiffening to attention again.

'At ease, corporal, at ease,' said the elderly man, putting on a pair of eyeglasses and looking at some papers on his desk. 'This is . . . er . . . Zentner . . . claim American citizen, eh?'

'The name is Williams, sir.'

'Ah, quite so . . . Joe Williams, seaman. . . .' He fixed his blue eyes confidentially on Joe. 'Is that your name, me boy?'

'Yessir.'

'Well, how do you come to be trying to get into England in wartime without passport or other identifying document?'

Joe told about how he had an American A.B. certificate and had been on the beach at B.A. . . . Buenos Aires.

'And why were you . . . er . . . in this condition in the Argentine?'

'Well, sir, I'd been on the Mallory Line and my ship sailed without me and I'd been painting the town red a little, sir, and the skipper pulled out ahead of schedule so that left me on the beach.'

'Ah . . . a hot time in the old town tonight . . . that sort of thing, eh?' The elderly man laughed; then suddenly he puckered up his brows. 'Let me see . . . er . . . what steamer of the Mallory Line were you travelling on?'

'The *Patagonia*, sir, and I wasn't travellin' on her, I was seaman on board of her.'

The elderly man wrote a long while on a sheet of paper, then he lifted Joe's cigarbox out of the desk drawer and began looking through the clippings and photographs. He brought out a photograph and turned it out so that Joe could see it. 'Quite a pretty girl . . . is that your best beloved, Williams?'

Joe blushed scarlet. 'That's my sister.'

'I say she looks like a ripping girl . . . don't you think so, corporal?'

'Quite so, sir,' said the corporal distantly.

'Now, me boy, if you know anything about the activities of German agents in South America . . . many of them are Americans or impostors masquerading as Americans . . . it'll be much better for you to make a clean breast of it.'

'Honestly, sir,' said Joe, 'I don't know a thing about it. I was only in B.A. for a few days.'

'Have you any parents living?'

'My father's a pretty sick man. . . . But I have my mother and sisters in Georgetown.'

'Georgetown . . . Georgetown . . . let me see . . . isn't that in British Guiana?'

'It's part of Washington, D.C.'

'Of course . . . ah, I see you were in the navy. . . .' The elderly man held off the picture of Joe and the two other gobs.

Joe's knees felt so weak he thought he was going to fall down. 'No, sir, that was in the naval reserve.'

The elderly man put everything back in the cigarbox. 'You can have these now, my boy . . . You'd better give him a bit of breakfast and let him have an airing in the yard. He looks a bit weak on his pins, corporal.'

'Very good, sir.' The corporal saluted, and they marched out.

The breakfast was watery oatmeal, stale tea, and two slices of bread with margarine on it. After it Joe felt hungrier than before. Still it was good to get out in the air, even if it was drizzling and the flagstones of the small courtyard where they put him were like ice to his bare feet under the thin slime of black mud that was over them.

There was another prisoner in the courtyard, a little fatfaced man in a derby hat and a brown overcoat, who came up to Joe immediately. 'Say, are you an American?'

'Sure,' said Joe.

'My name's Zentner . . . buyer in restaurant furnishings . . . from Chicago. . . . This is the tamnest outrage. Here I come to this tamned country to buy their tamned goods, to spend good American dollars. . . . Three days ago yet I placed a tentousand dollar order in Sheffield. And they arrest me for a spy and I been here all night yet and only this morning vill they let me telephone the consulate. It is outrageous and I hafe a passport and visa all they want. I can sue for this outrage. I shall take it to Vashington. I shall sue the British government for a hundred tousand dollars for defamation of character. Forty years an American citizen and my fader he came not from Chermany but from Poland. . . . And you, poor boy, I see that you haf no shoes. And they talk about the atrocious Chermans and if this ain't an atrocity, vat is it?'

Joe was shivering and running round the court at a jogtrot to try to keep warm. Mr Zentner took off his brown coat and handed it to him. 'Here, kid, you put that coat on.'

'But, jeez, it's too good; that's damn nice of you.'

'In adversity ve must help von anoder.'

'Dodgast it, if this is their spring, I hate to think what their winter's like. . . . I'll give the coat back to you when I go in. Jeez, my feet are cold. . . . Say, did they search you?'

Mr Zentner rolled up his eyes. 'Outrageous,' he spluttered . . . 'Vat indignities to a buyer from a neutral and friendly country. Vait till I tell the ambassador. I shall sue. I shall demand damages.'

'Same here,' said Joe, laughing.

The corporal appeared in the door and shouted, 'Williams.'

Joe gave back the coat and shook Mr Zentner's hand. 'Say for Gawd's sake, don't forget to tell the consul there's another American here. They're talkin' about sendin' me to a concentration camp for duration.'

'Sure, don't vorry, boy. I'll get you out,' said Mr Zentner, puffing out his chest.

This time Joe was taken to a regular cell that had a little light and room to walk around. The corporal gave him a pair of shoes and some wool socks full of holes. He couldn't get the shoes on, but the socks warmed his feet up a little. At noon they handed him a kind of stew that was mostly potatoes with eyes in them and some more bread and margarine.

The third day when the turnkey brought the noonday slum, he brought a brownpaper package that had been opened. In it was a suit of clothes, shirt, flannel underwear, socks, and even a necktie.

'There was a chit with it, but it's against the regulytions,' said the turnkey. 'That outfit'll make a bloomin' toff out of you.'

Late that afternoon the turnkey told Joe to come along and he put on the clean collar that was too tight for his neck and the necktie and hitched up the pants that were much too big for him around the waist and followed along corridors and across a court full of tommies into a little office with a sentry at the door and a sergeant at a desk. Sitting on a chair was a busylooking young man with a straw hat on his knees.

' 'Ere's your man, sir,' said the sergeant without looking at Joe. 'I'll let you question him.'

The busylooking young man got to his feet and went up to Joe. 'Well, you've certainly been making me a lot of trouble, but I've been over the records in your case and it looks as if you were what you represented yourself to be. . . . What's your father's name?'

'Same as mine, Joseph P. Williams. . . . Say, are you the American consul?'

'I'm from the consulate. . . . Say, what the hell do you want to come ashore without a passport for? Don't you think we have anything better to do than to take care of a lot of damn fools that don't know enough to come in when it rains? Damn it, I was goin' to play golf this afternoon and here I've been here two hours waiting to get you out of the cooler.'

'Jeez, I didn't come ashore. They come on and got me.'

'That'll teach you a lesson, I hope. . . . Next time you have your papers in order.'

'Yessirree . . . I shu will.'

Half an hour later Joe was out on the street, the cigarbox and his old clothes rolled up in a ball under his arm. It was a sunny afternoon; the redfaced people in dark clothes, longfaced women in crummy hats, the streets full of big buses and the tall trolleycars; everything looked awful funny, until he suddenly remembered it was England and he'd never been there before.

He had to wait a long time in an empty office at the consulate while the busylooking young man made up a lot of papers. He was hungry and kept thinking of beefsteak and frenchfried. At last he was called to the desk and given a paper and told that there was a berth all ready for him on the American steamer *Tampa*, out of Pensacola, and he'd better go right down to the agents and make sure about it and go on board and if they caught him around Liverpool again it would be the worse for him.

'Say, is there any way I can get anything to eat around here, Mr Consul?'

'What do you think this is, a restaurant? . . . No, we have no appropriations for any handouts. You ought to be grateful for what we've done already.'

'They never paid me off on the *Argyle* and I'm about starved in that jail, that's all.'

'Well, here's a shilling, but that's absolutely all I can do.'

Joe looked at the coin, 'Who's 'at – King George? Well, thank you, Mr Consul.'

He was walking along the street with the agent's address in one hand and the shilling in the other. He felt sore and faint and sick at his stomach. He saw Mr Zentner the other side of the street. He ran across through the jammed up traffic and went up to him with his hand held out.

'I got the clothes, Mr Zentner, it was damn nice of you to send them.' Mr Zentner was walking along with a small man in an officer's uniform. He waved a pudgy hand and said, 'Glad to be of service to a fellow citizen,' and walked on.

Joe went into a friedfish shop and spent sixpence on fried fish and spent the other sixpence on a big mug of beer in a saloon where he'd hoped to find free lunch to fill up on, but there wasn't any free lunch. By the time he'd found his way to the agent's office it was closed and there he was roaming round the streets in the white misty evening without any place to go. He asked several guys around the wharves if they knew where the *Tampa* was docked, but nobody did and they talked so funny he could hardly understand what they said anyway.

Then just when the streetlights were going on, and Joe was feeling pretty discouraged, he found himself walking down a side street behind three Americans. He caught up to them and asked them if they knew where the *Tampa* was. Why the hell shouldn't they know, weren't they off'n her and out to see the goddam town and he'd better come along. And if he wasn't tickled to meet some guys from home after those two months on the limejuicer and being in jail and everything. They went into a bar and drank some whiskey and he told all about the jail and how the damn bobbies had taken him off the *Argyle* and he'd never gotten his pay nor nutten and they set him up to drinks and one of the guys who was from Norfolk, Virginia, named Will Stirp pulled out a fivedollar bill and said to take that and pay him back when he could.

It was like coming home to God's country running into guys like that and they all had a drink all around; they were four of 'em Americans in this lousy limejuicer town and they each set up a round because they were four of 'em Americans ready to fight the world. Olaf was a Swede, but he had his first papers, so he counted too, and the other feller's name was Maloney. The hatchetfaced barmaid held back on the change, but they got it out of her; she'd only given 'em fifteen shillings instead of twenty for a pound, but they made her give the five shillings back. They went to another friedfish shop; couldn't seem to get a damn thing to eat in this country except fried fish, and then they all had some more drinks and were the four of them Americans feeling pretty good in this lousy limejuicer town. A runner got hold of them because it was closing time on account of the war and there wasn't a damn thing open and very few streetlights and funny little hats on the streetlights on account of the zeppelins. The runner was a pale ratfaced punk and said he knowed a house where they could 'ave a bit of beer and nice girls and a quiet social time. There was a big lamp with red roses painted on it in the parlor of the house and the girls were skinny and had horseteeth and there were some bloody limejuicers there who were pretty well under way and they were the four of them Americans. The limeys began to pick on Olaf for bein' a bloody 'un. Olaf said he was a Swede, but that he'd sooner be a bloody 'un than a limejuicer at that. Somebody poked somebody else and the first thing Joe knew he was fighting a guy bigger 'n he was and police whistles blew and there was the whole crowd of them piled up in the Black Maria.

Will Stirp kept saying they was the four of them Americans just havin' a pleasant social time and there was no call for the bobbies to interfere. But they were all dragged up to a desk and committed and all four of 'em Americans locked up in the same cell and the limeys in another cell. The police station was full of drunks yelling and singing. Maloney had a bloody nose. Olaf went to sleep. Joe couldn't sleep; he kept saying to Will Stirp he was scared they sure would send him to a concentration camp for the duration of the war this time, and each time Will Stirp said they were the four of them Americans and wasn't he a Freeborn American Citizen and there wasn't a damn thing they could do to 'em. Freedom of the seas, God damn it.

Next morning they were in court and it was funny as hell except that Joe was scared; it was solemn as Quakermeetin' and the magistrate wore a little wig and they were everyone of 'em fined three and six and costs. It came to about a dollar a head. Damned lucky they still had some jack on them.

And the magistrate in the little wig gave 'em a hell of a talking to about how this was wartime and they had no right being drunk and disorderly on British soil, but had ought to be fighting shoulder to shoulder with their brothers, Englishmen of their own blood and to whom the Americans owed everything, even their existence as a great nation, to defend civilization and free institutions and plucky little Belgium against the invading Huns who were raping women and sinking peaceful merchantmen.

When the magistrate had finished, the court attendants said, 'Hear, hear,' under their breath and they all looked very savage and solemn and turned the American boys loose after they'd paid their fines and the police sergeant had looked at their papers. They held Joe after the others on account of his paper being from the consulate and not having the stamp of the proper police station on it, but after a while they let him go with a warning not to come ashore again and that if he did it would be worse for him.

Joe felt relieved when he'd seen the skipper and had been taken on and had rigged up his bunk and gone ashore and gotten his bundle that he'd left with the nice flaxenhaired barmaid at the first pub he'd gone to the night before. At last he was on an American ship. She had an American flag painted on either side of the hull and her name *Tampa*, Pensacola, Florida, in white letters. There was a colored boy cooking and first thing they had cornmeal mush and karo syrup, and coffee instead of that lousy tea, and the food tasted awful good. Joe felt better than any time since he'd left home. The bunks were clean and a fine feeling it was when the *Tampa* left the dock with her whistle blowing and started easing down the slate-colored stream of the Mersey towards the sea.

Fifteen days to Hampton Roads, with sunny weather and a sea like glass every day up to the last two days and then a stiff northwesterly wind that kicked up considerable chop off the Capes. They landed the few bundles of cotton print goods that made up the cargo at the Union Terminal in Norfolk. It was a big day for Joe when he went ashore with his pay in his pocket to take a look around the town with Will Stirp, who belonged there.

They went to see Will Stirp's folks and took in a ballgame and after that hopped the trolley down to Virginia Beach with some girls Will Stirp knew. One of the girls' names was Della; and she was very dark and Joe fell for her, kind of. When they were putting on their bathing suits in the bathhouse he asked Will would she . . . ? And Will got sore and said, 'Ain't you got the sense to tell a good girl from a hooker?' And Joe said well, you never could tell nowadays.

They went in swimming and fooled around the beach in their bathingsuits and built a fire and toasted marshmallows and then they took the girls home. Della let Joe kiss her when they said goodnight and he began kinder planning that she'd be his steady girl.

Back in town they didn't know just what to do. They wanted some drinks and a couple of frails, but they were afraid of getting tanked up and spending all their money. They went to a poolroom Will knew and shot some pool and Joe was pretty good and cleaned up the local boys. After that they went and Joe set up a drink, but it was closing time and right away they were out on the street again. They couldn't find any hookers;

Will said he knew a house, but they soaked you too damn much, and they were just about going home to turn in when they ran into two high yellers who gave 'em the eye. They followed 'em down the street a long way and into a crossstreet where there weren't many lights. The girls were hot stuff, but they were scared and nervous for fear somebody might see 'em. They found an empty house with a back porch where it was black as pitch and took 'em up there and afterwards they went back and slept at Will Stirp's folks' house.

The *Tampa* had gone into drydock at Newport News for repairs on a started plate. Joe and Will Stirp were paid off and hung round Norfolk all day without knowing what to do with themselves. Saturday afternoons and Sundays, Joe played a little baseball with a scratch team of boys who worked in the Navy Yard, evenings he went out with Della Matthews. She was a stenographer in the First National Bank and used to say she'd never marry a boy who went to sea, you couldn't trust 'em and that it was a rough kind of a life and didn't have any advancement in it. Joe said she was right, but you were only young once and what the hell, things didn't matter so much anyway. She used to ask him about his folks and why he didn't go up to Washington to see them, especially as his dad was ill. He said the old man could choke for all he cared, he hated him, that was about the size of it. She said she thought he was terrible. That time he was setting her up to a soda after the movies. She looked cute and plump in a fluffy pink dress and her little black eyes all excited and flashing. Joe said not to talk about that stuff, it didn't matter, but she looked at him awful mean and mad and said she'd like to shake him and that everything mattered terribly and it was wicked to talk like that and that he was a nice boy and came from nice people and had been nicely raised and ought to be thinking of getting ahead in the world instead of being a bum and a loafer. Joe got sore and said was that so? and left her at her folks' house without saying another word. He didn't see her for four or five days after that.

Then he went by where Della worked, and waited for her to come out one evening. He'd been thinking about her more than he wanted to and what she'd said. First, she tried to walk past him, but he grinned at her and she couldn't help smiling back. He was pretty broke by that time, but he took her and bought her a box of candy. They talked about how hot it was and he said they'd go to the ballgame next week. He told her how the *Tampa* was pulling out for Pensacola to load lumber and then across to the other side.

They were waiting for the trolley to go to Virginia Beach, walking up and down fighting the mosquitoes. She looked all upset when he said he was going to the other side. Before Joe knew what he was doing he was saying that he wouldn't ship on the *Tampa* again, but that he'd get a job right here in Norfolk.

That night was full moon. They fooled around in their bathingsuits a long while on the beach beside a little smudgefire Joe made to keep the mosquitoes off. He was sitting crosslegged and she lay with her head on his knees and all the time he was stroking her hair and leaning over and kissing her; she said how funny his face looked upside down when he kissed her like that. She said they'd get married as soon as he got a steady job and between the two of them they'd amount to something. Ever since she'd graduated from highschool at the head of her class she'd felt she ought to work hard and amount to something. 'The folks round here are awful no-account, Joe, don't know they're alive half the time.'

'D'you know it, Del, you kinda remind me o' my sister Janey honest you do. Dodgast it, she's amounting to something all right. . . . She's awful pretty too . . .'

Della said she hoped she could see her some day and Joe said sure she would and he pulled her to her feet and drew her to him tight and hugged her and kissed her. It was late, and the beach was chilly and lonely under the big moon. Della got atrembling and said she'd have to get her clothes on or she'd catch her death. They had to run not to lose the last car.

The rails twanged as the car lurched through the moonlit pinebarrens full of tambourining dryflies and katydids. Della suddenly crumpled up and began to cry. Joe kept asking her what the matter was, but she wouldn't answer, only cried and cried. It was kind of a relief to leave her at her folks' house and walk alone through empty airless streets to the boardinghouse where he had a room.

All the next week he hoofed it around Norfolk and Portsmouth looking for a job that had a future to it. He even went over to Newport News. Coming back on the ferry, he didn't have enough jack to pay his fare and had to get the guy who took tickets to let him work his way over sweeping up. The landlady began to ask for next week's rent. All the jobs Joe applied for needed experience or training or you'd ought to have finished highschool and there weren't many jobs anyway, so in the end he had to go boating again, on a seagoing barge that was waiting for a towboat to take her down East to Rockport with a load of coal.

There were five barges in the tow; it wasn't such a bad trip, just him and an old man named Gaskin and his boy, a kid of about fifteen whose name was Joe too. The only trouble they had was a squall off Cape Cod when the towrope parted, but the towboat captain was right up on his toes and managed to get a new cable on board 'em before they'd straightened out on their anchor.

Up in Rockport they unloaded their coal and anchored out in the harbor waiting to be towed to another wharf to load granite blocks for the trip back. One night, when Gaskin and his boy had gone ashore and Joe was on watch, the second engineer of the tug, a thinfaced guy named Hart, came under the stern in a skiff and whispered to Joe did he want some c—t. Joe was stretched out in the house smoking a pipe and thinking about Della. The hills and the harbor and the rocky shore were fading into a warm pink twilight. Hart had a nervous stuttering manner. Joe held off at first, but after a while he said, 'Bring 'em along.'

'Got any cards?' said Hart.

'Yare I got a pack.'

Joe went below to clean up the cabin. He'd just kid 'em along, he was thinking. He'd oughtn't to have a rough time with girls and all that now that he was going to marry Della. He heard the sound of the oars and went out on deck. A fogbank was coming in from the sea. There was Hart and his two girls under the stern. They tripped and giggled and fell hard against him when he helped 'em over the side. They'd brought some liquor and a couple of pounds of hamburger and some crackers. They weren't much for looks, but they were pretty good sorts with big firm arms and shoulders and they sure could drink liquor. Joe'd never seen girls like that before. They were sports all right. They had four quarts of liquor between 'em and drank it in tumblers.

The other two barges were sounding their claxons every two minutes, but Joe forgot all about his. The fog was white like canvas nailed across the cabin ports. They played strip poker, but they didn't get very far with it. Him and Hart changed girls three times that night. The girls were cookoo, they never seemed to have enough, but round twelve the girls were darned decent, they cooked up the hamburger and served up a lunch and ate all old man Gaskin's bread and butter.

Then Hart passed out and the girls began to get worried about getting home on account of the fog and everything. All of 'em laughing like loons they hauled Hart up on deck and poured a bucket of water on him. That Maine water was so cold that he came to like sixty, sore as a pup and wanting to fight Joe. The girls quieted him down and got him into the boat and they went off into the fog singing *Tipperary*.

Joe was reeling himself. He stuck his head in a bucket of water and cleaned up the cabin and threw the bottles overboard and started working on the claxon regularly. To hell with 'em, he kept saying to himself, he wouldn't be a plaster saint for anybody. He was feeling fine, he wished he had something more to do than spin that damn claxon.

Old man Gaskin came on board about day. Joe could see he'd gotten wind of something, because after that he never would speak to him except to give orders and wouldn't let his boy speak to him; so that when they'd unloaded the granite blocks in East New York, Joe asked for his pay and said he was through. Old man Gaskin growled out it was a good riddance and that he wouldn't have no boozin' and whorin' on his barge. So there was Joe with fortyfive dollars in his pocket walking through Red Hook looking for a boardinghouse.

After he'd been a couple of days reading want ads and going around Brooklyn looking for a job he got sick. He went to a sawbones an oldtimer at the boardinghouse told him about. The doc, who was a little kike with a goatee, told him it was the gonawria and he'd have to come every afternoon for treatment. He said he'd guarantee to cure him up for fifty dollars, half payable in advance, and that he'd advise him to have a bloodtest taken to see if he had syphilis too and that would cost him fifteen dollars. Joe paid down twentyfive, but said he'd think about the test. He had a treatment and went out into the street. The doc had told him to be sure to walk as little as possible, but he couldn't seem to go home to the stinking boardinghouse and wandered aimlessly round the clattering Brooklyn streets. It was a hot afternoon. The sweat was pouring off him as he walked. If you catch it right the first day or two it ain't so bad, he kept saying to himself. He came out on a bridge under the Elevated; must be Brooklyn Bridge.

It was cooler walking across the bridge. Through the spiderwebbing of cables, the shipping and the pack of tall buildings were black against the sparkle of the harbor. Joe sat down on a bench at the first pier and stretched his legs out in front of him. Here he'd gone to work and caught a dose. He felt terrible and how was he going to write Del now; and his board to pay, and a job to get and these damn treatments to take. Jesus, he felt lousy.

A kid came by with an evening paper. He bought a *Journal* and sat with the paper on his lap looking at the headlines: RUSH MORE TROOPS TO MEX BORDER. What the hell could he do? He couldn't even join the National Guard and go to Mexico; they wouldn't take you if you were sick and even if they did it would be the goddam navy all over again. He sat reading the want ads, the ads about adding to your income with two hours' agreeable work at home evenings, the ads of Pelmanism and correspondence courses. What the hell could he do? He sat there until it was dark. Then he took a car to Atlantic Avenue and went up four flights to the room where he had a cot under the window and turned in.

That night a big thundersquall came up. There was a lot of thunder and lightning damned close. Joe lay flat on his back watching the lightning, so bright it dimmed the streetlights, flicker on the ceiling. The springs rattled every time the guy in the other cot turned in his sleep. It began to rain in, but Joe felt so weak and sick it was a long time before he had the gumption to sit up and pull down the window.

In the morning the landlady, who was a big raw-boned Swedish woman with wisps of flaxen hair down over her bony face, started bawling him out about the bed's being wet. 'I can't help it if it rains, can I?' he grumbled, looking at her big feet. When he caught her eye, it came over him that she was kidding him and they both laughed.

She was a swell woman, her name was Mrs Olsen and she'd raised six children, three boys who'd grown up and gone to sea, a girl who was a schoolteacher in St Paul and a pair of girl twins about seven or eight who were always getting into mischief. 'Yust one year more and I send them to Olga in Milwaukee. I know sailormen.' Pop Olsen had been on the beach somewhere in the South Seas for years. 'Yust as well he stay there. In Brooklyn he been always in de lockup. Every week cost me money to get him outa yail.'

Joe got to helping her round the house with the cleaning and did odd painting and carpentering jobs for her. After his money ran out, she let him stay on and even lent him twentyfive

bucks to pay the doctor when he told her about being sick.
She slapped him on the back when he thanked her; 'Every boy
I ever lend money to, he turn out yust one big bum,' she said
and laughed. She was a swell woman.

It was nasty sleety winter weather. Mornings Joe sat in the
steamy kitchen studying a course in navigation he'd started
getting from the Alexander Hamilton Institute. Afternoons he
fidgeted in the dingy doctor's office that smelt of carbolic,
waiting for his turn for treatment, looking through frayed
copies of the *National Geographic* for 1909. It was a glum-
looking bunch waited in there. Nobody ever said anything much
to anybody else. A couple of times he met guys on the street
he'd talked with a little waiting in there, but they always
walked right past him as if they didn't see him. Evenings he
sometimes went over to Manhattan and played checkers at the
Seamen's Institute or hung around the Seamen's Union getting
the dope on ships he might get a berth on when the doc dried
him up. It was a bum time except that Mrs Olsen was darn
good to him and he got fonder of her than he'd ever been of
his own mother.

The darn kike sawbones tried to hold him up for another
twentyfive bucks to complete the cure, but Joe said to hell with
it and shipped as an A.B. on a brandnew Standard Oil tanker,
the *Montana*, bound light for Tampico and then out east, some
of the boys said to Aden and others said to Bombay. He was
sick of the cold and the sleet and the grimy Brooklyn streets
and the logarithm tables in the course on navigation he couldn't
get through his head and Mrs Olsen's bullying jolly voice; she
was beginning to act like she wanted to run his life for him.
She was a swell woman, but it was about time he got the hell
out.

The *Montana* rounded Sandy Hook in a spiteful lashing
snowstorm out of the northwest, but three days later they were
in the Gulf Stream south of Hatteras rolling in a long swell
with all the crew's denims and shirts drying on lines rigged
from the shrouds. It was good to be on blue water again.

Tampico was a hell of a place; they said that mescal made
you crazy if you drank too much of it; there were big dance-
halls full of greasers dancing with their hats on and with guns
on their hips, and bands and mechanical pianos going full tilt
in every bar, and fights and drunk Texans from the oilwells.
The doors of all the cribhouses were open so that you could
see the bed with white pillows and the picture of the Virgin

over it and the lamps with fancy shades and the colored paper trimming; the broadfaced brown girls sat out in front in lace slips. But everything was so damned high that they spent up all their jack first thing and had to go back on board before it was hardly midnight. And the mosquitoes got into the fo'c'stle and the sandflies about day and it was hot and nobody could sleep.

When the tanks had been pumped full, the *Montana* went out into the Gulf of Mexico into a norther with the decks awash and the spray lashing the bridge. They hadn't been out two hours before they'd lost a man overboard off the monkey-walk and a boy named Higgins had had his foot smashed lashing the starboard anchor that had broken loose. It made 'em pretty sore down in the fo'c'stle that the skipper wouldn't lower a boat, though the older men said that no boat could have lived in a sea like that. As it was the skipper cruised in a wide curve and took a couple of seas on his beam that like to stove in the steel decks.

Nothing much else happened on that trip except that one night when Joe was at the wheel and the ship was dead quiet except for the irregular rustle of broken water as she plowed through the long flat seas eastward, he suddenly smelt roses or honeysuckle maybe. The sky was blue as a bowl of curdled milk with a waned scrap of moon bobbing up from time to time. It was honeysuckle, sure enough, and manured garden patches and moist foliage like walking past the open door of a florist's in winter. It made him feel soft and funny inside like he had a girl standing right beside him on the bridge, like he had Del there with her hair all smelly with some kind of perfume. Funny, the smell of dark girls' hair. He took down the binoculars, but he couldn't see anything on the horizon only the curdled scud drifting west in the faint moonlight. He found he was losing his course, good thing the mate hadn't picked out that moment to look aft at the wake. He got her back to E.N.E. by ¼E. When his trick was over and he rolled into his bunk, he lay awake a long time thinking of Del. God, he wanted money and a good job and a girl of his own instead of all these damn floosies when you got into port. What he ought to do was go down to Norfolk and settle down and get married.

Next day about noon they sighted the gray sugarloaf of Pico with a band of white clouds just under the peak and Fayal blue and irregular to the north. They passed between the two islands. The sea got very blue; it smelled like the country lanes outside of Washington when there was honeysuckle and laurel blooming in the runs. The bluegreen yellowgreen patchwork fields covered the steep hills like an oldfashioned quilt. That night they raised other islands to the eastward.

Five days of a heavy groundswell and they were in the Straits of Gibraltar. Eight days of dirty sea and chilly driving rain and they were off the Egyptian coast, a warm sunny morning, going into the port of Alexandria under one bell while the band of yellow mist ahead thickened up into masts, wharves, buildings, palmtrees. The streets smelt like a garbage pail, they drank arrack in bars run by Greeks who'd been in America and paid a dollar apiece to see three Jewishlooking girls dance a belly dance naked in a back room. In Alexandria they saw their first camouflaged ships, three British scout-cruisers striped like zebras and a transport all painted up with blue and green water-markings. When they saw them, all the watch on deck lined up along the rail and laughed like they'd split.

When he got paid off in New York a month later, it made him feel pretty good to go to Mrs Olsen and pay her back what he owed her. She had another youngster staying with her at the boardinghouse, a towheaded Swede who didn't know any English, so she didn't pay much attention to Joe. He hung around the kitchen a little while and asked her how things were and told her about the bunch on the *Montana*, then he went over to the Penn Station to see when he could catch a train to Washington. He sat dozing in the smoker of the daycoach half the night thinking of Georgetown and when he'd been a kid at school and the bunch in the poolroom on 4½ Street and trips on the river with Alec and Janey.

It was a bright wintry sunny morning when he piled out at the Union Station. He couldn't seem to make up his mind to go over to Georgetown to see the folks. He loafed around the Union Station, got a shave and a shine and a cup of coffee, read the Washington *Post*, counted his money; he still had more'n fifty iron men, quite a roll of lettuce for a guy like him. Then he guessed he'd wait and see Janey first, he'd wait around and maybe he'd catch her coming out from where she worked at noon. He walked around the Capitol Grounds and down Pennsylvania Avenue to the White House. On the Avenue he saw the same enlistment booth where he'd enlisted for the navy. Kinder gave him the creeps. He went and sat in the winter sunlight in Lafayette Square, looking at the little dressed-up kids playing and the nursemaids and the fat starlings hopping round the grass and the statue of Andrew Jackson, until he thought it was time to go catch Janey. His heart was beating so he could hardly see straight. It must have been later than he thought because none of the girls coming out of the elevator was her, though he waited about an hour in the vestibule of the Riggs Building until some lousy dick or other came up to him and asked him what the hell he was loitering around for.

So Joe had to go over to Georgetown after all to find out where Janey was. Mommer was in and his kid sisters and they were all talking about how they were going to have the house remodeled with the ten thousand dollars from the Old Man's insurance and they wanted him to go up to Oak Hill to see the grave, but Joe said what was the use and got away as soon as he could. They asked all kinds of questions about how he was getting on and he didn't know what the hell to tell 'em. They told him where Janey lived, but they didn't know when she got out of her office.

He stopped at the Belasco and bought some theater tickets and then went back to the Riggs Building. He got there just as Janey was stepping out of the elevator. She was nicely dressed and had her chin up with a new little cute independent tilt. He was so glad to see her he was afraid he was going to bawl. Her voice was different. She had a quick chilly way of talking and a kidding manner she'd never had before. He took her to supper and to the theater and she told him all about how well she was getting on at Dreyfus and Carroll and what interesting people she was getting to know. It made him feel like a bum going around with her.

Then he left her at the apartment she had with a girl friend and took the car back to the station. He settled down and smoked a cigar in the smoker of the daycoach. He felt pretty blue. Next day in New York he looked up a guy he knew and they went out and had a few drinks and found 'em some skirts and the day after that he was sitting on a bench in Union Square with a headache and not a red cent in his jeans. He found the stubs of the tickets to the show at the Belasco Theater he'd taken Janey to and put them carefully in the cigarbox with the other junk.

Next boat he shipped on was the *North Star* bound for St Nazaire with a cargo listed as canned goods that everybody knew was shellcaps, and bonuses for the crew on account of the danger of going through the zone. She was a crazy whaleback, had been an oreboat on the Great Lakes, leaked so they had to have the pumps going half the time, but Joe liked the bunch and the chow was darn good and old Cap'n Perry was as fine an old seadog as you'd like to see, had been living ashore for a couple of years down at Atlantic Highlands, but had come back on account of the big money to try to make a pile for his daughter; she'd get the insurance anyway, Joe heard him tell the mate with a wheezy laugh. They had a smooth winter crossing, the wind behind them all the way right till they were in the Bay of Biscay. It was very cold and the sea was dead calm when they came in sight of the French coast, low and sandy at the mouth of the Loire.

They had the flag up and the ship's name signal and Sparks was working overtime and they sure were nervous on account of mines until the French patrol boat came out and led the way through the winding channel into the river between the minefields.

When they saw the spires and the long rows of gray houses and the little clustered chimneypots of St Nazaire in the smoky dust the boys were going round slapping each other on the back and saying they sure would get cockeyed this night.

But what happened was that they anchored out in the stream and Cap'n Perry and the first mate went ashore in the dinghy and they didn't dock till two days later on account of there being no room at the wharves. When they did get ashore to take a look at the mademosels and the vin rouge, they all had to show their seamen's passports when they left the wharf to a redfaced man in a blue uniform trimmed with red who had a tremendous pair of pointed black mustaches. Blackie Flannagan had crouched down behind him and somebody was just going to give him a shove over his back when the Chief yelled at them from across the street, 'For Chris' sake, can't you c——s see that's a frog cop? You don't want to get run in right on the wharf, do you?'

Joe and Flannagan got separated from the others and walked around to look the town over. The streets were paved with cobblestones and awful little and funny and the old women all wore tight white lace caps and everything looked kinder falling down. Even the dogs looked like frog dogs. They ended up in a place marked American Bar, but it didn't look like any bar they'd ever seen in the States. They bought a bottle of cognac for a starter. Flannagan said the town looked like Hoboken, but Joe said it looked kinder like Villefranche where he'd been when he was in the navy. American dollars went pretty far if you knew enough not to let 'em gyp you.

Another American came into the dump and they got to talking and he said he'd been torpedoed on the *Oswego* right in the mouth of the Loire River. They gave him some of the cognac and he said how it had been, that Uboat had blowed the poor old *Oswego* clear outa the water and when smoke cleared away she'd split right in two and closed up like a jackknife. They had another bottle of cognac on that and then the feller took them to a house he said he knew and there they found some more of the bunch drinking beer and dancing around with the girls.

Joe was having a good time parleyvooing with one of the girls, he'd point to something and she'd tell him how to say it in French, when a fight started someway and the frog cops came and the bunch had to run for it. They all got back aboard ship ahead of the cops, but they came and stood on the dock and jabbered for about half an hour until old Cap'n Perry, who'd just gotten back from town in a horsecab, told 'em where to get off.

The trip back was slow but pretty good. They were only a week in Hampton Roads, loaded up with a cargo of steel ingots and explosives, and cleared for Cardiff. It was nervous work. The Cap'n took a northerly course and they got into a lot of fog. Then after a solid week of icy cold weather with a huge following sea they sighted Rockall. Joe was at the wheel. The green hand in the crowsnest yelled out, 'Battleship ahead,' and old Cap'n Perry stood on the bridge laughing, looking at the rock through his binoculars.

Next morning they raised the Hebrides to the south. Cap'n Perry was just pointing out the Butt of Lewis to the mate when the lookout in the bow gave a scared hail. It was a submarine all right. You could see first the periscope trailing a white feather of foam, then the dripping conning tower. The submarine had hardly gotten to the surface when she started firing across the *North Star*'s bows with a small gun that the squareheads manned while decks were still awash. Joe went running aft to run up the flag, although they had the flag painted amidships on either side of the boat. The engineroom bells jingled as Cap'n Perry threw her into full speed astern. The jerries stopped firing and four of them came on board in a collapsible punt. All hands had their life preservers on and some of the men were going below for their duffle when the fritz officer who came aboard shouted in English that they had five minutes to abandon the ship. Cap'n Perry handed over the ship's papers, the boats were lowered like winking as the blocks were well oiled. Something made Joe run back up to the boat deck and cut the lashings on the liferafts with his jackknife, so he and Cap'n Perry and the ship's cat were the last to leave the *North Star*. The jerries had planted bombs in the engineroom and were rowing back to the submarine like the devil was after them. The Cap'n's boat had hardly pushed off when the explosion lammed them a blow on the side of the head. The boat swamped and before they knew what had hit them they were swimming in the icy water among all kinds of planking and junk. Two of the boats were still afloat. The old *North Star* was sinking quietly with the flag flying and the signalflags blowing out prettily in the light breeze. They must have been half an hour or an hour in the water. After the ship had sunk they managed to get onto the liferafts and the mate's boat and the Chief's boat took them in tow. Cap'n Perry called the roll. There wasn't a soul missing. The submarine had submerged and gone some time ago. The men in the boats started pulling towards shore. Till nightfall the strong tide was carrying them in fast towards the Pentland Firth. In the last dusk they could see the tall headlands of the Orkneys. But when the tide changed they couldn't make headway against it. The men in the boats and the men in the rafts took turn and turn about at the oars, but they couldn't buck the terrible ebb. Somebody said the tide ran eight knots an hour in there. It was a pretty bad night. With the first dawn they caught sight of a scoutcruiser bearing down on them. Her searchlight glared suddenly in their faces making everything look black again. The Britishers took 'em on board and hustled them down into the engineroom to get warm. A redfaced steward came down with a bucket of steaming tea with rum in it and served it out with a ladle.

The scoutcruiser took 'em into Glasgow, pretty well shaken up by the chop of the Irish Sea, and they all stood around in the drizzle on the dock while Cap'n Perry went to find the American consul. Joe was getting numb in the feet standing still and tried to walk across to the iron gates opposite the wharfhouse to take a squint down the street, but an elderly man in a uniform poked a bayonet at his belly and he stopped. Joe went back to the crowd and told 'em how they were prisoners

there like they were fritzies. Jeez, it made 'em sore. Flannagan
started telling about how the frogs had arrested him one time
for getting into a fight with an orangeman in a bar in Marseilles
and had been ready to shoot him because they said the Irish
were all pro-German. Joe told about how the limeys had run
him in in Liverpool. They were all grousing about how the
whole business was a lousy deal when Ben Tarbell the mate
turned up with an old guy from the consulate and told 'em
to come along.

They had to troop half across town, through streets black
dark for fear of airraids and slimy with rain, to a long tarpaper
shack inside a barbedwire enclosure. Ben Tarbell told the boys
he was sorry, but they'd have to stay there for the present, and
that he was trying to get the consul to do something about it
and the Old Man had cabled the owners to try to get 'em some
pay. Some girls from the Red Cross brought them grub, mostly
bread and marmalade and meatpaste, nothing you could really
sink your teeth into, and some thin blankets. They stayed in
that damn place for twelve days, playing poker and yarning
and reading old newspapers. Evenings sometimes a frowzy
halfdrunk woman would get past the old guard and peek in the
door of the shack and beckon one of the men out into the foggy
darkness behind the latrines somewhere. Some of the guys were
disgusted and wouldn't go.

They'd been shut up in there so long that when the mate
finally came around and told 'em they were going home, they
didn't have enough spunk left in 'em to yell. They went across
the town packed with traffic and gasflare in the fog again and
on board a new 6000 ton freighter, the *Vicksburg*, that had
just unloaded a cargo of cotton. It felt funny being a passenger and being able to lay around all day on the trip home.

Joe was lying out on the hatchcover the first sunny day they'd
had when old Cap'n Perry came up to him. Joe got to his feet.
Cap'n Perry said he hadn't had a chance to tell him what he
thought of him for having the presence of mind to cut the
lashings on those rafts and that half the men on the boat owed
their lives to him. He said Joe was a bright boy and ought to
start studying how to get out of the fo'c'stle and that the
American merchant marine was growing every day on account
of the war and young fellers like him were just what they
needed for officers, 'You remind me, boy.' he said. 'when we get
to Hampton Roads and I'll see what I can do on the next ship
I get. You could get your third mate's ticket right now with a

little time in shore school.' Joe grinned and said he sure would like to. It made him feel good the whole trip. He couldn't wait to go and see Del and tell her he wasn't in the fo'c'stle any more. Dodgast it, he was tired of being treated like a jailbird all his life.

The *Vicksburg* docked at Newport News. Hampton Roads was fuller of shipping than Joe had ever seen it. Along the wharves everybody was talking about the *Deutschland* that had just unloaded a cargo of dyes in Baltimore. When Joe got paid off, he wouldn't even take a drink with his shipmates, but hustled down to the ferry station to get the ferry for Norfolk. Jeez, the old ferry seemed slow. It was about five o'clock a Saturday afternoon when he got into Norfolk. Walking down the street he was scared she wouldn't be home yet.

Del was home and seemed glad to see him. She said she had a date that night, but he teased her into breaking it off. After all, weren't they engaged to be married? They went out and had a sundae at an icecream parlor and she told him all about her new job with Duponts and how she was getting ten more a week and how all the boys she knew and several girls were working in the munition factories and how some of 'em were making fifteen dollars a day and they were buying cars and the boy she'd had a date with that night had a Packard. It took a long time for Joe to get around to tell her about what old Cap'n Perry had said and she was all excited about his having been torpedoed and said why didn't he go and get a job over at Newport News in the shipyard and make real money, she didn't like the idea of his being torpedoed every minute, but Joe said he hated to leave the sea now that there was a chance of getting ahead. She asked him how much he'd make as third mate on a freighter and he said a hundred and twentyfive a month, but there'd always be bonuses for the zone and there were a lot of new ships being built and he thought the prospects pretty good all around.

Del screwed her face up in a funny way and said she didn't know how she'd like having a husband who was away from home all the time, but she went into a phone booth and called the other boy up and broke off the date she had with him. They went back to Del's house and she cooked up a bite of supper. Her folks had gone over to Fortress Monroe to eat with an aunt of hers. It made Joe feel good to see her with an apron on bustling around the kitchen. She let him kiss her a couple of times, but when he went up behind her and hugged her and pulled her face back and kissed her, she said not to do that, it made her feel all out of breath. The dark smell of her hair and the feel of her skin that was white like milk against his lips made him feel giddy. It was a relief when they went out on the street in the keen northwest wind again. He bought her a box of Saturday night candies at a drugstore. They went to see a bill of vaudeville and movies at the Colonial. The Belgian war pictures were awful exciting and Del said wasn't it terrible and Joe started to tell her about what a guy he knew had told him about being in an airraid in London, but she didn't listen.

When he kissed her goodnight in the hall, Joe felt awful hot and pressed her up in the corner by the hatrack and tried to get his hand under her skirt, but she said not till they were married, and he said with his mouth against hers, when would they get married and she said they'd get married as soon as he got his new job.

Just then they heard the key in the latch just beside them and she pulled him into the parlor and whispered not to say anything about their being engaged just yet. It was Del's old man and her mother and her two kid sisters and the old man gave Joe a mean look and the kid sisters giggled and Joe went away feeling fussed. It was early yet, but Joe felt too hetup to sleep, so he walked around a little and then went by the Stirps' house to see if Will was in town. Will was in Baltimore looking for a job, but old Mrs Stirp said if he didn't have nowhere to go and wanted to sleep in Will's bed he was welcome, but he couldn't sleep for thinking of Del and how smart she was and how she felt in his arms and how the smell of her hair made him feel crazy and how much he wanted her.

First thing he did Monday morning was to go over to Newport News and see Cap'n Perry. The Old Man was darn nice to him, asked him about his schooling and his folks. When Joe said he was old Cap'n Joe Williams's son, Cap'n Perry couldn't do enough for him. Him and Joe's old man had been on the *Albert and Mary Smith* together in the old clippership days. He said he'd have a berth for Joe as junior officer on the *Henry B. Higginbotham* as soon as she'd finished repairs and he must go to work at shore school over in Norfolk and get ready to go before the licensing board and get his ticket. He'd coach him up on the fine points himself. When he left, the Old Man said, 'Ma boy, if you work like you oughter, bein' your dad's son, an' this war keeps up, you'll be master of your own vessel in five years, I'll guarantee it.'

Joe couldn't wait to get hold of Del and tell her about it. That night he took her to the movies to see the *Four Horsemen.* It was darned exciting, they held hands all through and he kept his leg pressed against her plump little leg. Seeing it with her and the war and everything flickering on the screen and the music like in church and her hair against his cheek and being pressed close to her a little sweaty in the warm dark like to went to his head. When the picture was over he felt he'd go crazy if he couldn't have her right away. She was kinder kidding him along and he got sore and said God damn it, they'd have to get married right away or else he was through. She'd held out on him just about long enough. She began to cry and turned her face up to him all wet with tears and said if he really loved her he wouldn't talk like that and that that was no way to talk to a lady and he felt awful bad about it. When they got back to her folks' house, everybody had gone to bed and they went out in the pantry back of the kitchen without turning the light on and she let him love her up. She said honestly she loved him so much she'd let him do anything he wanted, only she knew he wouldn't respect her if she did. She said she was sick of living at home and having her mother keep tabs on her all the time, and she'd tell her folks in the morning about how he'd got a job as a ship's officer and they had to get married before he left and that he must get him his uniform right away.

When Joe left the house to look around and find a flop, he was walking on air. He hadn't planned to get married that soon, but what the hell, a man had to have a girl of his own. He began doping out what he'd write Janey about it, but he decided she wouldn't like it and that he'd better not write. He wished Janey wasn't getting so kind of uppish, but after all she was making a big success of business. When he was skipper of his own ship she'd think it was all great.

Joe was two months ashore that time. He went to shore school every day, lived at the Y.M.C.A. and didn't take a drink or shoot pool or anything. The pay he had saved up from the two trips on the *North Star* was just about enough to swing it. Every week or so he went over to Newport News to talk it over with old Cap'n Perry who told him what kind of questions the examining board would ask him and what kind of papers he'd need. Joe was pretty worried about his original A.B. certificate, but he had another now and recommendations from captains of ships he'd been on. What the hell, he'd been at sea four years, it was about time he knew a little about running a ship. He almost worried himself sick over the examination, but when he was actually there standing before the old birds on the board it wasn't as bad as he thought it'd be. When he actually got the third mate's license and showed it to Del, they were both of them pretty tickled.

Joe bought his uniform when he got an advance of pay. From then on he was busy all day doing odd jobs round the drydock for old Cap'n Perry who hadn't gotten a crew together yet. Then in the evenings he worked painting up the little bedroom, kitchenette, and bath he'd rented for him and Del to live in when he was ashore. Del's folks insisted on having a church wedding and Will Stirp, who was making fifteen dollars a day in a shipyard in Baltimore, came down to be best man.

Joe felt awful silly at the wedding and Will Stirp had gotten hold of some whiskey and had a breath like a distillery wagon and a couple of the other boys were drunk and that made Del and her folks awful sore and Del looked like she wanted to crown him all through the service. When it was over Joe found he'd wilted his collar and Del's old man began pulling a lot of jokes and her sisters giggled so much in their white organdy dresses, he could have choked 'em. They went back to the Matthews' house and everybody was awful stiff except Will Stirp and his friends who brought in a bottle of whiskey and got old man Matthews cockeyed. Mrs Matthews ran 'em all out of the house and all the old cats from the Ladies' Aid rolled their eyes up and said, 'Could you imagine it?' And Joe and Del left in a taxicab a feller he knew drove and everybody threw rice at them and Joe found he had a sign reading Newlywed pinned on the tail of his coat and Del cried and cried and when they got to their apartment Del locked herself in the bathroom and wouldn't answer when he called and he was afraid she'd fainted.

Joe took off his new blue serge coat and his collar and necktie and walked up and down, not knowing what to do. It was six o'clock in the evening. He had to be aboard ship at midnight because they were sailing for France as soon as it was day. He didn't know what to do. He thought maybe she'd want something to eat, so he cooked up some bacon and eggs on the stove. By the time everything was cold and Joe was walking up and down cussing under his breath, Del came out of the bathroom looking all fresh and pink like nothing had happened. She said she couldn't eat anything, but let's go to a movie . . .

'But, honeybug,' said Joe, 'I've got to pull out at twelve.' She began to cry again and he flushed and felt awful fussed. She snuggled up to him and said, 'We won't stay for the feature. We'll come back in time.' He grabbed her and started hugging her, but she held him off firmly and said 'Later.'

Joe couldn't look at the picture. When they got back to the apartment, it was ten o'clock. She let him pull off her clothes, but she jumped into bed and wrapped the bedclothes around her and whimpered that she was afraid of having a baby, that he must wait till she found out what to do to keep from having a baby. All she let him do was rub up against her through the bedclothes and then suddenly it was ten of twelve and he had to jump into his clothes and run down to the wharf. An old colored man rowed him out to where his ship lay at anchor. It was a sweetsmelling spring night without any moon. He heard honking overhead and tried to squint up his eyes to see the birds passing against the pale stars. 'Them's geese, boss,' said the old colored man in a soft voice. When he climbed on board everybody started kidding him and declared he looked all wore out. Joe didn't know what to say, so he talked big and kidded back and lied like a fish.

# Newsreel 21

*Goodbye Broadway*
*Hello France*
*We're ten million strong*

EIGHTYEAROLD BOY SHOT BY LAD WITH RIFLE

the police have already notified us that any entertainment in Paris must be brief and quietly conducted and not in public view and that we have already had more dances than we ought

capitalization grown 104 per cent while business expands 250 per cent

HAWAIIAN SUGAR CONTROL LOST BY GERMANS

efforts of the Bolshevik Government to discuss the withdrawal of the U.S. and allied forces from Russia through negotiation for an armistice are attracting no serious attention

BRITISH AIRMAN FIGHTS SIXTY FOES

SERBIANS ADVANCE TEN MILES; TAKE TEN TOWNS; MENACE PRILEP

*Good morning*
*Mr Zip Zip Zip*
*You're surely looking fine*
*Good morning*
*Mr Zip Zip Zip*
*With your hair cut just as short as*
*With your hair cut just as short as*
*With your hair cut just as short as mine*

LENINE REPORTED ALIVE

### AUDIENCE AT HIPPODROME TESTIMONIALS MOVED TO CHEERS AND TEARS

several different stories have come to me well authenticated concerning the depth of Hindenburg's brutality; the details are too horrible for print. They relate to outraged womanhood and girlhood, suicide and blood of the innocent that wet the feet of Hindenburg

#### WAR DECREASES MARRIAGES AND BIRTHS

> *Oh ashes to ashes*
> *And dust ʃo dust*
> *If the shrapnel don't get you*
> *Then the eightyeights must*

## The Camera Eye (29)

the raindrops fall one by one out of the horsechestnut tree over the arbor onto the table in the abandoned beergarden and the puddly gravel and my clipped skull where my fingers move gently forward and back over the fuzzy knobs and hollows

spring and we've just been swimming in the Marne way off somewhere beyond the fat clouds on the horizon they are hammering on a tin roof     in the rain in the spring after a swim in the Marne with that hammering to the north pounding the thought of death into our ears

the winey thought of death stings in the spring blood that throbs in the sunburned neck     up and down the belly under the tight belt hurries like cognac into the tips of my toes and the lobes of my ears and my fingers stroking the fuzzy closecropped skull

shyly tingling fingers feel out the limits of the hard immortal skull under the flesh a deathshead and skeleton sits wearing glasses in the arbor under the lucid occasional raindrops inside the new khaki uniform inside my twentyoneyearold body that's been swimming in the Marne in red and whitestriped trunks in Chalons in the spring

## *Richard Ellsworth Savage*

The years Dick was little he never heard anything about his dad, but when he was doing his homework evenings up in his little room in the attic he'd start thinking about him sometimes; he'd throw himself on the bed and lie on his back trying to remember what he had been like and Oak Park and everything before Mother had been so unhappy and they had had to come East to live with Aunt Beatrice. There was the smell of bay rum and cigarsmoke and he was sitting on the back of an upholstered sofa beside a big man in a panama hat who shook the sofa when he laughed; he held on to Dad's back and punched his arm and the muscle was hard like a chair or a table and when Dad laughed he could feel it rumble in his back, 'Dicky, keep your dirty feet off my palmbeach suit,' and he was on his hands and knees in the sunlight that poured through the lace curtains of the window trying to pick the big purple roses off the carpet; they were all standing in front of a red automobile and Dad's face was red and he smelt of armpits and white steam was coming out around, and people were saying Safetyvalve. Downstairs Dad and Mummy were at dinner and there was company and wine and a new butler and it must be awful funny because they laughed so much and the knives and forks went click-click all the time; Dad found him in his nightgown peeking through the portières and came out awful funny and excited smelling like wine and whaled him and Mother came out and said, 'Henry, don't strike the child,' and they stood hissing at one another in low voices behind the portières on account of company and Mummy had picked Dick up and carried him upstairs crying in her evening dress all lacy and frizzly and with big puffy silk sleeves; touching silk put his teeth on edge, made him shudder all down his spine. He and Henry had had tan overcoats with pockets in them like grownup overcoats and tan caps and he'd lost the button off the top of his. Way back there it was sunny and windy; Dick got tired and sickyfeeling when he tried to remember back like that and it got him so he couldn't keep his mind on tomorrow's lessons and would pull out *Twenty Thousand Leagues Under the Sea* that he had under the mattress because Mother took books away when they weren't just about the lessons and would read just a little and then he'd forget everything reading and wouldn't know his lessons the next day.

All the same he got along very well at school and the teachers liked him, particularly Miss Teazle, the English teacher, because he had nice manners and said little things that weren't fresh but that made them laugh. Miss Teazle said he showed real feeling for English composition. One Christmas he sent her a little rhyme he made up about the Christ Child and the Three Kings and she declared he had a gift.

The better he liked it in school the worse it was at home. Aunt Beatrice was always nag nag nag from morning till night. As if he didn't know that he and Mother were eating her bread and sleeping under her roof; they paid board, didn't they? even if they didn't pay as much as Major and Mrs Glen or Doctor Kern did, and they certainly did enough work to pay for their keep anyway. He'd heard Mrs Glen saying when Doctor Atwood was calling and Aunt Beatrice was out of the room how it was a shame that poor Mrs Savage, such a sweet woman, and a good churchwoman too, and the daughter of a general in the army, had to work her fingers to the bone for her sister who was only a fussy old maid and overcharged so, though of course she did keep a very charming house and set an excellent table, not like a boardinghouse at all, more like a lovely refined private home, such a relief to find in Trenton, that was such a commercial city so full of workingpeople and foreigners; too bad that the daughters of General Ellsworth should be reduced to taking paying guests. Dick felt Mrs Glen might have said something about his carrying out the ashes and shovelling snow and all that. Anyway he didn't think a highschool student ought to have to take time from his studies to do the chores.

Doctor Atwood was the rector of Saint Gabriel's Episcopal Church where Dick had to sing in the choir every Sunday at two services while mother and his brother Henry S., who was three years older than he was and worked in a drafting office in Philadelphia and only came home weekends, sat comfortably in a pew. Mother loved Saint Gabriel's because it was so highchurch and they had processions and even incense. Dick hated it on account of choirpractice and having to keep his surplice clean and because he never had any pocketmoney to shoot craps with behind the bench in the vestry and he was always the one who had to stand at the door and whisper, 'Cheeze it,' if anybody was coming.

One Sunday, right after his thirteenth birthday, he'd walked home from church with his mother and Henry feeling hungry and wondering all the way if they were going to have fried chicken for dinner. They were all three stepping up onto the stoop, Mother leaning a little on Dick's arm and the purple and green poppies on her wide hat jiggling in the October sunlight, when he saw Aunt Beatrice's thin face looking worriedly out through the glass panel of the front door.

'Leona,' she said in an excited reproachful voice, 'he's here.'

'Who, Beatrice dear?'

'You know well enough . . . I don't know what to do . . . he says he wants to see you. I made him wait in the lower hall on account of . . . er . . . our friends.'

'Oh, God, Beatrice, haven't I borne enough from that man?'

Mother let herself drop onto the bench under the stag'shorn coatrack in the hall. Dick and Henry stared at the white faces of the two women. Aunt Beatrice pursed up her lips and said in a spiteful tone, 'You boys had better go out and walk round the block. I can't have two big hulks like you loafing round the house. You be back for Sunday dinner at onethirty sharp . . . run along now.'

'Why, what's the matter with Aunt Beatrice?' asked Dick as they walked off down the street.

'Got the pip, I guess . . . she gives me a pain in the neck,' Henry said in a superior tone.

Dick walked along kicking at the pavement with his toes.

'Say, we might go around and have a soda . . . they have awful good sodas at Dryer's.'

'Got any dough?'

Dick shook his head.

'Well, you needn't think I'm goin' to treat you. . . . Jimminy crickets, Trenton's a rotten town . . . In Philadelphia I seen a drugstore with a sodafountain half a block long.'

'Aw, you.'

'I bet you don't remember when we lived in Oak Park, Dick. . . . Now Chicago's a fine town.'

'Sure I do . . . and you an' me going to kindergarden and Dad being there and everything.'

'Hell's bells, I wanta smoke.'

'Mother'll smell it on you.'

'Don't give a damn if she does.'

When they got home Aunt Beatrice met them at the front door looking sore as a crab and told them to go down to the basement. Mother wanted to see them. The back stairs smelt of Sunday dinner and sage chickenstuffing. They hobbled down as slowly as possible, it must be about Henry's smoking. She was in the dark basement hall. By the light of the gasjet against the wall Dick couldn't make out who the man was. Mother came up to them and they could see that her eyes were red. 'Boys, it's your father,' she said in a weak voice. The tears began running down her face.

The man had a gray shapeless head and his hair was cut very short, the lids of his eyes were red and lashless and his eyes were the same color as his face. Dick was scared. It was somebody he'd known when he was little; it couldn't be Dad.

'For God's sake, no more waterworks, Leona,' the man said in a whining voice. As he stood staring into the boys' faces his body wobbled a little as if he was weak in the knees. 'They're good lookers both of them, Leona . . . I guess they don't think much of their poor old dad.'

They all stood there without saying anything in the dark basement hall in the rich close smell of Sunday dinner from the kitchen. Dick felt he ought to talk, but something had stuck in his throat. He found he was stuttering, 'Ha-ha-hav-have you been sick?'

The man turned to Mother. 'You'd better tell them all about it when I'm gone . . . don't spare me . . . nobody's ever spared me . . . Don't look at me as if I was a ghost, boys, I won't hurt you.' A nervous tremor shook the lower part of his face. 'All my life I've always been the one has gotten hurt. . . . Well, this is a long way from Oak Park . . . I just wanted to take a look at you, good-bye . . . I guess the likes of me had better go out the basement door . . . I'll meet you at the bank at eleven sharp, Leona, and that'll be the last thing you'll ever have to do for me.'

The gasjet went red when the door opened and flooded the hall with reflected sunlight. Dick was shaking for fear the man was going to kiss him, but all he did was give them each a little trembly pat on the shoulder. His suit hung loose on him and he seemed to have trouble lifting his feet in their soft baggy shoes up the five stone steps to the street.

Mother closed the door sharply.

'He's going to Cuba,' she said. 'That's the last time we'll see him. I hope God can forgive him for all this, your poor mother never can . . . at least he's out of that horrible place.'

'Where was he, Mom?' asked Henry in a businesslike voice.

'Atlanta.'

Dick ran away and up to the top floor and into his own room in the attic and threw himself on the bed sobbing.

They none of them went down to dinner although they were hungry and the stairs were rich with the smell of roast chicken. When Pearl was washing up, Dick tiptoed into the kitchen and coaxed a big heaping plate of chicken and stuffing and sweetpotatoes out of her; she said to run along and eat it in the backyard because it was her day out and she had the dishes to do. He sat on a dusty step ladder in the laundry eating. He could hardly get the chicken down on account of the funny stiffness in his throat. When he'd finished, Pearl made him help her wipe.

That summer they got him a job as bellboy in a small hotel at Bay Head that was run by a lady who was a parishioner of Doctor Atwood's. Before he left Major and Mrs Glen, who were Aunt Beatrice's starboarders, gave him a fivedollar bill for pocketmoney and a copy of the *Little Shepherd of Kingdom Come* to read on the train. Doctor Atwood asked him to stay after the Bibleclass his last Sunday and told him the parable of the talent, that Dick knew very well already because Doctor Atwood preached on it as a text four times every year, and showed him a letter from the headmaster of Kent accepting him for the next year as a scholarship pupil and told him that he must work hard because God expected from each of us according to our abilities. Then he told him a few things a growing boy ought to know and said he must avoid temptations and always serve God with a clean body and a clean mind, and keep himself pure for the lovely sweet girl he would some day marry, and that anything else led only to madness and disease. Dick went away with his cheeks burning.

It wasn't so bad at the Bayview, but the guests and help were all old people; about his own age there was only Skinny Murray, the other bellhop, a tall sandyhaired boy who never had anything to say. He was a couple of years older than Dick. They slept on two cots in a small airless room right up under the roof that would still be so hot from the sun by bedtime they could hardly touch it. Through the thin partition they could hear the waitresses in the next room rustling about and giggling as they went to bed. Dick hated that sound and the smell of girls and cheap facepowder that drifted in through the cracks in the wall. The hottest nights he and Skinny would take the screen out of the window and crawl out along the gutter to a piece of flat roof there was over one of the upper porches. There the mosquitoes would torment them, but it was better than trying to sleep on their cots. Once the girls were looking out of the window and saw them crawling along the gutter and made a great racket that they were peeping and that they'd report them to the manageress, and they were scared to death and made plans all night about what they'd do if they were fired, they'd go to Barnegat and get work on fishingboats; but the next day the girls didn't say anything about it. Dick was kinda disappointed because he hated waiting on people and running up and down stairs answering bells.

It was Skinny who got the idea they might make some extra money selling fudge, because when Dick got a package of fudge from his mother he sold it to one of the waitresses for a quarter. So Mrs Savage sent a package of fresh fudge and panocha every week by parcel post that Dick and Skinny sold to the guests in little boxes. Skinny bought the boxes and did most of the work, but Dick convinced him it wouldn't be fair for him to take more than ten per cent of the profits because he and his mother put up the original capital.

The next summer they made quite a thing of the fudge-selling. Skinny did the work more than ever because Dick had been to a private school and had been hobnobbing with rich boys all winter whose parents had plenty of money. Luckily none of them came to Bay Head for the summer. He told Skinny all about the school and recited ballads about Saint John Hospitaller and Saint Christopher he'd made up and that had been published in the school paper; he told him about serving at the altar and the beauty of the Christian Faith and about how he'd made the outfield in the junior baseballteam. Dick made Skinny go to church with him every Sunday to the little Episcopal chapel called Saint Mary's-by-the-Sea. Dick used to stay after the service and discuss points of doctrine and ceremony with Mr Thurlow, the young minister, and was finally invited to come home with him to dinner and meet his wife.

The Thurlows lived in an unpainted peakedroofed bungalow in the middle of a sandlot near the station. Mrs Thurlow was a dark girl with a thin aquiline nose and bangs, who smoked cigarettes and hated Bay Head. She talked about how bored she was and how she shocked the old lady parishioners and Dick thought she was wonderful. She was a great reader of the *Smart Set* and *The Black Cat* and books that were advanced, and poked fun at Edwin's attempts to restore primitive Christianity to the boardwalk, as she put it. Edwin Thurlow would look at her from under the colorless lashes of his pale eyes and whisper meekly, 'Hilda, you oughtn't to talk like that'; then he'd turn mildly to Dick and say, 'Her bark is worse than her bite, you know.' They got to be great friends and Dick took to running around to their house whenever he could get away from the hotel. He took Skinny around a couple of times, but Skinny seemed to feel that their talk was too deep for him and would never stay long, but would shuffle off after explaining that he had to sell some fudge.

The next summer it was mostly the hope of seeing the Thurlows that made Dick not mind going to work at the Bayview where Mrs Higgins gave him the job of roomclerk with an increase of pay on account of his gentlemanly manners. Dick was sixteen and his voice was changing; he had dreams about things with girls and thought a lot about sin and had a secret crush on Spike Culbertson, the yellowhaired captain of his school ballteam. He hated everything about his life, his aunt and the smell of her boardinghouse, the thought of his father, his mother's flowergarden hats, not having enough money to buy good clothes or go to fashionable summer resorts like the other fellows did. All kinds of things got him terribly agitated so that it was hard not to show it. The wobble of the waitresses' hips and breasts while they were serving meals, girls' underwear in store windows, the smell of the bathhouses and the salty tingle of a wet bathingsuit and the tanned skin of fellows and girls in bathingsuits lying out in the sun on the beach.

He'd been writing Edwin and Hilda long letters all winter about anything that came into his head, but when he actually saw them he felt funny and constrained. Hilda was using a new kind of perfume that tickled his nose; even when he was sitting at the table at lunch with them, eating cold ham and potato salad from the delicatessen and talking about the primitive litanies and Gregorian music he couldn't help undressing them in his mind, thinking of them in bed naked; he hated the way he felt.

Sunday afternoons Edwin went to Elberon to conduct services in another little summer chapel. Hilda never went and often invited Dick to go out for a walk with her or come to tea. He and Hilda began to have a little world between them that Edwin had nothing to do with, where they only talked about him to poke fun at him. Dick began to see Hilda in his queer horrid dream. Hilda began to talk about how she and Dick were really brother and sister, how passionless people who never really wanted anything couldn't understand people like them. Those times Dick didn't get much chance to say anything. He and Hilda would sit on the back stoop in the shade smoking Egyptian Deities until they felt a little sick. Hilda'd say she didn't care whether the damn parishioners saw her or not, and talk and talk about how she wanted something to happen in her life, and smart clothes and to travel to foreign countries and to have money to spend and not to have to fuss with the housekeeping and how she felt sometimes she could kill Edwin for his mild calfish manner.

Edwin usually got back on a train that got in at 10.53 and, as Dick had Sunday evenings off from the hotel, he and Hilda would eat supper alone together and then take a walk along the beach. Hilda would take his arm and walk close to him; he'd wonder if she felt him tremble whenever their legs touched.

All week he'd think about those Sunday evenings. Sometimes he'd tell himself that he wouldn't go another time. He'd stay up in his room and read Dumas or go out with fellows he knew; being alone with Hilda like that made him feel too rotten afterwards. Then one moonless night, when they'd walked way down the beach beyond the rosy fires of the picnickers, and were sitting side by side on the sand talking about India's Love Lyrics that Hilda had been reading aloud that afternoon, she suddenly jumped on him and mussed up his hair and stuck her knees into his stomach and began to run her hands over his body under his shirt. She was strong for a girl, but he'd just managed to push her off when he had to grab her by the shoulders and pull her down on top of him. They neither of them said anything, but lay there in the sand breathing hard. At last she whispered, 'Dick, I mustn't have a baby. . . . We can't afford it. . . . That's why Edwin won't sleep with me. Damn it, I want you, Dick. Don't you see how awful it all is?' While she was talking her hands were burning him, moving down across his chest, over his ribs, around the curve of his belly. 'Don't, Hilda, don't.' There were mosquitoes around their heads. The long hissing invisible wash of the surf came almost to their feet.

That night Dick couldn't go down to the train to meet Edwin the way he usually did. He went back to the Bayview with his knees trembling, and threw himself on his bed in his stuffy little room under the roof. He thought of killing himself, but he was afraid of going to hell; he tried to pray, at least to remember the Lord's Prayer. He was terribly scared when he found he couldn't even remember the Lord's Prayer. Maybe that was the sin against the Holy Ghost they had committed.

The sky was gray and the birds were chirping outside before he got to sleep. All next day, as he sat holloweyed behind the desk, passing on the guests' demands for icewater and towels, answering inquiries about rooms and traintimes, he was turning a poem over in his mind about the scarlet of my sin and the scarlet of thy sin and dark birds above the surging seawaves crying and damned souls passionately sighing. When it was finished he showed the poem to the Thurlows. Edwin wanted to know where he got such morbid ideas, but was glad that faith and the church triumphed in the end. Hilda laughed hysterically and said he was a funny boy, but that maybe he'd be a writer someday.

When Skinny came down for a two weeks' vacation to take the place of one of the new bellhops that was sick, Dick talked very big to him about women and sin and about how he was in love with a married woman. Skinny said that wasn't right, because there were plenty of easy women around who'd give a feller all the loving he wanted. But when Dick found out that he'd never been with a girl, although he was two years older, he put on so many airs about experience and sin, that one night when they'd gone down to the drugstore for a soda, Skinny picked up a couple of girls and they walked down the beach with them. The girls were thirtyfive if they were a day and Dick didn't do anything but tell his girl about his unhappy love affair and how he had to be faithful to his love even though she was being unfaithful to him at the very moment. She said he was too young to take things serious like that and that a girl ought to be ashamed of herself who made a nice boy like him unhappy. 'Jeez, I'd make a feller happy if I had the chanct,' she said and burst out crying.

Walking back to the Bayview, Skinny was worried for fear he might have caught something, but Dick said physical things didn't matter and that repentance was the key of redemption. It turned out that Skinny did get sick because later in the summer he wrote Dick that he was paying a doctor five dollars a week to cure him up and that he felt terrible about it. Dick and Hilda went on sinning Sunday evenings when Edwin was conducting services in Elberon and when Dick went back to school that fall he felt very much the man of the world.

In the Christmas vacation he went to stay with the Thurlows in East Orange where Edwin was the assistant to the rector of the church of Saint John, Apostle. There, at tea at the rector's he met Hiram Halsey Cooper, a Jersey City lawyer and politician who was interested in High Church and first editions of Huysmans and who asked Dick to come to see him. When Dick called, Mr Cooper gave him a glass of sherry, showed him first editions of Beardsley and Huysmans and Austin Dobson, sighed about his lost youth and offered him a job in his office as soon as school was over. It turned out that Mr Cooper's wife, who was dead, had been an Ellsworth and a cousin of Dick's mother. Dick promised to send him copies of all his poems, and the articles he published in the school paper.

All the week he was with the Thurlows he was trying to get to see Hilda alone, but she managed to avoid him. He'd heard about French letters and wanted to tell her about them, but it wasn't until the last day that Edwin had to go out and make parochial calls. This time it was Dick who was the lover and Hilda who tried to hold him off, but he made her take off her clothes and they laughed and giggled together while they were making love. This time they didn't worry so much about sin and when Edwin came home to supper he asked them what the joke was, they seemed in such a good humor. Dick started telling a lot of cockandbull stories about his Aunt Beatrice and her boarders and they parted at the train in a gale of laughter.

That summer was the Baltimore convention. Mr Cooper had rented a house there and entertained a great deal. Dick's job was to stay in the outer office and be polite to everybody and take down people's names. He wore a blue serge suit and made a fine impression on everybody with his wavy black hair that Hilda used to tell him was like a raven's wing, his candid blue eyes and his pink and white complexion. What was going on was rather over his head, but he soon discovered what people Mr Cooper really wanted to see and what people were merely to be kidded along. Then when he and Mr Cooper found themselves alone, Mr Cooper would get out a bottle of Amontillado and pour them each a glass and sit in a big leather chair rubbing his forehead as if to rub the politics out of his mind and start talking about literature and the nineties and how he wished he was young again. It was understood that he was going to advance Dick the money to go through Harvard with.

Dick had hardly gotten back to school as a senior the next fall when he got a telegram from his mother:

> COME HOME AT ONCE DARLING YOUR POOR
> FATHER IS DEAD

He didn't feel sorry, but kind of ashamed, afraid of meeting any of the masters or fellows who might ask him questions. At the railway station it seemed as if the train would never come. It was Saturday and there were a couple of fellows in his class at the station. Until the train came he thought of nothing else but dodging them. He sat stiff on his seat in the empty day-coach looking out at the russet October hills, all keyed up for fear somebody would speak to him. It was a relief to hurry out of the Grand Central Station into the crowded New York streets where nobody knew him, where he knew nobody. Crossing on the ferry he felt happy and adventurous. He began to dread getting home and deliberately missed the first train to Trenton. He went into the old dining room of the Pennsylvania Station and ate fried oysters and sweet corn for lunch and ordered a glass of sherry, half afraid the colored waiter wouldn't serve him. He sat there a long time reading *The Smart Set* and drinking the sherry feeling like a man of the world, a traveler on his own, but underneath it all was the memory of that man's trembling white hurt face, the way he'd walked up the area steps that day. The restaurant gradually emptied. The waiter must be thinking it was funny his sitting there that long. He paid his check, and before he wanted to found himself on the train for Trenton.

At Aunt Beatrice's house everything looked and smelt the same. His mother was lying on the bed with the shades down and a handkerchief soaked in eau de cologne on her forehead. She showed him a photograph that he'd sent from Havana, a withered man who looked too small for his palmbeach suit and panama hat. He'd been working in the consulate as a clerk and had left a tenthousanddollar life insurance in her favor. While they were talking Henry came in looking worried and sore. The two of them went out in the back yard and smoked cigarettes together. Henry said he was going to take Mother to live with him in Philadelphia, get her away from Aunt Beatrice's nagging and this damn boardinghouse. He wanted Dick to come too and go to the U. of P. Dick said no, he was going to Harvard. Henry asked him how he was going to get the money. Dick said he'd make out all right, he didn't want any of the damned insurance. Henry said he wasn't going to touch it, that was Mother's, and they went back upstairs feeling about ready to sock each other in the jaw. Dick felt better, though, he could tell the fellows at school that his father had been consul at Havana and had died of a tropical fever.

That summer Dick worked for Mr Cooper at twenty-five dollars a week getting up a prospectus for an art museum he wanted to found in Jersey City and delighted him so by dedicating to him a verse translation of Horace's poem about Maecenas that he worked up with the help of the trot, that Mr Cooper made him a present of a thousand dollars to take him through college; for the sake of form and so that Dick should feel his responsibilities he put it in the form of a note maturing in five years at four per cent interest.

He spent his two weeks' vacation with the Thurlows at Bay Head. He'd hardly been able to wait going down on the train to see how Hilda would be, but everything was different. Edwin didn't have the paperwhite look he used to have; he'd had a call as assistant in a rich church on Long Island where the only thing that worried him was that part of the congregation was low and wouldn't allow chanting or incense. He was comforting himself with the thought that they did allow candles on the altar. Hilda was changed too. Dick was worried to see that she and Edwin held hands during supper. When they got alone she told him that she and Edwin were very happy now and that she was going to have a baby and that bygones must be bygones. Dick stalked up and down and ran his hands through his hair and talked darkly about death and hellonearth and going to the devil as fast as he could, but Hilda just laughed and told him not to be silly, that he was a goodlooking attractive boy and would find many nice girls crazy to fall in love with him. Before he left they had a long talk about religion and Dick told them, with a bitter stare at Hilda, that he'd lost his faith and only believed in Pan and Bacchus, the old gods of lust and drink. Edwin was quite startled, but Hilda said it was all nonsense and only growing pains. After he'd left he wrote a very obscure poem full of classical references that he labeled, 'To a Common Prostitute,' and sent to Hilda, adding a postscript that he was dedicating his life to Beauty and Sin.

Dick had an exam to repeat in Geometry which he'd flunked in the spring and one in Advanced Latin that he was taking for extra credits, so he went up to Cambridge a week before college opened. He sent his trunk and suitcase out by the transfer company from the South Station and went out on the subway. He had on a new gray suit and a new gray felt hat and was afraid of losing the certified check he had in his pocket for deposit in the Cambridge bank. The glimpse of redbrick Boston and the State House with its gold dome beyond the slate-colored Charles as the train came out into the air to cross the bridge looked like the places in foreign countries he and Hilda had talked about going to. Kendall Square . . . Central Square . . . Harvard Square. The train didn't go any further; he had to get out. Something about the sign on the turnstile OUT TO THE COLLEGE YARD sent a chill down his spine. He hadn't been in Cambridge two hours before he discovered that his felt hat ought to have been brown and old instead of new and that getting a room in the Yard had been a grave mistake for a freshman.

Perhaps it was the result of living in the Yard that he got to know all the wrong people, a couple of Socialist Jews in first-year law, a graduate student from the Middle West who was taking his Ph.D. in Gothic, a Y.M.C.A. addict out from Dorchester who went to chapel every morning. He went out for freshman rowing, but didn't make any of the crews and took to rowing by himself in a wherry three afternoons a week. The fellows he met down at the boathouse were pleasant enough to him, but most of them lived on the Gold Coast or in Beck and he never got much further than hello and solong with them. He went to all the football rallies and smokers and beernights, but he never could get there without one of his Jewish friends or a graduate student, so he never met anybody there who was anybody.

One Sunday morning in the spring he ran into Freddy Wigglesworth in the Union just as they were both going in to breakfast; they sat down at the same table. Freddy, an old Kent man, was a junior now. He asked Dick what he was doing and who he knew, and appeared horrified by what he heard.

'My dear boy,' he said, 'there's nothing to do now but go out for the *Monthly* or the *Advocate*. . . . I don't imagine the *Crime* would be much in your line, would it?'

'I was thinking of taking some of my stuff around, but I hardly had the nerve.'

'I wish you'd come around to see me last fall. . . . Goodness, we owe it to the old school to get you started right. Didn't any-

body tell you that nobody lived in the Yard except seniors?'
Freddy shook his head sadly as he drank his coffee.

Afterwards they went around to Dick's room and he read
some poems out loud. 'Why, I don't think they're so bad,' said
Freddy Wigglesworth, between puffs at a cigarette. 'Pretty
purple I'd say, though. . . . You get a few of them typed and
I'll take them round to R.G. . . . Meet me at the Union at
eight o'clock a week from Monday night and we'll go around
to Copey's. . . . Well, solong, I must be going.' After he'd gone
Dick walked up and down his room, his heart thumping hard.
He wanted to talk to somebody, but he was sick of all the
people he knew around Cambridge, so he sat down and wrote
Hilda and Edwin a long letter with rhyming inserts about how
well he was getting on at college.

Monday night finally came around. Already trying to tell
himself not to be disappointed if Freddy Wigglesworth forgot
about the date, Dick was on his way to the Union a full hour
before the time. The cavernous clatter and smell of Mem, the
funny stories of the boneheads at his table, and Mr Kanrich's
sweaty bald head bobbing above the brass instruments of the
band in the gallery seemed particularly dreary that evening.

There were tulips in the trim Cambridge gardens, and now
and then a whiff of lilacs on the wind. Dick's clothes irked
him; his legs were heavy as he walked around and around the
blocks of yellow frame houses and grass dooryards that he
already knew too well. The blood pounding through his veins
seemed too fast and too hot to stand. He must get out of Cambridge or go crazy. Of course at eight sharp when he walked
slowly up the Union steps Wigglesworth hadn't come yet. Dick
went upstairs to the library and picked up a book, but he was
too nervous to even read the title. He went downstairs again
and stood around in the hall. A fellow who worked next to
him in Physics 1 lab. came up and started to talk about something, but Dick could hardly drag out an answer. The fellow
gave him a puzzled look and walked off. It was twenty past
eight. Of course he wasn't coming, God damn him, he'd been
a fool to expect he'd come, a stuckup snob like Wigglesworth
wouldn't keep a date with a fellow like him.

Freddy Wigglesworth was standing in front of him, with his
hands in his pockets. 'Well, shall we Copify?' he was saying.

There was another fellow with him, a dreamylooking boy
with fluffy light gold hair and very paleblue eyes. Dick couldn't
help staring at him he was so handsome. 'This is Blake. He's

my younger brother. . . . You're in the same class.' Blake Wigglesworth hardly looked at Dick when they shook hands, but his mouth twisted up into a lopsided smile. When they crossed the Yard in the early summer dusk, fellows were leaning out the windows yelling 'Rinehart O Rinehart' and grackles were making a racket in the elms, and you could hear the screech of streetcar wheels from Mass. Avenue; but there was a complete hush in the lowceiling room lit with candles where a scrubbylooking little man was reading aloud a story that turned out to be Kipling's 'The Man Who Would Be King.' Everybody sat on the floor and was very intent. Dick decided he was going to be a writer.

Sophomore year Dick and Blake Wigglesworth began to go around together. Dick had a room in Ridgely and Blake was always there. Dick suddenly found he liked college, that the weeks were flying by. The *Advocate* and the *Monthly* each published a poem of his that winter; he and Ned, as he took to calling Blake Wigglesworth, had tea and conversation about books and poets in the afternoons and lit the room with candles. They hardly ever ate at Mem any more, though Dick was signed up there. Dick had no pocketmoney at all once he'd paid for his board and tuition and the rent at Ridgely, but Ned had a pretty liberal allowance that went for both. The Wigglesworths were well off; they often invited Dick to have Sunday dinner with them at Nahant. Ned's father was a retired art critic and had a white Vandyke beard; there was an Italian marble fireplace in the drawingroom over which hung a painting of a madonna, two angels, and some lilies that the Wigglesworths believed to be by Botticelli, although B.B., out of sheer malice, Mr Wigglesworth would explain, insisted that it was by Botticini.

Saturday nights Dick and Ned took to eating supper at the Thorndike in Boston and getting a little tight on sparkling nebbiolo. Then they'd go to the theater or the Old Howard.

The next summer Hiram Halsey Cooper was campaigning for Wilson. In spite of Ned's kidding letters, Dick found himself getting all worked up about the New Freedom, Too Proud to Fight, Neutrality in Mind and Deed, Industrial Harmony between Capital and Labor, and worked twelve hours a day typing releases, jollying smalltown newspaper editors into giving more space to Mr Cooper's speeches, branding Privilege, flaying the Interests. It was a letdown to get back to the dying elms of the Yard, lectures that neither advocated anything, nor attacked anything, *The Hill of Dreams*, and tea in the afternoons. He'd gotten a scholarship from the English Department and he and Ned had a room together in a house on Garden Street. They had quite a bunch of friends who were interested in English and Fine Arts and things like that, who'd gather in their room in the late afternoon, and sit late in the candlelight and the cigarettesmoke and the incense in front of a bronze Buddha Ned had bought in Chinatown when he was tight once, drinking tea and eating cake and talking. Ned never said anything unless the talk came around to drinking or sailingships; whenever politics or the war or anything like that came up he had a way of closing his eyes and throwing back his head and saying Blahblahblahblah.

Election Day Dick was so excited he cut all his classes. In the afternoon he and Ned took a walk round the North End, and out to the end of T Wharf. It was a bitterly raw gray day. They were talking about a plan they had, that they never spoke about before people, of getting hold of a small yawl or ketch after they'd graduated and following the coast down to Florida and the West Indies and then through the Panama Canal and out into the Pacific. Ned had bought a book on navigation and started to study it. That afternoon Ned was sore because Dick couldn't seem to keep his mind on talk about sailing and kept wondering out loud how this state and that state was going to vote. They ate supper grumpily at the Venice, that was crowded for once, of cold scallopini and spaghetti; the service was wretched. As soon as they'd finished one bottle of white orvieto, Ned would order another; they left the restaurant walking stiffly and carefully, leaning against each other a little. Disembodied faces swirled past them against the pinkishgold dark of Hanover Street. They found themselves on the Common in the fringes of the crowd watching the bulletin board on the *Boston Herald* Building. 'Who's winning? Batter up. . . . Hurray for our side,' Ned kept yelling. 'Don't you know enough to know it's election night?' a man behind them said out of the corner of his mouth. 'Blahblahblahblah,' brayed Ned in the man's face.

Dick had to drag him off among the trees to avoid a fight. 'We'll certainly be pinched if you go on like this,' Dick was whispering earnestly in his ear. 'And I want to see the returns. Wilson might be winning.'

'Let's go to Frank Locke's and have a drink.'

Dick wanted to stay out with the crowd and see the returns;

he was excited and didn't want to drink any more. 'It means we won't go to war.' 'Razzer have a war,' said Ned thickly, 'be zo amuzing . . . but war or no war lez have a lil drink on it.'

The barkeep at Frank Locke's wouldn't serve them, though he'd often served them before, and they were disgruntledly on their way down Washington Street to another bar when a boy ran past with an extra in four-inch black type HUGHES ELECTED. 'Hurray,' yelled Ned. Dick put his hand over his mouth and they wrestled there in the street while a hostile group of men gathered around them. Dick could hear the flat unfriendly voices, 'College boys . . . Harvard men.' His hat fell off. Ned let go his hold to let him pick it up. A cop was elbowing his way through towards them. They both straightened up and walked off soberly, their faces red. 'It's all blahblahblahblah,' whispered Ned under his breath. They walked along toward Scollay Square. Dick was sore.

He didn't like the looks of the crowd around Scollay Square either and wanted to go home to Cambridge, but Ned struck up a conversation with a thuggylooking individual and a sailor whose legs were weaving. 'Say, Chub, let's take 'em along to Mother Bly's,' said the thuggylooking individual, poking the sailor in the ribs with his elbow. 'Take it easy now, feller, take it easy,' the sailor muttering unsteadily.

'Go anywhere they don't have all this blahblahblahblah,' Ned was shouting, seesawing from one foot to the other.

'Say, Ned, you're drunk, come along back to Cambridge,' Dick whined desperately in his ear and tugged at his arm, 'They want to get you drunk and take your money.'

'Can't get me drunk, I am drunk . . . blahblahblahblah,' whinnied Ned, and took the sailor's white cap and put it on his head instead of his own hat.

'Well, do what you damn please, I'm going.' Dick let go Ned's arm suddenly and walked away as fast as he could. He walked along across Beacon Hill, his ears ringing, his head hot and thumping. He walked all the way to Cambridge and got to his room shivering and tired, on the edge of crying. He went to bed, but he couldn't sleep and lay there all night cold and miserable even after he'd piled the rug on top of the blankets, listening for every sound in the street.

In the morning he got up with a headache and a sour burntout feeling all through him. He was having some coffee and a toasted roll at the counter under the *Lampoon* Building when Ned came in looking fresh and rosy with his mouth all twisted up in a smile, 'Well, my young politico, Professor Wilson was elected and we've missed out on the saber and epaulettes.' Dick grunted and went on eating. 'I was worried about you,' went on Ned airily, 'where did you disappear to?'

'What do you think I did? I went home and went to bed,' snapped Dick.

'That Barney turned out to be a very amusing fellow, a boxing instructor, if he didn't have a weak heart he'd be welterweight champion of New England. We ended up in a Turkish Bath . . . a most curious place.'

Dick felt like smashing him in the face. 'I've got a lab period,' he said hoarsely and walked out of the lunchcounter.

It was dusk before he went back to Ridgely. There was somebody in the room. It was Ned moving about the room in the blue dusk. 'Dick,' he began to mumble as soon as the door closed behind him, 'never be sore.' He stood in the middle of the room with his hands in his pockets swaying. 'Never be sore, Dick, at things fellows do when they're drunk. . . . Never be sore at anything fellows do. Be a good fellow and make me a cup of tea.' Dick filled the kettle and lit the alcohol flame under it. 'Fellow has to do lotta damn fool things, Dick.'

'But people like that . . . picking up a sailor in Scollay Square . . . so damn risky,' he said weakly.

Ned swung around towards him laughing easily and happily. 'And you always told me I was a damn Backbay snob.'

Dick didn't answer. He had dropped into the chair beside the table. He wasn't sore any more. He was trying to keep from crying. Ned had lain down on the couch and was lifting first one leg and then the other above his head. Dick sat staring at the blue alcohol flame of the lamp listening to the purring of the teakettle until the last dusk faded to darkness and ashy light from the street began to filter into the room.

That winter Ned was drunk every evening. Dick made the *Monthly* and the *Advocate*, had poems reprinted in the *Literary Digest* and the *Conning Tower*, attended meetings of the Boston Poetry Society, and was invited to dinner by Amy Lowell. He and Ned argued a good deal because Dick was a pacifist and Ned said, what the hell, he'd join the Navy, it was all a lot of blah anyway.

In the Easter vacation, after the Armed Ship Bill had passed, Dick had a long talk with Mr Cooper who wanted to get him a job in Washington, because he said a boy of his talent oughtn't to endanger his career by joining the army and already there was talk of conscription. Dick blushed becomingly and said he felt it would be against his conscience to help in the war in any way. They talked a long time without getting anywhere about duty to the state and party leadership and highest expediency. In the end Mr Cooper made him promise not to take any rash step without consulting him. Back in Cambridge everybody was drilling and going to lectures on military science. Dick was finishing up the fouryear course in three years and had to work hard, but nothing in the courses seemed to mean anything any more. He managed to find time to polish up a group of sonnets called *Morituri Te Salutant* that he sent to a prize competition run by the *Literary Digest*. It won the prize, but the editors wrote back that they would prefer a note of hope in the last sestet. Dick put in the note of hope and sent the hundred dollars to Mother to go to Atlantic City with. He discovered that if he went into war work he could get his degree that spring without taking any exams and went in to Boston one day without saying anything to anybody and signed up in the volunteer ambulance service.

The night he told Ned that he was going to France they got very drunk on orvieto wine in their room and talked a great deal about how it was the fate of Youth and Beauty and Love and Friendship to be mashed out by an early death, while the old fat pompous fools would make merry over their carcasses. In the pearly dawn they went out and sat with a last bottle on one of the old tombstones in the graveyard, on the corner of Harvard Square. They sat on the cold tombstone a long time without saying anything, only drinking, and after each drink threw their heads back and softly bleated in unison Blahblahblahblah.

Sailing for France on the *Chicago* in early June was like suddenly having to give up a book he'd been reading and hadn't finished. Ned and his mother and Mr Cooper and the literary lady considerably older than himself he'd slept with several times rather uncomfortably in her double-decker apartment on Central Park South, and his poetry and his pacifist friends and the lights of the Esplanade shakily reflected in the Charles, faded in his mind like paragraphs in a novel laid by unfinished. He was a little seasick and a little shy of the boat and the noisy boozing crowd and the longfaced Red Cross women workers giving each other gooseflesh with stories of spitted Belgian babies and Canadian officers crucified and elderly nuns raped; inside he was coiled up tight as an overwound clock with wondering what it would be like over there.

Bordeaux, the red Garonne, the pastelcolored streets of old tall mansardroofed houses, the sunlight and shadow so delicately blue and yellow, the names of the stations all out of Shakespeare, the yellowbacked novels on the bookstands, the bottles of wine in the buvettes, were like nothing he'd imagined. All the way to Paris the faintly bluegreen fields were spattered scarlet with poppies like the first lines of a poem; the little train jogged along in dactyls; everything seemed to fall into rhyme.

They got to Paris too late to report at the Norton-Harjes office. Dick left his bag in the room assigned him with two other fellows at the Hotel Mont Thabor and walked around the streets. It wasn't dark yet. There was almost no traffic, but the boulevards were full of strollers in the blue June dusk. As it got darker women leaned out towards them from behind all the trees, girls' hands clutched their arms, here and there a dirty word in English burst like a thrown egg above the nasal singsong of French. The three of them walked arm in arm, a little scared and very aloof, their ears still ringing from the talk on the dangers of infection with syphilis and gonorrhea a medical officer had given the last night on the boat. They went back to the hotel early.

Ed Schuyler, who knew French on account of having been to boardingschool in Switzerland, shook his head as he was cleaning his teeth at the washstand and spluttered out through his toothbrush, 'C'est la guerre.' 'Well, the first five years'll be the hardest,' said Dick, laughing. Fred Summers was an automobile mechanic from Kansas. He was sitting up in bed in his woolly underwear. 'Fellers,' he said, solemnly looking from one to the other, 'This ain't a war. . . . It's a goddam whorehouse.'

In the morning they were up early and hurried through their coffee and rolls and rushed out hot and cold with excitement to the rue François Premier to report. They were told where to get their uniforms and cautioned to keep away from wine and women and told to come back in the afternoon. In the afternoon they were told to come back next morning for their identity cards. The identity cards took another day's waiting around. In between they drove around the Bois in horsecabs, went to see Notre Dame and the Conciergerie and the Sainte Chapelle and out on the streetcar to Malmaison. Dick was furbishing up his prepschool French and would sit in the mild sunlight among the shabby white statues in the Tuileries Gardens reading *Les Dieux Ont Soif* and *L'Ile des Pingouins.* He and Ed Schuyler and Fred stuck together and after dining exceeding well every night for fear it might be their last chance at a Paris meal, took a turn around the boulevards in the crowded horizonblue dusk; they'd gotten to the point of talking to the girls now and kidding them along a little. Fred Summers had bought himself a prophylactic kit and a set of smutty postcards. He said the last night before they left he was going to tear loose. When they got to the front he might get killed and then what? Dick said he liked talking to the girls, but that the whole business was too commercial and turned his stomach. Ed Schuyler, who'd been nicknamed Frenchie and was getting very Continental in his ways, said that the streetgirls were too naïve.

The last night before they left was bright moonlight, so the Gothas came over. They were eating in a little restaurant in Montmartre. The cashlady and waiter made them all go down into the cellar when the sirens started wailing for the second time. There they met up with three youngish women named Suzette, Minette, and Annette. When the little honking fireengine went by to announce that the raid was over, it was already closing time and they couldn't get any more drinks at the bar; so the girls took them to a closely shuttered house where they were ushered into a big room with livercolored wallpaper that had green roses on it. An old man in a green baize apron brought up champagne and the girls began to sit on knees and ruffle up hair. Summers got the prettiest girl and hauled her right into the alcove where the bed was with a big mirror above the whole length of it. Then he pulled the curtain. Dick found himself stuck with the fattest and oldest one and got disgusted. Her flesh felt like rubber. He gave her ten francs and left.

Hurrying down the black sloping street outside he ran into some Australian officers who gave him a drink of whiskey out of a bottle and took him into another house where they tried to get a show put on, but the madam said the girls were all busy and the Australians were too drunk to pay attention anyway and started to wreck the place. Dick just managed to slip out before the gendarmes came. He was walking in the general direction of the hotel when there was another alert and he found himself being yanked down into a subway by a lot of Belgians. There was a girl down there who was very pretty and Dick was trying to explain to her that she ought to go to a hotel with him when the man she was with, who was a colonel of Spahis in a red cloak covered with gold braid, came up, his waxed mustaches bristling with fury. Dick explained that it was all a mistake and there were apologies all around and they were all brave allies. They walked around several blocks looking for some place to have a drink together, but everything was closed, so they parted regretfully at the door of Dick's hotel. He went up to the room in splendid humor; there he found the other two glumly applying argyrol and Metchnikoff paste. Dick made a good tall story out of his adventures. But the other two said he'd been a hell of a poor sport to walk out on a lady and hurt her sensitive feelings. 'Fellers,' began Fred Summers, looking in each of their faces with his round eyes, 'it ain't a war, it's a goddam . . .' He couldn't think of a word for it, so Dick turned out the light.

# Newsreel 22

COMING YEAR PROMISES REBIRTH OF RAILROADS

DEBS IS GIVEN THIRTY YEARS IN PRISON

*There's a long long trail awinding*
*Into the land of my dreams*
*Where the nightingales are singing*
*And the white moon beams*

future generations will rise up and call those men blessed who have the courage of their convictions, a proper appreciation of the value of human life as contrasted with material gain, and who, imbued with the spirit of brotherhood, will lay hold of the great opportunity

BONDS BUY BULLETS   BUY BONDS

COPPERS INFLUENCED BY UNCERTAIN OUTLOOK

WOMEN VOTE LIKE VETERAN POLITICIANS

restore timehonored meatcombination dishes such as hash, goulash, meat pies, and liver and bacon. Every German soldier carries a little clothesbrush in his pocket; first thing he does when he lands in a prisoncage is to get out his brush and start cleaning his clothes

EMPLOYER MUST PROVE WORKER IS ESSENTIAL

*There's a long long night of waiting*
*Until my dreams all come true*

AGITATORS CAN'T GET AMERICAN PASSPORTS

the two men out of the Transvaal district during the voyage expressed their opinion that the British and American flags expressed nothing and, as far as they were concerned, could be sunk to the bottom of the Atlantic, and acknowledged that they were socalled Nationalists, a type much resembling the I.W.W. here. 'I have no intention,' wrote Hearst, 'of meeting Governor Smith either publicly, privately, politically, or socially, as I do not find any satisfaction

### KILLS HERSELF AT SEA; CROWDER IN CITY AFTER SLACKERS

*Oh, old Uncle Sam*
  *He's got the infantree*
*He's got the cavalree*
  *He's got the artileree*
*And then, by God, we'll all go to Chermanee*
*God Help Kaiser Bill!*

## The Camera Eye (30)

remembering the gray crooked fingers the thick drip of blood off the canvas the bubbling when the lungcases try to breathe the muddy scraps of flesh you put in the ambulance alive and haul out dead

three of us sit in the dry cement fountain of the little garden with the pink walls in Récicourt

*No      there must be some way      they taught us      Land of the Free      conscience      Give me liberty or give me      Well they give us death*

sunny afternoon      through the faint aftersick of mustardgas I smell the box the white roses and the white phlox with a crimson eye      three brownandwhitestriped snails hang with infinite delicacy from a honeysucklebranch overhead up in the blue a sausageballoon grazes drowsily like a tethered cow      there are drunken wasps clinging to the tooripe pears that fall and squash whenever the near guns spew their heavy shells that go off rumbling through the sky

with a whir that makes you remember walking in the woods and starting a woodcock

welltodo country people carefully built the walls and the little backhouse with the cleanscrubbed seat and the

quartermoon in the door like the backhouse of an old farm
at home    carefully planted the garden and savored the
fruit and the flowers and carefully planned this war

    *to hell with 'em        Patrick Henry in khaki submits*
*to shortarm inspection and puts all his pennies in a Liberty*
*Loan      or give me*

    arrivés    shrapnel twanging its harps out of tiny
powderpuff clouds invites us delicately to glory    we happy
watching the careful movements of the snails in the afternoon sunlight talking in low voices about

    *La Libre Belgique        The Junius papers        Areo-*
*pagitica        Milton went blind for freedom of speech*
*If you hit the words Democracy will understand        even*
*the bankers and the clergymen        I        you        we*
        *must*

                When three men hold together
                The kingdoms are less by three

    we are happy talking in low voices in the afternoon
sunlight about après la guerre that our fingers our blood
our lungs our flesh under the dirty khaki feldgrau bleu
horizon might go on sweeten grow until we fall from the
tree ripe like the tooripe pears    the arrivés know and
singing éclats sizzling gas shells        theirs is the power and
the glory

    *or give me death*

## Randolph Bourne

Randolph Bourne
came as an inhabitant of this earth
without the pleasure of choosing his dwelling or his career.

    He was a hunchback, grandson of a congregational mini-
ster, born in 1886 in Bloomfield, New Jersey; there he attended
grammarschool and highschool.

    At the age of seventeen he went to work as secretary to
a Morristown businessman.

    He worked his way through Columbia working in a pianola
record factory in Newark, working as a proofreader, piano-
tuner, accompanist in a vocal studio in Carnegie Hall.

At Columbia he studied with John Dewey,
got a traveling fellowship that took him to England Paris
Rome Berlin Copenhagen,
wrote a book on the Gary schools.
In Europe he heard music, a great deal of Wagner and
Scriabine
and bought himself a black cape.

This little sparrowlike man,
tiny twisted bit of flesh in a black cape,
always in pain and ailing,
put a pebble in his sling
and hit Goliath in the forehead with it.
*War*, he wrote, *is the health of the state.*

Half musician, half educational theorist (weak health and
being poor and twisted in body and on bad terms with his
people hadn't spoiled the world for Randolph Bourne; he was
a happy man, loved die Meistersinger and playing Bach with
his long hands that stretched so easily over the keys and pretty
girls and good food and evenings of talk. When he was dying
of pneumonia a friend brought him an eggnog; Look at the
yellow, it's beautiful, he kept saying as his life ebbed into
delirium and fever. He was a happy man). Bourne seized with
feverish intensity on the ideas then going around at Columbia
he picked rosy glasses out of the turgid jumble of John Dewey's
teaching through which he saw clear and sharp
    the shining capitol of reformed democracy,
    Wilson's New Freedom;
    but he was too good a mathematician; he had to work the
equations out;

    with the result
    that in the crazy spring of 1917 he began to get unpopular
where his bread was buttered at the *New Republic*;
        for *New Freedom* read *Conscription*, for *Democracy, Win
the War*, for *Reform, Safeguard the Morgan Loans*
        for Progress Civilization Education Service,
        Buy a Liberty Bond,
        Strafe the Hun,
        Jail the Objectors.
    He resigned from the *New Republic*; only *The Seven Arts*
had the nerve to publish his articles against the war. The

backers of the *Seven Arts* took their money elsewhere; friends didn't like to be seen with Bourne, his father wrote him begging him not to disgrace the family name. The rainbowtinted future of reformed democracy went pop like a pricked soapbubble.

The liberals scurried to Washington;

some of his friends pled with him to climb up on Schoolmaster Wilson's sharabang; the war was great fought from the swivel chairs of Mr Creel's bureau in Washington.

He was cartooned, shadowed by the espionage service and the counterespionage service; taking a walk with two girl friends at Wood's Hole he was arrested, a trunk full of manuscript and letters was stolen from him in Connecticut. (Force to the utmost, thundered Schoolmaster Wilson)

He didn't live to see the big circus of the Peace of Versaille or the purplish normalcy of the Ohio Gang.

Six weeks after the armistice he died planning an essay on the foundations of future radicalism in America.

If any man has a ghost
Bourne has a ghost,
a tiny twisted unscared ghost in a black cloak
hopping along the grimy old brick and brownstone streets
still left in downtown New York,
crying out in a shrill soundless giggle:
*War is the health of the state.*

# Newsreel 23

*If you don't like your Uncle Sammy*
*If you don't like the red white and blue*

smiles of patriotic Essex County will be concentrated and recorded at Branch Brook Park, Newark, New Jersey, tomorrow afternoon. Bands will play while a vast throng marches happily to the rhythm of wartime anthems and airs. Mothers of the nation's sons will be there; wives, many of them carrying babes born after their fathers sailed for the front, will occupy a place in Essex County's graphic pageant; relatives and friends of the heroes who are carrying on the message of Freedom will file past a battery of cameras and all will smile a message recording installment number 7 of Smiles Across the Sea. The hour for these folks to start smiling is 2.30.

### MOBS PLUNDER CITIES

### NEWSPAPERMAN LEADS THROUGH BARRAGE

it was a pitiful sight at dusk every evening when the whole population evacuated the city, going to sleep in the fields until daylight. Old women and tiny children, cripples drawn in carts or wheeled in barrows, men carrying chairs bring those too feeble and old to walk

### JERSEY TROOPS TAKE WOMAN GUNNERS

the trouble had its origin with the demand of the marine workers for an eighthour day

*If you don't like the stars in Old Glory*
*Then go back to your land across the sea*
*To the land from which you came*
*Whatever be its name*

### G.P.O. LEADER ACCUSED OF DRAFT FRAUDS

*If you don't like the red white and blue*
*Then don't act like the cur in the story*
*Don't bite the hand that's feeding you*

## Eveline Hutchins

Little Eveline and Arget and Lade and Gogo lived on the top floor of a yellowbrick house on the North Shore Drive. Arget and Lade were little Eveline's sisters. Gogo was her little brother, littler than Eveline; he had such nice blue eyes, but Miss Matilda had horrid blue eyes. On the floor below was Doctor Hutchins's study where Yourfather mustn't be disturbed, and Dearmother's room where she stayed all morning painting dressed in a lavender smock. On the groundfloor was the drawingroom and diningroom, where parishioners came and little children must be seen and not heard, and at dinnertime you could smell good things to eat and hear knives and forks and tinkly companyvoices and Yourfather's booming scary voice and when Yourfather's voice was going all the companyvoices were quiet. Yourfather was Doctor Hutchins, but Our Father art in heaven. When Yourfather stood beside the bed at night to see that little girls said their prayers, Eveline would close her eyes tightscared. It was only when she'd hopped into bed and snuggled way down so that the covers were right across her nose that she felt cozy.

George was a dear, although Adelaide and Margaret teased him and said he was their Assistant like Mr Blessington was Father's assistant. George always caught things first and then they all had them. It was lovely when they had the measles and the mumps all at once. They stayed in bed and had hyacinths in pots and guinea pigs and Dearmother used to come up and read the *Jungle Book* and do funny pictures and Yourfather would come up and make funny birdbeaks that opened out of paper and tell stories he made up right out of his head and Dearmother said he had said prayers for you children in church and that made them feel fine and grownup.

When they were all up and playing in the nursery George caught something again and had monia on account of getting cold on his chest and Yourfather was very solemn and said not to grieve if God called little brother away. But God brought little George back to them, only he was delicate after that and had to wear glasses, and when Dearmother let Eveline help bathe him because Miss Mathilda was having the measles, too, Eveline noticed he had something funny there where she didn't have anything. She asked Dearmother if it was a mump, but Dearmother scolded her and said she was a vulgar little girl to have looked. 'Hush, child, don't ask questions.' Eveline got red all over and cried and Adelaide and Margaret wouldn't speak to her for days on account of her being a vulgar little girl.

Summers they all went to Maine with Miss Mathilda in a drawingroom. George and Eveline slept in the upper and Adelaide and Margaret slept in the lower; Miss Mathilda was trainsick and didn't close her eyes all night on the sofa opposite. The train went rumblebump chugchug and the trees and houses ran by, the front ones fast and those way off very slow and at night the engine wailed and the children couldn't make out why the strong nice tall conductor was so nice to Miss Mathilda who was so hateful and trainsick. Maine smelt all woodsy and Mother and Father were there to meet them and they all put on khaki jumpers and went camping with Father and the guides. It was Eveline who learned to swim quicker than anybody.

Going back to Chicago it would be autumn and Mother loved the lovely autumn foliage that made Miss Mathilda feel so traurig on account of winter coming on, and the frost on the grass beyond the shadows of the cars out of the train-window in the morning. At home Sam would be scrubbing the enamel paint and Phoebe and Miss Mathilda would be putting up curtains and the nursery would smell traurig of mothballs. One fall Father started to read aloud a little of the *Ideals of the King* every night after they were tucked into bed. All that winter Adelaide and Margaret were King Arthur and Queen Whenever. Eveline wanted to be Elaine the Fair, but Adelaide said she couldn't because her hair was mousey and she had a face like a pie, so she had to be the Maiden Evelina.

The Maiden Evelina used to go into Miss Mathilda's room when she was out and look at herself for a long time in the lookingglass. He hair wasn't mousey, it was quite fair if only they would let her have it curly instead of in pigtails, and even if her eyes weren't blue like George's they had little green specks in them. Her forehead was noble. Miss Mathilda caught her staring like that into the mirror one day.

'Look at yourself too much and you'll find you're looking at the devil,' said Miss Mathilda in her nasty stiff German way.

When Eveline was twelve years old they moved to a bigger house over on Drexel Boulevard. Adelaide and Margaret went East to boardingschool at New Hope and Mother had to go spend the winter with friends at Santa Fé on account of her health. It was fun eating breakfast every morning with just Dad and George and Miss Mathilda, who was getting elderly and paid more attention to running the house and to reading Sir Gilbert Parker's novels than to the children. Eveline didn't like school, but she liked having Dad help her with her Latin evenings and do algebra equations for her. She thought he was wonderful when he preached so kind and good from the pulpit and was proud of being the minister's daughter at Sunday afternoon Bibleclass. She thought a great deal about the father-hood of God and the woman of Samaria and Joseph of Arimathea and Baldur the beautiful and the Brotherhood of Man and the apostle that Jesus loved. That Christmas she took around a lot of baskets to poor people's houses. Poverty was dreadful and the poor were so scary and why didn't God do something about the problems and evils of Chicago, and the conditions, she'd ask her father. He'd smile and say she was too young to worry about those things yet. She called him Dad now and was his Pal.

On her birthday Mother sent her a beautiful illustrated book of the Blessed Damosel by Dante Gabriel Rossetti with colored illustrations from his paintings and those of Burne Jones. She used to say the name Dante Gabriel Rossetti over and over to herself like traurig she loved it so. She started painting and writing little verses about choirs of angels and little poor children at Christmastime. The first picture she did in oils was a portrait of Elaine the Fair, that she sent her mother for Christmas. Everybody said it showed great talent. When friends of Dad's came to dinner they'd say when they were introduced to her, 'So this is the talented one, is it?'

Adelaide and Margaret were pretty scornful about all that when they came home from school. They said the house looked dowdy and nothing had any style to it in Chicago, and wasn't it awful being minister's daughters, but of course Dad wasn't like an ordinary minister in a white tie, he was a Unitarian and very broad and more like a prominent author or scientist. George was getting to be a sulky little boy with dirty finger-nails who never could keep his necktie straight and was always breaking his glasses. Eveline was working on a portrait of him the way he had been when he was little with blue eyes and gamboge curls. She used to cry over her paints she loved him so and little poor children she saw on the street. Everybody said she ought to study Art.

It was Adelaide who first met Sally Emerson. One Easter they were going to put on *Aglavaine and Selizette* at the church for charity. Miss Rodgers, the French teacher at Doctor Grant's school, was going to coach them and said that they ought to ask Mrs Philip Payne Emerson, who had seen the original production abroad, about the scenery and costumes; and that besides her interest would be invaluable to make it *go*; everything that Sally Emerson was interested in *went*. The Hutchins girls were all excited when Doctor Hutchins called up Mrs Emerson on the telephone and asked if Adelaide might come over some morning and ask her advice about some amateur theatricals. They'd already sat down to lunch when Adelaide came back, her eyes shining. She wouldn't say much except that Mrs Philip Payne Emerson knew Matterlink intimately and that she was coming to tea, but kept declaring, 'She's the most stylish woman I ever met.'

*Aglavaine and Selizette* didn't turn out quite as the Hutchins girls and Miss Rodgers had hoped, though everybody said the scenery and costumes Eveline designed showed real ability, but the week after the performance, Eveline got a message one morning that Mrs Emerson had asked her to lunch that day and only her. Adelaide and Margaret were so mad they wouldn't speak to her. She felt pretty shaky when she set off into the icybright dusty day. At the last minute Adelaide had lent her a hat and Margaret her fur neckpiece, so that she wouldn't disgrace them, they said. By the time she got to the Emersons' house she was chilled to the bone. She was ushered into a little dressingroom with all kinds of brushes and combs and silver jars with powder and even rogue and toiletwaters in purple, green, and pink bottles and left to take off her things. When she saw herself in the big mirror she almost screamed, she looked so young and piefaced and her dress was so horrid. The only thing that looked any good was the foxfur, so she kept that on when she went into the big upstairs lounge with its deep gray carpet soft underfoot and the sunlight pouring in through French windows onto bright colors and the black polished grandpiano. There were big bowls of freezias on every table and yellow and pink French and German books of reproductions of paintings. Even the sootbitten blocks of Chicago houses flattened under the wind and the zero sunlight looked faintly exciting and foreign through the big pattern of the yellow lace curtains. In the rich smell of the freezias there was a little expensive wisp of cigarettesmoke.

Sally Emerson came in smoking a cigarette and said, 'Excuse me, my dear,' some wretched woman had had her impaled on the telephone like a butterfly on a pin for the last halfhour. They ate lunch at a little table the elderly colored man brought in all set and Eveline was treated just like a grownup woman and a glass of port poured out for her. She only dared take a sip, but it was delicious, and the lunch was all crispy and creamy with cheese grated on things and she would have eaten a lot if she hadn't felt so shy. Sally Emerson talked about how clever Eveline's costumes had been for the show and said she must keep up her drawing and talked about how there were as many people with artistic ability in Chicago as anywhere in the world and what was lacking was the milieu, the atmosphere my dear, and that the social leaders were all vicious numbskulls and that it was up to the few people who cared about Art to stick together and create the rich beautiful milieu they needed, and about Paris, and about Mary Garden, and Debussy. Eveline went home with her head reeling with names and pictures, little snatches out of operas, and in her nose the tickling smell of the freezias mixed with toasted cheese and cigarettesmoke. When she got home everything looked so cluttered and bare and ugly she burst out crying and wouldn't answer any of her sisters' questions; that made them madder than ever.

That June after school was over, they all went out to Santa Fé to see her mother. She was awfully depressed out at Santa Fé, the sun was so hot and the eroded hills were so dry and dusty and Mother had gotten so washedout-looking and was reading theosophy and talking about God and the beauty of soul of the Indians and Mexicans in a way that made the children uncomfortable. Eveline read a great many books that summer and hated going out. She read Scott and Thackeray and W. J. Locke and Dumas, and when she found an old copy of *Trilby* in the house she read it three times running. That started her seeing things in Du Maurier illustrations instead of in knights and ladies.

When she wasn't reading she was lying flat on her back dreaming out long stories about herself and Sally Emerson. She didn't feel well most of the time and would drop into long successions of horrid thoughts about people's bodies that made her feel nauseated. Adelaide and Margaret told her what to do about her trouble every month, but she didn't tell them how horrid it made her feel inside. She read the Bible and looked up *uterus* and words like that in encyclopaedias and dictionaries. Then one night she decided she wouldn't stand it any more and went through the medicine chest in the bathroom till she found a bottle marked POISON that had some kind of laudanum compound in it. But she wanted to write a poem before she died, she felt so lovely musically traurig about dying, but she couldn't seem to get the rhymes right and finally fell asleep with her head on the paper. When she woke up it was dawn and she was hunched up over the table by the window, stiff and chilly in her thin nightgown. She slipped into bed shivering. Anyway she promised herself that she'd keep the bottle and kill herself whenever things seemed too filthy and horrid. That made her feel better.

That fall Margaret and Adelaide went to Vassar. Eveline would have liked to go East too, but everybody said she was too young, though she'd passed most of her college board exams. She stayed in Chicago and went to artclasses and lectures of one sort or another and did churchwork. It was an unhappy winter. Sally Emerson seemed to have forgotten her. The young people around the church were so stuffy and conventional. Eveline got to hate the evenings at Drexel Boulevard, and all the vague Emerson her father talked in his rich preacher's boom. What she liked best was the work she did at Hull House. Eric Egstrom gave drawingclasses there in the evenings and she used to see him sometimes smoking a cigarette in the back passage, leaning against the wall, looking very Norse, she thought, in his gray smock full of bright fresh dabs of paint. She'd sometimes smoke a cigarette with him exchanging a few words about Manet or Claude Monet's innumerable haystacks, all the time feeling uneasy because the conversation wasn't more interesting and clever and afraid somebody would come and find her smoking.

Miss Mathilda said it was bad for a girl to be so dreamy and wanted her to learn to sew.

All Eveline thought about that winter was going to the Art Institute and trying to paint pictures of the Lake Front that would be colored like Whistlers, but be rich and full like Millet drawings. Eric didn't love her or else he wouldn't be so friendly and aloof. She'd had her great love; now her life was over and she must devote herself to Art. She began to wear her hair screwed up in a knot at the nape of her neck and when her sisters said it was unbecoming she said she wanted it to be unbecoming. It was at the Art Institute that her beautiful friendship with Eleanor Stoddard began. Eveline was wearing her new gray hat that she thought looked like something in a Manet portrait and got to talking with such an interesting girl. When she went home she was so excited she wrote George, who was at boardingschool, about it, saying she was the first girl she'd met who really seemed to *feel* painting, that she could *really* talk about things with. And then too she was *really* doing something, and so independent and told things so comically. After all if love was going to be denied her, she could build her life on a *beautiful friendship*.

Eveline was getting to like it so much in Chicago, she was really disappointed when the time came to leave for the year's trip abroad that Doctor Hutchins had been planning for his family for so many years. But New York and getting on the *Baltic* and making out the tags for their baggage and the funny smell of the staterooms made her forget all about that. They had a rough trip and the boat rolled a good deal, but they sat at the captain's table and the captain was a jovial Englishman and kept their spirits up so that they hardly missed a meal. They landed in Liverpool with twentythree pieces of baggage, but lost the shawlstrap that had the medicinechest in it on the way down to London and had to spend their first morning getting it from the Lost and Found Office at Saint Pancras. In London it was very foggy. George and Eveline went to see the Elgin Marbles and the Tower of London and ate their lunches in A B C restaurants and had a fine time riding in the tube. Doctor Hutchins let them stay only ten days in Paris and most of that time they were making side trips to see cathedrals. Notre Dame and Rheims and Beauvais and Chartres with their bright glass and their smell of incense in cold stone and the tall gray longfaced statues nearly made Eveline a Catholic. They had a firstclass compartment reserved all the way to Florence and a hamper with cold chicken in it and many bottles of Saint Galmier mineral water and they made tea on a little alcohol lamp.

That winter it rained a lot and the villa was chilly and the girls squabbled among themselves a good deal and Florence seemed to be full of nothing but old English ladies; still Eveline drew from life and read Gordon Craig. She didn't know any young men and she hated the young Italians with names out of Dante that hung around Adelaide and Margaret under the delusion that they were rich heiresses. On the whole she was glad to go home with Mother a little earlier than the others who were going to take a trip to Greece. They sailed from Antwerp on the *Kroonland*. Eveline thought it was the happiest moment of her life when she felt the deck tremble under her feet as the steamer left the dock and the long rumble of the whistle in her ears.

Her mother didn't go down to the diningsaloon the first night out, so that Eveline was a little embarrassed going in to table all alone and had sat down and started eating her soup before she noticed that the young man opposite her was an American and goodlooking. He had blue eyes and crisp untidy tow hair. It was too wonderful when he turned out to be from Chicago. His name was Dirk McArthur. He'd been studying a year at Munich, but said he was getting out before they threw him out. He and Eveline got to be friends right away; they owned the boat after that. It was a balmy crossing for April. They played shuffleboard and decktennis and spent a lot of time in the bow watching the sleek Atlantic waves curl and break under the lunge of the ship.

One moonlight night, when the moon was plunging westward through scudding spindrift the way the *Kroonland* was plunging through the uneasy swell, they climbed up to the crowsnest. This was an adventure; Eveline didn't want to show she was scared. There was no watch and they were alone, a little giddy in the snug canvas socket that smelt a little of sailors' pipes. When Dirk put his arm around her shoulders Eveline's head began to reel. She oughtn't to let him. 'Gee, you're a good sport, Eveline,' he said in a breathless voice. 'I never knew a nice girl who was a good sport before.' Without quite meaning to she turned her face towards his. Their cheeks touched and his mouth slid around and kissed her hard on her mouth. She pushed him away with a jerk.

'Hey, you're not trying to throw me overboard, are you?' he said, laughing. 'Look, Eveline, won't you give me a little tiny kiss to show there's no hard feeling. There's just you and me tonight on the whole broad Atlantic.'

She kissed him scaredly on the chin. 'Say, Eveline, I like you so much. You're the swellest girl.' She smiled at him and suddenly he was hugging her tight, his legs hard and strong against her legs, his hands spread over her back, his lips trying to open her lips. She got her mouth away from him. 'No, no, please don't,' she could hear her little creaky voice saying.

'All right, I'm sorry. . . . No more caveman stuff, honest injun, Eveline. But you mustn't forget that you're the most attractive girl on the boat. . . . I mean in the world, you know how a feller feels.'

He started down first. Letting herself down through the opening in the bottom of the crowsnest she began to get dizzy. She was falling. His arms tightened around her.

'That's all right, girly, your foot slipped,' he said gruffly in her ear. 'I've got you.'

Her head was swimming, she couldn't seem to make her arms and legs work, she could hear her little moaning voice, 'Don't drop me, Dirk, don't drop me.'

When they finally got down the ladder to the deck, Dirk leaned against the mast and let out a long breath, 'Whee . . . you certainly gave me a scare, young lady.'

'I'm so sorry,' she said. 'It was silly of me to suddenly get girlish like that. . . . I must have fainted for a minute.'

'Gosh, I oughtn't to have taken you up there.'

'I'm glad you did,' Eveline said; then she found herself blushing and hurried off down the maindeck to the first class entrance and the stateroom, where she had to make up a story to explain to Mother how she'd torn her stocking.

She couldn't sleep that night, but lay awake in her bunk listening to the distant rhythm of the engines and the creaking of the ship and the seethe of churned seas that came in through the open porthole. She could still feel the soft brush of his cheek and the sudden tightening muscles of his arms around her shoulder. She knew now she was terribly in love with Dirk and wished he'd propose to her. But next morning she was really flattered when Judge Ganch, a tall whitehaired lawyer from Salt Lake City with a young red face and a breezy manner, sat on the end of her deckchair and talked to her by the hour about his early life in the West and his unhappy marriage and politics and Teddy Roosevelt and the Progressive Party. She'd rather have been with Dirk, but it made her feel pretty and excited to see Dirk walk past with his nose out of joint while she listened to Judge Ganch's stories. She wished the trip would never end.

Back in Chicago she saw a lot of Dirk McArthur. He always kissed her when he brought her home and he held her very tight when he danced with her and sometimes used to hold her hand and tell her with a nice girl she was, but he never would say anything about getting married. Once she met Sally Emerson at a dance she'd gone to with Dirk she had to admit that she wasn't doing any painting and Sally Emerson looked so disappointed that Eveline felt quite ashamed and started talking fast about Gordon Craig and an exhibition of Matisse she'd seen in Paris. Sally Emerson was just leaving. A young man was waiting to dance with Eveline. Sally Emerson took her hand and said: 'But, Eveline, you mustn't forget that we have high hopes of you.' And while she was dancing everything that Sally Emerson stood for and how wonderful she used to think her came sweeping through Eveline's head; but driving home with Dirk all these thoughts were dazzled out of her in the glare of his headlights, the strong leap forward of the car on the pickup, the purr of the motor, his arm around her, the great force pressing her against him when they went around curves.

It was a hot night, he drove west through endless identical suburbs out into the prairie. Eveline knew that they ought to go home, everybody was back from Europe now and they'd notice how late she got in, but she didn't say anything. It was only when he stopped the car that she noticed that he was very drunk. He took out a flask and offered her a drink. She shook her head. They'd stopped in front of a white barn. In the reflection of the headlights his shirtfront and his face and his mussedup hair all looked chalky white. 'You don't love me, Dirk,' she said. 'Sure I do, love you better'n anybody . . . except myself . . . that's a trouble with me . . . love myself best.' She rubbed her knuckles through his hair, 'You're pretty silly, do you know it?' 'Ouch,' he said. It was starting to rain, so he turned the car around and made for Chicago.

Eveline never knew exactly where it was they smashed up, only that she was crawling out from under the seat and her dress was ruined and she wasn't hurt, only the rain was streaking the headlights of the cars that stopped along the road on either side of them. Dirk was sitting on the mudguard of the first car that had stopped. 'Are you all right, Eveline?' he called shakily. 'It's only my dress,' she said. He was bleeding from a gash in his forehead and he was holding his arm against his body as if he were cold. Then it was all nightmare, telephoning Dad, getting Dirk to the hospital, dodging the reporters, calling up Mr McArthur to get him to set to work to keep it out of the morning papers. It was eight o'clock of a hot spring morning when she got home wearing a raincoat one of the nurses had lent her over her ruined evening dress.

The family was all at breakfast. Nobody said anything. Then Dad got to his feet and came forward, with his napkin in his hand, 'My dear, I shan't speak of your behavior now, to say nothing of the pain and mortification you have caused all of us. . . . I can only say it would have served you right if you had sustained serious injuries in such an escapade. Go up and rest if you can.' Eveline went upstairs, doublelocked her door and threw herself sobbing on the bed.

As soon as they could, her mother and sisters hurried her off to Santa Fé. It was hot and dusty there and she hated it. She couldn't stop thinking of Dirk. She began telling people she believed in free love and lay for hours on the bed in her room reading Swinburne and Laurence Hope and dreaming Dirk was there. She got so she could almost feel the insistent fingers of his hands spread over the small of her back and his mouth like that night in the crowsnest on the *Kroonland*. It was a kind of relief when she came down with scarlet fever and had to lie in bed for eight weeks in the isolation wing of the hospital. Everybody sent her flowers and she read a lot of books on design and interior decorating and did watercolors.

When she went up to Chicago for Adelaide's wedding in October, she had a pale mature look. Eleanor cried out when she kissed her, 'My dear, you've grown stunningly handsome.' She had one thing on her mind, to see Dirk and get it over with. It was several days before they could arrange to meet because Dad had called him up and forbidden him to come to the house and they had a scene over the telephone. They met in the lobby of The Drake. She could see at a glance that Dirk had been hitting it up since she'd seen him. He was a little drunk now. He had a sheepish boyish look that made her feel like crying.

'Well, how's Barney Oldfield?' she said, laughing.

'Rotten, gee, you look stunning, Eveline. . . . Say, *The Follies of 1914* are in town, a big New York hit. . . . I got tickets, do you mind if we go?'

'No, it'll be bully.'

He ordered everything most expensive he could find on the bill of fare, and champagne. She had something in her throat that kept her from swallowing. She had to say it before he got too drunk.

'Dirk . . . this doesn't sound very ladylike, but like this it's too tiresome. . . . The way you acted last spring I thought you liked me . . . well, how much do you? I want to know.'

Dirk put his glass down and turned red. Then he took a deep breath and said, 'Eveline, you know I'm not the marrying kind . . . love 'em and leave 'em's more like it. I can't help how I am.'

'I don't mean I want you to marry me,' her voice rose shrilly out of control. She began to giggle. 'I don't mean I want to be made an honest woman. Anyway, there's no reason.' She was able to laugh more naturally. 'Let's forget it. . . . I won't tease you any more.'

'You're a good sport, Eveline. I always knew you were a good sport.'

Going down the aisle of the theater he was so drunk she had to put her hand under his elbow to keep him from staggering. The music and cheap colors and jiggling bodies of the chorusgirls all seemed to hit on some raw place inside her, so that everything she saw hurt like sweet on a jumpy tooth.

Dirk kept talking all through. 'See that girl . . . second from the left on the back row, that's Queenie Frothingham. . . . You understand, Eveline. But I'll tell you one thing, I never made a girl take the first misstep. . . . I haven't got that to reproach myself with.'

The usher came down and asked him to quit talking so loud, he was spoiling others' enjoyment of the show. He gave her a dollar and said he'd be quiet as a mouse, as a little dumb mouse and suddenly went to sleep.

At the end of the first act, Eveline said she had to go home, said the doctor had told her she'd have to have plenty of sleep. He insisted on taking her to her door in a taxicab and then went off to go back to the show and to Queenie. Eveline lay awake all night staring at her window. Next morning she was the first one down to breakfast. When Dad came down she told him she'd have to go to work and asked him to lend her a thousand dollars to start an interior decorating business.

The decorating business she started with Eleanor Stoddard in Chicago didn't make as much money as Eveline had hoped, and Eleanor was rather trying on the whole; but they met such interesting people and went to parties and firstnights and openings of art exhibitions, and Sally Emerson saw to it that they were very much in the vanguard of things in Chicago socially. Eleanor kept complaining that the young men Eveline collected were all so poor and certainly more of a liability than an asset to the business. Eveline had great faith in their all making names for themselves, so that when Freddy Seargeant, who'd been such a nuisance and had had to be lent money various times, came through with an actual production of *Tess of the d'Urbervilles* in New York, Eveline felt so triumphant she almost fell in love with him. Freddy was very much in love with her and Eveline couldn't decide what to do about him. He was a dear and she was very fond of him, but she couldn't imagine marrying him and this would be her first love affair and Freddy just didn't seem to carry her off her feet.

What she did like was sitting up late talking to him over Rhine wine and seltzer in the Brevoort café that was full of such interesting people. Eveline would sit there looking at him through the crinkling cigarettesmoke wondering whether she was going to have a love affair. He was a tall thin man of about thirty with some splashes of white in his thick black hair and a long pale face. He had a distinguished rather literary manner, used the broad 'a' so that people often thought he was from Boston, one of the Back Bay Seargeants.

One night they got to making plans for themselves and the American theater. If they could get backing they'd start a repertory theater and do real American plays. He'd be the American Stanislavsky and she'd be the American Lady Gregory, and maybe the American Bakst too. When the café closed she told him to go around by the other staircase and go up to her room. She was excited by the idea of being alone in a hotel room with a young man and thought how shocked Eleanor would be if she knew about it. They smoked cigarettes and talked about the theater a little distractedly, and at last Freddy put his arm around her waist and kissed her and asked if he could stay all night. She let him kiss her, but she could only think of Dirk and told him please not this time, and he was very contrite and begged her with tears in his eyes to forgive him for sullying a beautiful moment. She said she didn't mean that and to come back and have breakfast with her.

After he'd gone she half wished she'd made him stay. Her body tingled all over the way it used to when Dirk put his arms around her and she wanted terribly to know what making love was like. She took a cold bath and went to bed. When she woke up and saw Freddy again she'd decide whether she was in love with him. But the next morning she got a telegram calling her home. Dad was seriously ill with diabetes. Freddy put her on the train. She'd expected that the parting would carry her off her feet, but it didn't somehow.

Doctor Hutchins got better and Eveline took him down to Santa Fé to recuperate. Her mother was sick most of the time too, and as Margaret and Adelaide were both married and George had gotten a job abroad with Hoover's Belgian Relief, it seemed to be up to her to take care of the old people. She spent a dreamy unhappy year in spite of the great skeleton landscape and horseback trips and working at watercolors of Mexicans and Indian penitentes. She went around the house ordering meals, attending to housekeeping, irritated by the stupidity of servantgirls, making out laundry lists.

The only man she met there who made her seem alive was José O'Riely. He was a Spaniard in spite of his Irish name, a slender young man with a tobaccocolored face and dark green eyes, who had somehow gotten married to a stout Mexican woman who brought out a new squalling brown infant every nine months. He was a painter and lived by doing odd carpenter jobs and sometimes posing as a model. Eveline got to talk to him one day when he was painting the garage doors and asked him to pose for her. He kept looking at the pastel she was doing of him and telling her it was wretched, until she broke down and cried. He apologized in his stiff English and said she must not be upset, that she had talent and that he'd teach her to draw himself. He took her down to his house, an untidy little shack in the Mexican part of town, where he introduced her to Lola, his wife, who looked at her with scared suspicious black eyes, and showed her his paintings, big retablos painted on plaster that looked like Italian primitives. 'You see I paint martires,' he said, 'but not Christian. I paint the martires of the workingclass under exploitation. Lola does not understand. She want me to paint rich ladies like you and make plenty money. Which you think is best?' Eveline flushed; she didn't like being classed with the rich ladies. But the pictures thrilled her and she said she would advertise them among her friends; she decided she'd discovered a genius.

O'Riely was grateful and wouldn't take any money for posing or criticizing her paintings after that, instead he sometimes borrowed small sums as a friend. Even before he started making love to her, she decided that this time it must be a real affair. She'd go crazy if something didn't happen to her soon.

The main difficulty was finding somewhere they could go. Her studio was right back of the house and there was the danger that her father or mother or friends coming to call might break in on them any time. Then too Santa Fé was a

small place and people were already noticing how often he
went to her studio.

One night when the Hutchins' chauffeur was away, they
climbed up to his room above the garage. It was pitchblack
there and smelled of old pipes and soiled clothes. Eveline was
terrified to find that she'd lost control of her own self; it was
like going under ether. He was surprised to find she was a
virgin and was very kind and gentle, almost apologetic. But she
felt none of the ecstasy she had expected lying in his arms on
the chauffeur's bed; it was almost as if it had all happened
before. Afterwards they lay on the bed talking a long time in
low intimate voices. His manner had changed; he treated her
gravely and indulgently, like a child. He said he hated things
to be secret and sordid like that, it was brutalizing to them
both. He would find a place where they could meet in the open,
in the sun and air, not like criminals this way. He wanted to
draw her, the beautiful slenderness of her body would be the
inspiration of his painting and her lovely little round breasts.
Then he looked her over carefully to see if her dress looked
mussed and told her to run over to the house and go to bed;
and to take precautions if she didn't want to have a baby,
though he would be proud to have her bear a child of his,
particularly as she was rich enough to support it. The idea
horrified her and she felt it was coarse and unfeeling of him to
talk about it lightly that way.

They met all that winter a couple of times a week in a little
deserted cabin that lay off the trail in the basin of a small
stony cañon back of the town. She would ride over and he
would walk by a different road. They called it their desert
island. Then one day Lola looked in his portfolios and found
hundreds of drawings of the same naked girl; she came up to
the Hutchins' house shaking and screaming with the hair streaming down her face, looking for Eveline and crying that she was
going to kill her. Doctor Hutchins was thunderstruck; but
though she was terribly frightened inside, Eveline managed to
keep cool and tell her father that she had let O'Riely do drawings of her, but that there'd been nothing else between them,
and that his wife was a stupid ignorant Mexican and couldn't
imagine a man and a woman being alone in a studio together
without thinking something disgusting. Although he scolded
her for being so imprudent, Dad believed her and they managed to keep the whole thing from Mother, but she managed
to see José only once more after that. He shrugged his shoul-

ders and said what could he do, he couldn't abandon his wife and children to starve, poor as he was he had to live with them, and a man had to have a woman to work for him and cook; he couldn't live on romantic lifeclasses, he had to eat, and Lola was a good woman but stupid and untidy and had made him promise not to see Eveline again. Eveline turned on her heel and left him before he was through talking. She was glad she had a horse she could jump on and ride away.

## The Camera Eye (31)

a mattress covered with something from Vantine's makes a divan in the ladyphotographer's studio   we sit on the divan and on cushions on the floor and the longnecked English actor reads the Song of Songs in rhythms

and the ladyphotographer in breastplates and silk bloomers dances the Song of Songs in rhythms

the little girl in pink is a classical dancer with panpipes but the hennahaired ladyphotographer dances the Song of Songs in rhythms with winking bellybutton and clash of breastplates in more Oriental style

*stay muh with flahgons comfort muh with ahpples*

*for I am sick of loeuve*

*his left hand is under muh head and his rahght hand doth embrace muh*

the semiretired actress who lived upstairs let out a yell and then another   Burglars secondstory men   Good God she's being attacked   we men run up the stairs poor woman she's in hysterics   It's the wrong flat the stairs are full of dicks outside they're backing up the wagon   All right men on one side girls on the other what the hell kind of place is this anyway? Dicks coming in all the windows dicks coming out of the kitchenette

the hennahaired ladyphotographer holds them at bay draped in a portière waving the telephone   Is this Mr Wickersham's office?   District Attorney   trying experience

a few friends   a little dance recital in the most brutal manner   prominent actress upstairs in hysterics   allright officer talk to the District Attorney he'll tell you who I am who our friends are

Dicks slink away wagon jangles to another street the English actor is speaking    Only by the greatest control I kept muh temper the swine I'm terrible when I'm aroused terrible

and the Turkish consul and his friend who were there incog   belligerent nation Department of Justice Espionage hunting radicals proGermans slipped quietly out and the two of us ran down the stairs and walked fast downtown and crossed to Weehawken on the ferry

it was a night of enormous fog through which moved blunderingly the great blind shapes of steamboat sirens from the lower bay

in the bow of the ferry we breathed the rancid riverbreeze talking loud in a shouting laugh

out of the quiet streets of Weehawken incredible slanting viaducts lead up into the fog

## *Eveline Hutchins*

She felt halfcrazy until she got on the train to go back East. Mother and Dad didn't want her to go, but she showed them a telegram she'd wired Eleanor to send her offering her a high salary in her decorating business. She said it was an opening that wouldn't come again and she had to take it, and anyway, as George was coming home for a vacation, they wouldn't be entirely alone. The night she left she lay awake in her lower berth tremendously happy in the roar of the air and the swift pound of the wheels on the rails. But after St Louis she began to worry: she'd decided she was pregnant.

She was terribly frightened. The Grand Central Station seemed so immense, so full of blank faces staring at her as she passed following the redcap who carried her bag. She was afraid she'd faint before she got to the taxicab. All the way downtown the jolting of the cab and the jangling throb of the traffic in her ears made her head swim with nausea. At the Brevoort she had some coffee. Ruddy sunlight was coming in the tall windows, the place had a warm restaurant smell; she began to feel better. She went to the phone and called Eleanor.

A French maid answered that Mademoiselle was still asleep, but that she would tell her who had called as soon as she woke up. Then she called Freddy, who sounded very much excited and said he'd be there as soon as he could get over from Brooklyn.

When she saw Freddy it was just as if she hadn't been away at all. He almost had a backer for the Maya ballet and he was mixed up in a new musical show he wanted Eveline to do costumes for. But he was very gloomy about the prospects of war with Germany, said he was a pacifist and would probably have to go to jail, unless there was a revolution. Eveline told him about her talks with José O'Riely and what a great painter he was, and said she thought maybe she was an anarchist. Freddy looked worried and asked her if she was sure she hadn't fallen in love with him, and she blushed and smiled and said no, and Freddy said she was a hundred times betterlooking than last year.

They went together to see Eleanor whose house in the east thirties was very elegant and expensivelooking. Eleanor was sitting up in bed answering her mail. Her hair was carefully done and she had on a pink satin dressinggown with lace and ermine on it. They had coffee with her and hot rolls that the Martinique maid had baked herself. Eleanor was delighted to see Eveline and said how well she looked and was full of mysteries about her business and everything. She said she was on the edge of becoming a theatrical producer and spoke about 'my financial adviser' this and that, until Eveline didn't know what to think; still it was evident that things were going pretty well with her. Eveline wanted to ask her what she knew about birthcontrol, but she never got around to it, and perhaps it was just as well, as, when they got on the subject of the war, they quarreled at once.

That afternoon Freddy took her to tea with him at the house of a middleaged lady who lived on West Eighth Street and was an enthusiastic pacifist. The house was full of people arguing and young men and young women wagging their heads together in important whispers. There she got to talking with a haggardlooking brighteyed young man named Don Stevens. Freddy had to go off to a rehearsal and she stayed there talking to Don Stevens. Then all of a sudden they found that everybody had gone and that they were alone with the hostess, who was a stout puffy eager woman that Eveline decided was just too tiresome. She said Goodnight and left. She had hardly gotten down the front steps to the street when Stevens was after her with his lanky stride dragging his overcoat behind him; 'Where are you going to eat supper, Eveline Hutchins?' Eveline said she hadn't thought and before she knew it was eating with him in an Italian restaurant on Third Street. He ate a lot of spaghetti very fast and drank a lot of red wine and introduced her to the waiter, whose name was Giovanni. 'He's a maximalist and so am I,' he said. 'This young woman seems to be a philosophic anarchist, but we'll get her over that.'

Don Stevens came from South Dakota and had worked on smalltown papers ever since his highschool days. He'd also worked as a harvesthand back home and been in on several I.W.W. scraps. He showed Eveline his red card with considerable pride. He'd come to New York to work on *The Call*, but had just resigned because they were too damn lilylivered, he said. He also wrote for the *Metropolitan Magazine* and the *Masses*, and spoke at antiwar meetings. He said that there wasn't a Chinaman's chance that the U.S. would keep out of the war; the Germans were winning, the workingclass all over Europe was on the edge of revolt, the revolution in Russia was the beginning of the worldwide social revolution and the bankers knew it and Wilson knew it; the only question was whether the industrial workers in the East and the farmers and casual laborers in the Middle West and West would stand for war. The entire press was bought and muzzled. The Morgans had to fight or go bankrupt. 'It's the greatest conspiracy in history.'

Giovanni and Eveline listened, holding their breath, Giovanni occasionally looking nervously around the room to see if any of the customers at the other tables looked like detectives. 'God damn it, Giovanni, let's have another bottle of wine,' Don would cry out in the middle of a long analysis of Kühn, Loeb and Company's foreign holdings. Then suddenly he'd turn to Eveline, filling up her glass, 'Where have you been all these years? I've so needed a lovely girl like you. Let's have a splendid time tonight, may be the last good meal we ever get, we may be in jail or shot against a wall a month from now, isn't that so, Giovanni?'

Giovanni forgot to wait on his other tables and was bawled out by the proprietor. Eveline kept laughing. When Don asked her why, she said she didn't know except that he was so funny.

'But it really is Armageddon, God damn it.' Then he shook

his head: 'What's the use, there never was a woman living who could understand political ideas.'

'Of course I can . . . I think it's terrible. I don't know what to do.'

'I don't know what to do,' he said savagely, 'I don't know whether to fight the war and go to jail, or to get a job as a war correspondent and see the goddam mess. If you could rely on anybody to back you up, it 'ud be another thing . . . Oh, hell, let's get out of here.'

He charged the check, and asked Eveline to lend him half a dollar to leave for Giovanni, said he didn't have a cent in his jeans. She found herself drinking a last glass of wine with him in a chilly littered room up three flights of dirty wooden stairs in Patchin Place. He began to make love to her, and when she objected that she'd just known him for seven hours he said that was another stupid bourgeois idea she ought to get rid of. When she asked him about birthcontrol, he sat down beside her and talked for half an hour about what a great woman Margaret Sanger was and how birthcontrol was the greatest single blessing to mankind since the invention of fire. When he started to make love to her again in a businesslike way, she, laughing and blushing, let him take off her clothes. It was three o'clock when, feeling weak and guilty and bedraggled, she got back to her room at the Brevoort. She took a huge dose of castor oil and went to bed where she lay awake till daylight wondering what she could say to Freddy. She'd had a date to meet him at eleven for a bite of supper after his rehearsal. Her fear of being pregnant had disappeared, like waking up from a nightmare.

That spring was full of plans for shows and decorating houses with Eleanor and Freddy, but nothing came of them, and after a while Eveline couldn't keep her mind on New York, what with war declared, and the streets filling with flags and uniforms, and everybody going patriotic crazy around her and seeing spies and pacifists under every bed. Eleanor was getting herself a job in the Red Cross. Don Stevens had signed up with the Friends' Relief. Freddy announced a new decision every day, but finally said he wouldn't decide what to do till he was called for the draft. Adelaide's husband had a job in Washington in the new Shipping Board. Dad was writing her every few days that Wilson was the greatest President since Lincoln. Some days she felt that she must be losing her mind, people around her seemed so cracked. When she began talking about it to Eleanor, Eleanor smiled in a superior way and said she'd already asked to have her as assistant in her office in Paris.

'Your office in Paris, darling?' Eleanor nodded. 'I don't care what kind of work it is, I'll do it gladly,' said Eveline. Eleanor sailed one Saturday on the *Rochambeau*, and two weeks later Eveline herself sailed on the *Touraine*.

It was a hazy summer evening. She'd been almost rude cutting short the goodbyes of Margaret and Adelaide and Margaret's husband Bill, who was a Major by this time and teaching sharpshooting out on Long Island, she was so anxious to cut loose from this America she felt was just too tiresome. The boat was two hours late in sailing. The band kept playing *Tipperary* and *Auprès de ma Blonde* and *La Madelon*. There were a great many young men around in various uniforms, all rather drunk. The little French sailors with their red pompons and baby faces yelled back and forth in rolling twangy bordelais. Eveline walked up and down the deck until her feet were tired. It seemed as if the boat would never sail. And Freddy, who had turned up late, kept waving to her from the dock and she was afraid Don Stevens would come and she was sick of all her life in these last years.

She went down to her cabin and started reading Barbusse's *Le Feu* that Don had sent her. She fell asleep, and when the grayhaired skinny woman who was her cabinmate woke her up bustling around, the first thing she felt was the trembling pound of the ship's engines. 'Well, you missed dinner,' said the grayhaired woman.

Her name was Miss Eliza Felton and she was an illustrator of children's books. She was going to France to drive a truck. At first Eveline thought she was just too tiresome, but as the warm quiet days of the crossing wore on she got to like her. Miss Felton had a great crush on Eveline and was a nuisance, but she was fond of wine and knew a great deal about France, where she'd lived for many years. In fact she'd studied painting at Fontainebleau in the old days of the impressionists. She was bitter against the Huns on account of Rheims and Louvain and the poor little Belgian babies with their hands cut off, but she didn't have much use for any male government, called Wilson a coward, Clemenceau a bully, and Lloyd George a sneak. She laughed at the precautions against submarine attack and said she knew the French Line was perfectly safe because all the German spies traveled by it. When they landed in Bordeaux she was a great help to Eveline.

They stayed over a day to see the town instead of going up to Paris with all the other Red Cross people and Relief workers. The rows of gray eighteenthcentury houses were too lovely in the endless rosy summer twilight, and the flowers for sale and the polite people in the shops and the delicate patterns of the ironwork, and the fine dinner they had at the Chapon Fin.

The only trouble with going around with Eliza Felton was that she kept all the men away. They went up to Paris on the daytrain next day and Eveline could hardly keep from tears at the beauty of the country and the houses and the vines and the tall ranks of poplars. There were little soldiers in pale blue at every station and the elderly and deferential conductor looked like a collegeprofessor. When the train finally slid smoothly through the tunnel and into the Orléans station her throat was so tight she could hardly speak. It was as if she'd never been to Paris before.

'Now where are you going, dear? You see we have to carry our own traps,' said Eliza Felton in a businesslike way.

'Well, I suppose I should go to the Red Cross and report.'

'Too late for tonight, I can tell you that.'

'Well, I might try to call up Eleanor.'

'Might as well try to wake the dead as try to use the Paris telephone in wartime . . . what you'd better do, dear, is come with me to a little hotel I know on the Quai and sign up with the Red Cross in the morning; that's what I'm going to do.'

'I'd hate to get sent back home.'

'They won't know you're here for weeks. . . . I know those dumbbells.'

So Eveline waited with their traps while Eliza Felton fetched a little truck. They piled their bags on it and rolled them out of the station and through the empty streets in the last faint mauve of twilight to the hotel. There were very few lights and they were blue and hooded with tin hats so that they couldn't be seen from above. The Seine, the old bridges, and the long bulk of the Louvre opposite looked faint and unreal; it was like walking through a Whistler.

'We must hurry and get something to eat before everything closes up. . . . I'll take you to Adrienne's,' said Miss Felton.

They left their bags to be taken up to their rooms at the hôtel du Quai Voltaire and walked fast through a lot of narrow crisscross fastdarkening streets. They ducked into the door of the little restaurant just as someone was starting to pull the heavy iron shutter down. 'Tiens, c'est Mademoiselle Elise,' cried a woman's voice from the back of the heavily upholstered little room. A short Frenchwoman with a very large head and very large popeyes ran forward and hugged Miss Felton and kissed her a number of times. 'This is Miss Hutchins,' said Miss Felton in her dry voice. 'Verry plised . . . she is so prretty . . . beautiful eyes, hein?' It made Eveline uncomfortable the way the woman looked at her, the way her big powdered face was set like an egg in a cup in the frilly highnecked blouse. She brought out some soup and cold veal and bread, with many apologies on account of not having butter or sugar, complaining in a singsong voice about how severe the police were and how the profiteers were hoarding food and how bad the military situation was. Then she suddenly stopped talking; all their eyes lit at the same moment on the sign on the wall:

MEFIEZ VOUS LES OREILLES ENNEMIS VOUS
ECOUTENT

'Enfin c'est la guerre,' Adrienne said. She was sitting beside Miss Felton, patting Miss Felton's thin hand with her pudgy hand all covered with paste rings. She had made them coffee. They were drinking little glasses of Cointreau. She leaned over and patted Eveline on the neck. 'Faut pas s'en faire, hein?' Then she threw back her head and let out a shrill hysterical laugh. She kept pouring out more little glasses of Cointreau and Miss Felton seemed to be getting a little tipsy. Adrienne kept patting her hand. Eveline felt her own head swimming in the stuffy dark closedup little room. She got to her feet and said she was going back to the hotel, that she had a headache and was sleepy. They tried to coax her to stay, but she ducked out under the shutter.

Half the street outside was lit up by moonlight, the other half was in pitchblack shadow. All at once Eveline remembered that she didn't know the way back to the hotel, still she couldn't go into that restaurant again and that woman gave her the horrors, so she walked along fast, keeping in the moonlight, scared of the silence and the few shadowy people and the old gaunt houses with their wide inky doorways. She came out on a boulevard at last where there were men and women strolling, voices and an occasional automobile with blue lights running silently over the asphalt. Suddenly the nightmare scream of a siren started up in the distance, then another and another. Somewhere lost in the sky was a faint humming like a bee, louder, then fainter, then louder again. Eveline looked at the people around her. Nobody seemed alarmed or to hurry their strolling pace.

'Les avions . . . les boches . . . ' she heard people saying in unstartled tones. She found herself standing at the curb staring up into the milky sky that was fast becoming rayed with searchlights. Next to her was a fatherlylooking French officer with all kinds of lace on his képi and drooping mustaches. The sky overhead began to sparkle like with mica; it was beautiful and far away like fireworks seen across the lake on the Fourth. Involuntarily she said aloud, 'What's that?' 'C'est le shrapnel, mademoiselle. It is ourr ahnt-aircrahft cannons,' he said carefully in English, and then gave her his arm and offered to take her home. She noticed that he smelt rather strongly of cognac, but he was very nice and paternal in his manner and made funny gestures of things coming down on their heads and said they must get under cover. She said please to go to the hôtel du Quai Voltaire, as she'd lost her way.

'Ah, charmant, charmant,' said the elderly French officer. While they had stood there talking, everybody else on the street had melted out of sight. Guns were barking in every direction now. They were going down through the narrow streets again, keeping close to the wall. Once he pulled her suddenly into a doorway and something landed whang on the pavement opposite. 'It is the fragments of shrapnel, not good,' he said, tapping himself on the top of the képi. He laughed and Eveline laughed and they got along famously. They had come out on the riverbank. It seemed safe for some reason under the thickfoliaged trees. From the door of the hotel he suddenly pointed into the sky, 'Look, c'est les fokkers, ils s'en fichent de nous.' As he spoke the Boche planes wheeled overhead so that their wings caught the moonlight. For a second they were like seven tiny silver dragonflies, then they'd vanished. At the same moment came the rending snort of a bomb from somewhere across the river. 'Permettez, mademoiselle.' They went into the pitchblack hall of the hotel and felt their way down into the cellar. As he handed Eveline down the last step of the dusty wooden stairs, the officer gravely saluted the mixed group of people in bathrobes or overcoats over their nightclothes who were grouped around a couple of candles.

There was a waiter there and the officer tried to order a drink, but the waiter said, 'Ah, mon colonel, c'est defendu,' and the colonel made a wry face. Eveline sat up on a sort of table. She was so excited looking at the people and listening to the distant snort of the bombs that she hardly noticed that the colonel was squeezing her knee a little more than was necessary. The colonel's hands became a problem. When the airraid was over, something went by on the street making a funny seesaw noise between the quacking of a duck and a burro's bray. It struck Eveline so funny she laughed and laughed so that the colonel didn't seem to know what to make of her. When she tried to say goodnight to him to go up to her room and get some sleep, he wanted to go up too. She didn't know what to do. He'd been so nice and polite she didn't want to be rude to him, but she couldn't seem to make him understand that she wanted to go to bed and to sleep; he'd answer that so did he. When she tried to explain that she had a friend with her, he asked if the friend was as charming as mademoiselle, in that case he'd be delighted. Eveline's French broke down entirely. She wished to heavens Miss Felton would turn up, she couldn't make the concierge understand that she wanted the key to her room and that mon colonel wasn't coming up and was ready to break down and cry when a young American in civilian clothes with a red face and a turnedup nose appeared from somewhere out of the shadows and said with a flourish in very bad French, 'Monsieur, moi frère de madmosel, can't you see that the little girl is fatiguée and wants to say bon-soir?' He linked his arm in the colonel's and said, 'Vive la France. . . . Come up to my room and have a drink.' The colonel drew himself up and looked very angry. Without waiting to see what happened, Eveline ran up the stairs to her room, rushed in and double-locked the door.

# Newsreel 24

it is difficult to realize the colossal scale upon which Europe will have to borrow in order to make good the destruction of war

BAGS TWENTYEIGHT HUNS SINGLEHANDED

PEACE TALK BEGINNING TO HAVE ITS EFFECT ON SOUTHERN IRON MARKET

LOCAL BOY CAPTURES OFFICER

ONE THIRD WAR ALLOTMENTS FRAUDULENT

*There are smiles that make us happy*
*There are smiles that make us blue*

again let us examine into the matter of rates; let it be assumed that the United States is operating fleets aggregating 3000 freight and passenger vessels between U.S. and foreign ports

GANG LEADER SLAIN IN STREET

*There are smiles that wipe away the teardrops*
*Like the sunbeams dry away the dew*
*There are smiles that have a tender meaning*
*That the eyes of love alone can see*

SOLDIER VOTE CARRIED ELECTION

suppose now that into this delicate medium of economic law there is thrust the controlling factor of an owner of a third of the world's tonnage, who regards with equanimity both profit and loss, who does not count as a factor in the cost of operation the interest on capital investment, who builds vessels whether they may be profitably operated or not and who charges rates commensurate in no certain measure with the laws of supply and demand; how long would it be before the ocean transport of the whole world had broken down completely?

### CROWN PRINCE ON THE RUN

*But the smiles that fill my heart with sunshine*
             *Are*
                 *the*
                     *smiles*
                           *you*
                                *give*
                                      *to*
                                          *me*

persistent talk of peace is an unsettling factor and the epidemic of influenza has deterred country buyers from visiting the larger centers

## The Camera Eye (32)

à quatorze heures précisément the Boche diurnally shelled that bridge with their wellknown precision as to time and place  à quatorze heures précisément Dick Norton with his monocle in his eye lined up his section at a little distance from the bridge to turn it over to the American Red Cross

The Red Cross majors looked pudgy and white under their new uniforms in their shined Sam Browne belts in their shined tight leather puttees    so this was overseas

so this was the front    well    well

Dick Norton adjusted his monocle and began to talk about how as gentlemen volunteers he had signed us up and as gentlemen volunteers he bade us farewell  Wham the first arrivé the smell of almonds the sunday feeling of no traffic on the road not a poilu in sight  Dick Norton adjusted his monocle    the Red Cross majors felt the showering mud    sniffed the lyddite    swift whiff of latrines and of huddled troops

Wham Wham Wham like the Fourth of July    the shellfragments sing our ears ring

the bridge is standing and Dick Norton adjusting his

monocle is standing talking at length about gentlemen
volunteers and ambulance service and la belle France

The empty staffcar is standing
but where are the majors taking over command
who were to make a speech in the name of the Red
Cross? The slowest and pudgiest and whitest of the majors
is still to be seen on his hands and knees with mud all over
his puttees crawling into the abris and that's the last we saw
of the Red Cross majors
and the last we heard of gentlemen
or volunteers


# The Happy Warrior

The Roosevelts had lived for seven righteous generations
on Manhattan Island; they owned a big brick house on Twentieth Street, an estate up at Dobbs Ferry, lots in the city, a pew
in the Dutch Reformed Church, interests, stocks and bonds,
they felt Manhattan was theirs, they felt America was theirs.
Their son,
Theodore,
was a sickly youngster, suffered asthma, was very near-
sighted; his hands and feet were so small it was hard for him
to learn to box; his arms were very short;
his father was something of a humanitarian, gave Christmas dinners to newsboys, deplored conditions, slums, the East
Side, Hell's Kitchen.
Young Theodore had ponies, was encouraged to walk in
the woods, to go camping, was instructed in boxing and fencing (an American gentleman should know how to defend himself), taught Bible Class, did mission work (an American
gentleman should do his best to uplift those not so fortunately
situated);
righteousness was his by birth;
he had a passion for nature study, for reading about birds
and wild animals, for going hunting; he got to be a good shot
in spite of his glasses, a good walker in spite of his tiny feet
and short legs, a fair horseman, an aggressive scrapper in spite
of his short reach, a crack politician in spite of being the son

of one of the owning Dutch families of New York.

In 1876 he went up to Cambridge to study at Harvard, a wealthy talkative erratic young man with sidewhiskers and definite ideas about everything under the sun;

at Harvard he drove around in a dogcart, collected stuffed birds, mounted specimens he'd shot on his trips in the Adirondacks; in spite of not drinking and being somewhat of a christer, having odd ideas about reform and remedying abuses, he made Porcellian and the Dickey and the clubs that were his right as the son of one of the owning Dutch families of New York.

He told his friends he was going to devote his life to social service: *I wish to preach not the doctrine of ignoble ease, but the doctrine of the strenuous life, the life of toil and effort, of labor and strife.*

From the time he was eleven years old he wrote copiously, filled diaries, notebooks, loose leaves, with a big impulsive scrawl about everything he did and thought and said;

naturally he studied law.

He married young and went to Switzerland to climb the Matterhorn; his first wife's early death broke him all up. He went out to the badlands of western Dakota to become a rancher on the Little Missouri River;

when he came back to Manhattan he was Teddy, the straight shooter from the West, the elkhunter, the man in the Stetson hat, who'd roped steers, fought a grizzly hand to hand, acted as Deputy Sheriff

(a Roosevelt has a duty to his country; the duty of a Roosevelt is to uplift those not so fortunately situated, those who have come more recently to our shores);

in the West, Deputy Sheriff Roosevelt felt the white man's burden, helped to arrest malefactors, badmen; service was bully.

All this time he'd been writing, filling the magazines with stories of his hunts and adventures, filling political meetings with his opinions, his denunciations, his pat phrases: Strenuous Life, Realizable Ideals, Just Government, *when men fear work or fear righteous war, when women fear motherhood, they tremble on the brink of doom, and well it is that they should vanish from the earth, where they are fit subjects for the scorn of all men and women who are themselves strong and brave and highminded.*

T. R. married a wealthy woman and righteously raised a family at Sagamore Hill.

He served a term in the New York Legislature, was appointed by Grover Cleveland to the unremunerative job of Commissioner for Civil Service Reform

was Reform Police Commissioner of New York, pursued malefactors, stoutly maintained that white was white and black was black,

wrote the Naval History of the War of 1812,

was appointed Assistant Secretary of the Navy,

and when the *Maine* blew up resigned to lead the Rough Riders,

Lieutenant-Colonel.

This was the Rubicon, the Fight, the Old Glory, the Just Cause. The American public was not kept in ignorance of the Colonel's bravery when the bullets sang, how he charged without his men up San Juan Hill and had to go back to fetch them, how he shot a running Spaniard in the tail.

It was too bad that the regulars had gotten up San Juan Hill first from the other side, that there was no need to get up San Juan Hill at all. Santiago was surrendered. It was a successful campaign. T. R. charged up San Juan Hill into the governorship of the Empire State;

but after the fighting, volunteers warcorrespondents magazinewriters began to want to go home;

it wasn't bully huddling under puptents in the tropical rain or scorching in the morning sun of the seared Cuban hills with malaria mowing them down and dysentery and always yellowjack to be afraid of.

T. R. got up a roundrobin to the President and asked for the amateur warriors to be sent home and leave the dirtywork to the regulars

who were digging trenches and shovelling crap and fighting malaria and dysentery and yellowjack

to make Cuba cozy for the Sugar Trust

and the National City Bank.


When he landed at home, one of his first interviews was with Lemuel Quigg, emissary of Boss Platt who had the votes of upstate New York sewed into the lining of his vest;

he saw Boss Platt too, but he forgot about that afterwards. Things were bully. He wrote a life of Oliver Cromwell whom people said he resembled. As Governor he doublecrossed the

Platt machine (a righteous man may have a short memory);
Boss Platt thought he'd shelved him by nominating him for
the Vice-Presidency in 1900;

Czolgocz made him President.

T. R. drove like a fiend in a buckboard over the muddy
roads through the driving rain from Mount Marcy in the
Adirondacks to catch the train to Buffalo where McKinley was
dying.
As President
he moved Sagamore Hill, the healthy happy normal American home, to the White House, took foreign diplomats and fat
army officers out walking in Rock Creek Park, where he led
them a terrible dance through brambles, hopping across the
creek on steppingstones, wading the fords, scrambling up the
shaly banks,
and shook the Big Stick at malefactors of great wealth.
Things were bully.
He engineered the Panama revolution under the shadow
of which took place the famous hocuspocus of juggling the
old and new canal companies by which forty million dollars
vanished into the pockets of the international bankers,
but Old Glory floated over the Canal Zone
and the canal was cut through.
He busted a few trusts,
had Booker Washington to lunch at the White House,
and urged the conservation of wild life.
He got the Nobel Peace Prize for patching up the Peace
of Portsmouth that ended the Russo-Japanese War,
and sent the Atlantic Fleet around the world for everybody to see that America was a firstclass power. He left the
presidency to Taft after his second term leaving to that ele-
phantine lawyer the congenial task of pouring judicial oil on
the hurt feelings of the moneymasters.
and went to Africa to hunt big game.
Biggame hunting was bully.
Every time a lion or an elephant went crashing down into
the jungle underbrush, under the impact of a wellplaced mushroom bullet,
the papers lit up with headlines;
when he talked with the Kaiser on horseback
the world was not ignorant of what he said, or when he

lectured the Nationalists at Cairo telling them that this was a white man's world.

He went to Brazil where he traveled through the Matto Grosso in a dugout over waters infested with the tiny maneating fish, the piranha,

shot tapirs,

jaguars,

specimens of the whitelipped peccary.

He ran the rapids of the River of Doubt

down to the Amazon frontiers where he arrived sick, an infected abscess in his leg, stretched out under an awning in a dugout with a tame trumpeterbird beside him.

Back in the States he fought his last fight when he came out for the Republican nomination in 1912 a Progressive, champion of the Square Deal, crusader for the Plain People; the Bull Moose bolted out from under the Taft steamroller and formed the Progressive Party for righteousness' sake at the Chicago Colosseum while the delegates who were going to restore democratic government rocked with tears in their eyes as they sang

> On ward Christian so old gers
> March ing as to war

Perhaps the River of Doubt had been too much for a man of his age; perhaps things weren't so bully any more; T. R. lost his voice during the triangular campaign. In Duluth a maniac shot him in the chest, his life was saved only by the thick bundle of manuscript of the speech he was going to deliver. T. R. delivered the speech with the bullet still in him, heard the scared applause, felt the plain people praying for his recovery, but the spell was broken somehow.

The Democrats swept in, the World War drowned out the righteous voice of the Happy Warrior in the roar of exploding lyddite.

Wilson wouldn't let T.R. lead a division, this was no amateur's war (perhaps the regulars remembered the round-robin at Santiago). All he could do was write magazine articles against the Huns, send his sons; Quentin was killed.

It wasn't the bully amateur's world any more. Nobody knew that on Armistice Day, Theodore Roosevelt, happy amateur warrior with the grinning teeth, the shaking forefinger, naturalist, explorer, magazinewriter, Sundayschool

teacher, cowpuncher, moralist, politician, righteous orator
with a short memory, fond of denouncing liars (the Ananias
Club) and having pillowfights with his children, was taken to
the Roosevelt Hospital gravely ill with inflammatory rheumatism.

Things weren't bully any more;

T. R. had grit;

he bore the pain, the obscurity, the sense of being forgotten as he had borne the grilling portages when he was
exploring the River of Doubt, the heat, the fetid jungle mud,
the infected abscess in his leg,

and died quietly in his sleep
at Sagamore Hill
on January 6, 1919
and left on the shoulders of his sons
the white man's burden.


## The Camera Eye (33)

eleven thousand registered harlots said the Red Cross
Publicity Man infest the streets of Marseilles

the Ford stalled three times in the Rue de Rivoli   in
Fontainebleau we had our café au lait in bed   the Forest
was so achingly red yellow novemberbrown under the tiny
lavender rain   beyond the road climbed through dove-
colored hills   the air smelt of apples

Nevers (Dumas nom de dieu) Athos Porthos and
d'Artagnan had ordered a bisque at the inn   we wound
down slowly into red Maçon that smelt of winelees and the
vintage   fais ce que voudras   saute Bourgignon in the
Rhone valley the first strawcolored sunlight streaked the
white road with shadows of skeletal poplars   at every stop
we drank wine strong as beefsteaks rich as the palace of
François Premier bouquet of the last sleetlashed roses   we
didn't cross the river to Lyon where Jean-Jacques suffered
from greensickness as a youngster   the landscapes of
Provence were all out of the Gallic Wars the towns were
dictionaries of Latin roots Orange Tarascon Arles where
Van Gogh cut off his ear   the convoy became less of a conducted tour   we stopped to play craps in the estaminets

boys we're going south    to drink the red wine the popes
loved best    to eat fat meals in oliveoil and garlic    bound
south    cépes provençale the north wind was shrilling over
the plains of the Camargue hustling us into Marseilles
where the eleven thousand were dandling themselves in the
fogged mirrors of the promenoir at the Apollo

oysters and vin de Cassis petite fille tellement brune
tête de lune qui amait les veentair sports    in the end they
were all slot machines undressed as Phocean figurines
posted with their legs apart around the scummy edges of
the oldest port

the Riviera was a letdown, but there was a candy-
colored church with a pointed steeple on every hill beyond
San Remo    Porto Maurizio blue seltzerbottles standing in
the cinzanocolored sunlight beside a glass of VERMOUTH
TORINO    Savona was set for the Merchant of Venice
painted by Veronese    Ponte Decimo    in Ponte Decimo
ambulances were parked in a moonlit square of bleak stone
workingpeople's houses    hoarfrost covered everything    in
the little bar the Successful Story Writer taught us to drink
cognac and maraschino half and half

havanuzzerone

it turned out he was not writing what he felt he wanted
to be writing What can you tell them at home about the war?
it turned out he was not wanting what he wrote    he wanted
to be feeling    cognac and maraschino    was no longer
young    (It made us damn sore we greedy for what we felt
we wanted tell 'em all they lied see new towns go to Genoa)

havanuzzerone?    it turned out that he wished he was a
naked brown shepherd boy sitting on a hillside playing a
flute in the sunlight

going to Genoa was easy enough the streetcar went
there Genoa the new town we'd never seen full of marble
doges and breakneck stairs marble lions in the moonlight
Genoa    was the ancient ducal city burning? all the marble
palaces and the square stone houses and the campaniles
topping hills had one marble wall on fire

bonfire under the moon

the bars were full of Britishers overdressed civilians

strolling under porticoes outside the harbor under the Genoa moon the sea was on fire the member of His Majesty's Intelligence Service said it was a Yankee tanker had struck a mine? been torpedoed? why don't they scuttle her?

Genoa   eyes flared with the light of the burning tanker Genoa   what are you looking for? the flare in the blood under the moon down the midnight streets in boys' and girls' faces   Genoa   eyes the question in their eyes

through the crumbling stone courts under the Genoa moon up and down the breakneck stairs eyes on fire under the moon round the next corner full in your face the flare of the bonfire on the sea

eleven thousand registered harlots said the Red Cross Publicity Man infest the streets of Marseilles

## *Joe Williams*

It was a lousy trip. Joe was worried all the time about Del and about not making good and the deckcrew was a bunch of soreheads. The engines kept breaking down. The *Higginbotham* was built like a cheesebox and so slow there were days when they didn't make more'n thirty or forty miles against moderate headwinds. The only good times he had was taking boxing lessons from the second engineer, a fellow named Glen Hardwick. He was a little wiry guy, who was a pretty good amateur boxer, though he must have been forty years old. By the time they got to Bordeaux Joe was able to give him a good workout. He was heavier and had a better reach and Glen said he'd a straight natural right that would take him far as a lightweight.

In Bordeaux the first port official that came on board tried to kiss Cap'n Perry on both cheeks. President Wilson had just declared war on Germany. All over the town nothing was too good for Les Américains. Evenings when they were off Joe and Glen Hardwick cruised around together. The Bordeaux girls were damn pretty. They met up with a couple one afternoon in the public garden that weren't hookers at all. They were nicely dressed and looked like they came of good families, what the

hell it was wartime. At first Joe thought he ought to lay off
that stuff now that he was married, but hell, hadn't Del held
out on him. What did she think he was, a plaster saint? They
ended by going to a little hotel the girls knew and eating supper
and drinking beaucoup wine and champagne and having a big
party. Joe had never had such a good time with a girl in his
life. His girl's name was Marceline and when they woke up in
the morning the help at the hotel brought them in coffee and
rolls and they ate breakfast, both of 'em sitting up in bed and
Joe's French began to pick up and he learned how to say C'est
la guerre and On les aura and Je m'en fiche and Marceline
said she'd always be his sweetie when he was in Bordeaux and
called him petit lapin.

They stayed in Bordeaux only the four days it took 'em to
wait their turn to go up to the dock and unload, but they drank
wine and cognac all the time and the food was swell and nobody could do enough for them on account of America having
come into the war and it was a great old four days.

On the trip home the *Higginbotham* sprung leaks so bad the
old man stopped worrying about submarines altogether. It was
nip and tuck if they'd make Halifax. The ship was light and
rolled like a log so that even with fiddles on they couldn't keep
dishes on the messtable. One dirty night of driving fog somewhere south of Cape Race, Joe with his chin in his peajacket
was taking a turn on the deck amidship when he was suddenly
thrown flat. They never knew what hit 'em, a mine or a torpedo.
It was only that the boats were in darn good order and the sea
was smooth that they got off at all. As it was, the four boats
got separated. The *Higginbotham* faded into the fog and they
never saw her sink, though the last they could make out her
maindeck was awash.

They were cold and wet. In Joe's boat nobody said much.
The men at the oars had to work hard to keep her bow into
the little chop that came up. Each sea a little bigger than the
others drenched them with spray. They had on wool sweaters
and lifepreservers but the cold seeped through. At last the fog
grayed a little and it was day. Joe's boat and the captain's boat
managed to keep together until late that afternoon they were
picked up by a big fishing schooner, a Banker bound for
Boston.

When they were picked up, old Cap'n Perry was in a bad
way. The master of the fishing schooner did everything he
could for him, but he was unconscious when they reached

Boston four days later and died on the way to the hospital. The doctors said it was pneumonia.

Next morning Joe and the mate went to the office of the agent of Perkins and Ellerman, the owners, to see about getting themselves and the crew paid off. There was some kind of damn monkeydoodle business about the vessel's having changed owners in midAtlantic, a man named Rosenberg had bought her on a speculation and now he couldn't be found and the Chase National Bank was claiming ownership and the underwriters were raising cain. The agent said he was sure they'd be paid all right, because Rosenberg had posted bond, but it would be some time. 'And what the hell do they expect us to do all that time, eat grass?' The clerk said he was sorry, but they'd have to take it up direct with Mr Rosenberg.

Joe and the first mate stood side by side on the curb outside the office and cursed for a while, then the mate went over to South Boston to break the news to the Chief who lived there.

It was a warm June afternoon. Joe started to go around the shipping offices to see what he could do in the way of a berth. He got tired of that and went and sat on a bench on the Common, staring at the sparrows and the gobs loafing around and the shopgirls coming home from work, their little heels clattering on the asphalt paths.

Joe hung around Boston broke for a couple of weeks. The Salvation Army took care of the survivors, serving 'em beans and watery soup and a lot of hymns offkey that didn't appeal to Joe the way he felt just then. He was crazy to get enough jack to go to Norfolk to see Del. He wrote her every day, but the letters he got back to General Delivery seemed kinder cool. She was worried about the rent and wanted some spring clothes and was afraid they wouldn't like it at the office if they found out about her being married.

Joe sat on the benches on the Common and roamed around among the flowerbeds in the Public Garden, and called regularly at the agent's office to ask about a berth, but finally he got sick of hanging around and went down and signed on as quartermaster, on a United Fruit boat, the *Callao*. He thought it 'ud be a short run and by the time he got back in a couple of weeks he'd be able to get his money.

On the home trip they had to wait several days, anchored outside in the roads at Roseau in Dominica, for the limes they were going to load to be crated. Everybody was sore at the

port authorities, a lot of damn British niggers, on account of
the quarantine and the limes not being ready and how slow the
lighters were coming off from the shore. The last night in port
Joe and Larry, one of the other quartermasters, got kidding
some young coons in a bumboat that had been selling fruit and
liquor to the crew under the stern; first thing they knew they'd
offered 'em a dollar each to take 'em ashore and land 'em
down the beach so's the officers wouldn't see them. The town
smelt of niggers. There were no lights in the streets. A little
coalblack youngster ran up and asked did they want some
mountain chicken. 'I guess that means wild women, sure,' said
Joe. 'All bets are off tonight.' The little dinge took 'em into a
bar kept by a stout mulatto woman and said something to her
in the island lingo they couldn't understand, and she said they'd
have to wait a few minutes and they sat down and had a couple
of drinks of corn and oil. 'I guess she must be the madam,'
said Larry. 'If they ain't pretty good lookers they can go to
hell for all I care. I'm not much on the dark meat.' From out
back same a sound of sizzling and a smell of something frying.
'Dodgast it, I could eat something,' said Joe. 'Say, boy, tell her we
want something to eat.' 'By and by you eat mountain chicken.'
'What the hell?' They finished their drinks just as the woman
came back with a big platter of something fried up. 'What's
that?' asked Joe. 'That's mountain chicken, mister; that's how
we call froglegs down here, but they ain't like the frogs you
all has in the States. I been in the States and I know. We
wouldn't eat them here. These here is clean frogs just like
chicken. You'll find it real good if you eat it.' They roared.
'Jesus, the drinks are on us,' said Larry, wiping the tears out
of his eyes.

Then they thought they'd go pick up some girls. They saw a
couple leaving the house where the music was and followed 'em
down the dark street. They started to talk to 'em and the girls
showed their teeth and wriggled in their clothes and giggled.
But three or four nigger men came up sore as hell and began
talking in the local lingo. 'Jeez, Larry, we'd better watch our
step,' said Joe through his teeth. 'Those bozos got razors.' They
were in the middle of a yelling bunch of big black men when
they heard an American voice behind them, 'Don't say another word, boys, I'll handle this.' A small man in khaki riding-
breeches and a panama hat was pushing his way through the
crowd talking in the island lingo all the time. He was a little
man with a gray triangular face tufted with a goatee. 'My

name's Henderson, DeBuque Henderson of Bridgeport, Connecticut.' He shook hands with both of them.

'Well, what's the trouble, boys? It's all right now, everybody knows me here. You have to be careful on this island, boys, they're touchy, these people, very touchy. . . . You boys better come along with me and have a drink. . . .' He took them each by the arm and walked them hurriedly up the street. 'Well, I was young once . . . I'm still young . . . sure, had to see the island . . . damn right too, the most interesting island in the whole Caribbean, only lonely . . . never see a white face.'

When they got to his house he walked them through a big whitewashed room onto a terrace that smelt of vanilla flowers. They could see the town underneath with its few lights, the dark hills, the while hull of the *Callao* with the lighters around her lit up by the working lights. At intervals the rattle of winches came up to them and a crazy jigtime from somewhere.

The old feller poured them each a glass of rum; then another. He had a parrot on a perch that kept screeching. The landbreeze had come up full of heavy flowersmells off the mountains and blew the old feller's stringy white hair in his eyes. He pointed at the *Callao* all lit up with its ring of lighters. 'United Fruit . . . United Thieves Company . . . it's a monopoly . . . if you won't take their prices they let your limes rot on the wharf; it's a monopoly. You boys are working for a bunch of thieves, but I know it ain't your fault. Here's lookin' at you.'

Before they knew it Larry and Joe were singing. The old man was talking about cottonspinning machinery and canecrushers and pouring out drinks from a rumbottle. They were pretty goddam drunk. They didn't know how they got aboard. Joe remembered the dark fo'c'stle and the sound of snoring from the bunks spinning around, then sleep hitting him like a sandbag and the sweet, sicky taste of rum in his mouth.

A couple of days later Joe came down with a fever and horrible pains in his joints. He was out of his head when they put him ashore at St Thomas's. It was dengue and he was sick for two months before he had the strength even to write Del to tell her where he was. The hospital orderly told him he'd been out of his head five days and they'd given him up for a goner. The doctors had been sore as hell about it because this was post hospital; after all he was a white man and unconscious and they couldn't very well feed him to the sharks.

It was July before Joe was well enough to walk around the

steep little coraldust streets of the town. He had to leave the hospital and would have been in a bad way if one of the cooks at the marine barracks hadn't looked out for him and found him a flop in an unused section of the building. It was hot and there was never a cloud in the sky and he got pretty sick of looking at the niggers and the bare hills and the blue shutin harbor. He spent a lot of time sitting out on the old coalwharf in the shade of a piece of corrugatediron roof looking through the planking at the clear deep bluegreen water, watching shoals of snappers feeding around the piles. He got to thinking about Del and that French girl in Bordeaux and the war and how the United Fruit was a bunch of thieves and then the thoughts would go round and round in his head like the little silver and blue yellow fish round the swaying weeds on the piles and he'd find he'd dropped off to sleep.

When a northbound fruitsteamer came into the harbor he got hold of one of the officers on the wharf and told him his sad story. They gave him passage up to New York. First thing he did was try to get hold of Janey; maybe if she thought he ought to, he'd give up this dog's life and take a steady job ashore. He called up the J. Ward Moorehouse advertising office where she worked, but the girl at the other end of the line told him she was the boss's secretary and was out West on business.

He went over and got a flop at Mrs Olsen's in Redhook. Everybody over there was talking about the draft and how they rounded you up for a slacker if they picked you up on the street without a registration card. And sure enough, just as Joe was stepping out of the subway at Wall Street one morning, a cop came up to him and asked him for his card. Joe said he was a merchant seaman and had just got back from a trip and hadn't had time to register yet and that he was exempt, but the cop said he'd have to tell that to the judge. They were quite a bunch being marched down Broadway; smart guys in the crowd of clerks and counterjumpers along the sidewalks yelled 'Slackers' at them and the girls hissed and booed.

In the Custom House they were herded into some of the basement rooms. It was a hot August day. Joe elbowed his way through the sweating, grumbling crowd towards the window. Most of them were foreigners, there were longshoremen and waterfront loafers; a lot of the group were talking big, but Joe remembered the navy and kept his mouth shut and listened. He was in there all day. The cops wouldn't let anybody telephone and there was only one toilet and they had to go to that under guard. Joe felt pretty weak on his pins, he hadn't gotten over the effect of the dengue yet. He was about ready to pass out when he saw a face he knew. Damned if it wasn't Glen Hardwick.

Glen had been picked up by a Britisher and taken into Halifax. He'd signed as second on the *Chemang*, taking out mules to Bordeaux and a general cargo to Genoa, going to be armed with a threeinch gun and navy gunners, Joe ought to come along. 'Jesus, do you think I could get aboard her?' Joe asked. 'Sure, they're crazy for navigation officers; they'd take you on even without a ticket.' Bordeaux sounded pretty good, remember the girlfriends there? They doped out that when Glen got out he'd phone Mrs Olsen to bring over Joe's license that was in a cigarbox at the head of his bed. When they finally were taken up to the desk to be questioned, the guy let Glen go right away and said Joe could go as soon as they got his license over, but that they must register at once even if they were exempt from the draft. 'After all, you boys ought to remember that there's a war on,' said the inspector at the desk. 'Well, we sure ought to know,' said Joe.

Mrs Olsen came over all in a flurry with Joe's papers and Joe hustled over to the office in East New York and they took him on as bosun. The skipper was Ben Tarbell who'd been first mate on the *Higginbotham*. Joe wanted to go down to Norfolk to see Del, but hell, this was no time to stay ashore. What he did was to send her fifty bucks he borrowed from Glen. He didn't have time to worry about it anyway because they sailed the next day with sealed orders as to where to meet the convoy.

It wasn't so bad steaming in convoy. The navy officers on the destroyers and the *Salem* that was in command gave the orders, but the merchant captains kidded back and forth with wigwag signals. It was some sight to see the Atlantic Ocean full of long strings of freighters all blotched up with gray and white watermarkings like barberpoles by the camouflage artists. There were old tubs in that convoy that a man wouldn't have trusted himself in to cross to Staten Island in peacetime and one of the new wooden Shipping Board boats leaked so bad, jerrybuilt out of new wood – somebody musta been making money – that she had to be abandoned and scuttled halfway across.

Joe and Glen smoked their pipes together in Glen's cabin and chewed the fat a good deal. They decided that everything ashore was the bunk and the only place for them was blue water. Joe got damn fedup with bawling out the bunch of scum he had for a crew. Once they got in the zone, all the ships started steering a zigzag course and everybody began to get white around the gills. Joe never cussed so much in his life. There was a false alarm of submarines every few hours and seaplanes dropping depthbombs and excited guncrews firing at old barrels, bunches of seaweed, dazzle in the water. Steaming into the Gironde at night with the searchlights crisscrossing and the blinker signals and the patrolboats scooting around, they sure felt good.

It was a relief to get the dirty trampling mules off the ship and their stench out of everything, and to get rid of the yelling and cussing of the hostlers. Glen and Joe got ashore only for a few hours and couldn't find Marceline and Loulou. The Garonne was beginning to look like the Delaware with all the new Americanbuilt steel and concrete piers. Going out they had to anchor several hours to repair a leaky steampipe and saw a patrolboat go by towing five ships' boats crowded to the gunnels, so they guessed the fritzes must be pretty busy outside.

No convoy this time. They slipped out in the middle of a foggy night. When one of the deckhands came up out of the fo'c'stle with a cigarette in the corner of his mouth, the mate knocked him flat and said he'd have him arrested when he got back home for a damn German spy. They coasted Spain as far as Finisterre. The skipper had just changed the course to southerly when they saw a sure enough periscope astern. The skipper grabbed the wheel himself and yelled down the tube to the engineroom to give him everything they'd got, that wasn't much, to be sure, and the guncrew started blazing away.

The periscope disappeared, but a couple of hours later they overhauled a tubby kind of ketch, must be a Spanish fishingboat, that was heading for the shore, for Vigo probably, scudding along wing and wing in the half a gale that was blowing up west northwest. They'd no sooner crossed the wake of the ketch than there was a thud that shook the ship and a column of water shot up that drenched them all on the bridge. Everything worked like clockwork. Number 1 was the only compartment flooded. As luck would have it, the crew was all out of the fo'c'stle standing on deck amidships in their life preservers. The *Chemang* settled a little by the bow, that was all. The gunners were certain it was a mine dropped by the old black ketch that had crossed their bow and let them have a couple of shots, but the ship was rolling so in the heavy sea that the shots went wild. Anyway, the ketch went out of sight behind the island that blocks the mouth of the roadstead of Vigo. The *Chemang* crawled on in under one bell.

By the time they got into the channel opposite the town of Vigo, the water was gaining on the pumps in Number 2, and there was four feet of water in the engineroom. They had to beach her on the banks of hard sand to the right of the town.

So they were ashore again with their bundles standing around outside the consul's office, waiting for him to find them somewhere to flop. The consul was a Spaniard and didn't speak as much English as he might have, but he treated them fine. The Liberal Party of Vigo invited officers and crew to go to a bullfight there was going to be that afternoon. More monkeydoodle business, the skipper got a cable to turn the ship over to the agents of Gomez and Ca. of Bilboa who had bought her as she stood and were changing her registry.

When they got to the bullring half the crowd cheered them and yelled, 'Viva los Aliados,' and the rest hissed and shouted, 'Viva Maura.' They thought there was going to be a fight right there, but the bull came out and everybody quieted down. The bullfight was darn bloody, but the boys with the spangles were some steppers and the people sitting around made them drink wine all the time out of little black skins and passed around bottles of cognac so that the crew got pretty cockeyed and Joe spent most of his time keeping the boys in order. Then the officers were tendered a banquet by the local pro-allied society and a lot of bozos with mostachios made fiery speeches that nobody could understand and the Americans cheered and sang, *The Yanks are Coming* and *Keep the Home Fires Burning* and *We're Bound for the Hamburg Show*. The chief, an old fellow named McGillicuddy, did some cardtricks, and the evening was a big success. Joe and Glen bunked together at the hotel. The maid there was awful pretty, but wouldn't let 'em get away with any foolishness.

'Well, Joe,' said Glen, before they went to sleep, 'it's a great war.'

'Well, I guess that's strike three,' said Joe.

'That was no strike, that was a ball,' said Glen.

They waited two weeks in Vigo while the officials quarreled about their status and they got pretty fedup with it. Then they were all loaded on a train to take them to Gibraltar where they were to be taken on board a Shipping Board boat. They were three days on the train with nothing to sleep on but hard benches. Spain was just one set of great dusty mountains after another. They changed cars in Madrid and in Seville and a guy turned up each time from the consulate to take care of them. When they got to Seville they found it was Algeciras they were going to instead of Gib.

When they got to Algeciras they found that nobody had ever heard of them. They camped out in the consulate while the consul telegraphed all over the place and finally chartered two trucks and sent them over to Cadiz. Spain was some country, all rocks and wine and busty blackeyed women and olivetrees. When they got to Cadiz the consular agent was there to meet them with a telegram in his hand. The tanker *Gold Shell* was waiting in Algeciras to take them on board there, so it was back again cooped up on the trucks, bouncing on the hard benches with their faces powdered with dust and their mouths full of it and not a cent in anybody's jeans left to buy a drink with. When they got on board the *Gold Shell* around three in the morning a bright moonlight night, some of the boys were so tired they fell down and went to sleep right on the deck with their heads on their seabags.

The *Gold Shell* landed 'em in Perth Amboy in late October. Joe drew his back pay and took the first train connections he could get for Norfolk. He was fedup with bawling out that bunch of pimps in the fo'c'stle. Damn it, he was through with the sea; he was going to settle down and have a little married life.

He felt swell coming over on the ferry from Cape Charles, passing the Ripraps, out of the bay full of whitecaps into the smooth brown water of Hampton Roads crowded with shipping; four great battlewagons at anchor, subchasers speeding in and out and a white revenue cutter, camouflaged freighters and colliers, a bunch of red munitions barges anchored off by themselves. It was a sparkling fall day. He felt good; he had three hundred and fifty dollars in his pocket. He had a good suit on and he felt sunburned and he'd just had a good meal. God damn it, he wanted a little love now. Maybe they'd have a kid.

Things sure were different in Norfolk. Everybody in new uniforms, twominute speakers at the corner of Main and Granby, Liberty Loan posters, bands playing. He hardly knew the town walking up from the ferry. He'd written Del that he was coming, but he was worried about seeing her, hadn't had any letters lately. He still had a latchkey to the apartment, but he knocked before opening the door. There was nobody there.

He'd always pictured her running to the door to meet him. Still it was only four o'clock, she must be at her work. Must have another girl with her, don't keep the house so tidy. . . . Underwear hung to dry on a line, bits of clothing on all the chairs, a box of candy with half-eaten pieces in it on the table. . . . Jeez, they must have had a party last night. There was a half a cake, glasses that had had liquor in them, a plate full of cigarette butts and even a cigar butt. Oh, well, she'd probably had some friends in. He went to the bathroom and shaved and cleaned up a little. Sure Del was always popular, she probably had a lot of friends in all the time, playing cards and that. In the bathroom there was a pot of rouge and lipsticks, and face-powder spilt over the faucets. It made Joe feel funny shaving among all these women's things.

He heard her voice laughing on the stairs and a man's voice; the key clicked in the lock. Joe closed his suitcase and stood up. Del had bobbed her hair. She flew up to him and threw her arms around his neck. 'Why, I declare it's my hubby.' Joe could taste rouge on her lips. 'My, you look thin, Joe. Poor Boy, you musta been awful sick. . . . If I'd had any money at all I'd have jumped on a boat and come on down. . . . This is Wilmer Tayloe . . . I mean Lieutenant Tayloe, he just got his commission yesterday.'

Joe hesitated a moment and then held out his hand. The other fellow had red hair clipped close and a freckled face. He was all dressed up in a whipcord uniform, shiny Sam Browne belt and puttees. He had a silver bar on each shoulder and spurs on his feet.

'He's just going overseas tomorrow. He was coming by to take me out to dinner. Oh, Joe, I've got so much to tell you, honey.'

Joe and Lieutenant Tayloe stood around eyeing each other uncomfortably while Del bustled around tidying the place up, talking to Joe all the time. 'It's terrible I never get any chance to do anything and neither does Hilda . . . You remember Hilda Thompson, Joe? Well, she's been livin' with me to help make up the rent, but we're both of us doin' war work down at the Red Cross canteen every evening and then I sell Liberty Bonds. . . . Don't you hate the Huns, Joe! Oh, I just hate them, and so does Hilda. . . . She's thinking of changing her name on account of its being German. I promised to call her Gloria but I always forget. . . . You know, Wilmer, Joe's been torpedoed twice.'

'Well, I suppose the first six times is the hardest,' stammered Lieutenant Tayloe.

Joe grunted.

Del disappeared into the bathroom and closed the door. 'You boys make yourselves comfortable. I'll be dressed in a minute.'

Neither of them said anything. Lieutenant Tayloe's shoes creaked as he shifted his weight from one foot to the other. At last he pulled a flask out of his hip pocket. 'Have a drink,' he said. 'Ma outfit's goin' overseas any time after midnight.' 'I guess I'd better,' said Joe, without smiling. When Della came out of the bathroom all dressed up she certainly looked snappy. She was much prettier than last time Joe had seen her. He was all the time wondering if he ought to go up and hit that damn shavetail until at last he left, Del telling him to come by and get her at the Red Cross canteen.

When he'd left she came and sat on Joe's knee and asked him about everything and whether he'd got his second mate's ticket yet and whether he'd missed her and how she wished he could make a little more money because she hated to have another girl in with her this way but it was the only way she could pay the rent. She drank a little of the whiskey that the lieutenant had forgotten on the table and ruffled his hair and loved him up. Joe asked her if Hilda was coming in soon and she said no she had a date and she was going to meet her at the canteen. But Joe went and bolted the door anyway and for the first time they were really happy hugged in each other's arms on the bed.

Joe didn't know what to do with himself around Norfolk. Del was at the office all day and at the Red Cross canteen all the evening. He'd usually be in bed when she came home. Usually there'd be some damn army officer or other bringing her home, and he'd hear them talking and kidding outside the door and lie there in bed imagining that the guy was kissing her or loving her up. He'd be about ready to hit her when she'd come in and bawl her out and they'd quarrel and yell at each other and she'd always end by saying that he didn't understand her and she thought he was unpatriotic to be interfering with her war work and sometimes they'd make up and he'd feel crazy in love with her and she'd make herself little and cute in his arms and give him little tiny kisses that made him almost

cry they made him feel so happy. She was getting better looking every day and she sure was a snappy dresser.

Sunday mornings she'd be too tired to get up and he'd cook
breakfast for her and they'd sit up in bed together and eat
breakfast like he had with Marceline that time in Bordeaux.
Then she'd tell him she was crazy about him and what a smart
guy he was and how she wanted him to get a good shore job
and make a lot of money so that she wouldn't have to work
any more and how Captain Barnes whose folks were worth a
million had wanted her to get a divorce from Joe and marry
him and Mr Canfield in the Dupont office who made a cool
fifty thousand a year had wanted to give her a pearl necklace
but she hadn't taken it because she didn't think it was right.
Talk like that made Joe feel pretty rotten. Sometimes he'd
start to talk about what they'd do if they had some kids, but
Del 'ud always make a funny face and tell him not to talk like
that.

Joe went around looking for work and almost landed the
job of foreman in one of the repairshops over at the shipyard
in Newport News, but at the last minute another berry horned
in ahead of him and got it. A couple times he went out on
parties with Del and Hilda Thompson, and some army officers
and a midshipman off a destroyer, but they all high-hatted him,
and Del let any boy who wanted to kiss her and would disappear into a phone booth with anything she could pick up so
long as it had a uniform on and he had a hell of a time. He
found a poolroom where some boys he knew hung out and
where he could get corn liquor and started tanking up a good
deal. It made Del awful sore to come home and find him drunk
but he didn't care any more.

Then one night when Joe had been to a fight with some
guys and had gotten an edge on afterward, he met Del and
another damn shavetail walking on the street. It was pretty
dark and there weren't many people around and they stopped
in every dark doorway and the shavetail was kissing and hugging her. When he got them under a streetlight so's he made
sure it was Del, he went up to them and asked them what the
hell they meant. Del must have had some drinks because she
started tittering in a shrill little voice that drove him crazy and
he hauled off and let the shavetail have a perfect left right on
the button. The spurs tinkled and the shavetail went to sleep
right flat on the little grass patch under the streetlight. It began
to hit Joe kinder funny, but Del was sore as the devil and said

she'd have him arrested for insult to the uniform and assault and battery and that he was nothing but a yellow snivelling slacker and what was he doing hanging around home when all the boys were at the front fighting the Huns. Joe sobered up and pulled the guy up to his feet and told them both they could go straight to hell. He walked off before the shavetail, who musta been pretty tight, had time to do anything but splutter, and went straight home and packed his suitcase and pulled out.

Will Stirp was in town, so Joe went over to his house and got him up out of bed and said he'd busted up housekeeping and would Will lend him twentyfive bucks to go up to New York with. Will said it was a damn good thing and that love 'em and leave 'em was the only thing for guys like them. They talked till about day about one thing and another. Then Joe went to sleep and slept till late afternoon. He got up in time to catch the Washington boat. He didn't take a room but roamed around on deck all night. He got to cracking with one ot the officers and went and sat in the pilothouse that smelt comfortably of old last year's pipes. Listening to the sludge of water from the bow and watching the wabbly white finger of the searchlight pick up buoys and lighthouses, he began to pull himself together. He said he was going up to New York to see his sister and try for a second mate's ticket with the Shipping Board. His stories about being torpedoed went big because none of them on the *Dominion City* had even been across the pond.

It felt like old times standing in the bow in the sharp November morning, sniffing the old brackish smell of the Potomac water, passing redbrick Alexandria and Anacostia and the Arsenal and the Navy Yard, seeing the Monument stick up pink through the mist in the early light. The wharves looked about the same, the yachts and powerboats anchored opposite, the Baltimore boat just coming in, the ramshackle excursion steamers, the oystershells underfoot on the wharf, the nigger roustabouts standing around. Then he was hopping the Georgetown car and too soon he was walking up the redbrick street. While he rang the bell, he was wondering why he'd come home.

Mommer looked older, but she was in pretty good shape and all taken up with her boarders and how the girls were both engaged. They said that Janey was doing so well in her work, but that living in New York had changed her. Joe said he was going down to New York to try to get his second mate's ticket and that he sure would look her up. When they asked him

about the war and the submarines and all that, he didn't know
what to tell 'em so he kinder kidded them along. He was glad
when it was time to go over to Washington to get his train,
though they were darn nice to him and seemed to think that
he was making a big success getting to be a second mate so
young. He didn't tell 'em about being married.

Going down on the train to New York, Joe sat in the smoker
looking out of the window at farms and stations and billboards
and the grimy streets of factory towns through Jersey under
a driving rain, and everything he saw seemed to remind him of
Del and places outside of Norfolk and good times he'd had
when he was a kid. When he got to the Penn Station in New
York, first thing he did was check his bag, then he walked down
Eighth Avenue all shiny with rain to the corner of the street
where Janey lived. He guessed he'd better phone her first and
called from a cigarstore. Her voice sounded kinder stiff; she
said she was busy and couldn't see him till tomorrow. He came
out of the phone booth and walked down the street not knowing
where to go. He had a package under his arm with a couple
of Spanish shawls he'd bought for her and Del on the last trip.
He felt so blue he wanted to drop the shawls and everything
down a drain, but he thought better of it and went back to the
checkroom at the station and left them in his suitcase. Then
he went and smoked a pipe for a while in the waitingroom.

God damn it to hell he needed a drink. He went over to
Broadway and walked down to Union Square, stopping in
every place he could find that looked like a saloon, but they
wouldn't serve him anywhere. Union Square was all lit up and
full of navy recruiting posters. A big wooden model of a battleship filled up one side of it. There was a crowd standing
around and a young girl dressed like a sailor was making a
speech about patriotism. The cold rain came on again and the
crowd scattered. Joe went down a street and into a ginmill
called The Old Farm. He must have looked like somebody the
barkeep knew because he said hello and poured him out a
shot of rye.

Joe got to talking with two guys from Chicago who were
drinking whiskey with beer chasers. They said this wartalk was
a lot of bushwa propaganda and that if working stiffs stopped
working in munitions factories making shells to knock other
working stiffs' blocks off with, there wouldn't be no goddam
war. Joe said they were goddam right but look at the big money

you made. The guys from Chicago said they'd been working in a munitions factory themselves but they were through, goddam it, and that if the working stiffs made a few easy dollars it meant that the war profiteers were making easy millions. They said the Russians had the right idea, make a revolution and shoot the goddam profiteers and that 'ud happen in this country if they didn't watch out and a damn good thing too. The barkeep leaned across the bar and said they'd oughtn't to talk thataway, folks 'ud take 'em for German spies.

'Why, you're a German yourself, George,' said one of the guys.

The barkeep flushed and said, 'Names don't mean nothin' . . . I'm a patriotic American. I vas talking yust for your good. If you vant to land in de hoosgow it's not my funeral.' But he set them up to drinks on the house and it seemed to Joe that he agreed with 'em.

They drank another round and Joe said it was all true but what the hell could you do about it? The guys said what you could do about it was join the I.W.W. and carry a red card and be a classconscious worker. Joe said that stuff was only for foreigners, but if somebody started a white man's party to fight the profiteers and the goddam bankers he'd be with 'em. The guys from Chicago began to get sore and said the wobblies were just as much white men as he was and that political parties were the bunk and that all Southerners were scabs. Joe backed off and was looking at the guys to see which one of 'em he'd hit first when the barkeep stepped around from the end of the bar and came between them. He was fat, but he had shoulders and a meanlooking pair of blue eyes.

'Look here, you bums,' he said, 'you listen to me, sure I'm a Cherman but am I for de Kaiser? No, he's a schweinhunt, I am sokialist unt I live toity years in Union City unt own my home unt pay taxes unt I'm a good American, but dot don't mean dot I vill foight for Banker Morgan, not vonce. I know American vorkman in de sokialist party toity years unt all dey do is foight among each oder. Every sonofabitch denk him better den de next sonofabitch. You loafers getoutahere . . . closin' time . . . I'm goin' to close up an' go home.'

One of the guys from Chicago started to laugh, 'Well, I guess the drinks are on us, Oscar . . . it'll be different after the revolution.'

Joe still wanted to fight, but he paid for a round with his last greenback and the barkeep, who was still red in the face from his speech, lifted a glass of beer to his mouth. He blew the foam off it and said, 'If I talk like dot I lose my yob.'

They shook hands all around and Joe went out into the gusty northeast rain. He felt lit but he didn't feel good. He went up to Union Square again. The recruiting speeches were over. The model battleship was dark. A couple of ragged-looking youngsters were huddled in the lee of the recruiting tent. Joe felt lousy. He went down into the subway and waited for the Brooklyn train.

At Mrs Olsen's everything was dark. Joe rang and in a little while she came down in a padded pink dressinggown and opened the door. She was sore at being waked up and bawled him out for drinking, but she gave him a flop and next morning lent him fifteen bucks to tide him over till he got work on a Shipping Board boat. Mrs Olsen looked tired and a lot older, she said she had pains in her back and couldn't get through her work any more.

Next morning Joe put up some shelves in the pantry for her and carried out a lot of litter before he went over to the Shipping Board recruiting office to put his name down for the officers' school. The little kike behind the desk had never been to sea and asked him a lot of damfool questions and told him to come around next week to find out what action would be taken on his application. Joe got sore and told him to f—k himself and walked out.

He took Janey out to supper and to a show, but she talked just like everybody else did and bawled him out for cussing and he didn't have a very good time. She liked the shawls, though, and he was glad she was making out so well in New York. He never did get around to talking to her about Della.

After taking her home he didn't know what the hell to do with himself. He wanted a drink, but taking Janey out and everything had cleaned up the fifteen bucks he'd borrowed from Mrs Olsen. He walked west to a saloon he knew on Tenth Avenue, but the place was closed: wartime prohibition. Then he walked back towards Union Square, maybe that feller Tex he'd seen when he was walking across the square with Janey would still be sitting there and he could chew the rag awhile with him. He sat down on a bench opposite the cardboard battleship and began sizing it up: not such a bad job. Hell, I wisht I'd never seen the inside of a real battleship, he was thinking, when Tex slipped into the seat beside him and put his hand on his knee. The minute he touched him Joe knew he'd never liked the guy, eyes too close together: 'What you lookin' so blue about, Joe? Tell me, you're gettin' your ticket.'

Joe nodded and leaned over and spat carefully between his feet.

'What do you think of that for a model battleship, pretty nifty, ain't it? Jeez, us guys is lucky not to be overseas fightin' the fritzes in the trenches.'

'Oh, I'd just as soon,' growled Joe. 'I wouldn't give a damn.'

'Say, Joe, I got a job lined up. Guess I oughtn't to blab around about it, but you're regular. I know you won't say nothin'. I been on the bum for two weeks, somethin' wrong with my stomach. Man, I'm sick, I'm tellin' you. I can't do no heavy work no more. A punk I know works in a whitefront been slippin' me my grub, see. Well, I was sittin' on a bench right here on the square, a feller kinda welldressed sits down an' starts to chum up. Looked to me like one of these here sissies lookin' for rough trade, see, thought I'd roll him for some jack, what the hell, what can you do if you're sick an' can't work?'

Joe sat leaning back with his legs stuck out, his hands in his pockets staring hard at the outline of the battleship against the buildings. Tex was talking fast, poking his face into Joe's: 'Turns out the sonofabitch was a dick. S—t I was scared pissless. A secret service agent. Burns is his big boss . . . but what he's lookin' for's reds, slackers, German spies, guys that can't keep their trap shut . . . an' he turns around and hands me out a job, twentyfive smackers a week if little Willy makes good. All I got to do's bum around and listen to guys talk, see? If I hears anything that ain't a hundred per cent I slips the word to the boss and he investigates. Twentyfive a week servin' my country besides, and if I gets in any kind of jam, Burns gets me out. . . . What do you think of that for the gravy, Joe?'

Joe got to his feet. 'Guess I'll go back to Brooklyn.'

'Stick around . . . look here, you've always treated me white . . . you belong, I know that, Joe . . . I'll put you next to this guy if you want. He's a good scout, educated feller an' all that and he knows where you can get plenty liquor an' women if you want 'em.'

'Hell, I'm going to sea and get out of all this s—t,' said Joe, turning his back and walking towards the subway station.

## The Camera Eye (34)

his voice was three thousand miles away all the time
he kept wanting to get up outa bed     his cheeks were bright
pink and the choky breathing     No kid you better lay there
quiet we dont want you catching more cold that's why they
sent me down to stay with you to keep you from getting up
outa bed

the barrelvaulted room all smells fever and whitewash
carbolic sick wops outside the airraid siren's got a nightmare

(Mestre's a railhead and its moonlight over the Brenta
and the basehospital and the ammunition dump

carbolic blue moonlight)

all the time he kept trying to get up outa bed     Kiddo
you better lay there quiet     his voice was in Minnesota but
dontjaunerstandafellersgottogetup     I got a date animpor-
tantengagementtoseeabout those lots ought nevertohave-
stayedinbedsolate     I'll lose my deposit     For chrissake
dont you think I'm broke enough as it is?

Kiddo you gotto lay there quiet     we're in the hospital
in Mestre you got a little fever makes things seem funny

Cant you letafellerbe?     You're in cahoots withem
thaswhassematteris I know theyreouttorookme     they think
Imagoddamsucker tomadethatdeposit I'll showem Illknock-
yergoddamblockoff

my shadow on the vault bulkyclumsily staggering and
swaying from the one candle spluttering red in the raw
winterhospital carbolic night above the shadow on the cot
gotto keep his shoulders down to the cot Curley's husky
inspite of

(you can hear their motors now the antiaircraft batteries
are letting loose must be great up there in the moonlight out
of the smell of carbolic and latrines and sick wops)

sit back and light a macedonia by the candle he seems
to be asleep his breathing's so tough pneumonia breathing
can hear myself breathe     and the water tick in the

faucet    doctors and orderlies all down in the bombproof cant even hear a sick wop groan

Jesus is the guy dying?

they've cut off their motors    the little drums in my ears sure that's why they call em drums    (up there in the blue moonlight the Austrian observer's reaching for the string that dumps the applecart)    the candleflame stands up still

not that time but wham in the side of the head woke Curley and the glass tinkling in the upstairs windows the candle staggered but didnt go out the vault sways with my shadow and Curley's shadow dammit he's strong head's full of the fever reek    Kiddo you gotto stay in bed (they dumped the applecart allright) shellfragments hailing around outside Kiddo you gotto get back to bed

But I gotadate on christohsweetjesus cant you tell me how to get back to the outfit    haveaheart dad I didntmeanno harm itsonlyaboutthose lots

the voice dwindles into a whine.    I'm pulling the covers up to his chin again light the candle again smoke a macedonia again look at my watch again must be near day ten o'clock    they dont relieve me till eight

way off a voice goes up and up and swoops like the airraid siren ayayooOTO

# Newsreel 25

General Pershing's forces today occupied Belle Joyeuse Farm and the southern edges of the Bois des Loges. The Americans encountered but little machinegun opposition. The advance was in the nature of a linestraightening operation. Otherwise the activity along the front today consisted principally of artillery firing and bombing. Patrols are operating around Belluno having preceded the flood of allies pouring through the Quero pass in the Grappa region

### REBEL SAILORS DEFY ALLIES

> *Bonjour ma chérie*
> *Comment allez vous?*
> *Bonjour ma chérie*
> *how do you do?*

after a long conference with the Secretary of War and the Secretary of State President Wilson returned to the White House this afternoon apparently highly pleased that events are steadily pursuing the course which he had felt they would take

> *Avez vous fiancé?    cela ne fait rien*
> *Voulez vouz couchez avec moi ce soir?*
> *Wee, wee, combien?*

### HELP THE FOOD ADMINISTRATION BY
### REPORTING WAR PROFITEERS

Lord Roberts, who is Foreign Minister Balfour's right-hand man added, 'When victory comes the responsibility for America and Great Britain will rest not on statesmen but on the people.' The display of the red flag in our thoroughfares seems to be emblematic of unbridled license and an insignia for lawhating and anarchy, like the black flag it represents everything that is repulsive

## LENINE FLEES TO FINLAND

here I am snug as a bug in a rug on this third day of October. It was Sunday I went over and got hit in the left leg with a machinegun bullet above the knee. I am in a base hospital and very comfortable. I am writing with my left hand as my right one is under my head.

### STOCK MARKET STRONG BUT NARROW

*Some day I'm going to murder the bugler*
*Some day they're going to find him dead*
*I'll dislocate his reveille*
*And step upon it heavily*
*And spend*
*     the rest of my life in bed*


# A Hoosier Quixote

*Hibben, Paxton, journalist, Indianapolis, Ind., Dec. 5, 1880, s. Thomas Entrekin and Jeannie Merrill (Ketcham) H.; A.B. Princeton 1903, A.M. Harvard 1904*

Thinking men were worried in the Middle West in the years Hibben was growing up there, something was wrong with the American Republic, was it the Gold Standard, Privilege, The Interests, Wall Street?

The rich were getting richer, the poor were getting poorer, small farmers were being squeezed out, workingmen were working twelve hours a day for a bare living; profits were for the rich, the law was for the rich, the cops were for the rich;

was it for that the Pilgrims had bent their heads into the storm, filled the fleeing Indians with slugs out of their blunderbusses

and worked the stony farms of New England;

was it for that the pioneers had crossed the Appalachians, long squirrelguns slung across lean backs,

a fistful of corn in the pocket of the buckskin vest,

was it for that the Indiana farmboys had turned out to shoot down Johnny Red and make the black man free?

Paxton Hibben was a small cantankerous boy, son of one of the best families (the Hibbens had a wholesale drygoods

business in Indianapolis); in school the rich kids didn't like him
because he went around with the poor kids and the poor kids
didn't like him because his folks were rich,

but he was the star pupil of Short Ridge High
ran the paper,
won all the debates.


At Princeton he was the young collegian, editor of the
*Tiger*, drank a lot, didn't deny that he ran around after girls,
made a brilliant scholastic record, and was a thorn in the flesh
of the godly. The natural course for a bright young man of
his class and position was to study law, but Hibben wanted

travel and romance à la Byron and de Musset, wellgroomed
adventures in foreign lands,
so
as his family was one of the best in Indiana and friendly
with Senator Beveridge he was gotten a post in the diplomatic
service:

> *3rd sec and 2nd sec American Embassy St Petersburg
> and Mexico City 1905–6, sec Legation and Chargé
> d'affaires, Bogotá, Colombia, 1908–9; The Hague and
> Luxembourg 1909–12, Santiago de Chile 1912 (retired).*


Pushkin for de Musset; St Petersburg was a young dude's
romance:
goldencrusted spires under a platinum sky,
the icegray Neva flowing swift and deep under bridges
that jingled with sleighbells;
riding home from the Islands with the Grand Duke's
mistress, the most beautiful most amorous singer of Neapolitan
streetsongs;
staking a pile of rubles in a tall room glittering with
chandeliers, monocles, diamonds dripped on white shoulders;
white snow, white tablecloths, white sheets,
Kakhetian wine, vodka fresh as newmown hay, Astrakhan
caviar, sturgeon, Finnish salmon, Lapland ptarmigan, and the
most beautiful women in the world;


but it was 1905, Hibben left the Embassy one night and
saw a flare of red against the trampled snow of the Nevsky
and red flags,

blood frozen in the ruts, blood trickling down the car-tracks;

he saw the machineguns on the balconies of the Winter Palace, the Cossacks charging the unarmed crowds that wanted peace and food and a little freedom,

heard the throaty roar of the Russian *Marseillaise;*

some stubborn streak in the old American blood flared in revolt, he walked the streets all night with the revolutionists, got in wrong at the Embassy

and was transferred to Mexico City where there was no revolution yet, only peons and priests and the stillness of the great volcanos.

The Cientificos made him a member of the Jockey Club

where in the magnificent building of blue Puebla tile he lost all his money at roulette and helped them drink up the last few cases of champagne left over from the plunder of Cortez.

Chargé d'affaires in Colombia (he never forgot he owed his career to Beveridge; he believed passionately in Roosevelt, and righteousness and reform, and the antitrust laws, the Big Stick that was going to scare away the grafters and malefactors of great wealth and get the common man his due) he helped wangle the revolution that stole the Canal Zone from the Bishop of Bogotá; later he stuck up for Roosevelt in the Pulitzer libel suit; he was a Progressive, believed in the Canal and T. R.

He was shunted to The Hague where he went to sleep during the vague deliberations of the International Tribunal.

In 1912 he resigned from the Diplomatic Service and went home to campaign for Roosevelt,

got to Chicago in time to hear them singing *Onward, Christian Soldiers* at the convention in the Colosseum; in the closepacked voices and the cheers, he heard the trample of the Russian *Marseillaise,* the sullen silence of Mexican peons, Colombian Indians waiting for a deliverer, in the reverberance of the hymn he heard the measured cadences of the Declaration of Independence.

The talk of social justice petered out; T. R. was a windbag like the rest of 'em, the Bull Moose was stuffed with the same sawdust as the G.O.P.

Paxton Hibben ran for Congress as a Progressive in

Indiana, but the European war had already taken people's minds off social justice.

> *War Corr Collier's Weekly 1914–15; staff corr Associated Press in Europe, 1915–17; war corr Leslie's Weekly in Near East and sec Russian commn for Near East Relief, June– Dec 1921*

In those years he forgot all about diplomat's mauve silk bathrobe and the ivory toilet sets and the little tête-à-têtes with grandduchesses,

he went to Germany as Beveridge's secretary, saw the German troops goosestepping through Brussels,

saw Poincaré visiting the long doomed galleries of Verdun between ranks of bitter half-mutinous soldiers in blue,

saw the gangrened wounds, the cholera, the typhus, the little children with their bellies swollen with famine, the maggoty corpses of the Serbian retreat, drunk Allied officers chasing sick naked girls upstairs in the brothels in Saloniki, soldiers looting stores and churches, French and British sailors fighting with beerbottles in the bars;

walked up and down the terrace with King Constantine during the bombardment of Athens, fought a duel with a French commission agent who got up and left when a German sat down to eat in the diningroom at the Grande Bretagne; Hibben thought the duel was a joke until all his friends began putting on silk hats; he stood up and let the Frenchman take two shots at him and then fired into the ground; in Athens as everywhere he was always in hot water, a slightly built truculent man, always standing up for his friends, for people out of luck, for some idea, too reckless ever to lay down the careful stepping-stones of a respectable career.

> *Commd 1st lieut F.A. Nov 27–1917; capt May 31–1919; served at war coll camp Grant; in France with 332nd E.A.; Finance Bureau S.O.S.; at G.H.Q. in office of Insp Gen of A.E.F.; discharged Aug 21–1919; capt O.R.C. Feb 7th– 1920; recommd Feb 7–1925*

The war in Europe was bloody and dirty and dull, but the war in New York revealed such slimy depths of vileness and hypocrisy that no man who saw it can ever feel the same again; in the army training camps it was different, the boys believed

in a world safe for Democracy; Hibben believed in the Fourteen Points, he believed in The War to End War.

*With mil Mission to Armenia Aug–Dec 1919; staff corr
in Europe for the Chicago Tribune; with the Near East
Relief 1920–22; sec Russian Red Cross commn in America
1922; v dir for U.S. Nansen Relief Mission 1923; sec AM
Commn Relief Russian Children Apr 1922*

In the famine year the cholera year the typhus year Paxton
Hibben went to Moscow with a relief commission.

In Paris they were still haggling over the price of blood,
squabbling over toy flags, the riverfrontiers on reliefmaps, the
historical destiny of peoples, while behind the scenes the good
contractplayers, the Deterdings, the Zahkaroffs, the Stinnesses
sat quiet and possessed themselves of the raw materials.

In Moscow there was order,

in Moscow there was work,

in Moscow there was hope;

the *Marseilles* of 1905, *Onward, Christian Soldiers* of 1912,
the sullen passiveness of American Indians, of infantrymen
waiting for death at the front was part of the tremendous roar
of the Marxian *Internationale.*

Hibben believed in the new world.

Back in America

somebody got hold of a photograph of Captain Paxton
Hibben laying a wreath on Jack Reed's grave; they tried to
throw him out of the O.R.C.;

at Princeton at the twentieth reunion of his college class
his classmates started to lynch him; they were drunk and
perhaps it was just a collegeboy prank twenty years too late
but they had a noose around his neck,

lynch the goddam red,

no more place in America for change, no more place for
the old gags; social justice, progressivism, revolt against oppression, democracy; put the reds on the skids,

no money for them,

no jobs for them.

*Mem Authors League of America, Soc of Colonial Wars,
Vets Foreign Wars, Am Legion, fellow Royal and Am
Geog Socs. Decorated chevalier Order of St Stanislas
(Russian), Officer Order of the Redeemer (Greek), Order*

*of the Sacred Treasure (Japan). Clubs Princeton, Newspaper, Civic (New York)*

*Author: Constantine and the Greek People 1920, The Famine in Russia 1922, Henry Ward Beecher an American Portrait 1927.*

d. 1929.

# Newsreel 26

EUROPE ON KNIFE EDGE

*Tout le long de la Thamise*
*Nous sommes allés tout les deux*
*Gouter l'heure exquise.*

in such conditions is it surprising that the Department
of Justice looks with positive affection upon those who
refused service in the draft, with leniency upon convicted
anarchists and with something like indifference upon the
overwhelming majority of them still out of jail or unde-
ported for years after the organization of the U.S. Steel
Corporation Wall Street was busy on the problem of measuring the cubic yards of water injected into the property

FINISHED STEEL MOVES RATHER MORE FREELY

*Where do we go from here, boys,*
*Where do we go from here?*

WILD DUCKS FLY OVER PARIS

FERTILIZER INDUSTRY STIMULATED BY WAR

*Anywhere from Harlem*
*To a Jersey City pier*

the winning of the war is just as much dependent upon
the industrial workers as it is upon the soldiers. Our wonderful record of launching one hundred ships on Independence
Day shows what can be done when we put our shoulders to
the wheel under the spur of patriotism

SAMARITAINE BATHS SINK IN SWOLLEN SEINE

*I may not know*
*What the war's about*
*But you bet by gosh*
*I'll soon find out*

*And so my sweetheart*
*Don't you fear*
*I'll bring you a king*
*For a souvenir*
*And I'll get you a Turk*
*And the Kaiser too*
*And that's about all*
*One feller can do*

AFTER-WAR PLANS OF AETNA EXPLOSIVES

ANCIENT CITY IN GLOOM EVEN THE CHURCH
BELLS ON SUNDAY BEING STILLED

*Where do we go from here, boys,*
*Where do we go from here?*

## Richard Ellsworth Savage

It was at Fontainebleau lined up in the square in front of Francis I's palace they first saw the big gray Fiat ambulances they were to drive. Schuyler came back from talking with the French drivers who were turning them over with the news that they were sore as hell because it meant they had to go back into the front line. They asked why the devil the Americans couldn't stay home and mind their own business instead of coming over here and filling up all the good embusqué jobs. That night the section went into cantonment in tarpaper barracks that stank of carbolic, in a little town in Champagne. It turned out to be the Fourth of July, so the maréchale-de-logis served out champagne with supper and a general with white walrus whiskers came and made a speech about how with the help of Amérique héroique la victoire was certain, and proposed a toast to le président Veelson. The chef of the section, Bill Knickerbocker, got up a little nervously and toasted la France héroique, l'héroique Cinquième Armée, and la victoire by Christmas. Fireworks were furnished by the Boches who sent over an airraid that made everybody scuttle for the bombproof dugout.

Once they got down there Fred Summers said it smelt too bad and anyway he wanted a drink and he and Dick went out to find an estaminet, keeping close under the eaves of the houses to escape the occasional shrapnel fragments from the anticraft guns. They found a little bar all full of tobaccosmoke and French poilus singing *la Madelon*. Everybody cheered when they came in and a dozen glasses were handed to them. They smoked their first caporal ordinaire and everybody set them up to drinks so that at closing time, when the bugles blew the French equivalent of taps, they found themselves walking a little unsteadily along the pitchblack streets arm in arm with two poilus who'd promised to find them their cantonment. The poilus said la guerre was une saloperie and la victoire was une sale blague and asked eagerly if les américains knew anything about la révolution en Russie. Dick said he was a pacifist and was for anything that would stop the war and they all shook hands very significantly and talked about la révolution mondiale. When they were turning in on their folding cots, Fred Summers suddenly sat bolt upright with his blanket around him and said in a solemn funny way he had, 'Fellers, this ain't a war. It's a goddam madhouse.'

There were two other fellows in the section who liked to drink wine and chatter bad French; Steve Warner, who'd been a special student at Harvard, and Ripley, who was a freshman at Columbia. The five of them went around together, finding places to get omelettes and pommes frites in the villages within walking distance, making the rounds of the estaminets every night; they got to be known as the grenadine guards. When the section moved up onto the Voie Sacrée back of Verdun and was quartered for three rainy weeks in a little ruined village called Erize la Petite, they set up their cots together in the same corner of the old brokendown barn they were given for a cantonment. It rained all day and all night; all day and all night camions ground past through the deep liquid putty of the roads carrying men and munitions to Verdun. Dick used to sit on his cot looking out through the door at the jiggling mudspattered faces of the young French soldiers going up for the attack, drunk and desperate and yelling à bas la guerre, mort aux vaches, à bas la guerre. Once Steve came in suddenly, his face pale above the dripping poncho, his eyes snapping, and said in a low voice, 'Now I know what the tumbrils were like in the Terror, that's what they are, tumbrils.'

Dick was relieved to find out, when they finally moved up within range of the guns, that he wasn't any more scared than anybody else. The first time they went on post he and Fred lost their way in the shellshredded woods and were trying to turn the car around on a little rise naked as the face of the

moon when three shells from an Austrian eightyeight went
past them like three cracks of a whip. They never knew how
they got out of the car and into the ditch, but when the sparse
blue almondsmelling smoke cleared they were both lying flat in
the mud. Fred went to pieces and Dick had to put his arm
around him and keep whispering in his ear, 'Come on, boy, we
got to make it. Come on, Fred, we'll fool 'em.' It all hit him
funny and he kept laughing all the way back along the road
into the quieter section of the woods where the dressing station
had been cleverly located right in front of a battery of 405s,
so that the concussion almost bounced the wounded out of their
stretchers every time a gun was fired. When they got back to the
section after taking a load to the triage, they were able to
show three jagged holes from shellfragments in the side of
the car.

Next day the attack began and continual barrages and
counterbarrages and heavy gasbombardments; the section was
on twentyfour-hour duty for three days, at the end of it everybody had dysentery and bad nerves. One fellow got shellshock,
although he'd been too scared to go on post, and had to be
sent back to Paris. A couple of men had to be evacuated for
dysentery. The grenadine guards came through the attack
pretty well, except that Steve and Ripley had gotten a little
extra sniff of mustard gas up at P2 one night and vomited
whenever they ate anything.

In their twentyfour-hour periods off duty they'd meet in a
little garden at Récicourt that was the section's base. No one
else seemed to know about it. The garden had been attached
to a pink villa, but the villa had been mashed to dust as if a
great foot had stepped on it. The garden was untouched, only
a little weedy from neglect, roses were in bloom there and
butterflies and bees droned around the flowers on sunny afternoons. At first they took the bees for distant arrivés and went
flat on their bellies when they heard them. There had been a
cement fountain in the middle of the garden and there they
used to sit when the Germans got it into their heads to shell
the road and the nearby bridge. There was regular shelling
three times a day and a little scattering between times. Somebody would be detailed to stand in line at the Copé and buy
South-of-France melons and four-franc-fifty champagne. Then
they'd take off their shirts to toast their backs and shoulders
if it was sunny and sit in the dry fountain eating the melons
and drinking the warm cidery champagne and talk about how

they'd go back to the States and start an underground news-paper like *La Libre Belgique* to tell people what the war was really like.

What Dick liked best in the garden was the little backhouse, like the backhouse in a New England farm, with a clean scrubbed seat and a halfmoon in the door, through which on sunny days the wasps who had a nest in the ceiling hummed busily in and out. He'd sit there with his belly aching listening to the low voices of his friends talking in the driedup fountain. Their voices made him feel happy and at home while he stood wiping himself on a few old yellowed squares of a 1914 *Petit Journal* that still hung on the nail. Once he came back buckling his belt and saying, 'Do you know? I was thinking how fine it would be if you could reorganize the cells of your body into some other kind of life ... it's too damn lousy being a human ... I'd like to be a cat, a nice comfortable housecat sitting by the fire.'

'It's a hell of a note,' said Steve, reaching for his shirt and putting it on. A cloud had gone over the sun and it was suddenly chilly. The guns sounded quiet and distant. Dick felt suddenly chilly and lonely. 'It's a hell of a note when you have to be ashamed of belonging to your own race. But I swear I am, I swear I'm ashamed of being a man ... it will take some huge wave of hope like a revolution to make me feel any self-respect ever again. ... God, we're a lousy cruel vicious dumb type of tailless ape.'

'Well, if you want to earn your selfrespect, Steve, and the respect of us other apes, why don't you go down, now that they're not shelling, and buy us a bottle of champagny water?' said Ripley.

After the attack on Hill 304 the division went en repos back of Bar-le-Duc for a couple of weeks and then up into a quiet section of the Argonne called le Four de Paris where the French played chess with the Boches in the front line and where one side always warned the other before setting off a mine under a piece of trench. When they were off duty they could go into the inhabited and undestroyed town of Sainte Ménéhoulde and eat fresh pastry and pumpkin soup and roast chicken. When the section was disbanded and everybody sent back to Paris, Dick hated to leave the mellow autumn woods of the Argonne. The U.S. Army was to take over the ambulance service attached to the French. Everybody got a copy of the section's citation; Dick Norton made them a speech under shellfire, never dropping the monocle out of his eye, dismissing them as gentlemen volunteers and that was the end of the section.

Except for an occasional shell from the Bertha, Paris was quiet and pleasant that November. It was too foggy for airraids. Dick and Steve Warner got a very cheap room back of the Panthéon; in the daytime they read French and in the evenings roamed round cafés and drinking places. Fred Summers got himself a job with the Red Cross at twentyfive dollars a week and a steady girl the second day they hit Paris. Ripley and Ed Schuyler took lodgings in considerable style over Henry's bar. They all ate dinner together every night and argued themselves sick about what they ought to do. Steve said he was going home and C.O. and to hell with it; Ripley and Schuyler said they didn't care what they did as long as they kept out of the American army, and talked about joining the Foreign Legion or the Lafayette Escadrille.

Fred Summers said, 'Fellers, this war's the most gigantic cockeyed graft of the century and me for it and the cross red nurses.' At the end of the first week he was holding down two Red Cross jobs, each at twentyfive a week, and being kept by a middleaged French marraine who owned a big house in Neuilly. When Dick's money gave out, Fred borrowed some for him from his marraine, but he never would let any of the others see her. 'Don't want you fellers to know what I'm in for,' he'd say.

At lunchtime one day Fred Summers came round to say that everything was fixed up and that he had jobs for them all. The wops, he explained, were pretty well shot after Caporetto and couldn't get out of the habit of retreating. It was thought that sending an American Red Cross ambulance section down would help their morale. He was in charge of recruiting for the time being and had put all their names down. Dick immediately said he spoke Italian and felt he'd be a great help to the morale of the Italians, so the next morning they were all at the Red Cross office when it opened and were duly enrolled in Section 1 of the American Red Cross for Italy. There followed a couple more weeks waiting around during which Fred Summers took on a mysterious Serbian lady he picked up in a café back of the Place St Michel who wanted to teach them to take hashish, and Dick became friends with a drunken Montenegrin who'd been a barkeep in New York and who promised to get them all decorated by King Nicholas of Montenegro. But the day they were going to be received at Neuilly to have the decorations pinned on, the section left.

The convoy of twelve Fiats and eight Fords ran along the smooth macadam roads south through the Forest of Fontainebleau and wound east through the winecolored hills of central France. Dick was driving a Ford alone and was so busy trying to remember what to do with his feet he could hardly notice the scenery. Next day they went over the mountains and down into the valley of the Rhone, into a rich wine country with planetrees and cypresses, smelling of the vintage and late fall roses and the south. By Montélimar, the war, the worry about jail and protest and sedition all seemed a nightmare out of another century.

They had a magnificent supper in the quiet pink and white town with cèpes and garlic and strong red wine. 'Fellers,' Fred Summers kept saying, 'this ain't a war, it's a goddam Cook's tour.' They slept in style in the big brocadehung beds at the hotel, and when they left in the morning a little schoolboy ran after Dick's car shouting, Vive l'Amérique, and handed him a box of nougat, the local specialty; it was the land of Cockaigne.

That day the convoy fell to pieces running into Marseilles; discipline melted away; drivers stopped at all the wineshops along the sunny roads to drink and play craps. The Red Cross publicity man and the *Saturday Evening Post* correspondent, who was the famous writer, Montgomery Ellis, got hideously boiled and could be heard whooping and yelling in the back of the staffcar, while the little fat lieutenant ran up and down the line of cars at every stop red and hysterically puffing. Eventually they were all rounded up and entered Marseilles in formation. They'd just finished parking in a row in the main square and the boys were settling back into the bars and cafés roundabout, when a man named Ford got the bright idea of looking into his gasoline tank with a match and blew his car up. The local fire department came out in style and when car Number 8 was properly incinerated turned their high-pressure hose on the others, and Schuyler, who spoke the best French in the section, had to be dragged away from a conversation with the cigarette girl at the corner café to beg the fire chief for chrissake to lay off.

With the addition of a fellow named Sheldrake, who was an expert on folkdancing and had been in the famous section 7, the grenadine guards dined in state at the Bristol. They continued the evening at the promenoire at the Apollo, that was so full of all the petites femmes in the world, they never saw the show. Everything was cockeyed and full of women, the shrill bright main streets with their cafés and cabarets, and the black sweaty tunnels of streets back of the harbor full of rumpled beds and sailors and black skin and brown skin, wriggling bellies, flopping purple white breasts, grinding thighs.

Very late Steve and Dick found themselves alone in a little restaurant eating ham and eggs and coffee. They were drunk and sleepy and quarreling drowsily. When they paid, the middleaged waitress told them to put the tip on the corner of the table and blew them out of their chairs by calmly hoisting her skirts and picking up the coins between her legs.

'It's a hoax, a goddam hoax . . . Sex is a slotmachine,' Steve kept saying and it seemed gigantically funny, so funny that they went into an early morning bar and tried to tell the man behind the counter about it, but he didn't understand them and wrote out on a piece of paper the name of an establishment where they could faire rigajig, une maison, propre, convenable, et de haute moralité. Hooting with laughter they found themselves reeling and stumbling as they climbed endless stairways. The wind was cold as hell. They were in front of a crazylooking cathedral looking down on the harbor, steamboats, great expanses of platinum sea hemmed in by ashen mountains. 'By God, that's the Mediterranean.'

They sobered up in the cold jostling wind and the wide metallic flare of dawn and got back to their hotel in time to shake the others out of their drunken slumbers and be the first to report for duty at the parked cars. Dick was so sleepy he forgot what he ought to do with his feet and ran his Ford into the car ahead and smashed his headlights. The fat lieutenant bawled him out shrilly and took the car away from him and put him on a Fiat with Sheldrake, so he had nothing to do all day but look out of his drowse at the Corniche and the Mediterranean and the redroofed towns and the long lines of steamboats bound east hugging the shore for fear of U-boats, convoyed by an occasional French destroyer with its smokestacks in all the wrong places.

Crossing the Italian border they were greeted by crowds of schoolchildren with palmleaves and baskets of oranges, and a movie operator. Sheldrake kept stroking his beard and bowing and saluting at the cheers of evviva gli americani, until zowie. he got an orange between the eyes that pretty near gave him a nosebleed. Another man down the line came within an inch of having his eye put out by a palmbranch thrown by a delirious inhabitant of Vintimiglia. It was a great reception. That night in San Remo enthusiastic wops kept running up to the boys on the street, shaking their hands and congratulating them on il Presidente Veelson; somebody stole all the spare tires out of the camionette and the Red Cross publicity man's suitcase that had been left in the staffcar. They were greeted effusively and shortchanged in the bars. Evviva gli alleati.

Everybody in the section began to curse out Italy and the rubber spaghetti and the vinegary wine, except Dick and Steven, who suddenly became woplovers and bought themselves grammars to learn the language. Dick already gave a pretty good imitation of talking Italian, especially before the Red Cross officers, by putting an *o* on the end of all the French words he knew. He didn't give a damn about anything any more. It was sunny, vermouth was a great drink, the towns and the toy churches on the tops of hills and the vineyards and the cypresses and the blue sea were like a succession of backdrops for an oldfashioned opera. The buildings were stagy and ridiculously magnificent; on every blank wall the damn wops had painted windows and colonnades and balconies with fat Titianhaired beauties leaning over them and clouds and covies of dimpletummied cupids.

That night they parked the convoy in the main square of a godforsaken little burg on the outskirts of Genoa. They went with Sheldrake to have a drink in a bar and found themselves drinking with the *Saturday Evening Post* correspondent who soon began to get tight and to say how he envied them their good looks and their sanguine youth and idealism. Steve picked him up about everything and argued bitterly that youth was the lousiest time in your life, and that he ought to be goddam glad he was forty years old and able to write about the war instead of fighting in it. Ellis goodnaturedly pointed out that they weren't fighting either. Steve made Sheldrake sore by snapping out, 'No, of course not, we're goddamned embusqués.' He and Steve left the bar and ran like deer to get out of sight before Sheldrake could follow them. Around the corner they saw a streetcar marked Genoa and Steve hopped it without saying a word. Dick didn't have anything to do but follow.

The car rounded a block of houses and came out on the waterfront. "Judas Priest, Dick,' said Steve, 'the goddam town's on fire.' Beyond the black hulks of boats drawn up on the shore a rosy flame like a gigantic lampflame sent a broad shimmer towards them across the water. 'Gracious, Steve, do you suppose the Austrians are in there?'

The car went whanging along; the conductor who came and got their fare looked calm enough. 'Inglese?' he asked. 'Americani,' said Steve. He smiled and clapped them on the back and said something about the Presidente Veelson that they couldn't understand.

They got off the car in a big square surrounded by huge arcades that a raw bittersweet wind blew hugely through. Dressedup people in overcoats were walking up and down on the clean mosaic pavement. The town was all marble. Every façade that faced the sea was pink with the glow of the fire. 'Here the tenors and the baritones and the sopranos all ready for the show to begin,' said Dick. Steve grunted, 'Chorus'll probably be the goddam Austrians.'

They were cold and went into one of the shiny nickel and plateglass cafés to have a grog. The waiter told them in broken English that the fire was on an American tanker that had hit a mine and that she'd been burning for three days. A longfaced English officer came over from the bar and started to tell them how he was on a secret mission; it was all bloody awful about the retreat; it hadn't stopped yet; in Milan they were talking about falling back on the Po; the only reason the bloody Austrians hadn't overrun all bloody Lombardy was they'd been so disorganized by their rapid advance they were in almost as bad shape as the bloody Italians were. Damned Italian officers kept talking about the quadrilateral, and if it wasn't for the French and British troops behind the Italian lines they'd have sold out long ago. French morale was pretty shaky, at that. Dick told him about how the tools got swiped every time they took their eyes off their cars. The Englishman said the thievery in these parts was extraordinary; that was what his secret mission was about; he was trying to trace an entire carload of boots that had vanished between Vintimiglia and San Raphael. 'Whole bloody luggage van turns into thin air overnight . . . extraordinary. . . . See those blighters over there at that table, they're bloody Austrian spies every mother's son of them . . . but try as I can I can't get them arrested . . . extraordinary. It's a bloody melodrama that's what it is, just like Drury Lane. A jolly good thing you Americans have come in. If you hadn't you'd see the bloody German flag flying over Genoa at this minute.' He suddenly looked at his wristwatch, advised them to buy a bottle of whiskey at the bar if they wanted another bit of drink, because it was closing time, said cheeryoh, and hustled out.

They plunged out again into the empty marble town, down dark lanes and streets of stone steps with always the glare on some jutting wall overhead brighter and redder as they neared the waterfront. Time and again they got lost; at last they came out on wharves and bristle of masts of crowded feluccas and beyond the little crimsontipped waves of the harbor, the breakwater, and outside the breakwater the mass of flame of the burning tanker. Excited and drunk they walked on and on through the town: 'By God, these towns are older than the world,' Dick kept saying.

While they were looking at a marble lion, shaped like a dog, that stood polished to glassy smoothness by centuries of hands at the bottom of a flight of steps, an American voice hailed them, wanting to know if they knew their way around this goddam town. It was a young fellow who was a sailor on an American boat that had come over with a carload of mules. They said sure they knew their way and gave him a drink out of the bottle of cognac they'd bought. They sat there on the stone balustrade beside the lion that looked like a dog and swigged cognac out of the bottle and talked. The sailor showed them some silk stockings he'd salvaged off the burning oilship and told them about how he'd been jazzing an Eyetalian girl only she'd gone to sleep and he'd gotten disgusted and walked out on her. 'This war's hell ain't it de truth?' he said; they all got to laughing.

'You guys seem to be a couple of pretty good guys,' the sailor said. They handed him the bottle and he took a gulp. 'You fellers are princes,' he added, spluttering, 'and I'm goin' to tell you what I think, see. . . . This whole goddam war's a gold brick, it ain't on the level, it's crooked from A to Z. No matter how it comes out fellers like us gets the s—y end of the stick, see? Well, what I say is all bets is off . . . every man go to hell in his own way . . . and three strikes is out, see?' They finished up the cognac.

Singing out savagely, 'To hell wid 'em I say,' the sailor threw the bottle with all his might against the head of the stone lion. The Genoese lion went on staring ahead with glassy doglike eye.

Sourlooking loafers started gathering around to see what the trouble was, so they moved on, the sailor waving his silk stockings as he walked. They found him his steamer tied up to the dock and shook hands again and again at the gangplank.

Then it was up to Dick and Steve to get themselves back across the ten miles to Ponte Decimo. Chilly and sleepy they walked until their feet were sore, then hopped a wop truck the rest of the way. The cobbles of the square and the roofs of the cars were covered with hoarfrost when they got there. Dick made a noise getting into the stretcher beside Sheldrake's and Sheldrake woke up, 'What the hell?' he said. 'Shut up,' said Dick, 'don't you see you're waking people up?'

Next day they got to Milan, huge wintry city with its overgrown pincushion cathedral and its Galleria jammed with people and restaurants and newspapers and whores and Cinzano and Campari Bitters. There followed another period of waiting during which most of the section settled down to an endless crapgame in the back room at Cova's; then they moved out to a place called Dolo on a frozen canal somewhere in the Venetian plain. To get to the elegant carved and painted villa where they were quartered they had to cross the Brenta. A company of British sappers had the bridge all mined and ready to blow up when the retreat began again. They promised to wait till Section 1 had crossed before blowing the bridge up. In Dolo there was very little to do; it was raw wintry weather; while most of the section sat around the stove and swapped their jack at poker, the grenadine guards made themselves hot rum punches over a gasoline burner, read Boccaccio in Italian and argued with Steve about anarchism.

Dick spent a great deal of his time wondering how he was going to get to Venice. It turned out that the fat lieutenant was worried by the fact that the section had no cocoa and that the Red Cross commissary in Milan hadn't sent the section any breakfast foods. Dick suggested that Venice was one of the world's great cocoa markets, and that somebody who knew Italian ought to be sent over there to buy cocoa; so one frosty morning Dick found himself properly equipped with papers and seals boarding the little steamboat at Mestre.

There was a thin skim of ice on the lagoon that tore with a sound of silk on either side of the narrow bow where Dick stood leaning forward over the rail, tears in his eyes from the raw wind, staring at the long rows of stakes and the light red buildings rising palely out of the green water to bubblelike domes and square pointedtipped towers that etched themselves sharper and sharper against the zinc sky. The hunchback bridges, the greenslimy steps, the palaces, the marble quays were all empty. The only life was in a group of torpedoboats anchored in the Grand Canal. Dick forgot all about the cocoa walking through sculptured squares and the narrow streets and quays along the icefilled canals of the great dead city that lay there on the lagoon frail and empty as a cast snakeskin. To the north he could hear the tomtomming of the guns fifteen miles away on the Piave. On the way back it began to snow.

A few days later they moved up to Bassano behind Monte Grappa into a late Renaissance villa all painted up with cupids and angels and elaborate draperies. Back of the villa the Brenta roared day and night under a covered bridge. There they spent their time evacuating cases of frozen feet, drinking hot rum punches at Citadella where the base hospital and the whorehouses were, and singing *The Foggy Foggy Dew* and *The Little Black Bull Came Down from the Mountain* over the rubber spaghetti at chow. Ripley and Steve decided they wanted to learn to draw and spent their days off drawing architectural details or the covered bridge. Schuyler practiced his Italian talking about Nietzsche with the Italian lieutenant. Fred Summers had gotten a dose off a Milanese lady who he said must have belonged to one of the best families because she was riding in a carriage and picked him up, not he her, and spent most of his spare time brewing himself home remedies like cherry stems in hot water. Dick got to feeling lonely and blue, and in need of privacy, and wrote a great many letters home. The letters he got back made him feel worse than not getting any.

'You must understand how it is,' he wrote the Thurlows, answering an enthusiastic screed of Hilda's about the 'war to end war,' 'I don't believe in Christianity any more and can't argue from that standpoint, but you do, or at least Edwin does, and he ought to realize that in urging young men to go into this cockeyed lunatic asylum of war he's doing everything he can to undermine all the principles and ideals he most believes in. As the young fellow we had that talk with in Genoa that night said, it's not on the level, it's a dirty goldbrick game put over by governments and politicians for their own selfish interests, it's crooked from A to Z. If it wasn't for the censorship I could tell you things that would make you vomit.'

Then he'd suddenly snap out of his argumentative mood and all the phrases about liberty and civilization steaming up out of his head would seem damn silly too, and he'd light the gasoline burner and make a rum punch and cheer up chewing the rag with Steve about books or painting or architecture. Moonlight nights the Austrians made things lively by sending bombing planes over. Some nights Dick found that staying out of the dugout and giving them a chance at him gave him a sort of bitter pleasure, and the dugout wasn't any protection against a direct hit anyway.

Sometime in February Steve read in the paper that the Empress Taitu of Abyssinia had died. They held a wake. They drank all the rum they had and keened until the rest of the section thought they'd gone crazy. They sat in the dark round the open moonlit window wrapped in blankets and drinking warm zabaglione. Some Austrian planes that had been droning overhead suddenly cut off their motors and dumped a load of bombs right in front of them. The antiaircraft guns had been barking for some time and shrapnel sparkling in the moonhazy sky overhead, but they'd been too drunk to notice. One bomb fell geflump into the Brenta and the others filled the space in front of the window with red leaping glare and shook the villa with three roaring snorts. Plaster fell from the ceiling. They could hear the tiles scuttering down off the roof overhead.

'Jesus, that was almost goodnight,' said Summers. Steve started singing, *Come away from that window, my light and my life*, but the rest of them drowned it out with an out-of-tune *Deutschland, Deutschland Ueber Alles*. They suddenly all felt crazy drunk.

Ed Schuyler was standing on a chair giving a recitation of the *Erlkönig* when Feldmann, the Swiss hotelkeeper's son, who was now head of the section, stuck his head in the door and asked what in the devil they thought they were doing. 'You'd better go down in the abris, one of the Italian mechanics was killed and a soldier walking up the road had his legs blown off . . . no time for monkeyshines.' They offered him a drink and he went off in a rage. After that they drank marsala. Sometime in the early dawn grayness Dick got up and staggered to the window to vomit; it was raining pitchforks, the foaming rapids of the Brenta looked very white through the shimmering rain.

Next day it was Dick's and Steve's turn to go on post to Rova. They drove out of the yard at six with their heads like fireballoons, damn glad to be away from the big scandal there'd be at the section. At Rova the lines were quiet, only a few

pneumonia or venereal cases to evacuate, and a couple of poor
devils who'd shot themselves in the foot and were to be sent
to the hospital under guard; but at the officers' mess where
they ate things were very agitated indeed. Tenente Sardinaglia
was under arrest in his quarters for saucing the Coronele and
had been up there for two days making up a little march on
his mandolin that he called the march of the medical colonels.
Serrati told them about it giggling behind his hand while they
were waiting for the other officers to come to mess. It was all
on account of the macchina for coffee. There were only three
macchine for the whole mess, one for the colonel, one for the
major, and the other went around to the junior officers in
rotation; well, one day last week they'd been kidding the bella
ragazza, the niece of the farmer on whom they were quartered;
she hadn't let any of the officers kiss her and had carried on
like a crazy woman when they pinched her behind, and the
colonel had been angry about it, and angrier yet when Sardinaglia had bet him five lira that he could kiss her and he'd
whispered something in her ear and she'd let him and that had
made the colonel get purple in the face and he'd told the
ordinanza not to give the macchina to the tenente when his
turn came round; and Sardinaglia had slapped the ordinanza's
face and there'd been a row and as a result Sardinaglia was
confined to his quarters and the Americans would see what a
circus it was. They all had to straighten their faces in a hurry
because the colonel and the major and the two captains came
jingling in at that moment.

The ordinanza came and saluted, and said pronto spaghetti
in a cheerful tone, and everybody sat down. For a while the
officers were quiet sucking in the long oily tomatocoated strings
of spaghetti, the wine was passed around and the colonel had
just cleared his throat to begin one of his funny stories that
everybody had to laugh at, when from up above there came the
tinkle of a mandolin. The colonel's face got red and he put a
forkful of spaghetti in his mouth instead of saying anything.
As it was Sunday the meal was unusually long: at dessert the
coffee macchina was awarded to Dick as a courtesy to gli
americani and somebody produced a bottle of strega. The
colonel told the ordinanza to tell the bella ragazza to come
and have a glass of strega with him; he looked pretty sour at
the idea, Dick thought; but he went and got her. She turned
out to be a handsome stout oliveskinned countrygirl. Her
cheeks burning, she went timidly up to the colonel and said,

thank you very much, but please she never drank strong drinks. The colonel grabbed her and made her sit on his knee and tried to make her drink his glass of strega, but she kept her handsome set of ivory teeth clenched and wouldn't drink it. It ended by several of the officers holding her and tickling her and the colonel pouring the strega over her chin. Everybody roared with laughter except the ordinanza, who turned white as chalk, and Steve and Dick who didn't know where to look. While the senior officers were teasing and tickling her and running their hands into her blouse, the junior officers were holding her feet and running their hands up her legs. Finally the colonel got control of his laughter enough to say, 'Basta, now she must give me a kiss.' But the girl broke loose and ran out of the room.

'Go and bring her back,' the colonel said to the ordinanza. After a moment the ordinanza came back and stood at attention and said he couldn't find her. 'Good for him,' whispered Steve to Dick. Dick noticed that the ordinanza's legs were trembling. 'You can't, can't you?' roared the colonel, and gave the ordinanza a push; one of the lieutenants stuck his foot out and the ordinanza tripped over it and fell. Everybody laughed and the colonel gave him a kick; he had gotten to his hands and knees when the colonel gave him a kick in the seat of his pants that sent him flat to the floor again. The officers all roared, the ordinanza crawled to the door with the colonel running after him giving him little kicks first on one side and then on the other, like a soccerplayer with a football. That put everybody in a good humor and they had another drink of strega all around. When they got outside, Serrati, who'd been laughing with the rest, grabbed Dick's arm and hissed in his ear, 'Bestie, . . . sono tutti bestie.'

When the other officers had gone, Serrati took them up to see Sardinaglia, who was a tall longfaced young man who liked to call himself a futurista. Serrati told him what had happened and said he was afraid the Americans had been disgusted. 'A futurist must be disgusted at nothing except weakness and stupidity,' said Sardinaglia sententiously. Then he told them he'd found out who the bella ragazza was really sleeping with . . . with the ordinanza. That he said disgusted him; it showed that women were all pigs. Then he said to sit down on his cot while he played them the march of the medical colonels. They declared it was fine. 'A futurist must be strong and disgusted with nothing,' he said, still trilling on the mandolin;

'that's why I admire the Germans and American millionaires.'
They all laughed.

Dick and Steve went out to pick up some feriti to evacuate
to the hospital. Behind the barn where they parked the cars,
they found the ordinanza sitting on a stone with his head in
his hands, tears had made long streaks on the dirt of his face.
Steve went up to him and patted him on the back and gave him
a package of Mecca cigarettes, that had been distributed to
them at the Y.M.C.A. The ordinanza squeezed Steve's hand,
looked as if he was going to kiss it. He said after the war he
was going to America where people were civilized, not bestie
like here. Dick asked him where the girl had gone. 'Gone away,'
he said. 'Andata via.'

When they got back to the section they found there was
hell to pay. Orders had come for Savage, Warner, Ripley,
and Schuyler to report to the head office in Rome in order to
be sent back to the States. Feldmann wouldn't tell them what
the trouble was. They noticed at once that the other men in
the section were looking at them suspiciously and were nervous
about speaking to them, except for Fred Summers who said
he didn't understand it, the whole frigging business was a
madhouse anyway. Sheldrake, who'd moved his dufflebag and
cot into another room in the villa, came around with an I-told-
you-so air and said he'd heard the words 'seditious utterances'
and that an Italian intelligence officer had been around asking
about them. He wished them good luck and said it was too
bad. They left the section without saying goodbye to anybody.
Feldmann drove them and their dufflebags and bedrolls down
to Vicenza in the camionette. At the railroad station he handed
them their orders of movement to Rome, said it was too bad,
wished them good luck, and went off in a hurry without
shaking hands.

'The sonsofbitches,' growled Steve, 'you might think we had
leprosy.'

Ed Schuyler was reading the military passes, his face beaming. 'Men and brethren,' he said. 'I am moved to make a
speech . . . this is the greatest graft yet . . . do you gentlemen
realize that what's happening is that the Red Cross, otherwise
known as the goose that lays the golden egg, is presenting us
with a free tour of Italy? We don't have to get to Rome for
a year.'

'Keep out of Rome till the revolution,' suggested Dick.

'Enter Rome with the Austrians,' said Ripley.

A train came into the station. They piled into a firstclass compartment; when the conductor came and tried to explain that their orders read for secondclass transportation, they couldn't understand Italian, so finally he left them there. At Verona they piled off to check their dufflebags and cots to Rome. It was suppertime, so they decided to walk around the town and spend the night. In the morning they went to see the ancient theater and the great peachcolored marble church of San Zeno. Then they sat around the café at the station until a train came by for Rome. The train was jampacked with officers in paleblue and palegreen cloaks; by Bologna they'd gotten tired of sitting on the floor of the vestibule and decided they must see the leaning towers. Then they went to Pistoja, Lucca, Pisa, and back to the main line at Florence. When the conductors shook their heads over the orders of movement, they explained that they'd been misinformed and due to ignorance of the language had taken the wrong train. At Florence, where it was rainy and cold and the buildings all looked like the replicas of them they'd seen at home, the stationmaster put them forcibly on the express for Rome, but they sneaked out the other side after it had started and got into the local for Assisi. From there they got to Siena by way of San Gimignano, as full of towers as New York, in a hack they hired for the day, and ended up one fine spring morning full up to the neck with painting and architecture and oil and garlic and scenery, looking at the Signorelli frescoes in the cathedral at Orvieto. They stayed there all day looking at the great fresco of the Last Judgment, drinking the magnificent wine and basking in the sunny square outside. When they got to Rome, to the station next to the Baths of Diocletian, they felt pretty bad at the prospect of giving up their passes; they were amazed when the employee merely stamped them and gave them back, saying, 'Per il ritorno.'

They went to a hotel and cleaned up, and then, pooling the last of their money, went on a big bust with a highclass meal, Frascati wine and asti for dessert, a vaudeville show and a cabaret on the Via Roma, where they met an American girl they called the baroness who promised to show them the town. By the end of the evening nobody had enough money left to go home with the baroness or any of her charming ladyfriends, so they hired a cab with their last ten lire to take them out to see the Colosseum by moonlight. The great masses of ruins, the engraved stones, the names, the stately Roman names, the old cabdriver with his oilcloth stovepipe hat and his green soupstrainers recommending whorehouses under the last quarter of the ruined moon, the great masses of masonry full of arches and columns piled up everywhere into the night, the boom of the word Rome dying away in pompous chords into the past, sent them to bed with their heads whirling, Rome throbbing in their ears so that they could not sleep.

Next morning Dick got up while the others were still dead to the world and went round to the Red Cross; he was suddenly nervous and worried so that he couldn't eat his breakfast. At the office he saw a stoutish Bostonian major who seemed to be running things, and asked him straight out what the devil the trouble was. The major hemmed and hawed and kept the conversation in an agreeable tone, as one Harvard man to another. He talked about indiscretions and oversensitiveness of the Italians. As a matter of fact, the censor didn't like the tone of certain letters, etcetera, etcetera. Dick said he felt he ought to explain his position, and that if the Red Cross felt he hadn't done his duty they ought to give him a courtmartial, he said he felt there were many men in his position who had pacifist views, but now that the country was at war were willing to do any kind of work they could to help, but that didn't mean he believed in the war, he felt he ought to be allowed to explain his position. The major said Ah well he quite understood, etcetera, etcetera, but that the young should realize the importance of discretion, etcetera, etcetera, and that the whole thing had been satisfactorily explained as an indiscretion; as a matter of fact the incident was closed. Dick kept saying he ought to be allowed to explain his position, and the major kept saying the incident was closed, etcetera, etcetera, until it all seemed a little silly and he left the office. The major promised him transportation to Paris if he wanted to take it up with the office there. Dick went back to the hotel feeling baffled and sore.

The other two had gone out, so he and Steve walked around the town, looking at the sunny streets, that smelt of frying oliveoil and wine and old stones, and the domed baroque churches and the columns and the Pantheon and the Tiber. They didn't have a cent in their pockets to buy lunch or a drink with. They spent the afternoon hungry, napping glumly on the warm sod of the Pincian, and got back to the room famished and depressed to find Schuyler and Ripley drinking vermouth and soda and in high spirits. Schuyler had run into an old friend of his father's, Colonel Anderson, who was on a mission investigating the Red Cross, and had poured out his woes and given him dope about small graft at the office in Milan. Colonel Anderson had set him up to lunch and highballs at the Hotel de Russie, lent him a hundred dollars and fixed him up with a job in the publicity department. 'So men and brethren, evviva Italia and the goddamned Alleati, we're all set.' 'What about the dossier?' Steve asked savagely. 'Aw forget it, siamo tutti Italiani . . . who's a defeatist now?'

Schuyler set them all up to meals, took them out to Tivoli and the Lake of Nemi in a staffcar, and finally put them on the train to Paris with the rating of captain on their transport orders.

The first day in Paris Steve went off to the Red Cross office to get shipped home. 'To hell with, I'm going to C.O.,' was all he'd say. Ripley enlisted in the French artillery school at Fontainebleau. Dick got himself a cheap room in a little hotel on the Île St Louis and spent his days interviewing first one higherup and then another in the Red Cross; Hiram Halsey Cooper had suggested the names in a very guarded reply to a cable Dick sent him from Rome. The higherups sent him from one to the other. 'Young man,' said one baldheaded official in a luxurious office at the Hotel Crillon, 'your opinions, while showing a senseless and cowardly turn of mind, don't matter. The American people is out to get the Kaiser. We are bending every nerve and every energy towards that end; nobody who gets in the way of the great machine the energy and devotion of a hundred million patriots is building towards the stainless purpose of saving civilization from the Huns will be mashed like a fly. I'm surprised that a collegebred man like you hasn't more sense. Don't monkey with the buzzsaw.'

Finally he was sent to the army intelligence service where he found a young fellow named Spaulding he'd known in college who greeted him with a queazy smile. 'Old man,' he said, 'in a time like this we can't give in to our personal feelings can we . . . ? I think it's perfectly criminal to allow yourself the luxury of private opinions, perfectly criminal. It's wartime and we've all got to do our duty, it's people like you that are encouraging the Germans to keep up the fight, people like you and the Russians.' Spaulding's boss was a captain and wore spurs and magnificently polished puttees; he was a sternlooking young man with a delicate profile. He strode up to Dick, put his face close to his and yelled, 'What would you do

if two Huns attacked your sister? You'd fight, wouldn't you?
. . . if you're not a dirty yellow dawg. . . .' Dick tried to point
out that he was anxious to keep on doing the work he had been
doing, he was trying to get back to the front with the Red
Cross, he wanted an opportunity to explain his position. The
captain strode up and down, bawling him out, yelling that any
man who was still a pacifist after the President's declaration
of war was a moron or what was worse a degenerate and that
they didn't want people like that in the A.E.F. and that he was
going to see to it that Dick would be sent back to the States
and that he would not be allowed to come back in any capacity
whatsoever. 'The A.E.F. is no place for a slacker.'

Dick gave up and went to the Red Cross office to get his
transportation; they gave him an order for the *Touraine* sailing
from Bordeaux in two weeks. His last two weeks in Paris he
spent working as a volunteer stretcherbearer at the American
Hospital on the Avenue du Bois de Boulogne. It was June.
There were airraids every clear night and when the wind was
right you could hear the guns on the front. The German
offensive was on, the lines were so near Paris the ambulances
were evacuating wounded directly on the basehospitals. All
night the stretcher cases would spread along the broad pavements under the trees in fresh leaf in front of the hospital; Dick
would help carry them up the marble stairs into the reception
room. One night they put him on duty outside the operatingroom and for twelve hours he had the job of carrying out
buckets of blood and gauze from which protruded occasionally
a shattered bone or a piece of an arm or a leg. When he went
off duty he'd walk home achingly tired through the strawberry-
scented early Parisian morning, thinking of the faces and the
eyes and the sweatdrenched hair and the clenched fingers
clotted with blood and dirt and the fellows kidding and pleading
for cigarettes and the bubbling groans of the lung cases.

One day he saw a pocket compass in a jeweler's window on
the Rue de Rivoli. He went in and bought it; there was suddenly
a fullformed plan in his head to buy a civilian suit, leave his
uniform in a heap on the wharf at Bordeaux and make for
the Spanish border. With luck and all the old transport orders
he had in his inside pocket he was sure he could make it; hop
across the border and then, once in a country free from nightmare, decide what to do. He even got ready a letter to send
his mother.

All the time he was packing his books and other junk in his

dufflebag and carrying it on his back up the quais to the Gare
d'Orléans, Swinburne's *Song in Time of Order* kept going
through his head:

> *While three men hold together*
> *The kingdoms are less by three.*

By gum, he must write some verse: what people needed
was stirring poems to nerve them for revolt against their
cannibal governments. Sitting in the secondclass compartment
he was so busy building a daydream of himself living in a
sunscorched Spanish town, sending out flaming poems and
manifestoes, calling young men to revolt against their butchers,
poems that would be published by secret presses all over the
world, that he hardly saw the suburbs of Paris or the bluegreen
summer farmlands sliding by.

> *Let our flag run out straight in the wind*
> *The old red shall be floated again*
> *When the ranks that are thin shall be thinned*
> *When the names that were twenty are ten*

Even the rumblebump rumblebump of the French railroad
train seemed to be chanting as if the words were muttered low
in unison by a marching crowd:

> *While three men hold together*
> *The kingdoms are less by three.*

At noon Dick got hungry and went to the diner to eat a
last deluxe meal. He sat down at a table opposite a goodlooking
young man in a French officer's uniform. 'Good God, Ned,
is that you?'

Blake Wigglesworth threw back his head in the funny way
he had and laughed. 'Garçon,' he shouted, 'un verre pour le
monsieur.'

'But how long were you in the Lafayette Escadrille?' stammered Dick.

'Not long . . . they wouldn't have me.'

'And how about the Navy?'

'Threw me out, too, the damn fools think I've got T.B. . . .
garçon, une bouteille de champagne. . . . Where are you going?'

'I'll explain.'

'Well, I'm going home on the *Touraine*.' Ned threw back
his head laughing again and his lips formed the syllables
blahblahblahblah. Dick noticed that although his face was

very pale and thin, his skin under his eyes and up onto the temples was flushed and his eyes looked a little too bright.

'Well, so am I,' he heard himself say.

'I got into hot water,' said Ned.

'Me too,' said Dick. 'Very.'

They lifted their glasses and looked into each other's eyes and laughed. They sat in the diner all afternoon talking and drinking and got to Bordeaux boiled as owls. Ned had spent all his money in Paris and Dick had very little left, so they had to sell their bedrolls and equipment to a couple of American lieutenants just arrived they met in the Café de Bordeaux. It was almost like old days in Boston going around from bar to bar and looking for places to get drinks after closing. They spent most of the night in an elegant maison publique all upholstered in pink satin, talking to the madam, a dried up woman with a long upper lip like a llama's, wearing a black spangled evening dress, who took a fancy to them and made them stay and eat onion soup with her. They were so busy talking they forgot about the girls. She'd been in the Transvaal during the Boer War and spoke a curious brand of South African English. 'Vous comprennez ve had very find clientèle, every man jack officers, very much elegance, decorum. These johnnies off the veldt . . . get the hell outen here . . . bloody select don't you know. Ve had two salons, one salon English officers, one salon Boer officers, very select, never in all the war make any bloody row, no fight. . . . Vos compatriotes les Américains ce n'est pas comme ça, mes amis. Beaucoup sonofabeetch, make drunk, make bloody row, make sick, naturellement il y a aussi des gentils garçons comme vous, mes mignons, des véritables gentlemens,' and she patted them both on the cheeks with her horny ringed hands. When they left she wanted to kiss them and went with them to the door saying, 'Bonsoir, mes jolis petits gentlemens.'

All the crossing they were never sober after eleven in the morning; it was calm misty weather; they were very happy. One night, when he was standing alone in the stern beside the small gun, Dick was searching his pocket for a cigarette when his fingers felt something hard in the lining of his coat. It was the little compass he had bought to help him across the Spanish border. Guiltily, he fished it out and dropped it overboard.

# Newsreel 27

HER WOUNDED HERO OF WAR A FRAUD SAYS
WIFE IN SUIT

*Mid the wars great coise*
*Stands the red cross noise*
*She's the rose of no man's land*

according to the thousands who had assembled to see
the launching and were eyewitnesses of the disaster the
scaffold simply seemed to turn over like a gigantic turtle
precipitating its occupants into twentyfive feet of water. This
was exactly four minutes before the launching was scheduled

*Oh that battle of Paree*
*It's making a bum out of me*

BRITISH BEGIN OPERATION ON AFGHAN FRONTIER

the leading part in world trade, which the U.S. is now
confidently expected to take, will depend to a very great
extent upon the intelligence and success with which its
harbors are utilized and developed

*I wanta go home I wanta go home*
*The bullets they whistle the cannons they roar*
*I don't want to go to the trenches no more*
*Oh ship me over the sea*
*Where the Allemand can't get at me*

you have begun a crusade against toys, but if all the
German toys were commandeered and destroyed, the end
of German importations would not yet have been reached

HOLDS UP TWENTY DINERS IN CAFE

LAWHATING GATHERINGS NOT TO BE ALLOWED IN
CRITICAL TIME THREATENING SOCIAL UPHEAVAL

*Oh my     I'm too young to die*
*I wanna go home*

NANCY ENJOYS NIGHTLIFE DESPITE RAIDS

TATTOOED WOMAN SOUGHT BY POLICE IN
TRUNK MURDER

ARMY WIFE SLASHED BY ADMIRER

Young Man Alleged to Have Taken Money to Aid in
Promotion of a Reserve Officer. It appears that these men
were Chinese merchants from Irkutsk, Chita, and elsewhere
who were proceeding homeward to Harbin carrying their
profits for investment in new stocks

> *Oh that battle of Paree*
> *It's making a bum out of me*
> *Toujours la femme et combien*

THREE HUNDRED THOUSAND RUSSIAN NOBLES
SLAIN BY BOLSHEVIKI

BANKERS OF THIS COUNTRY, BRITAIN, AND
FRANCE TO SAFEGUARD FOREIGN INVESTORS

these three girls came to France thirteen months ago
and were the first concertparty to entertain at the front. They
staged a show for the American troops from a flatcar base
of a large naval gun three kilometers behind the line on the
day of the evening of the drive at Château Thierry. After
that they were assigned to the Aix-les-Bains leave area
where they acted during the day as canteen girls and entertained and danced at night

> *You never knew a place that was so short of men*
> *Beaucoup rum     beaucoup fun*
> *Mother'd never know her loving son*
> *Oh if you wan to see     that Statue of Libertee*
> *Keep away from that battle of Paree*

## The Camera Eye (35)

there were always two cats the color of hot milk with
a little coffee in it with aquamarine eyes and sootblack faces
in the window of the laundry opposite the little creamery

where we ate breakfast on the Montagne Sainte Geneviève huddled between the old squeezedup slate gray houses of the Latin Quarter leaning over steep small streets cozy under the fog    minute streets lit with different colored chalks cluttered with infinitesimal bars restaurants paintshops and old prints beds bidets faded perfumery microscopic sizzle of frying butter

the Bertha made a snapping noise no louder than a cannoncracker near the hotel where Oscar Wilde died we all run up stairs to see if the house was on fire but the old woman whose lard was burning was sore as a crutch

all the big new quarters near the Arc de Triomphe were deserted but in the dogeared yellowbacked Paris of the Carmagnole the Faubourg Saint Antoine the Commune we were singing

> *'suis dans l'axe*
> *'suis dans l'axe*
> *'suis dans l'axe du gros canon*

when the Bertha dropped in the Seine there was a concours de pêche in the little brightgreen skiffs among all the old whiskery fishermen scooping up in nets the minnows the concussion had stunned

## *Eveline Hutchins*

Eveline went to live with Eleanor in a fine apartment Eleanor had gotten hold of somehow on the Quai de la Tournelle. It was the mansard floor of a gray peelingfaced house built at the time of Richelieu and done over under Louis Quinze. Eveline never tired of looking out the window, through the delicate tracing of the wroughtiron balcony, at the Seine where toy steamboats bucked the current, towing shinyvarnished barges that had lace curtains and geraniums in the windows of their deckhouses painted green and red, and at the island opposite where the rocketing curves of the flying buttresses shoved the apse of Notre Dame dizzily upwards out of the trees of a little park. They had tea at a small Buhl table in the window almost every evening when they got home from the office on the Rue de Rivoli, after spending the day pasting pictures of ruined French farms and orphaned children and starving warbabies into scrapbooks to be sent home for use in Red Cross drives.

After tea she'd go out in the kitchen and watch Yvonne cook. With the groceries and sugar they drew at the Red Cross commissary, Yvonne operated a system of barter so that their food hardly cost them anything. At first Eveline tried to stop her, but she'd answer with a torrent of argument: did Mademoiselle think that President Poincaré or the generals or the cabinet ministers, ces salots de profiteurs, ces salots d'embusqués, went without their brioches? It was the système D, ils s'en fichent des particuliers, des pauvres gens . . . very well, her ladies would eat as well as any old camels of generals, if she had her way she'd have all the generals line up before a firingsquad and the embusqué ministers and the ronds de cuir too. Eleanor said her sufferings had made the old woman a little cracked, but Jerry Burnham said it was the rest of the world that was cracked.

Jerry Burnham was the little redfaced man who'd been such a help with the colonel the first night Eveline got to Paris. They often laughed about it afterwards. He was working for the U.P. and appeared every few days in her office on his rounds covering Red Cross activities. He knew all the Paris restaurants and would take Eveline out to dinner at the Tour d'Argent or to lunch at the Taverne Nicolas Flamel and they'd walk around the old streets of the Marais afternoons and get late to their work together. When they'd settle in the evening at a good quiet table in a café where they couldn't be overheard (all the waiters were spies he said), he'd drink a lot of cognac and soda and pour out his feelings, how his work disgusted him, how a correspondent couldn't get to see anything any more, how he had three or four censorships on his neck all the time and had to send out prepared stuff that was all a pack of dirty lies every word of it, how a man lost his self-respect doing things like that year after year, how a newspaperman had been little better than a skunk before the war, but that now there wasn't anything low enough you could call him. Eveline would try to cheer him up, telling him that when the war was over he ought to write a book like Le Feu and really tell the truth about it. 'But the war won't ever be over . . . too damn profitable, do you get me? Back home they're coining money, the British are coining money; even the French, look at Bordeaux and Toulouse and Marseilles, coining money and

the goddam politicians, all of 'em got bank accounts in Amsterdam or Barcelona, the sonsofbitches.' Then he'd take her hand
and get a crying jag and promise that if it did end he'd get
back his selfrespect and write the great novel he felt he had
in him.

Late that fall Eveline came home one evening tramping
through the mud and the foggy dusk to find that Eleanor had
a French soldier to tea. She was glad to see him, because she
was always complaining that she wasn't getting to know any
French people, nothing but professional relievers and Red Cross
women who were just too tiresome; but it was some moments
before she realized it was Maurice Millet. She wondered how
she could have fallen for him even when she was a kid, he
looked so middleaged and pasty and oldmaidish in his stained
blue uniform. His large eyes with their girlish long lashes had
heavy violet rings under them. Eleanor evidently thought he
was wonderful still, and drank up his talk about l'élan suprème
du sacrifice and l'harmonie mystérieuse de la mort. He was a
stretcherbearer in a basehospital at Nancy, had become very
religious and had almost forgotten his English. When they
asked him about his painting, he shrugged his shoulders and
wouldn't answer. At supper he ate very little and drank only
water. He stayed till late in the evening telling them about
miraculous conversions of unbelievers, extreme unction on the
firingline, a vision of the young Christ he'd seen walking among
the wounded in a dressingstation during a gasattack. Après la
guerre he was going into a monastery. Trappist, perhaps. After
he left, Eleanor said it had been the most inspiring
evening she'd ever had in her life; Eveline didn't argue with
her.

Maurice came back one other afternoon before his perme
expired, bringing a young writer who was working at the Quai
d'Orsay, a tall young Frenchman with pink cheeks who looked
like an English publicschool boy, whose name was Raoul
Lemonnier. He seemed to prefer to speak English than French.
He'd been at the front for two years in the Chasseurs Alpins
and had been réformé on account of his lungs or his uncle who
was a minister he couldn't say which. It was all very boring,
he said. He thought tennis was ripping, though, and went out to
Saint Cloud to row every afternoon. Eleanor discovered that
what she'd been wanting all fall had been a game of tennis.
He said he liked English and American women because they
liked sport. Here every woman thought you wanted to go to

bed with her right away; 'Love is very boring,' he said. He and
Eveline stood in the window talking about cocktails (he adored
American drinks) and looked out at the last purple shreds of
dusk settling over Notre Dame and the Seine, while Eleanor
and Maurice sat in the dark in the little salon talking about
Saint Francis of Assisi. She asked him to dinner.

The next morning Eleanor said she thought she was going
to become a Catholic. On their way to the office she made
Eveline stop into Notre Dame with her to hear Mass and they
both lit candles for Maurice's safety at the front before what
Eveline thought was a just too tiresomelooking Virgin near
the main door. But it was impressive all the same, the priests
moaning and the lights and the smell of chilled incense. She
certainly hoped poor Maurice wouldn't be killed.

For dinner that night Eveline invited Jerry Burnham, Miss
Felton who was back from Amiens, and Major Appleton who
was in Paris doing something about tanks. It was a fine dinner,
duck roasted with oranges, although Jerry, who was sore about
how much Eveline talked to Lemonnier, had to get drunk and
use a lot of bad language and tell about the retreat at Caporetto
and say that the Allies were in a bad way. Major Appleton said
he oughtn't to say it even if it was true and got quite red in
the face. Eleanor was pretty indignant and said he ought to
be arrested for making such a statement, and after everybody
had left she and Eveline had quite a quarrel. 'What will that
young Frenchman be thinking of us? You're a darling, Eveline
dear, but you have the vulgarest friends. I don't know where
you pick them up, and that Felton woman drank four cocktails,
a quart of beaujolais, and three cognacs, I kept tabs on her
myself.' Eveline started to laugh and they both got to laughing.
But Eleanor said that their life was getting much too bohemian
and that it wasn't right with the war on and things going so
dreadfully in Italy and Russia and the poor boys in the trenches
and all that.

That winter Paris gradually filled up with Americans in
uniform, and staffcars, and groceries from the Red Cross supply
store; and Major Moorehouse, who, it turned out, was an old
friend of Eleanor's, arrived straight from Washington to take
charge of the Red Cross publicity. Everybody was talking
about him before he came because he'd been one of the bestknown publicity experts in New York before the war. There
was no one who hadn't heard of J. Ward Moorehouse. There
was a lot of scurry around the office when word came around

that he'd actually landed in Brest and everybody was nervous worrying where the axe was going to fall.

The morning he arrived, the first thing Eveline noticed was that Eleanor had had her hair curled. Then just before noon the whole publicity department was asked into Major Wood's office to meet Major Moorehouse. He was a biggish man with blue eyes and hair so light it was almost white. His uniform fitted well and his Sam Browne belt and his puttees shone like glass. Eveline thought at once that there was something sincere and appealing about him, like about her father, that she liked. He looked young, too, in spite of the thick jowl, and he had a slight Southern accent when he talked. He made a little speech about the importance of the work the Red Cross was doing to keep up the morale of civilians and combatants, and that their publicity ought to have two aims, to stimulate giving among the folks back home and to keep people informed of the progress of the work. The trouble now was that people didn't know enough about what a valuable effort the Red Cross workers were making and were too prone to listen to the criticisms of pro-Germans working under the mask of pacifism and knockers and slackers always ready to carp and criticize; and that the American people and the warwracked populations of the Allied countries must be made to know the splendid sacrifice the Red Cross workers were making, as splendid in its way as the sacrifice of the dear boys in the trenches.

'Even at this moment, my friends, we are under fire, ready to make the supreme sacrifice that civilization shall not perish from the earth.' Major Wood leaned back in his swivelchair and let out a squeak that made everybody look up with a start and several people looked out of the window as if they expected to see a shell from Big Bertha hurtling right in on them. 'You see,' said Major Moorehouse eagerly, his blue eyes snapping, 'that is what we must make people feel . . . the catch in the throat, the wrench to steady the nerves, the determination to carry on.'

Eveline felt stirred in spite of herself. She looked a quick sideways look at Eleanor, who looked cool and lilylike as she had when she was listening to Maurice tell about the young Christ of the gasattack. Can't ever tell what she's thinking, though, said Eveline to herself.

That afternoon when J. W., as Eleanor called Major Moorehouse, came down to have a cup of tea with them, Eveline felt that she was being narrowly watched and minded her *p*'s and *q*'s as well as she could; it is the financial adviser; she was giggling about it inside. He looked a little haggard and didn't say much, and winced noticeably when they talked about air-raids moonlight nights, and how President Poincaré went around in person every morning to visit the ruins and condole with the survivors. He didn't stay long and went off some place in a staffcar to confer with some high official or other. Eveline thought he looked nervous and uneasy and would rather have stayed with them. Eleanor went out on the landing of the stairs with him and was gone some time. Eveline watched her narrowly when she came back into the room, but her face had its accustomed look of finely chiseled calm. It was on the tip of Eveline's tongue to ask her if Major Moorehouse was her . . . her . . . but she couldn't think of a way of putting it.

Eleanor didn't say anything for some time; then she shook her head and said, 'Poor Gertrude.'

'Who's that?'

Eleanor's voice was just a shade tinny, 'J. W.'s wife . . . she's in a sanitarium with a nervous breakdown . . . the strain, darling, this terrible war.'

Major Moorehouse went down to Italy to reorganize the publicity of the American Red Cross there, and a couple of weeks later Eleanor got orders from Washington to join the Rome office. That left Eveline alone with Yvonne in the apartment.

It was a chilly, lonely winter and working with all these relievers was just too tiresome, but Eveline managed to hold her job and to have some fun sometimes in the evening with Raoul, who would come around and take her out to some petite boîte or other that he'd always say was very boring. He took her to the Noctambules where you could sometimes get drinks after the legal hours; or up to a little restaurant on the Butte of Montmartre where one cold moonlit January night they stood on the porch of the Sacré Coeur and saw the Zeppelins come over. Paris stretched out cold and dead as if all the tiers of roofs and domes were carved out of snow and the shrapnel sparkled frostily overhead and the searchlights were antennae of great insects moving through the milky darkness. At intervals came red snorting flares of the incendiary bombs. Just once they caught sight of two tiny silver cigars overhead. They looked higher than the moon.

Eveline found that Raoul's arm that had been around her waist had slipped up and that he had his hand over her breast.

'C'est fou tu sais . . . c'est fou tu sais,' he was saying in a singsong voice, he seemed to have forgotten his English. After that they talked French and Eveline thought she loved him terribly much. After the breloque had gone through the streets, they walked home across dark silent Paris. At one corner a gendarme came up and asked Lemonnier for his papers. He read them through painfully in the faint blue glow of a corner light, while Eveline stood by breathless, feeling her heart pound. The gendarme handed back the papers, saluted, apologized profusely, and walked off. Neither of them said anything about it, but Raoul seemed to be taking it for granted he was going to sleep with her at her apartment. They walked home briskly through the cold black streets, their footsteps clacking sharply on the cobbles. She hung on his arm; there was something tight and electric and uncomfortable in the way their hips occasionally touched as they walked.

Her house was one of the few in Paris that didn't have a concierge. She unlocked the door and they climbed shivering together up the cold stone stairs. She whispered to him to be quiet, because of her maid. 'It is very boring,' he whispered; his lips brushed warm against her ear. 'I hope you won't think it's too boring.'

While he was combing his hair at her dressingtable, taking little connoisseur's sniffs at her bottles of perfume, preening himself in the mirror without haste and embarrassment, he said, 'Charmante Eveline, would you like to be my wife? It could be arranged, don't you know. My uncle who is the head of the family is very fond of Americans. Of course it would be very boring, the contract and all that.'

'Oh, no, that wouldn't be my idea at all,' she whispered, giggling and shivering from the bed. Raoul gave her a furious offended look, said goodnight very formally and left.

When the trees began to bud outside her window and the flowerwomen in the markets began to sell narcissuses and daffodils, the feeling that it was spring made her long months alone in Paris seem drearier than ever. Jerry Burnham had gone to Palestine; Raoul Lemonnier had never come to see her again; whenever he was in town Major Appleton came around and paid her rather elaborate attentions, but he was just too tiresome. Eliza Felton was driving an ambulance attached to a U.S. basehospital on the Avenue du Bois de Boulogne and would come around those Sundays when she was off duty and make Eveline's life miserable with her complaints that Eveline was not the free pagan soul she'd thought at first. She said that nobody loved her and that she was praying for the Bertha with her number on it that would end it all. It got so bad that Eveline wasn't able to stay in the house at all on Sunday and often spent the afternoon in her office reading Anatole France.

Then Yvonne's crotchets were pretty trying; she tried to run Eveline's life with her tightlipped comments. When Don Stevens turned up for a leave, looking more haggard than ever in the gray uniform of the Quaker outfit, it was a godsend, and Eveline decided maybe she'd been in love with him after all. She told Yvonne he was her cousin and that they'd been brought up like brother and sister and put him up in Eleanor's room.

Don was in a tremendous state of excitement about the success of the Bolsheviki in Russia, ate enormously, drank all the wine in the house, and was full of mysterious references to underground forces he was in touch with. He said all the armies were mutinous and that what had happened at Caporetto would happen on the whole front; the German soldiers were ready for revolt, too, and that would be the beginning of the world revolution. He told her about the mutinies at Verdun, about long trainloads of soldiers he'd seen going up to an attack, crying, 'À bas la guerre,' and shooting at the gendarmes as they went.

'Eveline, we're on the edge of gigantic events. . . . The workingclasses of the world won't stand for this nonsense any longer . . . damn it, the war will have been almost worth while if we get a new Socialist civilization out of it.' He leaned across the table and kissed her right under the thin nose of Yvonne, who was bringing in pancakes with burning brandy on them. He wagged his finger at Yvonne and almost got a smile out of her by the way he said, 'Après la guerre finie.'

That spring and summer things certainly did seem shaky, almost as if Don were right. At night she could hear the gigantic surf of the guns in continuous barrage on the crumpling front. The office was full of crazy rumors: the British Fifth Army had turned and run, the Canadians had mutinied and seized Amiens, spies were disabling all the American planes, the Austrians were breaking through in Italy again. Three times the Red Cross office had orders to pack up their records and be ready to move out of Paris. In the face of all that, it was hard for the publicity department to keep up the proper cheerful attitude in their releases, but Paris kept on filling up reassuringly with American faces, American M.P.'s, Sam Browne belts, and canned goods; and in July Major Moorehouse, who had just arrived back from the States, came into the office with a firsthand account of Château Thierry and announced that the war would be over in a year.

The same evening he asked Eveline to dine with him at the Café de la Paix and to do it she broke a date she had with Jerry Burnham, who had gotten back from the Near East and the Balkans and was full of stories of cholera and calamity. J. W. ordered a magnificent dinner; he said Eleanor had told him to see if Eveline didn't need a little cheering up. He talked about the gigantic era of expansion that would dawn for America after the war. America the good Samaritan healing the wounds of wartorn Europe. It was as if he was rehearsing a speech; when he got to the end of it he looked at Eveline with a funny deprecatory smile and said, 'And the joke of it is, it's true,' and Eveline laughed and suddenly found that she liked J. W. very much indeed.

She had on a new dress she'd bought at Paquin's with some money her father had sent her for her birthday, and it was a relief after the uniform. They were through eating before they had really gotten started talking. Eveline wanted to try to get him to talk about himself. After dinner they went to Maxim's, but that was full up with brawling drunken aviators, and the rumpus seemed to scare J. W. so that Eveline suggested to him that they go down to her place and have a glass of wine. When they got to the Quai de la Tournelle, just as they were stepping out of J. W.'s staffcar she caught sight of Don Stevens walking down the street. For a second she hoped he wouldn't see them, but he turned around and ran back. He had a young fellow with him in a private's uniform whose name was Johnson. They all went up and sat around glumly in her parlor. She and J. W. couldn't seem to talk about anything but Eleanor, and the other two sat glumly in their chairs looking embarrassed until J. W. got to his feet, went down to his staffcar, and left.

'God damn it, if there's anything I hate it's a Red Cross Major,' broke out Don as soon as the door closed behind J. W.

Eveline was angry. 'Well, it's no worse than being a fake Quaker,' she said icily.

'You must forgive our intruding, Miss Hutchins,' mumbled the doughboy who had a blond Swedish look.

'We wanted to get you to come out to a café or something, but it's too late now,' started Don crossly.

The doughboy interrupted him, 'I hope, Miss Hutchins, you don't mind our intruding, I mean my intruding . . . I begged Don to bring me along. He's talked so much about you and it's a year since I've seen a real nice American girl.'

He had a deferential way of talking and a whiny Minnesota accent that Eveline hated at first, but by the time he excused himself and left, she liked him and stood up for him when Don said, 'He's an awful sweet guy, but there's something sappy about him. I was afraid you wouldn't like him.' She wouldn't let Don spend the night with her as he'd expected and he went away looking very sullen.

In October Eleanor came back with a lot of antique Italian painted panels she'd picked up for a song. In the Red Cross office there were more people than were needed for the work and she and Eleanor and J. W. took a tour of the Red Cross canteens in the east of France in a staffcar. It was a wonderful trip, the weather was good for a wonder, almost like American October, they had lunch and dinner at regimental headquarters and army corps headquarters and divisional headquarters everywhere, and all the young officers were so nice to them, and J. W. was in such a good humor and kept them laughing all the time, and they saw field batteries firing and an airplane duel and sausage balloons and heard the shriek of an arrivé. It was during that trip that Eveline began to notice for the first time something cool in Eleanor's manner that hurt her; they'd been such good friends the first week Eleanor had gotten back from Rome.

Back in Paris it suddenly got very exciting, so many people they knew turned up, Eveline's brother George who was an interpreter at the headquarters of the S.O.S. and a Mr Robbins, a friend of J. W.'s who was always drunk and had a very funny way of talking, and Jerry Burnham and a lot of newspapermen and Major Appleton who was now a colonel. They had little dinners and parties and the main difficulty was sorting out ranks and getting hold of people who mixed properly. Fortunately their friends were all officers or correspondents who ranked as officers. Only once Don Stevens turned up just before they were having Major Appleton and Brigadier General Byng to dinner, and Eveline's asking him to stay made things very awkward because the General thought Quakers were slackers of the worst kind, and Don flared up and said a pacifist could be a better patriot than a staff officer in a soft job and that patriotism was a crime against humanity anyway. It would have been very disagreeable if Major Appleton who had drunk a great many cocktails hadn't broken through the little gilt chair he was sitting on and the General had laughed and kidded the Major with a bad pun about avoir due poise that took everybody's mind off the argument. Eleanor was very sore about Don, and after the guests had left she and Eveline had a stand-up quarrel. Next morning Eleanor wouldn't speak to her; Eveline went out to look for another apartment.

# Newsreel 28

*Oh the eagles they fly high*
*In Mobile, in Mobile*

Americans swim broad river and scale steep banks of canal in brilliant capture of Dun. It is a remarkable fact that the Compagnie Générale Transatlantique, more familiarly known as the French Line, has not lost a single vessel in its regular passenger service during the entire period of the war

RED FLAG FLIES ON BALTIC

'I went through Egypt to join Allenby,' he said. 'I flew in an aeroplane making the journey in two hours that it took the children of Israel forty years to make. That is something to set people thinking of the progress of modern science.'

*Lucky cows don't fly*
*In Mobile, in Mobile*

PERSHING FORCES FOE FURTHER BACK

SINGS FOR WOUNDED SOLDIERS; NOT SHOT
AS SPY

*Je donnerais Versailles*
*Paris et Saint Denis*
*Les tours de Notre Dame*
*Les clochers de mon pays*

HELP THE FOOD ADMINISTRATION BY REPORTING
WAR PROFITEERS

the completeness of the accord reached on most points by the conferees caused satisfaction and even some surprise among participants

REDS FORCE MERCHANT VESSELS TO FLEE

HUNS ON RUN

*Auprès de ma blonde*
*Qu'il fait bon fait bon fait bon*
*Auprès de ma blonde*
*Qu'il fait bon dormir*

CHEZ LES SOCIALISTES LES AVEUGLES SONT ROI

The German government requests the President of the United States of America to take steps for the restoration of peace, to notify all the belligerents of this request and to invite them to delegate plenipotentiaries for the purpose of taking up negotiations. The German government accepts, as a basis for the peace negotiations, the programme laid down by the President of the United States in his message to Congress of January 8th, 1918, and in his subsequent pronouncements, particularly in his address of September 27th, 1918. In order to avoid further bloodshed the German government requests the President of the United States to bring about the immediate conclusion of a general armistice on land, on the water, and in the air.

## Joe Williams

Joe had been hanging around New York and Brooklyn for a while, borrowing money from Mrs Olsen and getting tanked up all the time. One day she went to work and threw him out. It was damned cold and he had to go to a mission a couple of nights. He was afraid of getting arrested for the draft and he was fedup with every goddam thing; it ended by his going out as ordinary seaman on the *Appalachian*, a big new freighter bound for Bordeaux and Genoa. It kinder went with the way he felt being treated like a jailbird again and swobbing decks and chipping paint. In the fo'c'stle there was mostly country kids who'd never seen the sea and a few old bums who weren't good for anything. They got into a dirty blow four days out and shipped a small tidal wave that stove in two of the starboard lifeboats and the convoy got scattered and they found that the deck hadn't been properly caulked and the water kept coming down into the fo'c'stle. It turned out that Joe was the only man they had on board the mate could trust at the wheel, so they took him off scrubbing paint and in his four-hour tricks he had plenty of time to think about how lousy everything was. In Bordeaux he'd have liked to look up Marceline, but none of the crew got to go ashore.

The bosun went and got cockeyed with a couple of dough-boys and came back with a bottle of cognac for Joe, whom he'd taken a shine to, and a lot of latrine talk about how the frogs were licked and the limeys and the wops were licked something terrible and how if it hadn't been for us the Kaiser 'ud be riding into gay Paree any day and as it was it was nip and tuck. It was cold as hell. Joe and the bosun went and drank the cognac in the galley with the cook who was an oldtimer who'd been in the Klondike gold rush. They had the ship to themselves because the officers were all ashore taking a look at the mademosels and everybody else was asleep. The bosun said it was the end of civilization and the cook said he didn't give a f — k and Joe said he didn't give a f — k and the bosun said they were a couple of goddam Bolshevikis and passed out cold.

It was a funny trip round Spain and through the Straits and up the French coast to Genoa. All the way there was a single file of camouflaged freighters, Greeks and Britishers and Nor-wegians and Americans, all hugging the coast and creeping along with lifepreservers piled on deck and boats swung out on the davits. Passing 'em was another line coming back light, transports and colliers from Italy and Saloniki, white hospital ships, every kind of old tub out of the seven seas, rusty freighters with their screws so far out of the water you could hear 'em thrashing a couple of hours after they were hull down and out of sight. Once they got into the Mediterranean there were French and British battleships to seaward all the time and sillylooking destroyers with their long smokesmudges that would hail you and come aboard to see the ship's papers. Ashore it didn't look like the war a bit. The weather was sunny after they passed Gibraltar. The Spanish coast was green with bare pink and yellow mountains back of the shore and all scattered with little white houses like lumps of sugar that bunched up here and there into towns. Crossing the Gulf of Lyons in a drizzling rain and driving fog and nasty choppy sea, they came within an ace of running down a big felucca loaded with barrels of wine. Then they were bowling along the

French Riviera in a howling northwest wind, with the red-roofed towns all bright and shiny and the dry hills rising rocky behind them, and snowmountains standing out clear up above. After they passed Monte Carlo it was a circus, the houses were all pink and blue and yellow and there were tall poplars and tall pointed churchsteeples in all the valleys.

That night they were on the lookout for the big light marked on the chart for Genoa when they saw a red glare ahead. Rumor went around that the Heinies had captured the town and were burning it. The second mate put up to the skipper right on the bridge that they'd all be captured if they went any further and they'd better go back and put into Marseilles, but the skipper told him it was none of his goddam business and to keep his mouth shut till his opinion was asked. The glare got brighter as they got nearer. It turned out to be a tanker on fire outside the breakwater. She was a big new Standard Oil tanker, settled a little in the bows with fire pouring out of her and spreading out over the water. You could see the breakwater and the lighthouses and the town piling up the hills behind with red glitter in all the windows and the crowded ships in the harbor all lit up with red flare.

After they'd anchored, the bosun took Joe and a couple of the youngsters in the dinghy, and they went over to see what they could do aboard the tanker. The stern was way up out of water. So far as they could see there was no one on the ship. Some wops in a motorboat came up and jabbered at them, but they pretended not to understand what they meant. There was a fireboat standing by, too, but there wasn't anything they could do. 'Why the hell don't they scuttle her?' the bosun kept saying.

Joe caught sight of a ropeladder hanging into the water and pulled the dinghy over to it. Before the others had started yelling at him to come back, he was halfway up it. When he jumped down onto the deck from the rail he wondered what the hell he was doing up there. God damn it, I hope she does blow up, he said aloud to himself. It was bright as day up there. The forward part of the ship and the sea around it was burning like a lamp. He reckoned the boat had hit a mine or been torpedoed. The crew had evidently left in a hurry, as there were all sorts of bits of clothing and a couple of seabags by the davits aft where the lifeboats had been. Joe picked himself out a nice new sweater and then went down into the cabin. On a table he found a box of Havana cigars. He took out a cigar and lit one. It made him feel good to stand there and light a cigar with the goddam tanks ready to blow him to Halifax any minute. It was a good cigar, too. In a tissuepaper package on the table were seven pairs of ladies' silk stockings. Swell to take home to Del was his first thought. But then he remembered that he was through with all that. He stuffed the silk stockings into his pants pockets anyway, and went back on deck.

The bosun was yelling at him from the boat for chrissake to come along or he'd get left. He just had time to pick up a wallet on the companionway. 'It ain't gasoline, it's crude oil. She might burn for a week,' he yelled at the guys in the boat as he came slowly down the ladder pulling at the cigar as he came and looking out over the harbor, packed with masts and stacks and derricks, at the big marble houses and the old towers and porticoes and the hills behind all lit up in red. 'Where the hell's the crew?'

'Probably all cockeyed ashore by this time, where I'd like to be,' said the bosun. Joe divvied up the cigars, but he kept the silk stockings for himself. There wasn't anything in the wallet. 'Hellova note,' grumbled the bosun, 'haven't they got any chemicals?'

'These goddam wops wouldn't know what to do with 'em if they did have,' said one of the youngsters.

They rowed back to the *Appalachian* and reported to the skipper that the tanker had been abandoned and it was up to the port authorities to get rid of her.

All next day the tanker burned outside the breakwater. About nightfall another of her tanks went off like a roman candle and the fire began spreading more and more over the water. The *Appalachian* heaved her anchor and went up to the wharf.

That night Joe and the bosun went out to look at the town. The streets were narrow and had steps in them leading up the hill to broad avenues, with cafés and little tables out under the colonnades, where the pavements were all polished marble set in patterns. It was pretty chilly and they went into a bar and drank pink hot drinks with rum in them.

There they ran into a wop named Charley who'd been twelve years in Brooklyn and he took them to a dump where they ate a lot of spaghetti and fried veal and drank white wine. Charley told about how they treated you like a dog in the Eyetalian army and the pay was five cents a day and you didn't even get that, and Charley was all for il Presidente Veelson and the Fourteen Points and said soon they'd make peace without victory and bigga revoluzione in Italia and make bigga war on the Francese and the Inglese treata Eyetalian lika dirt. Charley brought in two girls he said were his cousins, Nedda and Dora, and one of 'em sat on Joe's knees and, boy, how she could eat spaghetti, and they all drank wine. It cost 'em all the money Joe had to pay for supper.

When he was taking Nedda up to bed up an outside staircase in the courtyard, he could see the flare of the tanker burning outside the harbor on the blank walls and tiled roofs of the houses.

Nedda wouldn't get undressed, but wanted to see Joe's money. Joe didn't have any money, so he brought out the silk stockings. She looked worried and shook her head, but she was darn pretty and had big black eyes and Joe wanted it bad and yelled for Charley and Charley came up the stairs and talked wop to the girl and said sure she'd take the silk stockings and wasn't America the greatest country in the world and tutti alleati and Presidente Veelson big man for Italia. But the girl wouldn't go ahead until they'd gotten hold of an old woman who was in the kitchen, who came wheezing up the stairs and felt the stockings, and musta said they were real silk and worth money, because the girl put her arm around Joe's neck and Charley said, 'Sure, pard, she sleepa with you all night, maka love good.'

But about midnight when the girl had gone to sleep, Joe got tired of lying there. He could smell the closets down in the court and a rooster kept crowing loud as the dickens like it was right under his ear. He got up and put on his clothes, and tiptoed out. The silk stockings were hanging on a chair. He picked 'em up and shoved them in his pockets again. His shoes creaked like hell. The street door was all bolted and barred and he had a devil of a time getting it open. Just as he got out in the street, a dog began to bark somewhere and he ran for it. He got lost in a million little narrow stone streets, but he figured that if he kept on going downhill he'd get to the harbor sometime. Then he began to see the pink glow from the burning tanker again on some of the housewalls and steered by that.

On some steep steps he ran into a couple of Americans in khaki uniforms and asked them the way and they gave him a drink out of a bottle of cognac and said they were on their way to the Eyetalian front and that there'd been a big retreat and that everything was cockeyed and they didn't know where the cockeyed front was and they were going to wait right there till the cockeyed front came right to them. He told 'em about the silk stockings and they thought it was goddam funny, and showed him the way to the wharf where the *Appalachian* was and they shook hands a great many times when they said goodnight and they said the wops were swine and he said they were princes to have shown him the way and they said he was a prince and they finished up the cognac and he went on board and tumbled into his bunk.

When the *Appalachian* cleared for home, the tanker was still burning outside the harbor. Joe came down with a dose on the trip home and he couldn't drink anything for several months and kinda steadied down when he got to Brooklyn. He went to the shoreschool run by the Shipping Board in Platt Institute and got his second mate's license and made trips back and forth between New York and St Nazaire all through that year on a new wooden boat built in Seattle called the *Owanda*, and a lot of trouble they had with her.

He and Janey wrote each other often. She was overseas with the Red Cross and very patriotic. Joe began to think that maybe she was right. Anyway, if you believed the papers the Heinies were getting licked, and it was a big opportunity for a young guy if you didn't get in wrong by being taken for a pro-German or a Bolshevik or some goddam thing. After all, as Janey kept writing, civilization had to be saved and it was up to us to do it. Joe started a savings account and bought him a Liberty bond.

Armistice night Joe was in St Nazaire. The town was wild. Everybody ashore, all the doughboys out of their camps, all the frog soldiers out of their barracks, everybody clapping everybody else on the back, pulling corks, giving each other drinks, popping champagne bottles, kissing every pretty girl, being kissed by old women, kissed on both cheeks by French veterans with whiskers. The mates and the skipper and the chief and a couple of naval officers they'd never seen before all started to have a big feed in a café, but they never got further than soup because everybody was dancing in the kitchen and they poured the cook so many drinks he passed out cold, and they all sat there singing and drinking champagne out of tumblers and cheering the Allied flags that girls kept carrying through.

Joe went cruising looking for Jeanette, who was a girl

he'd kinder taken up with whenever he was in St Nazaire. He wanted to find her before he got too zigzag. She'd promised to couchay with him that night before it turned out to be Armistice Day. She said she never couchayed with anybody else all the time the *Owanda* was in port and he treated her right and brought her beaucoup presents from L'Amérique, and du sucer and du cafay. Joe felt good, he had quite a wad in his pocket and, goddam it, American money was worth something these days; and a couple of pounds of sugar he'd brought in the pockets of his raincoat was better than money with the mademosels.

He went in back where there was a cabaret all red plush with mirrors and the music was playing *The Star-Spangled Banner* and everybody cried Vive L'Amérique and pushed drinks in his face as he came in and then he was dancing with a fat girl and the music was playing some damn foxtrot or other. He pulled away from the fat girl because he'd seen Jeanette. She had an American flag draped over her dress. She was dancing with a big sixfoot black Senegalese. Joe saw red. He pulled her away from the nigger who was a frog officer all full of gold braid and she said, 'Wazamatta chérie,' and Joe hauled off and hit the damn nigger as hard as he could right on the button, but the nigger didn't budge. The nigger's face had a black puzzled smiling look like he was just going to ask a question. A waiter and a coupla frog soldiers came up and tried to pull Joe away. Everybody was yelling and jabbering. Jeanette was trying to get between Joe and the waiter and got a sock in the jaw that knocked her flat. Joe laid out a couple of frogs and was backing off towards the door, when he saw in the mirror that a big guy in a blouse was bringing down a bottle on his head with both hands. He tried to swing around, but he didn't have time. The bottle crashed his skull and he was out.

# Newsreel 29

the arrival of the news caused the swamping of the city's telephone lines

> *Y fallait pas*
> *Y fallait pas*
> *Y fallait pas-a-a-a-a-yallez*

**BIG GUNS USED IN HAMBURG**

at the Custom House the crowd sang *The Star-Spangled Banner* under the direction of Byron R. Newton the Collector of the Port

**MORGAN ON WINDOWLEDGE**
**KICKS HEELS AS HE SHOWERS**
**CROWD WITH TICKERTAPE**

down at the battery the siren of the fireboat *New York* let out a shriek when the news reached there and in less time than it takes to say boo pandemonium broke loose all along the waterfront

> *Oh say can you see by the dawn's early light*

**WOMEN MOB CROWN PRINCE FOR KISSING**
**MODISTE**

> *Allons enfants de la patrie*
> *Le jour de gloire est arrivé*

> *It's the wrong way to tickle Mary*
> *It's the wrong place to go*

'We've been at war with the devil and it was worth all the suffering it entailed,' said William Howard Taft at a victory celebration here last night

> *Ka-ka-katee, beautiful Katee*
> *She's the only gu-gu-girl that I adore*
> *And when the moon shines*

Unipress, N.Y.

Paris urgent Brest Admiral Wilson who announced 16.00 (4 P.M.) Brest newspaper armistice been signed later notified unconfirmable meanwhile Brest riotously celebrating

TWO TROLLIES HELD UP BY GUNMAN IN QUEENS

*Over the cowshed*
*I'll be waiting at the ka-ka-kitchen door*

SPECIAL GRAND JURY ASKED TO INDICT
BOLSHEVISTS

the soldiers and sailors gave the only touch of color to the celebration. They went in wholeheartedly for having a good time, getting plenty to drink despite that fact that they were in uniform. Some of these returned fighters nearly caused a riot when they took an armful of stones and attemped to break an electric sign at Broadway and Fortysecond Street reading:

WELCOME HOME TO OUR HEROES

*Oh say can you see by the dawn's early light*
*What so proudly we hailed at the twilight's last gleaming*
*When the rocket's red glare the bombs bursting in air*
*Was proof to our eyes that the flag was still there*

## The Camera Eye (36)

when we emptied the rosies to leeward over the side every night after the last inspection we'd stop for a moment's gulp of the November gale the lash of spray in back of your ears for a look at the spume splintered off the leaping waves shipwreckers drowners of men (in their great purple floating mines rose and fell gently submarines traveled under them on an even keel) to glance at the sky veiled with scud to take our hands off the greasy handles of the cans full of slum they couldn't eat (nine meals nine dumpings of the leftover grub nine cussingmatches with the cockney steward who tried to hold out on the stewed apricots inspections AttenSHUN    click clack At Ease    shoot the flashlight in every corner of the tin pans    nine lineups along the heaving airless corridor of seasick seascared doughboys with their messkits in their hands)

Hey sojer tell me they've signed an armistice    tell me the war's over    they're takin' us home    latrine talk the hell you say    now I'll tell one    we were already leading the empty rosies down three flights of iron ladders into the heaving retching hold starting up with the full whenever the ship rolled a little slum would trickle out the side

## Meester Veelson

The year that Buchanan was elected President Thomas Woodrow Wilson

was born to a Presbyterian minister's daughter

in the manse at Staunton in the valley of Virginia; it was the old Scotch-Irish stock; the father was a Presbyterian minister, too, and a teacher of rhetoric in theological seminaries; the Wilsons lived in a universe of words linked into an incontrovertible firmament by two centuries of Calvinist divines,

God was the Word

and the Word was God.

Doctor Wilson was a man of standing who loved his home and his children and good books and his wife and correct syntax and talked to God every day at family prayers;

he brought his sons up

between the Bible and the dictionary.

The years of the Civil War

the years of life and drum and platoonfire and proclamations

the Wilsons lived in Augusta, Georgia; Tommy was a backward child, didn't learn his letters till he was nine, but when he learned to read, his favorite reading was Parson Weems's

*Life of Washington*

In 1870 Doctor Wilson was called to the Theological Seminary at Columbia, South Carolina; Tommy attended Davidson College,

where he developed a good tenor voice;

then he went to Princeton and became a debater and editor of the *Princetonian.* His first published article in the *Nassau Literary Magazine* was an appreciation of Bismarck.

Afterwards he studied law at the University of Virginia; young Wilson wanted to be a Great Man, like Gladstone and the eighteenth-century English Parliamentarians; he wanted to hold the packed benches spellbound in the cause of Truth; but law practice irked him; he was more at home in the booky air of libraries, lecturerooms, college chapel, it was a relief to leave his law practice at Atlanta and take a Historical Fellowship at Johns Hopkins; there he wrote *Congressional Government.*

At twentynine he married a girl with a taste for painting (while he was courting her he coached her in how to use the broad 'a') and got a job at Bryn Mawr teaching the girls History and Political Economy. When he got his Ph.D. from Johns Hopkins he moved to a professorship at Wesleyan, wrote articles, started a History of the United States,

spoke out for Truth Reform Responsible Government Democracy from the lecture platform, climbed all the steps of a brilliant university career; in 1901 the trustees of Princeton offered him the presidency;

he plunged into reforming the university, made violent friends and enemies, set the campus by the ears,

and the American people began to find on the front pages the name of Woodrow Wilson.

In 1909 he made addresses on Lincoln and Robert E. Lee and in 1910

the Democratic bosses of New Jersey, hardpressed by muckrakers and reformers, got the bright idea of offering the nomination for Governor to the stainless college president who attracted such large audiences

by publicly championing Right.

When Mr Wilson addressed the Trenton convention that nominated him for Governor he confessed his belief in the common man (the smalltown bosses and the wardheelers looked at each other and scratched their heads); he went on, his voice growing firmer:

*that is, the man by whose judgment I for one wish to be guided, so that as the tasks multiply, and as the days come when all will feel confusion and dismay, we may lift up our*

*eyes to the hills out of these dark valleys where the crags of
special privilege overshadow and darken our path, to where
the sun gleams through the great passage in the broken cliffs,
the sun of God,*

   *the sun meant to regenerate men,*

   *the sun meant to liberate them from their passion and
despair and lift us to those uplands which are the promised
land of every man who desires liberty and achievement.*

The smalltown bosses and the wardheelers looked at each
other and scratched their heads; then they cheered; Wilson
fooled the wiseacres and doublecrossed the bosses, was elected
by a huge plurality;

   so he left Princeton only halfreformed to be Governor of
New Jersey,

   and became reconciled with Bryan

   at the Jackson Day dinner: when Bryan remarked, 'I of
course knew that you were not with me in my position on the
currency,' Mr Wilson replied, 'All I can say, Mr Bryan, is
that you are a great big man.'

   He was introduced to Colonel House,

   that amateur Merlin of politics who was spinning his webs
at the Hotel Gotham,

   and at the convention in Baltimore the next July the
upshot of the puppetshow staged for sweating delegates by
Hearst and House behind the scenes, and Bryan booming in
the corridors with a handkerchief over his wilted collar, was
that Woodrow Wilson was nominated for the presidency.

   The bolt of the Progressives in Chicago from Taft to T.R.
made his election sure;

   so he left the State of New Jersey halfreformed

   (pitiless publicity was the slogan of the Shadow Lawn
Campaign)

   and went to the White House

   our twentyeighth President.

   While Woodrow Wilson drove up Pennsylvania Avenue
beside Taft, the great buttertub, who as President had been
genially undoing T.R.'s reactionary efforts to put business
under the control of the government,

   J. Pierpont Morgan sat playing solitaire in his back office
on Wall Street, smoking twenty black cigars a day, cursing the
follies of democracy.

   Wilson flayed the interests and branded privilege, refused

to recognize Huerta and sent the militia to the Rio Grande,
    to assume a policy of watchful waiting. He published *The New Freedom* and delivered his messages to Congress in person, like a college president addressing the faculty and students. At Mobile he said:
    *I wish to take this occasion to say that the United States will never again seek one additional foot of territory by conquest;*
    and he landed the marines at Vera Cruz.

    *We are witnessing a renaissance of public spirit, a re-awakening of sober public opinion, a revival of the power of the people, the beginning of an age of thoughtful reconstruction...*
    but the World had started spinning round Sarajevo.
    First it was *neutrality in thought and deed*, then *too proud to fight* when the *Lusitania* sinking and the danger to the Morgan loans and the stories of the British and French propagandists set all the financial centers in the East bawling for war, but the suction of the drumbeat and the guns was too strong; the best people took their fashions from Paris and their broad 'a's' from London, and T. R. and the House of Morgan.
    Five months after his re-election on the slogan *He kept us out of war*, Wilson pushed the Armed Ship Bill through Congress and declared that a state of war existed between the United States and the Central Powers:
    *Force without stint or limit, force to the utmost.*

    Wilson became the state (war is the health of the state), Washington his Versailles, manned the socialized government with dollar-a-year men out of the great corporations and ran the big parade
    of men munitions groceries mules and trucks to France. Five million men stood at attention outside of their tarpaper barracks every sundown while they played *The Star-Spangled Banner.*
    War brought the eighthour day, women's votes, prohibition, compulsory arbitration, high wages, high rates of interest, cost plus contracts, and the luxury of being a Gold Star Mother.
    If you objected to making the world safe for cost plus democracy you went to jail with Debs.
    Almost too soon the show was over, Prince Max of Baden was pleading for the Fourteen Points, Foch was occupying

the bridgeheads on the Rhine, and the Kaiser, out of breath, ran for the train down the platform at Potsdam wearing a silk hat and some say false whiskers.

With the help of *Almighty God, Right, Truth, Justice, Freedom, Democracy, the Selfdetermination of Nations, No indemnities no annexations,*

and Cuban sugar and Caucasian manganese and Northwestern wheat and Dixie cotton, the British blockade, General Pershing, the taxicabs of Paris and the seventyfive gun,

we won the war.

On December 4, 1918, Woodrow Wilson, the first President to leave the territory of the United States during his presidency, sailed for France on board the *George Washington,*

the most powerful man in the world.

In Europe they knew what gas smelt like and the sweet sick stench of bodies buried too shallow and the gray look of the skin of starved children; they read in the papers that Meester Veelson was for peace and freedom and canned goods and butter and sugar;

he landed at Brest with his staff of experts and publicists after a rough trip on the *George Washington.*

La France héroique was there with the speeches, the singing schoolchildren, the mayors in their red sashes. (Did Meester Veelson see the gendarmes at Brest beating back the demonstration of dockyard workers who came to meet him with red flags?)

At the station in Paris he stepped from the train onto a wide red carpet that led him, between rows of potted palms, silk hats, legions of honor, decorated busts of uniforms, frockcoats, rosettes, boutonnières, to a Rolls-Royce. (Did Meester Veelson see the women in black, the cripples in their little carts, the pale anxious faces along the streets; did he hear the terrible anguish of the cheers as they hurried him and his new wife to the Hôtel de Murat, where in rooms full of brocade, gilt clocks, Buhl cabinets, and ormolu cupids the presidential suite had been prepared?)

While the experts were organizing the procedure of the peace conference, spreading green baize on the tables, arranging the protocols,

the Wilsons took a tour to see for themselves: the day after Christmas they were entertained at Buckingham Palace; at Newyear's they called on the Pope and on the microscopic Italian King at the Quirinal. (Did Meester Veelson know that in the peasants' wargrimed houses along the Brenta and the Piave they were burning candles in front of his picture cut out of the illustrated papers?) (Did Meester Veelson know that the people of Europe spelled a challenge to oppression out of the Fourteen Points, as centuries before they had spelled a challenge to oppression out of the ninetyfive articles Martin Luther nailed to the churchdoor in Wittenberg?)

January 18, 1919, in the midst of serried uniforms, cocked hats, and gold braid, decorations, epaulettes, orders of merit and knighthood, the High Contracting Parties, the Allied and Associated Powers, met in the Salon de l'Horloge at the Quai d'Orsay to dictate the peace,

but the grand assembly of the peace conference was too public a place to make peace in,

so the High Contracting Parties

formed the Council of Ten, went into the Gobelin Room, and, surrounded by Rubens's History of Marie de Medici,

began to dictate the peace.

But the Council of Ten was too public a place to make peace in,

so they formed the Council of Four.

Orlando went home in a huff,

and then there were three:

Clemenceau,

Lloyd George,

Woodrow Wilson.

Three old men shuffling the pack,

dealing out the cards:

the Rhineland, Danzig, the Polish Corridor, the Ruhr, self-determination of small nations, the Saar, League of Nations, mandates, the Mespot, Freedom of the Seas, Transjordania, Shantung, Fiume, and the Island of Yap:

machinegun fire and arson

starvation, lice, cholera, typhus;

oil was trumps.

Woodrow Wilson believed in his father's God,

so he told the parishioners in the little Lowther Street Congregational Church where his grandfather had preached in Carlisle in Scotland, a day so chilly that the newspapermen sitting in the old pews all had to keep their overcoats on.

On April 7 he ordered the *George Washington* to be held

at Brest with steam up ready to take the American delegation
home;

but he didn't go.

On April 19 sharper Clemenceau and sharper Lloyd
George got him into their little cozy threecard game they
called the Council of Four.

On June 28 the Treaty of Versailles was ready

and Wilson had to go back home to explain to the
politicians, who'd been ganging up on him meanwhile in the
Senate and House, and to sober public opinion and to his
father's God how he'd let himself be trimmed and how far
he'd made the world safe

for democracy and the New Freedom.

From the day he landed in Hoboken, he had his back to
the wall of the White House, talking to save his faith in words,
talking to save his faith in the League of Nations, talking to
save his faith in himself, in his father's God.

He strained every nerve of his body and brain, every
agency of the government he had under his control (if anybody
disagreed he was a crook or a red; no pardon for Debs).

In Seattle the wobblies whose leaders were in jail, in
Seattle the wobblies whose leaders had been lynched, who'd
been shot down like dogs, in Seattle the wobblies lined four
blocks as Wilson passed, stood silent with their arms folded
staring at the great liberal as he was hurried past in his car,
huddled in his overcoat, haggard with fatigue, one side of his
face twitching. Then men in overalls, the workingstiffs let him
pass in silence after all the other blocks of handclapping and
patriotic cheers.

In Pueblo, Colorado, he was a gray man hardly able to
stand, one side of his face twitching:

*Now that the mists of this great question have cleared
away, I believe that men will see the Truth, eye for eye and
face to face. There is one thing the American People always
rise to and extend their hand to, that is, the truth of justice
and of liberty and of peace. We have accepted that truth and
we are going to be led by it, and it is going to lead us, and
through us the world, out into pastures of quietness and peace
such as the world never dreamed of before.*

That was his last speech;

on the train to Wichita he had a stroke. He gave up the
speaking tour that was to sweep the country for the League

of Nations. After that he was a ruined paralyzed man barely able to speak;

the day he gave up the presidency to Harding the joint committee of the Senate and House appointed Henry Cabot Lodge, his lifelong enemy, to make the formal call at the executive office in the Capitol and ask the formal question whether the President had any message for the Congress assembled in joint session;

Wilson managed to get to his feet, lifting himself painfully by the two arms of the chair. 'Senator Lodge, I have no further communication to make, thank you . . . Good morning,' he said.

In 1924 on February 3, he died.

# Newsreel 30

### MONSTER GUNS REMOVED?

*Longhaired preachers come out every night*
*Try to tell you what's wrong and what's right*
*But when asked about something to eat*
*They will answer in accents so sweet*

### PRESIDENT HAS SLIGHT COLD AT SEA

Special chef and staff of waiters and kitchen helpers drafted from the Biltmore

Every comfort provided

Orchestra to play during meals and Navy Yard Band to play for deck music

*You will eat bye and bye*
*In that glorious land above the sky*

the city presents a picture of the wildest destruction, especially around the General Post Office which had been totally destroyed by fire, nothing but ruins remaining

*Work and pray*
*Live on hay*

### THREE TRUCKLOADS OF RECORDS GATHERED HERE

eleven men were killed and twentythree injured, some of them seriously as the result of an explosion of fulminate of mercury in the priming unit of one of the cap works of the E. I. duPont de Nemours Powder Company; in the evening Mrs Wilson released carrier pigeons . . . *and through it all how fine the spirit of the nation was, what unity of purpose, what untiring zeal, what elevation of purpose ran through all its splendid display of strength, its untiring accomplishment. I have said that those of us who stayed at home to do the work of organization and supply would always wish*

*we had been with the men we sustained by our labor, but
we can never be ashamed* . . . in the diningroom music
was furnished by a quartet of sailors

> *You'll get pie*
> *In the sky*
> *When you die*

GORGAS WOULD PUT SOLDIERS IN HUTS

EIGHT HUNDRED FIGHTING MEN CHEER
BOLSHEVIKI

All the arrangements were well ordered but the crowd
was kept at a distance. The people gathered on the hills near
the pier raised a great shout when the President's launch
steamed up. A détour was made from the Champs Élysées
to cross the Seine over the Alexander III Bridge which
recalled another historic pageant when Paris outdid herself
to honor an absolute ruler in the person of the czar.

ADDRESSED FOURTEEN HUNDRED MAYORS
FROM PALACE BALCONY

BRITISH NAVY TO BE SUPREME, DECLARES
CHURCHILL

## The Camera Eye (37)

*alphabetically according to rank* tapped out with two
cold index fingers on the company Corona *Allots Class A
& B Ins prem C & D*

Atten—SHUN snap to the hooks and eyes at my throat
constricting the adamsapple bringing together the U.S. and
the Caduceus

At Ease

outside they're drilling in the purple drizzle of a winter
afternoon in Ferrières en Gatinais, Abbaye founded by
Clovis over the skeletons of three disciples of notre seigneur
Jésus-Christ *3rd Lib Loan Sec of Treas* Altian Politian and
Hermatian *4th Lib Loan Sec of Treas must be on CL E or*

*other form Q.M.C. 38* now it's raining hard and the gutters gurgle there's tinkling from all the little glassgreen streams

Alcuin was prior once    and millwheels grind behind the mossed stone walls and Clodhilde and Clodomir were buried here

*promotions only marked under gains* drowsily clacked out on the rusteaten Corona in the cantonment of O'Rielly's Traveling Circus alone except for the undertaker soldiering in his bunk and the dry hack of the guy that has TB that the MO was never sober enough to examine

> *Iodine will make you happy*
> *Iodine will make you well*

fourthirty    the pass comes alive among the CC pills in my pocket

the acting QM Sarge and the Topkicker go out through the gate of USAAS base camp in their slickers in the lamplit rain and make their way without a cent in their OD to the Cheval Blanc where by chevrons and parleyvooing they bum drinks and omelettes avec pommes frites and kid applecheeked Madeleine may wee

in the dark hallway to the back room the boys are lined up waiting to get in to the girl in black from out of town to drop ten francs and hurry to the propho station *sol viol sk not L D viol Go 41/14 rd. sent S C M*

outside it's raining on the cobbled town inside we drink vin rouge parlezvous froglegs may wee couchez avec and the old territorial at the next table drinks illegal pernod and remarks    Toute est bien fait dans la nature à la votre aux Américains

> *Après la guerre finee*
> *Back to the States for me*

Dans la mort il n'y a rien de terrible    Quand on va mourir on pense à tout mais vite

the first day in the year dismissed after rollcall I went walking with a fellow from Philadelphia along the purple wintryrutted roads under the purple embroidery of the pleached trees full of rooks cackling overhead over the

ruddier hills to a village    we're going to walk a long way
get good wine full of Merovingian names millwheels glassgreen streams where the water gurgles out of old stone
gargoyles Madeleine's red apples the smell of beech leaves
we're going to drink wine the boy from Philadelphia's got
beaucoup jack    wintry purpler wine    the sun breaks out
through the clouds on the first day in the year

    in the first village
    we stop in our tracks
    to look at a waxwork

the old man has shot the pretty peasant girl who looks
like Madeleine but younger she lies there shot in the left
breast in the blood in the ruts of the road pretty and plump
as a little quail

The old man then took off one shoe and put the shotgun under his chin pulled the trigger with his toe and blew
the top of his head off    we stand looking at the bare foot
and the shoe and the foot in the shoe and the shot girl and the
old man with a gunnysack over his head and the dirty bare
toe he pulled the trigger with    Faut pas toucher until the
commissaire comes procès verbale

    on this first day
    of the year the sun
    is shining

washing and dressing hastily they came to the ground-floor at the brusque call of the commissaries, being assembled in one of the rear rooms in the basement of the house. Here they were lined up in a semicircle along the wall, the young grandduchesses trembling at the unusual nature of the orders given and at the gloomy hour. They more than suspected the errand upon which the commissaries had come. Addressing the Czar, Yarodsky, without the least attempt to soften his announcement, stated that they must all die and at once. The revolution was in danger, he stated, and the fact that there were still the members of the reigning house living added to that danger. Therefore, to remove them was the duty of all Russian patriots. 'Thus your life is ended,' he said in conclusion.

'I am ready,' was the simple announcement of the Czar, while the Czarina, clinging to him, loosed her hold long enough to make the sign of the cross, an example followed by the Grandduchess Olga and by Doctor Botkin.

The Czarevitch, paralyzed with fear, stood in stupefaction beside his mother, uttering no sound either in supplication or protest, while his three sisters and the other granduchesses sank to the floor trembling.

Yarodsky drew his revolver and fired the first shot. A volley followed and the prisoners reeled to the ground. Where the bullets failed to find their mark the bayonet put the finishing touches. The mingled blood of the victims not only covered the floor of the room where the execution took place but ran in streams along the hallway.

## *Daughter*

The Trents lived in a house on Pleasant Avenue that was the finest street in Dallas that was the biggest and fastest growing town in Texas that was the biggest State in the Union and had the blackest soil and the whitest people and America was the greatest country in the world and Daughter was Dad's onlyest sweetest little girl. He real name was Anne Elizabeth Trent after poor dear mother who had died when she was a little tiny girl, but Dad and the boys called her Daughter. Buddy's real name was William Delaney Trent like Dad, who was a prominent attorney, and Buster's real name was Spencer Anderson Trent.

Winters they went to school and summers they ran wild on the ranch that Grandfather had taken up as a pioneer. When they'd been very little, there hadn't been any fences yet and still a few maverick steers out along the creekbottoms, but by the time Daughter was in highschool everything was fenced and they were building a macadam road out from Dallas and Dad went everywhere in the Ford instead of on his fine Arab stallion Mullah he'd been given by a stockman at the Fat Stock Show in Waco when the stockman had gone broke and hadn't been able to pay his lawyer's fee. Daughter had a creamcolored pony named Coffee who'd nod his head and paw with his hoof when he wanted a lump of sugar, but some of the girls she knew had cars, and Daughter and the boys kept after Dad to buy a car, a real car instead of that miserable old flivver he drove around the ranch.

When Dad bought a Pierce Arrow touringcar the spring Daughter graduated from highschool, she was the happiest girl in the world. Sitting at the wheel in a fluffy white dress the morning of Commencement outside the house waiting for Dad, who had just come out from the office and was changing his clothes, she had thought how much she'd like to be able to see herself sitting there in the not too hot June morning in the lustrous black shiny car among the shiny brass and nickel fixtures under the shiny paleblue big Texas sky in the middle of the big flat rich Texas country that ran for two hundred miles in every direction. She could see half her face in the little oval mirror on the mudguard. It looked red and sunburned under her sandybrown hair. If she only had red hair and a skin white like buttermilk like Susan Gillespie had, she was wishing when she saw Joe Washburn coming along the street dark and seriouslooking under his panama hat.

She fixed her face in a shy kind of smile just in time to have him say, 'How lovely you look, Daughter, you must excuse ma sayin' so.'

'I'm just waiting for Dad and the boys to go to the exercises. O Joe, we're late and I'm so excited. . . . I feel like a sight.' ~

'Well, have a good time.' He walked on hurriedly putting his hat back on his head as he went. Something hotter than the June sunshine had come out of Joe's very dark eyes and run in a blush over her face and down the back of her neck under her thin dress and down the middle of her bosom, where the little breasts that she tried never to think of were just beginning to be noticeable. At last Dad and the boys came out, all looking blond and dressedup and sunburned. Dad made her sit in the back seat with Bud who sat up stiff as a poker.

The big wind that had come up drove grit in their faces. After she caught sight of the brick buildings of the highschool and the crowd and the light dresses and the stands and the big flag with the stripes all wiggling against the sky, she got so excited she never remembered anything that happened.

That night, wearing her first evening dress at the dance, she came to in the feeling of tulle and powder and crowds, boys all stiff and scared in their dark coats, girls packing into the dressingroom to look at each other's dresses. She never said a word while she was dancing, just smiled and held her head a little to one side and hoped somebody would cut in. Half the time she didn't know who she was dancing with, just moved smiling in a cloud of pink tulle and colored lights; boys' faces bobbed in front of her, tried to say smarty ladykillerish things or else were shy and tonguetied, different colored faces on top of the same stiff bodies. Honestly, she was surprised when Susan Gillespie came up to her when they were getting their wraps to go home and giggled, 'My dear, you were the belle of the ball.' When Bud and Buster said so next morning and old black Emma who'd brought them all up after mother died came in from the kitchen and said, 'Lawsy, Miss Annie, folks is talkin' all over town about how you was the belle of the ball last night,' she felt herself blushing happily all over. Emma said she'd heard it from that noaccount yaller man on the milk route whose aunt worked at Mrs Washburn's, then she set down the popovers and went out with a grin as wide as a piano.

'Well, Daughter,' said Dad in his deep quiet voice, tapping
the top of her hand, 'I thought so myself, but I thought maybe
I was prejudiced.'

During the summer Joe Washburn, who'd just graduated
from law school at Austin and who was going into Dad's office
in the fall, came and spent two weeks with them on the ranch.
Daughter was just horrid to him, made old Hildreth give him
a mean little old oneeyed pony to ride, put horned toads in his
cot, would hand him hot chile sauce instead of catsup at table
or try to get him to put salt instead of sugar in his coffee. The
boys got so off her they wouldn't speak to her and Dad said
she was getting to be a regular tomboy, but she couldn't seem
to stop acting like she did.

Then one day they all rode over to eat supper on Clear Creek
and went swimming by moonlight in the deep hole there was
under the bluff. Daughter got a crazy streak in her after a
while and ran up and said she was going to dive from the edge
of the bluff. The water looked so good and the moon floated
shivering on top. They all yelled at her not to do it, but she
made a dandy dive right from the edge. But something was the
matter. She'd hit her head, it hurt terribly. She was swallowing
water, she was fighting a great weight that was pressing down
on her, that was Joe. The moonlight flowed out in a swirl,
leaving it all black, only she had her arms around Joe's neck,
her fingers were tightening around the ribbed muscles of his
arms. She came to with his face looking into hers and the moon
up in the sky again and warm stuff pouring over her forehead.
She was trying to say, 'Joe, I wanto, Joe, I wanto,' but it all
drained away into warm sticky black again, only she caught
his voice deep, deep . . . 'pretty near had me drowned too . . .'
and Dad, sharp and angry like in court, 'I told her she oughtn't
to dive off there.'

She came to herself again in bed with her head hurting
horribly and Doctor Winslow there, and the first thing she
thought was where was Joe and had she acted like a little silly
telling him she was crazy about him? But nobody said anything about it and they were all awful nice to her except Dad
came, still talking with his angry courtroom voice, and lectured
her for being foolhardy and a tomboy and having almost cost
Joe his life by the stranglehold she had on him when they'd
pulled them both out of the water. She had a fractured skull
and had to be in bed all summer and Joe was awful nice,
though he looked at her kinder funny out of his sharp black

eyes the first time he came in her room. As long as he stayed on the ranch he came to read to her after lunch. He read her all of *Lorna Doone* and half of *Nicholas Nickleby* and she lay there in bed, hot and cozy in her fever, feeling the rumble of his deep voice through the pain in her head and fighting all the time inside not to cry out like a little silly that she was crazy about him and why didn't he like her just a little bit. When he'd gone, it wasn't any fun being sick any more. Dad or Bud came and read to her sometimes, but most of the time she liked better reading to herself. She read all of Dickens, *Lorna Doone* twice, and Poole's *The Harbor*; that made her want to go to New York.

Next fall Dad took her North for a year in a finishing school in Lancaster, Pennsylvania. She was excited on the trip up on the train and loved every minute of it, but Miss Tyngs was horrid and the girls were all Northern girls and so mean and made fun of her clothes and talked about nothing but Newport, and Southampton, and matinée idols she'd never seen; she hated it. She cried every night after she'd gone to bed, thinking how she hated the school and how Joe Washburn would never like her now. When Christmas vacation came and she had to stay on with the two Miss Tyngs and some of the teachers who lived too far away to go home either, she just decided she wouldn't stand it any longer, and one morning before anybody was up she got out of the house, walked down to the station, bought herself a ticket to Washington, and got on the first westbound train with nothing but a toothbrush and a nightgown in her handbag. She was scared all alone on the train at first, but such a nice young Virginian who was a West Point Cadet got on at Havre de Grace where she had to change; they had the time of their lives together laughing and talking. In Washington he asked permission to be her escort in the nicest way and took her all around, to see the Capitol and the White House and the Smithsonian Institution and set her up to lunch at the New Willard and put her on the train for St Louis that night. His name was Paul English. She promised she'd write him every day of her life. She was so excited she couldn't sleep lying in her berth looking out of the window of the Pullman at the trees and the circling hills all in the faint glow of snow and now and then lights speeding by; she could remember exactly how he looked and how his hair was parted and the long confident grip of his hand when they said goodbye. She'd been a little nervous at first, but they'd been like old friends right from the beginning and he'd been so courteous and gentlemanly. He'd been her first pickup.

When she walked in on Dad and the boys at breakfast a sunny winter morning two days later, my, weren't they surprised; Dad tried to scold her, but Daughter could see that he was as pleased as she was. Anyway, she didn't care, it was so good to be home.

After Christmas she and Dad and the boys went for a week's hunting down near Corpus Christi and had the time of their lives and Daughter shot her first deer. When they got back to Dallas, Daughter said she wasn't going back to be finished, but that what she would like to do was go up to New York to stay with Ada Washburn, who was studying at Columbia, and to take courses where she'd really learn something. Ada was Joe Washburn's sister, an old maid but bright as a dollar, and was working for her Ph.D. in Education. It took a lot of arguing because Dad had set his heart on having Daughter go to a finishing school, but she finally convinced him and was off again to New York.

She was reading *Les Misérables* all the way up on the train and looking out at the grayishbrownish winter landscape that didn't seem to have any life to it after she left the broad hills of Texas, palegreen with winter wheat and alfalfa, feeling more and more excited and scared as hour by hour she got nearer New York. There was a stout motherly woman who'd lost her husband who got on the train at Little Rock and wouldn't stop talking about the dangers and pitfalls that beset a young woman's path in big cities. She kept such a strict watch on Daughter that she never got a chance to talk to the interesting-looking young man with the intense black eyes who boarded the train at St Louis and kept going over papers of some kind he had in a brown briefcase. She thought he looked a little like Joe Washburn. At last, when they were crossing New Jersey and there got to be more and more factories and grimy industrial towns, Daughter's heart got to beating so fast she couldn't sit still, but kept having to go out and stamp around in the cold raw air of the vestibule. The fat grayheaded conductor asked her with a teasing laugh if her beau was going to be down at the station to meet her, she seemed so anxious to get in. They were going through Newark then. Only one more stop. The sky was leadcolor over wet streets full of automobiles and a drizzly rain was pitting the patches of snow with gray. The train began to cross wide desolate saltmarshes, here and there broken by an uneven group of factory structures or a black river with steamboats on it. There didn't seem to be any people; it looked so cold over those marshes Daughter felt scared and lonely just looking at them and wished she was home. Then suddenly the train was in a tunnel, and the porter was piling all the bags in the front end of the car. She got into the fur coat Dad had bought her as a Christmas present and pulled her gloves on over her hands cold with excitement for fear that maybe Ada Washburn hadn't gotten her telegram or hadn't been able to come down to meet her.

But there she was on the platform in noseglasses and raincoat looking as oldmaidish as ever and a slightly younger girl with her who turned out to be from Waco and studying art. They had a long ride in a taxi up crowded streets full of slush with yellow and gray snowpiles along the sidewalks.

'If you'd have been here a week ago, Anne Elizabeth, I declare you'd have seen a real blizzard.'

'I used to think snow was like on Christmas cards,' said Esther Wilson, who was an interestinglooking girl with black eyes and a long face and a deep kind of tragicsounding voice. 'But it was just an illusion like a lot of things.'

'New York's no place for illusions,' said Ada sharply.

'It all looks kinder like a illusion to me,' said Daughter, looking out of the window of the taxicab.

Ada and Esther had a lovely big apartment on University Heights where they had fixed up the diningroom as a bedroom for Daughter. She didn't like New York, but it was exciting; everything was gray and grimy and the people all seemed to be foreigners and nobody paid any attention to you except now and then a man tried to pick you up on the street or brushed up against you in the subway, which was disgusting. She was signed up as a special student and went to lectures about Economics and English Literature and Art and talked a little occasionally with some boy who happened to be sitting next to her, but she was so much younger than anybody she met and she didn't seem to have the right line of talk to interest them. It was fun going to matinées with Ada sometimes or riding down all bundled up on top of the bus to go to the art museum with Esther on Sunday afternoons, but they were both of them so staid and grownup and all the time getting shocked by things she said and did.

When Paul English called up and asked her to go to a matinée with him one Saturday, she was very thrilled. They'd written a few letters back and forth, but they hadn't seen each other since Washington. She was all morning putting on first one dress and then the other, trying out different ways of doing her hair, and was still taking a hot bath when he called for her, so that Ada had to entertain him for the longest time. When she saw him all her thrill dribbled away, he looked so stiff and stuckup in his dress uniform. First thing she knew she was kidding him, and acting silly going downtown in the subway so that by the time they got to the Astor where he took her to lunch, he looked sore as a pup. She left him at the table and went to the ladies' room to see if she couldn't get her hair to look a little better than it did and got to talking with an elderly Jewish lady in diamonds who'd lost her pocketbook, and when she got back the lunch was standing cold on the table and Paul English was looking at his wristwatch uneasily. She didn't like the play and he tried to get fresh in the taxicab driving up Riverside Drive, although it was still broad daylight, and she slapped his face. He said she was the meanest girl he'd ever met and she said she liked being mean and if he didn't like it he knew what he could do. Before that she'd made up her mind that she'd crossed him off her list.

She went in her room and cried and wouldn't take any supper. She felt real miserable having Paul English turn out a pill like that. It was lonely not having anybody to take her out and no chance of meeting anybody because she had to go everywhere with those old maids. She lay on her back on the floor looking at the furniture from underneath like when she'd been little and thinking of Joe Washburn. Ada came in and found her in the silliest position lying on the floor with her legs in the air; she jumped up and kissed her all over her face and hugged her and said she'd been a little idiot, but it was all over now and was there anything to eat in the icebox.

When she met Edwin Vinal at one of Ada's Sunday evening parties that she didn't usually come out to on account of people sitting around so prim and talking so solemn and deep over their cocoa and cupcakes, it made everything different and she began to like New York. He was a scrawny kind of young fellow who was taking courses in sociology. He sat on a stiff chair with his cocoacup balanced uncomfortably in his hand and didn't seem to know where to put his legs. He didn't say anything all evening, but just as he was going, he picked up something Ada said about values and began to talk a blue streak, quoting all the time from a man named Veblen.

Daughter felt kind of attracted to him and asked who Veblen was, and he began to talk to her. She wasn't up on what he was talking about, but it made her feel lively inside to have him talking right to her like that. He had light hair and black eyebrows and lashes around very palegray eyes with little gold specks in them. She liked his awkward lanky way of moving around. Next evening he came to see her and brought her a volume of the *Theory of the Leisure Class* and asked her if she didn't want to go skating with him at the Saint Nicholas Rink. She went in her room to get ready and began to dawdle around powdering her face and looking at herself in the glass. 'Hey, Anne, for gosh sakes, we haven't got all night,' he yelled through the door. She had never had ice skates on her feet before, but she knew how to rollerskate, so with Edwin holding her arm she was able to get around the big hall with its band playing and all the tiers of lights and faces around the balcony. She had more fun than she'd had any time since she left home.

Edwin Vinal had been a social worker and lived in a settlement house and now he had a scholarship at Columbia, but he said the profs were too theoretical and never seemed to realize it was real people like you and me they were dealing with. Daughter had done churchwork and taken around baskets to poorwhite families at Christmas time and said she'd like to do some socialservice work right here in New York. As they were taking off their skates, he asked her if she really meant it and she smiled up at him and said, 'Hope I may die if I don't.'

So the next evening he took her downtown threequarters of an hour's ride in the subway and then a long stretch on a crosstown car to a settlement house on Grand Street where she had to wait while he gave an English lesson to a class of greasylooking young Lithuanians or Polaks or something like that. Then they walked around the streets and Edwin pointed out the conditions. It was like the Mexican part of San Antonio or Houston, only there were all kinds of foreigners. None of them looked as if they ever bathed and the streets smelt of garbage. There was laundry hanging out everywhere and signs in all kinds of funny languages. Edwin showed her some in Russian and Yiddish, one in Armenian and two in Arabic. The streets were awful crowded and there were pushcarts along the curb and peddlers everywhere and funny smells of cooking coming out of restaurants, and outlandish phonograph music. Edwin pointed out two tiredlooking painted girls who he said were streetwalkers, drunks stumbling out of a saloon, a young man

in a checked cap he said was a cadet drumming up trade for a
disorderly house, some sallowfaced boys he said were gunmen
and dope peddlers. It was a relief when they came up again out
of the subway way uptown where a springy wind was blowing
down the broad empty streets that smelt of the Hudson River.

'Well, Anne, how did you like your little trip to the under-
world?'

'All right,' she said after a pause. 'Another time I think I'll
take a gun in my handbag. . . . But all those people, Edwin,
how on earth can you make citizens out of them? We oughtn't
to let all these foreigners come over and mess up our country.'

'You're entirely wrong,' Edwin snapped at her. 'They'd all
be decent if they had a chance. We'd be just like them if we
hadn't been lucky enough to be born of decent families in small
prosperous American towns.'

'Oh, how can you talk so silly, Edwin; they're not white
people and they never will be. They're just like Mexicans or
somethin', or niggers.' She caught herself up and swallowed
the last word. The colored elevator boy was browsing on a
bench right behind her.

'If you're not the benightedest little heathen I ever saw,' said
Edwin teasingly. 'You're a Christian, aren't you, well, have
you ever thought that Christ was a Jew?'

'Well, I'm fallin' down with sleep and can't argue with you,
but I know you're wrong.' She went into the elevator and the
colored elevator boy got up yawning and stretching. The last
she saw of Edwin in the rapidly decreasing patch of light
between the floor of the elevator and the ceiling of the vestibule
he was shaking his fist at her. She threw him a kiss without
meaning to.

When she got in the apartment, Ada, who was reading in the
livingroom, scolded her a little for being so late, but she
pleaded that she was too tired and sleepy to be scolded. 'What
do you think of Edwin Vinal, Ada?'

'Why, my dear, I think he's a splendid young fellow, a little
restless, maybe, but he'll settle down. . . . Why?'

'Oh, I dunno,' said Daughter, yawning. 'Goodnight, Ada
darlin'.'

She took a hot bath and put a lot of perfume on and went
to bed, but she couldn't go to sleep. Her legs ached from the
greasy pavements and she could feel the walls of the tenements
sweating lust and filth and the smell of crowded bodies closing
in on her; in spite of the perfume she still had the rank garbagy

smell in her nose, and the dazzle of street lights and faces pricked her eyes. When she went to sleep, she dreamed she had rouged her lips and was walking up and down, up and down with a gun in her handbag; Joe Washburn walked by and she kept catching at his arm to try to make him stop, but he kept walking by without looking at her and so did Dad, and they wouldn't look when a big Jew with a beard kept getting closer to her and he smelt horrid of the East Side and garlic and waterclosets and she tried to get the gun out of her bag to shoot him and he had his arms around her and was pulling her face close to his. She couldn't get the gun out of the handbag and behind the roaring clatter of the subway in her ears was Edwin Vinal's voice saying, 'You're a Christian, aren't you? You're entirely wrong . . . a Christian, aren't you? Have you ever thought that Christ would have been just like them if he hadn't been lucky enough to have been born of decent people . . . a Christian, aren't you . . .'

Ada, standing over her in a nightgown, woke her up, 'What can be the matter, child?'

'I was having a nightmare . . . isn't that silly?' said Daughter and sat boltupright in bed. 'Did I yell bloody murder?'

'I bet you children were out eating Welsh Rabbit, that's why you were so late,' said Ada, and went back to her room laughing.

That spring Daughter coached a girls' basketball team at a Y.W.C.A. in the Bronx, and got engaged to Edwin Vinal. She told him she didn't want to marry anybody for a couple of years yet, and he said he didn't care about carnal marriage, but that the important thing was for them to plan a life of service together. Sunday evenings, when the weather got good, they would go and cook a steak together in Palisades Park and sit there looking through the trees at the lights coming on in the great toothed rockrim of the city and talk about what was good and evil and what real love was. Coming back, they'd stand hand in hand in the bow of the ferryboat among the crowd of Boy Scouts and hikers and picnickers and look at the great sweep of lighted buildings fading away into the ruddy haze down the North River and talk about all the terrible conditions in the city. Edwin would kiss her on the forehead when he said Goodnight and she'd go up in the elevator feeling that the kiss was a dedication.

At the end of June she went home to spend three months on the ranch, but she was very unhappy there that summer. Some-

how she couldn't get around to telling Dad about her engagement. When Joe Washburn came out to spend a week, the boys
made her furious teasing her about him and telling her that
he was engaged to a girl in Oklahoma City, and she got so
mad she wouldn't speak to them and was barely civil to Joe.
She insisted on riding a mean little pinto that bucked and
threw her once or twice. She drove the car right through a gate
one night and busted both lamps to smithereens. When Dad
scolded her about her recklessness, she'd tell him he oughtn't
to care because she was going back East to earn her own living
and he'd be rid of her. Joe Washburn treated her with the same
grave kindness as always, and sometimes when she was acting
crazy she'd catch a funny understanding kidding gleam in his
keen eyes that would make her feel suddenly all weak and silly
inside. The night before he left, the boys cornered a rattler on
the rockpile behind the corral and Daughter dared Joe to pick
it up and snap its head off. Joe ran for a forked stick and
caught the snake with a jab behind the head and threw it with
all his might against the wall of the little smokehouse. As it
lay wriggling on the grass with a broken back, Bud took its
head off with a hoe. It had six rattles and a button.

'Daughter,' Joe drawled, looking her in the face with his
steady smiling stare, 'sometimes you talk like you didn't have
good sense.'

'You're yaller, that's what's the matter with you,' she said.

'Daughter, you're crazy . . . you apologize to Joe,' yelled
Bud, running up red in the face with the dead snake in his
hand.

She turned and went into the ranchhouse and threw herself
on her bed. She didn't come out of her room till after Joe had
left in the morning.

The week before she left to go back to Columbia, she was
good as gold and tried to make it up to Dad and the boys by
baking cakes for them and attending to the housekeeping for
having acted so mean and crazy all summer. She met Ada in
Dallas and they engaged a section together. She'd been hoping
that Joe would come down to the station to see them off, but
he was in Oklahoma City on oil business. On her way North
she wrote him a long letter saying she didn't know what had
gotten into her that day with the rattler and wouldn't he please
forgive her.

Daughter worked hard that autumn. She'd gotten herself
admitted to the School of Journalism in spite of Edwin's dis-

approval. He wanted her to study to be a teacher or social worker, but she said journalism offered more opportunity. They more or less broke off over it; although they saw each other a good deal, they didn't talk so much about being engaged. There was a boy named Webb Cruthers studying journalism that Daughter got to be good friends with, although Ada said he was no good and wouldn't let her bring him to the house. He was shorter than she, had dark hair, and looked about fifteen, although he said he was twentyone. He had a creamy white skin that made people call him Babyface, and a funny confidential way of talking as if he didn't take what he was saying altogether seriously himself. He said he was an anarchist and talked all the time about politics and the war. He used to take her down to the East Side, too, but it was more fun than going with Edwin. Webb always wanted to go in somewhere to get a drink and talk to people. He took her to saloons and to Roumanian rathskellers and Arabian restaurants and more places than she'd ever imagined. He knew everybody everywhere and seemed to manage to make people trust him for the check, because he hardly ever had any money, and when they'd spent whatever she had with her, Webb would have to charge the rest. Daughter didn't drink more than an occasional glass of wine, and if he began to get too obstreperous, she'd make him take her to the nearest subway and go on home. The next day he'd be a little weak and trembly and tell her about his hangover and funny stories about adventures he'd had when he was tight. He always had pamphlets in his pockets about socialism and syndicalism and copies of *Mother Earth* or *The Masses*.

After Christmas Webb got all wrapped up in a strike of textile workers that was going on in a town over in New Jersey. One Sunday they went over to see what it was like. They got off the train at a grimy brick station in the middle of the empty business section, a few people standing around in front of lunchcounters, empty stores closed for Sunday; there seemed nothing special about the town until they walked out to the long low square brick buildings of the mills. There were knots of policemen in blue standing about in the wide muddy roadway outside and inside the wiremesh gates huskylooking young men in khaki. 'Those are special deputies, the sonsofbitches,' muttered Webb between his teeth. They went to Strike Headquarters to see a girl Webb knew who was doing publicity for them. At the head of a grimy stairway crowded with grayfaced foreign men and women in faded graylooking clothes, they found an office noisy with talk and click of typewriters. The hallway was piled with stacks of handbills that a tiredlooking young man was giving out in packages to boys in ragged sweaters. Webb found Sylvia Dalhart, a longnosed girl with glasses, who was typing madly at a desk piled with newspapers and clippings. She waved a hand and said, 'Webb, wait for me outside. I'm going to show some newspaper guys around and you'd better come.'

Out in the hall they ran into a fellow Webb knew, Ben Compton, a tall young man with a long thin nose and red-rimmed eyes, who said he was going to speak at the meeting and asked Webb if he wouldn't speak. 'Jeez, what could I say to those fellers? I'm just a bum of a college stoodjent, like you, Ben.' 'Tell 'em the workers have got to win the world, tell 'em this fight is part of a great historic battle. Talking's the easiest part of the movement. The truth's simple enough.' He had an explosive way of talking with a pause between each sentence, as if the sentence took some time to come up from some place way down inside. Daughter sized up that he was attractive even though he was probably a Jew. 'Well, I'll try to stammer out something about democracy in industry,' said Webb.

Sylvia Dalhart was already pushing them down the stairs. She had with her a pale young man in a raincoat and black felt hat who was chewing the end of a half of a cigar that had gone out. 'Fellowworkers, this is Joe Bigelow from the *Globe*,' she had a Western burr in her voice that made Daughter feel at home. 'We're going to show him around.'

They went all over town, to strikers' houses where tired-looking women in sweaters out at the elbows were cooking up lean Sunday dinners of corned beef and cabbage or stewed meat and potatoes, or in some houses they just had cabbage and bread, or just potatoes. Then they went to a lunchroom near the station and ate some lunch. Daughter paid the check, as nobody seemed to have any money, and it was time to go to the meeting.

The trolleycar was crowded with strikers and their wives and children. The meeting was to be held in the next town because in that town the Mills owned everything and there was no way of hiring a hall. It had started to sleet, and they got their feet wet wading through the slush to the mean frame building where the meeting was going to be held. When they got to the

door there were mounted police out in front. 'Half full,' a cop
told them at the streetcorner, 'no more allowed inside.'

They stood around in the sleet waiting for somebody with
authority. There were thousands of strikers, men and women
and boys and girls, the older people talking among themselves
in low voices in foreign languages. Webb kept saying, 'Jesus,
this is outrageous. Somebody ought to do something.' Daughter's feet were cold and she wanted to go home.

Then Ben Compton came around from the back of the
building. People began to gather around him. 'There's Ben . . .
there's Compton, good boy, Benny,' she heard people saying.
Young men moved around through the crowd whispering,
'Overflow meeting . . . stand your ground, folks.'

He began to speak hanging by one arm from a lamppost.
'Comrades, this is another insult flung in the face of the workingclass. There are not more than forty people in the hall and
they close the doors and tell us it's full . . .' The crowd began
swaying back and forth, hats, umbrellas bobbing in the sleety
rain. Then she saw the two cops were dragging Compton off
and heard the jangle of the patrolwagon. 'Shame, shame!'
people yelled. They began to back off from the cops; the flow
was away from the hall. People were moving quietly and
dejectedly down the street towards the trolley tracks with the
cordon of mounted police pressing them on. Suddenly Webb
whispered in her ear, 'Let me lean on your shoulder,' and
jumped on a hydrant.

'This is outrageous!' he shouted, 'you people had a permit
to use the hall and had hired it and no power on earth has a
right to keep you out of it. To hell with the Cossacks.'

Two mounted police were loping towards him, opening a
lane through the crowd as they came. Webb was off the hydrant
and had grabbed Daughter's hand, 'Let's run like hell,' he
whispered, and was off, doubling back and forth among the
scurrying people. She followed him laughing and out of breath.
A trolleycar was coming down the main street. Webb caught
it on the move, but she couldn't make it and had to wait for
the next. Meanwhile the cops were riding slowly back and forth
among the crowd breaking it up.

Daughter's feet ached from paddling in slush all afternoon
and she was thinking that she ought to get home before she
caught her death of cold. At the station waiting for the train
she saw Webb. He looked scared to death. He'd pulled his
cap down over his eyes and his muffler up over his chin and

pretended not to know Daughter when she went up to him. Once they got on the overheated train he sneaked up the aisle and sat down next to her.

'I was afraid some dick 'ud recognize me at the station,' he whispered. 'Well, what do you think of it?'

'I thought it was terrible . . . they're all so yaller . . . the only people looked good to me were those boys guardin' the mills, they looked like white men. . . . And as for you, Webb Cruthers, you ran like a deer.'

'Don't talk so loud. . . . Do you think I ought to have waited and gotten arrested like Ben?'

'Of course, it's none of my business.'

'You don't understand revolutionary tactics, Anne.'

Going over on the ferry they were both of them cold and hungry. Webb said he had the key to a room a friend of his had down on Eighth Street and that they'd better go there and warm their feet and make some tea before they went uptown. They had a long sullen walk, neither of them saying anything, from the ferry landing to the house. The room, that smelt of turpentine and was untidy, turned out to be a big studio heated by a gasburner. It was cold as Greenland, so they wrapped themselves in blankets and took off their shoes and stockings and toasted their feet in front of the gas. Daughter took her skirt off under the blanket and hung it up over the heater. 'Well, I declare,' she said, 'if your friend comes in, we sure will be compromised.'

'He won't,' said Webb, 'he's up at Cold Spring for the weekend.' Webb was moving around in his bare feet, putting on water to boil and making toast.

'You'd better take your trousers off, Webb, I can see the water dripping off them from here.' Webb blushed and pulled them off, draping the blanket around himself like a Roman senator.

For a long time they didn't say anything and all they could hear above the distant hum of traffic was the hiss of the gasflame and the intermittent purr of the kettle just beginning to boil. Then Webb suddenly began to talk in a nervous spluttering way. 'So you think I'm yellow, do you? Well, you may be right, Anne . . . not that I give a damn . . . I mean, you see, there's times when a fellow ought to be a coward and times when he ought to do the he-man stuff. Now don't talk for a minute, let me say something. . . . I'm hellishly attracted to you . . . and it's been yellow of me not to tell you about it

before, see? I don't believe in love or anything like that, all
bourgeois nonsense; but I think when people are attracted to
each other I think it's yellow of them not to . . . you know
what I mean.'

'No, I doan', Webb,' said Daughter after a pause.

Webb looked at her in a puzzled way as he brought her a
cup of tea and some buttered toast with a piece of cheese on
it. They ate in silence for a while; it was so quiet they could
hear each other gulping little swallows of tea.

'Now, what in Jesus Christ's name did you mean by that?'
Webb suddenly shouted out.

Daughter felt warm and drowsy in her blanket, with the hot
tea in her and the dry gasheat licking the soles of her feet.
'Well, what does anybody mean by anything?' she mumbled
dreamily.

Webb put down his teacup and began to walk up and down
the room trailing the blanket after him. 'S—t,' he suddenly
said, as he stepped on a thumbtack. He stood on one leg
looking at the sole of his foot that was black from the grime
of the floor. 'But, Jesus Christ, Anne . . . people ought to be
free and happy about sex . . . come ahead, let's.' His cheeks
were pink and his black hair that needed cutting was every
which way. He kept on standing on one leg and looking at the
sole of his foot.

Daughter began to laugh. 'You look awful funny like that,
Webb.' She felt a warm glow all over her. 'Give me another
cup of tea and make me some more toast.'

After she'd had the tea and toast, she said, 'Well, isn't it
about time we ought to be going uptown?'

'But Christ, Anne, I'm making indecent proposals to you,'
he said shrilly, half laughing and half in tears. 'For God's sake,
pay attention . . . Damn it, I'll make you pay attention, you little
bitch.' He dropped his blanket and ran at her. She could see
he was fighting mad. He pulled her up out of her chair and
kissed her on the mouth. She had quite a tussle with him, as
he was wiry and strong, but she managed to get her forearm
under his chin and to push his face away far enough to give
him a punch on the nose. His nose began to bleed.

'Don't be silly, Webb,' she said, breathing hard, 'I don't want
that sort of thing, not yet, anyway . . . go and wash your face.'

He went to the sink and began dabbling his face with water.
Daughter hurried into her skirt and shoes and stockings and
went over to the sink where he was washing his face.

'That was mean of me, Webb, I'm terribly sorry. There's something always makes me be mean to people I like.'

Webb wouldn't say anything for a long time. His nose was still bleeding.

'Go along home,' he said, 'I'm going to stay here. . . . It's all right . . . my mistake.'

She put on her dripping raincoat and went out into the shiny evening streets. All the way home on the express in the subway she was feeling warm and tender towards Webb, like towards Dad or the boys.

She didn't see him for several days; then one evening he called and asked her if she wanted to go out on the picket line next morning. It was still dark when she met him at the ferry station. They were both cold and sleepy and didn't say much going out on the train. From the train they had to run through the slippery streets to get to the mills in time to join the picket line. Faces looked cold and pinched in the blue early light. Women had shawls over their heads, few of the men or boys had overcoats. The young girls were all shivering in their cheap fancy topcoats that had no warmth to them. The cops had already begun to break up the head of the line. Some of the strikers were singing *Solidarity Forever*, others were yelling Scabs, Scabs, and making funny long jeering hoots. Daughter was confused and excited.

Suddenly everybody around her broke and ran and left her in a stretch of empty street in front of the wire fencing of the mills. Ten feet in front of her a young woman slipped and fell. Daughter caught the scared look in her eyes that were round and black. Daughter stepped forward to help her up, but two policemen were ahead of her swinging their nightsticks. Daughter thought they were going to help the girl up. She stood still for a second, frozen in her tracks when she saw one of the policemen's feet shoot out. He'd kicked the girl full in the face. Daughter never remembered what happened except that she was wanting a gun and punching into the policeman's big red face and against the buttons and the thick heavy cloth of his overcoat. Something crashed down on her head from behind; dizzy and sick she was being pushed into the police-wagon. In front of her was the girl's face all caved in and bleeding. In the darkness inside were other men and women cursing and laughing. But Daughter and the woman opposite looked at each other dazedly and said nothing. Then the door closed behind them and they were in the dark.

When they were committed, she was charged with rioting, felonious assault, obstructing an officer, and inciting to sedition. It wasn't so bad in the county jail. The women's section was crowded with strikers; all the cells were full of girls laughing and talking, singing songs and telling each other how they'd been arrested, how long they'd been in, how they were going to win the strike. In Daughter's cell the girls all clustered around her and wanted to know how she'd gotten there. She began to feel she was quite a hero. Towards evening her name was called and she found Webb and Ada and a lawyer clustered around the policesergeant's desk. Ada was mad, 'Read that, young woman, and see how that'll sound back home,' she said, poking an afternoon paper under her nose.

TEXAS BELLE ASSAULTS COP, said one headline. Then followed an account of her knocking down a policeman with a left on the jaw. She was released on a thousand dollars bail; outside the jail, Ben Compton broke away from the group of reporters around him and rushed up to her. 'Congratulations, Miss Trent,' he said, 'that was a darn nervy thing to do . . . made a very good impression in the press.'

Sylvia Dalhart was with him. She threw her arms around her and kissed her: 'That was a mighty spunky thing to do. Say, we're sending a delegation to Washington to see President Wilson and present a petition and we want you on it. The President will refuse to see the delegation and you'll have a chance to picket the White House and get arrested again.'

'Well, I declare,' said Ada when they were safely on the train for New York. 'I think you've lost your mind.'

'You'd have done the same thing, Ada darlin', if you'd seen what I saw . . . when I tell Dad and the boys about it they'll see red. It's the most outrageous thing I ever heard of.' Then she burst out crying.

When they got back to Ada's apartment they found a telegram from Dad saying

COMING AT ONCE   MAKE NO STATEMENT UNTIL
I ARRIVE

Late that night another telegram came; it read:

DAD SERIOUSLY ILL   COME ON HOME AT ONCE
HAVE ADA RETAIN BEST LAWYER OBTAINABLE

In the morning Daughter, scared and trembling, was on the first train south. At St Louis she got a telegram saying

DON'T WORRY CONDITION FAIR DOUBLE PNEUMONIA

Upset as she was it certainly did her good to see the wide Texas country, the spring crops beginning, a few bluebonnets in bloom. Buster was there to meet her at the depot. 'Well, Daughter,' he said after he had taken her bag, 'you've almost killed Dad.'

Buster was sixteen and captain of the highschool ballteam. Driving her up to the house in the new Stutz, he told her how things were. Bud had been tearing things up at the University and was on the edge of getting fired and had gotten balled up with a girl in Galveston who was trying to blackmail him. Dad had been very much worried because he'd gotten in too deep in the oil game and seeing Daughter spread all over the front page for knocking down a cop had about finished him; old Emma was getting too old to run the house for them any more and it was up to Daughter to give up her crazy ideas and stay home and keep house for them. 'See this car? A dandy, ain't it? . . . I bought it myself. . . . Did a little tradin' in options up near Amarillo on my own, jus' for the hell of it, and I made five thousand bucks.'

'Why, you smart kid. I tell you, Buster, it's good to be home. But about that policeman you'd have done the same yourself or you're not my brother. I'll tell you all about it sometime. Believe me, it does me good to see Texas faces after those mean weaselfaced Easterners.'

Doctor Winslow was in the hall when they came in. He shook hands warmly and told her how well she was looking and not to worry because he'd pull her dad through if it was the last thing he did on earth. The sickroom and Dad's restless flushed face made her feel awful, and she didn't like finding a trained nurse running the house.

After Dad began to get around a little, they both went down to Port Arthur for a couple of weeks for a change to stay with an old friend of Dad's. Dad said he'd give her a car if she'd stay on, and that he'd get her out of this silly mess she'd gotten into up North.

She began to play a lot of tennis and golf again and to go out a good deal socially. Joe Washburn had married and was living in Oklahoma getting rich on oil. She felt easier in Dallas when he wasn't there; seeing him upset her so. The next fall

Daughter went down to Austin to finish her journalism course, mostly because she thought her being there would keep Bud in the strait and narrow. Friday afternoons they drove back home together in her Buick sedan for the weekend. Dad had bought a new Tudor style house way out and all her spare time was taken up picking out furniture and hanging curtains and arranging the rooms. She had a great many beaux always coming around to take her out and had to start keeping an engagement book. Especially after the declaration of war social life became very hectic. She was going every minute and never got any sleep. Everybody was getting commissions or leaving for officers' training camps. Daughter went in for Red Cross work and organized a canteen, but that wasn't enough, and she kept applying to be sent abroad. Bud went down to San Antonio to learn to fly and Buster, who'd been in the militia, lied about his age and joined up as a private and was sent to Jefferson Barracks. At the canteen she lived in a whirl and had one or two proposals of marriage a week, but she always told them that she hadn't any intention of being a war bride.

Then one morning a War Department telegram came. Dad was in Austin on business, so she opened it. Bud had crashed, killed. First thing Daughter thought was how hard it would hit Dad. The phone rang; it was a longdistance call from San Antonio, sounded like Joe Washburn's voice.

'Is that you, Joe?' she said weakly.

'Daughter, I want to speak to your father,' came his grave drawl.

'I know . . . O Joe.'

'It was his first solo flight. He was a great boy. Nobody seems to know how it happened. Must have been defect in structure. I'll call Austin. I know where to get hold of him. . . . I've got the number . . . see you soon, Daughter.'

Joe rang off. Daughter went into her room and burrowed face down into the bed that hadn't been made up. For a minute she tried to imagine that she hadn't gotten up yet, that she dreamed the phone ringing and Joe's voice. Then she thought of Bud so sharply it was as if he'd come into the room, the way he laughed, the hard pressure of his long thin hand over her hands when he'd suddenly grabbed the wheel when they'd skidded going around a corner into San Antonio the last time she'd driven him down after a leave, the clean anxious lean look of his face above the tight khaki collar of the uniform.

Then she heard Joe's voice again: *Must have been some defect in structure.*

She went down and jumped into her car. At the filling-station where she filled up with gas and oil the garageman asked her how the boys liked it in the army. She couldn't stop to tell him about it now. 'Bully, they like it fine,' she said, with a grin that hurt her like a slap in the face. She wired Dad at his lawpartner's office that she was coming and pulled out of town for Austin. The roads were in bad shape, it made her feel better to feel the car plow through the muddy ruts and the water spraying out in a wave on either side when she went through a puddle at fifty.

She averaged fortyfive all the way and got to Austin before dark. Dad had already gone down to San Antonio on the train. Deadtired, she started off. She had a blowout and it took her a long time to get it fixed; it was midnight before she drew up at Menger. Automatically she looked at herself in the little mirror before going in. There were streaks of mud on her face and her eyes were red.

In the lobby she found Dad and Joe Washburn sitting side by side with burntout cigars in their mouths. Their faces looked a little alike. Must have been the gray drawn look that made them look alike. She kissed them both.

'Dad, you ought to go to bed,' she said briskly. 'You look all in.'

'I suppose I might as well . . . There's nothing left to do,' he said.

'Wait for me, Joe, until I get Dad fixed up,' she said in a low voice as she passed him.

She went up to the room with Dad, got herself a room adjoining, ruffled his hair and kissed him very gently and left him to go to bed.

When she got back down to the lobby, Joe was sitting in the same place with the same expression on his face. It made her mad to see him like that.

Her sharp brisk voice surprised her. 'Come outside a minute, Joe, I want to walk around a little.' The rain had cleared the air. It was a transparent early summer night. 'Look here, Joe, who's responsible for the condition of the planes? I've got to know.'

'Daughter, how funny you talk . . . what you ought to do is get some sleep, you're all overwrought.'

'Joe, you answer my question.'

'But Daughter, don't you see nobody's responsible. The army's a big institution. Mistakes are inevitable. There's a lot of money being made by contractors of one kind or another. Whatever you say, aviation is in its infancy . . . we all knew the risks before we joined up.'

'If Bud had been killed in France, I wouldn't have felt like this . . . but here . . . Joe, somebody's directly responsible for my brother's death. I want to go and talk to him, that's all. I won't do anything silly. You all think I'm a lunatic, I know, but I'm thinking of all the other girls who have brothers training to be aviators. The man who inspected those planes is a traitor to his country and ought to be shot down like a dog.'

'Look here, Daughter,' Joe said as he brought her back to the hotel, 'we're fightin' a war now. Individual lives don't matter; this isn't the time for lettin' your personal feelin's get away with you or embarrassin' the authorities with criticism. When we've licked the Huns'll be plenty of time for gettin' the incompetents and the crooks . . . that's how I feel about it.'

'Well, goodnight, Joe . . . you be mighty careful yourself. When do you expect to get your wings?'

'Oh, in a couple of weeks.'

'How's Gladys and Bunny?'

'Oh, they're all right,' said Joe; a funny constraint came into his voice and he blushed. 'They're in Tulsa with Mrs Higgins.'

She went to bed and lay there without moving, feeling desperately quiet and cool; she was too tired to sleep. When morning came, she went around to the garage to get her car. She felt in the pocket on the door to see if her handbag was there that always had her little pearlhandled revolver in it, and drove out to the aviation camp. At the gate the sentry wouldn't let her by, so she sent a note to Colonel Morrissey, who was a friend of Dad's, saying that she must see him at once. The corporal was very nice and got her a chair in the little office at the gate and a few minutes later said he had Colonel Morrissey on the wire. She started to talk to him, but she couldn't think what to say. The desk and the office and the corporal began swaying giddily and she fainted.

She came to in a staffcar with Joe Washburn who was taking her back to the hotel. He was patting her hand saying, 'That's all right, Daughter.' She was clinging to him and crying like a little tiny girl. They put her to bed at the hotel and gave her bromides and the doctor wouldn't let her get up until after the funeral was over.

She got a reputation for being a little crazy after that. She stayed on in San Antonio. Everything was very gay and tense. All day she worked in a canteen and evenings she went out, supper and dancing, every night with a different aviation officer. Everybody had taken to drinking a great deal. It was like when she used to go to highschool dances, she felt herself moving in a brilliantly lighted daze of suppers and lights and dancing and champagne and different colored faces and stiff identical bodies of men dancing with her, only now she had a kidding line and let them hug her and kiss her in taxicabs, in phonebooths, in people's backyards.

One night she met Joe Washburn at a party Ida Olsen was giving for some boys who were leaving for overseas. It was the first time she'd ever seen Joe drink. He wasn't drunk, but she could see that he'd been drinking a great deal. They went and sat side by side on the back steps of the kitchen in the dark. It was a clear hot night full of dryflies with a hard hot wind rustling the dry twigs of the trees. Suddenly she took Joe's hand: 'Oh, Joe, this is awful.'

Joe began to talk about how unhappy he was with his wife, how he was making big money through his oil leases and didn't give a damn about it, how sick he was of the army. They'd made him an instructor and wouldn't let him go overseas and he was almost crazy out there in camp.

'Oh, Joe, I want to go overseas too. I'm leading such a silly life here.'

'You have been actin' kinder wild, Daughter, since Bud died,' came Joe's soft deep drawling voice.

'Oh, Joe, I wisht I was dead,' she said and put her head on his knee and began to cry.

'Don't cry, Daughter, don't cry,' he began to say, then suddenly he was kissing her. His kisses were hard and crazy and made her go all limp against him.

'I don't love anybody but you, Joe,' she suddenly said quietly.

But he already had control of himself; 'Daughter, forgive me,' he said in a quiet lawyer's voice, 'I don't know what I was thinking of, I must be crazy . . . this war is making us all crazy . . . Goodnight . . . Say . . . er . . . erase this all from the record, will you?'

That night she couldn't sleep a wink. At six in the morning she got into her car, filled up with gas and oil and started for Dallas. It was a bright fall morning with blue mist in the hollows. Dry cornstalks rustled on the long hills red and yellow with fall. It was late when she got home. Dad was sitting up reading the war news in pajamas and bathrobe. 'Well, it won't be long now, Daughter,' he said. 'The Hindenburg Line is crumpling up. I knew our boys could do it, once they got started.' Dad's face was more lined and his hair whiter than she'd remembered it. She heated up a can of Campbell's soup, as she hadn't taken any time to eat. They had a cozy little supper together and read a funny letter of Buster's from Camp Merritt where his outfit was waiting to go overseas. When she went to bed in her own room, it was like being a little girl again; she'd always loved times when she got a chance to have a cozy chat with Dad all alone; she went to sleep the minute her head hit the pillow.

She stayed on in Dallas taking care of Dad; it was only sometimes when she thought of Joe Washburn that she felt she couldn't stand it another minute. The fake armistice came and then the real armistice; everybody was crazy for a week like a New Orleans Mardi Gras. Daughter decided that she was going to be an old maid and keep house for Dad. Buster came home looking very tanned and full of army slang. She started attending lectures at Southern Methodist, doing church work, getting books out of the circulating library, baking angelcake; when young girlfriends of Buster's came to the house, she acted as a chaperon.

Thanksgiving, Joe Washburn and his wife came to dinner with them. Old Emma was sick, so Daughter cooked the turkey herself. It was only when they'd all sat down to table, with the yellow candles lighted in the silver candlesticks and the salted nuts set out in the little silver trays and the decoration of pink and purple mapleleaves, that she remembered Bud. She suddenly began to feel faint and ran into her room. She lay face down on the bed listening to their grave voices. Joe came to the door to see what was the matter. She jumped up laughing, and almost scared Joe to death by kissing him square on the mouth. 'I'm all right, Joe,' she said. 'How's yourself?'

Then she ran to the table and started cheering everybody up, so that they all enjoyed their dinner. When they were drinking their coffee in the other room, she told them that she'd signed up to go overseas for six months with the Near East Relief, that had been recruiting at Southern Methodist. Dad was furious, and Buster said she ought to stay home now the war was over, but Daughter said, others had given their lives to save the world from the Germans and that she certainly could give up six months to relief work. When she said that, they all thought of Bud and were quiet.

It wasn't actually true that she'd signed up, but she did the next morning and got around Miss Frazier, a returned missionary from China who was arranging it, so that they sent her up to New York that week, with orders to sail immediately with the office in Rome as her first destination. She was so wildly excited all the time she was getting her passport and having her uniform fitted, she hardly noticed how glum Dad and Buster looked. She had only a day in New York. When the boat backed out of the dock with its siren screaming and started steaming down the North River, she stood on the front deck with her hair blowing in the wind, sniffing the funny steamboat harbor overseas smell and feeling like a twoyearold.

# Newsreel 32

GOLDEN VOICE OF CARUSO SWELLS IN VICTORY
SONG TO CROWDS ON STREETS

*Oh Oh Oh, it's a lovely war*
*Oo wouldn't be a sodger, ay*

from Pic Umbral to the north of the Stelvio it will
follow the crest of the Rhetian Alps up to the sources of
the Adige and the Eisah passing thence by Mounts Reschen
and Brenner and the heights of Oetz and Boaller; thence
south crossing Mount Toblach

*As soon as reveille has gone*
*We feel just as 'eavy as lead*
*But we never git up till the sergeant*
*Brings us a cup of tea in bed*

HYPNOTIZED BY COMMON-LAW WIFE

army casualties soar to 64,305 with 318 today; 11,760
have paid the supreme sacrifice in action and 6,193 are
severely wounded

*Oh Oh Oh, it's a lovely war*
*Oo wouldn't be a sodger, ay*
*Oh, it's a shyme to tyke the py*

in the villages in peasant houses the Americans are
treated as guests living in the best rooms and courteously
offered the best shining samovars or teaurns by the house-
wives

*Le chef de gare il est cocu*

in the largely populated districts a spectacular touch
was given the festivities by groups of aliens appearing in
costume and a carnival spirit prevailed

BRITISH SUPPRESS SOVIETS

*Le chef de gare il est cocu*
*Qui est cocu? Le chef de gare*
*Sa femme elle l'a voulut*

there can be no reason to believe these officers of an established news organization serving newspapers all over the country failed to realize their responsibilities at a moment of supreme significance to the people of this country. Even to anticipate the event in a matter of such moment would be a grave imposition for which those responsible must be called to account

*Any complaynts this morning?*
*Do we complayn? Not we*
*Wats the matter with lumps of onion*
*Floatin' around in the tea?*

PEACE DOVE IN JEWELS GIVEN MRS WILSON

and the watershed of the Cols di Polberdo, Podlaniscam, and Idria. From this point the line turns southeast towards the Schneeberg, excludes the whole basin of the Saave and its tributaries. From Schneeberg it goes down to the coast in such a way as to include Castna, Mattuglia and Volusca

## *The Camera Eye (38)*

sealed signed and delivered     all over Tours you can smell lindens in bloom     it's hot my uniform sticks     the OD chafes me under the chin

only four days ago A.W.O.L. crawling under the freight cars at the station of St Pierre-des-Corps     waiting in the buvette for the M.P. on guard to look away from the door so's I could slink out with a cigarette (and my heart) in my mouth     then in a tiny box of a hotel room changing the date on that old movement order

but today

my discharge sealed signed and delivered sends off sparks in my pocket like a romancandle

I walk past the headquarters of the S.O.S. Hay sojer

your tunic's unbuttoned (f—k you buddy) and down the
lindenshaded street to the bathhouse that has a court with
flowers in the middle of it   the hot water gushes green out
of brass swanheads into the whitemetal tub   I strip myself
naked   soap myself all over with the sour pink soap
slide into the warm deepgreen tub   through the white
curtain in the window a finger of afternoon sunlight leng-
thens on the ceiling   towel's dry and warm smells of steam

in the suitcase I've got a suit of civvies I borrowed from
a fellow I know   the buck private in the rear rank of
Uncle Sam's Medical Corps (serial number . . . never could
remember the number anyway I dropped it in the Loire)
goes down the drain with a gurgle and hiss and

having amply tipped and gotten the eye from the fat
woman who swept up the towels

I step out into the lindensmell of a July afternoon and
stroll up to the café where at the little tables outside only
officers may set their whipcord behinds   and order a drink
of cognac unservable to those in uniform while waiting for
the train to Paris and sit down firmly in long pants in the
iron chair

an anonymous civilian

# Newsreel 33

CAN'T RECALL KILLING SISTER; CLAIMS

*I've got the blues*
*I've got the blues*
*I've got the alcohoholic blues*

SOAP CRISIS THREATENED

with the gay sunlight and the resumption of racing
Paris has resumed its normal life. The thousands and
thousands of flags of all nations hang on dozens of lines
stretching from mast to mast making a fairylike effect that
is positively astonishing

THREAT LETTERS REVEALED

*I love my country indeed I do*
*But this war is making me blue*
*I like fightin' fightin's my name*
*But fightin' is the least about this fightin' game*

the police found an anteroom full of mysteriouslook-
ing packages which when opened were found full of pamphlets in Yiddish Russian and English and of membership
cards for the Industrial Workers of the World

HIGH WIND INCREASES DANGER OF MEN

WHILE PEACE IS TALKED OF WORLDWIDE
WAR RAGES

the agents said the arrests were ordered from the State
Department. The detention was so sudden neither of the
men had time to obtain his baggage from the vessel. Then
came a plaintive message from two businessmen at Lure;
the consignment had arrived, the sacks had been opened,
and their contents was ordinary building plaster. The huge
car remained suspended in some trees upside down while

the passengers were thrown into the torrent twenty feet
below

*Lordy, lordy, war is hell*
*Since he amputated my booze*

OUTRAGE PERPETRATED IN SEOUL

*I've got the alcohohoholic blues*

The Department of Justice Has the Goods on the
Packers According to Attorney General Palmer
L'Ecole du Malheur Nous Rend Optimistes
Unity of Free Peoples Will Prevent any Inequitable
Outcome of Peace of Paris
it is only too clear that the League of Nations lies in
pieces on the floor of the Hôtel Crillon and the modest
alliance that might with advantage occupy its place is but
a vague sketch

HOW TO DEAL WITH BOLSHEVISTS?
SHOOT THEM! POLES' WAY!

HAMBURG CROWDS FLOCK TO SEE FORD

HINTS AT BIG POOL TO DEVELOP ASIA

*When Mr Hoover said to cut our eatin' down*
*I did it and I didn't ever raise a frown*
*Then when he said to cut out coal,*
*But now he's cut right into my soul*

Allons-nous Assister à la Panique des Sots?
stones were clattering on the roof and crashing through
the windows and wild men were shrieking through the key-
hole while enormous issues depended on them that required
calm and deliberation at any rate the President did not
speak to the leaders of the democratic movements

LIEBKNECHT KILLED ON WAY TO PRISON

## Eveline Hutchins

Eveline had moved to a little place on the Rue de Bussy
where there was a street market every day. Eleanor, to show

that there was no hard feeling, had given her a couple of her Italian painted panels to decorate the dark parlor with. In early November rumors of an armistice began to fly around and then suddenly one afternoon Major Wood ran into the office that Eleanor and Eveline shared and dragged them both away from their desks and kissed them both and shouted, 'At last it's come.' Before she knew it, Eveline found herself kissing Major Moorehouse right on the mouth. The Red Cross office turned into a college dormitory the night of a football victory: it was the Armistice.

Everybody seemed suddenly to have bottles of cognac and to be singing, *There's a long long trail awinding* or *La Madellon pour nous n'est pas sévère.*

She and Eleanor and J. W. and Major Wood were in a taxicab going to the Café de la Paix.

For some reason they kept getting out of taxicabs and other people kept getting in. They had to get to the Café de la Paix, but whenever they got into a taxicab it was stopped by the crowd and the driver disappeared. But when they got there, they found every table filled and files of people singing and dancing streaming in and out all the doors. They were Greeks, Polish legionnaires, Russians, Serbs, Albanians in white kilts, a Highlander with bagpipes, and a lot of girls in Alsatian costume. It was annoying not being able to find a table. Eleanor said maybe they ought to go somewhere else. J. W. was preoccupied and wanted to get to a telephone.

Only Major Wood seemed to be enjoying himself. He was a grayhaired man with a little grizzled mustache and kept saying, 'Ah, the lid's off today.' He and Eveline went upstairs to see if they could find room there and ran into two Anzacs seated on a billiard table surrounded by a dozen bottles of champagne. Soon they were all drinking champagne with the Anzacs. They couldn't get anything to eat, although Eleanor said she was starving, and when J. W. tried to get into the phone booth he found an Italian officer and a girl tightly wedged together in it. The Anzacs were pretty drunk, and one of them was saying that the Armistice was probably just another bloody piece of lying propaganda; so Eleanor suggested they try to go back to her place to have something to eat. J. W. said yes, they could stop at the Bourse so that he could send some cables. He must get in touch with his broker. The Anzacs didn't like it when they left and were rather rude.

They stood around for a long time in front of the opera

in the middle of swirling crowds. The streetlights were on; the gray outlines of the opera were edged along the cornices with shimmering gasflames. They were jostled and pushed about. There were no buses, no automobiles; occasionally they passed a taxicab stranded in the crowd like a rock in a stream. At last on a side street they found themselves alongside a Red Cross staffcar that had nobody in it. The driver, who wasn't too sober, said he was trying to get the car back to the garage and said he'd take them down to the Quai de la Tournelle first.

Eveline was just climbing in when somehow she felt it was just too tiresome and she couldn't. The next minute she was marching arm in arm with a little French sailor in a group of people mostly in Polish uniform who were following a Greek flag and singing *la Brabançonne.*

A minute later she realized she'd lost the car and her friends and was scared. She couldn't recognize the streets even, in this new Paris full of arclights and flags and bands and drunken people. She found herself dancing with the little sailor in the asphalt square in front of a church with two towers, then with a French colonial officer in a red cloak, then with a Polish legionnaire who spoke a little English and had lived in Newark, New Jersey, and then suddenly some young French soldiers were dancing in a ring around her holding hands. The game was you had to kiss one of them to break the ring. When she caught on she kissed one of them and everybody clapped and cheered and cried Vive l'Amérique. Another bunch came and kept on and on dancing around her until she began to feel scared. Her head was beginning to whirl around when she caught sight of an American uniform on the outskirts of the crowd. She broke through the ring bowling over a little fat Frenchman and fell on the doughboy's neck and kissed him, and everybody laughed and cheered and cried encore. He looked embarrassed; the man with him was Paul Johnson, Don Stevens's friend. 'You see I had to kiss somebody,' Eveline said, blushing. The doughboy laughed and looked pleased.

'Oh, I hope you didn't mind, Miss Hutchins, I hope you don't mind this crowd and everything,' apologized Paul Johnson.

People spun around them dancing and shouting and she had to kiss Paul Johnson, too, before they'd let them go. He apologized solemnly again and said. 'Isn't it wonderful to be in Paris to see the armistice and everything, if you don't mind the crowd and everything . . . but honestly, Miss Hutchins,

they're awful goodnatured. No fights or nothin' . . . Say, Don's
in this café.'

Don was behind a little zinc bar in the entrance to the café
shaking up cocktails for a big crowd of Canadian and Anzac
officers, all very drunk. 'I can't get him out of there,' whispered
Paul. 'He's had more than he ought.'

They got Don out from behind the bar. There seemed to be
nobody there to pay for the drinks. In the door he pulled off
his gray cap and cried, 'Vive les quakers . . . à bas la guerre,'
and everybody cheered. They roamed around aimlessly for a
while; now and then they'd be stopped by a ring of people
dancing around her and Don would kiss her. He was noisy
drunk and she didn't like the way he acted as if she was his
girl. She began to feel tired by the time they got to the Place
de la Concorde and suggested that they cross the river and
try to get to her apartment where she had some cold veal and
salad.

Paul was embarrassedly saying perhaps he'd better not come,
when Don ran off after a group of Alsatian girls who were
hopping and skipping up the Champs Élysées.

'Now you've got to come,' she said. 'To keep me from being
kissed too much by strange men.'

'But Miss Hutchins, you mustn't think Don meant anything
running off like that. He's very excitable, especially when he
drinks.' She laughed and they walked on without saying
anything more.

When they got to her apartment the old concierge hobbled
out from her box and shook hands with both of them. 'Ah,
madame, c'est la victoire,' she said, 'but it won't make my
dead son come back to life, will it?' For some reason Eveline
could not think of anything to do but give her five francs and
she went back muttering a singsong, 'Merci, m'sieur, madame.'

Up in Eveline's tiny room Paul seemed terribly embarrassed.
They ate everything there was to the last crumb of stale bread
and talked a little vaguely. Paul sat on the edge of his chair
and told her about his travels back and forth with dispatches.
He said how wonderful it had been for him coming abroad and
seeing the army and European cities and meeting people like
her and Don Stevens and that he hoped she didn't mind his
not knowing much about all the things she and Don talked
about.

'If this really is the beginning of peace, I wonder what we'll
all do, Miss Hutchins.'

'Oh, do call me Eveline, Paul.'

'I really do think it is the peace, Eveline, according to Wilson's Fourteen Points. I think Wilson's a great man myself in spite of all Don says, I know he's a darn sight cleverer than I am, but still . . . maybe this is the last war there'll ever be. Gosh, think of that . . .'

She hoped he'd kiss her when he left, but all he did was shake hands awkwardly and say all in a breath, 'I hope you won't mind if I come to see you next time I can get to Paris.'

For the Peace Conference, J. W. had a suite at the Crillon, with his blond secretary, Miss Williams, at a desk in a little anteroom, and Morton, his English valet, serving tea in the late afternoon. Eveline liked dropping into the Crillon late in the afternoon after walking up the arcades of the Rue de Rivoli from her office. The antiquated corridors of the hotel were crowded with Americans coming and going. In J. W.'s big salon there'd be Morton stealthily handing around tea, and people in uniform and in frock coats and the cigarettesmoky air would be full of halftold anecdotes. J. W. fascinated her, dressed in gray Scotch tweeds that always had a crease on the trousers (he'd given up wearing his Red Cross major's uniform), with such an aloof agreeable manner, tempered by the preoccupied look of a very busy man always being called up on the phone, receiving telegrams or notes from his secretary, disappearing into the embrasure of one of the windows that looked out on the Place de la Concorde with someone for a whispered conversation, or being asked to step in to see Colonel House for a moment; and still, when he handed her a champagne cocktail just before they all went out to dinner on nights he didn't have to go to some official function, or asked if she wanted another cup of tea, she'd feel for a second in her eyes the direct glance of two boyish blue eyes with a funny candid partly humorous look that teased her. She wanted to know him better; Eleanor, she felt, watched them like a cat watching a mouse. After all, Eveline kept saying to herself, she hadn't any right. It wasn't as if there was anything really between them.

When J. W. was busy, they often went out with Edgar Robbins, who seemed to be a sort of assistant of J. W.'s. Eleanor couldn't abide him, said there was something insulting in his cynicism, but Eveline liked to hear him talk. He said the peace was going to be ghastlier than the war, said it was a good thing nobody ever asked his opinion about anything be-

cause he'd certainly land in jail if he gave it. Robbins's favorite
hangout was Freddy's up back of Montmartre. They'd sit there
all evening in the small smokycrowded rooms while Freddy,
who had a big white beard like Walt Whitman, would play on
the guitar and sing. Sometimes he'd get drunk and set the
company up to drinks on the house. Then his wife, a cross
woman who looked like a gypsy, would come out of the back
room and curse and scream at him. People at the tables would
get up and recite long poems about La Grand' route, La Misère,
L'Assassinat, or sing old French songs like *Les Filles de Nantes.*
If it went over, everybody present would clap hands in unison.
They called that giving a bon. Freddy got to know them and
would make a great fuss when they arrived, 'Ah, les belles
Américaines.' Robbins would sit there moodily drinking calvados after calvados, now and then letting out a crack about the
day's happenings at the Peace Conference. He said that the
place was a fake, that the calvados was wretched, and that
Freddy was a dirty old bum, but for some reason he always
wanted to go back.

J. W. went there a couple of times, and occasionally they'd
take some delegate from the Peace Conference who'd be
mightily impressed by their knowledge of the inner life of Paris.
J. W. was enchanted by the old French songs, but he said the
place made him feel itchy and that he thought there were fleas
there. Eveline liked to watch him when he was listening to a
song with his eyes halfclosed and his head thrown back. She
felt that Robbins didn't appreciate the rich potentialities of
his nature and always shut him up when he started to say something sarcastic about the big cheese, as he called him. She
thought it was disagreeable of Eleanor to laugh at things like
that, especially when J. W. seemed so devoted to her.

When Jerry Burnham came back from Armenia and found
that Eveline was going around with J. Ward Moorehouse all
the time, he was terribly upset. He took her out to lunch at
the Medicis Grill on the left bank and talked and talked about
it.

'Why, Eveline, I thought of you as a person who wouldn't
be taken in by a big bluff like that. The guy's nothing but a
goddam megaphone. . . . Honestly, Eveline, it's not that I
expect you to fall for me, I know very well you don't give a
damn about me, and why should you? . . . But Christ, a damn
publicity agent.'

'Now, Jerry,' said Eveline with her mouth full of hors

d'œuvres, 'you know very well I'm fond of you . . . It's just too tiresome of you to talk like that.'

'You don't like me the way I'd like you to . . . but to hell with that . . . Have wine or beer?'

'You pick out a nice Burgundy, Jerry, to warm us up a little. . . . But you wrote an article about J. W. yourself . . . I saw it reprinted in that column in the *Herald*.'

'Go ahead, rub it in . . . Christ, I swear, Eveline, I'm going to get out of this lousy trade and . . . that was all plain old-fashioned bushwa and I thought you'd have had the sense to see it. Gee, this is good sole.'

'Delicious . . . but, Jerry, you're the one ought to have more sense.'

'I dunno – I thought you were different from other upper-class women, made your own living and all that.'

'Let's not wrangle, Jerry, let's have some fun; here we are in Paris and the war's over and it's a fine wintry day and everybody's here. . . .'

'War over, my eye,' said Jerry rudely.

Eveline thought he was just too tiresome, and looked out the window at the ruddy winter sunlight and the old Medici fountain and the delicate violet lacework of the bare trees behind the high iron fence of the Luxembourg Garden. Then she looked at Jerry's red intense face with the turnedup nose and the crisp boyishly curly hair that was beginning to turn a little gray; she leaned over and gave the back of his hand a couple of little pats.

'I understand, Jerry, you've seen things that I haven't imagined . . . I guess it's the corrupting influence of the Red Cross.'

He smiled and poured her out some more wine and said with a sigh:

'You're the most damnably attractive woman I ever met, Eveline . . . but like all women what you worship is power, when money's the main thing it's money, when it's fame it's fame, when it's art, you're a goddamned artlover . . . I guess I'm the same, only I kid myself more.'

Eveline pressed her lips together and didn't say anything. She suddenly felt cold and frightened and lonely and couldn't think of anything to say. Jerry gulped down a glass of wine and started talking about throwing up his job and going to Spain to write a book. He said he didn't pretend to have any self-respect, but that being a newspaper correspondent was too damn much nowadays. Eveline said she never wanted to go back to America, she felt life would be just too tiresome there after the war.

When they'd had their coffee they walked through the gardens. Near the Senate Chamber some old gentlemen were playing croquet in the last purplish patch of afternoon sunlight. 'Oh, I think the French are wonderful,' said Eveline. 'Second childhood,' growled Jerry. They rambled aimlessly round the streets, reading palegreen, yellow, and pink theater notices on kiosks, looking into windows of antiqueshops.

'We ought both to be at our offices,' said Jerry.

'I'm not going back,' said Eveline, 'I'll call up and say I have a cold and have gone home to bed . . . I think I'll do that anyway.'

'Don't do that; let's play hookey and have a swell time.'

They went to the café opposite Saint-Germain-des-Prés. When Eveline came back from phoning, Jerry had bought her a bunch of violets and ordered cognac and seltzer.

'Eveline, let's celebrate,' he said. 'I think I'll cable the sonsobitches and tell 'em I've resigned.'

'Do you think you ought to do that, Jerry? After all, it's a wonderful opportunity to see the Peace Conference and everything.'

After a few minutes she left him and walked home. She wouldn't let him come with her. As she passed the window where they'd been sitting, she looked in; he was ordering another drink.

On the Rue de Bussy the market was very jolly under the gaslights. It all smelt of fresh greens, and butter and cheese. She bought some rolls for breakfast and a few little cakes in case somebody came in to tea. It was cozy in her little pink and white salon with the fire of briquettes going in the grate. Eveline wrapped herself up in a steamerrug and lay down on the couch.

She was asleep when her bell jingled. It was Eleanor and J. W. come to inquire how she was. J. W. was free tonight and wanted them to come to the opera with him to see *Castor and Pollux*. Eveline said she was feeling terrible, but she thought she'd go just the same. She put on some tea for them and ran into her bedroom to dress. She felt so happy she couldn't help humming as she sat at her dressingtable looking at herself in the glass. Her skin looked very white and her face had a quiet mysterious look she liked. She carefully put on very little lipstick and drew her hair back to a knot behind; her hair worried her, it wasn't curly and didn't have any particular color; for a moment she thought she wouldn't go. Then Eleanor came in with a cup of tea in her hand telling her to hurry because they had to go down and wait while she dressed herself and that the opera started early. Eveline didn't have any real evening wrap, so she had to wear an old rabbitfur coat over her evening dress. At Eleanor's they found Robbins waiting; he wore a tuxedo that looked a little the worse for wear. J. W. was in the uniform of a Red Cross major. Eveline thought he must have been exercising, because his jowl didn't curve out from the tight high collar as much as it had formerly.

They ate in a hurry at Poccardi's and drank a lot of badly made martinis. Robbins and J. W. were in fine feather, and kept them laughing all the time. Eveline understood now why they worked together so well. At the opera, where they arrived late, it was wonderful, glittering with chandeliers and uniforms. Miss Williams, J. W.'s secretary, was already in the box. Eveline thought how nice he must be to work for, and for a moment bitterly envied Miss Williams, even to her peroxide hair and her brisk chilly manner of talking. Miss Williams leaned back and said they'd missed it, that President and Mrs Wilson had just come in and had been received with a great ovation, and Marshal Foch was there and she thought President Poincaré.

Between the acts they worked their way as best they could into the crowded lobby. Eveline found herself walking up and down with Robbins; every now and then she'd catch sight of Eleanor with J. W. and feel a little envious.

'They put on a better show out here than they do on the stage,' said Robbins.

'Don't you like the production. . . . I think it's a magnificent production.'

'Well, I suppose looked at from the professional point of view . . .'

Eveline was watching Eleanor, she was being introduced to a French general in red pants; she looked handsome this evening in her hard chilly way. Robbins tried to pilot them in through the crowd to the little bar, but they gave it up, there were too many people ahead of them. Robbins started all at once to talk about Baku and the oil business. 'It's funny as a crutch,' he kept saying; 'while we sit here wrangling under schoolmaster Wilson, John Bull's putting his hands on all the world's future supplies of oil . . . just to keep it from the bolos. They've got

Persia and the Messpot and now I'll be damned if they don't want Baku.' Eveline was bored and thinking to herself that Robbins had been in his cups too much again, when the bell rang.

When they got back to their box a leanfaced man who wasn't in evening clothes was sitting in the back talking to J. W. in a low voice. Eleanor leaned over to Eveline and whispered in her ear, 'That was General Gouraud.' The lights went out; Eveline found she was forgetting herself in the deep stateliness of the music. At the next intermission she leaned over to J. W. and asked him how he liked it. 'Magnificent,' he said, and she saw to her surprise that he had tears in his eyes. She found herself talking about the music with J. W. and the man without a dresssuit, whose name was Rasmussen.

It was hot and crowded in the tall overdecorated lobby. Mr Rasmussen managed to get a window open and they went out on the balcony that opened on the serried lights that dimmed down the avenue into a reddish glow of fog.

'That's the time I'd like to have lived,' said J. W. dreamily.

'The court of the Sun King?' asked Mr Rasmussen. 'No, it must have been too chilly in the winter months and I bet the plumbing was terrible.

'Ah, it was a glorious time,' said J. W. as if he hadn't heard. Then he turned to Eveline, 'You're sure you're not catching cold . . . you ought to have a wrap, you know.'

'But as I was saying, Moorehouse,' said Rasmussen in a different tone of voice, 'I have positive information that they can't hold Baku without heavy reinforcements and there's no one they can get them from except from us.' The bell rang again and they hurried to their box.

After the opera they went to the Café de la Paix to drink a glass of champagne, except for Robbins who went off to take Miss Williams back to her hotel. Eveline and Eleanor sat on the cushioned bench on either side of J. W. and Mr Rasmussen sat on a chair opposite them. He did most of the talking, taking nervous gulps of champagne between sentences or else running his fingers through his spiky black hair. He was an engineer with Standard Oil. He kept talking about Baku and Mohommarah and Morsul, how the Anglo-Persian and the Royal Dutch were getting ahead of the U.S. in the Near East and trying to foist off Armenia on us for a mandate, which the Turks had pillaged to the last blade of grass, leaving nothing but a lot of starving people to feed.

'We'll probably have to feed 'em anyway,' said J. W.

'But my gosh, man, something can be done about it; even if the President has so far forgotten American interests to let himself be bulldozed by the British in everything, public opinion can be aroused. We stand to lose our primacy in world oil production.'

'Oh, well, the matter of mandates isn't settled yet.'

'What's going to happen is that the British are going to present a fait accompli to the Conference . . . findings keepings . . . why, it would be better for us for the French to have Baku.'

'How about the Russians?' asked Eveline.

'According to selfdetermination the Russians have no right to it. The population is mostly Turkish and Armenian,' said Rasmussen. 'But, by gorry, I'd rather have the Reds have it than the British; of course I don't suppose they'll last long.'

'No, I have reliable information that Lenine and Trotsky have split and the monarchy will be restored in Russia inside of three months.'

When they finished the first bottle of champagne, Mr Rasmussen ordered another. By the time the café closed, Eveline's ears were ringing. 'Let's make a night of it,' Mr Rasmussen was saying.

They went in a taxicab up to Montmartre to L'Abbaye where there was dancing and singing and uniforms everywhere and everything was hung with the flags of the Allies. J. W. asked Eveline to dance with him first and Eleanor looked a little sour when she had to go off in the arms of Mr Rasmussen who danced very badly indeed. Eveline and J. W. talked about the music of Rameau and J. W. said again that he would like to have lived in the times of the court at Versailles. But Eveline said what could be more exciting than to be in Paris right now with all the map of Europe being remade right under their noses, and J. W. said perhaps she was right. They agreed that the orchestra was too bad to dance to.

Next dance Eveline danced with Mr Rasmussen who told her how handsome she was and said he needed a good woman in his life; that he'd spent all his life out in the bush grubbing around for gold or testing specimens of shale and that he was sick of it, and if Wilson now was going to let the British bulldoze him into giving them the world's future supply of oil when we'd won the war for them, he was through.

'But can't you do something about it, can't you put your ideas before the public, Mr Rasmussen?' said Eveline, leaning a little against him; Eveline had a crazy champagneglass spinning in her head.

'That's Moorehouse's job, not mine, and there isn't any public since the war. The public'll damn well do what it's told, and, besides, like God Almighty it's far away . . . what we've got to do is make a few key men understand the situation. Moorehouse is the key to the key men.'

'And who's the key to Moorehouse?' asked Eveline recklessly. The music had stopped.

'Wish to heaven I knew,' said Rasmussen soberly in a low voice. 'You're not, are you?'

Eveline shook her head with a tightlipped smile like Eleanor's.

When they'd eaten onion soup and some cold meat, J. W. said, 'Let's go up to the top of the hill and make Freddy play us some songs.'

'I thought you didn't like it up there,' said Eleanor.

'I don't, my dear,' said J. W., 'but I like those old French songs.'

Eleanor looked cross and sleepy. Eveline wished she and Mr Rasmussen would go home; she felt if she could only talk to J. W. alone, he'd be so interesting.

Freddy's was almost empty; it was chilly in there. They didn't have any champagne and nobody drank the liqueurs they ordered. Mr Rasmussen said Freddy looked like an old prospector he'd known out in the Sangre de Cristo Mountains and began to tell a long story about Death Valley that nobody listened to. They were all chilly and sleepy and silent, going back across Paris in the old moldysmelling twocylinder taxi. J. W. wanted a cup of coffee, but there didn't seem to be any place open where he could get it.

Next day Mr Rasmussen called Eveline up at her office to ask her to eat lunch with him and she was hard put to it to find an excuse not to go. After that Mr Rasmussen seemed to be everywhere she went, sending her flowers and theater tickets, coming around with automobiles to take her riding, sending her little blue pneumatiques full of tender messages. Eleanor teased her about her new Romeo.

Then Paul Johnson turned up in Paris, having gotten himself into the Sorbonne detachment, and used to come around to her place on the Rue de Bussy in the late afternoons and sit watching her silently and lugubriously. He and Mr Rasmussen would sit there talking about wheat and the stockyards, while Eveline dressed to go out with somebody else, usually Eleanor and J. W.

Eveline could see that J. W. always liked to have her along as well as Eleanor when they went out in the evenings; it was just that welldressed American girls were rare in Paris at that time, she told herself, and that J. W. liked to be seen with them and to have them along when he took important people out to dinner. She and Eleanor treated each other with a stiff nervous sarcasm now, except occasionally when they were alone together, they talked like in the old days, laughing at people and happenings together. Eleanor would never let a chance pass to poke fun at her Romeos.

Her brother George turned up at the office one day with a captain's two silver bars on his shoulders. His whipcord uniform fitted like a glove, his puttees shone, and he wore spurs. He'd been in the Intelligence Service attached to the British and had just come down from Germany where he'd been an interpreter on General McAndrews's staff. He was going to Cambridge for the spring term and called everybody blighters or rotters and said the food at the restaurant where Eveline took him for lunch was simply ripping. After he'd left her, saying her ideas were not cricket, she burst out crying. When she was leaving the office that afternoon, thinking gloomily about how George had grown up to be a horrid little prig of a brasshat, she met Mr Rasmussen under the arcades of the Rue de Rivoli; he was carrying a mechanical canarybird. It was a stuffed canary and you wound it up underneath the cage. Then it fluttered its wings and sang. He made her stop on the corner while he made it sing. 'I'm going to send that back home to the kids,' he said. 'My wife and I are separated, but I'm fond of the kids; they live in Pasadena . . . I've had a very unhappy life.' Then he invited Eveline to step into the Ritz Bar and have a cocktail with him. Robbins was there with a redheaded newspaperwoman from San Francisco. They sat at a wicker table together and drank Alexanders. The bar was crowded.

'What's the use of a League of Nations if it's to be dominated by Great Britain and her colonies?' said Mr Rasmussen sourly.

'But don't you think any kind of a league's better than nothing?' said Eveline.

'It's not the name you give things, it's who's getting theirs underneath that counts,' said Robbins.

'That's a very cynical remark,' said the California woman. 'This isn't any time to be cynical.'

'This is a time,' said Robbins, 'when if we weren't cynical we'd shoot ourselves.'

In March Eveline's twoweeks leave came around. Eleanor was going to make a trip to Rome to help wind up the affairs of the office there, so they decided they'd go down on the train together and spend a few days in Nice. They needed to get the damp cold of Paris out of their bones. Eveline felt as excited as a child the afternoon when they were all packed and ready to go and had bought wagon-lit reservations and gotten their transport orders signed.

Mr Rasmussen insisted on seeing her off and ordered up a big dinner in the restaurant at the Gare de Lyon that Eveline was too excited to eat, what with the smell of the coalsmoke and the thought of waking up where it would be sunny and warm. Paul Johnson appeared when they were about half through, saying he'd come to help them with their bags. He'd lost one of the buttons off his uniform and he looked gloomy and mussed-up. He said he wouldn't eat anything, but nervously drank down several glasses of wine. Both he and Mr Rasmussen looked like thunderclouds when Jerry Burnham appeared drunk as a lord carrying a large bouquet of roses.

'Won't that be taking coals to Newcastle, Jerry?' said Eveline.

'You don't know Nice . . . you'll probably have skating down there . . . beautiful figure eights on the ice.'

'Jerry,' said Eleanor in her chilly little voice, 'you're thinking of St Moritz.'

'You'll be thinking of it too,' said Jerry, 'when you feel that cold wind.'

Meanwhile Paul and Mr Rasmussen had picked up their bags. 'Honestly, we'd better make tracks,' said Paul, nervously jiggling Eveline's suitcase. 'It's about traintime.' They all scampered through the station. Jerry Burnham had forgotten to buy a ticket and couldn't go out on the platform, they left him arguing with the officials and searching his pockets for his presscard. Paul put the bags in the compartment and shook hands hurriedly with Eleanor. Eveline found his eyes in hers serious and hurt like a dog's eyes.

'You won't stay too long, will you? There's not much time left,' he said. Eveline felt she'd like to kiss him, but the train was starting. Paul scrambled off. All Mr Rasmussen could do was hand some papers and Jerry's roses through the window and wave his hat mournfully from the platform. It was a relief the train had started. Eleanor was leaning back against the cushions laughing and laughing.

'I declare, Eveline. You're too funny with your Romeos.'

Eveline couldn't help laughing herself. She leaned over and patted Eleanor on the shoulder. 'Let's just have a wonderful time,' she said.

Next morning early when Eveline woke up and looked out they were in the station at Marseilles. It gave her a funny feeling because she'd wanted to stop off there and see the town, but Eleanor had insisted on going straight to Nice, she hated the sordidness of seaports she'd said. But later when they had their coffee in the diner, looking out at the pines and the dry hills and headlands cutting out blue patches of the Mediterranean, Eveline felt excited and happy again.

They got a good room in a hotel and walked through the streets in the cool sunshine among the wounded soldiers and officers of all the Allied armies and strolled along the Promenade des Anglais under the gray palmtrees, and gradually Eveline began to feel a chilly feeling of disappointment coming over her. Here was her twoweeks leave and she was going to waste it at Nice. Eleanor kept on being crisp and cheerful and suggested they sit down in the big café on the square where a brass band was playing and have a little dubonnet before lunch. After they'd sat there for some time, looking at the uniforms and the quantities of overdressed women who were no better than they should be, Eveline leaned back in her chair and said, 'And now that we're here, darling, what on earth shall we do?'

The next morning Eveline woke late; she almost hated to get up, as she couldn't imagine how she was going to pass the time all day. As she lay there looking at the stripes of sunlight on the wall that came through the shutters, she heard a man's voice in the adjoining room, that was Eleanor's. Eveline stiffened and listened. It was J. W.'s voice. When she got up and dressed, she found her heart was pounding. She was pulling on her best pair of transparent black silk stockings when Eleanor came in. 'Who do you think's turned up? J. W. just motored down to see me off to Italy . . . He said it was getting too stuffy for him around the Peace Conference and he had to get a change of air . . . Come on in, Eveline, dear, and have some coffee with us.'

She can't keep the triumph out of her voice, aren't women silly, thought Eveline. 'That's lovely, I'll be right in, darling,' she said in her most musical tones.

J. W. had on a light gray flannel suit and a bright blue necktie and his face was pink from the long ride. He was in fine spirits. He'd driven down from Paris in fifteen hours with only four hours' sleep after dinner in Lyons. They all drank a great deal of bitter coffee with hot milk and planned out a ride.

It was a fine day. The big Packard car rolled them smoothly along the Corniche. They lunched at Monte Carlo, took a look at the casino in the afternoon, and went on and had tea in an English tearoom in Mentone. Next day they went up to Grasse and saw the perfume factories, and the day after they put Eleanor on the rapide for Rome. J. W. was to leave immediately afterwards to go back to Paris. Eleanor's thin white face looked a little forlorn, Eveline thought, looking out at them through the window of the wagon-lit. When the train pulled out, Eveline and J. W. stood on the platform in the empty station with the smoke swirling milky with sunlight under the glass roof overhead and looked at each other with a certain amount of constraint.

'She's a great little girl,' said J. W.

'I'm very fond of her,' said Eveline. Her voice rang false in her ears. 'I wish we were going with her.'

They walked back out to the car. 'Where can I take you, Eveline, before I pull out, back to the hotel?'

Eveline's heart was pounding again. 'Suppose we have a little lunch before you go, let me invite you to lunch.'

'That's very nice of you . . . well, I suppose I might as well, I've got to lunch somewhere. And there's no place fit for a white man between here and Lyons.'

They lunched at the casino over the water. The sea was very blue. Outside there were three sailboats with lateen sails making for the entrance to the port. It was warm and jolly, smelt of wine and food sizzled in butter in the glassedin restaurant. Eveline began to like it in Nice.

J. W. drank more wine than he usually did. He began to talk about his boyhood in Wilmington and even hummed a little of a song he'd written in the old days. Eveline was thrilled. Then he began to tell her about Pittsburgh and his ideas about capital and labor. For dessert they had peaches flambé with rum; Eveline recklessly ordered a bottle of champagne. They were getting along famously.

They began to talk about Eleanor. Eveline told about how she'd met Eleanor in the Art Institute and how Eleanor had meant everything to her in Chicago, the only girl she'd ever met who was really interested in the things she was interested in, and how much talent Eleanor had, and how much business ability. J. W. told about how much she'd meant to him during the trying years with his second wife Gertrude in New York, and how people had misunderstood their beautiful friendship that had been always free from the sensual and the degrading.

'Really,' said Eveline, looking J. W. suddenly straight in the eye, 'I'd always thought you and Eleanor were lovers.'

J. W. blushed. For a second Eveline was afraid she'd shocked him. He wrinkled up the skin around his eyes in a comical boyish way. 'No, honestly not . . . I've been too busy working all my life ever to develop that side of my nature . . . People think differently about those things than they did.' Eveline nodded. The deep flush on his face seemed to have set her cheeks on fire. 'And now,' J. W. went on, shaking his head gloomily, 'I'm in my forties and it's too late.'

'Why too late?'

Eveline sat looking at him with her lips a little apart, her cheeks blazing.

'Maybe it's taken the war to teach us how to live,' he said. 'We've been too much interested in money and material things, it's taken the French to show us how to live. Where back home in the States could you find a beautiful atmosphere like this?' J. W. waved his arm to include in a sweeping gesture the sea, the tables crowded with women dressed in bright colors and men in their best uniforms, the bright glint of blue light on glasses and cutlery. The waiter mistook his gesture and slyly substituted a full bottle for the empty bottle in the champagnepail.

'By golly, Eveline, you've been so charming, you've made me forget the time and going back to Paris and everything. This is the sort of thing I've missed all my life until I met you and Eleanor . . . of course, with Eleanor it's been all on the higher plane . . . Let's take a drink to Eleanor . . . beautiful talented Eleanor . . . Eveline, women have been a great inspiration to me all my life, lovely charming delicate women. Many of my best ideas have come from women, not directly, you understand, but through the mental stimulation . . . People don't understand me, Eveline, some of the newspaper boys particularly have written some very hard things about me . . . why, I'm an old newspaperman myself . . . Eveline, permit me to say that you look so charming and understanding . . . this illness of my wife . . . poor Gertrude . . . I'm afraid she'll never be herself again . . . You see, it's put me in a most disagreeable position, if some member of her family is appointed guardian it might mean that the considerable sum of money invested by the Staple family in my business would be withdrawn . . . that would leave me with very grave embarrassments . . . then I've had to abandon my Mexican affairs . . . what the oil business down there needs is just somebody to explain its point of view to the Mexican public, to the American public, my aim was to get the big interests to take the public in . . .' Eveline filled his glass. Her head was swimming a little, but she felt wonderful. She wanted to lean over and kiss him, to make him feel how she admired and understood him. He went on talking with the glass in his hand, almost as if he were speaking to a whole Rotary Club. '. . . to take the public into its confidence . . . I had to throw overboard all that . . . when I felt the government of my country needed me. My position is very difficult in Paris, Eveline. . . . They've got the President surrounded by a Chinese wall . . . I fear that his advisers don't realize the importance of publicity, of taking the public into their confidence at every move. This is a great historical moment, America stands at the parting of the ways . . . without us the war would have ended in a German victory or a negotiated peace . . . And now our very allies are trying to monopolize the natural resources of the world behind our backs. . . . You remember what Rasmussen said . . . well, he's quite right. The President is surrounded by sinister intrigues. Why, even the presidents of the great corporations don't realize that now is the time to spend money, to spend it like water. I could have the French press in my pocket in a week with the proper resources, even in England I have a hunch that something could be done if it was handled the right way. And then the people are fully behind us everywhere, they are sick of autocracy and secret diplomacy, they are ready to greet American democracy, American democratic business methods with open arms. The only way for us to secure the benefits of the peace to the world is for us to dominate it. Mr Wilson doesn't realize the power of a modern campaign of scientific publicity . . . Why, for three weeks I've been trying to get an interview with him, and back in Washington I was calling him Woodrow, almost . . . It was at his personal request that I dropped everything in New York at great personal sacrifice, brought over a large part of my office staff . . . and now . . . but Eveline, my dear girl, I'm afraid I'm talking you to death.'

Eveline leaned over and patted his hand that lay on the edge of the table. Her eyes were shining. 'Oh, it's wonderful,' she said. 'Isn't this fun, J. W.?'

'Ah, Eveline, I wish I was free to fall in love with you.'

'Aren't we pretty free, J. W.? and it's wartime . . . I think all the conventional rubbish about marriage and everything is just too tiresome, don't you?'

'Ah, Eveline, if I was only free . . . let's go out and take a little air . . . Why, we've been here all afternoon.'

Eveline insisted on paying for the lunch, although it took all the money she had on her. They both staggered a little as they left the restaurant, Eveline felt giddy and leaned against J. W.'s shoulder. He kept patting her hand and saying. 'There, there, we'll take a little ride.'

Towards sunset they were riding around the end of the bay into Cannes. 'Well, well, we must pull ourselves together,' said J. W. 'You don't want to stay down here all alone, do you, little girl? Suppose you drive back to Paris with me, we'll stop off in some picturesque villages, make a trip of it. Too likely to meet people we know around here. I'll send back the staffcar and hire a French car . . . take no chances.'

'All right, I think Nice is just too tiresome anyway.'

J. W. called to the chauffeur to go back to Nice. He dropped her at her hotel, saying he'd call for her at ninethirty in the morning and that she must get a good night's sleep. She felt terribly let down after he'd gone; had a cup of tea that was cold and tasted of soap sent to her room; and went to bed. She lay in bed thinking that she was acting like a nasty little bitch; but it was too late to go back now. She couldn't sleep, her whole body felt jangled and twitching. This way she'd look like a wreck tomorrow, she got up and rustled around in her bag until she found some aspirin. She took a lot of the aspirin and got back in bed again and lay perfectly still, but she kept seeing faces that would grow clear out of the blur of a half-dream and then fade again, and her ears buzzed with long cadences of senseless talk. Sometimes it was Jerry Burnham's face that would bud out of the mists, changing slowly into Mr Rasmussen's or Edgar Robbins's or Paul Johnson's or Freddy Seargeant's. She got up and walked shivering up and down the room for a long time. Then she got into bed again and fell asleep and didn't wake up until the chambermaid knocked on the door saying that a gentleman was waiting for her.

When she got down, J. W. was pacing up and down in the sun outside the hotel door. A long lowslung Italian car was standing under the palms beside the geranium bed. They had coffee together without saying much at a little iron table outside the hotel. J. W. said he'd had a miserable room in a hotel where the service was poor.

As soon as Eveline got her bag down, they started off at sixty miles an hour. The chauffeur drove like a fiend through a howling north wind that increased as they went down the coast. They were in Marseilles stiff and dustcaked in time for a late lunch at a fish restaurant on the edge of the old harbor. Eveline's head was whirling again, with speed and lashing wind and dust and vines and olivetrees and gray rock mountains whirling past and now and then a piece of slateblue sea cut out with a jigsaw.

'After all, J. W., the war was terrible,' said Eveline. 'But it's a great time to be alive. Things are happening at last.'

J. W. muttered something about a surge of idealism between his teeth and went on eating his bouillabaisse. He didn't seem to be very talkative today. 'Now at home,' he said, 'they wouldn't have left all the bones in the fish this way.'

'Well, what do you think is going to happen about the oil situation?' Eveline started again.

'Blamed if I know,' said J. W. 'We'd better be starting if we're going to make that place before nightfall.'

J. W. had sent the chauffeur to buy an extra rug and they wrapped themselves up tight under the little hood in the back of the car. J. W. put his arm around Eveline and tucked her in. 'Now we're snug as a bug in a rug,' he said. They giggled cozily together.

The mistral got so strong the poplars were all bent double on the dusty plains before the car started to climb the winding road to Les Baux. Bucking the wind cut down their speed. It was dark when they got into the ruined town.

They were the only people in the hotel. It was cold there and the knots of olivewood burning in the grates didn't give any heat, only puffs of gray smoke when a gust of wind came down the chimney, but they had an excellent dinner and hot spiced wine that made them feel much better. They had to put on their overcoats to go up to their bedroom. Climbing the stairs J. W. kissed her under the ear and whispered, 'Eveline, dear little girl, you make me feel like a boy again.'

Long after J. W. had gone to sleep, Eveline lay awake beside him listening to the wind rattling the shutters, yelling around the corners of the roof, howling over the desert plain far below. The house smelt of dry dusty coldness. No matter how much she cuddled against him, she couldn't get to feel really warm. The same creaky carrousel of faces, plans, scraps of talk kept going round and round in her head. keeping her from thinking consecutively. keeping her from going to sleep.

Next morning when J. W. found he had to bathe out of a basin he made a face and said, 'I hope you don't mind roughing it this way, dear little girl.'

They went over across the Rhône to Nîmes for lunch, riding through Arles and Avignon on the way, then they turned back to the Rhône and got into Lyons late at night. They had supper sent up to their room in the hotel and took hot baths and drank hot wine again. When the waiter had taken away the tray, Eveline threw herself on J. W.'s lap and began to kiss him. It was a long time before she'd let him go to sleep.

Next morning it was raining hard. They waited around a couple of hours hoping it would stop. J. W. was preoccupied and tried to get Paris on the phone, but without any luck. Eveline sat in the dreary hotel salon reading old copies of *l'Illustration*. She wished she was back in Paris too. Finally they decided to start.

The rain went down to a drizzle, but the roads were in a bad shape and by dark they hadn't gotten any further than Nevers. J. W. was getting the sniffles and started taking quinine to ward off a cold. He got adjoining rooms with a bath between in the hotel at Nevers, so that night they slept in separate beds. At supper Eveline tried to get him talking about the Peace Conference, but he said, 'Why talk shop? We'll be back there soon enough. Why not talk about ourselves and each other?'

When they got near Paris, J. W. began to get nervous. His nose had begun to run. At Fontainebleau they had a fine lunch. J. W. went in from there on the train, leaving the chauffeur to take Eveline home to the Rue de Bussy and then deliver his baggage at the Crillon afterward. Eveline felt pretty forlorn riding in all alone through the suburbs of Paris. She was remembering how excited she'd been when they'd all been seeing her off at the Gare de Lyons a few days before and decided she was very unhappy indeed.

Next day she went around to the Crillon at about the usual time in the afternoon. There was nobody in J. W.'s anteroom but Miss Williams, his secretary. She stared Eveline right in the face with such cold hostile eyes that Eveline immediately thought she must know something. She said Mr Moorehouse had a bad cold and fever and wasn't seeing anybody.

'Well, I'll write him a little note,' said Eveline. 'No, I'll call him up later. Don't you think that's the idea, Miss Williams?' Miss Williams nodded her head dryly. 'Very well,' she said.

Eveline lingered. 'You see, I've just come back from leave . . . I came back a couple of days early because there was so much sightseeing I wanted to do near Paris. Isn't the weather miserable?'

Miss Williams puckered her forehead thoughtfully and took a step towards her. 'Very . . . It's most unfortunate, Miss Hutchins, that Mr Moorehouse should have gotten this cold at this moment. We have a number of important matters pending. And the way things are at the Peace Conference the situation changes every minute so that constant watchfulness is necessary . . . We think it is a very important moment from every point of view . . . Too bad Mr Moorehouse should get laid up just now. We feel very badly about it, all of us. He feels just terribly about it.'

'I'm so sorry,' said Eveline. 'I do hope he'll be better tomorrow.'

'The doctor says he will . . . but it's very unfortunate.'

Eveline stood hesitating. She didn't know what to say. Then she caught sight of a little gold star that Miss Williams wore on a brooch. Eveline wanted to make friends. 'Oh, Miss Williams,' she said, 'I didn't know you lost anyone dear to you.'

Miss Williams's face got more chilly and pinched than ever. She seemed to be fumbling for something to say. 'Er . . . my brother was in the navy,' she said and walked over to her desk where she started typing very fast. Eveline stood where she was a second watching Miss Williams's fingers twinkling on the keyboard. Then she said weakly, 'Oh, I'm so sorry,' and turned and went out.

When Eleanor got back, with a lot of old Italian damask in her trunk, J. W. was up and around again. It seemed to Eveline that Eleanor had something cold and sarcastic in her manner of speaking she'd never had before. When she went to the Crillon to tea, Miss Williams would hardly speak to Eveline, but put herself out to be polite to Eleanor. Even Morton, the valet, seemed to make the same difference. J. W. from time to time gave her a furtive squeeze of the hand, but they never got to go out alone any more. Eveline began to think of going home to America, but the thought of going back to Santa Fé or to any kind of life she'd lived before was hideous to her. She wrote J. W. long uneasy notes every day telling him how unhappy she was, but he never mentioned them when she saw him. When she asked him once why he didn't ever write her a few words, he said quickly, 'I never write personal letters,' and changed the subject.

In the end of April Don Stevens turned up in Paris. He was in civilian clothes as he'd resigned from the reconstruction unit. He asked Eveline to put him up as he was broke. Eveline was afraid of the concierge and of what Eleanor or J. W. might say if they found out, but she felt desperate and bitter and didn't care much what happened anyway; so she said all right, she'd put him up, but he wasn't to tell anybody where he was staying. Don teased her about her bourgeois ideas, said those sorts of things wouldn't matter after the revolution, that the first test of strength was coming on the first of May. He made her read *L'Humanité* and took her up to the Rue du Croissant to show her the little restaurant where Jaurès had been assassinated.

One day a tall longfaced young man in some kind of a uniform came into the office and turned out to be Freddy Seargeant, who had just got a job in the Near East Relief and was all excited about going out to Constantinople. Eveline was delighted to see him, but after she'd been with him all afternoon she began to feel that the old talk about the theater and decoration and pattern and color and form didn't mean much to her any more. Freddy was in ecstasy about being in Paris, and the little children sailing boats in the ponds in the Tuileries Gardens, and the helmets of the Garde Républicaine turned out to salute the King and Queen of the Belgians who happened to be going up the Rue de Rivoli when they passed. Eveline felt mean and teased him about not having gone through with it as a C.O.; he explained that a friend had gotten him into the camouflage service before he knew it and that he didn't care about politics anyway, and that before he could do anything the war was over and he was discharged. They tried to get Eleanor to go out to dinner with them, but she had a mysterious engagement to dine with J. W. and some people from the Quai d'Orsay, and couldn't come. Eveline went with Freddy to the Opéra Comique to see *Pélléas*, but she felt fidgety all through it and almost slapped him when she saw he was

crying at the end. Having an orangewater ice at the Café
Néapolitan afterwards, she upset Freddy terribly by saying
Debussy was old hat, and he took her home glumly in a taxi.
At the last minute she relented and tried to be nice to him;
she promised to go out to Chartres with him the next Sunday.

It was still dark when Freddy turned up Sunday morning.
They went out and got some coffee sleepily from an old
woman who had a little stand in the doorway opposite. They
still had an hour before traintime and Freddy suggested they
go and get Eleanor up. He'd so looked forward to going to
Chartres with both of them, he said; it would be old times all
over again, he hated to think how life was drawing them all
apart. So they got into a cab and went down to the Quai de la
Tournelle. The great question was how to get in the house, as the
street door was locked and there was no concierge. Freddy rang
and rang the bell until finally the Frenchman who lived on the
lower floor came out indignant in his bathrobe and let them in.

They banged on Eleanor's door. Freddy kept shouting,
'Eleanor Stoddard, you jump right up and come to Chartres
with us.' After a while Eleanor's face appeared, cool and white
and collected, in the crack of the door above a stunning blue
négligée.

'Eleanor, we've got just half an hour to catch the train for
Chartres, the taxi has full steam up outside and if you don't
come we'll all regret it to our dying day.'

'But I'm not dressed . . . it's so early.'

'You look charming enough to go just as you are.' Freddy
pushed through the door and grabbed her in his arms. 'Eleanor,
you've got to come...I'm off for the Near East tomorrow night.'

Eveline followed them into the salon. Passing the halfopen
door of the bedroom, she glanced in and found herself looking
J. W. full in the face. He was sitting bolt upright in the bed,
wearing pajamas with a bright blue stripe. His blue eyes looked
straight through her. Some impulse made Eveline pull the door
to.

Eleanor noticed her gesture. 'Thank you, darling,' she said
coolly, 'it's so untidy in there.'

'Oh, do come, Eleanor . . . after all you can't have forgotten
old times the way hardhearted Hannah there seems to have,'
said Freddy in a cajoling whine.

'Let me think,' said Eleanor, tapping her chin with the sharppointed nail of a white forefinger. 'I'll tell you what we'll do,
darlings, you two go out on the poky old train as you're ready

and I'll run out as soon as I'm dressed and call up J. W. at the Crillon and see if he won't drive me out. Then we can all come back together. How's that?'

'That would be lovely, Eleanor dear,' said Eveline in a singsong voice. 'Splendid, oh, I knew you'd come . . well, we've got to be off. If we miss each other, we'll be in front of the cathedral at noon . . . Is that all right?'

Eveline went downstairs in a daze. All the way out to Chartres, Freddy was accusing her bitterly of being absentminded and not liking her old friends any more.

By the time they got to Chartres it was raining hard. They spent a gloomy day there. The stained glass that had been taken away for safety during the war hadn't been put back yet. The tall twelfth-century saints had a wet, slimy look in the driving rain. Freddy said that the sight of the black Virgin surrounded by candles in the crypt was worth all the trouble of the trip for him, but it wasn't for Eveline. Eleanor and J. W. didn't turn up. 'Of course not in this rain,' said Freddy. It was a kind of relief to Eveline to find that she'd caught cold and would have to go to bed as soon as she got home. Freddy took her to her door in a taxi, but she wouldn't let him come up for fear he'd find Don there.

Don was there, and was very sympathetic about her cold and tucked her in bed and made her a hot lemonade with cognac in it. He had his pockets full of money, as he'd just sold some articles, and had gotten a job to go to Vienna for the *Daily Herald* of London. He was pulling out as soon after May 1 as he could . . . 'unless something breaks here,' he said impressively. He went away that evening to a hotel, thanking her for putting him up like a good comrade even if she didn't love him any more. The place felt empty after he'd gone. She almost wished she'd made him stay. She lay in bed feeling feverishly miserable, and finally went to sleep feeling sick and scared and lonely.

The morning of the first of May, Paul Johnson came around before she was up. He was in civilian clothes and looked young and slender and nice and lighthaired and handsome. He said Don Stevens had gotten him all wrought up about what was going to happen, what with the general strike and all that; he'd come to stick around if Eveline didn't mind. 'I thought I'd better not be in uniform, so I borrowed this suit from a feller,' he said.

'I think I'll strike too,' said Eveline. 'I'm so sick of that Red Cross office I could scream.'

'Gee, that 'ud be wonderful, Eveline. We can walk around and see the excitement. . . . It'll be all right if you're with me . . . I mean I'll be easier in my mind if I know where you are if there's trouble . . . You're awful reckless, Eveline.'

'My, you look handsome in that suit, Paul . . . I never saw you in civilian clothes before.'

Paul blushed and put his hands uneasily into his pockets. 'Lord, I'll be glad to get into civvies for keeps,' he said seriously. 'Even though it'll mean me goin' back to work. . . . I can't get a darn thing out of these Sorbonne lectures . . . everybody's too darn restless, I guess . . . and I'm sick of hearing what bums the Boches are, that's all the frog profs seem to be able to talk about.'

'Well, go out and read a book and I'll get up. . . . Did you notice if the old woman across the way had coffee out?'

'Yare, she did,' called Paul from the salon to which he'd retreated when Eveline stuck her toes out from under the bedclothes. 'Shall I go out and bring some in?'

'That's a darling, do. . . . I've got brioches and butter here . . . take that enameled milkcan out of the kitchen.'

Eveline looked at herself in the mirror before she started dressing. She had shadows under her eyes and faint beginnings of crowsfeet. Chillier than the damp Paris room came the thought of growing old. It was so horribly actual that she suddenly burst into tears. An old hag's tearsmeared face looked at her bitterly out of the mirror. She pressed the palms of her hands hard over her eyes. 'Oh, I lead such a silly life,' she whispered aloud.

Paul was back. She could hear him moving around awkwardly in the salon. 'I forgot to tell you . . . Don says Anatole France is going to march with the mutilays of la guerre. . . . I've got the cafay o lay whenever you're ready.'

'Just a minute,' she called from the basin where she was splashing cold water on her face. 'How old are you, Paul?' she asked him when she came out of her bedroom all dressed, smiling, feeling that she was looking her best.

'Free, white, and twentyone . . . we'd better drink up this coffee before it gets cold.'

'You don't look as old as that.'

'Oh, I'm old enough to know better,' said Paul, getting very red in the face.

'I'm five years older than that,' said Eveline. 'Oh, how I hate growing old.'

'Five years don't mean anything,' stammered Paul.

He was so nervous he spilt a lot of coffee over his trouserleg. 'Oh, hell, that's a dumb thing to do,' he growled.

'I'll get it out in a second,' said Eveline, running for a towel. She made him sit in a chair and kneeled down in front of him and scrubbed at the inside of his thigh with the towel. Paul sat there stiff, red as a beet, with his lips pressed together. He jumped to his feet before she'd finished. 'Well, let's go out and see what's happening. I wish I knew more about what it's all about.'

'Well, you might at least say thank you,' said Eveline, looking up at him.

'Thanks; gosh, it's awful nice of you, Eveline.'

Outside it was like Sunday. A few stores were open on the side streets, but they had their iron shutters halfway down. It was a gray day; they walked up the Boulevard Saint-Germain, passing many people out strolling in their best clothes. It wasn't until a squadron of the Garde Républicaine clattered past them in their shiny helmets and their tricolor plumes that they had any inkling of tenseness in the air.

Over on the other side of the Seine there were more people and little groups of gendarmes standing around.

At the crossing of several streets they saw a cluster of old men in workclothes with a red flag and a sign, L'UNION DES TRAVAILLEURS FERA LA PAIX DU MONDE. A cordon of republican guards rode down on them with their sabers drawn, the sun flashing on their helmets. The old men ran or flattened themselves in doorways.

On the Grands Boulevards there were companies of poilus in tin hats and grimy blue uniforms standing round their stacked rifles. The crowds on the streets cheered them as they surged past; everything seemed goodnatured and jolly. Eveline and Paul began to get tired; they'd been walking all morning. They began to wonder where they'd get any lunch. Then, too, it was starting to rain.

Passing the Bourse they met Don Stevens, who had just come out of the telegraph office. He was sore and tired. He'd been up since five o'clock. 'If they're going to have a riot, why the hell can't they have it in time to make the cables . . . Well, I saw Anatole France dispersed on the Place d'Alma. Ought to be a story in that except for all this damned censorship. Things are pretty serious in Germany . . . I think something's going to happen there.'

'Will anything happen here in Paris, Don?' asked Paul.

'Damned if I know . . . some kids busted up those gratings around the trees and threw them at the cops on the Avenue Magenta . . . Burnham in there says there are barricades at the end of the Place de la Bastille, but I'm damned if I'm going over till I get something to eat . . . I don't believe it anyway . . . I'm about foundered What are you two bourgeois doing out a day like this?'

'Hey, fellowworker, don't shoot,' said Paul, throwing up his hands. 'Wait till we get something to eat,' Eveline laughed. She thought how much better she liked Paul than she liked Don.

They walked around a lot of back streets in the drizzling rain and at last found a little restaurant from which came voices and a smell of food. They ducked in under the iron shutter of the door. It was dark and crowded with taxidrivers and workingmen. They squeezed into the end of a marble table where two old men were playing chess. Eveline's leg was pressed against Paul's. She didn't move; then he began to get red and moved his chair a little. 'Excuse me,' he said.

They all ate liver and onions, and Don got to talking with the old men in his fluent bad French. They said the youngsters weren't good for anything nowadays. In the old days when they descended into the street they tore up the pavings and grabbed the cops by the legs and pulled them off their horses. Today was supposed to be a general strike and what had they done? . . . nothing . . . a few urchins had thrown some stones and one café window had been broken. It wasn't like that that liberty defended itself and the dignity of labor. The old men went back to their chess. Don set them up to a bottle of wine.

Eveline was sitting back halflistening, wondering if she'd go around to see J. W. in the afternoon. She hadn't seen him or Eleanor since that Sunday morning; she didn't care anyway. She wondered, if Paul would marry her, how it would be to have a lot of little babies that would have the same young coltish fuzzy look he had. She liked it in this little dark restaurant that smelt of food and wine and caporal ordinaire, sitting back and letting Don lay down the law to Paul about the revolution.

'When I get back home, I guess I'll bum around the country a little, get a job as a harvesthand and stuff like that and find out about those things,' Paul said finally. 'Now I don't know a darn thing, just what I hear people say.'

After they had eaten they were sitting over some glasses of wine, when they heard an American voice. Two M.P.'s had come in and were having a drink at the zinc bar.

'Don't talk English,' whispered Paul. They sat there stiffly trying to look as French as possible until the two khaki uniforms disappeared, then Paul said, 'Whee, I was scared . . . they'd picked me up sure as hell if they'd found me without my uniform . . . Then it'd have been the Roo Saint Anne and goodbye Paree.'

'Why, you poor kid, they'd have shot you at sunrise,' said Eveline. 'You go right home and change your clothes at once . . . . I'm going to the Red Cross for a while anyway.'

Don walked over to the Rue de Rivoli with her. Paul shot off down another street to go to his room and get his uniform.

'I think Paul Johnson's an awfully nice boy; where did you collect him, Don?' Eveline said in a casual tone.

'He's kinder simple . . . unlicked cub kind of a kid . . . I guess he's all right . . . I got to know him when the transport section he was in was billeted near us up in the Marne . . . Then he got this cush job in the Post Dispatch Service and now he's studying at the Sorbonne. . . . By God, he needs it . . . no social ideas . . . Paul still thinks it was the stork.'

'He must come from near where you came from . . . back home, I mean.'

'Yare, his dad owns a grain elevator in some little tank town or other . . . petit bourgeois . . . bum environment . . . He's not a bad kid in spite of it . . . Damn shame he hasn't read Marx, something to stiffen his ideas up.' Don made a funny face. 'That goes with you too, Eveline, but I gave you up as hopeless long ago. Ornamental but not useful.'

They'd stopped and were talking on the streetcorner under the arcade.

'Oh, Don, I think your ideas are just too tiresome,' she began.

He interrupted, 'Well, solong, here comes a bus . . . I oughtn't to ride on a scab bus, but it's too damn far to walk all the way to the Bastille.' He gave her a kiss. 'Don't be sore at me.'

Eveline waved her hand, 'Have a good time in Vienna, Don.' He jumped on the platform of the bus as it rumbled past. The last Eveline saw the woman conductor was trying to push him off because the bus was complet.

She went up to her office and tried to look as if she'd been there all day. At a little before six she walked up the street to the Crillon and went to see J. W. Everything was as usual there,

Miss Williams looking chilly and yellowhaired at her desk, Morton stealthily handing around tea and petit fours, J. W. deep in talk with a personage in a cutaway in the embrasure of the window, halfhidden by the heavy champagnecolored drapes, Eleanor in a pearlgray afternoon dress Eveline had never seen before, chatting chirpily with three young staff-officers in front of the fireplace. Eveline had a cup of tea and talked about something or other with Eleanor for a moment, then she said she had an engagement and left.

In the anteroom she caught Miss Williams's eye as she passed. She stopped by her desk a moment: 'Busy as ever, Miss Williams,' she said.

'It's better to be busy,' she said. 'It keeps a person out of mischief . . . It seems to me that in Paris they waste a great deal of time . . . I never imagined that there could be a place where people could sit around idle so much of the time.'

'The French value their leisure more than anything.'

'Leisure's all right if you have something to do with it . . . but this social life wastes so much of our time . . . People come to lunch and stay all afternoon. I don't know what we can do about it . . . it makes a very difficult situation.' Miss Williams looked hard at Eveline. 'I don't suppose you have much to do down at the Red Cross any more, do you, Miss Hutchins?'

Eveline smiled sweetly. 'No, we just live for our leisure like the French.'

She walked across the wide asphalt spaces of the Place de la Concorde, without knowing quite what to do with herself, and turned up the Champs Élysées where the horsechestnuts were just coming into flower. The general strike seemed to be about over, because there were a few cabs on the streets. She sat down on a bench and a cadaverouslooking individual in a frock coat sat down beside her and tried to pick her up. She got up and walked as fast as she could. At the Rond Point she had to stop to wait for a bunch of French mounted artillery and two seventyfives to go past before she could cross the street. The cadaverous man was beside her; he turned and held out his hand, tipping his hat as he did so, as if he was an old friend. She muttered, 'Oh, it's just too tiresome,' and got into a horse-cab that was standing by the curb. She almost thought the man was going to get in, too, but he just stood looking after her scowling as the cab drove off following the guns as if she was part of the regiment. Once at home she made herself some cocoa on the gasstove and went lonely to bed with a book.

Next evening when she got back to her apartment Paul was waiting for her, wearing a new uniform and with a resplendent shine on his knobtoed shoes. 'Why, Paul, you look as if you'd been through a washing machine.'

'A friend of mine's a sergeant in the quartermaster's stores . . . coughed up a new outfit.'

'You look too beautiful for words.'

'You mean you do, Eveline.'

They went over to the boulevards and had dinner on the salmoncolored plush seats among the Pompeian columns at Noël Peter's to the accompaniment of slithery violinmusic. Paul had his month's pay and commutation of rations in his pocket and felt fine. They talked about what they'd do when they got back to America. Paul said his dad wanted him to go into a grainbroker's office in Minneapolis, but he wanted to try his luck in New York. He thought a young feller ought to try a lot of things before he settled down at a business so that he could find out what he was fitted for. Eveline said she didn't know what she wanted to do. She didn't want to do anything she'd done before, she knew that, maybe she'd like to live in Paris.

'I didn't like it much in Paris before,' Paul said, 'but like this, goin' out with you, I like it fine.'

Eveline teased him, 'Oh, I don't think you like me much, you never act as if you did.'

'But jeez, Eveline, you know so much and you've been around so much. It's mighty nice of you to let me come around at all, honestly I'll appreciate it all my life.'

'Oh, I wish you wouldn't be like that . . . I hate people to be humble,' Eveline broke out angrily.

They went on eating in silence. They were eating asparagus with grated cheese on it. Paul took several gulps of wine and looked at her in a hurt dumb way she hated.

'Oh, I feel like a party tonight,' she said a little later. 'I've been so miserable all day, Paul . . . I'll tell you about it sometime . . . you know the kind of feeling when everything you've wanted crumbles in your fingers as you grasp it.'

'All right, Eveline,' Paul said, banging with his fist on the table, 'let's cheer up and have a big time.'

When they were drinking coffee the orchestra began to play polkas and people began to dance among the tables encouraged by cries of Ah Polkaah aah from the violinist. It was a fine sight to see the middleaged diners whirling around under the beaming eyes of the stout Italian headwaiter who seemed to feel that la gaité was coming back to Paree at last. Paul and Eveline forgot themselves and tried to dance it too. Paul was very awkward, but having his arms around her made her feel better somehow, made her forget the scaring loneliness she felt.

When the polka had subsided a little, Paul paid the fat check and they went out arm in arm, pressing close against each other like all the Paris lovers, to stroll on the boulevards in the May evening that smelt of wine and hot rolls and wild strawberries. They felt lightheaded. Eveline kept smiling.

'Come on, let's have a big time,' whispered Paul occasionally as if to keep his courage up.

'I was just thinking what my friends 'ud think if they saw me walking up the Boulevard arm in arm with a drunken doughboy,' Eveline said.

'No, honest, I'm not drunk,' said Paul. 'I can drink a lot more than you think. And I won't be in the army much longer, not if this peace treaty goes through.'

'Oh, I don't care,' said Eveline, 'I don't care what happens.'

They heard music in another café and saw the shadows of dancers passing across the windows upstairs. 'Let's go up there,' said Eveline. They went in and upstairs to the dancehall that was a long room full of mirrors. There Eveline said she wanted to drink some Rhine wine. They studied the card a long while and finally, with a funny sideways look at Paul, suggested liebefraumilch.

Paul got red, 'I wish I had a liebe frau,' he said.

'Why, probably you have . . . one in every port,' said Eveline. He shook his head.

Next time they danced he held her very tight. He didn't seem so awkward as he had before.

'I feel pretty lonely myself, these days,' said Eveline when they sat down again.

'You, lonely . . . with the whole of the Peace Conference running after you, and the A.E.F. too . . . Why, Don told me you're a dangerous woman.'

She shrugged her shoulders. 'When did Don find that out? Maybe you could be dangerous too, Paul.'

Next time they danced, she put her cheek against his. When the music stopped, he looked as if he was going to kiss her, but he didn't.

'This is the most wonderful evening I ever had in my life,'

he said. 'I wish I was the kind of guy you really wanted to have take you out.'

'Maybe you could get to be, Paul . . . you seem to be learning fast. . . . No, but we're acting silly . . . I hate ogling and flirting around . . . I guess I want the moon . . . maybe I want to get married and have a baby.'

Paul was embarrassed. They sat silent watching the other dancers. Eveline saw a young French soldier lean over and kiss the little girl he was dancing with on the lips; kissing, they kept on dancing. Eveline wished she was that girl.

'Let's have a little more wine,' she said to Paul.

'Do you think we'd better? All right, what the heck, we're having a big time.'

Getting in the taxicab Paul was pretty drunk, laughing and hugging her. As soon as they were in the darkness of the back of the taxi, they started kissing.

Eveline held Paul off for a minute. 'Let's go to your place instead of mine,' she said. 'I'm afraid of my concierge.'

'All right . . . it's awful little,' said Paul, giggling. 'But ish gebibbel, we should worry get a wrinkle.'

When they had gotten past the bitter eyes that sized them up of the old man who kept the keys at Paul's hotel, they staggered up a long chilly winding stair and into a little room that gave on a court. 'It's a great life if you don't weaken,' said Paul, waving his arms after he'd locked and bolted the door. It had started to rain again and the rain made the sound of a waterfall on the glass roof at the bottom of the court. Paul threw his hat and tunic in the corner of the room and came towards her, his eyes shining.

They'd hardly gotten to bed when he fell asleep with his head on her shoulder. She slipped out of bed to turn the light off and open the window and then snuggled shivering against his body that was warm and relaxed like a child's. Outside the rain poured down on the glass roof. There was a puppy shut up somewhere in the building that whined and yelped desperately without stopping. Eveline couldn't get to sleep. Something shut up inside her was whining like the puppy. Through the window she began to see the dark peak of a roof and chimneypots against a fading purple sky. Finally she fell asleep.

Next day they spent together. She'd phoned in to the Red Cross that she was sick as usual and Paul forgot about the Sorbonne altogether. They sat all morning in the faint sunshine at a café near the Madeleine making plans about what they'd do. They'd get themselves sent back home as soon as they possibly could and get jobs in New York and get married. Paul was going to study engineering in his spare time. There was a firm of grain and feed merchants in Jersey City, friends of his father's he knew he could get a job with. Eveline could start up her decorating business again. Paul was happy and confident and had lost his apologetic manner. Eveline kept telling herself that Paul had stuff in him, that she was in love with Paul, that something could be made out of Paul.

The rest of the month of May they were both a little light-headed all the time. They spent all their pay the first few days so that they had to eat at little table d'hôte restaurants crowded with students and workingpeople and poor clerks, where they bought books of tickets that gave them a meal for two francs or two-fifty. One Sunday in June they went out to Saint-Germain and walked through the forest. Eveline had spells of nausea and weakness and had to lie down on the grass several times. Paul looked worried sick. At last they got to a little settlement on the bank of the Seine. The Seine flowed fast streaked with green and lilac in the afternoon light, brimming the low banks bordered by ranks of huge poplars. They crossed a little ferry rowed by an old man that Eveline called Father Time.

Halfway over she said to Paul, 'Do you know what's the matter with me, Paul? I'm going to have a baby.'

Paul let his breath out in a whistle. 'Well, I hadn't just planned for that . . . I guess I've been a stinker not to make you marry me before this . . . We'll get married right away. I'll find out what you have to do to get permission to get married in the A.E.F. I guess it's all right, Eveline . . . but, gee, it does change my plans.'

They'd reached the other bank and walked up through Conflans to the railroad station to get the train back to Paris. Paul looked worried.

'Well, don't you think it changes my plans too?' said Eveline dryly. 'It's going over Niagara Falls in a barrel, that's what it is.'

'Eveline,' said Paul seriously with tears in his eyes, 'what can I ever do to make it up to you? . . . honest, I'll do my best.'

The train whistled and rumbled into the platform in front of them. They were so absorbed in their thoughts they hardly saw it. When they'd climbed into a thirdclass compartment they sat silent bolt upright facing each other, their knees touching, looking out of the window without seeing the suburbs of Paris, not saying anything.

At last Eveline said with a tight throat, 'I want to have the little brat, Paul, we have to go through everything in life.' Paul nodded. Then she couldn't see his face any more. The train had gone into a tunnel.

# Newsreel 34

WHOLE WORLD IS SHORT OF PLATINUM

Il serait criminel de négliger les intérêts français dans les Balkans

KILLS SELF IN CELL

the quotation of United Cigar Stores made this month of $167 per share means $501 per share for the old stock upon which present stockholders are receiving 27 per cent per share as formerly held. Through peace and war it has maintained and increased its dividends

SIX TRAPPED ON UPPER FLOOR

*How are you goin' to keep 'em down on the farm*
*After they've seen Paree*

If Wall Street needed the treaty, which means if the business interests of the country properly desired to know to what extent we are being committed in affairs which do not concern us, why should it take the trouble to corrupt the tagrag and bobtail which forms Mr Wilson's following in Paris?

ALLIES URGE MAGYAR PEOPLE TO UPSET
BELA KUN REGIME

ELEVEN WOMEN MISSING IN BLUEBEARD
MYSTERY

Enfin la France achète les stocks américains

*How are you goin' to keep 'em away from Broadway*
*Jazzin' around*
*Paintin' the town*

the boulevards during the afternoon presented an un-wonted aspect. The café terraces in most cases were deserted and had been cleared of their tables and chairs. At some of the cafés customers were admitted one by one and served by faithful waiters, who, however, had discarded their aprons

### YEOMANETTE SHRIEKS FOR FORMER SUITOR AS SHE SEEKS DEATH IN DRIVE APARTMENT

### DESIRES OF HEDJAZ STIR PARIS CRITICS

in order not prematurely to show their colors a pretense is made of disbanding a few formations; in reality, however, these troops are being transferred lock stock and barrel to Kolchak

### I.W.W. IN PLOT TO KILL WILSON

### FIND TEN THOUSAND BAGS OF DECAYED ONIONS

### FALL ON STAIRS KILLS WEALTHY CITIZEN

the mistiness of the weather hid the gunboat from sight soon after it left the dock, but the President continued to wave his hat and smile as the boat headed towards the *George Washington*

### OVERTHROW OF SOVIET RULE SURE

## The House of Morgan

*I commit my soul into the hands of my savior,* wrote John Pierpont Morgan in his will, *in full confidence that having redeemed it and washed it in His most precious blood, He will present it faultless before my heavenly father, and I entreat my children to maintain and defend at all hazard and at any cost of personal sacrifice the blessed doctrine of complete atonement for sin through the blood of Jesus Christ once offered and through that alone,*

and into the hands of the House of Morgan represented by his son,

he committed,

when he died in Rome in 1913,

the control of the Morgan interests in New York, Paris, and London, four national banks, three trust companies, three life insurance companies, ten railroad systems, three streetrail-

way companies, an express company, the International Mercantile Marine,
power,
on the cantilever principle, through interlocking directorates,
over eighteen other railroads, U.S. Steel, General Electric, American Tel. and Tel., five major industries;
the interwoven cables of the Morgan-Stillman-Baker combination held credit up like a suspension bridge, thirteen per cent of the banking resources of the world.

The first Morgan to make a pool was Joseph Morgan, a hotelkeeper in Hartford, Connecticut, who organized stage-coach lines and bought up Aetna Life Insurance stock in a time of panic caused by one of the big New York fires in the 1830s;
his son Junius followed in his footsteps, first in the dry-goods business, and then as partner to George Peabody, a Massachusetts banker who built up an enormous underwriting and mercantile business in London and became a friend of Queen Victoria;
Junius married the daughter of John Pierpont, a Boston preacher, poet, eccentric, and abolitionist; and their eldest son,
John Pierpont Morgan,
arrived in New York to make his fortune
after being trained in England, going to school at Vevey, proving himself a crack mathematician at the University of Göttingen,
a lanky morose young man of twenty,
just in time for the panic of '57
(war and panics on the stock exchange, bankruptcies, war-loans, good growing weather for the House of Morgan).

When the guns started booming at Fort Sumter, young Morgan turned some money over reselling condemned muskets to the U.S. Army and began to make himself felt in the Gold Room in downtown New York; there was more in trading in gold than in trading in muskets; so much for the Civil War.
During the Franco-Prussian War Junius Morgan floated a huge bond issue for the French government at Tours.
At the same time young Morgan was fighting Jay Cooke and the German-Jew Bankers in Frankfort over the funding of

the American war debt (he never did like the Germans or the Jews).

The panic of '73 ruined Jay Cooke and made J. Pierpont Morgan the boss croupier of Wall Street; he united with the Philadelphia Drexels and built the Drexel Building where for thirty years he sat in his glassedin office, redfaced and insolent, writing at his desk, smoking great black cigars, or, if important issues were involved, playing solitaire in his inner office; he was famous for his few words, Yes or No, and for his way of suddenly blowing up in a visitor's face and for that special gesture of the arm that meant, *What do I get out of it?*

In '77 Junius Morgan retired; J. Pierpont got himself made a member of the board of directors of the New York Central Railroad and launched the first *Corsair*. He liked yachting and to have pretty actresses call him Commodore.

He founded the Lying-in Hospital on Stuyvesant Square, and was fond of going into Saint George's church and singing a hymn all alone in the afternoon quiet.

In the panic of '93

at no inconsiderable profit to himself

Morgan saved the U.S. Treasury; gold was draining out, the country was ruined, the farmers were howling for a silver standard, Grover Cleveland and his cabinet were walking up and down in the Blue Room at the White House without being able to come to a decision, in Congress they were making speeches while the gold reserves melted in the Subtreasuries; poor people were starving; Coxey's army was marching to Washington; for a long time Grover Cleveland couldn't bring himself to call in the representative of the Wall Street moneymasters; Morgan sat in his suite at the Arlington smoking cigars and quietly playing solitaire until at last the President sent for him;

he had a plan all ready for stopping the gold hemorrhage.

After that what Morgan said went; when Carnegie sold out he built the Steel Trust.

J. Pierpont Morgan was a bullnecked irascible man with small black magpie's eyes and a growth on his nose; he let his partners work themselves to death over the detailed routine of banking, and sat in his back office smoking black cigars; when there was something to be decided he said Yes or No or just turned his back and went back to his solitaire.

Every Christmas his librarian read him Dickens's *A Christmas Carol* from the original manuscript.

He was fond of canarybirds and pekinese dogs and liked to take pretty actresses yachting. Each *Corsair* was a finer vessel than the last.

When he dined with King Edward he sat at His Majesty's right; he ate with the Kaiser tête-à-tête; he liked talking to cardinals or the Pope, and never missed a conference of Episcopal bishops;

Rome was his favorite city.

He liked choice cookery and old wines and pretty women and yachting, and going over his collections, now and then picking up a jeweled snuffbox and staring at it with his magpie's eyes.

He made a collection of the autographs of the rulers of France, owned glass cases full of Babylonian tablets, seals, signets, statuettes, busts,

Gallo-Roman bronzes,

Merovingian jewels, miniatures, watches, tapestries, porcelains, cuneiform inscriptions, paintings by all the old masters, Dutch, Italian, Flemish, Spanish,

manuscripts of the Gospels and the Apocalypse,

a collection of the works of Jean-Jacques Rousseau,

and the letters of Pliny the Younger.

His collectors bought anything that was expensive or rare or had the glint of empire on it, and he had it brought to him and stared hard at it with his magpie's eyes. Then it was put in a glass case.

The last year of his life he went up the Nile on a dahabeeyah and spent a long time staring at the great columns of the Temple of Karnak.

The panic of 1907 and the death of Harriman, his great opponent in railroad financing, in 1909, had left him the undisputed ruler of Wall Street, most powerful private citizen in the world;

an old man tired of the purple, suffering from gout, he had deigned to go to Washington to answer the questions of the Pujo Committee during the Money Trust Investigation: Yes, I did what seemed to me to be for the best interests of the country.

So admirably was his empire built that his death in 1913 hardly caused a ripple in the exchanges of the world: the purple descended to his son, J. P. Morgan, who had been trained at Groton and Harvard and by associating with the British ruling class

to be a more constitutional monarch: *J. P. Morgan suggests . . .*

By 1917 the Allies had borrowed one billion, ninehundred million dollars through the House of Morgan: we went overseas for democracy and the flag;

and by the end of the Peace Conference the phrase *J. P. Morgan suggests* had compulsion over a power of seventyfour billion dollars.

J. P. Morgan is a silent man, not given to public utterances, but during the great steel strike he wrote Gary: *Heartfelt congratulations on your stand for the open shop, with which I am, as you know, absolutely in accord. I believe American principles of liberty are deeply involved, and must win if we stand firm.*

(Wars and panics on the stock exchange,
machinegunfire and arson,
bankruptcies, warloans,
starvation, lice, cholera and typhus:
good growing weather for the House of Morgan.)

# Newsreel 35

the Grand Prix de la Victoire, run yesterday for fifty-second time was an event that will long remain in the memories of those present, for never in the history of the classic race has Longchamps presented such a glorious scene

*Keep the home fires burning*
*Till the boys come home*

LEVIATHAN UNABLE TO PUT TO SEA

BOLSHEVIKS ABOLISH POSTAGE STAMPS

ARTIST TAKES GAS IN NEW HAVEN

FIND BLOOD ON ONE DOLLAR BILL

*While our hearts are yearning*

POTASH CAUSE OF BREAK IN PARLEY

MAJOR DIES OF POISONING

TOOK ROACH SALTS BY MISTAKE

riot and robbery developed into the most awful pogrom ever heard of. Within two or three days the Lemberg Ghetto was turned into heaps of smoking débris. Eyewitnesses estimate that the Polish soldiers killed more than a thousand Jewish men and women and children

LENIN SHOT BY TROTSKY IN DRUNKEN BRAWL

you know where I stand on beer, said Brisbane in seeking assistance

*Though the boys are far away*
*They long for home*
*There's a silver lining*
*Through the dark clouds shining*

## PRESIDENT EVOKES CRY OF THE DEAD

### LETTER CLUE TO BOMB OUTRAGE

Emile Deen in the preceding three installments of his interview described the situation between the Royal Dutch and the Standard Oil Company, as being the beginning of a struggle for the control of the markets of the world which was only halted by the war. 'The basic factors,' he said, 'are envy, discontent, and suspicion.' The extraordinary industrial growth of our nation since the Civil War, the opening-up of new territory, the development of resources, the rapid increase in population, all these things have resulted in the creation of many big and sudden fortunes. Is there a mother, father, sweetheart, relative, or friend of any one of the two million boys fighting abroad who does not thank God that Wall Street contributed H. P. Davidson to the Red Cross?

#### BOND THIEF MURDERED

*Turn the bright side inside out*
*Till the boys come home*

## The Camera Eye (39)

daylight enlarges out of ruddy quiet very faintly throbbing wanes into my sweet darkness broadens red through the warm blood weighting the lids warmsweetly then snaps on

enormously blue yellow pink

today is Paris    pink sunlight hazy on the clouds against patches of robinsegg    a tiny siren hoots shrilly traffic drowsily rumbles clatters over the cobbles taxis squawk    the yellow's the comforter through the open window the Louvre emphasizes its sedate architecture of greypink stone between the Seine and the sky

and the certainty of Paris

the towboat shiny green and red chugs against the current towing three black and mahoganyvarnished barges their deckhouse windows have green shutters and lace curtains and pots of geraniums in flower    to get under the bridge a fat man in blue had to let the little black stack drop flat to the deck

Paris comes into the room in the servantgirl's eyes the warm bulge of her breasts under the grey smock    the smell of chicory in coffee scalded milk and the shine that crunches on the crescent rolls stuck with little dabs of very sweet unsalted butter

in the yellow paperback of the book that halfhides the agreeable countenance of my friend

Paris of 1919

paris-mutuel

roulettewheel that spins round the Tour Eiffel red square white square a million dollars a billion marks a trillion roubles baisse du franc or a mandate for Montmarte

Cirque Médrano the steeplechase gravity of cellos tuning up on the stage at the Salle Gaveau oboes and a triangle  la musique s'en fou de moi says the old marchioness jingling with diamonds as she walks out on Stravinski   but the red colt took the jumps backwards and we lost all our money

la peinture opposite the Madeleine   Cézanne Picasso Modigliani

Nouvelle Athènes

la poesie of manifestos always freshtinted on the kiosks and slogans scrawled in chalk on the urinals L'UNION DES TRAVAILLEURS FLERA LA PAIX DU MONDE

revolution round the spinning Eiffel Tower

that burns up our last year's diagrams the dates fly off the calendar we'll make everything new today is the Year I   Today is the sunny morning of the first day of spring We gulp our coffee splash water on us jump into our clothes run downstairs step out wideawake into the first morning of the first day of the first year

# Newsreel 36

TO THE GLORY OF FRANCE ETERNAL

*Oh a German officer crossed the Rhine*
*Parleyvoo*

GERMANS BEATEN AT RIGA

GRATEFUL PARISIANS CHEER MARSHALS
OF FRANCE

*Oh a German officer crossed the Rhine*
*He liked the women and loved the wine*
*Hankypanky parleyvoo*

PITEOUS PLAINT OF WIFE TELLS OF RIVAL'S
WILES

Wilson's arrival in Washington starts trouble. Paris strikers hear harangues at picnic. Café wrecked and bombs thrown in Fiume streets. Parisians pay more for meat. Il serait dangereux d'augmenter les vivres. Bethmann Holweg's blood boils. Mysterious forces halt antibolshevist march.

HUN'S HAND SEEN IN PLOTS

*Oh Mademoiselle from Armentières*
*Parleyvoo*
*Oh Mademoiselle from Armentières*
*Parleyvoo*
*Hasn't been — for forty years*
*Hankypanky parleyvoo*

wrecks mark final day at La Baule; syndicated wageearners seize opportunity to threaten employers unprepared for change. LAYS WREATH ON TOMB OF LAFAYETTE. Richest negress is dead. Yale dormitories stormed by angry mob of soldiers. Goldmine in kinks.

TIGHTENS SCREW ON BERLIN

*Oh he took her upstairs and into bed*
*And there he cracked her maidenhead*
*Hankypanky parleyvoo*

NO DROP IN PRICES TO FOLLOW PEACE SAY
BUSINESSMEN

KILLS SELF AT DESK IN OFFICE

MODERN BLUEBEARD NOW VICTIM OF
MELANCHOLIA

He is none other than General Minus of the old Russian Imperial General Staff, who, during the Kerensky régime, was commander of troops in the region of Minsk. Paris policemen threaten to join strike movement, allow it to send into France barrels bearing the mystic word Mistelles. One speculator is said to have netted nearly five million francs within a week.

*Oh the first three months and all went well*
*But the second three months she began to swell*
*Hankypanky parleyvoo*

large financial resources, improved appliances and abundant raw materials of America should assist French genius in restoring and increasing industrial power of France, joining hands in the charming scenery, wonderful roads, excellent hotels, and good cookery makes site of Lyons fair crossed by the fortyfifth parallel. Favored by great mineral resources its future looms incalculably splendid. Any man who attempts to take over control of municipal functions here will be shot on sight, Mayor Ole Hanson remarked. He is a little man himself, but has big ideas; a big brain, and big hopes. Upon first meeting him one is struck by his resemblance to Mark Twain

## *Richard Ellsworth Savage*

Dick and Ned felt pretty rocky the morning they sighted Fire Island lightship. Dick wasn't looking forward to landing in God's Country with no money and the draft board to face, and he was worried about how his mother was going to make out. All Ned was complaining about was wartime prohibition. They were both a little jumpy from all the cognac they'd drunk on the trip over. They were already in the slategreen shallow seas off Long Island; no help for it now. The heavy haze to the west and then the low boxlike houses that looked as if they were drowned in water and then the white strip of beach of the Rockaways; the scenic-railways of Coney Island; the full green summer trees and the gray frame houses with their white trim on Staten Island; it was all heartbreakingly like home. When the immigration tug came alongside, Dick was surprised to see Hiram Halsey Cooper, in khaki uniform and puttees, clambering up the steps. Dick lit a cigarette and tried to look sober.

'My boy, it's a great relief to see you. . . . Your mother and I have been . . . er . . .' Dick interrupted to introduce him to Ned.

Mr Cooper, who was in the uniform of a major, took him by the sleeve and drew him up the deck. 'Better put on your uniform to land.'

'All right, sir, I thought it looked rather shabby.'

'All the better. . . . Well, I suppose it's hell over there . . . and no chance for courting the muse, eh? . . . You're coming up to Washington with me tonight. We've been very uneasy about you, but that's all over now . . . made me realize what a lonely old man I am. Look here, my boy, your mother was the daughter of Major General Ellsworth, isn't that so?' Dick nodded. 'Of course she must have been because my dear wife was his niece. . . . Well, hurry and put your uniform on and remember . . . leave all the talking to me.'

While he was changing into the old Norton-Harjes uniform, Dick was thinking how suddenly Mr Cooper had aged and wondering just how he could ask him to lend him fifteen dollars to pay the bill he'd run up at the bar.

New York had a funny lonely empty look in the summer afternoon sunlight; well, here he was home. At the Pennsylvania Station there were policemen and plainclothes men at all the entrances demanding the registration cards of all the young men who were not in uniform. As he and Mr Cooper ran for the train, he caught sight of a dejectedlooking group of men herded together in a corner hemmed by a cordon of sweating cops.

When they got in their seats in the parlorcar on the Congressional, Mr Cooper mopped his face with a handkerchief.

'You understand why I said to put your uniform on. Well, I suppose it was hell?'

'Some of it was pretty bad,' said Dick casually. 'I hated to come back, though.'

'I know you did, my boy. . . . You didn't expect to find your old mentor in the uniform of a major . . . well, we must all put our shoulders to the wheel. I'm in the purchasing department of Ordnance. You see the chief of our bureau of personnel is General Sykes; he turns out to have served with your grandfather. I've told him about you, your experience on two fronts, your knowledge of languages and . . . well . . . naturally he's very much interested. . . . I think we can get you a commission right away.'

'Mr Cooper, it's . . .' stammered Dick, 'it's extraordinarily decent . . . damn kind of you to interest yourself in me this way.'

'My boy, I didn't realize how I missed you . . . our chats about the muse and the ancients . . . until you had gone.' Mr Cooper's voice was drowned out by the roar of the train. Well, here I am home, something inside Dick's head kept saying to him.

When the train stopped at the West Philadelphia Station the only sound was the quiet droning of the electric fans; Mr Cooper leaned over and tapped Dick's knee, 'Only one thing you must promise . . . no more peace talk till we win the war. When peace comes, we can put some in our poems. . . . Then'll be the time for us all to work for a lasting peace. . . . As for that little incident in Italy . . . it's nothing . . . forget it . . . nobody ever heard of it.' Dick nodded; it made him sore to feel that he was blushing. They neither of them said anything until the waiter came through calling, 'Dinner now being served in the diningcar forward.'

In Washington (now you are home, something kept saying in Dick's head) Mr Cooper had a room in the Willard where he put Dick up on the couch as the hotel was full and it was impossible to get another room anywhere. After he'd rolled up in the sheet, Dick heard Mr Cooper tiptoe over and stand beside the couch breathing hard. He opened his eyes and grinned.

'Well, my boy,' said Mr Cooper, 'it's nice to have you home . . . sleep well,' and he went back to bed.

Next morning he was introduced to General Sykes: 'This is the young man who wants to serve his country,' said Mr Cooper with a flourish, 'as his grandfather served it. . . . In fact, he was so impatient that he went to war before his country did, and enlisted in the Volunteer Ambulance Service with the French and afterwards with the Italians.'

General Sykes was a little old man with bright eyes and a hawk nose and extremely deaf. 'Yes, Ellsworth was a great fellow; we campaigned against Hieronimo together . . . Ah, the Old West . . . I was only fourteen at Gettysburg and damme I don't think he was there at all. We went through West Point in the same class after the war, poor old Ellsworth. . . . So you've smelled powder have you, my boy?' Dick colored and nodded.

'You see, General,' shouted Mr Cooper, 'he feels he wants some more . . . er . . . responsible work than was possible in the Ambulance Service.'

'Yessiree, no place for a highspirited young fellow. . . . You know Andrews, Major . . .' The General was scribbling on a pad. 'Take him to see Colonel Andrews with this memorandum and he'll fix him up, has to decide on qualifications, etc. . . . You understand . . . good luck, my boy.'

Dick managed a passable salute and they were out in the corridor; Mr Cooper was smiling broadly. 'Well, that's done. I must be getting back to my office. You go and fill out the forms and take your medical examination . . . or perhaps that'll be at the camp . . . Anyway come and lunch with me at the Willard at one. Come up to the room.' Dick saluted, smiling.

He spent the rest of the morning filling out blanks. After lunch he went down to Atlantic City to see his mother. She looked just the same. She was staying in a boardinghouse at the Chelsea end and was very much exercised about spies. Henry had enlisted as a private in the infantry and was somewhere in France. Mother said it made her blood boil to think of the grandson of General Ellsworth being a mere private, but that she felt confident he'd soon rise from the ranks. Dick hadn't heard her speak of her father since she used to talk about him when he was a child, and asked her about him. He had died when she was quite a little girl leaving the family not too well off considering their station in life. All she remembered was a tall man in blue with a floppy felt hat caught up on one side and a white goatee; when she'd first seen a cartoon of Uncle Sam she'd thought it was her father. He always had hoarhound drops in a little silver bonbonnière in his pocket, she'd been so excited about the military funeral and a nice kind army officer giving her his handkerchief. She'd kept the bonbonnière for many years, but it had had to go with everything else when your poor father . . . er . . . failed.

A week later Dick received a War Department envelope addressed to Savage, Richard Ellsworth, 2nd Lieut. Ord. Dept., enclosing his commission and ordering him to proceed to Camp Merritt, N.J., within twentyfour hours. Dick found himself in charge of a casuals company at Camp Merritt and wouldn't have known what on earth to do if it hadn't been for the sergeant. Once they were on the transport it was better; he had what had been a firstclass cabin with two other second lieutenants and a major; Dick had the drop on them all because he'd been at the front. The transport was the *Leviathan*; Dick began to feel himself again when he saw the last of Sandy Hook; he wrote Ned a long letter in doggerel that began:

His father was a jailbird and his mother had no kale
He was much too fond of cognac and he drank it by the
pail
But now he's a Second Lieut and supported by the State
Sports a handsome uniform and a military gait
And this is the most terrific fate that ever can befall
A boy whose grandpa was a Major-General.

The other two shavetails in the cabin were nondescript youngsters from Leland Stanford, but Major Thompson was a West Pointer and stiff as a ramrod. He was a middleaged man with a yellow round face, thin lips and noseglasses. Dick thawed him out a little by getting him a pint of whiskey through his sergeant who'd gotten chummy with the stewards, when he got seasick two days out, and discovered that he was a passionate admirer of Kipling and had heard Copeland read *Danny Deever* and been very much impressed. Furthermore, he was an expert on mules and horseflesh, and the author of a monograph: 'The Spanish Horse.' Dick admitted that he'd studied with Copeland and somehow it came out that he was the grandson of the late General Ellsworth. Major Thompson began to take an interest in him and to ask him questions about the donkeys the French used to carry ammunition in the trenches, Italian cavalry horses, and the works of Rudyard Kipling. The night before they reached Brest when everybody was flustered and the decks were all dark and silent for the zone, Dick went into a toilet and reread the long kidding letter he'd written Ned first day out. He tore it up into small bits, dropped them in the can and then flushed it carefully: no more letters.

In Brest, Dick took three majors downtown and ordered them a meal and good wine at the hotel; during the evening Major Thompson told stories about the Philippines and the Spanish War; after the fourth bottle Dick taught them all to sing *Mademoiselle from Armentières*. A few days later he was detached from his casuals company and sent to Tours; Major Thompson, who felt he needed somebody to speak French for him and to talk about Kipling with, had gotten him transferred to his office. It was a relief to see the last of Brest, where everybody was in a continual grouch from the drizzle and the mud and the discipline and the saluting and the formations and the fear of getting in wrong with the brasshats.

Tours was full of lovely creamystone buildings buried in dense masses of bluegreen late summer foliage. Dick was on commutation of rations and boarded with an agreeable old woman who brought him up his café au lait in bed every morning. He got to know a fellow in the Personnel Department through whom he began to work to get Henry transferred out of the infantry. He and Major Thompson and old Colonel Edgecombe and several other officers dined together very often; they got so they couldn't do without Dick who knew how to order a meal comme il faut, and the proper vintages of wines and could parleyvoo with the French girls and make up limericks and was the grandson of the late General Ellsworth.

When the Post Dispatch Service was organized as a separate outfit, Colonel Edgecombe, who headed it, got him away from Major Thompson and his horsedealers; Dick became one of his assistants with the rank of Captain. Immediately he managed to get Henry transferred from the officers' school to Tours. It was too late, though, to get him more than a first lieutenancy.

When Lieutenant Savage reported to Captain Savage in his office, he looked brown and skinny and sore. That evening they drank a bottle of white wine together in Dick's room. The first thing Henry said when the door closed behind them was, 'Well, of all the goddam lousy grafts ... I don't know whether to be proud of the little kid brother or to sock him in the eye.'

Dick poured him a drink. 'It must have been Mother's

doing,' he said. 'Honestly, I'd forgotten that Grandpa was a general.'

'If you knew what us guys at the front used to say about the S.O.S.'

'But somebody's got to handle the supplies and the ordnance and . . .'

'And the mademosels and the vin blanc,' broke in Henry.

'Sure, but I've been very virtuous. . . . Your little brother's minding his *p*'s and *q*'s, and honestly I've been working like a nigger.

'Writing loveletters for ordnance majors, I bet. . . . Hell, you can't beat it. He lands with his nose in the butter every time. . . . Anyway, I'm glad there's one successful member of the family to carry on the name of the late General Ellsworth.'

'Have a disagreeable time in the Argonne?'

'Lousy . . . until they sent me back to officers' school.'

'We had a swell time there in the Ambulance Service in '17.'

'Oh, you would.'

Henry drank some more wine and mellowed up a little. Every now and then he'd look around the big room with its lace curtains and its scrubbed tile floor and its big fourposter bed and make a popping sound with his lips and mutter: 'Pretty soft.' Dick took him out and set him up to a fine dinner at his favorite bistro and then went around and fixed him up with Minette, who was the bestlooking girl at Madame Patou's.

After Henry had gone upstairs, Dick sat in the parlor a few minutes with a girl they called Dirty Gertie who had hair dyed red and a big floppy painted mouth, drinking the bad cognac and feeling blue. 'Vous triste?' she said, and put her clammy hand on his forehead. He nodded. 'Fièvre . . . trop penser . . . penser no good . . . moi aussi.' Then she said she'd kill herself, but she was afraid, not that she believed in God, but that she was afraid of how quiet it would be after she was dead. Dick cheered her up, 'Bientot guerre finée. Tout le monde content go back home.' The girl burst out crying and Madame Patou came running in screaming and clawing like a seagull. She was a heavy woman with an ugly jaw. She grabbed the girl by the hair and began shaking her. Dick was flustered. He managed to make the woman let the girl go back to her room, left some money and walked out. He felt terrible. When he got home he felt like writing some verse. He tried to recapture the sweet and heavy pulsing of feelings he used to have when he sat down to write a poem. But all he could do was just feel miserable so he went to bed. All night half-thinking half-dreaming he couldn't get Dirty Gertie's face out of his head. Then he began remembering the times he used to have with Hilda at Bay Head and had a long conversation with himself about love. Everything's so hellishly sordid . . . I'm sick of whores and chastity, I want to have love affairs. He began planning what he'd do after the war, probably go home and get a political job in Jersey; a pretty sordid prospect.

He was lying on his back staring at the ceiling that was livid with dawn when he heard Henry's voice calling his name down in the street outside; he tiptoed down the cold tiled stairs and let him in.

'Why the hell did you let me go with that girl, Dick? I feel like a louse . . . Oh Christ . . . mind if I have half this bed, Dick? I'll get me a room in the morning.'

Dick found him a pair of pajamas and made himself small on his side of the bed. 'The trouble with you, Henry,' he said, yawning, 'is that you're just an old Puritan . . . you ought to be more Continental.'

'I notice you didn't go with any of those bitches yourself.'

'I haven't got any morals, but I'm finicky, my dear, Epicurus' owne sonne,' Dick drawled sleepily.

'S — t, I feel like a dirty dishrag,' whispered Henry.

Dick closed his eyes and went to sleep.

Early in October, Dick was sent to Brest with a dispatch case that the Colonel said was too important to entrust to an enlisted man. At Rennes he had to wait two hours for the train, and was sitting eating in the restaurant when a dough-boy with his arm in a sling came up to him saying, 'Hello, Dick, for crying out loud.' It was Skinny Murray.

'By gosh, Skinny, I'm glad to see you . . . it must be five or six years . . . Gee, we're getting old. Look, sit down . . . no, I can't do that.'

'I suppose I ought to have saluted, sir,' said Skinny stiffly.

'Can that, Skinny . . . but we've got to find a place to talk . . . got any time before your train? You see it's me the M.P.'s would arrest if they saw me eating and drinking with an enlisted man. . . . Wait around till I've finished my lunch and we'll find a ginmill across from the station. I'll risk it.'

'I've got an hour . . . I'm going to the Grenoble leave area.'

'Lucky bastard . . . were you badly wounded, Skinny?'

'Piece of shrapnel in the wing, Captain,' said Skinny, coming to attention as a sergeant of M.P.'s stalked stiffly through the station restaurant. 'Those birds gimme the willies.'

Dick hurried through his lunch, paid, and walked across the square outside the station. One of the cafés had a back room that looked dark and quiet. They were just settling down to chat over two beers when Dick remembered the dispatch case. He'd left it at the table. Whispering breathlessly that he'd be back he ran across the square and into the station restaurant. Three French officers were at the table. 'Pardon, messieurs.' It was still where he'd left it under the table. 'If I'd lost that I'd have had to shoot myself,' he told Skinny. They chatted about Trenton and Philadelphia and Bay Head and Doctor Atwood. Skinny was married and had a good job in a Philadelphia bank. He had volunteered for the tanks and was winged by a bit of shrapnel before the attack started, damn lucky for him, because his gang had been wiped out by a black maria. He was just out of hospital today and felt pretty weak on his pins. Dick took down his service data and said he'd get him transferred to Tours; just the kind of fellow they needed for a courier. Then Skinny had to run for his train, and Dick, with the dispatch case tightly wedged under his arm, went out to stroll around the town daintily colored and faintly gay under the autumn drizzle.

The rumor of the fake armistice set Tours humming like a swarm of bees; there was a lot of drinking and backslapping and officers and enlisted men danced snakedances in and out of the officebuildings. When it turned out to be a false alarm Dick felt almost relieved. The days that followed everybody round the headquarters of the Dispatch Service wore a mysterious expression of knowing more than they were willing to tell. The night of the real armistice Dick ate supper a little deliriously with Colonel Edgecombe and some other officers. After dinner Dick happened to meet the Colonel in the courtyard out back. The Colonel's face was red and his mustache bristled.

'Well, Savage, it's a great day for the race,' he said, and laughed a great deal.

'What race?' said Dick shyly.

'The human race,' roared the colonel.

Then he drew Dick aside: 'How would you like to go to Paris, my boy? It seems that there's to be a Peace Conference in Paris and that President Wilson is going to attend it in person . . . seems incredible . . . and I've been ordered to put this outfit at the disposal of the American delegation that's coming soon to dictate the peace, so we'll be Peace Conference couriers. Of course, I suppose if you feel you have to go home it could be arranged.'

'Oh, no, sir,' broke in Dick hurriedly. 'I was just beginning to worry about having to go home and look for a job.... The Peace Conference will be a circus and any chance to travel around Europe suits me.'

The colonel looked at him with narrowed eyes. 'I wouldn't put it just that way ... service should be our first thought ... naturally what I said is strictly confidential.'

'Oh, strictly,' said Dick, but he couldn't help wearing a grin on his face when he went back to join the others at the table.

Paris again; and this time in a new whipcord uniform with silver bars at his shoulders and with money in his pockets. One of the first things he did was to go back to look at the little street behind the Pantheon where he'd lived with Steve Warner the year before. The tall chalkygray houses, the stores, the little bars, the bigeyed children in the black smocks, the youngsters in caps with silk handkerchiefs around their necks, the Parisian drawl of the argot; it all made him feel vaguely unhappy; he was wondering what had happened to Steve. It was a relief to get back to the office where the enlisted men were moving in newly arrived American rolltop desks and yellow varnished cardindex cases.

The hub of this Paris was the Hôtel de Crillon on the Place de la Concorde, its artery the Rue Royale where arriving dignitaries, President Wilson, Lloyd George, and the King and Queen of the Belgians were constantly parading escorted by the Garde Républicaine in their plumed helmets; Dick began living in a delirium of trips to Brussels on the night express, lobster cardinal washed down with Beaune on the red plush settees at Larue's, champagne cocktails at the Ritz Bar, talk full of the lowdown over a demie at the Café Weber; it was like the old days of the Baltimore Convention, only he didn't give a damn any more; it all hit him cockeyed funny.

One night soon after Christmas, Colonel Edgecombe took Dick to dinner at Voisin's with a famous New York publicity man who was said to be very near to Colonel House. They stood a moment on the pavement outside the restaurant to look at the tubby domed church opposite. 'You see, Savage, this fellow's the husband of a relative of mine, one of the Pittsburgh Staples ... smooth ... it seems to me. You look him over. For a youngster you seem to have a keen eye for character.'

Mr Moorehouse turned out to be a large quietspoken blue-eyed jowly man with occasionally a touch of the Southern Senator in his way of talking. With him were a man named Robbins and a Miss Stoddard, a frail-looking woman with very transparent alabaster skin and a sharp chirpy voice; Dick noticed that she was stunningly welldressed. The restaurant was a little too much like an Episcopal church; Dick said very little, was very polite to Miss Stoddard, and kept his eyes and ears open, eating the grandducal food and carefully tasting the mellow wine that nobody else seemed to pay any attention to. Miss Stoddard kept everybody talking, but nobody seemed to want to commit themselves to saying anything about the Peace Conference. Miss Stoddard told with considerable malice about the furnishings of the Hôtel de Murat and the Wilsons' colored maid and what kind of clothes the President's wife, whom she insisted on calling Mrs Galt, was wearing. It was a relief when they got to the cigars and liqueurs. After dinner Colonel Edgecombe offered to drop Mr Moorehouse at the Crillon, as his staffcar had come for him. Dick and Mr Robbins took Miss Stoddard home in a taxicab to her apartment opposite Notre Dame on the left bank. They left her at her door. 'Perhaps you'll come around some afternoon to tea, Captain Savage,' she said.

The taximan refused to take them any further, said it was late and that he was bound home to Noisy-le-sec and drove off.

Robbins took hold of Dick's arm. 'Now for crissake let's go and have a decent drink. . . . Boy, I'm sick of the bigwigs.'

'All right,' said Dick, 'where'll we go?'

Walking along the foggy quay, past the shadowy bulk of Notre Dame, they talked scatteringly about Paris and how cold it was. Robbins was a short man with an impudent bossy look on his red face. In the café it was only a little less chilly than in the street.

'This climate's going to be the death of me,' said Robbins, snuggling his chin down in his overcoat.

'Woolly underwear's the only answer; that's one thing I've learned in the army,' said Dick, laughing.

They settled on a plush bench near the stove at the end of the cigarsmoky giltornamented room. Robbins ordered a bottle of Scotch whiskey, glasses, lemon, sugar, and a lot of hot water. It took a long time to get the hot water, so Robbins poured them each a quarter of a tumbler of the whiskey straight. When he'd drunk his, his face that had been sagging and tired, smoothed out so that he looked ten years younger.

'Only way to keep warm in this goddam town's to keep stewed.'

'Still I'm glad to be back in little old Paree,' said Dick, smiling and stretching his legs out under the table.

'Only place in the world to be right at present,' said Robbins. 'Paris is the hub of the world . . . unless it's Moscow.'

At the word Moscow a Frenchman playing checkers at the next table brought his eyes up from the board and stared at the two Americans. Dick couldn't make out what there was in his stare; it made him uneasy. The waiter came with the hot water. It wasn't hot enough, so Robbins made a scene and sent it back. He poured out a couple of half-tumblers of straight whiskey to drink while they were waiting.

'Is the President going to recognize the soviets?' Dick found himself asking in a low voice.

'I'm betting on it . . . I believe he's sending an unofficial mission. Depends a little on oil and manganese . . . it used to be King Coal, but now it's Emperor Petroleum and Miss Manganese, queen consort of steel. That's all in the pink republic of Georgia . . . I hope to get there soon, they say that they have the finest wine and the most beautiful women in the world. By God, I got to get there. . . . But the oil . . . God damn it, that's what this damned idealist Wilson can't understand, while they're setting him up to big feeds at Buckingham Palace the jolly old British army is occupying Mosul, the Karun River, Persia . . . now the latrine news has it that they're in Baku . . . the future oil metropolis of the world.'

'I thought the Baku fields were running dry.'

'Don't you believe it . . . I just talked to a fellow who'd been there . . . a funny fellow, Rasmussen, you ought to meet him.'

Dick said hadn't we got plenty of oil at home. Robbins banged his fist on the table.

'You never can have plenty of anything . . . that's the first law of thermodynamics. I never have plenty of whiskey. . . . You're a young fellow, do you ever have plenty of tail? Well, neither Standard Oil nor the Royal Dutch-Shell can ever have plenty of crude oil.'

Dick blushed and laughed a little forcedly. He didn't like this fellow Robbins. The waiter finally came back with boiling water and Robbins made them each a toddy. For a while neither of them said anything. The checkerplayers had gone.

Suddenly Robbins turned to Dick and looked in his face with his hazy blue drunkard's eyes: 'Well, what do you boys think about it all? What do the fellers in the trenches think?'

'How do you mean?'

'Oh, hell, I don't mean anything. . . . But if they thought the war was lousy, wait till they see the peace . . . Oh, boy, wait till they see the peace.'

'Down at Tours I don't think anybody thought much about it either way . . . however, I don't think that anybody that's seen it considers war the prize way of settling international difficulties . . . I don't think Black Jack Pershing himself thinks that.'

'Oh, listen to him . . . can't be more than twentyfive and he talks like a book by Woodrow Wilson . . . I'm a sonofabitch and I know it, but when I'm drunk I say what I goddam please.'

'I don't see any good a lot of loud talk's going to do. It's a magnificent tragic show . . . the Paris fog smells of strawberries . . . the gods don't love us, but we'll die young just the same. . . . Who said I was sober?'

They finished up a bottle. Dick taught Robbins a rhyme in French:

> *Les marionettes font font font*
> *Trois petit tours et puis s'en vont*

and when the café closed they went out arm in arm. Robbins was humming,

> Cheer up, Napoleon you'll soon be dead
> A short life and a gay one

and stopping to talk with all the petites femmes they met on the Boul' Mich'. Dick finally left him talking to a cowlike woman in a flappy hat in front of the fountain on the Place Saint-Michel, and began the long walk home to his hotel that was opposite the Gare Saint-Lazare.

The broad asphalt streets were deserted under the pink arclights, but here and there on benches along the quais, under the bare dripping trees along the bank of the Seine, in spite of the raw night couples were still sitting huddled together in the strangleholds of l'amour. At the corner of the Boulevard Sébastopol a whitefaced young man who was walking the other way looked quickly into his face and stopped. Dick slackened his pace for a moment, but walked on past the string of marketcarts rumbling down the Rue de Rivoli, taking deep breaths to clear the reek of whiskey out of his head. The long brightlylighted avenue that led to the opera was empty. In front of the opera there were a few people, a girl with a lovely complexion who was hanging on the arm of a poilu gave him a long smile. Almost at his hotel he ran face to face into a girl who seemed remarkably pretty; before he knew it he was asking her what she was doing out so late. She laughed, charmingly he thought, and said she was doing the same thing he was. He took her to a little hotel on the back street behind his own. They were shown into a chilly room that smelt of furniture polish. There was a big bed, a bidet, and a lot of heavy claretcolored hangings. The girl was older than he'd thought and very tired, but she had a beautiful figure and very pale skin; he was glad to see how clean her underwear was, with a pretty lace edging. They sat a little while on the edge of the bed talking low.

When he asked her what her name was, she shook her head and smiled, 'Qu'est-ce que ça vous fait?'

'L'homme sans nom et la femme sans nom, vont faire l'amour à l'hôtel du néant,' he said.

'Oh qu'il est rigolo, celui-là,' she giggled. 'Dis, tu n'est pas malade?' He shook his head. 'Moi non plus,' she said, and started rubbing up against him like a kitten.

When they left the hotel they roamed around the dark streets until they found an earlymorning coffeebar. They ate coffee and croissants together in drowsy intimate quiet, leaning very close to each other as they stood against the bar. She left him to go up the hill towards Montmartre. He asked her if he couldn't see her again sometime. She shrugged her shoulders. He gave her thirty francs and kissed her and whispered in her ear a parody of his little rhyme:

> *Les petites marionettes font font font*
> *Un p'tit peu d'amour et puis s'en vont*

She laughed and pinched his cheek and the last he heard of her was her gruff giggle and 'Oh qu'il est rigolo, celui-là.'

He went back to his room feeling happy and sleepy and saying to himself: What's the matter with my life is I haven't got a woman of my own. He had just time to wash and shave and put on a clean shirt and to rush down to headquarters in order to be there when Colonel Edgecombe, who was a damnably early riser, got in. He found orders to leave for Rome that night.

By the time he got on the train his eyes were stinging with sleepiness. He and the sergeant who went with him had a compartment reserved at the end of a firstclass coach marked Paris–Brindisi. Outside of their compartment the train was packed; people were standing in the aisles.

Dick had taken off his coat and Sam Browne belt and was loosening his puttees, planning to stretch out on one of the seats and go to sleep even before the train left, when he saw a skinny American face in the door of the compartment. 'I beg your pardon, is this Ca-ca-captain Savage?' Dick sat up and nodded yawning. 'Captain Savage, my name is Barrow, G. H. Barrow, attached to the American delegation. . . . I have to go to Rome tonight and there's not a seat on the train. The transport officer in the station very kindly said that . . . er . . . er . . . although it wasn't according to Hoyle you might stretch a point and allow us to ride with you . . . I have with me a very charming young lady member of the Near East Relief . . .'

'Captain Savage, it certainly is mighty nice of you to let us ride with you,' came a drawling Texas voice, and a pinkcheeked girl in a dark gray uniform brushed past the man who said his name was Barrow and climbed up into the car. Mr Barrow, who was shaped like a string bean and had a prominent twitching Adam's apple and popeyes, began tossing up satchels and suitcases.

Dick was sore and began to say stiffly, 'I suppose you know that it's entirely against my orders . . .' but he heard his own voice saying it and suddenly grinned and said, 'All right, Sergeant Wilson and I will probably be shot at sunrise, but go ahead.' At that moment the train started.

Dick reluctantly scraped his things together into one corner and settled down there and immediately closed his eyes. He was much too sleepy to make the effort of talking to any damn relievers. The sergeant sat in the other corner and Mr Barrow and the girl occupied the other seat. Through his doze Dick could hear Mr Barrow's voice chugging along, now and then drowned out by the rattle of the express train. He had a stuttery way of talking like a badly running motorboat engine. The girl didn't say much except, 'Oh my,' and 'I declare,' now and then. It was the European situation: President Wilson says . . . new diplomacy . . . new Europe . . . permanent peace without annexations or indemnities. President Wilson says . . .

new understanding between capital and labor . . . President
Wilson appeals to . . . industrial democracy . . . plain people
all over the world behind the President. Covenant. League of
Nations . . . Dick was asleep dreaming of a girl rubbing her
breasts against him purring like a kitten, of a popeyed man
making a speech, of William Jennings Wilson speaking before
the Baltimore conflagration, of industrial democracy in a bathhouse on the Marne in striped trunks, with a young Texas boy
with pink cheeks who wanted to . . . like a string bean . . .
with a twitching adamsapple . . .

He woke up with a nightmarish feeling that somebody was
choking him. The train had stopped. It was stifling in the
compartment. The blue shade was drawn down on the lamp
overhead. He stepped over everybody's legs and went out in
the passage and opened a window. Cold mountain air cut into
his nostrils. The hills were snowy in the moonlight. Beside the
track a French sentry was sleepily leaning on his rifle. Dick
yawned desperately.

The Near East Relief girl was standing beside him, looking
at him smiling. 'Where are we gettin' to, Captain Savage? . . .
Is this Italy yet?'

'I guess it's the Swiss border . . . we'll have a long wait, I
guess . . . they take forever at these borders.'

'Oh jiminy,' said the girl, jumping up and down, 'it's the
first time I ever crossed a border.'

Dick laughed and settled back into his seat again. The train
pulled into a barny lonelylooking station, very dimly lit, and
the civilian passengers started piling out with their baggage.
Dick sent his papers by the sergeant to the military inspection
and settled back to sleep again.

He slept soundly and didn't wake up until the Mont Cenis.
Then it was the Italian frontier. Again cold air, snowy mountains, everybody getting out into an empty barn of a station.

Sleepysentimentally remembering the last time he'd gone
into Italy on the Fiat car with Sheldrake, he walked shivering
to the station bar and drank a bottle of mineral water and a
glass of wine. He took a couple of bottles of mineral water
and a fiasco of chianti back to the compartment, and offered
Mr Barrow and the girl drinks when they came back from
the customs and the police, looking very cross and sleepy. The
girl said she couldn't drink wine because she'd signed a pledge
not to drink or smoke when she joined the N.E.R., but she
drank some mineral water and complained that it tickled her

nose. Then they all huddled back into their corners to try to sleep some more. By the time they pulled into the Termi Station in Rome they were all calling each other by their first names. The Texas girl's name was Anne Elizabeth. She and Dick had spent the day standing in the corridor looking out at the saffronroofed towns and the peasants' houses each with a blue smear on the stucco behind the grapevine over the door, and the olives and the twisted shapes of the vines in their red-terraced fields; the pale hilly Italian landscape where the pointed cypresses stood up so dark they were like gashes in a canvas. She'd told him all about trying to get overseas all through the war and how her brother had been killed learning to fly at San Antonio, and how nice Mr Barrow had been on the boat and in Paris, but that he would try to make love to her and acted so silly, which was very inconvenient; Dick said well maybe it wasn't so silly. He could see that Anne Elizabeth felt fine about traveling to Rome with a real army officer who'd been to the front and could talk Italian and everything.

From the station he had to rush to the Embassy with his dispatch cases, but he had time to arrange to call up Miss Trent at the Near East Relief. Barrow, too, shook hands with him warmly and said he hoped they'd see something of each other; he was anxious to establish contacts with people who really knew what it was all about.

The only thing Dick thought of that night was to get through and get to bed. Next morning he called up Ed Schuyler at the Red Cross. They ate a big winey lunch together at an expensive restaurant near the Pincio Gardens. Ed had been leading the life of Riley; he had an apartment on the Spanish Stairs and took a lot of trips. He'd gotten fat. But now he was in trouble. The husband of an Italian woman he'd been running round with was threatening to challenge him to a duel and he was afraid there'd be a row and he'd lose his job with the Red Cross. 'The war was all right but it's the peace that really gets you,' he said. Anyway he was sick of Italy and the Red Cross and wanted to go home. The only thing was that they were going to have a revolution in Italy and he'd like to stay and see it. 'Well, Dick, for a member of the grenadine guards you seem to have done pretty well for yourself.'

'All a series of accidents,' said Dick, wrinkling up his nose. 'Things are funny, do you know it?'

'Don't I know it . . . I wonder what happened to poor old

Steve? Fred Summers was joining the Polish Legion, last I heard of him.'

'Steve's probably in jail,' said Dick, 'where we ought to be.'

'But it's not every day you get a chance to see a show like this.'

It was four o'clock when they left the restaurant. They went to Ed's room and sat drinking cognac in his window looking out over the yellow and verdigris roofs of the city and the baroque domes sparkling in the last sunlight, remembering how tremendously they'd felt Rome the last time they'd been there together, talking about what they'd be doing now that the war was over. Ed Schuyler said he wanted to get a foreign correspondent job that would take him out East; he couldn't imagine going back home to upstate New York; he had to see Persia and Afghanistan. Talking about what he was going to do made Dick feel hellishly miserable. He started walking back and forth across the tiled floor.

The bell rang and Schuyler went out in the hall. Dick heard whispering and a woman's voice talking Italian in a thin treble. After a moment Ed pushed a little longnosed woman with huge black eyes into the room. 'This is Magda,' he said; 'Signora Sculpi, meet Captain Savage.'

After that they had to talk in mixed French and Italian. 'I don't think it's going to rain,' said Ed. 'Suppose I get hold of a girl for you and we take a drive and eat supper at Caesar's palace . . . maybe it won't be too cold.'

Dick remembered Anne Elizabeth and called up the N.E.R. The Texas voice was delighted, said the relievers were awful and that she'd made a date with Mr Barrow, but would get out of it. Yes, she'd be ready if they called for her in half an hour. After a lot of bargaining between Signora Sculpi and a cabman they hired a twohorse landau, considerably elegant and decrepit. Anne Elizabeth was waiting for them at her door.

'Those old hens make me tired,' she said, jumping into the cab. 'Tell him to hurry or Mr Barrow'll catch us. . . . Those old hens say I have to be in by nine o'clock. I declare it's worse'n Sundayschool in there. . . . It was mighty nice of you to ask me out to meet your friends, Captain Savage. . . . I was just dying to get out and see the town. . . . Isn't it wonderful? Say, where does the Pope live?'

The sun had set and it had begun to get chilly. The Palazzo dei Cesari was empty and chilly, so they merely had a vermouth there and went back into town for dinner. After dinner they went to a show at the Apollo.

'My, I'll ketch it,' said Anne Elizabeth, 'but I don't care. I want to see the town.'

She took Dick's arm as they went into the theater. 'Do you know, Dick . . . all these foreigners make me feel kinder lonesome . . . I'm glad I got a white man with me . . . When I was at school in New York I used to go out to Jersey to see a textile strike . . . I used to be interested in things like that. I used to feel like I do now then. But I wouldn't miss any of it. Maybe it's the way you feel when you're having a really interesting time.'

Dick felt a little drunk and very affectionate. He squeezed her arm and leaned over her. 'Bad mans shan't hurt lil' Texas girl,' he crooned.

'I guess you think I haven't got good sense,' said Anne Elizabeth, suddenly changing her tone. 'But oh lawsie, how'm I going to get along with that Methodist Board of Temperance and Public Morals I've got to live with! I don't mean I don't think their work's fine . . . It's awful to think of poor little children starving everywhere. . . . We've won the war, now it's up to us to help patch things up in Europe just like the President says.' The curtain was going up and all the Italians around started shushing. Anne Elizabeth subsided. When Dick tried to get hold of her hand she pulled it away and flicked his with her fingers. 'Say, I thought you were out of highschool,' she said.

The show wasn't much, and Anne Elizabeth, who couldn't understand a word, kept letting her head drop on Dick's shoulder and going to sleep. In the intermission when they all went to the bar for drinks, Anne Elizabeth dutifully took lemonade. Going upstairs again to their seats, there was suddenly a scuffle. A little Italian with eyeglasses and a bald head had run at Ed Schuyler screaming, 'Traditore.' He ran at him so hard that they both lost their balance and rolled down the redcarpeted steps, the little Italian punching and kicking and Ed holding him off at arm's length as best he could. Dick and Anne Elizabeth, who turned out to be very strong, grabbed the little Italian, picked him up off the ground and locked his arms behind him while Signora Sculpi fell on his neck sobbing. It was the husband.

Ed meanwhile got to his feet looking very red and sheepish. By the time the Italian police appeared, everything had quieted down and the manager was nervously brushing the dust off

Ed's uniform. Anne Elizabeth found the little Italian his eye-glasses, that were badly bent, and he led his wife out, who was sobbing. He looked so funny, when he stopped in the door with his bent eyeglasses trembling on the end of his nose to shake his fist at Ed, that Dick couldn't help laughing. Ed was apologizing profusely to the manager, who seemed to take his side, explaining to the policemen in their shiny hats that the husband was pazzo. The bell rang and they all went back to their seats.

'Why, Anne Elizabeth, you're a jujutsu expert,' Dick whispered, his lips touching her ear. They got to giggling so they couldn't pay attention to the show and had to go out to a café.

'Now I suppose all the wops'll think I'm a coward if I don't challenge the poor little bugger to a duel.'

'Sure, it'll be cappistols at thirty paces now . . . or eggplants at five yards.' Dick was laughing so hard he was crying.

Ed began to get sore. 'It isn't funny,' he said, 'it's a hell of a thing to have happen . . . a guy never seems to be able to have any fun without making other people miserable . . . poor Magda . . . it's hellish for her. . . . Miss Trent, I hope you'll excuse this ridiculous exhibition.' Ed got up and went home.

'Well, what on earth was that about, Dick?' asked Anne Elizabeth, when they'd gotten out in the street and were walking towards the N.E.R. boardinghouse.

'Well, I suppose Signore husband was jealous on account of Ed's running around with Magda . . . or else it's a pretty little blackmail plot . . . poor Ed seems all cut up about it.'

'People sure do things over here they wouldn't do at home . . . I declare it's peculiar.'

'Oh, Ed gets in trouble everywhere. . . . He's got a special knack.'

'I guess it's the war and Continental standards and everything loosens up people's morals. . . . I never was prissy, but my goodness, I was surprised when Mr Barrow asked me to go to his hotel the first day we landed . . . I'd only spoken to him three or four times before on the boat. . . . Now at home he wouldn't have done that, not in a thousand years.'

Dick looked searchingly into Anne Elizabeth's face. 'In Rome do as the Romans do,' he said with a funny smirk.

She laughed, looking hard into his eyes as if trying to guess what he meant. 'Oh, well, I guess it's all part of life,' she said. In the shadow of the doorway he wanted to do some heavy kissing, but she gave him a quick peck in the mouth and shook her head. Then she grabbed his hand and squeezed it hard and said, 'Let's us be good friends.' Dick walked home with his head swimming with the scent of her sandy hair.

Dick had three or four days to wait in Rome. The President was to arrive on January 3 and several couriers were held at his disposition. Meanwhile he had nothing to do but walk around the town and listen to the bands practicing *The Star-Spangled Banner* and watch the flags and the stands going up.

The first of January was a holiday; Dick and Ed and Mr Barrow and Anne Elizabeth hired a car and went out to Hadrian's Villa and then on to Tivoli for lunch. It was a showery day and there was a great deal of mud on the roads. Anne Elizabeth said the rolling Campagna, yellow and brown with winter, made her think of back home along the Middle-buster. They ate fritto misto and drank a lot of fine gold Frascati wine at the restaurant above the waterfall. Ed and Mr Barrow agreed about the Roman Empire and that the ancients knew the art of life. Anne Elizabeth seemed to Dick to be flirting with Mr Barrow. It made him sore the way she let him move his chair close to hers when they sat drinking their coffee on the terrace afterwards, looking down into the deep ravine brimmed with mist from the waterfall. Dick sat drinking his coffee without saying anything.

When she'd emptied her cup, Anne Elizabeth jumped to her feet and said she wanted to go up to the little round temple that stood on the hillside opposite like something in an old engraving. Ed said the path was too steep for so soon after lunch. Mr Barrow said without enthusiasm – er, he'd go. Anne Elizabeth was off running across the bridge and down the path with Dick running after her slipping and stumbling in the loose gravel and the puddles. When they got to the bottom the mist was soppy and cold on their faces. The waterfall was right over their heads. Their ears were full of the roar of it. Dick looked back to see if Mr Barrow was coming.

'He must have turned back,' he shouted above the falls.

'Oh, I hate people who won't ever go anywhere,' yelled Anne Elizabeth. She grabbed his hand. 'Let's run up to the temple.'

They got up there breathless. Across the ravine they could see Ed and Mr Barrow still sitting on the terrace of the restaurant. Anne Elizabeth thumbed her nose at them and then waved. 'Isn't this wonderful?' she spluttered. 'Oh, I'm wild about ruins and scenery . . . I'd like to go all over Italy and see everything. . . . Where can we go this afternoon? . . . Let's not go back and listen to them mouthing about the Roman Empire.'

'We might get to Nemi . . . you know the lake where Caligula had his galleys . . . but I don't think we can get there without the car.'

'Then they'd come along. . . . No, let's take a walk.'

'It might rain on us.'

'Well, what if it does? We won't run.'

They went up a path over the hills above the town and soon found themselves walking through wet pastures and oakwoods with the Campagna stretching lightbrown below them and the roofs of Tivoli picked out with black cypresses like exclamation points. It was a showery springfeeling afternoon. They could see the showers moving in dark gray and whitish blurs across the Campagna. Underfoot little redpurple cyclamens were blooming. Anne Elizabeth kept picking them and poking them in his face for him to smell. Her cheeks were red and her hair was untidy and she seemed to feel too happy to walk, running and skipping all the way. A small sprinkle of rain wet them a little and made the hair streak on her forehead. Then there was a patch of chilly sunlight. They sat down on the root of a big beechtree and looked up at the long redbrown pointed buds that glinted against the sky. Their noses were full of the smell of the little cyclamens. Dick felt steamy from the climb and the wet underbrush and the wine he'd drunk and the smell of the little cyclamens. He turned and looked in her eyes. 'Well,' he said. She grabbed him by the ears and kissed him again and again. 'Say you love me,' she kept saying in a strangling voice. He could smell her sandy hair and warm body and the sweetness of the little cyclamens. He pulled her to her feet and held her against his body and kissed her on the mouth; their tongues touched. He dragged her through a break in the hedge into the next field. The ground was too wet. Across the field was a little hut made of brush. They staggered as they walked with their arms around each other's waists, their thighs grinding stiffly together. The hut was full of dry cornfodder. They lay squirming together among the dry crackling cornfodder. She lay on her back with her eyes closed, her lips tightly pursed. He had one hand under her head and with the other was trying to undo her clothes; something tore under his hand. She began pushing him away.

'No, no, Dick, not here . . . we've got to go back.'

'Darling girl . . . I must . . . you're so wonderful.'

She broke away from him and ran out of the hut. He sat up on the floor, hating her, brushing the dry shreds off his uniform.

Outside it was raining hard. 'Let's go back; Dick, I'm crazy about you, but you oughtn't to have torn my panties . . . oh, you're so exasperating.' She began to laugh.

'You oughtn't to start anything you don't want to finish,' said Dick. 'Oh, I think women are terrible . . . except prosti-tutes . . . there you know what you're getting.'

She went up to him and kissed him. 'Poor little boy . . . he feels so cross. I'm so sorry . . . I'll sleep with you, Dick . . . I promise I will. You see it's difficult . . . In Rome we'll get a room somewhere.'

'Are you a virgin?' His voice was constrained and stiff.

She nodded. 'Funny, isn't it? . . . in wartime . . . You boys have risked your lives. I guess I can risk that.'

'I guess I can borrow Ed's apartment. I think he's going to Naples tomorrow.'

'But you really love me, Dick?'

'Of course . . . it's only this makes me feel terrible . . . making love's so magnificent.'

'I suppose it is . . . Oh, I wish I was dead.'

They plodded along down the hill through the downpour that gradually slackened to a cold drizzle. Dick felt tired out and sodden; the rain was beginning to get down his neck. Anne Elizabeth had dropped her bunch of cyclamens.

When they got back, the restaurant keeper said that the others had gone to the Villa d'Este, but would come back soon. They drank hot rum and water and tried to dry themselves over a brazier of charcoal in the kitchen.

'We're a fine pair of drowned rats,' tittered Anne Elizabeth.

Dick growled, 'A pair of precious idiots.'

By the time the others came back they were warm but still wet. It was a relief to argue with Barrow who was saying that if the ruling classes of today knew as much about the art of life as those old Italians he wouldn't be a Socialist.

'I didn't think you were a Socialist any more,' broke in Anne Elizabeth. 'I'm sure I'm not; look how the German Socialists have acted in the war and now they try to crybaby and say they wanted peace all along.'

'It's possible . . . to rec . . . to reconcile being a Socialist with faith in our President and . . . er . . . in democracy,' stammered

Barrow, going close to her. 'We'll have to have a long talk about that, Anne Elizabeth.'

Dick noticed how his eyes goggled when he looked at her. I guess he's out after her, he said to himself. When they got into the car he didn't care whether Barrow sat next to her or not. They drove all the way back to Rome in the rain.

The next three days were very busy with President Wilson's visit to Rome. Dick got cards to various official functions, heard a great many speeches in Italian and French and English, saw a great many silk hats and decorations and saluted a great deal and got a pain in the back from holding a stiff military posture. In the Roman Forum he was near enough the President's party to hear the short man with black mustaches who was pointing out the ruins of the temple of Romulus, say in stiff English, 'Everything here bears relation to the events of the great war.' There was a hush as the people in the outer groups of dignitaries strained their ears to hear what Mr Wilson would say.

'That is true,' replied Mr Wilson in a measured voice. 'And we must not look upon these ruins as mere stones, but as immortal symbols.' A little appreciative murmur came from the group.

The Italian spoke a little louder next time. All the silk hats cocked at an angle as the dignitaries waited for the Italian's reply. 'In America,' he said with a little bow, 'you have something greater, and it is hidden in your hearts.'

Mr Wilson's silk hat stood up very straight against all the timeeaten columns and the endless courses of dressed stone.

'Yes,' replied Mr Wilson, 'it is the greatest pride of Americans to have demonstrated the immense love of humanity which they bear in their hearts.'

As the President spoke, Dick caught sight of his face past the cock's feathers of some Italian generals. It was a gray stony cold face grooved like the columns, very long under the silk hat. The little smile around the mouth looked as if it had been painted on afterwards. The group moved on and passed out of earshot.

That evening at five, when he met Anne Elizabeth at Ed's apartment, he had to tell her all about the official receptions. He said all he'd seen had been a gold replica of the wolf suckling Romulus and Remus up at the Capitol when the President had been made a Roman citizen, and his face in the Forum. 'A terrifying face, I swear it's a reptile's face, not warm-blooded, or else the face on one of those old Roman politicians on a tomb on the Via Appia. . . . Do you know what we are, Anne Elizabeth? we're the Romans of the Twentieth Century'; he burst out laughing, 'and I always wanted to be a Greek.'

Anne Elizabeth, who was a great admirer of Wilson, was annoyed at first by what he was saying. He was nervous and excited and went on talking and talking. For this once she broke her pledge and drank some hot rum with him, as the room was terribly chilly. In the light of the streetlamps on the little corner of the Spanish Stairs they could see from Ed's window, they could see the jumbled darkness of crowds continually passing and repassing.

'By God, Anne Elizabeth, it's terrible to think about it. . . . You don't know the way people feel, people praying for him in peasants' huts . . . oh, we don't know anything and we're grinding them all underfoot. . . . It's the sack of Corinth . . . they think he's going to give them peace, give them back the cozy beforethewar world. It makes you sick to hear all the speeches. . . . Oh, Christ, let's stay human as long as we can . . . not get reptile's eyes and stone faces and ink in our veins instead of blood. . . . I'm damned if I'll be a Roman.'

'I know what you mean,' said Anne Elizabeth, ruffling up his hair. 'You're an artist, Dick, and I love you very much . . . you're my poet, Dick.'

'To hell with them all,' said Dick, throwing his arms around her.

In spite of the hot rum, Dick was very nervous when he took his clothes off. She was trembling when he came to her on the bed. It was all right, but she bled a good deal and they didn't have a very good time. At supper afterwards they couldn't seem to find anything to say to each other. She went home early and Dick wandered desolately around the streets among the excited crowds and the flags and the illuminations and the uniforms. The Corso was packed; Dick went into a café and was greeted by a group of Italian officers who insisted on setting him up to drinks. One young fellow with an oliveskin and very long black eyelashes, whose name was Carlo Hugobuoni, became his special friend and entertainer and took him around to all the tables introducing him as Il capitan Salvaggio Ricardo. It was all asti spumante and Evviva gli americani and Italia irridenta and Meester Veelson who had saved civiltá and evviva la pace, and they ended by taking Dick to see the belle ragazze. To his great relief all the girls were busy at the house where they took him and Dick was able to slip away and go back to the hotel to bed.

The next morning when he came down to drink his coffee there was Carlo waiting for him in the hotel lobby. Carlo was very sleepy; he hadn't been able to find a ragazza until five in the morning, but now he was at the orders of his caro amico to show him round the town. All day Dick had him with him, in spite of his efforts to get rid of him without hurting his feelings. He waited while Dick went to get his orders from the military mission, had lunch with him and Ed Schuyler; it was all Ed could do to get him away so that Dick could go to Ed's apartment to meet Anne Elizabeth. Ed was very funny about it, said that, as he'd lost Magda, he wouldn't be able to do anything worth while there himself and was glad to have Dick using the room for venereal purposes. Then he linked his arm firmly in Carlo's and carried him off to a café.

Dick and Anne Elizabeth were very tender and quiet. It was their last afternoon together. Dick was leaving for Paris that night, and Anne Elizabeth expected to be sent to Constantinople any day. Dick promised he'd get himself out to see her there. That night Anne Elizabeth went with him to the station. There they found Carlo waiting with a huge salami wrapped in silver paper and a bottle of chianti. The fellow that was going with him had brought the dispatch cases, so there was nothing for Dick to do but get on the train. He couldn't seem to think of anything to say and it was a relief when the train pulled out.

As soon as he reported to Colonel Edgecombe, he was sent off again to Warsaw. Through Germany all the trains were late and people looked deathly pale and everybody talked of a Bolshevik uprising. Dick was walking up and down the snowy platform, stamping to keep his feet warm, during an endless wait at a station in East Prussia, when he ran into Fred Summers. Fred was a guard on a Red Cross supply car and invited Dick to ride with him a couple of stations. Dick fetched his dispatches and went along. Fred had the caboose fitted with an oilstove and a cot and a great store of wine, cognac, and Baker's chocolate. They rode all day together talking as the train joggled slowly across an endless gray frozen plain.

'It's not a peace,' said Fred Summers, 'it's a cockeyed massacre! Christ, you ought to see the pogroms.'

Dick laughed and laughed. 'Jeerusalem, it makes me feel good to hear you, you old bum, Fred. . . . It's like the old days of the grenadine guards.'

'Jeez, that was a circus,' said Fred. 'Out here it's too damn hellish to be funny . . . everybody starved and crazy.'

'You were damn sensible not to get to be an officer . . . you have to be so damn careful about everything you say and do you can't have any kind of good time.'

'Jeez, you're the last man I'd ever have expected to turn out a captain.'

'C'est la guerre,' said Dick.

They drank and talked and talked and drank so much that Dick could barely get back to his compartment with his dispatch case. When they got into the Warsaw Station Fred came running up with a package of chocolate bars. 'Here's a little relief, Dick,' he said. 'It's a fine for coucher avec. Ain't a woman in Warsaw won't coucher all night for a chocolate bar.'

When he got back to Paris, Dick and Colonel Edgecombe went to tea at Miss Stoddard's. Her drawingroom was tall and stately with Italian panels on the walls and yellow and orange damask hangings; through the heavy lace in the windows you could see the purple branches of the trees along the quai, the jade Seine and the tall stone lace of the apse of Notre Dame.

'What a magnificent setting you have arranged for yourself, Miss Stoddard,' said Colonel Edgecombe, 'and if you excuse the compliment, the gem is worthy of its setting.'

'They were fine old rooms,' said Miss Stoddard; 'all you need do with these old houses is to give them a chance.' She turned to Dick: 'Young man, what did you do to Robbins that night we all had supper together? He talks about nothing else but what a bright fellow you are.'

Dick blushed. 'We had a glass of uncommonly good scotch together afterwards . . . It must have been that.'

'Well, I'll have to keep my eye on you . . . I don't trust these bright young men.'

They drank tea sitting around an ancient wroughtiron stove. A fat major and a lanternjawed Standard Oil man named Rasmussen came in, and later a Miss Hutchins who looked very slender and welltailored in her Red Cross uniform. They talked about Chartres and about the devastated regions and the popular enthusiasm that was greeting Mr Wilson everywhere and why Clemenceau always wore gray lisle gloves. Miss

Hutchins said it was because he really had claws instead of hands and that was why they called him the tiger.

Miss Stoddard got Dick in the window: 'I hear you've just come from Rome, Captain Savage . . . I've been in Rome a great deal since the war began . . . Tell me what you saw . . . tell me about everything . . . I like it better than anywhere.'

'Do you like Tivoli?'

'Yes, I suppose so; it's rather a tourist place, though, don't you think?'

Dick told her the story of the fight at the Apollo without mentioning Ed's name, and she was very much amused. They got along very well in the window watching the streetlamps come into greenish bloom along the river as they talked; Dick was wondering how old she was, la femme de trente ans.

As he and the Colonel were leaving, they met Mr Moorehouse in the hall. He shook hands warmly with Dick, said he was so glad to see him again and asked him to come by late some afternoon, his quarters were at the Crillon and there were often some interesting people there. Dick was curiously elated by the tea, although he'd expected to be bored. He began to think it was about time he got out of the service, and, on the way back to the office, where they had some work to clean up, asked the Colonel what steps he ought to take to get out of the service in France. He thought he might get a position of some kind in Paris.

'Well, if you're looking for that, this fellow Moorehouse is the man for you . . . I believe he's to be in charge of some sort of publicity work for Standard Oil . . . Can you see yourself as a public relations counsel, Savage?' The Colonel laughed.

'Well, I've got my mother to think of,' said Dick seriously.

At the office Dick found two letters. One was from Mr Wigglesworth saying that Blake had died of tuberculosis at Saranac the week before, and the other was from Anne Elizabeth:

DARLING:

I'm working at a desk in this miserable dump that's nothing but a collection of old cats that make me tired. Darling, I love you so much. We must see each other soon. I wonder what Dad and Buster would say if I brought a goodlooking husband home from overseas. They'd be hopping mad at first, but I reckon they'd get over it. Goldarn it, I don't want to work at a desk, I want to travel around Europe and see the sights. The only thing I like here is a little bunch of cyclamens on my desk. Do you remember the cute little pink cyclamens? I've got a bad cold and I'm lonely as the dickens. This Methodist Board of Temperance and Public Morals are the meanest people I've ever seen. Ever been homesick, Dick? I don't believe you ever have. Do get yourself sent right back to Rome. I wish I hadn't been such a prissy silly little girl up there where the cyclamens bloomed. It's hard to be a woman, Dick. Do anything you like but don't forget me. I love you so.

ANNE ELIZABETH

When Dick got back to his hotel room with the two letters in the inside pocket of his tunic he threw himself down on the bed and lay a long time staring at the ceiling.

A little before midnight Henry knocked on the door. He was just in from Brussels. 'Why, what's the matter, Dick, you look all gray . . . are you sick or something?'

Dick got to his feet and washed his face at the washbasin. 'Nothing the matter,' he spluttered through the water. 'I'm fedup with this man's army, I guess.'

'You look like you'd been crying.'

'Crying over spilt milk,' said Dick, and cleared his throat with a little laugh.

'Say, Dick, I'm in trouble; you've got to help me out. . . . You remember that girl Olga, the one who threw the teapot at me?' Dick nodded. 'Well, she says she's going to have a baby and that I'm the proud parent. . . . It's ridiculous.'

'Well, things like that happen,' said Dick sourly.

'No, but Christ, man, I don't want to marry the bitch . . . or support the offspring . . . it's so silly. Even if she is going to have a baby, it's probably not mine . . . She says she'll write to General Pershing. Some of those poor devils of enlisted men they sent up for twenty years for rape . . . it's the same story.'

'They shot a couple. . . . Thank God I wasn't on that court-martial.'

'But think of how it 'ud upset Mother. . . . Look here, you can parleyvoo better'n I can . . . I want you to come and talk to her.'

'All right . . . but I'm deadtired and feel lousy . . .' Dick put on his tunic. 'Say, Henry, how are you off for jack? The franc's dropping all the time. We might be able to give her a little money, and we'll be going home soon, we'll be too far away for blackmail.'

Henry looked low. 'It's a hell of a thing to have to admit to your kid brother,' he said, 'but I played poker the other night and got cleaned out . . . I'm S.O.L. all down the line.'

They went around to the place on Montmartre where Olga was hatcheck girl. There was nobody there yet, so she was able to come out and have a drink with them at the bar. Dick rather liked her. She was a bleached blonde with a small, hard, impudent face and big brown eyes. Dick talked her around, saying that his brother couldn't marry a foreigner on account of la famille and not having a situation and that he would soon be out of the army and back at a drafting desk . . . did she know how little a draftsman in an architect's office was paid en Amérique? Nothing at all, and with la vie chère and la chute du franc and le dollar would go next maybe and la révolution mondiale would be coming on, and the best thing she could do was to be a good girl and not have the baby. She began to cry . . . she so wanted to get married and have children and as for an avortment . . . mais non, puis non. She stamped her foot and went back to her hatcheck booth. Dick followed her and consoled her and patted her cheek and said que voulez-vous it was la vie and wouldn't she consider a present of five hundred francs? She shook her head, but when he mentioned a thousand she began to brighten up and to admit that que voulez-vous it was la vie. Dick left her and Henry cheerfully making a date to go home together after the boîte closed.

'Well, I had a couple of hundred bucks saved up. I guess it'll have to go . . . try to hold her off until we can get a good exchange . . . and Henry, the next time you play poker, for goodness' sake watch yourself.'

The day before the first plenary session of the Peace Conference Dick was running into the Crillon to go up to see Mr Moorehouse who had promised to get cards for him and Colonel Edgecombe, when he saw a familiar face in a French uniform. It was Ripley, just discharged from the French artillery school at Fontainebleau. He said he was in there trying to find an old friend of his father's to see if he could get a job connected with the peace delegations. He was broke and Marianne the Third Republic wasn't keeping him any more unless he enlisted in the Foreign Legion and that was the last thing he wanted to do. After Dick had phoned Colonel Edgecombe that Mr Moorehouse had been unable to get them cards and that they must try again through military channels, they went and had a drink together at the Ritz Bar.

'Bigtime stuff,' said Ripley, looking around at the decorations on the uniforms and the jewels on the women.

'*How are you goin' to keep 'em down on the farm ... After they've seen Paree?*' Dick grunted. 'I wish to hell I knew what I was going to do after I got out of this man's army.'

'Ask me something easy ... oh, I guess I can get a job somewhere ... if the worst comes to the worst I'll have to go back and finish Columbia ... I wish the revolution 'ud come. I don't want to go back to the States ... hell, I dunno what I want to do.'

This kind of talk made Dick feel uneasy: 'Méfiez-vous,' he quoted. 'Les oreilles ennemis vous écoutent.'

'And that's not the half of it.'

'Say, have you heard anything from Steve Warner?' Dick asked in a low voice.

'I got a letter from Boston ... I think he got a year's sentence for refusing to register ... He's lucky ... A lot of those poor devils got twenty years.'

'Well, that comes of monkeying with the buzzsaw,' said Dick out loud. Ripley looked at him hard with narrowed eyes for a second; then they went on talking about other things.

That afternoon Dick took Miss Stoddard to tea at Rumpelmeyer's, and afterwards walked up to the Crillon with her to call on Mr Moorehouse. The corridors of the Crillon were lively as an anthill with scuttling khaki uniforms, marine yeomen, messenger boys, civilians; a gust of typewriter clicking came out from every open door. At every landing groups of civilian experts stood talking in low voices, exchanging glances with passersby, scribbling notes on scratchpads.

Miss Stoddard grabbed Dick's arm with her sharp white fingers. 'Listen ... it's like a dynamo ... what do you think it means?'

'Not peace,' said Dick.

In the vestibule of Mr Moorehouse's suite, she introduced him to Miss Williams, the tiredlooking sharpfaced blonde who was his secretary. 'She's a treasure,' Miss Stoddard whispered as they went through into the drawingroom; 'does more work than anybody in the whole place.'

There were a great many people standing around in the blue light that filtered in through the long windows. A waiter was making his way among the groups with a tray of glasses and a valetlooking person was tiptoeing around with a bottle of port. Some people had teacups and others had glasses in their hands, but nobody was paying much attention to them. Dick noticed at once from the way Miss Stoddard walked into the room and the way Mr Moorehouse came forward a little to meet her, that she was used to running the show in that room. He was introduced to various people and stood around for a while with his mouth shut and his ears open. Mr Moorehouse spoke to him and remembered his name, but at that moment a message came that Colonel House was on the phone and Dick had no further chance to talk to him.

As he was leaving, Miss Williams, the secretary, said: 'Captain Savage excuse me a moment . . . You're a friend of Mr Robbins's, aren't you?'

Dick smiled at her and said, 'Well, rather an acquaintance, I'd say. He seems a very interesting fellow.'

'He's a very brilliant man,' said Miss Williams, 'but I'm afraid he's losing his grip . . . as I look at it it's very demoralizing over here . . . for a man. How can anybody expect to get through their work in a place where they take three hours for lunch and sit around drinking in those miserable cafés the rest of the time?'

'You don't like Paris, Miss Williams.'

'I should say not.'

'Robbins does,' said Dick maliciously.

'Too well,' said Miss Williams. 'I thought if you were a friend of his you might help us straighten him out. We're very worried over him. He hasn't been here for two days at a most important time, very important contacts to be made. J. W.'s working himself to the bone. I'm so afraid he'll break down under the strain . . . And you can't get a reliable stenographer or an extra typewriter . . . I have to do all the typing besides my secretarial duties.'

'Oh, it's a busy time for all of us,' said Dick. 'Goodbye, Miss Williams.' She gave him a smile as he left.

In late February he came back from a long dismal run to Vienna to find another letter from Anne Elizabeth.

DICK DARLING:

Thanks for the fine postcards. I'm still at this desk job and so lonely. Try to come to Rome if you can. Something is happening that is going to make a great change in our lives. I'm terribly worried about it, but I have every confidence in you. I know you're straight, Dicky boy. Oh, I've got to see you. If you don't come in a day or two, I may throw up everything and come to Paris. Your girl,

ANNE ELIZABETH

Dick went cold all over when he read the letter in the Brasserie Weber where he'd gone to have a beer with an artillery second lieutenant named Staunton Wills who was studying at the Sorbonne. Then he read a letter from his mother complaining about her lonely old age and one from Mr Cooper offering him a job. Wills was talking about a girl he'd seen at the Théâtre Caumartin he wanted to get to know, and was asking Dick in his capacity of an expert in these matters, how he ought to go about it. Dick tried to keep talking about how he could certainly get to see her by sending her a note through the ouvreuse, tried to keep looking at the people with umbrellas passing up and down the Rue Royale and the wet taxis and shiny staffcars, but his mind was in a panic; she was going to have a baby; she expected him to marry her; I'm damned if I will. After they'd had their beer, he and Wills went walking down the left bank of the Seine, looking at old books and engravings in the secondhand bookstalls and ended up having tea with Eleanor Stoddard.

'Why are you looking so doleful, Richard?' asked Eleanor. They had gone into the window with their teacups. At the table Wills was sitting talking with Eveline Hutchins and a newspaper man.

Dick took a gulp of tea. 'Talking to you's a great pleasure to me, Eleanor,' he said.

'Well, then, it's not that that's making you pull such a long face?'

'You know . . . some days you feel as if you were stagnating . . . I guess I'm tired of wearing a uniform . . . I want to be a private individual for a change.'

'You don't want to go home, do you?'

'Oh, no. I've got to go, I guess, to do something about Mother, that is if Henry doesn't go . . . Colonel Edgecombe says he can get me released from the service over here, that is, if I waive my right to transportation home. God knows I'm willing to do that.'

'Why don't you stay over here? . . . We might get J. W. to fix up something for you . . . How would you like to be one of his bright young men?'

'It 'ud be better than ward politics in Joisey . . . I'd like to get a job that sent me traveling . . . It's ridiculous because I spend my life on the train in this service, but I'm not fedup with it yet.'

She patted the back of his hand: 'That's what I like about you, Richard, the appetite you have for everything . . . J. W. spoke several times about that keen look you have . . . he's like that, he's never lost his appetite, that's why he's getting to be a power in the world . . . you know Colonel House consults him all the time . . . You see, I've lost my appetite.' They went back to the teatable.

Next day orders came around to send a man to Rome; Dick jumped at the job. When he heard Anne Elizabeth's voice over the phone, chilly panic went through him again, but he made his voice as agreeable as he could. 'Oh, you were a darling to come, Dicky boy,' she was saying. He met her at a café at the corner of the Piazza Venezia. It made him feel embarrassed the uncontrolled way she ran up to him and threw her arms around his neck and kissed him. 'It's all right,' she said, laughing, 'they'll just think we're a couple of crazy Americans . . . Oh, Dick, lemme look at you . . . Oh, Dicky boy, I've been so lonesome for you.'

Dick's throat was tight. 'We can have supper tonight, can't we?' he managed to say. 'I thought we might get hold of Ed Schuyler.'

She'd picked out a small hotel on a back street for them to go to. Dick let himself be carried away by her; after all, she was quite pretty today with her cheeks so flushed, and the smell of her hair made him think of the smell of the little cyclamens on the hill above Tivoli; but all the time he was making love to her, sweating and straining in her arms, wheels were going round in his head; what can I do, can I do, can I do?

They were so late getting to Ed's place that he had given them up. He was all packed up to leave Rome for Paris and home the next day.

'That's fine,' said Dick, 'we'll go on the same train.'

'This is my last night in Rome, ladies and gentlemen,' said Ed, 'let's go and have a bangup supper and to hell with the Red Cross.'

They ate an elaborate supper with firstclass wines, at a place in front of Trajan's Column, but Dick couldn't taste anything. His own voice sounded tinnily in his ears. He could see that Ed was making mighty efforts to cheer things up, ordering fresh bottles, kidding the waiter, telling funny stories about his misadventures with Roman ladies. Anne Elizabeth drank a lot of wine, said that the N.E.R. dragons weren't as bad as she had painted them, that they'd given her a latchkey when she'd told them her fiancé was in Rome for just the evening. She kept nudging Dick's knee with hers under the table and wanting them to sing *Auld Lang Syne*. After dinner they rode around in a cab and stopped to drop coins in the Trevi Fountain. They ended up at Ed's place sitting on packingboxes, finishing up a bottle of champagne Ed suddenly remembered and singing *Auprès de ma blonde*.

All the time Dick felt sober and cold inside. It was a relief when Ed announced drunkenly that he was going to visit some lovely Roman ladies of his acquaintance for the last time and leave his flat to I promessi sposi for the night. After he'd gone, Anne Elizabeth threw her arms around Dick: 'Give me one kiss, Dicky boy, and then you must take me back to the Methodist Board of Temperance and Public Morals ... after all, it's private morals that count. Oh, I love our private morals.'

Dick kissed her, then he went and looked out of the window. It had started to rain again. Frail ribbons of light from a streetlamp shot along the stone treads of the corner of the Spanish Stairs he could see between the houses. She came and rested her head on his shoulder:

'What you thinking about, Dicky boy?'

'Look, Anne Elizabeth, I've been wanting to talk about it ... do you really think that ... ?'

'It's more than two months now ... It couldn't be anything else, and I have a little morning sickness now and then. I'd been feeling terrible today, only I declare seeing you's made me forget all about it.'

'But you must realize ... it worries me terribly. There must be something you can do about it.'

'I tried castor oil and quinine ... that's all I know ... you see I'm just a simple country girl.'

'Oh, do be serious ... you've got to do something. There are plenty of doctors would attend to it ... I can raise the money somehow ... It's hellish, I've got to go back tomorrow ... I wish I was out of this goddam uniform.'

'But I declare I think I'd kinda like a husband and a baby ... if you were the husband and the baby was yours.'

'I can't do it ... I couldn't afford it ... They won't let you get married in the army.'

'That's not so, Dick,' she said slowly.

They stood a long time side by side without looking at each

other, looking at the rain over the dark roofs and the faint
phosphorescent streaks of the streets. She spoke in a trembly
frail voice, 'You mean you don't love me any more.'

'Of course I do, I don't know what love is . . . I suppose I
love any lovely girl . . . and especially you, sweetheart.' Dick
heard his own voice, like somebody else's voice in his ears.
'We've had some fine times together.' She was kissing him all
around his neck above the stiff collar of the tunic. 'But, darling,
can't you understand I can't support a child until I have some
definite career, and I've got my mother to support; Henry's so
irresponsible I can't expect anything from him. But I've got
to take you home; it's getting late.

When they got down into the street, the rain had let up
again. All the waterspouts were gurgling and water glinted in
the gutters under the streetlamps. She suddenly slapped him,
shouted you're it, and ran down the street. He had to chase
her, swearing under his breath. He lost her in a small square
and was getting ready to give her up and go home when she
jumped out at him from behind a stone phoenix on the edge
of a fountain. He grabbed her by the arm, 'Don't be so damn
kittenish,' he said nastily. 'Can't you see I'm worried sick.' She
began to cry.

When they got to her door, she suddenly turned to him and
said seriously, 'Look, Dick, maybe we'll put off the baby . . .
I'll try horseback riding. Everybody says that works. I'll write
you . . . honestly, I wouldn't hamper your career in any way
. . . and I know you ought to have time for your poetry . . .
You've got a big future, boy, I know it . . . if we got married
I'd work too.'

'Anne Elizabeth, you're a wonderful girl, maybe if we didn't
have the baby we might wangle it somehow.' He took her by
the shoulders and kissed her on the forehead.

Suddenly she started jumping up and down, chanting like
a child, 'Goody, goody, goody, we're going to get married.'

'Oh, do be serious, kid.'

'I am . . . unto death,' she said slowly. 'Look, don't come to
see me tomorrow . . . I have a lot of supplies to check up. I'll
write you to Paris.'

Back at the hotel it gave him a curious feeling putting on
his pajamas and getting alone into the bed where he and Anne
Elizabeth had been together that afternoon. There were bedbugs and the room smelt and he spent a miserable night.

All the way down to Paris on the train, Ed kept making him

drink and talking about the revolution, saying he had it on good authority the syndicates were going to seize the factories in Italy the first of May. Hungary had gone red and Bavaria, next it would be Austria, then Italy, then Prussia and France; the American troops sent against the Russians in Archangel had mutinied: 'It's the world revolution, a goddam swell time to be alive, and we'll be goddam lucky if we come out of it with whole skins.'

Dick said grumpily that he didn't think so; the Allies had things well in hand.

'But, Dick, I thought you were all for the revolution, it's the only possible way to end this cockeyed war.'

'The war's over now and all these revolutions are just the war turned inside out . . . You can't stop war by shooting all your opponents. That's just more war.'

They got sore and argued savagely. Dick was glad they were alone in the compartment. 'But I thought you were a royalist, Ed.'

'I was . . . but since seeing the King of Italy I've changed my mind . . . I guess I'm for a dictator, the man on the white horse.'

They settled to sleep on either side of the compartment, sore and drunk. In the morning they staggered out with headaches into the crisp air of a frontier station and drank steaming hot chocolate a freshfaced Frenchwoman poured out for them into big white cups. Everything was frosty. The sun was rising bright vermilion. Ed Schuyler talked about la belle, la douce France, and they began to get along better. By the time they reached the banlieue, they were talking about going to see Spinelli in *Plus ça Change* that night.

After the office and details to attend to and the necessity of appearing stiff and military before the sergeants, it was a relief to walk down the left bank of the Seine, where the buds were bursting pink and palest green on the trees, and the bouquinistes were closing up their stalls in the deepening lavender twilight, to the Quai de la Tournelle where everything looked like two centuries ago, and to walk slowly up the chilly stone stairs to Eleanor's and to find her sitting behind the teatable in an ivorycolored dress with big pearls around her neck pouring tea and retailing, in her malicious gentle voice, all the latest gossip of the Crillon and the Peace Conference. It gave Dick a funny feeling when she said, as he was leaving, that they wouldn't see each other for a couple of weeks, as she was going to Rome to do some work at the Red Cross office there.

'What a shame we couldn't have been there at the same time,' said Dick.

'I'd have liked that too,' she said. 'Arrivederci, Richard.'

March was a miserable month for Dick. He didn't seem to have any friends any more and he was sick to death of everybody around the dispatch service. When he was off duty his hotel room was so cold that he'd have to go out to a café to read. He missed Eleanor and going to her cozy apartment in the afternoon. He kept getting worrying letters from Anne Elizabeth; he couldn't make out from them what had happened; she made mysterious references to having met a charming friend of his at the Red Cross who had meant so much. Then, too, he was broke because he kept having to lend Henry money to buy off Olga with.

Early in April he got back from one of his everlasting trips to Coblenz and found a pneumatique from Eleanor for him at his hotel. She was inviting him to go on a picnic to Chantilly with her and J. W. the next Sunday.

They left at eleven from the Crillon in J. W.'s new Fiat. There was Eleanor in her gray tailored suit and a stately lady of a certain age named Mrs Wilberforce, the wife of a vice-president of Standard Oil, and longfaced Mr Rasmussen. It was a fine day and everybody felt the spring in the air. At Chantilly they went through the château and fed the big carp in the moat. They ate their lunch in the woods, sitting on rubber cushions. J. W. kept everybody laughing, explaining how he hated picnics, asking everybody what it was that got into even the most intelligent women that they were always trying to make people go on picnics. After lunch they drove to Senlis to see the houses that the Uhlans had destroyed there in the battle of the Marne.

Walking through the garden of the ruined château, Eleanor and Dick dropped behind the others, 'You don't know anything about when they're going to sign peace, do you, Eleanor?' asked Dick.

'Why, it doesn't look now as if anybody would ever sign ... certainly the Italians won't; have you seen what d'Annunzio said?'

'Because the day after peace is signed I take off Uncle Sam's livery ... The only time in my life time has ever dragged on my hand has been since I've been in the army.'

'I got to meet a friend of yours in Rome,' said Eleanor, looking at him sideways.

Dick felt chilly all over. 'Who was that?' he asked. It was an effort to keep his voice steady.

'That little Texas girl . . . she's a cute little thing. She said you were engaged!' Eleanor's voice was cool and probing like a dentist's tool.

'She exaggerated a little' – he gave a little dry laugh – 'as Mark Twain said when they reported his death.' Dick felt that he was blushing furiously.

'I hope so . . . You see, Richard . . . I'm old enough to be – well, at least your maiden aunt. She's a cute little thing . . . but you oughtn't to marry just yet, of course it's none of my business . . . an unsuitable marriage has been the ruination of many a promising young fellow . . . I shouldn't say this.'

'But I like your taking an interest like that, honestly it means a great deal to me . . . I understand all about marry in haste and repent at leisure. In fact, I'm not very much interested in marriage anyway . . . but . . . I don't know . . . Oh, the whole thing is very difficult.'

'Never do anything difficult . . . It's never worth it,' said Eleanor severely. Dick didn't say anything. She quickened her step to catch up with the others. Walking beside her he caught sight of her coldly chiseled profile jiggling a little from the jolt of her high heels on the cobbles. Suddenly she turned to him laughing, 'Now I won't scold you any more, Richard, ever again.'

A shower was coming up. They'd hardly got back into the car before it started to rain. Going home the gimcrack Paris suburbs looked gray and gloomy in the rain. When they parted in the lobby of the Crillon, J. W. let Dick understand that there would be a job for him in his office as soon as he was out of the service. Dick went home and wrote his mother about it in high spirits:

. . . It's not that everything isn't intensely interesting here in Paris or that I haven't gotten to know people quite close to what's really going on, but wearing a uniform and always having to worry about army regulations and saluting and everything like that, seems to keep my mind from working. Inside I'll be in the doldrums until I get a suit of civvies on again. I've been promised a position in J. Ward Moorehouse's office here in Paris; he's a dollar-a-year expert, but as soon as peace is signed he expects to start his business up again. He's an adviser on public relations and publicity to big corporations like Standard Oil. It's the type of work that will allow me to continue my real work on the side. Everybody tells me it's the opportunity of a lifetime. . . .

Then next time he saw Miss Williams she smiled broadly and came right up to him holding out her hand. 'Oh, I'm so glad, Captain Savage. J. W. says you're going to be with us . . . I'm sure it'll be an enjoyable and profitable experience for all parties.'

'Well, I don't suppose I ought to count my chickens before they're hatched,' said Dick.

'Oh, they're hatched all right,' said Miss Williams, beaming at him.

In the middle of May, Dick came back from Cologne with a hangover after a party with a couple of aviators and some German girls. Going out with German girls was strictly against orders from G.H.Q. and he was nervous for fear they might have been conducting themselves in a manner unbecoming to officers and gentlemen. He could still taste the sekt with peaches in it when he got off the train at the Gare du Nord. At the office Colonel Edgecombe noticed how pale and shaky he looked and kidded him about what a tremendous time they must be having in the occupied area. Then he sent him home to rest up. When he got to his hotel he found a pneumatique from Anne Elizabeth:

I'M STAYING AT THE CONTINENTAL AND MUST SEE YOU AT ONCE.

He took a hot bath and went to bed and slept for several hours. When he woke up, it was already dark. It was some time before he remembered Anne Elizabeth's letter. He was sitting on the edge of the bed sullenly buckling his puttees to go around and see her when there was a knock on his door. It was the elevatorman telling him a lady was waiting for him downstairs. The elevatorman had hardly said it before Anne Elizabeth came running down the hall. She was pale and had a red bruise on one side of her face. Something cantankerous in the way she ran immediately got on Dick's nerves. 'I told them I was your sister and ran up the stairs,' she said, kissing him breathlessly.

Dick gave the elevatorman a couple of francs and whispered to her, 'Come in. What's the matter?' He left the room door halfopen.

'I'm in trouble . . . the N.E.R. is sending me home.'

'How's that?'

'Played hookey once too often, I guess . . . I'm just as glad; they make me tired.'

'How did you hurt yourself?'

'Horse fell with me down at Ostia . . . I've been having the time of my life riding Italian cavalry horses . . . they'll take anything.'

Dick was looking her hard in the face trying to make her out. 'Well,' he said, 'is it all right? . . . I've got to know . . . I'm worried sick about it.'

She threw herself face down on the bed. Dick tiptoed over and gently closed the door. She had her head stuck into her elbow and was sobbing. He sat on the edge of the bed and tried to get her to look at him. She suddenly got up and began walking around the room. 'Nothing does any good . . . I'm going to have the baby . . . Oh, I'm so worried about Dad. I'm afraid it'll kill him if he finds out . . . Oh, you're so mean . . . you're so mean.'

'But, Anne Elizabeth, do be reasonable . . . Can't we go on being friends? I've just been offered a very fine position when I get out of the service, but I can't take a wife and child at this stage of the game, you must understand that . . . and if you want to get married there are plenty of fellows who'd give their eyeteeth to marry you . . . You know how popular you are . . . I don't think marriage means anything anyway.'

She sat down in a chair and immediately got up again. She was laughing: 'If Dad or Buster was here it would be a shotgun wedding, I guess . . . but that wouldn't help much.' Her hysterical laugh got on his nerves; he was shaking from the effort to control himself and talk reasonably.

'Why not G. H. Barrow? He's a prominent man and has money . . . He's crazy about you, told me so himself when I met him at the Crillon the other day . . . After all, we have to be sensible about things . . . It's no more my fault than it is yours . . . if you'd taken proper precautions . . .'

She took her hat off and smoothed her hair in the mirror. Then she poured some water out in his washbasin, washed her face and smoothed her hair again. Dick was hoping she'd go, everything she did drove him crazy. There were tears in her eyes when she came up to him. 'Give me a kiss, Dick . . . don't worry about me . . . I'll work things out somehow.'

'I'm sure it's not too late for an operation,' said Dick. 'I'll find out an address tomorrow and drop you a line to the Continental . . . Anne Elizabeth . . . it's splendid of you to be so splendid about this.'

She shook her head, whispered goodbye and hurried out of the room.

'Well, that's that,' said Dick, aloud to himself. He felt terribly sorry about Anne Elizabeth. Gee, I'm glad I'm not a girl, he kept thinking. He had a splitting headache. He locked his door, got undressed and put out the light. When he opened the window, a gust of raw rainy air came into the room and made him feel better. It was just like Ed said, you couldn't do anything without making other people miserable. A hell of a rotten world. The streets in front of the Gare Saint-Lazare shone like canals where the streetlamps were reflected in them. There were still people on the pavements, a man calling InTRAN-sigeant, twangy honk of taxicabs. He thought of Anne Elizabeth going home alone in a taxicab through the wet streets. He wished he had a great many lives so that he might have spent one of them with Anne Elizabeth. Might write a poem about that and send it to her. And the smell of the little cyclamens. In the café opposite the waiters were turning the chairs upside down and setting them on the tables. He wished he had a great many lives so that he might be a waiter in a café turning the chairs upside down. The iron shutters clanked as they came down. Now was the time the women came out on the streets, walking back and forth, stopping, loitering, walking back and forth, and those young toughs with skin the color of mushrooms. He began to shiver. He got into bed, the sheets had a clammy glaze on them. All the same, Paris was no place to go to bed alone, no place to go home alone in a honking taxi, in the heartbreak of honking taxis. Poor Anne Elizabeth. Poor Dick. He lay shivering between the clammy sheets, his eyes were pinned open with safetypins.

Gradually he got warmer. Tomorrow. Seventhirty: shave, buckle puttees . . . café au lait, brioches, beurre. He'd be hungry, hadn't had any supper . . . deux oeufs sur le plat. Bonjour m'ssieurs mesdames. Jingling spurs to the office, Sergeant Ames at ease. Day dragged out in khaki; twilight tea at Eleanor's, make her talk to Moorehouse to clinch job after the signing of the peace, tell her about the late General Ellsworth, they'll laugh about it together. Dragged out khaki days until after the sign-ing of the peace. Dun, drab, khaki. Poor Dick got to go to work after the signing of the peace. Poor Tom's cold. Poor Dicky boy . . . Richard . . . He brought his feet up to where he could rub them. Poor Richard's feet. After the Signing of the Peace.

By the time his feet were warm, he'd fallen asleep.

# Newsreel 37

the American commander-in-chief paid tribute to the dead and wounded, urged the soldiers to thank God for the victory and declared that a new version of duty to God and Country had come to all. When the numbers were hoisted it was found that that of M. A. Aumont's Zimzizimi was missing. The colt had been seized with a fit of coughing in the morning and was consequently withdrawn almost at the last moment

REPUBLICANS GETTING READY FOR THE HECKLING OF WILSON

MOVE TO INDICT EX-KAISER IN CHICAGO

*Johnny get your gun*
*get your gun*
*get your gun*
*We've got 'em on the run*

we face a great change in the social structure of this great country, declared Mr Schwab, the man who becomes the aristocrat of the future will become so not because of birth or wealth but because he has done something for the good of the country

RUTHLESS WAR TO CRUSH REDS

*on the run*
*on the run*

at the same time several columns of soldiers and sailors appeared in front of the chancellor's palace. The situation in Germany is developing into a neck-and-neck race between American food and Bolshevism. Find Lloyd George Taking Both Sides in Peace Disputes.

*Oh that tattooed French Ladee*
*Tattooed from neck to knee*
*She was a sight to see*

## MACKAY OF POSTAL CALLS BURLESON BOLSHEVIK

popular demonstrations will mark the visits of the President and of the rulers of Great Britain and Belgium who will be entertained at a series of fêtes. The irony of the situation lies in the fact that the freedom of speech and the press for which the Social Democrats clamored is now proving the chief source of menace to the new government

*Right across her jaw*
*Was the Royal Flying Corps*
*On her back was the Union Jack*
*Now could you ask for more?*

the War Department today decided to give out a guarded bulletin concerning a near mutiny of some of the American troops in the Archangel sector and their refusal to go to the front when ordered in spite of police orders comparative quiet prevailed, but as the procession moved along the various avenues, Malakoff, Henri Martin, Victor Hugo, and the Trocadéro and through the district in the aristocratic quarter of Paris in which Jaurès lived, there was a feeling of walking over mined roads where the merest incident might bring about an explosion

### REINFORCEMENTS RUSHED TO REMOVE CAUSE OF ANXIETY

*All up and down her spine*
*Was the King's Own Guard in line*
*And all around her hips*
*Steamed a fleet of battleships*

the workers of Bavaria have overcome their party divisions and united in a mighty bloc against all domination and exploitation; they have taken over in Workers', Soldiers', and Peasants' Councils entire public authority

*Right above her kidney*
*Was a bird'seye view of Sydney*
*But what I loved best was across her chest*
*My home in Tennessee*

FORMER EASTSIDERS LARGELY RESPONSIBLE
FOR BOLSHEVISM, SAYS DOCTOR SIMONS

ORDERS HOUSING OF LABOR IN PALACES

UKRAINIANS FIRE ON ALLIED MISSION

it looks at present as if Landru would be held responsible for the deaths of all the women who have disappeared in France, not only for the past ten years but for many decades previously

## The Camera Eye (40)

I walked all over town general strike no buses no taxicabs    the gates of the Metro closed    Place d'Iéna I saw red flags Anatole France in a white beard placards MUTILÉS DE LA GUERRE and the nutcracker faces of the agents de sûreté

Mort aux vaches

at the Place de la Concorde the Republican Guards in christmastree helmets were riding among the crowd whacking the Parisians with the flat of their swords scraps of the *International* worriedlooking soldiers in their helmets lounging with grounded arms all along the Grands Boulevards

Vive les poilus

at the République    à bas la guerre MORT AUX VACHES à bas la Paix des Assassins    they've torn up the gratings from around the trees and are throwing stones and bits of castiron at the fancydressed Republican Guards hissing whistling poking at the horses with umbrellas scraps of the *International*

at the Gare de l'Est they're singing the *International* entire    the gendarmerie nationale is making its way slowly down Magenta into stones whistles bits of iron the *Inter-*

*national*     Mort aux vaches      Barricades we must build
barricades      young kids are trying to break down the
shutters of an arms shop      revolver shots an old woman in
a window was hit (Whose blood is that on the cobbles?)
we're all running down a side street dodging into courtyards
concierges trying to close the outside doors on cavalry
charging twelve abreast firecracker faces      scared and mean
behind their big mustaches under their Christmastree
helmets

        at a corner I run into a friend running too      Look out
They're shooting to kill and it's begun to rain hard so
we dive in together just before a shutter slams down on the
door of the little café      dark and quiet inside a few workingmen past middle age are grumblingly drinking at the bar

        Ah les salops      There are no papers      Somebody said
the revolution had triumphed in Marseilles and Lille      Ça
va taper dure      We drink grog américain      our feet are
wet      at the next table two elderly men are playing chess
over a bottle of white wine

        later we peep out from under the sliding shutter that's
down over the door into the hard rain on the empty streets
only a smashed umbrella and an old checked cap side by
side in the clean stone gutter and a torn handbill L'UNION
DES TRAVAILLEURS FERA

# Newsreel 38

*C'est la lutte finale*
  *Groupons-nous et demain*
*L'internationale*
  *Sera le genre humain*

## FUSILLADE IN THE DIET

## Y.M.C.A. WORKERS ARRESTED FOR STEALING FUNDS

declares wisdom of people alone can guide the nation in such an enterprise    SAYS U.S. MUST HAVE WORLD'S GREATEST FLEET    *when I was in Italy a little limping group of wounded Italian soldiers sought an interview with me. I could not conjecture what they were going to say to me, and with the greatest simplicity, with a touching simplicity, they presented me with a petition in favor of the League of Nations.* Soldiers Rebel at German Opera

## ORDERED TO ALLOW ALL GREEKS TO DIE

## CANADIANS RIOT IN BRITISH CAMP

*Arise ye pris'ners of starvation*
*Arise ye wretched of the earth*
*For justice thunders condemnation*

À qui la Faute si le Beurre est Cher?

## GAINS RUN HIGH IN WALL STREET

## MANY NEW RECORDS

## NE SOYONS PAS LES DUPES DU TRAVESTI BOLCHEVISTE

the opinion prevails in Washington that while it might be irksome to the American public to send troops to Asia

Minor people would be more willing to use an army to establish order south of the Rio Grande. Strikers menace complete tieup of New York City. Order restored in Lahore. Lille undertakers on strike

### THREAT OF MUTINY BY U.S. TROOPS

### CALIFORNIA JURY QUICKLY RENDERS VERDICT AGAINST SACRAMENTO WORKERS

> *'Tis the final conflict*
> *Let each stand in his place*
> *The international party*
> *Shall be the human race*

### BOLSHEVISM READY TO COLLAPSE, SAYS ESCAPED GENERAL

the French Censor will not allow the *Herald* to say what the Chinese delegation has done, but that there is serious unrest it would be idle to deny. Men who have been deprived of the opportunity to earn a living, who see their children crying for food, who face an indefinite shutdown of industries and a possible cessation of railway traffic with all the disorganization of national life therein implied, can hardly be expected to view the situation calmly and with equanimity.

### BRITISH TRY HARD TO KEEP PROMISE TO HANG KAISER

it is declared the Koreans are confident President Wilson will come in an aeroplane and listen to their views. A white flag set up on Seoul Hill is presumed to indicate the landing-place

## *Daughter*

She wasn't sick a bit and was very popular on the crossing that was very gay, although the sea was rough and it was bitter cold. There was a Mr Barrow who had been sent on a special mission by the President who paid her a great deal of attention.

He was a very interesting man and full of information about everything. He'd been a Socialist and very close to labor. He was so interested when she told him about her experiences in the textile strike over in Jersey. In the evenings they'd walk around and around the deck arm in arm, now and then being almost thrown off their feet by an especially heavy roll. She had a little trouble with him trying to make love to her, but managed to argue him out of it by telling him what she needed right now was a good friend, that she'd had a very unhappy love affair and couldn't think of anything like that any more. He was so kind and sympathetic, and said he could understand that thoroughly because his relation with women had been very unsatisfactory all his life. He said people ought to be free in love and marriage and not tied by conventions or inhibitions. He said what he believed in was passionate friendship. She said she did, too, but when he wanted her to come to his room in the hotel the first night they were in Paris, she gave him a terrible tonguelashing. But he was so nice to her on the trip down to Rome that she began to think that maybe if he asked her to marry him she might do it.

There was an American officer on the train, Captain Savage, so goodlooking and such a funny talker, on his way to Rome with important dispatches. From the minute she met Dick, Europe was wonderful. He talked French and Italian. and said how beautiful the old tumbledown towns were and screwed up his mouth so funnily when he told stories about comical things that happened in the war. He was a little like Webb onlyso much nicer and more selfreliant and betterlooking. From the minute she saw him she forgot all about Joe and as for G. H. Barrow, she couldn't stand the thought of him. When Captain Savage looked at her, it made her all melt up inside; by the time they'd gotten to Rome she'd admitted to herself she was crazy about him. When they went out walking together the day they all made an excursion to the ruins of the Emperor Hadrian's villa, and the little town where the waterfall was, she was glad that he'd been drinking. She wanted all the time to throw herself in his arms; there was something about the rainy landscape and the dark lasciviouseyed people and the old names of the towns and the garlic and oil in the food and the smiling voices and the smell of the tiny magenta wildflowers he said were called cyclamens that made her not care about anything anymore. She almost fainted when he started to make love to her. Oh, she wished he would, but No, No, she couldn't just then, but the next day she'd drink in spite of the pledge she'd signed with the N.E.R. and shoot the moon. It wasn't so sordid as she'd expected, but it wasn't so wonderful either; she was terribly scared and cold and sick, like when she'd told him she hadn't ever before. But the next day he was so gentle and strong, and she suddenly felt very happy. When he had to go back to Paris and there was nothing but office work and a lot of dreary old maids to talk to, it was too miserable.

When she found she was going to have a baby she was scared, but she didn't really care so much; of course he'd marry her. Dad and Buster would be sore at first, but they'd be sure to like him. He wrote poetry and was going to be a writer when he got out of the army; she was sure he was going to be famous. He didn't write letters very often and when she made him come back to Rome he wasn't nearly as nice about it as she expected; but of course it must have been a shock to him. They decided that perhaps it would be better not to have the baby just then or get married till he got out of the service, though there didn't seem to be any doubt in his mind about getting married then. She tried several things and went riding a great deal with Lieutenant Grassi, who had been educated at Eton and spoke perfect English and was so charming to her and said she was the best woman rider he'd ever known. It was on account of her going out riding so much with Lieutenant Grassi and getting in so late that the old cats at the N.E.R. got sore and sent her home to America.

Going to Paris on the train, Daughter really was scared. The horseback riding hadn't done any good, and she was sore all over from a fall she'd had when one of Lieutenant Grassi's cavalry horses fell with her and broke his leg when she took him over a stone wall. The horse had to be shot and the Lieutenant had been horrid about it; these foreigners always showed a mean streak in the end. She was worried about people's noticing how she looked because it was nearly three months now. She and Dick would have to get married right away, that's all there was to it. Perhaps it would even be better to tell people they'd been married in Rome by a fat little old priest.

The minute she saw Dick's face when she was running down the corridor towards him in his hotel, she knew it was all over; he didn't love her the least bit. She walked home to her hotel hardly able to see where she was going through the slimywet Paris streets. She was surprised when she got there because she expected she'd lose her way. She almost hoped she'd lose her way. She went up to her room and sat down in a chair without taking off her dripping wet hat and coat. She must think. This was the end of everything.

The next morning she went around to the office; they gave her her transportation back home and told her what boat she was going on and said she must sail in four days. After that she went back to the hotel and sat down in a chair again and tried to think. She couldn't go home to Dallas like this. A note from Dick came around giving the address of a doctor.

Do forgive me, he wrote. You're a wonderful girl and I'm sure it'll be all right.

She tore the thin blue letter up in little tiny pieces and dropped it out the window. Then she lay down on the bed and cried till her eyes burned. Her nausea came on and she had to go out in the hall to the toilet. When she lay down again, she went to sleep for a while and woke up feeling hungry.

The day had cleared; sunlight was streaming into the room. She walked downstairs to the desk and called up G. H. Barrow in his office. He seemed delighted and said if she'd wait for him half an hour, he'd come and fetch her out to lunch in the Bois; they'd forget everything except that it was spring and that they were beautiful pagans at heart. Daughter made a sour face, but said pleasantly enough over the phone that she'd wait for him.

When he came he wore a sporty gray flannel suit and a gray fedora hat. She felt very drab beside him in the darkgray uniform she hated so.

'Why, my dearest little girl . . . you've saved my life,' he said. 'Su-su-spring makes me think of suicide unless I'm in lu-lu-love . . . I was feeling . . . er . . . er . . . elderly and not in love. We must change all that.'

'I was feeling like that too.'

'What's the matter?'

'Well, maybe I'll tell you and maybe I won't.' She almost liked his long nose and his long jaw today. 'Anyway, I'm too starved to talk.'

'I'll do all the talking . . .' he said laughing. 'Alwa-wa-ways do anywa-wa-way . . . and I'll set you up to the bu-bu-best meal you ever ate.'

He talked boisterously all the way out in the cab about the Peace Conference and the terrible fight the President had had to keep his principles intact. 'Hemmed in by every sinister intrigue, by all the poisonous ghosts of secret treaties, with two of the cleverest and most unscrupulous manipulators out

of oldworld statecraft as his opponents . . . He fought on . . .
we are all of us fighting on . . . It's the greatest crusade in
history; if we win, the world will be a better place to live in; if
we lose, it will be given up to Bolshevism and despair . . . you
can imagine, Anne Elizabeth, how charming it was to have
your pretty little voice suddenly tickle my ear over the telephone and call me away if only for a brief space from all this
worry and responsibility . . . why, there's even a rumor that an
attempt has been made to poison the President at the Hôtel
Murat . . . it's the President alone with a few backers and
wellwishers and devoted adherents who is standing out for
decency, fairplay, and good sense, never forget that for an
instant. . . .'

He talked on and on as if he was rehearsing a speech.
Daughter heard him faintly like through a faulty telephone connection. The day, too, the little pagodas of bloom on the horsechestnuts, the crowds, the overdressed children, the flags against
the blue sky, the streets of handsome houses behind trees with
their carved stonework and their iron balconies and their
polished windows shining in the May sunshine; Paris was all
little and bright and far away like a picture seen through the
wrong end of a fieldglass. When the luncheon came on at the
big glittery outdoor restaurant, it was the same thing, she
couldn't taste what she was eating.

He made her drink quite a lot of wine and after a while she
heard herself talking to him. She'd never talked like this to a
man before. He seemed so understanding and kind. She found
herself talking to him about Dad and how hard it had been
giving up Joe Washburn, and how going over on the boat her
life had suddenly seemed all new . . . 'Somethin' funny's happened to me, I declare . . . I always used to get along with
everybody fine and now I can't seem to. In the N.E.R. office in
Rome I couldn't get along with any of those old cats, and I
got to be good friends with an Italian boy, used to take me
horseback riding, an' I couldn't get along with him, and you
know Captain Savage on the train to Italy who let us ride in his
compartment, we went out to Tivoli with him' – her ears began
to roar when she spoke of Dick. She was going to tell Mr
Barrow everything. 'We got along so well we got engaged and
now I've quarreled with him.'

She saw Mr Barrow's long knobbly face leaning towards
her across the table. The gap was very wide between his front
teeth when he smiled. 'Do you think, Annie girl, you could get

along with me a little?' He put his skinny puffyveined hand towards her across the table.

She laughed and threw her head to one side, 'We seem to be gettin' along all right right now.'

'It would make me very happy if you could . . . you make me very happy anyway, just to look at you . . . I'm happier at this moment than I've been for years, except perhaps for the mu-mu-moment when the Covenant for the League of Nations was signed.'

She laughed again. 'Well, I don't feel like any Peace Treaty, the fact is I'm in terrible trouble.' She found herself watching his face carefully; the upper lip thinned, he wasn't smiling any more.

'Why, what's the ma-ma-matter . . . if there was any wa-wa-way I could . . . er . . . be of any assistance . . . I'd be the happiest fellow in the world.'

'Oh, no . . . I hate losing my job, though, and having to go home in disgrace . . . that's about the size of it . . . it's all my fault for running around like a little nitwit.'

She was going to break down and cry, but suddenly the nausea came on again and she had to hurry to the ladies' room of the restaurant. She got there just in time to throw up. The shapeless leatherfaced woman there was very kind and sympathetic; it scared Daughter how she immediately seemed to know what was the matter. She didn't know much French, but she could see that the woman was asking if it was Madame's first child, how many months, congratulating her. Suddenly she decided she'd kill herself. When she got back, Barrow had paid the bill and was walking back and forth on the gravel path in front of the tables.

'You poor little girl,' he said. 'What can be the matter? You suddenly turned deathly pale.'

'It's nothing . . . I think I'll go home and lie down . . . I don't think all that spaghetti and garlic agreed with me in Italy . . . maybe it's that wine.'

'But perhaps I could do something about finding you a job in Paris. Are you a typist or stenographer?'

'Might make a stab at it,' said Daughter bitterly.

She hated Mr Barrow. All the way back in the taxi she couldn't get to say anything. Mr Barrow talked and talked. When she got back to the hotel, she lay down on the bed and gave herself up to thinking about Dick.

She decided she'd go home. She stayed in her room and

although Mr Barrow kept calling up asking her out and making suggestions about possible jobs, she wouldn't see him. She said she was having a bilious attack and would stay in bed. The night before she was to sail he asked her to dine with him and some friends and before she knew it she said she'd go along. He called for her at six and took her for cocktails at the Ritz Bar. She'd gone out and bought herself an evening dress at the Galeries Lafayette and was feeling fine, she was telling herself, as she sat drinking the champagne cocktail, that if Dick should come in now she wouldn't bat an eyelash. Mr Barrow was talking about the Fiume situation and the difficulties the President was having with Congress and how he feared that the whole great work of the League of Nations was in danger, when Dick came in looking very handsome in his uniform with a pale older woman in gray and a tall stoutish lighthaired man, whom Mr Barrow pointed out as J. Ward Moorehouse. Dick must have seen her, but he wouldn't look at her. She didn't care any more about anything. They drank down their cocktails and went out. On the way up to Montmartre she let Mr Barrow give her a long kiss on the mouth that put him in fine spirits. She didn't care; she had decided she'd kill herself.

Waiting for them at the table at the Hermitage Mr Barrow had reserved was a newspaper correspondent named Burnham and a Miss Hutchins who was a Red Cross worker. They were very much excited about a man named Stevens who had been arrested by the Army of Occupation, they thought accused of Bolshevik propaganda; he'd been courtmartialed and they were afraid he was going to be shot. Miss Hutchins was very upset and said Mr Barrow ought to go to the President about it as soon as Mr Wilson got back to Paris. In the meantime they had to get the execution stayed. She said Don Stevens was a newspaperman and although a radical not connected with any kind of propaganda and anyway it was horrible to shoot a man for wanting a better world. Mr Barrow was very embarrassed and stuttered and hemmed and hawed and said that Stevens was a very silly young man who talked too much about things he didn't understand, but that he supposed he'd have to do the best he could to try to get him out, but that after all, he hadn't shown the proper spirit. . . .

That made Miss Hutchins very angry. 'But they're going to shoot him . . . suppose it had happened to you . . .' she kept saying. 'Can't you understand that we've got to save his life?'

Daughter couldn't seem to think of anything to say, as she

didn't know what they were talking about; she sat there in the restaurant looking at the waiters and the lights and the people at the tables. Opposite there was a party of attractivelooking young French officers. One of them, a tall man with a hawk nose, was looking at her. Their eyes met and she couldn't help grinning. Those boys looked as if they were having a fine time. A party of Americans dressed up like plush horses crossed the floor between her and the Frenchmen. It was Dick and the pale woman and J. Ward Moorehouse and a big middleaged woman in a great many deep pink ruffles and emeralds. They sat down at the table next to Daughter's table where there had been a sign saying Réservée all evening. Everybody was introduced and she and Dick shook hands very formally, as if they were the merest acquaintances. Miss Stoddard, whom she'd been so friendly with in Rome, gave her a quick inquisitive cold stare that made her feel terrible.

Miss Hutchins immediately went over and began talking about Don Stevens and trying to get Mr Moorehouse to call up Colonel House right away and get him to take some action in his case. Mr Moorehouse acted very quiet and calm and said he was sure she need have no anxiety, he was probably only being held for investigation, and in any case he didn't think the court-martial in the Army of Occupation would take extreme measures against a civilian and an American citizen. Miss Hutchins said all she wanted was a stay because his father was a friend of La Follette's and would be able to get together considerable influence in Washington. Mr Moorehouse smiled when he heard that. 'If his life depended on the influence of Senator La Follette, I think you would have cause to be alarmed, Eveline, but I think I can assure you that it doesn't.' Miss Hutchins looked very cross when she heard that and settled back to glumly eating her supper. Anyway, the party was spoiled. Daughter couldn't imagine what it was that had made everybody so stiff and constrained; maybe she was imagining it on account of her and Dick. Now and then she gave him a sideways glance. He looked so different from the way she'd known him sitting there so prim and prissylooking, talking to the stout woman in pink in a low pompous whisper now and then. It made her want to throw a plate at him.

It was a relief when the orchestra started playing dance music. Mr Barrow wasn't a very good dancer and she didn't like the way he kept squeezing her hand and patting her neck. After they were through dancing they went into the bar to have a gin fizz. The ceiling was hung with tricolor decoration; the four French officers were in there; there were people singing *La Madelon de la Victoire* and all the tough little girls were laughing and talking loud shrill French.

Mr Barrow was whispering in her ear all the time: 'Darling girl, you must let me take you home tonight. . . . You mustn't sail . . . I'm sure I can arrange everything with the Red Cross or whatever it is. . . . I've led such an unhappy life and I think I'd kill myself if I had to give you up . . . couldn't you love me just a little . . . I've dedicated my life to unattainable ideals and here I am getting old without grasping true happiness for a moment. You're the only girl I've ever known who seemed really a beautiful pagan at heart . . . appreciate the art of life.' Then he kissed her wetly in the ear.

'But, George, I can't love anybody now . . . I hate everybody.'

'Let me teach you . . . just give me a chance.'

'If you knew about me, you wouldn't want me,' she said coldly. She caught again a funny scared look on his face and a thinning of his lips over his widely spaced teeth.

They went back to the table. She sat there fidgeting while everybody talked carefully, with long pauses, about the Peace Treaty, when it was going to be signed, whether the Germans would sign. Then she couldn't stand it any longer and went to the ladies' room to powder her nose. On the way back to the table she peeped into the bar to see what was going on in there.

The hawknosed French officer caught sight of her, jumped to his feet, clicked his heels together, saluted, bowed and said in broken English, 'Charming lady, will you not stay a moment and drink once with your umble servant?'

Daughter went to their table and sat down. 'You boys looked like you were having such a good time,' she said. 'I'm with the worst old set of plush horses . . . They make me tired.'

'Permettez, mademoiselle,' he said, and introduced her to his friends.

He was an aviator. They were all aviation officers. His name was Pierre. When she told them her brother had been an aviator and had been killed, they were very nice to her. She couldn't help letting them think Bud had been killed at the front.

'Mademoiselle,' said Pierre solemnly, 'allow me, with all possible respect, to be your brother.'

'Shake,' she said.

They all shook hands solemnly, they were drinking little

glasses of cognac, but after that they ordered champagne. She danced with them all. She was very happy and didn't care what happened. They were young goodlooking boys, all the time laughing and nice to her. They had clasped their hands and were dancing ring around the rosy in the middle of the floor while everybody around was clapping, when she saw Mr Barrow's face red and indignant in the door. Next time the doorway spun around she yelled over her shoulder, 'Be back in a minute, teacher.' The face disappeared. She was dizzy, but Pierre caught her and held her tight; he smelt of perfume, but still she liked having him hold her tight.

He suggested they go somewhere else. 'Mademoiselle Sistair,' he whispered, 'allow us to show you the mystères de Paree ... afterwards we can come back to your plus orsairs. They will probably become intoxicate ... plus orsairs invariably intoxicate.'

They laughed. He had gray eyes and light hair, he said he was a Norman. She said he was the nicest Frenchman she'd ever met. She had a hard time getting her coat from the checkroom because she didn't have any check, but she went in and picked it out while Pierre talked French to the checkgirl. They got into a long low gray car; Daughter had never seen such speeding. Pierre was a fine driver, though; he had a game of running full speed towards a gendarme and swerving just enough at the right moment. She said supposing he hit one; he shrugged his shoulders and said, 'It does not mattair ... they are ... ow do you call it? ... bloody cows.' They went to Maxim's, where it was too quiet for them, then to a little tough dancehall way across Paris. Daughter could see that Pierre was wellknown everywhere and an Ace. The other aviators met girls in different places and dropped away. Before she realized it she and Pierre were alone in the long gray car.

'Primo,' he was explaining, 'we will go to Les Halles to eat soupe à l'oignon ... and then I shall take you a little tour en avion.'

'Oh, please do. I've never been up in a plane ... I'd like to go up and loop the loop ... promise you'll loop the loop.'

'Entendu,' he said.

They sat a little sleepily in a small empty eatingplace and ate onion soup and drank some more champagne. He was still very kind and considerate, but he seemed to have exhausted his English. She thought vaguely about going back to the hotel and catching the boattrain, but all she seemed to be able to say was, 'Loop the loop, promise me you'll loop the loop.' His eyes had gotten a little glazy, 'With Mademoiselle Sistair,' he said, 'I do not make love . . . I make loop the loop.'

It was a long drive out to the aviation field. A little grayness of dawn was creeping over everything. Pierre couldn't drive straight any more, so that she had to grab the wheel once or twice to steady him. When they drew up with a jerk at the field, she could see the rows of hangars and three planes standing out in deepest blue and beyond, rows of poplartrees against the silver rim of the plain. Overhead the sky sagged heavily like a wet tent. Daughter got out of the car shivering.

Pierre was staggering a little. 'Perhaps you will go instead to bed . . . to bed it is very good,' he said, yawning.

She put her arm around him, 'You promised you'd take me up and loop the loop.'

'All right,' he said angrily and walked towards one of the planes.

He fumbled with the engine awhile and she could hear him swearing in French. Then he went into the hangar to wake up a mechanic. Daughter stood there shivering in the growing silvery light. She wouldn't think of anything. She wanted to go up in a plane. Her head ached, but she didn't feel nauseated. When the mechanic came back with Pierre, she could make out that he was arguing with him trying to make him give up the flight. She got very sore: 'Pierre, you've got to take me up,' she yelled at the two men sleepily arguing in French. 'Awright, Mademoiselle Sistair.' They wrapped a heavy army coat around her and strapped her very carefully in the observer's seat. Pierre climbed into the pilot seat. It was a Blériot monoplane, he said. The mechanic spun the propeller. The engine started. Everything was full of the roar of the engine. Suddenly she was scared and sober, thought about home and Dad and Buster and the boat she was going to take tomorrow, no, it was today. It seemed an endless time with the engine roaring. The light was brighter. She started to fumble with the straps to unstrap them. It was crazy going up like this. She had to catch that boat. The plane had started. It was bouncing over the field, bouncing along the ground. They were still on the ground rumbling bouncing along. Maybe it wouldn't go up. She hoped it wouldn't go up. A row of poplars swept past below them. The motor was a settled roar now, they were climbing. It was daylight; a cold silver sun shone in her face. Underneath them was a floor of thick white clouds like a beach.

She was terribly cold and stunned by the roar of the motor. The man in goggles in front of her turned around and yelled something. She couldn't hear. She'd forgotten who Pierre was. She stretched her hand out towards him and waved it around. The plane went on climbing steadily. She began to see hills standing up in the light on either side of the white beach of clouds, must be the valley of the Seine full of fog; where was Paris? They were plunging into the sun, no, no, don't, don't, now it's the end. The white clouds were a ceiling overhead, the sun spun around once, first fast then slowly, then the plane was climbing again. She felt terribly sick, she was afraid she was going to faint. Dying must be like this. Perhaps she'd have a miscarriage. Her body was throbbing with the roar of the engine. She had barely strength enough to stretch her hand towards him again and make the same motion. The same thing again. This time she didn't feel so bad. They were climbing again into blue sky, a wind must have come up because the plane was lunging a little, took an occasional sickening drop into a pocket. The face in the goggles turned around and swayed from side to side. She thought the lips formed the words, No good; but now she could see Paris like an embroidered pincushion, with all the steeples and the Eiffel Tower and the towers of the Trocadéro sticking up through a milky haze. The Sacré Coeur on Montmartre was very white and cast a shadow clear to the garden that looked like a map. Then it was behind them and they were circling over green country. It was rough and she began to feel sick again. There was a ripping sound of some kind. A little wire waving loose and glistening against the blue began to whine. She tried to yell to the man in goggles. He turned and saw her waving and went into another dive. This time. No. Paris, the Eiffel Tower, the Sacré Coeur, the green fields spun. They were climbing again. Daughter saw the shine of a wing gliding by itself a little way from the plane. The spinning sun blinded her as they dropped.

# Newsreel 39

spectacle of ruined villages and tortured earth 'the work of fiends' wrings hearts of Mr Hugh C. Wallace during his visit to wasted and shelltorn regions

### WHIPPET TANKS ON FIFTH AVENUE STIR LOAN ENTHUSIASM

### U.S. MOBILIZES IN ORIENT AGAINST JAP MENACE

*Rule Britannia, rule the waves*
*Britains never never shall be slaves*

### YOUNG WOMAN FOUND STRANGLED IN YONKERS

the socialrevolutionaries are the agents of Denekine, Kolchak, and the Allied Imperial Armies. I was one of the organizers of the Soldiers', Sailors', and Workmen's council in Seattle. There is the same sentiment in this meeting that appeared at our first meeting in Seattle when 5000 men in uniform attended. EX-KAISER SPENDS HOURS IN WRITING. Speaking broadly their choice is between revolutionary socialism and anarchy. England already has plunged into socialism, France hesitates, Belgium has gone, Italy is going, while Lenine's shadow grows stronger and stronger over the Conference.

### TEN SHIPS LAID BARRIERS OF SUDDEN DEATH FROM ORKNEYS TO SKAGGERAK

### NO COAL? TRY PEAT

*If you want to find the generals*
*I know where they are*
*If you want to find the generals*
*I know where they are*

masses still don't know how the war started, how it was conducted, or how it ended, declared Maximilian

Harden. The War Ministry was stormed by demonstrators who dragged out Herr Neuring and threw him into the Elbe where he was shot and killed as he tried to swim to the bank

### VICIOUS PRACTICES RESPONSIBLE FOR HIGH LIVING COSTS, WILSON TELLS CONGRESS

*I saw them*
*I saw them*
*Down in the*
*Deep dugout*


## *The Camera Eye (41)*

aren't you coming to the anarchist picnic    there's going to be an anarchist picnic sure you've got to come to the anarchist picnic this afternoon it was way out at Garches in a kind of park it took a long time to get out there we were late there were youngsters and young girls with glasses and old men with their whiskers and long white zits and everybody wore black artist ties    some had taken off their shoes and stockings and were wandering around in the long grass    a young man with a black artist tie was reading a poem. Voilà said a voice c'est plutôt le geste prolétaire it was a nice afternoon we sat on the grass and looked around le geste prolétaire

But God damn it they've got all the machineguns in the world all the printingpresses linotypes tickerribbon curling iron plushhorses Ritz and we    you    I?    barehands a few songs not very good songs plutôt le geste prolétaire

*Les bourgeois à la lanterne nom de dieu*

et l'humanité la futurité la lutte des classes l'inépuisable angoisse des foules la misère du travailleur tu sais mon vieux sans blague

it was chilly early summer gloaming among the eighteenth-centuryshaped trees when we started home    I sat on

the impériale of the thirdclass car with the daughter of the
Libertaire (that's Patrick Henry ours after all give me or
death) a fine girl her father she said never let her go out
alone never let her see any young men it was like being in a
convent she wanted liberty fraternity equality and a young
man to take her out    in the tunnels the coalgas made us
cough and she wanted l'Amérique la vie le théâtre le feev
o'clock le smoking le foxtrot    she was a nice girl we sat
side by side on the roof of the car and looked at the banlieue
de Paris a desert of little gingerbread brick maisonnettes
flattening out under the broad gloom of evening she and I
tu sais mon ami but what kind of goddam management is
this?

# Newsreel 40

Italians! against all and everything remember that the beacon is lighted at Fiume and that all harangues are contained in the words: Fiume or Death.

Criez aux quatre vents que je n'accepte aucune transaction. Le reste ici contre tout le monde et je prépare de très mauvais jours.

Criez cela je vous prie à tue-tête

the call for enlistments mentions a chance for gold service stripes, opportunities for biggame hunting and thrilling watersports added to the general advantages of travel in foreign countries

> *Chi va piano*
> *Va sano*
> *Chi va forte*
> *Va 'la morte*
> *Evviva la libertá*

### EARTHQUAKE IN ITALY DEVASTATES LIKE WAR

only way Y.M.C.A. girls can travel is on troopships; part of fleet will go seaward to help Wilson

### DEMPSEY KNOCKS OUT WILLARD IN THIRD ROUND

Ils sont sourds.
Je vous embrasse.
Le coeur de Fiume est à vous.

## Joe Hill

A young Swede named Hillstrom went to sea, got himself calloused hands on sailingships and tramps, learned English in the fo'c'stle of the steamers that make the run from Stockholm to Hull, dreamed the Swede's dream of the West;

when he got to America they gave him a job polishing cuspidors in a Bowery saloon.

He moved west to Chicago and worked in a machineshop.

He moved west and followed the harvest, hung around employment agencies, paid out many a dollar for a job in a construction camp, walked out many a mile when the grub was too bum, or the boss too tough, or too many bugs in the bunkhouse;

read Marx and the I.W.W. Preamble and dreamed about forming the structure of the new society within the shell of the old.

He was in California for the S.P. strike (*Casey Jones, two locomotives, Casey Jones*), used to play the concertina outside the bunkhouse door, after supper, evenings (*Longhaired preachers come out every night*), had a knack for setting rebel words to tunes (*And the union makes us strong*).

Along the coast in cookshacks flophouses jungles wobblies hoboes bindlestiffs began singing Joe Hill's songs. They sang 'em in the county jails of the State of Washington, Oregon, California, Nevada, Idaho, in the bullpens in Montana and Arizona, sang 'em in Walla Walla, San Quentin, and Leavenworth,

forming the structure of the new society within the jails of the old.

At Bingham, Utah, Joe Hill organized the workers of the Utah Construction Company in the One Big Union, won a new wagescale, shorter hours, better grub. (The angel Moroni didn't like labororganizers any better than the Southern Pacific did.)

The angel Moroni moved the hearts of the Mormons to decide it was Joe Hill shot a grocer named Morrison. The Swedish consul and President Wilson tried to get him a new trial, but the angel Moroni moved the hearts of the Supreme Court of the State of Utah to sustain the verdict of guilty. He was in jail a year, went on making up songs. In November 1915 he was stood up against the wall in the jail yard in Salt Lake City.

'Don't mourn for me    organize,' was the last word he sent out to the workingstiffs of the I.W.W. Joe Hill stood up against the wall of the jail yard, looked into the muzzles of the guns, and gave the word to fire.

They put him in a black suit, put a stiff collar around his neck and a bow tie, shipped him to Chicago for a bangup funeral, and photographed his handsome stony mask staring into the future.

The first of May they scattered his ashes to the wind.

## *Ben Compton*

> *The history of all hitherto existing society is the history of class struggles. . . .*

The old people were Jews, but at school Benny always said no he wasn't a Jew, he was an American, because he'd been born in Brooklyn and lived at 2531 Twentyfifth Avenue in Flatbush and they owned their home. The teacher in the seventh grade said he squinted and sent him home with a note, so Pop took an afternoon off from the jewelry store where he worked with a lens in his eye repairing watches, to take Benny to an optician who put drops in his eyes and made him read little teeny letters on a white card. Pop seemed tickled when the optician said Benny had to wear glasses. 'Vatchmaker's eyes . . . takes after his old man,' he said and patted his cheek. The steel eyeglasses were heavy on Benny's nose and cut into him behind the ears. It made him feel funny to have Pop telling the optician that a boy with glasses wouldn't be a bum and a baseballplayer like Sam and Isidore, but would attend to his studies and be a lawyer and a scholar like the men of old. 'A rabbi maybe,' said the optician, but Pop said rabbis were loafers and lived on the blood of the poor; he and the old woman still ate kosher and kept the sabbath like their fathers, but synagogue and the rabbis . . . he made a spitting sound with his lips. The optician laughed and said as for himself he was a freethinker, but religion was good for the commonpeople. When they got home, Momma said the glasses made Benny look awful old. Sam and Izzy yelled, 'Hello, foureyes,' when they came in from selling papers, but at school next day they told the other kids it was a statesprison offense to roughhouse a feller with glasses. Once he had the glasses Benny got to be very good at his lessons.

In highschool he made the debating team. When he was

thirteen Pop had a long illness and had to give up work for a year. They lost the house that was almost paid for and went to live in a flat on Myrtle Avenue. Benny got work in a drugstore evenings. Sam and Izzy left home, Sam to work in a furrier's in Newark; Izzy had gotten to loafing in poolparlors so Pop threw him out. He'd always been a good athlete and palled around with an Irishman named Pug Riley who was going to get him into the ring. Momma cried and Pop forbade any of the kids to mention his name; still they all knew that Gladys, the oldest one, who was working as a stenographer over in Manhattan, sent Izzy a fivedollar bill now and then. Benny looked much older than he was and hardly ever thought of anything except making money so the old people could have a house of their own again. When he grew up he'd be a lawyer and a businessman and make a pile quick so that Gladys could quit work and get married and the old people could buy a big house and live in the country. Momma used to tell him about how when she was a young maiden in the old country they used to go out in the woods after strawberries and mushrooms and stop by a farmhouse and drink milk all warm and foamy from the cow. Benny was going to get rich and take them all out in the country for a trip to a summer resort.

When Pop was well enough to work again, he rented half a twofamily house in Flatbush where at least they'd be away from the noise of the Elevated. The same year Benny graduated from highschool and won a prize for an essay on 'The American Government.' He'd gotten very tall and thin and had terrible headaches. The old people said he'd outgrown himself and took him to see Doctor Cohen who lived on the same block but had his office downtown near Borough Hall. The Doctor said he'd have to give up nightwork and studying too hard; what he needed was something that would keep him outdoors and develop his body. 'All work and no play makes Jack a dull boy,' he said, scratching the grizzled beard under his chin. Benny said he had to make some money this summer because he wanted to go to New York University in the fall. Doctor Cohen said he ought to eat plenty of milkdishes and fresh eggs and go somewhere where he could be out in the sun and take it easy all summer. He charged two dollars. Walking home, the old man kept striking his forehead with the flat of his hand and saying he was a failure; thirty years he had worked in America and now he was a sick old man all used up and couldn't provide for his children. Momma cried. Gladys told them not to be silly, Benny was a clever boy and a bright student and what was the use of all his booklearning if he couldn't think up some way of getting a job in the country. Benny went to bed without saying anything.

A few days later Izzy came home. He rang the doorbell as soon as the old man had gone to work one morning.

'You almost met Pop,' said Benny who opened the door.

'Nutten doin'. I waited round the corner till I seen him go. ... How's everybody?' Izzy had on a light gray suit and a green necktie and wore a fedora hat to match the suit. He said he had to get to Lancaster, Pennsylvania, to fight a Filipino featherweight on Saturday.

'You ain't tough enough, kid . . . too much the momma's boy.'

In the end Benny went with him. They rode on the L to Brooklyn Bridge and then walked across New York to the ferry. They bought tickets to Elizabeth. When the train stopped in a freightyard, they sneaked forward into the blind baggage. At West Philadelphia they dropped off and got chased by the yard detective. A brewery wagon picked them up and carried them along the road as far as West Chester. They had to walk the rest of the way. A Mennonite farmer let them spend the night in his barn, but in the morning he wouldn't let them have any breakfast until they'd chopped wood for two hours. By the time they got to Lancaster, Benny was all in. He went to sleep in the lockerroom at the Athletic Club and didn't wake up until the fight was over. Izzy had knocked out the Filipino featherweight in the third round and won a purse of twentyfive dollars. He sent Benny over to a lodginghouse with the shine who took care of the lockerroom and went out with the boys to paint the town red. Next morning he turned up with his face green and his eyes bloodshot; he'd spent all his money, but he'd gotten Benny a job helping a feller who did a little smalltime fightpromoting and ran a canteen in a construction camp up near Mauch Chunk.

It was a road job. Ben stayed there for two months earning ten dollars a week and his keep. He learned to drive a team and to keep books. The boss of the canteen, Hiram Volle, gypped the construction workers in their accounts, but Benny didn't think much about it because they were most of 'em wops, until he got to be friends with a young fellow named Nick Gigli who worked with the gang at the gravelpit. Nick used to hang around the canteen before closingtime in the evening; then they'd go out and smoke a cigarette together and talk. Sundays they'd walk out in the country with the Sunday paper and fool around all afternoon lying in the sun and talking about the articles in the magazine section. Nick was from North Italy and all the men in the gang were Sicilians, so he was lonely. His father and elder brothers were anarchists and he was too; he told Benny about Bakunin and Malatesta and said Benny ought to be ashamed of himself for wanting to get to be a rich businessman; sure he ought to study and learn, maybe he ought to get to be a lawyer, but he ought to work for the revolution and the workingclass; to be a business-man was to be a shark and a robber like that sonofabitch Volle. He taught Benny to roll cigarettes and told him about all the girls that were in love with him; that girl in the boxoffice of the movie in Mauch Chunk; he could have her any time he wanted, but a revolutionist ought to be careful about the girls he went with, women took a classconscious workingman's mind off his aims, they were the main seduction of capitalist society. Ben asked him if he thought he ought to throw up his job with Volle, because Volle was such a crook, but Nick said any other capitalist would be the same, all they could do was wait for the Day. Nick was eighteen with bitter brown eyes and a skin almost as dark as a mulatto's. Ben thought he was great on account of all he'd done; he'd shined shoes, been a sailor, a miner, a dishwasher, and had worked in textile mills, shoe-factories, and a cement factory and had had all kinds of women and been in jail for three weeks in the Paterson strike. Round the camp if any of the wops saw Ben going anywhere alone, he'd yell at him, 'Hey, kid, where's Nick?'

On Friday evening there was an argument in front of the window where the construction boss was paying the men off. That night, when Ben was getting into his bunk in the back of the tarpaper shack the canteen was in, Nick came around and whispered in his ear that the bosses had been gypping the men on time and that they were going on strike tomorrow. Ben said if they went out he'd go out too. Nick called him a brave comrade in Italian and hauled off and kissed him on both cheeks. Next morning only a few of the pick and shovel men turned out when the whistle blew. Ben hung around the door of the cookshack, not knowing what to do with himself. Volle noticed him and told him to hitch up the team to go down to the station after a box of tobacco. Ben looked at his feet and said he couldn't because he was on strike. Volle burst out laughing and told him to quit his kidding, funniest thing he'd ever heard of a kike walking out with a lot of wops. Ben felt himself go cold and stiff all over: 'I'm not a kike any more'n you are. . . . I'm an American born . . . and I'm goin' to stick with my class, you dirty crook.' Volle turned white and stepped up and shook a big fist under Ben's nose and said he was fired and that if he wasn't a little f—g shrimp of a foureyed kike he'd knock his goddam block off; anyway his brother sure would give him a whaling when he heard about it.

Ben went to his bunk and rolled his things into a bundle and went off to find Nick. Nick was a little down the road where the bunkhouses were, in the center of a bunch of wops all yelling and waving their arms. The superintendent and the gangbosses all turned out with revolvers in black holsters strapped around their waists and one of them made a speech in English and another one Sicilian saying that this was a squareshooting concern that had always treated laborers square and if they didn't like it they could get the hell out. They'd never had a strike and didn't propose to begin now. There was big money involved in this job and the company wasn't going to work and see it tied up by any goddam foolishness. Any man who wasn't on his job next time the whistle blew was fired and would have to get a move on and remember that the State of Pennsylvania had vagrancy laws. When the whistle blew again, everybody went back to work except Ben and Nick. They walked off down the road with their bundles. Nick had tears in his eyes and was saying, 'Too much gentle, too much patient . . . we do not know our strength yet.'

That night they found a brokendown schoolhouse a little off the road on a hill above a river. They'd bought some bread and peanut butter at a store and sat out in front eating it and talking about what they'd do. By the time they'd finished eating, it was dark. Ben had never been out in the country alone like that at night. The wind rustled the woods all around and the rapid river seethed down in the valley. It was a chilly August night with a heavy dew. They didn't have any covering so Nick showed Ben how to take his jacket off and put it over his head and how to sleep against the wall to keep from getting sore lying on the bare boards. He'd hardly gotten to sleep when he woke up icycold and shaking. There was a window broken; he could see the frame and the jagged bits of glass against the cloudy moonlight. He lay back, musta been dreaming. Something banged on the roof and rolled down the shingles over his head and dropped to the ground. 'Hey, Ben, for chrissake, wassat?' came Nick's voice in a hoarse whisper. They both got up and stared out through the broken windowframe.

'That was busted before,' said Nick. He walked over and opened the outside door. They both shivered in the chilly wind up the valley that rustled the trees like rain, the river down below made a creaking grinding noise like a string of carts and wagons.

A stone hit the roof above them and rolled off. The next one went between their heads and hit the cracked plaster of the wall behind. Ben heard the click of the blade as Nick opened his pocketknife. He strained his eyes till the tears came, but he couldn't make out anything but the leaves stirring in the wind.

'You come outa there . . . come up here . . . talk . . . you sonofabitch,' yelled Nick.

There was no answer.

'What you think?' whispered Nick over his shoulder to Ben.

Ben didn't say anything; he was trying to keep his teeth from chattering. Nick pushed him back in and pulled the door to. They piled the dusty benches against the door and blocked up the lower part of the window with boards out of the floor.

'Break in. I keell one of him anyhow,' said Nick. 'You don't believe in speerits?'

'Naw, no such thing,' said Ben.

They sat down side by side on the floor with their backs to the cracked plaster and listened. Nick had put the knife down between them. He took Ben's fingers and made him feel the catch that held the blade steady. 'Good knife . . . sailor knife,' he whispered. Ben strained his ears. Only the spattering sound of the wind in the trees and the steady grind of the river. No more stones came.

Next morning they left the schoolhouse at first day. Neither of them had had any sleep. Ben's eyes were stinging. When the sun came up they found a man who was patching up a broken spring on a truck. They helped him jack it up with a block of wood and he gave them a lift into Scranton where they got jobs washing dishes in a hashjoint run by a Greek.

> . . . all fixed fastfrozen relations, with their train of ancient and venerable prejudices and opinions, are swept away, all newformed ones become antiquated before they can ossify. . . .

Pearldiving wasn't much to Ben's taste, so at the end of a couple of weeks, as he'd saved up the price of the ticket, he said he was going back home to see the old people. Nick stayed on because a girl in a candystore had fallen for him. Later he'd go up to Allentown, where a brother of his had a job in a steelmill and was making big money. The last thing he said when he went down and put Ben on the train for New York was, 'Benny, you learn and study . . . be great man for workingclass and remember too much girls bad business.'

Ben hated leaving Nick, but he had to get home to find a job for the winter that would give him time to study. He took the exams and matriculated at the College of the City of New York. The old man borrowed a hundred dollars from the Morris Plan to get him started and Sam sent him twentyfive from Newark to buy books with. Then he made a little money himself working in Kahn's drugstore evenings. Sunday afternoons he went to the library and read Marx's *Capital*. He joined the Socialist Party and went to lectures at the Rand School whenever he got a chance. He was working to be a wellsharpened instrument.

The next spring he got sick with scarlet fever and was ten weeks in the hospital. When he got out, his eyes were so bad it gave him a headache to read for an hour. The old man owed the Morris Plan another hundred dollars besides the first hundred dollars and the interest and the investigation fees.

Ben had met a girl at a lecture at Cooper Union who had worked in a textile mill over in Jersey. She'd been arrested during the Paterson strike and had been blacklisted. Now she was a salesgirl at Wanamaker's, but her folks still worked in the Botany Mill at Passaic. Her name was Helen Mauer; she was five years older than Ben, a pale blonde, and already had lines in her face. She said there was nothing in the Socialist movement; it was the syndicalists had the right idea. After the lecture she took him to the Cosmopolitan Café on Second Avenue to have a glass of tea and introduced him to some people she said were real rebels; when Ben told Gladys and the old people about them, the old man said, 'Pfooy . . . radical Jews,' and made a spitting sound with his lips. He said Benny ought to cut out these monkeyshines and get to work. He was getting old and now he was in debt, and if he got sick it would be up to Benny to support him and the old woman. Ben said he was working all the time, but that your folks didn't count, it was the workingclass that he was working for. The old man got red in the face and said his family was sacred and next to that his own people. Momma and Gladys cried. The old man got to his feet; choking and coughing, he raised his hands above his head and cursed Ben and Ben left the house.

He had no money on him and was still weak from the scarlet fever. He walked across Brooklyn and across the Manhattan Bridge and up through the East Side, all full of ruddy lights and crowds and pushcarts with vegetables that smelt of the spring, to the house where Helen lived on East Sixth Street. The landlady said he couldn't go up to her room. Helen said it wasn't any of her business, but while they were arguing about it his ears began to ring and he fainted on the hall settee. When he came to with water running down his neck, Helen helped him up the four flights and made him lie down on her bed. She yelled down to the landlady, who was screaming about the police, that she would leave first thing in the morning and nothing in the world could make her leave sooner. She made Ben some tea and they sat up all night talking on her bed. They decided that they'd live in free union together and spent the rest of the night packing her things. She had mostly books and pamphlets.

Next morning they went out at six o'clock, because she had to be at Wanamaker's at eight, to look for a room. They didn't exactly tell the next landlady they weren't married, but when she said, 'So you're bride and groom?' they nodded and smiled. Fortunately Helen had enough money in her purse to pay the week in advance. Then she had to run off to work. Ben didn't have any money to buy anything to eat, so he lay on the bed reading *Progress and Poverty* all day. When she came back in the evening, she brought in some supper from a delicatessen. Eating the rye bread and salami they were very happy. She had such large breasts for such a slender little girl. He had to go out to a drugstore to buy some safeties because she said how could she have a baby just now when they had to give all their strength to the movement. There were bedbugs in the bed, but they told each other that they were as happy as they could be under the capitalist system, that some day they'd have a free society where workers wouldn't have to huddle in filthy lodginghouses full of bedbugs or row with landladies and lovers could have babies if they wanted to.

A few days later Helen was laid off from Wanamaker's because they were cutting down their personnel for the slack summer season. They went over to Jersey where she went to

live with her folks and Ben got a job in the shipping department of a worsted mill. They rented a room together in Passaic.
When a strike came he and Helen were both on the committee.
Ben got to be quite a speechmaker. He was arrested several
times and almost had his skull cracked by a policeman's billy
and got six months in jail out of it. But he'd found out that
when he got up on a soapbox to talk. he could make people
listen to him, that he could talk and say what he thought and
get a laugh or a cheer out of the massed upturned faces. When
he stood up in court to take his sentence, he started to talk
about surplus value. The strikers in the audience cheered
and the judge had the attendants clear the courtroom. Ben
could see the reporters busily taking down what he said: he
was glad to be a living example of the injustice and brutality
of the capitalist system. The judge shut him up by saying he'd
give him another six months for contempt of court if he didn't
keep quiet, and Ben was taken to the county jail in an automobile full of special deputies with riot guns. The papers spoke
of him as a wellknown Socialist agitator.

In jail Ben got to be friends with a wobbly named Bram
Hicks, a tall youngster from Frisco with light hair and blue
eyes who told him if he wanted to know the labormovement
he ought to get him a red card and go out to the Coast. Bram
was a boilermaker by profession, but had shipped as a sailor
for a change and landed in Perth Amboy broke. He'd been
working on the repairshift of one of the mills and had gone
out with the rest. He'd pushed a cop in the face when they'd
broken up a picketline and been sent up for six months for
assault and battery. Meeting him once a day in the prison
yard was the one thing kept Ben going in jail.

They were both released on the same day. They walked along
the street together. The strike was over. The mills were running.
The streets where there'd been picketlines, the halls where Ben
had made speeches, looked quiet and ordinary. He took Bram
around to Helen's. She wasn't there, but after a while she came
in with a little redfaced ferretnosed Englishman whom she introduced as Billy, an English comrade. First thing Ben guessed
that he was sleeping with her. He left Bram in the room with
the Englishman and beckoned her outside. The narrow upper
hall of the old frame house smelt of vinegar.

'You're through with me?' he asked in a shaky voice.

'Oh, Ben, don't act so conventional.'

'You mighta waited till I got outa jail.'

'But can't you see that we're all comrades? You're a brave
fighter and oughtn't to be so conventional, Ben. . . . Billy
doesn't mean anything to me. He's a steward on a liner. He'll
be going away soon.'

'Then I don't mean anything to you either.' He grabbed
Helen's wrist and squeezed it as hard as he could. 'I guess I'm
all wrong, but I'm crazy about you. . . . I thought you . . .'

'Ouch, Ben . . . you're talkin' silly, you know how much I
like you.'

They went back in the room and talked about the movement.
Ben said he was going West with Bram Hicks.

> *. . . he becomes an appendage of the machine and
> it is only the most simple, most monotonous, most
> easily required knack that is required of him. . . .*

Bram knew all the ropes. Walking, riding blind baggage or
on empty gondolas, hopping rides on deliverywagons and
trucks, they got to Buffalo. In a flophouse there Bram found
a guy he knew who got them signed on as deckhands on a
whaleback going back light to Duluth. In Duluth they joined
a gang being shipped up to harvest wheat for an outfit in
Saskatchewan. At first the work was very heavy for Ben and
Bram was scared he'd cave in, but the fourteenhour days out
in the sun and the dust, the copious grub, the dead sleep in
the lofts of the big barns began to toughen him up. Lying flat
on the straw in his sweaty clothes he'd still feel through his
sleep the tingle of the sun on his face and neck, the strain in
his muscles, the whir of the reapers and binders along the
horizon, the roar of the thresher, the grind of gears of the
trucks carrying the red wheat to the elevators. He began to
talk like a harvest stiff. After the harvest they worked in a
fruitcannery on the Columbia River, a lousy steamy job full
of the sour stench of rotting fruitpeelings. There they read in
*Solidarity* about the shingleweavers' strike and the free-speech
fight in Everett, and decided they'd go down and see what they
could do to help out. The last day they worked there Bram
lost the forefinger of his right hand repairing the slicing and
peeling machinery. The company doctor said he couldn't get
any compensation because he'd already given notice, and,
besides, not being a Canadian . . . A little shyster lawyer came
around to the boardinghouse where Bram was lying on the
bed in a fever, with his hand in a big wad of bandage, and

tried to get him to sue, but Bram yelled at the lawyer to get the hell out. Ben said he was wrong, the workingclass ought to have its lawyers too.

When the hand had healed a little, they went down on the boat from Vancouver to Seattle. I.W.W. headquarters there was like a picnic ground, crowded with young men coming in from every part of the U.S. and Canada. One day a big bunch went down to Everett on the boat to try to hold a meeting at the corner of Wetmore and Hewitt Avenues. The dock was full of deputies with rifles, and revolvers. 'The Commercial Club boys are waiting for us,' some guy's voice tittered nervously. The deputies had white handkerchiefs around their necks. 'There's Sheriff McRae,' said somebody. Bram edged up to Ben. 'We better stick together. . . . Looks to me like we was goin' to get tamped up some.' The wobblies were arrested as fast as they stepped off the boat and herded down to the end of the dock. The deputies were drunk, most of them. Ben could smell the whiskey on the breath of the redfaced guy who grabbed him by the arm. 'Get a move on there, you sonofabitch . . .' He got a blow from a riflebutt in the small of his back. He could hear the crack of saps on men's skulls. Anybody who resisted had his face beaten to a jelly with a club. The wobblies were made to climb up into a truck. With the dusk a cold drizzle had come on. 'Boys, we got to show 'em we got guts,' a redhaired boy said. A deputy who was holding on to the back of the truck aimed a blow at him with his sap, but lost his balance and fell off. The wobblies laughed. The deputy climbed on again, purple in the face. 'You'll be laughin' outa the other side of your dirty mugs when we get through with you,' he yelled.

Out in the woods where the country road crossed the railroad track they were made to get out of the trucks. The deputies stood around them with their guns leveled while the sheriff, who was reeling drunk, and two well-dressed middleaged men talked over what they'd do. Ben heard the word gantlet.

'Look here, sheriff,' somebody said, 'we're not here to make any kind of disturbance. All we want's our constitutional rights of free speech.'

The sheriff turned towards them waving the butt of his revolver, 'Oh, you do, do you, you c—s. Well, this is Snohomish County and you ain't goin' to forget it . . . if you come here again some of you fellers is goin' to die, that's all there is about it. . . . All right, boys, let's go.'

The deputies made two lines down towards the railroad track. They grabbed the wobblies one by one and beat them up. Three of them grabbed Ben.

'You a wobbly?'

'Sure I am, you dirty yellow . . .' he began.

The sheriff came up and hauled off to hit him. 'Look out, he's got glasses on.' A big hand pulled the glasses off. 'We'll fix that.' Then the sheriff punched him in the nose with his fist. 'Say you ain't.'

Ben's mouth was full of blood. He set his jaw. 'He's a kike, hit him again for me.'

'Say you ain't a wobbly.' Somebody whacked a riflebarrel against his shins and he fell forward. 'Run for it,' they were yelling. Blows with clubs and riflebutts were splitting his ears.

He tried to walk forward without running. He tripped on a rail and fell, cutting his arm on something sharp. There was so much blood in his eyes he couldn't see. A heavy boot was kicking him again and again in the side. He was passing out. Somehow he staggered forward. Somebody was holding him up under the arms and was dragging him free of the cattleguard on the track. Another fellow began to wipe his face off with a handkerchief. He heard Bram's voice way off somewhere, 'We're over the county line, boys.' What with losing his glasses and the rain and the night and the shooting pain all up and down his back Ben couldn't see anything. He heard shots behind them and yells from where other guys were running the gantlet. He was the center of a little straggling group of wobblies making their way down the railroad track. 'Fellowworkers,' Bram was saying in his deep quiet voice, 'we must never forget this night.'

At the interurban trolley station they took up a collection among the ragged and bloody group to buy tickets to Seattle for the guys most hurt. Ben was so dazed and sick he could hardly hold the ticket when somebody pushed it into his hand. Bram and the rest of them set off to walk the thirty miles back to Seattle.

Ben was in hospital three weeks. The kicks in the back had affected his kidneys and he was in frightful pain most of the time. The morphine they gave him made him so dopey he barely knew what was happening when they brought in the boys wounded in the shooting on the Everett dock on November 5th. When he was discharged he could just walk. Everybody he

knew was in jail. At General Delivery he found a letter from
Gladys enclosing fifty dollars and saying his father wanted
him to come home.

The Defense Committee told him to go ahead; he was just
the man to raise funds for them in the East. An enormous
amount of money would be needed for the defense of the
seventyfour wobblies held in the Everett jail charged with
murder. Ben hung around Seattle for a couple of weeks doing
odd jobs for the Defense Committee, trying to figure out a
way to get home. A sympathizer who worked in a shipping
office finally got him a berth as supercargo on a freighter that
was going to New York through the Panama Canal. The sea
trip and the detailed clerical work helped him to pull himself
together. Still there wasn't a night he didn't wake up with a
nightmare scream in his throat sitting up in his bunk dreaming
the deputies were coming to get him to make him run the gantlet.
When he got to sleep again, he'd dream he was caught in the
cattleguard and the teeth were tearing his arms and heavy boots
were kicking him in the back. It got so it took all his nerve to
lie down in his bunk to go to sleep. The men on the ship
thought he was a hophead and steered clear of him. It was a
great day when he saw the tall buildings of New York shining
in the brown morning haze.

> *... when in the course of development class distinc-*
> *tions have disappeared and all production has been*
> *concentrated in the hands of a vast association of the*
> *whole nation, the public power will lose its political*
> *character. ...*

Ben lived at home that winter because it was cheaper. When
he told Pop he was going to study law in the office of a radical
lawyer named Morris Stein whom he'd met in connection with
raising money for the Everett boys, the old man was delighted.
'A clever lawyer can protect the workers and the poor Jews
and make money too,' he said, rubbing his hands. 'Benny, I
always knew you were a good boy.' Momma nodded and
smiled. 'Because in this country it's not like over there under
the warlords, even a lazy bum's got constitootional rights,
that's why they wrote the constitootion for.' It made Ben feel
sick talking to them about it.

He worked as a clerk in Stein's office on lower Broadway
and in the evenings addressed protest meetings about the

Everett massacre. Morris Stein's sister Fanya, who was a thin dark wealthy woman about thirtyfive, was an ardent pacifist and made him read Tolstoy and Kropotkin. She believed that Wilson would keep the country out of the European war and sent money to all the women's peace organizations. She had a car and used to run him around town sometimes when he had several meetings in one evening. His heart would always be thumping when he went into the hall where the meeting was and began to hear the babble and rustle of the audience filing in, garment workers on the East Side, waterfront workers in Brooklyn, workers in chemical and metalproducts plants in Newark, parlor socialists and pinks at the Rand School or on lower Fifth Avenue, the vast anonymous mass of all classes, races, trades in Madison Square Garden. His hands would always be cold when he shook hands with the chairman and other speakers on the platform. When his turn came to speak, there'd be a moment when all the faces looking up at him would blur into a mass of pink, the hum of the hall would deafen him, he'd be in a panic for fear he'd forgotten what he wanted to say. Then all at once he'd hear his own voice enunciating clearly and firmly, feel its reverberance along the walls and ceiling, feel ears growing tense, men and women leaning forward in their chairs, see the rows of faces quite clearly, the groups of people who couldn't find seats crowding at the doors. Phrases like *protest, massaction, united workingclass of this country and the world, revolution*, would light up the eyes and faces under him like the glare of a bonfire.

After the speech he'd feel shaky, his glasses would be so misted he'd have to wipe them, he'd feel all the awkwardness of his tall gangling frame. Fanya would get him away as soon as she could, tell him with shining eyes that he'd spoken magnificently, take him downtown, if the meeting had been in Manhattan, to have some supper in the Brevoort basement or at the Cosmopolitan Café before he went home on the subway to Brooklyn. He knew that she was in love with him, but they rarely talked about anything outside of the movement.

When the Russian Revolution came in February, Ben and the Steins bought every edition of the papers for weeks, read all the correspondents' reports with desperate intentness; it was the dawning of The Day. There was a feeling of carnival all down the East Side and in the Jewish sections of Brooklyn. The old people cried whenever they spoke of it. 'Next Austria,

then the Reich, then England . . . freed peoples everywhere,'
Pop would say. 'And last, Uncle Sam,' Ben would add, grimly
setting his jaw.

The April day Woodrow Wilson declared war, Fanya went
to bed with an hysterical crying fit. Ben went up to see her at
the apartment Morris Stein and his wife had on Riverside
Drive. She'd come back from Washington the day before. She'd
been up there with a women's peace delegation trying to see
the President. The detectives had run them off the White House
lawn and several girls had been arrested. 'What did you expect?
. . . of course the capitalists want war. They'll think a little
different when they find what they're getting's a revolution.'
She begged him to stay with her, but he left, saying he had to
go see them down at *The Call.* As he left the house, he found
himself making a spitting noise with his lips like his father.
He told himself he'd never go there again.

He registered for the draft on Stein's advice, though he
wrote *conscientious objector* on the card. Soon after that he
and Stein quarreled. Stein said there was nothing to it but to
bow before the storm; Ben said he was going to agitate against
it until he was put in jail. That meant he was out of a job and
it was the end of his studying law. Kahn wouldn't take him
back in his drugstore because he was afraid the cops would
raid him if it got to be known he had a radical working for
him. Ben's brother Sam was working in a munitions factory
at Perth Amboy and making big money; he kept writing Ben
to stop his foolishness and get a job there too. Even Gladys
told him it was silly to ram his head against a stone wall. In
July he left home and went back to live with Helen Mauer
over in Passaic. His number hadn't been called yet, so it was
easy to get a job in the shipping department of one of the
mills. They were working overtime and losing hands fast by
the draft.

The Rand School had been closed up, *The Call* suspended,
every day new friends were going around to Wilson's way of
looking at things. Helen's folks and their friends were making
good money, working overtime; they laughed or got sore at
any talk of protest strikes or revolutionary movements; people
were buying washing machines, Liberty Bonds, vacuum
cleaners, making first payments on houses. The girls were
buying fur coats and silk stockings. Helen and Ben began to
plan to go out to Chicago, where the wobblies were putting up
a fight. September second came the roundup of I.W.W. officials

by government agents. Ben and Helen expected to be arrested, but they were passed over. They spent a rainy Sunday huddled on the bed in their dank room, trying to decide what they ought to do. Everything they trusted was giving way under their feet. 'I feel like a rat in a trap,' Helen kept saying. Every now and then Ben would jump up and walk up and down hitting his forehead with the palm of his hand. 'We gotta do something here, look what they're doing in Russia.'

One day a warworker came around to the shipping department to sign everybody up for a Liberty Bond. He was a cockylooking young man in a yellow slicker. Ben wasn't much given to arguments during working hours, so he just shook his head and went back to the manifest he was making out.

'You don't want to spoil the record of your department, do you? It's one hundred per cent perfect so far.'

Ben tried to smile. 'It seems too bad, but I guess it'll have to be.'

Ben could feel the eyes of the other men in the office on him. The young man in the slicker was balancing uneasily from one foot to the other. 'I don't suppose you want people to think you're a pro-German or a pacifist, do you?'

'They can suppose what they damn like, for all I care.'

'Let's see your registration card, I bet you're a slacker.'

'Look here, get me,' said Ben, getting to his feet. 'I don't believe in capitalist war and I'm not going to do anything I can help to support it.'

The young man in the slicker turned his back. 'Oh, if you're one of them yellow bastards, I won't even talk to you.'

Ben went back to work. That evening when he was punching the timeclock a cop stepped up to him. 'Let's see your registration card, buddy.' Ben brought the card out from his inside pocket. The cop read it over carefully, 'Looks all right to me,' he said reluctantly. At the end of the week Ben found he was fired; no reason given.

He went to the room in a panic. When Helen came back he said he was going to Mexico. 'They could get me under the Espionage Act for what I told that guy about fighting capitalism.' Helen tried to calm him down, but he said he wouldn't sleep in that room another night, so they packed their bags and went over to New York on the train. They had about a hundred dollars saved up between them. They got a room on East Eighth Street under the name of Mr and Mrs Gold. It was the next morning that they read in the *Times* that

the Maximalists had taken over the government in Petrograd
with the slogan 'All Power to the Soviets.' They were sitting
in a small pastry shop on Second Avenue drinking their morning coffee, when Ben, who had run around to the newsstand
for a paper, came back with the news.

Helen began to cry: 'Oh, darling, it's too good to be true.
It's the world revolution. . . . Now the workers'll see that they
were being deceived by false good times, that the war's really
aimed at them. Now the other armies'll start to mutiny.'

Ben took her hand under the table and squeezed it hard. 'We
gotta work now, darling. . . . I'll go to jail here before I'll
run away to Mexico. I'd acted like a yellow bastard if it
hadn't been for you, Helen. . . . A man's no good alone.'

They gulped their coffee and walked around to the Ferbers'
house on Seventeenth Street. Al Ferber was a doctor, a short
stout man with a big paunch; he was just leaving the house to go
to his office. He went back into the hall with them and yelled
upstairs to his wife: 'Molly, come down . . . Kerensky's run
out of Petrograd with a flea in his ear . . . . dressed as a woman
he ran.' Then he said in Yiddish to Ben that if the comrades
were going to hold a meeting to send greetings to the soldiers'
and peasants' government, he'd give a hundred dollars toward
expenses, but his name would have to be kept out of it or
else he'd lose his practice. Molly Ferber came downstairs in a
quilted dressinggown and said she'd sell something and add
another hundred. They spent the day going around to find
comrades they had the addresses of; they didn't dare use the
phone for fear of the wires being tapped.

The meeting was held at the Empire Casino in the Bronx
a week later. Two Federal agents with beefsteak faces sat in
the front row with a stenographer who took down everything
that was said. The police closed the doors after the first couple
of hundred people had come in. The speakers on the platform
could hear them breaking up the crowd outside with motorcycles. Soldiers and sailors in uniform were sneaking into the
gallery by ones and twos and trying to stare the speakers out
of countenance.

When the old whitehaired man who was chairman of the
meeting walked to the front of the stage and said, 'Comrades,
gentlemen of the Department of Justice, and not forgetting
our young wellwishers up in the gallery, we have met to send
a resolution of greetings from the oppressed workers of
America to the triumphant workers of Russia,' everybody stood

up and cheered. The crowd milling around outside cheered too. Somewhere they could hear a bunch singing the *International*. They could hear policewhistles and the dang-dang of a patrol wagon. Ben noticed that Fanya Stein was in the audience; she looked pale and her eyes held on to him with a fixed feverish stare. When his turn came to speak, he began by saying that on account of the kind sympathizers from Washington in the audience, he couldn't say what he wanted to say, but that every man and woman in the audience who was not a traitor to their class knew what he wanted to say. . . . 'The capitalist governments are digging their own graves by driving their people to slaughter in a crazy unnecessary war that nobody can benefit from except bankers and munition makers. . . . The American workingclass, like the workingclasses of the rest of the world, will learn their lesson. The profiteers are giving us instruction in the use of guns; the day will come when we will use it.'

'That's enough, let's go, boys,' yelled a voice from the gallery. The soldiers and sailors started hustling the people out of the seats. The police from the entrances converged on the speakers. Ben and a couple of others were arrested. The men in the audience who were of conscription age were made to show their registration cards before they could leave. Ben was hustled out into a closed limousine with the blinds drawn before he could speak to Helen. He'd hardly noticed who it was had clicked the handcuffs on his wrists.

They kept him for three days without anything to eat or drink in a disused office in the Federal Building on Park Row. Every few hours a new bunch of detectives would stamp into the room and question him. His head throbbing, and ready to faint with thirst, he'd face the ring of long yellow faces, jowly red faces, pimply faces, boozers' and hopheads' faces, feel the eyes boring into him; sometimes they kidded and cajoled him, and sometimes they bullied and threatened; one bunch brought in pieces of rubber hose to beat him up with. He jumped up and faced them. For some reason they didn't beat him up, but instead brought him some water and a couple of stale ham sandwiches. After that he was able to sleep a little.

An agent yanked him off his bench and led him out into a wellappointed office where he was questioned almost kindly by an elderly man at a mahogany desk with a bunch of roses on the corner of it. The smell of the roses made him feel sick. The elderly man said he could see his lawyer and Morris Stein came into the room.

'Benny,' he said, 'leave everything to me . . . Mr Watkins has consented to quash all charges if you'll promise to report for military training. It seems your number's been called.'

'If you let me out,' Ben said in a low trembling voice, 'I'll do my best to oppose capitalist war until you arrest me again.'

Morris Stein and Mr Watkins looked at each other and shook their heads indulgently.

'Well,' said Mr Watkins, 'I can't help but admire your spirit and wish it was in a better cause.'

It ended by his being let out on fifteen thousand dollars bail on Morris Stein's assurance that he would do no agitating until the date of his trial. The Steins wouldn't tell him who put up the bail.

Morris and Edna Stein gave him a room in their apartment; Fanya was there all the time. They fed him good food and tried to make him drink wine with his meals and a glass of milk before going to bed. He didn't have any interest in anything, slept as much as he could, read all the books he found in the place. When Morris would try to talk to him about his case he'd shut him up, 'You're doing this, Morris . . . do anything . . . why should I care. I might as well be in jail as like this.'

'Well, I must say that's a compliment,' Fanya said, laughing.

Helen Mauer called up several times to tell him how things were going. She'd always say she had no news to tell that she could say over the telephone, but he never asked her to come up to see him. About as far as he went from the Steins' apartment was to go out every day to sit for a while on a bench on the Drive and look out over the gray Hudson at the rows of frame houses on the Jersey side and the gray palisades.

The day his case came up for trial the press was full of hints of German victories. It was spring and sunny outside the broad grimy windows of the courtroom. Ben sat sleepily in the stuffy gloom. Everything seemed very simple. Stein and the Judge had their little jokes together and the Assistant District Attorney was positively genial. The jury reported 'guilty' and the judge sentenced him to twenty years' imprisonment. Morris Stein filed an appeal and the judge let him stay out on bail. The only moment Ben came to life was when he was allowed to address the court before being sentenced. He made a speech about the revolutionary movement he'd been preparing all

these weeks. Even as he said it, it seemed silly and weak. He
almost stopped in the middle. His voice strengthened and
filled the courtroom as he got to the end. Even the judge and
the old snuffling attendants sat up when he recited for his
peroration, the last words of the Communist Manifesto:

*In place of the old bourgeois society, with its classes
and class antagonisms, we shall have an association, in
which the free development of each is the condition
for the free development of all.*

The appeal dragged and dragged. Ben started studying law
again. He wanted to work in Stein's office to pay for his keep,
but Stein said it would be risky; he said the war would be over
soon and the red scare would die down, so that he could get
him off with a light sentence. He brought lawbooks up for
him to study and promised to take him into partnership if he
passed his bar exam, once he could get his citizenship restored.
Edna Stein was a fat spiteful woman and rarely spoke to him;
Fanya fussed over him with nervous doting attentions that
made him feel sick. He slept badly and his kidneys bothered
him. One night he got up and dressed and was tiptoeing down
the carpeted hall towards the door with his shoes in his hand,
when Fanya with her black hair down her back came out of
the door of her room. She was in a nightdress that showed her
skinny figure and flat breasts. 'Benny, where are you going?'
    'I'm going crazy here . . . I've got to get out.' His teeth
were chattering. 'I've got to get back into the movement. . . .
They'll catch me and send me to jail right away . . . it will be
better like that.'
    'You poor boy, you're in no condition.' She threw her arms
round his neck and pulled him into her room.
    'Fanya, you gotta let me go. . . . I might make it across the
Mexican border . . . other guys have.'
    'You're crazy . . . and what about your bail?'
    'What do I care . . . don't you see we gotta do something.'
    She'd pulled him down on her bed and was stroking his
forehead. 'Poor boy . . . I love you so, Benny, couldn't you
think of me a little bit . . . just a little teeny bit . . . I could
help you so much in the movement. . . . Tomorrow we'll talk
about it . . . I want to help you, Benny.' He let her untie his
necktie.
    The armistice came, and news of the Peace Conference,

revolutionary movements all over Europe. Trotsky's armies driving the Whites out of Russia. Fanya Stein told everybody she and Ben were married and took him to live with her at her studio apartment on Eighth Street, where she nursed him through the flu and double pneumonia. The first day the doctor said he could go out she drove up the Hudson in her Buick sedan. They came back in the early summer gloaming to find a special delivery letter from Morris. The circuit court had denied the appeal, but reduced the sentence to ten years. The next day at noon he'd have to report to be delivered by his bondsmen to the custody of the U.S. District Court. He'd probably go to Atlanta. Soon after the letter Morris himself turned up. Fanya had broken down and was crying hysterically. Morris looked pale. 'Ben,' he said, 'we're beaten . . . You'll have to go to Atlanta for a while . . . you'll have good company down there . . . but don't worry. We'll take your case to the President. Now that the war's over, they can't keep the liberal press muzzled any more.'

'That's all right,' said Ben, 'it's better to know the worst.'

Fanya jumped up from the couch where she'd been sobbing and started screaming at her brother. When Ben went out to walk around the block, he left them quarreling bitterly. He found himself looking carefully at the houses, the taxicabs, the streetlights, people's faces, a funny hydrant that had a torso like a woman's, some bottles of mineral oil stacked in a drugstore window. Nujol. He decided he'd better go over to Brooklyn to say goodbye to the old people. At the subway station he stopped. He hadn't the strength; he'd write them.

Next morning at nine he went down to Morris Stein's office with his suitcase in his hand. He'd made Fanya promise not to come. He had to tell himself several times he was going to jail; he felt as if he was going on a business trip of some kind. He had on a new suit of English tweed Fanya had bought him.

Lower Broadway was all streaked red, white, and blue with flags; there were crowds of clerks and stenographers and officeboys lining both pavements where he came up out of the subway. Cops on motorcycles were keeping the street clear. From down towards the Battery came the sound of a military band playing *Keep the Home Fires Burning*. Everybody looked flushed and happy. It was hard to keep from walking in step to the music in the fresh summer morning that smelt of the harbor and ships. He had to keep telling himself: those are the people who sent Debs to jail, those are the people who shot Joe Hill, who murdered Frank Little, those are the people who beat us up in Everett, who want me to rot for ten years in jail.

The colored elevatorboy grinned at him when he took him up in the elevator, 'Is they startin' to go past yet, mister?' Ben shook his head and frowned.

The lawoffice looked clean and shiny. The telephone girl had red hair and wore a gold star. There was an American flag draped over the door of Stein's private office. Stein was at his desk talking to an upperclasslooking young man in a tweed suit.

'Ben,' Stein said cheerily, 'meet Stevens Warner . . . He's just gotten out of Charlestown, served a year for refusing to register.'

'Not quite a year,' said the young man, getting up and shaking hands. 'I'm out on good behavior.'

Ben didn't like him, in his tweed suit and his expensive-looking necktie; all at once he remembered that he was wearing the same kind of suit himself. The thought made him sore. 'How was it?' he asked coldly.

'Not so bad; they had me working in the greenhouse . . . They treated me fairly well when they found out I'd already been to the front.'

'How was that?'

'Oh, in the ambulance service. . . . They just thought I was mildly insane. . . . It was a damned instructive experience.'

'They treat the workers different,' said Ben angrily.

'And now we're going to start a nationwide campaign to get all the other boys out,' said Stein, getting to his feet and rubbing his hands, 'starting with Debs . . . you'll see, Ben, you won't be down there long . . . people are coming to their senses already.'

A burst of brassy music came up from Broadway, and the regular tramp of soldiers marching. They all looked out of the window. All down the long gray canyon flags were stream-ing out, uncoiling tickertape and papers glinted all through the ruddy sunlight, squirmed in the shadows; people were yelling themselves hoarse.

'Damn fools,' said Warner; 'it won't make the doughboys forget about K.P.'

Morris Stein came back into the room with a funny bright-ness in his eyes. 'Makes me feel maybe I missed something.'

'Well, I've got to be going,' said Warner, shaking hands

again. 'You certainly got a rotten break, Compton . . . don't think for a minute we won't be working night and day to get you out . . . I'm sure public sentiment will change. We have great hopes of President Wilson . . . after all, his labor record was fairly good before the war.'

'I guess it'll be the workers will get me out, if I'm gotten out,' said Ben.

Warner's eyes were searching his face. Ben didn't smile. Warner stood before him uneasily for a moment and then took his hand again. Ben didn't return the pressure. 'Good luck,' said Warner and walked out of the office.

'What's that, one of these liberalminded college boys?' Ben asked of Stein.

Stein nodded. He'd gotten interested in some papers on his desk. 'Yes . . . great boy, Steve Warner . . . you'll find some books or magazines in the library . . . I'll be with you in a few minutes.'

Ben went into the library and took down a book on Torts. He read and read the fine print. When Stein came to get him, he didn't know what he'd been reading or how much time had passed. Walking up Broadway the going was slow on account of the crowds and the bands and the steady files of marching soldiers in khaki with tin hats on their heads. Stein nudged him to take his hat off as a regimental flag passed them in the middle of a fife and drum corps. He kept it in his hand so as not to have to take it off again. He took a deep breath of the dusty sunny air of the street, full of girls' perfumerysmells and gasoline from the exhaust of the trucks hauling the big guns, full of laughing and shouting and shuffle and tramp of feet; then the dark doorway of the Federal Building gulped them.

It was a relief to have it all over, alone with the deputy on the train for Atlanta. The deputy was a big morose man with bluish sacks under his eyes. As the handcuffs cut Ben's wrist, he unlocked them except when the train was in a station. Ben remembered it was his birthday; he was twentythree years old.

# Newsreel 41

in British Colonial Office quarters it is believed that Australian irritation will diminish as soon as it is realized that the substance is more important than the shadow. It may be stated that press representatives who are expeditious in sending their telegrams at an early hour, suffer because their telegrams are thrown into baskets. Others which come later are heaped on top of them and in the end the messages on top of the basket are dealt with first. But this must not be taken as an insult. Count von Brockdorf-Rantzau was very weak and it was only his physical condition that kept him from rising

### PRIVATES HOLD UP CABMAN

*Hold the fort for we are coming
Union men be strong;
Side by side we battle onward,
Victory will come.*

New York City Federation says evening gowns are demoralizing youth of the land

### SOLDIERS OVERSEAS FEAR LOSS OF GOLD V

### CONSCRIPTION A PUZZLE

Is there hostile propaganda at work in Paris?

*We meet today in Freedom's cause
And raise our voices high
We'll join our hands in union strong
To battle or to die*

### FRANCE YET THE FRONTIER OF FREEDOM

provision is made whereby the wellbeing and development of backward and colonial regions are regarded as the sacred trust of civilization over which the League of Nations exercises supervising care

REDS WEAKENING WASHINGTON HEARS

*Hold the fort for we are coming*
*Union men be strong*

the marine workers' affiliation meeting early last night at number 26 Park Place voted to start a general walkout at 6 A.M. tomorrow

BURLESON ORDERS ALL POSTAL TELEGRAPH
NEWS SUPPRESSED

his reply was an order to his followers to hang these two lads on the spot. They were placed on chairs under trees, halters fastened on the boughs were placed around their necks, and then they were maltreated until they pushed the chair away from them with their feet in order to finish their torments

## The Camera Eye (42)

four hours we casuals pile up scrapiron in the flatcars and four hours we drag the scrapiron off the flatcars and pile it on the side of the track   KEEP THE BOYS FIT TO GO HOME is the slogan of the Y.M.C.A.   in the morning the shadows of the poplars point west and in the afternoon they point out east where Persia is   the jagged bits of old iron cut into our hands through the canvas gloves a kind of gray slagdust plugs our noses and ears stings eyes
four hunkies   a couple of wops   a bohunk   dagoes
guineas   two little dark guys with blue chins nobody can talk to

spare parts no outfit wanted to use

mashed mudguards busted springs old spades and shovels entrenching tools twisted hospital cots   a mountain of nuts and bolts of all sizes   four million miles of barbedwire chickenwire rabbitfence   acres of tin roofing

square miles of parked trucks    long parades of locomotives strung along the yellow rails of the sidings

KEEP THE BOYS FIT TO GO    up in the office the
grumpy sergeants doing the paperwork don't know where
home is lost our outfits our service records our aluminum
numberplates no spika de Engliss no entiendo comprend
pas no capisco nyeh panimayoo

day after day the shadows of the poplars point west
northwest north northeast east    When they desoit they
always heads south the corporal said    Pretty tough but
if he ain't got a soivice record how can we make out his
discharge    KEEP OUR BOYS FIT for whatthehell the
war's over

scrap

# Newsreel 42

it was a gala day for Seattle. Enormous crowds not only filled the streets on the line of march from the pier, but finally later in the evening machineguns were placed in position, the guardsmen withstanding a shower of missiles until their inaction so endangered them the officers gave the order to fire.     WOULD CUT OFF LIGHT.     President Lowell of Harvard University has urged the students to serve as strikebreakers. 'In accordance with its tradition of public service, the university desires at this time of crisis to maintain order and support the laws of the Commonwealth.'

### THREE ARMIES FIGHT FOR KIEW

### CALLS SITUATION A CRIME AGAINST CIVILIZATION

### TO MAKE US INVULNERABLE

during the funeral services of Horace Traubel, literary executor and biographer of Walt Whitman, this afternoon, a fire broke out in the Unitarian Church of the Messiah. Periodicals, tugboats, and shipyards were affected. Two thousand passengers held up at Havre from which Mr Wilson embarked to review the Pacific fleet, but thousands were massed on each side of the street seemingly satisfied merely to get a glimpse of the President. As the *George Washington* steamed slowly to her berth in Hoboken through the crowded lower bay, every craft afloat gave welcome to King Albert and Queen Elizabeth by hoarse blasts of their whistles

### CRUCIBLE STEEL CONTINUES TO LEAD MARKET

*My country 'tis of thee*
*Sweet land of libertee*
*Of thee I sing*

## *Paul Bunyan*

When Wesley Everest came home from overseas and got his discharge from the army, he went back to his old job of logging. His folks were of the old Kentucky and Tennessee stock of woodsmen and squirrelhunters who followed the trail blazed by Lewis and Clark into the rainy giant forests of the Pacific slope. In the army Everest was a sharpshooter, won a medal for a crack shot.

(Since the days of the homesteaders the western promoters and the politicians and lobbyists in Washington had been busy with the rainy giant forests of the Pacific slope, with the result that:

*ten monopoly groups aggregating only one thousand eight hundred and two holders, monopolized one thousand two hundred and eight billion, eight hundred million,*

[1,208,800,000,000]

*square feet of standing timber, . . . enough standing timber . . . to yield the planks necessary [over and above the manufacturing wastage] to make a floating bridge more than two feet thick and more than five miles wide from New York to Liverpool;*

wood for scaffolding, wood for jerrybuilding residential suburbs, billboards, wood for shacks and ships and shantytowns, pulp for tabloids, yellow journals, editorial pages, advertising copy, mailorder catalogues, filingcards, army paperwork, handbills, flimsy.)

Wesley Everest was a logger like Paul Bunyan.

The lumberjacks, loggers, shingleweavers, sawmill workers were the helots of the timber empire; the I.W.W. put the idea of industrial democracy in Paul Bunyan's head; wobbly organizers said the forests ought to belong to the whole people, said Paul Bunyan ought to be paid in real money instead of in company scrip, ought to have a decent place to dry his clothes, wet from the sweat of a day's work in zero weather and snow, an eighthour day, clean bunkhouses, wholesome grub; when Paul Bunyan came back from making Europe safe for the democracy of the big Four, he joined the lumberjacks' local to help make the Pacific slope safe for the workingstiffs. The wobblies were reds. Not a thing in this world Paul Bunyan's ascared of.

(To be a red in the summer of 1919 was worse than being a Hun or a pacifist in the summer of 1917.)

The timberowners, the sawmill and shinglekings were patriots; they'd won the war (in the course of which the price of lumber had gone from $16 a thousand feet to $116; there are even cases where the government paid as high as $1200 a thousand for spruce); they set out to clean the reds out of the logging camps.

free American institutions must be preserved at any cost;

so they formed the Employers' Association and the Legion of Loyal Loggers; they made it worth their while for bunches of ex-soldiers to raid I.W.W. halls, lynch and beat up organizers, burn subversive literature.

On Memorial day 1918 the boys of the American Legion in Centralia led by a group from the Chamber of Commerce wrecked the I.W.W. hall, beat everybody they found in it, jailed some and piled the rest of the boys in a truck and dumped them over the county line, burned the papers and pamphlets and auctioned off the fittings for the Red Cross; the wobblies' desk still stands in the Chamber of Commerce.

The loggers hired a new hall and the union kept on growing. Not a thing in this world Paul Bunyan's ascared of.

Before Armistice Day, 1919, the town was full of rumors that on that day the hall would be raided for keeps. A young man of good family and pleasant manners, Warren O. Grimm, had been an officer with the American force in Siberia; that made him an authority on labor and Bolsheviks, so he was chosen by the businessmen to lead the hundred per cent forces in the Citizens' Protective League to put the fear of God into Paul Bunyan.

The first thing the brave patriots did was pick up a blind newsdealer and thrash him and drop him in a ditch across the county line.

The loggers consulted counsel and decided they had a right to defend their hall and themselves in case of a raid. Not a thing in this world Paul Bunyan's ascared of.

Wesley Everest was a crack shot; Armistice Day he put on his uniform and filled his pockets with cartridges. Wesley Everest was not much of a talker; at a meeting in the union hall the Sunday before the raid, there'd been talk of the chance of a lynching bee; Wesley Everest had been walking up and down the aisle with his O.D. coat on over a suit of overalls, distributing literature and pamphlets; when the boys said they wouldn't stand for another raid, he stopped in his tracks with the papers under his arm, rolled himself a brownpaper cigarette and smiled a funny quiet smile.

Armistice Day was raw and cold; the mist rolled in from Puget Sound and dripped from the dark boughs of the spruces and the shiny storefronts of the town. Warren O. Grimm commanded the Centralia section of the parade. The exsoldiers were in their uniforms. When the parade passed by the union hall without halting, the loggers inside breathed easier, but on the way back the parade halted in front of the hall. Somebody whistled through his fingers. Somebody yelled, 'Let's go . . . at 'em boys.' They ran towards the wobbly hall. Three men crashed through the door. A rifle spoke. Rifles cracked on the hills back of the town, roared in the back of the hall.

Grimm and an exsoldier were hit.

The parade broke in disorder, but the men with rifles formed again and rushed the hall. They found a few unarmed men hiding in an old icebox, a boy in uniform at the head of the stairs with his arms over his head.

Wesley Everest shot the magazine of his rifle out, dropped it and ran for the woods. As he ran he broke through the crowd in the back of the hall, held them off with a blue automatic, scaled a fence, doubled down an alley and through the back street. The mob followed. They dropped the coils of rope they had with them to lynch Britt Smith the I.W.W. secretary. It was Wesley Everest's drawing them off that kept them from lynching Britt Smith right there.

Stopping once or twice to hold the mob off with some scattered shots, Wesley Everest ran for the river, started to wade across. Up to his waist in water he stopped and turned.

Wesley Everest turned to face the mob with a funny quiet smile on his face. He'd lost his hat and his hair dripped with water and sweat. They started to rush him.

'Stand back,' he shouted, 'if there's bulls in the crowd I'll submit to arrest.'

The mob was at him. He shot from the hip four times, then his gun jammed. He tugged at the trigger, and taking cool aim shot the foremost of them dead. It was Dale Hubbard, another exsoldier, nephew of one of the big lumbermen of Centralia.

Then he threw his empty gun away and fought with his hands. The mob had him. A man bashed his teeth in with the butt of a shotgun. Somebody brought a rope and they started to hang him. A woman elbowed through the crowd and pulled the rope off his neck.

'You haven't the guts to hang a man in the daytime,' was what Wesley Everest said.

They took him to the jail and threw him on the floor of a cell. Meanwhile they were putting the other loggers through the third degree.

That night the city lights were turned off. A mob smashed in the outer door of the jail. 'Don't shoot, boys, here's your man,' said the guard. Wesley Everest met them on his feet, 'Tell the boys I did my best,' he whispered to the men in the other cells.

They took him off in a limousine to the Chehalis River Bridge. As Wesley Everest lay stunned in the bottom of the car, a Centralia businessman cut his penis and testicles off with a razor. Wesley Everest gave a great scream of pain. Somebody has remembered that after a while he whispered, 'For God's sake, men, shoot me . . . don't let me suffer like this.' Then they hanged him from the bridge in the glare of the headlights.

The coroner at his inquest thought it was a great joke.

He reported that Wesley Everest had broken out of jail and run to the Chehalis River Bridge and tied a rope around his neck and jumped off, finding the rope too short he'd climbed back and fastened on a longer one, had jumped off again, broke his neck and shot himself full of holes.

They jammed the mangled wreckage into a packing box and buried it.

Nobody knows where they buried the body of Wesley Everest, but the six loggers they caught they buried in the Walla Walla Penitentiary.

## Richard Ellsworth Savage

The pinnacles and buttresses of the apse of Notre Dame looked crumbly as cigarash in the late afternoon sunshine. 'But you've got to stay, Richard,' Eleanor was saying as she went about the room collecting the teathings on a tray for the maid to take out. 'I had to do something about Eveline and her husband before they sailed . . . after all, she's one of my oldest friends . . . and I've invited all her wildeyed hangerson to come in afterwards.' A fleet of big drays loaded with winebarrels rumbled along the quay outside. Dick was staring out into the gray ash of the afternoon. 'Do close that window, Richard, the dust is pouring in. . . . Of course, I realize that you'll have to leave early to go to J. W.'s meeting with the press. . . . If it hadn't been for that he'd have had to come, poor dear, but you know how busy he is.'

'Well, I don't exactly find the time hanging on my hands . . . but I'll stay and greet the happy pair. In the army I'd forgotten about work.' He got to his feet and walked back into the room to light a cigarette.

'Well, you needn't be so mournful about it.'

'I don't see you dancing in the streets yourself.'

'I think Eveline's made a very grave mistake . . . Americans are just too incredibly frivolous about marriage.'

Dick's throat got tight. He found himself noticing how stiffly he put the cigarette to his mouth, inhaled the smoke and blew it out. Eleanor's eyes were on his face, cool and searching. Dick didn't say anything, he tried to keep his face stiff.

'Were you in love with that poor girl, Richard?'

Dick blushed and shook his head.

'Well, you needn't pretend to be so hard about it . . . it's just young to pretend to be hard about things.'

'Jilted by army officer, Texas belle killed in plane wreck . . . but most of the correspondents know me and did their best to kill that story. . . . What did you expect me to do, jump into the grave like Hamlet? The Honorable Mr Barrow did all of that that was necessary. It was a frightfully tough break . . .' He let himself drop into a chair. 'I wish I was hard enough so that I didn't give a damn about anything. When history's walking on all our faces is no time for pretty sentiments.' He made a funny face and started talking out of the corner of his mouth. 'All I ask sister is to see de woild with Uncle Woodrow . . . le beau monde sans blague tu sais.'

Eleanor was laughing her little shrill laugh when they heard Eveline's and Paul Johnson's voice outside on the landing.

Eleanor had bought them a pair of little blue parakeets in a cage. They drank Montrachet and ate roast duck cooked with oranges. In the middle of the meal Dick had to go up to the

Crillon. It was a relief to be out in the air, sitting in an open taxi, running past the Louvre made enormous by the late twilight under which the Paris streets seemed empty and very long ago like the Roman Forum. All the way up past the Tuileries he played with an impulse to tell the taxidriver to take him to the opera, to the circus, to the fortifications, anywhere to hell and gone. He set his pokerface as he walked past the doorman at the Crillon.

Miss Williams gave him a relieved smile when he appeared in the door. 'Oh, I was afraid you'd be late, Captain Savage.'

Dick shook his head and grinned. 'Anybody come?'

'Oh, they're coming in swarms. It'll make the front pages,' she whispered. Then she had to answer the phone.

The big room was already filling up with newspapermen. Jerry Burnham whispered as he shook hands, 'Say, Dick, if it's a typewritten statement, you won't leave the room alive.'

'Don't worry,' said Dick with a grin.

'Say, where's Robbins?'

'He's out of the picture,' said Dick dryly, 'I think he's in Nice drinking up the last of his liver.'

J. W. had come in by the other door and was moving around the room shaking hands with men he knew, being introduced to others. A young fellow with untidy hair and his necktie crooked put a paper in Dick's hand. 'Say, ask him if he'd answer some of these questions.'

'Is he going home to campaign for the League of Nations?' somebody asked in his other ear.

Everybody was settled in chairs; J. W. leaned over the back of his and said that this was going to be an informal chat, after all, he was an old newspaperman himself. There was a pause. Dick glanced around at J. W.'s pale slightly jowly face just in time to catch a flash of his blue eyes around the faces of the correspondents. An elderly man asked in a grave voice if Mr Moorehouse cared to say anything about the differences of opinion between the President and Colonel House. Dick settled himself back to be bored. J. W. answered with a cool smile that they'd better ask Colonel House himself about that. When somebody spoke the word oil everybody sat up in their chairs. Yes, he could say definitely an accord, a working agreement had been reached between certain American oil producers and perhaps the Royal Dutch-Shell; oh, no, of course not to set prices, but a proof of a new era of international co-operation that was dawning in which great aggregations of capital

would work together for peace and democracy, against re-
actionaries and militarists on the one hand and against the
bloody forces of bolshevism on the other. And what about the
League of Nations? 'A new era,' went on J. W. in a confidential
tone, 'is dawning.'

Chairs scraped and squeaked, pencils scratched on pads,
everybody was very attentive. Everybody got it down that J. W.
was sailing for New York on the *Rochambeau* in two weeks.
After the newspapermen had gone off to make their cable
deadline, J. W. yawned and asked Dick to make his excuses to
Eleanor, that he was really too tired to get down to her place
tonight. When Dick got out on the streets again there was still
a little of the violet of dusk in the sky. He hailed a taxi; goddam it, he could take a taxi whenever he wanted to now.

It was pretty stiff at Eleanor's; people were sitting around in
the parlor and in one bedroom that had been fitted up as a sort
of boudoir with a tall mirror draped with lace, talking uncomfortably and intermittently. The bridegroom looked as if he
had ants under his collar. Eveline and Eleanor were standing
in the window talking with a gauntfaced man who turned out
to be Don Stevens who'd been arrested in Germany by the
Army of Occupation and for whom Eveline had made everybody scamper around so.

'And any time I get in a jam,' he was saying, 'I always find
a little Jew who helps get me out ... this time he was a tailor.'

'Well, Eveline isn't a little Jew or a tailor,' said Eleanor
icily, 'but I can tell you she did a great deal.'

Stevens walked across the room to Dick and asked him what
sort of man Moorehouse was.

Dick found himself blushing. He wished Stevens wouldn't
talk so loud. 'Why, he's a man of extraordinary ability,' he
stammered.

'I thought he was a stuffed shirt ... I didn't see what those
damn fools of the bourgeois press thought they were getting
for a story ... I was there for the *D.H.*'

'Yes, I saw you,' said Dick.

'I thought maybe, from what Steve Warner said, you were
the sort of guy who'd be boring from within.'

'Boring in another sense, I guess, boring and bored.'

Stevens stood over him glaring at him as if he was going to
hit him. 'Well, we'll know soon enough which side a man's on.
We'll all have to show our faces, as they say in Russia, before
long.'

Eleanor interrupted with a fresh smoking bottle of champagne. Stevens went back to talk to Eveline in the window. 'Why, I'd as soon have a Baptist preacher in the house,' Eleanor tittered.

'Damn it, I hate people who get their pleasure by making other people feel uncomfortable,' grumbled Dick under his breath.

Eleanor smiled a quick V-shaped smile and gave his arm a pat with her thin white hand, that was tipped by long nails pointed and pink and marked with halfmoons. 'So do I, Dick, so do I.'

When Dick whispered that he had a headache and thought he'd go home and turn in, she gripped his arm and pulled him into the hall. 'Don't you dare go home and leave me alone with this frost.' Dick made a face and followed her back into the salon. She poured him a glass of champagne from the bottle she still held in her hand: 'Cheer up Eveline,' she whispered squeakily. 'She's about ready to go down for the third time.'

Dick stood around for hours talking to Mrs Johnson about books, plays, the opera. Neither of them seemed to be able to keep track of what the other was saying. Eveline couldn't keep her eyes off her husband. He had a young cubbish look Dick couldn't help liking; he was standing by the sideboard getting tight with Stevens, who kept making ugly audible remarks about parasites and the lahdedah boys of the bourgeoisie. It went on for a long time. Paul Johnson got sick and Dick had to help him find the bathroom. When he came back into the salon he almost had a fight with Stevens, who, after an argument about the Peace Conference, suddenly hauled off with his fists clenched and called him a goddam fairy. The Johnsons hustled Stevens out. Eleanor came up to Dick and put her arm around his neck and said he'd been magnificent.

Paul Johnson came back upstairs after they'd gone to get the parakeets. He looked pale as a sheet. One of the birds had died and was lying on its back stiff with his claws in the air at the bottom of the cage.

At about three o'clock Dick rode home to his hotel in a taxi.

# Newsreel 43

the placards borne by the radicals were taken away from them, their clothing torn and eyes blackened before the service and exservice men had finished with them

Thirtyfour die after drinking wood alcohol   trains in France may soon stop

GERARD THROWS HIS HAT INTO THE RING

SUPREME COURT DASHES LAST HOPE OF MOIST MOUTH

LIFEBOAT CALLED BY ROCKET SIGNALS SEARCHES IN VAIN FOR SIXTEEN HOURS

*America I love you*
*You're like a sweetheart of mine*

LES GENS SAGES FUIENT LES REUNIONS POLITIQUES

WALL STREET CLOSES WEAK: FEARS TIGHT MONEY

*From ocean to ocean*
*For you my devotion*
*Is touching each boundary line*

LITTLE CARUSO EXPECTED

his mother, Mrs W. D. McGillicudy, said: 'My first husband was killed while crossing tracks in front of a train, my second husband was killed in the same way, and now it is my son

*Just like a little baby*
*Climbing its mother's knee*

MACHINEGUNS MOW DOWN MOBS IN KNOXVILLE

*America I love you*

AVIATORS LIVED FOR SIX DAYS ON SHELLFISH

the police compelled the demonstrators to lower these flags and ordered the convention not to exhibit any red emblems save the red in the starry banner of the United States; it may not be indiscreet to state, however, in any case it cannot dim his glory, that General Pershing was confined to his stateroom through seasickness when the message arrived. OLD FELLOW OF EIGHTYNINE TREASURES CHEWINGGUM AS PRECIOUS SOUVENIR COULDN'T MAINTAIN HIS SERENITY IN CLOSING LEAGUE DEBATES

*And there's a hundred million others like me*

## The Body of an American

Whereasthe Congressoftheunitedstates byaconcurrentresolutionadoptedon the4thdayofmarch lastauthorizedthe Secretaryofwar to cause to be brought to theunitedstatesthe body of an American whowasamemberoftheamericanexpeditionaryforce in europe who lost his life during the worldwarandwhoseidentityhasnotbeenestablished for burial inthememorialamphitheatreof thenationalcemetery atarlingtonvirginia

In the tarpaper morgue at Châlons-sur-Marne in the reek of chloride of lime and the dead, they picked out the pine box that held all that was left of

enie menie minie moe plenty other pine boxes stacked up there containing what they'd scraped up of Richard Roe

and other person or persons unknown. Only one can go. How did they pick John Doe?

Make sure he ain't a dinge, boys.

make sure he ain't a guinea or a kike,

how can you tell a guy's a hundredpercent when all you've got's a gunnysack full of bones, bronze buttons stamped with the screaming eagle and a pair of roll puttees?

. . . and the gagging chloride and the puky dirtstench of the yearold dead . . .

The day withal was too meaningful and tragic for applause. Silence, tears, songs and prayer, muffled drums and soft music were the instrumentalities today of national approbation.

John Doe was born (thudding din of blood in love into the shuddering soar of a man and a woman alone indeed together lurching into

and ninemonths sick drowse waking into scared agony and the pain and blood and mess of birth). John Doe was born

and raised in Brooklyn, in Memphis, near the lakefront in Cleveland, Ohio, in the stench of the stockyards in Chi, on Beacon Hill, in an old brick house in Alexandria, Virginia, on Telegraph Hill, in a halftimbered Tudor cottage in Portland, the city of roses,

in the Lying-In Hospital old Morgan endowed on Stuyvesant Square,

across the railroad tracks, out near the country club, in a shack cabin tenement apartmenthouse exclusive residential suburb;

scion of one of the best families in the social register, won first prize in the baby parade at Coronado Beach, was marbles champion of the Little Rock grammarschools, crack basketballplayer at the Booneville High, quarterback at the State Reformatory, having saved the sheriff's kid from drowning in the Little Missouri River was invited to Washington to be photographed shaking hands with the President on the White House steps;—

> though this was a time of mourning, such an assemblage necessarily has about it a touch of color. In the boxes are seen the court uniforms of foreign diplomats, the gold braid of our own and foreign fleets and armies, the black of the conventional morning dress of American statesmen, the varicolored furs and outdoor wrapping garments of mothers and sisters come to mourn, the drab and blue of soldiers and sailors, the glitter of musical instruments and the white and black of a vested choir

– busboy harveststiff hogcaller boyscout champeen cornshucker of Western Kansas bellhop at the United States

Hotel at Saratoga Springs officeboy callboy fruiter telephonelineman longshoreman lumberjack plumber's helper,

worked for an exterminating company in Union City, filled pipes in an opium joint in Trenton, New Jersey.

Y.M.C.A. secretary, express agent, truckdriver, fordmechanic, sold books in Denver, Colorado: Madam would you be willing to help a young man work his way through college?

President Harding, with a reverence seemingly more significant because of his high temporal station, concluded his speech:

*We are met today to pay the impersonal tribute;*
*the name of him whose body lies before us took flight*
*with his imperishable soul ...*

*as a typical soldier of this representative democracy*
*he fought and died believing in the indisputable justice of*
*his country's cause ...*

by raising his right hand and asking the thousands within the sound of his voice to join in the prayer:

*Our Father which art in heaven hallowed be thy*
*name ...*

Naked he went into the army;

they weighed you, measured you, looked for flat feet, squeezed your penis to see if you had clap, looked up your anus to see if you had piles, counted your teeth, made you cough, listened to your heart and lungs, made you read the letters on the card, charted your urine and your intelligence,

gave you a service record for a future (imperishable soul)

and an identification tag stamped with your serial number to hang around your neck, issued O.D. regulation equipment, a condiment can and a copy of the articles of war.

Atten'SHUN suck in your gut you c — r wipe that smile off your face eyes right wattja tink dis is a choirchsocial? For-war-D'ARCH.

John Doe

and Richard Roe and other person or persons unknown
drilled, hiked, manual of arms, ate slum, learned to
salute, to soldier, to loaf in the latrines, forbidden to smoke
on deck, overseas guard duty, forty men and eight horses,
shortarm inspection and the ping of shrapnel and the shrill
bullets combing the air and the sorehead woodpeckers the
machineguns mud cooties gasmasks and the itch.

*Say feller tell me how I can get back to my outfit.*

John Doe had a head
for twentyodd years intensely the nerves of the eyes the
ears the palate the tongue the fingers the toes the armpits,
the nerves warmfeeling under the skin charged the coiled
brain with hurt sweet warm cold mine must don't sayings
print headlines:
Thou shalt not the multiplication table long division,
Now is the time for all good men knocks but once at a
young man's door, It's a great life if Ish gebibbel, The first
five years'll be the Safety First, Suppose a Hun tried to rape
your my country right or wrong, Catch 'em young What he
don't know won't treat 'em rough, Tell 'em nothin', He got
what was coming to him he got his, This is a white man's
country, Kick the bucket, Gone west, If you don't like it
you can croaked him
*Say buddy can't you tell me how I can get back to my
outfit?*

Can't help jumpin' when them things go off, give me
the trots them things do. I lost my identification tag swimmin' in the Marne, roughhousin' with a guy while we was
waitin' to be deloused, in bed with a girl named Jeanne
(Love moving picture wet French postcard dream began
with saltpeter in the coffee and ended at the propho
station); –
*Say soldier for chrissake can't you tell me how I can
get back to my outfit?*

John Doe
heart pumped blood:

alive thudding silence of blood in your ears

down in the clearing in the Oregon forest where the punkins were punkincolor pouring into the blood through the eyes and the fallcolored trees and the bronze hoopers were hopping through the dry grass, where tiny striped snails hung on the underside of the blades and the flies hummed, wasps droned, bumblebees buzzed, and the woods smelt of wine and mushrooms and apples, honey smell of fall pouring into the blood,

and I dropped the tin hat and the sweaty pack and lay flat with the dogday sun licking my throat and adamsapple and the tight skin over the breastbone.

The shell had his number on it.

The blood ran into the ground.

The service record dropped out of the filing cabinet when the quartermaster sergeant got blotto that time they had to pack up and leave the billets in a hurry.

The identification tag was in the bottom of the Marne.

The blood ran into the ground, the brains oozed out of the cracked skull and were licked up by the trenchrats, the belly swelled and raised a generation of bluebottle flies,

and the incorruptible skeleton,

and the scraps of dried viscera and skin bundled in khaki

they took to Châlons-sur-Marne
and laid it out neat in a pine coffin
and took it home to God's Country on a battleship
and buried it in a sarcophagus in the Memorial Amphitheater in the Arlington National Cemetery
and draped the Old Glory over it
and the bugler played taps
and Mr Harding prayed to God and the diplomats and the generals and the admirals and the brasshats and the politicians and the handsomely dressed ladies out of the

society column of the *Washington Post* stood up solemn
    and thought how beautiful sad Old Glory God's Country
it was to have the bugler play taps and the three volleys
made their ears ring.

    Where his chest ought to have been they pinned
    the Congressional Medal, the D.S.C., the Médaille
Militaire, the Belgian Croix de Guerre, the Italian gold
medal, the Vitutea Militara sent by Queen Marie of
Rumania, the Czechoslovak War Cross, the Virtuti Militari
of the Poles, a wreath sent by Hamilton Fish, Jr., of New
York, and a little wampum presented by a deputation of
Arizona redskins in warpaint and feathers. All the Wash-
ingtonians brought flowers.

    Woodrow Wilson brought a bouquet of poppies.

# The Big Money

# Charley Anderson

Charley Anderson lay in his bunk in a glary red buzz. *Oh, Titine*, damn that tune last night. He lay flat with his eyes hot; the tongue in his mouth was thick warm sour felt. He dragged his feet out from under the blanket and hung them over the edge of the bunk, big white feet with pink knobs on the toes; he let them drop to the red carpet and hauled himself shakily to the porthole. He stuck his head out.

Instead of the dock, fog, little graygreen waves slapping against the steamer's scaling side. At anchor. A gull screamed above him hidden in the fog. He shivered and pulled his head in.

At the basin he splashed cold water on his face and neck. Where the cold water hit him his skin flushed pink.

He began to feel cold and sick and got back into his bunk and pulled the stillwarm covers up to his chin. Home. Damn that tune.

He jumped up. His head and stomach throbbed in time now. He pulled out the chamberpot and leaned over it. He gagged; a little green bile came. No, I don't want to puke. He got into his underclothes and the whipcord pants of his uniform and lathered his face to shave. Shaving made him feel blue. What I need's a ... He rang for the steward. 'Bonjour, m'sieur.' 'Say, Billy, let's have a double cognac tootsuite.'

He buttoned his shirt carefully and put on his tunic; looking at himself in the glass, his eyes had red rims and his face looked green under the sunburn. Suddenly he began to feel sick again; a sour gagging was welling up from his stomach to his throat. God, these French boats stink. A knock, the steward's frog smile and 'Voilà m'sieur,' the white plate slopped with a thin amber spilling out of the glass. 'When do we dock?' The steward shrugged and growled, 'La brume.'

Green spots were still dancing in front of his eyes as he went up the linoleumsmelling companionway. Up on deck the wet fog squeezed wet against his face. He stuck his hands in his pockets and leaned into it. Nobody on deck, a few trunks, steamerchairs folded and stacked. To windward everything was wet. Drops trickled down the brassrimmed windows of the smokingroom. Nothing in any direction but fog.

Next time around he met Joe Askew. Joe looked fine. His little mustache spread neat under his thin nose. His eyes were clear.

'Isn't this the damnedest note, Charley? Fog.'

'Rotten.'

'Got a head?'

'You look topnotch, Joe.'

'Sure, why not? I got the fidgets, been up since six o'clock. Damn this fog, we may be here all day.'

'It's fog all right.'

They took a couple of turns round the deck.

'Notice how the boat stinks, Joe?'

'It's being at anchor, and the fog stimulates your smellers, I guess. How about breakfast?'

Charley didn't say anything for a moment, then he took a deep breath and said, 'All right, let's try it.'

The diningsaloon smelt of onions and brasspolish. The Johnsons were already at the table. Mrs Johnson looked pale and cool. She had on a little gray hat Charley hadn't seen before, all ready to land. Paul gave Charley a sickly kind of smile when he said hello. Charley noticed how Paul's hand was shaking when he lifted the glass of orangejuice. His lips were white.

'Anybody seen Ollie Taylor?' asked Charley.

'The Major's feelin' pretty bad, I bet,' said Paul, giggling.

'And how are you, Charley?' Mrs Johnson intoned sweetly.

'Oh, I'm . . . I'm in the pink.'

'Liar,' said Joe Askew.

'Oh, I can't imagine,' Mrs Johnson was saying, 'what kept you boys up so late last night.'

'We did some singing,' said Joe Askew.

'Somebody I know,' said Mrs Johnson, 'went to bed in his clothes.' Her eye caught Charley's.

Paul was changing the subject: 'Well, we're back in God's country.'

'Oh, I can't imagine,' cried Mrs Johnson, 'what America's going to be like.'

Charley was bolting his wuffs avec du bakin and the coffee that tasted of bilge.

'What I'm looking forward to,' Joe Askew was saying, 'is a real American breakfast.'

'Grapefruit,' said Mrs Johnson.

'Cornflakes and cream,' said Joe.

'Hot cornmuffins,' said Mrs Johnson.

'Fresh eggs and real Virginia ham,' said Joe.

'Wheatcakes and country sausage,' said Mrs Johnson.

'Scrapple,' said Joe.

'Good coffee with real cream,' said Mrs Johnson, laughing.

'You win,' said Paul with a sickly grin as he left the table.

Charley took a last gulp of his coffee. Then he said he thought he'd go on deck to see if the immigration officers had come. 'Why, what's the matter with Charley?' He could hear Joe and Mrs Johnson laughing together as he ran up the companionway.

Once on deck he decided he wasn't going to be sick. The fog had lifted a little. Astern of the *Niagara* he could see the shadows of other steamers at anchor, and beyond, a rounded shadow that might be land. Gulls wheeled and screamed overhead. Somewhere across the water a foghorn groaned at intervals. Charley walked up forward and leaned into the wet fog.

Joe Askew came up behind him smoking a cigar and took him by the arm: 'Better walk, Charley,' he said. 'Isn't this a hell of a note? Looks like little old New York had gotten torpedoed during the late unpleasantness. . . . I can't see a damn thing, can you?'

'I thought I saw some land a minute ago, but it's gone now.'

'Musta been Atlantic Highlands; we're anchored off the Hook. . . . Goddam it, I want to get ashore.'

'Your wife'll be there, won't she, Joe?'

'She ought to be. . . . Know anybody in New York, Charley?'

Charley shook his head. 'I got a long ways to go yet before I go home. . . . I don't know what I'll do when I get there.'

'Damn it, we may be here all day,' said Joe Askew.

'Joe,' said Charley, 'suppose we have a drink . . . one final drink.'

'They've closed up the damn bar.'

They'd packed their bags the night before. There was nothing to do. They spent the morning playing rummy in the smokingroom. Nobody could keep his mind on the game. Paul kept dropping his cards. Nobody ever knew who had taken the last trick. Charley was trying to keep his eyes off Mrs Johnson's eyes, off the little curve of her neck where it ducked under the gray fur trimming of her dress.

'I can't imagine,' she said again, 'what you boys found to

talk about so late last night. . . . I thought we'd talked about everything under heaven before I went to bed.'

'Oh, we found topics, but mostly it came out in the form of singing,' said Joe Askew.

'I know I always miss things when I go to bed.' Charley noticed Paul beside him staring at her with pale loving eyes. 'But,' she was saying with her teasing smile, 'it's just too boring to sit up.'

Paul blushed, he looked as if he were going to cry; Charley wondered if Paul had thought of the same thing he'd thought of.

'Well, let's see; whose deal was it?' said Joe Askew briskly.

Round noon Major Taylor came into the smokingroom. 'Good morning, everybody. . . . I know nobody feels worse than I do. Commandant says we may not dock till tomorrow morning.'

They put up the cards without finishing the hand.

'That's nice,' said Joe Askew.

'It's just as well,' said Ollie Taylor. 'I'm a wreck. The last of the harddrinking hardriding Taylors is a wreck. We could stand the war, but the peace has done us in.'

Charley looked up in Ollie Taylor's gray face sagging in the pale glare of the fog through the smokingroom windows and noticed the white streaks in his hair and mustache. Gosh, he thought to himself, I'm going to quit this drinking.

They got through lunch somehow, then scattered to their cabins to sleep.

In the corridor outside his cabin Charley met Mrs Johnson. 'Well, the first ten days'll be the hardest, Mrs Johnson.'

'Why don't you call me Eveline; everybody else does?'

Charley turned red. 'What's the use? We won't ever see each other again.'

'Why not?' she said.

He looked into her long hazel eyes; the pupils widened till the hazel was all black.

'Jesus, I'd like it if we could,' he stammered. 'Don't think for a minute I . . .'

She'd already brushed silkily past him and was gone down the corridor. He went into his cabin and slammed the door. His bags were packed. The steward had put away the bedclothes. Charley threw himself face down on the striped mustysmelling ticking of the mattress. 'God damn that woman,' he said aloud.

The rattle of a steamwinch woke him, then he heard the jingle of the engineroom bell. He looked out the porthole and saw a yellow and white revenuecutter and, beyond, vague pink sunlight on frame houses. The fog was lifting; they were in the Narrows.

By the time he'd splashed the aching sleep out of his eyes and run up on deck, the *Niagara* was nosing her way slowly across the greengray glinting bay. The ruddy fog was looped up like curtains overhead. A red ferryboat crossed their bow. To the right there was a line of four- and five-masted schooners at anchor, beyond them a squarerigger and a huddle of squatty Shipping Board steamers, some of them still striped and mottled with camouflage. Then dead ahead, the up-and-down gleam in the blur of the tall buildings of New York.

Joe Askew came up to him with his trenchcoat on and his German fieldglasses hung over his shoulder. Joe's blue eyes were shining. 'Do you see the Statue of Liberty yet, Charley?'

'No . . . yes, there she is. I remembered her lookin' bigger.'

'There's Black Tom where the explosion was.'

'Things look pretty quiet, Joe.'

'It's Sunday, that's why.'

'It would be Sunday.'

They were opposite the Battery now. The long spans of the bridges to Brooklyn went off into smoky shadow behind the pale skyscrapers.

'Well, Charley, that's where they keep all the money. We got to get some of it away from 'em,' said Joe Askew, tugging at his mustache.

'Wish I knew how to start in, Joe.'

They were skirting a long row of roofed slips. Joe held out his hand. 'Well, Charley, write to me, kid, do you hear? It was a great war while it lasted.'

'I sure will, Joe.'

Two tugs were shoving the *Niagara* around into the slip against the strong ebbtide. American and French flags flew over the wharfbuilding, in the dark doorways were groups of people waving.

'There's my wife,' said Joe Askew suddenly. He squeezed Charley's hand. 'Solong, kid. We're home.'

First thing Charley knew, too soon, he was walking down the gangplank. The transportofficer barely looked at his papers; the customsman said, 'Well, I guess it's good to be home, Lieutenant,' as he put the stamps on his grip. He got past the Y man and the two reporters and the member of the mayor's committee; the few people and the scattered trunks looked lost and lonely in the huge yellow gloom of the wharfbuilding. Major Taylor and the Johnsons shook hands like strangers.

Then he was following his small khaki trunk to a taxicab. The Johnsons already had a cab and were waiting for a stray grip. Charley went over to them. He couldn't think of anything to say. Paul said he must be sure to come to see them if he stayed in New York, but he kept standing in the door of the cab, so that it was hard for Charley to talk to Eveline. He could see the muscles relax on Paul's jaw when the porter brought the lost grip. 'Be sure and look us up,' Paul said and jumped in and slammed the door.

Charley went back to his cab, carrying with him a last glimpse of long hazel eyes and her teasing smile. 'Do you know if they still give officers special rates at the McAlpin?' he asked the taximan.

'Sure, they treat you all right if you're an officer. . . . If you're an enlisted man you get your ass kicked,' answered the taximan out of the corner of his mouth and slammed the gears.

The taxi turned into a wide empty cobbled street. The cab rode easier than the Paris cabs. The big warehouses and marketbuildings were all closed up.

'Gee, things look pretty quiet here,' Charley said, leaning forward to talk to the taximan through the window.

'Quiet as hell. . . . You wait till you start to look for a job,' said the taximan.

'But, Jesus, I don't ever remember things bein' as quiet as this.'

'Well, why shouldn't they be quiet? . . . It's Sunday, ain't it?'

'Oh, sure, I'd forgotten it was Sunday.'

'Sure it's Sunday.'

'I remember now it's Sunday.'

# Newsreel 44

*Yankee Doodle that melodee*

COLONEL HOUSE ARRIVES FROM EUROPE

APPARENTLY A VERY SICK MAN

*Yankee Doodle that melodee*

TO CONQUER SPACE AND SEE DISTANCES

but has not the time come for newspaper proprietors to join in a wholesome movement for the purpose of calming troubled minds, giving all the news but laying less stress on prospective calamities

DEADLOCK UNBROKEN AS FIGHT SPREADS

they permitted the Steel Trust Government to trample underfoot the democratic rights which they had so often been assured were the heritage of the people of this country

SHIPOWNERS DEMAND PROTECTION

*Yankee doodle that melodee*
*Yankee doodle that melodee*
*Makes me stand right up and cheer*

only survivors of crew of schooner *Onato* are put in jail on arrival in Philadelphia

PRESIDENT STRONGER WORKS IN SICKROOM

*I'm coming U.S.A.*
*I'll say*

MAY GAG PRESS

*There's no land . . . so grand*

Charles M. Schwab, who has returned from Europe, was a luncheon guest at the White House. He stated that this country was prosperous but not so prosperous as it should be, because there were so many disturbing investigations on foot

> *... as my land*
> *From California to Manhattan Isle*

## *Charley Anderson*

The ratfaced bellboy put down the bags, tried the faucets of the washbowl, opened the window a little, put the key on the inside of the door and then stood at something like attention and said, 'Anything else, Lootenant?'

This is the life, thought Charley, and fished a quarter out of his pocket.

'Thank you, sir, Lootenant.' The bellboy shuffled his feet and cleared his throat. 'It must have been terrible overseas, Lootenant.'

Charley laughed. 'Oh, it was all right.'

'I wish I coulda gone, Lootenant.' The boy showed a couple of ratteeth in a grin. 'It must be wonderful to be a hero,' he said and backed out the door.

Charley stood looking out the window as he unbuttoned his tunic. He was high up. Through a street of grimy square buildings he could see some columns and the roofs of the new Penn Station and beyond, across the trainyards, a blurred sun setting behind high ground the other side of the Hudson. Overhead was purple and pink. An El train clattered raspingly through the empty Sundayevening streets. The wind that streamed through the bottom of the window had a gritty smell of coalashes. Charley put the window down and went to wash his face and hands. The hotel towel felt soft and thick with a little whiff of chloride. He went to the lookingglass and combed his hair. Now what?

He was walking up and down the room fidgeting with a cigarette, watching the sky go dark outside the window, when the jangle of the phone startled him.

It was Ollie Taylor's polite fuddled voice. 'I thought maybe you wouldn't know where to get a drink. Do you want to come around to the club?'

'Gee, that's nice of you, Ollie. I was jus' wonderin' what a feller could do with himself in this man's town.'

'You know it's quite dreadful here,' Ollie's voice went on.

'Prohibition and all that, it's worse than the wildest imagination could conceive. I'll come and pick you up with a cab.'

'All right, Ollie, I'll be in the lobby.'

Charley put on his tunic, remembered to leave off his Sam Browne belt, straightened his scrubby sandy hair again, and went down into the lobby. He sat down in a deep chair facing the revolving doors.

The lobby was crowded. There was music coming from somewhere in back. He sat there listening to the dancetunes, looking at the silk stockings and the high heels and the furcoats and the pretty girls' faces pinched a little by the wind as they came in off the street. There was an expensive jingle and crinkle to everything. Gosh, it was great. The girls left little trails of perfume and a warm smell of furs as they passed him. He started counting up how much jack he had. He had a draft for three hundred bucks he'd saved out of his pay, four yellow-backed twenties in the wallet in his inside pocket he'd won at poker on the boat, a couple of tens, and let's see how much change. The coins made a little jingle in his pants as he fingered them over.

Ollie Taylor's red face was nodding at Charley above a big camel'shair coat. 'My dear boy, New York's a wreck. . . . They are pouring icecream sodas in the Knickerbocker bar. . . .' When they got into the cab together he blew a reek of high-grade rye whiskey in Charley's face. 'Charley, I've promised to take you along to dinner with me. . . . Just up to ole Nat Benton's. You won't mind . . . he's a good scout. The ladies want to see a real flying aviator with palms.'

'You're sure I won't be buttin' in, Ollie?'

'My dear boy, say no more about it.'

At the club everybody seemed to know Ollie Taylor. He and Charley stood a long time drinking Manhattans at a dark-paneled bar in a group of whitehaired old gents with a barroom tan on their faces. It was Major this and Major that and Lieutenant every time anybody spoke to Charley. Charley was getting to be afraid Ollie would get too much of a load on to go to dinner at anybody's house.

At last it turned out to be seventhirty, and leaving the final-round of cocktails, they got into a cab again, each of them munching a clove, and started uptown. 'I don't know what to say to 'em,' Ollie said. 'I tell them I've just spent the most delightful two years of my life, and they make funny mouths at me, but I can't help it.'

There was a terrible lot of marble, and doormen in green, at the apartmenthouse where they went out to dinner, and the elevator was inlaid in different kinds of wood. Nat Benton, Ollie whispered while they were waiting for the door to open, was a Wall Street broker.

They were all in evening dress waiting for them for dinner in a pinkishcolored drawingroom. They were evidently old friends of Ollie's because they made a great fuss over him and they were very cordial to Charley and brought out cocktails right away, and Charley felt like the cock of the walk.

There was a girl named Miss Humphries who was as pretty as a picture. The minute Charley set eyes on her Charley decided that was who he was going to talk to. Her eyes and her fluffy palegreen dress and the powder in the little hollow between her shoulderblades made him feel a little dizzy so that he didn't dare stand too close to her.

Ollie saw the two of them together and came up and pinched her ear. 'Doris, you've grown up to be a raving beauty.' He stood beaming, teetering a little on his short legs. 'Hum . . . only the brave deserve the fair. . . . It's not every day we come home from the wars, is it, Charley me boy?'

'Isn't he a darling?' she said when Ollie turned away. 'We used to be great sweethearts when I was about six and he was a collegeboy.'

When they were all ready to go into dinner Ollie, who'd had a couple more cocktails, spread out his arms and made a speech. 'Look at them, lovely, intelligent, lively American women. . . . There was nothing like that on the other side, was there, Charley? Three things you can't get anywhere else in the world, a good cocktail, a decent breakfast, and an American girl, God bless 'em.'

'Oh, he's such a darling,' whispered Miss Humphries in Charley's ear.

There was silverware in rows and rows on the table and a Chinese bowl with roses in the middle of it, and a group of giltstemmed wineglasses at each plate. Charley was relieved when he found he was sitting next to Miss Humphries. She was smiling up at him.

'Gosh,' he said, grinning into her face, 'I hardly know how to act.'

'It must be a change . . . from over there. But just act natural. That's what I do.'

'Oh, no, a feller always gets into trouble when he acts natural.'

She laughed. 'Maybe you're right. . . . Oh, do tell me what it was really like over there. . . . Nobody'll ever tell me everything.' She pointed to the palms on his Croix de Guerre. 'Oh, Lieutenant Anderson, you must tell me about those.'

They had white wine with the fish and red wine with the roastbeef and a dessert all full of whippedcream. Charley kept telling himself he mustn't drink too much so that he'd be sure to behave right.

Miss Humphries' first name was Doris. Mrs Benton called her that. She'd spent a year in a convent in Paris before the war and asked him about places she'd known, the Church of the Madeleine and Rumpelmayer's and the pastryshop opposite the Comédie Française. After dinner she and Charley took their coffeecups into a windowbay behind a big pink begonia in a brass pot and she asked him if he didn't think New York was awful. She sat on the windowseat and he stood over her looking past her white shoulder through the window down at the traffic in the street below. It had come on to rain and the lights of the cars made long rippling streaks on the black pavement of Park Avenue. He said something about how he thought home would look pretty good to him all the same. He was wondering if it would be all right if he told her she had beautiful shoulders. He'd just about gotten around to it when he heard Ollie Taylor getting everybody together to go out to a cabaret. 'I know it's a chore,' Ollie was saying, 'but you children must remember it's my first night in New York and humor my weakness.'

They stood in a group under the marquee while the doorman called taxicabs. Doris Humphries in her long eveningwrap with fur at the bottom of it stood so close to Charley her shoulder touched his arm. In the lashing rainy wind off the street he could smell the warm perfume she wore and her furs and her hair. They stood back while the older people got into the cabs. For a second her hand was in his, very little and cool as he helped her into the cab. He handed out half a dollar to the doorman who had whispered 'Shanley's' to the taxidriver in a serious careful flunkey's voice.

The taxi was purring smoothly downtown between the tall square buildings. Charley was a little dizzy. He didn't dare look at her for a moment, but looked out at faces, cars, traffic-cops, people in raincoats and umbrellas passing against drugstore windows.

'Now tell me how you got the palms.'

'Oh, the frogs just threw those in now and then to keep the boys cheerful.'

'How many Huns did you bring down?'

'Why bring that up?'

She stamped her foot on the floor of the taxi. 'Oh, nobody'll ever tell me anything! . . . I don't believe you were ever at the front, any of you.'

Charley laughed. His throat was a little dry. 'Well, I was over it a couple of times.'

Suddenly she turned to him. There were flecks of light in her eyes in the dark of the cab. 'Oh, I understand. . . . Lieutenant Anderson, I think you flyers are the finest people there are.'

'Miss Humphries, I think you're a . . . humdinger. . . . I hope this taxi never gets to this dump . . . wherever it is we're goin'.'

She leaned her shoulder against his for a second. He found he was holding her hand. 'After all, my name is Doris,' she said in a tiny babytalk voice.

'Doris,' he said. 'Mine's Charley.'

'Charley, do you like to dance?' she asked in the same tiny voice.

'Sure,' Charley said, giving her hand a quick squeeze.

Her voice melted like a little tiny piece of candy. 'Me too. . . . Oh, so much.'

When they went in, the orchestra was playing *Dardanella*. Charley left his trenchcoat and his hat in the checkroom. The headwaiter's heavy grizzled eyebrows bowed over a white shirtfront. Charley was following Doris's slender back, the hollow between the shoulderblades where his hand would like to be, across the red carpet, between the white tables, the men's starched shirts, the women's shoulders, through the sizzly smell of champagne and welshrabbit and hot chafingdishes, across a corner of the dancefloor among the swaying couples to the round white table where the rest of them were already settled. The knives and forks shone among the stiff creases of the fresh tablecloth.

Mrs Benton was pulling off her white kid gloves looking at Ollie Taylor's purple face as he told a funny story. 'Let's dance,' Charley whispered to Doris. 'Let's dance all the time.'

Charley was scared of dancing too tough so he held her a little away from him. She had a way of dancing with her eyes closed. 'Gee, Doris, you are a wonderful dancer.' When the music stopped, the tables and the cigarsmoke and the people went on reeling a little round their heads. Doris was looking up at him out of the corners of her eyes. 'I bet you miss the French girls, Charley. How did you like the way the French girls danced, Charley?'

'Terrible.'

At the table they were drinking champagne out of breakfast coffeecups. Ollie had had two bottles sent up from the club by a messenger. When the music started again, Charley had to dance with Mrs Benton, and then with the other lady, the one with the diamonds and the spare tire around her waist. He and Doris only had two more dances together. Charley could see the others wanted to go home because Ollie was getting too tight. He had a flask of rye on his hip and a couple of times had beckoned Charley out to have a swig in the cloakroom with him. Charley tongued the bottle each time because he was hoping he'd get a chance to take Doris home.

When they got outside, it turned out she lived in the same block as the Bentons did; Charley cruised around on the outside of the group while the ladies were getting their wraps on before going out to the taxicab, but he couldn't get a look from her. It was just, 'Goodnight, Ollie dear, goodnight, Lieutenant Anderson,' and the doorman slamming the taxi door. He hardly knew which of the hands he had shaken had been hers.

# Newsreel 45

> *'Twarn't for powder and for storebought hair*
> *De man I love would not gone nowhere*

if one should seek a simple explanation of his career, it would doubtless be found in that extraordinary decision to forsake the ease of a clerkship for the wearying labor of a section hand. The youth who so early in life had so much of judgment and willpower could not fail to rise above the general run of men. He became the intimate of bankers

> *St Louis woman wid her diamon' rings*
> *Pulls dat man aroun' by her apron strings*

*Tired of walking, riding a bicycle or riding in streetcars, he is likely to buy a Ford.*

### DAYLIGHT HOLDUP SCATTERS CROWD

*Just as soon as his wife discovers that every Ford is like every other Ford and that nearly everyone has one, she is likely to influence him to step into the next social group, of which the Dodge is the most conspicuous example.*

### DESPERATE REVOLVER BATTLE FOLLOWS

*The next step comes when daughter comes back from college and the family moves into a new home. Father wants economy. Mother craves opportunity for her children, daughter desires social prestige and son wants travel, speed, get-up-and-go.*

### MAN SLAIN NEAR HOTEL MAJESTIC BY THREE FOOTPADS

> *I hate to see de evenin sun go down*
> *Hate to see de evenin sun go down*
> *'Cause my baby he done lef' dis town*

such exploits may indicate a dangerous degree of

bravado but they display the qualities that made a boy of highschool age the acknowledged leader of a gang that has been a thorn in the side of the State of

## The American Plan

Frederick Winslow Taylor (they called him Speedy Taylor in the shop) was born in Germantown, Pennsylvania, the year of Buchanan's election. His father was a lawyer, his mother came from a family of New Bedford whalers; she was a great reader of Emerson, belonged to the Unitarian Church and the Browning Society. She was a fervent abolitionist and believed in democratic manners; she was a housekeeper of the old school, kept everybody busy from dawn till dark. She laid down the rules of conduct:

selfrespect, selfreliance, selfcontrol

and a cold long head for figures.

But she wanted her children to appreciate the finer things, so she took them abroad for three years on the Continent, showed them cathedrals, grand opera, Roman pediments, the old masters under their brown varnish in their great frames of tarnished gilt.

Later Fred Taylor was impatient of these wasted years, stamped out of the room when people talked about the finer things; he was a testy youngster, fond of practical jokes, and a great hand at rigging up contraptions and devices.

At Exeter he was head of his class and captain of the ballteam, the first man to pitch overhand. (When umpires complained that overhand pitching wasn't in the rules of the game, he answered that it got results.)

As a boy he had nightmares; going to bed was horrible for him; he thought they came from sleeping on his back. He made himself a leather harness with wooden pegs that stuck into his flesh when he turned over. When he was grown he slept in a chair or in bed in a sitting position propped up with pillows. All his life he suffered from sleeplessness.

He was a crackerjack tennisplayer. In 1881, with his friend Clark, he won the National Doubles Championship. (He used a spoonshaped racket of his own design.)

At school he broke down from overwork, his eyes went back on him. The doctor suggested manual labor. So instead of going to Harvard he went into the machineshop of a small pumpmanufacturing concern, owned by a friend of the family's, to learn the trade of patternmaker and machinist. He learned to handle a lathe and to dress and cuss like a workingman.

Fred Taylor never smoked tobacco or drank liquor or used tea or coffee; he couldn't understand why his fellow-mechanics wanted to go on sprees and get drunk and raise cain Saturday nights. He lived at home; when he wasn't reading technical books he'd play parts in amateur theatricals or step up to the piano in the evening and sing a good tenor in *A Warrior Bold* or *A Spanish Cavalier*.

He served his first year's apprenticeship in the machineshop without pay; the next two years he made a dollar and a half a week, the last year two dollars.

Pennsylvania was getting rich off iron and coal. When he was twentytwo, Fred Taylor went to work at the Midvale Iron Works. At first he had to take a clerical job, but he hated that and went to work with a shovel. At last he got them to put him on a lathe. He was a good machinist, he worked ten hours a day and in the evenings followed an engineering course at Stevens. In six years he rose from machinist's helper to keeper of toolcribs to gangboss to foreman to mastermechanic in charge of repairs to chief draftsman and director of research to chief engineer of the Midvale Plant.

The early years he was a machinist with the other machinists in the shop, cussed and joked and worked with the rest of them, soldiered on the job when they did. Mustn't give the boss more than his money's worth. But when he got to be foreman, he was on the management's side of the fence, *gathering in on the part of those on the management's side all the great mass of traditional knowledge which in the past has been in the heads of the workmen and in the physical skill and knack of the workman.* He couldn't stand to see an idle lathe or an idle man.

Production went to his head and thrilled his sleepless nerves like liquor or women on a Saturday night. He never loafed and he'd be damned if anybody else would. Production was an itch under his skin.

He lost his friends in the shop; they called him nigger-driver. He was a stockily built man with a temper and a short tongue.

*I was a young man in years, but I give you my word I was a great deal older than I am now, what with the worry, meanness, and contemptibleness of the whole damn thing. It's a horrid life for any man to live, not being able to look any workman in the face without seeing hostility there, and a feeling that every man around you is your virtual enemy.*

That was the beginning of the Taylor System of Scientific Management.

He was impatient of explanations, he didn't care whose hide he took off in enforcing the laws he believed inherent in the industrial process.

*When starting an experiment in any field, question everything, question the very foundations upon which the art rests, question the simplest, the most selfevident, the most universally accepted facts; prove everything.*

except the dominant Quaker Yankee (the New Bedford skippers were the greatest niggerdrivers on the whaling seas) rules of conduct. He boasted he'd never ask a workman to do anything he couldn't do.

He devised an improved steamhammer; he standardized tools and equipment, he filled the shop with college students with stopwatches and diagrams, tabulating, standardizing. *There's the right way of doing a thing and the wrong way of doing it; the right way means increased production, lower costs, higher wages, bigger profits:* the American plan.

He broke up the foreman's job into separate functions, speedbosses, gangbosses, timestudy men, order-of-work men.

The skilled mechanics were too stubborn for him; what he wanted was a plain handyman who'd do what he was told. If he was a firstclass man and did firstclass work, Taylor was willing to let him have firstclass pay; that's where he began to get into trouble with the owners.

At thirtyfour he married and left Midvale and took a flyer for the big money in connection with a pulpmill started in Maine by some admirals and political friends of Grover Cleveland's;

the panic of '93 made hash of that enterprise,

so Taylor invented for himself the job of Consulting Engineer in Management and began to build up a fortune by careful investments.

The first paper he read before the American Society of Mechanical Engineers was anything but a success; they said he was crazy. *I have found*, he wrote in 1909, *that any improvement is not only opposed but aggressively and bitterly opposed by the majority of men.*

He was called in by Bethlehem Steel. It was in Bethlehem he made his famous experiments with handling pigiron; he taught a Dutchman named Schmidt to handle fortyseven tons instead of twelve and a half tons of pigiron a day and got Schmidt to admit he was as good as ever at the end of the day.

He was a crank about shovels, every job had to have a shovel of the right weight and size for that job alone; every job had to have a man of the right weight and size for that job alone; but when he began to pay his men in proportion to the increased efficiency of their work,

the owners, who were a lot of greedy smalleyed Dutchmen, began to raise Hail Columbia; when Schwab bought Bethlehem Steel in 1901

Fred Taylor

inventor of efficiency

who had doubled the production of the stampingmill by speeding up the main lines of shafting from ninetysix to twohundred and twentyfive revolutions a minute

was unceremoniously fired.


After that Fred Taylor always said he couldn't afford to work for money.

He took to playing golf (using golfclubs of his own design), doping out methods for transplanting huge boxtrees into the garden of his home.


At Boxly in Germantown he kept open house for engineers, factorymanagers, industrialists;

he wrote papers,

lectured in colleges,

appeared before a congressional committee,

everywhere preached the virtues of scientific management and the Barth slide rule, the cutting-down of waste and idleness, the substitution for skilled mechanics of the plain handyman (like Schmidt the pigiron handler) who'd move as he was told

and work by the piece:

production;

more steel rails more bicycles more spools of thread more armorplate for battleships more bedpans more barbedwire more needles more lightningrods more ballbearings more dollarbills;

(the old Quaker families of Germantown were growing rich, the Pennsylvania millionaires were breeding billionaires out of iron and coal)

production would make every firstclass American rich who was willing to work at piecework and not drink or raise cain or think or stand mooning at his lathe.

Thrifty Schmidt the pigiron handler can invest his money and get to be an owner like Schwab and the rest of the greedy smalleyed Dutchmen and cultivate a taste for Bach and have hundredyearold boxtrees in his garden at Bethlehem or Germantown or Chestnut Hill,

and lay down the rules of conduct;

the American plan.

But Fred Taylor never saw the working of the American plan;

in 1915 he went to the hospital in Philadelphia suffering from a breakdown.

Pneumonia developed; the nightnurse heard him winding his watch;

on the morning of his fiftyninth birthday, when the nurse went into his room to look at him at fourthirty,

he was dead with his watch in his hand.

# Newsreel 46

these are the men for whom the rabid lawless, anarchistic element of society in this country has been laboring ever since sentence was imposed, and of late they have been augmented by many good lawabiding citizens who have been misled by the subtle arguments of those propagandists

*The times are hard and the wages low*
*Leave her Johnny leave her*
*The bread is hard and the beef is salt*
*It's time for us to leave her*

**BANKERS HAIL ERA OF EXPANSION**

**PROSPERITY FOR ALL SEEN ASSURED**

Find German Love of Caviar a Danger to Stable Money

**EX-SERVICE MEN DEMAND JOBS**

*No one knows*
*No one cares if I'm weary*
*Oh how soon they forget Château-Thierry*

**WE FEEL VERY FRIENDLY TOWARDS THE TYPEWRITER USERS OF NEW YORK CITY**

**JOBLESS RIOT AT AGENCY**

*Ships in de oceans*
*Rocks in de sea*
*Blond-headed woman*
*Made a fool outa me*

## The Camera Eye (43)

throat tightens when the redstacked steamer churning the faintly heaving slate colored swell swerves slicking· in a long greenmarbled curve past the red lightship

spine stiffens with the remembered chill of the offshore Atlantic

and the jag of frame houses in the west above the invisible land and spiderweb rollercoasters and the chewinggum towers of Coney and the freighters with their stacks away aft and the blur beyond Sandy Hook

and the smell of saltmarshes warmclammysweet

remembered bays silvery inlets barred with trestles

the put-put before day of a gasolineboat way up the creek

raked masts of bugeyes against straight tall pines on the shellwhite beach

the limeycold reek of an oysterboat in winter

and creak of rockers on the porch of the scrollsaw cottage and uncles' voices pokerface stories told sideways out of the big mouth (from Missouri who took no rubber nickels) the redskin in the buffalorobe selling snakeroot in the flare of oratorical redfire the sulphury choke and the hookandladder clanging down the redbrick street while the clinging firemen with uncles' faces pull on their rubbercoats

and the crunch of whitecorn muffins and coffee with cream gulped in a hurry before traintime and apartmenthouse mornings stifling with newspapers and the smooth powdery feel of new greenbacks and the whack of a cop's billy cracking a citizen's skull and the faces blurred with newsprint of men in jail

the whine and shriek of the buzzsaw and the tipsy smell of raw lumber and straggling through slagheaps through fireweed through wasted woodlands the shantytowns the shantytowns

what good burying those years in the old graveyard by

the brokendown brick church that morning in the spring
when the sandy lanes were treated with blue puddles and
the air was violets and pineneedles

what good burying those hated years in the latrine-
stench at Brocourt under the starshells

if today the crookedfaced custominspector with the soft
tough talk the burring speech the funnypaper antics of thick
hands jerking thumb

(So you brought home French books didjer?)

is my uncle

# Newsreel 47

boy seeking future offered opportunity . . . good positions for bright . . . CHANCE FOR ADVANCEMENT . . . boy to learn . . . errand boy . . . office boy

### YOUNG MAN WANTED

*Oh tell me how long*
*I'll have to wait*

### OPPORTUNITY

in bank that chooses its officers from the ranks, for wideawake ambitious bookkeeper . . . architectural draftsman with experience on factory and industrial buildings in brick, timber, and reinforced concrete . . . bronzefitter . . . letterer . . . patternmaker . . . carriage painter . . . firstclass striper and finisher . . . young man for hosiery, underwear, and notion house . . . assistant in order department . . . firstclass penman accurate at figures . . . energetic hardworker for setting dies in powerpresses for metal parts

canvasser . . . flavor chemist . . . freightelevator man . . . housesalesman . . . insuranceman . . . insuranceman . . . invoice clerk . . . jeweler . . . laborer . . . machinist . . . millingmachine man . . shipping clerk . . . shipping clerk . . . shipping clerk . . . shoe salesman . . . signwriter . . . solicitor for retail fishmarket . . . teacher . . . timekeeper . . . tool and diemaker, tracer, toolroom foreman, translator, typist . . . windowtrimmer . . . wrapper

### OPPORTUNITY FOR

*Do I get it now*
*Or must I hesitate*

young man not afraid of hard work
young man for office
young man for stockroom

young man as stenographer<br>
young man to travel<br>
young man to learn

OPPORTUNITY

*Oh tell me how long*

 to superintend municipal light, water, and ice plant in beautiful growing, healthful town in Florida's highlands ... to take charge of underwear department in large wholesale mailhouse ... to assist in railroad investigation ... to take charge of about twenty men on tools, dies, gigs, and gauges ... as bookkeeper in stockroom ... for light porter work ... civil engineer ... machinery and die appraiser ... building estimator ... electrical and power-plant engineer

## The Camera Eye (44)

 the unnamed arrival

 (who had hung from the pommel of the unshod white stallion's saddle

 a full knapsack

 and leaving the embers dying in the hollow of the barren Syrian hills where the Agail had camped when dawn sharpshining cracked night off the ridged desert had ridden towards the dungy villages and the patches of sesame and the apricotgardens)

 shaved off his beard in Damascus

 and sat drinking hot milk and coffee in front of the hotel in Beirut staring at the white hulk of Lebanon fumbling with letters piled on the table and clipped streamers of newsprint

 addressed not to the unspeaker of arabic or the clumsy scramblerup on camelback so sore in the rump from riding

 but to someone

 who

 (but this evening in the soft nightclimate of the Levantine coast the kind officials are contemplating further improvements

scarcelybathed he finds himself cast for a role provided with a white tie carefully tied by the viceconsul stuffed into a boiled shirt a tailcoat too small a pair of dresstrousers too large which the kind wife of the kind official gigglingly fastens in the back with safetypins which immediately burst open when he bows to the High Commissioner's lady     faulty costuming makes the role of eminent explorer impossible to play     and the patent leather pumps painfully squeezing the toes got lost under the table during the champagne and speeches)

who arriving in Manhattan finds waiting again the forsomebodyelsetailored dress suit

the position offered the opportunity presented the collarbutton digging into the adamsapple while a wooden image croaks down a table at two rows of freshlypressed gentlemen who wear fashionably their tailored names

stuffed into shirts to caption miles lightyears of clipped streamers of newsprint

Gentlemen I apologize it was the wrong bell it was due to a misapprehension that I found myself on the stage when the curtain rose the poem I recited in a foreign language was not mine in fact it was somebody else who was speaking it's not me in uniform in the snapshot it's a lamentable error mistaken identity the servicerecord was lost the gentleman occupying the swivelchair wearing the red carnation is somebody else than

whoever it was who equipped with false whiskers was standing outside in the rainy street and has managed undetected to make himself scarce down a manhole

the pastyfaced young man wearing somebody else's readymade business opportunity

is most assuredly not

the holder of any of the positions for which he made application at the employmentagency

## *Charley Anderson*

The train was three hours late getting into St Paul. Charley had his coat on and his bag closed an hour before he got in. He sat fidgeting in the seat, taking off and pulling on a pair of new buckskin gloves. He wished they wouldn't all be down at the station to meet him. Maybe only Jim would be there. Maybe they hadn't got his wire.

The porter came and brushed him off, then took his bags. Charley couldn't see much through the driving steam and snow outside the window. The train slackened speed, stopped in a broad snowswept freightyard, started again with a jerk and a series of snorts from the forced draft in the engine. The bumpers slammed all down the train. Charley's hands were icy inside his gloves. The porter stuck his head in and yelled, 'St Paul'. There was nothing to do but get out.

There they all were. Old man Vogel and Aunt Hartmann with their red faces and their long noses looked just the same as ever, but Jim and Hedwig had both of them filled out. Hedwig had on a mink coat and Jim's overcoat looked darn prosperous. Jim snatched Charley's bags away from him and Hedwig and Aunt Hartmann kissed him and old man Vogel thumped him on the back. They all talked at once and asked him all kinds of questions. When he asked about Ma, Jim frowned and said she was in the hospital, they'd go around to see her this afternoon. They piled the bags into a new Ford sedan and squeezed themselves in after with a lot of giggling and squealing from Aunt Hartmann.

'You see I got the Ford agency now,' said Jim.

'To tell the truth, things have been pretty good out here.'

'Wait till you see the house, it's all been done over,' said Hedwig.

'Vell, my poy made de Cherman Kaiser run. Speaking for the Cherman-American commoonity of the Twin Cities, ve are pr'roud of you.'

They had a big dinner ready and Jim gave him a drink of whiskey and old man Vogel kept pouring him out beer and saying. 'Now tell us about it.' Charley sat there, his face all red, eating the stewed chicken and the dumplings and drinking the beer till he was ready to burst. He couldn't think what to tell them, so he made funny cracks when they asked him questions. After dinner old man Vogel gave him one of his best Havana cigars.

That afternoon Charley and Jim went to the hospital to see Ma. Driving over, Jim said she'd been operated on for a tumor, but that he was afraid it was cancer, but even that hadn't given Charley an idea of how sick she'd be. Her face was shrunken and yellow against the white pillow. When he leaned over to kiss her, her lips felt thin and hot. Her breath was very bad.

'Charley, I'm glad you came,' she said in a trembly voice. 'It would have been better if you'd come sooner. . . . Not that I'm not comfortable here . . . anyway, I'll be glad having my boys around me when I get well. God has watched over us all, Charley, we mustn't forget Him.'

'Now, Ma, we don't want to get tired and excited,' said Jim. 'We want to keep our strength to get well.'

'Oh, but He's been so merciful.' She brought her small hand, so thin it was blue, out from under the cover and dabbed at her eyes with a handkerchief. 'Jim, hand me my glasses, that's a good boy,' she said in a stronger voice. 'Let me take a look at the prodigal son.'

Charley couldn't help shuffling his feet uneasily as she looked at him.

'You're quite a man now and you've made quite a name for yourself over there. You boys have turned out better than I hoped. . . . Charley, I was afraid you'd turn out a bum like your old man.' They all laughed. They didn't know what to say.

She took her glasses off again and tried to reach for the bedside table with them. The glasses dropped out of her hand and broke on the concrete floor. 'Oh . . . my . . . never mind, I don't need 'em much here.'

Charley picked the pieces up and put them carefully in his vest pocket. 'I'll get 'em fixed, Ma.'

The nurse was standing in the door beckoning with her head. 'Well, goodbye, see you tomorrow,' they said.

Once they were out in the corridor, Charley felt that tears were running down his face.

'That's how it is,' said Jim, frowning. 'They keep her under dope most of the time. I thought she'd be more comfortable in a private room, but they sure do know how to charge in these damn hospitals.'

'I'll chip in on it,' said Charley. 'I got a little money saved up.'

'Well, I suppose it's no more than right you should,' Jim said.

Charley took a deep breath of the cold afternoon when they paused on the hospital steps, but he couldn't get the smell of ether and drugs and sickness out of his head. It had come fine with an icy wind. The snow on the streets and roofs was bright pink from the flaring sunset.

'We'll go down to the shop and see what's what,' said Jim. 'I told the guy works for me to call up some of the newspaperboys. I thought it would be a little free advertising if they came down to the salesroom to interview you.' Jim slapped Charley on the back. 'They eat up this returnedhero stuff. String 'em along a little, won't you?'

Charley didn't answer.

'Jesus Christ, Jim, I don't know what to tell 'em,' he said in a low voice when they got back in the car.

Jim was pressing his foot on the selfstarter. 'What do you think of comin' in the business, Charley? It's gettin' to be a good 'un, I can tell you that.'

'That's nice of you, Jim. Suppose I kinder think about it.'

When they got back to the house, they went around to the new salesroom Jim had built out from the garage, that had been a liverystable in the old days, back of old man Vogel's house. The salesroom had a big plateglass window with *Ford* slanting across it in blue letters. Inside stood a new truck all shining and polished. Then there was a green carpet and a veneered mahogany desk and a telephone that pulled out on a nickel accordion bracket and an artificial palm in a fancy jardiniere in the corner.

'Take your weight off your feet, Charley,' said Jim, pointing to the swivelchair and bringing out a box of cigars. 'Let's sit around and chew the rag a little.'

Charley sat down and picked himself out a cigar. Jim stood against the radiator with his thumbs in the armholes of his vest. 'What do you think of it, kid; pretty keen, ain't it?'

'Pretty keen, Jim.' They lit their cigars and scuffled around with their feet a little.

Jim began again: 'But it won't do. I got to get me a big new place downtown. This used to be central. Now it's out to hell and gone.'

Charley kinder grunted and puffed on his cigar. Jim took a couple of steps back and forth, looking at Charley all the time. 'With your connections in the Legion and aviation and all that kinder stuff, we'll be jake. Every other Ford dealer in the district's got a German name.'

'Jim, can that stuff. I can't talk to newspapermen.'

Jim flushed and frowned and sat down on the edge of the desk. 'But you got to hold up your end. . . . What do you think I'm taking you in on it for? I'm not doin' it for my kid brother's pretty blue eyes.'

Charley got to his feet. 'Jim, I ain't goin' in on it. I'm already signed up with an aviation proposition with my old C.O.'

'Twentyfive years from now you can talk to me about aviation. Ain't practical yet.'

'Well, we got a couple of tricks up our sleeve. . . . We're shootin' the moon.'

'That's about the size of it.' Jim got to his feet. His lips got thin. 'Well, you needn't think you can lay around my house all winter just because you're a war hero. If that's your idea you've got another think comin'.' Charley burst out laughing. Jim came up and put his hand wheedlingly on Charley's shoulder. 'Say, those birds'll be around here in a few minutes. You be a good feller and change into your uniform and put on all the medals. . . . Give us a break.'

Charley stood a minute staring at the ash on his cigar. 'How about givin' me a break? Haven't been in the house five hours and there you go pickin' on me just like when I was workin' back here. . . .'

Jim was losing control of himself, he was starting to shake. 'Well, you know what you can do about that,' he said, cutting his words off sharp.

Charley felt like smashing him one in his damn narrow jaw. 'If it wasn't for Ma, you wouldn't need to worry about that,' he said quietly.

Jim didn't answer for a minute. The wrinkles came out of his forehead. He shook his head and looked grave. 'You're right, Charley, you better stick around. If it gives her any pleasure . . .'

Charley threw his cigar halfsmoked into the brass spittoon and walked out the door before Jim could stop him. He went to the house and got his hat and coat and went for a long walk through the soggy snow of the late afternoon.

They were just finishing at the suppertable when Charley got back. His supper had been set out on a plate for him at his place. Nobody spoke but old man Vogel. 'Ve been tinking, dese airmen maybe dey live on air too,' he said and laughed wheezily.

Nobody else laughed. Jim got up and went out of the room. As soon as Charley had swallowed his supper, he said he was sleepy and went up to bed.

Charley stayed on while November dragged on towards Thanksgiving and Christmas. His mother never seemed to be any better. Every afternoon he went over to see her for five or ten minutes. She was always cheerful. It made him feel terrible the way she talked about the goodness of God and how she was going to get better. He'd try to get her talking about Fargo and old Lizzie and the old days in the boardinghouse, but she didn't seem to remember much about that, except about sermons she'd heard in church. He'd leave the hospital feeling weak and groggy. The rest of his time he spent looking up books on internalcombustion motors at the public library, or did odd jobs for Jim in the garage the way he used to when he was a kid.

One evening after Newyear's Charley went over to the Elks Ball in Minneapolis with a couple of fellows he knew. The big hall was full of noise and paper lanterns. He was cruising around threading his way between groups of people waiting for the next dance when he found himself looking into a thin face and blue eyes he knew. It was too late to make out he hadn't seen her. 'Hello, Emiscah,' he said, keeping his voice as casual as he could.

'Charley . . . my God.' He was afraid for a minute that she was going to faint.

'Let's dance,' he said.

She felt limp in his arms. They danced awhile without saying anything. She had too much rouge on her cheeks and he didn't like the perfume she had on. After the dance they sat in a corner and talked. She wasn't married yet. She worked in a departmentstore. No, she didn't live at home any more, she lived in a flat with a girlfriend. He must come up. It would be like old times. He must give her his phone number. She supposed things seemed pretty tame to him now after all those French girls. And imagine him getting a commission, the Andersons sure were going up in the world, she guessed they'd be forgetting their old friends. Emiscah's voice had gotten screechy and she had a way he didn't like of putting her hand on his knee.

As soon as he could Charley said he had a headache and had to go home. He wouldn't wait for the guys he'd come with. The evening was ruined for him anyway, he was thinking. He rode back all alone on the interurban trolley. It was cold as blazes. It was about time he got the hell out of this dump. He really did have a splitting headache and chills.

Next morning he was down with the flu and had to stay in bed. It was almost a relief. Hedwig brought him stacks of detective stories and Aunt Hartmann fussed over him and brought him toddies and eggflips, and all he had to do was lie there and read.

First thing he did when he got on his feet was to go over to the hospital. Ma had had another operation and hadn't come out of it very well. The room was darkened and she didn't remember when she'd seen him last. She seemed to think she was home in Fargo and that he'd just come back from his trip south. She held tight to his hand and kept saying, 'My son that was lost hath been returned to me . . thank God for my boy.' It took the strength out of him, so he had to sit down for a second in a wicker chair in the corridor when he left her.

A nurse came up to him and stood beside him fidgeting with a paper and pencil. He looked up at her, she had pink cheeks and pretty dark eyelashes. 'You mustn't let it get you,' she said.

He grinned. 'Oh, I'm all right. . . . I just got out of bed from a touch of flu, it sure pulls down your strength.'

'I hear you were an aviator,' she said. 'I had a brother in the Royal Flying Corps. We're Canadians.'

'Those were great boys,' said Charley. He wondered if he could date her up, but then he thought of Ma. 'Tell me honestly what you think, please do.'

'Well, it's against the rules, but judging from other cases I've seen her chances are not very good.'

'I thought so.'

He got to his feet. 'You're a peach, do you know it?'

Her face got red from the starched cap to the white collar of her uniform. She wrinkled up her forehead and her voice got very chilly. 'In a case like that it's better to have it happen quickly.'

Charley felt a lump rise in his throat. 'Oh, I know.'

'Well, goodbye, Lieutenant, I've got to go about my business.'

'Gee, thanks a lot,' said Charley.

When he got out in the air he kept remembering her pretty face and her nice lips.

One slushy morning of thaw in early March, Charley was

taking a scorched gasket out of a Buick when the garage helper came and said they wanted him on the phone from the hospital. A cold voice said Mrs Anderson was sinking fast and the family better be notified. Charley got out of his overalls and went to call Hedwig. Jim was out, so they took one of the cars out of the garage. Charley had forgotten to wash his hands and they were black with grease and carbon. Hedwig found him a rag to wipe them off with. 'Someday, Hedwig,' he said, 'I'm going to get me a clean job in a draftin' room.'

'Well, Jim wanted you to be his salesman,' Hedwig snapped crossly. 'I don't see how you're going to get anywheres if you turn down every opportunity.'

'Well, maybe there's opportunities I won't turn down.'

'I'd like to know where you're going to get 'em except with us,' she said.

Charley didn't answer. Neither of them said anything more in the long drive across town. When they got to the hospital, they found that Ma had sunk into a coma. Two days later she died.

At the funeral, about halfway through the service, Charley felt the tears coming. He went out and locked himself in the toilet at the garage and sat down on the seat and cried like a child. When they came back from the cemetery, he was in a black mood and wouldn't let anybody speak to him. After supper, when he found Jim and Hedwig sitting at the dining-room table figuring out with pencil and paper how much it had cost them, he blew up, and said he'd pay every damn cent of it and they wouldn't have to worry about his staying around the goddam house either. He went out slamming the door after him and ran upstairs and threw himself on his bed. He lay there a long time in his uniform without undressing, staring at the ceiling and hearing mealy voices saying, deceased, bereavement, hereafter.

The day after the funeral Emiscah called up. She said she was so sorry about his mother's death and wouldn't he come around to see her some evening? Before he knew what he was doing, he'd said he'd come. He felt blue and lonely and he had to talk to somebody besides Jim and Hedwig. That evening he drove over to see her. She was alone. He didn't like the cheap gimcracky look her apartment had. He took her out to the movies and she said did he remember the time they went to see *The Birth of a Nation* together. He said he didn't, though he remembered all right. He could see that she wanted to start things up with him again.

Driving back to her place, she let her head drop on his shoulder. When he stopped the car in front of where she lived, he looked down and saw that she was crying. 'Charley, won't you give me a little kiss for old times?' she whispered. He kissed her. When she said would he come up, he stammered that he had to be home early. She kept saying, 'Oh, come ahead. I won't eat you, Charley,' and finally he went up with her, though it was the last thing he'd intended to do.

She made them cocoa on her gasburner and told him how unhappy she was, it was so tiring being on your feet all day behind the counter and the women who came to buy things were so mean to you, and the floorwalkers were always pinching your seat and expecting you to cuddlecooty with them in the fittingbooths. Some day she was going to turn on the gas. It made Charley feel bad having her talk like that and he had to pet her a little to make her stop crying. Then he got hot and had to make love to her. When he left he promised to call her up next week.

Next morning he got a letter that she must have written right after he left, saying that she'd never loved anybody but him. That night after supper he tried to write her that he didn't want to marry anybody and least of all her; he couldn't get it worded right, so he didn't write at all. When she called up next day, he said he was very busy and that he'd have to go up into North Dakota to see about some property his mother had left. He didn't like the way she said, 'Of course I understand. I'll call you up when you get back, dear.'

Hedwig began to ask who that woman was who was calling him up all the time, and Jim said, 'Look out for the women, Charley. If they think you've got anything they'll hold on to you like a leech.'

'Yessir,' said old man Vogel, 'it's not like ven you're in the army yet and can say goodbye, mein schatz, I'm off to the vars; now they can find out vere you live.'

'You needn't worry,' growled Charley. 'I won't stay put.'

The day they went over to the lawyer's office to read Ma's will, Jim and Hedwig dressed up fit to kill. It made Charley sore to see them, Hedwig in a new black tailored dress with a little lace at the throat and Jim dressed up like an undertaker in the suit he'd bought for the funeral. The lawyer was a small elderly German Jew with white hair brushed carefully over the big baldspot on the top of his head and goldrimmed pincenez on his thin nose. He was waiting for them when they came into the office. He got up smiling solemnly behind his desk littered with blue bound documents and made a little bow. Then he sat down beaming at them with his elbows among the papers, gently rubbing the tips of his fingers together. Nobody spoke for a moment. Jim coughed behind his hand like in church.

'Now let me see,' said Mr Goldberg in a gentlesweet voice with a slight accent like an actor's. 'Oughtn't there to be more of you?'

Jim spoke up. 'Esther and Ruth couldn't come. They both live on the coast. . . . I've got their power of attorneys. Ruth had her husband sign hers too, in case there might be any realestate.'

Mr Goldberg made a little clucking noise with his tongue. 'Too bad. I'd rather have all parties present. . . . But in this case there will be no difficulty, I trust. Mr James A. Anderson is named sole executor. Of course you understand that in a case like this the aim of all parties is to avoid taking the will to probate. That saves trouble and expense. There is no need of it when one of the legatees is named executor. . . . I shall proceed to read the will.'

Mr Goldberg must have drafted it himself because he sure seemed to enjoy reading it. Except for a legacy of one thousand dollars to Lizzie Green who had run Ma's boardinghouse up in Fargo, all the estate, real and personal, the lots in Fargo, the Liberty Bonds and the fifteenhundred dollar savingsaccount were left to the children jointly to be administered by James A. Anderson, sole executor, and eventually divided as they should agree among themselves.

'Now are there any questions and suggestions?' asked Mr Goldberg genially.

Charley couldn't help seeing that Jim felt pretty good about it.

'It has been suggested,' went on Mr Goldberg's even voice that melted blandly among the documents like butter on a hot biscuit, 'that Mr Charles Anderson, who I understand is leaving soon for the East, would be willing to sign a power of attorney similar to those signed by his sisters. . . . The understanding is that the money will be invested in a mortgage on the Anderson Motor Sales Company.'

Charley felt himself go cold all over. Jim and Hedwig were

looking at him anxiously. 'I don't understand the legal talk,' he said, 'but what I want to do is get mine as soon as possible. . . . I have a proposition in the East I want to put some money in.'

Jim's thin lower lip began to tremble. 'You'd better not be a damn fool, Charley. I know more about business than you do.'

'About your business maybe, but not about mine.'

Hedwig, who'd been looking at Charley like she could kill him, began to butt in: 'Now, Charley, you let Jim do what he thinks best. He just wants to do what's best for all of us.'

'Aw, shut your face,' said Charley.

Jim jumped to his feet. 'Look here, kid, you can't talk to my wife in that tone of voice.'

'My friends, my dear friends,' the lawyer crooned, rubbing his fingers together till it looked like they'd smoke, 'we mustn't let ourselves be carried away, must we, not on a solemn occasion like this. . . . What we want is a quiet fireside chat . . . the friendly atmosphere of the home. . . .'

Charley let out a snorting laugh. 'That's what it's always been like in my home,' he said halfaloud and turned his back on them to look out of the window over white roofs and icicle-hung firescapes. The snow, thawing on the shingle roof of a frame house next door, was steaming in the early afternoon sun. Beyond it he could see blacklots deep in drifts and a piece of clean asphalt street where cars shuttled back and forth.

'Look here, Charley, snap out of it.' Jim's voice behind him took on a pleading singsong tone. 'You know the proposition Ford has put up to his dealers. . . . It's sink or swim for me. . . . But as an investment it's the chance of a lifetime. . . . The cars are there. . . . You can't lose, even if the company folds up.'

Charley turned around. 'Jim,' he said mildly, 'I don't want to argue about it. . . . I want to get my share of what Ma left in cash as soon as you and Mr Goldberg can fix it up. . . . I got somethin' about airplane motors that'll make any old Ford agency look like thirty cents.'

'But I want to put Ma's money in on a sure thing. The Ford car is the safest investment in the world, isn't that so, Mr Goldberg?'

'You certainly see them everywhere. Perhaps the young man would wait and think things over a little. . . . I can make the preliminary steps . . .'

'Preliminary nothing. I want to get what I can out right now. If you can't do it I'll go and get another lawyer who will.'

Charley picked up his hat and coat and walked out.

Next morning Charley turned up at breakfast in his overalls as usual. Jim told him he didn't want him doing any work in his business, seeing the way he felt about it. Charley went back upstairs to his room and lay down on the bed. When Hedwig came in to make it up she said, 'Oh, are you still here?' and went out slamming the door after her. He could hear her slamming and banging things around the house as she and Aunt Hartmann did the housework.

About the middle of the morning, Charley went down to where Jim sat worrying over his books at the desk in the office. 'Jim, I want to talk to you.'

Jim took off his glasses and looked up at him. 'Well, what's on your mind?' he asked, cutting off his words the way he had.

Charley said he'd sign a power of attorney for Jim if he'd lend him five hundred dollars right away. Then maybe later, if the airplane proposition looked good, he'd let Jim in on it. Jim made a sour face at that. 'All right,' said Charley. 'Make it four hundred. I got to get out of this dump.'

Jim rose to his feet slowly. He was so pale Charley thought he must be sick. 'Well, if you can't get it into your head what I'm up against . . . you can't and to hell with you. . . . All right, you and me are through. . . . Hedwig will have to borrow it at the bank in her name. . . . I'm up to my neck.'

'Fix it any way you like,' said Charley. 'I got to get out of here.'

It was lucky the phone rang when it did or Charley and Jim would have taken a poke at each other. Charley answered it. It was Emiscah. She said she'd been over in St Paul and had seen him on the street yesterday and that he'd just said he was going to be out of town to give her the air, and he had to come over tonight or she didn't know what she'd do, he wouldn't want her to kill herself, would he? He got all balled up, what with rowing with Jim and everything and ended by telling her he'd come. By the time he was through talking, Jim had walked into the salesroom and was chinning with a customer, all smiles.

Going over on the trolley he decided he'd tell her he'd got married to a French girl during the war, but when he got up to her flat he didn't know what to say, she looked so thin and pale. He took her out to a dancehall. It made him feel bad how happy she acted, as if everything was fixed up again between them. When he left her he made a date for the next week.

Before that day came, he was off for Chi. He didn't begin to feel really good until he'd transferred acrosstown and was on the New York train. He had a letter in his pocket from Joe Askew telling him Joe would be in town to meet him. He had what was left of the three hundred berries Hedwig coughed up after deducting his board and lodging all winter at ten dollars a week. But on the New York train he stopped thinking about all that and about Emiscah and the mean time he'd had and let himself think about New York and airplane motors and Doris Humphries.

When he woke up in the morning in the lower berth, he pushed up the shade and looked out; the train was going through the Pennsylvania hills, the fields were freshplowed, some of the trees had a little fuzz of green on them. In a farmyard a flock of yellow chickens were picking around under a peartree in bloom. 'By God,' he said aloud, 'I'm through with the sticks.'

# Newsreel 48

truly the Steel Corporation stands forth as a corporate colossus both physically and financially

*Now the folks in Georgia they done gone wild*
*Over that brand new dancin' style*
*Called      Shake      That      Thing*

CARBARNS BLAZE

GYPSY ARRESTED FOR TELLING THE TRUTH

Horsewhipping Hastens Wedding

that strength has long since become almost a truism as steel's expanding career progressed, yet the dimensions thereof need at times to be freshly measured to be caught in proper perspective

DAZED BY MAINE DEMOCRATS CRY FOR MONEY

*shake that thing*

Woman of Mystery Tries Suicide in Park Lake

*shake that thing*

OLIVE THOMAS DEAD FROM POISON

LETTER SAID GET OUT OF WALL STREET

BOMB WAGON TRACED TO JERSEY

*Shake      That      Thing*

Writer of Warnings Arrives

BODY FOUND LASHED TO BICYCLE

FIND BOMB CLOCKWORK

## Tin Lizzie

'*Mr Ford the automobileer,*' the featurewriter wrote in 1900,

'*Mr Ford the automobileer began by giving his steed three or four sharp jerks with the lever at the righthand side of the seat; that is, he pulled the lever up and down sharply in order, as he said, to mix air with gasoline and drive the charge into the exploding cylinder. . . . Mr Ford slipped a small electric switch handle and there followed a puff, puff, puff. . . . The puffing of the machine assumed a higher key. . . . She was flying along about eight miles an hour. The ruts in the road were deep, but the machine certainly went with a dreamlike smoothness. There was none of the bumping common even to a steamer. . . . By this time the boulevard had been reached, and the automobileer, letting a lever fall a little, let her out. Whiz! She picked up speed with infinite rapidity. As she ran on there was a clattering behind, the new noise of the automobile.*'

For twenty years or more,

ever since he'd left his father's farm when he was sixteen to get a job in a Detroit machineshop, Henry Ford had been nuts about machinery. First it was watches, then he designed a steamtractor, then he built a horseless carriage with an engine adapted from the Otto gasengine he'd read about in *The World of Science*, then a mechanical buggy with a onecylinder fourcycle motor, that would run forward but not back;

at last, in ninetyeight, he felt he was far enough along to risk throwing up his job with the Detroit Edison Company, where he'd worked his way up from night fireman to chief engineer, to put all his time into working on a new gasoline engine,

(in the late eighties he'd met Edison at a meeting of electriclight employees in Atlantic City. He'd gone up to Edison after Edison had delivered an address and asked him if he thought gasoline was practical as a motor fuel. Edison had said yes. If Edison said it, it was true. Edison was the great admiration of Henry Ford's life);

and in driving his mechanical buggy, sitting there at the lever jauntily dressed in a tightbuttoned jacket and a high collar and a derby hat, back and forth over the level illpaved streets of Detroit,

scaring the big brewery horses and the skinny trotting horses and the sleekrumped pacers with the motor's loud explosions,

looking for men scatterbrained enough to invest money in a factory for building automobiles.

He was the eldest son of an Irish immigrant who during the Civil War had married the daughter of a prosperous Pennsylvania Dutch farmer and settled down to farming near Dearborn in Wayne County, Michigan;

like plenty of other Americans, young Henry grew up hating the endless sogging through the mud about the chores, the hauling and pitching manure, the kerosene lamps to clean, the irk and sweat and solitude of the farm.

He was a slender, active youngster, a good skater, clever with his hands; what he liked was to tend the machinery and let the others do the heavy work. His mother had told him not to drink, smoke, gamble, or get into debt, and he never did.

When he was in his early twenties his father tried to get him back from Detroit, where he was working as mechanic and repairman for the Drydock Engine Company that built engines for steamboats, by giving him forty acres of land.

Young Henry built himself an uptodate square white dwellinghouse with a false mansard roof and married and settled down on the farm,

but he let the hired men do the farming;

he bought himself a buzzsaw and rented a stationary engine and cut the timber off the woodlots.

He was a thrifty young man who never drank or smoked or gambled or coveted his neighbor's wife, but he couldn't stand living on the farm.

He moved to Detroit, and in the brick barn behind his house tinkered for years in his spare time with a mechanical buggy that would be light enough to run over the clayey wagonroads of Wayne County, Michigan.

By 1900 he had a practicable car to promote.

He was forty years old before the Ford Motor Company was started and production began to move.

Speed was the first thing the early automobile manufacturers went after. Races advertised the makes of cars.

Henry Ford himself hung up several records at the track at Grosse Pointe and on the ice on Lake St Clair. In his .999 he did the mile in thirtynine and fourfifths seconds.

But it had always been his custom to hire others to do the heavy work. The speed he was busy with was speed in production, the records, records in efficient output. He hired Barney Oldfield, a stunt bicyclerider from Salt Lake City, to do the racing for him.

Henry Ford had ideas about other things than the designing of motors, carburetors, magnetos, jigs and fixtures, punches and dies; he had ideas about sales;

that the big money was in economical quantity production, quick turnover, cheap interchangeable easilyreplaced standardized parts;

it wasn't until 1909, after years of arguing with his partners, that Ford put out the first Model T.

Henry Ford was right.

That season he sold more than ten thousand tin lizzies, ten years later he was selling almost a million a year.

In these years the Taylor Plan was stirring up plantmanagers and manufacturers all over the country. Efficiency was the word. The same ingenuity that went into improving the performance of a machine could go into improving the performance of the workmen producing the machine.

In 1913 they established the assemblyline at Ford's. That season the profits were something like twentyfive million dollars, but they had trouble in keeping the men on the job, machinists didn't seem to like it at Ford's.

Henry Ford had ideas about other things than production.

He was the largest automobile manufacturer in the world; he paid high wages; maybe if the steady workers thought they were getting a cut (a very small cut) in the profits, it would give trained men an inducement to stick to their jobs,

wellpaid workers might save enough money to buy a tin lizzie; the first day Ford's announced that cleancut properly married American workers who wanted jobs had a chance to make five bucks a day (of course it turned out that there were strings to it; always there were strings to it)

such an enormous crowd waited outside the Highland Park plant all through the zero January night

that there was a riot when the gates were opened; cops broke heads, jobhunters threw bricks; property, Henry Ford's own property, was destroyed. The company dicks had to turn on the firehose to beat back the crowd.

The American Plan; automotive prosperity seeping down from above; it turned out there were strings to it.

But that five dollars a day

paid to good, clean American workmen

who didn't drink or smoke cigarettes or read or think,

and who didn't commit adultery

and whose wives didn't take in boarders,

made America once more the Yukon of the sweated workers of the world;

made all the tin lizzies and the automotive age, and incidentally,

made Henry Ford the automobileer, the admirer of Edison, the birdlover,

the great American of his time.

But Henry Ford had ideas about other things besides assemblylines and the livinghabits of his employees. He was full of ideas. Instead of going to the city to make his fortune, here was a country boy who'd made his fortune by bringing the city out to the farm. The precepts he'd learned out of McGuffey's Reader, his mother's prejudices and preconceptions, he had preserved clean and unworn as freshprinted bills in the safe in a bank.

He wanted people to know about his ideas, so he bought the *Dearborn Independent* and started a campaign against cigarettesmoking.

When war broke out in Europe, he had ideas about that too. (Suspicion of armymen and soldiering were part of the Mid-West farm tradition, like thrift, stickativeness, temperance, and sharp practice in money matters.) Any intelligent American mechanic could see that if the Europeans hadn't been a lot of ignorant underpaid foreigners who drank, smoked, were loose about women, and wasteful in their methods of production, the war could never have happened.

When Rosika Schwimmer broke through the stockade of secretaries and servicemen who surrounded Henry Ford and suggested to him that he could stop the war, he said sure they'd hire a ship and go over and get the boys out of the trenches by Christmas.

He hired a steamboat, the *Oscar II,* and filled it up with pacifists and socialworkers,

    to go over to explain to the princelings of Europe
    that what they were doing was vicious and silly.

It wasn't his fault that Poor Richard's commonsense no longer rules the world and that most of the pacifists were nuts,
    goofy with headlines.

When William Jennings Bryan went over to Hoboken to see him off, somebody handed William Jennings Bryan a squirrel in a cage; William Jennings Bryan made a speech with the squirrel under his arm. Henry Ford threw American Beauty roses to the crowd. The band played *I Didn't Raise My Boy to Be a Soldier.* Practical jokers let loose more squirrels. An eloping couple was married by a platoon of ministers in the saloon, and Mr Zero, the flophouse humanitarian, who reached the dock too late to sail,
    dove into the North River and swam after the boat.

The *Oscar II* was described as a floating Chautauqua; Henry Ford said it felt like a Middle-Western village, but by the time they reached Christiansand in Norway, the reporters had kidded him so that he had gotten cold feet and gone to bed. The world was too crazy outside of Wayne County, Michigan. Mrs Ford and the management sent an Episcopal dean after him who brought him home under wraps,
    and the pacifists had to speechify without him.

Two years later Ford's was manufacturing munitions, Eagle boats; Henry Ford was planning oneman tanks, and oneman submarines like the one tried out in the Revolutionary War. He announced to the press that he'd turn over his war profits to the government,
    but there's no record that he ever did.
    One thing he brought back from his trip
    was the Protocols of the Elders of Zion.

He started a campaign to enlighten the world in the *Dearborn Independent*; the Jews were why the world wasn't like Wayne County, Michigan, in the old horse-and-buggy days;

    the Jews had started the war, Bolshevism, Darwinism, Marxism, Nietzsche, short skirts and lipstick. They were behind Wall Street and the international bankers, and the whiteslave traffic and the movies and the Supreme Court and ragtime and the illegal liquor business.

Henry Ford denounced the Jews and ran for Senator and sued the *Chicago Tribune* for libel,
and was the laughingstock of the kept metropolitan press;
but when the metropolitan bankers tried to horn in on his business
he thoroughly outsmarted them.

In 1918 he had borrowed on notes to buy out his minority stockholders for the picayune sum of seventyfive million dollars.

In February, 1920, he needed cash to pay off some of these notes that were coming due. A banker is supposed to have called on him and offered him every facility if the bankers' representative could be made a member of the board of directors. Henry Ford handed the banker his hat,
and went about raising the money in his own way:
he shipped every car and part he had in his plant to his dealers and demanded immediate cash payment. Let the other fellow do the borrowing had always been a cardinal principle. He shut down production and canceled all orders from the supplyfirms. Many dealers were ruined, many supplyfirms failed, but when he reopened his plant,
he owned it absolutely,
the way a man owns an unmortgaged farm with the taxes paid up.

In 1922 there started the Ford boom for President (high wages, waterpower, industry scattered to the small towns) that was skillfully pricked behind the scenes
by another crackerbarrel philosopher,
Calvin Coolidge;
but in 1922 Henry Ford sold one million three hundred and thirtytwo thousand two hundred and nine tin lizzies; he was the richest man in the world.

Good roads had followed the narrow ruts made in the mud by the Model T. The great automotive boom was on. At Ford's production was improving all the time; less waste, more spotters, strawbosses, stoolpigeons (fifteen minutes for lunch, three minutes to go to the toilet, the Taylorized speedup everywhere, reachunder, adjustwasher, screwdown bolt, shove in cotterpin, reachunder, adjustwasher, screwdown bolt, reachunderadjustscrewdownreachunderadjust, until every ounce of life was sucked off into production and at night the workmen went home gray shaking husks).

Ford owned every detail of the process from the ore in

the hills until the car rolled off the end of the assemblyline under its own power; the plants were rationalized to the last tenthousandth of an inch as measured by the Johansen scale;

in 1926 the production cycle was reduced to eightyone hours from the ore in the mine to the finished salable car proceeding under its own power,

but the Model T was obsolete.

New Era prosperity and the American Plan
(there were strings to it, always there were strings to it)
had killed Tin Lizzie.
Ford's was just one of many automobile plants.
When the stockmarket bubble burst,
Mr Ford the crackerbarrel philosopher said jubilantly,
'I told you so.
Serves you right for gambling and getting in debt.
The country is sound.'
But when the country on cracked shoes, in frayed trousers, belts tightened over hollow bellies,
idle hands cracked and chapped with the cold of that coldest March day of 1932,
started marching from Detroit to Dearborn, asking for work and the American Plan, all they could think of at Ford's was machineguns.
The country was sound, but they mowed the marchers down.
They shot four of them dead.

Henry Ford as an old man
is a passionate antiquarian
(lives besieged on his father's farm embedded in an estate of thousands of millionaire acres, protected by an army of servicemen, secretaries, secret agents, dicks under orders of an English exprizefighter,
always afraid of the feet in broken shoes on the roads, afraid the gangs will kidnap his grandchildren,
that a crank will shoot him,
that Change and the idle hands out of work will break through the gates and the high fences;
protected by a private army against
the new America of starved children and hollow bellies and cracked shoes stamping on souplines,
that has swallowed up the old thrifty farmlands

of Wayne County, Michigan,
as if they had never been).
Henry Ford as an old man
is a passionate antiquarian.

He rebuilt his father's farmhouse and put it back exactly
in the state he remembered it in as a boy. He built a village
of museums for buggies, sleighs, coaches, old plows, water-
wheels, obsolete models of motorcars. He scoured the country
for fiddlers to play oldfashioned squaredances.

Even old taverns he bought and put back into their
original shape, as well as Thomas Edison's early laboratories.

When he bought the Wayside Inn near Sudbury, Massachusetts, he had the new highway where the newmodel cars
roared and slithered and hissed oilily past (*the new noise of the
automobile*)

moved away from the door,
put back the old bad road,
so that everything might be
the way it used to be,
in the days of horses and buggies.

# Newsreel 49

*Jack o' Diamonds Jack o' Diamonds*
*You rob my pocket     of silver and gold*

## WITNESSES OF MYSTERY IN SLUSH PROBE

## PHILADELPHIAN BEATEN TO DEATH IN HIS ROOM

the men who the workers had been told a short year before were fighting their battle for democracy upon the bloodstained fields of France and whom they had been urged to support by giving the last of their strength to the work of production – these men were coming to teach them democracy and with them came their instruments of murder, their automatic rifles, their machineguns, their cannon that could clear a street two miles long in a few minutes and the helmets that the workers of Gary had produced

*Yes we have no bananas*
*We have no bananas today*

## TRACTION RING KILLS BUS BILL

## DRUNKEN TROOPS IN SKIRTS DANCE AS HOUSES BURN

## GIRL SUICIDE WAS FRIEND OF OLIVE THOMAS

## KILLS SELF DESPITE WIFE WHO GOES MAD

## SEEKS FACTS OF HUNT FOR CASH IN THE EAST

the business consists in large part of financing manufacturers and merchants by purchasing evidences of indebtedness arising from the sale of a large variety of naturally marketed products such as automobiles, electrical appliances, machinery

## *Charley Anderson*

'Misser Andson Misser Andson, telegram for Misser Andson.'
Charley held out his hand for the telegram, and standing in the
swaying aisle read the strips of letters pasted on the paper:

DOWN WITH FLU    WIRE ME ADDRESS    SEE YOU
NEXT WEEK    JOE

'A hell of a note,' he kept saying to himself as he wormed
his way back to his seat past women closing up their bags,
a grayhaired man getting into his overcoat, the porter loaded
with suitcases. 'A hell of a note.' The train was already slowing
down for the Grand Central.

It was quiet on the gray underground platform when he
stepped out of the stuffy Pullman and took his bag from the
porter, lonelylooking. He walked up the incline swinging his
heavy suitcase. The train had given him a headache. The
station was so big it didn't have the crowded look he'd remembered New York had. Through the thick glass of the huge
arched windows he could see rain streaking the buildings
opposite. Roaming round the station, not knowing which way
to go, he found himself looking in the window of a lunchroom.

He went in and sat down. The waitress was a little dark
sourfaced girl with rings under her eyes. It was a muggy sort
of day, the smell of soap from the dishwashing and of hot
grease from the kitchen hung in streaks in the air. When the
waitress leaned over to set the place for him, he got a whiff of
damp underclothes and armpits and talcumpowder. He looked
up at her and tried to get a smile out of her. When she turned
to go get him some tomatosoup, he watched her square bottom
moving back and forth under her black dress. There was something heavy and lecherous about the rainy eastern day.

He spooned soup into his mouth without tasting it. Before
he'd finished, he got up and went to the phonebooth. He didn't
have to look up her number. Waiting for the call, he was so
nervous the sweat ran down behind his ears. When a woman's
voice answered, his voice dried up way down in his throat.
Finally he got it out. 'I want to speak to Miss Humphries,
please. . . . Tell her it's Charley Anderson . . . Lieutenant
Anderson.' He was still trying to clear his throat when her

voice came in an intimate caressing singsong. Of course she remembered him, her voice said, too sweet of him to call her up, of course they must see each other all the time, how thrilling, she'd just love to, but she was going out of t wn for the weekend, yes, a long weekend. But wouldn't he call her up next week, no, towards the end of the week? She'd just adore to see him.

When he went back to his table the waitress was fussing around it.

'Didn't you like your soup?' she asked him.

'Check. . . . Had to make some phonecalls.'

'Oh, phonecalls,' she said in a kidding voice. This time it was the waitress who was trying to get a smile out of him.

'Let's have a piece of pie and a cup of coffee,' he said, keeping his eyes on the bill-of-fare.

'They got lovely lemonmeringue pie,' the waitress said, with a kind of sigh that made him laugh.

He looked up at her laughing feeling horny and outafterit again: 'All right, sweetheart, make it lemonmeringue.'

When he'd eaten the pie, he paid his check and went back into the phonebooth. Some woman had been in there leaving a strong reek of perfume. He called up the Century Club to see if Ollie Taylor was in town. They said he was in Europe; then he called up the Johnsons; they were the only people left he knew. Eveline Johnson's voice had a deep muffled sound over the phone. When he told her his name, she laughed and said, 'Why, of course we'd love to see you. Come down to dinner tonight; we'll introduce you to the new baby.'

When he got out of the subway at Astor Place, it wasn't time to go to dinner yet. He asked the newsvendor which way Fifth Avenue was and walked up and down the quiet redbrick blocks. He felt stuffy from the movie he'd killed the afternoon in. When he looked at his watch, it was only halfpast six. He wasn't invited to the Johnsons' till seven. He'd already passed the house three times when he decided to go up the steps. Their names were scrawled out, Paul Johnson – Eveline Hutchins, on a card above the bell. He rang the bell and stood fidgeting with his necktie while he waited. Nobody answered. He was wondering if he ought to ring again when Paul Johnson came briskly down the street from Fifth Avenue with his hat on the back of his head, whistling as he walked.

'Why, hello, Anderson, where did you come from?' he asked in an embarrassed voice. He had several bags of groceries that he had to pile on his left arm before he could shake hands.

'Guess I ought to congratulate you,' said Charley.

Paul looked at him blankly for a moment; then he blushed. 'Of course . . . the son and heir. . . . Oh, well, it's a hostage to fortune, that's what they say. . . .'

Paul let him into a large bare oldfashioned room with flowing purple curtains in the windows. 'Just sit down for a minute. I'll see what Eveline's up to.' He pointed to a horsehair sofa and went through the sliding doors into a back room.

He came back immediately, carefully pulling the door to behind him. 'Why, that's great. Eveline says you're goin' to have supper with us. She said you just came back from out there. How'd things seem out there? I wouldn't go back if they paid me now. New York's a great life if you don't weaken. . . . Here, I'll show you where you can clean up. . . . Eveline's invited a whole mess of people to supper. I'll have to run around to the butcher's. . . . Want to wash up?'

The bathroom was steamy and smelt of bathsalts. Somebody had just taken a bath there. Babyclothes hung to dry over the tub. A red douchebag hung behind the door and over it a yellow lace négligée of some kind. It made Charley feel funny to be in there. When he'd dried his hands he sniffed them, and the perfume of the soap filled his head.

When he came out of the door, he found Mrs Johnson leaning against the white marble mantel with a yellowbacked French novel in her hand. She had on a long lacy gown with puff sleeves and wore tortoiseshell readingglasses. She took off the glasses and tucked them into the book and stood holding out her hand.

'I'm so glad you could come. I don't go out much yet, so I don't get to see anybody unless they come to see me.'

'Mighty nice of you to ask me. I been out in the sticks. I tell you it makes you feel good to see folks from the other side. . . . This is the nearest thing to Paree I've seen for some time.'

She laughed; he remembered her laugh from the boat. The way he felt like kissing her made him fidgety. He lit a cigarette.

'Do you mind not smoking? For some reason tobaccosmoke makes me feel sick ever since before I had the baby, so I don't let anybody smoke. Isn't it horrid of me?'

Charley blushed and threw his cigarette in the grate. He began to walk back and forth in the tall narrow room.

'Hadn't we better sit down?' she said with her slow irritating smile. 'What are you up to in New York?'

'Got me a job. I got plans. . . . Say, how's the baby? I'd like to see it.'

'All right, when he wakes up I'll introduce you. You can be one of his uncles. I've got to do something about supper now. Doesn't it seem strange us all being in New York?'

'I bet this town's a hard nut to crack.'

She went into the back room through the sliding doors and soon a smell of sizzling butter began to seep through them. Charley caught himself just at the point of lighting another cigarette, then roamed round the room, looking at the oldfashioned furniture, the three white lilies in a vase, the shelves of French books, until Paul, red in the face and sweating, passed through with more groceries and told him he'd shake up a drink.

Charley sat down on the couch and stretched out his legs. It was quiet in the highceilinged room. There was something cozy about the light rustle and clatter the Johnsons made moving around behind the sliding doors, the Frenchy smell of supper cooking. Paul came back with a tray piled with plates and glasses and a demijohn of wine. He laid a loaf of frenchbread on the marbletopped table and a plate of tunafish and a cheese. 'I'm sorry I haven't got anything to make a cocktail with. . . . I didn't get out of the office till late. . . . All we've got's this dago wine.'

'Check. . . . I'm keepin' away from that stuff a little. . . . Too much on my mind.'

'Are you round town looking for a job?'

'Feller goin' in on a proposition with me. You remember Joe Askew on the boat? Great, boy, wasn't he? The trouble is the damn fool's laid up with the flu and that leaves me high and dry until he gets down here.'

'Things are sure tighter than I expected. . . . My old man got me into a grainbroker's office over in Jersey City . . . just to tide me over. But gosh, I don't want to wear out a desk all my life. I wouldn'ta done it if it hadn't been for the little stranger.'

'Well, we've got something that'll be worth money if we ever get the kale to put in to develop it.'

Eveline opened the sliding doors and brought in a bowl of salad. Paul had started to talk about the grain business, but he shut his mouth and waited for her to speak.

'It's curious,' she said. 'After the war New York. . . . Nobody can keep away from it.'

A baby's thin squalling followed her out of the back room. 'That's his messcall,' said Paul.

'If you really want to see him,' said Eveline, 'come along now, but I should think it would be just too boring to look at other people's babies.'

'I'd like to,' said Charley. 'Haven't got any of my own to look at.'

'How are you so sure?' said Eveline, with a slow teasing smile. Charley got red and laughed.

They stood round the pink crib with their wineglasses in their hands. Charley found himself looking down into a toothless pink face and two little pudgy hands grabbing the air.

'I suppose I ought to say it looks like Daddy,' he said.

'The little darling looks more like our Darwinian ancestor,' said Eveline coldly. 'When I first saw him I cried and cried. Oh, I hope he grows a chin.'

Charley caught himself looking out of the corner of his eye at Paul's chin that wasn't so very prominent either. 'He's a cheerful little rascal,' he said.

Eveline brought the baby a bottle from the kitchenette next the bathroom, then they went into the other room.

'This layout sure makes me feel envious,' Charley was saying when he caught Eveline Johnson's eye. She shrugged her shoulders. 'You two and the baby all nicely set with a place to live and a glass of wine and everything. . . . Makes me feel the war's over. . . . What I've got to do is crack down an' get to work.'

'Don't worry,' said Paul. 'It'll happen soon enough.'

'Well, I wish people would come. The casserole's all ready,' said Eveline. 'Charles Edward Holden is coming. . . . He's always late.'

'He said maybe he'd come,' said Paul. 'Here's Al now. That's his knock.'

A lanky sallow individual came in the door from the street. Paul introduced him to Charley as his brother Al. The man looked at Charley with a peevish searching gray eye for a moment. 'Lieutenant Anderson . . . Say, we've met before someplace.'

'Were you over on the other side?'

The lanky man shook his head vigorously. 'No. . . . It must have been in New York. . . . I never forget a face.' Charley felt his face getting red.

A tall haggardfaced man named Stevens and a plump little girl came in. Charley didn't catch the girl's name. She had straight black bobbed hair. The man named Stevens paid no attention to anybody but Al Johnson. The little girl paid no attention to anybody but Stevens. 'Well, Al,' he said threateningly, 'have recent events changed your ideas any?'

'We've got to go slow, Don, we've got to go slow . . . we can't affront every decent human instinct. . . . We've got to stick close to the workingclass.'

'Oh, if you're all going to start about the workingclass, I think we'd better have supper and not wait for Holden,' said Eveline, getting to her feet. 'Don'll be so cross if he argues on an empty stomach.'

'Who's that? Charles Edward Holden?' asked Al Johnson with a tone of respect in his voice.

'Don't wait for him,' said Don Stevens. 'He's nothing but a bourgeois muckraker.'

Charley and Paul helped Eveline bring in another table that was all set in the bedroom. Charley managed to sit next to her. 'Gee, this is wonderful food. It all makes me think of old Paree,' he kept saying. 'My brother wanted me to go into a Ford agency with him out in the Twin Cities, but how can you keep them down on the farm after they've seen Paree?'

'But New York's the capital now.' It was teasing the way she leaned toward him when she spoke, the way her long eyes seemed to be all the time figuring out something about him.

'I hope you'll let me come around sometimes,' he said. 'It's goin' to be kinder hard sleddin' in New York till I get my feet on the ground.'

'Oh, I'm always here,' she said, 'and shall be till we can afford to get a reliable nurse for Jeremy. Poor Paul has to work late at the office half the time. . . . Oh, I wish we could all make a lot of money right away quick.'

Charley smiled grimly. 'Give the boys a chance. We ain't properly got the khaki off our skins yet.'

Charley couldn't keep up with the conversation very well, so he leaned back on the sofa looking at Eveline Johnson. Paul didn't say much either. After he'd brought in coffee he disappeared altogether. Eveline and the little girl at the head of the table both seemed to think Stevens was pretty wonderful, and Al Johnson, who sat next to Charley on the sofa, kept leaning across him to make a point with Eveline and shake his long forefinger. Part of the time it looked like Al Johnson and Stevens would take a poke at each other. What with not following their talk – after all, he wasn't onto the town yet – and the good food and the wine, Charley began to get sleepy. He finally had to get up to stretch his legs.

Nobody paid any attention to him, so he strolled into the kitchenette where he found Paul washing the dishes. 'Lemme help you wipe,' he said.

'Naw, I got a system,' said Paul. 'You see Eveline does all the cooking, so it's only fair for me to wash the dishes.'

'Say, won't those birds get in trouble if they talk like that?' Charley jerked his thumb in the direction of the front room.

'Don Stevens is a red, so he's a marked man anyway.'

'Mind you, I don't say they're wrong, but, Jesus, we got our livin's to make.'

'Al's on the *World*. They're pretty liberal down there.'

'Out our way a man can't open his face without stirrin' up a hornet'snest,' said Charley, laughing. 'They don't know the war's over.'

When the dishes were done, they went back to the front room.

Don Stevens strode up to Charley. 'Eveline says you are an aviator,' he said frowning. 'Tell us what aviators think about. Are they for the exploiting class or the workingclass?'

'That's a pretty big order,' drawled Charley. 'Most of the fellers I know are tryin' to get into the workin'class.'

The doorbell rang. Eveline looked up smiling. 'That's probably Charles Edward Holden,' said Al.

Paul opened the door.

'Hello, Dick,' said Eveline. 'Everybody thought you were Charles Edward Holden.

'Well, maybe I am,' said the nattilydressed young man with slightlybulging blue eyes who appeared in the doorway. 'I've been feeling a little odd all day.'

Eveline introduced the new guy by his military handle: 'Captain Savage, Lieutenant Anderson.'

'Humph,' said Stevens in the back of the room.

Charley noticed that Stevens and the young man who had just come in stared at each other without speaking. It was all getting very confusing. Eveline and the bobbedhaired girl began to make polite remarks to each other in chilly voices. Charley guessed it was about time for him to butt out. 'I've got to alley along, Mrs Johnson,' he said.

'Say, Anderson, wait for me a minute. I'll walk along the street with you,' Al Johnson called across the room at him.

Charley suddenly found himself looking right in Eveline's eyes. 'I sure enjoyed it,' he said.

'Come in to tea some afternoon,' she said.

'All right, I'll do that.' He squeezed her hand hard. While he was saying goodbye to the others, he heard Captain Savage and Eveline giggling together.

'I just came in to see how the other half lives,' he was saying. 'Eveline, you look too beautiful tonight.'

Charley felt good standing on the stoop in the spring evening. The city air had a cool rinsed smell after the rain. He was wondering if she . . . Well, you never can tell till you try.

Al Johnson came out behind him and took his arm. 'Say, Paul says you come from out home.'

'Sure,' said Charley. 'Don't you see the hayseed in my ears?'

'Gosh, when Eveline has two or more of her old beaux calling on her at once it's a bit heavy. . . . And she like to froze that poor little girl of Don's to death. . . . Say, how about you and me go have a drink of whiskey to take the taste of that damn red ink out of our mouths?'

'That 'ud be great,' said Charley.

They walked across Fifth Avenue and down the street until they got to a narrow black door. Al Johnson rang the bell and a man in shirtsleeves let them into a passage that smelt of toilets. They walked through that into a barroom.

'Well, that's more like it,' said Al Johnson. 'After all, I have only one night off a week.'

'It's like the good old days that never were,' said Charley.

They sat down at a small round table opposite the bar and ordered rye. Al Johnson suddenly waved his long forefinger across the table. 'I remember when it was I met you. It was the day war was declared. We were all drunk as coots down at Little Hungary.' Charley said jeez, he'd met a lot of people that night. 'Sure that's when it was,' said Al Johnson. 'I never forget a face,' and he called to the waiter to make it beer chasers.

They had several more ryes with beer chasers on the strength of old times. 'Why, New York's like any other dump,' Charley was saying, 'it's just a village.'

'Greenwich Village,' said Al Johnson.

They had a flock of whiskies on the strength of the good old times they'd had at Little Hungary. They didn't like it at the table any more, so they stood up at the bar. There were two pallid young men at the bar and a plump girl with stringy hair in a Bulgarian embroidered blouse. They were old friends of

Al Johnson's. 'An old newspaperman,' Al Johnson was saying, 'never forgets faces . . . or names.' He turned to Charley. 'Colonel, meet my very dear friends . . . Colonel . . . er . . .' Charley had put out his hand and was just about to say Anderson when Al Johnson came out with 'Charles Edward Holden, meet my artistical friends . . .'

Charley never got a chance to put a word in. The two young men started to explain the play they'd been to at the Washington Square Players. The girl had a turnedup nose and blue eyes with dark rings under them. The eyes looked up at him effusively while she shook his hand.

'Not really. . . . Oh, I've so wanted to meet you, Mr Holden. I read all your articles.'

'But I'm not really . . .' started Charley.

'Not really a colonel,' said the girl.

'Just a colonel for a night,' said Al with a wave of his hand and ordered some more whiskies.

'Oh, Mr Holden,' said the girl, who put her whiskey away like a trooper, 'isn't it wonderful that we should meet like this? . . . I thought you were much older and not so good-looking. Now, Mr Holden, I want you to tell me all about everything.'

'Better call me Charley.'

'My name's Bobbie . . . you call me Bobbie, won't you?'

'Check,' said Charley.

She drew him away from the bar a little. 'I was having a rotten time. . . . They are dear boys, but they won't talk about anything except how Philip drank iodine because Edward didn't love him any more. I hate personalities, don't you? I like to talk, don't you? Oh, I hate people who don't do things. I mean books and world conditions and things like that, don't you?'

'Sure,' said Charley.

They found themselves at the end of the bar. Al Johnson seemed to have found a number of other very dear friends to celebrate old times with.

The girl plucked at Charley's sleeve: 'Suppose we go somewhere quiet and talk. I can't hear myself think in here.'

'Do you know someplace we can dance?' asked Charley. The girl nodded.

One the street she took his arm. The wind had gone into the north, cold and gusty. 'Let's skip,' said the girl, 'or are you too dignified, Mr Holden?'

'Better call me Charley.'

They walked east and down a street full of tenements and crowded little Italian stores. The girl rang at a basement door. While they were waiting, she put her hand on his arm. 'I got some money ... let this be my party.'

'But I wouldn't like that.'

'All right, we'll make it fifty-fifty. I believe in sexual equality, don't you?' Charley leaned over and kissed her. 'Oh, this is a wonderful evening for me. . . . You are the nicest celebrity I ever met. . . . Most of them are pretty stuffy, don't you think so? No joie de vivre.'

'But,' stammered Charley, 'I'm not ...'

As he spoke, the door opened. 'Hello, Jimmy,' said the girl to a slicklooking young man in a brown suit who opened the door. 'Meet the boyfriend ... Mr Grady ... Mr Holden.'

The young man's eyes flashed. 'Not Charles Edward ...' The girl nodded her head excitedly, so that a big lock of her hair flopped over one eye. 'Well, sir, I'm very happy to meet you. ... I'm a constant reader, sir.'

Bowing and blushing, Jimmy found them a table next to the dancefloor in the stuffy little cabaret hot from the spotlights and the cigarettesmoke and the crowded dancers. They ordered more whiskey and welshrabbits. Then she grabbed Charley's hand and pulled him to his feet. They danced. The girl rubbed close to him till he could feel her little round breasts through the Bulgarian blouse.

'My . . . the boy can dance,' she whispered. 'Let's forget everything, who we are, the day of the week ...'

'Me ... I forgot two hours ago,' said Charley, giving her a squeeze.

'You're just a plain farmerlad and I'm a barefoot girl.'

'More truth than poetry to that,' said Charley through his teeth.

'Poetry ... I love poetry, don't you?'

They danced until the place closed up. They were staggering when they got out on the black empty streets. They stumbled past garbagepails. Cats ran out from under their feet. They stopped and talked about free love with a cop. At every corner they stopped and kissed. As she was looking for her latchkey in her purse, she said thoughtfully: 'People who really do things make the most beautiful lovers, don't you think so?'

Charley woke up first. Sunlight was streaming in through an uncurtained window. The girl was asleep, her face pressed into the pillow. Her mouth was open and she looked considerably older than she had the night before. Her skin was pasty and green and she had stringy hair.

Charley put his clothes on quietly. On big tables inches deep in dust and littered with drawings of funnylooking nudes, he found a piece of charcoal. On the back of a sheet of yellow paper that had a half a poem written on it he wrote: 'Had a swell time. . . . Goodbye . . . Goodluck. Charley.' He didn't put his shoes on until he got to the bottom of the creaky stairs.

Out on the street in the cold blowy spring morning he felt wonderful. He kept bursting out laughing. A great little old town. He went into a lunchroom at the corner of Eighth Street and ordered himself a breakfast of scrambled eggs and bacon and hotcakes and coffee. He kept giggling as he ate it. Then he went uptown to Fortysecond Street on the El. Grimy roofs, plateglass windows, grimy bulbs of electriclight signs, fireescapes, watertanks, all looked wonderful in the gusty sunlight.

At the Grand Central Station the clock said eleventhirty. Porters were calling the names of westbound trains. He got his bag from the checkroom and took a taxi to the Chatterton House. That was where Joe Askew had written he ought to stay, a better address than the Y. His suitcase cut into his hand, as it was heavy from blueprints and books on mechanical drawing, so he jumped into a taxi. When the clerk at the desk asked for a reference, he brought out his reserve commission.

The place had an elevator and baths and showers at the ends of the dimlylit halls, and a lot of regulations on the back of the door of the little shoebox of a room they showed him into. He threw himself on the cot with his clothes on. He was sleepy. He lay giggling looking up at the ceiling. A great little old town.

As it turned out, he lived a long time in that stuffy little greenpapered room with its rickety mission furniture. The first few days he went around to see all the aviation concerns he found listed in the phonebook to see if he could pick up some kind of temporary job. He ran into a couple of men he'd known overseas, but nobody could promise him a job; if he'd only come a couple of months sooner. Everybody said things were slack. The politicians had commercial aviation by the short hairs and there you were, that was that. Too damn many flyers around looking for jobs anyway.

At the end of the first week he came back from a trip to a motorbuilding outfit in Long Island City, where they half-promised him a drafting job later in the summer, that is, if they got the contract their Washington man was laying for, to find a letter from Mrs Askew: Joe was a very sick man, double pneumonia. It would be a couple of months before he could get to the city. Joe had insisted on her writing, though she didn't think he was well enough to worry about business matters, but she'd done it to ease his mind. He said for Charley to be sure not to let anybody else see his plans until he got a patent, better get a job to tide over until they could get the thing started right.

Tide over, hell; Charley sat on his sagging bed counting his money. Four tens, a two, a one, and fiftythree cents in change. With the room eight dollars a week that didn't make his summer's prospects look so hot.

At last one day he got hold of Doris Humphries on the phone and she asked him to come on up next afternoon. At the Humphries' apartment it was just like it had been at the Bentons' the night he went there with Ollie Taylor, except that there was a maid instead of a butler. He felt pretty uncomfortable because there were only women there. Doris's mother was a haggard dressedup woman who gave him a searching look that he felt went right through him into the wallet in his back pocket.

They had tea and cakes, and Charley wasn't sure if he ought to smoke or not. They said Ollie Taylor had gone abroad again, to the south of France, and as Ollie Taylor was the only thing he had in common with them to talk about, that pretty well dried up the conversation. Dressed in civvies it wasn't so easy talking to rich women as it had been in the uniform. Still Doris smiled at him nicely and talked in a friendly confidential way about how sick she was of this society whirl and everything, that she was going out and get her a job. That's not so easy, thought Charley. She complained she never met any interesting men. She said Charley and Ollie Taylor – of course Ollie was an old dear – were the only men she knew she could stand talking to. 'I guess it's the war and going overseas that's done something to you,' she said, looking up at him. 'When you've seen things like that, you can't take yourself so seriously as these miserable loungelizards I have to meet. They are nothing but clotheshangers.'

When Charley left the big apartmenthouse, his head was

swimming so he was almost bagged by a taxicab crossing the street. He walked down the broad avenue humming with traffic in the early dark. She'd promised to go to a show with him one of these nights.

When he went to get Doris to take her out to dinner one evening in early May, after the engagement had been put off from week to week – she was so terribly busy, she always complained over the phone, she'd love to come but she was so terribly busy – he only had twenty bucks left in his wallet. He waited for her some time alone in the drawingroom of the Humphries' apartment. White covers had been hung on the piano and the chairs and curtains and the big white room smelt of mothballs. It all gave him a feeling he'd come too late. Doris came in at last looking so pale and silky and golden in a lowcut eveningdress it made him catch his breath.

'Hello, Charley, I hope you're not starved,' she said in that intimate way that always made him feel he'd known her a long time. 'You know I never could keep track of time.'

'Gosh, Doris, you look wonderful.' He caught her looking at his gray business suit. 'Oh, forgive me,' she said. 'I'll run and change my clothes.' Something chilly came into her voice and left it at once. 'It'll take only a minute.'

He felt himself getting red. 'I guess I oughta have worn eveningclothes,' he said. 'But I've been so busy. I haven't had my trunk sent out from Minnesota yet.'

'Of course not. It's almost summer. I don't know what I was thinking about. Wits woolgathering again.'

'Couldn't you go like that, you look lovely.'

'But it looks so silly to see a girl dressed up like a plush horse with a man in a business suit. It'll be more fun anyway . . . less the social engagement, you know. . . . Honestly I'll be only five minutes by the clock.'

Doris went out and half an hour later came back in a pearl-gray streetdress. A maid followed her in with a tray with cock-tailshaker and glasses. 'I thought we might have a drink before we go out. Then we'll be sure to know what we are getting,' she said.

He took her to the McAlpin for supper; he didn't know any place else. It was already eight o'clock. The theatertickets were burning his pocket, but she didn't seem in any hurry. It was halfpast nine when he put her in a taxi to go to the show. The taxi filled up with the light crazy smell of her perfume and her hair.

'Dorris, lemme say what I want to say for a minute,' he blurted out suddenly. 'I don't know whether you like anybody else very much. I kinder don't think you do from what you said about the guys you know.'

'Oh, please don't propose,' she said. 'If you knew how I hated proposals, particularly in a cab caught in a traffic jam.'

'No, I don't mean that. You wouldn't want to marry me the way I am now anyway . . . not by a long shot. I gotta get on my hindlegs first. But I'm goin' to pretty soon. . . . You know aviation is the comin' industry. . . . Ten years from now . . . Well, us fellers have a chance to get in on the groundfloor. . . . I want you to give me a break, Doris, hold off the other guys for a little while . . .'

'Wait for you ten years, my, that's a romantic notion . . . my grandmother would have thought it was lovely.'

'I mighta known you'd kid about it. Well, here we are.'

Charley tried to keep from looking sour when he helped Doris out. She squeezed his hand just for a second as she leaned on it. His heart started pounding. As they followed the usher into the dark theater full of girls and jazz, she put her small hand very lightly on his arm. Above their heads was the long powdery funnel of the spotlight spreading to a tinselly glitter where a redlipped girl in organdy was dancing. He squeezed Doris's hand hard against his ribs with his arm.

'All right, you get what I mean,' he whispered. 'You think about it . . . I've never had a girl get me this way before, Doris.' They dropped into their seats. The people behind started shushing, so Charley had to shut up. He couldn't pay any attention to the show.

'Charley, don't expect anything, but I think you're a swell guy,' she said when, stuffy from the hot theater and the lights and the crowd, they got into a taxi as they came out. She let him kiss her, but terribly soon the taxi stopped at her apartmenthouse. He said goodnight to her at the elevator. She shook her head with a smile when he asked if he could come up.

He walked home weak in the knees through the afterthe-theater bustle of Park Avenue and Fortysecond Street. He could still feel her mouth on his mouth, the smell of her pale frizzy hair, the littleness of her hands on his chest when she pushed his face away from hers.

The next morning he woke late feeling pooped as if he'd been on a threeday drunk. He bought the papers and had a cup of coffee and a doughnut at the coffeebar that stank of stale swill. This time he didn't look in the Business Opportunities column but under Mechanics and Machinists. That afternoon he got a job in an automobile repairshop on First Avenue. It made him feel bad to go back to the overalls and the grease under your fingernails and punching the timeclock like that, but there was no help for it. When he got back to the house he found a letter from Emiscah that made him feel worse than ever.

The minute he'd read the letter he tore it up. Nothing doing, bad enough to go back to grinding valves without starting that stuff up again. He sat down on the bed with his eyes full of peeved tears. It was too goddamned hellish to have everything close in on him like this after getting his commission and the ambulance service and the Lafayette Escadrille and having a mechanic attend to his plane and do all the dirty work. Of all the lousy stinking luck. When he felt a little quieter he got up and wrote Joe for Christ's sake to get well as soon as he could, that he had turned down an offer of a job with Triangle Motors over in Long Island City and was working as a mechanic in order to tide over and that he was darn sick of it and darned anxious to get going on their little proposition.

He'd worked at the repairshop for two weeks before he found out that the foreman ran a pokergame every payday in a disused office in the back of the building. He got in on it and played pretty carefully. The first couple of weeks he lost half his pay, but then he began to find that he wasn't such a bad pokerplayer at that. He never lost his temper and was pretty good at doping out where the cards were. He was careful not to blow about his winnings either, so he got away with more of their money than the other guys figured. The foreman was a big loudmouthed harp who wasn't any too pleased to have Charley horning in on his winnings; it had been his habit to take the money away from the boys himself. Charley kept him oiled up with a drink now and then, and besides, once he got his hand in he could get through more work than any man there. He always changed into his good clothes before he went home.

He didn't get to see Doris before she went to New York Harbor for the summer. The only people he knew were the Johnsons. He went down there a couple of times a week. He built them bookshelves and one Sunday helped them paint the livingroom floor.

Another Sunday he called up early to see if the Johnsons

wanted to go down to Long Beach to take a swim. Paul was in
bed with a sorethroat but Eveline said she'd go. Well, if she
wants it she can have it, he was telling himself as he walked
downtown, through the empty grime of the hot Sundaymorn-
ing streets. She came to the door in a loose yellow silk and lace
négligée that showed where her limp breasts began. Before she
could say anything he'd pulled her to him and kissed her. She
closed her eyes and let herself go limp in his arms. Then she
pushed him away and put her finger on her lips.

He blushed and lit a cigarette. 'Do you mind?' he said in
a shaky voice.

'I'll have to get used to cigarettes again sometime, I suppose,'
she said, very low.

He walked over to the window to pull himself together. She
followed him and reached for his cigarette and took a couple
of puffs of it. Then she said aloud in a cool voice, 'Come on
back and say hello to Paul.'

Paul was lying back against the pillows looking pale and
sweaty. On a table beside the bed there was a coffeepot and a
flowered cup and saucer and a pitcher of hot milk.

'Hi, Paul, you look like you was leadin' the life of Riley,'
Charley heard himself say in a hearty voice.

'Oh, you have to spoil them a little when they're sick,' cooed
Eveline.

Charley found himself laughing too loud. 'Hope it's nothin'
serious, old top.'

'Naw, I get these damn throats. You kids have a good time
at the beach. I wish I could come too.'

'Oh, it may be horrid,' said Eveline. 'But if we don't like
it we can always come back.'

'Don't hurry,' said Paul. 'I got plenty to read. I'll be fine here.'

'Well, you and Jeremy keep bachelor hall together.'

Eveline had gotten up a luncheonbasket with some sandwiches and a thermos full of cocktails. She looked very stylish,
Charley thought, as he walked beside her along the dusty sunny
street carrying the basket and the Sunday paper, in her little
turnedup white hat and her lightyellow summer dress. 'Oh, let's
have fun,' she said. 'It's been so long since I had any fun.'

When they got out of the train at Long Beach, a great blue
wind was streaming off the sea blurred by little cool patches of
mist. There was a big crowd along the boardwalk. The two
of them walked a long way up the beach. 'Don't you think it
would be fun if we could get away from everybody?' she was

saying. They walked along, their feet sinking into the sand, their voices drowned in the pound and hiss of the surf. 'This is great stuff,' he kept saying.

They walked and walked. Charley had his bathingsuit on under his clothes; it had got to feel hot and itchy before they found a place they liked. They set the basket down behind a low dune and Eveline took her clothes off under a big towel she'd brought with her. Charley felt a little shy pulling off his shirt and pants right in front of her, but that seemed to be on the books.

'My, you've got a beautiful body,' she said.

Charley tugged uneasily at the end of his bathingsuit. 'I'm pretty healthy, I guess,' he said. He looked at his hands sticking out red and grimed from the white skin of his forearms that were freckled a little under the light fuzz. 'I sure would like to get a job where I could keep my hands clean.'

'A man's hands ought to show his work. . . . That's the whole beauty of hands,' said Eveline. She had wriggled into her suit and let drop the towel. It was a paleblue onepiece suit very tight.

'Gosh, you've got a pretty figure. That's what I first noticed about you on the boat.'

She stepped over and took his arm. 'Let's go in,' she said. 'The surf scares me, but it's terribly beautiful. . . . Oh, I think this is fun, don't you?'

Her arm felt very silky against his. He could feel her bare thigh against his bare thigh. Their feet touched as they walked out of the hot loose sand onto the hard cool sand. A foaming wide tongue of seawater ran up the beach at them and wet their legs to the knees. She let go his arm and took his hand.

He hadn't had much practice with surf and the first thing he knew a wave had knocked him galleywest. He came up spluttering with his mouth and ears full of water. She was on her feet laughing at him holding out her hand to help him to his feet. 'Come on out further,' she shouted. They ducked through the next wave and swam out. Just outside of the place where the waves broke they bobbed up and down treading water. 'Not too far out, on account of the seapussies. . . .'

'What?'

'Currents,' she shouted, putting her mouth close to his ear.

He got swamped by another roller and came up spitting and gasping. She was swimming on her back with her eyes closed and her lips pouted. He took two strokes towards her and kissed her cold wet face. He tried to grab her round the body but a wave broke over their heads.

She pushed him off as they came up sputtering. 'You made me loose my bathingcap. Look.'

'There it is. I'll get it.' He fought his way back through the surf and grabbed the cap just as the undertow was sucking it under. 'Some surf,' he yelled.

She followed him out and stood beside him in the shallow spume with her short hair wet over her eyes. She brushed it back with her hand. 'Here we are,' she said. Charley looked both ways down the beach. There was nobody to be seen in the earlyafternoon glare. He tried to put his arm around her.

She skipped out of his reach. 'Charley . . . aren't you starved?'

'For you, Eveline.'

'What I want's lunch.'

When they'd eaten up the lunch and drunk all the cocktails, they felt drowsy and a little drunk. They lay side by side in the sun on the big towel. She made him keep his hands to himself. He closed his eyes, but he was too excited to go to sleep. Before he knew it he was talking his head off. 'You see Joe's been workin' on the patent end of it, and he knows how to handle the lawyers and the big boys with the big wads. I'm afraid if I try to go into it alone, some bird'll go to work and steal my stuff. That's what usually happens when a guy invents anything.'

'Do women ever tell you how attractive you are, Charley?'

'Overseas I didn't have any trouble. . . You know, Aviat-err, lewtenong, Croix de Guerre, couchay, wee wee. . . . That was all right, but in this man's country no girl you want'll look at a guy unless he's loaded up with jack. . . . . Sure, they'll lead you on an' get you halfcrazy.' He was a fool to do it, but he went to work and told her all about Doris.

'But they're not all like that,' she said, stroking the back of his hand. 'Some women are square.'

She wouldn't let him do anything but cuddle a little with her under the towel. The sun began to get low. They got up chilly and sandy and with the sunburn starting to tease. As they walked back along the beach, he felt sour and blue. She was talking about the evening and the waves and the seagulls and squeezing his arm as she leaned on it. They went into a hotel on the boardwalk to have a little supper and that just about cleaned his last fivespot.

He couldn't think of much to say going home on the train.

He left her at the corner of her street, then walked over to the Third Avenue El and took the train uptown. The train was full of fellows and girls coming home from Sunday excursions. He kept his eye peeled for a pickup, but there was nothing doing. When he got up into his little stuffy greenpapered room, he couldn't stay in it. He went out and roamed up and down Second and Third Avenues. One woman accosted him but she was too fat and old. There was a pretty plump little girl he walked along beside for a long time, but she threatened to call a cop when he spoke to her, so he went back to his room and took a hot shower and a cold shower and piled into bed. He didn't sleep a wink all night.

Eveline called him up so often in the next weeks and left so many messages for him that the clerk at the desk took him aside and warned him that the house was only intended for young men of irreproachable Christian life.

He took to leaving the shop early to go out with her places, and towards the end of July the foreman bounced him. The foreman was getting sore anyway because Charley kept on winning so much money at poker. Charley moved away from the Chatterton House and took a furnished room way east on Fifteenth Street, explaining to the landlady that his wife worked out of town and could only occasionally get in to see him. The landlady added two dollars to the rent and let it go at that. It got so he didn't do anything all day but wait for Eveline and drink lousy gin he bought in an Italian restaurant. He felt bad about Paul, but after all Paul wasn't a particular friend of his and if it wasn't him he reckoned it would be somebody else. Eveline talked so much it made his head spin, but she was certainly a stylishlooking rib and in bed she was swell. It was only when she talked about divorcing Paul and marrying him that he began to feel a little chilly. She was a good sport about paying for dinners and lunches when the money he'd saved up working in the shop gave out, but he couldn't very well let her pay for his rent, so he walked out on the landlady early one morning in September and took his bag up to the Grand Central Station. That same day he went by the Chatterton House to get his mail and found a letter from Emiscah.

He sat on a bench in the park behind the Public Library along with the other bums and read it:

CHARLEY BOY,

You always had such a heart of gold I know if you knew about what awful luck I've been having you would do something to help me. First I lost my job and things have been so slack around here this summer I haven't been able to get another; then I was sick and had to pay the doctor fifty dollars and I haven't been really what you might call well since, and so I had to draw out my savingsaccount and now it's all gone. The family won't do anything because they've been listening to some horrid lying stories too silly to deny. But now I've got to have ten dollars this week or the landlady will put me out and I don't know what will become of me. I know I've never done anything to deserve being so unhappy. Oh, I wish you were here so that you could cuddle me in your strong arms like you used to do. You used to love your poor little Emiscah. For the sake of your poor mother that's dead send me ten dollars right away by special delivery so it won't be too late. Sometimes I think it would be better to turn on the gas. The tears are running down my face so that I can't see the paper any more. God bless you.

EMISCAH

My girlfriend's broke too. You make such big money ten dollars won't mean anything and I promise I won't ask you again.

Charley, if you can't make it ten send five.

Charley scowled and tore up the letter and put the pieces in his pocket. The letter made him feel bad, but what was the use? He walked over to the Hotel Astor and went down to the men's room to wash up. He looked at himself in one of the mirrors. Gray suit still looked pretty good, his straw hat was new and his shirt was clean. The tie had a frayed place, but it didn't show if you kept the coat buttoned. All right if it didn't rain; he'd already hocked his other suit and his trenchcoat and his officers' boots. He still had a couple of dollars in change so he had his shoes shined. Then he went up to the writingroom and wrote to Joe that he was on his uppers and please to send him twentyfive by mail P.D.Q. and for crissake to come to New York. He mailed the letter and walked downtown, walking slowly down Broadway.

The only place he knew where he could bum a meal was the Johnsons', so he turned into their street from Fifth Avenue.

Paul met him at the door and held out his hand. 'Hello, Charley,' he said. 'I haven't seen you for a dog's age.'

'I been movin',' stammered Charley, feeling like a louse. 'Too many bedbugs in that last dump. . . . Say, I just stopped in to say hello.'

'Come on in and I'll shake up a drink. Eveline'll be back in a minute.'

Charley was shaking his head. 'No, I just stopped to say hello. How's the kid? Give Eveline my best. I got a date.'

He walked to a newsstand at the corner of Eighth Street and bought all the papers. Then he went to a blindtiger he knew and had a session with the helpwanted columns over some glasses of needle beer. He drank the beer slowly and noted down the addresses on a piece of paper he'd lifted off the Hotel Astor. One of them was a usedcar dealer, where the manager was a friend of Jim's. Charley had met him out home.

The lights went on and the windows got dark with a stuffy latesummer night. When he'd paid for the beer he only had a quarter left in his pocket. 'Damn it, this is the last time I let myself get in a jam like this,' he kept muttering as he wandered round the downtown streets. He sat for a long time in Washington Square, thinking about what kind of a salestalk he could give the manager of that usedcar dump.

A light rain began to fall. The streets were empty by this time. He turned up his collar and started to walk. His shoes had holes in them and with each step he could feel the cold water squish between his toes. Under an arclight he took off his straw hat and looked at it. It was already gummy and the rim had a swollen pulpy look. 'Now how in Christ's name am I goin' to go around to get me a job tomorrow?'

He turned on his heel and walked straight uptown towards the Johnsons' place. Every minute it rained harder. He rang the bell under the card Paul Johnson – Eveline Hutchins until Paul came to the door in pajamas looking very sleepy.

'Say, Paul, can I sleep on your couch?'

'It's pretty hard. . . . Come in. . . . I don't know if we've got any clean sheets.'

'That's all right . . . just for tonight . . . You see I got cleaned out in a crapgame. I got jack comin' tomorrow. I thought I'd try the benches, but the sonofabitch started to rain on me. I got business to attend to tomorrow an' I got to keep this suit good, see?'

'Sure. . . . Say, you look wet . . . I'll lend you a pair of pajamas and a bathrobe. Better take those things off.'

It was dry and comfortable on the Johnsons' couch. After Paul had gone back to bed, Charley lay there in Paul's bathrobe looking up at the ceiling. Through the tall window he could see the rain flickering through the streetlights outside and hear its continuous beat on the pavement. The baby woke up and cried, there was a light in the other room. He could hear Paul's and Eveline's sleepy voices and the rustle of them stirring around.

Then the baby quieted down, the light went out. Everything was quiet in the beating rain again. He went off to sleep.

Getting up and having breakfast with them was no picnic nor was borrowing twentyfive dollars from Paul, though Charley knew he could pay it back in a couple of days. He left when Paul left to go to the office without paying attention to Eveline's sidelong kidding glances. Never get in a jam like this again, he kept saying to himself.

First he went to a tailor's and sat there behind a curtain reading the *American* while his suit was pressed. Then he bought himself a new straw hat, went to a barbershop and had a shave, a haircut, a facial massage and a manicure, and went to a cobbler's to get his shoes shined and soled.

By that time it was almost noon. He went uptown on the subway and talked himself into a job as salesman in the secondhand autosales place above Columbus Circle where the manager was a friend of Jim's. When the guy asked Charley about how the folks out in Minneapolis were getting on, he had to make up a lot of stuff. That evening he got his laundry from the Chinaman and his things out of hock and went back to a room, with brown walls this time, at the Chatterton House. He set himself up to a good feed and went to bed early deadtired.

A few days later a letter came from Joe Askew with the twentyfive bucks and the news that he was getting on his feet and would be down soon to get to work. Meanwhile Charley was earning a small amount on commissions, but winning or losing up to a century a night in a pokergame on Sixtythird Street one of the salesmen took him up to. They were mostly automobile salesmen and advertising men in the game and they were free spenders and rolled up some big pots. Charley mailed the twentyfive he owed him down to Paul, and when Eveline called him up on the telephone always said he was terribly busy and would call her soon. No more of that stuff, nosiree. Whenever he won, he put half of his winnings in a savingsbank account he'd opened. He carried the bankbook in his inside pocket. When he noticed it there it always made him feel like a wise guy.

He kept away from Eveline. It was hard for him to get so far downtown and he didn't need to anyway because one of the other salesmen gave him the phonenumber of an apartment in a kind of hotel on the West Side, where a certain Mrs Darling would arrange meetings with agreeable young women if she were notified early enough in the day. It cost twentyfive bucks a throw, but the girls were clean and young and there were no followups of any kind. The fact that he could raise twentyfive bucks to blow that way made him feel pretty good, but it ate into his poker winnings. After a session with one of Mrs Darling's telephone numbers, he'd go back to his room at the Chatterton House feeling blue and disgusted. The girls were all right, but it wasn't fun like it had been with Eveline or even with Emiscah. He'd think of Doris and say to himself goshdarn it, he had to get him a woman of his own.

He took to selling fewer cars and playing more poker as the weeks went on and by the time he got a wire from Joe Askew saying he was coming to town next day, his job had just about petered out. He could tell that it was only because the manager was a friend of Jim's that he hadn't fired him already. He'd hit a losing streak and had to draw all the money out of the savingsaccount. When he went down to the station to meet Joe, he had a terrible head and only a dime in his pocket. The night before they'd cleaned him out at red dog.

Joe looked the same as ever, only he was thinner and his mustache was longer. 'Well, how's tricks?'

Charley took Joe's other bag as they walked up the platform. 'Troubled with low ceilin's, air full of holes.'

'I bet it is. Say, you look like you'd been hitting it up, Charley. I hope you're ready to get to work.'

'Sure. All depends on gettin' the right C.O. . . . Ain't I been to nightschool every night?'

'I bet you have.'

'How are you feelin' now, Joe?'

'Oh, I'm all right now. I just about fretted myself into a nuthouse. What a lousy summer I've had. . . . What have you been up to, you big bum?'

'Well, I've been gatherin' information about the theory of the straight flush. And women . . . have I learned about women? Say, how's the wife and kids?'

'Fine. . . . You'll meet 'em. I'm goin' to take an apartment here this winter. . . . Well, boy, it's a case of up and at 'em. We are goin' in with Andy Merritt. . . . You'll meet him this noon. Where can I get a room?'

'Well, I'm stayin' at that kind of glorified Y over on Thirtyeighth Street.'

'That's all right.'

When they got into the taxi, Joe tapped him on the knee and leaned over and asked with a grin, 'When are you ready to start to manufacture?'

'Tomorrow mornin' at eight o'clock. Old Bigelow just failed over in Long Island City. I seen his shop. Wouldn't cost much to get it in shape.'

'We'll go over there this afternoon. He might take a little stock.'

Charley shook his head. 'That stock's goin' to be worth money, Joe . . . give him cash or notes or anythin'. He's a halfwit anyway. Last time I went over there it was to try to get a job as a mechanic. . . . Jeez, I hope those days are over. . . . The trouble with me is, Joe, I want to get married, and to get married like I want I got to have beaucoup kale. . . . Believe it or not, I'm in love.'

'With the entire chorus at the Follies, I'll bet. . . . That's a hot one . . . you want to get married.' Joe laughed like he'd split. While Joe went up to his room to clean up, Charley went round to the corner drugstore to get himself a bromoseltzer.

They had lunch with Merritt, who turned out to be a gray-faced young man with a square jaw, at the Yale Club. Charley still had a pounding headache and felt groggily that he wasn't making much of an impression. He kept his mouth shut and let Joe do the talking. Joe and Merritt talked Washington and War Department and Navy Department and figures that made Charley feel he ought to be pinching himself to see if he was awake.

After lunch Merritt drove them out to Long Island City in an open Pierce Arrow touringcar. When they actually got to the plant, walking through the long littered rooms looking at lathe and electric motors and stamping and diemaking machines Charley felt he knew his way around better. He took out a piece of paper and started making notes. As that seemed to go big with Merritt, he made a lot more notes. Then Joe started making notes too. When Merritt took out a little book and started making notes himself, Charley knew he'd done the right thing.

They had dinner with Merritt and spent the evening with him. It was heavy sledding because Merritt was one of those people who could size a man up at a glance, and he was trying to size up Charley. They ate at an expensive French speakeasy and sat there a long time afterwards drinking cognac and soda. Merritt was a great one for writing lists of officers and salaries and words like capitalization, depreciation, amortization down on pieces of paper, all of them followed by big figures with plenty of zeroes. The upshot of it seemed to be that Charley Anderson would be earning two hundred and fifty a week (payable in preferred stock), starting last Monday as supervising engineer and that the question of the percentage of capital stock he and Joe would have for their patents would be decided at a meeting of the board of directors next day. The top of Charley's head was floating. His tongue was a little thick from the cognac. All he could think of saying, and he kept saying it, was 'Boys, we mustn't go off halfcocked.'

When he and Joe finally got Merritt and his Pierce Arrow back to the Yale Club, they heaved a deep breath. 'Say, Joe, is that bird a financial wizard or is he a nut? He talks like greenbacks grew on trees.'

'He makes 'em grow there. Honestly . . .' Joe Askew took his arm and his voice sunk to a whisper, 'that bird is going to be the Durant of aviation financing.'

'He don't seem to know a Liberty motor from the hind end of a blimp.'

'He knows the Secretary of the Interior, which is a hell of a lot more important.'

Charley got to laughing so he couldn't stop. All the way back to the Chatterton House he kept bumping into people walking along the street. His eyes were full of tears. He laughed and laughed. When they went to the desk to ask for their mail and saw the long pale face of the clerk, Charley nudged Joe. 'Well, it's our last night in this funeral parlor.'

The hallway to their rooms smelt of old sneakers and showers and lockerrooms. Charley got to laughing again. He sat on his bed a long time giggling to himself. 'Jesus, this is more like it; this is better than Paree.' After Joe had gone to bed, Charley stuck his head in the door still giggling. 'Rub me, Joe,' he yelled. 'I'm lucky.'

Next morning they went and ate their breakfast at the Belmont. Then Joe made Charley go to Knox's and buy him a derby before they went downtown. Charley's hair was a little too wiry for the derby to set well, but the band had an expensive Englishleathery smell. He kept taking it off and sniffing it on the way downtown in the subway.

'Say, Joe, when my first paycheck comes I want you to take me round and get me outfitted in a soup an' fish. . . . This girl, she likes a feller to dress up.'

'You won't be out of overalls, boy,' growled Joe Askew, 'night or day for six months if I have anything to say about it. We'll have to live in that plant if we expect the product to be halfway decent, don't fool yourself about that.'

'Sure, Joe, sure, I was only kiddin'.'

They met at the office of a lawyer named Lilienthal. From the minute they gave their names to the elegantlyupholstered blonde at the desk, Charley could feel the excitement of a deal in the air. The blonde smiled and bowed into the receiver. 'Oh, yes, of course. . . . Mr Anderson and Mr Askew.' A scrawny officeboy showed them at once into the library, a dark long room filled with calfbound lawbooks. They hadn't had time to sit down before Mr Lilienthal himself appeared through a groundglass door. He was a dark oval neckless man with a jaunty manner. 'Well, here's our pair of aces right on time.'

When Joe introduced them, he held Charley's hand for a moment in the smooth fat palm of his small hand. 'Andy Merritt has just been singing your praises, young fellah, he says you are the coming contactman.'

'And here I was just telling him I wouldn't let him out of the factory for six months. He's the bird who's got the feel for the motors.'

'Well, maybe he meant you birdmen's kind of contact,' said Mr Lilienthal, lifting one thin black eyebrow.

The lawyer ushered them into a big office with a big empty mahogany desk in the middle of it and a blue Chinese rug on the floor. Merritt and two other men were ahead of them. To Charley they looked like a Kuppenheimer ad standing there amid the blue crinkly cigarettesmoke in their neatlycut dark suits with the bright gray light coming through the window behind them. George Hollis was a pale young man with his hair parted in the middle and the other was a lanky darkfaced Irish lawyer named Burke, who was an old friend of Joe Askew's and would put their patents through Washington for them, Joe explained. They all seemed to think Charley was a great guy, but he was telling himself all the time to keep his mouth shut and let Joe do the talking.

They sat round that lawyer's mahogany desk all morning smoking cigars and cigarettes and spoiling a great deal of yellow scratchpaper until the desk looked like the bottom of an uncleaned birdcage and the Luckies tasted sour on Charley's tongue. Mr Lilienthal was all the time calling in his stenographer, a little mouselike girl with big gray eyes, to take notes and then sending her out again. Occasionally the phone buzzed and each time he answered it in his bored voice, 'My dear young lady, hasn't it occurred to you that I might be in conference?'

The concern was going to be called the Askew-Merritt Company. There was a great deal of talk about what state to incorporate in and how the stock was to be sold, how it was going to be listed, how it was going to be divided. When they finally got up to go to lunch, it was already two o'clock and Charley's head was swimming. Several of them went to the men's room on their way to the elevator and Charley managed to get into the urinal beside Joe and to whisper to him, 'Say, for crissake, Joe, are we rookin' those guys or are they rookin' us?' Joe wouldn't answer. All he did was to screw his face up and shrug his shoulders.

# Newsreel 50

*Don't blame it all on Broadway*

with few exceptions the management of our government has been and is in honest and competent hands, that the finances are sound and well managed, and that the business interests of the nation, including the owners, managers, and employees, are representative of honorable and patriotic motives and that the present economic condition warrants a continuation of confidence and prosperity

> *You have yourself to blame*
> *Don't shame the name of dear old Broadway*

GRAND JURY WILL QUIZ BALLPLAYERS

IMPROVED LUBRICATING SYSTEM THAT INSURES POSITIVE AND CONSTANT OILING OVER THE ENTIRE BEARING SURFACES

> *I've got a longin' way down in my heart*
> *For that old gang that has drifted apart*

the Dooling Shipbuilding Corporation has not paid or agreed to pay and will not pay, directly or indirectly, any bribe of any sort or description to any employee or representative of the U.S. Shipping Board, the Emergency Fleet Corporation, or any other government agency

SLAIN RICH MAN BURIED IN CELLAR

> *I can't forget that old quartette*
> *That sang Sweet Adeline*
> *Goodbye forever old fellows and gals*
> *Goodbye forever old sweethearts and pals*

NEWLY DESIGNED GEARS AFFORDING NOT ONLY GREATER STRENGTH AND LONGER LIFE BUT INCREASED SMOOTHNESS

NEW CLUTCH – AN ENGINEERING ACHIEVEMENT
THAT ADDS WONDERFUL POSITIVENESS TO
POWER TRANSMISSION THAT MAKES
GEARSHIFTING EASY AND NOISELESS

NEW AND LARGER BULLET LAMPS AFFORD THE
MOST PERFECT ILLUMINATION EVER
DEVELOPED FOR MOTOR USE

GARY CALLS ROMANTIC PUBLIC RESPONSIBLE
FOR EIGHTHOUR DAY

the prices obtained for packinghouse products were
the results of purely economic laws. Official figures prove
that if wheat prices are to respond to the law of supply
and demand

PIGIRON OUTPUT SHARPLY CURBED

*And if you should be dining with a little stranger*
*Red lights seem to warn you of a danger*
*Don't blame it all on Broadway*

## The Bitter Drink

Veblen,
a grayfaced shambling man lolling resentful at his desk
with his cheek on his hand, in a low sarcastic mumble of
intricate phrases subtly paying out the logical inescapable rope
of matter-of-fact for a society to hang itself by,
dissecting out the century with a scalpel so keen, so
comical, so exact that the professors and students ninetenths
of the time didn't know it was there, and the magnates and
the respected windbags and the applauded loudspeakers never
knew it was there.
Veblen
asked too many questions, suffered from a constitutional
inability to say yes.
Socrates asked questions, drank down the bitter drink one
night when the first cock crowed,
but Veblen
drank it in little sips through a long life in the stuffiness of
classrooms, the dust of libraries, the staleness of cheap flats such

as a poor instructor can afford. He fought the bogy all right, pedantry, routine, timeservers at office desks, trustees, college-presidents, the plump flunkies of the ruling businessmen, all the good jobs kept for yesmen, never enough money, every broadening hope thwarted. Veblen drank the bitter drink all right.

The Veblens were a family of freeholding farmers.

The freeholders of the narrow Norwegian valleys were a stubborn hardworking people, farmers, dairymen, fishermen, rooted in their fathers' stony fields, in their old timbered farmsteads with carved gables they took their names from, in the upland pastures where they grazed the stock in summer.

During the early nineteenth century the towns grew; Norway filled up with landless men, storekeepers, sheriffs, moneylenders, bailiffs, notaries in black with stiff collars and briefcases full of foreclosures under their arms. Industries were coming in. The townsmen were beginning to get profits out of the country and to finagle the farmers out of the freedom of their narrow farms.

The meanspirited submitted as tenants, daylaborers; but the strong men went out of the country

as their fathers had gone out of the country centuries before when Harald the Fairhaired and Saint Olaf hacked to pieces the liberties of the Northern men, who had been each man lord of his own creek, to make Christians and serfs of them,

only in the old days it was Iceland, Greenland, Vineland the Northmen had sailed west to; now it was America.

Both Thorstein Veblen's father's people and his mother's people had lost their farmsteads and with them the names that denoted them free men.

Thomas Anderson for a while tried to make his living as a traveling carpenter and cabinetmaker, but in 1847 he and his wife, Kari Thorsteinsdatter, crossed in a whalingship from Bremen and went out to join friends in the Scandihoovian colonies round Milwaukee.

Next year his brother Haldor joined him.

They were hard workers; in another year they had saved up money to pre-empt a claim on a hundred and sixty acres of uncleared land in Sheboygan County, Wisconsin; when they'd gotten that land part cleared they sold it and moved to an all-Norway colony in Manitowoc County, near Cato, and a place named Valders after the valley they had all come from in the old country;

there in the house Thomas Anderson built with his own tools, the sixth of twelve children, Thorstein Veblen was born.

When Thorstein was eight years old, Thomas Anderson moved west again into the blacksoil prairies of Minnesota that the Sioux and the buffalo had only been driven off from a few years before. In the deed to the new farm Thomas Anderson took back the old farmstead name of Veblen.

He was a solid farmer, builder, a clever carpenter, the first man to import merino sheep and a mechanical reaper and binder; he was a man of standing in the group of Norway people farming the edge of the prairie, who kept their dialects, the manner of life of their narrow Norway valleys, their Lutheran pastors, their homemade clothes and cheese and bread, their suspicion and stubborn dislike of townsmen's ways.

The townspeople were Yankees mostly, smart to make two dollars grow where a dollar grew before, storekeepers, middlemen, speculators, moneylenders, with long heads for politics and mortgages; they despised the Scandihoovian dirtfarmers they lived off, whose daughters did their wives' kitchenwork.

The Norway people believed as their fathers had believed that there were only two callings for an honest man, farming or preaching.

Thorstein grew up a hulking lad with a reputation for laziness and wit. He hated the irk of everrepeated backbreaking chores round the farm. Reading he was happy. Carpentering he liked or running farmmachinery. The Lutheran pastors who came to the house noticed that his supple mind slid easily round the corners of their theology. It was hard to get farmwork out of him; he had a stinging tongue and was famous for the funny names he called people; his father decided to make a preacher out of him.

When he was seventeen he was sent for out of the field where he was working. His bag was already packed. The horses were hitched up. He was being sent to Carleton Academy in Northfield, to prepare for Carleton College.

As there were several young Veblens to be educated, their father built them a house on a lot near the campus. Their food and clothes were sent to them from the farm. Cash money was something they never saw.

Thorstein spoke English with an accent. He had a constitutional inability to say yes. His mind was formed on the Norse sagas and on the matter-of-fact sense of his father's farming and the exact needs of carpenterwork and threshingmachines.

He could never take much interest in the theology, sociology, economics of Carleton College where they were busy trimming down the jagged dogmas of the old New England Bibletaught traders to make stencils to hang on the walls of commissionmerchants' offices.

Veblen's collegeyears were the years when Darwin's assertions of growth and becoming were breaking the set molds of the Noah's Ark world,

when Ibsen's women were tearing down the portières of the Victorian parlors,

and Marx's mighty machine was rigging the countinghouse's own logic to destroy the countinghouse.

When Veblen went home to the farm, he talked about these things with his father, following him up and down at his plowing, starting an argument while they were waiting for a new load for the wheatthresher. Thomas Anderson had seen Norway and America; he had the squarebuilt mind of a carpenter and builder, and an understanding of tools and the treasured elaborated builtupseasonbyseason knowledge of a careful farmer,

a tough whetstone for the sharpening steel of young Thorstein's wits.

At Carleton College young Veblen was considered a brilliant unsound eccentric; nobody could understand why a boy of such attainments wouldn't settle down to the business of the day, which was to buttress property and profits with anything usable in the débris of Christian ethics and eighteenthcentury economics that cluttered the minds of collegeprofessors, and to reinforce the sacred, already shaky edifice with the new strong girderwork of science Herbert Spencer was throwing up for the benefit of the bosses.

People complained they never knew whether Veblen was joking or serious.

In 1880 Thorstein Veblen started to try to make his living by teaching. A year in an academy at Madison, Wisconsin, wasn't much of a success. Next year he and his brother Andrew started graduate work at Johns Hopkins. Johns Hopkins didn't suit, but boarding in an old Baltimore house with some ruined gentlewomen gave him a disdaining glimpse of an etiquette motheaten now but handed down through the lavish leisure of the slaveowning planters' mansions straight from the merrie England of the landlord cavaliers.

(The valleyfarmers had always been scornful of outlanders' ways.)

He was more at home at Yale, where in Noah Porter he found a New England roundhead granite against which his Norway granite rang in clear dissent. He took his Ph.D. there. But there was still some question as to what department of the academic world he could best make a living in.

He read Kant and wrote prize essays. But he couldn't get a job. Try as he would he couldn't get his mouth round the essential yes.

He went back to Minnesota with a certain intolerant knowledge of the amenities of the higher learning. To his slight Norwegian accent he'd added the broad 'a.'

At home he loafed about the farm and tinkered with inventions of new machinery and read and talked theology and philosophy with his father. In the Scandihoovian colonies the price of wheat and the belief in God and Saint Olaf were going down together. The farmers of the Northwest were starting their long losing fight against the parasite businessmen who were sucking them dry. There was a mortgage on the farm, interest on debts to pay, always fertilizer, new machines to buy to speed production to pump in a halfcentury the wealth out of the soil laid down in a million years of buffalograss. His brothers kept grumbling about this sardonic loafer who wouldn't earn his keep.

Back home he met again his college sweetheart, Ellen Rolfe, the niece of the president of Carleton College, a girl who had railroadmagnates and money in the family. People in Northfield were shocked when it came out that she was going to marry the drawling pernickety bookish badlydressed young Norwegian ne'erdowell.

Her family hatched a plan to get him a job as economist for the Santa Fe Railroad, but at the wrong moment Ellen Rolfe's uncle lost control of the line. The young couple went to live at Stacyville where they did everything but earn a living. They read Latin and Greek and botanized in the woods and along the fences and in the roadside scrub. They boated on the river and Veblen started his translation of the *Laxdaelasaga*. They read *Looking Backward* and articles by Henry George. They looked at their world from the outside.

In '91 Veblen got together some money to go to Cornell to do postgraduate work. He turned up there in the office of the head of the economics department wearing a coonskin cap and gray corduroy trousers and said in his low sarcastic drawl, 'I am Thorstein Veblen,'
but it was not until several years later, after he was established at the new University of Chicago that had grown up next to the World's Fair, and had published *The Theory of the Leisure Class*, put on the map by Howells's famous review, that the world of the higher learning knew who Thorstein Veblen was.

Even in Chicago as the brilliant young economist he lived pioneerfashion. (The valleyfarmers had always been scornful of outlanders' ways.) He kept his books in packingcases laid on their sides along the walls. His only extravagances were the Russian cigarettes he smoked and the red sash he sometimes sported. He was a man without smalltalk. When he lectured he put his cheek on his hand and mumbled out his long spiral sentences, reiterative like the eddas. His language was a mixture of mechanics' terms, scientific latinity, slang, and Roget's *Thesaurus*. The other profs couldn't imagine why the girls fell for him so.

The girls fell for him so that Ellen Rolfe kept leaving him. He'd take summer trips abroad without his wife. There was a scandal about a girl on an ocean liner.

Tongues wagged so (Veblen was a man who never explained, who never could get his tongue around the essential yes; the valleyfarmers had always been scornful of the outlanders' ways, and their opinions) that his wife left him and went off to live alone on a timberclaim in Idaho and the president asked for his resignation.

Veblen went out to Idaho to get Ellen Rolfe to go with him to California when he succeeded in getting a job at a better salary at Leland Stanford, but in Palo Alto it was the same story as in Chicago. He suffered from woman trouble and the constitutional inability to say yes and an unnatural tendency to feel with the workingclass instead of with the profittakers. There were the same complaints that his courses were not constructive or attractive to bigmoney bequests and didn't help his students to butter their bread, make Phi Beta Kappa, pick plums off the hierarchies of the academic grove. His wife left him for good. He wrote to a friend: 'The president doesn't approve of my domestic arrangements; nor do I.'

Talking about it he once said, 'What is one to do if the woman moves in on you?'

He went back up to the shack in the Idaho woods.

Friends tried to get him an appointment to make studies in Crete, a chair at the University of Pekin, but always the bogy, routine, businessmen's flunkies in all the university offices . . . for the questioner the bitter drink.

His friend Davenport got him an appointment at the University of Missouri. At Columbia he lived like a hermit in the basement of the Davenports' house, helped with the work round the place, carpentered himself a table and chairs. He was already a bitter elderly man with a gray face covered with a net of fine wrinkles, a Vandyke beard and yellow teeth. Few students could follow his courses. The college authorities were often surprised and somewhat chagrined that when visitors came from Europe, it was always Veblen they wanted to meet.

These were the years he did most of his writing, trying out his ideas on his students, writing slowly at night in violet ink with a pen of his own designing. Whenever he published a book, he had to put up a guarantee with the publishers. In *The Theory of Business Enterprise, The Instinct of Workmanship, The Vested Interests and the Common Man,*

he established a new diagram of a society dominated by monopoly capital,

etched in irony

the sabotage of production by business,

the sabotage of life by blind need for money profits,

pointed out the alternatives: a warlike society strangled by the bureaucracies of the monopolies forced by the law of diminishing returns to grind down more and more the common man for profits,

or a new matter-of-fact commonsense society dominated by the needs of the men and women who did the work and the incredibly vast possibilities for peace and plenty offered by the progress of technology.

These were the years of Debs's speeches, growing labor-unions, the I.W.W. talk about industrial democracy: these years Veblen still held to the hope that the workingclass would take over the machine of production before monopoly had pushed the western nations down into the dark again.

War cut across all that: under the cover of the bunting of Woodrow Wilson's phrases the monopolies cracked down. American democracy was crushed.

The war at least offered Veblen an opportunity to break out of the airless greenhouse of academic life. He was offered a job with the Food Administration, he sent the Navy Department a device for catching submarines by trailing lengths of stout bindingwire. (Meanwhile the government found his books somewhat confusing. The postoffice was forbidding the mails to *Imperial Germany and the Industrial Revolution* while propaganda agencies were sending it out to make people hate the Huns. Educators were denouncing *The Nature of Peace* while Washington experts were clipping phrases out of it to add to the Wilsonian smokescreen.)

For the Food Administration Thorstein Veblen wrote two reports: in one he advocated granting the demands of the I.W.W. as a wartime measure and conciliating the working-class instead of beating up and jailing all the honest leaders; in the other he pointed out that the Food Administration was a businessman's racket and was not aiming for the most efficient organization of the country as a producing machine. He suggested that, in the interests of the efficient prosecution of the war, the government step into the place of the middle-man and furnish necessities to the farmers direct in return for raw materials;

but cutting out business was not at all the Administration's idea of making the world safe for democracy,

so Veblen had to resign from the Food Administration.

He signed the protests against the trial of the hundred and one wobblies in Chicago.

After the armistice he went to New York. In spite of all the oppression of the war years, the air was freshening. In Russia the great storm of revolt had broken, seemed to be sweeping west; in the strong gusts from the new world in the east the warsodden multitudes began to see again. At Versailles allies and enemies, magnates, generals, flunkey politicians were slamming the shutters against the storm, against the new, against hope. It was suddenly clear for a second in the thundering glare what war was about, what peace was about.

In America, in Europe, the old men won. The bankers in their offices took a deep breath, the bediamonded old ladies of the leisure class went back to clipping their coupons in the refined quiet of their safedeposit vaults,

the last puffs of the ozone of revolt went stale
in the whisper of speakeasy arguments.

Veblen wrote for the *Dial*,
lectured at the New School for Social Research.

He still had a hope that the engineers, the technicians, the nonprofiteers whose hands were on the switchboard might take up the fight where the workingclass had failed. He helped form the Technical Alliance. His last hope was the British general strike.

Was there no group of men bold enough to take charge of the magnificent machine before the pigeyed speculators and the yesmen at office desks irrevocably ruined it

and with it the hopes of four hundred years?

No one went to Veblen's lectures at the New School. With every article he wrote in the *Dial* the circulation dropped.

Harding's normalcy, the new era was beginning;
even Veblen made a small killing on the stockmarket.
He was an old man and lonely.

His second wife had gone to a sanitarium suffering from delusions of persecution.

There seemed no place for a masterless man

Veblen went back out to Palo Alto
to live in his shack in the tawny hills and observe from outside the last grabbing urges of the profit system taking on, as he put, the systematized delusions of dementia praecox.

There he finished his translation of the *Laxdaelasaga*.

He was an old man. He was much alone. He let the woodrats take what they wanted from his larder. A skunk that hung round the shack was so tame he'd rub up against Veblen's leg like a cat.

He told a friend he'd sometimes hear in the stillness about him the voices of his boyhood talking Norwegian as clear as on the farm in Minnesota where he was raised. His friends found him harder than ever to talk to, harder than ever to interest in anything. He was running down. The last sips of the bitter drink.

He died on August 3, 1929.

Among his papers a penciled note was found:

*It is also my wish, in case of death, to be cremated if it can conveniently be done, as expeditiously and inexpensively as may be, without ritual or ceremony of any kind; that my ashes be thrown loose into the sea or into some sizable stream running into the sea; that no tombstone, slab, epitaph, effigy, tablet, inscription or monument of any name or nature, be set up to my memory or name in any place or at any time; that no obituary, memorial, portrait or biography of me, nor any letters written to or by me be printed or published, or in any way reproduced, copied or circulated;*

but his memorial remains
riveted into the language:
the sharp clear prism of his mind.

# Newsreel 51

*The sunshine drifted from our alley*

HELP WANTED: ADVANCEMENT

positions that offer quick, accurate, experienced, well-recommended young girls and young women . . . good chance for advancement

*Ever since the day*
*Sally went away*

GIRLS GIRLS GIRLS

canvassers . . . caretakers . . . cashiers . . . chambermaids . . . waitresses . . . cleaners . . . file clerks . . . companions . . . comptometer operators . . . collection correspondents . . . cooks . . . dictaphone operators . . . gentlewomen . . . multigraph operators . . . Elliott Fisher operators . . . bill and entry clerks . . . gummers . . . glove buyers . . . governesses . . . hairdressers . . . models . . . good opportunity for stylish young ladies . . . intelligent young women

*Went down to St James Infirmary*
*Saw my baby there*
*All stretched out on a table*
*So pale, so cold, so fair*

*Went up to see the doctor*

WE HAVE HUNDREDS OF POSITIONS OPEN

we are anxious to fill vacancies, we offer good salaries, commissions, bonuses, prizes, business opportunities, training, advancement, educational opportunities, hospital service . . . restroom and lunchroom where excellent lunch is served at less than cost

*Let her go let her go God bless her*
*Wherever she may be*
*She may roam this wide world over*
*She'll never find a sweet man like me*

## Mary French

Poor Daddy never did get tucked away in bed right after supper the way he liked with his readinglight over his left shoulder and his glasses on and the paper in his hand and a fresh cigar in his mouth that the phone didn't ring, or else it would be a knocking at the back door and Mother would send little Mary to open it and she'd find a miner standing there white-faced with his eyelashes and eyebrows very black from the coaldust saying, 'Doc French, pliz . . . heem coma queek,' and poor Daddy would get up out of bed yawning in his pajamas and bathrobe and push his untidy gray hair off his forehead and tell Mary to go get his instrumentcase out of the office for him, and be off tying his necktie as he went, and half the time he'd be gone all night.

Mealtimes it was worse. They never seemed to get settled at the table for a meal, the three of them, without that awful phone ringing. Daddy would go and Mary and Mother would sit there finishing the meal alone, sitting there without saying anything, little Mary with her legs wrapped around the chairlegs staring at the picture of two dead wild ducks in the middle of the gingercolored wallpaper above Mother's trim black head. Then Mother would put away the dishes and clatter around the house muttering to herself that if poor Daddy ever took half the trouble with his paying patients that he did with those miserable foreigners and miners he would be a rich man today and she wouldn't be killing herself with housework. Mary hated to hear Mother talk against Daddy the way she did.

Poor Daddy and Mother didn't get along. Mary barely remembered a time when she was very very small when it had been different and they'd lived in Denver in a sunny house with flowering bushes in the yard. That was before Brother was taken and Daddy lost that money in the investment. Whenever anybody said Denver it made her think of sunny. Now they lived in Trinidad where everything was black like coal, the scrawny hills tall, darkening the valley full of rows of sooty shanties, the minetipples, the miners most of them greasers and hunkies and the awful saloons and the choky smeltersmoke and the little black trains. In Denver it was sunny, and white people lived there, real clean American children like Brother who was taken, and Mother said if poor Daddy cared for his own flesh and blood the way he cared for those miserable foreigners and miners Brother's life might have been saved. Mother had made her go into the parlor, she was so scared, but Mother held her hand so tight it hurt terribly, but nobody paid any attention, they all thought it was on account of Brother she was crying, and Mother made her look at him in the coffin under the glass.

After the funeral Mother was very sick and had a night and a day nurse and they wouldn't let Mary see her and Mary had to play by herself all alone in the yard. When Mother got well, she and poor Daddy didn't get along and always slept in separate rooms and Mary slept in the little hallroom between them. Poor Daddy got gray and worried and never laughed round the house any more after that and then it was all about the investment and they moved to Trinidad and Mother wouldn't let her play with the minechildren and when she came back from school she had nits in her hair.

Mary had to wear glasses and was good at her studies and was ready to go to highschool at twelve. When she wasn't studying she read all the books in the house. 'The child will ruin her eyes,' Mother would say to poor Daddy across the breakfasttable when he would come down with his eyes puffy from lack of sleep and would have to hurry through his breakfast to be off in time to make his calls. The spring Mary finished the eighth grade and won the prizes in French and American history and English, Miss Parsons came around specially to call on Mrs French to tell her what a good student little Mary French was and such a comfort to the teachers after all the miserable ignorant foreigners she had to put up with.

'My dear,' Mother said, 'don't think I don't know how it is.' Then suddenly she said, 'Miss Parsons, don't tell anybody, but we're going to move to Colorado Springs next fall.'

Miss Parsons sighed. 'Well, Mrs French, we'll hate to lose you, but it certainly is best for the child. There's a better element in the schools there.' Miss Parsons lifted her teacup with her little finger crooked and let it down again with a dry click in the saucer.

Mary sat watching them from the little tapestry stool by the fireplace. 'I hate to admit it,' Miss Parsons went on, 'because I was born and bred here, but Trinidad's no place to bring up a sweet clean little American girl.'

Granpa Wilkins had died that spring in Denver and Mother was beneficiary of his life insurance, so she carried off things with a high hand. Poor Daddy hated to leave Trinidad and they hardly even spoke without making Mary go and read in the library while they quarreled over the dirty dishes in the kitchen. Mary would sit with an old red embossedleather *Ivanhoe* in her hand and listen to their bitter wrangling voices coming through the board partition. 'You've ruined my life and now I'm not going to let you ruin the child's,' Mother would yell in that mean voice that made Mary feel so awful and Mary would sit there crying over the book until she got started reading again and after a couple of pages had forgotten everything except the yeomen in Lincoln Green and the knights on horseback and the castles. That summer, instead of going camping in Yellowstone like Daddy had planned, they moved to Colorado Springs.

At Colorado Springs they stayed first in a boardinghouse and then when the furniture came they moved to the green shingled bungalow where they were going to live that was set way back from the red gravel road in a scrawny lawn among tall poplartrees.

In the long grass Mary found the scaled remains of a croquetset. While Daddy and Mother were fussing about the furnishings that the men were moving in from a wagon, she ran around with a broken mallet slamming at the old cracked balls that hardly had any paint left on their red and green and yellow and blue bands. When Daddy came out of the house looking tired and gray with his hair untidy over his forehead, she ran up to him waving the mallet and wanted him to play croquet. 'No time for games now,' he said.

Mary burst out crying and he lifted her on his shoulder and carried her round the back porch and showed her how by climbing on the roof of the little toolhouse behind the kitchen door you could see the mesa and beyond, behind a tattered fringe of racing cheesecloth clouds, the blue sawtooth ranges piling up to the towering smooth mass of mountains where Pike's Peak was. 'We'll go up there some day on the cogwheel railroad,' he said in his warm cozy voice close to her ear. The mountains looked so far away and the speed of the clouds

made her feel dizzy. 'Just you and me,' he said; 'but you
mustn't ever cry . . . it'll make the children tease you in school,
Mary.'

In September she had to go to highschool. It was awful going
to a new school where she didn't have any friends. The girls
seemed so welldressed and stuckup in the firstyear high. Going
through the corridors hearing the other girls talk about parties
and the Country Club and sets of tennis and summer hotels
and automobiles and friends in finishingschools in the East,
Mary, with her glasses and the band to straighten her teeth
Mother had had the dentist put on, that made her lisp a little,
and her freckles and her hair that wasn't red or blond but just
sandy, felt a miserable foreigner like the smelly bawling miners'
kids back in Trinidad.

She liked the boys better. A redheaded boy grinned at her
sometimes. At least they let her alone. She did well in her
classes and thought the teachers were lovely. In English they
read *Ramona*, and one day Mary, scared to death all alone,
went to the cemetery to see the grave of Helen Hunt Jackson.
It was beautifully sad that spring afternoon in Evergreen
Cemetery. When she grew up, she decided, she was going to be
like Helen Hunt Jackson.

They had a Swedish girl named Anna to do the housework
and Mother and Daddy were hardly ever home when she came
back from school. Daddy had an office downtown in a new officebuilding and Mother was always busy with churchwork or at
the library reading up for papers she delivered at the women's
clubs. Half the time Mary had her supper all alone reading a
book or doing her homework. Then she would go out in the
kitchen and help Anna tidy up and try to keep her from going
home and leaving her alone in the house. When she heard the
front door opening, she would run out breathless. Usually it
was only Mother, but sometimes it was Daddy with his cigar
and his tired look and his clothes smelling of tobacco and
iodoform and carbolic, and maybe she could get him to sit on
her bed before she went to sleep to tell her stories about the
old days and miners and prospectors and the war between the
sheepherders and the ranchers.

At highschool Mary's best friend was Ada Cohn whose
father was a prominent Chicago lawyer who had had to come
out for his health. Mother did everything she could to keep her
from going to the Cohns' and used to have mean arguments
with Daddy about how it was only on account of his being so

shiftless that her only daughter was reduced to going around with Jews and every Tom Dick and Harry, and why didn't he join the Country Club and what was the use of her struggling to get a position for him among the better element by church activities and women's clubs and communitychest work if he went on being just a poor man's doctor and was seen loafing around with all the scum in poolrooms and worse places for all she knew instead of working up a handsome practice in a city where there were so many wealthy sick people; wasn't it to get away from all that sort of thing they'd left Trinidad?

'But, Hilda,' Daddy would say, 'be reasonable. It's on account of Mary's being a friend of the Cohns' that they've given me their practice. They are very nice kindly people.'

Mother would stare straight at him and hiss through her teeth: 'Oh, if you only had a tiny bit of ambition.'

Mary would run away from the table in tears and throw herself on her bed with a book and lie there listening to their voices raised and then Daddy's heavy slow step and the slam of the door and the sound of him cranking the car to start off on his calls again. Often she lay there with her teeth clenched wishing if Mother would only die and leave her and Daddy living alone quietly together. A cold shudder would go through her at the thought of how awful it was to have thoughts like that, and she'd start reading, hardly able to see the printed page through her tears at first, but gradually forgetting herself in the story in the book.

One thing that Mother and Daddy agreed about was that they wanted Mary to go to a really good Eastern college. The year before she graduated from highschool Mary had passed all the College Board exams except solid geometry. She was crazy to go.

Except for a few days camping every summer with Daddy and one summer month she spent answering the phone and making out the cards of the patients and keeping his accounts and sending out his bills at his office, she hated it in Colorado Springs. Her only boyfriend was a young fellow with a clubfoot named Joe Denny, the son of a saloonkeeper in Colorado City. He was working his way through Colorado College. He was a bitter slowspoken towheaded boy with a sharp jaw, a wizard in math. He hated liquor and John D. Rockefeller more than anything in the world. She and Joe and Ada would go out on picnics Sunday to the Garden of the Gods or Austin

Bluffs or one of the canyons and read poetry together. Their favorites were *The Hound of Heaven* and *The City of Dreadful Night*. Joe thrilled the girls one day standing on a flat rock above the little fire they were frying their bacon over and reciting *The Man with the Hoe*. At first they thought he'd written it himself.

When they got in, feeling sunburned and happy after a day in the open, Mary would so wish she could take her friends home the way Ada did. The Cohns were kind and jolly and always asked everybody to stay to dinner in spite of the fact that poor Mr Cohn was a very sick man. But Mary didn't dare take anybody home to her house for fear Mother would be rude to them, or that there'd be one of those yelling matches that started up all the time between Mother and Daddy. The summer before she went to Vassar, Mother and Daddy weren't speaking at all after a terrible argument when Daddy said one day at supper that he was going to vote for Eugene V. Debs in November.

At Vassar the girls she knew were better dressed than she was and had uppity finishingschool manners, but for the first time in her life she was popular. The instructors liked her because she was neat and serious and downright about everything and the girls said she was as homely as a mud fence but a darling.

It was all spoiled the second year when Ada came to Vassar. Ada was her oldest friend and Mary loved her dearly, so she was horrified to catch herself wishing Ada hadn't come. Ada had gotten so lush and Jewish and noisy, and her clothes were too expensive and never just right. They roomed together and Ada bought most of Mary's clothes and books for her because her allowance was so tiny. After Ada came, Mary wasn't popular the way she'd been, and the most successful girls shied off from her. Mary and Ada majored in sociology and said they were going to be socialworkers.

When Mary was a junior Mother went to Reno and got a divorce from Daddy, giving intemperance and mental cruelty as the cause. It had never occurred to Mary that poor Daddy drank. She cried and cried when she read about it in a newspaper clipping marked in red pencil some nameless wellwisher sent her from Colorado Springs. She burned the clipping in the fireplace so that Ada shouldn't see it, and when Ada asked her why her eyes were so red said it was because it had made her cry to read about all those poor soldiers being killed in the war in Europe. It made her feel awful having told Ada a lie and she lay awake all night worrying about it.

The next summer the two of them got jobs doing settlement-work at Hull House in Chicago. Chicago was scary and poor Ada Cohn couldn't keep on with the work and went up to Michigan to have a nervous breakdown; it was so awful the way poor people lived and the cracked red knuckles of the women who took in washing and the scabby heads of the little children and the clatter and the gritty wind on South Halstead Street and the stench of the stockyards; but it made Mary feel like years back in Trinidad when she was a little girl, the way she'd felt the summer she worked in Daddy's office.

When she went back to Colorado Springs for two weeks before Vassar opened, she found Mother staying in style in a small suite at the Broadmoor. Mother had inherited a block of stocks in American Smelting and Refining when Uncle Henry was killed in a streetcar accident in Denver, and had an income of twenty thousand a year. She had become a great bridge-player and was going round the country speaking at women's clubs against votes for women. She spoke of Daddy in a sweet cold acid voice as 'your poor dear father,' and told Mary she must dress better and stop wearing those awful spectacles. Mary wouldn't take any money from her mother because she said nobody had a right to money they hadn't earned, but she did let her fit her out with a new tailored tweed suit and a plain afternoondress with a lace collar and cuffs. She got along better with her mother now, but there was always a cold feeling of strain between them.

Mother said she didn't know where Daddy was living, so Mary had to go down to the office to see him. The office was dingier than she remembered it, and full of patients, downand-outlooking people mostly, and it was an hour before he could get away to take her to lunch.

They ate perched on stools at the counter of the little lunch-room next door. Daddy's hair was almost white now and his face was terribly lined and there were big gray pouches under his eyes. Mary got a lump in her throat every time she looked at him.

'Oh, Daddy, you ought to take a rest.'

'I know . . . I ought to get out of the altitude for a while. The old pump isn't so good as it was.'

'Daddy, why don't you come East at Christmas?'

'Maybe I will if I can raise the kale and get somebody to take over my practice for a month.'

She loved the deep bass of his voice so. 'It would do you so much good. . . . It's so long since we had a trip together.'

It was late. There was nobody in the lunchroom except the frozenmouthed waitress who was eating her own lunch at a table in the back. The big tiredfaced clock over the coffeeurn was ticking loud in the pauses of Daddy's slow talk.

'I never expected to neglect my own little girl . . . you know how it is . . . that's what I've done. . . . How's your mother?'

'Oh, Mother's on top of the world,' she said, with a laugh that sounded tinny in her ears. She was working to put Daddy at his ease, like a charity case.

'Oh, well, that's all over now. . . . I was never the proper husband for her,' said Daddy.

Mary felt her eyes fill with tears. 'Daddy, after I've graduated will you let me take over your office? That awful Miss Hylan is so slipshod. . . .'

'Oh, you'll have better things to do. It's always a surprise to me how many people pay their bills anyway . . . I don't pay mine.'

'Daddy, I'm going to have to take you in hand.'

'I reckon you will, daughter . . . your settlementwork is just trainin' for the reform of the old man, eh?' She felt herself blushing.

She'd hardly settled down to being with him when he had to rush off to see a woman who had been in labor five days and hadn't had her baby yet. She hated going back to the Broadmoor and the bellhops in monkeyjackets and the overdressed old hens sitting in the lobby. That evening Joe Denny called up to see if he could take her out for a drive. Mother was busy at bridge, so she slipped out without saying anything to her and met him on the hotel porch. She had on her new dress and had taken off her glasses and put them in her little bag. Joe was all a blur to her, but she could make out that he looked well and prosperous and was driving a new little Ford roadster.

'Why, Mary French,' he said, 'why, if you haven't gone and got goodlooking on me. . . . I guess there's no chance now for a guy like me.'

They drove slowly round the park for a while and then he parked the car in a spot of moonlight over a culvert. Down the little gully beyond the quakingaspens you could see the plains dark and shimmery stretching way off to the moonlit horizons. 'How lovely,' she said.

He turned his serious face with its pointed chin to hers and said, stammering a little: 'Mary, I've got to spit it out. . . . I want you and me to be engaged. . . . I'm going to Cornell to take an engineering course . . . scholarship. . . . When I get out I ought to be able to make fair money inside of a couple of years and be able to support a wife. . . . It would make me awful happy . . . if you'd say maybe . . . if by that time . . . there wasn't anybody else. . . .' His voice dwindled away.

Mary had a glimpse of the sharp serious lines of his face in the moonlight. She couldn't look at him.

'Joe, I always felt we were friends like Ada and me. It spoils everything to talk like that . . . When I get out of college I want to do socialservice work and I've got to take care of Daddy. . . . Please don't . . . anything like that makes me feel awful.'

He held his square hand out and they shook hands solemnly over the dashboard. 'All right, sister, what you say goes,' he said and drove her back to the hotel without another word. She sat a long time on the porch looking out at the September moonlight, feeling awful.

A few days later when she left to go back to school it was Joe who drove her to the station to take the train East because Mother had an important committeemeeting and Daddy had to be at the hospital. When they said goodbye and shook hands, he tapped her nervously on the shoulder a couple of times and acted like his throat was dry, but he didn't say anything more about getting engaged. Mary was so relieved.

On the train she read Ernest Poole's *The Harbor* and reread *The Jungle* and lay in the Pullman berth that night too excited to sleep, listening to the rumble of the wheels over the rails, the clatter of crossings, the faraway spooky wails of the locomotive, remembering the overdressed women putting on airs in the ladies' dressingroom who'd elbowed her away from the mirror and the heavyfaced businessmen snoring in their berths, thinking of the work there was to be done to make the country what it ought to be, the social conditions, the slums, the shanties with filthy tottering backhouses, the miners' children in grimy coats too big for them, the overworked women stooping over stoves, the youngsters struggling for an education in nightschools, hunger and unemployment and drink, and the police and the lawyers and the judges always ready to take it out on the weak; if the people in the Pullman cars could only be made to understand how it was; if she sacrificed her life, like Daddy taking care of his patients night and day, maybe she, like Miss Addams . . .

She couldn't wait to begin. She couldn't stay in her berth. She got up and went and sat tingling in the empty dressing-room trying to read *The Promise of American Life*. She read a few pages, but she couldn't take in the meaning of the words; thoughts were racing across her mind like the tatters of cloud pouring through the pass and across the dark bulk of the mountains at home. She got cold and shivery and went back to her berth.

Crossing Chicago she suddenly told the taximan to drive her to Hull House. She had to tell Miss Addams how she felt. But when the taxi drew up to the curb in the midst of the familiar squalor of South Halstead Street and she saw two girls she knew standing under the stone porch talking, she suddenly lost her nerve and told the driver to go on to the station.

Back at Vassar that winter everything seemed awful. Ada had taken up music and was studying the violin and could think of nothing but getting down to New York for concerts. She said she was in love with Doctor Muck of the Boston Symphony and wouldn't talk about the war or pacifism or social work or anything like that. The world outside – the submarine campaign, the war, the election – was so vivid Mary couldn't keep her mind on her courses or on Ada's gabble about musical celebrities. She went to all the lectures about current events and social conditions.

The lecture that excited her most that winter was G. H. Barrow's lecture on 'The Promise of Peace.' He was a tall thin man with bushy gray hair and a red face and a prominent adam'sapple and luminous eyes that tended to start out of his head a little. He had a little stutter and a warm confidential manner when he talked. He seemed so nice somehow Mary felt sure he had been a workingman. He had red gnarled hands with long fingers and walked up and down the room with a sinewy stride, taking off and putting on a pair of tortoiseshell glasses. After the lecture he was at Mr Hardwick's house and Mrs Hardwick served lemonade and cocoa and sandwiches and the girls all gathered round and asked questions. He was shyer than on the platform, but he talked beautifully about Labor's faith in Mr Wilson and how Labor would demand peace and how the Mexican Revolution (he'd just been to

Mexico and had had all sorts of adventures there) was just a beginning. Labor was going to get on its feet all over the world and start cleaning up the mess the old order had made, not by violence but by peaceful methods. Wilsonian methods. That night when Mary got to bed she could still feel the taut appealing nervous tremble that came into Mr Barrow's voice sometimes. It made her crazy anxious to get out of this choky collegelife and out into the world. She'd never known time to drag so as it did that winter.

One slushy day of February thaw she'd gone back to the room to change her wet overshoes between classes when she found a yellow telegram under the door:

BETTER COME HOME FOR A WHILE YOUR MOTHER NOT VERY WELL

It was signed DADDY. She was terribly worried, but it was a relief to have an excuse to get away from college. She took a lot of books with her, but she couldn't read on the train. She sat there too hot in the greenplush Pullman with a book on her knees, staring out at the flat snowcovered fields edged with tangles of bare violet trees and the billboards and the shanties and redbrick falsefront stores along new concrete highways and towns of ramshackle frame houses sooty with factorysmoke and the shanties and the barns and the outhouses slowly turning as the train bored through the Mid West, and thought of nothing.

Daddy met her at the station. His clothes looked even more rumpled than usual and he had a button off his overcoat. His face was full of new small fine wrinkles when he smiled. His eyes were redrimmed as if he hadn't slept for nights.

'It's all right, Mary,' he said. 'I oughtn't to have wired you to come . . . just selfindulgence . . . gettin' lonely in my old age.' He grabbed her bag from the porter and went on talking as they walked out of the station. 'Your mother's goin' along fine . . . I pulled her through. . . . Lucky I got wind that she was sick. That damn housephysician at the hotel would have killed her in another day. This Spanish influenza is tricky stuff.'

'Is it bad there, Daddy?'

'Very. . . . I want you to be very careful to avoid infection. . . . Hop in, I'll drive you out there.' He cranked the rusty touringcar and motioned her into the front. 'You know how your poor mother feels about liquor? . . . Well, I kept her drunk for four days.'

He got in beside her and started, talking as he drove. The iron cold made her feel better after the dusty choking plushsmell of the sleeper. 'She was nicer than I've ever known her. By God, I almost fell in love with her all over again. . . . You must be very careful not to let her do too much when she gets up . . . you know how she is. . . . It's the relapses that kill in this business.'

Mary felt suddenly happy. The bare twigs of the trees rosy and yellow and purple spread against the blue over the broad quiet streets. There were patches of frozen snow on the lawns. The sky was tremendously tall and full of yellow sunlight. The cold made the little hairs in her nose crisp.

Out at the Broadmoor Mother was lying in her bed in her neat sunny room with a pink bedjacket on over her nightgown and a lace boudoircap on her neatly combed black hair. She looked pale but so young and pretty and sort of foolish that for a second Mary felt that she and Daddy were the grownup people and Mother was their daughter. Right away Mother started talking happily about the war and the Huns and the submarine campaign and what could Mr Wilson be thinking of not teaching those Mexicans a lesson. She was sure it wouldn't have been like that if Mr Hughes had been elected; in fact she was sure that he had been elected legally and that the Democrats had stolen the election by some skulduggery or other. And that dreadful Bryan was making the country a laughingstock. 'My dear, Bryan is a traitor and ought to be shot.'

Daddy grinned at Mary, shrugged his shoulders, and went off saying, 'Now, Hilda, just stay in bed, and please, no alcoholic excess.'

When Daddy had gone, Mother suddenly started to cry. When Mary asked her what was the matter she wouldn't say. 'I guess it's the influenza makes me weak in the head,' she said. 'My dear, it's only by the mercy of God that I was spared.'

Mary couldn't sit all day listening to her mother go on about preparedness, it made her feel too miserable; so she went down to Daddy's office next morning to see if she could catch a glimpse of him. The waitingroom was crowded. When she peeped into his consultingroom, she could see at a glance that he hadn't been to bed all night. It turned out that Miss Hylan had gone home sick the day before. Mary said she'd take her place, but Daddy didn't want to let her. 'Nonsense,' said Mary, 'I can say doctor's office over the phone as well as that awful

Miss Hylan can.' He finally gave her a gauze mask and let her stay.

When they'd finished up the last patient, they went over to the lunchroom for something to eat. It was three o'clock. 'You'd better go out and see your mother,' he said. 'I've got to start on my rounds. They die awful easy from this thing. I've never seen anything like it.'

'I'll go back and tidy up the desk first,' said Mary firmly.

'If anybody calls up, tell them that if they think it's the flu, the patient must be put right to bed, keep their feet warm with a hotwaterbottle and plenty of stimulants. No use trying to go to the hospital because there's not a bed in a radius of a hundred miles.'

Mary went back to the office and sat down at the desk. There seemed to be an awful lot of new patients; on the last day Miss Hylan had run out of indexcards and had written their names on a scratchpad. They were all flu cases. While she sat there the phone rang constantly. Mary's fingers were cold and she felt trembly all over when she heard the anxious voices, men's, women's, asking for Doc French. It was five before she got away from the office. She took the streetcar out to the Broadmoor.

It gave her quite a turn to hear the band playing in the casino for the teadance and to see the colored lights and feel the quiet warmth of the hotel halls and the air of neat luxury in her mother's room. Mother was pretty peevish and said what was the use of her daughter's coming home if she neglected her like this. 'I had to do some things for Daddy,' was all Mary said. Mother started talking a blue streak about her campaign to put German women out of the Women's Tuesday Lunch Club. It went on all through supper. After supper they played cribbage until Mother began to feel sleepy.

The next day Mother said she felt fine and would sit up in a chair. Mary tried to get Daddy on the phone to see if she ought to, but there was no answer from the office. Then she remembered that she'd said she'd be there at nine and rushed downtown. It was eleven o'clock and the waitingroom was full before Daddy came in. He'd evidently just been to a barbershop to get shaved, but he looked deadtired.

'Oh, Daddy, I bet you haven't been to bed.'

'Sure, I got a couple of hours in one of the interne's rooms at the hospital. We lost a couple of cases last night.'

All that week Mary sat at the desk in the waitingroom of

Daddy's office, answering the phone through the gauze mask, telling frightened flushed men and women who sat there feeling the aches beginning in their backs, feeling the rising fever flush their cheeks, not to worry, that Doc French would be right back. At five she'd knock off and go to the hotel to eat supper and listen to her mother talk, but Daddy's work would be just beginning. She tried hard to get him to take a night off for sleep every other night.

'But how can I? McGuthrie's laid up and I've got all his practice to handle as well as my own. . . . This damn epidemic can't last indefinitely. . . . When it lets up a little we'll go out to the Coast for a couple of weeks. How about it?' He had a hacking cough and looked gray under the eyes, but he insisted he was tough and felt fine.

Sunday morning she got downtown late because she'd had to go to church with Mother and found Daddy dozing hunched up in a chair. When she came into the office he jumped up with a guilty look and she noticed that his face was very flushed.

'Been to church, eh, you and your mother?' he said in a curious rasping voice. 'Well, I've got to be gettin' about my business.' As he went out the door with his soft felt hat pushed far down over his eyes, it crossed Mary's mind that perhaps he'd been drinking.

There didn't seem to be many calls that Sunday so she went back home in time to take a drive with her mother in the afternoon. Mrs French was feeling fine and talking about how Mary ought to make her début next fall. 'After all, you owe it to your parents to keep up their position, dear.' Talk like that made Mary feel sick in the pit of her stomach. When they got back to the hotel, she said she felt tired and went to her room and lay on the bed and read *The Theory of the Leisure Class*.

Before she went out next morning she wrote a letter to Miss Addams telling her about the flu epidemic and saying that she just couldn't go back to college, with so much misery going on in the world, and couldn't they get her something to do at Hull House? She had to feel she was doing something real. Going downtown in the streetcar she felt rested and happy at having made up her mind; at the ends of streets she could see the range of mountains white as lumps of sugar in the brilliant winter sunshine. She wished she was going out for a hike with Joe Denny. When she put her key in the office door the carbolic iodoform alcohol reek of the doctor's office caught her throat. Daddy's hat and coat were hanging on the rack. Funny, she hadn't noticed his car at the curb. The groundglass door to the consultingroom was closed. She tapped on it. 'Daddy,' she called. There was no answer. She pushed the door open. Oh, he was asleep. He was lying on the couch with the laprobe from the car over his knees. The thought crossed her mind, how awful if he was deaddrunk. She tiptoed across the room. His head was jammed back between the pillow and the wall. His mouth had fallen open. His face, rough with the gray stubble, was twisted and strangled, eyes open. He was dead.

Mary found herself going quietly to the telephone and calling up the emergency hospital to say Doctor French had collapsed. She was still sitting at the telephone when she heard the ambulance bell outside. An interne in a white coat came in. She must have fainted because she next remembered being taken in a big car out to the Broadmoor. She went right to her room and locked herself in. She lay down on her bed and began to cry. Some time in the night she called up her mother's room on the phone. 'Please, Mother, I don't want to see anybody. I don't want to go to the funeral. I want to go right back to college.'

Mother made an awful rumpus, but Mary didn't listen to what she said and at last next morning Mother gave her a hundred dollars and let her go. She didn't remember whether she'd kissed her mother when she left or not. She went down to the depot alone and sat two hours in the waitingroom because the train East was late. She didn't feel anything. She seemed to be seeing things unusually vividly, the brilliant winter day, the etched faces of people sitting in the waitingroom, the colors on the magazines on the newsstand. The porter came to get her for the train. She sat in the Pullman looking out at the snow, the yellow grass, the red badlands, the wire fences, the stockcorrals along the track standing up gray and yellowish out of the snow, the watertanks, the little stations, the grain elevators, the redfaced trainmen with their earflaps and gauntlets. Early in the morning going through the industrial district before Chicago she looked out at the men, young men old men with tin dinnerpails, faces ruddy and screwed up with the early cold, crowding the platforms waiting to go to work. She looked in their faces carefully, studying their faces; they were people she expected to get to know, because she was going to stay in Chicago instead of going back to college.

## *The Camera Eye (45)*

the narrow yellow room teems with talk under the low ceiling and crinkling tendrils of cigarettesmoke twine blue and fade round noses behind ears under the rims of women's hats in arch looks changing arrangements of lips the toss of a bang the wise I-know-it wrinkles round the eyes all scrubbed stroked clipped scraped with the help of lipstick rouge shavingcream razorblades into a certain pattern that implies

this warmvoiced woman who moves back and forth with a throaty laugh head tossed a little back distributing with teasing looks the parts in the fiveoclock drama

every man his pigeonhole

the personality must be kept carefully adjusted over the face

to facilitate recognition she pins on each of us a badge today entails tomorrow

Thank you but why me? Inhibited? Indeed goodbye

the old brown hat flopped faithful on the chair beside the door successfully snatched

outside the clinking cocktail voices face

even in this elderly brick dwellinghouse made over with green paint orange candles a little tinted calcimine into

Greenwich Village

the stairs go up and down

lead through a hallway ranked with bells names evoking lives tangles unclassified

into the rainy twoway street where cabs slither slushing footsteps plunk slant lights shimmer on the curve of a wet cheek a pair of freshcolored lips a weatherlined neck a gnarled grimed hand an old man's bloodshot eye

street twoway to the corner of the roaring avenue where in the lilt of the rain and the din the four directions

(the salty in all of us ocean the protoplasm throbbing through cells growing dividing sprouting into the billion diverse not yet labeled not yet named

always they slip through the fingers
the changeable the multitudinous lives)
box dizzyingly the compass

## *Mary French*

For several weeks the announcement of a lecture had caught
Mary French's eye as she hurried past the bulletinboard at Hull
House: 'May 15 G. H. Barrow, Europe: Problems of Postwar
Reconstruction.' The name teased her memory, but it wasn't
until she actually saw him come into the lecturehall that she
remembered that he was the nice skinny redfaced lecturer
who talked about how it was the workingclass that would keep
the country out of war at Vassar that winter. It was the same
sincere hesitant voice with a little stutter in the beginning of
the sentences sometimes, the same informal way of stalking
up and down the lecturehall and sitting on the table beside the
waterpitcher with his legs crossed. At the reception afterwards
she didn't let on that she'd met him before. When they were
introduced she was happy to be able to give him some information he wanted about the chances exsoldiers had of finding
jobs in the Chicago area. Next morning Mary French was all
of a fluster when she was called to the phone and there was
Mr Barrow's voice asking her if she could spare him an hour
that afternoon as he'd been asked by Washington to get some
unofficial information for a certain bureau. 'You see, I thought
you would be able to give me the real truth because you are
in daily contact with the actual people.' She said she'd be
delighted and he said would she meet him in the lobby of the
Auditorium at five.

At four she was up in her room curling her hair, wondering
what dress to wear, trying to decide whether she'd go without
her glasses or not. Mr Barrow was so nice.

They had such an interesting talk about the employment
situation which was not at all a bright picture and when Mr
Barrow asked her to go to supper with him at a little Italian
place he knew in the Loop, she found herself saying yes without
a quiver in spite of the fact that she hadn't been out to dinner
with a man since she left Colorado Springs after her father's
death three years ago. She felt somehow that she'd known Mr
Barrow for years.

Still she was a bit surprised at the toughlooking place with sawdust on the floor he took her to, and that they sold liquor there and that he seemed to expect her to drink a cocktail. He drank several cocktails himself and ordered red wine. She turned down the cocktails, but did sip a little of the wine not to seem too oldfashioned. 'I admit,' he said, 'that I'm reaching the age where I have to have a drink to clear the work out of my head and let me relax. . . . That was the great thing about the other side . . . having wine with your meals. . . . They really understand the art of life over there.'

After they'd had their spumoni Mr Barrow ordered himself brandy and she drank the bitter black coffee and they sat in the stuffy noisy restaurant, smelly of garlic and sour wine and tomatosauce and sawdust, and forgot the time and talked. She said she'd taken up socialservice work to be in touch with something real, but now she was beginning to feel coopedup and so institutional that she often wondered if she wouldn't have done better to join the Red Cross overseas or the Friends Reconstruction Unit as so many of the girls had, but she so hated war that she didn't want to do anything to help even in the most peaceful way. If she'd been a man she would have been a C.O., she knew that.

Mr Barrow frowned and cleared his throat: 'Of course I suppose they were sincere, but they were very much mistaken and probably deserved what they got.'

'Do you still think so?'

'Yes, dear girl, I do. . . . Now we can ask for anything; nobody can refuse us, wages, the closed shop, the eighthour day. But it was hard differing with old friends . . . my attitude was much misunderstood in certain quarters. . . .'

'But you can't think it's right to give them these dreadful jail sentences.'

'That's just to scare the others. . . . You'll see they'll be getting out as soon as the excitement quiets down . . . Debs's pardon is expected any day.'

'I should hope so,' said Mary.

'Poor Debs,' said Mr Barrow, 'one mistake has destroyed the work of a lifetime, but he has a great heart, the greatest heart in the world.' Then he went on to tell her about how he'd been a railroadman himself in the old days, a freight agent in South Chicago; they'd made him the business agent of his local and he had worked for the Brotherhood, he'd had a hard time getting an education and suddenly he'd waked up, when he was more than thirty, in New York City writing a set of articles for the *Evening Globe*, to the fact that there was no woman in his life and that he knew nothing of the art of life and the sort of thing that seemed to come natural to them over there and to the Mexicans now. He'd married unwisely and gotten into trouble with a chorusgirl, and a woman had made his life a hell for five years, but now that he'd broken away from all that, he found himself lonely getting old wanting something more substantial than the little pickups of a man traveling on missions to Mexico and Italy and France and England, little international incidents, he called them with a thinlipped grin, that were nice affairs enough at the time but were just dust and ashes. Of course he didn't believe in bourgeois morality, but he wanted understanding and passionate friendship in a woman.

When he talked he showed the tip of his tongue sometimes through the broad gap in the middle of his upper teeth. She could see in his eyes how much he had suffered. 'Of course I don't believe in conventional marriage either,' said Mary. Then Mr Barrow broke out that she was so fresh so young so eager so lovely so what he needed in his life and his speech began to get a little thick and she guessed it was time she was getting back to Hull House because she had to get up so early. When he took her home in a taxi, she sat in the furthest corner of the seat, but he was very gentlemanly, although he did seem to stagger a little when they said goodnight.

After that supper the work at Hull House got to be more and more a chore, particularly as George Barrow, who was making a lecturetour all over the country in defense of the President's policies, wrote her several times a week. She wrote him funny letters back, kidding about the oldmaids at Hull House and saying that she felt it in her bones that she was going to graduate from there soon, the way she had from Vassar. Her friends at Hull House began to say how pretty she was getting to look now that she was curling her hair.

For her vacation that June Mary French had been planning to go up to Michigan with the Cohns, but when the time came she decided she really must make a break; so instead she took the *Northland* around to Cleveland and got herself a job as countergirl in the Eureka Cafeteria on Lakeside Avenue near the depot.

It was pretty tough. The manager was a fat Greek who pinched the girls' bottoms when he passed behind them along the counter. The girls used rouge and lipstick and were mean to Mary, giggling in corners about their dates or making dirty jokes with the busboys. At night she had shooting pains in her insteps from being so long on her feet and her head spun from the faces the asking mouths the probing eyes jerking along in the rush hours in front of her like beads on a string. Back in the rattly brass bed in the big yellowbrick roominghouse a girl she talked to on her boat had sent her to, she couldn't sleep or get the smell of cold grease and dishwashing out of her nose; she lay there scared and lonely listening to the other roomers stirring behind the thin partitions, tramping to the bathroom, slamming doors in the hall.

After she'd worked two weeks at the cafeteria, she decided she couldn't stand it another minute, so she gave up the job and went and got herself a room at the uptown Y.W.C.A. where they were very nice to her when they heard she'd come from Hull House and showed her a list of socialservice jobs she might want to try for, but she said No, she had to do real work in industry for once, and took the train to Pittsburgh where she knew a girl who was an assistant librarian at Carnegie Institute.

She got into Pittsburgh late on a summer afternoon. Crossing the bridge she had a glimpse of the level sunlight blooming pink and orange on a confusion of metalcolored smokes that jetted from a wilderness of chimneys ranked about the huge corrugatediron and girderwork structures along the riverbank. Then right away she was getting out of the daycoach into the brownish dark gloom of the station with her suitcase cutting into her hand. She called up her friend from a dirty phonebooth that smelled of cigarsmoke.

'Mary French, how lovely!' came Lois Speyer's comical burbling voice. 'I'll get you a room right here at Mrs Gansemeyer's, come on out to supper. It's a boardinghouse. Just wait till you see it. . . . But I just can't imagine anybody coming to Pittsburgh for their vacation.'

Mary found herself getting red and nervous right there in the phonebooth. 'I wanted to see something different from the socialworker angle.'

'Well, it's so nice the idea of having somebody to talk to that I hope it doesn't mean you've lost your mind . . . you know they don't employ Vassar graduates in the openhearth furnaces.'

'I'm not a Vassar graduate,' Mary French shouted into the

receiver, feeling the near tears stinging her eyes. 'I'm just like any other workinggirl. . . . You ought to have seen me working in that cafeteria in Cleveland.'

'Well, come on out, Mary darling, I'll save some supper for you.'

It was a long ride out on the streetcar. Pittsburgh was grim all right.

Next day she went around to the employment offices of several of the steelcompanies. When she said she'd been a socialworker, they looked at her awful funny. Nothing doing; not taking on clerical or secretarial workers now. She spent days with the newspapers answering helpwanted ads.

Lois Speyer certainly laughed in that longfaced sarcastic way she had when Mary had to take a reporting job that Lois had gotten her because Lois knew the girl who wrote the society column on the *Times-Sentinel*.

As the Pittsburgh summer dragged into August, hot and choky with coalgas and the strangling fumes from blastfurnaces, bloomingmills, rollingmills that clogged the smoky Y where the narrow rivervalleys came together, there began to be talk around the office about how red agitators had gotten into the mills. A certain Mr Gorman, said to be one of the head operatives for the Sherman Service, was often seen smoking a cigar in the managingeditor's office. The paper began to fill up with news of alien riots and Russian Bolshevists and the nationalization of women and the defeat of Lenin and Trotzky.

Then one afternoon in early September Mr Healy called Mary French into his private office and asked her to sit down. When he went over and closed the door tight, Mary thought for a second he was going to make indecent proposals to her, but instead he said in his most tired fatherly manner: 'Now, Miss French, I have an assignment for you that I don't want you to take unless you really want to. I've got a daughter myself, and I hope when she grows up she'll be a nice simple wellbroughtup girl like you are. So honestly if I thought it was demeaning I wouldn't ask you to do it . . . you know that. We're strictly the family newspaper . . . we let the other fellers pull the rough stuff. . . . You know an item never goes through my desk that I don't think of my own wife and daughters; how would I like to have them read it.'

Ted Healy was a large round blackhaired man with a rolling gray eye like a codfish's eye.

'What's the story, Mr Healy?' asked Mary briskly; she'd made up her mind it must be something about the whiteslave traffic.

'Well, these damned agitators, you know they're trying to start a strike. . . . Well, they've opened a publicity office downtown. I'm scared to send one of the boys down . . . might get into some trouble with those gorillas . . . I don't want a dead reporter on my front page. . . . But sending you down . . . You know you're not working for a paper, you're a social-service worker, want to get both sides of the story. . . . A sweet innocentlooking girl can't possibly come to any harm. . . . Well, I want to get the lowdown on the people working there . . . what part of Russia they were born in, how they got into this country in the first place . . . where the money comes from . . . prisonrecords, you know. . . . Get all the dope you can. It'll make a magnificent Sunday feature.'

'I'm very much interested in industrial relations . . . it's a wonderful assignment. . . . But, Mr Healy, aren't conditions pretty bad in the mills?'

Mr Healy jumped to his feet and began striding up and down the office. 'I've got all the dope on that. . . . Those damn guineas are making more money than they ever made in their lives, they buy stocks, they buy washingmachines and silk stockings for their women and they send money back to the old folks. While our boys were risking their lives in the trenches, they held down all the good jobs and most of 'em are enemy aliens at that. Those guineas are welloff, don't you forget it. The one thing they can't buy is brains. That's how those agitators get at 'em. They talk their language and fill 'em up with a lot of notions about how all they need to do is stop working and they can take possession of this country that we've built up into the greatest country in the world. . . . I don't hold it against the poor devils of guineas, they're just ignorant; but those reds who accept the hospitality of our country and then go around spreading their devilish propaganda . . . My God, if they were sincere I could forgive 'em, but they're just in it for the money like anybody else. We have absolute proof that they're paid by Russian reds with money and jewels they've stole over there; and they're not content with that, they go around shaking down those poor ignorant guineas . . . Well, all I can say is shooting's too good for 'em.' Ted Healy was red in the face. A boy in a green eyeshade burst in with a big bunch of flimsy.

Mary French got to her feet. 'I'll get right after it, Mr Healy,' she said.

She got off the car at the wrong corner and stumbled up the uneven pavement of a steep broad cobbled street of little gimcrack stores poolrooms barbershops and Italian spaghettiparlors. A gusty wind whirled dust and excelsior and old papers. Outside an unpainted doorway foreignlooking men stood talking in low voices in knots of three or four. Before she could get up her nerve to go up the long steep dirty narrow stairs, she looked for a minute into the photographer's window below at the tinted enlargements of babies with toopink cheeks and the family groups and the ramrodstiff bridal couples. Uptairs she paused in the littered hall. From offices on both sides came a sound of typing and arguing voices.

In the dark she ran into a young man. 'Hello,' he said in a gruff voice she liked, 'are you the lady from New York?'

'Not exactly. I'm from Colorado.'

'There was a lady from New York comin' to help us with some publicity. I thought maybe you was her.'

'That's just what I came for.'

'Come in, I'm just Gus Moscowski. I'm kinder the officeboy.' He opened one of the closed doors for her into a small dusty office piled with stackedup papers and filled up with a large table covered with clippings at which two young men in glasses sat in their shirtsleeves. 'Here are the regular guys.' All the time she was talking to the others she couldn't keep her eyes off him. He had blond closecropped hair and very blue eyes and a big bearcub look in his cheap serge suit shiny at the elbows and knees. The young men answered her questions so politely that she couldn't help telling them she was trying to do a feature story for the *Times-Sentinel*. They laughed their heads off.

'But Mr Healy said he wanted a fair wellrounded picture. He just thinks the men are being misled.' Mary found herself laughing too.

'Gus,' said the older man, 'you take this young lady around and show her some of the sights. . . . After all, Ted Healy may have lost his mind. First here's what Ted Healy's friends did to Fanny Sellers.'

She couldn't look at the photograph that he poked under her nose. 'What had she done?'

'Tried to organize the workingclass; that's the worst crime you can commit in this country.'

It was a relief to be out on the street again, hurrying along while Gus Moscowski shambled grinning beside her. 'Well, I guess I'd better take you first to see how folks live on fortytwo cents an hour. Too bad you can't talk Polish. I'm a Polack myself.'

'You must have been born in this country.'

'Sure, highschool graduate. If I can get the dough I want to take engineering at Carnegie Tech. . . . I dunno why I string along with these damn Polacks.' He looked her straight in the face and grinned when he said that.

She smiled back at him. 'I understand why,' she said.

He made a gesture with his elbow as they turned a corner past a group of ragged kids making mudpies; they were pale flabby filthy little kids with pouches under their eyes. Mary turned her eyes away, but she'd seen them, as she'd seen the photograph of the dead woman with her head caved in.

'Git an eyeful of cesspool alley the land of opportunity,' Gus Moscowski said way down in his throat.

That night when she got off the streetcar at the corner nearest Mrs Gansemeyer's, her legs were trembling and the small of her back ached. She went right up to her room and hurried into bed. She was too tired to eat or to sit up listening to Lois Speyer's line of sarcastic gossip. She couldn't sleep. She lay in her sagging bed listening to the voices of the boarders rocking on the porch below and to the hooting of engines and the clank of shunted freightcars down in the valley, seeing again the shapeless broken shoes and the worn hands folded over dirty aprons and the sharp anxious beadiness of women's eyes, feeling the quake underfoot of the crazy stairways zigzagging up and down the hills black and bare as slagpiles where the steelworkers lived in jumbled shanties and big black rows of smokegnawed clapboarded houses, in her nose the stench of cranky backhouses and kitchens with cabbage cooking and clothes boiling and unwashed children and drying diapers. She slept by fits and starts and would wake up with Gus Moscowski's warm tough voice in her head, and her whole body tingling with the hard fuzzy bearcub feel of him when his arm brushed against her arm or he put out his big hand to steady her at a place where the boardwalk had broken through and she'd started to slip in the loose shaly slide underneath. When she fell solidly asleep she went on dreaming about him. She woke up early feeling happy because she was going to meet him again right after breakfast.

That afternoon she went back to the office to write the piece. Just the way Ted Healy had said, she put in all she could find out about the boys running the publicity bureau. The nearest to Russia any of them came from was Canarsie, Long Island. She tried to get in both sides of the question, even called them 'possibly misguided.'

About a minute after she'd sent it in to the Sunday editor, she was called to the city desk. Ted Healy had on a green eyeshade and was bent over a swirl of galleys. Mary could see her copy on top of the pile of papers under his elbow. Somebody had scrawled across the top of it in red pencil: 'Why wish this on me?'

'Well, young lady,' he said, without looking up, 'you've written a firstrate propaganda piece for the *Nation* or some other parlorpink sheet in New York, but what the devil do you think we can do with it? This is Pittsburgh.' He got to his feet and held out his hand. 'Goodbye, Miss French, I wish I had some way of using you because you're a mighty smart girl . . . and smart girl reporters are rare. . . . I've sent your slip to the cashier. . . .' Before Mary French could get her breath, she was out on the pavement with an extra week's salary in her pocketbook, which after all was pretty white of old Ted Healy.

That night Lois Speyer looked aghast when Mary told her she'd been fired, but when Mary told Lois that she'd gone down and gotten a job doing publicity for the Amalgamated, Lois burst into tears. 'I said you'd lost your mind and it's true. . . . Either I'll have to move out of this boardinghouse or you will . . . and I won't be able to go around with you like I've been doing.'

'How ridiculous, Lois.'

'Darling, you don't know Pittsburgh. I don't care about those miserable strikers, but I absolutely have got to hold on to my job. . . . You know I just have to send money home. . . . Oh, we were just beginning to have such fun and now you have to go and spoil everything.'

'If you'd seen what I've seen you'd talk differently,' said Mary French coldly. They were never very good friends again after that.

Gus Moscowski found her a room with heavy lace curtains in the windows in the house of a Polish storekeeper who was a cousin of his father's. He escorted her solemnly back there from the office nights when they worked late, and they always did work late.

Mary French had never worked so hard in her life. She wrote releases, got up statistics on t.b., undernourishment of children, sanitary conditions, crime, took trips on interurban trolleys and slow locals to Rankin and Braddock and Homestead and Bessemer and as far as Youngstown and Steubenville and Gary, took notes on speeches of Foster and Fitzpatrick, saw meetings broken up and the troopers in their darkgray uniforms moving in a line down the unpaved alleys of company batches, beating up men and women with their clubs, kicking children out of their way, chasing old men off their front stoops. 'And to think,' said Gus of the troopers, 'that the sonsabitches are lousy Polacks themselves most of 'em. Now ain't that just like a Polack?'

She interviewed metropolitan newspapermen, spent hours trying to wheedle A.P. and U.P. men into sending straight stories, smoothed out the grammar in the Englishlanguage leaflets. The fall flew by before she knew it. The Amalgamated could only pay the barest expenses, her clothes were in awful shape, there was no curl in her hair, at night she couldn't sleep for the memory of the things she'd seen, the jailings, the bloody heads, the wreck of some family's parlor, sofa cut open, chairs smashed, chinacloset hacked to pieces with an axe, after the troopers had been through looking for 'literature'. She hardly knew herself when she looked at her face in the greenspotted giltframed mirror over the washstand as she hurriedly dressed in the morning. She had a haggard desperate look. She was beginning to look like a striker herself.

She hardly knew herself either when Gus's voice gave her cold shivers or when whether she felt good or not that day depended on how often he smiled when he spoke to her; it didn't seem like herself at all the way that, whenever her mind was free for a moment, she began to imagine him coming close to her, putting his arms around her, his lips his big hard hands. When that feeling came on, she would have to close her eyes and would feel herself dizzily reeling. Then she'd force her eyes open and fly at her typing and after a while would feel cool and clear again.

The day Mary French admitted to herself for the first time that the highpaid workers weren't coming out and that the lowpaid workers were going to lose their strike, she hardly dared look Gus in the face when he called for her to take her home. It was a muggy drizzly outofseason November night. As they walked along the street without saying anything, the fog suddenly glowed red in the direction of the mills.

'There they go,' said Gus. The glow grew and grew, first pink then orange. Mary nodded and said nothing. 'What can you do when the woikin'class won't stick together! Every kind of damn foreigner thinks the others is bums and the 'Mericans they think everybody's a bum 'cept you an' me. Wasn't so long ago we was all foreigners in this man's country. Christ, I dunno why I string along wid 'em.'

'Gus, what would you do if we lost the strike? I mean you personally.'

'I'll be on the black books all right. Means I couldn't get me another job in the metaltrades, not if I was the last guy on earth. . . . Hell, I dunno. Take a false name an' join the Navy, I guess. They say a guy kin get a real good eddication in the Navy.'

'I guess we oughtn't to talk about it. . . . Me, I don't know what I'll do.'

'You kin go anywheres and git a job on a paper like you had. . . . I wish I had your schoolin'. . . . I bet you'll be glad to be quit of this bunch of hunkies.'

'They are the workingclass, Gus.'

'Sure, if we could only git more sense into our damn heads. . . . You know I've got an own brother scabbin' right to this day.'

'He's probably worried about his wife and family.'

'I'd worry him if I could git my hands on him. . . . A woikin'man ain't got no right to have a wife and family.'

'He can have a girl. . . .' Her voice failed. She felt her heart beating so hard as she walked along beside him over the uneven pavement she was afraid he'd hear it.

'Girls aplenty,' Gus laughed. 'They're free and easy, Polish girls are. That's one good thing.'

'I wish . . .' Mary heard her voice saying.

'Well, goodnight. Rest good, you look all in.' He'd given her a pat on the shoulder and he'd turned and gone off with his long shambling stride. She was at the door of her house. When she got in her room she threw herself on the bed and cried.

It was several weeks later that Gus Moscowski was arrested distributing leaflets in Braddock. She saw him brought up before the squire, in the dirty courtroom packed close with the gray uniforms of statetroopers, and sentenced to five years. His arm was in a sling and there was a scab of clotted blood on the towy stubble on the back of his head. His blue eyes caught hers in the crowd and he grinned and gave her a jaunty wave of a big hand.

'So that's how it is, is it?' snarled a voice beside her. 'Well, you've had the last piece of c—k you get outa dat baby.'

There was a hulking gray trooper on either side of her. They hustled her out of court and marched her down to the interurban trolleystop. She didn't say anything, but she couldn't keep back the tears. She hadn't known men could talk to women like that. 'Come on now, loosen up, me an' Steve here we're twice the men . . . You ought to have better sense than to be spreadin' your legs for that punk.'

At last the Pittsburgh trolley came and they put her on it with a warning that if they ever saw her around again they'd have her up for soliciting. As the car pulled out she saw them turn away slapping each other on the back and laughing. She sat there hunched up in the seat in the back of the car with her stomach churning and her face set. Back at the office all she said was that the cossacks had run her out of the courthouse.

When she heard that George Barrow was in town with the Senatorial Investigating Commission, she went to him at once. She waited for him in the lobby of the Schenley. The still winter evening was one block of black iron cold. She was shivering in her thin coat. She was deadtired. It seemed weeks since she'd slept. It was warm in the big quiet hotel lobby, through her thin paper soles she could feel the thick nap of the carpet. There must have been a bridgeparty somewhere in the hotel because groups of welldressed middleaged women that reminded her of her mother kept going through the lobby. She let herself drop into a deep chair by a radiator and started at once to drowse off.

'You poor little girl, I can see you've been working. . . . This is different from socialservice work, I'll bet.' She opened her eyes. George had on a furlined coat with a furcollar out of which his thin neck and long knobby face stuck out comically like the head of a marabou stork.

She got up. 'Oh, Mr Barrow . . . I mean George.' He took her hand in his left hand and patted it gently with his right. 'Now I know what the frontline trenches are like,' she said, laughing at his kind comical look.

'You're laughing at my furcoat.... Wouldn't help the Amalgamated if I got pneumonia, would it? . . . Why haven't you got a warm coat? . . . Sweet little Mary French. . . . Just exactly the person I wanted to see. . . . Do you mind if we go up to the room? I don't like to talk here, too many eavesdroppers.'

Upstairs in his square warm room with pink hangings and pink lights he helped her off with her coat. He stood there frowning and weighing it in his hand. 'You've got to get a warm coat,' he said. After he'd ordered tea for her from the waiter, he rather ostentatiously left the door into the hall open. They settled down on either side of a little table at the foot of the bed that was littered with newspapers and typewritten sheets. 'Well, well well,' he said. 'This is a great pleasure for a lonely old codger like me. What would you think of having dinner with the Senator? . . . To see how the other half lives.'

They talked and talked. Now and then he slipped a little whiskey in her tea. He was very kind, said he was sure all the boys could be gotten out of jail as soon as the strike was settled and that it virtually was settled. He'd just been over in Youngstown talking to Fitzpatrick. He thought he'd just about convinced him that the only thing to do was to get the men back to work. He had Judge Gary's own private assurance that nobody would be discriminated against and that experts were working on the problem of an eighthour day. As soon as the technical difficulties could be overcome, the whole picture of the steelworker's life would change radically for the better. Then and there he offered to put Mary French on the payroll as his secretary. He said her actual experience with conditions would be invaluable in influencing legislation. If the great effort of the underpaid steelworkers wasn't to be lost, it would have to be incorporated in legislation. The center of the fight was moving to Washington. He felt the time was ripe in the Senate. She said her first obligation was to the strike committee. 'But, my dear sweet child,' George Barrow said, gently patting the back of her hand, 'in a few days there won't be any strike-committee.'

The Senator was a Southerner with irongray hair and white spats who looked at Mary French when he first came in the room as if he thought she was going to plant a bomb under the big bulge of his creamcolored vest, but his fatherly respectful delicate flowerofwomanhood manner was soothing. They ordered dinner brought up to George's room. The Senator kidded George in a heavy rotund way about his dangerous

Bolsheviki friends. They'd been putting away a good deal of rye and the smoky air of George's room was rich with whiskey. When she left them to go down to the office again, they were talking about taking in a burlesque show.

The bunch down at the office looked haggard and sour. When she told them about G. H. Barrow's offer, they told her to jump at it; of course it would be wonderful to have her working for them in Washington and besides they wouldn't be able to pay even her expenses any more. She finished her release and glumly said goodnight. That night she slept better than she had for weeks, though all the way home she was haunted by Gus Moscowski's blue eyes and his fair head with the blood clotted on it and his jaunty grin when his eyes met hers in the courtroom. She had decided that the best way to get the boys out of jail was to go to Washington with George.

Next morning George called her up at the office first thing and asked her what about the job. She said she'd take it. He said would fifty a week be all right; maybe he could raise it to seventyfive later. She said it was more than she'd ever made in her life. He said he wanted her to come right around to the Schenley; he had something important for her to do. When she got there he met her in the lobby with a hundreddollar bill in his hand. 'The first thing I want you to do, sweet girl, is to go buy yourself a warm overcoat. Here's two weeks' salary in advance. . . . You won't be any good to me as a secretary if you catch your death of pneumonia the first day.'

On the parlorcar going to Washington he handed over to her two big square black suitcases full of testimony.

'Don't think for a moment there's no work concerned with this job,' he said, fishing out manila envelope after manila envelope full of closely typed stenographers' notes on onionskin paper. 'The other stuff was more romantic,' he said, sharpening a pencil, 'but this in the longrange view is more useful.'

'I wonder,' said Mary.

'Mary dear, you are very young . . . and very sweet.' He sat back in his greenplush armchair looking at her a long time with his bulging eyes while the snowy hills streaked with green of lichened rocks and laced black with bare branches of trees filed by outside. Then he blurted out, Wouldn't it be fun if they got married when they got to Washington. She shook her head and went back to the problem of strikers' defense, but she couldn't help smiling at him when she said she didn't want to get married just yet; he'd been so kind. She felt he was a real friend.

In Washington she fixed herself up a little apartment in a house on H Street that was being sublet cheap by Democratic officeholders who were moving out. She often cooked supper for George there. She'd never done any cooking before except camp cooking, but George was quite an expert and knew how to make Italian spaghetti and chiliconcarne and oysterstew and real French bouillabaisse. He'd get wine from the Rumanian Embassy and they'd have very cozy meals together after long days working in the office. He talked and talked about love and the importance of a healthy sexlife for men and women, so that at last she let him. He was so tender and gentle that for a while she thought maybe she really loved him. He knew all about contraceptives and was very nice and humorous about them. Sleeping with a man didn't make as much difference in her life as she'd expected it would.

The day after Harding's inauguration two seedylooking men in shapeless gray caps shuffled up to her in the lobby of the little building on G Street where George's office was. One of them was Gus Moscowski. His cheeks were hollow and he looked tired and dirty.

'Hello, Miss French,' he said. 'Meet the kid brother . . . not the one that scabbed, this one's on the up and up. . . . You sure do look well.'

'Oh, Gus, they let you out.'

He nodded. 'New trial, cases dismissed. . . . But I tell you it's no fun in that cooler.'

She took them up to George's office. 'I'm sure Mr Barrow'll want to get firsthand news of the steelworkers.'

Gus made a gesture of pushing something away with his hand. 'We ain't steelworkers, we're bums. . . . Your friends the Senators sure sold us out pretty. Every sonofabitch ever walked across the street with a striker's blacklisted. The old man got his job back, way back at fifty cents instead of a dollar-ten after the priest made him kiss the book and promise not to join the union. . . . Lots of people goin' back to the old country. Me an' the kid we pulled out, went down to Baltimore to git a job on a boat somewheres, but the seamen are piled up ten deep on the wharf. . . . So we thought we might as well take in the 'nauguration and see how the fat boys looked.'

Mary tried to get them to take some money, but they shook their heads and said, 'We don't need a handout, we can woik.'

They were just going when George came in. He didn't seem any too pleased to see them, and began to lecture them on violence; if the strikers hadn't threatened violence and allowed themselves to be misled by a lot of Bolshevik agitators, the men who were really negotiating a settlement from the inside would have been able to get them much better terms.

'I won't argue with you, Mr Barrow. I suppose you think Father Kazinski was a red and that it was Fanny Sellers that bashed in the head of a statetrooper. An' then you say you're on the side of the workin'man.'

'And, George, even the Senate committee admitted that the violence was by the deputies and statetroopers. . . . I saw it myself after all,' put in Mary.

'Of course, boys . . . I know what you're up against. . . . I hold no brief for the Steel Trust. . . . But, Mary, what I want to impress on these boys is that the workingman is often his own worst enemy in these things.'

'The woikin'man gits f'rooked whatever way you look at it,' said Gus, 'and I don't know whether it's his friends or his enemies does the worst rookin'. . . . Well, we got to git a move on.'

'Boys, I'm sorry I've got so much pressing business to do. I'd like to hear about your experiences. Maybe some other time,' said George, settling down at his desk.

As they left, Mary French followed them to the door and whispered to Gus, 'And what about Carnegie Tech?'

His eyes didn't seem so blue as they'd seemed before he went to jail. 'Well, what about it?' said Gus, without looking at her and gently closed the groundglass door behind him.

That night while they were eating supper Mary suddenly got to her feet and said, 'George, we're as responsible as anybody for selling out the steelworkers.'

'Nonsense, Mary, it's the fault of the leaders who picked the wrong minute for the strike and then let the bosses hang a lot of crazy revolutionary notions on them. Organized Labor gets stung every time it mixes in politics. Gompers knows that. We all did our best for 'em.'

Mary French started to walk back and forth in the room. She was suddenly bitterly uncontrollably angry. 'That's the way they used to talk back in Colorado Springs. I might better go back and live with Mother and do charitywork. It would be better than making a living off the workingclass.'

She walked back and forth. He went on sitting there at the

table she'd fixed so carefully with flowers and a white cloth, drinking little sips of wine and putting first a little butter on the corner of a cracker and then a piece of Roquefort cheese and then biting it off and then another bit of butter and another piece of cheese, munching slowly all the time. She could feel his bulging eyes traveling over her body. 'We're just laborfakers,' she yelled in his face, and ran into the bedroom.

He stood over her still chewing on the cheese and crackers as he nervously patted the back of her shoulder. 'What a spiteful thing to say. . . . My child, you mustn't be so hysterical. . . . This isn't the first strike that's ever come out badly. . . . Even this time there's a gain. Fairminded people all over the country have been horrified by the ruthless violence of the steelbarons. It will influence legislation. . . . Sit up and have a glass of wine. . . . Now, Mary, why don't we get married? It's too silly living like this. I have some small investments. I saw a nice little house for sale in Georgetown just the other day. This is just the time now to buy a house when prices are dropping . . . personnel being cut out of all the departments. . . . After all, I've reached an age when I have a right to settle down and have a wife and kids . . . I don't want to wait till it's too late.'

Mary sat up sniveling. 'Oh, George, you've got plenty of time. . . . I don't know why I've got a horror of getting married. . . . Everything gives me the horrors tonight.'

'Poor little girl, it's probably the curse coming on,' said George and kissed her on the forehead. After he'd gone home to his hotel, she decided she'd go back to Colorado Springs to visit her mother for a while. Then she'd try to get some kind of newspaper job.

Before she could get off for the West, she found that a month had gone by. Fear of having a baby began to obsess her. She didn't want to tell George about it because she knew he'd insist on their getting married. She couldn't wait. She didn't know any doctor she could go to. Late one night she went into the kitchenette to stick her head in the oven and tried to turn on the gas, but it seemed so inconvenient somehow and her feet felt so cold on the linoleum that she went back to bed.

Next day she got a letter from Ada Cohn all about what a wonderful time Ada was having in New York where she had the loveliest apartment and was working so hard on her violin and hoped to give a concert in Carnegie Hall next season.

Without finishing reading the letter, Mary French started packing her things. She got to the station in time to get the teno'clock to New York. From the station she sent George a wire:

FRIEND SICK   CALLED TO NEW YORK   WRITING

She'd wired Ada and Ada met her at the Pennsylvania Station in New York looking very handsome and rich. In the taxicab Mary told her that she had to lend her the money to have an abortion. Ada had a crying fit and said of course she'd lend her the money, but who on earth could she go to? Honestly she wouldn't dare ask Doctor Kirstein about it because he was such a friend of her father's and mother's that he'd be dreadfully upset. 'I won't have a baby. I won't have a baby,' Mary was muttering.

Ada had a fine threeroom apartment in the back of a building on Madison Avenue with a light tancolored carpet and a huge grandpiano and lots of plants in pots and flowers in vases. They ate their supper there and strode up and down the livingroom all evening trying to think. Ada sat at the piano and played Bach preludes to calm her nerves, she said, but she was so upset she couldn't follow her music. At last Mary wrote George a specialdelivery letter asking him what to do. Next evening she got a reply. George was brokenhearted, but he enclosed the address of a doctor.

Mary gave the letter to Ada to read. 'What a lovely letter! I don't blame him at all. He sounds like a fine sensitive beautiful nature.'

'I hate him,' said Mary, driving her nails into the palms of her hands. 'I hate him.'

Next morning she went down all alone to the doctor's and had the operation. After it she went home in a taxicab and Ada put her to bed. Ada got on her nerves terribly tiptoeing in and out of the bedroom with her face wrinkled up. After about a week Mary French got up. She seemed to be all right, and started to go around New York looking for a job.

## The Camera Eye (46)

walk the streets and walk the streets inquiring of Coca-Cola signs Lucky Strike ads pricetags in storewindows

scraps of overheard conversations stray tatters of newsprint
yesterday's headlines sticking out of ashcans

for a set of figures a formula of action an address you
don't quite know you've forgotten the number the street
may be in Brooklyn a train leaving for somewhere a steamboat whistle stabbing your ears a job chalked up in front of
an agency

to do to make there are more lives than walking desperate the streets hurry underdog do   make

a speech urging action in the crowded hall after handclapping the pats and smiles of others on the platform the
scrape of chairs the expectant hush the few coughs during
the first stuttering attempt to talk straight tough going the
snatch for a slogan they are listening and then the easy
climb slogan by slogan to applause (if somebody in your
head didn't say liar to you and on Union Square

that time you leant from a soapbox over faces   avid
young opinionated old the middleaged numb with overwork
eyes bleared with newspaperreading   trying to tell them
the straight dope   make them laugh tell them what they
want to hear wave a flag whispers the internal agitator crazy
to succeed)

you suddenly falter ashamed flush red break out in
sweat   why not tell these men stamping in the wind that
we stand on a quicksand?   that doubt is the whetstone of
understanding is too hard hurts instead of urging   picket
John D. Rockefeller the bastard if the cops knock your
blocks off it's all for the advancement of the human race
while I go home after a drink and a hot meal and read
(with some difficulty in the Loeb Library trot) the epigrams
of Martial and ponder the course of history and what leverage might pry the owners loose from power and bring back
(I too Walt Whitman) our storybook democracy

and all the time in my pocket that letter from that
collegeboy asking me to explain why being right which he
admits   the radicals are in their private lives such shits

lie abed underdog (peeling the onion of doubt) with
the book unread in your hand and swing on the seesaw
maybe after all maybe topdog   make

money  you understand what he meant the old party
with the white beard beside the crystal inkpot at the cleared
varnished desk in the walnut office in whose voice boomed
all the clergymen of childhood and shrilled the hosannahs
of the offkey female choirs. All you say is very true but
there's such a thing as sales    And I have daughters    I'm
sure you too will end by thinking differently   make

money in New York (lipstick kissed off the lips of a
girl fashionablydressed fragrant at five o'clock in a taxicab
careening down Park Avenue went at the end of each crosstown street the west is flaming with gold and white smoke
billows from the smokestacks of steamboats leaving port
and the sky is lined with greenbacks

the riveters are quiet the trucks of the producers are
shoved off onto the marginal avenues

winnings sing from every streetcorner

crackle in the ignitions of the cars swish smooth in
ballbearings sparkle in the lights going on in the showwindows croak in the klaxons tootle in the horns of imported millionaire shining towncars

dollars are silky in her hair soft in her dress sprout in
the elaborately contrived rosepetals that you kiss become
pungent and crunchy in the speakeasy dinner sting shrill in
the drinks

make loud the girlandmusic show set off the laughing
jag in the cabaret swing in the shufflingshuffling orchestra
click sharp in the hatcheck girl's goodnight)

if not why not? walking the streets rolling on your
bed eyes sting from peeling the speculative onion of doubt
if somebody in your head    topdog?   underdog?   didn't
(and on Union Square) say liar to you

# Newsreel 52

*assembled to a service for the dear departed, the last half hour of devotion and remembrance of deeds done and work undone; the remembrance of friendship and love; of what was and what could have been. Why not use well that last half hour, why not make that last service as beautiful as Frank E. Campbell can make it at the funeral church (nonsectarian)*

### BODY TIED IN BAG IS FOUND FLOATING

*Chinatown my Chinatown where the lights are low*
*Hearts that know no other land*
*Drifting to and fro*

### APOPLEXY BRINGS END WHILE WIFE READS TO HIM

Mrs Harding was reading to him in a low soothing voice. It had been hoped that he would go to sleep under that influence

### DAUGHERTY IN CHARGE

*All alone*
*By the telephone*
*Waiting for a ring*

### TWO WOMEN'S BODIES IN SLAYER'S BAGGAGE

### WORKERS MARCH ON REICHSTAG CITY IN DARKNESS

### RACE IN TAXI TO PREVENT SUICIDE ENDS IN FAILURE AT THE BELMONT

### PERSHING DANCES TANGO IN THE ARGENTINE

### HARDING TRAIN CRAWLS FIFTY MILES THROUGH MASSED CHICAGO CROWDS

GIRL OUT OF WORK DIES FROM POISON

MANY SEE COOLIDGE BUT FEW HEAR HIM

*If you knew Susie*
*Like I know Susie*
*Oh oh oh what a girl*

## Art and Isadora

In San Francisco in eighteen-seventyeight Mrs Isadora O'Gorman Duncan, a highspirited lady with a taste for the piano, set about divorcing her husband, the prominent Mr Duncan, whose behavior we are led to believe had been grossly indelicate; the whole thing made her so nervous that she declared to her children that she couldn't keep anything on her stomach but a little champagne and oysters; in the middle of the bitterness and recriminations of the family row,

into a world of gaslit boardinghouses kept by ruined Southern belles and railroadmagnates and swinging doors and whiskery men nibbling cloves to hide the whiskey on their breaths and brass spittoons and fourwheel cabs and basques and bustles and long ruffled trailing skirts (in which lecturehall and concertroom, under the domination of ladies of culture, were the centers of aspiring life)

she bore a daughter whom she named after herself Isadora.

The break with Mr Duncan and the discovery of his duplicity turned Mrs Duncan into a bigoted feminist and an atheist, a passionate follower of Bob Ingersoll's lectures and writings; for God read Nature; for duty beauty, *and only man is vile.*

Mrs Duncan had a hard struggle to raise her children in the love of beauty and the hatred of corsets and conventions and manmade laws. She gave pianolessons, she did embroidery and knitted scarves and mittens.

The Duncans were always in debt.

The rent was always due.

Isadora's earliest memories were of wheedling grocers and butchers and landlords and selling little things her mother had made from door to door,

helping handvalises out of back windows when they had to jump their bills at one shabbygenteel boardinghouse after another in the outskirts of Oakland and San Francisco.

The little Duncans and their mother were a clan; it was the Duncans against a rude and sordid world. The Duncans weren't Catholics any more or Presbyterians or Quakers or Baptists; they were Artists.

When the children were quite young they managed to stir up interest among their neighbors by giving theatrical performances in a barn; the older girl Elizabeth gave lessons in society dancing; they were Westerners, the world was a goldrush; they weren't ashamed of being in the public eye. Isadora had green eyes and reddish hair and a beautiful neck and arms. She couldn't afford lessons in conventional dancing, so she made up dances of her own.

They moved to Chicago. Isadora got a job dancing to *The Washington Post* at the Masonic Temple Roof Garden for fifty a week. She danced at clubs. She went to see Augustin Daly and told him she'd discovered
the Dance
and went on in New York as a fairy in cheesecloth in a production of *Midsummer Night's Dream* with Ada Rehan.

The family followed her to New York. They rented a big room in Carnegie Hall, put mattresses in the corners, hung drapes on the wall and invented the first Greenwich Village Studio.

They were never more than one jump ahead of the sheriff, they were always wheedling the tradespeople out of bills, standing the landlady up for the rent, coaxing handouts out of rich philistines.

Isadora arranged recitals with Ethelbert Nevin
danced to reading of Omar Khayyám for society women at Newport. When the Hotel Windsor burned they lost all their trunks and the very long bill they owed and sailed for London on a cattleboat
to escape the materialism of their native America.

In London at the British Museum
they discovered the Greeks;
the Dance was Greek.
Under the smoky chimneypots of London, in the sootcoated squares, they danced in muslin tunics, they copied poses from Greek vases, went to lectures, artgalleries, concerts, plays, sopped up in a winter fifty years of Victorian culture.

Back to the Greeks.

Whenever they were put out of their lodgings for non-payment of rent, Isadora led them to the best hotel and engaged a suite and sent the waiters scurrying for lobsters and champagne and fruits outofseason; nothing was too good for Artists, Duncans, Greeks;

and the nineties London liked her gall.

In Kensington and even in Mayfair she danced at parties in private houses,

the Britishers, Prince Edward down,

were carried away by her preraphaelite beauty

her lusty American innocence

her California accent.

After London, Paris during the great exposition of nineteen-hundred. She danced with Loïe Fuller. She was still a virgin too shy to return the advances of Rodin the great master, completely baffled by the extraordinary behavior of Loïe Fuller's circle of crackbrained invert beauties. The Duncans were vegetarians, suspicious of vulgarity and men and materialism. Raymond made them all sandals.

Isadora and her mother and her brother Raymond went about Europe in sandals and fillets and Greek tunics

staying at the best hotels leading the Greek life of nature in a flutter of unpaid bills.

Isadora's first solo recital was at a theater in Budapest;

after that she was the diva, had a loveaffair with a leading actor; in Munich the students took the horses out of her carriage. Everything was flowers and handclapping and champagne suppers. In Berlin she was the rage.

With the money she made on her German tour she took the Duncans all to Greece. They arrived on a fishingboat from Ithaca. They posed in the Parthenon for photographs and danced in the Theater of Dionysus and trained a crowd of urchins to sing the ancient chorus from the *Suppliants* and built a temple to live in on a hill overlooking the ruins of ancient Athens, but there was no water on the hill and their money ran out before the temple was finished

so they had to stay at the Hôtel d'Angleterre and run up a bill there. When credit gave out, they took their chorus back to Berlin and put on the *Suppliants* in ancient Greek. Meeting Isadora in her peplum marching through the Tiergarten at the

head of her Greek boys marching in order, all in Greek tunics,
the Kaiserin's horse shied,

and Her Highness was thrown.


Isadora was the vogue.

She arrived in St Petersburg in time to see the night
funeral of the marchers shot down in front of the Winter Palace
in 1905. It hurt her. She was an American like Walt Whitman;
the murdering rulers of the world were not her people; the
marchers were her people; artists were not on the side of the
machineguns; she was an American in a Greek tunic; she was
for the people.

In St Petersburg, still under the spell of the eighteenth-
century ballet of the court of the Sunking,

her dancing was considered dangerous by the authorities.

In Germany she founded a school with the help of her
sister Elizabeth who did the organizing, and she had a baby
by Gordon Craig.

She went to America in triumph as she'd always planned
and harried the home philistines with a tour; her followers were
all the time getting pinched for wearing Greek tunics; she found
no freedom for Art in America.


Back in Paris it was the top of the world; Art meant
Isadora. At the funeral of the Prince de Polignac she met the
mythical millionaire (sewingmachine king) who was to be her
backer and to finance her school. She went off with him in his
yacht (whatever Isadora did was Art)

to dance in the Temple at Paestum

only for him,

but it rained and the musicians all got drenched. So they
all got drunk instead.

Art was the millionaire life. Art was whatever Isadora did.
She was carrying the millionaire's child to the great scandal of
the oldlady clubwomen and spinster artlovers when she danced
on her second American tour;

she took to drinking too much and stepping to the footlights and bawling out the boxholders.

Isadora was at the height of glory and scandal and power
and wealth, her school going, her millionaire was about to
build her a theater in Paris, the Duncans were the priests of a
cult (Art was whatever Isadora did),

when the car that was bringing her two children home

from the other side of Paris stalled on a bridge across the Seine. Forgetting that he'd left the car in gear the chauffeur got out to crank the motor. The car started, knocked down the chauffeur, plunged off the bridge into the Seine.

The children and their nurse were drowned.

The rest of her life moved desperately on
in the clatter of scandalized tongues, among the kidding faces of reporters, the threatening of bailiffs, the expostulations of hotelmanagers bringing overdue bills.

Isadora drank too much, she couldn't keep her hands off goodlooking young men, she dyed her hair various shades of brightred, she never took the trouble to make up her face properly, was careless about her dress, couldn't bother to keep her figure in shape, never could keep track of her money
but a great sense of health
filled the hall
when the pearshaped figure with the beautiful great arms tramped forward slowly from the back of the stage.

She was afraid of nothing; she was a great dancer.

In her own city of San Francisco the politicians wouldn't let her dance in the Greek Theater they'd built under her influence. Wherever she went she gave offense to the philistines. When the war broke out she danced the *Marseillaise*, but it didn't seem quite respectable and she gave offense by refusing to give up Wagner or to show the proper respectable feelings
of satisfaction at the butchery.

On her South American tour
she picked up men everywhere,
a Spanish painter, a couple of prizefighters, a stoker on the boat, a Brazilian poet,
brawled in tangohalls, bawled out the Argentines for niggers from the footlights, lushly triumphed in Montevideo and Brazil; but if she had money she couldn't help scandalously spending it on tangodancers, handouts, afterthetheater suppers, the generous gesture, no, all on my bill. The managers gypped her. She was afraid of nothing, never ashamed in the public eye of the clatter of scandalized tongues, the headlines in the afternoon papers.

When October split the husk off the old world, she remembered St Petersburg, the coffins lurching through the silent streets, the white faces, the clenched fists that night in St Petersburg, and danced the *Marche Slave*,

and waved red cheesecloth under the noses of the Boston old ladies in Symphony Hall;

but when she went to Russia full of hope of a school and work and a new life in freedom, it was too enormous, it was too difficult: cold, vodka, lice, no service in the hotels, new and old still piled pellmell together, seedbed and scrapheap, she hadn't the patience, her life had been too easy;

she picked up a yellowhaired poet

and brought him back

to Europe and the grand hotels.

Yessenin smashed up a whole floor of the Adlon in Berlin in one drunken party, he ruined a suite at the Continental in Paris. When he went back to Russia he killed himself. It was too enormous, it was too difficult.


When it was impossible to raise any more money for Art, for the crowds eating and drinking in the hotel suites and the rent of Rolls-Royces and the board of her pupils and disciples,

Isadora went down to the Riviera to write her memoirs to scrape up some cash out of the American public that had awakened after the war to the crassness of materialism and the Greeks and scandal and Art, and still had dollars to spend.

She hired a studio in Nice, but she could never pay the rent. She'd quarreled with her millionaire. Her jewels, the famous emerald, the ermine cloak, the works of art presented by the artists, had all gone into the pawnshops or been seized by hotelkeepers. All she had was the old blue drapes that had seen her great triumphs, a redleather handbag, and an old furcoat that was split down the back.

She couldn't stop drinking or putting her arms round the neck of the nearest young man; if she got any cash she threw a party or gave it away.

She tried to drown herself, but an English naval officer pulled her out of the moonlit Mediterranean.


One day at a little restaurant at Golfe Juan she picked up a goodlooking young wop who kept a garage and drove a little Bugatti racer.

Saying that she might want to buy the car, she made him go to her studio to take her out for a ride;

her friends didn't want her to go, said he was nothing but

a mechanic; she insisted, she'd had a few drinks (there was nothing left she cared for in the world but a few drinks and a goodlooking young man);

she got in beside him and

she threw her heavilyfringed scarf round her neck with a big sweep she had and

turned back and said,

with the strong California accent her French never lost: Adieu, mes amis, je vais à la gloire.

The mechanic put his car in gear and started.

The heavy trailing scarf caught in a wheel, wound tight. Her head was wrenched against the side of the car. The car stopped instantly; her neck was broken, her nose crushed, Isadora was dead.

# Newsreel 53

*Bye bye blackbird*

ARE YOU NEW YORK'S MOST BEAUTIFUL
GIRL STENOGRAPHER?

*No one here can love and understand me*
*Oh what hard luck stories they all hand me*

BRITAIN DECIDES TO GO IT ALONE

you too can quickly learn dancing at home without music
and without a partner . . . produces the same results as an
experienced masseur only quicker, easier, and less expensive.
Remember only marriageable men in the full possession of
unusual physical strength will be accepted as the Graphic
Apollos

*Make my bed and light the light*
*I'll arrive late tonight*

WOMAN IN HOME SHOT AS BURGLAR

GRAND DUKE HERE TO ENJOY HIMSELF

ECLIPSE FOUR SECONDS LATE

DOWNTOWN GAZERS SEE CORONA

others are more dressy being made of rich ottoman
silks, heavy satins, silk crêpe or côte de cheval with ornamen-
tation of ostrich perhaps

MAD DOG PANIC IN PENN STATION

UNHAPPY WIFE TRIES TO DIE

the richly blended beauty of the finish, both interior
and exterior, can come only from the hand of an artist
working towards an idea. *Substitutes good normal solid*

*tissue for that disfiguring fat.* He touches every point in the entire compass of human need. It may look a little foolish in print, but he can show you how to grow brains. If you are a victim of physical ill-being he can liberate you from pain. He can show you how to dissolve marital or conjugal problems. He is an expert in matters of sex.

*Blackbird bye bye*

SKYSCRAPERS BLINK ON EMPTY STREETS.

    it was a very languid, a very pink and white Peggy Joyce in a very pink and white boudoir who held out a small white hand

# Margo Dowling

    When Margie got big enough she used to go across to the station to meet Fred with a lantern dark winter nights when he was expected to be getting home from the city on the ninefourteen. Margie was very little for her age, Agnes used to say, but her red broadcloth coat with the fleece collar tickly round her ears was too small for her all the same, and left her chapped wrists out nights when the sleety wind whipped round the corner of the station and the wire handle of the heavy lantern cut cold into her hand. Always she went with a chill creeping down her spine and in her hands and feet for fear Fred wouldn't be himself and would lurch and stumble the way he sometimes did and be so red in the face and talk so awful. Mr Bemis the stoopshouldered station agent used to kid about it with big Joe Hines the sectionhand who was often puttering around in the station at traintime, and Margie would stand outside in order not to listen to them saying, 'Well, here's bettin' Fred Dowlin' comes in stinkin' again tonight.' It was when he was that way that he needed Margie and the lantern on account of the plankwalk over to the house being so narrow and slippery. When she was a very little girl she used to think that it was because he was so tired from the terrible hard work in the city that he walked so funny when he got off the train, but by the time she was eight or nine Agnes had told her all about how getting drunk was something men did and that they hadn't ought to. So every night she felt the same awful feeling when she saw the lights of the train coming towards her across the long trestle from Ozone Park.

Sometimes he didn't come at all and she'd go back home crying; but the good times he would jump springily off the train, square in his big overcoat that smelt of pipes, and swoop down on her and pick her up lantern and all: 'How's Daddy's good little girl?' He would kiss her and she would feel so proudhappy riding along there and looking at mean old Mr Bemis from up there, and Fred's voice deep in his big chest would go rumbling through his muffler, 'Goodnight, chief,' and the yellowlighted windows of the train would be moving and the red caterpillar's eyes in its tail would get little and draw together as the train went out of sight across the trestle towards Hammels. She would bounce up and down on his shoulder and feel the muscles of his arm hard like oars tighten against her when he'd run with her down the plankwalk shouting to Agnes, 'Any supper left, girlie?' and Agnes would come to the door grinning and wiping her hands on her apron and the big pan of hot soup would be steaming on the stove, and it would be so cozywarm and neat in the kitchen, and they'd let Margie sit up till she was nodding and her eyes were sandy and there was the sandman coming in the door, listening to Fred tell about pocket billiards and sweepstakes and racehorses and terrible fights in the city. Then Agnes would carry her into bed in the cold room and Fred would stand over her smoking his pipe and tell her about shipwrecks at Fire Island when he was in the Coast Guard, till the chinks of light coming in through the door from the kitchen got more and more blurred, and in spite of Margie's trying all the time to keep awake because she was so happy listening to Fred's burring voice, the sandman she'd tried to pretend had lost the train would come in behind Fred, and she'd drop off.

As she got older and along in gradeschool at Rockaway Park, it got to be less often like that. More and more Fred was drunk when he got off the train or else he didn't come at all. Then it was Agnes who would tell her stories about the old days and what fun it had been, and Agnes would sometimes stop in the middle of a story to cry, about how Agnes and Margie's mother had been such friends and both of them had been salesladies at Siegel Cooper's at the artificialflower counter and used to go to Manhattan Beach, so much more refined than Coney, Sundays, not to the Oriental Hotel of course, that was too expensive, but to a little beach near there, and how Fred was lifeguard there.

'You should have seen him in those days, with his strong tanned limbs he was the handsomest man . . .'

'But he's handsome now, isn't he, Agnes?' Margie would put in anxiously.

'Of course, dearie, but you ought to have seen him in those days.'

And Agnes would go on about how lucky he was at the races and how many people he'd saved from drowning and how all the people who owned the concessions chipped in to give him a bonus every year and how much money he always had in his pocket and a wonderful laugh and was such a cheery fellow. 'That was the ruination of him,' Agnes would say. 'He never could say no.' And Agnes would tell about the wedding and the orangeblossoms and the cake and how Margie's mother Margery died when she was born. 'She gave her life for yours, never forget that'; it made Margie feel dreadful, like she wasn't her own self, when Agnes said that.

And then one day when Agnes came out of work, there he'd been standing on the sidewalk wearing a derby hat and all dressed in black and asking her to marry him because she'd been Margery Ryan's best friend, and so they were married, but Fred never got over it and never could say no and that was why Fred took to drinking and lost his job at Holland's and nobody would hire him on any of the beaches on account of his fighting and drinking and so they'd moved to Broad Channel, but they didn't make enough with bait and rowboats and an occasional shoredinner so Fred had gotten a job in Jamaica in a saloon keeping bar because he had such a fine laugh and was so goodlooking and everybody liked him so. But that was the ruination of him worse than ever.

'But there's not a finer man in the world than Fred Dowling when he's himself. . . . Never forget that, Margie.' And they'd both begin to cry, and Agnes would ask Margie if she loved her as much as if she'd been her own mother and Margie would cry and say, 'Yes, Agnes darling.' 'You must always love me,' Agnes would say, 'because God doesn't seem to want me to have any little babies of my own.'

Margie had to go over on the train every day to go to school at Rockaway Park. She got along well in the gradeschool and liked the teachers and the books and the singing, but the children teased because her clothes were all homemade and funnylooking and because she was a mick and a Catholic and lived in a house on stilts. After she'd been Goldilocks in the school play one Christmas, that was all changed and she began to have a better time at school than at home.

At home there was always so much housework to do. Agnes was always washing and ironing and scrubbing because Fred hardly ever brought in any money any more. He'd lurch into the house drunk and dirty and smelling of stale beer and whiskey and curse and grumble about the food and why didn't Agnes ever have a nice piece of steak any more for him like she used to when he got home from the city and Agnes would break down, blubbering, 'What am I going to use for money?' Then he would call her dirty names, and Margie would run into her bedroom and slam the door and sometimes even pull the bureau across it and get into bed and lie there shaking. Sometimes when Agnes was putting breakfast on the table, always in a fluster for fear Margie would miss the train to school, Agnes would have a black eye and her face would be swollen and puffy where he'd hit her and she'd have a meek sorryforherself look Margie hated. And Agnes would be muttering all the time she watched the cocoa and condensed milk heating on the stove, 'God knows I've done my best and worked my fingers to the bone for him. . . . Holy saints of God, things can't go on like this.'

All Margie's dreams were about running away.

In summer they would sometimes have had fun if it hadn't been for always dreading that Fred would take a bit too much. Fred would get the rowboats out of the boathouse for the first sunny day of spring and work like a demon calking and painting them a fresh green and whistle as he worked, or he would be up before day digging clams or catching shiners for bait with a castingnet, and there was money around and big pans of chowder Long Island style and New England style simmering on the back of the stove, and Agnes was happy and singing and always in a bustle fixing shoredinners and sandwiches for fishermen, and Margie would go out sometimes with fishingparties, and Fred taught her to swim in the clear channel up under the railroad bridge and took her with him barefoot over the muddy flats clamming and after softshell crabs, and sportsmen with fancy vests who came down to rent a boat would often give her a quarter. When Fred was in a sober spell it was lovely in summer, the warm smell of the marshgrass, the freshness of the tide coming in through the inlet, the itch of saltwater and sunburn, but then as soon as he'd gotten a little money together Fred would get to drinking and Agnes's eyes would be red all the time and the business would go to pot. Margie hated the way Agnes's face got ugly and red when she cried; she'd tell herself that she'd never cry no matter what happened when she grew up.

Once in a while during the good times Fred would say he was going to give the family a treat and they'd get all dressedup and leave the place with old man Hines, Joe Hines's father, who had a wooden leg and big bushy white whiskers, and go over on the train to the beach and walk along the boardwalk to the amusementpark at Holland's.

It was too crowded and Margie would be scared of getting something on her pretty dress and there was such a glare and men and women with sunburned arms and legs and untidy hair lying out in the staring sun with sand over them, and Fred and Agnes would romp around in their bathingsuits like the others. Margie was scared of the big spuming surf crashing over her head; even when Fred held her in his arms she was scared and then it was terrible he'd swim so far out.

Afterwards they'd get back itchy into their clothes and walk along the boardwalk shrilling with peanutwagons and reeking with the smell of popcorn and saltwater taffy and hotdogs and mustard and beer all mixed up with the surf and the clanking roar of the rollercoaster and the steamcalliope from the merry-goround and so many horrid people pushing and shoving, stepping on your toes. She was too little to see over them. It was better when Fred hoisted her on his shoulder, though she was too old to ride on her father's shoulder in spite of being so small for her age and kept pulling at her pretty paleblue frock to keep it from getting above her knees.

What she liked at the beach was playing the game where you rolled a little ball over the clean narrow varnished boards into holes with numbers, and there was a Jap there in a clean starched white coat and shelves and shelves of the cutest little things for prizes: teapots, little china men that nodded their heads, vases for flowers, rows and rows of the prettiest Japanese dolls with real eyelashes some of them, and jar and jugs and pitchers. One time Margie won a little teapot shaped like an elephant that she kept for years. Fred and Agnes didn't seem to think much of the little Jap who gave the prizes, but Margie thought he was lovely, his face was so smooth and he had such a funny little voice and his lips and eyelids were so clearly marked just like the dolls' and he had long black eyelashes too.

Margie used to think she'd like to have him to take to bed with her like a doll. She said that and Agnes and Fred laughed and laughed at her so that she felt awful ashamed.

But what she liked best at Holland's Beach was the vaudeville theater. They'd go in there and the crowds and laughs and racket would die away as the big padded doors closed behind them. There'd be a movingpicture going on when they went in. She didn't like that much, but what she liked best in all the world were the illustrated songs that came next, the pictures of lovely ladies and gentlemen in colors like tinted flowers and such lovely dresses and big hats and the words with pansies and forgetmenots around them and the lady or gentleman singing them to the dark theater. There were always boats on ripply streams and ladies in lovely dresses being helped out of them, but not like at Broad Channel where it was so glary and there was nothing but mudflats and the slimysmelly piles and the boatlanding lying on the ooze when the tide went out, but lovely blue ripply rivers with lovely green banks and weeping-willowtrees hanging over them. After that it was vaudeville. There were acrobats and trained seals and men in straw hats who told funny jokes and ladies that danced. The Merry Widow Girls it was once, in their big black hats tipped up so wonderfully on one side and their sheathdresses and trains in blue and green and purple and yellow and orange and red, and a handsome young man in a cutaway coat waltzing with each in turn.

The trouble with going to Holland's Beach was that Fred would meet friends there and keep going in through swinging doors and coming back with his eyes bright and a smell of whiskey and pickled onions on his breath, and halfway through the good time, Margie would see that worried meek look coming over Agnes's face, and then she'd know that there would be no more fun that day. The last time they all went over together to the beach they lost Fred, although they looked everywhere for him, and had to go home without him. Agnes sobbed so loud that everybody stared at her on the train and Ed Otis the conductor, who was a friend of Fred's, came over and tried to tell her not to take on so, but that only made Agnes sob the worse. Margie was so ashamed she decided to run away or kill herself as soon as she got home so that she wouldn't have to face the people on the train ever again.

That time Fred didn't turn up the next day the way he usually did. Joe Hines came in to say that a guy had told him he'd seen Fred on a bat over in Brooklyn and that he didn't think he'd come home for a while. Agnes made Margie go to bed and she could hear her voice and Joe Hines's in the kitchen talking low for hours. Margie woke up with a start to find Agnes in her nightgown getting into bed with her.

Her cheeks were fiery hot and she kept saying, 'Imagine his nerve and him a miserable trackwalker. . . . Margie. . . . We can't stand this life any more, can we, little girl?'

'I bet he'd come here fussing, the dreadful old thing,' said Margie.

'Something like that. . . . Oh, it's too awful, I can't stand it any more. God knows I've worked my fingers to the bone.'

Margie suddenly came out with, 'Well, when the cat's away the mice will play,' and was surprised at how long Agnes laughed, though she was crying too.

In September, just when Agnes was fixing up Margie's dresses for the opening of school, the rentman came round for the quarter's rent. All they'd heard from Fred was a letter with a fivedollar bill in it. He said he'd gotten into a fight and gotten arrested and spent two weeks in jail, but that he had a job now and would be home as soon as he'd straightened things out a little. But Margie knew they owed the five dollars and twelve dollars more for groceries. When Agnes came back into the kitchen from talking to the rentman with her face streaky and horrid with crying, she told Margie that they were going into the city to live. 'I always told Fred Dowling the day would come when I couldn't stand it any more. Now he can make his own home after this.'

It was a dreadful day when they got their two bags and the awful old dampeaten trunk up to the station with the help of Joe Hines, who was always doing odd jobs for Agnes when Fred was away, and got on the train that took them into Brooklyn. They went to Agnes's father's and mother's, who lived in the back of a small paperhanger's store on Fulton Street under the El. Old Mr Fisher was a paperhanger and plasterer and the whole house smelt of paste and turpentine and plaster. He was a small little gray man and Mrs Fisher was just like him except that he had drooping gray mustaches and she didn't. They fixed up a cot for Margie in the parlor, but she could see that they thought she was a nuisance. She didn't like them either and hated it in Brooklyn.

It was a relief when Agnes said one evening when she came home before supper looking quite stylish, Margie thought, in her city clothes, that she'd taken a position as cook with a family on Brooklyn Heights and that she was going to send Margie to the Sisters' this winter.

Margie was a little scared all the time she was at the convent, from the minute she went in the door of the graystone vestibule with a whitemarble figure standing up in the middle of it. Margie hadn't ever had much religion, and the Sisters were scary in their dripping black with their faces and hands looking so pale always edged with white starched stuff, and the big dark church full of candles and the catechismclass and confession, and the way the little bell rang at Mass for everybody to close their eyes when the Saviour came down among angels and doves in a glare of amber light onto the altar. It was funny, after the way Agnes had let her run round the house without any clothes on, that when she took her bath once a week the Sister made her wear a sheet right in the tub and even soap herself under it.

The winter was a long slow climb to Christmas, and after all the girls had talked about what they'd do at Christmas so much Margie's Christmas was awful, a late gloomy dinner with Agnes and the old people and only one or two presents. Agnes looked pale, she was deadtired from getting the Christmas dinner for the people she worked for. She did bring a net stocking full of candy and a pretty goldenhaired dolly with eyes that opened and closed, but Margie felt like crying. Not even a tree. Already sitting at the table she was busy making up things to tell the other girls anyway.

Agnes was just kissing her goodnight and getting ready putting on her little worn furpiece to go back to Brooklyn Heights when Fred came in very much under the influence and wanted to take them all out on a party. Of course they wouldn't go and he went away mad and Agnes went away crying, and Margie lay awake half the night on the cot made up for her in the old peoples' parlor thinking how awful it was to be poor and have a father like that.

It was dreary, too, hanging round the old people's house while the vacation lasted. There was no place to play and they scolded her for the least little thing. It was bully to get back to the convent where there was a gym and she could play basketball and giggle with the other girls at recess. The winter term began to speed up towards Easter. Just before, she took her first communion. Agnes made the white dress for her and all the Sisters rolled up their eyes and said how pretty and pure she looked with her golden curls and blue eyes like an angel, and Minette Hardy, an older girl with a snubnose, got a crush on her and used to pass her chocolatepeppermints in the playground wrapped in bits of paper with little messages scrawled on them: 'To Goldilocks with love from her darling Minette,' and things like that.

She hated it when commencement came, and there was nothing about summer plans she could tell the other girls. She grew fast that summer and got gawky and her breasts began to show. The stuffy gritty hot weather dragged on endlessly at the Fishers'. It was awful there cooped up with the old people. Old Mrs Fisher never let her forget that she wasn't really Agnes's little girl and that she thought it was silly of her daughter to support the child of a noaccount like Fred. They tried to get her to do enough housework to pay for her keep and every day there were scoldings and tears and tantrums.

Margie was certainly happy when Agnes came in one day and said that she had a new job and that she and Margie would go over to New York to live. She jumped up and down yelling, 'Goody goody. . . . Oh, Agnes, we're going to get rich.'

'A fat chance,' said Agnes, 'but anyway it'll be better than being a servant.'

They gave their trunks and bags to an expressman and went over to New York on the El and then uptown on the subway. The streets of the uptown West Side looked amazingly big and wide and sunny to Margie. They were going to live with the Francinis in a little apartment on the corner on the same block with the bakery they ran on Amsterdam Avenue where Agnes was going to work. They had a small room for the two of them, but it had a canarybird in a cage and a lot of plants in the window and the Francinis were both of them fat and jolly and they had cakes with icing on them at every meal. Mrs Francini was Grandma Fisher's sister.

They didn't let Margie play with the other children on the block; the Francinis said it wasn't a safe block for little girls. She only got out once a week and that was Sunday evening; everybody always had to go over to the Drive and walk up to Grant's Tomb and back. It made her legs ache to walk so slowly along the crowded streets the way the Francinis did. All summer she wished for a pair of rollerskates, but the way the

Francinis talked and the way the nuns talked about dangers made her scared to go out on the streets alone. What she was so scared of she didn't quite know. She liked it, though, helping Agnes and the Francinis in the bakery.

That fall she went back to the convent. One afternoon soon after she'd gone back from the Christmas holidays Agnes came over to see her; the minute Margie went in the door of the visitors' parlor she saw that Agnes's eyes were red and asked what was the matter. Things had changed dreadfully at the bakery. Poor Mr Francini had fallen dead in the middle of his baking from a stroke and Mrs Francini was going out to the country to live with Uncle Joe Fisher.

'And then there's something else,' Agnes said and smiled and blushed. 'But I can't tell you about it now. You mustn't think that poor Agnes is bad and wicked, but I couldn't stand it being so lonely.'

Margie jumped up and down. 'Oh, goody, Fred's come back.'

'No, darling, it's not that,' Agnes said and kissed her and went away.

That Easter Margie had to stay at the convent all through the vacation. Agnes wrote she didn't have any place to take her just then. There were other girls there and it was rather fun. Then one day Agnes came over to get her to go out, bringing in a box right from the store a new darkblue dress and a little straw hat with pink flowers on it. It was lovely the way the tissuepaper rustled when she unpacked them. Margie ran up to the dormitory and put on the dress with her heart pounding, it was the prettiest and grownupest dress she'd ever had. She was only twelve, but from what little she could see of herself in the tiny mirrors they were allowed it made her look quite grownup. She ran down the empty graystone stairs, tripped and fell into the arms of Sister Elizabeth.

'Why such a hurry?'

'My mother's come to take me out on a party with my father and this is my new dress.'

'How nice,' said Sister Elizabeth, 'but you mustn't . . .'

Margie was already off down the passage to the parlor and was jumping up and down in front of Agnes hugging and kissing her. 'It's the prettiest dress I ever had.' Going over to New York on the Elevated Margie couldn't talk about anything else but the dress.

Agnes said they were going to lunch at a restaurant where theatrical people went. 'How wonderful! I've never had lunch in a real restaurant. . . . He must have made a lot of money and gotten rich.'

'He makes lots of money,' said Agnes in a funny stammering way as they were walking west along Thirtyeighth Street from the El station.

Instead of Fred it was a tall dark man with a dignified manner and a long straight nose who got up from the table to meet them. 'Margie,' said Agnes, 'this is Frank Mandeville.' Margie never let on she hadn't thought all the time that that was how it would be.

The actor shook hands with her and bowed as if she was a grownup young lady. 'Aggie never told me she was such a beauty . . . what eyes . . . what hair!' he said in his solemn voice.

They had a wonderful lunch and afterwards they went to Keith's and sat in orchestra seats. Margie was breathless and excited at being with a real actor. He'd said that the next day he was leaving for a twelveweeks' tour with a singing and piano act and that Agnes was going with him. 'And after that we'll come back and make a home for my little girl,' said Agnes. Margie was so excited that it wasn't till she was back in bed in the empty dormitory at the convent that she doped out that what it would mean for her was she'd have to stay at the Sisters' all summer.

The next fall she left the convent for good and went to live with Mr and Mrs Mandeville, as they called themselves, in two front rooms they sublet from a chiropractor. It was a big old brownstone house with a high stoop and steps way west on Seventyninth Street. Margie loved it there and got on fine with the theater people, all so welldressed and citifiedlooking, who lived in the apartments upstairs. Agnes said she must be careful not to get spoiled, because everybody called attention to her blue eyes and her curls like Mary Pickford's and her pert frozenface way of saying funny things.

Frank Mandeville always slept till twelve o'clock and Agnes and Margie would have breakfast alone quite early, talking in whispers so as not to wake him and looking out of the window at the trucks and cabs and movingvans passing in the street outside and Agnes would tell Margie about vaudeville houses and onenight stands and all about how happy she was and what a free-and-easy life it was and so different from the daily grind at Broad Channel and how she'd first met Frank Mandeville when he was broke and blue and almost ready to turn on the gas. He used to come into the bakery every day for his breakfast at two in the afternoon just when all the other customers had gone. He lived around the corner on Onehundredandfourfh Street. When he was completely flat, Agnes had let him charge his meals and had felt so sorry for him on account of his being so gentlemanly about it and out of a job, and then he got pleurisy and was threatened with t.b. and she was so lonely and miserable that she didn't care what anybody thought, she'd just moved in with him to nurse him and had stayed ever since, and how they were Mr and Mrs Mandeville to everybody and he was making big money with his act The Musical Mandevilles. And Margie would ask about Frank Mandeville's partners, Florida Schwartz, a big hardvoiced woman with titian hair, 'Of course she dyes it,' Agnes said 'henna,' and her son, a horrid waspwaisted young man of eighteen who paid no attention to Margie at all. The chiropractor downstairs whom everybody called Indian was Florida's affinity and that was why they'd all come to live in his house. 'Stagepeople are odd, but I think they have hearts of gold,' Agnes would say.

The Musical Mandevilles used to practice afternoons in the front room where there was a piano. They played all sorts of instruments and sang songs and Mannie whose stage name was Eddy Keller did an eccentric dance and an imitation of Hazel Dawn. It all seemed wonderful to Margie, and she was so excited she thought she'd die when Mr Mandeville said suddenly one day when they were all eating supper brought in from a delicatessen that the child must take singing and dancing lessons.

'You'll be wasting your money, Frank,' said Mannie through a chickenbone he was gnawing.

'Mannie, you're talking out of turn,' snapped Florida.

'Her father was a great one for singing and dancing in the old days,' put in Agnes in her breathless timid manner.

A career was something everybody had in New York and Margie decided she had one too. She walked down Broadway every day to her lesson in a studio in the same building as the Lincoln Square Theater. In October The Musical Mandevilles played there two weeks. Almost every day Agnes would come for her after the lesson and they'd have a sandwich and a glass of milk in a dairy lunch and then go to see the show. Agnes could never get over how pretty and young Mrs Schwartz looked behind the footlights and how sad and dignified Frank looked when he came in in his operacloak.

During the winter Agnes got a job too, running an artistic tearoom just off Broadway on Seventysecond Street, with a Miss Franklyn, a redhaired lady who was a theosophist and was putting in the capital. They all worked so hard they only met in the evenings when Frank and Florida and Mannie would be eating a bite in a hurry before going off to their theater.

The Musical Mandevilles were playing Newark the night Margie first went on. She was to come out in the middle of an *Everybody's Doing It* number rolling a hoop, in a blue muslin dress she didn't like because it made her look about six and she thought she ought to look grownup to go on the stage, and do a few steps of a ragtime dance and then curtsy like they had taught her at the convent and run off with her hoop. Frank had made her rehearse it again and again. She'd often burst out crying in the rehearsals on account of the mean remarks Mannie made.

She was dreadfully scared and her heart pounded waiting for the cue, but it was over before she knew what had happened. She had run on from the grimy wings into the warm glittery glare of the stage. They'd told her not to look out into the audience. Just once she peeped out into the blurry light-powdered cave of ranked white faces. She forgot part of her song and skimped her business and cried in the dressingroom after the act was over, but Agnes came round back saying she'd been lovely, and Frank was smiling, and even Mannie couldn't seem to think of anything mean to say; so the next time she went on her heart wasn't pounding so hard. Every littlest thing she did got an answer from the vague cave of faces. By the end of the week she was getting such a hand that Frank decided to run the *Everybody's Doing It* number just before the finale.

Florida Schwartz had said that Margery was too vulgar a given name for the stage, so she was billed as Little Margo.

All winter and the next summer they toured on the Keith circuit, sleeping in Pullmans and in all kinds of hotels and going to Chicago and Milwaukee and Kansas City and so many towns that Margie couldn't remember their names. Agnes came along as wardrobemistress and attended to the transportation and fetched and carried for everybody. She was always washing and ironing and heating up canned soup on an alcohol stove. Margie got to be ashamed of how shabby Agnes looked on the street beside Florida Schwartz. Whenever she met other stagechildren and they asked her who she thought the best matinee idol was, she'd answer Frank Mandeville.

When the war broke out The Musical Mandevilles were back in New York looking for new bookings. One evening Frank was explaining his plan to make the act a real headliner by turning it into a vestpocket operetta, when he and the Schwartzes got to quarreling about the war. Frank said the Mandevilles were descended from a long line of French nobility and that the Germans were barbarian swine and had no idea of art. The Schwartzes blew up and said that the French were degenerates and not to be trusted in money matters and that Frank was holding out receipts on them. They made such a racket that the other boarders banged on the wall and a camelfaced lady came up from the basement wearing a dressinggown spattered with red and blue poppies and with her hair in curlpapers to tell them to keep quiet. Agnes cried and Frank in a ringing voice ordered the Schwartzes to leave the room and not to darken his door again, and Margie got an awful fit of giggling. The more Agnes scolded at her the more she giggled. It wasn't until Frank took her in the arms of his rakishlytailored checked suit and stroked her hair and her forehead that she was able to quiet down. She went to bed that night still feeling funny and breathless inside with the whiff of bay rum and energine and Egyptian cigarettes that had teased her nose when she leaned against his chest.

That fall it was hard times again, vaudeville bookings were hard to get and Frank didn't have a partner for his act. Agnes went back to Miss Franklyn's teashop and Margie had to give up her singing and dancing lessons. They moved into one room, with a curtained cubicle for Margie to sleep in.

October was very warm that year. Margie was miserable hanging round the house all day, the steamheat wouldn't turn off altogether and it was too hot even with the window open. She felt tired all the time. The house smelled of frizzing hair and beautycreams and shavingsoap. The rooms were all rented to theater people and there was no time of the day that you could go up to the bathroom without meeting heavyeyed people in bathrobes or kimonos on the stairs. There was something hot and sticky in the way the men looked at Margie when she brushed past them in the hall that made her feel awful funny.

She loved Frank best of anybody. Agnes was always peevish, in a hurry to go to work or else deadtired just back from work, but Frank always spoke to her seriously as if she were a grownup young lady. The rare afternoons when he was in, he coached her on elocution and told her stories about the time he'd toured with Richard Mansfield. He'd give her bits of parts to learn and she had to recite them to him when he came home. When she didn't know them, he'd get very cold and stride up and down and say, 'Well, it's up to you, my dear, if you want a career you must work for it. . . . You have the godgiven gifts . . . but without hard work they are nothing. . . . I suppose you want to work in a tearoom like poor Agnes all your life.'

Then she'd run up to him and throw her arms round his neck and kiss him and say, 'Honest, Frank, I'll work terrible hard.' He'd be all flustered when she did that or mussed his hair and would say, 'Now, child, no liberties,' and suggest they go out for a walk up Broadway. Sometimes when he had a little money they'd go skating at the St Nicholas rink. When they spoke of Agnes they always called her poor Agnes as if she were a little halfwitted. There was something a little hick about Agnes.

But most of the time Margie just loafed or read magazines in the room or lay on the bed and felt the hours dribble away so horribly slowly. She'd dream about boys taking her out to the theater and to restaurants and what kind of a house she would live in when she became a great actress, and the jewelry she'd have, or else she'd remember how Indian the chiropractor had kneaded her back the time she had the sick headache. He was strong and brown and wiry in his shirtsleeves working on her back with his bigknuckled hands. It was only his eyes made her feel funny; eyes like Indian's would suddenly be looking at her when she was walking along Broadway, she'd hurry and wouldn't dare turn back to see if they were still looking, and get home all breathless and scared.

One warm afternoon in the late fall, Margie was lying on the bed reading a copy of the *Smart Set* Frank had bought that Agnes had made her promise not to read. She heard a shoe creak and jumped up popping the magazine under the pillow.

Frank was standing in the doorway looking at her. She didn't need to look at him twice to know that he'd been drinking. His eyes had that look and there was a flush on his usually white face. 'Haha, caught you that time, Little Margo,' he said.

'I bet you think I don't know my part,' said Margie.

'I wish I didn't know mine,' he said. 'I've just signed the lousiest contract I ever signed in my life. . . . The world will soon see Frank Mandeville on the filthy stage of a burlesque house.' He sat down on the bed with his felt hat still on his head and put a hand over his eyes. 'God, I'm tired. . . . ' Then he looked up at her with his eyes red and staring. 'Little Margo, you don't know what it is yet to buck the world.'

Margie said with a little giggle that she knew plenty and sat down beside him on the bed and took his hat off and smoothed his sweaty hair back from his forehead. Something inside of her was scared of doing it, but she couldn't help it.

'Let's go skating, Frank, it's so awful to be in the house all day.'

'Everything's horrible,' he said. Suddenly he pulled her to him and kissed her lips. She felt dizzy with the smell of bay rum and cigarettes and whiskey and cloves and armpits that came from him. She pulled away from him. 'Frank, don't, don't.' He had tight hold of her. She could feel his hands trembling, his heart thumping under his vest. He had grabbed her to him with one arm and was pulling at her clothes with the other. His voice wasn't like Frank's voice at all. 'I won't hurt you. I won't hurt you, child. Just forget. It's nothing. I can't stand it any more.' The voice went on and on whining in her ears. 'Please. Please.'

She didn't dare yell for fear the people in the house might come. She clenched her teeth and punched and scratched at the big wetlipped face pressing down hers. She felt weak like in a dream. His knee was pushing her legs apart.

When it was over, she wasn't crying. She didn't dare. He was walking up and down the room sobbing. She got up and straightened her dress.

He came over to her and shook her by the shoulders. 'If you ever tell anybody I'll kill you, you damn little brat. . . . Are you bleeding?' She shook her head.

He went over to the washstand and washed his face.

'I couldn't help it, I'm not a saint. . . . I've been under a terrible strain.'

Margie heard Agnes coming, the creak of her steps on the stairs. Agnes was puffing as she fumbled with the doorknob.

'Why, what on earth's the matter?' she said, coming in all out of breath.

'Agnes, I've had to scold your child,' Frank was saying in his tragedy voice. 'I come in deadtired and find the child reading that filthy magazine. . . . I won't have it. . . . Not while you are under my protection.'

'Oh, Margie, you promised you wouldn't. . . . But what did you do to your face?'

Frank came forward into the center of the room, patting his face all over with the towel. 'Agnes, I have a confession to make. . . . I got into an altercation downtown. I've had a very trying day downtown. My nerves have all gone to pieces. What will you think of me when I tell you I've signed a contract with a burlesque house?'

'Why, that's fine,' said Agnes. 'We certainly need the money. . . . How much will you be making?'

'It's shameful . . . twenty a week.'

'Oh, I'm so relieved . . . I thought something terrible had happened. Maybe Margie can start her lessons again.'

'If she's a good girl and doesn't waste her time reading trashy magazines.'

Margie was trembly like jelly inside. She felt herself breaking out in a cold sweat. She ran upstairs to the bathroom and doublelocked the door and stumbled to the toilet and threw up. Then she sat a long time on the edge of the bathtub. All she could think of was to run away.

But she couldn't seem to get to run away. At Christmas some friends of Frank's got her a job in a children's play. She made twentyfive dollars a performance and was the pet of all the society ladies. It made her feel quite stuckup. She almost got caught with the boy who played the Knight doing it behind some old flats when the theater was dark during a rehearsal.

It was awful living in the same room with Frank and Agnes. She hated them now. At night she'd lie awake with her eyes hot in the stuffy cubicle and listen to them. She knew that they were trying to be quiet, that they didn't want her to hear, but she couldn't help straining her ears and holding her breath when the faint rattle of springs from the rickety old iron bed they slept in began. She slept late after those nights in a horrible deep sleep she never wanted to wake up from. She began to be saucy and spiteful with Agnes and would never do anything she said. It was easy to make Agnes cry. 'Drat the child,' she'd say, wiping her eyes. 'I can't do anything with her. It's that little bit of success that went to her head.'

That winter she began to find Indian in the door of his consultationroom when she went past, standing there brown and sinewy in his white coat, always wanting to chat or show her a picture or something. He'd even offer her treatments free, but she'd look right into those funny blue-black eyes of his and kid him along. Then one day she went into the office when there were no patients and sat down on his knee without saying a word.

But the boy she liked best in the house was a Cuban named Tony Garrido, who played the guitar for two South Americans who danced the maxixe in a Broadway cabaret. She used to pass him on the stairs and knew all about it and decided she had a crush on him long before they ever spoke. He looked so young with his big brown eyes and his smooth oval face a very light coffeecolor with a little flush on the cheeks under his high long cheekbones. She used to wonder if he was the same color all over. He had polite bashful manners and a low grownup voice. The first time he spoke to her, one spring evening when she was standing on the stoop wondering desperately what she could do to keep from going up to the room, she knew he was going to fall for her. She kidded him and asked him what he put on his eyelashes to make them so black. He said it was the same thing that made her hair so pretty and golden and asked her to have an icecream soda with him.

Afterwards they walked on the Drive. He talked English fine with a little accent that Margie thought was very distinguished. Right away they'd stopped kidding and he was telling her how homesick he was for Havana and how crazy he was to get out of New York, and she was telling him what an awful life she led and how all the men in the house were always pinching her and jostling her on the stairs, and how she'd throw herself in the river if she had to go on living in one room with Agnes and Frank Mandeville. And as for that Indian, she wouldn't let him touch her not if he was the last man in the world.

She didn't get home until it was time for Tony to go downtown to his cabaret. Instead of supper they ate some more icecream sodas. Margie went back happy as a lark. Coming out of the drugstore, she'd heard a woman say to her friend, 'My, what a handsome young couple.'

Of course Frank and Agnes raised cain. Agnes cried and Frank lashed himself up into a passion and said he'd punch the damn greaser's head in if he so much as laid a finger on a pretty, pure American girl. Margie yelled out that she'd do what she damn pleased and said everything mean she could

think of. She'd decided that the thing for her to do was to
marry Tony and run away to Cuba with him.

Tony didn't seem to like the idea of getting married much,
but she'd go up to his little hall bedroom as soon as Frank
was out of the house at noon and wake Tony up and tease
him and pet him. He'd want to make love to her but she
wouldn't let him. The first time she fought him off he broke
down and cried and said it was an insult and that in Cuba
men didn't allow women to act like that. 'It's the first time
in my life a woman has refused my love.'

Margie said she didn't care, not till they were married and
had gotten out of this awful place. At last one afternoon she
teased him till he said all right. She put her hair up on top
of her head and put on her most grownuplooking dress and
they went down to the marriagebureau on the subway. They
were both of them scared to death when they had to go up to
the clerk he was twentyone and she said she was nineteen and
got away with it. She'd stolen the money out of Agnes's purse
to pay for the license.

She almost went crazy the weeks she had to wait for Tony
to finish out his contract. Then one day in May, when she
tapped on his bedroom door he showed her two hundred
dollars in bills he'd saved up and said, 'Today we get married.
. . . Tomorrow we sail for La 'Avana. We can make very much
money there. You will dance and I will sing and play the
guitar.' He made the gesture of playing the guitar with the
thinpointed fingers of one of his small hands. Her heart started
beating hard. She ran downstairs. Frank had already gone out.
She scribbled a note to Agnes on the piece of cardboard that had
come back from the laundry in one of Frank's boiled shirts:

AGNES DARLING:
Don't be mad. Tony and I got married today and we're going
to Havana, Cuba, to live. Tell Father if he comes around. I'll write
lots. Love to Frank.

> Your grateful daughter,
> MARGERY

Then she threw her clothes into an English pigskin suitcase
of Frank's that he'd just got back from the hockshop and ran
down the stairs three at a time. Tony was waiting for her on
the stoop, pale and trembling with his guitarcase and his suitcase beside him. 'I do not care for the money. Let's take a
taxi,' he said.

In the taxi she grabbed his hand, it was icy cold. At City

Hall he was so fussed he forgot all his English and she had to do everything. They borrowed a ring from the justice of the peace. It was over in a minute, and they were back in the taxi again going uptown to a hotel. Margie never could remember afterwards what hotel it was, only that they'd looked so fussed that the clerk wouldn't believe they were married until she showed him the marriagelicense, a big sheet of paper all bordered with forgetmenots. When they got up to the room they kissed each other in a hurry and washed up to go out to a show. First they went to Shanley's to dinner. Tony ordered expensive champagne and they both got to giggling on it.

He kept telling her what a rich city La 'Avana was and how the artists were really appreciated there and rich men would pay him fifty, one hundred dollars a night to play at their parties, 'And with you, darling Margo, it will be two three six time that much. . . . And we shall rent a fine house in the Vedado, very exclusive section, and servants very cheap there, and you will be like a queen. You will see I have many friends there, many rich men like me very much.' Margie sat back in her chair, looking at the restaurant and the welldressed ladies and gentlemen and the waiters so deferential and the silver dishes everything came in and at Tony's long eyelashes brushing his pink cheek as he talked about how warm it was and the cool breeze off the sea, and the palms and the roses, and parrots and singing birds in cages, and how everybody spent money in La 'Avana. It seemed the only happy day she'd ever had in her life.

When they took the boat the next day, Tony had only enough money to buy secondclass passages. They went over to Brooklyn on the El to save taxifare. Margie had to carry both bags up the steps because Tony said he had a headache and was afraid of dropping his guitarcase.

# Newsreel 54

there was nothing significant about the morning's trading. The first hour consisted of general buying and selling to even up accounts, but soon after eleven o'clock prices did less fluctuating and gradually firmed

TIMES SQUARE PATRONS LEFT HALF-SHAVED

Will Let Crop Rot In Producers' Hands Unless Prices Drop

RUSSIAN BARONESS SUICIDE AT MIAMI

*... the kind of a girl that men forget*
*Just a toy to enjoy for a while*

Coolidge Pictures Nation Prosperous Under His Policies

HUNT JERSEY WOODS FOR ROVING LEOPARD

PIGWOMAN SAW SLAYING

It had to be done and I did it, says Miss Ederle

FORTY-TWO INDICTED IN FLORIDA DEALS

Saw a Woman Resembling Mrs Hall Berating Couple Near Murder Scene, New Witness Says

several hundred tents and other light shelters put up by campers on a hill south of Front Street, which overlooks Hempstead Harbor, were laid in rows before the tornado as grass falls before a scythe

*When they play    Here    comes    the    bride*
*You'll stand outside*

THREE THOUSAND AMERICANS FOUND PENNILESS IN PARIS

*I am a poor girl*
*My fortune's been sad*

*I always was courted*
*By the wagoner's lad*

NINE DROWNED IN UPSTATE FLOODS

SHEIK SINKING

Rudolph Valentino, noted screen star, collapsed suddenly yesterday in his apartment at the Hotel Ambassador. Several hours later he underwent

# Adagio Dancer

The nineteenyearold son of a veterinary in Castellaneta in the south of Italy was shipped off to America like a lot of other unmanageable young Italians when his parents gave up trying to handle him, to sink or swim and maybe send a few lire home by international postal moneyorder. The family was through with him. But Rodolfo Guglielmi wanted to make good.

He got a job as assistant gardener in Central Park, but that kind of work was the last thing he wanted to do; he wanted to make good in the brightlights; money burned his pockets.

He hung around cabarets doing odd jobs, sweeping out for the waiters, washing cars; he was lazy handsome wellbuilt slender goodtempered and vain; he was a born tangodancer.

Lovehungry women thought he was a darling. He began to get engagements dancing the tango in ballrooms and cabarets; he teamed up with a girl named Jean Acker on a vaudeville tour and took the name of Rudolph Valentino.

Stranded on the Coast he headed for Hollywood, worked for a long time as an extra for five dollars a day; directors began to notice he photographed well.

He got his chance in *The Four Horsemen*
and became the gigolo of every woman's dreams.

Valentino spent his life in the colorless glare of klieg lights, in stucco villas obstructed with bricabrac, Oriental rugs, tigerskins, in the bridalsuites of hotels, in silk bathrobes in private cars.

He was always getting into limousines or getting out of limousines, or patting the necks of fine horses.

Wherever he went the sirens of the motorcyclecops screeched ahead of him,

flashlights flared,

the streets were jumbled with hysterical faces, waving hands, crazy eyes; they stuck out their autographbooks, yanked his buttons off, cut a tail off his admirablytailored dress-suit; they stole his hat and pulled at his necktie; his valets removed young women from under his bed; all night in nightclubs and cabarets actresses leching for stardom made sheepseyes at him under their mascaraed lashes.

He wanted to make good under the glare of the million-dollar searchlights

of El Dorado:

the Sheik, the Son of the Sheik;

personal appearances.


He married his old vaudeville partner, divorced her, married the adopted daughter of a millionaire, went into lawsuits with the producers who were debasing the art of the screen, spent a million dollars on one European trip;

he wanted to make good in the brightlights.

When the Chicago *Tribune* called him a pink powderpuff

and everybody started wagging their heads over a slavebracelet he wore that he said his wife had given him and his taste for mushy verse of which he published a small volume called *Daydreams* and the whispers grew about the testimony in his divorce case that he and his first wife had never slept together,

it broke his heart.

He tried to challenge the Chicago *Tribune* to a duel;

he wanted to make good

in heman twofisted broncobusting pokerplaying stockjuggling America. (He was a fair boxer and had a good seat on a horse; he loved the desert like the sheik and was tanned from the sun of Palm Springs.) He broke down in his suite in the Hotel Ambassador in New York: gastric ulcer.

When the doctors cut into his elegantlymolded body, they found that peritonitis had begun; the abdominal cavity contained a large amount of fluid and food particles; the viscera were coated with a greenishgray film; a round hole a centimeter in diameter was seen in the anterior wall of the stomach; the tissue of the stomach for one and onehalf centimeters immediately surrounding the perforation was necrotic. The appendix was inflamed and twisted against the small intestine.

When he came to from the ether, the first thing he said was, 'Well, did I behave like a pink powderpuff?'

His expensivelymassaged actor's body fought peritonitis for six days.

The switchboard at the hospital was swamped with calls, all the corridors were piled with flowers, crowds filled the street outside, filmstars who claimed they were his betrothed entrained for New York.

*Late in the afternoon a limousine drew up at the hospital door* (where the grimyfingered newspapermen and photographers stood around bored tired hoteyed smoking too many cigarettes making trips to the nearest speak exchanging wisecracks and deep dope waiting for him to die in time to make the evening papers), *and a woman, who said she was a maid employed by a dancer who was Valentino's first wife, alighted. She delivered to an attendant an envelope addressed to the filmstar and inscribed 'From Jean,' and a package. The package contained a white counterpane with lace ruffles and the word 'Rudy' embroidered in the four corners. This was accompanied by a pillowcover to match over a blue silk scented cushion.*

Rudolph Valentino was only thirtyone when he died.

His managers planned to make a big thing of his highlypublicized funeral, but the people in the streets were too crazy.

While he lay in state in a casket covered with a cloth of gold, tens of thousands of men, women, and children packed the streets outside. Hundreds were trampled, had their feet hurt by policehorses. In the muggy rain the cops lost control. Jammed masses stampeded under the clubs and the rearing hoofs of the horses. The funeral chapel was gutted, men and women fought over a flower, a piece of wallpaper, a piece of the broken plateglass window. Showwindows were burst in. Parked cars were overturned and smashed. When finally the mounted police after repeated charges beat the crowd off Broadway, where traffic was tied up for two hours, they picked up twentyeight separate shoes, a truckload of umbrellas, papers, hats, tornoff sleeves. All the ambulances in that part of the city were busy carting off women who'd fainted, girls who'd been stepped on. Epileptics threw fits. Cops collected little groups of abandoned children.

The fascisti sent a guard of honor and the antifascists drove them off. More rioting, cracked skulls, trampled feet. When the public was barred from the undertaking parlors, hundreds of women groggy with headlines got in to view the poor body,

claiming to be exdancingpartners, old playmates, relatives from the old country, filmstars; every few minutes a girl fainted in front of the bier and was revived by the newspapermen who put down her name and address and claim to notice in the public prints. Frank E. Campbell's undertakers and pallbearers, dignified wearers of black broadcloth and tackers-up of crape, were on the verge of a nervous breakdown. Even the boss had his fill of publicity that time.

It was two days before the cops could clear the streets enough to let the flowerpieces from Hollywood be brought in and described in the evening papers.

The church service was more of a success. The police-commissioner barred the public for four blocks around.

Many notables attended.

America's Sweetheart, sobbing bitterly in a small black straw with a black band and a black bow behind, in black georgette over black with a white lace collar and white lace cuffs, followed the coffin that was

covered by a blanket of pink roses

sent by a filmstar who appeared at the funeral heavily veiled, and swooned and had to be taken back to her suite at the Hotel Ambassador after she had shown the reporters a message allegedly written by one of the doctors alleging that Rudolph Valentino had spoken of her at the end

as his bridetobe.

A young woman committed suicide in London.

Relatives arriving from Europe were met by police reserves and Italian flags draped with crape. Exchamp Jim Jeffries said, 'Well, he made good.' The champion allowed himself to be quoted that the boy was fond of boxing and a great admirer of the champion.

The funeral train left for Hollywood.

In Chicago a few more people were hurt trying to see the coffin, but only made the inside pages.

The funeral train arrived in Hollywood on page 23 of the *New York Times*.

# Newsreel 55

LUNATIC BLOWS UP PITTSBURGH BANK

KRISHNAMURTI HERE SAYS HIS MESSAGE IS
WORLD HAPPINESS

*Close the doors*
*They are coming*
*Through the windows*

AMERICAN MARINES LAND IN NICARAGUA TO
PROTECT ALIENS

PANGALOS CAUGHT; PRISONER IN ATHENS

*Close the windows*
*They are coming through the doors*

SAW PIGWOMAN, THE OTHER SAYS, BUT NEITHER
CAN IDENTIFY ACCUSED

FUNDS ACCUMULATE IN NEW YORK

the desire for profits and more profits kept on increasing and the quest for easy money became well nigh universal. All of this meant an attempt to appropriate the belongings of others without rendering a corresponding service

'PHYSICIAN' WHO TOOK PROMINENT PART IN
VALENTINO FUNERAL EXPOSED AS FORMER
CONVICT

NEVER SAW HIM SAYS MANAGER

*Close the doors they are coming through the windows*
*My God they're coming through the floor*

## *The Camera Eye (47)*

    sirens bloom in the fog over the harbor    horns of all colors everyshaped whistles reach up from the river and the churn of screws the throb of engines    bells

    the steady broken swish of waves cut by prows    out of the unseen stirring tumblingly through the window tentacles stretch tingling

    to release the spring

    tonight start out ship somewhere join up sign on the dotted line enlist become one of

    hock the old raincoat of incertitude (in which you hunch alone    from the upsidedown image on the retina painstakingly out of color shape words remembered light and dark straining

    to rebuild yesterday    to clip out paper figures to stimulate growth    warp newsprint into faces smoothing and wrinkling in the various barelyfelt velocities of time)

    tonight now    the room fills with the throb and hubbub of departure    the explorer gets a few necessities together coaches himself on a beginning

    better the streets    first a stroll    uptown downtown along the wharves under the el peering into faces in taxicabs at the drivers of trucks at old men chewing in lunchrooms at drunk bums drooling puke in alleys what's the newsvendor reading?    what did the elderly wop selling chestnuts whisper to the fat woman behind the picklejars? where is she going the plain girl in a red hat running up the subway steps and the cop joking the other cop across the street?    and the smack of a kiss from two shadows under the stoop of the brownstone house and the grouchy faces at the streetcorner suddenly gaping black with yells at the thud of a blow a whistle scampering feet    the event?

    tonight now

    but instead you find yourself (if self is the bellyaching malingerer so often the companion of aimless walks) the jobhunt forgotten    neglected the bulletinboard where the futures are scrawled in chalk

among nibbling chinamen at the Thalia
ears dazed by the crash of alien gongs the chuckle of
rattles the piping of incomprehensible flutes the swing and
squawk of ununderstandable talk     otherworld music antics
postures costumes
    an unidentified stranger
    destination unknown
    hat pulled down over the     has he any?     face

## Charley Anderson

It was a bright metalcolored January day when Charley went
downtown to lunch with Nat Benton. He got to the broker's
office a little early, and sat waiting in an empty office looking
out through the broad steelframed windows at the North River
and the Statue of Liberty and the bay beyond all shiny ruffled
green in the northwest wind, spotted with white dabs of smoke
from tugboats, streaked with catspaws and the churny wakes
of freighters bucking the wind, checkered with lighters and
flatboats, carferries, barges, and the red sawedoff passenger-
ferries. A schooner with gray sails was running out before the
wind.

Charley sat at Nat Benton's desk smoking a cigarette and
being careful to get all his ashes in the polished brass ash-
receiver that stood beside the desk. The phone buzzed. It was
the switchboard girl. 'Mr Anderson . . . Mr Benton asked me
to beg you to excuse him for a few more minutes. He's out on
the floor. He'll be over right away.' A little later Benton stuck
in the crack of the door his thin pale face on a long neck
like a chicken's. 'Hullo, Charley . . . be right there.' Charley
had time to smoke one more cigarette before Benton came
back. 'I bet you're starved.'

'That's all right, Nat, I been enjoyin' the view.'

'View? . . . Sure . . . Why, I don't believe I look out of that
window from one week's end to the other. . . . Still it was on one
of those darned red ferries that old Vanderbilt got his start. . . .
I guess if I took my nose out of the ticker now and then I'd be
better off. . . . Come along, let's get something to eat,' Going
down in the elevator Nat Benton went on talking. 'Why, you are
certainly a difficult customer to get hold of.'

'The first time I've had my overalls off in a year,' said Charley, laughing.

The cold stung when they stepped out of the revolving doors. 'You know, Charley, there's been quite a little talk about you fellers on the street. . . . Askew-Merritt went up five points yesterday. The other day there was a feller from Detroit, a crackerjack feller . . . you know the Tern outfit . . . looking all over for you. We'll have lunch together next time he's in town.'

When they got to the corner under the El, an icy blast of wind lashed their faces and brought tears to their eyes. The street was crowded; men, errandboys, pretty girl stenographers, all had the same worried look and pursed lips Nat Benton had. 'Plenty cold today.' Benton was gasping, tugging at his coatcollar. 'These steamheated offices soften a feller up.' They ducked into a building and went down into the warm hotrolls smell of a basement restaurant. Their faces were still tingling from the cold when they had sat down and were studying the menucards.

'Do you know,' Benton said, 'I've got an idea you boys stand in the way of making a little money out there.'

'It's sure been a job gettin' her started,' said Charley as he put his spoon into a plate of peasoup. He was hungry. 'Every time you turn your back somethin' breaks down and everythin' goes cockeyed. But now I've got a wonderful guy for a foreman. He's a Heinie, used to work for the Fokker outfit.'

Nat Benton was eating rawroastbeef sandwiches and buttermilk. 'I've got no more digestion than . . .'

'Than John D. Rockefeller,' put in Charley. They laughed.

Benton started talking again. 'But as I was saying, I don't know anything about manufacturing, but it's always been my idea that the secret of moneymaking in that line of business was discovering proper people to work for you. They work for you or you work for them. That's about the size of it. After all, you fellers turn out the product there in Long Island City, but if you want to make the money you've got to come down here to make it. . . . Isn't that true?'

Charley looked up from the juicy sirloin he was just about to cut. He burst out laughing. 'I guess,' he said. 'A man 'ud be a damn fool to keep his nose on his draftin'board all his life.'

They talked about golf for a while, then, when they were having their coffee, Nat Benton said, 'Charley, I just wanted to pass the word along, on account of you being a friend of old Ollie's and the Humphries and all that sort of thing . . . don't you boys sell any of your stock. If I were you, I'd scrape up all the cash you could get ahold of for a margin and buy up any that's around loose. You'll have the chance soon.'

'You think she'll keep on risin'?'

'Now keep this under your hat . . . Merritt and that crowd are worried. They're selling, so you can expect a drop. That's what these Tern people in Detroit are waiting for to get in cheap, see, they like the looks of your little concern. . . . They think your engine is a whiz. . . . If it's agreeable to you, I'd like to handle your brokerage account, just for old times' sake, you understand.'

Charley laughed. 'Gosh, I hadn't pictured myself with a brokerage account . . . but, by heck, you may be right.'

'I wouldn't like to see you wake up one morning and find yourself out on the cold cold pavement, see, Charley?'

After they'd eaten, Nat Benton asked Charley if he'd ever seen the stock exchange operating. 'It's interesting to see if a feller's never seen it,' he said, and led Charley across Broadway where the lashing wind cut their faces and down a narrow street shaded by tall buildings into a crowded vestibule.

'My, that cold nips your ears,' he said.

'You ought to see it out where I come from,' said Charley.

They went up in an elevator and came out in a little room where some elderly parties in uniform greeted Mr Benton with considerable respect. Nat signed in a book and they were let out through a small door into the visitors' gallery and stood a minute looking down into a great greenish hall like a railroadstation onto the heads of a crowd of men, some in uniform, some with white badges, slowly churning around the tradingposts. Sometimes the crowd knotted and thickened at one booth and sometimes at another. The air was full of shuffle and low clicking machinesounds in which voices were lost.

'Don't look like much,' said Nat, 'but that's where it all changes hands.' Nat pointed out the booths where different classes of stocks were traded.

'I guess they don't think much about aviation stocks,' said Charley.

'No, it's all steel and oil and the automotive industries,' said Nat.

'We'll give 'em a few years . . . what do you say, Nat?' said Charley boisterously.

Charley went uptown on the Second Avenue El and out

across the Queensboro Bridge. At Queens Plaza he got off and walked over to the garage where he kept his car, a Stutz roadster he'd bought secondhand. The traffic was heavy and he was tired and peevish before he got out to the plant. The sky had become overcast and dry snow drove on the wind. He turned in and jammed on his brakes in the crunching ash of the yard in front of the office, then he pulled off his padded aviator's helmet and sat there a minute in the car after he'd switched off the motor listening to the hum and whirr and clatter of the plant. 'The sonsabitches are slackenin' up,' he muttered under his breath.

He stuck his head in Joe's office for a moment, but Joe was busy talking to a guy in a coonskin coat who looked like a bond salesman. So he ran down the hall to his own office, said, 'Hello, Ella, get me Mr Stauch,' and sat down at his desk which was covered with notes on blue and yellow sheets. 'A hell of a note,' he was thinking, 'for a guy to be glued to a desk all his life.'

Stauch's serious square pale face topped by a brush of colorless hair sprouting from a green eyeshade was leaning over him.

'Sit down Julius,' he said. 'How's tricks? . . . Burnishin' room all right?'

'Ach, yes, but we haf two stampingmachines broken in one day.'

'The hell you say. Let's go look at them.'

When Charley got back to the office, he had a streak of grease on his nose. He still had an oily micrometer in his hand. It was six o'clock. He called up Joe. 'Hello, Joe, goin' home?'

'Sure, I was waiting for you; what was the trouble?'

'I was crawlin' around on my belly in the grease as usual.'

Charley washed his hands and face in the lavatory and ran down the rubbertreaded steps.

Joe was waiting for him in the entry. 'My wife's got my car, Charley, let's take yours,' said Joe.

'It'll be a bit drafty, Joe.'

'We can stand it.'

'Goodnight, Mr Askew, goodnight, Mr Anderson,' said the old watchman in his blue cap with earflaps, who was closing up behind them.

'Say, Charley,' Joe said when they'd turned into the stream of traffic at the end of the alley, 'why don't you let Stauch do more of the routine work? He seems pretty efficient.'

'Knows a hell of a lot more than I do,' said Charley, squinting through the frosted windshield.

The headlights coming the other way made big sparkling blooms of light in the driving snow. On the bridge the girders were already all marked out with neat streaks of white. All you could see of the river and the city was a shadowy swirl, now dark, now glowing. Charley had all he could do to keep the car from skidding on the icy places on the bridge.

'Attaboy, Charley,' said Joe as they slewed down the ramp into the crosstown street full of golden light.

Across Fiftyninth they had to go at a snail's pace. They were stiff with cold and it was seven-thirty before they drove up to the door of the apartment house on Riverside Drive where Charley had been living all winter with the Askews. Mrs Askew and two yellowhaired little girls met them at their door.

Grace Askew was a bleachedlooking woman with pale hair and faint crowsfeet back of her eyes and on the sides of her neck that gave her a sweet crumpled complaining look. 'I was worried,' she said, 'about your not having the car in this blizzard.'

Jean, the oldest girl, was jumping up and down singing, 'Snowy snowy snowy, it's going to be snowy.'

'And, Charles,' said Grace in a teasing voice as they went into the parlor, that smelt warm of dinner cooking, to spread their hands before the gaslogs, 'if she called up once she called up twenty times. She must think I'm trying to keep you away from her.'

'Who . . . Doris?'

Grace pursed up her lips and nodded. 'But, Charles, you'd better stay home to dinner. I've got a wonderful leg of lamb and sweetpotatoes. You know you like our dinners better here than all those fancy fixin's over there . . .'

Charley was already at the phone. 'Oh, Charley,' came Doris's sweet lisping voice, 'I was afraid you'd been snowed in over on Long Island. I called there but nobody answered. . . . I've got an extra place . . . I've got some people to dinner you'd love to meet. . . . He was an engineer under the Czar. We're all waiting for you.'

'But honestly, Doris, I'm all in.'

'This'll be a change. Mother's gone south and we'll have the house to ourselves. We'll wait . . .'

'It's those lousy Russians again,' muttered Charley as he ran to his room and hopped into his dinnerclothes.

'Why, look at the loungelizard,' kidded Joe from the easy-chair where he was reading the evening paper with his legs stretched out towards the gaslogs.

'Daddy, what's a loungelizard?' intoned Jean.

'Grace, would you mind?' Charley went up to Mrs Askew blushing, with the two ends of his black tie hanging from his collar.

'Well, it's certainly devotion,' Grace said, getting up out of her chair – to tie the bow she had to stick the tip of her tongue out of the corner of her mouth – 'on a night like this.'

'I'd call it dementia if you asked me,' said Joe.

'Daddy, what's dementia?' echoed Jean, but Charley was already putting on his overcoat as he waited for the elevator in the fakemarble hall full of sample whiffs of all the dinners in all the apartments on the floor.

He pulled on his woolly gloves as he got into the car. In the park the snow hissed under his wheels. Turning out of the driveway at Fiftyninth, he went into a skid, out of it, into it again. His wheels gripped the pavement just beside a cop who stood at the corner beating his arms against his chest. The cop glared. Charley brought his hand up to his forehead in a snappy salute. The cop laughed. 'Naughty, naughty,' he said and went on thrashing his arms.

When the door of the Humphries' apartment opened, Charley's feet sank right away into the deep nap of a Baluchistan rug. Doris came out to meet him. 'Oh, you were a darling to come in this dreadful weather,' she cooed. He kissed her. He wished she didn't have so much greasy lipstick on. He hugged her to him so slender in the palegreen eveninggown. 'You're the darling,' he whispered.

From the drawingroom he could hear voices, foreign accents, and the clink of ice in a shaker. 'I wish we were goin' to be alone,' he said huskily.

'Oh, I know, Charley, but they were some people I just had to have. Maybe they'll go home early.' She straightened his necktie and patted down his hair and pushed him before her into the drawingroom.

When the last of Doris's dinnerguests had gone, the two of them stood in the hall facing each other. Charley drew a deep breath. He had drunk a lot of cocktails and champagne. He was crazy for her. 'Jesus, Doris, they were pretty hard to take.'

'It was sweet of you to come, Charley.'

Charley felt bitter smoldering anger swelling inside him. 'Look here, Doris, let's have a talk . . .'

'Oh, now we're going to be serious.' She made a face as she let herself drop on the settee.

'Now look here, Doris . . . I'm crazy about you, you know that . . .'

'Oh, but, Charley, we've had such fun together . . . we don't want to spoil it yet. . . . You know marriage isn't always so funny. . . . Most of my friends who've gotten married have had a horrid time.'

'If it's a question of jack, don't worry. The concern's goin' to go big. . . . I wouldn't lie to you. Ask Nat Benton. Just this after' he was explainin' to me how I could start gettin' in the money right away.'

Doris got up and went over to him and kissed him. 'Yes, he was a poor old silly. . . . You must think I'm a horrid mercenary little bitch. I don't see why you'd want to marry me if you thought I was like that. Honestly, Charley, what I'd love more than anything in the world would be to get out and make my own living. I hate this plushhorse existence.'

He grabbed her to him. She pushed him away. 'It's my dress, darling, yes, that costs money, not me. . . . Now you go home and go to bed like a good boy. You look all tiredout.'

When he got down to the street, he found the snow had drifted in over the seat of the car. The motor would barely turn over. No way of getting her to start. He called his garage to send somebody to start the car. Since he was in the phonebooth he might as well call up Mrs Darling. 'What a dreadful night, dearie. Well, since it's Mr Charley, maybe we can fix something up, but it's dreadfully short notice and the end of the week too. Well . . . in about an hour.'

Charley walked up and down in the snow in front of the apartmenthouse waiting for them to come round from the garage. The black angry bile was still rising in him. When they finally came and got her started, he let the mechanic take her back to the garage. Then he walked around to a speak he knew.

The streets were empty. Dry snow swished in his face as he went down the steps to the basement door. The bar was full of men and girls halftight and bellowing and tittering. Charley felt like wringing their goddam necks. He drank off four whiskies one after another and went around to Mrs Darling's. Going up in the elevator he began to feel tight. He gave the elevatorboy a dollar and caught out of the corner of his eye the black boy's happy surprised grin when he shoved the bill into his pocket. Once inside he let out a whoop. 'Now, Mr Charley,' said the colored girl in starched cap and apron who had opened the door, 'you know the missis don't like no noise . . . and you're such a civilspoken young gentleman.'

'Hello, dearie.' He hardly looked at the girl. 'Put out the light,' he said. 'Remember your name's Doris. Go in the bathroom and take your clothes off and don't forget to put on lipstick, plenty lipstick.' He switched off the light and tore off his clothes. In the dark it was hard to get the studs out of his boiled shirt. He grabbed the boiled shirt with both hands and ripped out the buttonholes. 'Now come in here, goddam you. I love you, you bitch Doris.' The girl was trembling. When he grabbed her to him she burst out crying.

He had to get some liquor for the girl to cheer her up and that started him off again. Next day he woke up late feeling too lousy to go out to the plant, he didn't want to go out, all he wanted to do was drink, so he hung around all day drinking gin and bitters in Mrs Darling's draperychoked parlor. In the afternoon Mrs Darling came in and played Russian bank with him and told him about how an operasinger had ruined her life, and wanted to get him to taper off on beer. That evening he got her to call up the same girl again. When she came he tried to explain to her that he wasn't crazy. He woke up alone in the bed feeling sober and disgusted.

The Askews were at breakfast when he got home Sunday morning. The little girls were lying on the floor reading the funny papers. There were Sunday papers on all the chairs.

Joe was sitting in his bathrobe smoking a cigar over his last cup of coffee. 'Just in time for a nice cup of fresh coffee,' he said.

'That must have been quite a dinnerparty,' said Grace, giggling.

'I got in on a little pokergame,' growled Charley.

When he sat down his overcoat opened and they saw his torn shirtfront. 'I'd say it was quite a pokergame,' said Joe.

'Everything was lousy,' said Charley. 'I'll go and wash my face.'

When he came back in his bathrobe and slippers he began to feel better.

Grace got him some country sausage and hot cornbread.

'Well, I've heard about these Park Avenue parties before, but never one that lasted two days.'

'Oh, lay off, Grace.'

'Say, Charley, did you read that article in the financial section of the *Evening Post* last night tipping off about a boom in airplane stocks?'

'No . . . but I had a talk with Nat Benton, you know he's a broker I told you about, a friend of Ollie Taylor's . . . Well, he said . . . '

Grace got to her feet. 'Now you know if you boys talk shop on Sundays I leave the room.' Joe took his wife's arm and gently pulled her back into her chair. 'Just let me say one thing and then we'll shut up. . . . I hope we keep out of the hands of the operators for at least five years. I'm sorry the damned stuff's listed. I wish I trusted Merritt and them as much as I do you and me.'

'We'll talk about that,' said Charley.

Joe handed him a cigar. 'All right, Gracie,' he said. 'How about a selection on the victrola?'

Charley had been planning all winter to take Doris with him to Washington when he flew down one of the sample planes to show off some of his patents to the experts at the War Department, but she and her mother sailed for Europe the week before. That left him with nothing to do one springy Saturday night, so he called up the Johnsons. He'd met Paul in the subway during the winter and Paul had asked him in a hurt way why he never came down any more. Charley had answered honestly he hadn't stuck his nose out of the plant in months. Now it made him feel funny calling up, listening to the phone ring and then Eveline's teasing voice that always seemed to have a little jeer in it: What fun, he must come down at once and stay to supper, she had a lot of funny people there, she said.

Paul opened the door for him. Paul's face had a tallowy look Charley hadn't noticed before. 'Welcome, stranger,' he said in a forced boisterous tone and gave him a couple of pats on the back as he went into the crowded room. There were some very pretty girls, and young men of different shapes and sizes, cocktailglasses, trays of little things to eat on crackers, cigarettesmoke. Everybody was talking and screeching like a lot of lathes in a turningplant.

At the back of the room Eveline, looking tall and pale and beautiful, sat on a marbletopped table beside a small man with a long yellow nose and pouches under his eyes. 'Oh, Charley, how prosperous you look. . . . Meet Charles Edward Holden

. . . Holdy, this is Charley Anderson; he's in flyingmachines. . . . Why, Charley, you look filthy rich.'

'Not yet,' said Charley. He was trying to keep from laughing.

'Well, what are you looking so pleased about? Everybody is just too dreary about everything this afternoon.'

'I'm not dreary,' said Holden. 'Now don't tell me I'm dreary.'

'Of course, Holdy, you're never dreary, but your remarks tend toward murder and suicide.'

Everybody laughed a great deal. Charley found himself pushed away from Eveline by people trying to listen to what Charles Edward Holden was saying. He found himself talking to a plain young woman in a shiny gray hat that had a big buckle set in it like a headlight.

'Do tell me what you do,' she said.

'How do you mean?'

'Oh, I mean almost everybody here does something, writes or paints or something.'

'Me? No, I don't do anything like that . . . I'm in airplane motors.'

'A flyer, oh my, how thrilling. . . . I always love to come to Eveline's, you never can tell who you'll meet. . . . Why, last time I was here Houdini had just left. She's wonderful on celebrities. But I think it's hard on Paul, don't you? . . . Paul's such a sweet boy. She and Mr Holden . . . it's all so public. He writes about her all the time in his column. . . . Of course I'm very oldfashioned. Most people don't seem to think anything of it. . . . Of course it's grand to be honest. . . . Of course he's such a celebrity too. . . . I certainly think people ought to be honest about their sexlife, don't you? It avoids all those dreadful complexes and things. . . . But it's too bad about Paul, such a nice cleancut young fellow. . . .'

When the guests had thinned out a little, a Frenchspeaking colored maid served a dinner of curry and rice with lots of little fixings. Mr Holden and Eveline did all the talking. It was all about people Charley hadn't ever heard of. He tried to break it up by telling about how he'd been taken for Charles Edward Holden in that saloon that time, but nobody listened, and he guessed it was just as well anyway. They had just come to the salad when Holden got up and said, 'My dear, my only morals consist in never being late to the theater, we must run.' He and Eveline went out in a hurry leaving Charley and Paul to talk to a quarrelsome middleaged man and his wife that Charley had never been introduced to. It wasn't much use trying to talk to them because the man was too tight to listen to anything anybody said and the woman was set on some kind of a private row with him and couldn't be got off it. When they staggered out, Charley and Paul were left alone. They went out to a moving picture house for a while, but the film was lousy, so Charley went uptown glum and tumbled into bed.

Next day Charley went by early for Andy Merritt and sat with him in the big antisepticlooking diningroom at the Yale Club while he ate his breakfast.

'Will it be bumpy?' was the first thing he asked.

'Weather report was fine yesterday.'

'What does Joe say?'

'He said for us to keep our goddam traps shut an' let the other guys do the talkin'.'

Merritt was drinking his last cup of coffee in little sips. 'You know Joe's a little overcautious sometimes. . . . He wants to have a jerkwater plant to run himself and hand down to his grandchildren. Now that was all very well in upstate New York in the old days . . . but now if a business isn't expanding it's on the shelf.'

'Oh, we're expandin' all right,' said Charley, getting to his feet to follow Merritt's broadshouldered tweed suit to the door of the diningroom. 'If we weren't expandin', we wouldn't be at all.'

While they were washing their hands in the lavatory Merritt asked Charley what he was taking along for clothes. Charley laughed and said he probably had a clean shirt and a toothbrush somewhere.

Merritt turned a square serious face to him: 'But we might have to go out. . . . I've engaged a small suite for us at the Waldman Park. You know in Washington those things count a great deal.'

'Well, if the worst comes to the worst, I can rent me a soup an' fish.'

As the porter was putting Merritt's big pigskin suitcase and his hatbox into the rumbleseat of the car, Merritt asked with a worried frown if Charley thought it would be too much weight. 'Hell, no, we could carry a dozen like that,' said Charley, putting his foot on the starter. They drove fast through the empty streets and out across the bridge and along the wide avenues bordered by low gimcrack houses out toward Jamaica. Bill Cermak had the ship out of the hangar and all tunedup.

Charley put his hand on the back of Bill's greasy leather

jerkin. 'Always on the dot, Bill,' he said. 'Meet Mr Merritt. . . . Say, Andy . . . Bill's comin' with us, if you don't mind . . . he can rebuild this motor out of old hairpins and chewin'gum if anythin' goes wrong.'

Bill was already hoisting Merritt's suitcase into the tail. Merritt was putting on a big leather coat and goggles like Charley had seen in the windows of Abercrombie and Fitch.

'Do you think it will be bumpy?' Merritt was asking again.

Charley gave him a boost. 'May be a little bumpy over Pennsylvania . . . but we ought to be there in time for a good lunch. . . . Well, gents, this is the first time I've ever been in the Nation's Capital.'

'Me neither,' said Bill.

'Bill ain't never been outside of Brooklyn,' said Charley, laughing.

He felt good as he climbed up to the controls. He put on his goggles and yelled back at Merritt, 'You're in the observer's seat, Andy.'

The Askew-Merritt starter worked like a dream. The motor sounded smooth and quiet as a sewingmachine. 'What do you think of that, Bill?' Charley kept yelling at the mechanic behind him. She taxied smoothly across the soft field in the early spring sunshine, bounced a couple of times, took the air and banked as he turned out across the slatecolored squares of Brooklyn. The light northwest wind made a million furrows on the opaque green bay. Then they were crossing the gutted factory districts of Bayonne and Elizabeth. Beyond the russet saltmeadows, Jersey stretched in great flat squares, some yellow, some red, some of them misted with the green of new crops.

There were ranks of big white cumulus clouds catching the sunlight beyond the Delaware. It got to be a little bumpy and Charley rose to seven thousand feet where it was cold and clear with a fiftymile wind blowing from the northwest. When he came down again it was noon and the Susquehanna shone bright blue in a rift in the clouds. Even at two thousand feet he could feel the warm steam of spring from the plowed land. Flying low over the farms he could see the white fluff of orchards in bloom. He got too far south, avoiding a heavy squall over the head of the Chesapeake, and had to follow the Potomac north up toward the glinting white dome of the Capitol and the shining sliver of the Washington Monument. There was no smoke over Washington. He circled around for half an hour before he found the flyingfield. There was so much green it all looked like flyingfield.

'Well, Andy,' said Charley when they were stretching their legs on the turf, 'when those experts see that starter their eyes'll pop out of their heads.'

Merritt's face looked pale and he tottered a little as he walked. 'Can't hear,' he shouted. 'I got to take a leak.'

Charley followed him to the hangar, leaving Bill to go over the motor. Merritt was phoning for a taxi. 'Christamighty, am I hungry?' roared Charley.

Merritt winced. 'I got to get a drink to settle my stomach first.'

When they got into the taxi with their feet on Merritt's enormous pigskin suitcase, 'I'll tell you one thing, Charley,' Merritt said, 'we've got to have a separate corporation for that starter . . . might need a separate productionplant and everything. Standard Airparts would list well.'

They had two rooms and a large parlor with pink easychairs in it at the huge new hotel. From the windows you could look down into the fresh green of Rock Creek Park. Merritt looked around with considerable satisfaction. 'I like to get into a place on Sunday,' he said. 'It gives you a chance to get settled before beginning work.' He added that he didn't think there'd be anybody in the diningroom he knew, not on a Sunday, but as it turned out it took them quite a while to get to their table. Charley was introduced on the way to a senator, a corporation lawyer, the youngest member of the House of Representatives and a nephew of the Secretary of the Navy. 'You see,' explained Merritt, 'my old man was a senator once.'

After lunch Charley went out to the field again to take a look at the ship. Bill Cermak had everything bright as a jeweler's window. Charley brought Bill back to the hotel to give him a drink. There were waiters in the hall outside the suite and cigarsmoke and a great sound of social voices pouring out the open door. Bill laid a thick finger against his crooked nose and said maybe he'd better blow.

'Gee, it does sound like the socialregister. Here, I'll let you in my bedroom an' I'll bring you a drink if you don't mind waiting a sec.'

'Sure, it's all right by me, boss.'

Charley washed his hands and straightened his necktie and went into the sittingroom all in a rush like a man diving into a cold pool.

Andy Merritt was giving a cocktailparty with dry martinis, chickensalad, sandwiches, a bowl of caviar, strips of smoked fish, two old silverhaired gentlemen, three huskyvoiced Southern belles with too much makeup on, a fat senator and a very thin senator in a high collar, a sprinkling of pale young men with Harvard accents and a sallow man with a gold tooth who wrote a syndicated column called *Capitol Small Talk*. There was a young publicityman named Savage he'd met at Eveline's. Charley was introduced all around and stood first on one foot and then on the other until he got a chance to sneak into the bedroom with two halftumblers of rye and a plate of sandwiches. 'Gosh, it's terrible in there. I don't dare open my mouth for fear of puttin' my foot in it.'

Charley and Bill sat on the bed eating the sandwiches and listening to the jingly babble that came in from the other room. When he'd drunk his whiskey Bill got to his feet, wiped his mouth on the back of his hand and asked what time Charley wanted him to report in the morning.

'Nine o'clock will do. You sure you don't want to stick around? . . . I don't know what to say to those birds . . . we might fix you up with a Southern belle.'

Bill said he was a quiet family man and would get him a flop and go to bed. When he left, it meant Charley had to go back to the cocktailparty.

When Charley went back into Merritt's room, he found the black eyes of the fat senator fixed on him from between the two cute bobbing hats of two pretty girls. Charley found himself saying goodbye to them. The browneyed one was a blonde and the blueeyed one had very black hair. A little tang of perfume and kid gloves lingered after them when they left.

'Now which would you say was the prettiest, young man?' The fat senator was standing beside him looking up at him with a tooconfidential smile.

Charley felt his throat stiffen, he didn't know why. 'They're a couple of beauties,' he said.

'They leave you like the ass between two bundles of hay,' said the fat senator with a soft chuckle that played smoothly in and out of the folds of his chin.

'Buridan's ass died of longing, Senator,' said the thin senator putting the envelope back in his pocket on which he and Andy Merritt had been doping out figures of some kind.

'And so do I, Senator,' said the fat one, pushing back the streak of black hair from his forehead, his loose jowls shaking.

'I die daily. . . . Senator, will you dine with me and these young men? I believe old Horace is getting us up a little terrapin.' He put a small plump hand on the thin senator's shoulder and another on Charley's.

'Sorry, Senator, the missus is having some friends out at the Chevy Chase Club.'

'Then I'm afraid these youngsters will have to put up with eating dinner with a pair of old fogies. I'd hoped you'd bridge the gap between the generations. . . . General Hicks is coming.'

Charley saw a faint pleased look come over Andy Merritt's serious wellbred face. The fat senator went on with his smooth ponderous courtroom voice. 'Perhaps we had better be on our way. . . . He's coming at seven and those old warhorses tend to be punctual.'

A great black Lincoln was just coming to a soundless stop at the hotel entry when the four of them, Charley and Andy Merritt and Savage and the fat senator, came out into the Washington night that smelt of oil on asphalt and the exhausts of cars and of young leaves and of wistariablossoms. The senator's house was a continuation of his car, big and dark and faintly gleaming and soundless. They sprawled in big black-leather chairs and an old whitehaired mulatto brought around manhattans on an engraved silver tray.

The senator took each of the men separately to show them where to wash up. Charley didn't much like the little pats on the back he got from the senator's small padded hands as he was ushered into a big oldfashioned bathroom with a setin marble tub. When he came back from washing his hands the folding doors were open to the diningroom and a halelooking old gentleman with a white mustache and a slight limp was walking up and down in front of them impatiently. 'I can smell that terrapin, Bowie,' he was saying. 'Ole Horace is still up to his tricks.'

With the soup and the sherry the general began to talk from the head of the table. 'Of course all this work with flyin'-machines is very interestin' for the advancement of science . . . I tell you, Bowie, you're one of the last people in this town who sets a decent table . . . perhaps it points to vast possibilities in the distant future. . . . But speakin' as a military man, gentlemen, you know some of us don't feel that they have proved their worth. . . . The terrapin is remarkable, Bowie. . . . I mean we don't put the confidence in the flyin'machine that they seem to have over at the Navy Department. . . . A good glass of burgundy, Bowie, nothin' I like so much. . . . Experiment is a great thing, gentlemen, and I don't deny that perhaps in the distant future . . .'

'In the distant future,' echoed Savage, laughing, as he followed Merritt and Charley out from under the stone portico of Senator Planet's house. A taxi was waiting for him. 'Where can I drop you, gentlemen? . . . The trouble with us is we are in the distant future and don't know it.'

'They certainly don't know it in Washington,' said Merritt as they got into the cab.

Savage giggled. 'The senator and the general were pricelessly archaic . . . like something dug up. . . . But don't worry about the general . . . once he knows he's dealing with . . . you know . . . presentable people, he's gentle as Santa Claus. . . . He believes in a government of gentlemen, for gentlemen and by gentlemen.'

'Well, don't we all?' said Merritt sternly.

Savage let out a hooting laugh. 'Nature's gentlemen . . . been looking for one for years.' Then he turned his bulging alcoholic eyes and his laughing pugface to Charley. 'The senator thinks you're the whiteheaded boy. . . . He asked me to bring you around to see him . . . the senator is very susceptible, you know.' He let out another laugh.

The guy must be pretty tight, thought Charley. He was a little woozy himself from the Napoleon brandy drunk out of balloonshaped glasses they'd finished off the dinner with. Savage let them out at the Waldman Park and his taxi went on. 'Say, who is that guy, Andy?'

'He's a wild man,' said Merritt. 'He is one of Moorehouse's bright young men. He's bright enough, but I don't like the stories I hear about him. He wants the Askew-Merritt contract, but we're not in that class yet. Those publicrelations people will eat you out of house and home.'

As they were going up in the elevator, Charley said, yawning, 'Gee, I hoped those pretty girls were comin' to dinner.'

'Senator Planet never has women to dinner. . . . He's got a funny reputation. . . . There are some funny people in this town.'

'I guess there are,' said Charley. He was all in; he'd hardly got his clothes off before he was asleep.

At the end of the week Charley and Bill flew back to New York leaving Andy Merritt to negotiate contracts with the government experts. When they'd run the ship into the hangar,

Charley said he'd wheel Bill home to Jamaica in his car. They stopped off in a kind of hofbrau for a beer. They were hungry and Bill thought his wife would be through supper, so they ate noodlesoup and schnitzels. Charley found they had some fake Rhinewine and ordered it. They drank the wine and ordered another set of schnitzels. Charley was telling Bill how Andy Merritt said the government contracts were going through and Andy Merritt was always right and he'd said it was a patriotic duty to capitalize production on a broad base. 'Bill, goddam it, we'll be in the money. How about another bottle? . . . Good old Bill, the pilot's nothin' without his mechanic, the promoter's nothin' without production. . . . You and me, Bill, we're in production, and by God I'm goin' to see we don't lose out. If they try to rook us we'll fight, already I've had offers, big offers from Detroit . . . in five years now we'll be in the money and I'll see you're in the big money too.'

They ate applecake and then the proprietor brought out a bottle of kümmel. Charley bought the bottle. 'Cheaper than payin' for it drink by drink, don't you think so, Bill?' Bill began to start saying he was a family man and had better be getting along home. 'Me,' said Charley, pouring out some kümmel into a tumbler, 'I haven't got no home to go to. . . . If she wanted she could have a home. I'd make her a wonderful home.'

Charley discovered that Bill Cermak had gone and that he was telling all this to a stout blond lady of uncertain age with a rich German accent. He was calling her Aunt Hartmann and telling her that if he ever had a home she'd be his housekeeper. They finished up the kümmel and started drinking beer. She stroked his head and called him her vandering yunge. There was an orchestra in Bavarian costume and a thicknecked man that sang. Charley wanted to yodel for the company, but she pulled him back to the table. She was very strong and pushed him away with big red arms when he tried to get friendly, but when he pinched her seat she looked down into her beer and giggled. It was all like back home in the old days, he kept telling her, only louder and funnier. It was dreadfully funny until they were sitting in the car and she had her head on his shoulder and was calling him schatz and her long coils of hair had come undone and hung down over the wheel. Somehow he managed to drive.

He woke up next morning in a rattletrap hotel in Coney Island. It was nine o'clock; he had a frightful head and Aunt

Hartmann was sitting up in bed looking pink, broad, and beefy and asking for kaffee und schlagsahne. He took her out to breakfast at a Vienna bakery. She ate a great deal and cried a great deal and said he mustn't think she was a bad woman, because she was just a poor girl out of work and she'd felt so badly on account of his being a poor homeless boy. He said he'd be a poor homeless boy for fair if he didn't get back to the office. He gave her all the change he had in his pocket and a fake address and left her crying over a third cup of coffee in the Vienna bakery and headed for Long Island City. About Ozone Park he had to stop to upchuck on the side of the road. He just managed to get into the yard of the plant with his last drop of gas. He slipped into his office. It was ten minutes of twelve.

His desk was full of notes and letters held together with clips and blue papers marked IMMEDIATE ATTENTION. He was scared Miss Robinson or Joe Askew would find out he was back. Then he remembered he had a silver flask of old bourbon in his desk drawer that Doris had given him the night before she sailed, to forget her by she'd said, kidding him. He'd just tipped his head back to take a swig when he saw Joe Askew standing in front of his desk.

Joe stood up with his legs apart with a worn frowning look on his face. 'Well, for Pete's sake, where have you been? We been worried as hell about you. . . . Grace waited dinner an hour.'

'Why didn't you call up the hangar?'

'Everybody had gone home. . . . Stauch's sick. Everything's tied up.'

'Haven't you heard from Merritt?'

'Sure . . . but that means we've got to reorganize production. . . . And frankly, Charley, that's a hell of an example to set the employees . . . boozing around the office. Last time I kept my mouth shut, but my god . . .'

Charley walked over to the cooler and drew himself a couple of papercupfuls of water. 'I got to celebratin' that trip to Washington last night. . . . After all, Joe, these contracts will put us on the map. . . . How about havin' a little drink?'

Joe frowned. 'You look like you'd been having plenty . . . and how about shaving before you come into the office? We expect our employees to do it, we ought to do it too. . . . For craps' sake, Charley, remember that the war's over.' Joe turned on his heel and went back to his own office.

Charley took another long pull on the flask. He was mad. 'I won't take it,' he muttered, 'not from him or anybody else.' Then the phone rang. The foreman of the assemblyroom was standing in the door. 'Please, Mr Anderson,' he said.

That was the beginning of it. From then everything seemed to go haywire. At eight o'clock that night Charley hadn't yet had a shave. He was eating a sandwich and drinking coffee out of a carton with the mechanics of the repaircrew over a busted machine. It was midnight and he was all in before he got home to the apartment. He was all ready to give Joe a piece of his mind, but there wasn't an Askew in sight.

Next morning at breakfast Grace's eyebrows were raised when she poured out the coffee. 'Well, if it isn't the lost battalion,' she said.

Joe Askew cleared his throat. 'Charley,' he said nervously, 'I didn't have any call to bawl you out like that . . . I guess I'm getting cranky in my old age. The plant's been hell on wheels all week.'

The two little girls began to giggle.

'Aw, let it ride,' said Charley.

'Little pitchers, Joe,' said Grace, rapping on the table for order. 'I guess we all need a rest. Now this summer, Joe, you'll take a vacation. I need a vacation in the worst way myself, especially from entertaining Joe's dead cats. He hasn't had anybody to talk to since you've been away, Charley, and the house has been full of dead cats.'

'That's just a couple of guys I've been trying to fix up with jobs. Grace thinks they're no good because they haven't much social smalltalk.'

'I don't think, I know they are dead cats,' said Grace. The little girls started to giggle some more.

Charley got to his feet and pushed back his chair.

'Comin', Joe?' he said. 'I've got to get back to my wreckin'-crew.'

It was a couple of weeks before Charley got away from the plant except to sleep. At the end of that time Stauch was back with his quiet regretful manner like the manner of an assisting physician in a hospital operatingroom, and things began to straighten out. The day Stauch finally came to Charley's office door saying, 'Production is now again smooth, Mr Anderson,' Charley decided he'd knock off at noon. He called up Nat Benton to wait for him for lunch and slipped out by the employees' entrances so that he wouldn't meet Joe in the entry.

In Nat's office they had a couple of drinks before going out to lunch. At the restaurant after they'd ordered, he said, 'Well, Nat, how's the intelligence service going?'

'How many shares have you got?'

'Five hundred.'

'Any other stock, anything you could put up for margin?'

'A little. . . . I got a couple of grand in cash.'

'Cash,' said Nat scornfully. 'For a rainy day . . . stuff and nonsense. . . . Why not put it to work?'

'That's what I'm talkin' about.'

'Suppose you try a little flyer in Auburn just to get your hand in.'

'But how about Merritt?'

'Hold your horses. . . . What I want to do is get you a little capital so you can fight those birds on an equal basis. . . . If you don't they'll freeze you out sure as fate.'

'Joe wouldn't,' said Charley.

'I don't know the man personally, but I do know men, and there are darn few who won't look out for number one first.'

'I guess they'll all rook you if they can.'

'I wouldn't put it just that way, Charley. There are some magnificent specimens of American manhood in the business world.'

That night Charley got drunk all by himself at a speak in the fifties.

By the time Doris landed from Europe in the fall, Charley had made two killings in Auburn and was buying up all the Askew-Merritt stock he could lay his hands on. At the same time he discovered he had credit, for a new car, for suits at Brooks Brothers, for meals at speakeasies. The car was a Packard sports phaeton with a long low custombody upholstered in red leather. He drove down to the dock to meet Doris and Mrs Humphries when they came in on the *Leviathan*. The ship had already docked when Charley got to Hoboken. Charley parked his car and hurried through the shabby groups at the thirdclass to the big swirl of welldressed people chattering round piles of pigskin suitcases, patent-leather hatboxes, wardrobetrunks with the labels of Ritz hotels on them, in the central part of the wharfbuilding. Under the H he caught sight of old Mrs Humphries. Above the big furcollar her face looked like a faded edition of Doris's, he had never before noticed how much.

She didn't recognize him for a moment. 'Why, Charles Anderson, how very nice.' She held her hand out to him without smiling. 'This is most trying. Doris, of course, had to leave her jewelcase in the cabin. . . . You are meeting someone, I presume.'

Charley blushed. 'I thought I might give you a lift . . . I got a big car now. I thought it would take your bags better than a taxi.'

Mrs Humphries wasn't paying much attention. 'There she is. . . .' She waved a gloved hand with an alligatorskin bag in it. 'Here I am.'

Doris came running through the crowd. She was flushed and her lips were very red. Her little hat and her fur were just the color of her hair. 'I've got it, Mother . . . what a silly girl.'

'Every time I go through this,' sighed Mrs Humphries, 'I decide I'll never go abroad again.'

Doris leaned over to tuck a piece of yellow something into a handbag that had been opened.

'Here's Mr Anderson, Doris,' said Mrs Humphries.

Doris turned with a jump and ran up to him and threw her arms round his neck and kissed him on the cheek. 'You darling to come down.' Then she introduced him to a redfaced young Englishman in an English plaid overcoat who was carrying a big bag of golfclubs. 'I know you'll like each other.'

'Is this your first visit to this country?' asked Charley.

'Quite the contrary,' said the Englishman, showing his yellow teeth in a smile. 'I was born in Wyoming.'

It was chilly on the wharf. Mrs Humphries went to sit in the heated waitingroom.

When the young man with the golfsticks went off to attend to his own bags, Doris said: 'How do you like George Duquesne? He was born here and brought up in England. His mother comes from people in the Doomsday Book. I went to stay with them at the most beautiful old abbey. . . . I had the time of my life in England. I think George is a duck. The Duquesnes have copper interests. They are almost like the Guggenheims except, of course, they are not Jewish. . . . Why, Charley, I believe you're jealous. . . . Silly . . . George and I are just like brother and sister, really . . . It's not like you and me at all, but he's such fun.'

It took the Humphries family a couple of hours to get through the customs. They had a great many bags and Doris had to pay duty on some dresses. When Mrs Humphries found she was to drive uptown in an open car with the top down, she looked black indeed, the fact that it was a snakylooking Packard didn't seem to help.

'Why, it's a regular rubberneck wagon,' said Doris. 'Mother, this is fun . . . Charley'll point out all the tall buildings.'

Mrs Humphries was grumbling as, surrounded by handbaggage, she settled into the back seat, 'Your dear father, Doris, never liked to see a lady riding in an open cab, much less in an open machine.'

When he'd taken them uptown, Charley didn't go back to the plant. He spent the rest of the day till closing at the Askews' apartment on the telephone talking to Benton's office. Since the listing of Standard Airparts there'd been a big drop in Askew-Merritt. He was hocking everything and waiting for it to hit bottom before buying. Every now and then he'd call up Benton and say, 'What do you think, Nat?'

Nat still had no tips late that afternoon, so Charley spun a coin to decide; it came heads. He called up the office and told them to start buying at the opening figure next day. Then he changed his clothes and cleared out before Grace brought the little girls home from school; he hardly spoke to the Askews these days. He was fed up out at the plant and he knew Joe thought he was a slacker.

When he changed his wallet from one jacket to the other, he opened it and counted his cash. He had four centuries and some chickenfeed. The bills were crisp and new, straight from the bank. He brought them up to his nose to sniff the new sweet sharp smell of the ink. Before he knew what he'd done he'd kissed them. He laughed out loud and put the bills back in his wallet. Jesus, he was feeling good. His new blue suit fitted nicely. His shoes were shined. He had clean socks on. His belly felt hard under his belt. He was whistling as he waited for the elevator.

Over at Doris's there was George Duquesne saying how ripping the new buildings looked on Fifth Avenue.

'Oh, Charley, wait till you taste one of George's alexanders, they're ripping,' said Doris. 'He learned to make them out in Constant after the war. . . . You see he was in the British army. . . . Charley was one of our star aces, George.'

Charley took George and Doris to dinner at the Plaza and to a show and to a nightclub. All the time he was feeding highpower liquor into George in the hope he'd pass out, but all George did was get redder and redder in the face and quieter and quieter, and he hadn't had much to say right at the beginning. It was three o'clock and Charley was sleepy and pretty tight himself before he could deliver George at the Saint Regis where he was staying.

'Now what shall we do?'

'But, darling, I've got to go home.'

'I haven't had a chance to talk to you.... Jeez, I haven't even had a chance to give you a proper hug since you landed.' They ended by going to the Columbus Circle Childs and eating scrambled eggs and bacon.

Doris was saying there ought to be beautiful places where people in love could go where they could find privacy and bed in beautiful surroundings. Charley said he knew plenty of places, but they weren't so beautiful.

'I'd go, Charley, honestly, if I wasn't afraid it would be sordid and spoil everything.'

Charley squeezed her hand hard. 'I wouldn't have the right to ask you, kid, not till we was married.'

As they walked up the street to where he'd parked his car, she let her head drop on his shoulder. 'Do you want me, Charley?' she said in a little tiny voice. 'I want you too . . . but I've got to go home or Mother'll be making a scene in the morning.'

Next Saturday afternoon Charley spent looking for a walkup furnished apartment. He rented a livingroom, kitchenette, and bath, all done in gray, from a hennahaired artist lady in flowing batiks who said she was going to Capri for six months of sheer beauty, and called up an agency for a Japanese houseboy to take care of it. Next day at breakfast he told the Askews he was moving.

Joe didn't say anything at first, but after he'd drunk the last of his cup of coffee, he got up frowning and walked a couple of times across the livingroom. Then he went to the window, saying quietly, 'Come here, Charley, I've got something to show you.' He put a hand on Charley's arm.... 'Look here, kid, it isn't on account of me being so sour all the time, is it? You know I'm worried about the damn business . . . seems to me we're getting in over our heads . . . but you know Grace and I both think the world of you.... I've just felt that you were putting in too much time on the stockmarket.... I don't suppose it's any of my damn business.... Anyway, us fellows from the old outfit, we've got to stick together.'

'Sure, Joe, sure.... Honestly, the reason I want this damn apartment has nothin' to do with that.... You're a married man with kids and don't need to worry about that sort of thing . . . but me, I got woman trouble.'

Joe burst out laughing. 'The old Continental sonofagun, but for crying out loud, why don't you get married?'

'God damn it, that's what I want to do,' said Charley. He laughed and so did Joe.

'Well, what's the big joke?' said Grace from behind the coffee-urn.

Charley nodded his head toward the little girls. 'Smokin'room stories,' he said.

'Oh, I think you're mean,' said Grace.

One snowy afternoon before Christmas, a couple of weeks after Charley had moved into his apartment, he got back to town early and met Doris at the Biltmore. She said, 'Let's go somewhere for a drink,' and he said he had drinks all laid out and she ought to come up to see the funny little sandwiches Taki made, all in different colors. She asked if the Jap was there now. He grinned and shook his head. It only took the taxi a couple of minutes to get them around to the converted brownstone house.

'Why, isn't this cozy?' Doris panted a little breathless from the stairs, as she threw open her furcoat. 'Now I feel really wicked.'

'But it's not like it was some guy you didn't know,' said Charley, 'or weren't fond of.' She let him kiss her. Then she took off her coat and hat and dropped down beside him on the windowseat warm from the steamheat.

'Nobody knows the address, nobody knows the phonenumber,' said Charley. When he put his arm around her thin shoulders and pulled her to him, she gave in to him with a little funny shudder and let him pull her on his knee. They kissed for a long time and then she wriggled loose and said, 'Charley, darling, you invited me here for a drink.'

He had the fixings for oldfashioneds in the kitchenette and a plate of sandwiches. He brought them in and set them out on the round wicker table.

Doris bit into several sandwiches before she decided which she liked best. 'Why, your Jap must be quite an artist, Charley,' she said.

'They're a clever little people,' said Charley.

'Everything's lovely, Charley, except this light hurts my eyes.'

When he switched off the lights the window was brightblue. The lights and shadows of the taxis moving up and down the snowy street and the glare from the stores opposite made shifting orange oblongs on the ceiling.

'Oh, it's wonderful here,' said Doris. 'Look how oldtimy the streets look with all the ruts in the snow.'

Charley kept refilling the oldfashioneds with whiskey. He got her to take her dress off. 'You know you told me about how dresses cost money.'

'Oh, you big silly. . . . Charley, do you like me a little bit?'

'What's the use of talking . . . I'm absolutely cuckoo about you . . you know I want us to be always together. I want us to get mar—'

'Don't spoil everything, this is so lovely, I never thought anything could be like this. . . . Charley, you're taking precautions, aren't you?'

'Sure thing,' said Charley through clenched teeth and went to his bureau for a condom.

At seven o'clock she got dressed in a hurry, said she had a dinner engagement and would be horribly late. Charley took her down and put her in a taxi. 'Now, darling,' he said, 'we won't talk about what I said. We'll just do it.' Walking back up the steep creaky stairs, he could taste her mouth, her hair, his head was bursting with the perfume she used. A chilly bitter feeling was getting hold of him, like the feeling of seasickness. 'Oh, Christ,' he said aloud and threw himself face down on the windowseat.

The apartment and Taki and the bootlegger and the payments on his car and the flowers he sent Doris every day all ran into more money than he expected every month. As soon as he made a deposit in the bank, he drew it out again. He owned a lot of stock, but it wasn't paying dividends. At Christmas he had to borrow five hundred bucks from Joe Askew to buy Doris a present. She'd told him he mustn't give her jewelry, so he asked Taki what he thought would be a suitable present for a very rich and beautiful young lady and Taki had said a silk kimono was very suitable, so Charley went out and bought her a mandarincoat. Doris made a funny face when she saw it, but she kissed him with a little quick peck in the corner of the mouth, because they were at her mother's, and said in a singsongy tone, 'Oh, what a sweet boy.'

Mrs Humphries had asked him for Christmas dinner. The house smelt of tinsel and greens, there was a lot of tissuepaper and litter on the chairs. The cocktails were weak and everybody stood around, Nat and Sally Benton, and some nephews and

nieces of Mrs Humphries, and her sister Eliza who was very
deaf, and George Duquesne who would talk of nothing but
wintersports, waiting for a midafternoon dinner to be announced. People seemed sour and embarrassed, except Ollie
Taylor who was just home from Italy full of the Christmas
spirit. He spent most of the time out in the pantry with his coat
off manufacturing what he called an oldtime Christmas punch.
He was so busy at it that it was hard to get him to the table
for dinner. Charley had to spend all his time taking care of
him and never got a word with Doris all day. After dinner and
the Christmas punch he had to take Ollie back to his club. Ollie
was absolutely blotto and huddled fat and whitefaced in the
taxi, bubbling 'Damn good Christmas' over and over again.

When he'd put Ollie in the hands of the doorman, Charley
couldn't decide whether to go back to the Humphries' where
he'd be sure to find Doris and George with their heads together
over some damnfool game or other or to go up to the Askews'
as he'd promised to. Bill Cermak had asked him out to take a
look at the bohunks in Jamaica, but he guessed it wouldn't be
the thing, he'd said. Charley said sure he'd come, anyplace to
get away from the stuffedshirts. From the Penn station he sent
a wire wishing the Askews a Merry Christmas. Sure the Askews
would understand he had to spend his Christmas with Doris.
On the empty train to Jamaica, he got to worrying about Doris,
maybe he oughtn't to have left her with that guy.

Out in Jamaica, Bill Cermak and his wife and their elderly
inlaws and friends were all tickled and a little bit fussed by
Charley's turning up. It was a small frame house with a green
papertile roof in a block of identical little houses with every
other roof red and every other roof green. Mrs Cermak was a
stout blonde, a little fuddled from the big dinner and the wine
that had brought brightened spots to her cheeks. She made
Charley eat some of the turkey and the plumpudding they'd
just taken off the table. Then they made hot wine with cloves
in it and Bill played tunes on the piano accordion while everybody danced and the kids yelled and beat on drums and got
underfoot.

When Charley said he had to go, Bill walked to the station
with him. 'Say, boss, we sure do appreciate your comin' out,'
began Bill.

'Hell, I ain't no boss,' said Charley. 'I belong with the
mechanics .. don't I, Bill? You and me, Bill, the mechanics
against the world ... and when I get married you're comin' to

play that damned accordeen of yours at the weddin' . . . get me, Bill . . . it may not be so long.'

Bill screwed up his face and rubbed his long crooked nose. 'Women is fine once you got 'em pinned down, boss, but when they ain't pinned down they're hell.'

'I got her pinned down, I got her pinned down all right so she's got to marry me to make an honest man of me.'

'Thataboy,' said Bill Cermak. They stood laughing and shaking hands on the drafty station platform till the Manhattan train came in.

During the automobile show Nat called up one day to say Farrell who ran the Tern outfit was in town and wanted to see Charley and Charley told Nat to bring him around for a cocktail in the afternoon. This time he got Taki to stay.

James Yardly Farrell was a roundfaced man with sandygray hair and a round bald head. When he came in the door, he began shouting, 'Where is he? Where is he?'

'Here he is,' said Nat Benton, laughing.

Farrell pumped Charley's hand. 'So this is the guy with the knowhow, is it? I've been trying to get hold of you for months . . . ask Nat if I haven't made his life miserable. . . . Look here, how about coming out to Detroit . . . Long Island City's no place for a guy like you. We need your knowhow out there . . . and what we need we're ready to pay for.'

Charley turned red. 'I'm pretty well off where I am, Mr Farrell.'

'How much do you make?'

'Oh, enough for a young feller.'

'We'll talk about that . . . but don't forget that in a new industry like ours the setup changes fast. . . . We got to keep our eyes open or we'll get left. . . . Well, we'll let it drop for the time being. . . . But I can tell you one thing, Anderson, I'm not going to stand by and see this industry ruined by being broken up in a lot of little onehorse units all cutting each other's throats. Don't you think it's better for us to sit around the table and cut the cake in a spirit of friendship and mutual service, and I tell you, young man, it's going to be a whale of a big cake.' He let his voice drop to a whisper.

Taki, with his yellow face drawn into a thin diplomatic smile, came around with a tray of bacardi cocktails.

'No, thanks, I don't drink,' said Farrell. 'Are you a bachelor, Mr Anderson?'

'Well, something like that. ... I don't guess I'll stay that way long.'

'You'd like it out in Detroit, honestly. ... Benton tells me you're from Minnesota.'

'Well, I was born in North Dakota.' Charley talked over his shoulder to the Jap. 'Taki, Mr Benton wants another drink.'

'We got a nice sociable crowd out there,' said Farrell.

After they'd gone, Charley called up Doris and asked her right out if she'd like to live in Detroit after they were married. She gave a thin shriek at the other end of the line. 'What a dreadful idea! ... and who said anything about that dreadful ... you know, state ... I don't like even to mention the horrid word. ... Don't you think we've had fun in New York this winter?'

'Sure,' answered Charley. 'I guess I'd be all right here if ... things were different. ... I thought maybe you'd like a change, that's all. ... I had an offer from a concern out there, see.'

'Now, Charley, you must promise not to mention anything so silly again.'

'Sure ... if you'll have dinner with me tomorrow night.'

'Darling, tomorrow I couldn't.'

'How about Saturday then?'

'All right, I'll break an engagement. Maybe you can come by for me at Carnegie Hall after the concert.'

'I'll even go to the damn concert if you like.'

'Oh, no, Mother's asked a lot of old ladies.' She was talking fast, her voice twanging in the receiver. 'There won't be any room in the box. You wait for me at the little tearoom, the Russian place where you waited and got so cross the time before.'

'All right, anyplace. ... Say, you don't know how I miss you when you're not with me.'

'Do you? Oh, Charley, you're a dear.' She rang off.

Charley put the receiver down and let himself slump back in his chair. He couldn't help feeling all of a tremble when he talked to her on the telephone. 'Hey, Taki, bring me that bottle of Scotch. ... Say, tell me, Taki,' Charley went on, pouring himself a stiff drink, 'in your country ... is it so damn difficult for a guy to get married?'

The Jap smiled and made a little bow. 'In my country everything much more difficult.'

Next day when Charley got back from the plant he found a wire from Doris saying Saturday absolutely impossible. 'Damn the bitch,' he said aloud. All evening he kept calling up on the phone and leaving messages, but she was never in. He got to hate the feel of the damn mouthpiece against his lips. Saturday he couldn't get any word to her either. Sunday morning he got Mrs Humphries on the phone. The cold creaky oldwoman's voice shrieked that Doris had suddenly gone to Southampton for the weekend. 'I know she'll come back with a dreadful cold,' Mrs Humphries added. 'Weekends in this weather.'

'Well, goodbye, Mrs Humphries,' said Charley and rang off.

Monday morning when Taki brought him a letter in Doris's hand, a big blue envelope that smelt of her perfume, the minute he opened it he knew before he read it what it would say.

CHARLEY DEAR,

You are such a dear and I'm so fond of you and do so want you for a friend [underlined]. You know the silly life I lead, right now I'm on the most preposterous weekend and I've told everybody I have a splitting headache and have gone to bed just to write to you. But, Charley, please forget all about weddings and things like that. The very idea makes me physically sick and besides I've promised George I'd marry him in June and the Duquesnes have a public-relations counsel – isn't it just too silly – but his business is to keep the Duquesnes popular with the public and he's given the whole story to the press, how I was courted among the Scotch moors and in the old medieval abbey and everything. And that's why I'm in such a hurry to write to you, Charley darling, because you're the best friend [twice underlined] I've got and the only one who lives in the real world of business and production and labor and everything like that, which I'd so love to belong to, and I wanted you to know first thing. Oh, Charley darling, please don't think horrid things about me.

Your loving friend [three times underlined]     D

Be a good boy and burn up this letter, won't you?

The buzzer was rattling. It was the boy from the garage with his car. Charley got on his hat and coat and went downstairs. He got in and drove out to Long Island City, walked up the rubbertreaded steps to his office, sat down at his desk, rustled papers, talked to Stauch over the phone, lunched in the employees' lunchroom with Joe Askew, dictated letters to the new towhaired stenographer, and suddenly it was six o'clock and he was jockeying his way through the traffic home.

Crossing the bridge he had an impulse to give a wrench to the wheel and step on the gas, but the damn car wouldn't clear the rail anyway, it would just make a nasty scrapheap of piledup traffic and trucks.

He didn't want to go home or to the speakeasy he and Doris had been having dinner in several times a week all winter, so he turned down Third Avenue. Maybe he'd run into somebody at Julius's. He stood up at the bar. He didn't want to drink any more than he wanted to do anything else. A few raw shots of rye made him feel better. To hell with her. Nothing like a few drinks. He was alone, he had money on him, he could do any goddam thing in the world.

Next to Charley at the bar stood a couple of fattish dowdy-looking women. They were with a redfaced man who was pretty drunk already. The women were talking about clothes and the man was telling about Belleau Wood. Right away he and Charley were old buddies from the A.E.F. 'The name is De Vries. Profession ... bonvivant,' said the man and tugged at the two women until they faced around toward Charley. He put his arm around them with a flourish and shouted, 'Meet the wife.'

They had drinks on Belleau Wood, the Argonne, the St Mihiel salient, and the battle of Paree. The women said goodness, how they wanted to go to Hoboken to the hofbrau. Charley said he'd take them all in his car. They sobered up a little and were pretty quiet crossing on the ferry. At the restaurant in the chilly dark Hoboken street they couldn't get anything but beer. After they'd finished supper De Vries said he knew a place where they could get real liquor. They circled round blocks and blocks and ended in a dump in Union City. When they'd drunk enough to start them doing squaredances, the women said wouldn't it be wonderful to go to Harlem. This time the ferry didn't sober them up so much because they had a bottle of Scotch with them. In Harlem they were thrown out of a dancehall and at last landed in a nightclub. The bonvivant fell down the redcarpeted stairs and Charley had a time laughing that off with the management. They ate fried chicken and drank some terrible gin the colored waiter sent out for, and danced. Charley kept thinking how beautifully he was dancing. He couldn't make out why he didn't have any luck picking up any of the highyallers.

Next morning he woke up in a room in a hotel. He looked around. No, there wasn't any woman in the bed. Except that his head ached and his ears were burning, he felt good. Stomach all right. For a moment he thought he'd just landed from France. Then he thought of the Packard, where the hell had he left it? He reached for the phone. 'Say, what hotel is this?' It was the McAlpin, goodmorning. He remembered Joe Turbino's number and phoned him to ask what the best thing for a hangover was. When he was through phoning, he didn't feel so good. His mouth tasted like the floor of a chickencoop. He went back to sleep. The phone woke him. 'A gentleman to see you.' Then he remembered all about Doris. The guy from Turbino's brought a bottle of Scotch. Charley took a drink of it straight, drank a lot of icewater, took a bath, ordered up some breakfast. But it was time to go out to lunch. He put the bottle of Scotch in his overcoat pocket and went round to Frank and Joe's for a cocktail.

That night he took a taxi up to Harlem. He went from joint to joint dancing with the highyallers. He got in a fight in a breakfastclub. It was day when he found himself in another taxi going downtown to Mrs Darling's. He didn't have any money to pay the taximan and the man insisted on going up in the elevator while he got the money. There was nobody in the apartment but the colored maid and she shelled out five dollars. She tried to get Charley to lie down, but he wanted to write her out a check. He could sign his name all right, but he couldn't sign it on the check. The maid tried to get him to take a bath and go to bed. She said he had blood all over his shirt.

He felt fine and was all cleaned up, had been asleep in a barberchair while the barber shaved him and put an icebag on his black eye, and he had gone back to Frank and Joe's for a pickup when there was Nat Benton. Good old Nat was worried asking him about his black eye and he was showing Nat where he'd skinned his knuckles on the guy, but Nat kept talking about the business and Askew-Merritt and Standard Airparts and said Charley'd be out on the sidewalk if it wasn't for him. They had some drinks, but Nat kept talking about buttermilk and wanted Charley to come around to the hotel and meet Farrell. Farrell thought Charley was about the best guy in the world, and Farrell was the coming man in the industry, you could bet your bottom dollar on Farrell. And right away there was Farrell and Charley was showing him his knuckle and telling him he'd socked the guy in that lousy pokergame and how he'd have cleaned 'em all up if somebody hadn't batted him back of the ear with a stocking full of sand. Detroit, sure. He was ready to go to Detroit any time, Detroit or anywhere else. Goddam it, a guy don't like to stay in a town where he's just been rolled. And that damn highyaller had his pocketbook with all his addresses in it. Papers? Sure. Sign anythin' you like, anythin' Nat says. Stock, sure. Swap every last share. What the hell would a guy want stock for in a plant in a town where he'd been rolled in a clipjoint. Detroit, sure, right away. Nat, call a taxi, we're goin' to Detroit.

Then they were back at the apartment and Taki was chattering and Nat attended to everything and Farrell was saying, 'I'd hate to see the other guy's eye,' and Charley could sign his name all right this time. First time he signed it on the table, but then he got it on the contract, and Nat fixed it all up about swapping his Askew-Merritt stock for Tern stock and then Nat and Farrell said Charley must be sleepy and Taki kept squeaking about how he had to take right away a hot bath.

Charley woke up the next morning feeling sober and dead like a stiff laid out for the undertaker. Taki brought him orangejuice, but he threw it right up again. He dropped back on the pillow. He'd told Taki not to let anybody in, but there was Joe Askew standing at the foot of the bed. Joe looked paler than usual and had a worried frown like at the office, and was pulling at his thin blond mustache. He didn't smile. 'How are you coming?' he said.

'Soso,' said Charley.

'So it's the Tern outfit, is it?'

'Joe, I can't stay in New York now. I'm through with this burg.'

'Through with a lot of other things, it looks like to me.'

'Joe, honest I wouldn'ta done it if I hadn't had to get out of this town . . . and I put as much into this as you did, some people think a little more.'

Joe's thin lips were clamped firmly together. He started to say something, stopped himself, and walked stiffly out of the room.

'Taki,' called Charley, 'try squeezin' out half a grapefruit, will you?'

his first move was to board a fast train for Miami to
see whether the builders engaged in construction financed
by his corporation were speeding up the work as much as
they might and to take a look at things in general

*Pearly early in the mornin'*

### LUTHERANS DROP HELL FOR HADES

*Oh joy*
*Feel that boat arockin'*
*Oh boy*
*See those darkies flockin'*
*What's that whistle sayin'*
*All aboard toot toot*

### AIR REJECTION BLAMED FOR WARSHIP DISASTER

*You're in Ken-tucky just as sure as you're born*

### LINER AFIRE

### POSSE CLOSING IN ON AIRMAIL BANDITS

*Down beside the summer sea*
*Along Miami Shore*
*Some one waits alone for me*
*Along Miami Shore*

### SINCE THIS TIME YESTERDAY NEARLY TWO THOUSAND MEN HAVE CHANGED TO CHESTERFIELDS

### PEACHES FLED WITH FEW CLOTHES

*Saw a rosebud in a store*
*So I'm goin' where there's more*
*Good-bye blues*

the three whites he has with him appear to be of primitive Nordic stock. Physically they are splendid creatures.

They have fine flaxen hair, blue-green eyes and white skins. The males are covered with a downlike hair

*Let me lay me down to sleep in Carolina*
*With a peaceful pillow 'neath my weary head*
*For a rolling stone like me there's nothing finer*
*Oh Lordy what a thrill*
*To hear that whip-poor-will*
*In Carolina*

## The Camera Eye (48)

westbound to Havana Puerto-Mexico Galveston out of Santander (the glassy estuary the feeling of hills hemming the moist night an occasional star drips chilly out of the rainy sky a row of lights spills off the muffled shore) the twinscrews rumble

at last westbound away from pension spinsters tasty about watercolors the old men with crocodile eyes hiding their bloody claws under neat lisle gloves the landscapes corroded with literature        westbound

*for an old man he is old*
*for an old man he is gray*
*but a young man's heart is full of love*
*get away old man get away*

at the dinnertable westbound in the broadlit saloon the amplybosomed broadbeamed   la bella cubana in a yellow lowcut dress archly with the sharp rosy nail of her littlest finger points

the curlyhaired young bucks from Bilbao (louder and funnier) in such tightwaisted icecreamcolored suits silk shirts striped ties (westbound to Havana for the sugarboom) the rich one has a diamond ring   tooshiny eyes look the way her little finger jabs

*but a young man's heart is full of love*

she whispers   He came out of her cabin when I was on the way to the bath   Why was she giggling in number sixtysix? the rich one from Bilbao orders champagne

to echo the corks that pop in an artillery salute from
the long table where the Mexican general tall solemnfaced
with a black mustache and five tall solemnfaced bluejowled
sons a fat majordomo and a sprinkling of blank henshaped
ladies who rustle out hurriedly in black silk with their handkerchiefs to their mouths as soon as we round the cape
where the lighthouse is

westbound (out of old into new inordinate new un-
deciphered new) southerly summertime crossing (towards
events) the roar in the ears the deep blue heaving the sun
hot on the back of your hand the feel of wet salt on the
handrails the smell of brasspolish and highpressure steam
the multitudinous flickering dazzle of light

and every noon we overeat hors d'oeuvres drink too
much wine while gigglingly with rolling eyes la bella to
indicate who slept with who sharply jabs with littlest pin-
sharpened finger

la juerga

alas the young buck from Bilbao the one with the
diamond ring suffers amidships (westbound the ancient
furies follow in our wake) a kick from Venus's dangerous
toe     retires to bed     we take our coffee in his cabin instead of the fumoir     the ladies interest themselves in his
plight

two gallegos loosemouthed frognecked itinerant are
invited up from the steerage to sing to the guitar (Vichy
water and deep song argyrol rhymes with rusiñol)

> si quieres qu'el carro cante
> mójele y déjele en rio
> que después de buen moja'o
> canta com' un silbí'o

and funny stories a thousand and one Havana nights
the dance of the millions     the fair cubanas a ellas les gustan
los negros

but stepping out on deck to get a breath of briny afternoon there's more to be seen than that rusty freighter
wallowing in indigo  el rubio  the buck from Bilbao who
has no diamond ring beset with yelling cubans  la bella

leads with heaving breast a small man with gray sideburns is pushed out at el rubio they shove at him from behind

escándalo

alternately the contestants argue with their friends who hold them back   break loose   fly at each other with threshing arms   are recaptured   pulled apart

ships officers intervene

pale and trembling the champions are led away   he of the sideburns to the ladies' drawingroom   el rubio aft to fumoir

there we masticate the insults   what was it all about?

no señor no   el rubio grabs   a sheet of the notepaper of the Compagnie Générale Transatlantique but fingers refuse to hold the pen   while he twined them in his long curly hair an unauthorized observer who had become involved in the broil misspelled glibly to his dictation

a challenge

and carried it frozenfaced to the parties in the ladies' drawingroom   coño

then we walk el rubio back and forth across the palpitating stern discuss rapiers pistols fencingpractice

now only the westbound observer appears at meals   el rubio mopes at the end of the bunk of his beclapped friend and prepares for doom   the ship's agog with duel talk until mon commandant a redfaced Breton visits all parties and explains that this kind of nonsense is expressly forbidden in the regulations of the Compagnie Générale Transatlantique and that the musical gallegos must go back to the steerage from whence they sprang   despair

enter with martial tread mi general expert he says in affairs of honor un militar   coño   vamos may he try to conciliate the parties

all to the fumoir where already four champagnebottles are ranked cozily iced in their whitemetal pails   coño sandwiches are served   mi general clears up the misunderstanding something about los negros and las cubanas overheard in the cabin of the bucks from Bilbao by listening vamos   down the ventilator   many things were that better were unsaid   but in any case honor insulated by the ventilator was intact gingerly the champions take each others hands coño palmas sombreros música   mi general is awarded the ear

in the steerage the gallegos sing and strum

el rubio at the bar confides to me   that it was from la bella of the pink jabbing finger and the dainty ear at ventilators that he with the diamond ring received the   and that he himself has fears   coño una puta indecente

arrival in Havana   an opulentlydressed husband in a panama hat receives la bella   the young bucks from Bilbao go to the Sevilla-Biltmore and I

dance of the millions or not lackofmoney has raised its customary head inevitable as visas

in the whirl of sugarboom prices in the Augustblistering sun yours truly tours the town and the sugary nights with twenty smackers fifteen eightfifty dwindling in the jeans in search of lucrative

and how to get to Mexico

or anywhere

## Margo Dowling

Margo Dowling was sixteen when she married Tony. She loved the trip down to Havana on the boat. It was very rough, but she wasn't sick a minute; Tony was. He turned very yellow and lay in his bunk all the time and only groaned when she tried to make him come on deck to breathe some air. The island was in sight before she could get him into his clothes. He was so weak she had to dress him like a baby. He lay on his bunk with his eyes closed and his cheeks hollow while she buttoned his shoes for him. Then she ran up on deck to see Havana, Cuba. The sea was still rough. The waves were shooting columns of spray up the great rocks under the lighthouse. The young thin-faced third officer who'd been so nice all the trip showed her Morro Castle back of the lighthouse and the little fishingboats with tiny black or brown figures in them swinging up and down on the huge swells outside it. The other side the pale caramelcolored houses looked as if they were standing up right out of the breakers. She asked him where Vedado was and he pointed up beyond into the haze above the surf. 'That's the fine residential section,' he said. It was very sunny and the sky was full of big white clouds.

By that time they were in the calm water of the harbor passing a row of big schooners anchored against the steep hill under the sunny forts and castles, and she had to go down into the bilgy closeness of their cabin to get Tony up and close their bags. He was still weak and kept saying his head was spinning. She had to help him down the gangplank.

The ramshackle dock was full of beadyeyed people in white and tan clothes bustling and jabbering. They all seemed to have come to meet Tony. There were old ladies in shawls and pimplylooking young men in straw hats and an old gentleman with big bushy white whiskers wearing a panama hat. Children with dark circles under their eyes got under everybody's feet. Everybody was yellow or coffeecolored and had black eyes, and there was one grayhaired old niggerwoman in a pink dress. Everybody cried and threw up their arms and hugged and kissed Tony and it was a long time before anybody noticed Margo at all. Then all the old women crowded around kissing her and staring at her and making exclamations in Spanish about her hair and her eyes and she felt awful silly not understanding a word and kept asking Tony which his mother was, but Tony had forgotten his English. When he finally pointed to a stout old lady in a shawl and said la mamá she was very much relieved it wasn't the colored one.

If this is the fine residential section, Margo said to herself when they all piled out of the streetcar, after a long ride through yammering streets of stone houses full of dust and oily smells and wagons and mulecarts, into the blisteringhot sun of a cobbled lane, I'm a milliondollar heiress.

They went through a tall doorway in a scabby peeling pinkstucco wall cut with narrow barred windows that went right down to the ground, into a cool rankishsmelling vestibule set with wicker chairs and plants. A parrot in a cage squawked and a fat piggy little white dog barked at Margo and the old lady who Tony had said was la mamá came forward and put her arm around her shoulders and said a lot of things in Spanish. Margo stood there standing first on one foot and then on the other. The doorway was crowded with the neighbors staring at her with their monkeyeyes.

'Say, Tony, you might at least tell me what she's saying,' Margo whined peevishly.

'Mother says this is your house and you are welcome, things like that. Now you must say muchas gracias, mamá.'

Margo couldn't say anything. A lump rose in her throat and she burst out crying.

She cried some more when she saw her room, a big dark alcove hung with torn lace curtains mostly filled up by a big iron bed with a yellow quilt on it that was all spotted with a brown stain. She quit crying and began to giggle when she saw the big cracked chamberpot with roses on it peeping out from under.

Tony was sore. 'Now you must behave very nice,' he said. 'My people they say you are very pretty but not wellbred.'

'Aw, you kiss my foot,' she said.

All the time she was in Havana she lived in that alcove with only a screen in front of the glass door to the court. Tony and the boys were always out. They'd never take her anywhere. The worst of it was when she found she was going to have a baby. Day after day she lay there all alone staring up at the cracked white plaster of the ceiling, listening to the shrill jabber of the women in the court and the vestibule and the parrot and the yapping of the little white dog that was named Kiki. Roaches ran up and down the wall and ate holes in any clothes that weren't put away in chests.

Every afternoon a hot square of sunlight pressed in through the glass roof of the court and ran along the edge of the bed and across the tiled floor and made the alcove glary and stifling.

Tony's family never let her go out unless one of the old women went along, and then it was usually just to market or to church. She hated going to the market that was so filthy and rancidsmelling and jammed with sweaty jostling Negroes and Chinamen yelling over coops of chickens and slimy stalls of fish. La mamá and Tia Feliciana and Carná the old niggerwoman seemed to love it. Church was better; at least people wore better clothes there and the tinsel altars were often full of flowers, so she went to confession regularly, though the priest didn't understand the few Spanish words she was beginning to piece together, and she couldn't understand his replies. Anyway, church was better than sitting all day in the heat and the rancid smells of the vestibule trying to talk to the old women who never did anything but fan and chatter, while the little white dog slept on a dirty cushion on a busted gilt chair and occasionally snapped at a fly.

Tony never paid any attention to her any more; she could

hardly blame him, her face looked so redeyed and swollen from crying. Tony was always around with a middleaged babyfaced fat man in a white suit with an enormous double gold watch-chain looped across his baywindow whom everybody spoke of very respectfully as el señor Manfredo. He was a sugarbroker and was going to send Tony to Paris to study music. Sometimes he'd come and sit in the vestibule on a wicker chair with his goldheaded cane between his fat knees. Margo always felt there was something funny about Señor Manfredo, but she was as nice to him as she could be. He paid no attention to her either. He never took his eyes off Tony's long black lashes.

Once she got desperate and ran out alone to Central Park to an American drugstore she'd noticed there one evening when the old women had taken her to hear the military band play. Every man she passed stared at her. She got to the drugstore on a dead run and bought all the castoroil and quinine she had money for. Going home she couldn't seem to go a block without some man following her and trying to take her arm. 'You go to hell,' she'd say to them in English and walk all the faster. She lost her way, was almost run over by a car, and at last got to the house breathless. The old women were back and raised cain.

When Tony got home they told him and he made a big scene and tried to beat her up, but she was stronger than he was and blacked his eye for him. Then he threw himself on the bed sobbing and she put cold compresses on his eye to get the swelling down and petted him and they were happy and cozy together for the first time since they'd come to Havana. The trouble was the old women found out about how she'd blacked his eye and everybody teased him about it. The whole street seemed to know and everybody said Tony was a sissy. La mamá never forgave Margo and was mean and spiteful to her after that.

If she only wasn't going to have the baby, Margo would have run away. All the castoroil did was to give her terrible colic and the quinine just made her ears ring. She stole a sharppointed knife from the kitchen and thought she'd kill herself with it, but she didn't have the nerve to stick it in. She thought of hanging herself by the bedsheet, but she couldn't seem to do that either. She kept the knife under the mattress and lay all day on the bed dreaming about what she'd do if she ever got back to the States and thinking about Agnes and Frank and vaudeville shows and the Keith Circuit and the Saint Nicholas

Rink. Sometimes she'd get herself to believe that this was all a long nightmare and that she'd wake up in bed at home at Indian's.

She wrote Agnes every week and Agnes would sometimes send her a couple of dollars in a letter. She'd saved fifteen dollars in a little alligatorskin purse Tony had given her when they first got to Havana, when he happened to look into it one day and pocketed the money and went out on a party. She was so sunk that she didn't even bawl him out about it when he came back after a night at a rumbajoint with dark circles under his eyes. Those days she was feeling too sick to bawl anybody out.

When her pains began, nobody had any idea of taking her to the hospital. The old women said they knew just what to do, and two Sisters of Mercy with big white butterfly headdresses began to bustle in and out with basins and pitchers of hot water. It lasted all day and all night and some of the next day. She was sure she was going to die. At last she yelled so loud for a doctor that they went out and fetched an old man with yellow hands all knobbed with rheumatism and a tobaccostained beard they said was a doctor. He had goldrimmed eyeglasses on a ribbon that kept falling off his long twisted nose. He examined her and said everything was fine and the old women grinning and nodding stood around behind him. Then the pains grabbed her again; she didn't know anything but the pain.

After it was all over, she lay back so weak she thought she must be dead. They brought it to her to look at, but she wouldn't look. Next day when she woke up she heard a thin cry beside her and couldn't imagine what it was. She was too sick to turn her head to look at it. The old women were shaking their heads over something, but she didn't care. When they told her she wasn't well enough to nurse it and that it would have to be raised on a bottle, she didn't care either.

A couple of days passed in blank weakness. Then she was able to drink a little orangejuice and hot milk and could raise her head on her elbow and look at the baby when they brought it to her. It looked dreadfully little. It was a little girl. Its poor little faced looked wrinkled and old like a monkey's. There was something the matter with its eyes.

She made them send for the old doctor and he sat on the edge of her bed looking very solemn and wiping and wiping his eyeglasses with his big clean silk handkerchief. He kept calling her a poor little niña and finally made her understand that the baby was blind and that her husband had a secret disease and that as soon as she was well enough she must go to a clinic for treatments. She didn't cry or say anything, but just lay there staring at him with her eyes hot and her hands and feet icy. She didn't want him to go, that was all she could think of. She made him tell her all about the disease and the treatment and made out to understand less Spanish than she did, just so that he wouldn't go away.

A couple of days later the old women put on their best black silk shawls and took the baby to the church to be christened. Its little face looked awful blue in the middle of all the lace they dressed it in. That night it turned almost black. In the morning it was dead. Tony cried and the old women all carried on and they spent a lot of money on a little white casket with silver handles and a hearse and a priest for the funeral. Afterwards the Sisters of Mercy came and prayed beside her bed and the priest came and talked to the old women in a beautiful tragedy voice like Frank's voice when he wore his morningcoat, but Margo just lay there in the bed hoping she'd die too, with her eyes closed and her lips pressed tight together. No matter what anybody said to her, she wouldn't answer or open her eyes.

When she got well enough to sit up, she wouldn't go to the clinic the way Tony was going. She wouldn't speak to him or to the old women. She pretended not to understand what they said. La mamá would look into her face in a spiteful way she had and shake her head and say, 'Loca.' That meant crazy.

Margo wrote desperate letters to Agnes: for God's sake she must sell something and send her fifty dollars so that she could get home. Just to get to Florida would be enough. She'd get a job. She didn't care what she did if she could only get back to God's Country. She just said that Tony was a bum and that she didn't like it in Havana. She never said a word about the baby or being sick.

Then one day she got an idea; she was an American citizen, wasn't she? She'd go to the consul and see if they wouldn't send her home. It was weeks before she could get out without one of the old women. The first time she got down to the consulate all dressed up in her one good dress only to find it closed. The next time she went in the morning when the old women were out marketing and got to see a clerk who was a towheaded American collegeboy. My, she felt good talking American again.

She could see he thought she was a knockout. She liked him, too, but she didn't let him see it. She told him she was sick and had to go back to the States and that she'd been gotten down there on false pretenses on the promise of an engagement at the Alhambra.

'The Alhambra,' said the clerk. 'Gosh, you don't look like that kind of a girl.'

'I'm not,' she said.

His name was George. He said that if she'd married a Cuban there was nothing he could do, as you lost your citizenship if you married a foreigner. She said suppose they weren't really married. He said he thought she'd said she wasn't that kind of a girl. She began to blubber and said she didn't care what kind of a girl she was, she had to get home. He said to come back next day and he'd see what the consulate could do, anyway wouldn't she have tea with him at the Miami that afternoon.

She said it was a date and hurried back to the house feeling better than she had for a long time. The minute she was by herself in the alcove, she took the marriagelicense out of her bag and tore it up into little tiny bits and dropped it into the filthy yellow bowl of the old watercloset in the back of the court. For once the chain worked and every last bit of forget-menotspotted paper went down into the sewer.

That afternoon she got a letter from Agnes with a fiftydollar draft on the National City Bank in it. She was so excited her heart almost stopped beating. Tony was out gallivanting around somewhere with the sugarbroker. She wrote him a note saying it was no use looking for her, she'd gone home, and pinned it on the underpart of the pillow on the bed. Then she waited until the old women had drowsed off for their siesta, and ran out.

She wasn't coming back. She just had the clothes she had on, and a few little pieces of cheap jewelry Tony had given her when they were first married, in her handbag. She went to the Miami and ordered an icecreamsoda in English so that everybody would know she was an American girl, and waited for George.

She was so scared every minute she thought she'd keel over. Suppose George didn't come. But he did come and he certainly was tickled when he saw the draft, because he said the consulate didn't have any funds for a case like hers. He said he'd get the draft cashed in the morning and help her buy her ticket and everything. She said he was a dandy and then suddenly leaned over and put her hand in its white kid glove on his arm and looked right into his eyes that were blue like hers were and whispered, 'George, you've got to help me some more. You've got to help me hide. . . . I'm so scared of that Cuban. You know they are terrible when they're jealous.'

George turned red and began to hem and haw a little, but Margo told him the story of what happened on her street just the other day, how a man, an armyofficer, had come home and found, well, his sweetheart, with another man, well, she might as well tell the story the way it happened, she guessed George wasn't easily shocked anyway, they were in bed together and the armyofficer emptied all the chambers of his revolver into the other man and then chased the woman up the street with a carvingknife and stabbed her five times in the public square. She began to giggle when she got that far, and George began to laugh. 'I know it sounds funny to you . . . but it wasn't so funny for her. She died right there without any clothes on in front of everybody.'

'Well, I guess we'll have to see what we can do,' said George, 'to keep you away from that carvingknife.'

What they did was to go over to Matanzas on the Hershey electriccar and get a room at a hotel. They had supper there and a lot of ginfizzes and George, who'd told her he'd leave her to come over the next day just in time for the boat, got romantic over the ginfizzes and the moonlight and dogs barking and the roosters crowing. They went walking with their arms round each other down the quiet chalkycolored moonstruck streets, and he missed the last car back to Havana. Margo didn't care about anything except not to be alone in that creepy empty whitewalled hotel with the moon so bright and everything. She liked George anyway.

The next morning at breakfast he said she'd have to let him lend her another fifty so that she could go back firstclass and she said honestly she'd pay it back as soon as she got a job in New York and that he must write to her every day.

He went over on the early car because he had to be at the office and she went over later all alone through the glary green countryside shrilling with insects, and went in a cab right from the ferry to the boat. George met her there at the dock with her ticket and a little bunch of orchids, the first she'd ever had, and a roll of bills that she tucked into her purse without counting. The stewards seemed awful surprised that she didn't have any baggage, so she made George tell them that she'd had to leave home at five minutes' notice because her father, who was a very wealthy man, was sick in New York. She and George went right down to her room, and he was very sad about her going away and said she was the loveliest girl he'd ever seen and that he'd write her every day too, but she couldn't follow what he was saying she was so scared Tony would come down to the boat looking for her.

At last the gong rang and George kissed her desperate hard and went ashore. She didn't dare go up on deck until she heard the engineroom bells and felt the shaking of the boat as it began to back out of the dock. Out of the porthole, as the boat pulled out, she got a glimpse of a dapper dark man in a white suit, that might have been Tony, who broke away from the cops and ran yelling and waving his arms down to the end of the wharf.

Maybe it was the orchids or her looks or the story about her father's illness, but the captain asked her to his table and all the officers rushed her, and she had the time of her life on the trip up. The only trouble was that she could only come on deck in the afternoon because she had only that one dress.

She'd given George a cable to send, so when they got to New York Agnes met her at the dock. It was late fall and Margo had nothing on but a light summer dress, so she said she'd set Agnes up to a taxi to go home. It was only when they got into the cab that she noticed Agnes was wearing black. When she asked her why, Agnes said Fred had died in Bellevue two weeks before. He'd been picked up on Twentythird Street deaddrunk and had died there without coming to.

'Oh, Agnes, I knew it . . . I had a premonition on the boat,' sobbed Margo.

When she'd wiped her eyes, she turned and looked at Agnes. 'Why, Agnes dear, how well you look,' she said. 'What a pretty suit. Has Frank got a job?'

'Oh, no,' said Agnes. 'You see Miss Franklyn's teashops are doing quite well. She's branching out and she's made me manageress of the new branch on Thirtyfourth Street at seventy-five dollars a week. Wait till you see our new apartment just off the Drive. . . . Oh, Margie, you must have had an awful time.'

'Well,' said Margo, 'it was pretty bad. His people are pretty

well off and prominent and all that, but it's hard to get on to
their ways. Tony's a bum and I hate him more than anything
in the world. But after all it was quite an experience . . . I
wouldn't have missed it.'

Frank met them at the door of the apartment. He looked
fatter than when Margo had last seen him and had patches of
silvery hair on either side of his forehead that gave him a
distinguished look like a minister or an ambassador. 'Little
Margo. . . . Welcome home my child. . . . What a beautiful
young woman you have become.' When he took her in his arms
and kissed her on the brow, she smelt again the smell of bayrum
and energine she'd remembered on him. 'Did Agnes tell you
that I'm going on the road with Mrs Fiske? . . . Dear Minnie
Maddern and I were children together.'

The apartment was a little dark, but it had a parlor, a
diningroom and two bedrooms, and a beautiful big bathroom
and kitchen. 'First thing I'm goin' to do,' said Margo, 'is take
a hot bath. . . . I don't believe I've had a hot bath since I left
New.York.'

While Agnes, who had taken the afternoon off from the tearoom, went out to do some marketing for supper, Margo went
into her neat little bedroom with chintz curtains on the walls
and took off her chilly rumpled summer dress and got into
Agnes's padded dressinggown. Then she sat back in the morrischair in the parlor and strung Frank along when he asked her
questions about her life in Havana.

Little by little he sidled over to the arm of her chair, telling
her how attractivelooking she'd become. Then suddenly he
made a grab for her. She'd been expecting it and gave him
a ringing slap on the face as she got to her feet. She felt herself
getting hysterical as he came toward her across the room
panting.

'Get away from me, you old buzzard,' she yelled, 'get away
from me or I'll tell Agnes all about you and Agnes and me
we'll throw you out on your ear.' She wanted to shut up, but
she couldn't stop yelling. 'Get away from me. I caught a disease
down there; if you don't keep away from me you'll catch it
too.'

Frank was so shocked he started to tremble all over. He let
himself drop into the morrischair and ran his long fingers
through his slick silverandblack hair. She slammed her bedroom
door on him and locked it. Sitting in there alone on the bed,
she began to think how she would never see Fred again, and

could it have been a premonition when she'd told them on the boat that her father was sick. Tears came to her eyes. Certainly she'd had a premonition. The steamheat hissed cozily. She lay back on the bed that was so comfortable with its clean pillows and silky comforter, and still crying fell asleep.

# Newsreel 57

the psychic removed all clothing before séances at Harvard. Electric torches, bells, large megaphones, baskets, all illuminated by phosphorescent paint, formed the psychic's equipment

*My brother's coming*
          *with pineapples*
     *Watch the circus begin*

IS WILLING TO FACE PROBERS

the psychic's feet were not near the professor's feet when his trouser leg was pulled. An electric bulb on the ceiling flashed on and off. Buzzers rang. A teleplasmic arm grasped objects on the table and pulled Doctor B.'s hair. Doctor B. placed his nose in the doughnut and encouraged Walter to pull as hard as possible. His nose was pulled.

*Altho' we both agreed to part*
*It left a sadness in my heart*

UNHAPPY WIFE TRIES TO DIE

SHEIK DENTIST RECONCILED

FINANCING ONLY PROBLEM

*I thought that I'd get along*
               *and now*
*I find that I was wrong*
               *somehow*

SOCIETY WOMEN SEEK JOBS IN VAIN AS
MAIDS TO QUEEN

NUN WILL WED GOB

*I'm brokenhearted*

QUEEN HONORS UNKNOWN SOLDIER

POLICE GUARD QUEEN IN MOB

*Beneath a dreamy Chinese moon*
*Where love is like a haunting tune*

PROFESSOR TORTURES RIVAL

QUEEN SLEEPS AS HER TRAIN DEPARTS

SOCIAL STRIFE BREWS

COOLIDGE URGES ADVERTISING

*I found her beneath the setting sun*
*When the day was done*

COP FEEDS CANARY ON FIVE HUNDRED
DOLLARS RICH BRIDE LEFT

*While the twilight deepened*
*The sky above*
*I told my love*
*In o-o-old Ma-an-ila-a-a*

ABANDONED APOLLO STILL HOPES FOR
RETURN OF WEALTHY BRIDE

## Margo Dowling

Agnes was a darling. She managed to raise money through the Morris Plan for Margo's operation when Doctor Dennison said it was absolutely necessary if her health wasn't to be seriously impaired, and nursed her the way she'd nursed her when she'd had measles when she was a little girl. When they told Margo she never could have a baby, Margo didn't care so much, but Agnes cried and cried.

By the time Margo began to get well again and think of getting a job, she felt as if she and Agnes had just been living together always. The Old Southern Waffle Shop was doing very well and Agnes was making seventyfive dollars a week; it was lucky that she did because Frank Mandeville hardly ever seemed able to get an engagement any more, there's no demand for real entertainment since the war, he'd say. He'd become very sad and respectable since he and Agnes had been married at the Little Church Around the Corner, and spent most of his time playing bridge at the Lambs Club and telling about the old days when he'd toured with Richard Mansfield. After Margo got on her feet, she spent a whole dreary winter hanging around the agencies and in the castingoffices of musical shows, before Flo Ziegfeld happened to see her one afternoon sitting in the outside office in a row of other girls. By chance she caught his eye and made a faint ghost of a funny face when he passed; he stopped and gave her a onceover; next day Mr Herman picked her for first row in the new show. Rehearsals were the hardest work she'd ever done in her life.

Right from the start Agnes said she was going to see to it that Margo didn't throw herself away with a trashy crowd of chorusgirls; so, although Agnes had to be at work by nine o'clock sharp every morning, she always came by the theater every night after late rehearsals or evening performances to take Margo home. It was only after Margo met Tad Whittlesea, a Yale halfback who spent his weekends in New York once the football season was over, that Agnes missed a single night. The nights Tad met her, Agnes stayed home. She'd looked Tad over carefully and had him to Sunday dinner at the apartment and decided that for a millionaire's son he was pretty steady and that it was good for him to feel some responsibility about Margo.

Those nights Margo would be in a hurry to give a last pat to the blond curls under the blue velvet toque and to slip into the furcape that wasn't silver fox but looked a little like it at a distance, and to leave the dusty stuffy dressingroom and the smells of curling irons and cocoabutter and girls' armpits and stagescenery and to run down the flight of drafty cement stairs and past old grayfaced Luke who was in his little glass box pulling on his overcoat getting ready to go home himself. She'd take a deep breath when she got out into the cold wind of the street. She never would let Tad meet her at the theater with the other stagedoor Johnnies. She liked to find him standing with his wellpolished tan shoes wide apart and his coonskin coat thrown open so that you could see his striped tie and soft rumpled shirt, among people in eveningdress in the lobby of the Astor.

Tad was a simple kind of redfaced boy who never had much to say. Margo did all the talking from the minute he handed her into the taxi to go to the nightclub. She'd keep him laughing with stories about the other girls and the wardrobewomen and the chorusmen. Sometimes he'd ask her to tell him a story over again so that he could remember it to tell his friends at college. The story about how the chorusmen, who were most of them fairies, had put the bitches' curse on a young fellow who was Maisie De Mar's boyfriend, so that he'd turned into a fairy too, scared Tad half to death.

'A lot of things sure do go on that people don't know about,' he said.

Margo wrinkled up her nose. 'You don't know the half of it, dearie.'

'But it must be just a story.'

'No, honestly, Tad, that's how it happened . . . we could hear them yelling and oohooing like they do down in their dressingroom. They all stood around in a circle and put the bitches' curse on him. I tell you we were scared.'

That night they went to the Columbus Circle Childs for some ham and eggs.

'Gee, Margo,' said Tad with his mouth full as he was finishing his second order of buttercakes. 'I don't think this is the right life for you. . . . You're the smartest girl I ever met and damn refined too.'

'Don't worry, Tad, little Margo isn't going to stay in the chorus all her life.'

On the way home in the taxi Tad started to make passes at her. It surprised Margo because he wasn't a fresh kind of a boy. He wasn't drunk either, he'd only had one bottle of Canadian ale.

'Gosh, Margo, you're wonderful. . . . You won't drink and you won't cuddlecooty.'

She gave him a little pecking kiss on the cheek.

'You ought to understand, Tad,' she said, 'I've got to keep my mind on my work.'

'I guess you think I'm just a dumb cluck.'

'You're a nice boy, Tad, but I like you best when you keep your hands in your pockets.'

'Oh, you're marvelous,' sighed Tad, looking at her with round eyes from out of his turnedup fuzzy collar from his own side of the cab.

'Just a woman men forget,' she said.

Having Tad to Sunday dinner got to be a regular thing. He'd come early to help Agnes lay the table, and take off his coat and roll up his shirtsleeves afterwards to help with the dishes, and then all four of them would play hearts and each drink a glass of beefironandwine tonic from the drugstore. Margo hated those Sunday afternoons, but Frank and Agnes seemed to love them, and Tad would stay till the last minute before he had to rush off to meet his father at the Metropolitan Club, saying he'd never had such a good time in his life.

One snowy Sunday afternoon, when Margo had slipped away from the cardtable saying she had a headache, and had lain on the bed all afternoon listening to the hissing of the steamheat, almost crying from restlessness and boredom, Agnes said with her eyes shining when she came in in her négligée after Tad was gone: 'Margo, you've got to marry him. He's the sweetest boy. He was telling us how this place is the first time in his life he's ever had any feeling of home. He's been brought up by servants and ridingmasters and people like that. . . . I never thought a millionaire could be such a dear. I just think he's a darling.'

'He's no millionaire,' said Margo, pouting.

'His old man has a seat on the stockexchange,' called Frank from the other room. 'You don't buy them with cigarstore coupons, do you, dear child?'

'Well,' said Margo, stretching and yawning, 'I certainly wouldn't be getting a spendthrift for a husband. . . .' Then she sat up and shook her finger at Agnes. 'I can tell you right now why he likes to come here Sundays. He gets a free meal and it doesn't cost him a cent.'

Jerry Herman, the yellowfaced bald shriveledup little castingdirector, was a man all the girls were scared to death of. When Regina Riggs said she'd seen Margo having a meal with him at Keene's Chophouse between performances, one Saturday, the girls never quit talking about it. It made Margo sore and gave her a sick feeling in the pit of her stomach to hear them giggling and whispering behind her back in the dressingroom.

Regina Riggs, a broadfaced girl from Oklahoma whose real given name was Queenie and who'd been in the Ziegfeld choruses since the days when they had horsecars on Broadway, took Margo's arm when they were going down the stairs side by side after a morning rehearsal. 'Look here, kiddo,' she said, 'I just want to tip you off about that guy, see? You know me, I been through the mill an' I don't give a hoot in hell for any of 'em . . . but let me tell you somethin'. There never been a girl got a spoken word by givin' that fourflusher a lay. Plenty of 'em have tried it. Maybe I've tried it myself. You can't beat the game with that guy an' a beautiful white body's about the cheapest thing there is in this town. . . . You got a kinda peart innocent look and I thought I'd put you wise.'

Margo opened her blue eyes wide. 'Why, the idea. . . . What made you think I'd . . .' She began to titter like a schoolgirl.

'All right, baby, let it ride. . . . I guess you'll hold out for the weddin'bells.' They both laughed. They were always good friends after that.

But not even Queenie knew about it when, after a long wearing rehearsal late one Saturday night of a new number that was coming in the next Monday, Margo found herself stepping into Jerry Herman's roadster. He said he'd drive her home, but when they reached Columbus Circle, he said wouldn't she drive out to his farm in Connecticut with him and have a real rest. Margo went into a drugstore and phoned Agnes that there'd be rehearsals all day Sunday and that she'd stay down at Queenie Riggs's flat that was nearer the theater.

Driving out, Jerry kept asking Margo about herself. 'There's something different about you, little girl,' he said. 'I bet you don't tell all you know. . . . You've got mystery.'

All the way out, Margo was telling about her early life on a Cuban sugarplantation and her father's great townhouse in the Vedado and Cuban music and dances, and how her father had been ruined by the sugartrust and she'd supported the family as a child actress in Christmas pantomimes in England and about her early unfortunate marriage with a Spanish nobleman, and how all that life was over now and all she cared about was her work.

'Well, that story would make great publicity,' was what Jerry Herman said about it.

When they drew up at a lighted farmhouse under a lot of tall trees, they sat in the car a moment, shivering a little in the chilly mist that came from a brook somewhere. He turned to her in the dark and seemed to be trying to look in her face. 'You know about the three monkeys, dear?'

'Sure,' said Margo. 'See no evil, hear no evil, speak no evil.'

'Correct,' he said. Then she let him kiss her.

Inside it was the prettiest farmhouse with a roaring fire and two men in checked lumberman's shirts and a couple of funny-looking women in Paris clothes with Park Avenue voices who turned out to be in the decorating business. The two men were scenic artists. Jerry cooked up ham and eggs in the kitchen for everybody and they drank hard cider and had quite a time, though Margo didn't quite know how to behave. To have something to do she got hold of a guitar that was hanging on the wall and picked out *Siboney* and some other Cuban songs Tony had taught her.

When one of the women said something about how she ought to do a Cuban specialty, her heart almost stopped beating. Blue daylight was coming through the mist outside of the windows before they got to bed. They all had a fine country breakfast giggling and kidding in their dressinggowns and Sunday afternoon Jerry drove her into town and let her out on the Drive near Seventyninth Street.

Frank and Agnes were in a great stew when she got home. Tad had been calling up all day. He'd been to the theater and found out that there weren't any rehearsals called. Margo said spitefully that she had been rehearsing a little specialty and that if any young collegeboy thought he could interfere with her career he had another think coming. The next weekend when he called up she woudn't see him.

But a week later, when she came out of her room about two o'clock on Sunday afternoon just in time for Agnes's big Sunday dinner, Tad was sitting there hanging his head, with his thick hands dangling between his knees. On the chair beside him was a green florist's box that she knew when she looked at it was American Beauty roses.

He jumped up. 'Oh, Margo ... don't be sore ... I just can't seem to have a good time going around without you.'

'I'm not sore, Tad,' she said. 'I just want everybody to understand that I won't let my life interfere with my work.'

'Sure, I get you,' said Tad.

Agnes came forward, all smiles, and put the roses in water.

'Gosh, I forgot,' said Tad, and pulled a redleather case out of his pocket. He was stuttering. 'You see D-d-dad g-g-gave me some s-s-stocks to play around with an' I made a little killing last week and I bought these, only we can't wear them except when we both go out together, can we?' It was a string of pearls, small and not very well matched, but pearls all right.

'Who else would take me anyplace where I could wear them, you mut?' said Margo. Margo felt herself blushing. 'And they're not Teclas?' Tad shook his head. She threw her arms around his neck and kissed him.

'Gosh, you honestly like them,' said Tad, talking fast. 'Well, there's one other thing ... Dad's letting me have the *Antoinette* – that's his boat, you know – for a two weeks' cruise this summer with my own crowd. I want you and Mrs Mandeville to come. I'd ask Mr Mandeville, too, but . . .'

'Nonsense,' said Agnes. 'I'm sure the party will be properly chaperoned without me. . . . I'd just get seasick. . . . It used to be terrible when poor Fred used to take me out fishing.'

'That was my father,' said Margo. 'He loved being out on the water . . . yachting . . . that kind of thing . . . I guess that's why I'm such a good sailor.'

'That's great,' said Tad.

At that minute Frank Mandeville came in from his Sunday walk, dressed in his morningcoat and carrying a silverheaded cane, and Agnes ran into the kitchenette to dish up the roast stuffed veal and vegetables and the strawberrypie from which warm spicy smells had been seeping through the air of the small apartment for some time.

'Gosh, I like it here,' said Tad, leaning back in his chair after they'd sat down to dinner.

The rest of that spring Margo had quite a time keeping Tad and Jerry from bumping into each other. She and Jerry never saw each other at the theater; early in the game she'd told him she had no intention of letting her life interfere with her work and he'd looked sharply at her with his shrewd boiled-looking eyes and said, 'Humph . . . I wish more of our young ladies felt like you do. . . . I spend most of my time combing them out of my hair.'

'Too bad about you,' said Margo. 'The Valentino of the castingoffice.'

She liked Jerry Herman well enough. He was full of dope about the theater business. The only trouble was that when they got confidential he began making Margo pay her share of the check at restaurants and showed her pictures of his wife and children in New Rochelle. She worked hard on the Cuban songs, but nothing ever came of the specialty.

In May the show went on the road. For a long time she couldn't decide whether to go or not. Queenie Riggs said absolutely not. It was all right for her, who didn't have any ambition any more except to pick her off a travelingman in a onehorse town and marry him before he sobered up, but for Margo Dowling, who had a career ahead of her, nothing doing. Better be at liberty all summer than a chorine on the road.

Jerry Herman was sore as a crab when she wouldn't sign the roadcontract. He blew up right in front of the officeforce and all the girls waiting in line and everything.

'All right, I seen it coming . . . now she's got a swelled head and thinks she's Peggy Joyce. . . . All right, I'm through.'

Margo looked him straight in the eye. 'You must have me confused with somebody else, Mr Herman. I'm sure I never started anything for you to be through with.'

All the girls were tittering when she walked out, and Jerry Herman looked at her like he wanted to choke her. It meant no more jobs in any company where he did the casting.

She spent the summer in the hot city hanging round Agnes's apartment with nothing to do. And there was Frank always waiting to make a pass at her, so that she had to lock her door when she went to bed. She'd lie around all day in the horrid stuffy little room with furry green wallpaper and an unwashed window that looked out on cindery backyards and a couple of ailanthus trees and always washing hung out. Tad had gone to Canada as soon as college was over. She spent the days reading magazines and monkeying with her hair and manicuring her fingernails and dreaming about how she could get out of this miserable sordid life. Sordid was a word she'd just picked up. It was in her mind all the time, sordid, sordid, sordid. She decided she was crazy about Tad Whittlesea.

When August came, Tad wrote from Newport that his mother was sick and the yachting trip was off till next winter. Agnes cried when Margo showed her the letter. 'Well, there are other fish in the sea,' said Margo.

She and Queenie, who had resigned from the roadtour when she had a runin with the stagemanager, started making the rounds of the castingoffices again. They rehearsed four weeks for a show that flopped the opening night. Then they got jobs in the Greenwich Village Follies. The director gave Margo a chance to do her Cuban number and Margo got a special costume made and everything, only to be cut out before the dressrehearsal because the show was too long.

She would have felt terrible if Tad hadn't turned up after Thanksgiving to take her out every Saturday night. He talked a lot about the yachting trip they were going to take during his midwinter vacation. It all depended on when his exams came.

After Christmas she was at liberty again. Frank was sick in bed with kidney trouble and Margo was crazy to get away from the stuffy apartment and nursing Frank and doing the housekeeping for Agnes, who often didn't get home from her job till ten or eleven o'clock at night. Frank lay in bed, his face looking drawn and yellow and pettish, and needed attention all the time. Agnes never complained, but Margo was so fed up with hanging around New York she signed a contract for a job as entertainer in a Miami cabaret, though Queenie and Agnes carried on terrible and said it would ruin her career.

She hadn't yet settled her wrangle with the agent about who was going to pay her transportation South when one morning in February Agnes came in to wake her up.

Margo could see that it was something because Agnes was beaming all over her face. It was Tad calling her on the phone. He'd had bronchitis and was going to take a month off from college with a tutor on his father's boat in the West Indies. The boat was in Jacksonville. Before the tutor got there, he'd be able to take anybody he liked for a little cruise. Wouldn't Margo come and bring a friend? Somebody not too gay. He wished Agnes could go, he said, if that was impossible on account of Mr Mandeville's being sick, who else could she take? Margo was so excited she could hardly breathe.

'Tad, how wonderful,' she said. 'I was planning to go South this week, anyway. You must be a mindreader.'

Queenie Riggs arranged to go with her, though she said she'd never been on a yacht before and was scared she wouldn't act right.

'Well, I spent a lot of time in rowboats when I was a kid. . . . It's the same sort of thing,' said Margo.

When they got out of the taxicab at the Penn Station there was Tad and a skinny little sleekhaired boy with him waiting to meet them. They were all very much excited and the boys' breaths smelled pretty strong of gin.

'You girls buy your own tickets,' said Tad, taking Margo by the arm and pushing some bills down into the pocket of her furcoat. 'The reservations are in your name, you'll have a drawingroom and we'll have one.'

'A couple of wiseguys,' whispered Queenie in her ear as they stood in line at the ticketwindow.

The other boy's name was Dick Rogers. Margo could see right away that he thought Queenie was too old and not refined enough. Margo was worried about their baggage too. Their bags looked awful cheap beside the boys' pigskin suitcases. She felt pretty down in the mouth when the train pulled out of the station. Here I am pulling a boner the first thing, she thought. And Queenie was throwing her head back and showing her gold tooth and yelling and shrieking already like she was at a fireman's picnic.

The four of them settled down in the girls' stateroom with the little table between them to drink a snifter of gin and began to feel more relaxed. When the train came out of the tunnel and lights began flashing by in the blackness outside, Queenie pulled down the shade. 'My, this is real cozy,' she said.

'Now the first thing I got to worry about is how to get you girls out on the boat. Dad won't care if he thinks we met you in Jacksonville, but if he knew we'd brought you down from New York he'd raise Hail Columbia.'

'I think we've got a chaperon all lined up in Jacksonville,' said young Rogers. 'She's a wonder. She's deaf and blind and she can't speak English.'

'I wish we had Agnes along,' said Tad. 'That's Margo's stepmother. My, she's a good sport.'

'Well, girls,' said young Rogers, taking a noisy swig from the ginbottle, 'when does the necking start?'

After they'd had dinner in the diningcar, they went lurching back to the drawingroom and had some more gin and young Rogers wanted them to play strip poker, but Margo said no.

'Aw, be a sport,' Queenie giggled. Queenie was pretty tight already.

Margo put on her furcoat. 'I want Tad to turn in soon,' she said. 'He's just out of a sickbed.'

She grabbed Tad's hand and pulled him out into the passage. 'Come on, let's give the kids a break. . . . The trouble with you collegeboys is that the minute a girl's unconventional you think she's an easy mark.'

'Oh, Margo . . .' Tad hugged her through her furcoat as they stepped out into the cold clanging air of the observation platform. 'You're grand.'

That night after they'd gotten undressed, young Rogers came in the girls' room in his bathrobe and said there was somebody asking for Margo in the other stateroom.

She slept in the same stateroom with Tad, but she wouldn't let him get into the bunk with her. 'Honest, Tad, I like you fine,' she said, peeking from under the covers in the upper berth, 'but you know . . . Heaven won't protect a workinggirl unless she protects herself. . . . And in my family we get married before the loving instead of after.'

Tad sighed and rolled over with his face to the wall on the berth below. 'Oh, heck . . . I'd been thinking about that.'

She switched off the light. 'But, Tad, aren't you even going to kiss me goodnight?'

In the middle of the night there was a knock on the door. Young Rogers came in, looking pretty rumpled. 'Time to switch,' he said. 'I'm scared the conductor'll catch us.'

'The conductor'll mind his own damn business,' said Tad grumpily, but Margo had already slipped out and gone back to her own stateroom.

Next morning at breakfast in the diningcar, Margo wouldn't stop kidding the other two about the dark circles under their eyes. Young Rogers ordered a plate of oysters and they thought they'd never get over the giggles. By the time they got to Jacksonville, Tad had taken Margo back to the observation platform and asked her why the hell they didn't get married anyway, he was free white and twentyone, wasn't he? Margo began to cry and grinned at him through her tears and said she guessed there were plenty reasons why not.

'By gum,' said Tad when they got off the train into the sunshine of the station, 'we'll buy us an engagement ring anyway.'

First thing on the way to a hotel in a taxi they went to a jeweler's and Tad bought her a solitaire diamond set in platinum and paid for it with a check. 'My, his old man must be some millionaire,' whispered Queenie into Margo's ear in a voice like a church.

After they'd been to the jeweler's, the boys drove the girls to the Mayflower Hotel. They got a room there and went upstairs to fix up a little. The girls washed their underclothes and took hot baths and laid out their dresses on the beds.

'If you want my opinion,' Queenie was saying while she was helping Margo wash her hair, 'those two livewires are gettin' cold feet. . . . All my life I've wanted to go on a yachtin' trip an' now we're not gettin' to go any more than a rabbit. . . . Oh, Margo, I hope it wasn't me gummed the game.'

'Tad'll do anything I say,' said Margo crossly.

'You wait and see,' said Queenie. 'But here we are squabblin' when we ought to be enjoyin' ourselves. . . . Isn't this the swellest room in the swellest hotel in Jacksonville, Florida?'

Margo couldn't help laughing. 'Well, whose fault is it?'

'That's right,' said Queenie, flouncing out of the shampoo-steaming bathroom where they were washing their hair, and slamming the door on Margo. 'Have the last word.'

At one o'clock the boys came by for them, and made them get all packed up and check out of the hotel. They went down to the dock in a Lincoln car Tad had hired. It was a beautiful sunny day. The *Antoinette* was anchored out in the St John's River, so they had to go out in a little speedboat.

The sailor was a goodlooking young fellow all in white; he touched his cap and held out his arm to help the girls in. When Margo put her hand in his arm to step into the boat, she felt the hard muscles under the white duck sleeve and noticed how the sun shone on the golden hairs on his brown hand. Sitting on the darkblue soft cushion she looked up at Tad handing the bags down to the sailor. Tad looked pale from being sick and had that funny simple broadfaced look, but he was a husky wellbuilt boy too. Suddenly she wanted to hug him.

Tad steered and the speedboat went through the water so fast it took the girls' breath away and they were scared for fear the spray would spoil the new sportdresses they were wearing for the first time. 'Oh, what a beauty,' they both sighed when they saw the *Antoinette* so big and white with a mahogany deckhouse and a broad yellow chimney.

'Oh, I didn't know it was a steamyacht,' crooned Queenie. 'Why, my lands, you could cross the ocean in it.'

'It's a diesel,' said Tad.

'Aren't we all?' said Margo.

Tad was going so fast they crashed right in the little mahogany stairway they had for getting on the boat, and for a second it cracked and creaked like it would break right off, but the sailors managed to hold on somehow.

'Hold her, Newt,' cried young Rogers, giggling.

'Damn,' said Tad, and he looked very sore as they went on board.

The girls were glad to get up onto the beautiful yacht and out of the tippy little speedboat where they were afraid of getting their dresses splashed.

The yacht had goodlooking officers in white uniforms and a table was all ready for lunch out under an awning on deck and a Filipino butler was standing beside it with a tray of cocktails and all kinds of little sandwiches cut into fancy shapes. They settled down to lunch in a hurry, because the boys said they were starved. They had broiled Florida lobster in a pink sauce and cold chicken and salad and they drank champagne. Margo had never been so happy in her life.

While they were eating, the yacht started to move slowly down the river, away from the ramshackle wharves and the dirtylooking old steamboats into the broad reaches of brown river that was splotched with green floating patches of water-hyacinths. A funny damp marshy smell came on the wind off the tangled trees that hid the banks. Once they saw a dozen big white birds with long necks fly up that Tad said were egrets. 'I bet they're expensive,' said Queenie. 'They're protected by the federal government,' said young Rogers.

They drank little glasses of brandy with their coffee. By the time they got up from the table, they were all pretty well spiffed. Margo had decided that Tad was the swellest boy she'd ever known and that she wouldn't hold out on him any longer, no matter what happened.

After lunch Tad showed them all over the boat. The dining-room was wonderful, all mirrors paneled in white and gold, and the cabins were the coziest things. The girls' cabin was just like an oldfashioned drawingroom. Their things had been all hung out for them while they'd been eating lunch.

While they were looking at the boat, young Rogers and Queenie disappeared somewhere, and the first thing Margo knew she and Tad were alone in a cabin looking at a photograph of a sailboat his father had won the Bermuda race with. Looking at the picture his cheek brushed against hers and there they were kissing.

'Gee, you're great,' said Tad. 'I'm kind of clumsy at this . . . no experience, you know.'

She pressed against him. 'I bet you've had plenty.' With his free hand he was bolting the door. 'Will you do like the ring said, Tad?'

When they went up on deck afterwards, Tad was acting kind of funny; he wouldn't look her in the eye and talked all the time to young Rogers. Queenie looked flushed and all rumpled-up like she'd been through a wringer, and staggered when she walked. Margo made her fix herself up and do her hair. She sure was wishing she hadn't brought Queenie. Margo looked fresh as a daisy herself, she decided, when she looked in the big mirror in the upstairs saloon.

The boat had stopped. Tad's face looked like a thunder-cloud when he came back from talking to the captain.

'We've got to go back to Jacksonville, burned out a bearing on the oilpump,' he said. 'A hell of a note.'

'That's great,' said young Rogers. 'We can look into the local nightlife.'

'And what I want to know is,' said Queenie, 'where's that chaperon you boys were talkin' about?'

'By gum,' said Tad, 'we forgot Mrs Vinton. . . . I bet she's been waiting down at the dock all day.'

'Too late for herbicide.' said Margo, and they all laughed except Tad who looked sourer than ever.

It was dark when they got to Jacksonville. They'd had to pack their bags up again and they'd changed into different dresses.

While they were changing their clothes, Queenie had talked awful silly. 'You mark my words, Margo, that boy wants to marry you.'

'Let's not talk about it,' Margo said several times.

'You treat him like he was dirt.'

Margo heard her own voice whining and mean: 'And who's business is it?'

Queenie flushed and went on with her packing. Margo could see she was sore.

They ate supper grumpily at the hotel. After supper young Rogers made them go out to a speakeasy he'd found. Margo didn't want to go and said she had a headache, but everybody said now be a sport and she went. It was a tough kind of a place with oilcloth on the tables and sawdust on the floor. There were some foreigners, wops or Cubans or something, standing against a bar in another room. Queenie said she didn't think it was the kind of place Mother's little girl ought to be seen in.

'Who the hell's going to see us?' said Tad still in his grouch.

'Don't we want to see life?' Rogers said, trying to cheer everybody up.

Margo lost track of what they were saying. She was staring through the door into the barroom. One of the foreigners standing at the bar was Tony. He looked older and his face was kind of puffy, but there was no doubt that it was Tony. He looked awful. He wore a rumpled white suit frayed at the cuffs of the trousers and he wiggled his hips like a woman as he talked. The first thing Margo thought was how on earth she could ever have liked that fagot. Out of the corner of her eye she could see Tad's sullen face and his nice light untidy hair and the cleancut collegeboy way he wore his clothes. She had to work fast. She was just opening her mouth to say honestly she had to go back to the hotel, when she caught sight of Tony's big black eyes and dark lashes. He was coming toward the table with his mincing walk, holding out both hands. 'Querida mia. . . . Why are you here?'

She introduced him as Antonio de Garrido, her partner in a Cuban dance number on the Keith Circuit, but he let the cat out of the bag right away by calling her his dear wife. She could feel the start Tad gave when he heard that. Then suddenly Tad began to make a great fuss over Tony and to order up drinks for him. He and Rogers kept whispering and laughing together about something. Then Tad was asking Tony to come on the cruise with them.

She could see Tad was acting drunker than he really was. She was ready for it when the boys got up to go. Tad's face was red as a beet.

'We got to see the skipper about that engine trouble,' he said. 'Maybe Señor de Garrido will see you girls back to the hotel. ... Now don't do anything I wouldn't do.'

'See you in the morning, cuties,' chimed in young Rogers.

After they'd gone, Margo got to her feet. 'Well, no use waiting around this dump. . . . You sure put your foot in it, Tony.'

Tony had tears in his eyes. 'Everything is very bad with me,' he said. 'I thought maybe my little Margo remembered . . . you know we used to be very fond. Don Manfredo, you remember my patron, Margo, had to leave Havana very suddenly. I hoped he would take me to Paris, but he brought me to Miami with him. Now we are no more friends. We have been unlucky at roulette. . . . He has only enough money for himself.'

'Why don't you get a job?'

'In these clothes . . . I am ashamed to show my face . . . maybe your friends . . .'

'You lay off them, do you hear?' Margo burst out.

Queenie was blubbering, 'You should have bought us return tickets to New York. Another time you remember that. Never leave the homeplate without a return ticket.'

Tony took them home to the hotel in a taxi and insisted on paying for it. He made a big scene saying goodnight. 'Little Margo, if you never see me again, remember I loved you. . . . I shall keel myself.' As they went up in the elevator, they could see him still standing on the sidewalk where they had left him.

In the morning they were waked up by a bellboy bringing an envelope on a silver tray. It was a letter to Margo from Tad. The handwriting was an awful scrawl. All it said was that the trip was off because the tutor had come and they were going to have to pick up Dad in Palm Beach. Enclosed there were five twenties.

'Oh, goody goody,' cried Queenie, sitting up in bed when she saw them. 'It sure would have been a long walk home. . . . Honest, that boy's a prince.'

'A damn hick,' said Margo. 'You take fifty and I take fifty. . . . Lucky I have an engagement fixed up in Miami.'

It was a relief when Queenie said she'd take the first train back to little old New York. Margo didn't want ever to see any of that bunch again.

They hadn't finished packing their bags when there was Tony at the door. He sure looked sick. Margo was so nervous she yelled at him, 'Who the hell let you in?'

Tony let himself drop into a chair and threw back his head with his eyes closed. Queenie closed up her travelingbag and came over and looked at him. 'Say, that bozo looks halfstarved. Better let me order up some coffee or something. . . . Was he really your husband like he said?'

Margo nodded.

'Well, you've got to do something about him. Poor boy, he sure does look down on his uppers.'

'I guess you're right,' said Margo, staring at them both with hot dry eyes.

She didn't go down to Miami that day. Tony was sick and threw up everything he ate. It turned out he hadn't had anything to eat for a week and had been drinking hard. 'I bet you that boy dopes,' Queenie whispered in Margo's ear.

They both cried when it was time for Queenie to go to her train. 'I've got to thank you for a wonderful time while it lasted,' she said.

Margo put Tony to bed after Queenie had gone off to her train. When they objected down at the desk, she said he was her husband. They had to register again. It made her feel awful to have to write down in the book Mr and Mrs Antonio de Garrido. Once it was written it didn't look so bad, though.

It was three days before Tony could get up. She had to have a doctor for him. The doctor gave him bromides and hot milk. The room was seven-fifty a day and the meals sent up and the doctor and medicine and everything ran into money. It began to look like she'd have to hock the ring Tad had given her.

It made her feel like she was acting in a play living with Tony again. She was kind of fond of him after all, but it sure wasn't what she'd planned. As he began to feel better, he began to talk confidently about the magnificent act they could put on together. Maybe they could sell it to the cabaret she'd signed an engagement with in Miami. After all, Tony was a sweet-tempered kind of a boy.

The trouble was that whenever she went out to get her hair curled or something, she'd always find one of the bellhops, a greasylooking blackhaired boy who was some kind of a spick himself, in the room with Tony. When she asked Tony what about it, he'd laugh and say, 'It is nothing. We talk Spanish together. That is all. He has been very attentive.'

'Yes, yes,' said Margo. She felt so damn lousy about everything she didn't give a damn anyway.

One morning when she woke up, Tony was gone. The roll of bills in her pocketbook was gone and all her jewelry except the solitaire diamond she wore on her finger was gone, too. When she called up the desk to ask if he'd paid the bill, they said that he had left word for her to be called at twelve and that was all. Nobody had seen him go out. The spick bellhop had gone, too.

All that Margo had left was her furcoat and fifteen cents. She didn't asked for the bill, but she knew it must be about fifty or sixty bucks. She dressed thoughtfully and carefully and decided to go out to a lunchroom for a cup of coffee. That was all the breakfast she had the price of.

Outside it was a warm spring day. The sunshine glinted on the rows of parked cars. The streets and the stores and the newsstands had a fresh sunny airy look. Margo walked up and down the main street of Jacksonville with an awful hollow feeling in the pit of her stomach. She looked in haberdashery store windows and in the windows of cheap jewelers and hockshops and read over carefully all the coming attractions listed at the moving picture houses. She found herself in front of a busstation. She read the fares and the times buses left for Miami and New Orleans and Tallahassee and Orlando and Tampa and Atlanta, Georgia, and Houston, Texas, and Los Angeles, California. In the busstation there was a lunchcounter. She went in to spend her fifteen cents. She'd get more for the ring at a hockshop if she didn't barge in on an empty stomach, was what she was thinking as she sat down at the counter and ordered a cup of coffee and a sandwich.

# Newsreel 58

*In my dreams it always seems*
*I hear you softly call to me*
*Valencia!*
*Where the orange trees forever scent the*
*Breeze beside the sea*

which in itself typifies the great drama of the Miami we have today. At the time only twenty years ago when the site of the Bay of Biscayne Bank was a farmer's hitching-yard and that of the First National Bank a public barbecue-ground, the ground here where this ultramodern hotel and club stands was isolated primeval forest. My father and myself were clearing little vegetable patches round it and I was peddling vegetables at the hotel Royal Palm, then a magnificent hotel set in a wild frontier. Even eight years ago I was growing tomatoes

*Valencia!*

SEEK MISSING LOOT

WOMAN DIRECTS HIGHWAY ROBBERY

*Lazy River flowing to the southland*
*Down where I long to be*

RADIUM VICTIMS TIPPED BRUSHES IN MOUTHS

this peninsula has been white every month though there have been some months when West Florida was represented as only fair

GIRL EVANGELS AWAIT CHRIST IN NEW YORK

*When the red red robin*
*Comes bob bob bobbin' along along*

We Want You to Use Our Credit System to Your

Utmost Advantage. Only a Small Down Payment and the Balance in Small Amounts to Suit Your Convenience.

*There'll be no more sobbin'*
*When he starts throbbin'*

### URGES STRIKES BE TERMED FELONIES

*When he starts throbbin'*
*His old sweet song*
*When the red red robin*

bright and early he showed no signs of fatigue or any of the usual evidences of a long journey just finished. There was not a wrinkle on his handsome suit of silken material, the weave and texture and color of which were so suitable for tropic summer days. His tie with its jeweled stickpin and his finger ring were details in perfect accord with his immaculate attire. Though small in stature and unassuming in manner, he disposed of twenty million dollars worth of building operations with as little fuss or flurry as ordinarily accompanies the act of a passenger on a trolley car in handing a nickel to the conductor.

## The Campers at Kitty Hawk

On December seventeenth, nineteen hundred and three, Bishop Wright, of the United Brethren, onetime editor of the *Religious Telescope*, received in his frame house on Hawthorn Street in Dayton, Ohio, a telegram from his boys Wilbur and Orville who'd gotten it into their heads to spend their vacations in a little camp out on the dunes of the North Carolina coast tinkering with a homemade glider they'd knocked together themselves. The telegram read:

SUCCESS FOUR FLIGHTS THURSDAY MORNING ALL AGAINST TWENTYONE-MILE WIND STARTED FROM LEVEL WITH ENGINE-POWER ALONE AVERAGE SPEED THROUGH AIR THIRTYONE MILES LONGEST FIFTYSEVEN SECONDS INFORM PRESS HOME CHRISTMAS

The figures were a little wrong because the telegraph operator misread Orville's hasty penciled scrawl,

but the fact remains

that a couple of young bicycle mechanics from Dayton, Ohio,

had designed, constructed, and flown

for the first time ever a practical airplane.

*After running the motor a few minutes to heat it up, I released the wire that held the machine to the track and the machine started forward into the wind. Wilbur ran at the side of the machine holding the wing to balance it on the track. Unlike the start on the fourteenth, made in a calm, the machine facing a twentyseven-mile wind started very slowly.... Wilbur was able to stay with it until it lifted from the track after a forty-foot run. One of the lifesaving men snapped the camera for us, taking a picture just as it reached the end of the track and the machine had risen to a height of about two feet.... The course of the flight up and down was extremely erratic, partly due to the irregularities of the air, partly to lack of experience in handling this machine. A sudden dart when a little over a hundred and twenty feet from the point at which it rose in the air ended the flight.... This flight lasted only twelve seconds, but it was nevertheless the first in the history of the world in which a machine carrying a man had raised itself by its own power into the air in full flight, had sailed forward without reduction of speed, and had finally landed at a point as high as that from which it started.*

A little later in the day the machine was caught in a gust of wind and turned over and smashed, almost killing the coast-guardsman who tried to hold it down;

it was too bad,

but the Wright brothers were too happy to care;

they'd proved that the damn thing flew.

*When these points had been definitely established, we at once packed our goods and returned home, knowing that the age of the flyingmachine had come at last.*

They were home for Christmas in Dayton, Ohio, where they'd been born in the seventies of a family who had been settled west of the Alleghenies since eighteen-fourteen; in Dayton, Ohio, where they'd been to grammarschool and highschool and joined their father's church and played baseball and hockey and worked out on the parallel bars and the flying swing and sold newspapers and built themselves a printingpress out of odds and ends from the junkheap and flown kites and tinkered with mechanical contraptions and gone around town as boys doing odd jobs to turn an honest penny.

The folks claimed it was the Bishop's bringing home a helicopter, a fiftycent mechanical toy made of two fans worked by elastic bands that was supposed to hover in the air, that had got his two youngest boys hipped on the subject of flight

so that they stayed home instead of marrying the way the other boys did, and puttered all day about the house picking up a living with jobprinting,

bicyclerepair work,

sitting up late nights reading books on aerodynamics.

Still they were sincere churchmembers, their bicycle business was prosperous, a man could rely on their word. They were popular in Dayton.

In those days flyingmachines were the big laugh of all the crackerbarrel philosophers. Langley's and Chanute's unsuccessful experiments had been jeered down with an I-told-you-so that rang from coast to coast. The Wrights' big problem was to find a place secluded enough to carry on their experiments without being the horselaugh of the countryside. Then they had no money to spend;

they were practical mechanics; when they needed anything they built it themselves.

They hit on Kitty Hawk,

on the great dunes and sandy banks that stretch south toward Hatteras seaward of Albemarle Sound,

a vast stretch of seabeach,

empty except for a coastguard station, a few fishermen's shacks, and the swarms of mosquitos and the ticks and chiggers in the crabgrass behind the dunes,

and overhead the gulls and swooping terns, in the evening fishhawks and cranes flapping across the saltmarshes, occasionally eagles

that the Wright brothers followed soaring with their eyes
as Leonardo watched them centuries before,
straining his sharp eyes to apprehend
the laws of flight.

Four miles across the loose sand from the scattering of shacks, the Wright brothers built themselves a camp and a shed for their gliders. It was a long way to pack their groceries, their tools, anything they happened to need; in summer it was hot as blazes, the mosquitoes were hell;

but they were alone there,

and they'd figured out that the loose sand was as soft as anything they could find to fall in.

There with a glider made of two planes and a tail in which they lay flat on their bellies and controlled the warp of the planes by shimmying their hips, taking off again and again all day from a big dune named Kill Devil Hill,

they learned to fly.

Once they'd managed to hover for a few seconds
and soar ever so slightly on a rising aircurrent,
they decided the time had come
to put a motor in their biplane.

Back in the shop in Dayton, Ohio, they built an airtunnel, which is their first great contribution to the science of flying, and tried out model planes in it.

They couldn't interest any builders of gasoline engines, so they had to build their own motor.

It worked; after that Christmas of nineteen-three the Wright brothers weren't doing it for fun any more; they gave up their bicycle business, got the use of a big old cowpasture belonging to the local banker for practice flights, spent all the time when they weren't working on their machine in promotion, worrying about patents, infringements, spies, trying to interest government officials, to make sense out of the smooth involved heartbreaking remarks of lawyers.

In two years they had a plane that would cover twenty-four miles at a stretch round and round the cowpasture.

People on the interurban car used to crane their necks out of the windows when they passed along the edge of the field, startled by the clattering pop-pop of the old Wright motor and the sight of the white biplane like a pair of ironingboards one on top of the other chugging along a good fifty feet in the air. The cows soon got used to it.

As the flights got longer,
the Wright brothers got backers,

engaged in lawsuits,
lay in their beds at night sleepless with the whine of
phantom millions, worse than the mosquitoes at Kitty Hawk.

In nineteen-seven they went to Paris,
allowed themselves to be togged out in dress suits and silk
hats,
learned to tip waiters,
talked with government experts, got used to gold braid
and postponements and Vandyke beards and the outspread
palms of politicos. For amusement
they played diabolo in the Tuileries Gardens.

They gave publicized flights at Fort Myers, where they
had their first fatal crackup, St Petersburg, Paris, Berlin; at
Pau they were all the rage,
such an attraction that the hotelkeeper
wouldn't charge them for their room.
Alfonso of Spain shook hands with them and was photographed sitting in the machine.
King Edward watched a flight,
the Crown Prince insisted on being taken up,
the rain of medals began.

They were congratulated by the Czar
and the King of Italy and the amateurs of sport, and the
society climbers and the papal titles,
and decorated by a society for universal peace.

Aeronautics became the sport of the day.
The Wrights don't seem to have been very much impressed
by the upholstery and the braid and the gold medals and the
parades of plush horses;
they remained practical mechanics
and insisted on doing all their own work themselves,
even to filling the gasolinetank.

In nineteen-eleven they were back on the dunes
at Kitty Hawk with a new glider.
Orville stayed up in the air for nine and a half minutes,
which remained a long time the record for motorless flight.
The same year Wilbur died of typhoidfever in Dayton.
In the rush of new names: Farman, Blériot, Curtiss,
Ferber, Esnault-Peltrie, Delagrange;

in the snorting impact of bombs and the whine and rattle
of shrapnel and the sudden stutter of machineguns after the
motor's been shut off overhead,

and we flatten into the mud

and make ourselves small cowering in the corners of
ruined walls,

the Wright brothers passed out of the headlines;

but not even headlines or the bitter smear of newsprint or
the choke of smokescreen and gas or chatter of brokers on the
stockmarket or barking of phantom millions or oratory of
brasshats laying wreaths on new monuments

can blur the memory

of the chilly December day

two shivering bicycle mechanics from Dayton, Ohio,

first felt their homemade contraption,

whittled out of hickory sticks,

gummed together with Arnstein's bicycle cement,

stretched with muslin they'd sewn on their sister's sewingmachine in their own backyard on Hawthorn Street in Dayton,
Ohio,

soar into the air

above the dunes and the wide beach

at Kitty Hawk.

# Newsreel 59

the stranger first coming to Detroit, if he be interested in the busy economic side of modern life, will find a marvelous industrial beehive; if he be a lover of nature, he will take notice of a site made forever remarkable by the waters of that noble strait that gives the city its name; if he be a student of romance and history, he will discover legends and records as entertaining and as instructive as the continent can supply

*I've a longing for my Omaha town*
*I long to go there and settle down*

DETROIT LEADS THE WORLD IN THE
MANUFACTURE OF AUTOMOBILES

*I want to see my pa*
*I want to see my ma*
*I want to go to dear old Omaha*

DETROIT IS FIRST
IN PHARMACEUTICALS
STOVES RANGES FURNACES
ADDING MACHINES
PAINTS AND VARNISHES
MARINE MOTORS
OVERALLS
SODA AND SALT PRODUCTS
SPORT SHOES
TWIST DRILLS
SHOWCASES
CORSETS
GASOLINE TORCHES
TRUCKS

*Mr Radio Man won't you do what you can*
*'Cause I'm so lonely*

*Tell my Mammy to come back home*
*Mr Radio Man*

DETROIT THE DYNAMIC RANKS HIGH

IN FOUNDRY AND MACHINE SHOP PRODUCTS
IN BRASS AND BRASS PRODUCTS
IN TOBACCO AND CIGARS
IN ALUMINUM CASTINGS
IN IRON AND STEEL
IN LUBRICATOR TOOLS
MALLEABLE IRON
METAL BEDS

*Back to the land that gave me birth*
*The grandest place on God's green earth*
*California! That's where I belong*

'DETROIT THE CITY WHERE LIFE IS WORTH
LIVING'

## Charley Anderson

First thing Charley heard when he climbed down from the controls was Farrell's voice shouting, 'Charley Anderson, the boy with the knowhow. Welcome to little old Detroit'; and then he saw Farrell's round face coming across the green grass of the field and his big mouth wide open. 'Kind of bumpy, wasn't it?'

'It was cold as hell,' said Charley. 'Call this a field?'

'We're getting the Chamber of Commerce het up about it. You can give 'em an earful about it, maybe.'

'I sure did slew around in that mud. Gosh, I pulled out in such a hurry I didn't even bring a toothbrush.'

Charley pulled off his gloves that were dripping with oil from a leak he'd had trouble with in the bumpy going over the hills. His back ached. It was a relief that Bill Cermak was there to get the boat into the hangar.

'All right, let's go,' he said.

'Thataboy,' roared Farrell and put his hand on Charley's shoulder. 'We'll stop by the house and see if I can fit you into a change of clothes.'

At that moment a taxi rolled out onto the field and out of it stepped Taki. He came running over with Charley's suitcase. He reached the car breathless. 'I hope you have a nice journey, sir.'

'Check,' said Charley. 'Did you get me a walkup?'

'Very nice inexpensive elevator apartment opposed to the Museum of Municipal Art,' panted Taki in his squeaky voice.

'Well, that's service,' Farrell said, and put his foot on the starter of his puttycolored Lincoln towncar. The motor purred silkily.

Taki put the suitcase in back and Charley hopped in beside Farrell. 'Taki thinks we lack culture,' said Charley, laughing. Farrell winked.

It was pleasant sitting slumped in the seat beside Farrell's welldressed figure behind the big softpurring motor, letting a little drowsiness come over him as they drove down broad straight boulevards with here and there a construction job that gave them a whiff of new bricks and raw firboards and fresh cement as they passed. A smell of early spring came off the fields and backlots on a raw wind that had little streaks of swampy warmth in it.

'Here's our little shanty,' said Farrell and swerved into a curving graded driveway and jammed on the brakes at the end of a long graystone house with narrow pointed windows and Gothic pinnacles like a cathedral. They got out and Charley followed Farrell across a terrace down an avenue of boxtrees in pots and through a frenchwindow into a billiardroom with a heavilycarved ceiling.

'This is my playroom,' said Farrell. 'After all, a man's got to have someplace to play.... Here's a bathroom you can change in. I'll be back for you in ten minutes.'

It was a big bathroom all in jadegreen with a couch, an easychair, a floorlamp, and a set of chestweights and indianclubs in the corner. Charley stripped and took a hot shower and changed his clothes.

He was just putting on his bestlooking striped tie when Farrell called through the door. 'Everything O.K.?'

'Check,' said Charley as he came out. 'I feel like a million dollars.'

Farrell looked him in the eye in a funny way and laughed. 'Why not?' he said.

The office was in an unfinished officebuilding in a ring of unfinished officebuildings round Grand Circus Park.

'You won't mind if I run you through the publicity department first, Charley,' said Farrell. 'Eddy Sawyer's a great boy. Then we'll all get together in my office and have some food.'

'Check,' said Charley.

'Say, Eddy, here's your birdman,' shouted Farrell, pushing Charley into a big bright office with orange hangings. 'Mr Sawyer, meet Mr Anderson . . . the Charley Anderson, our new consulting engineer. . . . Give us a buzz when you've put him through a course of sprouts.'

Farrell hurried off, leaving Charley alone with a small yellow-faced man with a large towhead who had the talk and manners of a highschool boy with the cigarette habit. Eddy Sawyer gave Charley's hand a tremendous squeeze, asked him how he liked the new offices, explained that orange stood for optimism, asked him if he ever got airsick, explained that he did terribly, wasn't it the damnedest luck seeing the business he was in, brought out from under his desk a bottle of whiskey. 'I bet J. Y. didn't give you a drink. . . . That man lives on air, a regular salamander.'

Charley said he would take a small shot and Eddy Sawyer produced two glasses that already had the ice in them and a siphon. 'Say when.' Charley took a gulp, then Eddy leaned back in his swivelchair having drained off his drink and said, 'Now Mr Anderson, if you don't mind let's have the old lifehistory, or whatever part of it is fit to print. . . . Mind you, we won't use anything right away, but we like to have the dope so that we can sort of feed it out as occasion demands.'

Charley blushed. 'Well,' he said, 'there's not very much to tell.'

'Thataboy,' said Eddy Sawyer, pouring out two more drinks and putting away the whiskeybottle. 'That's how all the best stories begin.' He pressed a buzzer and a curlyhaired stenographer with a pretty pink dollface came in and sat down with her notebook at the other side of the desk.

While he was fumbling through his story, Charley kept repeating to himself in the back of his head, 'Now, bo, don't make an ass of yourself the first day.' Before they were through, Farrell stuck his head in the door and said to come along, the crowd was waiting.

'Well, did you get all fixed up? . . . Charley, I want you to meet our salesmanager . . . Joe Stone, Charley Anderson. And Mr Frank and Mr O'Brien, our battery of legal talent, and Mr Bledsoe, he's in charge of output . . . that's your department.'

Charley shook a number of hands; there was a slick black head with hair parted in the middle, a pair of bald heads and a steelgray head with hair bristling up like a shoebrush, noseglasses, tortoiseshell glasses, one small mustache. 'Sure, mike,' Eddy Sawyer was stuttering away nervously. 'I've got enough on him to retire on the blackmail any time now.'

'That's a very good starter, young man,' said Cyrus Bledsoe, the grayhaired man, gruffly. 'I hope you've got some more notions left in the back of your head.'

'Check,' said Charley.

They all, except Bledsoe who growled that he never ate lunch, went out with him to the Athletic Club where they had a private diningroom and cocktails set out. Going up in the elevator a voice behind him said, 'How's the boy, Charley?' and Charley turned round to find himself face to face with Andy Merritt. Andy Merritt's darkgray suit seemed to fit him even better than usual. His sour smile was unusually thin.

'Why, what are you doing here?' Charley blurted out.

'Detroit,' said Andy Merritt, 'is a town that has always interested me extremely.'

'Say, how's Joe making out?'

Andy Merritt looked pained and Charley felt he ought to have kept his mouth shut. 'Joe was in excellent health when I last saw him,' said Andy. It turned out that Andy was lunching with them too.

When they were working on the filetmignon, Farrell got up and made a speech about how this luncheon was a beginning of a new spirit in the business of manufacturing airplane parts and motors and that the time had come for the airplane to quit hanging on the apronstrings of the automotive business because airplanes were going to turn the automobilemen into a lot of bicycle manufacturers before you could say Jack Robinson. A milliondollar business had to be handled in a milliondollar way. Then everybody yelled and clapped and Farrell held up his hand and described Charley Anderson's career as a war ace and an inventor and said it was a very happy day, a day he'd been waiting for a long time, when he could welcome him into the Tern flock. Then Eddy Sawyer led a cheer for Anderson and Charley had to get up and say how he was glad to get out there and be back in the great open spaces and the real manufacturing center of this country, and when you said manufacturing center of this country what you meant was manufacturing center of the whole bloody world. Eddy Sawyer led another cheer and then they all settled down to eat their peachmelba.

When they were getting their hats from the checkroom downstairs, Andy Merritt tapped Charley on the shoulder and said, 'A very good speech.... You know I'd felt for some time we ought to make a break.... You can't run a bigtime business with smalltown ideas. That's the trouble with poor old Joe, who's a prince, by the way ... smalltown ideas ...'

Charley went around to see the apartment. Taki had everything fixed up in great shape, flowers in the vases and all that sort of thing.

'Well, this is slick,' said Charley. 'How do you like it in Detroit?'

'Very interesting,' said Taki. 'Mr Ford permits to visit Highland Park.'

'Gosh, you don't lose any time.... Nothing like that assemblyline in your country, is there?'

Taki grinned and nodded. 'Very interesting,' he said with more emphasis.

Charley took off his coat and shoes and lay down on the couch in the sittingroom to take a nap, but it seemed he'd just closed his eyes when Taki was grinning and bowing from the door.

'Very sorry, sir, Mr Benton, longdistance.'

'Check,' said Charley.

Taki had his slippers there for him to stick his feet into and had discreetly laid his bathrobe on a chair beside the couch. At the phone Charley noticed that it was already dusk and that the streetlights were just coming on.

'Hello, Nat.'

'Hey, Charley, how are you making out?'

'Great,' said Charley.

'Say, I just called up to let you know you and Andy Merritt were going to be elected vicepresidents at the next meeting of Tern stockholders.'

'How do you know?' Nat laughed into the phone. 'Some intelligence service,' said Charley.

'Well, service is what we're here for,' said Nat. 'And Charley, there's a little pool down here.... I'm taking a dip myself and I thought you might like to come in.... I can't tell you the details over the phone, but I wrote you this afternoon.'

'I haven't got any cash.'

'You could put up about ten grand of stock to cover. The stock won't be tied up long.'

'Check,' said Charley. 'Shoot the moon . . . this is my lucky year.'

The plant was great. Charley drove out there in a new Buick sedan he bought himself right off the dealer's floor the next morning. The dealer seemed to know all about him and wouldn't even take a downpayment. 'It'll be a pleasure to have your account, Mr Anderson,' he said.

Old Bledsoe seemed to be on the lookout for him and showed him around. Everything was lit with skylights. There wasn't a belt in the place. Every machine had its own motor. 'Farrell thinks I'm an old stickinthemud because I don't talk high finance all the time, but goddamn it, if there's a more uptodate plant than this anywhere, I'll eat a goddamned dynamo.'

'Gee, I thought we were in pretty good shape out at Long Island City. . . . But this beats the Dutch.'

'That's exactly what it's intended to do,' growled Bledsoe.

Last Bledsoe introduced Charley to the engineering force and then showed him into the office off the draftingroom that was to be his. They closed the groundglass door and sat down facing each other in the silvery light from the skylight. Bledsoe pulled out a stogie and offered one to Charley. 'Ever smoke these? . . . They clear the head.'

Charley said he'd try anything once. They lit the stogies and Bledsoe began to talk between savage puffs of stinging blue smoke. 'Now look here, Anderson, I hope you've come out here to work with us and not to juggle your damned stock. . . . I know you're a war hero and all that and are slated for windowdressing, but it looks to me like you might have somep'n in your head too. . . . I'm saying this once and I'll never say it again. . . . If you're workin' with us, you're workin' with us, and if you're not, you'd better stick around your broker's office where you belong.'

'But, Mr Bledsoe, this is the chance I've been lookin' for,' stammered Charley. 'Hell, I'm a mechanic, that's all. I know that.'

'Well, I hope so. . . . If you are, and not a goddamned bondsalesman, you know that our motor's lousy and the ships they put it in are lousy. We're ten years behind the rest of the world in flyin' and we've got to catch up. Once we get the designs, we've got the production apparatus to flatten 'em all out. Now I want you to go home and get drunk or go wenchin' or whatever you do when you're worried and think about this damn business.'

'I'm through with that stuff,' said Charley. 'I had enough of that in New York.'

Bledsoe got to his feet with a jerk, letting the ash from his stogie fall on his alpaca vest. 'Well, you better get married then.'

'I been thinkin' of that.... But I can't find the other name to put on the license,' said Charley, laughing.

Bledsoe smiled. 'You design me a decent light dependable sixteencylinder aircooled motor and I'll get my little girl to introduce you to all the bestlookin' gals in Detroit. She knows 'em all.... And if it's money you're lookin' for, they sweat money.'

The phone buzzed. Bledsoe answered it, muttered under his breath, and stamped out of the office.

At noon Farrell came by to take Charley out to lunch. 'Did old Bledsoe give you an earful?' he asked. Charley nodded. 'Well, don't let him get under your skin. His bark is worse than his bite. He wouldn't be in the outfit if he wasn't the best plant-manager in the country.'

It was at the Country Club dance that Farrell and his wife, who was a thin oldish blonde, haggard and peevish under a festoon of diamonds, took him out to, that Charley met old Bledsoe's daughter Anne. She was a squareshouldered girl in pink with a large pleasantlysmiling mouth and a firm handshake. Charley cottoned to her first thing. They danced to *Just a Girl That Men Forget*, and she talked about how crazy she was about flying and had five hours toward her pilot's license. Charley said he'd take her up any time if she wasn't too proud to fly a Curtiss-Robin. She said he'd better not make a promise if he didn't intend to keep it because she always did what she said she'd do. Then she talked about golf and he didn't let on that he'd never had a golfclub in his hand in his life.

At supper when he came back from getting a couple of plates of chickensalad, he found her sitting at a round table under a Japanese lantern with a pale young guy, who turned out to be her brother Harry, and a girl with beautiful ashenblond hair and a touch of Alabama in her talk whose name was Gladys Wheatley. She seemed to be engaged or something to Harry Bledsoe, who had a silver flask and kept pouring gin into the fruitpunch and held her hand and called her Glad. They were all younger than Charley, but they made quite a fuss over him and kept saying what a godawful town Detroit was. When Charley got a little gin inside of him, he started telling war yarns for the first time in his life.

He drove Anne home and old Bledsoe came out with a copy of the *Engineering Journal* in his hand and said, 'So you've got acquainted, have you?'

'Oh, yes, we're old friends, Dad,' she said. 'Charley's going to teach me to fly.'

'Humph,' said Bledsoe and closed the door in Charley's face with a growling: 'You go home and worry about that motor.'

All that summer everybody thought that Charley and Anne were engaged. He'd get away from the plant for an hour or two on quiet afternoons and take a ship up at the flyingfield to give her a chance to pile up flying hours and on Sundays they'd play golf. Charley would get up early Sunday mornings to take a lesson with the golf pro out at the Sunnyside Club where he didn't know anybody. Saturday nights they'd often have dinner at the Bledsoes' house and go out to the Country Club to dance. Gladys Wheatley and Harry were usually along and they were known as a foursome by all the younger crowd. Old Bledsoe seemed pleased that Charley had taken up with his youngsters and began to treat him as a member of the family. Charley was happy, he enjoyed his work; after the years in New York being in Detroit was like being home. He and Nat made some killings in the market. As vicepresident and consulting engineer of the Tern Company he was making twenty-five thousand dollars a year.

Old Bledsoe grumbled that it was too damn much money for a young engineer, but it pleased him that Charley spent most of it on a small experimental shop where he and Bill Cermak were building a new motor on their own. Bill Cermak had moved his family out from Long Island and was full of hunches for mechanical improvements. Charley was so busy he didn't have time to think of women or take anything but an occasional drink in a social way. He thought Anne was a peach and enjoyed her company, but he never thought of her as a girl he might someday go to bed with.

Over the Labor Day weekend the Farrells invited the young Bledsoes and Gladys Wheatley out for a cruise. When he was asked, Charley felt that this was highlife at last and suggested he bring Taki along to mix drinks and act as steward. He drove the Bledsoes down to the yachtclub in his Buick.

Anne couldn't make out why he was feeling so good. 'Nothing to do for three days but sit around on a stuffy old boat and let the mosquitoes bite you,' she was grumbling in a gruff tone like her father's. 'Dad's right when he says he doesn't mind working over his work but he's darned if he'll work over his play.'

'But look at the company we'll have to suffer in, Annie.' Charley put his arm round her shoulders for a moment as she sat beside him on the front seat.

Harry, who was alone in the back, let out a giggle. 'Well, you needn't act so smart, Mister,' said Anne, without turning back. 'You and Gladys certainly do enough public petting to make a cat sick.'

'The stern birdman's weakening,' said Harry.

Charley blushed. 'Check,' he said.

They were already at the yachtclub and two young fellows in sailorsuits were taking the bags out of the back of the car.

Farrell's boat was a fast fiftyfoot cruiser with a diningroom on deck and wicker chairs and a lot of freshvarnished mahogany and polished brass. Farrell wore a yachtingcap and walked up and down the narrow deck with a worried look as the boat nosed out into the little muggy breeze. The river in the late afternoon had a smell of docks and weedy swamps.

'It makes me feel good to get out on the water, don't it you, Charley? . . . The one place they can't get at you.'

Meanwhile Mrs Farrell was apologizing to the ladies for the cramped accommodations. 'I keep trying to get Yardly to get a boat with some room in it, but it seems to me every one he gets is more cramped up than the last one.'

Charley had been listening to a light clinking sound from the pantry. When Taki appeared with a tray of manhattan cocktails, everybody cheered up. As he watched Taki bobbing with the tray in front of Gladys, Charley thought how wonderful she looked all in white with her pale abundant hair tied up in a white silk handkerchief.

Smiling beside him was Anne with her brown hair blowing in her eyes from the wind of the boat's speed. The engine made so much noise and the twinscrews churned up so much water that he could talk to her without the others hearing.

'Annie,' he said suddenly, 'I been thinking it's about time I got married.'

'Why, Charley, a mere boy like you.'

Charley felt warm all over. All at once he wanted a woman terribly bad. It was hard to control his voice.

'Well, I suppose we're both old enough to know better, but what would you think of the proposition? I've been pretty lucky this year as far as dough goes.'

Anne sipped her cocktail, looking at him and laughing with

her hair blowing across her face. 'What do you want me to do, ask for a statement of your bankdeposit?'

'But I mean you.'

'Check,' she said.

Farrell was yelling at them, 'How about a little game of penny ante before supper? ... It's gettin' windy out here. We'd be better off in the saloon.'

'Aye, aye, cap,' said Anne.

Before supper they played penny ante and drank manhattans and after supper the Farrells and the Bledsoes settled down to a game of auction. Gladys said she had a headache and Charley, after watching the game for a while, went out on deck to get the reek of the cigar he'd been smoking out of his lungs.

The boat was anchored in a little bay, near a lighted wharf that jutted out from shore. A halfmoon was setting behind a rocky point where one tall pine reached out of a dark snarl of branches above a crowd of shivering whitebirches. At the end of the wharf there was some sort of clubhouse that spilt ripples of light from its big windows; dancemusic throbbed and faded from it over the water. Charley sat in the bow. The boys who ran the boat for Farrell had turned in. He could hear their low voices and catch a smell of cigarettesmoke from the tiny hatch forward of the pilothouse. He leaned over to watch the small gray waves slapping against the bow. 'Bo, this is the bigtime stuff,' he was telling himself.

When he turned around, there was Gladys beside him. 'I thought you'd gone to bed, young lady,' he said.

'Thought you'd gotten rid of me for one night?' She wasn't smiling.

'Don't you think it's a pretty night, Glad?'

He took her hand; it was trembling and icecold. 'You don't want to catch cold, Glad,' he said.

She dug her long nails into his hand. 'Are you going to marry Anne?'

'Maybe.... Why? You're goin' to marry Harry, aren't you?'

'Nothing in this world would make me marry him.'

Charley put his arms round her. 'You poor little girl, you're cold. You ought to be in bed.' She put her head on his chest and began to sob. He could feel the tears warm through his shirt. He didn't know what to say. He stood there hugging her with the smell of her hair giddy, like the smell of Doris's hair used to be, in his nostrils.

'I wish we were off this damn boat,' he whispered. Her face

was turned up to his, very round and white. When he kissed her lips, she kissed him too. He pressed her to him hard. Now it was her little breasts he could feel against his chest. For just a second she let him put his tongue between her lips, then she pushed him away.

'Charley, we oughtn't to be acting like this, but I suddenly felt so lonely.'

Charley's voice was gruff in his throat. 'I'll never let you feel like that again.... Never, honestly . . . never....' 'Oh, you darling Charley.' She kissed him again very quickly and deliberately and ran away from him down the deck.

He walked up and down alone. He didn't know what to do. He was crazy for Gladys now. He couldn't go back and talk to the others. He couldn't go to bed. He slipped down the forward hatch and through the galley, where Taki sat cool as a cucumber in his white coat reading some thick book, into the cabin where his berth was and changed into his bathingsuit and ran up and dove over the side. The water wasn't as cold as he'd expected. He swam around for a while in the moonlight. Pulling himself up the ladder aft, he felt cold and goosefleshy. Farrell with a cigar in his teeth leaned over, grabbed his hand and hauled him on deck.

'Ha, ha, the iron man,' he shouted. 'The girls beat us two rubbers and went to bed with their winnings. Suppose you get into your bathrobe and have a drink and half an hour of red dog or something silly before we turn in.'

'Check,' said Charley, who was jumping up and down on the deck to shake off the water.

While Charley was rubbing himself down with a towel below, he could hear the girls chattering and giggling in their stateroom. He was so embarrassed when he sat down next to Harry, who was a little drunk and silly that he drank off half a tumbler of rye and lost eighty dollars. He was glad to see that it was Harry who won. 'Lucky at cards, unlucky in love,' he kept saying to himself after he'd turned in.

A week later, Gladys took Charley to see her parents after they'd had tea together at his flat chaperoned by Taki's grin and his bobbing black head. Horton B. Wheatley was a power, so Farrell said, in the Security Trust Company, a redfaced man with grizzled hair and a small silvery mustache. Mrs Wheatley was a droopy woman with a pretty Alabama voice and a face faded and pouchy and withered as a spent toyballoon.

Mr Wheatley started talking before Gladys had finished the

introductions: 'Well, sir, we'd been expectin' somethin' like that to happen. Of course, it's too soon for us all to make up our minds, but I don't see how I kin help tellin' you, ma boy, that I'd rather see ma daughter wedded to a boy like you that's worked his way up in the world, even though we don't know much about you yet, than to a boy like Harry who's a nice enough kid in his way, but who's never done a thing in his life but take the schoolin' his father provided for him. Ma boy, we are mighty proud, my wife and me, to know you and to have you and our little girl . . . she's all we've got in this world, so she's mighty precious to us . . .'

'Your parents are . . . have been called away, I believe, Mr Anderson,' put in Mrs Wheatley. Charley nodded. 'Oh, I'm so sorry. . . . They were from St Paul, Gladys says . . .'

Mr Wheatley was talking again. 'Mr Anderson, Mother, was one of our most prominent war aces; he won his spurs fightin' for the flag, Mother, an' his whole career seems to me to be an example . . . now I'm goin' to make you blush, ma boy . . . of how American democracy works at its very best pushin' forward to success the most intelligent and best-fitted and weedin' out the weaklin's. . . . Mr Anderson, there's one thing I'm goin' to ask you to do right now. I'm goin' to ask you to come to church with us next Sunday an' address ma Sundayschool class. I'm sure you won't mind sayin' a few words of inspiration and guidance to the youngsters there.'

Charley blushed and nodded. 'Aw, Daddy,' sang Gladys, putting her arms around both their necks, 'don't make him do that. Sunday's the only day the poor boy gets any golf. . . . You know I always said I never would marry a Sundayschool teacher.'

Mr Wheatley laughed and Mrs Wheatley cast down her eyes and sighed. 'Once won't hurt him, will it, Charley?'

'Of course not,' Charley found himself saying. 'It would be an inspiration.'

Next day Charley and Mr Wheatley had lunch alone at the University Club. 'Well, son, I guess the die is cast,' said Mr Wheatley when they met in the lobby. 'The Wheatley women have made up their minds, there's nothin' for us to do but bow to the decision. I certainly wish you children every happiness, son. . . .' As they ate, Mr Wheatley talked about the bank and the Tern interests and the merger with Askew-Merritt that would a little more than double the capitalization of the new Tern Aviation Company. 'You're surprised that I know all about this, Charley ... that's what I'd been thinkin', that boy's a mechanical genius, but he don't keep track of the financial end ... he don't realize what his holdin's in that concern mean to him and the financial world.'

'Well, I know some pretty good guys who give me the low-down,' said Charley.

'Fair enough, fair enough,' said Mr Wheatley, 'but now that it's in the family maybe some of ma advice, the result of twenty years of bankin' experience at home in Birmingham and here in this great new dazzlin' city of Detroit ...'

'Well, I sure will be glad to take it, Mr Wheatley,' stammered Charley.

Mr Wheatley went on to talk about a lot on the waterfront with riparian rights at Grosse Pointe he was planning to turn over to the children for a weddingpresent and how they ought to build on it right away if only as an investment in the most restricted residential area in the entire United States of America. 'And, son, if you come around to ma office after lunch, you'll see the plans for the prettiest little old English house to set on that lot you ever did see. I've been havin' 'em drawn up as a surprise for Mother and Gladys, by Ordway and Ordway.... Half-timbered Tudor they call it. I thought I'd turn the whole thing over to you children, as it'll be too big for Mother and me now that Gladys is gettin' married. I'll chip in the lot and you chip in the house and we'll settle the whole thing on Gladys for any children.'

They finished their lunch. As they got up, Mr Wheatley took Charley's hand and shook it. 'And I sincerely hope and pray that there'll be children, son.'

Just after Thanksgiving the society pages of all the Detroit papers were full of a dinnerdance given by Mr and Mrs Horton B. Wheatley to announce the approaching marriage of their daughter Gladys to Mr Charles Anderson, inventor war ace and head of the research department at the great Tern Airplane Plant.

Old Bledsoe never spoke to Charley after the day the engagement was announced, but Anne came over to Charley and Gladys the night of the Halloween dance at the Country Club and said she thoroughly understood and wished them every happiness.

A few days before the wedding, Taki gave notice. 'But I thought you would stay on.... I'm sure my wife would like it, too. Maybe we can give you a raise.'

Taki grinned and bowed. 'It is regrettable,' he said, 'that I experience only bachelor establishments ... but I wish you hereafter every contentment.'

What hurt Charley most was that when he wrote Joe Askew asking him to be his bestman, he wired back only one word: 'No.'

The wedding was at the Emmanuel Baptist Church. Charley wore a cutaway and new black shoes that pinched his toes. He kept trying to remember not to put his hand up to his tie. Nat Benton came on from New York to be bestman and was a great help. While they were waiting in the vestry, Nat pulled a flask out of his pants pocket and tried to get Charley to take a drink. 'You look kinda green around the gills, Charley.' Charley shook his head and made a gesture with his thumb in the direction from which the organ music was coming. 'Are you sure you got the ring?' Nat grinned and took a drink himself. He cleared his throat. 'Well, Charley, you ought to congratulate me for picking a winner.... If I could spot the market like I can spot a likely youngster, I'd be in the money right now.'

Charley was so nervous he stammered. 'Did ... don't worry, Nat, I'll take care of you.' They both laughed and felt better. An usher was already beckoning wildly at them from the vestry door.

Gladys in so many satinwhite frills and the lace veil and the orangeblossoms, with a little boy in white satin holding up her train, looked like somebody Charley had never seen before. They both said, 'I will' rather loud without looking at each other. At the reception afterwards there was no liquor in the punch on account of the Wheatleys. Charley felt halfchoked with the smell of the flowers and of women's furs and with trying to say something to all the overdressed old ladies he was introduced to, who all said the same thing about what a beautiful wedding. He'd just broken away to go upstairs to change his clothes when he saw Ollie Taylor, very tight, trip on a Persian rug in the hall and measure his length at the feet of Mrs Wheatley who'd just come out of the receptionroom looking very pale and weepy in lavender and orchids. Charley kept right on upstairs.

In spite of the wedding's being dry, Nat and Farrell had certainly had something, because their eyes were shining and there was a moist look round their mouths when they came into the room where Charley was changing into a brown suit for traveling.

'Lucky bastards,' he said. 'Where did you get it? . . . Gosh, you might have kept Ollie Taylor out.'

'He's gone,' said Nat. They added in chorus, 'We attend to everything.'

'Gosh,' said Charley, 'I was just thinkin' it's a good thing I sent my brother in Minneapolis and his gang invitations too late for 'em to get here. I can just see my old Uncle Vogel runnin' around pinchin' the dowagers in the seat and cryin' hochheit.'

'It's too bad about Ollie,' said Nat. 'He's one of the best-hearted fellers in the world.'

'Poor old Ollie,' echoed Charley. 'He's lost his grip.'

There was a knock on the door. It was Gladys, her little face pale and goldenhaired and wonderful-looking in the middle of an enormous chinchilla collar. 'Charley, we've got to go. You naughty boy, I don't believe you've looked at the presents yet.'

She led them into an upstairs sittingroom stacked with glassware and silver table articles and flowers and smokingsets and toiletsets and cocktailshakers until it looked like a department store. 'Aren't they sweet?' she said.

'Never saw anythin' like it in my life,' said Charley. They saw more guests coming in at the other end and ran out into the back hall again.

'How many detectives have they got?' asked Charley.

'Four,' said Gladys.

'Well, now,' said Charley, 'we vamoose.'

'Well, it's time for us to retire,' chorused Farrell, and Nat suddenly doubled up laughing. 'Or may we kiss the bride?'

'Check,' said Charley. 'Thank all the ushers for me.'

Gladys fluttered her hand. 'You are dears . . . go away now.'

Charley tried to hug her to him, but she pushed him away. 'Daddy's got all the bags out the kitchen door. . . . Oh, let's hurry. . . . Oh, I'm almost crazy.'

They ran down the backstairs and got into a taxi with their baggage. His was pigskin; hers was shiny black. The bags had a new expensive smell. Charley saw Farrell and Nat come out from under the columns of the big colonial porch, but before they could throw the confetti the taxidriver had stepped on the gas and they were off.

At the depot there was nobody but the Wheatleys, Mrs Wheatley crying in her baggy mink coat, Mr Wheatley orating about the American home whether anybody listened or not. By the time the train pulled out, Gladys was crying too and

Charley was sitting opposite her feeling miserable and not knowing how the hell to begin.

'I wish we'd flown.'

'You know it wouldn't have been possible in this weather,' said Gladys, and then burst out crying again.

To have something to do, Charley ordered some dinner from the diningcar and sent the colored porter to get a pail of ice for the champagne.

'Oh, my nerves,' moaned Gladys, pressing her gloved hands over her eyes.

'After all, kid, it isn't as if it was somebody else... It's just you and me,' said Charley gently.

She began to titter. 'Well, I guess I'm a little silly.'

When the porter, grinning and respectfully sympathetic, opened the champagne, she just wet her lips with it. Charlie drank off his glass and filled it up again. 'Here's how, Glad, this is the life.' When the porter had gone, Charley asked her why she wouldn't drink. 'You used to be quite a rummy out at the countryclub, Glad.'

'I don't want you to drink either.'

'Why?'

She turned very red. 'Mother says that if the parents get drunk, they have idiot children.'

'Oh, you poor baby,' said Charley, his eyes filling with tears. They sat for a long time looking at each other while the fizz went out of the champagne in the glasses and the champagne slopped out onto the table with the jolting of the train. When the broiled chicken came, Gladys couldn't eat a bite of it. Charley ate both portions and drank up the champagne and felt he was acting like a hog.

The train clanked and roared in their ears through the snowy night. After the porter had taken away the supperdishes, Charley took off his coat and sat beside her and tried to make love to her. She'd only let him kiss her and hug her like they'd done before they were married. When he tried to undo her dress, she pushed him away. 'Wait, wait.'

She went into the lavatory to get into her nightdress. He thought he'd go crazy she took so long. He sat in his pajamas in the icy gritty flaw of wind that came in through the crack of the window until his teeth were chattering. At last he started to bang on the door of the toilet. 'Anything wrong, Glad? What's the matter, darlin'?'

She came out in a fluffy lace négligée. She'd put on too much makeup. Her lips were trembling under the greasy lipstick. 'Oh, Charley, don't let's tonight on the train, it's so awful like this.'

Charley felt suddenly uncontrollably angry. 'But you're my wife. I'm your husband, goddam it.' He switched off the light. Her hands were icy in his. As he grabbed her to him, he felt the muscles of his arms swelling strong behind her slender back. It felt good the way the lace and silk tore under his hands.

Afterwards she made him get out of bed and lie on the couch wrapped in a blanket. She bled a great deal. Neither of them slept. Next day she looked so pale and the bleeding hadn't stopped and they were afraid they'd have to stop somewhere to get a doctor. By evening she felt better, but still she couldn't eat anything. All afternoon she lay halfasleep on the couch while Charley sat beside her holding her hand with a pile of unread magazines on his knees.

It was like getting out of jail when they got off the train at Palm Beach and saw the green grass and the palmtrees and the hedges of hibiscus in flower. When she saw the big rooms of their corner suite at the Royal Poinciana, where she'd wanted to go because that was where her father and mother had gone on their weddingtrip, and the flowers friends had sent that filled up the parlor, Gladys threw her arms around his neck and kissed him even before the last bellboy had got out of the room. 'Oh, Charley, forgive me for being so horrid.' Next morning they lay happy in bed side by side after they'd had their breakfast and looked out of the window at the sea beyond the palmtrees, and smelt the freshness of the surf and listened to it pounding along the beach. 'Oh, Charley,' Gladys said, 'let's have everything always just like this.'

Their first child was born in December. It was a boy. They named him Wheatley. When Gladys came back from the hospital, instead of coming back to the apartment she went into the new house out at Grosse Pointe that still smelt of paint and raw plaster. What with the hospital expenses and the furniture bills and Christmas, Charley had to borrow twenty thousand from the bank. He spent more time than ever talking over the phone to Nat Benton's office in New York. Gladys bought a load of new clothes and kept tiffanyglass bowls full of freezias and narcissus all over the house. Even on the dressingtable in her bathroom she always had flowers. Mrs Wheatley said she got her love of flowers from her grandmother Randolph, because the Wheatleys had never been able to tell one flower from another. When the next child turned out to be a girl, Gladys said, as she lay in the hospital, her face looking drawn and yellow against the white pillows, beside the great bunch of glittering white orchids Charley had ordered from the florist at five dollars a bloom, she wished she could name her Orchid. They ended by naming her Marguerite after Gladys's grandmother Randolph.

Gladys didn't recover very well after the little girl's birth and had to have several small operations that kept her in bed three months. When she got on her feet, she had the big room next to the nursery and the children's nurse's room redecorated in white and gold for her own bedroom. Charley groused about it a good deal because it was in the other wing of the house from his room. When he'd come over in his bathrobe before turning in and try to get into bed with her, she would keep him off with a cool smile, and when he insisted, she would give him a few pecking kisses and tell him not to make a noise or he would wake the babies. Sometimes tears of irritation would start into his eyes. 'Jesus, Glad, don't you love me at all?' She would answer that if he really loved her he'd have come home the night she had the Smyth Perkinses to dinner instead of phoning at the last minute that he'd have to stay at the office.

'But, Jesus, Glad, if I didn't make the money how would I pay the bills?'

'If you loved me you'd be more considerate, that's all,' she would say, and two curving lines would come on her face from her nostrils to the corners of her mouth like the lines on her mother's face and Charley would kiss her gently and say poor little girl and go back to his room feeling like a louse. Times she did let him stay she lay so cold and still and talked about how he hurt her, so that he would go back to the tester bed in his big bedroom feeling so nervous and jumpy it would take several stiff whiskies to get him in shape to go to sleep.

One night when he'd taken Bill Cermak, who was now a foreman at the Flint plant, over to a roadhouse the other side of Windsor to talk to him about the trouble they were having with molders and diemakers, after they'd had a couple of whiskies, Charley found himself instead asking Bill about married life. 'Say, Bill, do you ever have trouble with your wife?'

'Sure, boss,' said Bill, laughing. 'I got plenty trouble. But the old lady's all right, you know her, nice kids good cook, all time want me to go to church.'

'Say, Bill, when did you get the idea of callin' me boss? Cut it out.'

'Too goddam rich,' said Bill.

'Hell, have another whiskey.' Charley drank his down. 'And beer chasers like in the old days.... Remember that Christmas party out in Long Island City and that blonde at the beer-parlor.... Jesus, I used to think I was a little devil with the women.... But my wife she don't seem to get the idea.'

'You have two nice kids already; what the hell, maybe you're too ambitious.'

'You wouldn't believe it . . . only once since little Peaches was born.'

'Most women gets hotter when they're married awhile.... That's why the boys are sore at your damned efficiency expert.'

'Stauch? Stauch's a genius at production.'

'Maybe, but he don't give the boys any chance for repro-duction.' Bill laughed and wiped the beer off his mouth.

'Good old Bill,' said Charley. 'By god, I'll get you on the board of directors yet.'

Bill wasn't laughing any more. 'Honestly, no kiddin'. That damn squarehead make the boys work so hard they can't get a hardon when they go to bed, an' their wives raise hell with 'em. I'm strawboss and they all think sonofabitch too, but they're right.'

Charley was laughing. 'You're a squarehead yourself, Bill, and I don't know what I can do about it, I'm just an employee of the company myself.... We got to have efficient production or they'll wipe us out of business. Ford's buildin' planes now.'

'You'll lose all your best guys.... Slavedrivin' may be all right in the automobile business, but buildin' an airplane motor's skilled labor.'

'Aw, Christ, I wish I was still tinkerin' with that damn motor and didn't have to worry about money all the time.... Bill, I'm broke.... Let's have another whiskey.'

'Better eat.'

'Sure, order up a steak . . . anythin' you like. Let's go take a piss. That's one thing they don't charge for.... Say, Bill, does it seem to you that I'm gettin' a potbelly? . . . Broke, a potbelly, an' my wife won't sleep with me.... Do you think I'm a rummy, Bill. I sometimes think I better lay off for keeps. I never used to pull a blank when I drank.'

'Hell, no, you smart young feller, one of the smartest, a fool for a threepoint landing and a pokerplayer . . . my God.'

'What's the use if your wife won't sleep with you?'

Charley wouldn't eat anything. Bill ate up both their steaks. Charley kept on drinking whiskey out of a bottle he had under the table and beer for chasers. 'But tell me . . . your wife, does she let you have it any time you want it? . . . The guys in the shop, their wives won't let 'em alone, eh?'

Bill was a little drunk too. 'My wife she do what I say.'

It ended by Bill's having to drive Charley's new Packard back to the ferry. In Detroit, Bill made Charley drink a lot of soda-water in a drugstore, but when he got back in the car he just slumped down at the wheel. He let Bill drive him home to Grosse Pointe. Charley could hear Bill arguing with the guards along the road, each one really had to see Mr Anderson passed out in the back of the car before he'd let Bill through, but he didn't give a hoot, struck him so funny he began to giggle. The big joke was when the houseman had to help Bill get him up to his bedroom. 'The boss a little sick, see, overwork,' Bill said each time, then he'd tap his head solemnly. 'Too much brain-work.'

Charley came to up in his bedroom and was able to articulate muzzily: 'Bill, you're a prince. . . . George, call a taxi to take Mr Cermak home . . . lucky bastard go home to his wife.' Then he stretched out on the bed with one shoe on and one shoe off and went quietly to sleep.

When he came back from his next trip to New York and Washington, he called up Bill at the plant. 'Hey, Bill, how's the boy? Your wife still do what you say, ha ha? Me, I'm terrible, very exhaustin' business trip, understand . . . never drank so much in my life or with so many goddam crooks. Say, Bill, don't worry if you get fired, you're on my private payroll, understand. . . . We're goin' to fire the whole outfit. . . . Hell, if they don't like it workin' for us, let 'em try to like it workin' for somebody else. . . . This is a free country. I wouldn't want to keep a man against his will. . . . Look, how long will it take you to tune up that little Moth type, you know, number 16 . . . yours truly's Mosquito? . . . Check. . . . Well, if we can get her in shape soon enough so they can use her as a model, see, for their specifications . . . Jesus, Bill, if we can do that . . . we're on easy-street . . . You won't have to worry about if the kids can go to college or not . . . goddam it, you an' the missis can go to college yourselves. . . . Check.'

Charley put the receiver back on the desk. His secretary, Miss Finnegan, was standing in the door. She had red hair and a beautiful complexion with a few freckles round her little sharp nose. She was a snappy dresser. She was looking at Charley with her lightbrown eyes all moist and wide as he was laying down the law over the phone. Charley felt his chest puff out a little. He pulled in his belly as hard as he could. 'Gosh,' he was saying at the back of his head, 'maybe I could lay Elsie Finnegan.' Somebody had put a pot of blue hyacinths on his desk; a smell of spring came from them that all at once made him remember Bar-le-Duc, and troutfishing up the Red River.

It was a flowerysmelling spring morning again when Charley drove out to the plant from the office to give the Anderson Mosquito its trial spin. He had managed to give Elsie Finnegan a kiss for the first time and had left her crumpled and trembling at her desk. Bill Cermak had said over the phone that the tiny ship was tuned up and in fine shape. It was a relief to get out of the office where he'd been fidgeting for a couple of hours trying to get through a call to Nat Benton's office about some stock he'd wired them to take a profit on. After he'd kissed her, he'd told Elsie Finnegan to switch the call out to the trial field for him. It made him feel good to be driving out through the half-built town, through the avenue jammed with trucks full of construction materials, jockeying his car among the trucks with a feeling of shine and strength at the perfect action of his clutch and the smooth response of the gears. The gatekeeper had the New York call for him. The connection was perfect. Nat had banked thirteen grand for him. As he hung up the receiver, he thought, Poor little Elsie, he'd have to buy her something real nice. 'It's a great day, Joe, ain't it?' he said to the gatekeeper.

Bill was waiting for him beside the new ship at the entrance to the hangar, wiping grease off his thick fingers with a bunch of waste.

Charley slapped him on the back. 'Good old Bill... Isn't this a great day for the race?' Bill fell for it. 'What race, boss?'

'The human race, you fathead.... Say, Bill,' he went on as he took off his gloves and his welltailored spring overcoat, 'I don't mind tellin' you I feel wonderful today ... made thirteen grand on the market yesterday ... easy as rollin' off a log.'

While Charley pulled a suit of overalls on, the mechanics pushed the new ship out onto the grass for Bill to make his general inspection. 'Jesus, she's pretty.' The tiny aluminum ship glistened in the sun out on the green grass like something in a jeweler's window. There were dandelions and clover on the grass and a swirling flight of little white butterflies went up right from under his black clodhoppers when Bill came back to Charley and stood beside him.

Charley winked at Bill Cermak standing beside him in his blue denims stolidly looking at his feet. 'Smile, you sonofabitch,' he said. 'Don't this weather make you feel good?'

Bill turned a square bohunk face toward Charley. 'Now look here, Mr Anderson, you always treat me good . . . from way back Long Island days. You know me, do work, go home, keep my face shut.'

'What's on your mind, Bill? . . . Want me to try to wangle another raise for you? Check.'

Bill shook his heavy square face and rubbed his nose with a black forefinger. 'Tern Company used to be good place to work – good work, good pay. You know me, Mr Anderson, I'm no bolshayvik . . . but no stoolpigeon either.'

'But damn it, Bill, why can't you tell those guys to have a little patience . . . we're workin' out a profitsharin' scheme. I've worked on a lathe myself. . . . I've worked as a mechanic all over this goddam country. . . . I know what the boys are up against, but I know what the management's up against too. . . . Gosh, this thing's in its infancy; we're pouring more capital into the business all the time. . . . We've got a responsibility toward our investors. Where do you think that jack I made yesterday's goin' but the business of course? The oldtime shop was a great thing, everybody kidded and smoked and told smutty stories, but the pressure's too great now. If every department don't click like a machine, we're rooked. If the boys want a union, we'll give 'em a union. You get up a meeting and tell 'em how we feel about it, but tell 'em we've got to have some patriotism. Tell 'em the industry's the first line of national defense. We'll send Eddy Sawyer down to talk to 'em . . . make 'em understand our problems.'

Bill Cermak shook his head. 'Plenty other guys do that.'

Charley frowned. 'Well, let's see how she goes,' he snapped impatiently. 'Gosh, she's a honey.'

The roar of the motor kept them from saying any more. The mechanic stepped from the controls and Charley climbed in. Bill Cermak got in behind. She started taxiing fast across the green field. Charley turned her into the wind and let her have the gas. At the first soaring bounce there was a jerk. As he pitched forward, Charley switched off the ignition.

They were carrying him across the field on a stretcher. Each step of the men carrying the stretcher made two jagged things grind together in his leg. He tried to tell 'em that he had a piece of something in his side, but his voice was very small and hoarse. In the shadow of the hangar he was trying to raise himself on his elbow. 'What the devil happened? Is Bill all right?' The men shook their heads. Then he passed out again like the juice failing in a car.

In the ambulance he tried to ask the man in the white jacket about Bill Cermak and to remember back exactly what had happened, but the leg kept him too busy trying not to yell. 'Hey, doc,' he managed to croak, 'can't you get these aluminum splinters out of my side?' The damn ship must have turned turtle on them. Wings couldn't take it, maybe, but it's time they got the motor lifted off me. 'Hey, doc, why can't they get a move on?'

When he got the first whiff of the hospital, there were a lot of men in white jackets moving and whispering round him. The hospital smelt strong of ether. The trouble was he couldn't breathe. Somebody must have spilt that damned ether. No, not on my face. The motor roared. He must have been seeing things. The motor's roar swung into an easy singsong. Sure, she was taking it fine, steady as one of those big old bombers. When he woke up, a nurse was helping him puke into a bowl.

When he woke up again, for chrissake no more ether, no, it was flowers, and Gladys was standing beside the bed with a big bunch of sweetpeas in her hand. Her face had a pinched look.

'Hello, Glad, how's the girl?'

'Oh, I've been so worried, Charley. How do you feel? Oh, Charley, for a man of your standing to risk his life in practice flights . . . Why don't you let the people whose business it is do it, I declare.'

There was something Charley wanted to ask. He was scared about something. 'Say, are the kids all right?'

'Wheatley skinned his knee and I'm afraid the baby has a little temperature. I've phoned Doctor Thompson. I don't think it's anything, though.'

'Is Bill Cermak all right?'

Gladys's mouth trembled. 'Oh, yes,' she said, cutting the words off sharply. 'Well, I suppose this means our dinnerdance is off. . . . The Edsel Fords were coming.'

'Hell, no, why not have it, anyway? Yours truly can attend in a wheelchair. Say, they sure have got me in a straitjacket. . . . I guess I busted some ribs.'

Gladys nodded; her mouth was getting very small and thin. Then she suddenly began to cry.

The nurse came in and said reproachfully, 'Oh, Mrs Anderson.'

Charley was just as glad when Gladys went out and left him alone with the nurse. 'Say, nurse, get hold of the doctor, will you? Tell him I'm feeling fine and want to look over the extent of the damage.'

'Mr Anderson, you mustn't have anything on your mind.'

'I know, tell Mrs Anderson I want her to get in touch with the office.'

'But it's Sunday, Mr Anderson. A great many people have been downstairs, but I don't think the doctor is letting them up yet.' The nurse was a freshfaced girl with a slightly Scotch way of talking.

'I bet you're a Canadian,' said Charley.

'Right, that time,' said the nurse.

'I knew a wonderful nurse who was a Canadian once. If I'd had any sense, I'd have married her.'

The housephysician was a roundfaced man with a jovial smooth manner almost like a headwaiter at a big hotel.

'Say, doc, ought my leg to hurt so damn much?'

'You see we haven't set it yet. You tried to puncture a lung, but didn't quite get away with it. We had to remove a few little splinters of rib.'

'Not from the lung . . .'

'Luckily not.'

'But why the hell didn't you set the leg at the same time?'

'Well, we're waiting for Doctor Roberts to come on from New York. . . . Mrs Anderson insisted on him. Of course, we are all very pleased, as he's one of the most eminent men in his profession. . . . It'll be another little operation.'

It wasn't until he'd come to from the second operation that they told him that Bill Cermak had died of a fractured skull.

Charley was in the hospital three months with his leg in a Balkan frame. The fractured ribs healed up fast, but he kept on having trouble with his breathing. Gladys handled all the house bills and came every afternoon for a minute. She was always in a hurry and always terribly worried. He had to turn over a power of attorney to Moe Frank, his lawyer, who used to come to see him a couple of times a week to talk things over. Charley couldn't say much, he couldn't say much to anybody he was in so much pain.

He liked it best when Gladys sent Wheatley to see him. Wheatley was three years old now and thought it was great in the hospital. He liked to see the nurse working all the little weights and pulleys of the frame the leg hung in. 'Daddy's living in a airplane,' was what he always said about it. He had tow hair and his nose was beginning to stick up and Charley thought he took after him.

Marguerite was still too little to be much fun. The one time Gladys had the governess bring her, she bawled so at the look of the scarylooking frame she had to be taken home. Gladys wouldn't let her come again. Gladys and Charley had a bitter row about letting Wheatley come, as she said she didn't want the child to remember his father in the hospital.

'But, Glad, he'll have plenty of time to get over it, get over it a damn sight sooner than I will.'

Gladys pursed her lips together and said nothing. When she'd gone, Charley lay there hating her and wondering how they could ever have had children together.

Just about the time he began to see clearly that they all expected him to be a cripple the rest of his life, he began to mend, but it was winter before he was able to go home on crutches. He still suffered sometimes from a sort of nervous difficulty in breathing. The house seemed strange as he dragged himself around in it. Gladys had had every room redecorated while he was away and all the servants were different. Charley didn't feel it was his house at all. What he enjoyed best was the massage he had three times a week. He spent his days playing with the kids and talking to Miss Jarvis, their stiff and elderly English governess. After they'd gone to bed, he'd sit in his sittingroom drinking Scotch-and-soda and feeling puffy and nervous. Goddam it, he was getting too fat. Gladys was always cool as a cucumber these days; even when he went into fits of temper and cursed at her, she'd stand there looking at him with a cold look of disgust on her carefully madeup face. She entertained a great deal, but made the servants understand that Mr Anderson wasn't well enough to come down. He began to feel like a poor relation in his own house. Once, when the Farrells were coming, he put on his tuxedo and hobbled down to dinner on his crutches. There was no place set for him and everybody looked at him like he was a ghost.

'Thataboy!' shouted Farrell in his yapping voice. 'I was expecting to come up and chin with you after dinner.' It turned out that what Farrell wanted to talk about was the suit for five hundred thousand some damn shyster had induced Cermak's widow to bring against the company. Farrell had an idea that if Charley went and saw her he could induce her to be reasonable and settle for a small annuity. Charley said he'd be damned if he'd go. At dinner Charley got tight and upset the afterdinner coffeecups with his crutch and went off to bed in a rage.

What he enjoyed outside of playing with the kids was buying and selling stocks and talking to Nat over the longdistance. Nat kept telling him he was getting the feel of the market. Nat warned him and Charley knew damn well that he was slipping at Tern and that if he didn't do something he'd be frozen out, but he felt too rotten to go to directors' meetings; what he did do was to sell out about half his stocks in small parcels. Nat kept telling him if he'd only get a move on, he could get control of the whole business before Andy Merritt pulled off his new reorganization, but he felt too damn nervous and miserable to make the effort. All he could seem to do was to grumble and call Julius Stauch and raise hell about details. Stauch had taken over his work on the new monoplane and turned out a little ship that had gone through all tests with flying colors. When he'd put down the receiver, Charley would pour himself a little Scotch and settle back on the couch in his window and mutter to himself, 'Well, you're dished this time.'

One evening Farrell came around and had a long talk and said what Charley needed was a fishing trip; he'd never get well if he kept on this way. He said he'd been talking to Doc Thompson and that he recommended three months off and plenty of exercise if he ever expected to throw away his crutches.

Gladys couldn't go because old Mrs Wheatley was sick, so Charley got into the back of his Lincoln towncar alone with the chauffeur to drive him, and a lot of blankets to keep him warm, and a flask of whiskey and a thermosbottle of hot coffee, to go down all alone to Miami.

At Cincinnati he felt so bum he spent a whole day in bed in the hotel there. He got the chauffeur to get him booklets about Florida from a travel agency, and finally sent a wire to Nat Benton asking him to spend a week with him down at the Key Largo fishingcamp. Next morning he started off again early. He'd had a good night's sleep and he felt better and began to enjoy the trip. But he felt a damn fool sitting there being driven like an old woman all bundled up in rugs. He was lonely, too, because the chauffeur wasn't the kind of bird you could talk to. He was a sourlooking Canuck Gladys had hired because she thought it was classy to give her orders in French through the speakingtube; Charley was sure the bastard gypped him on the price of gas and oil and repairs along the road; that damn Lincoln was turning out a bottomless pit for gas and oil.

In Jacksonville the sun was shining. Charley gave himself the satisfaction of firing the chauffeur as soon as they'd driven up to the door of the hotel. Then he went to bed with a pint of bum corn the bellboy sold him and slept like a log.

In the morning he woke up late feeling thirsty but cheerful. After breakfast he checked out of the hotel and drove around the town a little. It made him feel good to pack his own bag and get into the front seat and drive his own car.

The town had a cheerful rattletrap look in the sunlight under the big white clouds and the blue sky. At the lunchroom next to the busstation he stopped to have a drink. He felt so good that he got out of the car without his crutches and hobbled across the warm pavement. The wind was fluttering the leaves of the magazines and the pink and palegreen sheets of the papers outside the lunchroom window. Charley was out of breath from the effort when he slid onto a stool at the counter. 'Give me a limeade and no sweetnin' in it, please,' he said to the ratfaced boy at the fountain.

The sodajerker didn't pay any attention, he was looking down the other way. Charley felt his face get red. His first idea was, I'll get him fired. Then he looked where the boy was looking. There was a blonde eating a sandwich at the other end of the counter. She certainly was pretty. She wore a little black hat and a neat bluegray suit and a little white lace around her neck and at her wrists. She had an amazed look on her face like she'd just heard something extraordinarily funny. Forgetting to favor his game leg Charley slipped up several seats toward her.

'Say, bo, how about that limeade?' he shouted cheerfully at the sodajerker.

The girl was looking at Charley. Her eyes really were a perfectly pure blue. She was speaking to him. 'Maybe you know how long the bus takes to Miami, Mister. This boy thinks he's a wit, so I can't get any data.'

'Suppose we try it out and see,' said Charley.

'They surely come funny in Florida. . . . Another humorist.'

'No, I mean it. If you let me drive you down, you'll be doing a sick man a great favor.'

'Sure it won't mean a fate worse than death?'

'You'll be perfectly safe with me, young lady. I'm almost a cripple. I'll show you my crutches in the car.'

'What's the trouble?'

'Cracked up in a plane.'

'You a pilot?'

Charlie nodded.

'Not quite skinny enough for Lindbergh,' she said, looking him up and down.

Charley turned red. 'I am a little overweight. It's being cooped up with this lousy leg.'

'Well, I guess I'll try it. If I step into your car and wake up in Buenos Aires, it'll be my bad luck.'

Charley tried to pay for her coffee and sandwich, but she wouldn't let him. Something about her manner kept him laughing all the time.

When he got up and she saw how he limped, she pursed her mouth up. 'Gee, that's too bad.' When she saw the car, she stopped in her tracks. 'Zowie,' she said, 'we're bloomin' millionaires.'

They were laughing as they got into the car. There was something about the way she said things that made him laugh. She wouldn't say what her name was. 'Call me Madame X,' she said.

'Then you'll have to call me Mr A,' said Charley.

They laughed and giggled all the way to Daytona Beach where they stopped off and went into the surf for a dip. Charley felt ashamed of his pot and his pale skin and his limp as he walked across the beach with her looking brown and trim in her blue bathingsuit. She had a pretty figure, although her hips were a little big.

'Anyway, it's not as if I'd come out of it with one leg shorter than the other. The doc says I'll be absolutely O.K. if I exercise it right.'

'Sure, you'll be great in no time. And me thinkin' you was an elderly sugardaddy in the drugstore there.'

'I think you're a humdinger, Madame X.'

'Be sure you don't put anything in writing, Mr A.'

Charley's leg ached like blazes when he came out of the water, but it didn't keep him from having a whale of a good appetite for the first time in months. After a big fishdinner they started off again. She went to sleep in the car with her neat little head on his shoulder. He felt very happy driving down the straight smooth concrete highway, although he felt tired already. When they got into Miami that night, she made him take her to a small hotel back near the railroad tracks and wouldn't let him come in with her. 'But gosh, couldn't we see each other again?'

'Sure, you can see me any night at the Palms. I'm an entertainer there.'

'Honest . . . I knew you were an entertainer, but I didn't know you were a professional.'

'You sure did me a good turn, Mr A. Now it can be told . . . I was flat broke with exactly the price of that ham sandwich and if you hadn't brought me down I'd alost the chance of working here. . . . I'll tell you about it sometime.'

'Tell me your name. I'd like to call you up.'

'You tell me yours.'

'Charles Anderson. I'll be staying bored to death at the Miami-Biltmore.'

'So you really are Mr A. . . . Well, goodbye, Mr A, and thanks a million times.' She ran into the hotel.

Charley was crazy about her already. He was so tired he just barely made his hotel. He went up to his room and tumbled into bed and for the first time in months went to sleep without getting drunk first.

A week later, when Nat Benton turned up, he was surprised to find Charley in such good shape. 'Nothin' like a change,' said Charley, laughing. They drove on down toward the Keys together. Charley had Margo Dowling's photograph in his pocket, a professional photograph of her dressed in Spanish costume for her act. He'd been to the Palms every night, but he hadn't managed to get her to go out with him yet. When he'd suggest anything, she'd shake her head and make a face and say, 'I'll tell you all about it sometime.' But the last night she had given him a number where he could call her up.

Nat kept trying to talk about the market and the big reorganization of Tern and Askew-Merritt that Merritt was engineering, but Charley would shut him up with, 'Aw, hell, let's talk about somethin' else.'

The camp was all right, but the mosquitoes were fierce. They spent a good day on the reef fishing for barracuda and grouper. They took a jug of bacardi out in the motorboat and fished and drank and ate sandwiches. Charley told Nat all about the crackup. 'Honestly, I don't think it was my fault. It was one of those damn things you can't help. . . . Now I feel as if I'd lost the last friend I had on earth. Honest, I'd a given anythin' I had in the world if that hadn't happened to Bill.'

'After all,' said Nat, 'he was only a mechanic.'

One day when they got in from fishing, drunk and with their hands and pants fishy, and their faces burned by the sun and glare, and dizzy from the sound and smell of the motor and the choppy motion of the boat, they found waiting for them a wire from Benton's office.

UNKNOWN UNLOADING TERN STOP DROPS FOUR
AND A HALF POINTS STOP WIRE INSTRUCTIONS

'Instructions hell,' said Benton, jamming his stuff into his suitcase. 'We'll go up and see. Suppose we charter a plane at Miami.'

'You take the plane,' said Charley coolly. 'I'm going to ride on the train.'

In New York he sat all day in the back room of Nat Benton's office smoking too many cigars, watching the ticker, fretting and fuming, riding up and down town in taxicabs, getting the lowdown from various sallowfaced friends of Nat's and Moe Frank's. By the end of the week he'd lost four hundred thousand dollars and had let go every airplane stock he had in the world.

All the time he was sitting there putting on a big show of business he was counting the minutes, the way he had when he was a kid in school, for the market to close so that he could go uptown to a speakeasy on Fiftysecond Street to meet a henna-haired girl named Sally Hogan he'd met when he was out with Nat at the Club Dover. She was the first girl he'd picked up when he got to New York. He didn't give a damn about her, but he had to have some kind of a girl. They were registered at the hotel as Mr and Mrs Smith.

One morning when they were having breakfast in bed there was a light knock on the door. 'Come in,' yelled Charley, thinking it was the waiter. Two shabbylooking men rushed into the room, followed by O'Higgins, a shyster lawyer he'd met a couple of times back in Detroit. Sally let out a shriek and covered her head with the pillow.

'Howdy, Charley,' said O'Higgins. 'I'm sorry to do this, but it's all in the line of duty. You don't deny that you are Charles Anderson, do you? Well, I thought you'd rather hear it from me than just read the legal terms. Mrs Anderson is suing you for divorce in Michigan. . . . That's all right, boys.'

The shabby men bowed meekly and backed out the door.

'Of all the lousy stinkin' tricks . . .'

'Mrs Anderson's had the detectives on your trail ever since you fired her chauffeur in Jacksonville.'

Charley had such a splitting headache and felt so weak from a hangover that he couldn't lift his head. He wanted to get up and sock that sonofabitch O'Higgins, but all he could do was lie there and take it. 'But she never said anything about it in her letters. She'd been writin' me right along. There's never been any trouble between us.'

O'Higgins shook his curly head. 'Too bad,' he said. 'Maybe if you can see her you can arrange it between you. You know my advice about these things is always keep 'em out of court. Well, I'm heartily sorry, old boy, to have caused you and your charming friend any embarrassment . . . no hard feelings I hope, Charley, old man. . . . I thought it would be pleasanter, more open and aboveboard, if I came along, if you saw a friendly face, as you might say. I'm sure this can all be amicably settled.' He stood there awhile rubbing his hands and nodding and then tiptoed to the door. Standing there with one hand on the doorknob he waved the other big flipper toward the bed. 'Well, so long, Sally. . . . Guess I'll be seein' you down at the office.'

Then he closed the door softly after him. Sally had jumped out of bed and was running toward the door with a terrified look on her face. Charley began to laugh in spite of his splitting headache. 'Aw, never mind, girlie,' he said. 'Serves me right for bein' a sucker. . . . I know we all got our livin's to make. . . . Come on back to bed.'

# Newsreel 60

Was Céline to blame? To young Scotty marriage seemed just a lark, a wild time in good standing. But when she began to demand money and the extravagant things he couldn't afford, did Céline meet him halfway? Or did she blind herself to the very meaning of the sacred word: wife?

**CROOK FROZEN OUT OF SHARE IN BONDS TELLS MURDER PLOT**

**TO REPEAL DECISION ON CASTIRON PIPE**

*In a little Spanish town*
*'Twas on a night like this*

speculative sentiment was encouraged at the opening of the week by the clearer outlook. Favorable weather was doing much to eliminate the signs of hesitation lately evinced by several trades

*I'm in love again*
*And the Spring*
*Is comin'*
*I'm in love again*
*Hear my heart strings*
*Strummin'*

**ITCHING GONE IN ONE NIGHT**

thousands of prosperous happy women began to earn double and treble their former wages and sometimes even more immediately

*Yes sir that's my baby*
*That's my baby na-ow!*

**APE TRIAL GOAT TO CONFER WITH ATTORNEYS**

**MYSTERIOUS MR Y TO TESTIFY**

an exquisite replica in miniature of a sunlit French

country home on the banks of the Rhone boldly built on the crest of Sunset Ridge overlooking the most beautiful lakeland in New Jersey where every window frames a picture of surprising beauty

> *And the tune I'm hummin'*
> *I'll not go roamin' like a kid again*
> *I'll stay home and be a kid again*

### NEIGHBOURS ENJOIN NOCTURNAL SHOUTS IN TURKISH BATH

### ALL CITY POLICE TURN OUT IN BANDIT HUNT

### CONGOLEUM BREAK FEATURES OPENING

for the sixth week freightcar loadings have passed the million mark in this country, indicating that prosperity is general and that records are being established and broken everywhere

> *Good-bye east and good-bye west*
> *Good-bye north and all the rest*
> *Hello Swan-ee Hello*

## Margo Dowling

When Margo got back to the city after her spring in Miami, everybody cried out how handsome she looked with her tan and her blue eyes and her hair bleached out light by the Florida sun. But she sure found her work cut out for her. The Mandevilles were in a bad way. Frank had spent three months in the hospital and had had one kidney removed in an operation. When he got home he was still so sick that Agnes gave up her position to stay home and nurse him; she and Frank had taken up Science and wouldn't have the doctor any more. They talked all the time about having proper thoughts and about how Frank's life had been saved by Miss Jenkins, a practitioner Agnes had met at her tearoom. They owed five hundred dollars in doctor's bills and hospital expenses, and talked about God all the time. It was lucky that Mr Anderson the new boyfriend was a very rich man.

Mr A, as she called him, kept offering to set Margo up in an apartment on Park Avenue, but she always said nothing doing, what did he think she was, a kept woman? She did let him play the stockmarket a little for her, and buy her clothes and jewelry and take her to Atlantic City and Long Beach weekends. He'd been an airplane pilot and decorated in the war and had big investments in airplane companies. He drank more than was good for him; he was a beefy florid guy who looked older than he was, a big talker, and hard to handle when he'd been drinking, but he was openhanded and liked laughing and jokes when he was feeling good. Margo thought that he was a pretty good egg.

'Anyway, what can you do when a guy picks up a telephone and turns over a thousand dollars for you?' was what she'd tell Agnes when she wanted to tease her.

'Margie, dear, you mustn't talk like that,' Agnes would say. 'It sounds so mercenary.'

Agnes talked an awful lot about Love and right thoughts and being true and good these days. Margo liked better to hear Mr Anderson blowing about his killings on the stockmarket and the planes he'd designed, and how he was going to organize a net of airways that would make the Pennsylvania Railroad look like a suburban busline.

Evening after evening she'd have to sit with him in speakeasies in the Fifties drinking whiskey and listening to him talk about this business and that and big deals in stocks down on the Street, and about how he was out to get that Detroit crowd that was trying to ease him out of Standard Airparts and about his divorce and how much it was costing him. One night at the Stork Club, when he was showing her pictures of his kids, he broke down and started to blubber. The court had just awarded the custody of the children to his wife.

Mr A had his troubles all right. One of the worst was a redheaded girl he'd been caught with in a hotel by his wife's detectives who was all the time blackmailing him, and threatening to sue for breach of promise and give the whole story to the Hearst papers.

'Oh, how awful,' Agnes would keep saying, when Margo would tell her about it over a cup of coffee at noon. 'If he only had the right thoughts. . . . You must talk to him and make him try and see. . . . If he only understood I know everything would be different. . . . A successful man like that should be full of right thoughts.'

'Full of Canadian Club, that's what's the matter with him. . . .

You ought to see the trouble I have getting him home nights.'
'You're the only friend he has,' Agnes would say, rolling up her eyes. 'I think it's noble of you to stick by him.'

Margo was paying all the back bills up at the apartment and had started a small account at the Bowery Savings Bank, just to be on the safe side. She felt she was getting the hang of the stockmarket a little. Still it made her feel trashy not working and it gave her the creeps sitting around in the apartment summer afternoons while Agnes read Frank *Science and Health* in a singsong voice, so she started going around the dress shops to see if she could get herself a job as a model.

'I want to learn some more about clothes . . . mine always look like they were made of old floursacks,' she explained to Agnes.

'Are you sure Mr Anderson won't mind?'

'If he don't like it he can lump it,' said Margo, tossing her head.

In the fall they finally took her on at Piquot's new French gownshop on Fiftyseventh Street. It was tiresome work, but it left her evenings free. She confided to Agnes that if she ever let Mr A out of her sight in the evening some little floosey or other would get hold of him sure as fate.

Agnes was delighted that Margo was out of the show business. 'I never felt it was right for you to do that sort of thing and now I feel you can be a real power for good with poor Mr Anderson,' Agnes said. Whenever Margo told them about a new plunger he had taken on the market, Agnes and Frank would hold the thought for Mr Anderson.

Jules Piquot was a middleaged roundfaced Frenchman with a funny waddle like a duck who thought all the girls were crazy about him. He took a great fancy to Margo, or maybe it was that he'd found out somewhere that her protector, as he called it, was a millionaire. He said she must always keep that beautiful golden tan and made her wear her hair smooth on her head instead of in the curls she'd worn it in since she had been a Follies girl. 'Vat is te use to make beautiful clothes for American women if tey look so healty like from milkin' a cow?' he said. 'Vat you need to make interestin' a dress is 'ere,' and he struck himself with a pudgy ringed fist on the bosom of his silk pleated shirt. 'It is drama. . . . In America all you care about is te perfect tirtysix.'

'Oh, I guess you think we're very unrefined,' said Margo.

'If I only 'ad some capital,' groaned Piquot, shaking his head as he went back to his office on the mezzanine that was all glass and eggshell-white with aluminum fittings. 'I could make New York te most stylish city in te vorld.'

Margo liked it parading around in the Paris models and in Piquot's own slinky contraptions over the deep puttycolored rugs. It was better than shaking her fanny in the chorus all right. She didn't have to get down to the showrooms till late. The showrooms were warm and spotless, with a faint bitter smell on the air of new materials and dyes and mothballs, shot through with a whiff of scented Egyptian cigarettes. The models had a little room in the back where they could sit and read magazines and talk about beauty treatments and the theatres and the football season, when there were no customers. There were only two other girls who came regularly and there weren't too many customers either. The girls said that Piquot was going broke.

When he had his sale after Christmas, Margo got Agnes to go down one Monday morning and buy her three stunning gowns for thirty dollars each; she tipped Agnes off on just what to buy and made out not to know her when she pranced out to show the new spring models off.

There wasn't any doubt any more that Piquot was going broke. Billcollectors stormed in the little office on the mezzanine and everybody's pay was three weeks in arrears, and Piquot's moonshaped face drooped in tiny sagging wrinkles. Margo decided she'd better start looking around for another job, especially as Mr A's drinking was getting harder and harder to handle. Every morning she studied the stockmarket reports. She didn't have the faith she had at first in Mr A's tips after she'd bought Sinclair one day and had had to cover her margin and had come out three hundred dollars in the hole.

One Saturday there was a great stir around Piquot's. Piquot himself kept charging out of his office waving his short arms, sometimes peevish and sometimes cackling and giggling, driving the salesladies and models before him like a new rooster in a henyard. Somebody was coming to take photographs for *Vogue*. The photographer when he finally came was a thinfaced young Jewish boy with a pasty skin and dark circles under his eyes. He had a regular big photographer's camera and a great many flashlight bulbs all silvercrinkly inside that Piquot kept picking up and handling in a gingerly kind of way and exclaiming over. 'A vonderful invention. . . . I vould never 'ave photographs taken before because I detest explosions and ten te danger of fire.'

It was a warm day in February and the steamheated showrooms were stifling hot. The young man who came to take the
pictures was drenched in sweat when he came out from under
the black cloth. Piquot wouldn't leave him alone for a second.
He had to take Piquot in his office, Piquot at the draftingboard,
Piquot among the models. The girls thought their turn would
never come. The photographer kept saying, 'You let me alone,
Mr Piquot. . . . I want to plan something artistic.' The girls all
got to giggling. At last Piquot went off and locked himself in his
office in a pet. They could see him in there through the glass partition, sitting at his desk with his head in his hands. After that
things quieted down. Margo and the photographer got along
very well. He kept whispering to her to see what she could do to
keep the old gent out of the pictures. When he left to go up to
the loft upstairs where the dresses were made, the photographer
handed her his card and asked her if she wouldn't let him take
her picture at his studio some Sunday. It would mean a great
deal to him and it wouldn't cost her anything. He was sure he
could get something distinctively artistic. She took his card and
said she'd be around the next afternoon. On the card it said
Margolies, Art Photographer.

That Sunday Mr A took her out to lunch at the Hotel Pennsylvania and afterwards she managed to get him to drive her
over to Margolies' studio. She guessed the young Jewish boy
wasn't so well off and thought Mr A might just as well pay for a
set of photographs. Mr A was sore about going because he'd
gotten his big car out and wanted to take her for a drive up the
Hudson. Anyway he went. It was funny in Margolies' studio.
Everything was hung with black velvet and there were screens
of different sizes in black and white and yellow and green and
silver standing all over the big dusty room under the grimy skylights. The young man acted funny, too, as if he hadn't expected
them.

'All this is over,' he said. 'This is my brother Lee's studio. I'm
attending to his clientèle while he's abroad. . . . My interests are
in the real art of the future.'

'What's that?' asked Mr A, grumpily clipping the end off a
cigar as he looked around for a place to sit down.

'Motionpictures. You see I'm Sam Margolies. . . . You'll hear
of me if you haven't yet.'

Mr A sat down grouchily on a dusty velvet modelstand. 'Well,
make it snappy. . . . We want to go driving.'

Sam Margolies seemed sore because Margo had just come in

her streetclothes. He looked her over with his petulant gray eyes for a long time. 'I may not be able to do anything . . . I can't create if I'm hurried. . . . I had seen you stately in Spanish black.'

Margo laughed. 'I'm not exactly the type.'

'The type for a small infanta by Velasquez.' He had a definite foreign accent when he spoke earnestly.

'Well, I was married to a Spaniard once. . . . That was enough of Spanish grandees and all that kind of thing to last me a lifetime.'

'Wait, wait,' said Sam Margolies, walking all round her. 'I see it, first in streetclothes and then . . .' He ran out of the room and came back with a black lace shawl. 'An infanta in the court of old Spain.'

'You don't know what it's like to be married to one,' said Margo. 'And to live in a house full of noble spick relatives.'

While Sam Margolies was posing her in her streetclothes Mr A was walking up and down fidgeting with his cigar. It must have been getting cloudy out because the overhead skylight grew darker and darker. When Sam Margolies turned the floodlights on her, the skylight went blue, like on the stage. Then, when he got to posing her in the Spanish shawl and made her take her things off and let her undies down so that she had nothing on but the shawl above the waist, she noticed that Mr A had let his cigar go out and was watching intently. The reflection from the floodlight made his eyes glint.

After the photographer was through, when they were walking down the gritty wooden stairs from the studio, Mr A said, 'I don't like that guy . . . makes me think of a pimp.'

'Oh, no, it's just that he's very artistic,' said Margo. 'How much did he say the photographs were?'

'Plenty,' said Mr A.

In the unlighted hall that smelt of cabbage cooking somewhere, he grabbed her to him and kissed her. Through the glass front door she could see a flutter of snow in the street that was empty under the lamps.

'Aw, to hell with him,' he said, stretching his fingers out across the small of her back. 'You're a great little girl, do you know it? Gosh, I like this house. It makes me think of the old days.'

Margo shook her head and blinked. 'Too bad about our drive,' she said. 'It's snowing.'

'Drive, hell,' said Mr A. 'Let's you and me act like we was fond of each other for tonight at least. . . . First we'll go to the

Meadowbrook and have a little bite to drink. . . . Jesus, I wish I'd met you before I got in on the dough, when I was livin' in bedbug alley and all that sort of thing.'

She let her head drop on his chest for a moment. 'Charley, you're number one,' she whispered.

That night he got Margo to say that when Agnes took Frank out to his sister's house in New Jersey like she was planning, to try if a little country air wouldn't do him good, she'd go and live with him.

'If you knew how I was sick of this hellraisin' kind of life,' he told her.

She looked straight up in his boiled blue eyes. 'Do you think I like it, Mr A?' She was fond of Charley Anderson that night.

After that Sunday, Sam Margolies called up Margo about every day, at the apartment and at Piquot's, and sent her photographs of herself all framed for hanging, but she would never see him. She had enough to think of, what with being alone in the apartment now, because Agnes had finally got Frank away to the country with the help of a practitioner and a great deal of reading of *Science and Health*, and all the bills to pay and daily letters from Tony who'd found out her address, saying he was sick and begging for money and to be allowed to come around to see her.

Then one Monday morning she got down to Piquot's late and found the door locked and a crowd of girls milling shrilly around in front of it. Poor Piquot had been found dead in his bathtub from a dose of cyanide of potassium and there was nobody to pay their back wages.

Piquot's being dead gave Margo the creeps so that she didn't dare go home. She went down to Altman's and did some shopping and at noon called up Mr A's office to tell him about Piquot and to see if he wouldn't have lunch with her. With poor old Piquot dead and her job gone, there was nothing to do but to strike Mr A for a lump sum. About two grand would fix her up, and she could get her solitaire diamond Tad had given her out of hock. Maybe if she teased him he would put her up to something good on the market. When she called up, they said Mr Anderson wouldn't be in his office until three. She went to Schrafft's and had chickenpatties for lunch all by herself in the middle of the crowd of cackling women shoppers.

She already had a date to meet Mr A that evening at a French speakeasy on Fiftysecond Street where they often ate dinner. When she got back from having her hair washed and waved, it was too early to get dressed, but she started fiddling around with her clothes anyway because she didn't know what else to do, and it was so quiet and lonely in the empty apartment. She took a long time doing her nails and then started trying on one dress after another. Her bed got all piled with rumpled dresses. Everything seemed to have spots on it. She was almost crying when she at last slipped her furcoat over a paleyellow eveningdress that had come from Piquot's, but that she wasn't sure about, and went down in the shabby elevator into the smelly hallway of the apartmenthouse. The elevatorboy fetched her a taxi.

There were white columns in the hall of the oldfashioned wealthy family residence converted into a restaurant, and a warm expensive pinkish glow of shaded lights. She felt cozier than she'd felt all day as she stepped in on the thick carpet. The headwaiter bowed her to a table and she sat there sipping an oldfashioned, feeling the men in the room looking at her and grinning a little to herself when she thought what the girls at Piquot's would have said about a dame who got to a date with the boyfriend ahead of time. She wished he'd hurry up and come, so that she could tell him the story and stop imagining how poor old Piquot must have looked slumped down in his bathtub, dead from cyanide. It was all on the tip of her tongue ready to tell.

Instead of Mr A a freshlooking youngster with a long sandy head and a lantern jaw was leaning over her table. She straightened herself in her chair to give him a dirty look, but smiled up at him when he leaned over and said in a Brooklyn confidential kind of voice, 'Miss Dowlin' . . . excuse it . . . I'm Mr Anderson's secretary. He had to hop the plane to Detroit on important business. He knew you were crazy to go to the Music Box opening, so he sent me out to get tickets. Here they are. I pretty near had to blackjack a guy to get 'em for you. The boss said maybe you'd like to take Mrs Mandeville.' He had been talking fast, like he was afraid she'd shut him up; he drew a deep breath and smiled.

Margo took the two green tickets and tapped them peevishly on the tablecloth. 'What a shame . . . I don't know who I could get to go now, it's so late. She's in the country.'

'My, that's too bad. . . . I don't suppose I could pinchhit for the boss?'

'Of all the gall . . .' she began; then suddenly she found herself laughing. 'But you're not dressed.'

'Leave it to me, Miss Dowlin'. . . . You eat your supper and I'll come back in a soup an' fish and take you to the show.'

Promptly at eight there he was back with his hair slicked, wearing a rustylooking dinnerjacket that was too short in the sleeves. When they got in the taxi, she asked him if he'd hijacked a waiter and he put his hand over his mouth and said, 'Don't say a woid, Miss Dowlin' . . . it's hired.'

Between the acts, he pointed out all the celebrities to her, including himself. He told her that his name was Clifton Wegman and that everybody called him Cliff and that he was twentythree years old and could play the mandolin and was a little demon with pocket billiards.

'Well, Cliff, you're a likely lad,' she said.

'Likely to succeed?'

'I'll tell the world.'

'A popular graduate of the New York School of Business . . . opportunities wanted.'

They had the time of their lives together. After the show Cliff said he was starved, because he hadn't had his supper, what with chasing the theatertickets and the tuck and all, and she took him to the Club Dover to have a bite to eat. He surely had an appetite. It was a pleasure to see him put away a beefsteak with mushrooms. They had some drinks there and laughed their heads off at the floorshow, and, when he tried to get fresh in the taxicab, she slapped his face, but not very hard. That kid could talk himself out of anything.

When they got to her door, he said could he come up, and before she could stop herself she'd said yes, if he acted like a gentleman. He said that wasn't so easy with a girl like her, but he'd try, and they were laughing and scuffling so in front of her door she dropped her key. They both stooped to pick it up. When she got to her feet flushing from the kiss he'd given her, she noticed that the man sitting all hunched up on the stairs beside the elevator was Tony.

'Well, goodnight, Cliff, thanks for seeing a poor little workinggirl home,' Margo said cheerily.

Tony got to his feet and staggered over toward the open door of the apartment. His face had a green pallor and his clothes looked like he'd lain in the gutter all night.

'This is Tony,' said Margo. 'He's a . . . a relative of mine . . . not in very good repair.'

Cliff looked from one to the other, let out a low whistle and walked down the stairs.

'Well, now you can tell me what you mean by hanging around my place. . . . I've a great mind to have you arrested for a burglar.'

Tony could hardly talk. His lip was bloody and all puffed up. 'No place to go,' he said. 'A gang beat me up.' He was teetering so she had to grab the sleeve of his filthy overcoat to keep him from falling.

'Oh, Tony,' she said, 'you sure are a mess. Come on in, but if you pull any tricks like you did last time . . . I swear to God I'll break every bone in your body.'

She put him to bed. Next morning he was so jittery she had to send for a doctor. The sawbones said he was suffering from dope and exposure and suggested a cure in a sanatorium. Tony lay in bed white and trembling. He cried a great deal, but he was as meek as a lamb and said yes, he'd do anything the doctor said. Once he grabbed her hand and kissed it and begged her to forgive him for having stolen her money so that he could die happy.

'You won't die, not you,' said Margo, smoothing the stiff black hair off his forehead with her free hand. 'No such luck.' She went out for a little walk on the Drive to try to decide what to do. The dizzysweet clinging smell of the paraldehyde the doctor had given Tony for a sedative had made her feel sick.

At the end of the week when Charley Anderson came back from Detroit and met her at the place on Fiftysecond Street for dinner, he looked worried and haggard. She came out with her sad story and he didn't take it so well. He said he was hard up for cash, that his wife had everything tied up on him, that he'd had severe losses on the market; he could raise five hundred dollars for her, but he'd have to pledge some securities to do that. Then she said she guessed she'd have to go back to her old engagement as entertainer at the Palms at Miami and he said, swell, if she didn't look out he'd come down there and let her support him.

'I don't know why everybody's got to thinkin' I'm a lousy millionaire. All I want is get out of the whole business with enough jack to let me settle down to work on motors. If it hadn't been for this sonofabitchin' divorce I'd been out long ago. This winter I expect to clean up and get out. I'm only a dumb mechanic anyway.'

'You want to get out and I want to get in,' said Margo, looking him straight in the eye. They both laughed together.

'Aw, let's go up to your place, since the folks are away. I'm tired of these lousy speakeasies.'

She shook her head, still laughing. 'It's swarming with Spanish relatives,' she said. 'We can't go there.'

They got a bag at his hotel and went over to Brooklyn in a taxi, to a hotel where they were wellknown as Mr and Mrs Dowling. On the way over in the taxi she managed to get the ante raised to a thousand.

Next day she took Tony to a sanatorium up in the Catskills. He did everything she said like a good little boy and talked about getting a job when he got out and about honor and manhood. When she got back to town, she called up the office and found that Mr A was back in Detroit, but he'd left instructions with his secretary to get her her ticket and a drawingroom and fix up everything about the trip to Miami. She closed up her apartment and the office attended to storing the furniture and the packing and everything.

When she went down to the train there was Cliff waiting to meet her with his wiseguy grin and his hat on the back of his long thin head.

'Why, this certainly is sweet of him,' said Margo, pinning some liliesofthevalley Cliff had brought her to her furcoat as two redcaps rushed forward to get her bags.

'Sweet of who?' Cliff whispered. 'Of the boss or of me?'

There were roses in the drawingroom, and Cliff had bought her *Theatre* and *Variety* and *Zit's Weekly* and *Town Topics* and *Shadowland*. 'My, this is grand,' she said.

He winked. 'The boss said to send you off in the best possible style.' He brought a bottle out of his overcoat pocket. 'That's Teacher's Highland Cream. . . . Well, so long.' He made a little bow and went off down the corridor.

Margo settled herself in the drawingroom and almost wished Cliff hadn't gone so soon. He might at least have taken longer to say goodbye. My, that boy was fresh. The train had no sooner started when there he was back, with his hands in his pants pockets, looking anxious and chewing gum at a great rate.

'Well,' she said, frowning, 'now what?'

'I bought me a ticket to Richmond. . . . I don't travel enough . . . freedom from office cares.'

'You'll get fired.'

'Nope . . . this is Saturday. I'll be back bright and early Monday morning.'

'But he'll find out.'

Cliff took his coat off, folded it carefully and laid it on the rack, then he sat down opposite her and pulled the door of the drawingroom to. 'Not unless you tell him.'

She started to get to her feet. 'Well, of all the fresh kids.'

He went on in the same tone of voice. 'And you won't tell him and I won't tell him about . . . er . . .'

'But, you damn fool, that's just my exhusband.'

'Well, I'm lookin' forward to bein' the exboyfriend. . . . No, honestly, I know you'll like me . . . they all like me.' He leaned over to take her hand. His hand was icycold. 'No, honest, Margo, why's it any different from the other night? Nobody'll know. You just leave it to me.'

Margo began to giggle. 'Say, Cliff, you ought to have a sign on you.'

'Sayin' what?'

'Fresh paint.'

She went over and sat beside him. Through the shaking rumble of the train she could feel him shaking. 'Why, you funny kid,' she said. 'You were scared to death all the time.'

## Newsreel 61

*High high high*
*Up in the hills*
*Watching the clouds roll by*

genius, hard work, vast resources, and the power and will to achieve something distinctive, something more beautiful, something more appealing to the taste and wise judgment of the better people than are the things which have made the Coral Gables of today, and that tomorrow may be better, bigger, more compellingly beautiful

*High high high up in the hills*

GIANT AIRSHIP BREAKS IN TWO IN MIDFLIGHT

here young and old will gather to disport themselves in fresh invigorating salt water, or to exchange idle gossip in the loggias which overlook the gleaming pool, and at night the tinkle of music will tempt you to dance the hours away.

*Shaking hands with the sky*

*It is the early investor who will share to the fullest extent in the large and rapid enhancement of values that will follow such characterful development*

*Who's the big man with gold in his mouth?*
*Where does he come from? he comes from the south*

TOWN SITE OF JUPITER SOLD FOR
TEN MILLION DOLLARS

*like Aladdin with his magic lamp, the Capitalist, the Investor, and the Builder converted what was once a desolate swamp into a wonderful city linked with a network of glistening boulevards*

*Sleepy head sleepy head*
*Open your eyes*

*Sun's in the skies*
*Stop yawnin'*
*It's mornin'*

### ACRES OF GOLD NEAR TAMPA

*like a magnificent shawl of sapphire and jade, studded*
*with a myriad of multicolored gems, the colorful waters of*
*the lower Atlantic weave a spell of lasting enchantment. The*
*spot where your future joy, contentment, and happiness is so*
*sure that to deviate is to pass up the outstanding opportunity*
*of your lifetime*

### MATE FOLLOWS WIFE IN LEAP FROM WINDOW

### BATTLE DRUG-CRAZED KILLERS

*Lulu always wants to do*
*What we boys don't want her to*

A detachment of motorcycle police led the line of march
and cleared the way for the whiteclad columns. Behind the
police rode A. P. Schneider, grand marshal. He was followed
by Mr Sparrow's band and members of the painters' union.
The motionpicture operators were next in line and the
cigarworkers, the glaziers, the musicians, the signpainters
and the Brotherhood of Railway Trainmen followed in the
order named. The meatcutters brought up the rear of the first
division.

The second division was composed of more than thirtyfive hundred carpenters. The third division was led by the
Clown Band and consisted of electricians, blacksmiths,
plasterers, printers, pressmen, elevator constructors, postoffice clerks, and plumbers and steamfitters.

The fourth division was led by ironworkers, brick-
masons, the Brotherhood of Locomotive Engineers, steam
and operating engineers, the Typographical Union, lathers,
composition roofers, sheetmetal workers, tailors and
machinists

*Don't bring Lulu*
*I'll bring her myself*

## Charley Anderson

'You watch, Cliff. . . We'll knock 'em higher than a kite,'
Charley said to his secretary, as they came out of the crowded
elevator into the humming lobby of the Woolworth Building.
'Yessiree,' said Cliff, nodding wisely. He had a long face with
a thin parchment skin drawn tightly from under his brown felt
hat over high cheekbones and thin nose. The lipless mouth
never opened very wide above the thin jaw. He repeated out of
the corner of his mouth, 'Yessiree, bobby . . . higher than a kite.'

They went through the revolving doors into the fiveo'clock
crowd that packed the lower Broadway sidewalks to the curbs
in the drizzly dusk of a raw February day.

Charley pulled a lot of fat envelopes out of the pockets of his
English waterproof and handed them to Cliff. 'Take these up to
the office and be sure they get into Nat Benton's personal safe.
They can go over to the bank in the mornin' . . . then you're
through. Call me at nine, see? You were a little late yesterday.
. . . I'm not goin' to worry about anythin' till then.'

'Yessir, get a good night's sleep, sir,' said Cliff and slid out of
sight in the crowd.

Charley stopped a cruising taxicab and let himself drop into
the seat. Weather like this his leg still ached. He swallowed a
sigh; what the hell was the number? 'Go on uptown to Park
Avenue,' he yelled at the driver. He couldn't think of the
number of the damn place. . . . 'To East Fiftysecond Street. I'll
show you the house.' He settled back against the cushions.
Christ, I'm tired, he whispered to himself. As he sat slumped
back jolted by the stopping and starting of the taxi in the traffic,
his belt cut into his belly. He loosened the belt a notch, felt
better, brought a cigar out of his breastpocket and bit the end
off.

It took him some time to light the cigar. Each time he had the
match ready the taxi started or stopped. When he did light it, it
didn't taste good. 'Hell, I've smoked too much today . . . what I
need's a drink,' he muttered aloud.

The taxi moved jerkily uptown. Now and then out of the
corner of his eye he caught gray outlines of men in other taxis
and private cars. As soon as he'd made out one group of figures,
another took its place. On Lafayette Street the traffic was
smoother. The whole stream of metal, glass, upholstery, over-

coats, haberdashery, flesh and blood was moving uptown. Cars
stopped, started, shifted gears in unison as if they were run by
one set of bells. Charley sat slumped in the seat feeling the layer
of fat on his belly against his trousers, feeling the fat of his jowl
against his stiff collar. Why the hell couldn't he remember that
number? He'd been there every night for a month. A vein in his
left eyelid kept throbbing.

'Bonjour, monsieur,' said the plainclothes doorman. 'How do
you do, mon capitaine,' said Freddy the rattoothed proprietor,
nodding a sleek black head. 'Monsieur dining with Mademoiselle tonight?'

Charley shook his head. 'I have a feller coming to dinner
with me at seven.'

'Bien, monsieur.'

'Let's have a Scotch-and-soda while I'm waitin' and be sure it
ain't that rotgut you tried to palm off on me yesterday.'

Freddy smiled wanly. 'It was a mistake, Mr Anderson. We
have the veritable pinchbottle. You see the wrappings. It is still
wet from the saltwater.' Charley grunted and dropped into an
easy chair in the corner of the bar.

He drank the whiskey off straight and sipped the soda afterwards. 'Hey, Maurice, bring me another,' he called to the grayhaired old wrinklefaced Swiss waiter. 'Bring me another. Make
it double, see? ... in a regular highball glass. I'm tired this
evenin'.'

The shot of whiskey warmed his gut. He sat up straighter. He
grinned up at the waiter. 'Well, Maurice, you haven't told me
what you thought about the market today.'

'I'm not sure, sir. ... But you know, Mr Anderson. ... If you
only wanted to you could tell me.'

Charley stretched his legs out and laughed. 'Flyin' higher than
a kite, eh. ... Oh, hell, it's a bloody chore. I want to forget it.'

By the time he saw Eddy Sawyer threading his way toward
him through the faces, the business suits, the hands holding
glasses in front of the cocktailbar, he felt good.

He got to his feet. 'How's the boy, Eddy? How's things in
little old Deetroit? They all think I'm pretty much of a sonofabitch, don't they? Give us the dirt, Eddy.'

Eddy sighed and sank into the deep chair beside him. 'Well,
it's a long story, Charley.'

'What would you say to a bacardi with a touch of absinthe in
it? ... All right, make it two, Maurice.'

Eddy's face was yellow and wrinkled as a summer apple that's hung too long on the tree. When he smiled, the deepening wrinkles shot out from his mouth and eyes over his cheeks. 'Well, Charley, old man, it's good to see you. . . . You know they're calling you the boy wizard of aviation financing?'

'Is that all they're callin' me?' Charley tapped his dead cigar against the brass rim of the ashtray. 'I've heard worse things than that.'

By the time they'd had their third cocktail, Charley got so he couldn't stop talking. 'Well, you can just tell J. Y. from me that there was one day I could have put him out on his ass and I didn't do it. Why didn't I do it? Because I didn't give a goddam. I really owned my stock. They'd hocked everythin' they had an' still they couldn't cover, see. . . . I thought, hell, they're friends of mine. Good old J. Y. Hell, I said to Nat Benton when he wanted me to clean up while the cleanin' was good . . . they're friends of mine. Let 'em ride along with us. An' now look at 'em gangin' up on me with Gladys. Do you know how much alimony Gladys got awarded her? Four thousand dollars a month. Judge is a friend of her old man . . . probably gets a rakeoff. Stripped me of my children . . . every damn thing I've got they've tied up on me. . . . Pretty, ain't it, to take a man's children away from him? Well, Eddy, I know you had nothin' to do with it, but when you get back to Detroit and see those yellow bastards who had to get behind a woman's skirts because they couldn't outsmart me any other way . . . you tell 'em from me that I'm out to strip 'em to their shirts every last one of 'em. . . . I'm just beginnin' to get the hang of this game. I've made some dust fly . . . the boy wizard, eh? . . . Well, you just tell 'em they ain't seen nothin' yet. They think I'm just a dumb cluck of an inventor . . . just a mechanic like poor old Bill Cermak. . . . Hell, let's eat.'

They were sitting at the table and the waiter was putting differentcoloured horsd'oeuvres on Charley's plate. 'Take it away . . . I'll eat a piece of steak, nothing else.'

Eddy was eating busily. He looked up at Charley and his face began to wrinkle into a wisecrack. 'I guess it's another case of the woman always pays.'

Charley didn't laugh. 'Gladys never paid for anythin' in her life. You know just as well as I do what Gladys was like. All of those Wheatleys are skinflints. She takes after the old man. . . . Well, I've learned my lesson. . . . No more rich bitches. . . . Why, a goddam whore wouldn't have acted the way that bitch has acted. . . . Well, you can just tell 'em, when you get back to your employers in Detroit . . . I know what they sent you for. . . . To see if the old boy could still take his liquor. . . . Drinkin' himself to death, so that's the story, is it? Well, I can still drink you under the table, good old Eddy, ain't that so? You just tell 'em Eddy, that the old boy's as good as ever, a hell of a lot wiser. . . . They thought they had him out on his can after the divorce, did they? Well, you tell 'em to wait an' see. An' you tell Gladys the first time she makes a misstep . . . just once, she needn't think I haven't got my operatives watchin' her . . . Tell her I'm out to get the kids back, an' strip her of every goddam thing she's got. . . . Let her go out on the streets, I don't give a damn.'

Eddy was slapping him on the back. 'Well, oldtimer, I've got to run along. . . . Sure good to see you still riding high, wide, and handsome.'

'Higher than a kite,' shouted Charley, bursting out laughing. Eddy had gone. Old Maurice was trying to make him eat the piece of steak he'd taken out to heat up. Charley couldn't eat. 'Take it home to the wife and kiddies,' he told Maurice. The speak had cleared for the theatertime lull. 'Bring me a bottle of champagne, Maurice, old man, and then maybe I can get the steak down. That's how they do it in the old country, eh? Don't tell me I been drinkin' too much . . . I know it. . . . When everybody you had any confidence in has rooked you all down the line, you don't give a damn, do you, Maurice?'

A man with closecropped black hair and a closecropped black mustache was looking at Charley, leaning over a cocktailglass on the bar. 'I say you don't give a damn,' Charley shouted at the man when he caught his eye. 'Do you?'

'Hell, no, got anything to say about it?' said the man, squaring off toward the table.

'Maurice, bring this gentleman a glass.' Charley got to his feet and swayed back and forth bowing politely across the table. The bouncer, who'd come out from a little door in back wiping his red hands on his apron, backed out of the room again. 'Anderson my name is. . . . Glad to meet you, Mr . . .'

'Budkiewitz,' said the blackhaired man, who advanced scowling and swaying a little to the other side of the table.

Charley pointed to a chair. 'I'm drunk . . . beaucoup champagny water . . . have a glass.'

'With pleasure if you put it that way. . . . Always rather drink than fight. . . . Here's to the old days of the Rainbow Division.'

'Was you over there?'

'Sure. Put it there, buddy.'

'Those were the days.'

'And now you come back and over here there's nothin' but a lot of doublecrossin' bastards.'

'Businessmen . . . to hell wid 'em . . . doublecrossin' bastards I call 'em.'

Mr Budkiewitz got to his feet, scowling again. 'To what kind of business do you refer?'

'Nobody's business. Take it easy, buddy.' Mr Budkiewitz sat down again. 'Oh, hell, bring out another bottle, Maurice, and have it cold. Ever drunk that wine in Saumur, Mr Budkibbitzer?'

'Have I drunk Saumur? Why shouldn't I drink it? Trained there for three months.'

'That's what I said to myself. That boy was overseas,' said Charley.

'I'll tell the cockeyed world.'

'What's your business, Mr Buchanan?'

'I'm an inventor.'

'Just up my street. Ever heard of the Askew-Merritt starter?'

He'd never heard of the Askew-Merritt starter and Charley had never heard of the Autorinse washingmachine, but soon they were calling each other Charley and Paul. Paul had had trouble with his wife too, said he was going to jail before he'd pay her any more alimony. Charley said he'd go to jail too.

Instead they went to a nightclub where they met two charming girls. Charley was telling the charming girls how he was going to set Paul, good old Paul, up in business, in the washingmachine business. They went places in taxicabs under the El with the girls. They went to a place in the Village. Charley was going to get all the girls, the sweet pretty little girls, jobs in the chorus. Charley was explaining how he was going to take the shirts off those bastards in Detroit. He'd get the girls jobs in the chorus so that they could take their shirts off. It was all very funny.

In the morning light he was sitting alone in a place with torn windowshades. Good old Paul had gone and the girls had gone and he was sitting at a table covered with cigarettestubs and spilt dago red looking at the stinging brightness coming through the worn places in the windowshade. It wasn't a hotel or a callhouse, it was some kind of a dump with tables, and it stank of old cigarsmoke and last night's spaghetti and tomatosauce and dago red.

Somebody was shaking him. 'What time is it?'

A fat wop and a young slickhaired wop in their dirty shirtsleeves were shaking him. 'Time to pay up and get out. Here's your bill.'

A lot of things were scrawled on a card. Charley could only read it with one eye at a time. The total was seventyfive dollars. The wops looked threatening.

'You tell us give them girls twentyfive dollars each on account.'

Charley reached for his billroll. Only a dollar. Where the hell had his wallet gone? The young wop was playing with a small leather blackjack he'd taken out of his back pocket.

'A century ain't high for what you spent an' the girls an' all. . . . If you f—k around it'll cost you more. . . . You got your watch, ain't you? This ain't no clipjoint.'

'What time is it?'

'What time is it, Joe?'

'Let me call up the office. I'll get my secretary to come up.'

'What's the number? What's his name?' The young wop tossed up the blackjack and caught it. 'I'll talk to him. We're lettin' you out of this cheap. We don't want no hard feelin's.'

After they'd called up the office and left word that Mr Anderson was sick and to come at once, they gave him some coffee with rum in it that made him feel sicker than ever. At last Cliff was standing over him looking neat and wellshaved. 'Well, Cliff, I'm not the drinker I used to be.'

In the taxicab he passed out cold.

He opened his eyes in his bed at the hotel. 'There must have been knockout drops in the coffee,' he said to Cliff who sat by the window reading the paper.

'Well, Mr Anderson, you sure had us worried. A damn lucky thing it was they didn't know who they'd bagged in that clipjoint. If they had, it would have cost us ten grand to get out of there.'

'Cliff, you're a good boy. After this you get a raise.'

'Seems to me I've heard that story before, Mr Anderson.'

'Benton know?'

'I had to tell him some. I said you'd eaten some bad fish and had ptomaine poisoning.'

'Not so bad for a young feller. God, I wonder if I'm gettin' to be a rummy. . . . How are things downtown?'

'Lousy. Mr Benton almost went crazy trying to get in touch with you yesterday.'

'Christ, I got a head. . . . Say, Cliff, you don't think I'm gettin' to be a rummy, do you?'

'Here's some dope the sawbones left.'

'What day of the week is it?'

'Saturday.'

'Jesus Christ, I thought it was Friday.'

The phone rang. Cliff went over to answer it. 'It's the massageman.'

'Tell him to come up. . . . Say, is Benton stayin' in town?'

'Sure he's in town, Mr Anderson, he's trying to get hold of Merritt and see if he can stop the slaughter. . . . Merritt . . .'

'Oh, hell, I'll hear about it soon enough. Tell this masseur to come in.'

After the massage, that was agony, especially the cheerful German-accent remarks about the weather and the hockey season made by the big curlyhaired Swede who looked like a doorman, Charley felt well enough to go to the toilet and throw up some green bile. Then he took a cold shower and went back to bed and shouted for Cliff, who was typing letters in the drawingroom, to ring for the bellhop to get cracked ice for a rubber icepad to put on his head.

He lay back on the pillows and began to feel a little better.

'Hey, Cliff, how about lettin' in the light of day? What time is it?'

'About noon.'

'Christ. . . . Say, Cliff, did any women call up?' Cliff shook his head. 'Thank God.'

'A guy called up, said he was a taxidriver, said you'd told him you'd get him a job in an airplane factory . . . I told him you'd left for Miami.'

Charley was beginning to feel a little better. He lay back in the soft comfortable bed on the crisplylaundered pillows and looked around the big clean hotel bedroom. The room was high up. Silvery light poured in through the broad window. Through the A between the curtains in the window he could see a piece of sky bright and fleecy as milkweed silk. Charley began to feel a vague sense of accomplishment, like a man getting over the fatigue of a long journey or a dangerous mountainclimb.

'Say, Cliff, how about a small gin and bitters with a lot of ice in it? . . . I think that 'ud probably be the makin' of me.'

'Mr Anderson, the doc said to swear off and to take some of that dope whenever you felt like taking a drink.'

'Every time I take it, that stuff makes me puke. What does he think I am, a hophead?'

'All right, Mr Anderson, you're the boss,' said Cliff, screwing up his thin mouth.

'Thataboy, Cliff. . . . Then I'll try some grapefruitjuice and if that stays down I'll take a good breakfast and to hell wid 'em. . . . Why aren't the papers here?'

'Here they are, Mr Anderson . . . I've got 'em all turned to the financial section.'

Charley looked over the reports of trading. His eyes wouldn't focus very well yet. He still did better by closing one eye. A paragraph in *News and Comment* made him sit up.

'Hey, Cliff,' he yelled, 'did you see this?'

'Sure,' said Cliff. 'I said things were bad.'

'But if they're goin' ahead, it means Merritt and Farrell have got their proxies sure.'

Cliff nodded wisely with his head a little to one side.

'Where the hell's Benton?'

'He just phoned, Mr Anderson, he's on his way uptown now.'

'Hey, give me that drink before he comes and then put all the stuff away and order up a breakfast.'

Benton came in the bedroom behind the breakfasttray. He wore a brown suit and a derby. His face looked like an old dishcloth in spite of his snappy clothes.

Charley spoke first, 'Say, Benton, am I out on my fanny?'

Benton carefully and slowly took off his gloves and hat and overcoat and set them on the mahogany table by the window.

'The sidewalk is fairly well padded,' he said.

'All right, Cliff. . . . Will you finish up that correspondence?' Cliff closed the door behind him gently. 'Merritt outsmarted us?'

'He and Farrell are playing ball together. All you can do is take a licking and train up for another bout.'

'But damn it, Benton . . .'

Benton got to his feet and walked up and down the room at the foot of the bed. 'No use cussing at me. . . . I'm going to do the cussing today. What do you think of a guy who goes on a bender at a critical moment like this? Yellow, that's what I call it. . . . You deserved what you got . . . and I had a hell of a time saving my own hide, I can tell you. Well, I picked you for a winner, Anderson, and I still think that if you cut out the funny business you could be in the real money in ten years. Now let me tell you something, young man, you've gone exactly as far as you can go on your record overseas, and that was certainly a hell of a lot further than most. As for this invention racket . . . you know as well as I do there's no money in it unless you have the genius for promotion needed to go with it. You had a big initial success and thought you were the boy wizard and could put over any damn thing you had a mind to.'

'Hey, Nat, for Pete's sake don't you think I've got brains enough to know that? . . . This darn divorce and bein' in hospital so long kinder got me, that's all.'

'Alibis.'

'What do you think I ought to do?'

'You ought to pull out of this town for a while. . . . How about your brother's business out in Minnesota?'

'Go back to the sticks and sell tin lizzies . . . that's a swell future.'

'Where do you think Henry Ford made his money?'

'I know. But he keeps his dealers broke. . . . What I need's to get in good physical shape. I always have a good time in Florida. I might go down there and lay around in the sun for a month.'

'O.K. if you keep out of that landboom.'

'Sure, Nat, I won't even play poker . . . I'm goin' down there for a rest. Get my leg in real good shape. Then when I come back we'll see the fur fly. After all, there's still that Standard Airparts stock.'

'No longer listed.'

'Check.'

'Well, optimist, my wife's expecting me for lunch. . . . Have a good trip.'

Benton went out. 'Hey, Cliff,' Charley called through the door. 'Tell 'em to come and get this damn breakfastray. It didn't turn out so well. And phone Parker to get the car in shape. Be sure the tires are all O.K. I'm pullin' out for Florida Monday.'

In a moment Cliff stuck his head in the door. His face was red. 'Are you . . . will you be needing me down there, sir?'

'No, I'll be needin' you here to keep an eye on the boys downtown. . . . I got to have somebody here I can trust. . . . I'll tell you what I will have you do, though . . . go down to Trenton and accompany Miss Dowlin' down to Norfolk. I'll pick her up there. She's in Trenton visitin' her folks. Her old man just died or somethin'. You'd just as soon do that, wouldn't you? It'll give you a little trip.'

Charley was watching Cliff's face. He screwed his mouth

further to one side and bowed like a butler. 'Very good, sir,' he said.

Charley lay back on the pillows again. His head was throbbing, his stomach was still tied up in knots. When he closed his eyes dizzy red lights bloomed in front of them. He began to think about Jim and how Jim had never paid over his share of the old lady's money he'd put into the business. Anyway, he ain't got a plane, two cars, a suite at the Biltmore, and a secretary that'll do any goddam thing in the world for you, and a girl like Margo. He tried to remember how her face looked, the funny amazed way she opened her eyes wide when she was going to make a funny crack. He couldn't remember a damn thing, only the sick feeling he had all over and the red globes blooming before his eyes. In a little while he fell asleep.

He was still feeling so shaky when he started South that he took Parker along to drive the car. He sat glumly in his new camel'shair coat with his hands hanging between his knees staring ahead through the roaring blank of the Holland Tunnel, thinking of Margo and Bill Edwards, the patent lawyer he had to see in Washington about a suit, and remembering the bills in Cliff's deskdrawer and wondering where the money was coming from to fight this patent suit against Askew-Merritt. He had a grand in bills in his pocket and that made him feel good, anyway. Gosh, money's a great thing, he said to himself.

They came out of the tunnel into a rainygray morning and the roar and slambanging of trucks through Jersey City. Then the traffic gradually thinned and they were going across the flat farmlands of New Jersey strawcolored and ruddy with winter. At Philadelphia Charley made Parker drive him to Broad Street. 'I haven't got the patience to drive, I'll take the afternoon train. Come to the Waldman Park when you get in.'

He hired a drawingroom in the parlorcar and went and lay down to try to sleep. The train clattered and roared so and the gray sky and the lavender fields and yellow pastures and the twigs of the trees beginning to glow red and green and pale-yellow with a foretaste of spring made him feel so blue, so like howling like a dog, that he got fed up with being shutup in the damn drawingroom and went back to the clubcar to smoke a cigar.

He was slumped in the leather chair fumbling for the cigar-clipper in his vest pocket when the portly man in the next chair looked up from a bluecovered sheaf of lawpapers he was poring over. Charley looked into the black eyes and the smooth bluejowled face and at the bald head still neatly plastered with a patch of black hair shaped like a bird's wing, without immediately recognizing it.

'Why, Charley, ma boy, I reckon you must be in love.'

Charley straightened up and put out his hand. 'Hello, senator,' he said, stammering a little like he used to in the old days. 'Goin' to the nation's capital?'

'Such is my unfortunate fate.' Senator Planet's eyes went searching all over him. 'Charley, I hear you had an accident.'

'I've had a series of them,' said Charley, turning red.

Senator Planet nodded his head understandingly and made a clucking noise with his tongue. 'Too bad . . . too bad. . . . Well, sir, a good deal of water has run under the bridge since you and young Merritt had dinner with me that night in Washington. . . . Well, we're none of us gettin' any younger.'

Charley got the feeling that the senator's black eyes got considerable pleasure from exploring the flabby lines where his neck met his collar and the bulge of his belly against his vest. 'Well, we're none of us getting any younger,' the senator repeated.

'You are, senator. I swear you look younger than you did the last time I saw you.'

The senator smiled. 'Well, I hope you'll forgive me for makin' the remark . . . but it's been one of the most sensational careers I have had the luck to witness in many years of public life.'

'Well, it's a new industry. Things happen fast.'

'Unparalleled,' said the senator. 'We live in an age of unparalleled progress . . . everywhere except in Washington. . . . You should come down to our quiet little village more often. . . . . You have many friends there. I see by the papers, as Mr Dooley used to say, that there's been considerable reorganization out with you folks in Detroit. Need a broader capital base, I suppose.'

'A good many have been thrown out on their broad capital bases,' said Charley.

He thought the senator would never quit laughing. The senator pulled out a large initialed silk handkerchief to wipe the tears from his eyes and brought his small pudgy hand down on Charley's knee. 'Godalmighty, we ought to have a drink on that.'

The senator ordered whiterock from the porter and mysteriously wafted a couple of slugs of good rye whiskey into it from a bottle he had in his Gladstone bag. Charley began to feel better. The senator was saying that some very interesting developments were to be expected from the development of airroutes. The need for subsidies was pretty generally admitted if this great nation was to catch up on its lag in air transportation. The question would be of course which of a number of competing concerns enjoyed the confidence of the Administration. There was more in this airroute business than there ever had been in supplying ships and equipment. 'A question of the confidence of the Administration, ma boy.' At the word confidence, Senator Planet's black eyes shone. 'That's why, ma boy, I'm glad to see you up here. Stick close to our little village on the Potomac, ma boy.'

'Check,' said Charley.

'When you're in Miami, look up my old friend Homer Cassidy.... He's got a nice boat ... he'll take you fishin' ... I'll write him, Charley. If I could get away I might spend a week down there myself next month. There's a world of money bein' made down there right now.'

'I sure will, senator, that's mighty nice of you, senator.'

By the time they got into the Union Station Charley and the senator were riding high. They were talking trunklines and connecting lines, airports and realestate. Charley couldn't make out whether he was hiring Senator Planet for the lobbying or whether Senator Planet was hiring him. They parted almost affectionately at the taxistand.

Next afternoon he drove down through Virginia. It was a pretty, sunny afternoon. The judastrees were beginning to come out red on the sheltered hillsides. He had two bottles of that good rye whiskey Senator Planet had sent up to the hotel for him. As he drove, he began to get sore at Parker the chauffeur. All the bastard did was get rakeoffs on the spare parts and gas and oil. Here he'd charged up eight new tires in the last month; what did he do with tires, anyway, eat them? By the time they were crossing the tollbridge into Norfolk, Charley was sore as a crab. He had to hold himself in to keep from hauling off and giving the bastard a crack on the sallow jaw of his smooth flunkey's face. In front of the hotel he blew up.

'Parker, you're fired. Here's your month's wages and your trip back to New York. If I see your face around this town tomorrow, I'll have you run in for theft. You know what I'm referrin' to just as well as I do. You damn chauffeurs think you're too damn smart. I know the whole racket, see.... I have to work

for my dough just as hard as you do. Just to prove it I'm goin'
to drive myself from now on.' He hated the man's smooth un-
moving face.

'Very well, sir,' Parker said coolly. 'Shall I return you the
uniform?'

'You can take the uniform and shove it up your . . .' Charley
paused. He was stamping up and down red in the face on the
pavement at the hotel entrance in a circle of giggling colored
bellboys. 'Here, boy, take those bags in and have my car taken
around to the garage. . . . All right, Parker, you have your
instructions.'

He strode into the hotel and ordered the biggest double suite
they had. He registered in his own name. 'Mrs Anderson will
be here directly.' Then he called up the other hotels to find out
where the hell Margo was. 'Hello, kid,' he said when at last it
was her voice at the end of the wire. 'Come on over. You're
Mrs Anderson and no questions asked. Aw, to hell with 'em;
nobody's goin' to dictate to me what I'll do or who I'll see or
what I'm goin' to do with my money. I'm through with all
that. Come right around. I'm crazy to see you . . .'

When she came in, followed by the bellhop with the bags, she
certainly looked prettier than ever.

'Well, Charley,' she said, when the bellhop had gone out, 'this
sure is the cream de la cream. . . . You must have hit oil.' After
she'd run all around the rooms, she came back and snuggled up
to him. 'I bet you been giving 'em hell on the market.'

'They tried to put somethin' over on me, but it can't be done.
Take it from me. . . . Have a drink Margo. . . . Let's get a little
bit cockeyed, you and me, Margo. . . . Christ, I was afraid you
wouldn't come.'

She was doing her face in the mirror. 'Me? Why, I'm only
a pushover,' she said in that gruff low tone that made him shiver
all up his spine.

'Say, where's Cliff?'

'Our hatchetfaced young friend who was kind enough to accompany me to the meeting with the lord and master? He
pulled out on the six o'clock train.'

'The hell he did. I had some instructions for him.'

'He said you said be in the office Tuesday morning and he'd
do it if he had to fly. Say, Charley, if he's a sample of your
employees, they must worship the ground you walk on. He
couldn't stop talking about what a great guy you were.'

'Well, they know I'm regular, been through the mill . . .

understand their point of view. It wasn't so long ago I was workin' at a lathe myself.'

Charley felt good. He poured them each another drink. Margo took his and poured half of the rye back into the bottle. 'Don't want to get too cockeyed, Mr A,' she said in that new low caressing voice.

Charley grabbed her to him and kissed her hard on the mouth. 'Christ, if you only knew how I've wanted to have a really swell woman all to myself. I've had some awful bitches . . . Gladys, God, what a bitch she was! She pretty near ruined me . . . tried to strip me of every cent I had in the world . . . ganged up on me with guys I thought were my friends. . . . But you just watch, little girl. I'm goin' to show 'em. In five years they'll come crawlin' to me on their bellies. I don't know what it is, but I got a kind of feel for the big money . . . Nat Benton says I got it . . . I know I got it. I can travel on a hunch, see. Those bastards all had money to begin with.'

After they'd ordered their supper and while they were having just one little drink waiting for it, Margo brought out some bills she had in her handbag.

'Sure, I'll handle 'em right away,' Charley shoved them into his pocket without looking at them.

'You know, Mr A, I wouldn't have to worry you about things like that if I had an account in my own name.'

'How about ten grand in the First National Bank when we get to Miami?'

'Suit yourself, Charley . . . I never did understand more money than my week's salary, you know that. That's all any real trouper understands. I got cleaned out fixing the folks up in Trenton. It certainly costs money to die in this man's country.'

Charley's eyes filled with tears. 'Was it your dad, Margery?'

She made a funny face. 'Oh, no. The old man bumped off from too much Keeley cure when I was a little twirp with my hair down my back. . . . This was my stepmother's second husband. I'm fond of my stepmother, believe it or not. . . . She's been the only friend I had in this world. I'll tell you about her someday. It's quite a story.'

'How much did it cost? I'll take care of it.'

Margo shook her head. 'I never loaded my relations on any man's back,' she said.

When the waiter came in with a tray full of big silver dishes followed by a second waiter pushing in a table already set,

Margo pulled apart from Charley. 'Well, this is the life,' she whispered in a way that made him laugh.

Driving down was a circus. The weather was good. As they went further south there began to be a green fuzz of spring on the woods. There were flowers in the pinebarrens. Birds were singing. The car ran like a dream. Charley kept her at sixty on the concrete roads, driving carefully, enjoying the driving, the good fourwheel brakes, the easy whir of the motor under the hood. Margo was a smart girl and crazy about him and kept making funny cracks. They drank just enough to keep them feeling good. They made Savannah late that night and felt so good they got so tight there the manager threatened to run them out of the big old hotel. That was when Margo threw an ashtray through the transom.

They'd been too drunk to have much fun in bed that night and woke up with a taste of copper in their mouths and horrible heads. Margo looked haggard and green and saggy under the eyes before she went in to take her bath. Charley made her a prairie oyster for breakfast like he said the English aviators used to make over on the other side, and she threw it right up without breaking the eggyolk. She made him come and look at it in the toilet before she pulled the chain. There was the raw eggyolk looking up at them like it had just come out of the shell. They couldn't help laughing about it in spite of their heads.

It was eleven o'clock when they pulled out. Charley drove kind of easy along the winding road through the wooded section of southern Georgia, cut with inlets and saltmarshes from which cranes flew up and once a white flock of egrets. They felt pretty pooped by the time they got to Jacksonville. Neither of them could eat anything but a lambchop washed down with some lousy gin they paid eight dollars a quart for to the colored bellboy who claimed it was the best English gin imported from Nassau the night before. They drank the gin with bitters and went to bed.

Driving down from Jax to Miami, the sun was real hot. Charley wanted to have the top down to get plenty of air, but Margo wouldn't hear of it. She made him laugh about it. 'A girl'll sacrifice anything for a man except her complexion.' They couldn't eat on the way down, though Charley kept tanking up on the gin. When they got into Miami they went right to the old Palms where Margo used to work and got a big ovation from Joe Kantor and Eddy Palermo and the boys of the band. They all said it looked like a honeymoon and kidded about seeing the

marriagelicense. 'Merely a chance acquaintance . . . something
I picked up at the busstation in Jax,' Margo kept saying. Charley
ordered the best meal they had in the house and drinks all
around and champagne. They danced all evening in spite of his
game leg. When he passed out, they took him upstairs to Joe
and Mrs Kantor's own room. When he began to wake up,
Margo was sitting fully dressed looking fresh as a daisy on the
edge of the bed. It was late in the morning. She brought him
up breakfast on a tray herself.

'Look here, Mr A,' she said. 'You came down here for a rest.
No more nightclubs for a while. I've rented us a little bungalow
down on the beach and we'll put you up at the hotel to avoid
the breath of scandal and you'll like it. What we need's the
influence of the home. . . . And you and me, Mr A, we're on the
wagon.'

The bungalow was in Spanishmission style, and cost a lot,
but they sure had a good time at Miami Beach. They played
the dograces and the roulettewheels and Charley got in with a
bunch of allnight pokerplayers through Homer Cassidy, Senator
Planet's friend, a big smiling cultured whitehaired Southerner
in a baggy linen suit, who came round to the hotel to look him
up. After a lot of talking about one thing and another, Cassidy
got around to the fact that he was buying up options on
property for the new airport and would let Charley in on it for
the sake of his connections, but he had to have cash right away.
At poker Charley's luck was great, he always won enough to
have a big roll of bills on him, but his bankaccount was a dog
of a different stripe. He began burning up the wires to Nat
Benton's office in New York.

Margo tried to keep him from drinking; the only times he
could really get a snootful were when he went out fishing with
Cassidy. Margo wouldn't go fishing; she said she didn't like the
way the fish looked at her when they came up out of the water.
One day he'd gone down to the dock to go fishing with Cassidy,
but found that the norther that had come up that morning
was blowing too hard. It was damn lucky because just as Charley
was leaving the dock a Western Union messengerboy came up
on his bike. The wind was getting sharper every minute and
blew the chilly dust in Charley's face as he read the telegram.
It was from the senator:

ADMINISTRATION PREPARES OATS FOR PEGASUS

As soon as he got back to the beach, Charley talked to Benton over longdistance. Next day airplane stocks bounced when the news came over the wires of a bill introduced to subsidize airlines. Charley sold everything he had at the top, covered his margins, and was sitting pretty when the afternoon papers killed the story.

A week later he started to rebuy at twenty points lower. Anyway, he'd have the cash to refinance his loans and go in with Cassidy on the options. When he told Cassidy he was ready to go in with him, they went out on the boat to talk things over. A colored boy made them mintjuleps. They sat in the stern with their rods and big straw hats to keep the sun out of their eyes, and the juleps on a table behind them. When they got to the edge of the blue water they began to troll for sailfish.

It was a day of blue sky with big soft pinkishwhite clouds lavender underneath drifting in the sun. There was enough wind blowing against the current out in the Gulf Stream to make sharp choppy waves green where they broke and blue and purple in the trough. They followed the long streaks of mustardcolored weed, but they didn't see any sailfish. Cassidy caught a dolphin and Charley lost one. The boat pitched so that Charley had to keep working on the juleps to keep his stomach straight.

Most of the morning they cruised back and forth in front of the mouth of the Miami River. Beyond the steep dark waves they could see the still sunny brown water of the bay and against the horizon the new buildings sparkling white among a red web of girder construction.

'Buildin', that's what I like to see,' said Homer Cassidy, waving a veined hand that had a big old gold sealring on it toward the city. 'And it's just beginnin'.... Why, boy, I kin remember when Miamah was the jumpin'off place, a little collection of brokendown shacks between the railroad and the river, and I tell you the mosquitoes were fierce. There were a few crackers down here growin' early tomatoes and layin' abed half the time with chills and fever ... and now look at it ... an' up in New York they try to tell you the boom ain't sound.' Charley nodded without speaking. He was having a tussle with a fish on his line. His face was getting red and his hand was cramped from reeling. 'Nothin' but a small bonito,' said Cassidy. '. . . The way they try to tell you the fishin' ain't any good . . . that's all propaganda for the West Coast.... Boy, I must admit that I saw it comin' years ago when I was workin' with old Flagler. There was a man with vision.... I went down

with him on the first train that went over the overseas extension
into Key West . . . I was one of the attorneys for the road at the
time. Schoolchildren threw roses under his feet all the way from
his private car to the carriage. . . . We had nearly a thousand
men carried away in hurricanes before the line was completed . . . and now the new Miamah . . . an' Miamah Beach,
what do you think of Miamah Beach? It's Flagler's dream come
true.'

'Well, what I'd like to do . . .' Charley began, and stopped to
take a big swig of the new julep the colored boy had just handed
him. He was beginning to feel wonderful now that the little
touch of seasickness had gone. Cassidy's fishing guide had taken
Charley's rod up forward to put a new hook on it, so Charley
was sitting there in the stern of the motorboat feeling the sun
eat into his back and little flecks of salt spray drying on his
face with nothing to do but sip the julep, with nothing to worry
about. 'Cassidy, this sure is the life . . . why can't a guy do what
he wants to with his life? I was just goin' to say what I want to
do is get out of this whole racket . . . investments, all that
crap. . . . I'd like to get out with a small pile and get a house and
settle down to monkeyin' around with motors and designin'
planes and stuff like that. . . . I always thought if I could
pull out with enough jack I'd like to build me a windtunnel
all my own . . . you know that's what they test out model
planes in.'

'Of course,' said Cassidy, 'it's aviation that's goin' to make
Miamah. . . . Think of it, eighteen, fourteen, ten hours from
New York. . . . I don't need to tell you . . . and you and me and
the senator . . . we're right in among the foundin' fathers with
that airport. . . . Well, boy, I've waited all ma life to make a
real killin'. All ma life I been servin' others . . . on the bench,
railroad lawyer, all that sort of thing. . . . Seems to me about
time to make a pile of ma own.'

'Suppose they pick some other place, then we'll be holdin' the
bag. After all, it's happened before,' said Charley.

'Boy, they can't do it. You know yourself that that's the ideal
location, and then . . . I oughtn't to be tellin' you this, but you'll
find it out soon anyway . . . well, you know our Washington
friend, well, he's one of the forwardestlookin' men in this
country. . . . That money I put up don't come out of Homer
Cassidy's account because Homer Cassidy's broke. That's what's
worryin' me right this minute. I'm merely his agent. And in all
the years I've been associated with Senator Planet, upon ma

soul and body I've never seen him put up a cent unless it was a sure thing.'

Charley began to grin. 'Well, the old sonofabitch.'

Cassidy laughed. 'You know the one about a nod's as good as a wink to a blind mule. How about a nice Virginia ham sandwich?'

They had another drink with the sandwiches. Charley got to feeling like talking. It was a swell day. Cassidy was a prince. He was having a swell time. 'Funny,' Charley said, 'when I first saw Miami it was from out at sea like this. I never would have thought I'd be down here shovelin' in the dough.... There weren't all those tall buildin's then either. I was goin' up to New York on a coastin' boat. I was just a kid and I'd been down to New Orleans for the Mardi Gras and I tell you I was broke. I got on the boat to come up to New York and got to pallin' with a Florida cracker ... he was a funny guy.... We went up to New York together. He said the thing to do was get over an' see the war, so him and me like a pair of damn fools we enlisted in one of those volunteer ambulance services. After that I switched to aviation. That's how I got started in my line of business. Miami didn't mean a thing to me then.'

'Well, Flagler gave me ma start,' said Cassidy. 'And I'm not ashamed to admit it ... buyin' up rightofway for the Florida East Coast.... Flagler started me and he started Miamah.'

That night, when they got in sunburned and a little drunk from the day on the Gulf Stream, they tucked all the options away in the safe in Judge Cassidy's office and went over to the Palms to relax from business cares. Margo wore her silver dress and she certainly looked stunning. There was a thin dark Irishlooking girl there named Eileen who seemed to know Cassidy from way back. The four of them had dinner together, Cassidy got good and tight and opened his mouth wide as a grouper's talking about the big airport and saying how he was going to let the girls in on some lots on the deal. Charley was drunk, but he wasn't too drunk to know Cassidy ought to keep his trap shut. When he danced with Eileen, he talked earnestly in her ear telling her she ought to make the boyfriend keep his trap shut until the thing was made public from the proper quarters. Margo saw them with their heads together and acted the jealous bitch and started making over Cassidy to beat the cars. When Charley got her to dance with him, she played dumb and wouldn't answer when he spoke to her.

He left her at the table and went over to have some drinks

at the bar. There he got into an argument with a skinny guy who looked like a cracker. Eddy Palermo, with an oily smile on his face the shape and color of an olive, ran over and got between them. 'You can't fight this gentleman, Mr Anderson, he's our county attorney.... I know you gentlemen would like each other ... Mr Pappy, Mr Anderson was one of our leading war aces.'

They dropped their fists and stood glaring at each other with the little wop nodding and grinning between them. Charley put out his hand. 'All right, put it there, pal,' he said. The county attorney gave him a mean look and put his hands in his pockets. 'County attorney, s – t,' said Charley. He was reeling. He had to put his hand against the wall to steady himself. And he turned and walked out the door. Outside he found Eileen who'd just come out of the ladies' room and was patting back her sleek hair in front of the mirror by the hatchecking stand. He felt choked with the whiskey and the cigarsmoke and the throbbing hum of the band and the shuffle of feet. He had to get outdoors. 'Come on, girlie, we're goin' for a ride, get some air.' Before the girl could open her mouth, he'd dragged her out to the parkinglot.

'Oh, but I don't think we ought to leave the others,' she kept saying.

'They're too goddam drunk to know. I'll bring you back in five minutes. A little air does a little girl good, especially a pretty little girl like you.'

The gears shrieked because he didn't have the clutch shoved out. The car stalled; he started the motor again and immediately went into high. The motor knocked for a minute, but began to gather speed. 'See,' he said, 'not a bad little bus.' As he drove, he talked out of the corner of his mouth to Eileen. 'That's the last time I go into that dump.... Those little cracker politicians fresh out of the turpentine camps can't get fresh with me. I can buy and sell 'em too easy like buyin' a bag of peanuts. Like that bastard Farrell. I'll buy and sell him yet. You don't know who he is, but all you need to know is he's a crook, one of the biggest crooks in the country, an' he thought, the whole damn lot of 'em thought, they'd put me out like they did poor old Joe Askew. But the man with the knowhow, the boy who thinks up the gadgets, they can't put him out. I can outsmart 'em at their own game too. We got somethin' bigger down here than they ever dreamed of. And the Administration all fixed up. This is goin' to be big, little girl, the biggest thing you ever saw and I'm goin' to let you in on it. We'll be on easystreet from now on. And when you're on easystreet you'll all forget poor old Charley Anderson the boy that put you wise.'

'Oh, it's so cold,' moaned Eileen. 'Let's go back. I'm shivering.' Charley leaned over and put his arm round her shoulders. As he turned, the car swerved. He wrenched it back onto the concrete road again. 'Oh, please do be careful, Mr Anderson.... You're doing eightyfive now.... Oh, don't scare me, please.'

Charley laughed. 'My, what a sweet little girl! Look, we're down to forty, just bowlin' pleasantly along at forty. Now we'll turn and go back, it's time little chickens were in bed. But you must never be scared in a car when I'm driving. If there's one thing I can do, it's drive a car. But I don't like to drive a car. Now if I had my own ship here. How would you like to take a nice trip in a plane? I'da had it down here before this, but it was in hock for the repair bills. Had to put a new motor in. But now I'm on easystreet. I'll get one of the boys to fly it down to me. Then we'll have a real time. You an' me an' Margo. Old Margo's a swell girl, got an awful temper, though. That's one thing I can do, I know how to pick the women.'

When they turned to run back toward Miami, they saw the long streak of the dawn behind the broad barrens dotted with dead pines and half-built stucco houses and closed servicestations and dogstands.

'Now the wind's behind us. We'll have you back before you can say Jack Robinson.' They were running along beside a railroad track. They were catching up on two red lights. 'I wonder if that's the New York train.' They were catching up on it, past the lighted observation car, past the sleepers with no light except through the groundglass windows of the dressingrooms at the ends of the cars. They were creeping up on the baggagecar and mailcars and the engine, very huge and tall and black with a little curling shine from Charley's headlights in the dark. The train had cut off the red streak of the dawn. 'Hell, they don't make no speed.' As they passed the cab, the whistle blew. 'Hell, I can beat him to the crossin'.' The lights of the crossing were ahead of them and the long beam of the engine's headlight, that made the red and yellow streak of the dawn edging the clouds very pale and far away. The bar was down at the crossing. Charley stepped on the gas. They crashed through the bar, shattering their headlights. The car swerved around sideways. Their eyes were full of the glare of the locomotive headlight and the shriek of the whistle. 'Don't be scared, we're through!'

Charley yelled at the girl. The car swerved around on the tracks and stalled.

He was jabbing at the starter with his foot. The crash wasn't anything. When he came to, he knew right away he was in a hospital. First thing he began wondering if he was going to have a hangover. He couldn't move. Everything was dark. From way down in a pit he could see the ceiling. Then he could see the peak of a nurse's cap and a nurse leaning over him. All the time he was talking. He couldn't stop talking.

'Well, I thought we were done for. Say, nurse, where did we crack up? Was it at the airport? I'd feel better if I could remember. It was this way, nurse . . . I'd taken that little girl up to let her get the feel of that new Boeing ship . . . you know the goldarned thing. . . . I was sore as hell at somebody, must have been my wife, poor old Gladys, did she give me a dirty deal? But now after this airport deal I'll be buyin' an' sellin' the whole bunch of them. Say, nurse, what happened? Was it at the airport?'

The nurse's face and her hair were yellow under the white cap. She had a thin face without lips and thin hands that went past his eyes to smooth the sheet under his chin.

'You must try and rest,' she said. 'Or else I'll have to give you another hypodermic.'

'Say, nurse, are you a Canadian? I bet you're a Canadian.'

'No, I'm from Tennessee . . . Why?'

'My mistake. You see always when I've been in a hospital before the nurses have been Canadians. Isn't it kinder dark in here? I wish I could tell you how it happened. Have they called the office? I guess maybe I drink too much. After this I attend strictly to business. I tell you a man has to keep his eyes open in this game. . . . Say, can't you get me some water?'

'I'm the night nurse. It isn't day yet. You try and get some sleep.'

'I guess they've called up the office. I'd like Stauch to take a look at the ship before anything's touched. Funny, nurse. I don't feel much pain, but I feel so terrible.'

'That's just the hypodermics,' said the nurse's brisk low voice. 'Now you rest quietly and in the morning you'll wake up feeling a whole lot better. You can only rinse out your mouth with this.'

'Check.'

He couldn't stop talking. 'You see it was this way. I had some sort of a wrangle with a guy. Are you listenin', nurse? I guess I've got a kind of a chip on my shoulder since they've been gangin' up on me so. In the old days I used to think everybody was a friend of mine, see. Now I know they're all crooks . . . even Gladys, she turned out the worst crook of the lot. . . . I guess it's the hangover makes me so terribly thirsty.'

The nurse was standing over him again. 'I'm afraid we'll have to give you a little of the sleepy stuff, brother. . . . Now just relax. Think of somethin' nice. That's a good boy.'

He felt her dabbing at his arm with something cold and wet. He felt the prick of the needle. The hard bed where he lay awake crumbled gradually under him. He was sinking, without any sweetness of sleep coming on, he was sinking into dark.

This time it was a stout starched woman standing over him. It was day. The shadows were different. She was poking some papers under his nose. She had a hard cheerful voice. 'Good morning, Mr Anderson, is there anything I can do for you?'

Charley was still down in a deep well. The room, the stout starched woman, the papers were far away above him somewhere. All around his eyes was stinging hot.

'Say, I don't feel as if I was all there, nurse.'

'I'm the superintendent. There are a few formalities if you don't mind . . . if you feel well enough.'

'Did you ever feel like it had all happened before? . . . Say, where, I mean what town . . . ? Never mind, don't tell me, I remember it all now.'

'I'm the superintendent. If you don't mind, the office would like a check for your first week in advance and then there are some other fees.'

'Don't worry. I've got money. . . . For God's sake, get me a drink.'

'It's just the regulations.'

'There must be a checkbook in my coat somewhere. . . . Or get hold of Cliff . . . Mr Wegman, my secretary. . . . He can make out a check for you.'

'Now don't you bother about anything, Mr Anderson. . . . The office has made out a blank check. I'll fill in the name of the bank. You sign it. That will be two hundred and fifty dollars on account.'

'Bankers' Trust, New York. . . . Gosh, I can just about sign my name.'

'The questionnaire we'll get the nurse to fill out later . . . for our records. . . . Well, goodbye, Mr Anderson, I hope you have

a very pleasant stay with us and wishing you a quick recovery.'
The stout starched woman had gone.

'Hey, nurse,' called Charley. He suddenly felt scared. 'What
is this dump, anyway? Where am I? Say, nurse, nurse.' He
shouted as loud as he could. The sweat broke out all over
his face and neck and ran into his ears and eyes. He could
move his head and his arms, but the pit of his stomach was
gone. He had no feeling in his legs. His mouth was dry with
thirst.

A new pretty pink nurse was leaning over him. 'What can I
do for you, Mister?' She wiped his face and showed him where
the bell was hanging just by his hand.

'Nurse, I'm terribly thirsty,' he said in a weak voice.

'Now you must just rinse out your mouth. The doctor doesn't
want you to eat or drink anything until he's established the
drainage.'

'Where is this doctor? . . . Why isn't he here now? . . . Why
hasn't he been here right along? If he isn't careful I'll fire him
and get another.'

'Here's Doctor Snyder right now,' said the nurse in an awed
whisper.

'Well, Anderson, you surely had a narrow squeak. You probably thought you were in a plane all the time. . . . Funny, I've
never known an airplane pilot yet who could drive a car. My
name's Snyder. Doctor Ridgely Snyder of New York. Doctor
Booth the housephysician here has called me in as a consultant.
It's possible we may have to patch up your inside a little. You
see when they picked you up, as I understand it, a good deal
of the car was lying across your middle . . . a very lucky break
that it didn't finish you right there. . . . You understand me,
don't you?'

Doctor Snyder was a big man with flat closeshaven cheeks
and square hands ending in square nails. A song old man Vogel
used to sing ran across Charley's faint mind as he looked at the
doctor standing there big and square and paunchy in his white
clothes: he looked like William Kaiser the butcher, but they
don't know each other.

'I guess it's the dope, but my mind don't work very good. . . .
You do the best you can, doc . . . and don't spare any expense. I
just fixed up a little deal that'll make their ears ring. . . . Say,
doctor, what about that little girl? Wasn't there a little girl in
the car?'

'Oh, don't worry about her. She's fine. She was thrown absolutely clear. A slight concussion, a few contusions, she's coming along splendidly.'

'I was scared to ask.'

'We've got to do a little operating . . . suture of the intestine, a very interesting problem. Now I don't want you to have anything on your mind, Mr Anderson. . . . It'll just be a stitch here and a stitch there . . . we'll see what we can do. This was supposed to be my vacation, but of course I'm always glad to step in in an emergency.'

'Well, thank you, doc, for whatever you can do. . . . I guess I ought not to drink so much. . . . Say, why won't they let me drink some water? . . . It's funny, when I first came to in here I thought I was in another of them clipjoints. Now Doris, she wouldn'ta liked me to talk like that, you know, bad grammar, conduct unbecoming an officer and a gentleman. But you know, doc, when you get so you can buy 'em and sell 'em like an old bag of peanuts, a bag of stale goobers, you don't care what they think. You know, doc, it may be a great thing for me bein' laid up, give me a chance to lay off the liquor, think about things. . . . Ever thought about things, doc?'

'What I'm thinking right now, Mr Anderson, is that I'd like you to be absolutely quiet.'

'All right, you do your stuff, doc . . . you send that pretty nurse in an' lemme talk to her. I want to talk about old Bill Cermak. . . . He was the only straight guy I ever knew, him an' Joe Askew. . . . I wonder how he felt when he died. . . . You see the last time I was – well, call it constitutionally damaged . . . him and me smashed up in a plane . . . the new Mosquito . . . there's millions in it now, but the bastards got the stock away from me. . . . Say, doc, I don't suppose you ever died, did you?'

There was nothing but the white ceiling above him, brighter where the light came from the window. Charley remembered the bell by his hand. He rang and rang it. Nobody came. Then he yanked at it until he felt the cord pull out somewhere. The pretty pink nurse's face bloomed above him like a closeup in a movie. Her young rarelykissed mouth was moving. He could see it making clucking noises, but a noise like longdistance in his ears kept him from hearing what she said. It was only when he was talking he didn't feel scared. 'Look here, young woman . . .' he could hear himself talking. He was enjoying hearing himself talking. 'I'm payin' the bills in this hospital and I'm goin' to have everythin' just how I want it. . . . I want you to sit here an' listen while I talk, see. Let's see, what was I tellin' that bird

about? He may be a doctor, but he looks like William Kaiser
the butcher to me. You're too young to know that song.'

'There's somebody to see you, Mr Anderson. Would you like
me to freshen your face up a little?'

Charley turned his eyes. The screen had been pushed open.
In the gray oblong of the door there was Margo. She was in
yellow. She was looking at him with eyes round as a bird's.

'You're not mad, Margery, are you?'

'I'm worse than mad, I'm worried.'

'Everythin's goin' to be oke, Margo. I got a swell sawbones
from New York. He'll patch me up. He looks like William
Kaiser the butcher all except the mustaches . . . what do you
know about that, I forgot the mustaches. . . . Don't look at me
funny like that. I'm all right, see. I just feel better if I talk, see.
I bet I'm the talkin'est patient they ever had in this hospital. . . .
Margo, you know I mighta gotten to be a rummy if I'd kept on
drinkin' like that. It's just as well to be caught up short.'

'Say, Charley, are you well enough to write out a check? I've
got to have some jack. You know you were goin' to give me a
commission on that airport deal. And I've got to hire a lawyer
for you. Eileen's folks are going to sue. That county attorney's
sworn out a warrant. I brought your New York checkbook.'

'Jesus, Margo, I've made a certain amount of jack, but I'm
not the Bank of England.'

'But, Charley, you said you'd open an account for me.'

'Gimme a chance to get out of the hospital.'

'Charley, you poor unfortunate Mr A . . . you don't think it's
any fun for me to worry you at a time like this . . . but I've got to
eat like other people . . . an' if I had some jack I could fix that
county attorney up . . . and keep the stuff out of the papers and
everything. You know the kind of story they'll make out of
it . . . but I got to have money quick.'

'All right, make out a check for five thousand. . . . Damn
lucky for you I didn't break my arm.'

The pretty pink nurse had come back. Her voice was cold
and sharp and icy. 'I'm afraid it's time,' she said.

Margo leaned over and kissed him on the forehead. Charley
felt like he was in a glass case. There was the touch of her lips,
the smell of her dress, her hair, the perfume she used, but he
couldn't feel them. Like a scene in a movie he watched her walk
out, the sway of her hips under the tight dress, the little nervous
way she was fluttering the check under her chin to dry the ink
on it.

'Say, nurse, it's like a run on a bank ... I guess they think the old institution's not so sound as it might be. ... I'm givin' orders now, see, tell 'em down at the desk, no more visitors, see? You and me an' Doctor Kaiser William there, that's enough, see.'

'Anyway, now it's time for a little trip across the hall,' said the pretty pink nurse, in a cheerful voice like it was a show or a baseball game they were going to.

An orderly came in. The room started moving away from the cot, a gray corridor was moving along, but the moving made blind spasms of pain rush up through his legs. He sank into sour puking blackness again. When it was light again, it was very far away. His tongue was dry in his mouth he was so thirsty. Reddish mist was over everything. He was talking, but way off somewhere. He could feel the talk coming out of his throat, but he couldn't hear it. What he heard was the doctor's voice saying peritonitis like it was the finest party in the world, like you'd say Merry Christmas. There were other voices. His eyes were open, there were other voices. He must be delirious. There was Jim sitting there with a puzzled sour gloomy look on his face like he used to see him when he was a kid on Sunday afternoons going over his books.

'That you, Jim? How did you get here?'

'We flew,' answered Jim. It was a surprise to Charley that people could hear him, his voice was so far away. 'Everything's all right, Charley ... you mustn't exert yourself in the least way. I'll attend to everything.'

'Can you hear me, Jim? It's like a bum longdistance phone connection.'

'That's all right, Charley. ... We'll take charge of everything. You just rest quiet. Say, Charley, just as a precaution I want to ask you, did you make a will?'

'Say, was it peritonitis I heard somebody say? That's bad, ain't it?'

Jim's face was white and long. 'It's ... it's just a little operation. I thought maybe you'd better give me power of attorney superseding all others, so that you won't have anything on your mind, see. I have it all made out, and I have Judge Grey here as a witness and Hedwig'll come in a minute. ... Tell me, are you married to this woman?'

'Me married? Never again. ... Good old Jim, always wantin' people to sign things. Too bad I didn't break my arm. Well, what do you think about planes now, Jim? Not practical yet ... eh? But practical enough to make more money than you ever

made sellin' tin lizzies.... Don't get sore, Jim.... Say, Jim, be
sure to get plenty of good doctors . . . I'm pretty sick, do you
know it? . . . It makes you so hoarse . . . make 'em let me have
some water to drink, Jim. Don't do to save on the doctors....
I want to talk like we used to when, you know, up the Red River
fishin' when there wasn't any. We'll try the fishin' out here . . .
swell fishin' right outside of Miami here.... I feel like I was
passin' out again. Make that doctor give me somethin'. That
was a shot. Thank you, nurse, made me feel fine, clears everythin' up. I tell you, Jim, things are hummin' in the air . . . mail
subsidies . . . airports . . . all these new airlines . . . we'll be the
foundin' fathers on all that.... They thought they had me out
on my ass, but I fooled 'em.... Jesus, Jim, I wish I could stop
talkin' and go to sleep. But this passin' out's not like sleep, it's
like a . . . somethin' phony.'

   He had to keep on talking, but it wasn't any use. He was too
hoarse. His voice was a faint croak, he was so thirsty. They
couldn't hear him. He had to make them hear him. He was too
weak. He was dropping spinning being sucked down into

# Newsreel 62

STARS PORTEND EVIL FOR COOLIDGE

*If you can't tell the world*
*She's a good little girl*
*Then just say nothing at all*

the elder Way had been attempting for several years to get a certain kind of celery spray on the market. The investigation of the charges that he had been beaten revealed that Way had been warned to cease writing letters, but it also brought to light the statement that the leading celery growers were using a spray containing deadly poison

*As long as she's sorree*
*She needs sympathee*

MINERS RETAIL HORRORS OF DEATH PIT

inasmuch as banks are having trouble in Florida at this time, checks are not going through as fast as they should. To prevent delay please send us express money order instead of certified check

*Just like a butterfly that's caught in the rain*
*Longing for flowers*
*Dreaming of hours*
*Back in that sun-kissed lane*

TOURISTS ROB GAS STATION

PROFIT TAKING FAILS TO CHECK STOCK RISE

the climate breeds optimism and it is hard for pessimism to survive the bright sunshine and balmy breezes that blow from the Gulf and the Atlantic

*Oh it ain't gonna rain no more*

HURRICANE SWEEPS SOUTH FLORIDA

SOUTH FLORIDA DEVASTATED

ONE THOUSAND DEAD, THIRTY-EIGHT THOUSAND
DESTITUTE

BROADWAY BEAUTY BEATEN

*Fox he got a bushy tail*
*Possum's tail is bare*
*Rabbit got no tail at all*
*But only a tuft o'hair*

FLORIDA RELIEF FUND FAR SHORT

MARTIAL LAW LOOMS

*It ain't gonna rain no more*

according to the police the group spent Saturday evening at Hillside Park, a Belleville amusement resort, and
about midnight went to the bungalow. The Bagley girls retired, they told the police, and when the men entered their
room one of the girls jumped from a window

*But how in hell kin the old folks tell*
*It ain't gonna rain no more?*

## Margo Dowling

Agnes got off the sleeper dressed from head to foot in black
crape. She had put on weight and her face had a gray rumpled
look Margo hadn't noticed on it before. Margo put her head on
Agnes's shoulder and burst out crying right there in the sunny
crowded Miami station. They got into the Buick to go out to
the beach. Agnes didn't even notice the car or the uniformed
chauffeur or anything. She took Margo's hand and they sat
looking away from each other out into the sunny streets full of
slowlymoving people in light clothes. Margo was patting her
eyes with her lace handkerchief.

'Oughtn't you to wear black?' Agnes said. 'Wouldn't you
feel better if you were wearing black?'

It wasn't until the blue Buick drew up at the door of the
bungalow on the beach and Raymond, the thinfaced mulatto
chauffeur, hopped out smiling respectfully to take the bags, that
Agnes began to notice anything. She cried out, 'Oh, what a
lovely car.'

Margo showed her through the house and out on the screened porch under the palms facing the purpleblue sea and the green water along the shore and the white breakers. 'Oh, it's too lovely,' Agnes said and let herself drop into a Gloucester hammock, sighing. 'Oh, I'm so tired.' Then she began to cry again. Margo went to do her face at the long mirror in the hall. 'Well,' she said when she came back looking freshpowdered and rosy, 'how do you like the house? Some little shack, isn't it?'

'Oh, we won't be able to stay here now. . . . What'll we do now?' Agnes was blubbering. 'I know it's all the wicked unreality of matter. . . . Oh, if he'd only had proper thoughts.'

'Anyway, the rent's paid for another month,' said Margo.

'Oh, but the expense,' sobbed Agnes.

Margo was looking out through the screendoor at a big black tanker on the horizon. She turned her head and talked peevishly over her shoulder. 'Well, there's nothing to keep me from turning over a few options, is there? I tell you what they are having down here's a boom. Maybe we can make some money. I know everybody who is anybody in this town. You just wait and see, Agnes.'

Eliza, the black maid, brought in a silver coffeeservice and cups and a plate of toast on a silver tray covered by a lace doily. Agnes pushed back her veil, drank some coffee in little gulps and began to nibble at a piece of toast.

'Have some preserves on it,' said Margo, lighting herself a cigarette. 'I didn't think you and Frank believed in mourning.'

'I couldn't help it. It made me feel better. Oh, Margo, have you ever thought that if it wasn't for our dreadful unbelief they might be with us this day.' She dried her eyes and went back to the coffee and toast. 'When's the funeral?'

'It's going to be in Minnesota. His folks have taken charge of everything. They think I'm ratpoison.'

'Poor Mr Anderson. . . . You must be prostrated, you poor child.'

'You ought to see 'em. His brother Jim would take the pennies off a dead man's eyes. He's threatening to sue to get back some securities he claims were Charley's. Well, let him sue. Homer Cassidy's my lawyer and what he says goes in this town. . . . Agnes, you've got to take off those widow's weeds and act human. What would Frank think if he was here?'

'He is here,' Agnes shrieked and went all to pieces and started sobbing again. 'He's watching over us right now. I know that!' She dried her eyes and sniffed. 'Oh, Margie, coming down on the train I'd been thinking that maybe you and Mr Anderson had been secretly married. He must have left an enormous estate.'

'Most of it is tied up.... But Charley was all right, he fixed me up as we went along.'

'But just think of it, two such dreadful things happening in one winter.'

'Agnes,' said Margo, getting to her feet, 'if you talk like that I'm going to send you right back to New York.... Haven't I been depressed enough? Your nose is all red. It's awful.... Look, you make yourself at home. I'm going out to attend to some business.'

'Oh, I can't stay here. I feel too strange,' sobbed Agnes.

'Well, you can come along if you take off that dreadful veil. Hurry up, I've got to meet somebody.'

She made Agnes fix her hair and put on a white blouse. The black dress really was quite becoming to her. Margo made her put on a little makeup. 'There, dearie. Now you look lovely,' she said and kissed her.

'Is this really your car?' sighed Agnes as she sank back on the seat of the blue Buick sedan. 'I can't believe it.'

'Want to see the registration papers?' said Margo. 'All right, Raymond, you know where the broker's office is.'

'I sure do, Miss,' said Raymond, touching the shiny visor of his cap as the motor started to hum under the unscratched paint of the hood.

At the broker's office there was the usual welldressed elderly crowd in sportclothes filling up the benches, men with panamahats held on knees of palmbeach suits and linen plusfours, women in pinks and greens and light tan and white crisp dresses. It always affected Margo a little like church, the whispers, the deferential manners, the boys quick and attentive at the long blackboards marked with columns of symbols, the click of the telegraph, the firm voice reading the quotations off the ticker at a desk in the back of the room. As they went in, Agnes in an awed voice whispered in Margo's ear hadn't she better go and sit in the car until Margo had finished her business. 'No, stick around,' said Margo. 'You see those boys are chalking up the stockmarket play by play on those blackboards.... I'm just beginning to get on to this business.' Two elderly gentlemen with white hair and broadflanged Jewish noses smilingly made room for them on a bench in the back of the room. Several people turned and stared at Margo. She heard a woman's voice hissing something about Anderson to the man beside her. There was a little stir of whispering and nudging. Margo felt well-dressed and didn't care.

'Well, ma dear young lady,' Judge Cassidy's voice purred behind her, 'buyin' or sellin' today?'

Margo turned her head. There was the glint of a gold tooth in the smile on the broad red face under the thatch of silvery hair the same color as the gray linen suit which was crossed by another glint of gold in the watchchain looped double across the ample bulge of the judge's vest. Margo shook her head. 'Nothing much doing today,' she said. Judge Cassidy jerked his head and started for the door. Margo got up and followed, pulling Agnes after her. When they got out in the breezy sunshine of the short street that ran to the bathingbeach, Margo introduced Agnes as her guardian angel.

'I hope you won't disappoint us today the way you did yesterday, ma dear young lady,' began Judge Cassidy. 'Perhaps we can induce Mrs Mandeville . . .'

'I'm afraid not,' broke in Margo. 'You see the poor darling's so tired. . . . She's just gotten in from New York. . . . You see, Agnes dear, we are going to look at some lots. Raymond will take you home, and lunch is all ordered for you and everything. . . . You just take a nice rest.'

'Oh, of course I do need a rest,' said Agnes, flushing. Margo helped her into the Buick that Raymond had just brought around from the parkingplace, kissed her, and then walked down the block with the judge to where his Pierce Arrow touringcar stood shiny and glittery in the hot noon sunlight.

The judge drove his own car. Margo sat with him in the front seat. As soon as he'd started the car, she said, 'Well, what about that check?'

'Why, ma dear young lady, I'm very much afraid that no funds means no funds. . . . I presume we can recover from the estate.'

'Just in time to make a first payment on a cemetery lot.'

'Well, those things do take time . . . the poor boy seems to have left his affairs in considerable confusion.'

'Poor guy,' said Margo, looking away through the rows of palms at the brown reaches of Biscayne Bay. Here and there on the green islands new stucco construction stuck out raw, like stagescenery out on the sidewalk in the daytime. 'Honestly I did the best I could to straighten him out.'

'Of course. . . . Of course he had very considerable holdings.

... It was that crazy New York life. Down here we take things easily, we know how to let the fruit ripen on the tree.'

'Oranges,' said Margo, 'and lemons.' She started to laugh, but the judge didn't join in.

Neither of them said anything for a while. They'd reached the end of the causeway and turned past yellow frame wharf-buildings into the dense traffic of the Miami waterfront. Everywhere new tall buildings iced like layercake were standing up out of scaffolding and builder's rubbish.

Rumbling over the temporary wooden bridge across the Miami River in a roar of concretemixers and a drive of dust from the construction work, Margo said, turning a roundeyed pokerface at the judge, 'Well, I guess I'll have to hock the old sparklers.'

The judge laughed and said, 'I can assure you the bank will afford you every facility. . . . Don't bother your pretty little head about it. You hold some very considerable options right now if I'm not mistaken.'

'I don't suppose you could lend me a couple of grand to run on on the strength of them, judge.'

They were running on a broad new concrete road through dense tropical scrub. 'Ma dear young lady,' said Judge Cassidy in his genial drawl, 'I couldn't do that for your own sake . . . think of the false interpretations . . . the idle gossip. We're a little oldfashioned down here. We're easygoin', but once the breath of scandal . . . Why, even drivin' with such a charmin' passenger through the streets of Miamah is a folly, a very pleasant folly. But you must realize, ma dear young lady . . . A man in ma position can't afford . . . Don't misunderstand ma motive, ma dear young lady. I never turned down a friend in ma life. . . . But ma position would unfortunately not be understood that way. Only a husband or a . . .'

'Is this a proposal, judge?' she broke in sharply. Her eyes were stinging. It was hard keeping back the tears.

'Just a little advice to a client. . . .' The judge sighed. 'Unfortunately I'm a family man.'

'How long is this boom going to last?'

'I don't need to remind you what type of animal is born every minute.'

'No need at all,' said Margo gruffly.

They were driving into the parkinglot behind the great new caramelcolored hotel.

As she got out of the car, Margo said, 'Well, I guess some of them can afford to lose their money, but we can't, can we, judge?'

'Ma dear young lady, there's no such word in the bright lexicon of youth.' The judge was ushering her into the diningroom in his fatherly way. 'Ah, there are the boys now.'

At a round table in the center of the crowded diningroom sat two fatfaced young men with big mouths wearing pinkstriped shirts and nilegreen wash neckties and white suits. They got up still chewing and pumped Margo's hand when the judge presented them. They were twins. As they sat down again, one of them winked and shook a fat forefinger. 'We used to see you at the Palms, girlie, naughty, naughty.'

'Well, boys,' said the judge, 'how's tricks?'

'Couldn't be better,' one of them said with his mouth full.

'You see, boys,' said the judge, 'this young lady wants to make a few small investments with a quick turnover. . . .' The twins grunted and went on chewing.

After lunch the judge drove them all down to the Venetian Pool where William Jennings Bryan sitting in an armchair on the float under a striped awning was talking to the crowd. From where they were they couldn't hear what he was saying, only the laughter and handclapping of the crowd in the pauses. 'Do you know, judge,' said one of the twins, as they worked their way through the fringes of the crowd around the pool, 'if the old boy hadn't wasted his time with politics, he'da made a great auctioneer.'

Margo began to feel tired and wilted. She followed the twins into the realestateoffice full of perspiring men in shirtsleeves. The judge got her a chair. She sat there tapping with her white kid foot on the tiled floor with her lap full of blueprints. The prices were all so high. She felt out of her depth and missed Mr A to buy for her, he'd have known what to buy sure. Outside, the benches on the lawn were crowded. Bawling voices came from everywhere. The auction was beginning. The twins on the stand were waving their arms and banging with their hammers. The judge was striding around behind Margo's chair talking boom to anybody who would listen.

When he paused for breath, she looked up at him and said, 'Judge Cassidy, could you get me a taxi?'

'Ma dear young lady, I'll drive you home myself. It'll be a pleasure.'

'O.K.,' said Margo.

'You are very wise,' whispered Judge Cassidy in her ear.

As they were walking along the edge of the crowd, one of the twins they'd had lunch with left the auctioneer's stand and dove through the crowd after them. 'Miss Dowlin',' he said, 'kin me an' Al come to call?'

'Sure,' said Margo, smiling. 'Name's in the phonebook under Dowling.'

'We'll be around.' And he ran back to the stand where his brother was pounding with his hammer. She'd been afraid she hadn't made a hit with the twins. Now she felt the tired lines smoothing out of her face.

'Well, what do you think of the great development of Coral Gables?' said the judge as he helped her into the car.

'Somebody must be making money,' said Margo dryly.

Once in the house she pulled off her hat and told Raymond, who acted as butler in the afternoons, to make some martini cocktails, found the judge a cigar, and then excused herself for a moment. Upstairs she found Agnes sitting in her room in a lavender négligée manicuring her nails at the dressingtable. Without saying a word Margo dropped on the bed and began to cry.

Agnes got up looking big and flabby and gentle and came over to the bed. 'Why, Margie, you never cry. . . .'

'I know I don't,' sobbed Margo, 'but it's all so awful. . . . Judge Cassidy's down there, you go and talk to him. . . .'

'Poor little girl. Surely I will, but it's you he'll be wanting to see. . . . You've been through too much.'

'I won't go back to the chorus . . . I won't,' Margo sobbed.

'Oh, no, I wouldn't like that. . . . But I'll go down now. . . . I feel really rested for the first time in months,' said Agnes.

When Margo was alone, she stopped bawling at once. 'Why, I'm as bad as Agnes,' she muttered to herself as she got to her feet. She turned on the water for a bath. It was late by the time she'd gotten into an afternoondress and come downstairs. The judge looked pretty glum. He sat puffing at the butt of a cigar and sipping at a cocktail while Agnes talked to him about Faith.

He perked up when he saw Margo coming down the stairs. She put some dancemusic on the phonograph.

'When I'm in your house I'm like that famed Grecian sage in the house of the sirens . . . I forget hometies, engagements, everything,' said the judge, coming toward her onestepping.

They danced. Agnes went upstairs again. Margo could see that the judge was just on the edge of making a pass at her. She was wondering what to do about it when Cliff Wegman was suddenly ushered into the room. The judge gave the young man a scared suspicious look. Margo could see he thought he was going to be framed.

'Why, Mr Wegman, I didn't know you were in Miami.' She took the needle of the record and stopped the phonograph. 'Judge Cassidy, meet Mr Wegman.'

'Glad to meet you, judge. Mr Anderson used to talk about you. I was his personal secretary.' Cliff looked haggard and nervous. 'I just pulled into this little old town,' he said. 'I hope I'm not intruding.' He grinned at Margo. 'Well, I'm woiking for the Charles Anderson estate now.'

'Poor fellow,' said Judge Cassidy, getting to his feet. 'I had the honor of bein' quite a friend of Lieutenant Anderson's. . . .' Shaking his head he walked across the soft plumcolored carpet to Margo. 'Well, ma dear young lady, you must excuse me. But duty calls. This was indeed delightful.'

Margo went out with him to his car. The rosy evening was fading into dusk. A mockingbird was singing in a peppertree beside the house. 'When can I bring the jewelry?' Margo said, leaning toward the judge over the front seat of the car.

'Perhaps you better come to my office tomorrow noon. We'll go over to the bank together. Of course, the appraisal will have to be at the expense of the borrower.'

'O.K. and by that time I hope you'll have thought of some way I can turn it over quick. What's the use of having a boom if you don't take advantage of it?' The judge leaned over to kiss her. His wet lips brushed against her ear as she pulled her head away. 'Be yourself, judge,' she said.

In the livingroom Cliff was striding up and down fit to be tied. He stopped in his tracks and came toward her with his fists clenched as if he were going to hit her. He was chewing gum; the thin jaw moving from side to side gave him a face like a sheep. 'Well, the boss soitenly done right by little Orphan Annie.'

'Well, if that's all you came down here to tell me you can just get on the train and go back home.'

'Look here, Margo, I've come on business.'

'On business?' Margo let herself drop into a pink overstuffed chair. 'Sit down, Cliff . . . but you didn't need to come barging in here like a process-server. Is it about Charley's estate?'

'Estate hell . . . I want you to marry me. The pickin's are slim right now, but I've got a big career ahead.'

Margo let out a shriek and let her head drop on the back of

the chair. She got to laughing and couldn't stop laughing. 'No, honestly, Cliff,' she spluttered. 'But I don't want to marry anybody just now. . . . Why, Cliff, you sweet kid. I could kiss you.' He came over and tried to hug her. She got to her feet and pushed him away. 'I'm not going to let things like that interfere with my career either.'

Cliff frowned. 'I won't marry an actress. . . . You'd have to can that stuff.'

Margo got to laughing again. 'Not even a movingpicture actress?'

'Aw, hell, all you do is kid and I'm nuts about you.' He sat down on the davenport and wrung his head between his hands. She moved over and sat down beside him. 'Forget it, Cliff.'

Cliff jumped up again. 'I can tell you one thing, you won't get anywheres fooling around with that old buzzard Cassidy. He's a married man and so crooked he has to go through a door edgeways. He gypped hell out of the boss in that airport deal. Hell. . . . That's probably no news to you. You probably were in on it and got your cut first thing. . . . And then you think it's a whale of a joke when a guy comes all the way down to the jumpingoff place to offer you the protection of his name. All right, I'm through. Good . . . night.' He went out slamming the glass doors into the hall so hard that a pane of glass broke and tinkled down to the floor.

Agnes rushed in from the diningroom. 'Oh, how dreadful,' she said. 'I was listening. I thought maybe poor Mr Anderson had left a trustfund for you.'

'That boy's got bats in his belfry,' said Margo.

A minute later the phone rang. It was Cliff with tears in his voice, apologizing, asking if he couldn't come back to talk it over. 'Not on your tintype,' said Margo and hung up. 'Well, Agnes,' said Margo as she came from the telephone, 'that's that. . . . We've got to figure these things out. . . . Cliff's right about that old fool Cassidy. He never was in the picture anyways.'

'Such a dignified man,' said Agnes, making clucking noises with her tongue.

Raymond announced dinner. Margo and Agnes ate alone, each at one end of the long mahogany table covered with doilies and silverware. The soup was cold and too salty. 'I've told that damn girl a hundred times not to do anything to the soup but take it out of the can and heat it,' Margo said peevishly. 'Oh, Agnes, please do the housekeeping . . . I can't get 'em to do anything right.'

'Oh, I'd love to,' said Agnes. 'Of course I've never kept house on a scale like this.'

'We're not going to, either,' said Margo. 'We've got to cut down.'

'I guess I'd better write Miss Franklyn to see if she's got another job for me.'

'You just wait a little while,' said Margo. 'We can stay on here for a coupla months. I've got an idea it would do Tony good down here. Suppose we send him his ticket to come down? Do you think he'd sell it on me and hit the dope again?'

'But he's cured. He told me himself he'd straightened out completely.' Agnes began to blubber over her plate. 'Oh, Margo, what an openhanded girl you are . . . just like your poor mother . . . always thinking of others.'

When Tony got to Miami, he looked pale as a mealyworm, but lying on the beach in the sun and dips in the breakers soon got him into fine shape. He was good as gold and seemed very grateful and helped Agnes with the housework, as they'd let the maids go; Agnes declared she couldn't do anything with them and would rather do the work herself. When men Margo knew came around, she introduced him as a Cuban relative. But he and Agnes mostly kept out of sight when she had company. Tony was tickled to death when Margo suggested he learn to drive the car. He drove fine right away, so they could let Raymond go. One day when he was getting ready to drive her over to meet some big realtors at Cocoanut Grove, Margo suggested, just as a joke, that Tony try to see if Raymond's old uniform wouldn't fit him. He looked fine in it. When she suggested he wear it when he drove her, he went into a tantrum, and talked about honor and manhood. She cooled him down saying that the whole thing was a joke and he said, well, if it was a joke, and wore it. Margo could tell he kinder liked the uniform because she saw him looking at himself in it in the pierglass in the hall.

Miami realestate was on the skids, but Margo managed to make a hundred thousand dollars profit on the options she held; on paper. The trouble was that she couldn't get any cash out of her profits.

The twins she'd met at Coral Gables gave her plenty of advice, but she was leery, and advice was all they did give her. They were always around in the evenings and Sundays, eating up everything Agnes had in the icebox and drinking all the liquor and talking big about the good things they were going to put youall onto. Agnes said she never shook the sand out of her beachslippers without expecting to find one of the twins in it. And they never came across with any parties either, didn't even bring around a bottle of Scotch once in a while. Agnes was kinder soft on them because Al made a fuss over her while Ed was trying to make Margo. One Sunday when they'd all been lying in the sun on the beach and sopping up cocktails all afternoon Ed broke into Margo's room when she was dressing after they'd come in to change out of their bathingsuits and started tearing her wrapper off her. She gave him a poke, but he was drunk as a fool and came at her worse than ever. She had to yell for Tony to come in and play the heavy husband. Tony was white as a sheet and trembled all over, but he managed to pick up a chair and was going to crown Ed with it when Al and Agnes came in to see what the racket was about. Al stuck by Ed and gave Tony a poke and yelled that he was a pimp and that they were a couple of goddam whores. Margo was scared. They never would have got them out of the house if Agnes hadn't gone to the phone and threatened to call the police. The twins said nothing doing, the police were there to run women like them out of town, but they got into their clothes and left and that was the last Margo saw of them.

After they'd gone, Tony had a crying fit and said that he wasn't a pimp and that his life was impossible and that he'd kill himself if she didn't give him money to go back to Havana. To get Tony to stay, they had to promise to get out of Miami as soon as they could. 'Now, Tony, you know you want to go to California,' Agnes kept saying and petting him like a baby. 'Sandflies are getting too bad on the beach, anyway,' said Margo. She went down in the living room and shook up another cocktail for them all. 'The bottom's dropped out of this dump. Time to pull out,' she said. 'I'm through.'

It was a sizzling hot day when they piled the things in the Buick and drove off up U.S. 1 with Tony, not in his uniform, but in a new waspwaisted white linen suit, at the wheel. The Buick was so piled with bags and household junk there was hardly room for Agnes in the back seat. Tony's guitar was slung from the ceiling. Margo's wardrobetrunk was strapped on behind. 'My goodness,' said Agnes when she came back from the restroom of the fillingstation in West Palm Beach where they'd stopped for gas, 'we look like a traveling tentshow.'

Between them they had about a hundred dollars in cash that Margo had turned over to Agnes to keep in her black handbag.

The first day Tony would talk about nothing but the hit he'd make in the movies. 'If Valentino can do it, it will be easy for me,' he'd say, craning his neck to see his clear brown profile in the narrow drivingmirror at the top of the windshield.

At night they stopped in touristcamps, all sleeping in one cabin to save money, and ate out of cans. Agnes loved it. She said it was like the old days when they were on the Keith Circuit and Margo was a child actress. Margo said child actress, hell, it made her feel like an old crone. Toward afternoon Tony would complain of shooting pains in his wrists and Margo would have to drive.

Along the gulf coast of Alabama, Mississippi, and Louisiana the roads were terrible. It was a relief when they got into Texas, though the weather there was showery. They thought they never would get across the State of Texas, though. Agnes said she didn't know there was so much alfalfa in the world. In El Paso they had to buy two new tires and get the brakes fixed. Agnes began to look worried when she counted over the roll of bills in her purse. The last couple of days across the desert to Yuma they had nothing to eat but one can of baked beans and a bunch of frankfurters. It was frightfully hot, but Agnes wouldn't even let them get Coca-Cola at the dustylooking drugstores in the farbetween little towns because she said they had to save every cent if they weren't going to hit Los Angeles deadbroke. As they were wallowing along in the dust of the unfinished highway outside of Yuma, a shinylooking S.P. expresstrain passed them, big new highshouldered locomotive Pullmancars, diner, clubcar with girls and men in light suits lolling around on the observation platform. The train passed slowly and the colored porters leaning out from the Pullmans grinned and waved. Margo remembered her trips to Florida in a drawingroom and sighed.

'Don't worry, Margie,' chanted Agnes from the back seat. 'We're almost there.'

'But where? Where? That's what I want to know,' said Margo, with tears starting into her eyes. The car went over a bump that almost broke the springs.

'Never mind,' said Tony, 'when I make the orientations I shall be making thousands a week and we shall travel in a private car.'

In Yuma they had to stop in the hotel because the camps were all full and that set them back plenty. They were all in, the three of them, and Margo woke up in the night in a high fever from the heat and dust and fatigue. In the morning the fever was gone, but her eyes were puffed up and red and she looked a sight. Her hair needed washing and was stringy and dry as a handful of tow.

The next day they were too tired to enjoy it when they went across the high fragrant mountains and came out into the San Bernardino Valley full of wellkept fruittrees, orangegroves that still had a few flowers on them, and coolsmelling irrigation ditches. In San Bernardino Margo said she'd have to have her hair washed if it was the last thing she did on this earth. They still had twentyfive dollars that Agnes had saved out of the housekeeping money in Miami, that she hadn't said anything about. While Margo and Agnes went to a beautyparlor, they gave Tony a couple of dollars to go around and get the car washed. That night they had a regular fiftycent dinner in a restaurant and went to a movingpicture show. They slept in a nice roomy cabin on the road to Pasadena in a camp the woman at the beautyparlor had told them about, and the next morning they set out early before the white clammy fog had lifted.

The road was good and went between miles and miles of orangegroves. By the time they got to Pasadena the sun had come out and Agnes and Margo declared it was the loveliest place they'd ever seen in their lives. Whenever they passed a particularly beautiful residence Tony would point at it with his finger and say that was where they'd live as soon as he had made the orientations.

They saw signs pointing to Hollywood, but somehow they got through the town without noticing it, and drew up in front of a small rentingoffice in Santa Monica. All the furnished bungalows the man had listed were too expensive and the man insisted on a month's rent in advance, so they drove on. They ended up in a dusty stucco bungalow court in the outskirts of Venice where the man seemed impressed by the blue Buick and the wardrobe trunk and let them take a place with only a week paid in advance. Margo thought it was horrid, but Agnes was in the highest spirits. She said Venice reminded her of Holland's in the old days. 'That's what gives me the sick,' said Margo. Tony went in and collapsed on the couch and Margo had to get the neighbors to help carry in the bags and wardrobetrunk. They lived in that bungalow court for more months than Margo ever liked to admit even at the time.

Margo registered at the agency as Margo de Garrido. She got taken on in society scenes as extra right away on account of her good clothes and a kind of a way of wearing them she had that she'd picked up at old Piquot's. Tony sat in the agency and loafed around outside the gate of any studio where there was a Spanish or South American picture being cast, wearing a broad-brimmed Cordoba hat he'd bought at a costumer's and tight-waisted trousers and sometimes cowboy boots and spurs, but the one thing there always seemed to be enough of was Latin types. He turned morose and peevish and took to driving the car around filled up with simpering young men he'd picked up, until Margo put her foot down and said it was her car and nobody else's, and not to bring his fagots around the house either. He got sore at that and walked out, but Agnes, who did the housekeeping and handled all the money Margo brought home, wouldn't let him have any pocketmoney until he'd apologized. Tony was away two days and came back looking hungry and hangdog.

After that Margo made him wear the old chauffeur's uniform when he drove her to the lot. She knew that if he wore that he wouldn't go anywhere after he'd left her except right home to change and then Agnes could take the car key. Margo would come home tired from a long day on the lot to find that he'd been hanging round the house all day strumming *It Ain't Gonna Rain No More* on his guitar, and sleeping and yawning on all the beds and dropping cigaretteashes everywhere. He said Margo had ruined his career. What she hated most about him was the way he yawned.

One Sunday, after they had been three years in the outskirts of L.A., moving from one bungalow to another, Margo getting on the lots fairly consistently as an extra, but never getting noticed by a director, managing to put aside a little money to pay the interest, but never getting together enough in a lump sum to bail out her jewelry at the bank in Miami, they had driven up to Altadena in the afternoon; on the way back they stopped at a garage to get a flat fixed; out in front of the garage there were some secondhand cars for sale. Margo walked up and down looking at them to have something to do while they were waiting.

'You wouldn't like a Rolls-Royce, would you, lady?' said the garage attendant kind of kidding as he pulled the jack out from under the car.

Margo climbed into the big black limousine with a red coatof-arms on the door and tried the seat. It certainly was comfort-able. She leaned out and said, 'How much is it?'

'One thousand dollars . . . it's a gift at the price.'

'Cheap at half the price,' said Margo.

Agnes had gotten out of the Buick and come over. 'Are you crazy, Margie?'

'Maybe,' said Margo and asked how much they'd allow her if she traded in the Buick. The attendant called the boss, a toad-faced young man with a monogram on his silk shirt. He and Margo argued back and forth for an hour about the price. Tony tried driving the car and said it ran like a dream. He was all pepped up at the idea of driving a Rolls, even an old one. In the end the man took the Buick and five hundred dollars in ten-dollar weekly payments. They signed the contract then and there, Margo gave Judge Cassidy's and Tad Whittlesea's names as references; they changed the plates and drove home that night in the Rolls-Royce to Santa Monica where they were living at the time. As they turned into Santa Monica Boulevard at Beverly Hills, Margo said carelessly, 'Tony, isn't that mailed hand holding a sword very much like the coatofarms of the Counts de Garrido?'

'These people out here are so ignorant they wouldn't know the difference,' said Tony.

'We'll just leave it there,' said Margo.

'Sure,' said Tony, 'it looks good.'

The other extras surely stared when Tony in his trim gray uniform drove her down to the lot next day, but Margo kept her pokerface. 'It's just the old family bus,' she said when a girl asked her about it. 'It's been in hock.'

'Is that your mother?' the girl asked again, pointing with her thumb at Agnes who was driving away sitting up dressed in her best black in the back of the huge shiny car with her nose in the air.

'Oh, no,' said Margo coldly. 'That's my companion.'

Plenty of men tried to date Margo up, but they were mostly extras or cameramen or propertymen or carpenters and she and Agnes didn't see that it would do her any good to mix up with them. It was a lonely life after all the friends and the guys crazy about her and the business deals and everything in Miami. Most nights she and Agnes just played Russian bank or threehanded bridge if Tony was in and not too illtempered to accommodate. Sometimes they went to the movies or to the beach if it was warm enough. They drove out through the crowds on Hollywood Boulevard nights when there was an opening at Grauman's Chinese Theater. The Rolls looked so

fancy and Margo still had a good eveningdress not too far
out of style so that everybody thought they were filmstars.

One dusty Saturday afternoon in midwinter Margo was
feeling particularly desperate because styles had changed so she
couldn't wear her old dresses any more and didn't have any
money for new; she jumped up from her seat knocking the
pack of solitaire cards onto the floor and shouted to Agnes
that she had to have a little blowout or she'd go crazy. Agnes
said why didn't they drive to Palm Springs to see the new resort
hotel. They'd eat dinner there if it wouldn't set them back
too much and then spend the night at a touristcamp down near
the Salton Sea. Give them a chance to get the chill of the Los
Angeles fog out of their bones.

When they got to Palm Springs, Agnes thought everything
looked too expensive and wanted to drive right on, but Margo
felt in her element right away. Tony was in his uniform and
had to wait for them in the car. He looked so black in the face
Margo thought he'd burst when she told him to go and get
himself some supper at a dogwagon, but he didn't dare answer
back because the doorman was right there.

They'd been to the ladies' room to freshen their faces up
and were walking up and down under the big datepalms looking
at the people to see if they could recognize any movie actors,
when Margo heard a voice that was familiar. A dark thinfaced
man in white serge who was chatting with an importantlooking
baldheaded Jewish gentleman was staring at her. He left his
friend and came up. He had a stiff walk like an officer review-
ing a company drawn up at attention.

'Miss Dowling,' he said, 'how very lucky for both of us.'

Margo looked smiling into the twitching sallow face with
dark puffs under the eyes. 'You're the photographer,' she said.

He stared at her hard. 'Sam Margolies,' he said. 'Well, I've
searched all over America and Europe for you. . . . Please be
in my office for a screentest at ten o'clock tomorrow. . . . Irwin
will give you the details.' He waved his hand lackadaisically
toward the fat man. 'Meet Mr Harris . . . Miss Dowling . . .
forgive me, I never take upon myself the responsibility of
introducing people. . . . But I want Irwin to see you . . . this
is one of the most beautiful women in America, Irwin.' He
drew his hand down in front of Margo a couple of inches from
her face working the fingers as if he were modeling something
out of clay. 'Ordinarily it would be impossible to photograph
her. Only I can put that face on the screen. . . .'

Margo felt cold all up her spine. She heard Agnes's mouth come open with a gasp behind her. She let a slow kidding smile start in the corners of her mouth.

'Look, Irwin,' cried Margolies, grabbing the fat man by the shoulder. 'It is the spirit of comedy. . . . But why didn't you come to see me?' He spoke a strong foreign accent of some kind. 'What have I done that you should neglect me?'

Margo looked bored. 'This is Mrs Mandeville, my . . . companion. . . . We are taking a little look a California.'

'What's there here except the studios?'

'Perhaps you'd show Mrs Mandeville around a moving-picture studio. She's so anxious to see one, and I don't know a soul in this part of the world . . . not a soul.'

'Of course, I'll have someone take you to all you care to see tomorrow. Nothing to see but dullness and vulgarity. . . . Irwin, that's the face I've been looking for for the little blond girl . . . you remember. . . . You talk to me of agencies, extras, nonsense, I don't want actors . . . But, Miss Dowling, where have you been? I halfexpected to meet you at Baden-Baden last summer. . . . You are the type for Baden-Baden. It's a ridiculous place, but one has to go somewhere. . . . Where have you been?'

'Florida . . . Havana . . . that sort of thing.' Margo was thinking to herself that the last time she met him he hadn't been using the broad 'a.'

'And you've given up the stage?'

Margo gave a little shrug. 'The family were so horrid about it.'

'Oh, I never liked her being on the stage,' cried Agnes who'd been waiting for a chance to put a word in.

'You'll like working in pictures,' said the fat man soothingly.

'My dear Margo,' said Margolies, 'it is not a very large part, but you are perfect for it, perfect. I can bring out in you the latent mystery. . . . Didn't I tell you, Irwin, that the thing to do was to go out of the studio and see the world . . . open the book of life? . . . In this ridiculous caravanserai we find the face, the spirit of comedy, the smile of the Mona Lisa. . . . That's a famous painting in Paris said to be worth five million dollars. . . . Don't ask me how I knew she would be here. . . . But I knew. Of course we cannot tell definitely until after the screentest. . . . I never commit myself . . .'

'But, Mr Margolies, I don't know if I can do it,' Margo said, her heart pounding. 'We're in a rush . . . We have important business to attend to in Miami . . . family matters, you understand.'

'That's of no importance. I'll find you an agent . . . we'll send somebody. . . . Petty details are of no importance to me. Realestate, I suppose.'

Margo nodded vaguely.

'A couple of years ago the house where we'd been living, it was so lovely, was washed clear out to sea,' said Agnes breathlessly.

'You'll get a better house . . . Malibu Beach, Beverly Hills. . . . I hate houses. . . . But I have been rude, I have detained you. . . . But you will forget Miami. We have everything out here. . . . You remember, Margo dearest, I told you that day that pictures had a great future . . . you and . . . you know, the great automobile magnate, I have forgotten his name . . . I told you you would hear of me in the pictures. . . . I rarely make predictions, but I am never wrong. They are based on belief in a sixth sense.'

'Oh, yes,' interrupted Agnes, 'it's so true, if you believe you're going to succeed you can't fail, that's what I tell Margie . . .'

'Very beautifully said, dear lady. . . . Miss Dowling darling, Continental Attractions at ten. . . . I'll have somebody stationed at the gate so that they'll let your chauffeur drive right to my office. It is impossible to reach me by phone. Even Irwin can't get at me when I am working on a picture. It will be an experience for you to see me at work.'

'Well, if I can manage it and my chauffeur can find the way.'

'You'll come,' said Margolies and dragged Irwin Harris away by one short white flannel arm into the diningroom. Welldressed people stared after them as they went. Then they were staring at Margo and Agnes.

'Let's go to the dogwagon and tell Tony. They'll just think we are eccentric,' whispered Margo in Agnes's ear. 'I declare I never imagined the Margolies was him.'

'Oh, isn't it wonderful!' said Agnes.

They were so excited they couldn't eat. They drove back to Santa Monica that night and Margo went straight to bed so as to be rested for the next morning.

Next morning when they got to the lot at a quarter of ten Mr Margolies hadn't sent word. Nobody had heard of an appointment. They waited half an hour. Agnes was having trouble keeping back the tears. Margo was laughing. 'I bet that

bozo was full of hop or something and forgot all about it.'
But she felt sick inside.

Tony had just started the motor and was about to pull
away because Margo didn't like being seen waiting at the gate
like that when a white Pierce Arrow custombuilt towncar with
Margolies all in white flannel with a white béret sitting alone
in the back drove up alongside. He was peering into the Rolls-
Royce and she could see him start with surprise when he
recognized her. He tapped on the window of his car with a
porcelainheaded cane. Then he got out of his car and reached
in and took Margo by the hand. 'I never apologize. . . . It is
often necessary for me to keep people waiting. You will come
with me. Perhaps your friend will call for you at five o'clock.
. . . I have much to tell you and to show you.'

They went upstairs in the elevator in a long plainfaced
building. He ushered her through several offices where young
men in their shirtsleeves were working at draftingboards, stenographers were typing, actors were waiting on benches. 'Frieda, a
screentest for Miss Dowling right away, please,' he said, as he
passed a secretary at a big desk in the last room. Then he
ushered her into his own office hung with Chinese paintings
and a single big carved Gothic chair set in the glare of a baby-
spot opposite a huge carved Gothic desk. 'Sit there, please.
. . . Margo darling, how can I explain to you the pleasure of
a face unsmirched by the camera? I can see that there is no
strain. . . . You do not care. Celtic freshness combined with
insouciance of noble Spain. . . . I can see that you've never
been before a camera before. . . . Excuse me.' He sank in the
deep chair behind his desk and started telephoning. Every now
and then a stenographer came and took notes that he recited
to her in a low voice. Margo sat and sat. She thought Margolies
had forgotten her. The room was warm and stuffy and began
to make her feel sleepy. She was fighting to keep her eyes open
when Margolies jumped up from his desk and said, 'Come,
darling, we'll go down now.'

Margo stood around for a while in front of some cameras in
a plastery-smelling room in the basement and then Margolies
took her to lunch at the crowded restaurant on the lot. She
could feel that everybody was looking up from their plates
to see who the new girl was that Margolies was taking to lunch.
While they ate, he asked her questions about her life on a great
sugarplantation in Cuba, and her débutante girlhood in New
York. Then he talked about Carlsbad and Baden-Baden and

Marienbad and how Southern California was getting over its
early ridiculous vulgarity: 'We have everything here that you
can find anywhere,' he said.

After lunch they went to see the rushes in the projectionroom.
Mr Harris turned up, too, smoking a cigar. Nobody said anything as they looked at Margo's big gray and white face,
grinning, turning, smirking, mouth opening and closing, head
tossing, eyes rolling. It made Margo feel quite sick looking at
it, though she loved still photographs of herself. She couldn't
get used to its being so big. Now and then Mr Harris would
grunt and the end of his cigar would glow red. Margo felt
relieved when the film was over and they were in the dark
again. Then the lights were on and they were filing out of the
projectionroom past a redfaced operator in shirtsleeves who
had thrown open the door to the little black box where the
machine was and gave Margo a look as she passed. Margo
couldn't make out whether he thought she was good or not.

On the landing of the outside staircase, Margolies put out
his hand coldly and said, 'Goodbye, dearest Margo. . . . There
are a hundred people waiting for me.' Margo thought it was
all off. Then he went on: 'You and Irwin will make the
business arrangements . . . I have no understanding of those
matters. . . . I'm sure you'll have a very pleasant afternoon.'

He turned back into the projectionroom swinging his cane
as he went. Mr Harris explained that Mr Margolies would let
her know when he wanted her and that meanwhile they would
work out the contract. Did she have an agent? If she didn't he
would recommend that they call in his friend Mr Hardbein to
protect her interests.

When she got into the office with Mr Harris sitting across
the desk from her and Mr Hardbein, a hollowfaced man with
a tough kidding manner, sitting beside her, she found herself
reading a threeyear contract at three hundred a week. 'Oh,
dear,' she said, 'I'm afraid I'd be awfully tired of it after that
length of time. . . . Do you mind if I ask my companion Mrs
Mandeville to come around? . . . I'm so ignorant about these
things.' Then she called up Agnes and they fiddled around
talking about the weather until Agnes got there.

Agnes was wonderful. She talked about commitments and
important business to be transacted and an estate to care for,
and said that at that figure it would not be worth Miss
Dowling's while to give up her world cruise, would it, darling,
if she appeared in the picture, anyway, it was only to accom-

modate an old friend Mr Margolies, and of course Miss Dowling had always made sacrifices for her work, and that she herself made sacrifices for it, and if necessary would work her fingers to the bone to give her a chance to have the kind of success she believed in and that she knew she would have because if you believed with an unsullied heart God would bring things about the way they ought to be. Agnes went on to talk about how awful unbelief was and at five o'clock just as the office was closing they went out to the car with a contract for three months at five hundred a week in Agnes's handbag. 'I hope the stores are still open,' Margo was saying. 'I've got to have some clothes.'

A toughlooking grayfaced man in ridingclothes with light tow hair was sitting in the front seat beside Tony. Margo and Agnes glared at the flat back of his head as they got into the car.

'Take us down to Tasker and Harding's on Hollywood Boulevard . . . the Paris Gown Shop,' Agnes said. 'Oh, goody, it'll be lovely to have you have some new clothes,' she whispered in Margo's ear.

When Tony let the stranger off at the corner of Hollywood and Sunset, he bowed stiffly and started off up the broad sidewalk. 'Tony, I don't know how many times I've told you you couldn't pick up your friends in my car,' began Margo.

She and Agnes nagged at him so that when he got home he was in a passion and said that he was moving out next day. 'You have done nothing but exploit me and interfere with my career. That was Max Hirsch. He's an Austrian count and a famous poloplayer.' Next day, sure enough, Tony packed his things and left the house.

The five hundred a week didn't go as far as Agnes and Margo thought it would. Mr Hardbein the agent took ten per cent of it first thing, then Agnes insisted on depositing fifty to pay off the loan in Miami so that Margo could get her jewelry back. Then moving into a new house in the nice part of Santa Monica cost a lot. There was a cook and a housemaid's wages to pay and they had to have a chauffeur now that Tony had gone. And there were clothes and a publicityman and all kinds of charities and handouts around the studio that you couldn't refuse. Agnes was wonderful. She attended to everything. Whenever any business matter came up, Margo would press her fingers to the two sides of her forehead and let her eyes close for a minute and groan. 'It's too bad, but I just haven't got a head for business.'

It was Agnes who picked out the new house, a Puerto Rican cottage with the cutest balconies, jampacked with antique Spanish furniture. In the evening Margo sat in an easychair in the big livingroom in front of an open fire playing Russian bank with Agnes. They got a few invitations from actors and people Margo met on the lot, but Margo said she wasn't going out until she found out what was what in this town.

'First thing you know we'll be going around with a bunch of bums who'll do us more harm than good.'

'How true that is,' sighed Agnes. 'Like those awful twins in Miami.'

They didn't see anything of Tony until, one Sunday night that Sam Margolies was coming to the house for the first time, he turned up drunk at about six o'clock and said that he and Max Hirsch wanted to start a polo school and that he had to have a thousand dollars right away.

'But Tony,' said Agnes, 'where's Margie going to get it? . . . You know just as well as I do how heavy our expenses are.'

Tony made a big scene, stormed and cried and said Agnes and Margo had ruined his stage career and that now they were out to ruin his career in pictures. 'I have been too patient,' he yelled, tapping himself on the chest. 'I have let myself be ruined by women.'

Margo kept looking at the clock on the mantel. It was nearly seven. She finally shelled out twentyfive bucks and told him to come back during the week. 'He's hitting the hop again,' she said after he'd gone. 'He'll go crazy one of these days.'

'Poor boy,' sighed Agnes, 'he's not a bad boy, only weak.'

'What I'm scared of is that that Heinie'll get hold of him and make us a lot of trouble. . . . That bird had a face like state's prison . . . guess the best thing to do is get a lawyer and start a divorce.'

'But think of the publicity,' wailed Agnes.

'Anyway,' said Margo, 'Tony's got to pass out of the picture. I've taken all I'm going to take from that greaser.'

Sam Margolies came an hour late. 'How peaceful,' he was saying. 'How can you do it in delirious Hollywood?'

'Why, Margie's just a quiet little workinggirl,' said Agnes, picking up her sewingbasket and starting to sidle out.

He sat down in the easychair without taking off his white béret and stretched out his bowlegs toward the fire. 'I hate the artificiality of it.'

'Don't you now?' said Agnes from the door.

Margo offered him a cocktail, but he said he didn't drink. When the maid brought out the dinner that Agnes had worked on all day, he wouldn't eat anything but toast and lettuce. 'I never eat or drink at mealtimes. I come only to look and to talk.'

'That's why you've gotten so thin,' kidded Margo.

'Do you remember the way I used to be in those old days? My New York period. Let's not talk about it. I have no memory. I live only in the present. Now I am thinking of the picture you are going to star in. I never go to parties, but you must come with me to Irwin Harris's tonight. There will be people there you'll have to know. Let me see your dresses. I'll pick out what you ought to wear. After this you must always let me come when you buy a dress.' Following her up the creaking stairs to her bedroom, he said, 'We must have a different setting for you. This won't do. This is suburban.'

Margo felt funny driving out through the avenues of palms of Beverly Hills sitting beside Sam Margolies. He'd made her put on the old yellow eveningdress she'd bought at Piquot's years ago that Agnes had recently had done over and lengthened by a little French dressmaker she'd found in Los Angeles. Her hands were cold and she was afraid Margolies would hear her heart knocking against her ribs. She tried to think of something funny to say, but what was the use, Margolies never laughed. She wondered what he was thinking. She could see his face, the narrow forehead under his black bang, the pouting lips, the beaklike profile very dark against the streetlights as he sat stiffly beside her with his hands on his knees. He still had on his white flannels and a white stock with a diamond pin in it in the shape of a golfclub. As the car turned into a drive toward a row of bright tall frenchwindows through the trees, he turned to her and said, 'You are afraid you will be bored. . . . You'll be surprised. You'll find we have something here that matches the foreign and New York society you are accustomed to.' As he turned his face toward her the light glinted on the whites of his eyes and sagging pouches under them and the wet broad lips. He went on whispering, squeezing her hand as he helped her out of the car. 'You will be the most elegant woman there, but only as one star is brighter than the other stars.'

Going into the door past the butler, Margo caught herself starting to giggle. 'How you do go on,' she said. 'You talk like a . . . like a genius.'

'That's what they call me,' said Margolies in a loud voice,

drawing his shoulders back and standing stiffly at attention to let her go past him through the large glass doors into the vestibule.

The worst of it was going into the dressingroom to take off her wraps. The women who were doing their faces and giving a last pat to their hair all turned and gave her a quick once-over that started at her slippers, ran up her stockings, picked out every hook and eye of her dress, ran round her neck to see if it was wrinkled and up into her hair to see if it was dyed. At once she knew that she ought to have an ermine wrap. There was one old dame standing smoking a cigarette by the lavatory door in a dress all made of cracked ice who had X-ray eyes; Margo felt her reading the pricetag on her stepins. The colored maid gave Margo a nice toothy grin as she laid Margo's coat over her arm that made her feel better. When she went out, she felt the stares clash together on her back and hang there like a tin can on a dog's tail. Keep a stiff upper lip, they can't eat you, she was telling herself as the door of the ladies' room closed behind her. She wished Agnes was there to tell her how lovely everybody was.

Margolies was waiting for her in the vestibule full of sparkly chandeliers. There was an orchestra playing and they were dancing in a big room. He took her to the fireplace at the end. Irwin Harris and Mr Hardbein, who looked as alike as a pair of eggs in their tight dress suits, came up and said goodevening. Margolies gave them each a hand without looking at them and sat down by the fireplace with his back to the crowd in a big carved chair like the one he had in his office. Mr Harris asked her to dance with him. After that it was like any other collection of dressedup people. At least until she found herself dancing with Rodney Cathcart.

She recognized him at once from the pictures, but it was a shock to find that his face had color in it, and that there was warm blood and muscle under his rakish eveningdress. He was a tall tanned young man with goldfishyellow hair and an English way of mumbling his words. She'd felt cold and shivery until she started to dance with him. After he'd danced with her once, he asked her to dance with him again. Between dances he led her to the buffet at the end of the room and tried to get her to drink. She held a Scotch-and-soda in a big blue glass each time and just sipped it while he drank down a couple of Scotches straight and ate a large plate of chicken salad. He seemed a little drunk, but he didn't seem to be getting any drunker. He didn't say anything, so she didn't say anything either. She loved dancing with him.

Every now and then when they danced round the end of the room, she caught sight of the whole room in the huge mirror over the fireplace. Once when she got just the right angle she thought she saw Margolies' face staring at her from out of the carved highbacked chair that faced the burning logs. He seemed to be staring at her attentively. The firelight playing on his face gave it a warm lively look she hadn't noticed on it before. Immediately blond heads, curly heads, bald heads, bare shoulders, black shoulders got in her way and she lost sight of that corner of the room.

It must have been about twelve o'clock when she found him standing beside the table where the Scotch was.

'Hello, Sam,' said Rodney Cathcart. 'How's every little thing?'

'We must go now, the poor child is tired in all this noise. . . . Rodney, you must let Miss Dowling go now.'

'O.K., pal,' said Rodney Cathcart and turned his back to pour himself another glass of Scotch.

When Margo came back from getting her wraps, she found Mr Hardbein waiting for her in the vestibule. He bowed as he squeezed her hand. 'Well, I don't mind telling you, Miss Dowling, that you made a sensation. The girls are all asking what you use to dye your hair with.' A laugh rumbled down into his broad vest. 'Would you come by my office? We might have a bite of lunch and talk things over a bit.'

Margo gave a little shudder. 'It's sweet of you, Mr Hardbein, but I never go to offices . . . I don't understand business. . . . You call us up, won't you?'

When she got out to the colonial porch there was Rodney Cathcart sitting beside Margolies in the long white car. Margo grinned and got in between them as cool as if she'd expected to find Rodney Cathcart there all the while. The car drove off. Nobody said anything. She couldn't tell where they were going, the avenues of palms and the strings of streetlamps all looked alike. They stopped at a big restaurant.

'I thought we'd better have a little snack. . . . You didn't eat anything all evening,' Margolies said, giving her hand a squeeze as he helped her out of the car.

'That's the berries,' said Rodney Cathcart who'd hopped out first. 'This dawncing makes a guy beastly 'ungry.'

The headwaiter bowed almost to the ground and led them

through the restaurant full of eyes to a table that had been reserved for them on the edge of the dancefloor. Margolies ate shreddedwheat biscuits and milk, Rodney Cathcart ate a steak, and Margo took on the end of her fork a few pieces of a lobsterpatty.

'A blighter needs a drink after that,' grumbled Rodney Cathcart, pushing back his plate after polishing off the last fried potato.

Margolies raised two fingers. 'Here it is forbidden.... How silly we are in this country! ... How silly they are!' He rolled his eyes toward Margo. She caught a wink in time to make it just a twitch of the eyelid and gave him that slow stopped smile he'd made such a fuss over at Palm Springs.

Margolies got to his feet. 'Come, Margo darling ... I have something to show you.' As she and Rodney Cathcart followed him out across the red carpet, she could feel ripples of excitement go through the people in the restaurant the way she'd felt it when she went places in Miami after Charley Anderson had been killed.

Margolies drove them to a big creamcolored apartmenthouse. They went up in an elevator. He opened a door with a latchkey and ushered them in. 'This,' he said, 'is my little bachelor flat.'

It was a big dark room with a balcony at the end hung with embroideries. The walls were covered with all kinds of oilpaintings, each lit by a little overhead light of its own. There were Oriental rugs piled one on the other on the floor and couches round the walls covered with zebra and lion skins.

'Oh, what a wonderful place!' said Margo.

Margolies turned to her smiling. 'A bit baronial, eh? The sort of thing you're accustomed to see in the castle of a Castilian grandee.'

'Absolutely,' said Margo.

Rodney Cathcart lay down full length on one of the couches. 'Say, Sam, old top,' he said, 'have you got any of that good Canadian ale? 'Ow about a little Guinness in it?'

Margolies went out into a pantry and the swinging door closed behind him. Margo roamed around looking at the brightcolored pictures and the shelves of wriggling Chinese figures. It made her feel spooky.

'Oh, I say,' Rodney Cathcart called from the couch. 'Come over here, Margo.... I like you.... You've got to call me Si.... My friends call me that. It's more American.'

'All right by me,' said Margo, sauntering toward the couch.

Rodney Cathcart put out his hand. 'Put it there, pal,' he said. When she put her hand in his, he grabbed it and tried to pull her toward him on the couch. 'Wouldn't you like to kiss me, Margo?' He had a terrific grip. She could feel how strong he was.

Margolies came back with a tray with bottles and glasses and set it on an ebony stand near the couch. 'This is where I do my work,' he said. 'Genius is helpless without the proper environment. . . . Sit there.' He pointed to the couch where Cathcart was lying. 'I shot that lion myself. . . . Excuse me a moment.' He went up the stairs to the balcony and a light went on up there. Then a door closed and the light was cut off. The only light in the room was over the pictures.

Rodney Cathcart sat up on the edge of the couch. 'For crissake, sister, drink something. . . .'

Margo started to titter. 'All right, Si, you can give me a spot of gin,' she said, and sat down beside him on the couch.

He was attractive. She found herself letting him kiss her, but right away his hand was working up her leg and she had to get up and walk over to the other side of the room to look at the pictures again. 'Oh, don't be silly,' he sighed, letting himself drop back on the couch.

There was no sound from upstairs. Margo began to get the jeebies wondering what Margolies was doing up there. She went back to the couch to get herself another spot of gin and Rodney Cathcart jumped up all of a sudden and put his arms around her from behind and bit her ear.

'Quit that caveman stuff,' she said, standing still. She didn't want to wrestle with him for fear he'd muss her dress.

'That's me,' he whispered in her ear. 'I find you most exciting.'

Margolies was standing in front of them with some papers in his hand. Margo wondered how long he'd been there. Rodney Cathcart let himself drop back on the couch and closed his eyes.

'Now sit down, Margo darling.' Margolies was saying in an even voice. 'I want to tell you a story. See if it awakens anything in you.' Margo felt herself flushing. Behind her Rodney Cathcart was giving long deep breaths as if he were asleep.

'You are tired of the giddy whirl of the European capitals,' Margolies was saying. 'You are the daughter of an old army-officer. Your mother is dead. You go everywhere, dances, dinners, affairs. Proposals are made for your hand. Your father is a French or perhaps a Spanish general. His country calls him. He is to be sent to Africa to repel the barbarous Moors. He

wants to leave you in a convent, but you insist on going with
him. You are following this?'

'Oh, yes,' said Margo eagerly. 'She'd stow away on the ship
to go with him to the war.'

'On the same boat there's a young American collegeboy who
has run away to join the Foreign Legion. We'll get the reason
later. That'll be your friend Si. You meet.... Everything is
lovely between you. Your father is very ill. By this time you are
in a mud fort besieged by natives, howling bloodthirsty savages.
Si breaks through the blockade to get the medicine necessary
to save your father's life.... On his return he's arrested as a
deserter. You rush to Tangier to get the American consul to
intervene. Your father's life is saved. You ride back just in time
to beat the firingsquad. Si is an American citizen and is decorated. The general kisses him on both cheeks and hands his
lovely daughter over into his strong arms.... I don't want you
to talk about this now.... Let it settle deep into your mind. Of
course, it's only a rudimentary sketch. The story is nonsense,
but it affords the director certain opportunities. I can see you
risking all, reputation, life itself, to save the man you love. Now
I'll take you home.... Look, Si's asleep. He's just an animal, a
brute blond beast.'

When Margolies put her wrap around her, he let his hands
rest for a moment on her shoulders. 'There's another thing I
want you to let sink into your heart ... not your intelligence ...
your heart.... Don't answer me now. Talk it over with your
charming companion. A little later, when we have this picture
done, I want you to marry me. I am free. Years ago in another
world I had a wife as men have wives, but we agreed to misunderstand and went our ways. Now I shall be too busy. You
have no conception of the intense detailed work involved. When
I am directing a picture, I can think of nothing else, but when
the creative labor is over, in three months' time perhaps, I want
you to marry me.... Don't reply now.'

They didn't say anything as he sat beside her on the way
home to Santa Monica driving slowly through the thick white
clammy morning mist. When the car drove up to her door, she
leaned over and tapped him on the cheek. 'Sam,' she said,
'you've given me the loveliest evening.'

Agnes was all of a twitter about where she'd been so late. She
was walking around in her dressinggown and had the lights on
all over the house. 'I had a vague brooding feeling after you'd
left, Margie. So I called up Madame Esther to ask her what she

thought. She had a message for me from Frank. You know she said last time he was trying to break through unfortunate influences.'

'Oh, Agnes, what did it say?'

'It said success is in your grasp, be firm. Oh, Margie, you've just got to marry him. . . . That's what Frank's been trying to tell us.'

'Jiminy crickets,' said Margo, falling on her bed when she got upstairs, 'I'm all in. Be a darling and hang up my clothes for me, Agnes.'

Margo was too excited to sleep. The room was too light. She kept seeing the light red through her eyelids. She must get her sleep. She'd look a sight if she didn't get her sleep. She called to Agnes to bring her an aspirin.

Agnes propped her up in bed with one hand and gave her the glass of water to wash the aspirin down with the other; it was like when she'd been a little girl and Agnes used to give her medicine when she was sick. Then suddenly she was dreaming that she was just finishing the *Everybody's Doing It* number and the pink cave of faces was roaring with applause and she ran off into the wings where Frank Mandeville was waiting for her in his black cloak with arms stretched wide open, and she ran into his arms and the cloak closed about her and she was down with the cloak choking her and he was on top of her clawing at her dress and past his shoulder she could see Tony laughing, Tony all in white with a white béret and a diamond golfclub on his stock jumping up and down and clapping. It must have been her yelling that brought Agnes. No, Agnes was telling her something. She sat up in bed shuddering.

Agnes was all in a fluster. 'Oh, it's dreadful. Tony's down there. He insists on seeing you, Margie. He's been reading in the papers. You know it's all over the papers about how you are starring with Rodney Cathcart in Mr Margolies' next picture. Tony's wild. He says he's your husband and he ought to attend to your business for you. He says he's got a legal right.'

'The little rat,' said Margo. 'Bring him up here. . . . What time is it?' She jumped out of bed and ran to the dressingtable to fix her face. When she heard them coming up the stairs, she pulled on her pink lace bedjacket and jumped back into bed. She was very sleepy when Tony came in the room. 'What's the trouble, Tony?' she said.

'I'm starving and here you are making three thousand a week. . . . Yesterday Max and I had no money for dinner. We are going to be put out of our apartment. By rights everything you make is mine.... I've been too soft ... I've let myself be cheated.'

Margo yawned. 'We're not in Cuba, dearie.' She sat up in bed. 'Look here, Tony, let's part friends. The contract isn't signed yet. Suppose when it is, we fix you up a little so that you and your friend can go and start your polo school in Havana. The trouble with you is you're homesick.'

'Wouldn't that be wonderful!' chimed in Agnes. 'Cuba would be just the place ... with all the tourists going down there and everything.'

Tony drew himself up stiffly. 'Margo, we are Christians. We believe. We know that the church forbids divorce.... Agnes, she doesn't understand.'

'I'm a lot better Christian than you are ... you know that, you ...' began Agnes shrilly.

'Now, Agnes, we can't argue about religion before breakfast.' Margo sat up and drew her knees up to her chin underneath the covers. 'Agnes and I believe that Mary Baker Eddy taught the truth, see, Tony. Sit down here, Tony.... You're getting too fat, Tony, the boys won't like you if you lose your girlish figure.... Look here, you and me we've seen each other through some tough times.' He sat on the bed and lit a cigarette. She stroked the spiky black hair off his forehead. 'You're not going to try to gum the game when I've got the biggest break I ever had in my life.'

'I been a louse. I'm no good,' Tony said. 'How about a thousand a month? That's only a third of what you make. You'll just waste it. Women don't need money.'

'Like hell they don't. You know it costs money to make money in this business.'

'All right ... make it five hundred. I don't understand the figures, you know that. You know I'm only a child.'

'Well, I don't either. You and Agnes go downstairs and talk it over while I get a bath and get dressed. I've got a dressmaker coming and I've got to have my hair done. I've got about a hundred appointments this afternoon.... Good boy, Tony.' She patted him on the cheek and he went away with Agnes meek as a lamb.

When Agnes came upstairs again after Margo had had her bath, she said crossly, 'Margie, we ought to have divorced Tony long ago. This German who's got hold of him is a bad egg. You know how Mr Hays feels about scandals.'

'I know I've been a damn fool.'

'I've got to ask Frank about this. I've got an appointment with Madame Esther this afternoon. Frank might tell us the name of a reliable lawyer.'

'We can't go to Vardaman. He's Mr Hardbein's lawyer and Sam's lawyer too. A girl sure is a fool ever to put anything in writing.'

The phone rang. It was Mr Hardbein calling up about the contract. Margo sent Agnes down to the office to talk to him. All afternoon, standing there in front of the long pierglass while the dressmaker fussed around her with her mouth full of pins, she was worrying about what to do. When Sam came around at five to see the new dresses, her hair was still in the dryer.

'How attractive you look with your head in that thing,' Sam said, 'and the lacy négligée and the little triangle of Brussels lace between your knees.... I shall remember it. I have total recall. I never forget anything I've seen. That is the secret of visual imagination.'

When Agnes came back for her in the Rolls, she had trouble getting away from Sam. He wanted to take them wherever they were going in his own car. 'You must have no secrets from me, Margo darling,' he said gently. 'You will see I understand every-thing ... everything.... I know you better than you know your-self. That's why I know I can direct you. I have studied every plane of your face and of your beautiful little girlish soul so full of desire.... Nothing you do can surprise or shock me.'

'That's good,' said Margo.

He went away sore.

'Oh, Margie, you oughtn't to treat Mr Margolies like that,' whined Agnes.

'I can do without him better than he can do without me,' said Margo. 'He's got to have a new star. They say he's pretty near on the skids, anyway.'

'Mr Hardbein says that's just because he's fired his publicity-man,' said Agnes.

It was late when they got started. Madame Esther's house was way downtown in a dilapidated part of Los Angeles. They had the chauffeur let them out two blocks from the house and walked to it down an alley between dusty bungalow courts like the places they'd lived in when they first came out to the Coast years ago.

Margo nudged Agnes. 'Remind you of anything?'

Agnes turned to her, frowning. 'We must only remember the pleasant beautiful things, Margie.'

Madame Esther's house was a big old frame house with wide porches and cracked shingle roofs. The blinds were drawn on all the grimy windows. Agnes knocked at a little groundglass door in back. A thin spinsterish woman with gray bobbed hair opened it immediately. 'You are late,' she whispered. 'Madame's in a state. They don't like to be kept waiting. It'll be difficult to break the chain.'

'Has she had anything from Frank?' whispered Agnes.

'He's very angry. I'm afraid he won't answer again.... Give me your hand.'

The woman took Agnes's hand and Agnes took Margo's hand and they went in single file down a dark passageway that had only a small red bulb burning in it, and through a door into a completely dark room that was full of people breathing and shuffling.

'I thought it was going to be private,' whispered Margo.

'Shush,' hissed Agnes in her ear.

When her eyes got accustomed to the darkness she could see Madame Esther's big puffy face swaying across a huge round table and faint blurs of other faces around it. They made way for Agnes and Margo and Margo found herself sitting down with somebody's wet damp hand clasped in hers. On the table in front of Madame Esther were a lot of little pads of white paper. Everything was quiet except for Agnes's heavy breathing next to her.

It seemed hours before anything happened. Then Margo saw that Madame Esther's eyes were open, but all she could see was the whites. A deep baritone voice was coming out of her lips talking a language she didn't understand. Somebody in the ring answered in the same language, evidently putting questions.

'That's Sidi Hassan the Hindu,' whispered Agnes. 'He's given some splendid tips on the stockmarket.'

'Silence!' yelled Madame Esther in a shrill woman's voice that almost scared Margo out of her wits. 'Frank is waiting. No, he has been called away. He left a message that all would be well. He left a message that tomorrow he would impart the information the parties desired and that his little girl must on no account take any step without consulting her darling Agnes.'

Agnes burst into hysterical sobs and a hand tapped Margo on the shoulder. The same grayhaired woman led them to the back door again. She had some smellingsalts that she made

Agnes sniff. Before she opened the groundglass door she said, 'That'll be fifty dollars, please. Twentyfive dollars each. . . . And Madame says that the beautiful girl must not come any more, it might be dangerous for her, we are surrounded by hostile influences. But Mrs Mandeville must come and get the messages. Nothing can harm her, Madame says, because she has the heart of a child.'

As they stepped out into the dark alley to find that it was already night and the lights were on everywhere, Margo pulled her fur up round her face so that nobody could recognize her.

'You see, Margie,' Agnes said as they settled back into the deep seat of the old Rolls, 'everything is going to be all right, with dear Frank watching over us. He means that you must go ahead and marry Mr Margolies right away.'

'Well, I suppose it's no worse than signing a threeyear contract,' said Margo. She told the chauffeur to drive as fast as he could because Sam was taking her to an opening at Grauman's that night.

When they drove up round the drive to the door, the first thing they saw was Tony and Max Hirsch sitting on the marble bench in the garden.

'I'll talk to them,' said Agnes.

Margo rushed upstairs and started to dress. She was sitting looking at herself in the glass in her stepins when Tony rushed into the room. When he got into the light over the dressingtable, she noticed that he had a black eye. 'Taking up the gentle art, eh, Tony?' she said, without turning around.

Tony talked breathlessly. 'Max blacked my eye because I did not want to come. Margo, he will kill me if you don't give me one thousand dollars. We will not leave the house till you give us a check and we got to have some cash, too, because Max is giving a party tonight and the bootlegger will not deliver the liquor until he's paid cash. Max says you are getting a divorce. How can you? There is no divorce under the church. It's a sin that I will not have on my soul. You cannot get a divorce.'

Margo got up and turned around to face him. 'Hand me my négligée on the bed there . . . no use catching my death of cold. . . . Say, Tony, do you think I'm getting too fat? I gained two pounds last week. . . . Look here, Tony, that squarehead's going to be the ruination of you. You better cut him out and go away for another cure somewhere. I'd hate to have the federal dicks get hold of you on a narcotic charge. They made a big raid in San Pedro only yesterday.'

Tony burst into tears. 'You've got to give it to me. He'll break every bone in my body.'

Margo looked at her wristwatch that lay on the dressingtable beside the big powderbox. Eight o'clock. Sam would be coming by any minute now.

'All right,' she said, 'but next time this house is going to be guarded by detectives. . . . Get that,' she said. 'And any monkeybusiness and you birds land in jail. If you think Sam Margolies can't keep it out of the papers, you've got another think coming. Go downstairs and tell Agnes to make you out a check and give you any cash she has in the house.' Margo went back to her dressing.

A few minutes later, Agnes came up crying. 'What shall we do? I gave them the check and two hundred dollars. . . . Oh, it's awful. Why didn't Frank warn us? I know he's watching over us, but he might have told us what to do about that dreadful man.'

Margo went into her dresscloset and slipped into a brandnew eveninggown. 'What we'll do is stop that check first thing in the morning. You call up the homeprotection office and get two detectives out here on day and night duty right away. I'm through, that's all.'

Margo was mad, she was striding up and down the room in her new white spangly dress with a trimming of ostrich feathers. She caught sight of herself in the big triple mirror standing between the beds. She went over and stood in front of it. She looked at the three views of herself in the white spangly dress. Her eyes were a flashing blue and her cheeks were flushed. Agnes came up behind her bringing her the rhinestone band she was going to wear in her hair. 'Oh, Margie,' she cried, 'you never looked so stunning.'

The maid came up to say that Mr Margolies was waiting. Margo kissed Agnes and said, 'You won't be scared with the detectives, will you, dearie?' Margo pulled the ermine wrap that they'd sent up on approval that afternoon round her shoulders and walked out to the car. Rodney Cathcart was there lolling in the back seat in his dressclothes. A set of perfect teeth shone in his long brown face when he smiled at her.

Sam had got out to help her in. 'Margo darling, you take our breaths away, I knew that was the right dress,' he said. His eyes were brighter than usual. 'Tonight's a very important night. It is the edict of the stars. I'll tell you about it later. I've had our horoscopes cast.'

In the crowded throbbing vestibule, Margo and Rodney Cathcart had to stop at the microphone to say a few words about their new picture and their association with Sam Margolies as they went in through the beating glare of lights and eyes to the lobby. When the master of ceremonies tried to get Margolies to speak, he turned his back angrily and walked into the theater as if it was empty, not looking to the right or the left. After the show they went to a restaurant and sat at a table for a while. Rodney Cathcart ordered kidneychops.

'You mustn't eat too much, Si,' said Margolies. 'The pièce de résistance is at my flat.'

Sure enough, there was a big table set out with cold salmon and lobstersalad and a Filipino butler opening champagne for just the three of them when they went back there after the restaurant had started to thin out. This time Margo tore loose and ate and drank all she could hold. Rodney Cathcart put away almost the whole salmon, muttering that it was topping, and even Sam, saying he was sure it would kill him, ate a plate of lobstersalad.

Margo was dizzygiggly drunk when she found that the Filipino and Sam Margolies had disappeared and that she and Si were sitting together on the couch that had the lionskin on it.

'So you're going to marry Sam,' said Si, gulping down a glass of champagne. She nodded. 'Good girl.' Si took off his coat and vest and hung them carefully on a chair. 'Hate clothes,' he said. 'You must come to my ranch. . . . Hot stuff.'

'But you wear them so beautifully,' said Margo.

'Correct,' said Si.

He reached over and lifted her onto his knee.

'But, Si, we oughtn't to, not on Sam's lionskin.'

Si put his mouth to hers and kissed her. 'You find me exciting? You ought to see me stripped.'

'Don't, don't,' said Margo. She couldn't help it, he was too strong, his hands were all over her under her dress.

'Oh, hell, I don't give a damn,' she said. He went over and got her another glass of champagne. For himself he filled a bowl that had held cracked ice earlier in the evening.

'As for that lion it's bloody rot. Sam shot it, but the blighter shot it in a zoo. They were sellin' off some old ones at one of the bloody lionfarms and they had a shoot. Couldn't miss 'em. It was a bloody crime.' He drank down the champagne and suddenly jumped at her. She fell on the couch with his arms crushing her.

She was dizzy. She walked up and down the room trying to catch her breath. 'Goodnight, hot sketch,' Si said and carefully put on his coat and vest again and was gone out the door. She was dizzy.

Sam was back and was showing her a lot of calculations on a piece of paper. His eyes bulged shiny into her face as she tried to read. His hands were shaking. 'It's tonight,' he kept saying, 'it's tonight that our lifelines cross.... We are married, whether we wish it or not. I don't believe in free will. Do you, darling Margo?'

Margo was dizzy. She couldn't say anything. 'Come, dear child, you are tired.' Margolies' voice burred soothingly in her ears. She let him lead her into the bedroom and carefully take her clothes off and lay her between the black silk sheets of the big poster bed.

It was broad daylight when Sam drove her back to the house. The detective outside touched his hat as they turned into the drive. It made her feel good to see the man's big pugface as he stood there guarding her house. Agnes was up and walking up and down in a padded flowered dressinggown in the livingroom with a newspaper in her hand.

'Where have you been?' she cried. 'Oh, Margie, you'll ruin your looks if you go on like this and you're just getting a start too.... Look at this ... now don't be shocked ... remember it's all for the best.'

She handed the *Times* to Margo, pointing out a headline with the sharp pink manicured nail of her forefinger. 'Didn't I tell you Frank was watching over us?'

### HOLLYWOOD EXTRA SLAIN AT PARTY
#### NOTED POLO PLAYER DISAPPEARS
#### SAILORS HELD

Two enlisted men in uniform, George Cook and Fred Costello, from the battleship *Kenesaw* were held for questioning when they were found stupefied with liquor or narcotics in the basement of an apartmenthouse at 2234 Higueras Drive, San Pedro, where residents allege a drunken party had been in progress all night. Near them was found the body of a young man whose skull had been fractured by a blow from a blunt instrument who was identified as a Cuban, Antonio Garrido, erstwhile extra on several prominent studio lots. He was still breathing when the police broke in in response to telephoned complaints from the neighbors. The fourth member of the party, a German citizen named Max Hirsch, supposed by some to be an Austrian nobleman, who shared an apartment at Mimosa in a fashionable bungalow court with the handsome young Cuban, had fled before police reached the scene of the tragedy. At an early hour this morning he had not yet been located by the police.

Margo felt the room swinging in great circles around her head. 'Oh, my God!' she said. Going upstairs she had to hold tight to the baluster to keep from falling. She tore off her clothes and ran herself a hot bath and lay back in it with her eyes closed.

'Oh, Margie,' wailed Agnes from the other room, 'your lovely new gown is a wreck.'

Margo and Sam Margolies flew to Tucson to be married. Nobody was present except Agnes and Rodney Cathcart. After the ceremony Margolies handed the justice of the peace a new hundreddollar bill. The going was pretty bumpy on the way back and the big rattly Ford trimotor gave them quite a shakingup crossing the desert. Margolies' face was all colors under his white béret, but he said it was delightful. Rodney Cathcart and Agnes vomited frankly into their cardboard containers. Margo felt her pretty smile tightening into a desperate grin, but she managed to keep the wedding breakfast down. When the plane came to rest at the airport at last, they kept the cameramen waiting half an hour before they could trust themselves to come down the gangplank flushed and smiling into a rain of streamers and confetti thrown by the attendants and the whir of the motionpicture cameras. Rodney Cathcart had to drink most of a pint of Scotch before he could get his legs not to buckle under him. Margo wore her smile over a mass of yellow orchids that had been waiting for her in the refrigerator at the airport, and Agnes looked tickled to death because Sam had bought her orchids too, lavender ones, and insisted that she stride down the gangplank into the cameras with the rest of them.

It was a relief after the glare of the desert and the lurching of the plane in the airpockets to get back to the quiet dressingroom of the lot. By three o'clock they were in their makeup. In a small room in the groundfloor Margolies went right back to work taking closeups of Margo and Rodney Cathcart in a clinch against the background of a corner of a mud fort. Si was stripped to the waist with two cartridgebelts crossed over his chest and a canvas legionnaire's képi on his head and Margo was in a white eveningdress with highheeled satin slippers. They were having trouble with the clinch on account of the cartridgebelts. Margolies with his porcelainhandled cane thrashing in front of him kept strutting back and forth from the little box he stood on behind the camera into the glare of the klieg light where Margo and Si clinched and unclinched a dozen times before they hit a position that suited him.

'My dear Si,' he was saying, 'you must make them feel it. Every ripple of your muscles must make them feel passion . . . you are stiff like a wooden doll. They all love her, a piece of fragile beautiful palpitant womanhood ready to give all for the man she loves. . . . Margo, darling, you faint, you let yourself go in his arms. If his strong arms weren't there to catch you, you would fall to the ground. Si, my dear fellow, you are not an athletic instructor teaching a young lady to swim, you are a desperate lover facing death. . . . They all feel they are you, you are loving her for them, the millions who want love and beauty and excitement, but forget them, loosen up, my dear fellow, forget that I'm here and the camera's here, you are alone together snatching a desperate moment, you are alone except for your two beating hearts, you and the most beautiful girl in the world, the nation's newest sweetheart. . . . All right . . . hold it. . . . Camera.'

# Newsreel 63

but a few minutes later this false land disappeared as quickly and as mysteriously as it had come and I found before me the long stretch of the silent sea with not a single sign of life in sight

> *Whippoorwills call*
> *And evening is nigh*
> *I hurry to . . . my blue heaven*

LINDBERGH IN PERIL AS WAVE TRAPS HIM IN CRUISER'S BOW

> *Down in the Tennessee mountains*
> *Away from the sins of the world*
> *Old Dan Kelly's son there he leaned on his gun*
> *Athinkin' of Zeb Turney's girl*

ACCLAIMED BY HUGE CROWDS IN THE STREETS

SNAPS PICTURES FROM DIZZY YARDARM

> *Dan was a hotblooded youngster*
> *His Dad raised him up sturdy an' right*

ENTHRALLED BY DARING DEED CITY CHEERS FROM DEPTHS OF ITS HEART

FLYER SPORTS IN AIR

> *His heart in a whirl with his love for the girl*
> *He loaded his doublebarreled gun*

LEADERS OF PUBLIC LIFE BREAK INTO UPROAR AT SIGHT OF FLYER

CONFUSION IN HOTEL

AVIATOR NEARLY HURLED FROM AUTO AS IT LEAPS FORWARD THROUGH GAP IN CROWD

> *Over the mountains he wandered*
> *This son of a Tennessee man*

*With fire in his eye and his gun by his side*
*Alooking for Zeb Turney's clan*

SHRINERS PARADE IN DELUGE OF RAIN

PAPER BLIZZARD CHOKES BROADWAY

*Shots ringin' out through the mountain*
*Shots ringin' out through the breeze*

LINDY TO HEAD BIG AIRLINE

*The story of Dan Kelly's moonshine*
*Is spread far and wide o'er the world*
*How Dan killed the clan shot them down to a man*
*And brought back old Zeb Turney's girl*

a short, partly bald man, his face set in tense emotion, ran out from a mass of people where he had been concealed and climbed quickly into the plane as if afraid he might be stopped. He had on ordinary clothes and a leather vest instead of a coat. He was bareheaded. He crowded down beside Chamberlin, looking neither at the crowd nor at his own wife who stood a little in front of the plane and at one side, her eyes big with wonder. The motor roared and the plane started down the runway, stopped and came back again and then took off perfectly

## *Architect*

A muggy day in late spring in eighteen-eightyseven a tall youngster of eighteen, with fine eyes and a handsome arrogant way of carrying his head, arrived in Chicago with seven dollars left in his pocket from buying his ticket from Madison with some cash he'd got by pawning Plutarch's *Lives*, a Gibbon's *Decline and Fall of the Roman Empire*, and an old furcollared coat.

Before leaving home to make himself a career in an architect's office (there was no architecture course at Wisconsin to clutter his mind with stale Beaux-Arts drawings), the youngster had seen the dome of the new State Capitol in Madison collapse on account of bad rubblework in the piers, some thieving contractors' skimping materials to save the politicians their rakeoff, and perhaps a trifling but deadly error in the architect's plans;

he never forgot the roar of burst masonry, the flying plaster, the soaring dustcloud, the mashed bodies of the dead and dying being carried out, set faces livid with plasterdust.

Walking round downtown Chicago, crossing and recrossing the bridges over the Chicago River in the jingle and clatter of traffic, the rattle of vans and loaded wagons and the stamping of big drayhorses and the hooting of towboats with barges and the rumbling whistle of lakesteamers waiting for the draw,

he thought of the great continent stretching a thousand miles east and south and north, three thousand miles west, and everywhere, at mineheads, on the shores of newlydredged harbors, along watercourses, at the intersections of railroads, sprouting

shacks roundhouses tipples grainelevators stores warehouses tenements, great houses for the wealthy set in broad treeshaded lawns, domed statehouses on hills, hotels churches operahouses auditoriums.

He walked with long eager steps

toward the untrammeled future opening in every direction for a young man who'd kept his hands to his work and his wits sharp to invent.

The same day he landed a job in an architect's office.

Frank Lloyd Wright was the grandson of a Welsh hatter and preacher who'd settled in a rich Wisconsin valley, Spring Valley, and raised a big family of farmers and preachers and schoolteachers there. Wright's father was a preacher too, a restless illadjusted New Englander who studied medicine, preached in a Baptist church in Weymouth, Massachusetts, and then as a Unitarian in the Middle West, taught music, read Sanskrit and finally walked out on his family.

Young Wright was born on his grandfather's farm, went to school in Weymouth and Madison, worked summers on a farm of his uncle's in Wisconsin.

His training in architecture was the reading of Viollet le Duc, the apostle of the thirteenth century and of the pure structural mathematics of Gothic stonemasonry, and the seven years he worked with Louis Sullivan in the office of Adler and Sullivan in Chicago. (It was Louis Sullivan who, after Richardson, invented whatever was invented in nineteenthcentury architecture in America.)

When Frank Lloyd Wright left Sullivan, he had already launched a distinctive style, prairie achitecture. In Oak Park he

built broad suburban dwellings for rich men that were the first
buildings to break the hold on American builders' minds of
centuries of pastward routine, of the wornout capital and plinth
and pediment dragged through the centuries from the Acropolis,
and the jaded traditional stencils of Roman masonry, the half-
obliterated Palladian copybooks.

Frank Lloyd Wright was cutting out a new avenue that led
toward the swift constructions in glassbricks and steel
foreshadowed today.

Delightedly he reached out for the new materials, steel in
tension, glass, concrete, the million new metals and alloys.

The son and grandson of preachers, he became a preacher
in blueprints,
projecting constructions in the American future instead of
the European past.

Inventor of plans,
plotter of tomorrow's girderwork phrases,
he preaches to the young men coming of age in the time
of oppression, cooped up by the plasterboard partitions of
finance routine, their lives and plans made poor by feudal levies
of parasite money standing astride every process to shake down
progress for the cutting of coupons:

*The properly citified citizen has become a broker, dealing
chiefly in human frailties or the ideas and inventions of others,
a puller of levers, a presser of buttons of vicarious power, his
by way of machine craft . . . and over beside him and beneath
him, even in his heart as he sleeps, is the taximeter of rent, in
some form to goad this anxious consumer's unceasing struggle
for or against more or less merciful or merciless money incre-
ment.*

To the young men who spend their days and nights drafting the plans for new *rented aggregates of rented cells upended
on hard pavements,*
he preaches
the horizons of his boyhood,
a future that is not the rise of a few points in a hundred
selected stocks, or an increase in carloadings, or a multiplication
of credit in the bank or a rise in the rate on callmoney,
but a new clean construction, from the ground up, based on
uses and needs,
toward the American future instead of toward the pain-

smeared past of Europe and Asia. Usonia he calls the broad teeming band of this new nation across the enormous continent between Atlantic and Pacific. He preaches a project for Usonia:

> *It is easy to realize how the complexity of crude utilitarian construction in the mechanical infancy of our growth, like the crude scaffolding for some noble building, did violence to the landscape. . . . The crude purpose of pioneering days has been accomplished. The scaffolding may be taken down and the true work, the culture of a civilization, may appear.*

Like the life of many a preacher, prophet, exhorter, Frank Lloyd Wright's life has been stormy. He has raised children, had rows with wives, overstepped boundaries, got into difficulties with the law, divorcecourts, bankruptcy, always the yellow press yapping at his heels, his misfortunes yelled out in headlines in the evening papers: affairs with women, the nightmare horror of the burning of his house in Wisconsin.

By a curious irony

the building that is most completely his is the Imperial Hotel in Tokyo that was one of the few structures to come unharmed through the earthquake of 1923 (the day the cable came telling him that the building had stood saving so many hundreds of lives he writes was one of his happiest days)

and it was reading in German that most Americans first learned of his work.

His life has been full of arrogant projects unaccomplished. (How often does the preacher hear his voice echo back hollow from the empty hall, the draftsman watch the dust fuzz over the carefullycontrived plans, the architect see the rolledup blueprints curl yellowing and brittle in the filingcabinet.)

Twice he's rebuilt the house where he works in his grandfather's valley in Wisconsin after fires and disasters that would have smashed most men forever.

He works in Wisconsin,

an erect spare whitehaired man, his sons are architects, apprentices from all over the world come to work with him,

drafting the new city (he calls it Broadacre City).

Near and Far are beaten (to imagine the new city you must blot out every ingrained habit of the past, build a nation from the ground up with the new tools). For the architect there are only uses:

the incredible multiplication of functions, strength and tensions in metal, the dynamo, the electric coil, radio, the photoelectric cell, the internalcombustion motor,

glass

concrete;

and needs. (Tell us, doctors of philosophy, what are the needs of a man. At least a man needs to be notjailed notafraid nothungry notcold not'without love, not a worker for a power he has never seen

that cares nothing for the uses and needs of a man or a woman or a child.)

Building a building is building the lives of the workers and dwellers in the building.

The buildings determine civilization as the cells in the honeycomb the functions of bees.

Perhaps in spite of himself the arrogant draftsman, the dilettante in concrete, the bohemian artist for wealthy ladies desiring to pay for prominence with the startling elaboration of their homes has been forced by the logic of uses and needs, by the lifelong struggle against the dragging undertow of money in mortmain,

to draft plans that demand for their fulfillment a new life;

only in freedom can we build the Usonian city. His plans are coming to life. His blueprints, as once Walt Whitman's words, stir the young men:—

Frank Lloyd Wright,

patriarch of the new building,

not without honor except in his own country.

# Newsreel 64

WEIRD FISH DRAWN FROM SARGASSO SEA

by night when the rest of the plant was still dim figures ugly in gasmasks worked in the long low building back of the research laboratory

RUM RING LINKS NATION

*All around the water tank
Waitin' for a train*

WOMAN SLAIN MATE HELD

BUSINESS MEN NOT ALARMED OVER COMING ELECTION

GRAVE FOREBODING UNSETTLES MOSCOW

LABOUR CHIEFS RULED OUT OF PULPITS

imagination boggles at the reports from Moscow. These murderers have put themselves beyond the pale. They have shown themselves to be the mad dogs of the world

WALLSTREET EMPLOYERS BANISH CHRISTMAS WORRIES AS BONUSES ROLL IN

*Left my girl in the mountains
Left her standin' in the rain*

OUR AIR SUPREMACY ACCLAIMED

LAND SO MOUNTAINOUS IT STANDS ON END

*Got myself in trouble
An' shot a county sheriff down*

In the stealth of the night have you heard padded feet creeping toward you?

TROTZKY OPENS ATTACK ON STALIN

STRANGLED MAN DEAD IN STREET

*Moanin' low . . .*
*My sweet man's gonna go*

HUNT HATCHET WOMAN WHO ATTACKED
SOCIETY MATRON

CLASPS HANDS OF HEROES

GIRL DYING IN MYSTERY PLUNGE

*He's the kind of man that needs the kind of woman like me*

COMPLETELY LOST IN FOG OVER MEXICO

ASSERT RUSSIA RISING

*For I'm dancin' with tears in my eyes*
*'Cause the girl in my arms isn't you*

SIX HUNDRED PUT TO DEATH AT ONCE
IN CANTON

SEE BOOM YEAR AHEAD

this checking we do for you in our investors consulting
service, we analyze every individual security you own and
give you an impartial report and rating thereon. Periodically
through the year we keep you posted on important developments. If danger signals suddenly develop, we advise you
promptly

## The Camera Eye (49)

walking from Plymouth to North Plymouth through the
raw air of Massachusetts Bay at each step a small cold
squudge through the sole of one shoe

looking out past the gray frame houses under the
robin'segg April sky across the white dories anchored in the
bottleclear shallows across the yellow sandbars and the slaty
bay ruffling to blue to the eastward

this is where the immigrants landed the roundheads the
sackers of castles the kingkillers haters of oppression this is
where they stood in a cluster after landing from the crowded
ship that stank of bilge    on the beach that belonged to no

one    between the ocean that belonged to no one and the
enormous forest that belonged to no one that stretched over
the hills where the deertracks were up the green rivervalleys
where the redskins grew their tall corn in patches forever
into the incredible west

for threehundred years the immigrants toiled into the
west

and now today

walking from Plymouth to North Plymouth suddenly
round a bend in the road beyond a little pond and yellow-
twigged willows hazy with green you see the Cordage    huge
sheds and buildings companyhouses all the same size all
grimed the same color a great square chimney long roofs
sharp ranked squares and oblongs cutting off the sea in
Plymouth Cordage    this is where another immigrant
worked hater of oppression who wanted a world unfenced

when they fired him from the cordage he peddled fish
the immigrants in the dark framehouses knew him    bought
his fish listened to his talk following his cart around from
door to door    you ask them    What was he like?    why
are they scared to talk of Bart scared because they knew him
scared eyes narrowing black with fright?    a barber the
man in the little grocerystore the woman he boarded with
in scared voices they ask Why won't they believe?    We
knew him    We seen him every day Why won't they believe
that day we buy the eels?

only the boy isn't scared

pencil scrawls in my notebook the scraps of recollection
the broken halfphrases the effort to intersect word with word
to dovetail clause with clause to rebuild out of mangled
memories unshakably (Old Pontius Pilate) the truth

the boy walks shyly browneyed beside me to the station
talks about how Bart helped him with his homework wants
to get ahead    why should it hurt him to have known Bart?

wants to go to Boston University    we shake hands
don't let them scare you

accustomed the smokingcar accustomed the jumble of
faces rumble cozily homelike toward Boston through the
gathering dark    how can I make them feel how our fathers

our uncles haters of oppression came to this coast      how
say     Don't let them scare you      make them feel who are
your oppressors America

rebuild the ruined words worn slimy in the mouths of
lawyers districtattorneys collegepresidents judges      without
the old words the immigrants haters of oppression brought
to Plymouth how can you know who are your betrayers
America

or that this fishpeddler you have in Charlestown Jail is
one of your founders Massachusetts?

# Newsreel 65

*Love oh love oh careless love*
*Like a thief comes in the night*

*Bring me a pillow for my poor head*
*A hammer for to knock out my brains*
*For the whiskey has ruined this body of mine*
*And the red lights have run me insane*

*But I'll love my baby till the sea runs dry*

This great new searchlight sunburns you two miles
away

*Till the rocks all dissolve by the sun*
*Oh ain't it hard?*

Smythe according to the petition was employed testing
the viscosity of lubricating oil in the Okmulgee plant of the
company on July 12, 1924. One of his duties was to pour
benzol on a hot vat where it was boiled down so that the
residue could be examined. Day after day he breathed the
not unpleasant fumes from the vat.

One morning about a year later Smythe cut his face
while shaving and noticed that the blood flowed for hours
in copious quantities from the tiny wound. His teeth also
began to bleed when he brushed them and when the flow

failed to stop after several days he consulted a doctor. The diagnosis was that the benzol fumes had broken down the walls of his blood vessels.

After eighteen months in bed, during which he slept only under the effect of opiates, Smythe's spleen and tonsils were removed. Meanwhile the periodic blood transfusions were resorted to in an effort to keep his blood supply near normal.

In all more than thirty-six pints of blood were infused through his arms until when the veins had been destroyed it was necessary to cut into his body to open other veins. During the whole time up to eight hours before his death, the complaint recited, he was conscious and in pain.

## Mary French

The first job Mary French got in New York she got through one of Ada's friends. It was sitting all day in an artgallery on Eighth Street where there was an exposition of sculpture and answering the questions of ladies in flowing batiks who came in in the afternoons to be seen appreciating art. After two weeks of that, the girl she was replacing came back and Mary, who kept telling herself she wanted to be connected with something real, went and got herself a job in the ladies' and misses' clothing department at Bloomingdale's. When the summer layoff came, she was dropped, but she went home and wrote an article about departmentstore workers for *The Freeman* and on the strength of it got herself a job doing research on wages, living-costs, and the spread between wholesale and retail prices in the dress industry for the International Ladies' Garment Workers. She liked the long hours digging out statistics, the talk with the organizers, the wisecracking radicals, the workingmen and girls who came into the crowded dingy office she shared with two or three other researchers. At last she felt what she was doing was real.

Ada had gone to Michigan with her family and had left Mary in the apartment on Madison Avenue. Mary was relieved to have her gone; she was still fond of her, but their interests were so different and they had silly arguments about the relative importance of art and social justice that left them tired and cross at each other so that sometimes they wouldn't speak for several days; and then they hated each other's friends. Still, Mary couldn't help being fond of Ada. They were such old friends and Ada forked out so generously for the strikers' defense committees, legal-aid funds and everything that Mary suggested; she was a very openhanded girl, but her point of view was hopelessly rich, she had no social consciousness. The apartment got on Mary French's nerves, too, with its pastelcolored knickknacks and the real Whistler and the toothick rugs and the toosoft boxsprings on the bed and the horrid little satin tassels on everything; but Mary was making so little money that not paying rent was a great help.

Ada's apartment came in very handy the night of the big meeting in Madison Square Garden to welcome the classwar prisoners released from Atlanta. Mary French, who had been asked to sit on the platform, overheard some members of the committee saying that they had no place to put up Ben Compton. They were looking for a quiet hideout where he could have a rest and shake the D. J. operatives who'd been following him around everywhere since he'd gotten to New York. Mary went up to them and in a whisper suggested her place. So after the meeting she waited in a yellow taxicab at the corner of Twentyninth and Madison until a tall pale man with a checked cap pulled way down over his face got in and sat down shakily beside her.

When the cab started, he put his steelrimmed glasses back on.

'Look back and see if a gray sedan's following us,' he said.

'I don't see anything,' said Mary.

'Oh, you wouldn't know it if you saw it,' he grumbled.

To be on the safe side they left the cab at the Grand Central Station and walked without speaking a way up Park Avenue and then west on a cross-street and down Madison again. Mary plucked his sleeve to stop him in front of the door. Once in the apartment he made Mary shoot the bolt and let himself drop into a chair without taking off his cap or his overcoat.

He didn't say anything. His shoulders were shaking. Mary didn't like to stare at him. She didn't know what to do. She puttered around the livingroom, lit the gaslogs, smoked a cigarette, and then she went into the kitchenette to make coffee. When she got back he'd taken off his things and was warming his bigknuckled hands at the gaslogs.

'You must excuse me, comrade,' he said in a dry hoarse voice. 'I'm all in.'

'Oh, don't mind me,' said Mary. 'I thought you might want some coffee.'

'No coffee . . . hot milk,' he said hurriedly. His teeth were chattering as if he were cold. She came back with a cup of hot milk. 'Could I have some sugar in it?' he said, and almost smiled.

'Of course,' she said. 'You made a magnificent speech, so restrained and kind of fiery. . . . It was the best in the whole meeting.'

'You didn't think I seemed agitated? I was afraid I'd go to pieces and not be able to finish. . . . You're sure nobody knows this address, or the phone number? You're sure we weren't followed?'

'I'm sure nobody'll find you here on Madison Avenue. . . . It's the last place they'd look.'

'I know they are trailing me,' he said with a shudder and dropped into a chair again.

They were silent for a long time. Mary could hear the gaslogs and the little sucking sips he drank the hot milk with. Then she said: 'It must have been terrible.'

He got to his feet and shook his head as if he didn't want to talk about it. He was a young man lankilybuilt, but he walked up and down in front of the gaslogs with a strangely elderly dragging walk. His face was white as a mushroom, with sags of brownish skin under his eyes.

'You see,' he said, 'it's like people who've been sick and have to learn to walk all over again . . . don't pay any attention.'

He drank several cups of hot milk and then he went to bed. She went into the other bedroom and closed the door and lay down on the bed with a pile of books and pamphlets. She had some legal details to look up.

She had just gotten sleepy and crawled under the covers herself when a knocking woke her. She snatched at her bathrobe and jumped up and opened the door. Ben Compton stood there trembling wearing a long unionsuit. He'd taken off his glasses and they'd left a red band across the bridge of his nose. His hair was rumpled and his knobby feet were bare.

'Comrade,' he stammered, 'd'you mind if I . . . d'you mind if I . . . d'you mind if I lie on the bed beside you? I can't sleep. I can't stay alone.'

'You poor boy. . . . Get into bed, you are shivering,' she said. She lay down beside him, still wearing her bathrobe and slippers.

'Shall I put out the light?' He nodded. 'Would you like some aspirin?' He shook his head. She pulled the covers up under his chin as if he were a child. He lay there on his back staring with wideopen black eyes at the ceiling. His teeth were clenched. She put her hand on his forehead as she would on a child's to see if he was feverish. He shuddered and drew away. 'Don't touch me,' he said.

Mary put out the light and tried to compose herself to sleep on the bed beside him. After a while he grabbed her hand and held it tight. They lay there in the dark side by side staring up at the ceiling. Then she felt his grip on her hand loosen; he was dropping off to sleep. She lay there beside him with her eyes open. She was afraid the slightest stir might wake him. Every time she fell asleep, she dreamed that detectives were breaking in the door and woke up with a shuddering start.

Next morning when she went out to go to the office, he was still asleep. She left a latchkey for him and a note explaining that there was food and coffee in the icebox. When she got home that afternoon, her heart beat fast as she went up in the elevator.

Her first thought after she'd opened the door was that he'd gone. The bedroom was empty. Then she noticed that the bathroom door was closed and that a sound of humming came from there.

She tapped. 'That you, Comrade Compton?' she said.

'Be right out.' His voice sounded firmer, more like the deep rich voice he'd addressed the meeting in. He came out smiling, long pale legs bristling with black hairs sticking oddly out from under Mary's lavender bathrobe.

'Hello, I've been taking a hot bath. This is the third I've taken. Doctor said they were a good thing. . . . You know, relax. . . .' He pulled out a pinkleather edition of Oscar Wilde's *Dorian Grey* from under his arm and shook it in front of her. 'Reading this tripe. . . . I feel better. . . . Say, comrade, whose apartment is this, anyway?'

'A friend of mine who's a violinist. . . . She's away till fall.'

'I wish she was here to play for us. I'd love to hear some good music. . . . Maybe you're musical.' Mary shook her head.

'Could you eat some supper? I've brought some in.'

'I'll try . . . nothing too rich . . . I've gotten very dyspeptic. . . . So you thought I spoke all right?'

'I thought it was wonderful,' she said.

'After supper I'll look at the papers you brought in. . . . If the kept press only wouldn't always garble what we say.'

She heated some peasoup and made toast and bacon and eggs

and he ate up everything she gave him. While they were eating, they had a nice cozy talk about the movement. She told him about her experiences in the great steelstrike. She could see he was beginning to take an interest in her. They'd hardly finished eating before he began to turn white. He went to the bathroom and threw up.

'Ben, you poor kid,' she said, when he came back looking haggard and shaky. 'It's awful.'

'Funny,' he said in a weak voice. 'When I was in the Bergen County jail over there in Jersey I came out feeling fine . . . but this time it's hit me.'

'Did they treat you badly?'

His teeth clenched and the muscles of his jaw stiffened, but he shook his head. Suddenly he grabbed her hand and his eyes filled with tears. 'Mary French, you're being too good to me,' he said. Mary couldn't help throwing her arms around him and hugging him. 'You don't know what it means to find a . . . to find a sweet girl comrade,' he said, pushing her gently away. 'Now let me see what the papers did to what I said.'

After Ben had been hiding out in the apartment for about a week, the two of them decided one Saturday night that they loved each other. Mary was happier than she'd ever been in her life. They romped around like kids all Sunday and went out walking in the park to hear the band play in the evening. They threw sponges at each other in the bathroom and teased each other while they were getting undressed; they slept tightly clasped in each other's arms.

In spite of never going out except at night, in the next few days Ben's cheeks began to have a little color in them and his step began to get some spring into it.

'You've made me feel like a man again, Mary,' he'd tell her a dozen times a day. 'Now I'm beginning to feel like I could do something again. After all, the revolutionary labor movement's just beginning in this country. The tide's going to turn, you watch. It's begun with Lenin and Trotzky's victories in Russia.' There was something moving to Mary in the way he pronounced those three words: Lenin, Trotzky, Russia.

After a couple of weeks he began to go to conferences with radical leaders. She never knew if she'd find him in or not when she got home from work. Sometimes it was three or four in the morning before he came in tired and haggard. Always his pockets bulged with literature and leaflets. Ada's fancy livingroom gradually filled up with badlyprinted newspapers and pamphlets and mimeographed sheets. On the mantelpiece among Ada's Dresdenchina figures playing musical instruments were stacked the three volumes of *Capital* with places marked in them with pencils. In the evening he'd read Mary pieces of a pamphlet he was working on, modeled on Lenin's *What's to Be Done?* and ask with knitted brows if he was clear, if simple workers would understand what he meant.

One Sunday in August he made her go with him to Coney Island where he'd made an appointment to meet his folks; he'd figured it would be easier to see them in a crowded place. He didn't want the dicks to trail him home and then be bothering the old people or his sister who had a good job as secretary to a prominent businessman. When they met, it was some time before the Comptons noticed Mary at all. They sat at a big round table at Stauch's and drank nearbeer. Mary found it hard to sit still in her chair when the Comptons all turned their eyes on her at once. The old people were very polite with gentle manners, but she could see that they wished she hadn't come. Ben's sister Gladys gave her one hard mean stare and then paid no attention to her. Ben's brother Sam, a stout prosperous-looking Jew who Ben had said had a small business, a sweatshop probably, was polite and oily. Only Izzy, the youngest brother, looked anything like a workingman and he was more likely a gangster. He treated her with kidding familiarity; she could see he thought of her as Ben's moll. They all admired Ben, she could see; he was the bright boy, the scholar, but they felt sorry about his radicalism as if it was an unfortunate sickness he had contracted. Still his name in the paper, the applause in Madison Square Garden, the speeches calling him a working-class hero, had impressed them.

After Ben and Mary had left the Comptons and were going into the subwaystation, Ben said bitterly in her ear, 'Well, that's the Jewish family. . . . What do you think of it? Some strait-jacket. . . . It 'ud be the same if I killed a man or ran a string of whorehouses. . . . even in the movement you can't break away from them.'

'But, Ben, it's got it's good side . . . they'd do anything in the world for you . . . my mother and me, we really hate each other.'

Ben needed clothes and so did Mary; she never had any of the money from the job left over from week to week, so for the first time in her life she wrote her mother asking for five hundred dollars. Her mother sent back a check with a rather

nice letter saying that she'd been made Republican State
Committeewoman and that she admired Mary's independence
because she'd always believed women had just as much right
as men to earn their own living and maybe women in politics
would have a better influence than she'd once thought, and
certainly Mary was showing grit in carving out a career for
herself, but she did hope she'd soon come around to seeing that
she could have just as interesting a career if she'd come back
to Colorado Springs and occupy the social position her mother's
situation entitled her to. Ben was so delighted when he saw the
check, he didn't ask what Mary had got the money for.

'Five hundred bucks is just what I needed,' he said. 'I hadn't
wanted to tell you, but they want me to lead a strike over in
Bayonne . . . rayonworkers . . . you know the old munition-
plants made over to make artificial silk. . . . It's a tough town
and the workers are so poor they can't pay their union dues
. . . but they've got a fine radical union over there. It's important to get a foothold in the new industries . . . that's where
the old sellout organizations of the A.F. of L. are failing. . . .
Five hundred bucks'll take care of the printing bill.'

'Oh, Ben, you are not rested yet. I'm so afraid they'll arrest
you again.'

He kissed her. 'Nothing to worry about.'

'But, Ben, I wanted you to get some clothes.'

'This is a fine suit. What's the matter with this suit? Didn't
Uncle Sam give me this suit himself? . . . Once we get things
going, we'll get you over to do publicity for us . . . enlarge your
knowledge of the clothing industry. Oh, Mary, you're a wonderful girl to have raised that money.'

That fall, when Ada came back, Mary moved out and got
herself a couple of small rooms on West Fourth Street in the
Village, so that Ben could have some place to go when he came
over to New York. That winter she worked tremendously hard,
still handling her old job and at the same time doing publicity
for the strikes Ben led in several Jersey towns. 'That's nothing
to how hard we'll have to work when we have soviets in
America,' Ben would say when she'd ask him didn't he think
they'd do better work if they didn't always try to do so many
things at once.

She never knew when Ben was going to turn up. Sometimes
he'd be there every night for a week and sometimes he would
be away for a month and she'd only hear from him through
newsreleases about meetings, picketlines broken up, injunctions

fought in the courts. Once they decided they'd get married and have a baby, but the comrades were calling for Ben to come and organize the towns around Passaic and he said it would distract him from his work and that they were young and that there'd be plenty of time for that sort of thing after the revolution. Now was the time to fight. Of course she could have the baby if she wanted to, but it would spoil her usefulness in the struggle for several months and he didn't think this was the time for it. It was the first time they'd quarreled. She said he was heartless. He said they had to sacrifice their personal feelings for the workingclass, and stormed out of the house in a temper. In the end she had an abortion, but she had to write her mother again for money to pay for it.

She threw herself into her work for the strikecommittee harder than ever. Sometimes for weeks she slept only four or five hours a night. She took to smoking a great deal. There was always a cigarette resting on a corner of her typewriter. The fine ash dropped into the pages as they came from the multigraph machine. Whenever she could be spared from the office, she went around collecting money from wealthy women, inducing prominent liberals to come and get arrested on the picketline, coaxing articles out of newspapermen, traveling around the country to find charitable people to go on bailbonds. The strikers, the men and women and children on picketlines, in soupkitchens, being interviewed in the dreary front parlors of their homes stripped of furniture they hadn't been able to make the last payment on, the buses full of scabs, the cops and deputies with sawedoff shotguns guarding the tall palings of the silent enormouslyextended oblongs of the blackwindowed millbuildings, passed in a sort of dreamy haze before her, like a show on the stage, in the middle of the continuous typing and multigraphing, the writing of letters and workingup of petitions, the long grind of officework that took up her days and nights.

She and Ben had no life together at all any more. She thrilled to him the way the workers did at meetings when he'd come to the platform in a tumult of stamping and applause and talk to them with flushed cheeks and shining eyes, talking clearly directly to each man and woman, encouraging them, warning them, explaining the economic setup to them. The millgirls were all crazy about him. In spite of herself Mary French would get a sick feeling in the pit of her stomach at the way they looked at him and at the way some big buxom freshlooking woman would stop him sometimes in the hall outside the office and put her hand on his arm and make him pay attention to her. Mary working away at her desk, with her tongue bitter and her mouth dry from too much smoking, would look at her yellowstained fingers and push her untidy uncurled hair off her forehead and feel badlydressed and faded and unattractive. If he'd give her one smile just for her before he bawled her out before the whole office because the leaflets weren't ready, she'd feel happy all day. But mostly he seemed to have forgotten that they'd been lovers.

After the A.F. of L. officials from Washington, in expensive overcoats and silk mufflers who smoked twentyfivecent cigars and spat on the floor of the office, had taken the strike out of Ben's hands and settled it, he came back to the room on Fourth Street late one night just as Mary was going to bed. His eyes were redrimmed from lack of sleep and his cheeks were sunken and gray. 'Oh, Ben,' she said and burst out crying. He was cold and bitter and desperate. He sat for hours on the edge of her bed telling her in a sharp monotonous voice about the sellout and the wrangles between the leftwingers and the old-line Socialists and laborleaders, and how now that it was all over here was his trial for contempt of court coming up.

'I feel so bad about spending the workers' money on my defense. . . . I'd as soon go to jail as not . . . but it's the precedent. . . . We've got to fight every case and it's the one way we can use the liberal lawyers, the lousy fakers. . . . And it costs so much and the union's broke and I don't like to have them spend the money on me . . . but they say that if we win my case, then the cases against the other boys will all be dropped. . . .'

'The thing to do,' she said, smoothing his hair off his forehead, 'is to relax a little.'

'You should be telling me?' he said and started to unlace his shoes.

It was a long time before she could get him to get into bed. He sat there halfundressed in the dark shivering and talking about the errors that had been committed in the strike. When at last he'd taken his clothes off and stood up to lay them on a chair, he looked like a skeleton in the broad swath of gray glare that cut across the room from the streetlight outside her window. She burst out crying all over again at the sunken look of his chest and the deep hollows inside his collarbone.

'What's the matter, girl?' Ben said gruffly. 'You crying because you haven't got a Valentino to go to bed with you?'

'Nonsense, Ben, I was just thinking you need fattening up
... you poor kid, you work so hard.'

'You'll be going off with a goodlooking young bondsalesman
one of these days, like you were used to back in Colorado
Springs. . . . I know what to expect . . . I don't give a damn
. . . I can make the fight alone.'

'Oh, Ben, don't talk like that . . . you know I'm heart and
soul . . .' She drew him to her. Suddenly he kissed her.

Next morning they quarreled bitterly while they were dressing, about the value of her researchwork. She said that after
all he couldn't talk; the strike hadn't been such a wild success.
He went out without eating his breakfast. She went uptown in
a clenched fury of misery, threw up her job, and a few days
later went down to Boston to work on the Sacco-Vanzetti case
with the new committee that had just been formed.

She'd never been in Boston before. The town these sunny
winter days had a redbrick oldtime steelengraving look that
pleased her. She got herself a little room on the edge of the
slums back of Beacon Hill and decided that when the case
was won, she'd write a novel about Boston. She bought some
school copybooks in a little musty stationers' shop and started
right away taking notes for the novel. The smell of the new
copybook with its faint blue lines made her feel fresh and new.
After this she'd observe life. She'd never fall for a man again.
Her mother had sent her a check for Christmas. With that she
bought herself some new clothes and quite a becoming hat.
She started to curl her hair again.

Her job was keeping in touch with newspapermen and
trying to get favorable items into the press. It was uphill work.
Although most of the newspapermen who had any connection
with the case thought the two had been wrongly convicted,
they tended to say that they were just two wop anarchists, so
what the hell! After she'd been out to Dedham jail to talk to
Sacco and to Charlestown to talk to Vanzetti, she tried to tell
the U.P. man what she felt about them one Saturday night when
he was taking her out to dinner at an Italian restaurant on
Hanover Street.

He was the only one of the newspapermen she got really
friendly with. He was an awful drunk, but he'd seen a great
deal and he had a gentle detached manner that she liked. He
liked her for some reason, though he kidded her unmercifully
about what he called her youthful fanaticism. When he'd ask
her out to dinner and make her drink a lot of red wine, she'd

tell herself that it wasn't really a waste of time, that it was important for her to keep in touch with the press services. His name was Jerry Burnham.

'But, Jerry, how can you stand it? If the State of Massachusetts can kill those two innocent men in the face of the protest of the whole world, it'll mean that there never will be any justice in America ever again.'

'When was there any to begin with?' he said with a mirthless giggle, leaning over to fill up her glass. 'Ever heard of Tom Mooney?' The curly white of his hair gave a strangely youthful look to his puffy red face.

'But there's something so peaceful, so honest about them; you get such a feeling of greatness out of them. Honestly they are great men.'

'Everything you say makes it more remarkable that they weren't executed years ago.'

'But the workingpeople, the common people, they won't allow it.'

'It's the common people who get most fun out of the torture and execution of great men. . . . If it's not going too far back, I'd like to know who it was demanded the execution of our friend Jesus H. Christ?'

It was Jerry Burnham who taught her to drink. He lived himself in a daily alcoholic haze carrying his drinks carefully and circumspectly like an acrobat walking across a tight wire with a tableful of dishes balanced on his head. He was so used to working his twentyfourhour newsservice that he attended to his wires and the business of his office as casually as he'd pay the check in one speakeasy before walking around the corner to another. His kidneys were shot and he was on the winewagon he said, but she often noticed whiskey on his breath when she went into his office. He was so exasperating that she'd swear to herself each time she went out with him it was the last. No more wasting time when every minute was precious. But the next time he'd ask her out, she'd crumple up at once and smile and say yes and waste another evening drinking wine and listening to him ramble on. 'It'll all end in blindness and sudden death,' he said one night as he left her in a taxi at the corner of her street. 'But who cares? Who in hell cares . . . Who on the bloody louseinfested globe gives one little small microscopic vestigial hoot?'

As courtdecision after courtdecision was lost and the rancid Boston spring warmed into summer and the governor's commission reported adversely and no hope remained but a pardon from the governor himself, Mary worked more and more desperately hard. She wrote articles, she talked to politicians and ministers and argued with editors, she made speeches in unionhalls. She wrote her mother pitiful humiliating letters to get money out of her on all sorts of pretexts. Every cent she could scrape up went into the work of her committee. There were always stationery and stamps and telegrams and phonecalls to pay for. She spent long evenings trying to coax communists, socialists, anarchists, liberals into working together. Hurrying along the stonepaved streets, she'd be whispering to herself, 'They've got to be saved, they've got to be saved.' When at last she got to bed, her dreams were full of impossible tasks; she was trying to glue a broken teapot together and as soon as she got one side of it mended the other side would come to pieces again; she was trying to mend a rent in her skirt and by the time the bottom was sewed the top had come undone again; she was trying to put together pieces of a torn typewritten sheet, the telegram was of the greatest importance, she couldn't see, it was all a blur before her eyes; it was the evidence that would force a new trial, her eyes were too bad, when she had spelled out one word from the swollen throbbing letters she'd forgotten the last one; she was climbing a shaky hillside among black guttedlooking houses pitching at crazy angles where steelworkers lived, at each step she slid back, it was too steep, she was crying for help, yelling, sliding back. Then warm reassuring voices like Ben Compton's when he was feeling well were telling her that Public Opinion wouldn't allow it, that after all Americans had a sense of Justice and Fair Play, that the Workingclass would rise; she'd see crowded meetings, slogans, banners, glary billboards with letters pitching into perspective saying: *Workers of the World Unite*, she'd be marching in the middle of crowds in parades of protest. They Shall Not Die.

She'd wake up with a start, bathe and dress hurriedly, and rush down to the office of the committee, snatching up a glass of orangejuice and a cup of coffee on the way. She was always the first there; if she slackened her work for a moment, she'd see their faces, the shoemaker's sharplymodeled pale face with the flashing eyes and the fishpeddler's philosophical mustaches and his musing unscared eyes. She'd see behind them the electric chair as clear as if it were standing in front of her desk in the stuffy crowded office.

July went by all too fast. August came. A growing crowd of all sorts of people began pouring through the office: old friends, wobblies who'd hitchhiked from the Coast, politicians interested in the Italian vote, lawyers with suggestions for the defense, writers, outofwork newspapermen, cranks and phonies of all kinds attracted by rumors of an enormous defensefund. She came back one afternoon from speaking in a union hall in Pawtucket and found G. H. Barrow sitting at her desk. He had written a great pile of personal telegrams to senators, congressmen, ministers, laborleaders, demanding that they join in the protest in the name of justice and civilization and the workingclass, long telegrams and cables at top rates. She figured out the cost as she checked them off. She didn't know how the committee could pay for them, but she handed them to the messengerboy waiting outside. She could hardly believe that those words had made her veins tingle only a few weeks before. It shocked her to think how meaningless they seemed to her now like the little cards you get from a onecent fortune-telling machine. For six months now she'd been reading and writing the same words every day.

Mary didn't have time to be embarrassed meeting George Barrow. They went out together to get a plate of soup at a cafeteria talking about nothing but the case as if they'd never known each other before. Picketing the State House had begun again, and as they came out of the restaurant Mary turned to him and said, 'Well, George, how about going up and getting arrested. . . . There's still time to make the afternoon papers. Your name would give us back and front page.'

He flushed red, and stood there in front of the restaurant in the noontime crowd looking tall and nervous and popeyed in his natty lightgray suit. 'But, my dear g-g-girl, I . . . if I thought it would do the slightest good I would . . . I'd get myself arrested or run over by a truck . . . but I think it would rob me of whatever usefulness I might have.'

Mary French looked him straight in the eye, her face white with fury. 'I didn't think you'd take the risk,' she said, clipping each word off and spitting it in his face. She turned her back on him and hurried to the office.

It was a sort of relief when she was arrested herself. She'd planned to keep out of sight of the cops, as she had been told her work was too valuable to lose, but she'd had to run up the Hill with a set of placards for a new batch of picketers who had gone off without them. There was nobody in the office she could send.

She was just crossing Beacon Street when two large polite cops suddenly appeared, one on each side of her. One of them said, 'Sorry, Miss, please come quietly,' and she found herself sitting in the dark patrolwagon. Driving to the policestation, she had a soothing sense of helplessness and irresponsibility. It was the first time in weeks she had felt herself relax. At the Joy Street Station they booked her, but they didn't put her in a cell. She sat on a bench opposite the window with two Jewish garmentworkers and a welldressed woman in a flowered summer dress with a string of pearls round her neck and watched the men picketers pouring through into the cells. The cops were polite, everybody was jolly; it seemed like a kind of game, it was hard to believe anything real was at stake.

In a crowd that had just been unloaded from the wagon on the steep street outside the policestation, she caught sight of a tall man she recognized as Donald Stevens from his picture in *The Daily*. A redfaced cop held on to each of his arms. His shirt was torn open at the neck and his necktie had a stringy look as if somebody had been yanking on it. The first thing Mary thought was how handsomely he held himself. He had steelgray hair and a brown outdoorlooking skin and luminous gray eyes over high cheekbones. When he was led away from the desk, she followed his broad shoulders with her eyes into the gloom of the cells. The woman next to her whispered in an awed voice that he was being held for inciting to riot instead of sauntering and loitering like the rest. Five thousand dollars bail. He had tried to hold a meeting on Boston Common.

Mary had been there about a halfhour when little Mr Feinstein from the office came round with a tall fashionablydressed man in a linen suit who put up the bail for her. At the same time Donald Stevens was bailed out. The four of them walked down the hill from the policestation together. At the corner the man in the linen suit said, 'You two were too useful to leave in there all day. . . . Perhaps we'll see you at the Bellevue . . . suite D, second floor.' Then he waved his hand and left them. Mary was so anxious to talk to Donald Stevens she didn't think to ask the man's name. Events were going past her faster than she could focus her mind on them.

Mary plucked at Donald Stevens's sleeve, she and Mr Feinstein both had to hurry to keep up with his long stride. 'I'm Mary French,' she said. 'What can we do? . . . We've got to do something.'

He turned to her with a broad smile as if he'd seen her for the first time. 'I've heard of you,' he said. 'You're a plucky little girl . . . you've been putting up a real fight in spite of your liberal committee.'

'But they've done the best they could,' she said.

'We've got to get the entire workingclass of Boston out on the streets,' said Stevens in his deep rattling voice.

'We've gotten out the garmentworkers, but that's all.'

He struck his open palm with his fist. 'What about the Italians? What about the North End? Where's your office? Look what we did in New York. Why can't you do it here?' He leaned over toward her with a caressing confidential manner. Right away the feeling of being tired and harassed left her, without thinking she put her hand on his arm. 'We'll go and talk to your committee; then we'll talk to the Italian committee. Then we'll shake up the unions.'

'But, Don, we've only got thirty hours,' said Mr Feinstein in a dry tired voice. 'I have more confidence in political pressure being applied to the governor. You know he has presidential aspirations. I think the governor's going to commute the sentences.'

At the office Mary found Jerry Burnham waiting for her. 'Well, Joan of Arc,' he said, 'I was just going down to bail you out. But I see they've turned you loose.'

Jerry and Donald Stevens had evidently known each other before. 'Well, Jerry,' said Donald Stevens savagely, 'doesn't this shake you out of your cynical pose a little?'

'I don't see why it should. It's nothing new to me that collegepresidents are skunks.'

Donald Stevens drew off against the wall as if he were holding himself back from giving Jerry a punch in the jaw. 'I can't see how any man who has any manhood left can help getting red . . . even a pettybourgeois journalist.'

'My dear Don, you ought to know by this time that we hocked our manhood for a brass check about the time of the First World War . . . that is if we had any . . . I suppose there'd be various opinions about that.'

Donald Stevens had already swung on into the inner office. Mary found herself looking into Jerry's reddening face, not knowing what to say. 'Well, Mary, if you have a need for a pickup during the day . . . I should think you would need it . . . I'll be at the old stand.'

'Oh, I won't have time,' Mary said coldly. She could hear

Donald Stevens's deep voice from the inner office. She hurried on after him.

The lawyers had failed. Talking, wrangling, arguing about how a lastminute protest could be organized, Mary could feel the hours ebbing, the hours of these men's lives. She felt the minutes dripping away as actually as if they were bleeding from her own wrists. She felt weak and sick. She couldn't think of anything. It was a relief to be out in the street trotting to keep up with Donald Stevens's big stride. They made a round of the committees. It was nearly noon, nothing was done.

Down on Hanover Street a palefaced Italian in a shabby Ford sedan hailed them. Stevens opened the door of the car. 'Comrade French, this is Comrade Strozzi . . . he's going to drive us around.'

'Are you a citizen?' she asked with an anxious frown.

Strozzi shook his head and smiled a thinlipped smile. 'Maybe they give me a free trip back to Italy,' he said.

Mary never remembered what they did the rest of the day. They drove all over the poorer Boston suburbs. Often the men they were looking for were out. A great deal of the time she spent in phonebooths calling wrong numbers. She couldn't seem to do anything right. She looked with numb staring eyes out of eyelids that felt like sandpaper at the men and women crowding into the office. Stevens had lost the irritated stinging manner he'd had at first. He argued with tradeunion officials, socialists, ministers, lawyers, with an aloof sarcastic coolness. 'After all, they are brave men. It doesn't matter whether they are saved or not any more, it's the power of the workingclass that's got to be saved,' he'd say. Everywhere there was the same opinion. A demonstration will mean violence, will spoil the chance that the governor will commute at the last moment. Mary had lost all her initiative. Suddenly she'd become Donald Stevens's secretary. She was least unhappy when she was running small errands for him.

Late that night she went through all the Italian restaurants on Hanover Street looking for an anarchist Stevens wanted to see. Every place was empty. There was a hush over everything. Deathwatch. People kept away from each other as if to avoid some contagion. At the back of a room in a little upstairs speakeasy she saw Jerry Burnham sitting alone at a table with a jigger of whiskey and a bottle of gingerale in front of him. His face was white as a napkin and he was teetering gently in his chair. He stared at her without seeing her. The waiter was bending over him shaking him. He was hopelessly drunk.

It was a relief to run back to the office where Stevens was still trying to line up a general strike. He gave her a searching look when she came in. 'Failed again,' she said bitterly. He put down the telephone receiver, got to his feet, strode over to the line of hooks on the grimy yellow wall and got down his hat and coat. 'Mary French, you're deadtired. I'm going to take you home.'

They had to walk around several blocks to avoid the cordon of police guarding the State House.

'Ever played tug of war?' Don was saying. 'You pull with all your might, but the other guys are heavier and you feel yourself being dragged their way. You're being pulled forward faster than you're pulling back. . . . Don't let me talk like a defeatist. . . . We're not a couple of goddamned liberals,' he said, and burst into a dry laugh. 'Don't you hate lawyers?'

They were standing in front of the bowfronted brick house where she had her room.

'Goodnight, Don,' she said.

'Goodnight, Mary, try and sleep.'

Monday was like another Sunday. She woke late. It was an agony getting out of bed. It was a fight to put on her clothes, to go down to the office and face the defeated eyes. The people she met on the street seemed to look away from her when she passed them. Deathwatch. The streets were quiet, even the traffic seemed muffled as if the whole city were under the terror of dying that night. The day passed in a monotonous mumble of words, columns in newspapers, telephone calls. Deathwatch. That night she had a moment of fierce excitement when she and Don started for Charlestown to join the protest parade. She hadn't expected they'd be so many. Gusts of singing, scattered bars of the *International*, burst and faded above the packed heads between the blank windows of the dingy houses. Deathwatch. On one side of her was a little man with eyeglasses who said he was a musicteacher, on the other a Jewish girl, a member of the Ladies' Fullfashioned Hosiery Workers. They linked arms. Don was in the front rank, a little ahead. They were crossing the bridge. They were walking on cobbles on a badly-lighted street under an elevated structure. Trains roared overhead. 'Only a few blocks from Charlestown jail,' a voice yelled. This time the cops were using their clubs. There was the clatter of the horses' hoofs on the cobbles and the whack thud whack thud of the clubs. And way off the jangle of patrolwagons. Mary was terribly scared. A big truck was bearing down on her. She jumped to one side out of the way behind one of the girder supports. Two cops had hold of her. She clung to the grimy girder. A cop was cracking her on the hand with his club. She wasn't much hurt, she was in a patrolwagon, she'd lost her hat and her hair had come down. She caught herself thinking that she ought to have her hair bobbed if she was going to do much of this sort of thing.

'Anybody know where Don Stevens is?'

Don's voice came a little shakily from the blackness in front. 'That you, Mary?'

'How are you, Don?'

'O.K. Sure. A little battered round the head an' ears.'

'He's bleedin' terrible,' came another man's voice.

'Comrades, let's sing,' Don's voice shouted.

Mary forgot everything as her voice joined his voice, all their voices, the voices of the crowds being driven back across the bridge in singing:

*Arise, ye prisoners of starvation . . .*

# Newsreel 66

HOLMES DENIES STAY

*A better world's in birth*

Tiny wasps imported from Korea in battle to death with Asiatic beetle

BOY CARRIED MILE DOWN SEWER; SHOT
OUT ALIVE

CHICAGO BARS MEETINGS

*For justice thunders condemnation*

WASHINGTON KEEPS EYE ON RADICALS

*Arise rejected of the earth*

PARIS BRUSSELS MOSCOW GENEVA
ADD THEIR VOICES

*It is the final conflict*
*Let each stand in his place*

GEOLOGIST LOST IN CAVE SIX DAYS

*The international Party*

SACCO AND VANZETTI MUST DIE

*Shall be the human race.*

*Much I thought of you when I was lying in the death house – the singing, the kind tender voices of the children from the playground where there was all the life and the joy of liberty – just one step from the wall that contains the buried agony of three buried souls. It would remind me so often of you and your sister and I wish I could see you every moment, but I feel better that you will not come to the death house so that you could not see the horrible picture of three living in agony waiting to be electrocuted.*

## *The Camera Eye (50)*

they have clubbed us off the streets     they are stronger
they are rich      they hire and fire the politicians the
newspapereditors the old judges the small men with reputa-
tions the collegepresidents the wardheelers (listen businessmen collegepresidents judges     America will not forget her
betrayers) they hire the men with guns      the uniforms the
policecars the patrolwagons

all right you have won      you will kill the brave men
our friends tonight

there is nothing left to do     we are beaten     we the
beaten crowd together in these old dingy schoolrooms on
Salem Street     shuffle up and down the gritty creaking
stairs sit hunched with bowed heads on benches and hear
the old words of the haters of oppression     made new in
sweat and agony tonight

our work is over      the scribbled phrases      the nights
typing releases the smell of the printshop the sharp reek of
newprinted leaflets the rush for Western Union stringing
words into wires the search for stinging words to make you
feel who are your oppressors America

America our nation has been beaten by strangers who
have turned our language inside out who have taken the
clean words our fathers spoke and made them slimy and
foul

their hired men sit on the judge's bench they sit back
with their feet on the tables under the dome of the State
House they are ignorant of our beliefs they have the dollars
the guns the armed forces the powerplants

they have built the electricchair and hired the executioner to throw the switch

all right we are two nations

America our nation has been beaten by strangers who
have bought the laws and fenced off the meadows and cut
down the woods for pulp and turned our pleasant cities into
slums and sweated the wealth out of our people and when

they want to they hire the executioner to throw the switch

but do they know that the old words of the immigrants are being renewed in blood and agony tonight do they know that the old American speech of the haters of oppression is new tonight in the mouth of an old woman from Pittsburgh of a husky boilermaker from Frisco who hopped freights clear from the Coast to come here in the mouth of a Back Bay socialworker in the mouth of an Italian printer of a hobo from Arkansas   the language of the beaten nation is not forgotten in our ears tonight

the men in the deathhouse made the old words new before they died

*If it had not been for these things, I might have lived out my life talking at streetcorners to scorning men. I might have died unknown, unmarked, a failure. This is our career and our triumph. Never in our full life can we hope to do such work for tolerance, for justice, for man's understanding of man as now we do by an accident.*

now their work is over   the immigrants haters of oppression lie quiet in black suits in the little undertaking parlor in the North End   the city is quiet   the men of the conquering nation are not to be seen on the streets

they have won why are they scared to be seen on the streets?   on the streets you see only the downcast faces of the beaten   the streets belong to the beaten nation all the way to the cemetery where the bodies of the immigrants are to be burned   we line the curbs in the drizzling rain we crowd the wet sidewalks elbow to elbow silent pale looking with scared eyes at the coffins

we stand defeated America

# Newsreel 67

when things are upset, there's always chaos, said Mr Ford. Work can accomplish wonders and overcome chaotic conditions. When the Russian masses will learn to want more than they have, when they will want white collars, soap, better clothes, better shoes, better housing, better living conditions

> *I lift up my finger and I say tweet tweet*
> >                         *slush slush*
> >                         *now now*
> >                         *come come*

REPUBLIC-TRUMBULL STEEL MERGER VOTED

> *There along the dreamy Amazon*
> *We met upon the shore*
> *Tho' the love I knew is ever gone*

WHEAT OVERSOLD REACHES NEW HIGH

> *Dreams linger on*

the first thing the volunteer firefighters did was to open the windows to let the smoke out. This created a draft and the fire with a good thirty mile wind right from the ocean did the rest

RECORD TURNOVER IN INSURANCE SHARES AS
TRADING PROGRESSES

outside the scene was a veritable bedlam. Well-dressed women walked up and down wringing their hands, helpless to save their belongings, while from the windows of the upper stories there rained a shower of trunks, suitcases and clothing hurled out indiscriminately. Jewelry and bricabrac valued at thousands was picked up by the spectators from the lawn, who thrust the objects under their coats and disappeared

### BROKERS LOANS HIT NEW HIGH

*Change all of your gray skies*
*Turn them into gay skies*
*And keep sweeping the cobwebs off the moon*

### MARKETS OPTIMISTIC

learn new uses for cement. How to develop profitable concrete business. How to judge materials. How to figure jobs. How to reinforce concrete. How to build forms, roads, sidewalks, floors, foundations, culverts, cellars

*And even tho' the Irish and the Dutch*
*Say it don't amount to much*
*Fifty million Frenchmen can't be wrong*

### STAR-SPANGLED BANDIT GANG ROBS DINERS

### MURDER BARES QUAKER STATE FANTASIES

### POKER SLAYER PRAISED

*Poor little Hollywood Rose*
*so all alone*
*No one in Hollywood knows*
*how sad she's grown*

### FIVE HUNDRED MILLIONS IN BANK DEAL

*Sure I love the dear silver that shines in your hair*
*And the brow that's all furrowed*
*And wrinkled with care*
*I kiss the dear fingers so toil worn for me*

### CARBONIC BUYS IN DRY ICE

### GAB MARATHON RUN FOR GOLD ON BROADWAY

the broad advertising of the bull markets, the wide extension of the ticker services, the equipping of branch brokerage offices with tickers, transparent, magnified translux stockquotation rolls have had the natural result of stirring up nation-wide interest in the stockmarket

## *Poor Little Rich Boy*

William Randolph Hearst was an only son, the only chick in the richlyfeathered nest of George and Phebe Hearst.

In eighteen-fifty George Hearst had left his folks and the farm in Franklin County, Missouri, and driven a team of oxen out to California. (In fortynine the sudden enormous flares of gold had filled the West;

the young men couldn't keep their minds on their plowing, on feeding the swill to the pigs, on threshing the wheat

when the fires of gold were sweeping the Pacific Slope. Cholera followed in the ruts of the oxcarts, they died of cholera round the campfires, in hastilybuilt chinchinfested cabins, they were picked off by hostile Indians, they blew each other's heads off in brawls.)

George Hearst was one of the few that made it;

he developed a knack for placermining;

as a prospector he had an accurate eye for picking a gold-bearing vein of quartz;

after seven years in El Dorado County he was a million-aire, Anaconda was beginning, he owned onesixth of the Ophir Mine, he was in on Comstock Lode.

In sixtyone he went back home to Missouri with his pockets full of nuggets and married Phebe Apperson and took her back by boat and across Panama to San Francisco the new hilly capital of the millionaire miners and bought a mansion for her beside the Golden Gate on the huge fogbound coast of the Pacific.

He owned vast ranges and ranches, raised cattle, ran race-horses, prospected in Mexico, employed five thousand men in his mines, on his estates, lost and won fortunes in mining deals, played poker at a century a chip, never went out without a bag of clinkers to hand out to old friends down on their uppers,

and died in Washington

a senator,

a rough diamond, a lusty beloved whitebearded old man with the big beak and sparrowhawk eyes of a breaker of trails, the beetling brows under the black slouch hat

of an oldtimer.

Mrs Hearst's boy was born in sixtythree.

Nothing too good for the only son.

The Hearsts doted on their boy;

the big lanky youngster grew up solemneyed and self-willed among servants and hired men, factotums, overseers, hangerson, old pensioners; his grandparents spoiled him; he always did everything he wanted. Mrs Hearst's boy must have everything of the best.

No lack of gold nuggets, twentydollar goldpieces, big silver cartwheels.

The boy had few playmates; he was too rich to get along with the others in the roughandtumble democracy of the boys growing up in San Francisco in those days. He was too timid and too arrogant; he wasn't liked.

His mother could always rent playmates with icecream, imported candies, expensive toys, ponies, fireworks always ready to set off. The ones he could buy he despised, he hankered always after the others.

He was great on practical jokes and pulling the leg of the grownups; when the new Palace Hotel was opened with a reception for General Grant he and a friend had themselves a time throwing down handfuls of birdshot on the glass roof of the court to the consternation of the bigwigs and stuffedshirts below.

Wherever they went royally the Hearsts could buy their way,

up and down the California coast, through ranches and miningtowns

in Nevada and in Mexico,

in the palace of Porfirio Diaz;

the old man had lived in the world, had rubbed shoulders with rich and poor, had knocked around in miners' hells, pushed his way through unblazed trails with a packmule. All his life Mrs Hearst's boy was to hanker after that world

hidden from him by a mist of millions;

the boy had a brain, appetites, an imperious will,

but he could never break away from the gilded apron-strings;

adventure became slumming.

He was sent to boardingschool at Saint Paul's, in Concord, New Hampshire. His pranks kept the school in an uproar. He was fired.

He tutored and went to Harvard

where he cut quite a swath as businessmanager of the *Lampoon*, a brilliant entertainer; he didn't drink much himself, he was softspoken and silent; he got the other boys drunk and paid the bills, bought the fireworks to celebrate Cleveland's election, hired the brassbands,

bought the creampies to throw at the actors from the box at the Old Howard,

the cannon crackers to blow out the lamps of herdic cabs with,

the champagne for the chorines.

He was rusticated and finally fired from Harvard, so the story goes, for sending to each of a number of professors a chamberpot with the professor's portrait tastefully engraved on it.

He went to New York. He was crazy about newspapers. Already he'd been hanging around the Boston newspaperoffices. In New York he was taken by Pulitzer's newfangled journalism. He didn't want to write; he wanted to be a newspaperman. (Newspapermen were part of that sharpcontoured world he wanted to see clear, the reallife world he saw distorted by a haze of millions, the ungraded lowlife world of American Democracy.)

Mrs Hearst's boy would be a newspaperman and a Democrat. (Newspapermen saw heard ate drank touched horsed kidded rubbed shoulders with real men, whored; that was life.)

He arrived home in California, a silent soft smiling solemneyed young man

dressed in the height of the London fashion.

When his father asked him what he wanted to do with his life,

he said he wanted to run the *Examiner* which was a moribund sheet in San Francisco which his father had taken over for a bad debt. It didn't seem much to ask. The old man couldn't imagine why Willie wanted the old rag instead of a mine or a ranch, but Mrs Hearst's boy always had his way.

Young Hearst went down to the *Examiner* one day

and turned the office topsyturvy. He had a knack for finding and using bright young men, he had a knack for using his own prurient hanker after the lusts and envies of plain unmonied lowlife men and women (the slummer sees only the streetwalkers, the dopeparlors, the strip acts and goes back uptown saying he knows the workingclass districts); the lowest common denominator;

manure to grow a career in,

the rot of democracy. Out of it grew rankly an empire of print. (Perhaps he liked to think of himself as the young Caius Julius flinging his millions away, tearing down emblems and traditions, making faces at togaed privilege, monopoly, stuffedshirts in office;

Caesar's life like his was a millionaire prank. Perhaps W. R. had read of republics ruined before;

Alcibiades, too, was a practical joker.)

The San Francisco *Examiner* grew in circulation, tickled the prurient hankers of the moneyless man

became *The Monarch of the Dailies.*

When the old man died, Mrs Hearst sold out of Anaconda for seven and a half millions of dollars. W. R. got the money from her to enter the New York field; he bought the *Morning Journal*

and started his race with the Pulitzers

as to who should cash in most

on the geewhizz emotion.

In politics he was the people's Democrat; he came out for Bryan in ninetysix; on the Coast he fought the Southern Pacific and the utilities and the railroad lawyers who were grabbing the state of California away from the first settlers; on election day in ninetysix his three papers in New York put out between them more than a million and a half copies, a record

that forced the *World* to cut its price to a penny.

When there's no news make news.

'You furnish the pictures and I'll furnish the war,' he's supposed to have wired Remington in Havana. The trouble in Cuba was a goldmine for circulation when Mark Hanna had settled national politics by planting McKinley in the White House.

Hearst had one of his bright young men engineer a jailbreak for Evangelina Cisneros, a fair Cuban revolutionist shoved into a dungeon by Weyler, and put on a big reception for her in Madison Square.

*Remember the 'Maine.'*

When McKinley was forced to declare war on Spain W. R.

had his plans all made to buy and sink a British steamer in the Suez Canal

but the Spanish fleet didn't take that route.

He hired the *Sylvia* and the *Buccaneer* and went down to Cuba himself with a portable press and a fleet of tugs

and brandishing a sixshooter went in with the longboat through the surf and captured twentysix unarmed halfdrowned Spanish sailors on the beach and forced them to kneel and kiss the American flag

in front of the camera.

Manila Bay raised the circulation of the *Morning Journal* to one million six hundred thousand.

When the Spaniards were licked, there was nobody left to heckle but the Mormons. Polygamy titillated the straphangers, and the sexlife of the rich, and penandink drawings of women in underclothes and prehistoric monsters in four colors. He discovered the sobsister: Annie Laurie, Dorothy Dix, Beatrice Fairfax. He splurged on comics, the Katzenjammer Kids, Buster Brown, Krazy Kat. Get excited when the public is excited;

his editorials hammered at malefactors of great wealth, trusts, the G.O.P., Mark Hanna and McKinley so shrilly that when McKinley was assassinated most Republicans in some way considered Hearst responsible for his death.

Hearst retorted by renaming the *Morning Journal* the *American*

and stepping into the limelight

wearing a black frockcoat and a tengallon hat, presidential timber,

the millionaire candidate of the common man.

Bryan made him president of the National Association of Democratic Clubs and advised him to start a paper in Chicago.

After Bryan's second defeat Hearst lined up with Charles F. Murphy in New York and was elected to Congress.

His headquarters were at the Holland House; the night of his election he gave a big free show of fireworks in Madison Square Garden; a mortar exploded and killed or wounded something like a hundred people; that was one piece of news the Hearst men made that wasn't spread on the front pages of the Hearst papers.

In the House of Representatives he was unpopular; it was

schooldays over again. The limp handshake, the solemn eyes set close to the long nose, the small flabby scornful smile were out of place among the Washington backslappers. He was ill at ease without his hired gang around him.

He was happier entertaining firstnighters and footlight favorites at the Holland House. In those years, when Broadway still stopped at Fortysecond Street,

Millicent Willson was a dancer in *The Girl from Paris;* she and her sister did a sister act together; she won a popularity contest in the *Morning Telegraph*

and the hand of

William Randolph Hearst.

In nineteen-four he spent a lot of money putting his name up in electric lights at the Chicago Convention to land the Democratic nomination, but Judge Parker and Wall Street got it away from him.

In nineteen-five he ran for Mayor of New York on a muni-cipalownership ticket.

In nineteen-six he very nearly got the governorship away from the solemnwhiskered Hughes There were Hearst for President clubs all over the country. He was making his way in politics spending millions to the tune of *Waltz Me Around Again, Willie.*

He managed to get his competitor James Gordon Bennett up in court for running indecent ads in the New York *Herald* and fined twentyfive thousand dollars, a feat which hardly con-tributed to his popularity in certain quarters.

In nineteen-eight he was running revelations about Stand-ard Oil, the Archbold letters that proved that the trusts were greasing the palms of the politicians in a big way. He was the candidate of the Independence Party, made up almost exclu-sively, so his enemies claimed, of Hearst employees.

(His fellowmillionaires felt he was a traitor to his class but when he was taxed with his treason he answered:

*You know I believe in property, and you know where I stand on personal fortunes, but isn't it better that I should represent in this country the dissatisfied than have somebody else do it who might not have the same real property relations that I may have?*)

By nineteen-fourteen, although he was the greatest news-paperowner in the country, the proprietor of hundreds of square

miles of ranching and mining country in California and Mexico,
 his affairs were in such a scramble he had trouble borrowing a million dollars,
 and politically he was ratpoison.


 All the millions he signed away
 all his skill at putting his own thoughts
 into the skull of the straphanger
 failed to bridge the tiny Rubicon between amateur and professional politics (perhaps he could too easily forget a disappointment buying a firstrate writer or an embroidered slipper attributed to Charlemagne or the gilded bed a king's mistress was supposed to have slept in).
 Sometimes he was high enough above the battle to see clear. He threw all the powers of his papers, all his brilliance as a publisher into an effort to keep the country sane and neutral during the first world war;
 he opposed loans to the Allies, seconded Bryan in his lonely fight to keep the interests of the United States as a whole paramount over the interests of the Morgan banks and the anglophile businessmen of the East;
 for his pains he was razzed as a pro-German,
 and when war was declared had detectives placed among his butlers,
 secretserviceagents ransacking his private papers, gumshoeing round his diningroom on Riverside Drive to investigate rumors of strange colored lights seen in his windows.
 He opposed the Peace of Versailles and the league of victorious nations
 and ended by proving that he was as patriotic as anybody
 by coming out for conscription
 and printing his papers with red white and blue borders and with little American flags at either end of the dateline and continually trying to stir up trouble across the Rio Grande
 and inflating the Yankee Doodle bogey,
 the biggest navy in the world.


 The people of New York City backed him up by electing Hearst's candidate for Mayor, Honest John Hylan,
 but Al Smith while he was still the sidewalks' hero rapped Hearst's knuckles when he tried to climb back onto the Democratic soundtruck.

In spite of enormous expenditures on forged documents he failed to bring about war with Mexico.

In spite of spraying hundreds of thousands of dollars into moviestudios he failed to put over his favorite moviestar as America's sweetheart.

And more and more the emperor of newsprint retired to his fief of San Simeon on the Pacific Coast, where he assembled a zoo, continued to dabble in movingpictures, collected warehouses full of tapestries, Mexican saddles, bricabrac, china, brocade, embroidery, old chests of drawers, tables and chairs, the loot of dead Europe,

built an Andalusian palace and a Moorish banquethall and there spends his last years amid the relaxing adulations of screenstars, admen, screenwriters, publicitymen, columnists, millionaire editors,

a monarch of that new El Dorado

where the warmedover daydreams of all the ghettos

are churned into an opiate haze

more scarily blinding to the moneyless man

more fruitful of millions

than all the clinking multitude of double eagles

the older Hearst minted out of El Dorado County in the old days (the empire of the printed word continues powerful by the inertia of bigness; but this power over the dreams

of the adolescents of the world

grows and poisons like a cancer),

and out of the westcoast haze comes now and then an old man's querulous voice

advocating the salestax,

hissing dirty names at the defenders of civil liberties for the workingman;

jail the reds,

praising the comforts of Baden-Baden under the blood and bludgeon rule of Handsome Adolph (Hearst's own loved invention, the lowest common denominator come to power

out of the rot of democracy)

complaining about the California incometaxes,

shrilling about the dangers of thought in the colleges.

Deport; jail.

Until he dies

the magnificent endlesslyrolling presses will pour out print for him, the whirring everywhere projectors will spit images for him,

a spent Caesar grown old with spending
never man enough to cross the Rubicon.

## Richard Ellsworth Savage

Dick Savage walked down Lexington to the office in the
Graybar Building. The December morning was sharp as steel,
bright glints cut into his eyes, splintering from storewindows,
from the glasses of people he passed on the street, from the
chromium rims of the headlights of automobiles. He wasn't
quite sure whether he had a hangover or not. In a jeweler's
window he caught sight of his face in the glass against the
black velvet backing, there was a puffy boiled look under the
eyes like in the photographs of the Prince of Wales. He felt sour
and gone in the middle like a rotten pear. He stepped into a
drugstore and ordered a bromoseltzer. At the sodafountain he
stood looking at himself in the mirror behind the glass shelf
with the gingeralebottles on it; his new darkblue broadcloth
coat looked well, anyway.

The black eyes of the sodajerker were seeking his eyes out.
'A heavy evening, eh?' Dick nodded and grinned. The sodajerker passed a thin redknuckled hand over his patentleather
hair. 'I didn't get off till one-thirty an' it takes me an hour to get
home on the subway. A whale of a chance I got to ...'

'I'm late at the office now,' said Dick and paid and walked
out, belching a little, into the sparkling morning street. He
walked fast, taking deep breaths. By the time he was standing
in the elevator with a sprinkling of stoutish fortyish welldressed
men, executives like himself getting to their offices late, he had
a definite sharp headache.

He'd hardly stretched his legs out under his desk when the
interoffice phone clicked. It was Miss Williams's voice: 'Good
morning, Mr Savage. We've been waiting for you . . . Mr
Moorehouse says please step into his office, he wants to speak
with you a minute before the staff conference.'

Dick got up and stood a second with his lips pursed, rocking
on the balls of his feet looking out the window over the ash-
colored blocks that stretched in a series of castiron molds east
to the chimneys of powerplants, the bridge, the streak of river
flashing back steel at the steelblue sky. Riveters shrilly clattered
in the new huge construction that was jutting up girder by
girder at the corner of Fortysecond. They all seemed inside his

head like a dentist's drill. He shuddered, belched, and hurried along the corridor into the large corner office.

J. W. was staring at the ceiling with his big jowly face as expressionless as a cow's. He turned his pale eyes on Dick without a smile. 'Do you realize there are seventyfive million people in this country unwilling or unable to go to a physician in time of sickness?' Dick twisted his face into a look of lively interest. He's been talking to Ed Griscolm, he said to himself. 'Those are the people the Bingham products have got to serve. He's touched only the fringes of this great potential market.'

'His business would be to make them feel they're smarter than the bigbugs who go to Battle Creek,' said Dick.

J. W. frowned thoughtfully.

Ed Griscolm had come in. He was a sallow long man with an enthusiastic flash in his eye that flickered on and off like an electriclight sign. He had a way of carrying his arms like a cheerleader about to lead a college yell.

Dick said 'Hello' without warmth.

'Top of the morning, Dick . . . a bit overhung I see. . . . Too bad, old man, too bad.'

'I was just saying, Ed,' J. W. went on in his slow even voice, 'that our talkingpoints should be, first, that they haven't scratched the top of their potential market of seventyfive million people and, second, that a properlyconducted campaign can eradicate the prejudice many people feel against proprietary medicines and substitute a feeling of pride in their use.'

'It's smart to be thrifty . . . that sort of thing,' shouted Ed.

'Selfmedication,' said Dick. 'Tell them the average sodajerker knows more about medicine today than the family physician did twentyfive years ago.'

'They think there's something hick about patent medicines,' yelled Ed Griscolm. 'We got to put patent medicines on Park Avenue.'

'Proprietary medicines,' said J. W. reprovingly.

Dick managed to wipe the smile off his face. 'We've got to break the whole idea,' he said, 'into its component parts.'

'Exactly.' J. W. picked up a carvedivory papercutter and looked at it in different angles in front of his face. The office was so silent they could hear the traffic roaring outside and the wind whistling between the steel windowframe and the steel window. Dick and Ed Griscolm held their breath. J. W. began to talk. 'The American public has become sophisticated . . . when I was a boy in Pittsburgh, all we thought of was display advertising, the appeal to the eye. Now with the growth of sophistication we must think of the other types of appeal, and the eradication of prejudice.... Bingo ... the name is out of date, it's all wrong. A man would be ashamed to lunch at the Metropolitan Club with a bottle of Bingo at his table ... that must be the talkingpoint.... Yesterday Mr Bingham seemed inclined to go ahead. He was balking a little at the cost of the campaign....'

'Never mind,' screeched Ed Griscolm, 'we'll nail the old buzzard's feet down yet.'

'I guess he has to be brought around gently, just as you were saying last night, J. W.,' said Dick in a low bland voice. 'They tell me Halsey of Halsey O'Connor's gone to bed with a nervous breakdown tryin' to get old Bingham to make up his mind.'

Ed Griscolm broke into a tittering laugh.

J. W. got to his feet with a faint smile. When J. W. smiled, Dick smiled too. 'I think he can be brought to appreciate the advantages connected with the name ... dignity ... established connections. ...' Still talking, J. W. led the way down the hall into the large room with a long oval mahogany table in the middle of it where the whole office was gathered. J. W. went first with his considerable belly waggling a little from side to side as he walked, and Dick and Ed Griscolm, each with an armful of typewritten projects in paleblue covers, followed a step behind him. Just as they were settling down after a certain amount of coughing and honking and J. W. was beginning about how there were seventyfive million people, Ed Griscolm ran out and came back with a neatlydrawn chart in blue and red and yellow lettering showing the layout of the proposed campaign. An admiring murmur ran round the table.

Dick caught a triumphant glance in his direction from Ed Griscolm. He looked at J. W. out of the corner of his eye. J. W. was looking at the chart with an expressionless face. Dick walked over to Ed Griscolm and patted him on the shoulder. 'A swell job, Ed, old man,' he whispered. Ed Griscolm's tense lips loosened into a smile. 'Well, gentlemen, what I'd like now is a snappy discussion,' said J. W. with a mean twinkle in his paleblue eye that matched for a second the twinkle of the small diamonds in his cufflinks.

While the others talked, Dick sat staring at J. W.'s hands spread out on the sheaf of typewritten papers on the table in front of him. Oldfashioned starched cuffs protruded from the sleeves of the perfectlyfitting doublebreasted gray jacket and out of them hung two pudgy strangely hicklooking hands with liverspots on them. All through the discussion Dick stared at the hands, all the time writing down phrases on his scratchpad and scratching them out. He couldn't think of anything. His brains felt boiled. He went on scratching away with his pencil at phrases that made no sense at all. On the fritz at the Ritz . . . Bingham's products cure the fits.

It was after one before the conference broke up. Everybody was congratulating Ed Griscolm on his layout. Dick heard his own voice saying it was wonderful, but it needed a slightly different slant.

'All right,' said J. W. 'How about finding that slightly different slant over the weekend? That's the idea I want to leave with every man here. I'm lunching with Mr Bingham Monday noon. I must have a perfected project to present.'

Dick Savage went back to his office and signed a pile of letters his secretary had left for him. Then he suddenly remembered he'd told Reggie Talbot he'd meet him for lunch at '63' to meet the girlfriend, and ran out, adjusting his blue muffler as he went down in the elevator. He caught sight of them at a table with their heads leaning together in the crinkled cigarettesmoke in the back of the crowded Saturdayafternoon speakeasy.

'Oh, Dick, hello,' said Reggie, jumping to his feet with his mild smile, grabbing Dick's hand and drawing him toward the table. 'I didn't wait for you at the office because I had to meet this one. . . . Jo, this is Mr Savage. The only man in New York who doesn't give a damn. . . . What'll you have to drink?'

The girl certainly was a knockout. When Dick let himself drop on the redleather settee beside her, facing Reggie's slender ashblond head and his big inquiring lightbrown eyes, he felt boozy and tired.

'Oh, Mr Savage, what's happened about the Bingham account? I'm so excited about it. Reggie can't talk about anything else. I know it's indiscreet to ask.' She looked earnestly in his face out of longlashed black eyes. They certainly made a pretty couple.

'Telling tales out of school, eh?' said Dick, picking up a breadstick and snapping it into his mouth.

'But you know, Dick, Jo and me . . . we talk about everything . . . it never goes any further. . . . And honestly, all the younger guys in the office think it's a damn shame J. W. didn't use your first layout. . . . Griscolm is going to lose the account for us if he isn't careful . . . it just don't click. . . . I think the old man's getting softening of the brain.'

'You know I've thought several times recently that J. W. wasn't in very good health. . . . Too bad. He's the most brilliant figure in the publicrelations field.' Dick heard an oily note come into his voice and felt ashamed in front of the youngsters and shut up suddenly. 'Say, Tony,' he called peevishly to the waiter. 'How about some cocktails? Give me a bacardi with a little absinthe in it, you know, my special. . . . Gosh, I feel a hundred years old.'

'Been burning the candle at both ends?' asked Reggie.

Dick twisted his face into a smirk. 'Oh, that candle,' he said. 'It gives me a lot of trouble.' They all blushed. Dick chuckled. 'By God, I don't think there are three other people in the city that have a blush left in them.'

They ordered more cocktails. While they were drinking, Dick felt the girl's eyes serious and dark fixed on his face. She lifted her glass to him. 'Reggie says you've been awfully sweet to him at the office. . . . He says he'd have been fired if it wasn't for you.'

'Who could help being sweet to Reggie? Look at him.' Reggie got red as a beet.

'The lad's got looks,' said the girl. 'But has he any brains?'

Dick began to feel better with the onionsoup and the third cocktail. He began to tell them how he envied them being kids and getting married. He promised he'd be bestman. When they asked him why he didn't get married himself, he confusedly had some more drinks and said his life was a shambles. He made fifteen thousand a year, but he never had any money. He knew a dozen beautiful women, but he never had a girl when he needed her. All the time he was talking, he was planning in the back of his head a release on the need for freedom of self-medication. He couldn't stop thinking about that damned Bingham account.

It was beginning to get dark when they came out of '63'. A feeling of envy stung him as he put the young people into a taxi. He felt affectionate and amorous and nicely buoyed up by the radiating warmth of food and alcohol in his belly. He stood for a minute on the corner of Madison Avenue watching the lively before-Christmas crowd pour along the sidewalk against the bright showwindows, all kinds of faces flushed and healthy-looking for once in the sharp cold evening in the slanting lights. Then he took a taxi down to Twelfth Street.

The colored maid who let him in was wearing a pretty lace apron. 'Hello, Cynthia.' 'How do you do, Mr Dick.' Dick could feel the impatient blood pounding in his temples as he walked up and down the old uneven parquet floor waiting. Eveline was smiling when she came out from the back room. She'd put too much powder on her face in too much of a hurry and it brought out the drawn lines between her nostrils and her mouth and gave her nose a floury look.

Her voice still had a lovely swing to it. 'Dick, I thought you'd given me up.'

'I've been working like a dog.... I've gotten so my brain won't work. I thought it would do me good to see you.' She handed him a Chinese porcelain box with cigarettes in it. They sat down side by side on a rickety oldfashioned horsehair sofa. 'How's Jeremy?' asked Dick in a cheerful tone.

Her voice went flat. 'He's gone out West with Paul for Christmas.'

'You must miss him . . . I'm disappointed myself. I love the brat.'

'Paul and I have finally decided to get a divorce . . . in a friendly way.'

'Eveline, I'm sorry.'

'Why?'

'I dunno. . . . It does seem silly. . . . But I always liked Paul.'

'It all got just too tiresome.... This way it'll be much better for him.'

There was something coolly bitter about her as she sat beside him in her a little too frizzy afternoondress He felt as if he was meeting her for the first time. He picked up her long blueveined hand and put it on the little table in front of them and patted it. 'I like you better . . . anyway.' It sounded phony in his ears, like something he'd say to a client. He jumped to his feet. 'Say, Eveline, suppose I call up Settignano and get some gin around? I've got to have a drink.... I can't get the office out of my head.'

'If you go back to the icebox you'll find some perfectly lovely cocktails all mixed. I just made them. There are some people coming in later.'

'How much later?'

'About seven o'clock . . . why?' Her eyes followed him teasingly as he went back through the glass doors.

In the pantry the colored girl was putting on her hat. 'Cynthia, Mrs Johnson alleges there are cocktails out here.'

'Yes, Mr Dick, I'll get you some glasses.'

'Is this your afternoon out?'

'Yessir, I'm goin' to church.'

'On Saturday afternoon?'

'Yessir, our church we have services every Saturday afternoon . . . lots of folks don't get Sunday off nowadays.'

'It's gotten so I don't get any day off at all.'

'It shoa is too bad, Mr Dick.'

He went back into the front room shakily, carrying a tray with the shaker jiggling on it. The two glasses clinked.

'Oh, Dick, I'm going to have to reform you. Your hands are shaking like an old graybeard's.'

'Well, I am an old graybeard. I'm worrying myself to death about whether the bastardly patentmedicine king will sign on the dotted line Monday.'

'Don't talk about it. . . . It sounds just too awful. I've been working myself . . . I'm trying to put on a play.'

'Eveline, that's swell! Who's it by?'

'Charles Edward Holden. . . . It's a magnificent piece of work. I'm terribly excited about it. I think I know how to do it. . . . I don't suppose you want to put a couple of thousand dollars in, do you, Dick?'

'Eveline, I'm flat broke. . . . They've got my salary garnisheed and Mother has to be supported in the style to which she is accustomed and then there's Brother Henry's ranch in Arizona . . . he's all balled up with a mortgage. . . . I thought Charles Edward Holden was just a columnist.'

'This is a side of him that's never come out. . . . I think he's the real poet of modern New York . . . you wait and see.'

Dick poured himself another cocktail. 'Let's talk about just us for a minute. . . . I feel so frazzled. . . . Oh, Eveline, you know what I mean. . . . We've been pretty good friends.' She let him hold her hand, but she did not return the squeeze he gave it. 'You know we always said we were just physically attractive to each other . . . why isn't that the swellest thing in the world?' He moved up close to her on the couch, gave her a little kiss on the cheek, tried to twist her face around. 'Don't you like this miserable sinner a little bit?'

'Dick, I can't.' She got to her feet. Her lips were twitching and she looked as if she was going to burst into tears. 'There's somebody I like very much . . . very, very much. I've decided to make some sense out of my life.'

'Who? That damn columnist?'

'Never mind who.'

Dick buried his face in his hands. When he took his hands

away, he was laughing. 'Well, if that isn't my luck.... Just Johnny on the spot and me full of speakeasy Saturdayafternoon amorosity.'

'Well, Dick, I'm sure you won't lack for partners.'

'I do today.... I feel lonely and hellish. My life is a shambles.'

'What a literary phrase!'

'I thought it was pretty good myself, but honestly I feel every whichway.... Something funny happened to me last night. I'll tell you about it someday when you like me better.'

'Dick, why don't you go to Eleanor's? She's giving a party for all the boyars.'

'Is she really going to marry that horrid little prince?' Eveline nodded with that same cold bitter look in her eyes. 'I suppose a title is the last word in the decorating business.... Why won't Eleanor put up some money?'

'I don't want to ask her. She's filthy with money, though, she's had a very successful fall. I guess we're all getting grasping in our old age.... What does poor Moorehouse think about the prince?'

'I wish I knew what he thought about anything. I've been working for him for years now and I don't know whether he's a genius or a stuffed shirt.... I wonder if he's going to be at Eleanor's. I want to get hold of him this evening for a moment.... That's a very good idea.... Eveline, you always do me good one way or another.'

'You'd better not go without phoning.... She's perfectly capable of not letting you in if you come uninvited and particularly with a houseful of émigrée Russians in tiaras.'

Dick went to the phone and called up. He had to wait a long time for Eleanor to come. Her voice sounded shrill and rasping. At first she said why didn't he come to dinner next week instead.

Dick's voice got very coaxing. 'Please let me see the famous prince, Eleanor.... And I've got something very important to ask you about.... After all, you've always been my guardian angel, Eleanor. If I can't come to you when I'm in trouble, who can I come to?'

At last she loosened up and said he could come, but he mustn't stay long. 'You can talk to poor J. Ward ... he looks a little forlorn.' Her voice ended in a screechy laugh that made the receiver jangle and hurt his ear.

When he went back to the sofa, Eveline was lying back

against the pillows soundlessly laughing. 'Dick,' she said, 'you're a master of blarney.' Dick made a face at her, kissed her on the forehead and left the house.

Eleanor's place was glittering with chandeliers and cutglass. When she met him at the drawingroom door, her small narrow face looked smooth and breakable as a piece of porcelain under her carefullycurled hair and above a big rhinestone brooch that held a lace collar together. From behind her came the boom and the high piping of Russian men's and women's voices and a smell of tea and charcoal. 'Well, Richard, here you are,' she said in a rapid hissing whisper. 'Don't forget to kiss the grand-duchess's hand . . . she's had such a dreadful life. You'd like to do any little thing that would please her, wouldn't you? . . . And, Richard, I'm worried about Ward . . . he looks so terribly tired . . . I hope he isn't beginning to break up. He's the type you know that goes off like that. . . . You know these big shortnecked blonds.'

There was a tall silver samovar on the Buhl table in front of the marble fireplace and beside it sat a large oldish woman in a tinsel shawl with her hair in a pompadour and the powder flaking off a tired blotchy face. She was very gracious and had quite a twinkle in her eye and she was piling caviar out of a heaped cutglass bowl onto a slice of blackbread and laughing with her mouth full. Around her were grouped Russians in all stages of age and decay, some in tunics and some in cheap business suits and some frowstylooking young women and a pair of young men with slick hair and choirboy faces. They were all drinking tea or little glasses of vodka. Everybody was ladling out caviar. Dick was introduced to the prince, who was an olivefaced young man with black brows and a little pointed mustache who wore a black tunic and black soft leather boots and had a prodigiously small waist. They were all merry as crickets chirping and roaring in Russian, French, and English. Eleanor sure is putting out, Dick caught himself thinking, as he dug into the mass of big graygrained caviar.

J. W. looking pale and fagged was standing in the corner of the room with his back to an icon that had three candles burning in front of it. Dick distinctly remembered having seen the icon in Eleanor's window some weeks before, against a piece of purple brocade. J. W. was talking to an ecclesiastic in a black cassock with purple trimmings, who when Dick went up to them turned out to have a rich Irish brogue.

'Meet the Archimandrite O'Donnell, Dick,' said J. W. 'Did I

get it right?' The Archimandrite grinned and nodded. 'He's been telling me about the monasteries in Greece.'

'You mean where they haul you up in a basket?' said Dick.

The Archimandrite jiggled his grinning, looselipped face up and down. 'I'm goin' to have the honorr and pleasurr of introducin' dear Eleanor into the mysteries of the true church. I was tellin' Mr Moorehouse the story of my conversion.' Dick found an impudent rolling eye looking him over. 'Perhaps you'd be carin' to come someday, Mr Savage, to hear our choir. Unbelief dissolves in music like a lump of sugar in a glass of hot tay.'

'Yes, I like the Russian choir,' said J. W.

'Don't you think that our dear Eleanor looks happier and younger for it?' The Archimandrite was beaming into the crowded room. J. W. nodded doubtfully. 'Och, a lovely graceful little thing she is, clever too.... Perhaps, Mr Moorehouse and Mr Savage, you'd come to the service and to lunch with me afterwards.... I have some ideas about a little book on my experiences at Mount Athos ... We could make a little parrty of it.'

Dick was amazed to find the Archimandrite's fingers pinching him in the seat and hastily moved away a step, but not before he'd caught from the Archimandrite's left eye a slow vigorous wink.

The big room was full of clinking and toasting, and there was the occasional crash of a broken glass. A group of younger Russians were singing in deep roaring voices that made the crystal chandelier tinkle over their heads. The caviar was all gone, but two uniformed maids were bringing in a table set with horsd'oeuvres in the middle of which was a large boiled salmon.

J. W. nudged Dick. 'I think we might go someplace where we can talk.'

'I was just waiting for you, J. W. I think I've got a new slant. I think it'll click this time.'

They'd just managed to make their way through the crush to the door when a Russian girl in black with fine black eyes and arched brows came running after them. 'Oh, you mustn't go. Leocadia Pavlovna likes you so much. She likes it here, it is informal ... the bohème. That is what we like about Leonora Ivanovna. She is bohème and we are bohème. We luff her.'

'I'm afraid we have a business appointment,' said J. W. solemnly.

The Russian girl snapped her fingers with, 'Oh, business, it is disgusting. . . . America would be so nice without the business.'

When they got out on the street, J. W. sighed. 'Poor Eleanor, I'm afraid she's in for something. . . . Those Russians will eat her out of house and home. Do you suppose she really will marry this Prince Mingraziali? I've made inquiries about him. . . . He's all that he says he is. But heavens!'

'With crowns and everything,' said Dick, 'the date's all set.'

'After all, Eleanor knows her own business. She's been very successful, you know.'

J. W.'s car was at the door. The chauffeur got out with a laprobe over his arm and was just about to close the door on J. W. when Dick said, 'J. W., have you a few minutes to talk about this Bingham account?'

'Of course, I was forgetting,' said J. W. in a tired voice. 'Come on out to supper at Great Neck. . . . I'm alone out there except for the children.' Smiling, Dick jumped in and the chauffeur closed the door of the big black towncar behind him.

It was pretty lugubrious eating in the diningroom with its painted Italian panels at the Moorehouses' with the butler and the secondman moving around silently in the dim light and only Dick and J. W. and Miss Simpson, the children's so very refined longfaced governess, at the long candlelit table. Afterwards, when they went into J. W.'s little white den to smoke and talk about the Bingham account, Dick thanked his stars when the old butler appeared with a bottle of Scotch and ice and glasses.

'Where did you find that, Thompson?' asked J. W.

'Been in the cellar since before the war, sir . . . those cases Mrs Moorehouse bought in Scotland. . . . I knew Mr Savage liked a bit of a spot.'

Dick laughed. 'That's the advantage of having a bad name,' he said.

J. W. drawled solemnly, 'It's the best to be had, I know that. . . . Do you know I never could get much out of drinking, so I gave it up, even before prohibition.'

J. W. had lit himself a cigar. Suddenly he threw it in the fire. 'I don't think I'll smoke tonight. The doctor says three cigars a day won't hurt me . . . but I've been feeling seedy all week. . . . I ought to get out of the stockmarket. . . . I hope you keep out of it, Dick.'

'My creditors don't leave me enough to buy a ticket to a raffle with.'

J. W. took a couple of steps across the small room lined with unscratched sets of the leading authors in morocco, and then stood with his back to the Florentine fireplace with his hands behind him. 'I feel chilly all the time. I don't think my circulation's very good.... Perhaps it was going to see Gertrude.... The doctors have finally admitted her case is hopeless. It was a great shock to me.'

Dick got to his feet and put down his glass. 'I'm sorry, J. W.... Still, there have been surprising cures in brain troubles.'

J. W. was standing with his lips in a thin tight line, his big jowl trembling a little. 'Not in schizophrenia.... I've managed to do pretty well in everything except that.... I'm a lonely man,' he said. 'And to think once upon a time I was planning to be a songwriter.' He smiled.

Dick smiled too and held out his hand. 'Shake hands, J. W.,' he said, 'with the ruins of a minor poet.'

'Anyway,' said J. W., 'the children will have the advantages I never had.... Would it bore you, before we get down to business, to go up and say goodnight to them? I'd like to have you see them.'

'Of course not, I love kids,' said Dick. 'In fact, I've never yet quite managed to grow up myself.'

At the head of the stairs Miss Simpson met them with her finger to her lips. 'Little Gertrude's asleep.' They tiptoed down the allwhite hall. The children were in bed, each in a small hospitallike room cold from an open window, on each pillow was a head of pale strawcolored hair.

'Staple's the oldest . . . he's twelve,' whispered J. W. 'Then Gertrude, then Johnny.'

Staple said goodnight politely. Gertrude didn't wake up when they turned the light on. Johnny sat up in a nightmare with his bright blue eyes open wide, crying, 'No, no,' in a tiny frightened voice.

J. W. sat on the edge of the bed petting him for a moment until he fell asleep again. 'Goodnight, Miss Simpson,' and they were tiptoeing down the stairs. 'What do you think of them?' J. W. turned beaming to Dick.

'They sure are a pretty sight.... I envy you,' said Dick.

'I'm glad I brought you out . . . I'd have been lonely without you . . . I must entertain more,' said J. W.

They settled back into their chairs by the fire and started to go over the layout to be presented to Bingham Products. When the clock struck ten, J. W. began to yawn.

Dick got to his feet. 'J. W., do you want my honest opinion?'

'Go ahead, boy, you know you can say anything you like to me.'

'Well, here it is.' Dick tossed off the last warm weak remnant of his Scotch. 'I think we can't see the woods for the trees ... we're balled up in a mass of petty detail. You say the old gentleman's pretty pigheaded ... one of these from newsboy to president characters.... Well, I don't think that this stuff really sets in high enough relief the campaign you outlined to us a month ago ...'

'I'm not very well satisfied with it, to tell the truth.'

'Is there a typewriter in the house?'

'I guess Thompson or Morton can scrape one up somewhere.'

'Well, I think that I might be able to bring your fundamental idea out a little more. To my mind it's one of the biggest ideas ever presented in the business world.'

'Of course it's the work of the whole office.'

'Let me see if I can take this to pieces and put it together again over the weekend. After all, there'll be nothing lost.... We've got to blow that old gent clean out of the water or else Halsey'll get him.'

'They're around him every minute like a pack of wolves,' said J. W., getting up yawning. 'Well, I leave it in your hands.' When he got to the door J. W. paused and turned. 'Of course, those Russian aristocrats are socially the top. It's a big thing for Eleanor that way.... But I wish she wouldn't do it.... You know, Dick, Eleanor and I have had a very beautiful relationship.... That little woman's advice and sympathy have meant a great deal to me.... I wish she wasn't going to do it.... Well, I'm going to bed.'

Dick went up to the big bedroom hung with English hunting-scenes. Thompson brought him up a new noiseless typewriter and the bottle of whiskey. Dick sat there working all night in his pajamas and bathrobe smoking and drinking the whiskey. He was still at it when the windows began to get blue with day and he began to make out between the heavy curtains black lacy masses of sleetladen trees grouped round a sodden lawn. His mouth was sour from too many cigarettes. He went into the bathroom frescoed with dolphins and began to whistle as he let the hot water pour into the tub. He felt bleary and dizzy, but he had a new layout.

Next day at noon when J. W. came back from church with the children, Dick was dressed and shaved and walking up and down the flagged terrace in the raw air. Dick's eyes felt hollow and his head throbbed, but J. W. was delighted with the work.

'Of course selfservice, independence, individualism is the word I gave the boys in the beginning. This is going to be more than a publicity campaign, it's going to be a campaign for Americanism.... After lunch I'll send the car over for Miss Williams to get her to take some dictation. There's more meat in this yet, Dick.'

'Of course,' said Dick, reddening. 'All I've done is restore your original conception, J. W.'

At lunch the children sat up at the table and Dick had a good time with them, making them talk to him and telling them stories about the bunnies he'd raised when he was a little boy in Jersey. J. W. was beaming. After lunch Dick played pingpong in the billiardroom in the basement with Miss Simpson and Staple and little Gertrude while Johnny picked up the balls for them. J. W. retired to his den to take a nap.

Later they arranged the prospectus for Miss Williams to type. The three of them were working there happily in front of the fire when Thompson appeared in the door and asked reverently if Mr Moorehouse cared to take a phonecall from Mr Griscolm. 'All right, give it to me on this phone here,' said J. W.

Dick froze in his chair. He could hear the voice at the other end of the line twanging excitedly. 'Ed, don't you worry,' J. W. was drawling. 'You take a good rest, my boy, and be fresh as a daisy in the morning so that you can pick holes in the final draft that Miss Williams and I were working over all last night. A few changes occurred to me in the night.... You know sleep brings council.... How about a little handball this afternoon? A sweat's a great thing for a man, you know. If it wasn't so wet I'd be putting in eighteen holes of golf myself. All right, see you in the morning, Ed.' J. W. put down the receiver. 'Do you know, Dick,' he said, 'I think Ed Griscolm ought to take a couple of weeks off in Nassau or some place like that. He's losing his grip a little.... I think I'll suggest it to him. He's been a very valuable fellow in the office, you know.'

'One of the brightest men in the publicrelations field,' said Dick flatly. They went back to work.

Next morning Dick drove in with J. W., but stopped off on Fiftyseventh to run round to his mother's apartment on Fiftysixth to change his shirt. When he got to the office, the switchboard operator in the lobby gave him a broad grin. Everything was humming with the Bingham account. In the vestibule he ran into the inevitable Miss Williams. Her sour lined oldmaidish face was twisted into a sugary smile. 'Mr Savage, Mr Moorehouse says would you mind meeting him and Mr Bingham at the Plaza at twelvethirty when he takes Mr Bingham to lunch?'

He spent the morning on routine work. Round eleven, Eveline Johnson called him up and said she wanted to see him. He said how about toward the end of the week. 'But I'm right in the building,' she said in a hurt voice.

'Oh, come on up, but I'm pretty busy.... You know Mondays.'

Eveline had a look of strain in the bright hard light that poured in the window from the overcast sky. She had on a gray coat with a furcollar that looked a little shabby and a prickly gray straw hat that fitted her head tight and had a kind of last-year's look. The lines from the flanges of her nose to the ends of her mouth looked deeper and harder than ever.

Dick got up and took both her hands. 'Eveline, you look tired.'

'I think I'm coming down with the grippe.' She talked fast. 'I just came in to see a friendly face. I have an appointment to see J. W. at eleven-fifteen.... Do you think he'll come across? If I can raise ten thousand, the Shuberts will raise the rest. But it's got to be right away because somebody has some kind of an option on it that expires tomorrow.... Oh, I'm so sick of not doing anything.... Holden has wonderful ideas about the production and he's letting me do the sets and costumes ... and if some Broadway producer does it he'll ruin it.... Dick, I know it's a great play.'

Dick frowned. 'This isn't such a very good time ... we're all pretty preoccupied this morning.'

'Well, I won't disturb you any more.' They were standing in the window. 'How can you stand those riveters going all the time?'

'Why, Eveline, those riveters are music to our ears, they make us sing like canaries in a thunderstorm. They mean business.... If J. W. takes my advice, that's where we're going to have our new office.'

'Well, goodbye.' She put her hand in its worn gray glove in his. 'I know you'll put in a word for me.... You're the white-haired boy around here.'

She went out leaving a little frail scent of cologne and furs in the office. Dick walked up and down in front of his desk frowning. He suddenly felt nervous and jumpy. He decided he'd run out to get a breath of air and maybe a small drink before he went to lunch. 'If anybody calls,' he said to his secretary, 'tell them to call me after three. I have an errand and then an appointment with Mr Moorehouse.'

In the elevator there was J. W. just going down in a new overcoat with a big furcollar and a new gray fedora. 'Dick,' he said, 'if you're late at the Plaza, I'll wring your neck.... You're slated for the blind bowboy.'

'To shoot Bingham in the heart?' Dick's ears hummed as the elevator dropped.

J. W. nodded, smiling. 'By the way, in strict confidence what do you think of Mrs Johnson's project to put on a play? ... Of course, she's a very lovely woman.... She used to be a great friend of Eleanor's.... Dick, my boy, why don't you marry?'

'Who? Eveline? She's married already.'

'I was thinking aloud, don't pay any attention to it.' They came out of the elevator and walked across the Grand Central together in the swirl of the noontime crowd. The sun had come out and sent long slanting motefilled rays across under the great blue ceiling overhead. 'But what do you think of this play venture? You see I'm pretty well tied up in the market.... I suppose I could borrow the money at the bank.'

'The theater's always risky,' said Dick. 'Eveline's a great girl and all that and full of talent, but I don't know how much of a head she has for business. Putting on a play's a risky business.'

'I like to help old friends out ... but it occurred to me that if the Shuberts thought there was money in it they'd be putting it in themselves.... Of course Mrs Johnson's very artistic.'

'Of course,' said Dick.

At twelve-thirty he was waiting for J. W. in the lobby of the Plaza chewing sensen to take the smell of the three whiskies he'd swallowed at Tony's on the way up off his breath. At twelve-fortyfive he saw coming from the checkroom J. W.'s large pearshaped figure with the paleblue eyes and the sleek strawgray hair, and beside him a tall gaunt man with untidy white hair curling into ducktails over his ears. The minute they stepped into the lobby, Dick began to hear a rasping opinionated boom from the tall man.

'... never one of those who could hold my peace while injustice ruled in the marketplace. It has been a long struggle and one which from the vantage of those threescore and ten years that the prophets of old promised to man upon this earth I can admit to have been largely crowned with material and spiritual success. Perhaps it was my early training for the pulpit, but I have always felt, and that feeling, Mr Moorehouse, is not rare among the prominent businessmen in this country, that material success is not the only thing . . . there is the attainment of the spirit of service. That is why I say to you frankly that I have been grieved and wounded by this dark conspiracy. Who steals my purse steals trash, but who would . . . what is it? . . . my memory's not what it was . . . my good name . . . Ah, yes, how do you do, Mr Savage?'

Dick was surprised by the wrench the handshake gave his arm. He found himself standing in front of a gaunt loosejointed old man with a shock of white hair and a big prognathous skull from which the sunburned skin hung in folds like the jowls of a birddog. J. W. seemed small and meek beside him.

'I'm very glad to meet you, sir,' E. R. Bingham said. 'I have often said to my girls that had I grown up in your generation I would have found happy and useful work in the field of public-relations. But alas, in my day the path was harder for a young man entering life with nothing but the excellent tradition of moral fervor and natural religion I absorbed if I may say so with my mother's milk. We had to put our shoulders to the wheel in those days and it was the wheel of an old muddy wagon drawn by mules, not the wheel of a luxurious motorcar.'

E. R. Bingham boomed his way into the diningroom. A covey of palefaced waiters gathered round, pulling out chairs, setting the table, bringing menucards.

'Boy, it is no use handing me the bill of fare,' E. R. Bingham addressed the headwaiter. 'I live by Nature's law. I eat only a few nuts and vegetables and drink raw milk. . . . Bring me some cooked spinach, a plate of grated carrots and a glass of unpasteurized milk. . . . As a result, gentlemen, when I went a few days ago to a great physician at the request of one of the great lifeinsurance companies in this city he was dumbfounded when he examined me. He could hardly believe that I was not telling a whopper when I told him I was seventyone. "Mr Bingham," he said, "you have the magnificent physique of a healthy athlete of fortyfive" . . . Feel that, young man.' E. R. Bingham flexed his arm under Dick's nose.

Dick gave the muscle a prod with two fingers. 'A sledge-hammer,' Dick said, nodding his head.

E. R. Bingham was already talking again: 'You see I practice what I preach, Mr Moorehouse . . . and I expect others to do the same. . . . I may add that in the entire list of remedies and pro-

prietary medicines controlled by Bingham Products and the
Rugged Health Corporation, there is not a single one that contains a mineral, a drug, or any other harmful ingredient. I have
sacrificed time and time again hundreds of thousands of dollars
to strike from my list a concoction deemed injurious or habit-
forming by Doctor Gorman and the rest of the splendid men
and women who make up our research department. Our medicines and our systems of diet and cure are Nature's remedies,
herbs and simples culled in the wilderness in the four corners
of the globe according to the tradition of wise men and the
findings of sound medical science.'

'Would you have coffee now, Mr Bingham, or later?'

'Coffee, sir, is a deadly poison, as are alcohol, tea, and
tobacco. If the shorthaired women and the longhaired men and
the wildeyed cranks from the medical schools, who are trying
to restrict the liberties of the American people to seek health
and wellbeing, would restrict their activities to the elimination
of these dangerous poisons that are sapping the virility of our
young men and the fertility of our lovely American womanhood, I would have no quarrel with them. In fact, I would do
everything I could to aid and abet them. Someday I shall put
my entire fortune at the disposal of such a campaign. I know
that the plain people of this country feel as I do because I'm one
of them, born and raised on the farm of plain Godfearing farming folk. The American people need to be protected from
cranks.'

'That, Mr Bingham,' said J. W., 'will be the keynote of the
campaign we have been outlining.' The fingerbowls had arrived.
'Well, Mr Bingham,' said J. W., getting to his feet, 'this has
been indeed a pleasure. I unfortunately shall have to leave you
to go downtown to a rather important directors' meeting, but
Mr Savage here has everything right at his fingertips and can,
I know, answer any further questions. I believe we are meeting
with your sales department at five.'

As soon as they were alone, E. R. Bingham leaned over the
table to Dick and said: 'Young man, I very much need a little
relaxation this afternoon. Perhaps you could come to some entertainment as my guest. . . . All work and no play . . . you know
the adage. Chicago has always been my headquarters and whenever I've been in New York I've been too busy to get around. . . .
Perhaps you could suggest some sort of show or musical extra-
vaganza. I belong to the plain people, let's go where the plain
people go.'

Dick nodded understandingly. 'Let's see, Monday afternoon
... I'll have to call up the office.... There ought to be vaudeville.... I can't think of anything but a burlesque show.'

'That's the sort of thing, music and young women.... I have
high regard for the human body. My daughters, thank God,
are magnificent physical specimens.... The sight of beautiful
female bodies is relaxing and soothing. Come along, you are
my guest. It will help me to make up my mind about this
matter.... Between you and me Mr Moorehouse is a very
extraordinary man. I think he can lend the necessary dignity....
But we must not forget that we are talking to the plain
people.'

'But the plain people aren't so plain as they were, Mr Bingham. They like things a little ritzy now,' said Dick, following
E. R. Bingham's rapid stride to the checkroom.

'I never wear hat or coat, only that muffler, young lady,'
E. R. Bingham was booming.

'Have you any children of your own, Mr Savage?' asked E. R.
Bingham when they were settled in the taxicab.

'No, I'm not married at the moment,' said Dick shakily, and
lit himself a cigarette.

'Will you forgive a man old enough to be your father for
pointing something out to you?' E. R. Bingham took Dick's
cigarette between two long knobbed fingers and dropped it out
of the window of the cab. 'My friend, you are poisoning yourself
with narcotics and destroying your virility. When I was around
forty years old, I was in the midst of a severe economic struggle.
All my great organization was still in its infancy. I was a physical wreck. I was a slave to alcohol and tobacco. I had parted
with my first wife and had I had a wife I wouldn't have been
able to ... behave with her as a man should. Well, one day I
said to myself: "Doc Bingham" – my friends called me Doc in
those days – "like Christian of old you are bound for the City
of Destruction, and when you're gone, you'll have neither chick
nor child to drop a tear for you." I began to interest myself in
the proper culture of the body ... my spirit, I may say, was
already developed by familiarity with the classics in my youth
and a memory that many have called prodigious.... The result has been success in every line of endeavor.... Someday you
shall meet my family and see what sweetness and beauty there
can be in a healthy American home.'

E. R. Bingham was still talking when they went down the
aisle to seats beside the gangplank at a burlesque show. Before

he could say Jack Robinson, Dick found himself looking up a series of bare jiggling female legs spotted from an occasional vaccination. The band crashed and blared, the girls wiggled and sang and stripped in a smell of dust and armpits and powder and greasepaint in the glare of the moving spot that kept lighting up E. R. Bingham's white head. E. R. Bingham was particularly delighted when one of the girls stooped and cooed, 'Why, look at Grandpa,' and sang into his face and wiggled her geestring at him. E. R. Bingham nudged Dick and whispered, 'Get her telephone number.' After she'd moved on he kept exclaiming, 'I feel like a boy again.'

In the intermission Dick managed to call Miss Williams at the office and to tell her to suggest to people not to smoke at the conference. 'Tell J. W. the old buzzard thinks cigarettes are coffinnails,' he said.

'Oh, Mr Savage,' said Miss Williams reprovingly.

At five Dick tried to get him out, but he insisted on staying till the end of the show. 'They'll wait for me, don't worry,' he said.

When they were back in a taxi on the way to the office, E. R. Bingham chuckled. 'By gad, I always enjoy a good legshow, the human form divine.... Perhaps we might, my friend, keep the story of our afternoon under our hats.' He gave Dick's knee a tremendous slap. 'It's great to play hookey.'

At the conference Bingham Products signed on the dotted line. Mr Bingham agreed to anything and paid no attention to what went on. Halfway through, he said he was tired and was going home to bed and left yawning, leaving Mr Goldmark and a representative of the J. Winthrop Hudson Company that did the advertising for Bingham Products to go over the details of the project. Dick couldn't help admiring the quiet domineering way J. W. had with them. After the conference Dick got drunk and tried to make a girl he knew in a taxicab, but nothing came of it, and he went home to the empty apartment feeling frightful.

The next morning Dick overslept. The telephone woke him. It was Miss Williams calling from the office. Would Mr Savage get himself a bag packed and have it sent down to the station so as to be ready to accompany Mr Moorehouse to Washington on the Congressional. 'And, Mr Savage,' she added, 'excuse me for saying so, but we all feel at the office that you were responsible for nailing the Bingham account. Mr Moorehouse was saying you must have hypnotized them.'

'That's very nice of you, Miss Williams,' said Dick in his sweetest voice.

Dick and J. W. took a drawingroom on the train. Miss Williams came, too, and they worked all the way down. Dick was crazy for a drink all afternoon, but he didn't dare take one, although he had a bottle of Scotch in his bag, because Miss Williams would be sure to spot him getting out the bottle and say something about it in that vague acid apologetic way she had, and he knew J. W. felt he drank too much. He felt so nervous he smoked cigarettes until his tongue began to dry up in his mouth and then took to chewing chiclets.

Dick kept J. W. busy with new slants until J. W. lay down to take a nap, saying he felt a little seedy; then Dick took Miss Williams to the diner to have a cup of tea and told her funny stories that kept her in a gale. By the time they reached the smoky Baltimore tunnels, he felt about ready for a padded cell. He'd have been telling people he was Napoleon before he got to Washington if he hadn't been able to get a good gulp of Scotch while Miss Williams was in the ladies' room and J. W. was deep in a bundle of letters E. R. Bingham had given him between Bingham Products and their Washington lobbyist Colonel Judson on the threat of purefood legislation.

When Dick finally escaped to his room in the corner suite J. W. always took at the Shoreham, he poured out a good drink to take quietly by himself, with soda and ice, while he prepared a comic telegram to send the girl he had a date for dinner with that night at the Colony Club. He'd barely sipped the drink when the phone rang. It was E. R. Bingham's secretary calling up from the Willard to see if Dick would dine with Mr and Mrs Bingham and the Misses Bingham.

'By all means go,' said J. W. when Dick inquired if he'd need him. 'First thing you know, I'll be completing the transaction by marrying you off to one of the lovely Bingham girls.'

The Bingham girls were three strapping young women named Hygeia, Althea, and Myra, and Mrs Bingham was a fat faded flatfaced blonde who wore round steel spectacles. The only one of the family who didn't wear glasses and have buckteeth was Myra, who seemed to take more after her father. She certainly talked a blue streak. She was the youngest, too, and E. R. Bingham, who was striding around in oldfashioned carpet-slippers with his shirt open at the neck and a piece of red flannel undershirt showing across his chest, introduced her as the artistic member of the family. She giggled a great deal about how she was going to New York to study painting. She told Dick he looked as if he had the artistic temperament.

They ate in some confusion because Mr Bingham kept sending back the dishes, and flew into a towering passion because the cabbage was overcooked and the raw carrots weren't ripe, and cursed and swore at the waiters and finally sent for the manager. About all they'd had was potatosoup and boiled onions sprinkled with hazelnuts and peanutbutter spread on wholewheat bread, all washed down with Coca-Cola, when two young men appeared with a microphone from N.B.C. for E. R. Bingham to broadcast his eighto'clock health talk. He was suddenly smiling and hearty again and Mrs Bingham reappeared from the bedroom to which she'd retreated crying, with her hands over her ears not to hear the old man's foul language. She came back with her eyes red and a little bottle of smelling-salts in her hand, just in time to be chased out of the room again. E. R. Bingham roared that women distracted his attention from the mike, but he made Dick stay and listen to his broadcast on health and diet and exercise hints and to the announcement of the annual crosscountry hike from Washington to Louisville sponsored by *Rugged Health*, the Bingham Products houseorgan, which he was going to lead in person for the first three days, just to set the pace for the youngsters, he said.

After the broadcast Mrs Bingham and the girls came in all rouged and powdered up, wearing diamond earrings and pearl necklaces and chinchilla coats. They invited Dick and the radio young men to go to Keith's with them, but Dick explained that he had work to do. Before Mrs Bingham left, she made Dick promise to come to visit them at their home in Eureka.

'You come and spend a month, young feller,' boomed E. R. Bingham, interrupting her. 'We'll make a man out of you there. The first week orangejuice and high irrigations, massage, rest. . . . After that we build you up with crackedwheat and plenty of milk and cream, a little boxing or trackwork, plenty of hiking out in the sun without a lot of stifling clothes on, and you'll come back a man. Nature's richest handiwork, the paragon of animals . . . you know the lines of the immortal bard . . . and you'll have forgotten all about that unhealthy New York life that's poisoning your system. You come out, young man. . . . Well, goodnight. By the time I've done my deep breathing it'll be my bedtime. When I'm in Washington I get up at six every morning and break the ice in the Basin. . . . How about coming down for a little dip tomorrow? Pathé

Newsreel is going to be there. . . . It would be worth your while in your business.'

Dick excused himself hastily, saying, 'Another time, Mr Bingham.'

At the Shoreham he found J. W. finishing dinner with Senator Planet and Colonel Judson, a smooth pink toadfaced man with a caressingly amiable manner.

The senator got to his feet and squeezed Dick's hand warmly. 'Why, boy, we expected to see you come back wearin' a tigerskin. . . . Did the old boy show you his chestexpansion?' J. W. was frowning.

'Not this time, senator,' said Dick quietly.

'But, senator,' J. W. said with some impatience, evidently picking up a speech where it had been broken off, 'it's the principle of the thing. Once government interference in business is established as a precedent, it means the end of liberty and private initiative in this country.'

'It means the beginning of red Russian bolshevistic tyranny,' added Colonel Judson, with angry emphasis.

Senator Planet laughed. 'Aren't those rather harsh words, Joel?'

'What this bill purports to do is to take the right of selfmedication from the American people. A set of lazy government employees and remittancemen will be able to tell you what laxative you may take and what not. Like all such things, it'll be in the hands of cranks and busybodies. Surely the American people have the right to choose what products they want to buy. It's an insult to the intelligence of our citizens.'

The senator tipped up an afterdinner coffeecup to get the last dregs of it. Dick noticed that they were drinking brandy out of big balloonglasses. 'Well,' said the senator slowly, 'what you say may be true, but the bill has a good deal of popular support and you gentlemen mustn't forget that I am not entirely a free agent in this matter. I have to consult the wishes of my constituents . . .'

'As I look at it,' interrupted Colonel Judson, 'all these socalled pure food and drug bills are class legislation in favor of the medical profession. Naturally the doctors want us to consult them before we buy a toothbrush or a package of licorice powder.'

J. W. picked up where he left off: 'The tendency of the growth of scientificallyprepared proprietary medicine has been to make the layman free and selfsufficient, able to treat many minor ills without consulting a physician.'

The senator finished his brandy without answering.

'Bowie,' said Colonel Judson, reaching for the bottle and pouring out some more, 'you know as well as I do that the plain people of your state don't want their freedom of choice curtailed by any Washington snoopers and busybodies. . . . And we've got the money and the organization to be of great assistance in your campaign. Mr Moorehouse is about to launch one of the biggest educational drives the country has ever seen to let the people know the truth about proprietary medicines, both in the metropolitan and the rural districts. He will roll up a great tidal wave of opinion that Congress will have to pay attention to. I've seen him do it before.'

'Excellent brandy,' said the senator. 'Fine Armagnac has been my favorite for years.' He cleared his throat and took a cigar from a box in the middle of the table and lit it in a leisurely fashion. 'I've been much criticized of late, by irresponsible people, of course, for what they term my reactionary association with big business. You know the demagogic appeal.'

'It is particularly at a time like this that an intelligentlyrun organization can be of most use to a man in public life,' said Colonel Judson earnestly.

Senator Planet's black eyes twinkled and he passed a hand over the patch of spiky black hair that had fallen over his low forehead, leaving a segment of the top of his head bald. 'I guess it comes down to how much assistance will be forthcoming,' he said, getting to his feet. 'The parallelogram of forces.'

The other men got to their feet too. The senator flicked the ash from his cigar.

'The force of public opinion, senator,' said J. W. portentously. 'That is what we have to offer.'

'Well, Mr Moorehouse, you must excuse me, I have some speeches to prepare. . . . This has been most delightful. . . . Dick, you must come to dinner while you're in Washington. We've been missing you at our little dinners. . . . Goodnight, Joel, see you tomorrow.' J. W.'s valet was holding the senator's furlined overcoat for him.

'Mr Bingham,' said J. W., 'is a very publicspirited man, senator; he's willing to spend a very considerable sum of money.'

'He'll have to,' said the senator.

After the door had closed on Senator Planet, the rest of them sat silent a moment. Dick poured himself a glass of the Armagnac.

'Well, Mr Bingham don't need to worry,' said Colonel Judson. 'But it's going to cost him money. Bowie an' his friends are just trying to raise the ante. You know I can read 'em like a book. . . . After all, I been around this town for fifteen years.'

'It's humiliating and absurd that legitimate business should have to stoop to such methods,' said J. W.

'Sure, J. W., you took the words right out of my mouth. . . . If you want my opinion, what we need is a strong man in this country to send all these politicians packing. . . . Don't think I don't know 'em. . . . But this little dinnerparty has been very valuable. You are a new element in the situation. . . . A valuable air of dignity, you know. . . . Well, goodnight.'

J. W. was already standing with his hand outstretched, his face white as paper.

'Well, I'll be running along,' said Colonel Judson. 'You can assure your client that that bill will never pass. . . . Take a good night's rest, Mr Moorehouse . . . Goodnight, Captain Savage. . . .' Colonel Judson patted both J. W. and Dick affectionately on the shoulder with his two hands in the same gesture. Chewing his cigar he eased out of the door leaving a broad smile behind him and a puff of rank blue smoke.

Dick turned to J. W. who had sunk down in a red plush chair. 'Are you sure you're feeling all right, J W.?'

'It's just a little indigestion,' J. W. said in a weak voice, his face twisted with pain, gripping the arms of the chair with both hands.

'Well, I guess we'd better all turn in,' said Dick. 'But J. W., how about getting a doctor in to take a look at you in the morning?'

'We'll see, goodnight,' said J. W., talking with difficulty with his eyes closed.

Dick had just got to sleep when a knocking on his door woke him with a start. He went to the door in his bare feet. It was Morton, J. W.'s elderly cockney valet. 'Beg pardon, sir, for waking you, sir,' he said. 'I'm worried about Mr Moorehouse, sir. Doctor Gleason's with him. . . . I'm afraid it's a heart attack. He's in pain something awful, sir.'

Dick put on his purple silk bathrobe and his slippers and ran into the drawingroom of the suite where he met the doctor. 'This is Mr Savage, sir,' said the valet. The doctor was a grayhaired man with a gray mustache and a portentous manner. He looked Dick fiercely in the eye as he spoke: 'Mr Moorehouse must be absolutely quiet for some days. It's a very light angina pectoris . . . not serious this time, but a thorough rest for a few months is indicated. He ought to have a thorough physical examination . . . talk him into it in the morning. I believe you are Mr Moorehouse's business partner, aren't you, Mr Savage?'

Dick blushed. 'I'm one of Mr Moorehouse's collaborators.'

'Take as much off his shoulders as you can.'

Dick nodded. He went back to his room and lay on his bed the rest of the night without being able to sleep.

In the morning when Dick went in to see him, J. W. was sitting up in bed propped up with pillows. His face was a rumpled white and he had violet shadows under his eyes. 'Dick, I certainly gave myself a scare.' J. W.'s voice was weak and shaking; it make Dick feel almost tearful to hear it.

'Well, what about the rest of us?'

'Well, Dick, I'm afraid I'm going to have to dump E. R. Bingham and a number of other matters on your shoulders. . . . And I've been thinking that perhaps I ought to change the whole capital structure of the firm. What would you think of Moorehouse, Griscolm and Savage?'

'I think it would be a mistake to change the name, J. W. After all, J. Ward Moorehouse is a national institution.'

J. W.'s voice quavered up a little stronger. He kept having to clear his throat. 'I guess you're right, Dick,' he said. 'I'd like to hold on long enough to give my boys a start in life.'

'What do you want to bet you wear a silk hat at my funeral, J. W.? In the first place, it may have been an attack of acute indigestion just as you thought. We can't go on merely one doctor's opinion. What would you think of a little trip to the Mayo clinic? All you need's a little overhauling, valves ground, carburetor adjusted, that sort of thing. . . . By the way, J. W., we wouldn't want Mr Bingham to discover that a mere fifteen-thousand a year man was handling his sacred proprietary medicines, would we?'

J. W. laughed weakly. 'Well, we'll see about that. . . . I think you'd better go on down to New York this morning and take charge of the office. Miss Williams and I will hold the fort here. . . . She's sour as a pickle, but a treasure, I tell you.'

'Hadn't I better stick around until we've had a specialist look you over?'

'Doctor Gleason filled me up with dope of some kind so that I'm pretty comfortable. I've wired my sister, Hazel, she teaches school over in Wilmington, she's the only one of the family I've seen much of since the old people died. . . . She'll be over this afternoon. It's her Christmas vacation.'

'Did Morton get you the opening quotations?'

'Skyrocketing. . . . Never saw anything like it. . . . But do you know, Dick, I'm going to sell out and lay on my oars for a while. . . . It's funny how an experience like this takes the heart out of you.'

'You and Paul Warburg,' said Dick.

'Maybe it's old age,' said J. W., and closed his eyes for a minute. His face seemed to be collapsing into a mass of gray and violet wrinkles as Dick looked.

'Well, take it easy, J. W.,' said Dick and tiptoed out of the room.

He caught the eleveno'clock train and got to the office in time to straighten things out. He told everybody that J. W. had a light touch of grippe and would be in bed for a few days. There was so much work piled up that he gave Miss Hilles his secretary a dollar for her supper and asked her to come back at eight. For himself he had some sandwiches and a carton of coffee sent up from a delicatessen. It was midnight before he got through. In the empty halls of the dim building he met two rusty old women coming with pails and scrubbingbrushes to clean the office. The night elevatorman was old and pastyfaced. Snow had fallen and turned to slush and gave Lexington Avenue a black gutted look like a street in an abandoned village. A raw wind whipped his face and ears as he turned uptown. He thought of the apartment on Fiftysixth Street full of his mother's furniture, the gilt chairs in the front room, all the dreary objects he'd known as a small boy, the *Stag at Bay* and the engravings of the Forum Romanorum in his room, the bird'seyemaple beds; he could see it all sharply as if he was there as he turned into the wind. Bad enough when his mother was there, but when she was in St Augustine, frightful. 'God damn it, it's time I was making enough money to reorganize my life,' he said to himself.

He jumped into the first taxi he came to and went to '63.' It was warm and cozy in '63.' As she helped him off with his coat and muffler, the platinumhaired checkgirl carried on an elaborate kidding that had been going on all winter about how he was going to take her to Miami and make her fortune at the races at Hialeah. Then he stood a second peering through the doorway into the low room full of wellgroomed heads, tables, glasses, cigarettesmoke spiraling in front of the pink lights. He caught sight of Pat Doolittle's black bang. There she was sitting in the alcove with Reggie and Jo.

The Italian waiter ran up, rubbing his hands. 'Good evening, Mr Savage, we've been missing you.'

'I've been in Washington.'

'Cold down there?'

'Oh, kind of medium,' said Dick and slipped into the redleather settee opposite Pat.

'Well, look who we have with us,' she said. 'I thought you were busy poisoning the American public under the dome of the Capitol.'

'Wouldn't be so bad if we poisoned some of those western legislators,' said Dick.

Reggie held out his hand. 'Well, put it there, Alec Borgia.... I reckon you're on the bourbon if you've been mingling with the conscript fathers.'

'Sure, I'll drink bourbon ... kids, I'm tired ... I'm going to eat something. I didn't have any supper. I just left the office.'

Reggie looked pretty tight; so did Pat. Jo was evidently sober and sore. I must fix this up, thought Dick, and put his arm round Pat's waist. 'Say, did you get my 'gram?'

'Laughed myself sick over it,' said Pat. 'Gosh, Dick, it's nice to have you back among the drinking classes.'

'Say, Dick,' said Reggie, 'is there anything in the rumor that old doughface toppled over?'

'Mr Moorehouse had a little attack of acute indigestion ... he was better when I left,' said Dick in a voice that sounded a little too solemn in his ears.

'Not drinking gets 'em in the end,' said Reggie. The girls laughed. Dick put down three bourbons in rapid succession, but he wasn't getting any lift from them. He just felt hungry and frazzled. He had his head twisted around trying to flag the waiter to find out what the devil had happened to his filetmignon when he heard Reggie drawling, 'After all J. Ward Moorehouse isn't a man ... it's a name.... You can't feel sorry when a name gets sick.'

Dick felt a rush of anger flush his head: 'He's one of the sixty most important men in this country,' he said. 'After all, Reggie, you're taking his money ...'

'Good God!' cried Reggie. 'The man on the high horse.'

Pat turned to Dick, laughing. 'They seem to be getting mighty holy down there in Washington.'

'No, you know I like to kid as well as anybody. . . . But when a man like J. W., who's perhaps done more than any one living man, whether you like what he does or not, to form the public mind in this country, is taken ill, I think sophomore wisecracks are in damn bad taste.'

Reggie was drunk. He was talking in phony Southern dialect. 'Wha, brudder, Ah didn't know as you was Mista Moahouse in pussen. Ah thunked you was juss a lowdown wageslave like the rest of us pickaninnies.'

Dick wanted to shut up, but he couldn't. 'Whether you like it or not, the molding of the public mind is one of the most important things that goes on in this country. If it wasn't for that, American business would be in a pretty pickle. . . . Now we may like the way American business does things or we may not like it, but it's a historical fact like the Himalaya Mountains and no amount of kidding's going to change it. It's only through publicrelations work that business is protected from wildeyed cranks and demagogues who are always ready to throw a monkeywrench into the industrial machine.'

'Hear, hear,' cried Pat.

'Well, you'll be the first to holler when they cut the income from your old man's firstmortgage bonds,' said Dick snappishly.

'Senator,' intoned Reggie, strengthened by another old-fashioned, 'allow me to congrat'late you . . . ma soul 'n body, senator, 'low me to congrat'late you . . . upon your val'able services to this great commonwealth that stretches from the great Atlantical Ocean to the great and glorious Pacifical.'

'Shut up, Reggie,' said Jo. 'Let him eat his steak in peace.'

'Well, you certainly made the eagle scream, Dick,' said Pat, 'but seriously, I guess you're right.'

'We've got to be realists,' said Dick.

'I believe,' said Pat Doolittle, throwing back her head and laughing, 'that he's come across with that raise.'

Dick couldn't help grinning and nodding. He felt better since he'd eaten. He ordered another round of drinks and began to talk about going up to Harlem to dance at Small's Paradise. He said he couldn't go to bed, he was too tired, he had to have some relaxation. Pat Doolittle said she loved it in Harlem, but that she hadn't brought any money.

'My party,' said Dick. 'I've got plenty of cash on me.'

They went up with a flask of whiskey in each of the girls'

handbags and in Dick's and Reggie's back pockets. Reggie and Pat sang *The Fireship* in the taxi. Dick drank a good deal in the taxi to catch up with the others. Going down the steps to Small's was like going underwater into a warm thicklygrown pool. The air was dense with musky smells of mulatto powder and perfume and lipstick and dresses and throbbed like flesh with the smoothlybalanced chugging of the band. Dick and Pat danced right away, holding each other very close. Their dancing seemed smooth as cream. Dick found her lips under his and kissed them. She kissed back. When the music stopped, they were reeling a little. They walked back to their table with drunken dignity. When the band started again, Dick danced with Jo. He kissed her too.

She pushed him off a little. 'Dick, you oughtn't to.'

'Reggie won't mind. It's all in the family. . . .' They were dancing next to Reggie and Pat hemmed in by a swaying blur of couples. Dick dropped Jo's hand and put his hand on Reggie's shoulder. 'Reggie, you don't mind if I kiss your future wife for you just once.'

'Go as far as you like, senator,' said Reggie. His voice was thick. Pat was having trouble keeping him on his feet. Jo gave Dick a waspish look and kept her face turned away for the rest of the dance. As soon as they got back to the table, she told Reggie that it was after two and she'd have to go home, she for one had to work in the morning.

When they were alone and Dick was just starting to make love to Pat, she turned to him and said, 'Oh, Dick, do take me someplace low . . . nobody'll ever take me any place really low.'

'I should think this would be quite low enough for a juniorleaguer,' he said.

'But this is more respectable than Broadway, and I'm not a juniorleaguer . . . I'm the new woman.'

Dick burst out laughing. They both laughed and had a drink on it and felt fond of each other again and Dick suddenly asked her why couldn't they be together always.

'I think you're mean. This isn't any place to propose to a girl. Imagine remembering all your life that you'd got engaged in Harlem. . . . I want to see life.'

'All right, young lady, we'll go . . . but don't blame me if it's too rough for you.'

'I'm not a sissy,' said Pat angrily. 'I know it wasn't the stork.'

Dick paid and they finished up one of the pints. Outside it

was snowing. Streets and stoops and pavements were white, innocent, quiet, glittering under the streetlights with freshfallen snow. Dick asked the whiteeyed black doorman about a dump he'd heard of and the doorman gave the taximan the address.

Dick began to feel good. 'Gosh, Pat, isn't this lovely,' he kept crying.

'Those kids can't take it. Takes us grownups to take it. . . . Say, Reggie's getting too fresh, do you know it?' Pat held his hand tight. Her cheeks were flushed and her face had a taut look. 'Isn't it exciting?' she said. The taxi stopped in front of an unpainted basement door with one electriclightbulb haloed with snowflakes above it.

They had a hard time getting in. There were no white people there at all. It was furnaceroom set around with plain kitchen tables and chairs. The steampipes overhead were hung with colored paper streamers. A big brown woman in a pink dress, big eyes rolling loose in their dark sockets and twitching lips, led them to a table. She seemed to take a shine to Pat. 'Come right on in, darlin',' she said. 'Where's you been all my life?'

Their whiskey was gone, so they drank gin. Things got to whirling round in Dick's head. He couldn't get off the subject of how sore he was at that little squirt Reggie. Here Dick had been nursing him along in the office for a year and now he goes smartaleck on him. The little twirp.

The only music was a piano where a slimwaisted black man was tickling the ivories. Dick and Pat danced and danced and he whirled her around until the sealskin browns and the high-yallers cheered and clapped. Then Dick slipped and dropped her. She went spinning into a table where some girls were sitting. Dark heads went back, pink rubber lips stretched, mouths opened. Gold teeth and ivories let out a roar.

Pat was dancing with a pale pretty mulatto girl in a yellow dress. Dick was dancing with a softhanded brown boy in a tightfitting suit the color of his skin. The boy was whispering in Dick's ear that his name was Gloria Swanson. Dick suddenly broke away from him and went over to Pat and pulled her away from the girl. Then he ordered drinks all around that changed sullen looks into smiles again. He had trouble getting Pat into her coat. The fat woman was very helpful. 'Sure, honey,' she said, 'you don't want to go on drinkin' tonight, spoil your lovely looks.' Dick hugged her and gave her a ten-dollar bill.

In the taxi Pat had hysterics and punched and bit at him

when he held her tight to try to keep her from opening the door and jumping out into the snow.

'You spoil everything. . . . You can't think of anybody except yourself,' she yelled. 'You'll never go through with anything.'

'But, Pat, honestly,' he was whining, 'I thought it was time to draw the line.'

By the time the taxi drew up in front of the big square apartmenthouse on Park Avenue where she lived, she was sobbing quietly on his shoulder. He took her into the elevator and kissed her for a long time in the upstairs hall before he'd let her put the key in the lock of the door. They stood there tottering clinging to each other, rubbing up against each other through their clothes, until Dick heard the swish of the rising elevator and opened her door for her and pushed her in.

When he got outside the door he found the taxi waiting for him. He'd forgotten to pay the driver. He couldn't stand to go home. He didn't feel drunk, he felt immensely venturesome and cool and innocently excited. Patricia Doolittle he hated more than anybody in the world. 'The bitch,' he kept saying aloud. He wondered how it would be to go back to the dump and see what happened and there he was being kissed by the fat woman who wiggled her breasts as she hugged him and called him her own lovin' chile, with a bottle of gin in his hand pouring drinks for everybody and dancing cheek to cheek with Gloria Swanson who was humming in his ear: Do I get it now . . . or must I he . . . esitate.

It was morning. Dick was shouting the party couldn't break up, they must all come to breakfast with him. Everybody was gone and he was getting into a taxicab with Gloria and a strapping black buck he said was his girlfriend Florence. He had a terrible time getting his key in the lock. He tripped and fell toward the paleblue light seeping through his mother's lace curtains in the windows. Something very soft tapped him across the back of the head.

He woke up undressed in his own bed. It was broad daylight. The phone was ringing. He let it ring. He sat up. He felt lightheaded, but not sick. He put his hand to his ear and it came away all bloody. It must have been a stocking full of sand that hit him. He got to his feet. He felt tottery, but he could walk. His head began to ache like thunder. He reached for the place on the table he usually left his watch. No watch. His clothes were neatly hung on a chair. He found the wallet in its usual place, but the roll of bills was gone. He sat down on the edge

of the bed. Of all the damn fools. Never never never take a risk
like that again. Now they knew his name, his address, his
phonenumber. Blackmail, oh Christ. How would it be when
Mother came home from Florida to find her son earning
twentyfive thousand a year, junior partner of J. Ward Moorehouse, being blackmailed by two nigger whores, male prostitutes
receiving males? Christ. And Pat Doolittle and the Bingham
girls. It would ruin his life. For a second he thought of going
into the kitchenette and turning on the gas.

He pulled himself together and took a bath. Then he dressed
carefully and put on his hat and coat and went out. It was only
nine o'clock. He saw the time in a jeweler's window on Lexington. There was a mirror in the same window. He looked at
his face. Didn't look so bad, would look worse later, but he
needed a shave and had to do something about the clotted blood
on his ear.

He didn't have any money, but he had his checkbook. He
walked to a Turkish bath near the Grand Central. The attendants kidded him about what a fight he'd been in. He began
to get over his scare a little and to talk big about what he'd
done to the other guy. They took his check all right and he
even was able to buy a drink to have before his breakfast. When
he got to the office, his head was still splitting, but he felt in
fair shape. He had to keep his hands in his pockets so that
Miss Hilles shouldn't see how they shook. Thank God, he
didn't have to sign any letters till afternoon.

Ed Griscolm came in and sat on his desk and talked about
J. W.'s condition and the Bingham account and Dick was sweet
as sugar to him. Ed Griscolm talked big about an offer he'd had
from Halsey, but Dick said, of course, he couldn't advise him,
but that as for him the one place in the country he wanted to
be was right here, especially now as there were bigger things in
sight than there had ever been before, he and J. W. had had
a long talk going down on the train.

'I guess you're right,' said Ed. 'I guess it was sour grapes
a little.'

Dick got to his feet. 'Honestly, Ed, old man, you mustn't
think for a minute J. W. doesn't appreciate your work. He even
let drop something about a raise.'

'Well, it was nice of you to put in a word for me, old man,'
said Ed, and they shook hands warmly.

As Ed was leaving the office he turned and said, 'Say, Dick,
I wish you'd give that youngster Talbot a talking to. . . . I know

he's a friend of yours, so I don't like to do it, but, Jesus Christ, he's gone and called up again saying he's in bed with the grippe. That's the third time this month.'

Dick wrinkled up his brows. 'I don't know what to do about him, Ed. He's a nice kid all right, but if he won't knuckle down to serious work . . . I guess we'll have to let him go. We certainly can't let drinking acquaintance stand in the way of the efficiency of the office. These kids all drink too much, anyway.'

After Ed had gone, Dick found on his desk a big lavender envelope marked Personal. A whiff of strong perfume came out when he opened it. It was an invitation from Myra Bingham to come to the housewarming of her studio on Central Park South.

He was still reading it when Miss Hilles's voice came out of the interoffice phone. 'There's Mr Henry B. Furness of the Furness Corporation says he must speak to Mr Moorehouse at once.'

'Put him on my phone, Miss Hilles. I'll talk to him . . . and, by the way, put a social engagement on my engagement pad . . . January fifteenth at five o'clock . . . reception Miss Myra Bingham, 36 Central Park South.'

# Newsreel 68

WALL STREET STUNNED

*This is not Thirtyeight but it's old Ninetyseven*
*You must put her in Center on time*

MARKET SURE TO RECOVER FROM SLUMP

DECLINE IN CONTRACTS

POLICE TURN MACHINE GUNS ON COLORADO
MINE STRIKERS KILL 5 WOUND 40

sympathizers appeared on the scene just as thousands of office workers were pouring out of the buildings at the lunch hour. As they raised their placard high and started an indefinite march from one side to the other, they were jeered and hooted not only by the office workers but also by workmen on a building under construction

NEW METHODS OF SELLING SEEN

RESCUE CREWS TRY TO UPEND ILL-FATED
CRAFT WHILE WAITING FOR PONTOONS

*He looked 'round an' said to his black greasy fireman*
*Jus' shovel in a little more coal*
*And when we cross that White Oak Mountain*
*You can watch your Ninety-seven roll*

I find your column interesting and need advice. I have saved four thousand dollars which I want to invest for a better income. Do you think I might buy stocks?

POLICE KILLER FLICKS CIGARETTE AS HE
GOES TREMBLING TO DOOM

PLAY AGENCIES IN RING OF SLAVE
GIRL MARTS

MAKER OF LOVE DISBARRED AS LAWYER

*Oh the right wing clothesmakers*
*And the Socialist fakers*
*They make by the workers . . .*
*Double cross*

*They preach Social-ism*
*But practice Fasc-ism*
*To keep capitalism*
*By the boss*

#### MOSCOW CONGRESS OUSTS OPPOSITION

*It's a mighty rough road from Lynchburg to Danville*
　*An' a line on a three mile grade*
*It was on that grade he lost his average*
　*An' you see what a jump he made*

#### MILL THUGS IN MURDER RAID

here is the most dangerous example of how at the decisive moment the bourgeois ideology liquidates class solidarity and turns a friend of the workingclass of yesterday into a most miserable propagandist for imperialism today

#### RED PICKETS FINED FOR PROTESTS HERE

*We leave our home in the morning*
*We kiss our children goodbye*

#### OFFICIALS STILL HOPE FOR RESCUE OF MEN

*He was goin' downgrade makin' ninety miles an hour*
　*When his whistle broke into a scream*
*He was found in the wreck with his hand on the throttle*
　*An' was scalded to death with the steam*

#### RADICALS FIGHT WITH CHAIRS AT UNITY MEETING

#### PATROLMEN PROTECT REDS

#### U.S. CHAMBER OF COMMERCE URGES CONFIDENCE

#### REAL VALUES UNHARMED

*While we slave for the bosses*
*Our children scream an' cry*

*But when we draw our money*
*Our grocery bills to pay*

### PRESIDENT SEES PROSPERITY NEAR

*Not a cent to spend for clothing*
*Not a cent to lay away*

### STEAMROLLER IN ACTION AGAINST
### MILITANTS

### MINERS BATTLE SCABS

*But we cannot buy for our children*
*Our wages are too low*
*Now listen to me you workers*
*Both you women and men*
*Let us win for them the victory*
*I'm sure it ain't no sin*

### CARILLON PEALS IN SINGING TOWER

the President declared it was impossible to view the increased advantages for the many without smiling at those who a short time ago expressed so much fear lest our country might come under the control of a few individuals of great wealth.

### HAPPY CROWDS THRONG CEREMONY

on a tiny island nestling like a green jewel in the lake that mirrors the singing tower, the President today participated in the dedication of a bird sanctuary and its pealing carillon, fulfilling the dream of an immigrant boy

## *The Camera Eye (51)*

at the head of the valley in the dark of the hills on the broken floor of a lurchedover cabin a man halfsits halflies propped up by an old woman two wrinkled girls that might be young    chunks of coal flare in the hearth flicker in his face white and sagging as dough    blacken the cavedin mouth the taut throat the belly swelled enormous with the wound he got working on the minetipple the barefoot girl brings him a tincup of water     the woman wipes sweat off his streaming face with a dirty denim sleeve     the firelight flares in his eyes stretched big with fever in the women's scared eyes and in the blanched faces of the foreigners

without help in the valley hemmed by dark strikesilent hills the man will die (my father died we know what it is like to see a man die) the women will lay him out on the rickety cot the miners will bury him

in the jail it's light too hot the steamheat hisses we talk through the greenpainted iron bars to a tall white mustachioed old man some smiling miners in shirtsleeves a boy

faces white from mining have already the tallowy look of jailfaces

foreigners what can we say to the dead?     foreigners what can we say to the jailed?     the representative of the political party talks fast through the bars join up with us and no other union we'll send you tobacco candy solidarity our lawyers will write briefs speakers will shout your names at meetings they'll carry your names on cardboards on picketlines     the men in jail shrug their shoulders smile thinly our eyes look in their eyes through the bars     what can I say?     (in another continent I have seen the faces looking out through the barred basement windows behind the ragged sentry's boots I have seen before day the straggling footsore prisoners herded through the streets limping between bayonets     heard the volley

I have seen the dead lying out in those distant deeper valleys) what can we say to the jailed?

in the law's office we stand against the wall the law is a big man with eyes angry in a big pumpkinface     who sits and stares at us meddling foreigners through the door the deputies crane with their guns     they stand guard at the mines     they blockade the miners' soupkitchens     they've cut off the road up the valley     the hiredmen with guns stand ready to shoot (they have made us foreigners in the land where we were born they are the conquering army that has filtered into the country unnoticed they have taken the

hilltops by stealth they levy toll they stand at the minehead
     they stand at the polls   they stand by when the bailiffs
carry the furniture of the family evicted from the city tenement out on the sidewalk they are there when the bankers
foreclose on a farm they are ambushed and ready to shoot
down the strikers marching behind the flag up the switch-
back road to the mine      those that the guns spare they jail)
     the law stares across the desk out of angry eyes his
face reddens in splotches like a gobbler's neck with the
strut of the power of submachineguns sawedoffshotguns
teargas and vomitinggas the power that can feed you or
leave you to starve
     sits easy at his desk his back is covered he feels
strong behind him he feels the prosecutingattorney the
judge an owner himself the political boss the minesuperin-
tendent the board of directors      the president of the utility
the manipulator of the holdingcompany
     he lifts his hand towards the telephone
     the deputies crowd in the door
     we have only words against


## Power Superpower

     In eighteen-eighty when Thomas Edison's agent was hook-
ing up the first telephone in London, he put an ad in the paper
for a secretary and stenographer. The eager young cockney
with sprouting muttonchop whiskers who answered it
     had recently lost his job as officeboy. In his spare time he
had been learning shorthand and bookkeeping and taking dictation from the editor of the English *Vanity Fair* at night and
jotting down the speeches in Parliament for the papers. He came
of temperance smallshopkeeper stock; already he was butting
his bullethead against the harsh structure of caste that doomed
boys of his class to a life of alpaca jackets, penmanship, sub-
ordination. To get a job with an American firm was to put a
foot on the rung of a ladder that led up into the blue.
     He did his best to make himself indispensable; they let
him operate the switchboard for the first halfhour when the
telephone service was opened. Edison noticed his weekly
reports on the electrical situation in England

and sent for him to be his personal secretary.

Samuel Insull landed in America on a raw March day in eightyone. Immediately he was taken out to Menlo Park, shown about the little group of laboratories, saw the strings of electric-lightbulbs shining at intervals across the snowy lots, all lit from the world's first central electric station. Edison put him right to work and he wasn't through till midnight. Next morning at six he was on the job; Edison had no use for any nonsense about hours or vacations. Insull worked from that time on until he was seventy without a break; no nonsense about hours or vacations. Electric power turned the ladder into an elevator.

Young Insull made himself indispensable to Edison and took more and more charge of Edison's business deals. He was tireless, ruthless, reliable as the tides, Edison used to say, and fiercely determined to rise.

In ninetytwo he induced Edison to send him to Chicago and put him in as president of the Chicago Edison Company. Now he was on his own. *My engineering*, he said once in a speech, when he was sufficiently czar of Chicago to allow himself the luxury of plain speaking, *has been largely concerned with engineering all I could out of the dollar.*

He was a stiffly arrogant redfaced man with a closecropped mustache; he lived on Lake Shore Drive and was at the office at 7.10 every morning. It took him fifteen years to merge the five electrical companies into the Commonwealth Edison Company. *Very early I discovered that the first essential, as in other public utility business, was that it should be operated as a monopoly.*

When his power was firm in electricity he captured gas, spread out into the surrounding townships in northern Illinois. When politicians got in his way, he bought them, when labor-leaders got in his way he bought them. Incredibly his power grew. He was scornful of bankers, lawyers were his hired men. He put his own lawyer in as corporation counsel and through him ran Chicago. When he found to his amazement that there were men (even a couple of young lawyers, Richberg and Ickes) in Chicago that he couldn't buy, he decided he'd better put on a show for the public;

Big Bill Thompson, the Builder:
*punch King George in the nose,*
the hunt for the treeclimbing fish,
the Chicago Opera.

It was too easy; the public had money, there was one of them born every minute, with the founding of Middlewest Utilities in nineteen twelve Insull began to use the public's money to spread his empire. His companies began to have open stockholders' meetings, to ballyhoo service, the small investor could sit there all day hearing the bigwigs talk. It's fun to be fooled. Companyunions hypnotized his employees; everybody had to buy stock in his companies, employees had to go out and sell stock, officeboys, linemen, trolleyconductors. Even Owen D. Young was afraid of him. *My experience is that the greatest aid in the efficiency of labor is a long line of men waiting at the gate.*

War shut up the progressives (no more nonsense about trustbusting, controlling monopoly, the public good) and raised Samuel Insull to the peak.

He was head of the Illinois State Council of Defense. *Now,* he said delightedly, *I can do anything I like.* With it came the perpetual spotlight, the purple taste of empire. If anybody didn't like what Samuel Insull did he was a traitor. Chicago damn well kept its mouth shut.

The Insull companies spread and merged put competitors out of business until Samuel Insull and his stooge brother Martin controlled through the leverage of holdingcompanies and directorates and blocks of minority stock

light and power, coalmines and tractioncompanies

in Illinois, Michigan, the Dakotas, Nebraska, Arkansas, Oklahoma, Missouri, Maine, Kansas, Wisconsin, Virginia, Ohio, North Carolina, Indiana, New York, New Jersey, Texas, in Canada, in Louisiana, in Georgia, in Florida and Alabama.

(It has been figured out that one dollar in Middle West Utilities controlled seventeen hundred and fifty dollars invested by the public in the subsidiary companies that actually did the work of producing electricity. With the delicate lever of a voting trust controlling the stock of the two top holdingcompanies he controlled a twelfth of the power output of America.)

Samuel Insull began to think he owned all that the way a man owns the roll of bills in his back pocket.

Always he'd been scornful of bankers. He owned quite a few in Chicago. But the New York bankers were laying for him; they felt he was a bounder, whispered that this financial structure was unsound. Fingers itched to grasp the lever that so delicately moved this enormous power over lives, superpower, Insull liked to call it.

A certain Cyrus S. Eaton of Cleveland, an exBaptist-minister, was the David that brought down this Goliath. Whether it was so or not he made Insull believe that Wall Street was behind him.

He started buying stock in the three Chicago utilities. Insull in a panic for fear he'd lose his control went into the market to buy against him. Finally the Reverend Eaton let himself be bought out, shaking down the old man for a profit of twenty million dollars.

The stockmarket crash.

Paper values were slipping. Insull's companies were intertwined in a tangle that no bookkeeper has ever been able to unravel.

The gas hissed out of the torn balloon. Insull threw away his imperial pride and went on his knees to the bankers.

The bankers had him where they wanted him. To save the face of the tottering czar he was made a receiver of his own concerns. But the old man couldn't get out of his head the illusion that the money was all his. When it was discovered that he was using the stockholders' funds to pay off his brother's brokerage accounts it was too thick even for a federaljudge. Insull was forced to resign.

He held directorates in eightyfive companies, he was chairman of sixtyfive, president of eleven: it took him three hours to sign his resignations.

As a reward for his services to monopoly his companies chipped in on a pension of eighteen thousand a year. But the public was shouting for criminal prosecution. When the handouts stopped newspapers and politicians turned on him. Revolt against the moneymanipulators was in the air. Samuel Insull got the wind up and ran off to Canada with his wife.

Extradition proceedings. He fled to Paris. When the authorities began to close in on him there he slipped away to Italy, took a plane to Tirana, another to Salonika and then the train to Athens. There the old fox went to earth. Money talked as sweetly in Athens as it had in Chicago in the old days.

The American ambassador tried to extradite him. Insull hired a chorus of Hellenic lawyers and politicos and sat drinking coffee in the lobby of the Grande Bretagne, while they proceeded to tie up the ambassador in a snarl of chicanery as complicated as the bookkeeping of his holdingcompanies. The successors of Demosthenes were delighted. The ancestral itch in

many a Hellenic palm was temporarily assuaged. Samuel Insull
settled down cozily in Athens, was stirred by the sight of the
Parthenon, watched the goats feeding on the Pentelic slopes,
visited the Areopagus, admired marble fragments ascribed to
Phidias, talked with the local bankers about reorganizing the
public utilities of Greece, was said to be promoting Macedonian
lignite. He was the toast of the Athenians; Madame Kouryoumdjouglou, the vivacious wife of a Bagdad datemerchant,
devoted herself to his comfort. When the first effort at extradition failed, the old gentleman declared in the courtroom, as
he struggled out from the embraces of his four lawyers: *Greece
is a small but great country.*

The idyll was interrupted when the Roosevelt Administration began to put the heat on the Greek Foreign Office. Government lawyers in Chicago were accumulating truckloads of
evidence and chalking up more and more drastic indictments.

Finally after many a postponement (he had hired physi-
cians as well as lawyers, they cried to high heaven that it would
kill him to leave the genial climate of the Attic plain),

he was ordered to leave Greece as an undesirable alien, to
the great indignation of Balkan society and of Madame Kouryoumdjouglou.

He hired the *Maiotis* a small and grubby Greek freighter
and panicked the foreignnews services by slipping off for an
unknown destination.

It was rumored that the new Odysseus was bound for
Aden, for the islands of the South Seas, that he'd been invited
to Persia. After a few days he turned up rather seasick in the
Bosporus on his way, it was said, to Rumania where Madame
Kouryoumdjouglou had advised him to put himself under the
protection of her friend la Lupescu.

At the request of the American ambassador the Turks
were delighted to drag him off the Greek freighter and place
him in a not at all comfortable jail. Again money had been
mysteriously wafted from England, the healing balm began to
flow, lawyers were hired, interpreters expostulated, doctors
made diagnoses;

but Angora was boss

and Insull was shipped off to Smyrna to be turned over to
the assistant federal districtattorney who had come all that way
to arrest him.

The Turks wouldn't even let Madame Kouryoumdjouglou,
on her way back from making arrangements in Bucharest, go

ashore to speak to him. In a scuffle with the officials on the steamboat the poor lady was pushed overboard
and with difficulty fished out of the Bosporus.

Once he was cornered the old man let himself tamely be taken home on the *Exilona*, started writing his memoirs, made himself agreeable to his fellow passengers, was taken off at Sandy Hook and rushed to Chicago to be arraigned.

In Chicago the government spitefully kept him a couple of nights in jail; men he'd never known, so the newspapers said, stepped forward to go on his twohundredandfiftythousanddollar bail. He was moved to a hospital that he himself had endowed. Solidarity. The leading businessmen in Chicago were photographed visiting him there. Henry Ford paid a call.

The trial was very beautiful. The prosecution got bogged in finance technicalities. The judge was not unfriendly. The Insulls stole the show.

They were folks, they smiled at reporters, they posed for photographers, they went down to the courtroom by bus. Investors might have been ruined but so, they allowed it to be known, were the Insulls; the captain had gone down with the ship.

Old Samuel Insull rambled amiably on the stand, told his lifestory: from officeboy to powermagnate, his struggle to make good, his love for his home and the kiddies. He didn't deny he'd made mistakes; who hadn't, but they were honest errors. Samuel Insull wept. Brother Martin wept. The lawyers wept. With voices choked with emotion headliners of Chicago business told from the witnessstand how much Insull had done for business in Chicago. There wasn't a dry eye in the jury.

Finally driven to the wall by the prosecutingattorney Samuel Insull blurted out that yes, he had made an error of some ten million dollars in accounting but that it had been an honest error.

Verdict: Not Guilty.

Smiling through their tears the happy Insulls went to their towncar amid the cheers of the crowd. Thousands of ruined investors, at least so the newspapers said, who had lost their life savings sat crying over the home editions at the thought of how Mr Insull had suffered. The bankers were happy, the bankers had moved in on the properties.

In an odor of sanctity the deposed monarch of superpower, the officeboy who made good, enjoys his declining years spending the pension of twentyone thousand a year that the directors of his old companies dutifully restored to him. *After fifty years of work*, he said, *my job is gone.*

## Mary French

Mary French had to stay late at the office and couldn't get to the hall until the meeting was almost over. There were no seats left, so she stood in the back. So many people were standing in front of her that she couldn't see Don, she could only hear his ringing harsh voice and feel the tense attention in the silence during his pauses. When a roar of applause answered his last words and the hall filled suddenly with voices and the scrape and shuffle of feet, she ran out ahead of the crowd and up the alley to the back door. Don was just coming out of the black sheetiron door talking over his shoulder as he came to two of the miners' delegates. He stopped a second to hold the door open for them with a long arm. His face had the flushed smile, there was the shine in his eye he often had after speaking, the look, Mary used to tell herself, of a man who had just come from a date with his best girl. It was some time before Don saw her in the group that gathered round him in the alley. Without looking at her, he swept her along with the men he was talking to and walked them fast toward the corner of the street. Eyes looked after them as they went from the groups of furworkers and garmentworkers that dotted the pavement in front of the hall. Mary tingled with the feeling of warm ownership in the looks of the workers as their eyes followed Don Stevens down the street.

It wasn't until they were seated in a small lunchroom under the El that Don turned to Mary and squeezed her hand. 'Tired?'

She nodded. 'Aren't you, Don?'

He laughed and drawled, 'No, I'm not tired. I'm hungry.'

'Comrade French, I thought we'd detailed you to see that Comrade Stevens ate regular,' said Rudy Goldfarb with a flash of teeth out of a dark Italianlooking face.

'He won't ever eat anything when he's going to speak,' Mary said.

'I make up for it afterwards,' said Don. 'Say, Mary, I hope you have some change. I don't think I've got a cent on me.'

Mary nodded, smiling. 'Mother came across again,' she whispered.

'Money,' broke in Steve Mestrovich. 'We got to have money or else we're licked.'

'The truck got off today,' said Mary. 'That's why I was so late getting to the meeting.'

Mestrovich passed the grimed bulk of his hand across his puttycolored face that had a sharply turnedup nose peppered with black pores. 'If cossack don't git him.'

'Eddy Spellman's a smart kid. He gets through like a shadow. I don't know how he does it.'

'You don't know what them clothes means to women and kids and . . . listen, Miss French, don't hold back nothin' because too raggedy. Ain't nothin' so ragged like what our little kids got on their backs.'

'Eddy's taking five cases of condensed milk. We'll have more as soon as he comes back.'

'Say, Mary,' said Don suddenly, looking up from his plate of soup, 'how about calling up Sylvia? I forgot to ask how much we collected at the meeting.'

Young Goldfarb got to his feet. 'I'll call. You look tired, Comrade French. . . . Anybody got a nickel?'

'Here, I got nickel,' said Mestrovich. He threw back his head and laughed. 'Damn funny . . . miner with nickel. Down our way miner got nickel put in frame send to Meester Carnegie Museum . . . very rare.' He got up roaring laughter and put on his black longvisored miner's cap. 'Goodnight, comrade, I walk Brooklyn. Reliefcommittee nine o'clock . . . right, Miss French?'

As he strode out of the lunchroom the heavy tread of his black boots made the sugarbowls jingle on the tables. 'Oh, Lord,' said Mary, with tears suddenly coming to her eyes. 'That was his last nickel.'

Goldfarb came back saying that the collection hadn't been so good. Sixtynine dollars and some pledges. 'Christmas time coming on . . . you know. Everybody's always broke at Christmas.'

'Henderson made a lousy speech,' grumbled Don. 'He's more of a socialfascist every day.'

Mary sat there feeling the tiredness in every bone of her body waiting until Don got ready to go home. She was too sleepy to follow what they were talking about, but every now and then the words centralcommittee, expulsions, oppositionists, splitters, rasped in her ears. Then Don was tapping her on the shoulder and she was waking up and walking beside him through the dark streets.

'It's funny, Don,' she was saying, 'I always go to sleep when you talk about party discipline. I guess it's because I don't want to hear about it.'

'No use being sentimental about it,' said Don savagely.

'But is it sentimental to be more interested in saving the miners' unions?' she said, suddenly feeling wide awake again.

'Of course that's what we all believe, but we have to follow the party line. A lot of those boys . . . Goldfarb's one of them . . . Ben Compton's another . . . think this is a debatingsociety. If they're not very careful indeed they'll find themselves out on their ear. . . . You just watch.'

Once they'd staggered up the five flights to their dingy little apartment where Mary had always planned to put up curtains but had never had time, Don suddenly caved in with fatigue and threw himself on the couch and fell asleep without taking off his clothes. Mary tried to rouse him, but gave it up. She unlaced his shoes for him and threw a blanket over him and got into bed herself and tried to sleep.

She was staring wide awake, she was counting old pairs of trousers, torn suits of woolly underwear, old armyshirts with the sleeves cut off, socks with holes in them that didn't match. She was seeing the rickety children with puffy bellies showing through their rags, the scrawny women with uncombed hair and hands distorted with work, the boys with their heads battered and bleeding from the clubs of the Coal and Iron Police, the photograph of a miner's body shot through with machinegun bullets. She got up and took two or three swigs from a bottle of gin she kept in the medicinecloset in the bathroom. The gin burned her throat. Coughing she went back to bed and went off into a hot dreamless sleep.

Toward morning Don woke her getting into the bed. He kissed her. 'Darling, I've set the alarm for seven. . . . Be sure to get me up. I've got a very important committeemeeting. . . . Be sure and do it.' He went off to sleep again right away like a child. She lay beside his bigboned lanky body, listening to his regular breathing, feeling happy and safe there in the bed with him.

Eddy Spellman got through with his truck again and distributed his stuff to several striking locals U.M.W. in the Pittsburgh district, although he had a narrow squeak when the deputies tried to ambush him near Greensburg. They'd have nabbed him if a guy he knew who was a bootlegger hadn't tipped him off. The same bootlegger helped him out when he skidded into a snowdrift on the hill going down into Johnstown on the way back. He was laughing about it as he helped Mary pack up the new shipment.

'He wanted to give me some liquor. . . . He's a good feller, do you know it, Miss Mary? . . . Tough kinder . . . that racket hardens a feller up . . . but a prince when you know him. . . . "Hell, no, Ed," his name's Eddy too, I says to him when he tries to slip me a pint, "I ain't goin' to take a drink until after the revolution and then I'll be ridin' so high I won't need to." '

Mary laughed. 'I guess we all ought to do that, Eddy. . . . But I feel so tired and discouraged at night sometimes.'

'Sure,' said Eddy, turning serious. 'It gits you down thinkin' how they got all the guns an' all the money an' we ain't got nothin'.'

'One thing you're going to have, Comrade Spellman, is a pair of warm gloves and a good overcoat before you make the next trip.'

His freckled face turned red to the roots of his red hair. 'Honest, Miss Mary, I don't git cold. To tell the truth the motor heats up so much in the old pile of junk it keeps me warm in the coldest weather. . . . After the next trip we got to put a new clutch in her and that'll take more jack than we kin spare from the milk. . . . I tell you things are bad up there in the coalfields this winter.'

'But those miners have got such wonderful spirit,' said Mary.

'The trouble is, Miss Mary, you kin only keep your spirit up a certain length of time on an empty stumick.'

That evening Don came by to the office to get Mary for supper. He was very cheerful and his gaunt bony face had more color in it than usual. 'Well, little girl, what would you think of moving up to Pittsburgh? After the plenum I may go out to do some organizing in western Pennsylvania and Ohio. Mestrovich says they need somebody to pep 'em up a little.'

Eddy Spellman looked up from the bale of clothes he was tying up. 'Take it from me, Comrade Stevens, they sure do.'

Mary felt a chill go through her. Don must have noticed the pallor spreading over her face. 'We won't take any risks,' he added hurriedly. 'Those miners take good care of a feller, don't they, Eddy?'

'They sure do. . . . Wherever the locals is strong you'll be safer than you are right here in New York.'

'Anyway,' said Mary, her throat tight and dry, 'if you've got to go, you've got to go.'

'You two go out an' eat,' said Eddy. 'I'll finish up . . . I'm bunkin' here anyway. Saves the price of a flop. . . . You feed Miss Mary up good, Comrade Stevens. We don't want her gettin' sick. . . . If all the real partymembers worked like she does, we'd have . . . hell, we'd have the finest kind of a revolution by the spring of the year.'

They went out laughing, and walked down to Bleecker Street and settled happily at a table in an Italian restaurant and ordered up the seventyfivecent dinner and a bottle of wine. 'You've got a great admirer in Eddy,' Don said, smiling at her across the table.

A couple of weeks later Mary came home one icy winter evening to find Don busy packing his grip. She couldn't help letting out a cry, her nerves were getting harder and harder to control. 'Oh, Don, it's not Pittsburgh yet?' Don shook his head and went on packing.

When he had closed up his wicker suitcase, he came over to her and put his arm round her shoulder. 'I've got to go across to the other side with . . . you know who . . . essential party business.'

'Oh, Don, I'd love to go, too. I've never been to Russia or anywhere.'

'I'll only be gone a month. We're sailing at midnight . . . and Mary darling . . . if anybody asks after me I'm in Pittsburgh, see?'

Mary started to cry. 'I'll have to say I don't know where you are . . . I know I can't ever get away with a lie.'

'Mary dear, it'll just be a few days . . . don't be a little silly.'

Mary smiled through her tears. 'But I am . . . I'm an awful little silly.'

He kissed her and patted her gently on the back. Then he picked up his suitcase and hurried out of the room with a big checked cap pulled down over his eyes.

Mary walked up and down the narrow room with her lips twitching, fighting to keep down the hysterical sobs. To give herself something to do, she began to plan how she could fix up the apartment so that it wouldn't look so dreary when Don came back. She pulled out the couch and pushed it across the window like a windowseat. Then she pulled the table out in front of it and grouped the chairs round the table. She made up her mind she'd paint the woodwork white and get turkeyred for the curtains.

Next morning she was in the middle of drinking her coffee out of a cracked cup without a saucer, feeling bitterly lonely in the empty apartment when the telephone rang. At first she didn't recognize whose voice it was. She was confused and kept stammering, 'Who is it, please?' into the receiver.

'But, Mary,' the voice was saying in an exasperated tone, 'you must know who I am. It's Ben Compton. . . bee ee enn . . . Ben. I've got to see you about something. Where could I meet you? Not at your place.'

Mary tried to keep her voice from sounding stiff and chilly. 'I've got to be uptown today. I've got to have lunch with a woman who may give some money to the miners. It's a horrible waste of time, but I can't help it. She won't give a cent unless I listen to her sad story. How about meeting me in front of the Public Library at twothirty?'

'Better say inside. . . . It's about zero out today. I just got up out of bed from the flu.'

Mary hardly knew Ben, he looked so much older. There was gray in the hair spilling out untidily from under his cap. He stooped and peered into her face querulously through his thick glasses. He didn't shake hands.

'Well, I might as well tell you . . . you'll know it soon enough if you don't know it already . . . I've been expelled from the party . . . oppositionist . . . exceptionalism . . . a lot of nonsense. . . . Well, that doesn't matter, I'm still a revolutionist . . . I'll continue to work outside of the party.'

'Oh, Ben, I'm so sorry,' was all Mary could find to say. 'You know I don't know anything except what I read in the *Daily*. It all seems too terrible to me.'

'Let's go out, that guard's watching us.'

Outside Ben began to shiver from the cold. His wrists stuck out red from his frayed green overcoat with sleeves much too short for his long arms.

'Oh, where can we go?' Mary kept saying.

Finally they went down into a basement automat and sat talking in low voices over a cup of coffee. 'I didn't want to go to your place because I didn't want to meet Stevens. . . . Stevens and me have never been friends, you know that. . . . Now he's in with the comintern crowd. He'll make the centralcommittee when they've cleaned out all the brains.'

'But, Ben, people can have differences of opinion, and still . . .'

'A party of yesmen . . . that'll be great. . . . But, Mary, I had to see you . . . I feel so lonely suddenly . . . you know, cut off from everything. . . . You know if we hadn't been fools we'd

have had that baby that time . . . we'd still love each other. . . .
Mary, you were very lovely to me when I first got out of jail. . . .
Say, where's your friend Ada, the musician who had that fancy
apartment?'

'Oh, she's as silly as ever . . . running around with some fool
violinist or other.'

'I've always liked music. . . . I ought to have kept you, Mary.'

'A lot of water's run under the bridge since then,' said Mary
coldly.

'Are you happy with Stevens? I haven't any right to ask.'

'But, Ben, what's the use of raking all this old stuff up?'

'You see, often a young guy thinks, I'll sacrifice everything,
and then, when he is cut off all that side of his life, he's not as
good as he was, do you see? For the first time in my life I have
no contact. I thought maybe you could get me in on reliefwork
somehow. The discipline isn't so strict in the relief organizations.'

'I don't think they want any disrupting influences in the
I.L.D.,' said Mary.

'So I'm a disrupter to you too. . . . All right, in the end the
workingclass will judge between us.'

'Let's not talk about it, Ben.'

'I'd like you to put it up to Stevens and ask him to sound out
the proper quarters . . . that's not much to ask, is it?'

'But Don's not here at present.' Before she could catch herself she'd blurted it out.

Ben looked her in the eye with a sudden sharp look.

'He hasn't by any chance sailed for Moscow with certain
other comrades?'

'He's gone to Pittsburgh on secret partywork and, for God's
sake, shut up about it. You just got hold of me to pump me.' She
got to her feet, her face flaming. 'Well, goodbye, Mr Compton.
. . . You don't happen to be a stoolpigeon as well as a disrupter,
do you?'

Ben Compton's face broke in pieces suddenly the way a child's
face does when it is just going to bawl. He sat there staring at
her, senselessly scraping the spoon round and round in the
empty coffeemug. She was halfway up the stairs when on an
impulse she went back and stood for a second looking down at
his bowed head. 'Ben,' she said in a gentler voice, 'I shouldn't
have said that . . . without proof. . . . I don't believe it.' Ben
Compton didn't look up. She went up the stairs again out into
the stinging wind and hurried down Fortysecond Street in the

afternoon crowd and took the subway down to Union Square.

The last day of the year Mary French got a telegram at the office from Ada Cohn.

PLEASE PLEASE COMMUNICATE YOUR MOTHER IN TOWN AT PLAZA  SAILING SOON  WANTS TO SEE YOU DOESN'T KNOW ADDRESS  WHAT SHALL I TELL HER

Newyear'sday there wasn't much doing at the office. Mary was the only one who had turned up, so in the middle of the morning she called up the Plaza and asked for Mrs French. No such party staying there. Next she called up Ada. Ada talked and talked about how Mary's mother had married again, a Judge Blake, a very prominent man, a retired federal circuit judge, such an attractive man with a white Vandyke beard, and Ada had to see Mary and Mrs Blake had been so sweet to her and Ada asked her to dinner at the Plaza and wanted to know all about Mary and that she'd had to admit that she never saw her, although she was her best friend, and she'd been to a New-year'seve party and had such a headache she couldn't practice and she'd invited some lovely people in that afternoon and wouldn't Mary come, she'd be sure to like them.

Mary almost hung up on her, Ada sounded so silly, but she said she'd call her back right away after she'd talked to her mother. It ended by her going home and getting her best dress on and going uptown to the Plaza to see Judge and Mrs Blake. She tried to find some place she could get her hair curled, because she knew the first thing her mother would say was that she looked a fright, but everything was closed on account of its being Newyear'sday.

Judge and Mrs Blake were getting ready to have lunch in a big private drawingroom on the corner looking out over the humped snowy hills of the park bristly with bare branches and interwoven with fastmoving shining streams of traffic. Mary's mother didn't look as if she'd aged a day; she was dressed in darkgreen and really looked stunning with a little white ruffle round her neck sitting there so at her ease, with rings on her fingers that sparkled in the gray winter light that came in through the big windows. The judge had a soft caressing voice. He talked elaborately about the prodigal daughter and the fatted calf until her mother broke in to say that they were going to Europe on a spree; they'd both of them made big killings on the stockexchange on the same day and they felt they owed themselves a little rest and relaxation. And she went on about how worried she'd been because all her letters had been returned from Mary's last address, and that she'd written Ada again and again and Ada had always said Mary was in Pittsburgh or Fall River or some horrible place doing social work and that she felt it was about time she gave up doing everything for the poor and unfortunate and devoted a little attention to her own kith and kin.

'I hear you are a very dreadful young lady, Mary, my dear,' said the judge, blandly, ladling some creamofcelery soup into her plate. 'I hope you didn't bring any bombs with you.' They both seemed to think that that was a splendid joke and laughed and laughed. 'But to be serious,' went on the judge, 'I know that social inequality is a very dreadful thing and a blot on the fair name of American democracy. But as we get older, my dear, we learn to live and let live, that we have to take the bad with the good a little.'

'Mary dear, why don't you go abroad with Ada Cohn and have a nice rest? . . . I'll find the money for the trip. I know it'll do you good. . . . You know I've never approved of your friendship with Ada Cohn. Out home we are probably a little old-fashioned about those things. Here she seems to be accepted everywhere. In fact, she seems to know all the prominent musical people. Of course how good a musician she is herself I'm not in a position to judge.'

'Hilda, dear,' said the judge, 'Ada Cohn has a heart of gold. I find her a very sweet girl. Her father was a very distinguished lawyer. You know we decided we'd lay aside our prejudices a little . . . didn't we, dear?'

'The judge is reforming me,' laughed Mary's mother coyly.

Mary was so nervous she felt she was going to scream. The heavy buttery food, the suave attentions of the waiter and the fatherly geniality of the judge made her almost gag.

'Look, Mother,' she said, 'if you really have a little money to spare, you might let me have something for our milkfund. After all, miners' children aren't guilty of anything.'

'My dear, I've already made substantial contributions to the Red Cross. . . . After all, we've had a miners' strike out in Colorado on our hands much worse than in Pennsylvania. . . . I've always felt, Mary dear, that if you were interested in labor conditions the place for you was home in Colorado Springs. If you must study that sort of thing there was never any need to come East for it.'

'Even the I.W.W. has reared its ugly head again,' said the judge.

'I don't happen to approve of the tactics of the I.W.W.,' said Mary stiffly.

'I should hope not,' said her mother.

'But, Mother, don't you think you could let me have a couple of hundred dollars?'

'To spend on those dreadful agitators; they may not be I Won't Works, but they're just as bad.'

'I'll promise that every cent goes into milk for the babies.'

'But that's just handing the miners over to these miserable Russian agitators. Naturally, if they can give milk to the children it makes them popular, puts them in a position where they can mislead these poor miserable foreigners worse than ever.'

The judge leaned forward across the table and put his blue-veined hand in its white starched cuff on Mary's mother's hand. 'It's not that we lack sympathy with the plight of the miners' women and children, or that we don't understand the dreadful conditions of the whole mining industry . . . we know altogether too much about that, don't we, Hilda? But . . .'

Mary suddenly found that she'd folded her napkin and gotten trembling to her feet. 'I don't see any reason for further prolonging this interview, that must be painful to you, Mother, as it is to me . . .'

'Perhaps I can arbitrate,' said the judge, smiling, getting to his feet with his napkin in his hand.

Mary felt a desperate tight feeling like a metal ring round her head. 'I've got to go, Mother . . . I don't feel very well today. Have a nice trip. . . . I don't want to argue.' Before they could stop her, she was off down the hall and on her way down in the elevator.

Mary felt so upset she had to talk to somebody, so she went to a telephone booth and called up Ada. Ada's voice was full of sobs, she said something dreadful had happened and that she'd called off her party and that Mary must come up to see her immediately. Even before Ada opened the door of the apartment on Madison Avenue, Mary got a whiff of the Forêt Vierge perfume Ada had taken to using when she first came to New York. Ada opened the door wearing a green and pink flowered silk wrapper with all sorts of little tassels hanging from it. She fell on Mary's neck. Her eyes were red and she sniffed as she talked.

'Why, what's the matter, Ada?' asked Mary coolly.

'Darling, I've just had the most dreadful row with Hjalmar. We have parted forever. . . . Of course I had to call off the party because I was giving it for him.'

'Who's Hjalmar?'

'He's somebody very beautiful . . . and very hateful. . . . But let's talk about you, Mary darling . . . I do hope you've made it up with your mother and Judge Blake.'

'I just walked out. . . . What's the use of arguing? They're on one side of the barricades and I'm on the other.'

Ada strode up and down the room. 'Oh, I hate talk like that. . . . It makes me feel awful. . . . At least you'll have a drink. . . . I've got to drink, I've been too nervous to practice all day.'

Mary stayed all afternoon at Ada's drinking ginrickeys and eating the sandwiches and little cakes that had been laid out in the kitchenette for the party and talking about old times and Ada's unhappy loveaffair. Ada made Mary read all his letters and Mary said he was a damn fool and good riddance. Then Ada cried and Mary told her she ought to be ashamed of herself, she didn't know what real misery was. Ada was very meek about it and went to her desk and wrote out a check in a shaky hand for a hundred dollars for the miners' milkfund. Ada had some supper sent up for them from the uptown Longchamps and declared she'd spent the happiest afternoon in years. She made Mary promise to come to her concert in the small hall at the Aeolian the following week. When Mary was going, Ada made her take a couple of dollars for a taxi. They were both reeling a little in the hall waiting for the elevator. 'We've just gotten to be a pair of old topers,' said Ada gaily. It was a good thing Mary had decided to take a taxi because she found it hard to stand on her feet.

That winter the situation of the miners in the Pittsburgh district got worse and worse. Evictions began. Families with little children were living in tents and in brokendown unheated tarpaper barracks. Mary lived in a feeling of nightmare, writing letters, mimeographing appeals, making speeches at meetings of clothing and fur workers, canvassing wealthy liberals. The money that came in was never enough. She took no salary for her work, so she had to get Ada to lend her money to pay her rent. She was thin and haggard and coughed all the time. Too many cigarettes, she'd explain. Eddy Spellman and Rudy Goldfarb worried about her. She could see they'd decided she wasn't eating enough because she was all the time finding on the corner of her desk a paper bag of sandwiches or a carton of coffee that one of them had brought in. Once Eddy brought her a big package of smearcase that his mother had made up home near Scranton. She couldn't eat it; she felt guilty every time she saw it sprouting green mold in the icebox that had no ice in it because she'd given up cooking, now that Don was away.

One evening Rudy came into the office with smiles all over his face. Eddy was leaning over packing the old clothes into bales as usual for his next trip. Rudy gave him a light kick in the seat of the pants.

'Hey you, Trotzkyite,' said Eddy, jumping at him and pulling out his necktie.

'Smile when you say that,' said Rudy, pummeling him.

They were all laughing. Mary felt like an oldmaid school-teacher watching the boys roughhousing in front of her desk. 'Meeting comes to order,' she said.

'They tried to hang it on me, but they couldn't,' said Rudy, panting, straightening his necktie and his mussed hair. 'But what I was going to say, Comrade French, was that I thought you might like to know that a certain comrade is getting in on the *Aquitania* tomorrow . . . tourist class.'

'Rudy, are you sure?'

'Saw the cable.'

Mary got to the dock too early and had to wait two hours. She tried to read the afternoon papers, but her eyes wouldn't follow the print. It was too hot in the receptionroom and too cold outside. She fidgeted around miserably until at last she saw the enormous black sheetiron wall sliding with its rows of lighted portholes past the openings in the wharfbuilding. Her hands and feet were icy. Her whole body ached to feel his arms around her, for the rasp of his deep voice in her ears. All the time a vague worry flitted in the back of her head, because she hadn't had a letter from him while he'd been away.

Suddenly there he was coming down the gangplank alone, with the old wicker suitcase in his hand. He had on a new belted German raincoat, but the same checked cap. She was face to face with him. He gave her a little hug but he didn't kiss her. There was something odd in his voice.

'Hello, Mary . . . I didn't expect to find you here. . . . I don't want to be noticed, you know.' His voice had a low furtive sound in her ears. He was nervously changing his suitcase from one hand to the other. 'See you in a few days. . . . I'm going to be pretty busy.'

She turned without a word and ran down the wharf. She

hurried breathless along the crosstown street to the Ninth Avenue El. When she opened her door, the new turkeyred curtains were like a blow from a whip in her face.

She couldn't go back to the office. She couldn't bear the thought of facing the boys and the people she knew, the people who had known them together. She called up and said she had a bad case of grippe and would have to stay in bed a couple of days. She stayed all day in the blank misery of the narrow rooms. Toward evening she dozed off to sleep on the couch. She woke up with a start thinking she heard a step in the hall outside. It wasn't Don, the steps went on up the next flight. After that she didn't sleep any more.

The next morning the phone woke her just when she settled herself in bed to drowse a little. It was Sylvia Goldstein saying she was sorry Mary had the grippe and asking if there was anything she could do. Oh, no, she was fine, she was just going to stay in bed all day, Mary answered in a dead voice.

'Well, I suppose you knew all the time about Comrade Stevens and Comrade Lichfield . . . you two were always so close . . . they were married in Moscow . . . she's an English comrade . . . she spoke at the big meeting at the Bronx Casino last night . . . she's got a great shock of red hair . . . stunning, but some of the girls think it's dyed. Lots of comrades didn't know you and Comrade Stevens had broken up . . . isn't it sad things like that have to happen in the movement?'

'Oh, that was a long time ago. . . . Goodbye, Sylvia,' said Mary harshly, and hung up. She called up a bootlegger she knew and told him to send her up a bottle of gin.

The next afternoon there was a light rap on the door and when Mary opened it a crack there was Ada wreathed in silver fox and breathing out a great gust of Forêt Vierge. 'Oh, Mary darling, I knew something was the matter. . . . You know sometimes I'm quite psychic. And when you didn't come to my concert, first I was mad, but then I said to myself I know the poor darling's sick. So I just went right down to your office. There was the handsomest boy there and I just made him tell me where you lived. He said you were sick with the grippe and so I came right over. My dear, why aren't you in bed? You look a sight.'

'I'm all right,' mumbled Mary numbly, pushing the stringy hair off her face. 'I been . . . making plans . . . about how we can handle this relief situation better.'

'Well, you're just coming up right away to my spare bedroom and let me pet you up a little. . . . I don't believe it's grippe, I think it's overwork. . . . If you're not careful you'll be having a nervous breakdown.'

'Maybe sumpen like that.' Mary couldn't articulate her words. She didn't seem to have any will of her own any more; she did everything Ada told her. When she was settled in Ada's clean lavendersmelling spare bed, they sent out for some barbital and it put her to sleep. Mary stayed there several days eating the meals Ada's maid brought her, drinking all the drinks Ada would give her, listening to the continual scrape of violin practice that came from the other room all morning. But at night she couldn't sleep without filling herself up with dope. She didn't seem to have any will left. It would take her half an hour to decide to get up to go to the toilet.

After she'd been at Ada's a week, she began to feel she ought to go home. She began to be impatient of Ada's sly references to unhappy loveaffairs and broken hearts and the beauty of abnegation and would snap Ada's head off whenever she started it.

'That's fine,' Ada would say. 'You are getting your meanness back.'

For some time Ada had been bringing up the subject of somebody she knew who'd been crazy about Mary for years and who was dying to see her again. Finally Mary gave in and said she would go to a cocktail party at Eveline Johnson's where Ada said she knew he'd be. 'And Eveline gives the most wonderful parties. I don't know how she does it because she never has any money, but all the most interesting people in New York will be there. They always are. Radicals too, you know. Eveline can't live without her little group of reds.'

Mary wore one of Ada's dresses that didn't fit her very well and went out in the morning to have her hair curled at Sak's where Ada always had hers curled. They had some cocktails at Ada's place before they went. At the last minute Mary said she wouldn't go because she'd finally got it out of Ada that it was George Barrow who was going to be at the party. Ada made Mary drink another cocktail and a reckless feeling came over her and she said all right, let's get a move on.

There was a smiling colored maid in a fancy lace cap and apron at the door of the house who took them down the hall to a bedroom full of coats and furs where they were to take off their wraps.

As Ada was doing her face at the dressingtable, Mary whispered in her ear, 'Just think what our reliefcommittee could do with the money that woman wastes on senseless entertaining.'

'But she's a darling,' Ada whispered back excitedly. 'Honestly, you'll like her.'

The door had opened behind their backs letting in a racketing gust of voices, laughs, tinkle of glasses, a whiff of perfume and toast and cigarettesmoke and gin.

'Oh, Ada,' came a ringing voice.

'Eveline, darling, how lovely you look! . . . This is Mary French, you know I said I'd bring her. . . . She's my oldest friend.' Mary found herself shaking hands with a tall slender woman in a pearlgray dress. Her face was very white and her lips were very red and her long large eyes were exaggerated with mascara.

'So nice of you to come,' Eveline Johnson said and sat down suddenly among the furs and wraps on the bed.

'It sounds like a lovely party,' cried Ada.

'I hate parties. I don't know why I give them,' said Eveline Johnson. 'Well, I guess I've got to go back to the menagerie. . . . Oh, Ada, I'm so tired.'

Mary found herself studying the harsh desperate lines under the makeup round Mrs Johnson's mouth and the strained tenseness of the cords of her neck. Their silly life tells on them, she was saying to herself.

'What about the play?' Ada was saying. 'I was so excited when I heard about it.'

'Oh, that's ancient history now,' said Eveline Johnson sharply. 'I'm working on a plan to bring over the ballet . . . turn it into something American. . . . I'll tell you about it sometime.'

'Oh, Eveline, did the screenstar come?' asked Ada, giggling.

'Oh, yes, they always come.' Eveline Johnson sighed. 'She's beautiful. . . . You must see her.'

'Of course, anybody in the world would come to your parties, Eveline.'

'I don't know why they should . . . they seem just too boring to me,'

Eveline Johnson was ushering them through some sliding doors into a highceilinged room dusky from shaded lights and cigarettesmoke where they were swallowed up in a jam of welldressed people talking and making faces and tossing their heads over cocktail glasses. There seemed no place to stand, so Mary sat down at the end of a couch beside a little marbletopped table. The other people on the couch were jabbering away among themselves and paid no attention to her. Ada and the

hostess had disappeared behind a wall of men's suits and after-
noongowns.

Mary had had time to smoke an entire cigarette before Ada
came back followed by George Barrow, whose thin face looked
flushed and whose adam'sapple stuck out further than ever over
his collar. He had a cocktail in each hand.

'Well well well, little Mary French, after all these years,' he
was saying with a kind of forced jollity. 'If you knew the trouble
we'd had getting these through the crush.'

'Hello, George,' said Mary casually. She took the cocktail he
handed her and drank it off. After the other drinks she'd had,
it made her head spin. Somehow George and Ada managed to
squeeze themselves in on the couch on either side of Mary.

'I want to hear all about the coalstrike,' George was saying,
knitting his brows. 'Too bad the insurgent locals had to choose
a moment when a strike played right into the operators' hands.'

Mary got angry. 'That's just the sort of remark I'd expect
from a man of your sort. If we waited for a favorable moment
there wouldn't be any strikes. . . . There never is any favorable
moment for the workers.'

'What sort of a man is a man of my sort?' said George
Barrow with fake humility, so Mary thought. 'That's what I
often ask myself.'

'Oh, I don't want to argue . . . I'm sick and tired of arguing.
. . . Get me another cocktail, George.'

He got up obediently and started threading his way across
the room. 'Now, Mary, don't row with poor George. . . .
He's so sweet. . . . Do you know, Margo Dowling really is here
. . . and her husband and Rodney Cathcart . . . they're always
together. They're on their way to the Riviera,' Ada talked into
her ear in a loud stage whisper.

'I'm sick of seeing movie actors on the screen,' said Mary,
'I don't want to see them in real life.'

Ada had slipped away. George was back with two more
cocktails and a plate of cold salmon and cucumbers. She
wouldn't eat anything.

'Don't you think you'd better, with all the drinks?' She shook
her head. 'Well, I'll eat it myself. . . . You know, Mary,' he
went on, 'I often wonder these days if I wouldn't have been a
happier man if I'd just stayed all my life an expressagent in
South Chicago and married some nice workinggirl and had a
flock of kids. . . . I'd be a wealthier and a happier man today
if I'd gone into business even.'

'Well, you don't look so badly off,' said Mary.

'You know it hurts me to be attacked as a laborfaker by you reds.... I may believe in compromise, but I've gained some very substantial dollarsandcents victories. . . . What you communists won't see is that there are sometimes two sides to a case.'

'I'm not a partymember,' said Mary.

'I know . . . but you work with them. . . . Why should you think you know better what's good for the miners than their own tried and true leaders?'

'If the miners ever had a chance to vote in their unions you'd find out how much they trust your sellout crowd.'

George Barrow shook his head. 'Mary, Mary . . . just the same headstrong warmhearted girl.'

'Rubbish, I haven't any feelings at all any more. I've seen how it works in the field. . . . It doesn't take a good heart to know which end of a riotgun's pointed at you.'

'Mary, I'm a very unhappy man.'

'Get me another cocktail, George.'

Mary had time to smoke two cigarettes before George came back. The nodding jabbering faces, the dresses, the gestures with hands floated in a smoky haze before her eyes.

The crowd was beginning to thin a little when George came back all flushed and smiling. 'Well, I had the pleasure of exchanging a few words with Miss Dowling, she was most charming. . . . But do you know what Red Haines tells me? I wonder if it's true. . . . It seems she's through; it seems that she's no good for talkingpictures . . . voice sounds like the croaking of an old crow over the loudspeaker,' he giggled a little drunkenly. 'There she is now, she's just leaving.'

A hush had fallen over the room. Through the dizzy swirl of cigerettesmoke Mary saw a small woman with blue eyelids and features regular as those of a porcelain doll under a mass of paleblond hair turn for a second to smile at somebody before she went out through the sliding doors. She had on a yellow dress and a lot of big sapphires. A tall bronzefaced actor and a bowlegged sallowfaced little man followed her out, and Eveline Johnson talking and talking in her breathless hectic way swept after them.

Mary was looking at it all through a humming haze like seeing a play from way up in a smoky balcony.

Ada came and stood in front of her rolling her eyes and opening her mouth wide when she talked. 'Oh, isn't it a wonderful party. . . . I met her. She had the loveliest manners . . . I don't know why, I expected her to be kinda tough. They say she came from the gutter.'

'Not at all,' said George. 'Her people were Spaniards of noble birth who lived in Cuba '

'Ada, I want to go home,' said Mary.

'Just a minute . . . I haven't had a chance to talk to dear Eveline. . . . She looks awfully tired and nervous today, poor dear.'

A lilypale young man brushed past them laughing over his shoulder at an older woman covered with silver lamé who followed him, her scrawny neck, wattled under the powder, thrust out and her hooknose quivering and eyes bulging over illconcealed pouches.

'Ada, I want to go home.'

'I thought you and I and George might have dinner together.'

Mary was seeing blurred faces getting big as they came towards her; changing shape as they went past, fading into the gloom like fish opening and closing their mouths in an aquarium.

'How about it? Miss Cohn, have you seen Charles Edward Holden around? He's usually quite a feature of Eveline's parties.' Mary hated George Barrow's doggy popeyed look when he talked. 'Now there's a sound intelligent fellow for you. I can talk to him all night.'

Ada narrowed her eyes as she leaned over and whispered shrilly in George Barrow's ear. 'He's engaged to be married to somebody else. Eveline's cut up about it. She's just living on her nerve.'

'George, if we've got to stay . . .' Mary said, 'get me another cocktail.'

A broadfaced woman in spangles with very red cheeks who was sitting on the couch beside Mary leaned across and said in a stage whisper, 'Isn't it dreadful? . . . You know I think it's most ungrateful of Holdy after all Eveline's done for him . . . in a social way . . . since she took him up . . . now he's accepted everywhere. I know the girl . . . a little bitch if there ever was one . . . not even wealthy.'

'Shush,' said Ada. 'Here's Eveline now. . . . Well, Eveline dear, the captains and the kings depart. Soon there'll be nothing but us smallfry left.'

'She didn't seem awful bright to me,' said Eveline, dropping into a chair beside them.

'Let me get you a drink, Eveline, dear,' said Ada. Eveline shook her head.

'What you need, Eveline, my dear,' said the broadfaced woman, leaning across the couch again, '. . . is a good trip abroad. New York's impossible after January . . . I shan't attempt to stay. . . . It would just mean a nervous breakdown if I did.'

'I thought maybe I might go to Morocco sometime if I could scrape up the cash,' said Eveline.

'Try Tunis, my dear. Tunis is divine.'

After she'd drunk the cocktail Barrow brought, Mary sat there seeing faces, hearing voices in a blank hateful haze. It took all her attention not to teeter on the edge of the couch. 'I really must go.' She had hold of George's arm crossing the room. She could walk very well, but she couldn't talk very well. In the bedroom Ada was helping her on with her coat.

Eveline Johnson was there with her big hazel eyes and her teasing singsong voice. 'Oh, Ada, it was sweet of you to come, I'm afraid it was just too boring. . . . Oh, Miss French, I so wanted to talk to you about the miners . . . I never get a chance to talk about things I'm really interested in any more. Do you know, Ada, I don't think I'll ever do this again. . . . It's just too boring.' She put her long hand to her temple and rubbed the fingers slowly across her forehead. 'Oh, Ada, I hope they go home soon. . . . I've got such a headache.'

'Oughtn't you to take something for it?'

'I will. I've got a wonderful painkiller. Ask me up next time you play Bach, Ada . . . I'd like that. You know it does seem too silly to spend your life filling up rooms with illassorted people who really hate each other.' Eveline Johnson followed them all the way down the hall to the front door as if she didn't want to let them go. She stood in her thin dress in the gust of cold wind that came from the open door while George went to the corner to get a cab.

'Eveline, go back in, you'll catch your death,' said Ada.

'Well, goodbye . . . you were darlings to come.' As the door closed slowly behind her, Mary watched Eveline Johnson's narrow shoulders. She was shivering as she walked back down the hall.

Mary reeled, suddenly feeling drunk in the cold air and Ada put her arm round her to steady her. 'Oh, Mary,' Ada said in her ear, 'I wish everybody wasn't so unhappy.'

'It's the waste,' Mary cried out savagely, suddenly able to

articulate. Ada and George Barrow were helping her into the cab. 'The food they waste and the money they waste while our people starve in tarpaper barracks.'

'The contradictions of capitalism,' said George Barrow with a knowing leer. 'How about a bite to eat?'

'Take me home first. No, not to Ada's,' Mary almost yelled. 'I'm sick of this parasite life. I'm going back to the office tomorrow. . . . I've got to call up tonight to see if they got in all right with that load of condensed milk. . . .' She picked up Ada's hand, suddenly feeling like old times again, and squeezed it. 'Ada, you've been sweet, honestly you've saved my life.'

'Ada's the perfect cure for hysterical people like us,' said George Barrow. The taxi had stopped beside the row of garbagecans in front of the house where Mary lived.

'No, I can walk up alone,' she said harshly and angrily again. 'It's just that being tiredout a drink makes me feel funny. Goodnight. I'll get my bag at your place tomorrow.'

Ada and Barrow went off in the taxicab with their heads together chatting and laughing. They've forgotten me already, thought Mary as she made her way up the stairs. She made the stairs all right, but had some trouble getting the key in the lock. When the door finally would open, she went straight to the couch in the front room and lay down and fell heavily asleep.

In the morning she felt more rested than she had in years. She got up early and ate a big breakfast with bacon and eggs at Childs on the way to the office. Rudy Goldfarb was already there, sitting at her desk.

He got up and stared at her without speaking for a moment. His eyes were red and bloodshot and his usually sleek black hair was all over his forehead. 'What's the matter, Rudy?'

'Comrade French, they got Eddy.'

'You mean they arrested him.'

'Arrested him, nothing, they shot him.'

'They killed him.' Mary felt a wave of nausea rising in her. The room started to spin around. She clenched her fists and the room fell into place again. Rudy was telling her how some miners had found the truck wrecked in a ditch. At first they thought that it had been an accident, but when they picked up Eddy Spellman he had a bullethole through his temple.

'We've got to have a protest meeting . . . do they know about it over at the Party?'

'Sure, they're trying to get Madison Square Garden. But,

Comrade French, he was one hell of a swell kid.' Mary was
shaking all over. The phone rang. Rudy answered it. 'Comrade
French, they want you over there right away. They want you to
be secretary of the committee for the protest meeting.'

Mary let herself drop into the chair at her desk for a moment
and began noting down the names of organizations to be notified.
Suddenly she looked up and looked Rudy straight in the eye.
'Do you know what we've got to do . . . we've got to move the
reliefcommittee to Pittsburgh. I knew all along we ought to
have been in Pittsburgh.'

'Risky business.'

'We ought to have been in Pittsburgh all along,' Mary said
firmly and quietly.

The phone rang again.

'It's somebody for you, Comrade French.'

As soon as the receiver touched Mary's ear, there was Ada
talking and talking. At first Mary couldn't make out what it
was about. 'But Mary darling, haven't you read the papers?'

'No, I said I hadn't. You mean about Eddy Spellman?'

'No, darling, it's too awful; you remember we were just there
yesterday for a cocktail party . . . you must remember Eveline
Johnson, it's so awful. I've sent out and got all the papers.
Of course the tabloids all say it's suicide.'

'Ada, I don't understand.'

'But, Mary, I'm trying to tell you . . . I'm so upset I can't
talk . . . she was such a lovely woman, so talented, an artist
really. . . . Well, when the maid got there this morning she
found her dead in her bed and we were just there twelve
hours before. It gives me the horrors. Some of the papers say
it was an overdose of a sleeping medicine. She couldn't have
meant to do it. If we'd only known, we might have been able
to do something, you know she said she had a headache.
Don't you think you could come up, I can't stay here alone I
feel so terrible.'

'Ada, I can't. . . . Something very serious has happened in
Pennsylvania. I have a great deal of work to do organizing a
protest. Goodbye, Ada.' Mary hung up, frowning.

'Say, Rudy, if Ada Cohn calls up again, tell her I'm out of
the office. . . . I have too much to do to spend my time taking
care of hysterical women a day like this.' She put on her hat,
collected her papers, and hurried over to the meeting of the
committee.

## *Vag*

The young man waits at the edge of the concrete, with one hand he grips a rubbed suitcase of phony leather, the other hand almost making a fist, thumb up

that moves in ever so slight an arc when a car slithers past, a truck roars, clatters; the wind of cars passing ruffles his hair, slaps grit in his face.

Head swims, hunger has twisted the belly tight,

he has skinned a heel through the torn sock, feet ache in the broken shoes, under the threadbare suit carefully brushed off with the hand, the torn drawers have a crummy feel, the feel of having slept in your clothes; in the nostrils lingers the staleness of discouraged carcasses crowded into a transient camp, the carbolic stench of the jail, on the taut cheeks the shamed flush from the boring eyes of cops and deputies, rail-roadbulls (they eat three squares a day, they are buttoned into wellmade clothes, they have wives to sleep with, kids to play with after supper, they work for the big men who buy their way, they stick their chests out with the sureness of power behind their backs). Git the hell out, scram! Know what's good for you, you'll make yourself scarce. Gittin' tough, eh? Think you kin take it, eh?

The punch in the jaw, the slam on the head with the night-stick, the wrist grabbed and twisted behind the back, the big knee brought up sharp into the crotch,

the walk out of town with sore feet to stand and wait at the edge of the hissing speeding string of cars where the reek of ether and lead and gas melts into the silent grassy smell of the earth.

Eyes black with want seek out the eyes of the drivers, a hitch, a hundred miles down the road.

Overhead in the blue a plane drones. Eyes follow the silver Douglas that flashes once in the sun and bores its smooth way out of sight into the blue.

(The transcontinental passengers sit pretty, big men with bankaccounts, highly paid jobs, who are saluted by doormen; telephonegirls say goodmorning to them. Last night after a fine dinner, drinks with friends, they left Newark. Roar of climbing motors slanting up into the inky haze. Lights drop away. An hour staring along a silvery wing at a big lonesome moon hurrying west through curdling scum. Beacons flash in a line across Ohio.

At Cleveland the plane drops banking in a smooth spiral, the string of lights along the lake swings in a circle. Climbing roar of the motors again; slumped in the soft seat drowsing through the flat moonlight night.

Chi. A glimpse of the dipper. Another spiral swoop from cool into hot air thick with dust and the reek of burnt prairies.

Beyond the Mississippi dawn creeps up behind through the murk over the great plains. Puddles of mist go white in the Iowa hills, farms, fences, silos, steel glint from a river. The blinking eyes of the beacons reddening into day. Watercourses vein the eroded hills.

Omaha. Great cumulus clouds, from coppery churning to creamy to silvery white, trail brown skirts of rain over the hot plains. Red and yellow badlands, tiny horned shapes of cattle.

Cheyenne. The cool high air smells of sweetgrass.

The tightbaled clouds to westward burst and scatter in tatters over the strawcolored hills. Indigo mountains jut rimrock. The plane breasts a huge crumbling cloudbank and toboggans over bumpy air across green and crimson slopes into the sunny dazzle of Salt Lake.

The transcontinental passenger thinks contracts, profits, vacationtrips, mighty continent between Atlantic and Pacific, power, wires humming dollars, cities jammed, hills empty, the indiantrail leading into the wagonroad, the macadamed pike, the concrete skyway; trains, planes: history the billiondollar speedup,

and in the bumpy air over the desert ranges towards Las Vegas

sickens and vomits into the carton container the steak and mushrooms he ate in New York. No matter, silver in the pocket, greenbacks in the wallet, drafts, certified checks, plenty restaurants in L. A.)

The young man waits on the side of the road; the plane has gone; thumb moves in a small arc when a car tears hissing past. Eyes seek the driver's eyes. A hundred miles down the road. Head swims, belly tightens, wants crawl over his skin like ants:

went to school, books said opportunity, ads promised speed, own your home, shine bigger than your neighbor, the radiocrooner whispered girls, ghosts of platinum girls coaxed from the screen, millions in winnings were chalked up on the boards in the offices, paychecks were for hands willing to work, the cleared desk of an executive with three telephones on it;

waits with swimming head, needs knot the belly, idle hands numb, beside the speeding traffic.

A hundred miles down the road.